Mind to Mind

Mind to Mind

A NOVEL

Seikan Hasegawa

GREAT OCEAN PUBLISHERS
ARLINGTON, VIRGINIA

Mind to Mind is the third in a series of books by Seikan Hasegawa to be published by Great Ocean Publishers. The first book in the series is *The Cave of Poison Grass, Essays on the Hannya Sutra*, the second *Essays on Marriage*. The books deal with various subjects, but their common theme and purpose is that of Zen training: the practical study of how to live best in each and every situation. The series is entitled COMPANIONS OF ZEN TRAINING.

Cover and text illustrations by Taiyo Hasegawa

Copyright © 1999 by Seikan Hasegawa
Cover and text illustrations copyright © 1999 by Taiyo Hasegawa

For further information contact:
Great Ocean Publishers
1823 North Lincoln Street
Arlington, Virginia 22207-3746

First Printing

Library of Congress Cataloging in Publication Data
Hasegawa, Seikan, 1945 –
    Mind to mind : a novel / Seikan Hasegawa.
        p. cm. — (Companions of Zen training)
    ISBN 0-915556-35-9 (alk. paper)
    I. Title. II. Series: Hasegawa, Seikan, 1945 – Companions of Zen training
PS3558.A72285M56   1999   98-47120
813'.54—dc21   CIP

Printed in the United States of America   10 9 8 7 6 5 4 3 2 1

With the everlasting wish of well-being for the readers still unknown I wrote this book. First I wrote it in Japanese and then in English. With my English far from perfect, the writing resembled the sight of a garden untended after the loss of its landholder or a beach with washed-ashore nets half buried after a storm. My wife, Elizabeth, corrected and polished it and every word, phrase, sentence began to shine like those items with dewdrops attached in the moonlight. Further, my disciple, editor as well as publisher, Mark Esterman, polished and corrected it. The Reverend Taiyo Hasegawa made the cover paintings and the illustrations. Their love goes through the book to all of you readers still unmet.

Contents

VI: YELLOW SEDIMENT

VII: PATH ALONG THE PEAKS

EPILOGUE

Mind to Mind

I

Scudding Clouds

1

Prologue

Life once triggered to begin repeats its cell cleavage with tremendous vigor, its precise operation vitalized by its own excellent purity, furious, transcendental, as if beyond interpretation, unless to say its purpose is to function, no less than the sun and the stars as they continue to burn in the deep and wide universe. Life has extremely sharp eyes to detect and ingest nourishment from all surrounding miscellaneous elements. What fierce bird can seize its food from amid a tornado that pulls up, tosses, and twirls trees, houses, haystacks, and fat swine too, sucking in the shrieks and squeals in a moment of insanity between raging earth and condensed black clouds? Only a creature who does not perish even as it is engulfed can live on in the rough wave of this world.

'Yet, this baby who came out with the gush of my amniotic fluid looks so weak! Such a wrinkled face, and tight-shut eyes and hands. Though he cries with all his might, it's not as bright, sharp, or powerful as the rooster's crow coming through the forest. How fragile and pitiful, if I compare it with the snow and wind constantly threatening the storm doors, breaking the pine branches, and bending the heads of the bamboos, their trunks, though said to be as strong as iron rods, splitting.

'In ancient India, I was told, Buddha heard a baby's cry as a declaration — "I am my own lord throughout heaven and earth!"[1] How I too wish to hear it like that! What mother wouldn't respect this baby's dear life intense with the desire to live on? My sour emotion of love and pity races in my chest quicker than the gusts of slanting snow or white water in a ravine, runs through my mind, washes my bones as if to bleach them of flesh.

'Aren't my breasts more dismal and a greater disillusionment than a costly pardon obtained from a church, or a false paycheck received at the end of enormous toil?

'I risked my life to hide a handful each of rice and soybeans from his father and his grandmother, and, how terrible, from his sister and brother. In their absence I stealthily and patiently cooked it over the brazier and fed the broth to the baby. I could do so yesterday and today, but what about tomorrow? His desire to live increases tenfold with every spoonful, while his ability decreases as much. Losing vitality but having unignorable desire —

3

what an optimistic contradiction, like a rocket that shoots into the sky and falls back to earth or burns up! And my ability to satisfy it is as insignificant as a firefly. Catch one in the hand and there's no warmth at all, only a trace of cooled enthusiasm....

'Alas, how I long for the bridge in my native village! — the thread-like branches of the willow refreshingly swaying and flashing in the dark with the pale white lights of fireflies. Dad was a trifle clumsy, but he mounted the wooden parapet and proclaimed, "I'll catch one for Micha!" Mama said, "Be careful, don't fall in the river. In the daytime you feel properly scared. Now you're taking false advantage of the night shadows and the sake you drank." There was suddenly a great explosive sound. I wonder why my heart was so surprised. Big, vivid, colorful chrysanthemum flowers over the hill — the fire-works had begun, an adventure in beauty that seemed to draw on the sky and stop the flow of time. The image and the moment were plucked from the dark and transported to the storehouse of the mind....

'Dad with me on his back walked through the crowd to find a good spot. Mama bought cotton candy and saw that I held it tight. He didn't complain when the pink fluffy bits dropped and turned to syrup on his ear, neck, and shoulder, no doubt unpleasant....How old was I? It must have been 1915, so I was four, yes, after supper they would talk about the slaying of many nuns by that dreadful priest, Ryoun — six in succession, it was said — or about the German occupation of Warsaw....

'All night my baby cried for hunger. I planned to give thin rice gruel at dawn, but I found there was no rice. I can't just keep lying here — I must secure some food by any means! A child's happiness utterly depends on what parents it has, in what circumstances. Is there some meaning in my having no possibility of giving my own child even half or a tenth the joy I received as a child, sheltered and tenderly nursed by my parents?' Facing her question, Micha was bewildered, chagrined, exasperated, as if kindly offered a bowl of frost with the words "Eat this for warmth and nourishment."

She must have been dozing. Beside her the baby was sleeping quietly.

'Fleeting sleep...as peaceful as the scent of damp spring grass or of sunlit hay....But I can't be like this — I must do something!...How is Kiku? She said as she left, "I'll see Gyodo too gets a bellyful."'

Kiku was eight and in second grade of elementary school. Taking advantage of winter vacation, she went every morning early until the hour after supper to work at a house keeping a fish shop. She cleaned the shop and the house, but mainly tended a six-month-old girl yet unweaned while tending her own brother Gyodo, aged three. She thought it odd to be making such an effort for another home when she had her young brother and now another just in his fourth day. But she saw the merit in what she was doing despite her feelings.

As long as she worked, three meals a day for her and Gyodo were secured. And more, the wife promised to provide all her school necessities — notebook, pencil, eraser, shoes, and sweater.

His round eyes were set deep behind sharp cheeks and a sharp nose. His teeth were crooked, and the red of his face was like frost burn — 'a doll face made from an open pinecone,' thought Kiku. He never gave her a head, bones, or even a tail, rejected by his customers but still having an amount of flesh. His only concern was to sell fish. Often she imagined him saying, "Hey, Kiku, wrap this in newspaper, take it home." But really it was like expecting a flower to bloom on a dead branch. 'How joyous if I could take home that thick head!' she thought as she swept the passageway, sensing on her back a warm and rather large quantity of urine from the baby tied up behind. No dog or cat got such a head either. Along with the guts, air bladders, fins, and tails he dumped it into a garbage barrel with a heavy lid, except for when he kept some for his own table.

His wife, whom Kiku served, had a stolid face and the full look of a woman close to term, though she had already delivered. She stood behind the shelves laid with various fish and managed the cash register. There was actually not much for her to do because her little husband promptly did everything, his diligence obviously due to her overwhelming pressure.

When she happened to hear the baby cry she simply left the shop, even during a customer's order, and appeared at the corner where Kiku was cleaning and arranging kitchen utensils. She stood and regarded Kiku busily working with the baby on her back and Gyodo playing nearby as he liked. Was she looking for some complaint, or merely observing? Kiku was never sure. She did not find her hard to serve. Her performance was judged mainly on whether or not the baby cried, and the baby was generally content if only she carried it and often changed its diaper. She was not required to be perfectly fastidious about cleaning; the wife ignored such details as the fine whitish dust on the window frames and the chair rungs and in the corners of the cupboards, and the brown on the spout of the teapot.

Kiku was stalwart and cheerful. Those who met her coming and going with her little brother were willing to be sympathetic about her circumstances and ready to admire her contribution. But seeing her bright, laughing face denying any problem, they quickly realized that such feelings had been obliterated like rime touched by sun.

5

Her secret for maintaining her brightness was to deny herself even a moment's worry when she was not busily moving about. There were distresses, such as that children her age gathered in merry groups to play, and could read as many books as they liked, given books and time by their parents. They even made family visits to the zoo, museums, theaters, and art galleries. Distressful also was that she had to give priority to the fish-shop baby even when Gyodo slipped and hit his head or was crying from boredom. There were also the matters at home: her parents blaming each other, their arguing, and then his violence.

Only when she was actively moving her limbs did she reflect. After moving about all day and exhausting herself, she could fall asleep as soon as she lay down.

Seeing her daughter forced to endure a suffering that she herself had never had to experience, Micha could do nothing but look on in the same manner as she regarded the sky thinly covered with snow clouds. Day and night a mass of air way below freezing surged across from Siberia, greedily sucking up moisture from the stormy sea and breaking against the formidable mountain walls that ran the length of the Japanese Archipelago, ranges crowned with the names Ou, Echigo, Mikuni, Hida, and still more, many more, hilly highlands.

'Just as I have no power against this weather, I am incapable before the incomprehensible suffering life of my daughter. For instance, I have less confidence in my ability and wisdom to deal with the cold than do thick-furred creatures who burrow into the earth. Almost more than me, this immature girl is able to live on.

'At her age I never considered the difficulty of life. I spent every day idle under my parents' care. Kiku is not only earning her daily food but tending Gyodo as well. How empty to sympathize with her and pity her, for I, lacking the experience, am unqualified to feel those emotions. Giving her such a situation, how I regret being her mother!

'Isn't one of the worst of our numerous sins the sin of making ourselves parents of a child who must be loved? We do so only by the superiority of a mature body, and with neither the confidence nor the ability to insure the child's nourishment and happiness however difficult the situation. Isn't it the sin of being powerless and ignorant?

'Killing is a great sin for stealing the pleasure that a life could have enjoyed. But isn't giving birth also a great sin if it tortures a new life? Is there any difference between giving birth to a baby who must live in torture and inventing, unaware of the consequences, the atomic bombs we learned this

6

summer were dropped on Hiroshima and Nagasaki, where hundreds of thousands died in the blaze?

'I wish a bomb would fall here too! People would reproach me for saying so, especially those who are so busy investigating the damage or devising remedial measures that they can find life worth living. "You're ungrateful!" they'd say. "Be thankful your life was spared!" But the ones who can reproach me aren't the ones who died. Those who can reproach me should be capable of blaming the Japanese capitalists and military who designed the war, and the Americans, called "the enemy," who dropped the bombs.

'Those who can reproach me can find the cause of their misery outside themselves. And as they are putting the dead and the dying into some kind of order they can cherish the illusion that they are performing a great deed, when actually they are only earning their living and satisfying their desire for recognition. What simple, unfair, happy people!

'Throughout the world there must be those who think they're better off dead, but knowing their children would be left behind, they live on. How helpful to them if everything could be instantly called off! Isn't the flash of an atomic bomb gospel itself? Not blessed with such gospel, I must take the only possible way to avoid giving more misery to my baby. Yes, I must stop his life as early as I can and commit the sin of killing, in addition to the sin of giving birth.

'Sleeping baby..."Mokuzu"...His life should be stopped even a day earlier, even an hour! One day's delay only increases his suffering and couldn't advance his ability to overcome it. Aren't hunger symptoms already beginning? — swollen belly, slowing pulse, anemia, diarrhea, emaciation? His weakened body lacks resistance and before long will be invaded by terrible things like pneumonia, dysentery, TB, typhoid fever...

'Now he looks perfectly beautiful. His hands are as fresh and delicate as new maple leaves, his feet smooth and elastic...shapely head with tender rich hair and eyebrows, bridge of the nose, mouth too, yes, every feature promises to be clear and distinctive. Yet, my only performable kindness and what I ought to do for him above all is to stop his life, and do it without spoiling the perfect beauty of his orderly body. Let no ugly spot appear! Just with his perfection as it is now, let him enjoy the freedom of the angels in heaven!'

Micha resolutely left her bed, taking pains not to wake the baby. Her surroundings seemed to whirl and darken, and a heaviness pulled at the back of her head. She nearly fell backward but caught herself, stooped, and rested her elbows on the tatami and her brow on her fists. Her postpartum bleeding must not have finished. Her heart pounded, and she was swept with nausea.

With greatest caution she wrapped the baby in a little blanket and carefully lifted him. So that he would not be awakened or harmed, she rested enough between movements to insure that she would not fall. She slid open the door, made her way through the adjoining room, slid open another door, and stepped down onto the earth of the yet colder entry room. There was no sign of life. She advanced to the service entrance, managed to slide open its heavy wooden door, and went out toward the side of the well. The snow had stopped and lay deep and expressionless. There was neither sunlight nor wind.

Carefully she continued along under the tile roof by the well. Underfoot was slippery with snow blown in and now melting. She could at last enter the kitchen cottage. A range with earthen furnaces now cold as ice sat dignified, absorbing every long-established custom. Set into it were five pots from small and shallow to large and deep. The visible portion and supporting rim of the middle pot radiated a silvery light. Its bottom could easily hold a dry measure of five or six liters of rice. The lid was a thick wood disk with a pair of wood bars for grips, which even an adult needed some vitality to lift with one hand. A basic condition for tasty rice was that the lid not be heaved up during the boiling stage.

For several days the rice pot had remained unused, keeping the polished look of its last cleaning by Micha before her delivery. While inside it was cavernous, the effect outside was tranquil but alerting, for the metal gleamed with the light of a sword.

As if laying him in state, Micha quietly lowered the baby wrapped in the blanket into the pot. He was received entirely with space remaining. Then she securely put on the lid.

The baby would be unable to reach as high as the top — he could not even stand. 'He can't possibly push this lid heavier than himself even if he could reach it. Soon he will consume all the oxygen, and after a brief spell of convulsions his life will be extinguished. It is only a matter of time!'

☙

He returned at the hour when the surroundings were bright beyond day-time, in the interval of snow light with the coming of evening. Throughout the short winter day the sun had been obscured by clouds.

He wore a simplified priest's robe known as a "robe to accompany the troops," convenient for activity, over which he wore a black cloak, and home-made pantaloons to protect the long pleats of his skirts from muddy snow. He was coming home bearing on his shoulder a hemp sack of twenty kilograms of rice. For him it was shameful to be dressed in the robe of a priest and yet be carrying a laborer's burden; it was also painful, and his hands were numbed by the long carry. But the thought of his wife's face and their new baby awaiting him in hunger made a hot joy rise in his chest.

His wife abused him and pronounced him incompetent to support and shelter his family, whence he was no longer expected to secure their livelihood. Is it not odd to coexist day after day while being considered incompetent as a husband and a father? What then was his relation? The answer was simple: he never doubted that he was both a husband and a father.

Certainly he was not so cruel as to enjoy people's unhappiness or easily push them toward misfortune. He never hoped to abandon his duty to his wife and children, who were without food. On the contrary he had much compassion, and the more he saw his family's distress, the more his pity increased, with the result that his love was not inferior to the love of other husbands and fathers; indeed it must have been inimitably deeper and sharper. The difference was that although it was based on compassion, it was not an exclusive love for family or for any specific persons, but was rather more universal in character. Naturally he did not see his family's troubles as the only noteworthy point on the horizon, like an island flooded with brilliance in the South Pacific.

He could not, in other words, use his suffering and that of his old mother and wife and children — no matter how they cried — as an excuse to decrease the income of other families so as to increase his own. He saw his family's gain as another's loss.

Not once, for instance, did he ask a decided compensation for his work. He drew and lettered signboards and advertisements, made designs for cloth, painted hanging scrolls, and so forth, when requests came from such places as groceries, meat shops, sake shops, bookstores, schools, and municipal offices, for he was a master of sumi painting and calligraphy, talented from boyhood.

Often he was offered only a bottle of sake for writing as many as three hundred New Year's cards. But he was content with the single fact that his art skill was useful to these folk. He did not care if an uncivil, calculating fellow with little sense of value remunerated him merely with transparent

9

compliments, such as "How wonderful, Reverend! Just to view your match-less brushwork purifies my mind. All my weariness and soil from living in this world are dispersing like mist!" Nor did he heed the sort who was truly impressed and forgot himself and his place as if absorbed in the moment after ejaculation.

Besides, there were some who brought extra paper, or a new brush, or a stick of sumi to request only one drawing or calligraphy — extras he much enjoyed. Basic, indispensable, they insured him another six months or more to relish his art. His joy on that account was not owing to so minor a matter as some kind of innocence or foolish lack of desire, even if others supposed so. It was just that to run out of paper, brush, sumi, and sumi stone — honored as an artist's "four treasures" — was as dire, he thought, as for a mouse to run out of rice, wheat, potatoes, and beans.

So he considered such compensation to be generally sufficient. Expect-ing and taking money as well for each piece of art was to behave like a merchant, which to him seemed as dirty as the maggots squirming in the pit of the latrine. 'How alien,' he thought, '— equal to living by selling one's own dear child!'

He let down the rice sack beside the range, dusted off the white powder that had sifted onto the shoulder of his robe, and went in by the service entrance.

"Oii! I'm back! You can be glad, I was given rice! We need worry no more, at least not for a while....What's the matter, are you sick?"

He looked closely at his wife, at her face partly hidden by the coverlet, and at the sleeping baby held snug in her arm. Her eyes were puffed and red.

"Crying? Why? People don't die from going hungry for a week or two... though I don't know about a baby. Anyway, we can ease our minds — I have rice. We'll celebrate New Year's Day, and our life for the coming month is secure."

"I put him in the rice pot and put on the lid!"

"Nnh? He's here, sleeping well. Show me his face. Look, he's peaceful with a smile, if maybe a bit undernourished."

"It was past noon, you were out. I thought having no food only tortures him, that I should kill him as my best kindness. How much time went by after I set him in the pot and came back I don't know. But the cry! It was frantic as if he was burning. It reached to here and pierced the air so I thought it would split the pillars, walls, doors, and more, the trees on the mountain and bamboos in the grove. It was sharp as lightning and went everywhere. Our chickens flapped and made unusual sounds."

Micha reported it all at once, her tears flooding and her throat choking.

Doyu was irritated because nothing had yet settled in his brain. All sorts of feelings and sights kept coming and going in his mind — the matter of his wife and baby and her conduct during his absence, his own parents, the priest who raised him in his acolyte days and under whom he had been continuing his Zen practice, today's Buddhist Association meeting, the members' faces and speeches, his eldest son, Bunyu, hiding his whereabouts, Kiku off with Gyodo to baby-sit, his expected earning from his chestnut harvest, his new calligraphy deriving its theme from *Linji lu* (Recorded words of Linji), and so on.

At last he fixed on one notion, though possibly it had no profound meaning: 'Phew, she cries like a woman!'

"Desperate, I rushed to the kitchen cottage and found the lid far off on the mud floor. It must have been thrown and rolled. By the wind? How could a baby push it off? Even if he struggled with his hands and feet, he couldn't reach — he can't stand. I know the great force when there's steam — how could his strength be superior? He's only four days old."

"'Eyebrows one foot two inches long grew from the chin,'[2] and, 'Though its looks be humble as mud, its nobility is like a gold ball.'"[3]

"Why bring up such obscurities? I assume you're quoting the ancients as usual. You'd better know I'll not be impressed no matter how fine the words, unless I'm shown their practice before my eyes. That aside, can you guess what I thought when I saw him with the lid heaved away and crying with all his might?"

"Can I guess? — such a matter belongs to a person's ever-changing mind, as hard to grasp as the clouds. In any case you should be ashamed of your superficial thinking and your rash decision to kill the baby — an outrageous idea!"

"Why should I be ashamed? I performed the most difficult kindness. But now I realize a baby's life doesn't entirely depend on the kindness and protection of its parents and other nearby people. That is to say, its life belongs to it more than to anyone else, and it will die if its life wishes to die, regardless of its parents' desperate care, or it will live if its life wishes to live, even if they try to kill it. Not having the final authority over their baby's life and death, parents have no cause to fly about in every direction, changing color. They must entrust the baby's life to the baby.

"I'm also now convinced a baby comes into this world and grows because there already was its original life, and not the other way around, which is the usual belief — that parents give it life and raise it. So we parents shouldn't invade such a basic matter as the creation of a life."

Doyu thought his wife spoke as if to overturn heaven and earth about

11

what for him was common sense. But he could not help venerating her conviction gained through her own experience. 'She'll not forget it, and all her days it will influence her view of herself and others and the world. After all, truth has no value in itself. Its dignity can be expressed only through the personality of each who understands it.'

2

Micha's Resolution

After New Year's Day, Micha's bleeding finally stopped and she recovered from her delivery. To obtain food somehow and enable her family to survive was her only concern. It was not so different from the life of a beast, but was the state most Japanese were in directly after the war.

There were people whose concern and effort day and night was not only for themselves and their families but for the whole of society and its course, for Japan's reconstruction and method of surviving in the world. But they were a limited number, the uppermost statesmen, businessmen, and academics, with whom Micha had no contact because first, they were fortunate to have little trouble for their daily life; second, they were highly educated, with careers that enabled them to be useful; and third — perhaps the foremost element — they still felt a passionate love for their country, or for mankind, even after defeat in battle.

'In the old days,' thought Micha, 'they were "the people above the clouds." What now should they be called? Administrators? cultured persons? intelligentsia? Whatever, they are almost totally unrelated to me. Their world is as awesome, noisy, conspicuous, and majestic as fireworks or thunder, yet it has nothing to do with me in terms of merit.

'When they touch down to earth they often bring bad news, just like lightning. I wish they'd stay above the clouds with their associates, and display their ability as they like and enjoy their game, and not move their venue to here.

'But I've heard rumors that make them worthy of pity. It's said they're running about in confusion under the orders of the armed occupier. To sum up, they as the leading class began the war as they wished, and they were un-shapely and were completely defeated. And even now they are running about, shouting "Reconstruction!" "Rehabilitation!" "No more war!" "World peace!" I presume they're not the same individuals, not the same faces, hands, and feet, but they're the same sort who have continued from the beginning of mankind, taking over the lead and boasting they are acting "for the people," "for the world," when nobody asked them to do so.

'As to that, my husband is a better man; at least I can understand his way of life, though he's disqualified as a husband and a father. He was born the child of a landowner who was vice-abbot of the head temple, and was given the highest education and trained himself as a priest. He had the culture, status, wealth, and connections suitable for governing this district, to say the least. In fact till very recently he was, despite his youth, the appointed president of the All-Kyoto Buddhist Association, and of the Agricultural Commission, and was assigned to other important posts. The day I attempted to kill Mokuzu he came home with rice given as a small honorarium for his four years of service to the Association. "Good news! At last I'm relieved of the presidency!" he reported. Were he a usual man of the leading class he might have lamented. But he enjoyed it: "I've no inclination to care about society, much less about Japan and the world. Of course I will help to a certain extent within my capacity if someone is in trouble, though it isn't a pleasurable task. I am a priest, but I've begun to feel I shouldn't sacrifice my family and myself so much for others. It is beyond my ability to practice philanthropy or free service at the very time my own family is crying for hunger. If only my family can keep going and I can continue to draw and paint, I can be fairly happy....In any case, you can enjoy my release from that half-obligatory post." Since then his mood has improved.'

Seated on the south veranda lit by the morning sun, Micha was thinking how to obtain money and food as she nursed Mokuzu wrapped in a blanket. Her thoughts did not arrive at the main point and circled incoherent nearby. Her brain was avoiding the most difficult and yet most concrete and practicable thought, as is the cunning of the brain to dwell on what is already done.

'My brother inherited my native house, and he died all too soon seven years ago in the Nomonhan Incident. How kind a brother he was! During my dormitory life he often called on me with fruit and sweets. The only girls from our area who went on to senior high school in those years were Okei and me....My husband performed a splendid funeral, and everyone was grateful, as was I, and I was proud to have married a man who could be so helpful at such a time.

'But as the war intensified, the field tenants were grudging with their rent and our income began to drop. The government ordered my husband to do

13

this or that official work, and by submitting himself so loyally he actually increased our expenses. We still had money, but no goods could be bought. Black-marketing prospered and became the common practice. Even during daylight hours peasants and grocers outrageously overcharged. Then the peasants actually stopped selling food. "What good are these paper scraps? We want substance — clothing — tools —" "Your trashy money is as useless as the knowledge of scholars of agriculture!" They declared their mind so nakedly and with abusive language, as is usual of people in the stronger position.

'I had no choice but to carry my clothes, which filled the drawers of my three paulownia chests, to the houses of peasants to gain a handful of food for the day. Day after day I exchanged them for rice, wheat, beans, potatoes, sesame seeds, carrots, and daikon radishes. But it wasn't trade, or far more than enough for necessities would have remained in my hand. What nonsense — my pure silk Nishijin brocade kimono was valued at two kilos of rice! My overkimono naturally dyed yellowish green was traded for even less, and my scarlet cotton underkimono went for three sweet potatoes!

'In that way most of my valuable trousseau prepared by my parents, who stayed awake late to figure the financing over and over, fell into the hands of peasants here and there.

'What could they do with such fancy clothes? Dress up their wives and daughters? It's unsuitable, like dressing up a wild boar or a fox. Or did they resell them at a higher price to richer folk through the hands of a black marketer? Either way, exchanging costly goods for so little of their crops could hardly be called business. Yet without it we would have died long since. Bunyu, son of my husband by his former wife, and Kiku and Gyodo survived, thanks to my kimonos. Leaving at dawn, crossing the far hills, climbing up and down, finally reaching possible farmhouses — it was no easy task, especially when most peasants too were distressed and unwilling to trade a single grain of rice or wheat. I was disdained, abused...There was such a detestable one, exposing yellow teeth and laughing, "Sure I'll offer a tad of rice in exchange for you!" Dreadful, ignoble man! We live fundamentally to perfect our purity. If we surrender it to live, what's the point of living? Stupid guy!

'Originally peasants hadn't even their own family name. They have been a people who sent their daughters to spinning mills, raking in the advance salary, and the girls were fated to die of TB or other illnesses from the cruel hard labor. Many sold their wives or daughters into prostitution, cast their newborns into the river, and abandoned their parents after carrying them deep into the mountains. What is the value of living by paying such a price? But is my attempt to kill Mokuzu out of my kindness the same? If so, then my

14

face too must have the degraded look of a queer human species — nasty, hopeless, cowardly, base, bent on instant profit and desperate just to live on as an organic creature, with no care for the pleasures of life and no appreciation. Is this why my husband is irritated and regards me with grief and contempt?

'At the onset of autumn two years ago, I returned to my native house to ask help from my sister-in-law, carrying my shame. My brother would have given me rice or anything else before I was forced to confess the extent of my plight. After all, my native house is a wholesale rice business. What was the state of her brain? — like the innards of a clock, complex and luminous with pale oil?

'After hearing my entire story, she slapped me with a cold argument, "It is shameful that the one who went out to marry should return with the sole thought of enhancing her new house at the expense of impoverishing the house she left. A person sensitive to shame and a person dead to shame are as opposite as day and night. I, though a widow, am in charge here. You by marriage are an outsider. And the responsible one in your home is your husband. Are you a widow? As long as you have him, entrust to him the task of requesting help. You who are not responsible should not intrude. Moreover, it is unjust that he does not appear. Had he come to consult, I might have considered."

'I further appealed, "Rather than stoop to beg, he prefers to see his wife and children, himself too, starve to death. Please understand his pride and lend us rice or wheat as a temporary measure." She replied, "If that's his way, you should follow him. It is a wife's duty. Or divorce him outright and gain your responsibility. Then I can consider you." "Divorce is unthinkable — the children would suffer without both parents!" I said, but she had already shut her ears. Is she made of ice? The house, the business, everything was built up by my parents. There I was born and grew up. My brother inherited it all. None of it was built up by her!

'On the way home I was so mortified I wept. At night I persuaded him, "If you just utter a word, my sister-in-law will help us. Please do! It can only help you and Bunyu...Kiku and Gyodo too. Please with patience go and bow your head!"

'His response was unexpected: "Is that so? What she says is reasonable. The most responsible one should properly do the asking. If it is as you report, I am willing to bow my head." He too must have been worrying about the children, after all. "It will be most fortunate for everyone to have our request granted. To ask a possible matter is not at all shameful, but is as bright and natural as the opening of a dew-speckled morning glory in the sun. How unlike asking the impossible, which is to grind dirt into a wound. Well, we are lucky. Tomorrow

15

we shall visit your sister-in-law." He withdrew to his study and rubbed down a stick of sumi to prepare for painting. As it was autumn, he chose to make a scene of sunlit chestnuts ripening in an opening bur, the branch bent low by their weight. The focus, he explained, was a thin patch of clouds driven by a quick breeze, seemingly disappearing and reappearing in the far sky between the branches. He inscribed a vertical legend in running style, "Scudding clouds," which resembled a dragon ascending to heaven.

He rolled it up and wrapped it carefully in a purple silk. "We can't go empty-handed. We'll take this as a gift."

'Next morning we went out as a couple in our best dress, leaving the children with his mother. The mist was dense, only the far mountaintops were visible, pale blue as if floating. The near surroundings were cold and pure white. As the mist began to clear, we found ourselves walking along the highway with the wide rice fields on either side ripening gold. Whenever a spike rose as it shed its dew, the grains brushed together with a light sound. Cicadas and grasshoppers flew out to the roadside. Rare it was to be going out together. I recalled how I felt at the start of our marriage. The sky cleared and became broad and high. A horse whinnied in a field.

'We were led to the best room and offered tea. My sister-in-law was leisurely in her appreciation of the painting.

'"Is there a profound Zen meaning in 'Scudding clouds'?" He earnestly responded, "Most things for a Zen priest are nothing other than the expression of the mind from beginning to end. If we thus interpret these clouds, there are many meanings both deep and shallow."

'She quoted various Zen phrases, as many as she happened to know, and asked for his comments. About forty minutes were wasted. Oh, how it vexed me! He too could not open the case and responded with rugged honesty to her every inquiry.

'The talk at last ended, and silence pervaded the room. Abruptly the shrill cries of shrikes reached our ears from the area of the persimmon at the garden corner; they were likely catching tree frogs or crickets in their sharp beaks and impaling them on twigs.

'"Now then, what was your purpose in coming here today?" Condescending and intimidating are suitable words, I suppose, to describe her manner.

'He was surprised and nonplused, having felt reassured that he would not need to explain and literally bow down, for seemingly she was understanding. But he reconsidered, and finding no alternative began to explain in a tone like the groping of the blind.

'"My appeal is, to be frank, er...the distress under the great war has been excessive. I have been reluctantly tolerating our field tenants' refusal to pay, and certainly I have been trying to find other ways to increase our income, with no result. Only my obligatory donation of labor has increased, that is, to see the soldiers off to the front, to care for the families, to perform services for those who returned as the souls of the departed war heroes, and, again, to comfort the grieving families. But it is evident that such work only demands my labor and brings no income, though my private expenditure mounts....

"'Moreover, as head of the Buddhist Association, I have put my energy into various tasks, particularly, and again, caring for the soldiers and their families — discipline, morals, mental health — and helping them out of their difficulties. But the post is honorary and brings no income, and the increasing expense is hard to dismiss, though I never tried to commit it to memory. Additionally I was ordered to head the Agricultural Commission, with the tasks of elaborating on and effecting the plan to reform the farmland for the coexistence and coprosperity of landowner and tenant. The character of this work too is that the more fairly I serve, the more I am disadvantaged as a landowner; yet so far I have been promoting the reform, and I can expect no income from there. Only the expense is sure.

"'On top of that remains the work of promoting chestnut culture in our region. For years I have been doing this out of my wish, and clearly it has begun to profit the local farmers now that the harvest is becoming more extensive — which is splendid, but it gives me no income other than what I receive from the few trees I planted on my own mountain. To be more precise, fifteen years ago I directed the farmers to clear their hills and mountains and plant chestnut seedlings, and during those years I invited specialists on chestnut culture to come and lecture to the villagers. I too investigated suitable varieties for the region; and the right fertilizer — type, amount, when to apply; and pruning, grafting, spraying — what chemicals and when for each disease and insect; and finally, how to sell the harvest. I have been the leading figure in these matters, and the related cost has been paid by me alone. Even now other localities too ask my practical advice. I try to go as much as I can, but expecting a certain honorarium is as futile as expecting to fill one's stomach with snow. The farmers or mountain owners are enjoying this new income and believing it is theirs alone, which is very natural but, to conclude, nothing comes to me.

"'Such are the facts broadly outlined. I hope you can understand the fatigue and misery of the six family members — my mother, wife, and children, and me. Please, I beg of you a temporary expedient." He deeply bowed with great formality. With stiff countenance my sister-in-law then spoke,

"'I cannot understand, absolutely not."

17

'"What? Yes, I mean, in sum, we are facing difficulty even in having three meals a day, and, disregarding ourselves as parents, we wish at least for the children, who are at a growing age. Therefore, please..." He attempted further explanation, but she stopped him,

'"No, what I don't understand is not how you got your distress nor how much you are suffering from it, but why I should practice so foolish a move when the result would threaten my own family. It is hard to find reason to shave off my bone and dig my grave even after considering that as a priest you might offer me a free burial service. We each have family to whom we are responsible. And after all you are a respectable man. You are of the landed class, you are educated, you can maintain your honor, and above all, you are a priest. I am but a merchant, and furthermore, a helpless widow."

'My husband's face suddenly turned blue. His eyes widened and emitted a strange light like a blue flame. Veins stood out on his temples. Abruptly he stood up and left the room with a vigor that shook the fixtures of the house, and, stepping into his clogs, he departed, slamming the lattice door.

'The long trail of his fury came to my ears — "Damnation! I was imposed upon!" As I hurried to follow, I saw from the corner of my eye my sister-in-law shrug and stick out her tongue like an impish schoolgirl.

'Walking the road straight through the rice fields, isolated from human habitation, tripping, I followed. When we came to where the Hokke River draws close to the road, where a dense grove of thin bamboo hides the bank, he wheeled about and kicked me in the thigh. Being slight, I was easily knocked to the ground and sent rolling to the grass of the roadside. With queer swift motions he never displayed before, he kicked me two or three more times in the back as I lay on my face. Then he deserted me and hastened on his way home.

'His words throughout were snatches of his unbearable indignation — "Slack woman! Abomination! Made me the fool, plotting together!" or "Stupid! What's so bad about dying if there's no food?"

'I thought as I lay there abandoned, "His words weren't uttered to be constructive — that would have required him to think through the whole situation in order, with fairness, and with loyalty to the law of causation. Instead he was refusing to see the reality in front of him and spoiling himself with his emotion, respecting it as some absolute being. By yielding to his anger he must have felt his joy.

'"Meeting difficulty and unable to keep calm, and, to avoid the great pain to himself, he yielded to his emotion. But as his emotion can ensure only his pleasure and cannot distinguish good from bad, right from wrong, propriety from impropriety, the difficulty he should stand up to is made yet more difficult. What self-destructive behavior! Regarded from another angle, he is a person who can't help creating enjoyment for himself even in the face of difficulty, that is, he's indulging in a lunatic inclination to immerse himself in a feeling of pleasure even when he's but a step from the ruin of his nearest relationships, including his relationship with himself.

'"I can understand with active sympathy his suffering, irritation, shame, and fury regarding my sister-in-law, and his distrust of me, and his self-pity. By kicking me, he cleared up all such uncomfortable feelings. Then I want to know how I am to clear up my uncomfortable feelings, which I have more than he, at least not less, and in addition I suffered his kicks. Who should be kicked by me — my children? How silly! Should I pull out the grass here by my face? That's stupid! Or kick the bamboo? It's also ridiculous, and useless. However uncomfortable I feel, no children of mine, no grass, no bamboo, nor anything else deserves my kick, and above all, that way our situation won't be improved."'

'When I got home I found him gulping sake, and he hit and kicked me more — on the head, back, legs, and buttocks too. I escaped and hid for the night in a shed by a rice field, where a peasant keeps a hoe, sickle, and plow. I left my children where he was raging. What absurd confusion!'

'Since then he drinks whenever even a minor pain or unpleasant feeling arises, and at such times he's violent with me, though he never used to be, even when he was angry. He loved to drink, but it always made him mellow. Now the sake conspires with his propensity to indulge in emotion, with the result that the material distress of our having no food is debased to the level of mental distress....'

Micha lifted the baby now satisfied by her milk and laid him against her shoulder to pat up air. She changed his diaper, tied him on her back, and put on a cotton-wadded coat that covered all of him but his head.

'It's getting so I have to think of my husband's unjust treatment whenever I think of my past and my married life — like the surety of coming on a garbage pit if I keep walking any path. The past was as dear and beautiful as autumn with its unlimited ceiling and visibility, the golden rice fields, the mountains like brocade, and from their depths the river starting thin as a thread and flowing forth in a leisurely curve. I can no longer see my past without crossing the scene of my husband's first violence....But to regret my injured past is the same as his self-pity that drives him to hit and kick to gain a momentary sweetness.

'Self-pity never brings good to other people near about who are waiting to bloom. Regardless of its various forms of expression, self-pity is laziness about finding a solution to a present difficulty and seeing only one's own

19

sadness enlarged as if through a magnifying glass; and more, shedding tears of sympathy at the sight of one's magnified poor self, and protecting and nursing it till one's whole body and mind are burnt up. He vents the stream of his self-pity in the form of violence. Mine I evaporate by regret. Others may dream up a future, or blame society by pointing out how it should be, or go to the extreme of worshiping God or Buddha. But if one is motivated by self-pity, nothing can fill the blank made by the laziness to overcome the real difficulty.

'So I mustn't spoil myself. I must swim through reality like a fish lightly and quietly rounding such obstacles as rocky grottoes, coral forests, and sea-weeds swayed by the tide.

'If I dismiss my self-pity, my mind and body can act without stagnation and I can live a life meaningful in its activity. Then my body will assume the most fitting form and my mind the most fitting character, slim and streamlined like a fish, so to speak, for action.

'Yes, I'll peddle clothes as my sister suggested — get stock from wholesale and walk the back country to earn our daily cash. That way I can secure our daily needs, taking Mokuzu on my back, Gyodo by the hand, going village to village, house to house.'

As the sun rose, the ice frozen fast to the earth began to melt, and from the seepage a seemingly warm steam began to rise.

3

The Quarrel between Fumi and Her Husband

"What? Are you telling me I should go out to see patients with a baby on my back? A doctor commonly takes a nurse, but I've never seen or heard of any who examined patients while tending his own child!"

"Please don't use that trick, I never suggested such a thing! What I'm asking is reasonable — that you love and take care of her as a father. You're trying to justify yourself by switching from a general consideration to a false specific!"

"You said neglecting the home and only working earns no respect or thanks from you — especially when you're tired."

"Certainly I did, but I meant...oh well, it's useless to talk with you. You're a cruel and cunning man, making much of yourself and seeing everything according to your own convenience. How it infuriates me! If only she would quickly grow up!"

Fumi, a slender housewife aged twenty-nine, drew near Ena and held her close. Ena, aged four, had soft, large eyes, now filmed with anxiety. Fumi pressed her brow to the back of her daughter's head. Ena sensed her mother's tears on her hair and bit her lip, about to cry. She stole a fearful look at her father, standing on the far side of the table.

He ran his hand frequently through his black hair glossy with pomade. It hung at his temples, disturbing his ears. He shot glances sharp as arrows and full of hate at his wife, who was lowering her head — at her hair done up in a snail shape and held with a tortoise shell clasp, at the many stray hairs on her white nape, at the clean lines of her ears, at her delicate shoulders. He turned his eyes to the south garden beyond the glass doors, to the southeast corner with its artificial pond and arranged rocks. He did not see things as meaningful objects; his eyes no more than unconsciously expressed his fury.

The effort to find words to hurl at each other was like scooping and hurling buckets of muddy water from a poor spring as each attempted to dispel his or her own gloom and stand with even the slightest advantage in the marital quarrel. After hurling a bucketful in the other's face, each had to await new issue from the ooze to make up another.

This time his bucket was the first to refill — "You say you wish she'd quickly grow up? If it's divorce you want, why not now, this very minute?"

"How dare you? You have absolutely no right! Only I am qualified to decide such a thing and when. You are the cause — you already had a wife and children when you married me. What woman can be calm treated like that? It's an insult, contempt for human life. And worse, I was waiting faithfully, keeping my purity until you could marry me." Fumi gazed at her husband with eyes red from weeping, burning with a flame of hate.

"Don't exaggerate! I never married her. That's why the children are called 'illegitimate.' They're worthy of pity. It's true — they should receive sympathy, and there's no reason they should be blamed. The person I married is obviously you, and therefore my lawful child is Ena."

"Either way it's the same — that nurse and those two are your woman and children. Well, aren't they? Whether or not you resort to legal terms, you can't decrease your evil deed and mean spirit. Furthermore, I never blamed them, because they too, as you just said, are victims of your bottomless cruelty. Your talent for meanness contorts my words as if I spoke ill of them, while you pose as a fair judge, pretending to protect them by accusing me. I'm blaming you alone, thoroughly, from one to ten, from beginning to end. You're hateful. You shift the problem to protect yourself, but that trick works only on your patients — ignorant peasants and merchants, who don't know your inside and are dazzled by your occupation and status, and by your pedantic, hypocritical posture."

"You don't understand anything. You think I'm far more cruel and wicked than I really am, because you're obsessed with the notion that your situation should be different. I understand your position. Therefore I never told you to go away. Nor did I consider taking Mitsu and going away myself. You lack perseverance. You haven't the composure and fortitude to do your best when you encounter unmovable realities. So you're convinced I'm responsible for everything as if I'm a kind of devil who can control human lives. It's a gross oversimplification, a complete misunderstanding, no more than a narrow, egoistic view.

"I assure you it's not my preference to have two families. I wish I could unite them in harmony. But there's what is called fate. We can't choose where to be born and raised. Many things we can't change by our effort, such as the people we happen to meet and associate with. If, like you, I blame such realities, I'll be forced to blame even my birth. You will too. And we'll end up with a grudge against the appearance of human beings and the environment in which they must live, on this earth, in this solar system.

"I've told you repeatedly that when I grew to a young man I attended medical school thanks to a scholarship left by Priest Kakkan of Tangenji. Your father, putting his trust in me, promised to build me a medical office when I graduated, and, following our parents' agreement, you and I became engaged. There was no dissatisfaction. The event was truly as joyous as seeing peach blossoms in spring.

"But at the same time, my tie with Mitsu was developing to the point where we were inseparable. Encouraging and helping each other, we found it as natural as the prospering of weeds under the flowering peach, and so it too was an inevitable, joyous event. Remember, in those days I was a self-supporting student who couldn't easily buy even medical books, despite Kakkan's aid and your father's promise. The fees for lectures and for the use of many expensive instruments, plus all the other costs — it added up. It was Mitsu who paid. Wasn't it natural that she and I became of one mind, though of different bodies? While time thus passed, your father began building the office and you were waiting with neck craned for my internship to finish, wishing it even a day earlier....

"At the time, then, not only I but all the people involved met to discuss the best way so that no one would cry for disappointment. The conclusion was that you would be my lawful wife and Mitsu and I would live in the practical sense in the office — an excellent plan as long as you, Mitsu, and I

22

in charge endeavored to make it work and followed the dictate that temperance is the best physic. In short, it would be peaceful if only we lived with some patience. Even you haven't found it disagreeable day after day. As a matter of fact, you rarely get hysterical like today.

"The point is, be patient, endure, and everything will be fine. In the main, you have too much luxury. Think of the Taiwanese or the Arabs. Even our own emperors until very recently kept one lawful wife and many concubines, at least four, commonly fifty to a hundred, sometimes even three hundred. Did they fight among themselves or make sarcastic remarks to their master? No, each served him with her unique character. Fortunately Mitsu has little desire and never speaks of removing you. You are the lawful wife. Her concern is always Ena, and your health too. If you are a little more calm, tolerant, and persevering, you'll find no problem. When you shut your eyes to your own faults, you blame me as if I'm the sole offender. This is our common fate — Mitsu's, yours, and mine. Welcome it, don't fight it, and surely it will embrace us as sweetly as we can dream. You understand?"

Seeing his wife's profile, Kenji was surprised. His mood had improved with his chance to speak whatever came to mind without her retort and interruption. He had not been looking at her. He had been only noting the ceiling, the floor, the few dishes on the table, the moons of his thumbnails, his yellow, knobby knuckles, the backs of his fists.

Her cheeks had no color, her eyes no life; even the expression of hate had left her face. She did not see the trees through the glass nor see Ena in her embrace. Her mind was in a state of abstraction. Her arms lacked strength and flexibility. One was against Ena's back, the other against her elbow, but they remained like the bones of a skeleton, there simply because they were there, and if Ena were to have moved and escaped, they no doubt would have kept their form. Fumi was stupefied and stiff. She was breathing, but was inhaling a minimum of oxygen and scarcely renewing it. Neither as cold as ice nor as lively as an animal, she was in a state closer to that of a plant. What was infant Ena thinking and doing all the while in the lap of a mother who was like the shed puparium of a cicada?

Ena feared her father and pitied her mother. To her their quarrel must have resembled a ringing in the ears, beyond her power to stop. She could do nothing but wish that peace and quiet would return like the calming of a storm. However, she felt she was a big element in their quarrel, if not its cause.

"Were there no Ena I'd have divorced you long ago!" her mother would say. And he: "What's wrong with having her? You're both living as you like!" "She'd be despised and shunned growing up fatherless! I'll just have to wait, at least till she's fourteen or fifteen and knows what she thinks and can open her way to live. If only she'd quickly grow up!" They fought like dog and monkey with no way to avoid hating and hurting each other. What if they separated? Then they could live in peace. But it was impossible because of her! Ena wanted to cry out, "Mother, don't mind about me — do as you like and live without having to fight!"

Kenji feigned a smile to comfort his daughter. Under his eyes she was buttoning and unbuttoning the navy blue cardigan her stiffened mother wore over a white blouse. She was looking at her mother's bosom and did not respond.

He glanced at his watch. It was well past nine. 'I'm late! Many patients must be already waiting, and Mitsu is wondering what's wrong and telling them I'll arrive very soon. I can no longer waste my time — I'll go. But can I leave Fumi in this state, and Ena, who doesn't understand a thing? What can I do? Well, time will solve it naturally. Quick, I must go!' Kenji went to the entrance and stepped into his black leather shoes.

As he walked away he thought with sympathy about his distraught wife, temporarily ceasing to feel and to think in her state of grief and helplessness, and about Ena with no one to turn to except such a mother. Still, he could not help fearing there was danger in leaving Ena with his wife. 'By some chance she could kill the girl. Sleeping in the same room I fear I too will be pierced in the throat by a pointed knife — that's precisely why I prefer to sleep at Mitsu's. But how about Ena? Well, it's her mother's responsibility. Things would be better if she actually committed such an outrage. She'd be reproached by everyone; no one would sympathize, and even if they did, it would be no more than sympathy. Crime must be feared, and punished as evident crime. From my position I have no reason to do my best to prevent such a tragedy from occurring in my absence.

'At any rate I'm obliged to go to my office. What a woman, she didn't prepare my breakfast, just made me feel unpleasant! She should imagine being in my place. I'm the one who must go out. Mitsu never makes me feel unpleasant; she knows my work would suffer for it. What a contrast! — my lawful wife neglects such uxorial duties as serving breakfast and seeing her husband off in a good mood. She only loves and pities her own feelings!'

Reminding himself of his wife's neglect that came of her preoccupation with hating and despising him, Kenji was minimizing, even trying to nullify, his own self-recognized weakness and cruelty, and so he kept thinking more or less the same thing all the way to his office, and no sight of anything along the route entered his eyes.

Ena slipped from her mother's arms and went to the sink. She pulled up a chair, mounted it, and turned the faucet to wet a towel. Her hands were too small and tender to wring it properly, which caused her some frustration.

She tried to make her mother take hold of it, but her mother's hands lay rigidly half closed on her lap. Ena pulled on the fingers and wedged the cold towel into a palm. Little by little the hands that had looked like clay images began to return to life, an effect like ice beginning to melt, though had she been ice, she would have spread over the chair and floor, leaving only wetness here and there. As it was, she began to emit a brightness as if a light had been turned on within. Her heart too regained its vitality, driving blood to her extremities and circulating well, and her vacant, unblinking eyes regained expression. The trace of tears alongside her nose shone with new tears reflecting the sunlight. 'Crying is better than not crying,' Ena decided. Were she a little older she might have thought, 'She is like a movie film stopping unexpectedly and restarting from the same place.' Ena must have more or less imagined so, for she could feel a rise of amusement, which joined with relief. She innocently smiled. Her mother responded with a smile like a flower beginning to open. Then mother and daughter embraced and laughed, and the room got back its life. Table, cupboard, doors, even the lawn and plants and rocks — each began to radiate its usual fresh vitality and individual character.

"I'm so sorry your parents' concerns are making it unpleasant for you — you could have spent a cheerful morning."

Fumi believed children in particular should not have to suffer and grieve on account of others — even a day, even a minute less was better — and she believed a mother's role was to protect her child from the external world whenever it brought unpleasantness and suffering. She regretted that she had just contradicted her belief, not only by making her child suffer but also by receiving help from one so innocent. Fumi recognized that she herself ought to become stronger, enough not to care a straw about a husband armed with lies and cruelties, enough to see him as a lower being to whom pity not hate was due.

"My father," said Ena as if to lecture her mother, though she was on her lap, "is a doctor outside the house and not a doctor inside the house. Maybe you aren't a mother outside, but you definitely are a mother inside!"

Fumi enjoyed this and was encouraged, yet being taught in this way by one so young made her smile wryly. She never tried to explain the quarrels to Ena, nor spoke ill to her of her father. 'It's something she must judge by herself according to her growth. Even if I tried to explain in a fair way, it would unavoidably be my view, no doubt exaggerated and self-justifying. A child shouldn't be taught either parent's private view, for neither can be objective. Certainly each wants a child's understanding and sympathy, but we must quickly destroy such urges, because a child's independent pure eyes and life must be respected.'

By way of an apology for the morning's gloom, Fumi wished to give Ena some joy. Fortunately the thin rain of the previous days had ceased, so the grass would no longer be wet. The sky was bright, and the cleanly washed trees were fresh and sensitively responding to the sunlight. From the garden they could see east to the far mountain range extending north. Steam was rising from its valleys. Mist buried the trees and villages at its foot. Only the faint blue but clear ridgeline stood in relief. Through such mist the massive and complex range appeared simple, two-dimensional, like the world of a picture. 'Things without depth are unsurpassably peaceful. Isn't peace the ideal we should seek and enjoy? I wonder why the wise have always sought depth and have venerated deep thinkers, whom common people can't fathom. Isn't it true that to deepen one's character means to make oneself queer, complicated, and full of contradictions whereby truth is mixed with lies, which mix with more lies in an endless process of lying? I can't understand such a world as Saint Shinran spoke of, "The worse you are, the more you shall be saved,"[1] or Zen Teacher Dogen, "There is enlightenment upon enlighten-ment and illusion upon illusion"[2]....

'Well, never mind! Today I shall take Ena to that mountain creek. The gregarious hydrangeas beside the modest and yet sharp, clean waterfall must be in bloom. The path in behind Tangenji too will be a pleasure for her. I'll buy her some treats on the way....'

"Yay, yay, a picnic!" Ena clasped her hands at her chest and raised her arms in a circle above her head like a ballet dancer. She was bright by nature.

"I'll make sandwiches and prepare the canteen, so you play by yourself for a while."

Into a little wisteria basket Ena put her favorite toys — a Western doll with various changes of clothes, a glass swan, a plush duck white as snow, and many tiny pots, pans, plates, cups, spoons, and forks. She could not determine whether to take her precious vermilion-lacquered music box, its top slightly arched to be soft to the touch. When opened, it revealed a mirror that reflected a little pile of imitation jewelry and it began to play Beethoven's "Bagatelle for Elise" at a rather quick tempo.

"Mother, may I take the music box?"

"Yes, but you'd better leave out the jewels; if they dropped in the grass, you'd never find them."

"But without them it will be empty!" Ena was disconcerted.

"You can put in something else, say, flowers, or pretty pebbles..."

"Oh..." Ena flew out from the kitchen to the lawn. The grass after the rain felt pleasant, almost ticklish, under her bare feet. She went to the pond. It was fed by a rill that came from behind the house, from a cliff there at the west. New water steadily flowed in, and the outflow was directed away from the premises. The pond was so clear as to reveal the pebbles on the bottom and the colorful carp swimming about, as well as their shadows. *Ayame* and *kakitsubata* irises grew out of the water by the edge, and a little school of medakas, preferring to swim in the narrow spaces between the stems, were highly visible. The ayame had finished their season. Some lingering blooms of the kakitsubata in white, yellow, and purple were reflected on the surface. There was no wind, but the flower reflections trembled with the movement of the carp and the incoming water.

Ena was not fond of the large flowers of the kakitsubata. 'Can't I find something small?' she mused. Grasping the rocks and shrubs, she pulled herself onto an artificially-made hillock. Its grassy sides were drier, and the sun-heated rocks were almost too hot to touch. Between some rocks she

found a clump of blue-eyed grass, its charming six-petaled flowers half open. This plant, native to North America, with tiny mauve flowers lasting but a day, was regarded as a weed when it appeared in the lawn. Yet its flower fit Ena's taste far more than any formal flower. She picked just one and put it in her music box.

☙

"Hold on," her mother cautioned. By now they had experienced many rides together on the bicycle, but Fumi never forgot to issue a warning each time. Her skirt was pressed tidily against the seat, and to Ena on the child's seat behind, her waistline appeared clean and emphatic, assuring her of her mother's reliability.

From their house, the highest on the mountainside, the dirt path gently sloped. The bicycle produced an occasional shrill from its brake, especially when they passed by a large irrigation pond and down a lane with clustered houses. Ena summoned melodies and words like a rummage of toys in a basket and let forth a stream of made-up songs like a silkworm spinning. Then, noticing children around her age playing in knots by a house or nearby, she would abruptly pipe down and stare in fascination, turning her head over her shoulder as the bicycle passed and not resuming to sing until well after.

She almost never played with the town or village children. Mostly she was with no one but her mother, except for rare times when cousins dropped in.

Where the road leveled were many more houses and many shops. Fumi turned onto the main street, a stretch of the Sasayama Highway. Since the Edo period this highway had been the main route from Kyoto in the east to Maizuru on the coast far in the west. Now it was replaced in importance by a new state road, though buses of the Tanba line and some trucks continued to pass through in decreased numbers. Most vehicles used the state road, which went directly toward Maizuru from an intersection in Kameoka, so the towns along the highway were declining after having prospered as post towns.

Fumi with Ena passed quickly by a lumber mill on the right and a large poultry farm on the left at the village outskirts and went straight on east. Ena was scared by the total impression of the mill — the circular saw, shining white and nearly as tall as the worker feeding in timber, the shadows of other workers within the dark interior, the terrible noise, and the smell of the black smoke from burning sawdust. From the poultry farm a stench constricted her chest and made her head feel heavy as lead.

The road then entered an expanse of rice fields. The green blades were being softly pressed and bent in waves, a sight that showed where the wind was, almost as if one could grasp it.

Up close the plants could be seen to be grown to a height of fifteen centimeters, their stems yet in field water. Ena could see the clouds and the bicycle with herself and her mother reflected. As the bicycle progressed, several thousand frogs quieted in turn, and in turn resumed their chorus. The clayey soil of the road was well packed, freeing the bicycle to run lightly. Fumi rode through the occasional puddles, providing Ena the joy of the sight and sound of the spray.

Near the end of the rice fields they came to a fine wooden bridge with tall pilings and elegant parapets, where the Sasayama Highway and the biggest river of the area, the Sakura, intersected in the shape of the Roman numeral ten. The road, built by human design to connect two points in the shortest way, conformed to a block style, whereas the river insisted on an italic style, meandering according to the mountains and fields.

Fumi stopped there and lifted Ena from the bicycle to take a slight rest. The river was turbid and quick, and apparently had shallow and deep places in its bed, for the water flowed in bundled lines that sometimes twisted like huge ropes. A white foam issued with a seemingly accusing sound. 'Does the river hesitate to speak up?' Fumi wondered. 'Did it once, but after all decide no word is better? Or is it already expressing as it is enough of its will and feeling?' Ena was picking up small stones and tossing them from the parapet. Soundlessly and instantly they were sucked into the roils, and the being of each one was thereby totally denied.

Back along the road in the direction from which they had come, the mountain with their house on it and the steeper back mountains overlapping in ranges were buried in mist and vapor. 'We don't realize we are living in such mist. At home we saw it heavy at the mountains to the east and north, but as we approach we can see each fold and tree, and our mountain, clear we thought, appears misty.

'Considering this kind of phenomenon — the relation between us and the nature we view — some preachers make up their ambiguous, sophistic, and acrobatic preaching. The priest of Tangenji isn't like that; he just paints the scenery, far better than other priests. I suppose priests generally refer too much to natural appearances to describe our mind and morals, taking advantage of the fact that nature charges no fee and claims no patents or royalties....'

North from the bridge they could see across the rice fields to Tangenji. The two-storied gate and the wall extending from it on either side were imposing. The wall, like that of a castle, was a high retaining wall of rocks topped by a white plaster wall with black-tiled coping.

Fumi thought about Priest Doyu and his wife, Micha, who dwelled in Tangenji. 'She has a hard time. The revenue from their field tenants declined toward the war's end and thereafter stopped because of the farmland reform. In essence he is too honest and too little tempted by money. He engages only in work that brings no return. More, he was rather losing money by advancing many reforms as head of the Buddhist Association and of the Agricultural Commission, while others have been using their posts to the utmost and seizing opportunities during the war confusion and postwar days to increase their land and income.

'I've heard that if she complains in the least and urges him to earn even a bit, he high-handedly scolds her and says she's a disgrace, the epitome of a merchant's daughter. Refusing to back down, she asks how they're to raise

29

their children. Already frenzied, he beats and kicks her and drinks till he gets sick. He was taught to live a noble life unsullied by mercenary concerns. But if he practices such a life, he falls into the awkward state of being unable to provide for his family, which weakens his credibility at home. Facing this plight, he is puzzled, worried, loses his bearings, and can't sustain his spirit to break through the antinomy. So he's violent with his wife and drinks to excess to gain momentary relief. Is it really true?

'Until recent years he could live nobly without troubling his family, for Tangenji had profitable lands. Now he can't without sacrificing them to poverty. So I guess the peace of the Tangenji family depends on how much he can give up his selfish desire to live a noble life. Or there's the solution which she is sort of practicing. Though unsuitable work for a priest's wife, peddling clothes is what she's doing, and if she continues, she can support her noble husband in addition to her children. And spontaneously she can feel toward him more love and respect. Oh well, who can be sure of what will happen; sure now is that their children would have died were it not for her peddling.

'Seeing it objectively, the discord of the Tangenji family, however she suffers and cries, is caused by material poverty. She blames, scorns, and insults him for his incapacity to live apart from a clean stream. He is ashamed and dishonored by her vitality to live in a muddy stream, and so he hates her. But is it that simple? In my observation, she doesn't think his nobility makes him entirely weak and useless; indeed she feels a measure of admiration, inspiration, even affection. He too can't insult and wholeheartedly deny her for her vitality to live as she soils her face to raise her children. He must partly feel astonishment, admiration, thanks, even love. Their problem can thus be solved as soon as they obtain some income. It's a kind of lover's quarrel. They blame each other because they love and respect each other. The only true problem is that they don't realize this matter of fact.

'As for me, my marital problem can't be solved by material means, because its cause is lack of love and affection. The Tangenji couple have a material problem owing to nobility and love. Their temple has a tradition of cultural leadership. My husband and I, laymen in the secular world, have no material problem, in fact we are rather well-to-do. Our problem is personal, cultural, spiritual.

'My husband, for instance, is a doctor, but he regards his practice as a means to rake in money like fallen leaves. To him it's only a business, nothing more. As proof look at that poor lone woman who died without his treatment. It's rumored he sells far more medicine than his patients need. He occupies himself with a whirl of requests from the rich, calling on them day

30

and night even for a minor cold, and so makes himself too busy to see anyone dying in poor circumstances.

'Above all, who can imagine the priest of Tangenji keeping two families? How ironic that my husband was given the chance to live a devil's life because of a scholarship left through the mercy of Priest Kakkan, father of the present priest of Tangenji....'

"Mother, what is it — are you thinking something again? Can't we go to the waterfall?" Ena looked up anxiously at her mother and pulled at the hem of her cardigan.

"Oh, I'm so sorry! Let's go. There must be many wild hydrangeas in bloom by the waterfall and along the creek."

4

Ena Pities Mokuzu

Instead of continuing on the Sasayama Highway, the bicycle took a crooked path, a route from the bridge to Tangenji. Down the middle and sides, where no wagon had made ruts, was a profusion of such weeds as clover, plantain, and galingale.

Ahead, houses straggled in twos and threes, most belonging to farmers who were once Tangenji field tenants. By the recent next-to-free land transfer they were now independent and fairly wealthy. They had been poor peasants, working the land and delivering sixty percent of the crops to the temple since the early Edo period. Now they were meeting such great fortune as their ancestors had never met, and it had come, in a word, by war. The land was theirs, with every crop they planted returning to them. So they said to one another without reserve that war was something to be thankful for – indeed it was the most interesting, intriguing, even amusing, thing in the world. More surprising yet was to hear these joyous words from the mouths of those who had lost one or more sons in the battle of the South Pacific islands.

Although ordered to deliver to the government their harvests of rice, wheat, and vegetables, they, being not so foolish, hid most of it under the floor and in mountain huts or dugouts to sell later at seven to ten times the controlled price to non-farming families or to black marketers. They could not supress their mirth over having been able to obtain a lavish kimono of silver

31

and gold brocade in exchange for only two kilos of rice, and a professor's one-month's salary for a bag of sweet potatoes. Some drank sake even in the day, and their ugly, slack faces looked yet uglier as they grinned and turned red.

Their forebears had been suppressed, hard-driven, and exploited for a thousand or possibly two thousand years. They now were fully partaking of the enjoyment they counted as rightfully owed their forebears and adding it to their own. Vengefully they denounced and scorned the former landowners and capitalists, and freely expressed what people who had belonged to the higher classes considered blasphemies. They laughed, for instance, at all who engaged in the fields of religion, philosophy, and art. But oddly, they were soon hunting after the paintings, ceramics, tea utensils, and kimonos still owned by the ruined elite. With these they decorated their alcoves regardless of system or harmony as they shed tears of joy.

Having neither the eye nor the composure to appreciate art, they based their judgment on the price; and above all they enjoyed the fact of ownership, which gave them the tyrannical right to do as they liked with their newly-got acquisitions.

"Look what's mine for just twenty kilos of rice! It's a sign of the times when a wife of gentle birth will undress and bed with me — and for so little! Eh? What's good about the picture? It's obvious, er, let's see, look at the 'subtle and profound,' er...'equilibrium of left and right'...well, no matter — but guess where it comes from. Handed through generations of a former peer family of Kyoto, and one day a professor gets hold of it, and then his wife, well, like I said. So now it's mine! I've got absolute freedom to drink, sleep, flirt, or fart before it, and if anyone starts quibbling about hard ideas like appreciation or value, I'll take and drop it in the toilet, he he he!"

Fumi with Ena passed a hedge in front of some farmhouses, approached the gate of Tangenji, and took a side path leading to the mountain behind the temple. There was a forest of chestnuts. The canopy of young leaves looked yellowish green filtering the sunlight.

The path went along the contours of the mountain foot toward the inner mountains. Beyond the chestnut forest was untended by human hand and was thickly wooded with such evergreens as camellia, blue oak, and camphor, which darkened the narrow path. It also steepened, so Fumi got off and pushed the bicycle.

"Mother, I smell something strange!"

"So do I. What could it be?...gold-banded lily would be sweeter....Oh, it must be pesticide!"

As they rounded another bend the view partially opened to terraced fields and gardens with some clustered farmhouses, the last of the village. From that point the path entered deep mountains along a fairly rapid stream. A machine had been making such a loud noise that it trampled the joy and spirit of conversing, but it ceased. From behind the farmhouses a white smoke began to drift toward the path, and out of it emerged two young men in straw hats. Each had a towel tied over his nose and mouth, and carried on his back a motor and in his hand a hose for spraying.

"What are you spraying for?" Fumi stopped to ask. Surprised to meet a refined lady so suddenly in such a place, they took off their towels and offered their greetings. The layers of powder on their towels scattered. It was all over their hats and eyebrows.

"We're spraying DDT. We belong to the youth association of this village and were asked by Public Health," answered the shorter one, whose soft, round face looked smiley. Actually he was serious; it was just that his eyes and eyebrows slanted down, and together with the dimples in his lower cheeks they made him seem to smile. 'What is his face like when he angers?' Fumi wondered, but asked,

"Won't it affect your health to spray so much with only a towel for protection?" The taller one replied as he cleaned the powder from his glasses with the inside of his shirt,

"Well, ma'am, the officer from the health center said it couldn't be good for us either. But we're built strong, so we don't mind and just keep spraying. He said to spray everywhere lavishly, especially around the sink, toilet, well, and drains. I don't know, but it's said dysentery or typhoid fever broke out in town, so the U.S. Occupation forces ordered the health center to spray DDT...."

"Yes, yes, he said it's not sure if it's harmful to us, but we know all the frogs and fish in the area are immediately dying," echoed the one with the seeming smile. The tall, spectacled one was known by his fellows to grow talkative whenever he met a woman he considered a beauty. His face was shapely; but he never read any books, which was too bad, for his eyes looked sleepy and not so unlike an old goat's.

"The health officer was muttering, 'Orders are orders if they come from Occupation.' Oh, yeah, like what recently happened to him." He indicated his companion with his chin and continued, "It turned into a big deal. He was bit on the butt by a dog — just teeth marks, you know, and it healed in a week without care. But Dr. Okada — you must know him — he reported it to Health and they contacted Occupation." The young men had no idea they were speaking with the very wife of the doctor, which was not unreasonable as Fumi never assisted his work.

33

"Three officials came to our village — someone from the health center in town, and a U.S. Army surgeon, and an interpreter. The surgeon was even taller than me and stood straight as a pole. Megu here surely couldn't have seen anything of him above his shaved trace of a heavy beard under his chin to his Adam's apple, and maybe a couple of razor nicks."

"Aw, Sen, you're exaggerating. His eyes were blue and seemed to spin. He had this habit of wetting his lip before speaking." Megu was truly smiling.

"What then?" Fumi was irritated but was listening kindly.

"Oh, the American surgeon insisted the dog who bit Megu must have rabies. At that, the health officer said, 'It can't be so. There's no case of hydrophobia in all of Japan. Even if the virus came in with the Occupation forces it couldn't possibly spread to this remote countryside.' They argued on the road at length through the interpreter, and by then Megu's ma and pa and me and everyone else from the village were gathered about as if to enjoy a monkey show or something. Nothing was being settled, so Megu's pa, who's apt to stutter, especially with strangers, screwed up his nerve to speak to the surgeon through the interpreter, and he says, 'My b-boy was b-bit on the b-b-butt, b-but it's nothing, right, Son? See? He's f-full of life. Hey, drop your pants and show 'em those teeth marks.' Megu was put in a fix. Was he really to expose before everyone's eyes his fat white butt, soft like a woman's? Megu, I truly sympathized."

Megu reddened and only kept smiling and looking aside.

Ena on the bicycle directed at him her sharp, candid stare.

"The surgeon was taken aback, but he did glance at the teeth marks, but only because they were there before his eyes. He must have been thinking, 'There's no way to know if it's rabies.' Then he gave Megu's butt a slap, which made everyone laugh, and straightened his face and spoke a lot through the interpreter — 'The present condition of the victim doesn't guarantee he hasn't hydrophobia. It has a long incubation period, from three weeks to over three months.'

"Then he detailed the symptoms — 'It starts with a local ache and the brain gets a bit queer, that is, the patient acts odd and finds it hard to breathe and drink, though he's thirsty. In the mid stage his throat convulses at the sight of water, and he drools and suffers convulsions, and hallucinates and talks in delirium. At last he's totally paralyzed and becomes a perfect lunatic. The death rate is one hundred percent.'

"Megu when he heard all this shouted, 'Uwaah!' and ran and jumped on a black bull and pounded it like riding a horse. The bull was surprised and bolted away. Megu with his body flying gripped the horns and cried something incomprehensible to drive the bull on even more. Unlike a horse a bull runs in circles, and Megu soon was dumped off and fell senseless onto the old mud of a field not yet planted.

"Everyone was astonished and only kept watching. But when we realized we'd better do something, he abruptly stood and ran without distinguishing the fields from the footways, and he ran and rolled and ran to the brook and scrambled up one of the sawtooth oaks planted there as a windbreak. He went right to the top — thin as the arm of your girl."

"It bent like a bow, and just when we were fearing he'd fall, he did, headfirst into a new-planted field! Well, the water was at eighteen centimeters. There wouldn't be a single stone, and the mud is at least thirty centimeters deep. You can't get hurt — it's like falling into marshmallow. The difference is, if Megu fell into marshmallow he'd savor it. As it was, he could only bite a couple of mud snails in addition to getting jet black with mud."

"Ha ha ha!" The person laughing was Megu, the very one presented as a fool. Not only Fumi but also the infant Ena felt uneasy, 'He couldn't be counted among the wise, and perhaps he's still touched by lunacy.'

"And what about the hydrophobia? I expect you also must be busy with your spraying. Why don't you tell just the conclusion." Impatient, Fumi addressed the garrulous Sen.

"Oh, well, the health officer turned pale and said to the surgeon, 'As you said — it's hydrophobia. What can we do?' The surgeon responded rather jokingly, 'It isn't symptomatic of hydrophobia. The boy was bitten just yesterday. Not enough time has passed for incubation. What he's showing is symptoms of a phobia against hydrophobia.' 'Oh, no, he's suffering from hydrophobia,' the officer insisted, though he'd been denying the presence of the virus in Japan. You see, their views became exactly reversed. At a loss, the surgeon spoke in perfectly intelligible Japanese, 'The Japanese are impossible to understand!' and he shrugged and shook his head as if to set it fast in his mechanical body. Then he said, 'Hunt up every dog, wild or domestic, and burn 'em all,' and he got into the jeep.

"At that moment Dr. Okada arrived, being very much delayed, and after hearing everything from the health officer, he said nothing. Meanwhile, Megu's pa was washing Megu and taking him into the house to be put to bed, and he now hesitatingly came out and consulted with Dr. Okada, 'W-what'll happen to my son?' Dr. Okada only said, 'Each man has his fate,' and he left without even looking at Megu.

"Fortunately Megu soon recovered, and as you see, he's living his normal life as much as he can hope. So, to conclude, nothing is made clear, and as for this DDT, no one knows if it's more baneful to us than good for killing mosquitoes, flies, dysentery and typhoid germs, and worse, no one's taking any responsibility. The fact is, Occupation orders Health, and Health orders our youth association. And that's it, ma'am."

Fumi resumed pushing the bicycle. They ascended alongside the torrent. Again the motor noise came from below. Fumi stopped where it was replaced by the roar of the waterfall and the sound of splashing. The water was breaking against the rocks and hastening on downward.

"From here you can walk," she said and lifted Ena from the bicycle. The cedars growing straight up here and there had reddish bark and were as wide around as a couple of stretches of a person's arms. Beneath them maples with fresh green leaves and cherries past flowering spread their branches in the shape of cast nets. Their roots grew down in insecure locations as if these smaller trees preferred such places. Both sides of the valley were covered with seemingly endless flowering hydrangeas. The slanting sunlight where it came through the cedars scattered across the maple leaves, causing the tiny dewdrops on each to sparkle and seem to dance. Some shafts reached the hydrangeas and illuminated a rising vapor. The lit flower clusters looked slightly blanched among those retaining their deeper blue, a blue of concentrated indigo, quiet, dignified, and yet vivid with boundless inner vitality.

Sighting the gregarious hydrangeas, Fumi was reminded of the profound, infinitely extending space between stars on a clear night. The pure power issuing from their stillness was composing an absolute world. She could not help longing, 'I too wish someday to be received as one of these hydrangea clusters in this valley and live in its eternal, much richer inner world.'

She pulled Ena by the hand, and they climbed along the wet slippery rocks and wound their way through the hydrangeas up to a height level with the brink of the waterfall. There Fumi's awe, with fear now added, came to a peak, as if she too would be swept into the depths of the basin.

Seen through the maples and pines clinging to the cliff, the falling water looked like a white belt ever running with furious speed. The basin was too dark and obscured by spray to be seen, but living there, it was reputed, were giant salamanders, officially designated a national treasure of nature.

The banks that contained the flow after it paused at the basin were dead silent in the blue of the hydrangeas, visible among the maples, cherries, and tall cedars they had seen on the way up.

Though moving, how quiet was the water at the brink the moment before it dropped. The brink was the only place where the huge volume of lake water could be released, that is, all water entering the lake, regardless of distance, would inevitably be drawn to the fall and dashed into the basin.

The far shore also burgeoned with hydrangeas, and rose to become a mountain of pine forest. Only the nearer hydrangeas were visible, for a mist was rising and drifting above the lake. Their flowers, fully exposed to the brilliant sun, showed gradations of color from fresh indigo nearby to whitish blue and almost only white shadows in the distance. No water surface, no pine forest, and even no sky could be seen beyond the center of the lake, from where the mist was rising the most. But the sky above was a thrusting clear blue. A pair of kites circled, riding an air current.

The shore where Fumi and Ena stood was also buried with hydrangeas. As they climbed onward, pines took over, and at that point the ridgeline was not far. 'There must be two kinds of reaction to encountering natural beauty far from human habitation. Some people are frankly impressed and think it's their birthplace, and they long to be someday united with it. Others are fearful before its bottomless mystery or spirit and try to escape, or they provoke it or fight against it. To which group does Ena belong?' Fumi looked at Ena.

"Mother, where can we have our picnic?"

Fumi laughed aloud as she thought, 'What a healthy, realistic child!'

"Wait a little more. We'll have it up ahead. The pine needles are dry and will make a nice place to sit."

Nature either vast or microscopic was beyond Ena's concern. She was intently observing a little crab moving at the moist base of some hydrangea stalks. Its legs and fine-grown but unequal claws were dark orange, its back, dark brown. It moved faster than she expected, and she nudged it with her foot to make it return to where it had been. She wanted to pick it up but was afraid of its claws.

As Fumi stooped to pick it up for her, there arose a commotion. Startled, Fumi stood and turned, but could see nothing strange. Yet surely the hydrangea flowers were moving as if by the approach of something. However big and fierce, it could conceal itself, for the hydrangeas were over human height.

Fumi drew Ena close. Ena clung to her mother, alarmed at the sight of her face — the color had ebbed and her eyes were fixed grimly on the locus of the noise. The large flower clusters swayed with a steadily approaching movement. 'Is it a wild boar?...or a bear? The disturbance is too big for a fox or a raccoon dog. A rock snake? — the villagers were saying one thick as a person's neck lives up here. I also heard a woodcutter was attacked by a bear. Or is it an atrocious criminal fleeing society, living in the mountains? There are numerous escaped convicts. What a fool I was to come this far alone with a little girl! We have no protection! There's that American soldier who

37

escaped from an Army jail and killed an innocent man, assaulted the wife and child, and raped even a seven-year-old girl....Yes — I must dive with Ena into the lake! We can cleanly die as we're sucked into the basin — far better than being attacked by a beast or an evildoer filthier than a beast. Come out, whatever you are — we're prepared for the worst!'

Filtering the hydrangeas, the mist over the lake looked whitish blue, and here and there, because of the sunlight it contained, it was tinted even purple or red. The movement in the hydrangeas slowly neared, but to those waiting with the strain of fear and resignation it seemed horribly slow.

What appeared from the bushes immediately eased their minds. Rather ludicrous, it was a boy, likely seven or eight years old, carrying on his back another, who looked no more than three or four. He was straddling the slope to keep from slipping. His face was congested by the tug of his shirt against his throat, his teeth were clenched. In the hand turned back to support his burden he gripped a paper bag.

"Oh, my! What are you doing up here?" Fumi asked. The boy, who had been fixing his eyes on the earth, looked up but showed no surprise at seeing so suddenly a woman and a girl. He had well-defined features.

"I've got to hurry — it's an emergency! My brother Mokuzu seems like he'll die. Lady, get out of the way, quick, please, I can't get through."

"Wait, I'll help. You're too little to carry him all the way down — you're sure to slip and fall. Let me see, what's the matter? Oh, what a fever!" Fumi took Mokuzu into her arms. He faintly opened lifeless eyes but shut them again, and, with no strength to raise his head, sank onto her bosom. His breath was smelly. His shorts were wet at the seat. When she held him more securely, a bit of orange diarrhea was squeezed out at the cuff.

Ena tried to see the profile of the boy who rested his head lifeless on her mother's bosom, breathing hard. His face was pale, his consciousness seemed dim.

"What a pity!" she said, with large tears forming in her large eyes. She took from her breast pocket a handkerchief with a floral design and wiped his thigh.

"Mother, please help him somehow. Will he be all right?"

"We've got to get him down. We'll wet a towel for his head. You can carry our basket."

The brother received the picnic basket and followed behind. As he descended he thought, 'How remorseful — I could've gone down much faster! She's so cautious — what an unwelcome favor!' And further, 'I must quickly tell Ma! It'll be okay if I can get him to her. Then he'll be at peace whether he lives or dies.'

Fumi picked her way down the narrow rocky path, turning sideways to keep her balance. She was frantic. Ena too was frantic trying to keep up. She used her hands and feet and crawled down like an animal. Even so, she slipped and scraped her elbow. But her concern was only the dimly conscious boy. 'Please, Buddha, save his life! Bear up, Mother! Please help him! Is he already dying?'

The brother was anxious. 'What an awkward case, caught by a strange, gracious lady at this important time! I'm sure Mokuzu was better off with me. I can't see why she and her appendix are dawdling. Why don't they run? Here's an easy path.

'The steep slope from the peak is so difficult, the soil slides, stones roll, roots interfere, and the hydrangeas block the view ahead. Here I can dash down, and could even if I had Mokuzu on my back. Look at her bottom sticking out, and her stiff leg reaching for a footing with great hesitation! Why doesn't she run? So what if she rolls? I'd not let a speck of dust get on Mokuzu even if I happened to roll. I can race down without fear. If need be, what's wrong with dragging him even if he's groaning with a high fever? Most important for him now is to return even a second earlier to Ma's bosom. It must be his wish to die there. It's much too pitiful to let him die on the way!' The words to express his frustration and resentment came only as far as his throat. What he actually said was, "Lady, thanks, I'll carry him now!" But neither Fumi nor Ena heard.

At last Fumi with Mokuzu in her arms arrived at the relatively level spot where she had left the bicycle. She laid him on the grass and ordered his brother to take the towel from the basket and go to the stream to wet it. Ena looked into the face of the sick boy being called Mokuzu and tried calling him, "Mokuzu, Mokuzu!" He slightly opened his eyes but shut them as soon as he vaguely saw mere air. He turned his face, half buried it in the grass, and seemed to smile, but it was the twitch of a facial muscle. Ena pulled out a stem of a weed played with by children to catch crabs; the hairy caterpillar-like ear was brushing his cheek. He was breathing fast, then holding his breath and releasing it with a long groan.

Fumi wiped his face with the wringing-wet towel and put it on his brow. "Which house are you from?" she asked his brother.

"Tangenji."

"Oh, then you must be Master Gyodo. Please run home and get your father."

"Dad? He went off early to Kyoto, to a memorial service at a subtemple in the head temple, Nanzenji."

"Then get your mother."

39

"Ma's in bed. She's not doing well after childbirth. So I came up to get hydrangea flowers — they're in this bag."

"What will you do with them?"

"Make a decoction. It's an antipyretic. She asked me to get them. I was just going when Mokuzu begged to come. He refused my advice to stay home. Ma has a high fever and a severe headache. When she tries to move, the bleeding starts again. The newborn girl cries and cries. Ma has so many troubles her head is full of pain and worry. So I took him."

"Was he all right when you left home?"

"Considerably better than now. He had diarrhea but tottered along as best he could. When we reached the waterfall I picked the flowers and tried to return, but he badgered me to take him to the top. Sure, it commands a fine view and is our private place to spend hours playing. We can see everything at a glance — the whole lake, all the fields, the highway with buses passing, the far mountains too. Mokuzu loves to count how many buses and trucks go left and right. The ones going left are his, the ones going right are mine. Whoever gets the most wins.

"Today too we were playing that game, but I urged him to go home quick because of Ma. He didn't rise, and when I checked I saw his red face was turning pale and his eyes were vacant, but looking toward the highway. I said let's go. He just sat there absent-minded. I thought something was greatly wrong — his brow was fiery, though oddly he was pale, and then all at once his body convulsed and he fell onto the pine needles. I thought he was dead because he didn't move. I shook him and held him up and tried like mad to squeeze a bunch of hydrangea flowers. I couldn't extract any juice, so I madly chewed them and put them in his mouth.

"He opened his eyes and said he wanted Ma. Then he fell asleep again. I carried him wildly by the shortest cut. I was upset but kept thinking, 'I won't let you die till you're with Ma!' Then we met you. So that's why I must hurry home with him even a second earlier and not keep him in this sort of place!"

Fumi was amazed by Gyodo's outpouring, by its order and varied vocabulary for his age. What amazed her more was his judgment and cool-headed but strong brotherly love. From the moment he met his brother's danger, his concern was to let him die in peace and not so much to keep him alive, and there was no fear or hesitancy regarding death. Fumi found herself asking,

"How old are you? Are you attending elementary school?"

"I'm six. I begin school next year, I was told."

'Imagine! Only two years older than Ena and yet possessing such independence and courage to do his best in his given situation! Is he a kind of prodigy? Or the product of the particular and to me unfathomable circumstances of Tangenji? Or is it a peculiarity of children, for whom nature is intensely pure, and thus they can confront things without letting various misty and irrelevant thoughts and distresses intervene? This boy strikes me as having nerves and bones made of steel.

'And look at Ena. This sick boy is for her an utter stranger, but she goes to and from the creek with her handkerchief and is cleaning his thighs without being asked. Isn't she frightened and revolted by the foamy and obviously blood-mixed, nauseating feces?

'Instead of shunning him in fear of contagion, she's tending him with devotion and tears, saying, "Poor Mokuzu, you mustn't die." How and where did she get such kindness? Is it too a gift of purity peculiar to children?' Fumi examined her own weakness as she concerned herself with Mokuzu, kneeling at his side. 'Children are as pure and intense as the hydrangeas we just saw. They're spirit itself...yes, spirit isn't an abstraction at all....

'But what illness is attacking him? Though a doctor's wife, I've nothing to do with medical work and I lack knowledge of that sort. Those two villagers were told of an outbreak of dysentery or typhoid fever and are going about spraying DDT. They don't know its effect, they even suspect it's more harmful than good. Dysentery? Sudden fever — this child has a high fever and had a convulsion...there's blood, he's but dimly conscious...it could be children's dysentery — he may really die! I'm required by law to report it to the health center. I have no choice but to enlist the aid of a doctor, my brutal, hateful husband!'

Mokuzu's face observed by Ena that day must have left an impression as if from a carved seal on every cell of her body, so to speak. It was seemingly floating, suffering but visited by occasional peace, pale but not ugly. While functioning with his heart and pulse, he was entrusting his body and mind to his surroundings. His face looked pitiful but lovely, weak but beautiful. She had received from it the strongest impression in all her tender years. Wherever she was and whatever she thought or did, she would recall it as a primary image throughout her days. By the sight of its expression, its state, the core of her spiritual life was established and would not be invaded or dimmed by any knowledge she later learned, such as that the capital of Japan is Tokyo or the center of the solar system is the sun.

That day she gave her best possession, a vermilion music box, to Mokuzu. With its lid open, there was to be found a single flower of blue-eyed grass picked by her at the pondside that morning.

5

Zen Master Tengai and His Attendant

Zen Master Tengai and his attendant, Bokuon, left at dawn from Shoshinji, a monastery temple deep in the mountains of Gifu Prefecture. They arrived at Kyoto Station by the Tokaido line, made their way through the crowded central hall to the west platform for the Sanin line, and boarded an antiquated train.

It being already past noon, few passengers were on the platform or waiting in the coaches of this local line. In the morning and evening here too would be crowded with commuters who worked in the city. Now there was no one for whom an appointed time was an important element, but only the self-employed or those with private matters to tend to, and each had the face, dress, and language that made their mode of life easy to discern.

The Zen master and his attendant took facing window seats and sat sternly just as in meditation hours, spines parallel to and at a slight distance from the wooden seat backs shining with layers of varnish.

Their relationship was obviously one of master and disciple. Both had shaven heads, but the master's was tan and naturally almost bald, while the disciple's was an oily blue. They wore black robes, and on the chest a *rakusu*, a rectangular cloth held at the upper corners by a band that went around the neck, a simplification of the *kasaya*, or surplice. The master's robe was of pure silk, and the weave of his rakusu had a fine arabesque of honeysuckle vine, noticeable only to the observant eye and further obscure because the purple had faded. A ring of real ivory joined the rectangle to its band on one side, to symbolize the perfect unity of wisdom and compassion. The disciple wore a rough cotton robe poorly dyed and a slightly smaller black rayon rakusu, its ring too a poor imitation.

The master had white tabi socks with white-thonged, leather-soled sandals, the disciple only rice-straw sandals, and his feet looked red and rough. Moreover, the master was short but splendidly stout, with a coercive mien, beyond comparison with the lanky bean sprout who was his disciple. And he occupied and pressed down more space as his domain.

With a thump to the passengers' backs the train started up.

"Ladies and gentlemen, we are limited to a shuttle between Kyoto and Kameoka owing to flood conditions between Kameoka and Sonobe. Passengers caring to proceed to points beyond must detrain at Kameoka and await resumption of regular service. Thank you." Although the announcement was made without emotion, some passengers raised a stir.

"Master, we are lucky we plan to get off at Kameoka anyway."

"Well then?" Zen Master Tengai fixed his eyes on Bokuon's to extract his further notion.

"Well...I have nothing to say other than we are lucky." Not expecting pursuit, Bokuon was thrown into a confusion that exposed his weakness.

"How can you tell what's lucky and what's not, especially concerning travel to request a certain favor? There's more opportunity to make a good impression and prove yourself sincere when the journey is hard."

Bokuon felt ashamed as if he had received a slap. "Yes," he assented simply. In half his mind he encouraged himself by recalling that adversity makes a man wise — one of the master's frequent sayings. In the other half he thought, 'Tut! It's impossible to converse with him even about a simple daily fact!'

Bokuon had been working under the order for mobilization of students in a Yokohama munitions factory making airplane parts. The factory was burned up in an air raid just before the war's end, and his parents, living nearby, succumbed in the fire. Ignorant of how to obtain food, and thinking that his first concern was to arrange a memorial service for his parents, Bokuon began to wander. At last he found his way to Shoshinji in Gifu, two years ago. Many youths were in similar straits, as were many young war veterans returned from the lands formerly under Japanese domination, and altogether as many as four hundred found their way to Shoshinji.

Even as he received them as his disciples, Zen Master Tengai well knew they were coming not to train to become priests but to supplicate aid from the Zen sect, which in expression of its beneficent aspect, provided welfare and relief work to society. The master hence turned his mind first to saving these arrivals from starvation while encouraging them to pursue whatever path they liked.

It was said that since old times Shoshinji maintained a fief as wide as 150 square kilometers, though most of it was mountain and forest. Zen Master Tengai therefore began to put his Zen trainees — vagabonds, to be exact — to the work of bringing timber from the mountains to be sold for building materials, and he directed them to make charcoal from the assorted deciduous oaks and cart it to town to peddle. In addition he taught them how to implant the spore of shiitake into oak logs to produce marketable mushrooms.

As he expected, his several enterprises went well, considering the amount of mountain and forest and the steady supply of laborers whose only wish was to be fed. More, all income went to the temple as pure profit because the master did not countenance paying anyone he received as a Zen trainee. Each was provided very simple food, and simple tools for mountain work — just a hatchet and a saw. And because of his abundant free labor, he could sell the timber, charcoal, and mushrooms at a price lower than that of his competitors, and sell a great quantity, for demand was well above supply during the postwar reconstruction years.

Day after day the coming and going of these laborer-trainees continued. After all most went away because even though their daily food was secured, the mountain work was too hard. Or there were those who could bear the work and actually did not dislike it, but they too left because they were dissatisfied with the minimum recompense and were occupied with worry over their future or longing for their families.

Yet some youths knew the leniency of one rule of the sect to which Shoshinji belonged. It was that whoever stayed three years in the monastery after finishing high school under the old education system could be certified as a priest, with the right to dwell in and preside over a local temple; and six years was required of whoever had not finished high school. Naturally there were those who, to gain a temple, would put in the time with great patience, and with no regard for the profound philosophy and noble research of the spiritual world or the great compassion or faith essential to religious practice.

Faced with this situation, Zen Master Tengai decided he would first secure food for whoever dropped in, second, use them as laborers for as long as they stayed, and third, not mind when they left — though his real concern was nothing other than to raise men of true Zen ability.

Thus it was that during the first year after the war and continuing for several years, Shoshinji always had some hundred trainees who generated cash and savings for the monastery.

The peak finally came around when Bokuon straggled in, and as the days, weeks, and months passed, the number dwindled until there were finally less than thirty such persons.

The master enjoyed the ebbing tide. 'It's a sign of world revival,' he thought. 'At last only men wishing to train will come and stay. How fortunate that the temple was left a considerable profit by those transients. From now on I can devote myself for the first time to tempering Zen talent to benefit the true reconstruction and development of Japan.

'After all, I am a priest and not a mushroom farmer or a merchant to make a profit. If once I wrestle with such agricultural work or related business, I can easily manage far better than any professional in the field; indeed I have proved it. But such work is suited only to worldlings.

44

'Frankly, who paid the highest income tax on timber, charcoal, and mushrooms? I did. The peasants and merchants petitioned the prefectural office and the tax office because I earned so much and paid so high a tax. "Shoshinji is making an unjust profit by using free labor. It's depressing the competitive power of us who are engaging in the same business. Furthermore, our tax shouldn't be aligned with theirs, but theirs with ours by making them report higher production costs." Their protest puzzled me. They were saying there's no virtue in my earning well, and no virtue in my paying so much tax. In effect they wanted to say a temple isn't a place to do business. It's a fair criticism. Worldly matters should be left to worldly men.'

Bokuon had entered Shoshinji at age twenty-three and already spent two years under the master's direction. Even so, he was not fixing his passion on Zen training. He also had no particular affection for the air of Shoshinji as a professional Zen training hall, or for his master's character, or for the communal life. As a lone orphan he felt no obligation to care about others. During his high school years he had not found any favorite study; and, being required to spend more time in the munitions factory than in school, he did not study much. He had never read any books on religion. He was in Shoshinji simply because he had nothing else to do, and was an attendant to the master because the master was using him in that way.

When during the first interview he related that he had lost his parents, the master had congratulated him instead of showing sympathy: "What a happy state you attained! For over two thousand years Buddhist priests have experienced great difficulty in severing the ties of blood. Examples abound of failures who spent the talent they were blessed with on their narrow, animal love. You were given the same state as that of Sakyamuni Buddha when with determination he left his father's castle and gave up all egoistic affairs to enter the priesthood. Your state is the same as that of a religious genius. From now on, grind yourself into flour and devote yourself to ascetic practice."

Truly the Zen master was enjoying the appearance of this summer moth who had flown into the fire; such a youth with no private encumbrances heightened his will to train him to be an excellent Zen priest. 'Another good condition to make a Zennist of him is that he has no various bits of half-knowledge, which means he hasn't a flourishing critical attitude. A Zennist must not toy with ideas but must be able to practice his pure actions without losing a moment. To be a Zennist, a disciple, such as I was, must efface himself and faithfully obey his master, and engage in his master's training-by-fire whatever form it takes. To train is to bury oneself into the personality of the master, absorb everything of him, and then develop one's own character yet better than the master's.'

When the train stopped at Nijo Station, three men and one manlike woman rudely boarded together. They wore rubber boots and had a towel about their necks, and each carried several empty hempen rice sacks. They had muscular shoulders, weather-burned faces, and irregular teeth oddly shining white. The woman was indistinguishable from the men with her untidy hair, clothes, gestures, and speech. They took seats directly across the aisle from the Zen master and his disciple.

"I worry the sack I bought and left in someone's custody could've washed away," a loud voice reverberated. The woman as soon as she sat down unwrapped a cloth on her knees and began to eat. Rice ball in hand she asked, "So where's it at?"

"At a house by the river, ya know, at Kasugabe. Fellow's name's Saiki —"

"Ahh, that spot is lower 'n the river — it may well be gone."

"Not necessarily. Saiki's kind in his way, though he only blasts a fowling piece all year round. He must've thrown it on the roof," opined the tallest man, whose face had no vigor of health.

"I'm impressed by yer magnanimity, Boss — didn't ya fear he'd open it and eat up the rice?" the smallest man inquired, taking out a cigarette and offering the pack around.

"Nah! Anyone a done that, he'd be half killed. I bet ya wanted him to eat it, right, Boss? That way ya can take twice over as penalty," the woman said and laughed with open mouth, exposing what she was eating.

"Don't be silly! I ain't no bonze. I never used such subtle tricks. Since old times it's a known fact they're the worst plotters, the second worst are pols, the third, cops."

"Careful, Boss — there's them across the way!"

"Eh? Oh! — excuse me! What I was saying is, ya know, a so-called generalization." The boss, pretending to notice them for the first time, tossed his words across the aisle to the two priests facing each other with erect posture.

Zen Master Tengai kept looking straight ahead. Bokuon looked over with a timorous smile.

"Hey, I don't care what kinda classy baldhead ya are. Why don't ya say something instead of acting snobbish?"

The master quietly turned his head and nailed his lynx eyes on the speaker.

The boss was built large. His eyes were a turbid red, and from the ridge of his coarse nose to his cheek ran a white scar, as if from a sword cut. Evidently he was short-tempered; a sensitive tic showed at his cheekbones, and his eyes had the intensity of a beast's.

46

The master with countenance unchanged gazed into his eyes. The man's fists trembled. The companion who had offered cigarettes crushed his out with a quick motion, shifted to the window, drew in his knees, and stared edgily about. Across from him the woman freely spoke — to restrain or to incite the boss was undeterminable.

"What's the profit dealing with them? Well, we have thirty minutes before Kameoka, time enough to enjoy it if ya like!"

Next to her the tall man with the pallid but somewhat handsome face continued to savor his cigarette with a faint smile. 'Fighting with bonzes ain't no fun,' he thought. 'Gangs or sleuths are more interesting.'

The boss, locked into the Zen master's gaze, had his own, personally formed concept. 'A bonze refused me my wife's funeral. I earnestly asked a nearby temple, "Please do a normal service free of charge. I got no faith or money, but without a service people will talk, plus she won't forgive me neither." He told me, "Wait a moment," and then disappeared. After making me wait nearly two hours he reappeared and said, "Please approach another temple. Tomorrow he must travel far on official business." I was too dumbstruck to speak — indeed I wanted to thunder something but couldn't decide what. At last I decided on "Why'd ya make me wait so long to tell me that?" and "What temple do ya recommend?" And as I was deciding which to say first, he said, "It's closing time." I begged his pardon like a fool. He put his hand on my shoulder so gentle I remembered her touch, and he pressed me along the path, and as soon as he got me out the gate he slammed the heavy zelkova doors. I stood there like an idiot. Then a storm rose from my gut and I banged and kicked the gate. Folks stared and gave me suspicious looks. I worried if I went on like that I'd get reported to the cops and my shady trade get exposed and my stupid sons and foolish daughters get in trouble, so with almost unbearable patience I left....

'Anyhow, this one who insists on pulling my eyes like a magnet without fear of my scar ain't him, at least he did me no wrong, and maybe he's better and greater. But a bonze is a bonze, like a catfish is a catfish whether it lives in Lake Biwa or the Amazon. So why, like a portrait on the wall, is he eyeing me? Should I biff him in the noodle? The likes of Hyosuke next to me can't stop me — what, ya rat, shaking? It's jiggling me and jolting my heart. And her? — amazing! eating, and acting unaware. Well, I never knew none but my wife and her, who's too brawny, vulgar, and shameless to be called a woman. Yet, inside she's got a good nature and sad nature as much as anyone. Bedding with me ain't recommendable, nor is doing black-market business, but she does it for her husband, white as a skinned tree root with TB. Ain't she admirable?

'Gnnn, even when I look away he's still looking! I can't stand it, he's getting my fist! Though...why would I wanna get caught by a railway guard and be checked by the cops for beating him down? But if that shadow of his comes out with some word to provoke me...Wow, he's staring in wonder. He's shaking! Just like Hyosuke! Well, Hyosuke had bad luck and came under me just to eat. Maybe this pale shaveling too, only he was a bit luckier to be picked up like he was and can act holy with bald head and black robe. Yeah! I'll scare him off even if he don't deserve it. He'll flap around and make just the blunder I need to smack his master.'

Like a bulldog he lowered his brow, where beads of sweat now stood out, and with a growl he leaned toward Bokuon. Reflexively Bokuon went to the window, and barely maintained his posture. He seemed thirsty, he licked his lips.

"See?" In triumph the boss glanced up at the Zen master, whom he expected to find still gazing at him. He was in for a surprise. The master was smiling.

'Who ever gave me such a smile...? Long ago...I was a little devil, but even then Ma rarely gave me a smile so warm it could wrap my whole body! Damnation! What's going on? This bonze I was taking for a stern, snow-covered mountain is kindly smiling at me. Is he a monster, or a crazily high-class bonze my kind can never meet except through newspaper or radio?'

"Hey, you." The Zen master's mouth opened for the first time as he addressed the man evenly. The little man stopped shaking, the tall one stopped his nihilistic smile, and the woman too, about to take up her last rice ball, stopped her hand, and all poured their attention to the odd scene created by the priest and their boss, known as Kaku.

"Have you children?" the master asked.

"Eh? Yeah, sure. So?" Kaku was irritated. He had blundered and could not force out his naturally vital, rough voice. He was moved close to tears.

"How many, and where are they now?"

"Why, of course they'd be in school about now, or dashing someplace, maybe into a warehouse, getting into mischief while the market's near and the park's far...two girls, two boys. I told ya, and so what?"

"Your children are not in school or in the market."

"Eh? Ya crazy? Strange bonze! So how can ya tell? Where are they?"

"In your bosom, in your mind. It is a fact that your children are in school or at the market or elsewhere. But that's not all. They are also in your mind. When you ride the train they ride with you. They are always with you in your mind whether you eat, do business, fight, or whatever. Incidentally, what is your wife doing?"

"She died. That's the problem."

"Truly she who died and was turned to ash by incineration or was returned to the soil by burial is your wife. But that is not all of her. The most important part is in your mind: she is always with you whatever you do, without exception.

"Like that, your wife and four children are living with you all the time. When you get up they get up, when you lie down, they lie down, and they feel with you every joy and sorrow.

"Therefore! —" Zen Master Tengai suddenly raised his real voice, concealed till then in the pit of his stomach. It pierced the air and shook the window glass. In a quieter tone he concluded,

"You should not forget the truth that you are always with your wife and four children. Consult well with them in your mind before you do or think anything."

The master took his former posture and paid no heed to the man or his fellows or to the scenes out the window. With slit-eyes he kept his meditation form.

Kaku bit his lip and ignored the tears joining the sweat from his brow and trailing down his cheeks. His companions too kept silent.

Bokuon sighed with relief and turned his eyes to the window. The train was running at full speed as if to hide from the passengers the poor and their dwellings, shacks with zinc roofs held down by stones, straw mats for walls, supported by leaning stakes. But the speed did not hide the repeating figures of housewives fanning clay braziers or hanging laundry in the sun with bantlings on their backs. 'Phew! If that bully had used violence, I'd have been called an unworthy attendant for not intervening. Even so, my master is great for not moving even an eyebrow and for making him shed tears. After all, I ought to follow him as long as I have nothing else to do.'

Leaving the shantytown behind, the train came to suburbs where a meadow displayed an unusual flowering of cosmos. It waved in the wind in red, pink, white, and even yellow, all the way to the mountain foot. The stems bending and fallen from the banks of a brook completely hid the water.

Just when he was thinking it would be pleasant to sit and rest there, Bokuon was invaded by darkness. When his eyes adjusted he could see in the window his face and the profile of the master with a queer sense of reality, or contrariwise, of unreality; behind them a white smoke was curling. The stink of coal began to float.

"Oi-i-! Shut those windows or we'll be smoked out like raccoon dogs!" Here and there came the sound of pulling down the heavy wooden window frames. Then came a white light, and the passengers before they realized it

49

were well beyond the tunnel. Beneath, a tremendous flow of muddy water twisted in many lines. Boughs of pines and maples on the far shore were immersed in the current and being tossed about.

But the water was down two or three meters from its peak. A large quantity of straw, clothing, utensils, and whatnot was caught in the trees, especially where they branched. Trees extirpated by the current were exposing fresh roots. Most of the passengers leaned on the sills to look, as if at a hero, at the trace of the absurd flood already settling as a fact of the past.

"Look at all the logs!" "Oi, did you see? A dog bobbing in the waves!" "I heard many cows and horses were washed away. Pigs too. It must be horrible upstream." "Many people too must have died." "Look, a roof — what a disaster!"

The train entered a series of short tunnels as the track followed the contour of a winding ravine. When it made a large curve, the passengers in the rear cars could see the steam locomotive and the front cars coursing vitally ahead. Where the precipice was cut to allow minimum passage, hundreds of reinforced concrete pilings stood high from the rocks of the valley to support the track, thus giving the outer side of the train the appearance of running along an iron bridge. On this day after a typhoon, however, the pilings were submerged almost to their tops, and between the train and the spray of surging muddy water the distance was less than one or two meters. On the previous day the track must have been underwater.

"This area is called Arashiyama, or the Hozu Gorge. Usually a thin clear indigo stream flows through and it's a pleasure to glide by boat and admire the luxuriant precipices, which look like naturally made screens. Cherries in spring, maples in autumn — an elegant tour.

"Around May the indigenous azaleas and rhododendrons compete in beauty. With the fine, cold rains of November, all but the faint figures of the peaks are enveloped in mist and you can hear only the chattering of monkeys and the belling of deer. The mountains covered in snow are indescribably stately and simple. Arashiyama, beautiful through all four seasons, will some-day become a place of international repute. But at times like now, as you see, it fearfully floods as if wishing to sweep away years of accumulated hatred and grudge. Which is its true face is hard to determine, which is why Zennists are fond of Arashiyama."

Zen Master Tengai explained in soft tones to Bokuon, perhaps out of pity for his ignorance, or because he was reminded of his long-ago training in the monastery of Daitokuji, when he was taken down these same rapids by his Zen master. Or perchance the sight of the wildly reversing muddy water turned his thoughts to human weakness.

50

Detonated by the tender words, Bokuon relaxed and summoned his courage to air his own thought, though in a restrained voice lest he be overheard across the aisle.

"Master, departing today from Shoshinji and passing through like this, I've seen so many dispossessed people living like cats and dogs. In Gifu City masked public health officers were spraying every nook and corner. They told me those dead by Japanese encephalitis already number above two thousand this year alone, and those with venereal disease come close to half a million nationwide. What thrives in these shantytowns is only vagabonds, gangs, and such black marketers as we see before us. Still more, in a province like this, flooded just prior to harvest, only disease and crime will spread."

The master, his face again stern, next-to-expressionless, pressed Bokuon to go on, "Well then?"

'Tut! Again he says "Well then?" He'll slap me as soon as I'm invited to speak out! But I opened my mouth, so I can only go on — and once for all I will!' With resolve he continued,

"That means the most urgent task is to help. Relief work is needed, and the priesthood should take the lead!"

"Well then?"

"Then, in other words, my master has been busy devoting himself and taking pains day and night to found a college to raise Zennists. But I think such work is quite a roundabout way of solving the general public distress...I mean, what we should do right away is directly extend a helping hand, isn't that so? For example, look at that Portuguese Catholic, Father Zenon. He was quick to build his 'town of ants' in Tokyo. I heard he's really dedicating himself...."

"Who thinks it is better to do such work?"

"Who? Those various religious men, of course, and..."

"I am asking, who is it who thinks so here and now?" The master was emphatic.

"Well, in such case, it's me...and...well then?"

"Then do so. From this moment. No one will stop you."

Bokuon, recognizing he had again been slapped, tried to hang on: "I understand...but if only you use your immeasurable wisdom and many connections..."

"Fool! Without invitation don't meddle in my affairs! Concern yourself with your own and make the habit of acting like a pioneer in whatever you do. Don't think in so weak and mean a manner, wishing others would do this or that, or thinking they should instead of you." Zen Master Tengai shut up Bokuon's words as well as his thought.

51

Kaku, who had been attending the master's admonition, now leaned across reverently, though the master, but for a glance, looked straight ahead.

"Er, should I say...'Zen Master'? Thanks for the words back there. I appreciate it — how I'm always with my kids and wife, even this minute or when I'm about my business. It truly bolstered me and made me ashamed, and gave me joy. Now I wish to be taught one more thing if ya don't mind — "

"Tell me."

"See, I'm living by doing a black-market business with my kind. We live in fear of the cops but have enough pluck when they ain't about to pit ourselves against the town gangs and blackmailers so we can do our business. We buy up rice, vegetables, fish, and so on from the country and sell it a little higher in the city. It's a fact the controlled distribution don't provide enough food. We do our dark work real well even in the daylight — we have to 'cause we got no other know-how, and of course got no fields....We got nothing but — and it's a great 'but' — our kids 'n such, and they'd starve without our work. Say, if we had to stop, we could only join a gang or turn into lumpen. But who wants to do our illegal work — watched by cops and sleuths, and scorned and feared? Here I'd like to ask just how to think — with what idea should we live day after day? This is the question — "

"'Mo-ji-chyu!'"[1] Zen Master Tengai cut in.

"Huh...?"

"Go straight on, devote yourself, don't look aside, don't loiter. If you are a black marketer, don't mind that you are, but aim to be the best black marketer in all Japan!"

Kaku was amazed. The tall, nihilistic-faced man, the timid man small as a money pouch, and the bold woman, were also amazed and looked at one another with open mouths.

Kaku's eyes shone as if the morning sun were rising in his brain. He nodded deeply, and of a sudden he roughly scratched his dirty cropped hair. Dandruff scattered and fell like snow about his thick round thighs, where his pants were threadbare.

When the train arrived at Kameoka Station, he awkwardly joined his palms, thanked the Zen master, and got off ahead. His companions each in turn followed suit. The master did not move except to join his palms in response.

6

Yosetsu on the Bus

When the passengers got off the train at the old wood-built Kameoka Station, they could see eight or more buses of the Tanba line waiting in front to carry people farther into the country. The drivers and conductors were talking idly, some leaning on the hoods of their buses, others squatting on the paved earth.

Passengers with business in Kameoka went off on foot along the various streets that branched from the station front, while those going to the rural districts had to choose the right bus.

Though it was early September, a temporary cool replaced the lingering summer heat as a result of the previous day's typhoon. The feathery tips of eulalia freshly shooting up swayed in the breeze between the National Railway Station and the Tanba-line bus company, while most sights were blocked by service sheds and warehouses.

Zen Master Tengai and his attendant were unsure of which bus to take to Tangenji.

"Why aren't you prompt to go ask those fellows?" Vexed by his attendant's dull wit, the master motioned with his chin toward the group of drivers and conductors gathered in a loose circle.

"Excuse me, which is the bus to Tangenji?" asked Bokuon to no one in particular in the group.

"Isn't that Bunyu's temple?" remarked one leaning on a hood. "Oi, Bunyu, why do you clean your bus so much? You make mine look bad when it's already good enough," he yelled to Bunyu two buses away polishing a window.

"He cleans like an idiot. I tell you it's a love affair with his bus. He should've been employed as a mechanic."

"Oh, he's happy as a conductor. Ride with him and you'll be stunned. Like a girl guide he lectures about the houses, the rivers, the mountains, and he's too kind to the passengers, or rather, meddles with them beyond his duty to sell tickets. He should work as a tour guide."

"I know — he terrifies me. Days he's on my bus it's dangerous to drive. He distracts me with his chat and sees I don't miss any of it — even introduces me and my career, exaggerated, of course. He tells how I got my license, how hard the training was, how I passed, like it was an aviator's license I was after!

"'Your driver's our best,' he says. 'So take it easy, ladies and gents, and enjoy the ride.' Moments later my right front wheel goes into a soft shoulder and I can't move out either way. So he says, 'Well, folks, we're having a little

53

drill and must practice how to avoid injury in the event of a fall into the valley. But that being too risky, please be satisfied with this childish substitute. Don't get upset or angry, just file off nicely and help push. Let's prove what a great task can be achieved by cooperation.'"

Bunyu approached their horse-laughter, but not before stopping to wipe his hands and slick back his hair. His blue flat-topped visor cap and serge uniform fit him perfectly, and he wore them without a flaw, whereas others tilted their caps, or wore no cap at all, or no shirt. Some even kept their jackets unbuttoned to show a bare chest. Bunyu by his own choice wore a red neckerchief. He seemed suited to a better occupation. He was tall, with clean-cut features.

"Hey, seems these priests are going to your temple. That's your route today, it should work out."

For an instant Bunyu lowered his thick, long eyelashes and furrowed his brow with a look of discomfort. Then right away he became garrulous, "Well, well, passengers, you must be tired coming this far. I'm the eldest son of Tangenji, and a conductor of the Tanba line, and yes, today my commitment is along the Sasayama Highway. We will head west for sixteen kilometers, stopping at Midoribashi, Yasumachi, Amarube, Yoshikawa, and on to Hatta, Rurikei, and finally the town of Sonobe. I can therefore see you safely to Tangenji if that's your aim. However, one thing you ought to know. I'm the eldest son there as well as a conductor here, so I should be set to welcome you doubly. But the point is, I'm now on duty and must give priority to my work for the Tanba line, if that's agreeable with you.

"Frankly, I'm given bed, board, uniform, and salary here, while there I get not even the space of a bed, nor so much as a handkerchief or a vine of sweet potato. People say I'm disowned, but that's not quite true. I wish it to be understood that my father and I never held any disownment ceremony, though for several years our opinions have differed and we've had no close contact, so of course no shared accommodation."

Bokuon thought Bunyu was abominable. Evidently no more than five or six years younger than himself, he was overly particular about his appearance, and too talkative, utterly unsuitable as a country bus conductor. With a bitter glance he concluded, 'But he's the type what charms the girls.'

Zen Master Tengai narrowed his eyes and firmed his mouth as if regarding a stand-up comedian in a vaudeville show. "Ho ho ho!...Then, conductor, tell us which bus to get on."

"Rely on me, this way please, Reverend." Bunyu guided with his hand on the back of the master, who was considerably shorter and fatter than he. Zen Master Tengai was an old-style priest, sternly denying himself and his disciples meat and matrimony. He was thus on his guard with women but lenient with handsome young men, and he now took a liking to Bunyu.

There came the deafening sound of the bus company bell to signal departure time, followed by an announcement by a young woman; but she could not contain a giggle and that too was broadcast over the loudspeaker. The cause was Bunyu, who had dashed into the office for his black cowhide bag of tickets and coins, and, slinging it around his neck as he left, had made as if to kiss her, then offer her his heart.

The driver had a grotesquely protruding brow. He seemed a rude fellow, starting off without properly engaging the gears and raising a grinding sound. Then as he tried to pull out faster than anyone else, the bus stalled after two or three meters of diagonal progress, which happened to be the best position to block the other buses.

The buses, using neither heavy oil nor of course gasoline, were made to run on charcoal gas. Once the engine stopped, much as great trouble had been taken to start it, the conductor needed to get off and insert an L-shaped crank into a hole in the front and turn it vigorously until the engine restarted. Volumes of black smoke rose from the chimney in back. The office girls were thankful to be behind glass. Passengers standing nearby began to gasp.

The engine going again, Bunyu with ruddy face hopped aboard and explained the entire route, "Ladies and gents, apologies for the delay. We are making the following stops..." Then directly he commenced to introduce the driver,

"Today the man taking you to your destinations safe and sound is called Harbin, our pet name, and he has the sunniest character.

"Everyone, please picture to yourselves a family under a five-watt bulb, the parents worrying how to obtain tomorrow's food. The several children can't sleep after only a cup of thin potato soup, and worse, the youngest has a high fever. It's a cold rainy autumn night, wind is shaking the storm doors, but if Harbin's there, how secure and cheered they feel! Note his incomparable brow, and his teeth jumbled like an open pomegranate, downright laughing at all sensitive and elegant culture.

"Shape, expression, and, most faithfully representative, his character allow nothing grave or noble to exist without its feeling shame. Such a brow and teeth make anyone recognize the impropriety of earnestly wrestling with affliction, hardship, strife, illness. To explain why by using the example of Harbin, let me say that dealing with these life problems to find a way out is equal to scraping off his excellent brow and kicking away his extraordinary teeth — a foolish violence.

"After all, changing that abnormal brow or those ugliest-ever teeth as one would bulldoze a mountain or pour agar into a mold is impossible and even if possible, the new brow and teeth wouldn't be his. Naturally his character couldn't coexist and would have to change. You see, he'd no longer be him but a different person. Would it be wise to lose himself by reason of a little too salient a brow and some ill-mannered teeth?

"Rather than worry about such things, he should live with them proudly. His brow is as fine a sight as a rock atop a beach cliff. His teeth are not unlike the thorns of raspberry or wild rose — effective, practical, and thus even beautiful."

Considering that the Zen master and his attendant were among the passengers, Bunyu was offering his best performance by imitating the preaching manner of one of his priest-professors at the Zen-related religious college he had attended for two years and then quit. In fact he often drew from what he regarded as his uninteresting college experience.

As it happened, Zen Master Tengai had served as president of that college for three years, just before and amid the postwar confusion. The year he resigned and returned to Shoshinji, Bunyu entered. So, unknown to both, they had almost run into a relationship of teacher and student.

"Now wouldn't you like to know why we call him Harbin? His name is Haruhei, but in point of fact his family was living in Harbin, capital of Heilungchiang Province in China. On the south bank of the Sung'hua River they daily made and sold eight hundred to fifteen hundred bean-jam buns in the Chinese style. Then as the war worsened and the Japanese Army was forced to withdraw, they too determined to return to their native Kameoka.

"Well, human habit is not to be slighted. They arose at three in the morning on the day after their return and made eight hundred Chinese buns. But not a one was sold. At three the next day they arose, and the next day too, and each day they made eight hundred buns, and not a one was sold. Twenty-four hundred buns filled their tiny house, yet they continued, and on the seventh day the number came to fifty-six hundred. Why, they couldn't even lay out their beds! But that very day they were blessed by great fortune. Nearly two thousand Japanese soldiers were repatriated from Taiwan, and in less than an hour all fifty-six hundred buns were sold and Harbin's parents made a fortune. To conclude, for everyone's sense our driver's name can't be Haruhei but must be Harbin."

"Ho ho ho!" ringingly laughed Zen Master Tengai. But to Bokuon it was not funny at all. He imagined the buns, so many as to make no space to lie down, and he felt sick.

'My master is too mild with worldly youths. We Shoshinji trainees get up at three-thirty and after two long hours of chanting and meditation, we breakfast on thin barley gruel and then must directly labor in the mountains or walk to town to beg. After a lunch of nothing but hard-cooked barley-and-rice, miso soup, and daikon pickle, we again must labor till evening chanting; and after the bath we can sup only if there's food left from lunch. Yet, we must meditate till ten. In addition we are summoned by the bell to the master's room to answer the koan he has given us, at least twice a day....Our life is so simple and hard, but never does he admire or comfort us. We are scolded, whipped with a bamboo stick, abused, and treated like idiots or crazies.

'In Shoshinji anyone who attempts to speak trifles like this squirt conductor will be thundered at by the master or by those big seniors, who with great patience are following his way in hopes of inheriting his position, like earthworms trying to ease out from under a rock. "Fool! While you don't know what your life is, don't speak nonsense! You're but 'a ghost that adheres to the grasses and leans on the trees.'[1] Whatever you say is bound to be harmful. Restrain your tongue, enlighten yourself, and possess brilliant awakened eyes!"

'Then how does that same master respond when he sees a worldly youth living as he likes? "Ho ho ho!" as if to condone his character, behavior, and words like a genial old man — how kind, soft, and spoiling!

'If I cautiously even so much as try to point out his different treatment, he suddenly looks glum. I'm sure he's immediately displeased and feels a pressure in his chest from knowing that such inconsistency is unsuitable in a Zen master, who should be consistent from morning to night, front to back.

'But he'll retort with full power, as if to inform the world that his feeling is the opposite — while thinking his true feeling is well hidden — "You damn fool! Of course the trainees under my direction are like my own children and grandchildren. How can I hold the same affection for all other youths in this vast world, especially when they don't come to me to be taught? Because I so love my respectable trainees, I harden my heart against pity and spare no pains to issue my hot shouts, earnest fist, and thirty beatings of the stick. Children don't appreciate their parents' sincere affection — it's said of the likes of you!"

'So I can only turn my complaints inward like a turtle pulling in its head. After all, what he says is reasonable and certainly contains the heat of molten iron....Yet I can't sweep from a corner of my brain the queer suspicion that his words harbor a falsehood and a sophism. He believes he accomplishes his severe teaching by reasonable words and actions. But aren't those merely his tools to use others as harshly as he likes and an excuse to express his authority? I wonder. If so, then the reason he acts grand and gentle before worldly youths is that they are beyond his influence. And he abuses his trainees because they are under his control. It could be so, and it's a grave human weakness. A man can be cruel to those close by and kind to those who are distant.

'To my regret I have little experience and no sure knowledge, and I haven't progressed at all in "seeing my original nature" — the koan imposed on me by him. And because I have nothing, I can't even tell if my thought is correct. I can't judge people, especially my master and senior monks — are they true Zen trainees as well as true Zen teachers? I'd be utterly lost in the outside world if I left Shoshinji. Everything is uncertain, and I can judge nothing clearly. I'm like an appendage, like the drooping excrement of a goldfish. I'm attending the master as a handyman though I'm already twenty-five and ashamed of myself...an unwelcome state. But since I can't find a more pleasant way of life, or way to reform myself, I can do nothing but go along like this for a while.'

As he thought thus and so, Bokuon was maintaining the appearance of a training monk in black robe. But his eyes lacked the expected pure and intense light of a trainee's, and had no air of piety, nor of mercy to softly enwrap and tenderly nurse creatures nearby. Indeed they showed less of confidence and well-being than a normal man's, and more of vague complaint, displeasure, and enervation.

The disparity between his composed and respectable outer state as a training monk and his inner state, inferior to that of any bright, earnest social person, which his eyes conveyed, gave Yosetsu, who chanced to be a passenger on the bus, occasion to smile. He was working his way up the aisle toward Bokuon to get acquainted with the Zen master.

The bus had passed along a paved street of Kameoka and was continuing west on the dirt-tamped Sasayama Highway, heading for various small towns and villages. The jolting in all directions was becoming violent. Occasionally the bus went into a deep pothole, startling the passengers and almost causing their heads to hit the ceiling. The driver, introduced as Harbin, enjoyed shaking his passengers from their seats by accelerating at the sight of any unevenness in the road. His prime joy during work was in fact to make a travesty of his duty to drive in the safest and most comfortable way. Bunyu was gracefully balancing his lithe body and ignoring the passengers bearing the jolts and some even emitting shrieks.

Yosetsu, having stood up from his seat and now nearing the master and attendant, was gripping the seat backs and stooping even more than was his custom, to avoid tumbling, and yet he kept smiling. The smile had begun over the noticeable contradiction in Bokuon. It now came of seeing him flailing his limbs as his astringent posture was disarrayed during the rapid passage of the bus into and out of a pothole. Zen Master Tengai kept his perfect meditation form regardless, which Yosetsu did not fail to note as proof of long years of training. He smiled whenever Bokuon lost his composure and whenever passengers shrieked. No doubt he also smiled because he was stooping uncommonly low as he advanced to the master, and because he was at last so close to Bokuon that he was almost butting him on the chin at each jolt.

Thus the reason for his smile kept changing. But while to the observer he seemed always to smile, the reasons why were indeterminable, whence he was thought to be a creepy and suspicious character.

Yosetsu was short and of poor build. His head was shaped like a taro potato or a light bulb, and was bald up toward the middle of the crown. He had glabrous skin. Only his nose for some reason was as tall and splendid as a Russian's. Despite these given features he was cultivating a small, grizzled mustache, which he clearly prized, for he was striving to keep every hair of it and even adding hairs from his nostrils. His deep-set eyes glittered like the eyes of a cornered mouse. They had no brightness or warmth, and beneath them were double or triple crescent wrinkles like moats or walls to keep out invaders, nay, to keep his secrets within.

'His looks are poor and decrepit, but I bet he's stubborn, tenacious as a snake that never loses its prey once it fixes its eye on it.' So thought a master mason sitting in the rear with gaitered legs spread wide, feet turned outward, in split-toed, heavy-cotton footwear. His mate, likely suffering from a stomach ulcer, for his face looked dark but pale, was regarding the wide spectacle of flattened, mud-sodden rice plants. The masons were being summoned to repair stone walls destroyed by the flood.

A middle-aged woman in somber dress, seated ahead of them across the aisle, and across from Yosetsu's vacant seat, was sizing him up. 'I should have nothing to do with his ilk. He's unworthy of attention and probably mean.' Her work was to call on the villages to repair umbrellas and shoes. Rain or shine she made her rounds, carrying her findings in a grimy canvas sack frayed on the bottom but once white. Her husband had returned from the battle-front after losing a leg, a hand, and an eye. Her joy was to get orders that required more time and patience than she had on the spot; these she took home to him waiting in his gloomy workroom.

Her saddest hours were when she thought of her eighteen-year-old son, disabled by infantile paralysis. She was affected by Bunyu's talk about the driver's forehead and teeth. 'My son, around the same age as this elegant conductor, needs diapers and help with eating even now. Yet he thinks and tries to say such nice thoughts that it doesn't matter that his body and voice are considered strange. "Mother, I'm sorry — I'm old enough to practice filial piety, but I'm exactly as always! I think I should die, but I fear death. Forgive me, Father, you too — by me you both have been ruined!" His father tells him, "Nonsense, you give us the courage and purpose to go on day after day, or what would be the meaning of our life? What would be our pleasure, for what our pain? It's we who should apologize for giving you such a body."

'This conductor's talk helps me better understand we've always thought correctly. Struggling to change one's defect or given fate is slighting one's inherent original pleasure of life, and could even be life-threatening.

'I heard he's a son of the Tangenji priest and he quit a religious college. But as might be expected, he says some good things. For me it's like seeing a sunrise over a hill.'

She noticed Yosetsu at the front of the bus. 'Why is he standing there? He's smiling at me! He must be amused, figuring I was encouraged by that talk, and he's taking it as proof of my weakness, my sad circumstances. I'd better ignore him completely.' As she coldly looked aside, she saw him from the corner of her eye, smiling anew.

Yosetsu persisted to cling to Bokuon's seat back, as if intending to lick his shoulder. He directed his eyes to a fat granny with a toddler two seats ahead of the repair woman. He smiled. The granny was protecting the child from hitting her head on the window or falling from the seat as she stood to stare at the passing scenery. The granny too was staring. Why would he smile at the sight of them? He was unaware of his smile, and no one else smiled. Did he smile because to him the old woman appeared to have risen above worldly desires to devote herself to an innocent child? It would have been incorrect to assume that of Yosetsu; well, not entirely, but it would have been too shallow, and shallowness breeds misconception.

This time Yosetsu's brain, aided by his mouse-like eyes, took at least three steps to produce his smile. First, he saw the similarity of the granny and the child in their both being 'powerless and far more injurious than beneficial to this hard world of struggle for existence.' Second, he saw their defenseless yet absorbed state as they took pleasure in the sights out the window, whether or not they were aware of the similarity stated by him. Third, he reexamined their being 'powerless and far more injurious than beneficial...,' and in place of 'to this hard world of struggle for existence' he put — 'to me.' In short, he also smiled whenever he saw something of little or no possible benefit to himself.

Of course he also smiled when he saw his possible benefit. There was a passenger well aware of this smile. He was Zosan, head of the town's board of education.

'I'm lucky,' he thought as he noticed Yosetsu boarding the bus, 'because his habit of taking a seat behind the left rear wheel is contrary to my preference for the right side behind the driver. How odd he doesn't fancy this seat, it being the most comfortable and safe. Doesn't he realize the driver will turn the wheel to his advantage if he faces a head-on collision? Too bad the conductor has to stand opposite — the most dangerous spot. Today I see priests are seated just behind him. Anyway, I'm lucky I don't have to confront Yosetsu, owing to our different habits...though he has the coign of vantage to observe me and others as he likes with that odious smile.'

Zosan, of portly figure, was neat in a tailored dark suit, the trousers silver pin-stripped. His silver-rim glasses and black hair glittered. His mustache too was groomed, taking its part in showing him to be possessed of some authority, culture, and learning.

He could make no sense of Yosetsu's mustache. 'It doesn't sort with his build, and he can't compose it without adding nostril hairs. I wouldn't know if he cares, but it looks scruffy. There's no harmonious architectonic effect from the macroscopic view, nor from the microscopic. For our education board too the foremost issue is to maintain a harmonious, unified view. Frankly, his mustache does nothing but lower the public esteem of mustaches, most unwelcome to us who wear ours with pride. Maybe that's why he keeps it, which would accord with his anfractious psychology.'

Sensing movement in the aisle, Zosan tried to look back. His neck had shortened with the fattening of his torso, and while still serving as a linkage, it was of small use as a pivot. He shifted his hefty thighs, and his striped trousers grew taut.

Yosetsu was smiling directly at Zosan even as he was turned astoop toward Bokuon. 'What's with him? — again smiling, after all!' Zosan slightly bowed and quickly turned away.

'He's likely smiling even now at my back!' Zosan could not help thinking about Yosetsu's smile. 'He coolly sees everyone and their affairs and smiles when people normally wouldn't, and when they're happily smiling, he disappears. He chances to appear only when others meet trouble or disaster. In a sunny spot he'd melt away. He's a man of the shade, turning up whether it's the shade of a city or prefectural assembly, a police station, or a temple. He's a slug.

'Once the Tangenji priest told me, "He's the child of a mistress and fated to see everything through her eyes" — presumably well said. That's why I'm careful not to impregnate Ikuko. People are wrong to condemn the idea of keeping a mistress. They say it can lead to an unhappy and tricky conception. But if there's no conception, how can a mistress be cause for woe? A woman who conceives isn't qualified to be a mistress, and a man who keeps a woman who conceives isn't gifted at keeping a mistress.'

Zosan never taxed his ingenuity over birth control or availed himself of the fruits of professional research. 'Natural prevention is what's important. If a man can keep enjoying sexual relations fair and square in a secret place without application of cunning or device and achieve it free of conception, it proves he has the talent to keep a woman. Is there any greater test of his qualification than to let him behave as he pleases while admiring heaven's gifts?

'Yosetsu is entirely wrong if he's smiling by spotting I'm on my way to Ikuko's at this time of day. I am, but he should know she is no source of woe but the very fountain of my pleasure! Fool!

'But wait, his smile shows some reserve. He must have a scheme to profit from my visiting her. Yes, he'll connect it with my position as head of the board: that would bring his smile to full margin. I see why I felt I had to bow to him just now — it was to calm his evil intention, or why should I bow to one so unworthy?

'But look! — while keeping the relation cordial enough to bow, I too can begin to grasp his tail! By all accounts he's running a money-lending business, and I'm getting word he's charging a high interest without a business license and without paying any income tax....'

Smiling, Yosetsu at last spoke to Bokuon in a voice so low that Zen Master Tengai and even Bokuon could hardly hear it. "How sorrowful an age, when the hearts of the people are devastated, when parents are bent on securing their children's daily food, stopping at nothing to gain their end and losing both confidence and principles to lead the young. Hence the young disregard both reason and *hetu-phala* and impulsively seek after pleasures at each *ksana*. In such an age how admirable to be setting your aim on training. Your soul is the 'soul of Japan,' and like the *candana*, fragrant even as it rots. You are a model to youth, a lighthouse for the world. Please stay on your guard and press on with your training, for nothing is more respectable than the practice of Buddhistic austerities."

He smiled as he spoke. Being short, he normally faced his listeners from below, giving them the sense that a caterpillar or ants were crawling on them, inchmeal from neck to nose to eyes. But since his audience was seated, Yosetsu could not show his full talent, and that made him impatient.

By praising and stimulating the attendant, he aimed to position himself higher than Bokuon; that is, he was posing as a protector of Buddhist trainees. At the same time, he aimed to put himself close to the master by humoring him through his attendant. Bokuon could not possibly intuit Yosetsu's smile. Praised, he smiled back and straightened up all the more, though he was embarrassed by the highfalutin language. "From all appearances you and your master have come a great way, but from where?"

"Shoshinji in Gifu. We are calling on Tangenji in Tanba."

"Oh, my! just as I guessed!"

"Did the priest of Tangenji inform you of my coming?" Zen Master Tengai spoke rapidly.

"No, er...yes — now that you mention it. So-o-o — indeed, he must have been awaiting you. To tell the truth, my name is Yosetsu Fujii and I am head representative of the Tangenji laymen. Laymen, I say, but we are few — just nineteen families. You see, in the early Edo period my ancestor Goemon Fujii, governor of the locality, built Tangenji as his private temple. Now the protection of Tangenji depends entirely on us few, on our pygmy effort after Tangenji lost its customary revenue."

"I am asking you — you layman — were you advertised of my coming today? Answer me." Zen Master Tengai carried his question with force.

"No, that's why..., I mean..." Here Yosetsu surmised that the master intended to judge the reliability of the character of the Tangenji priest by whether or not he had exposed to his laymen the master's coming. In fact Yosetsu knew nothing of it, and he answered, "I've had no word." Yet he pondered why the master was so intent on knowing, and he presumed that the master had a grave reason for visiting Tangenji, which he wished to keep covered. And he concluded that to know the reason would be equal to knowing the master, and to having some profit shared, to the degree that he involved himself. So he added,

"But, Master, I am a layman, the head layman, and sparing no pains for Tangenji. I know what concerns the Tangenji priest whether he expresses it to me or not."

"Well then?"

"So my first concern as head layman is to cause the least trouble to the Tangenji priest. Say, I suppose you plan to spend the night in Tangenji. Look, it is well past two. Then please consider their pecuniary distress. In the age when the Tangenji economy was steady, they could prepare all proper meals and bedding for their finer guests, whereas now, well, it is miserable — his sick wife and five children, though one finally became independent, as you see before you, the conductor...To make a long story short, let me say you will feel uncomfortable receiving even a grain of rice, a sip of soup, a single quilt, if you know the present situation. Yet he, who happens to be a proud person, will surely try to offer his best. But surely, too, his lavish hospitality will affect the quality and quantity of his infant children's meals for days. I on the other hand have the honor of being head layman for such occasions. Fortunately I have only three family members, my wife, my daughter — who teaches elementary school — and myself. We are not rich, but we have enough food,

63

bedding, and gardens, so please stay tonight in our home, I beg you. I know it's an impolite offer from a mere worldling to a Zen master so distinguished throughout the Empire, but my wish is to reduce the burden of our priest."

Yosetsu thought it propitious to his future to have the Zen master stay the night in his home. He would give him ample hospitality, talk at some length, and get acquainted. Shoshinji was a training monastery famous nationwide, and Zen Master Tengai had a great many connections with the central political and financial world and with various universities and even with the Imperial Palace. 'Whatever can it be, this secret matter that he came to discuss with our priest? All Tangenji profit ought to go through me, oughtn't it?'

Zen Master Tengai and his attendant decided to take off their travel attire at Yosetsu's house, visit Tangenji from there, and return to Yosetsu's around suppertime and spend the night.

At the bus stop Yosetsu's wife, Chiyo, not yet forty, in a quiet-colored kimono, and even smaller than her husband, bowed low to receive Yosetsu home. After he introduced his guests, she said without hesitance,

"You must be tired coming from so far. I shall ready the bath at once," and she invited them into the house. Bokuon was impressed that the wife should await the husband at the bus stop, and he was rather suspicious because she showed no surprise at sudden guests, as if they were expected.

Yosetsu's house stood right in front of the bus stop, receiving the cloud of dust after the bus drove on.

7

Acolyte Days

Zen Master Tengai and Doyu were Dharma brothers for having entered the Buddhist priesthood under the same priest, Mukai, of Toyoin, one of the subtemples in Nanzenji. By him they had been nursed as acolytes before advancing to monastic training.

Tengai had entered Toyoin at age twelve and at fifteen gone to the monastery at Daitokuji to train under Zen Master Shutan, and he was eight years older than Doyu. They had spent only countable days and nights together under Priest Mukai, when Tengai returned for some temple affairs. Tengai had already moved to Daitokuji as a Zen trainee when Doyu entered Toyoin at age eight. Doyu did not hurry to train in a monastery, and while staying under Priest Mukai he attended senior high school and then an imperial university, under the old education system. After graduation he chose to enter the monastery at Nanzenji, where luckily for him Mukai was then serving as Zen master. So Doyu followed Mukai from age eight to about twenty-five.

Zen Master Tengai, who had spent only three years under Mukai, later had occasion to speak of his experience to Doyu.

"Two things he severely taught me. The first was to understand ten by hearing one. He ordered, 'Bring tobacco!' When I did, he cried, 'Fool! Understand ten by hearing one!' Being just twelve and a very new acolyte, I could make no sense of his words and raised and lowered my eyes and stood there blankly. Suddenly I was given a fist that sent lights flashing in my eyeballs. I shed tears and kept standing there flustered. 'It is essential that a Zen priest "know the presence of fire by seeing smoke over the mountain, know it is a cow by seeing horns over the fence, know all corners of a box when shown just one. The professional can measure weight and worth by eye alone."'[1] Thus he scolded and spoke no further.

"I was stumped. More large tears came out, and at last I begged, 'I can't understand anything. I'm a novice. Please teach me more kindly.' He shouted and gave me another fist. 'Fool! If I tell you, it's mine. If you think it through by yourself, it's yours!' He meant, 'The real treasure of the house comes not through the gate.'[2]

"I directly realized tobacco needs a match, just as when asked to lend a chisel, one must also lend a mallet. I hastened to fetch the matchbox, and an ashtray. For the first time, he beamed with delight and reproved me gently, 'So, so. Manage everything like that, Shinichi' — my infant name.

"Since then I've always exerted my ingenuity to understand ten by hearing one. It might be a trifling teaching for someone else, but in truth for me it was gospel. Why? Because my constitution was so poor that our family doctor called me 'a wholesale of infirmity,' and everyone whispered that I would die young. Yet I had begun to wish for a long life, and oh, how my heart ached because I didn't know how to attain it. Then came the teaching, Understand ten by hearing one. I thought, 'Doesn't it mean to live ten times as much as he who understands one by hearing one?' I danced for joy and cried, 'This is the key to longevity! If I thus understand everything, I will be living a hundred years by living ten, three hundred by living thirty! How could I wish for more? At once I was able to dissolve my unease over the possibility of an early death, and since then I have been merrily doing my best to combust my life completely. I am deeply indebted to Mukai of Toyoin for his severe teaching.

"I owe him a second great debt of gratitude for Any excuse is an incompetent's complaint. 'Oi, buy tofu!' he ordered. I promptly went out with the little tin pan, but the shopkeeper and the people on the way spoke to me, 'Say, acolyte, what's your teacher doing today?' or 'Zen training must be hard for a tender child like you, eh?' I duly responded to each, and when I got back he inquired, 'Why so late just to buy tofu?' I tried to explain that I couldn't be curt, but he gave me a clout and scolded, 'Idiot! Don't you know that any excuse is an incompetent's complaint?' It was like that whenever I delayed even the least and for however unavoidable a reason.

"Another time he had a guest. I served them tea, and when the guest reached for his cup, it tipped over. 'Hey, Shinichi!' Heedless of the guest he summoned me and demanded, 'Why did you cause his tea to spill?'

"I was at a loss and thought, 'What the devil? The guest spilled it — why am I responsible?' He too was embarrassed and came to my rescue, 'It's my fault, please don't blame your acolyte.' But our teacher raised his voice all the more, 'Fool! You're wrong! Don't think up an excuse!' and he punched me in the brow. I couldn't bear the strain and my tears began to ooze out. Then he preached, 'Don't you yet understand? Our guest was discommoded because you improperly placed his cup. Setting it beyond his reach is inviting him to be careless. Not too far and not too near is correct, you fool! Nonetheless you're agonizing to find an excuse. Didn't you ever hear me say Any excuse is an incompetent's complaint?' and he punched me again. I could only shrink and apologize, 'I was wrong, please forgive me!'

"Since then I resolved never to make an excuse for any impropriety, even if it related to me only a little, and regardless of whether it was caused by others or of course by me, and I've taken my responsibility. Moreover, I am extra careful: I double- and triple-check against error so I can fulfill my first responsibility.

"Ah, yes, there was another such affair...Our teacher was accommodating this and that Kyoto merchant with some extra money, and my work was to retrieve it on the promised dates. I was sent on one such errand to a shop making and selling pickles, where many apprentices, clerks, and the owner himself were at work. When I said why I came, I was told, 'Come in the evening, we're too busy now.' I reported this to our teacher, and as I expected he scolded, 'Dumbbell! You went only to be repaid the money — go get it without grumbling to me with excuses!' With no choice I went back, but the owner was out and I returned to the temple to be scolded again. He had said to come in the evening, so I went then, and still he was out and no one could say when he'd be in. Our teacher when I told him roared, 'Any excuse is an incompetent's complaint!' and he gave me a buffet.

"I called on the shop next morning, and the owner said, 'I haven't the money now — I'll return it the day after tomorrow.' I was cheered to have a definite day. But our teacher scolded, 'Idiot! The dyer always promises to finish the job the day after tomorrow, a saying particularly true of Kyoto!' and he beat me more. I was at sea and my anxiety cost me my appetite. But he kept scolding, 'You went to retrieve it; your work is to return with it by any means. No need for excuses! Incompetent!'

"'The day after tomorrow' arrived. When I went to the shop I was again told the same thing. At that I was awakened and hit on an idea: 'I'll be made a sample of a fool if I don't somehow get it back right away. Endlessly he'll say the day after tomorrow and I'll be abused as incompetent. So I said, "'I am here because you said to come the day after tomorrow, which is today. If I let you extend to the day after tomorrow, you will extend to another day after tomorrow. I won't budge from your shop till I'm paid back. What's the point of returning to the temple just to be scolded?' I then sat down amid the bustle of workers and customers and commenced to meditate.

"At last outdone in patience, the owner returned the money. Our teacher rewarded me with the words 'Well done' and reminded me: 'No excuses from now on.'"

Zen Master Tengai often spoke of his acolyte days and the Zen training period that followed, possibly because he had many juniors to educate. Priest Doyu in contrast scarcely spoke of his — not to his wife, children, laymen, or anyone else — possibly because painting and making calligraphy was his interest.

In addition Doyu thought it unaccountable that the teacher portrayed by Tengai was so different, as if another person, from the teacher of his own experience.

In his heart he thought, 'Priest Mukai wasn't the stern teacher Tengai describes; I never received his fist. He must have scolded me uncountable times, but it wasn't so severe as to be printed on my mind to this day. In fact early on he was more affectionate with me than my real father, Priest Kakkan. Later too he was approachable whenever I went to consult him about my troubles.

'I wonder why our impressions are so different — there were, by the way, several other acolytes. It's unlikely Tengai is exaggerating or creating a new image of him; that would be taking undue liberty and be impolite to our teacher, who lived in his way, and Tengai would only be proving a thinness of love.

'On an afternoon of strong sunlight with lingering summer heat, when I had been less than ten days in Toyoin, Priest Mukai took me along when he went to a layman's house to perform a memorial service. On the way home we walked by the zoo. The deep moat along the south border, fed by the canal from Lake Biwa, was full of fresh green water, and the surface was dazzling. Beads of sweat stood on his tanned brow, on mine too. On the other shore, dark green boughs extended over the black iron fence, covering the fence and part of the moat. Mixed in were the pink flowers of crepe myrtle and oleander and the purifying white of althea.

'"Ken" — my infant name — "have you ever seen a lion?" "No." "A tiger?" "No." "Hmmm...you've never seen a lion, called 'king of the beasts,' nor a tiger, renowned for Buddha's having fed it his own body when it hungered, as you've read in the Jataka? You should see at an early age those beings who are our respectable companions. Then you will know how weak is the human body and how we are narrow-minded and shallow, living in a society that ranks human beings above all others. And you will vividly under-stand the folk saying, A tyrannical government is far fiercer than a tiger — recorded in Liji. Then how about an elephant or a giraffe?"

'Teasingly he asked, though I was but a child and he could suppose I hadn't seen an elephant or a giraffe if I hadn't seen a lion or a tiger. I could only say "No."

'We were walking along the paved road in the hot sun, the air shimmering with heat, and were soaked with sweat by the time we neared the southeast corner of the zoo. I longed to enter, and hadn't he just said I'd better see those animals at an early age? My expectation rose. "Nor a hippopotamus or a rhinoceros?"

'I turned to look back with reproach at the zoo as it receded from sight. I could still see the net dome of an aviary above the luxuriant trees. "Hmm, you haven't seen anything and you don't know anything."

'His words made me wistfully remember my native Tangenji and its environs, the pine mountain behind, the songs of the many insects, the variety of fish in the river...

'Abruptly he turned and briskly began to walk back. I wondered what was the matter with him. Then he made me cry for joy — "We're going in!"

'Another time, equally hot, perhaps nearer midsummer, we were also returning from a memorial service, a year after our visit to the zoo, so I was nine. As he stood by the moat he said, "How hot! Aren't you hot too?" as if it weren't obvious. "Of course I am, Reverend Teacher." "Then why don't you swim? Here's water! But you can't, can you, being a mountain boy?" In my native land the Sakura River curves through the rice fields. I could swim adequately from infancy. "I can, but here with all these people is it allowed?" "Why not? Consider it our garden in Kyoto. Shouldn't one swim in one's own garden? The water's clean, there's no sign to prohibit it, swim! swim!"

'He sat on the edge and eased his feet toward the water. I took off my black gossamer silk robe and white underrobe, and naked but for my loincloth I dived in. "Wet this!" he called, tossing me a towel from his wisteria basket. As I halted to receive it, I was surprised to realize how deep the water was and how cold it was below my knees as I tread it with my feet, and the flow seemed rather rapid. Directly I was seized with a cramp in my calf. I had swum only in a small river. Watching this development my teacher cried, "What a pretty pass!" and he dived in fully robed and brought me to land. As he scrambled up the bank, many pedestrians cast looks of suspicion.

'I remember another time; it must have been the autumn when I was ten. In front of the houses were potted chrysanthemums, or spindly ones with few flowers growing by the hedges. Again we were on the way home from a memorial service. On the red-tinged road our shadows were long, Priest Mukai's, mine, and the smaller, younger acolyte Nangaku's. From the dark and narrow lanes chilly winds like water streamed across us. It was a quiet, elite neighborhood, where, our teacher explained, there was the mansion of a certain zaibatsu or the house of a renowned scientist.

'Nangaku was perhaps on his first outing with our teacher, and much was new to him, coming from Hyogo Prefecture. He had the furrowed brow of an old man, in fact an ugly face and a weak appearance, yet he was stalwart and tenderhearted.

'We approached a mansion enclosed by a high wood wall along the top of which ran an elaborately spiked wire against burglars. Conspicuous amid the dense overspreading trees was one whose green foliage framed countless glossy yellow fruits, some catching the last red of the sun — not persimmons, for sure, nor apples or pears.

'"Say, Nangaku, what's that?" I asked. "Pomegranate?" he ventured, expressing ignorance not only of the fruit overhead. I laughed, and he said, "Oh! I see, Senior Brother, it must be chestnut!"

'His attempt to redeem his honor made me pity him, and I thought — "This fresh acolyte who doesn't know even chestnut must have grown up in a horribly poor situation. I have to look after him all the more." Yet I too didn't know what it was. "Look here, you both, how can you know so little? There ought to be a limit to everything, even ignorance. Well, there's no way but to accept with thanks one or two for you."

'So saying, our teacher tucked up his flowing sleeves and skirts and got down on all fours on the earth by the wall.

'Nangaku and I, having thought he would trouble to knock to get permission, couldn't understand his behavior and stood there in dumb surprise. "Oi, why so slow? Quick, Ken! get on my back — but take off your clogs!"

'At last figuring out his intent, I got on his back and reached up along the wall. "No, no, I see you can't do it alone, Nangaku must mount your shoulders!"

'Nangaku merrily complied, and I winced as I straightened up on our teacher's back. Looking down with his belly almost touching the earth, he cried in a labored voice, "Oii! Nangaku! Quick, pick five! Make sure! One's for me! Choose them big and well exposed to the sun."

'When we had them, he shook the dirt from his robes and demonstrated how to peel the skin as we walked on. From the neat segments he took one, put it in his mouth, and exclaimed, "Hm! Sweet! Now remember, this is the mandarin orange and not so unusual. Go to the villages along the Shizuoka coast and you'll find them more than persimmons in Kyoto. At the foot of Mt. Fuji the hills are all mandarin orchard and the ocean spreads greenish blue. One day I may take you there." As I tasted the sweet-sour juice, I pictured the bright sight of Shizuoka.'

Doyu thus remembered Priest Mukai as a father more kindly than his own, and not the sharp, severe teacher often referred to by Zen Master Tengai.

But he did not suspect his Dharma brother of lying; simply he decided that Tengai remembered in his own way how he was taught and how he received what he was taught.

And further he thought, 'First of all, Priest Mukai was great to the extent of later becoming Zen master of Nanzenji. He was far beyond ordinary people. He couldn't have been of simple quality like jelly, but must have been polyhedric, with front, back, top, bottom, right, left. He wouldn't practice such inept and imperfect mercy as to teach in the same way all who sought his guidance. He must have become each one in state and character and taught each in the most effective and suitable way. He was free as water, didn't rigidly insist, "This is me!" That would be unlike a Buddhist. He well perceived the truth that every existence is devoid of atman, and he instantly became round when round appeared, or whatever, according to the vessel to be filled. He performed the essence of the saying, Adapt your speech to your audience.

'Second,' though it was only another way of saying the same thing, 'Tengai and I were very different in character and background. Our common teacher taught us differently to develop our distinctive qualities. Naturally our impressions would differ. A severe method nurtured Tengai's nature, whereas mine benefited from a gentler method.

'Third,' Doyu advanced his thought, though it too was no more than a supplement to his "first" and "second," 'Tengai was the youngest of seven children in a poor, worldly family that had suffered bankruptcy, and his parents at the family home in Nagoya were in constant discord. I was the eldest son of an affluent family with a proud history, and my father was then vice-abbot of Nanzenji. Of course our teacher adjusted not only the method but also the content of his education.

'Fourth' — though this too was but an additional explanation — 'Tengai studied with him for three years starting at age twelve, when Mukai was relatively younger — the period when he was forty-three to forty-six — whereas I entered at eight and continued to study directly under him until my first marriage, at twenty-seven. Even after remarrying, I often and closely served him until he died — when I was thirty-two. So my study with him began when he was forty-seven, and it lasted until he was sixty-eight and on to his end — at seventy-one — the period of his maturity as a teacher. Well, Tengai was under him an incomparably short time, so there's no point in comparing how much we long for and understand our teacher. To conclude, Tengai is by any means my senior Dharma brother, and our impressions of our teacher are quite reasonably different, albeit the difference is great.'

Doyu thought about the subject no further. He was not a deep thinker, and besides, his interest was spent. After all, he was more emotional than cerebral, more of an artist than a philosopher.

8

Zen Master Tengai and Mokuzu

Chiyo offered frothy bitter tea and a thin-sliced bean confection to Zen Master Tengai and Bokuon and withdrew toward the kitchen leaving the words, "I shall ready the bath at once." The bath water was drawn from the well since before noon to save firewood even a little; she had only to start a fire with pine needles and add wood.

But Zen Master Tengai wished to call on Tangenji right away and did not touch the offered tea. He told her, "No, you needn't care about a bath for us." Yet she began to raise a smoke, and Yosetsu did not come out of whatever inner room he had entered.

The guest room where they were let in had in its alcove a scroll painting of bamboo signed by the priest Rinso. 'He taught Doyu's painting teacher, didn't he?' thought Zen Master Tengai.

'Doyu must have given this scroll to the head layman out of thanks for something. While I don't well understand painting and calligraphy, it's generally agreed that Rinso's paintings are so valuable as to merit proper care in an art museum and not be hung in this sort of private house. Priest Doyu isn't avaricious, yet why should he part with such a precious work? This head layman must have done him some extraordinary favor.'

Bokuon was looking up with curiosity at a pair of spears set along a lintel. The heads were wrapped in velvet, but apparently one was diamond-shaped, the other three-pronged. The shafts were two meters long and murky with soot. 'Without their covers they would gleam, for I bet they're well polished.'

"We can't afford to waste time in this manner. Tell our host we'll be off."

"Yes." Bokuon stood up but could not determine where to find the host. He stepped down to the black earth of the passage, found his way to the rear of the house, and went out to the back yard, where he heard some noise coming from a corner of a vegetable garden. Yosetsu was just leaving a chicken coop with a bird slung from his hand. Intending to give the Zen master a chicken dinner, he had finally captured one out of the ten or so, forced its rust brown wings one over the other, and bound its legs with a straw rope. The legs, tied tight, looked blanched.

The upside-down hen flopped her puffy red comb as she crooked a pensive-looking head to one side and then to the other, repeating the gesture that was her only remaining freedom.

"Er-r, excuse me, my master says he will start out now?"

Yosetsu approached smiling, and with an abrupt motion he thrust the chicken up almost against Bokuon's nose.

"It's no more than a ten-minute walk to Tangenji. Now, I don't know what grave and secret business your master has, but he'd better go after a bath. While he's visiting, I'll butcher this hen so when he comes back he can enjoy his supper."

"Uh...uh, I'm sorry but he never touches meat or fish...besides, he isn't going there on any secret business."

"Hooouu, he's practicing vegetarianism? Fancy such a formal priestly way!...Look, our Tangenji priest says, 'Fish tastes better than vegetables and meat tastes better than fish,' and he's living his honest life....Hey, biddy, you made a narrow escape!" He freed the hen and tossed it back into the coop.

"There's no use you and me eating chicken while your important Zen master abstains — you can eat meat, eh?"

"Yes, but it's prohibited within Shoshinji."

"That's just right for you while you're training. Eat stimulating foods and assuredly you'll never be delivered from *panca-visaya*, he he he!"

"Well, my master and I must be going." Bokuon turned, but Yosetsu said,

"Apparently he's in a hurry, but for what reason? I tell you, he'd better go after a bath. Our priest is poor, but he favors cleanliness — why, he bathes morning and evening. I will take your master properly to Tangenji after I change my clothes, got it?" Yosetsu walked away toward the bath room, off an end of the kitchen.

When Bokuon returned to the guest room and reported what their host had told him, Zen Master Tengai shouted,

"You fool! Go back and refuse the offer with a bang! Now we'll go! What is called 'human kindness' is good only to waste another's time." Seeing that his master was leaving for the entryway, Bokuon sped out toward the bath room. Yosetsu was now seated on a pile of firewood at the fuel hole talking with his wife as she fed the fire.

"You know, he isn't normal. I heard he eats nothing but shiitake, bamboo shoot, and such other as I hardly know of. Without eating stimulating food, a man can't give pleasure."

"My! the things you say!" His petite wife, squatting before the fuel hole, raised a florid face. Her neat mouth with even teeth smiled and her modest nostrils faintly twitched. She tightened the collar of her kimono, but had no way to conceal her generous posterior frankly exposing its shape, and Yosetsu turned his eyes there with a grin.

"I'm looking forward to the sight of your attentions, such as, you'll make him take a bath, and, in only your underwear you'll wash his back, belly, hands, feet, and more...conscientiously...he, he, he!"

73

"Dear me! Must I do the Zen master?"

"Of course! You seem not wholly averse to it. The other day as you served the prefectural governor I saw you stop your hands, rapt as a virgin."

"No, it was because — though I don't see how he could be so mistaken — he fervently entreated, 'Please, with your pious devotion, for mercy's sake, wash there a little more, more slowly, please, I beg you,' and he even tried to touch — oh, it was well beyond the hospitality of offering a guest a bath and washing his back where he can't reach."

"You say so and put on the airs of a lady, but I caught on...to the fact of your pleasure. Don't misunderstand, I'm not saying you were wrong; only I could see you had a hard time sitting proper because you were so aroused."

"No, no, I put up with such shameful work because I respectfully obey whatever my husband says. You too were pleased — you said your task went smoothly thanks to my assistance..."

Yosetsu sensed an intruder and, raising his eyes from his wife's rear end, saw at the sliding door of the back entrance Bokuon standing with squinting eyes.

Yosetsu blinked, embarrassed; he supposed his talk with his wife had been overheard. But spotting at once Bokuon's thick cheeks gone slack and his mouth hanging open, he chose the tactic of pointing at Bokuon's awkward position so as to detract from his own.

"What's the matter with you? Did he order you to eavesdrop, to sneak up on us? Keep on like that and you'll never be a fine independent priest! Or have you the backdoor trots?" Yosetsu while smiling thus spoke stingy words, slowly, as if to himself.

"No, uh, I came to say my master already went out, and, er-r, that's all!" Bokuon spun on his heel and retreated lest he receive further sarcasm or words impossible to respond to.

Zen Master Tengai was waiting in the shade of the garden trees before the house, where the western sun was shining.

"Now we'll go, and you, look sharp! Which way?"

"Which? What?"

"What? Didn't you ask him even the way to Tangenji? It will become night if I keep dealing with you and that layman. You both waste time and energy for nothing and you slight essentials." The master set into a brisk walk. Bokuon followed, but disliking to proceed with the unpleasant feeling of being equated with Yosetsu, he opened his mouth,

"Please, Master, is this the right way?"

"You ask me now after losing the chance to ask a suitable guy at a suitable time! To men who can't understand without asking, I've always taught, Ask freely, keep asking — it brings no shame. Haven't I? But if you can't practice

74

even that, shut up and stick by me. Ahead are mountains, the road is narrowing, we're leaving the private houses. Certainly we'll come to high land commanding a fine view. Look, the road is ascending along a stream; we'll find the temple up there."

The thin stream was increased by the flood of the day before and showed traces where the overflow had flattened the weeds of the banks and invaded the road. But the quick water was clear. All mud and soil that could make it turbid had washed away over the long years, leaving only rocks and stones, a sight indicating the source to be fairly near. Chestnut branches with burs not yet grown as big as a man's fist were lodged in the stream, evidence that the heavy rain had come with strong winds.

Persimmon leaves and branches too had been blown over the hedges of Chinese juniper or Chinese hawthorn before the houses and lay scattered on the road. The hard, green fruits were cracked and exposing their white astringent flesh, and the leaves were freshly green.

They continued toward the mountains on a road with straggling farmhouses alongside, clustered in threes or fives, single households originally, which must have divided for offspring. They now could see an expanse of green rice fields lit by sunset and the Sasayama Highway passing straight through. 'We came on that road by a country bus,' thought Bokuon. The road crossed a river, and a rolling path leading in their direction from the bridge could be detected. When they came to where the path met the road they were on, they were forced to a halt by the splendid sight of Tangenji, the weathered two-storied wooden gate, the huge thatched roof of the main building, and extending from the sides of the gate like the wall of a castle, a stone retaining wall surmounted by a white wall, against a chestnut mountain.

"Tangenji was founded by a priest, Togu Jyakuei, from Nanzenji, at the beginning of the Kanei era. 'Founded,' we say, but he built himself just a little retreat hermitage here at the mouth of Tanba, far enough from the capital yet near enough to observe the phases of the life and culture of the time transmitted like reflections off a mirror.

"It was about the time the shrine to Lord Tokugawa Ieyasu was erected at Edo Castle and then at Nikko; the age when the shogunate passed to the third shogun, Iemitsu, from the second, Hidetada; when Christianity was proscribed and the early Christians were executed; when the stubborn national isolation policy was on the way to being perfected; when all Buddhist temples and Shinto shrines were under the power of the military junta and all provincial lords were forced into absolute obedience by the policy of alternate-year residence in Edo. All commoners were assigned to temples as laymen and were forbidden to travel freely or to trade in land. In effect all people, organizations, and culture were controlled by the centralized government, or Bakufu, and only so far as they served it were they recognized. Such was the age. There is a close resemblance between the Tokugawa Bakufu and our Showa-era government that crashed its way into the Pacific War and was defeated.

"Tangenji's founding priest, Togu, had been an acolyte under Tenkai of the Tendai sect and later got acquainted with Suden Konchiin of Nanzenji. But he shunned those political power scrambles and came here. It was said he was an ingenious painter and calligrapher, and thereafter such priests who chose to avoid the front lines of worldly action customarily became the head priest of Tangenji. Here they could enjoy their preference for communing with birds and flowers in quiet circumstances. Their way is also one way to live in this world."

Zen Master Tengai closed his mouth because Bokuon had a beggarly amount of learning about history as well as present society, and furthermore, he showed no interest. 'This one has no spirit or desire for anything. Well, he is better than those with brains, though not an interesting youth to teach. He will perform only what is asked of him by his seniors and become the sort of priest who has squeezed himself into a mold to spend his days practicing what is neither good nor bad....' So thought Zen Master Tengai without any sentiment.

Bokuon could not forget the rear end of Yosetsu's wife, so round as she squatted, rich in comparison to her other parts, such as her fine-shaped, rather girlish face. Her eyes as she looked up at him were smiling coyly, like a beckoning female cat.

For Bokuon it was enough to stop all thought and imagination, as if he had been struck on the head with a hammer: she was to wash the naked body of his teacher, Zen Master Tengai! '...Would she do me, too? Will she...?' The path began to waver up and down and from side to side.

When they arrived at the granite steps leading up to the gate, they were attracted by a child seated on the threshold intent on something he held in his hand. He did not notice them even when they ascended. He was using the broken-off tip of a sword to carve on a white object. Above his head a large bell hung from the rafters, its dark cavernous interior showing through a lattice coffer.

The child noticed the intrusion of feet at the edge of his working field of vision and with a cry of surprise he instantly jumped back, surprising the master and his attendant.

"Oi, oi, young fellow, no need for surprise. It's just us," said Zen Master Tengai. The boy was instinctively pulling himself into a fighting stance against foreign invaders. But when he realized they were only priests, who could not be harmful, his body relaxed and his heart calmed; and his face began to redden, for he was ashamed of his hyperbolic reaction.

"What are you carving? Let me see...oh! are you using ivory just for your amusement? How extravagant...though I understood Tangenji to have been the wealthiest temple in all of Tanba from old times...."

Mokuzu did not know ivory or the word for it, but he supposed the priest meant the bone he was carving.

"There's as much as you want. The laymen's graveyard had a landslide in yesterday's typhoon and a lot of this came out." He turned and indicated the foot of the mountain at the western end of Tangenji.

"What? from a tomb? Oh, indeed, it is a human bone. Why are you carving such a thing?"

"Why? It's likely from Hirotaro, who died last spring before the cherry blossoms. From above the knee, a femur, but it's broken, you see, because he was buried alive. There's a mountain with soft, red soil. It has red pines and looks mild, but inside is a network of tunnels left from digging whetstones. There's even a track, and handcars came and went. The tunnels go every which way and are cut to pieces. But if all were put in a straight line, the length would go from here to Kameoka Station."

Zen Master Tengai was enjoyably listening to this talk, which he supposed was an echo of the father. Bokuon felt uncomfortable at the sight of the kid coolly toying with the bone of a dead man, and more, like his brother Bunyu he was garrulous.

"You know, Hirotaro went to the war. But he soon came back because he lost an eye. Everyone else served a long time in the army or returned as war dead. Only Hirotaro came back healthy except for his eye. So his house felt small against the public — even his wife said he should have served longer, according to Grandma. True or not, Hirotaro was humiliated in this village and was getting to be taciturn and shutting himself in the mountain of whetstones and digging from morning to night, day after day. Grandma was sure he was donating them all to the army as soon as he dug them up, because he was always thinking, 'I can't apologize enough to His Majesty the Emperor.'

"Then the war ended. It wasn't a simple ending, Dad says. Our country was utterly defeated and crippled. But Hirotaro kept going to the mountain. He got into the habit of digging, Ma says. Scarcely any good whetstones come out anymore. They're mostly odds and ends, used to fix the road. Lots of good ones can be got with little effort from Wakayama Prefecture, so no one else around here almost ever goes in there. After all, they dug in the mountain since the Edo period. Other men now farm the fields, or fix the riverbanks, or do trade or other things. Only Hirotaro entered every day, tap, tap, tap, digging whetstones. He took a lantern, and if it went out he would have to escape quickly to fresh air. The villagers told him, 'Don't go in on rainy days, the mountain will slide.' But he went on in with his mandrel and wisteria basket."

Apprehensive of being stopped with "That's good enough for now, boy," Mokuzu delayed taking a breath for as long as he could manage. His voice grew hoarse, and when he could no longer bear it, he raised his shoulders to snatch a breath.

"His parents were so old they couldn't walk well. They said, 'You served enough! The war is over and our Emperor declared he's a living god no more.' His wife said, 'My dear, I was ashamed over your brief service and your coming home alive, but it wasn't my true mind — I just spoke for appearances. You need no longer strive so hard.'

"But Hirotaro silently left for the mountain every day. Grandma said, and it seems quite accurate, 'He was convinced Japan lost the war because he didn't serve enough.'

"Then on one of those days of heavy rain before the cherry blossoms last spring, he didn't come back. The villagers had to dig all over the mountain, and they found him under a landslide.

"Dad and others gave him a funeral and buried him here in the laymen's graveyard at the mountain foot. But by yesterday's rain it was partly destroyed and his bones came out. Everyone said it's awful and they gathered and performed a mortuary service this morning. They also reerected his tomb. I got this bone before they did all that."

"Why did you get such a thing?"

"Well, isn't it clear to you? Remember, Grandma said Hirotaro wished to serve the Emperor. But Hirotaro couldn't perfectly do it. Now, Emperor means, look at this gate. Don't you see the Chrysanthemum Crest?" Mokuzu touched a panel of the zelkova gate for Zen Master Tengai.

"See? Here it is. Did you never hear my grandma say? — 'These are the Imperial Crests and this gate should be respected as you respect His Majesty the Emperor.' Now then, I feel sorry for Hirotaro who couldn't serve the Emperor and who had to live with grief and die with lament. It was good fortune that yesterday his bones were disinterred, though they were reinterred before with some trouble. So, on one of them I decided to carve the Imperial Crests."

Zen Master Tengai without comment received the bone. Four chrysanthemums each fashioned like the Imperial Crest were enchased, and were of quite exquisite workmanship. He showed it to his attendant,

"Look! Isn't this fine work?"

78

"Gee! Did you do it all by yourself? What skill!"

"I started this morning right after barley gruel. I had to sharpen my sword, but I've been working ever since, even skipping lunch. I have to carve three more crests and also fix up these hanging clouds a bit more...."

Zen Master Tengai was impressed by Mokuzu's carving skill, and by his orderly talk. 'Perhaps he inherited some talent from his father and has already had some education. Anyway, he's a child well suited to this temple with its tradition of artistic priests.'

"How old are you?"

"I'm five."

He had thick eyebrows and sharp, rather elongate eyes in a slender face.

"Are you studying how to draw and carve from your father?"

"There's no reason to be taught such things. Dad says the most hateful task is to teach others. Therefore — oh! Zen Master Tengai!"

The Zen master was surprised to be so addressed all of a sudden.

"You're wasting your time coming to ask him to take that post. He says, 'On no-o-o account would I place myself where I'd have to teach others.'"

Zen Master Tengai was put out of countenance as if given a blow in swordsmanship, 'What's this? I can't be unprepared even before a child!' and his heart darkened at the realization that his request to Doyu to become dean of the college he was going to found would be hardly likely to succeed. Bokuon, seeing that his master was given a blow, which was most rare, and from a mere child, was delighted and started to grow fond of the boy.

"Be that as it may, where is your father? Please tell him of my arrival." The master used a slightly keen tone.

"He performed a service this morning, as I said, for the bones of Hirotaro. After noon he went with my senior brother Gyodo to clean up the chestnut branches broken by the typhoon."

"And is not back yet? He must have known of my coming."

"Oh, sure, he came back and asked me if you'd come. Then I was given this job of waiting here for you while he and Gyodo are off with a bamboo basket to the mountain and to the river beach to hunt up the makings for your dinner. They should be back soon."

"Hey, little pal, you mean they're off to the mountain for hare and to the river for eel? My Zen master never eats flesh, not even in stock or sauce." Reminded of Yosetsu about to kill a chicken, Bokuon hoped to show his prudence and concern.

"Of course. We know he's a Zen master, and Dad says a Zen master is like Jizo Bodhisattva for being able to save everyone who has absurd and deluded ideas. However, it's too bad his enlightenment is like the menu of a feast for hungry ghosts who can't eat though they're famished. A Zen master deserves to be reproached for 'seeing the tree peonies as if in a dream.'"[1]

Bokuon could make no sense of the priest of Tangenji's definition of a Zen master as presented by his infant son. 'I bet the kid parrots his father's words without comprehension but with a triumphant air.' But Zen Master Tengai well understood from Mokuzu's presentation what Mokuzu's father meant. 'Indeed he's referring to Nanchyuan's reproach of those who are only superficially enlightened. It appears in case 40 of *Biyan lu*. Nanchyuan is my great ancestral senior in the transmission of the Dharma, and like him I must admonish my laymen. Yet Doyu chooses Nanchyuan's words to admonish me, a Zen master, who ought to be as great at educating the public in present-day Japan as Nanchyuan was in ancient China. Doyu must be pitying me, estimating me as one who knows only desk theory, who has in hand a fabulous menu but can't savor its offerings, who sees the real world as if living in a dream.'

Suppressing his discomfort, Zen Master Tengai asked,

"Hey, priestling, tell me the relation between my being a vegetarian and what your father says."

"Well, he says it's natural to eat enjoyably any available food. But Zen Master Tengai can't eat all good foods in the world, possibly because he has a delicate stomach, or is possessed by such a rigid idea as the Buddhist precept against killing. So they are digging kudzu roots and lily bulbs. They gathered some of the small early kind of chestnut and some maple and chrysanthemum leaves. Now they must be picking bamboo seeds. The bamboo by the river beach bloomed, so rare it happens once in a hundred twenty years. What they're gathering is only from plants, and it won't be mixed with any meat or fish. Dad can boil, bake, steam, fry — he knows every way to prepare those things. He says the amount of each is small but the taste is excellent. A Zen master is a pitiable creature, so it's best to offer the best vegetarian dishes."

"Really? It's a thankful matter. Your father speaks severe words, but is kind to the one he speaks of. Incidentally, where is your mother?"

"She went to sell clothes as usual with my sister Ran on her back. Dad said she needn't welcome the guest, because he isn't a friend or acquaintance of hers. And she can't cook those things, which she already pointed out. She says not working even a day makes less food and clothes for the children and she hasn't time to receive him, though she doesn't know whether he's a great person — and her clothes to wear before a guest are all gone."

"Your mother went to sell clothes? Is she peddling?"

"It's called something like that."

Quickly Zen Master Tengai had to understand the economic state of Tangenji, so dire as to depend on the peddling of the priest's wife. He envisioned the process of economic decay. The temple formerly had large landholdings. He sensed the sight of thick, slanting snow incessantly falling.

"Tell me, how old is your grandma and what is she doing?"

"She is seventy-one and so healthy she says she'll live to a hundred. She stays almost independent of us next to the main hall. We use the retreat cottage. The laymen complain if we use the main building. They say we children will tear the shojis and scribble on the walls, though Dad said, 'What's wrong if children scribble and doodle as much as they please?' and Ma cried, 'We became poor, we eat only unpalatable food, if any, and dress in patched clothes, so the laymen despise us and they sent us to the retreat cottage.'"

"How do you think about it?" Zen Master Tengai asked gently.

"Anywhere's the same. It's only a place to sleep. But what I detest —" Mokuzu shut his mouth. He disliked the effect of the problem of where they lived. It was a four-cornered battle between his parents and various laymen, his father and his mother, his parents and his grandmother, and his family and all the laymen. But he thought nothing could be done about it and there was no point in complaining; it was like the rainy season of June, the mists of November, no matter how he disliked it.

All the discords that came into his world through his senses he had decided could be dealt with only by refusing to allow them to invade his innermost mind. Or if he let them enter that far, he converted them to useful material for his world of imagination.

The world of reality was like the life of a fisherman who rows out to rough seas to catch fish: cheerless, cruel, hard. But just as the fisherman's catch is sorted and sent to market and finally reaches the kitchen, Mokuzu brought all matters to the kitchen of his brain and cooked them as he pleased to compose his fantasy, like a housewife making an enjoyable meal for her family.

Thus he submitted his body to the world of reality while using his mind for it very little. But when he entered the world of fantasy he freely and fully exerted his mind while his body stayed relatively inactive. Reality offered nothing worthy of notice. Fantasy was a sweet, delightful, charming world; so he spent the larger share of his ability there, and economized on the time and energy he needed for reality.

Now he was looking up at the sharply outlined sun about to set behind the top of the tall cypress at the southwest corner of the front garden. Soon many beams of light came through the fan-shaped leaves and reached the forward area of the garden, where the shade was increasing. The contrast between the shady and the bright earth became very clear.

"Oh!" Mokuzu spoke up. The two priests regarded him with raised eyebrows.

"I was told to lead the Zen master straight to the best room from the west garden as soon as he showed up," he announced and began to walk ahead.

They came to the front of the main building. The storm doors were drawn fully aside. Beyond the veranda was a wide, square, tatami-floored main hall. Deep in the back was a Buddhist sanctum decorated above and on either side with drapery.

In the depths of the sanctum an altar enshrined the temple's principle image, though from the garden it could not be seen for the scarcity of light reaching there. On the altar was in fact a shrine with its leaves shut fast, within which was a statue of the Eleven-Faced Kannon.

Zen Master Tengai stopped in the center of the front garden, from where he could directly face the principal image. With joined palms he bowed. Then Bokuon did the same.

Tangenji stood on an eminence and commanded a wide view of rice fields extending east, south, and west, through which the Sasayama Highway passed and the Sakura River meandered. Where the rice fields ended, small, round, overlapping mountains ranged to faraway soaring mountains so distant that their color was a simple pale blue without solidity like a paper cutout against the clear azure sky.

The master halted. "What a splendid sight! It expands the mind. The sky exactly fits the phrase 'There is only nothingness, no holiness exists,'[2] and the river, how like 'The willows are green, the flowers are red.'[3] Hey, kid! You have a pure and wide natural world, even if nothing else, eh?"

Mokuzu walked ahead, turned to the right off the path, went through a small gate with a cypress-bark roof, and stepped into a moss garden that led to the west veranda of the best guest room. The guests were still standing in the front garden admiring the view.

"Don't you think so, kid? Most important for human beings is where they grow up. Our surroundings are of first importance, for we see them day and night and they become our flesh and blood." The master spoke partly to comfort Mokuzu and partly to keep him from taking them ahead so quickly.

Mokuzu disliked the trouble of going back. He stepped up to the veranda, kicking his straw sandals onto the large stepping stone. From the veranda he responded,

"There couldn't be anything bigger or more important than our mind!" and he pushed aside the shojis and was gone into the guest room. The room was filled with the aroma of fine incense.

A low table and cushions were placed neatly before the alcove, and to the side a tea set had been prepared by Mokuzu's father so that tea could be offered as soon as hot water was brought in.

Zen Master Tengai in the garden clicked his tongue, "What precocious conceit!" Bokuon chuckled in spite of himself. At once the master glared at him fiercely and scolded away, "What's funny? You're a fool! How can a dullard like you possibly understand the true heart of a genius?"

In the alcove a scroll depicted a thin-colored crooked stem of wild chrysanthemum growing pendent from a cliff under white moonlight, painted by Mokuzu's father at age fifteen.

Mokuzu went out leaving the words, "If the last of the sun is bothersome, you can roll down the reed screen at the eaves of the veranda." He then set off to look for his father and brother Gyodo.

9

Divergent Views on Education

Zen Master Tengai's passion for education began not after the war, when he was in his fifties, but much earlier in his priestly career.

After studying with Priest Mukai he went to train under Zen Master Shutan at Daitokuji. There he was awakened to his original nature and at age twenty-nine was authorized by the master for his "perfection of the important study."

Subsequently, while acting as head priest of a small temple in Kyoto, he devoted his attention to educational good works, such as raising scholarships for university students and offering them lodging. During this time, however, Zen Master Shutan could not successfully refuse the request that he assume the Zen mastership of Shoshinji to revive its professional Zen training monastery, and he moved into the depths of the Gifu mountains, ordering Tengai to accompany him. There he soon died, and in his place he left his highest disciple, Ishin. As the new Zen master, Ishin devoted himself to the inherited task of reviving Shoshinji, assisted by the junior priest Tengai. But Ishin had a delicate constitution, and he too, burdened with the anxiety of responsibility, soon died. So at last Tengai became chief priest of Shoshinji and Zen master of its monastery.

Tengai was forty-five at the time, late in 1941, the year the Tojo Cabinet was formed and Pearl Harbor was attacked by the Japanese Imperial Navy.

From then he carried on with Shutan's and Ishin's cherished desire to revive Shoshinji, and he was also elected president of a college founded by the sect to which he belonged. But thinking it essential to start his own ideal education from the beginning, he resigned this latter post and began strenuous efforts to found his own college.

Whereas Shutan and Ishin had tried to accomplish the revival of Shoshinji through repair and remodeling of the buildings and grounds, Tengai thought, 'There's no point in pouring my energy into visible renovation, fated as it is to rise and ruin according to the currents of the time and regardless of my effort. Above all, my concern must be content, not form, which means, education for the purpose of issuing men of splendid talent into the world. To that end I must found my professional college and raise the present training monastery to a higher level like a graduate school.'

Hence he disregarded the worn tile roofs and rotting verandas and did not perfectly maintain the gardens, once applauded as fine specimens of the Zen garden. In addition, he rather attempted to discard the cultures of the tea ceremony, flower arrangement, calligraphy, sumi painting, Noh play, haiku, and so on, which had developed with Zen in Japan and could hardly be separated from it. And he kept himself at a trot to make his trainees aware of their original nature and to fulfill his earnest wish to found his college. His course of action was therefore to impose severe sitting meditation on his disciples and to assign them hard physical tasks, such as cutting and hauling timber, to form an economic base. At the same time, he courted men of good breeding and substantial means for donations while gathering professors to compose the faculty he would direct to teach the students and trainees.

Now then, though he was pondering it and rushing about as if possessed by it, what education had he in mind? This was Doyu's simple question. Did he feel highly honored to be asked to assume the deanship of Shoshin College to be founded by Zen Master Tengai? No, rather he felt uncomfortable.

"Zen Master, you seem to be consecrating your all to education, but could you explain to me its content and importance?"

"Tangenji Priest, listen, there are no more important beings than human beings in this human world. People, people, people, you meet them every-where as if they were the most plentiful beings, and yet how rare is a human being who is helpful to society, to the world of human beings. After all, the fundamental force to improve the human world in the direction in which people can live happily is neither the natural mountains and rivers nor machines, but only human beings. If there are able men, all systems and contents of society and the world can be changed for the better.

"At a glance you can find examples in our Buddhist and Zen history of the appearance of great men who helped many people over long years and in a wide area. And we needn't confine our sight to the East, to Buddhist society, for we can see the fact that human happiness was increased by the meritorious deeds of a few great people the world over and in every field — politics, the arts, medicine, science, industry. Indeed, for human beings no being is more important than the human being.

"Here we have to realize that even those able and beneficial men — if we trace them to their origins — were born naked and mewling. No one can be a prime minister at birth; everyone is dependent on the education of family, school, and society. So it's perfectly possible that the son of a poor stonecutter can become a prime minister.

"Education is of gravest importance. A man can turn either good or bad according to his education. He must be educated to be useful to the world. Education must be a long-range project to benefit posterity. The peace, prosperity, and happiness of future mankind utterly depend on how we educate the newborn from now on. Then, you can understand that nothing is more important than education, can't you?"

Zen Master Tengai enforced his words with so much stress and rising intonation that his delivery approached a shout.

"Ah, yes...education, and talented men...you mean..." Doyu took shredded tobacco from a caddy kept near at hand, as if intending to soften the atmosphere produced by the tone of his guest. Slowly he filled his pipe and lit it with a coal dug up from the ash in the hibachi. Undeniably Zen Master Tengai was impressive with his brimful rigor.

Doyu, having received his letters, was acquainted with his handwriting. 'What an ignorant hand!' he had been thinking. 'He gives his might to every line and corner of every character so the paper will almost tear at any moment from the pressure of the brush and stain of the ink. Does he wish to express the grandeur and strength of his characters by mere brawn? It's a crazy misconception. Such effects should be expressed to the best of one's ability by tactful use of tone and line, by compositional balance and contrast, by treatment of space. Brushwork produced by so much force as to endanger the paper or scatter the ink like fresh blood might impress the untrained eye as art of tremendous spirit. But whoever has had some training in art will estimate it to be shameless and unscrupulous ignorance and savagery, and the artist to be of rigid, narrow, and humble character.'

Doyu had sufficient, even unstrained, confidence in his eye for art. After all, at age four he had enjoyably received his first lessons in calligraphy from his father; and he was raised in so blest a situation as to be provided two private teachers by Priest Mukai. They were a high priest of the Tendai sect,

Kawachi Gyokusui, considered one of the best contemporary calligraphers, and at the same time Nomura Keishun, a leading sumi painter of the Kyoto-Shijo school. By each Doyu had been congratulated: 'I have nothing more I can teach you. Henceforth cultivate your character and improve your skill on your own. My wish is that you steadily seek what I have been steadily seeking.' This verbal certification, commonly called 'initiation into the mysteries of art,' Doyu had received when he was only around twenty-five.

Since then until his present age of forty-six, he had daily amused himself with the brush in spite of disruption from various circumstances, such as inheriting Tangenji at his father's death, meeting the death of his first wife, remarrying, fathering five children, and being compelled to live in a penurious state.

To talk about his confidence to judge art was therefore too silly; he could judge it as easily as he could judge the right path to take to any building or rock in his familiar abode with his eyes shut.

But for that very reason he did not train himself in Zen practice as much as to qualify as a Zen master, and he found it hard to judge how fine a Zen master Tengai was. 'As for his calligraphy, he is altogether misunderstanding. But possibly the profession of Zen educator is unlike the way of painting and calligraphy, though some part could be alike....I remember our teacher Mukai telling me one day, "You haven't the character for a first-class Zen priest. Yet your talent with the brush is beyond my tether and is respectable, as your teachers Kawachi and Nomura recognize. Therefore, much as I am your Zen teacher, I shan't teach you Zen in a way that interferes with your path." And, incidentally, he commented on Tengai, at the time training under Zen Master Shutan, "He has the talent to be a national figure as a Zen master. When the world of Zen meets distress, only men like him can save and revive it. The more the country is disordered, the more his greatness will be expressed. Such he is, though he can become nothing other than a Zen master or a politician. If he turns to politics, he could likely become a prime minister....."'

"I am convinced that the most fatal cause of our defeat in the war was the shortage of able men. Exceedingly great was the ambition to establish the Greater East Asia Coprosperity Sphere to unite the minds of a hundred million people as the mind of one nation to be presided over by our preeminent Emperor, descended from an unbroken line of sovereigns. But in reality how many politicians, military personnel, and civilians did their best from the bottom of their heart? Didn't their conduct differ from their word? Isn't it an evident fact that most were lacking in spirit and from day to day fitting themselves out for surface appearance — as if to prove they too were decent Japanese — while they were hating it and only striving after selfish desires?

"I had occasion to see this in detail. During the war I lectured throughout Japan and thrice visited the Chinese mainland on the pretext of encouraging and comforting the soldiers at the front. It was a disaster; they were reciting the 'Imperial Directive to Military Personnel,' while in reality they lacked spiritual enlightenment and peace even in their personal lives, to say nothing of loyalty to our Emperor. Fearful of their own death, how could they protect their country and its people? The same can be said of most politicians and government officials; they couldn't make head or tail of their lives or of the world. They led the people while their prime concern was to protect their position, salary, and honor. With such as they how could we implement our Holy War to build the Greater East Asia Coprosperity Sphere? We deserved to fail and should have expected to be beaten down. The reason for our defeat was, in the first place, and in the second too, the shortage of able men, and not a shortage of weapons, petroleum, food, and money.

"Tangenji Priest, you can understand, for you too experienced acolyte life and monastic life. Don't you think with regret, 'If only those statesmen, generals, scholars, and industrialists had worked at least a third as hard as we Zen trainees!'?

"Don't we rise at three during the exclusive meditation terms, and elsewise at three-thirty? We finish a good part of the day's work by the time common people wake around seven. In those early hours we finish our chanting, sitting meditation, koan combat, and indoor and outdoor cleaning. We eat no fish or meat, yet live an energetic life. We sleep four hours when six are allowed, and we have no Sundays. We get a day's rest about once a month to mend our clothes, cure our ills, wash our laundry, and write our kin, so as to put in order our personal affairs should we meet an unexpected death.

"Zen monks never complain but enjoy such a life, for they recognize the greatest task is to study the Dharma, and they believe they had better die if they can't become enlightened. They suffer not over the prospect of death but over living without knowing the meaning of their life, their death, the world, the universe. Indeed we Zen trainees are gladly living each day all day by risking our life for the Truth.

"But look at the world. In what field is anyone risking his life for and entirely devoting himself to the study of so honorable a matter? During the war too, numerous brass hats came to our monastery, calling it a study trip. But they couldn't bear even a week of our training and raised a howl and escaped. They complained of leg pain from the sitting meditation, dizziness from hunger, stupor from so little sleep. Alas, those very men were occupying

87

the country's most important military and civilian posts! But for us monks they were like babies or weak-kneed, snot-nosed kids!

"Don't you feel chagrined? We passed to them the helm that was to steer Japan into the future, and we watched from the side because they assured us that we could depend on them. But they were nothing, and as we feared, they overturned the country. How we must repent for letting such incompetents take the lead! I knew the moment the war began that Japan would fail, for I saw who they were: excellent at nothing but the art of lying, and they deceived even themselves for a while. I understood that to carry out the Holy War was an impossibility for them because they hadn't cleared up their fear of death, and so they were incapable of offering themselves.

"Never did I more regret not entering politics myself than when I saw our fate was defeat. Were I prime minister then, I would not have kept such leaders. It would have been better for them to sweep up trash in a local office. And the prime minister should have made the proper educational reforms to hammer out able men. When it first became apparent that our Holy War would fail, those former princes, peers, and higher officials began coming to Zen Master Shutan at Daitokuji. But by then he was too old and his highest disciple, Ishin, ailing...When they turned to me, it was the final moment of the war. All I could do was advise them on how to finish the war and how to reconstruct Japan.

"The misfortune of our Emperor and his people was the shortage of talent to serve the country. Instead, mere masters of the lie took over all the important posts.

"However, we Zen Buddhist priests must share some responsibility. From old times our Zen sect has raised and assisted the emperors, shoguns, and leading class. But since the Meiji era all sects, especially our Zen sect, directly received waves of agitation from the exclusion of Buddhism, and our Zen talent dried up. How could Zen priests who had turned cowardly and doltish guide society? Who can refrain from shedding tears if they know the brilliant history of Japan and of Zen, and the wretched history from the Meiji era on down? What corruption! Alas, where can we now see a Zen priest worthy of the name National Teacher, like Daio, Daito, and Muso, and where such Zen Teachers as Eisai and Dogen, where the likes of Hakuin, Takuan, and Suden? It is a grave matter! The fate of Zen talent is the fate of Japan, and by effect not only the fate of our Japanese Zen community but of the world, despite what people may wish.

"Tangenji Priest, from my talk so far, please understand how education is important, especially education based on Zen spirit. It may help your understanding if I discuss the history of East and West and the future of the world and the fate of the earth, but there is no time. We are in a burning house! The matter is that urgent! We must issue out able men who have solved their life problems and can sacrifice themselves for Japan. There is no point in regretting the past. Now is the time not to be sorry but to reconstruct our destroyed country. There is no way but to reconstruct our Zen sect. Indeed there is no way but for Zennists to lead the leading class.

"I have vowed to devote my remaining life to the reconstruction of Japan, making my base Shoshinji in Gifu under the slogan 'Reconstruction of Japan from Shoshinji!' That is the essential place to train great Zennists who will scatter across the country and the world to teach Zen. Under their tutelage, leaders will dedicate themselves to their people. In the last analysis the purpose of founding my college is to raise Zennists, to build up a Zen-spirited nation, and to establish a Zen-spirited world."

Zen Master Tengai was not a great speaker; his talk was neither closely reasoned nor rich in vocabulary; nor was he capable of the well-turned phrase that could scratch, as it were, the itch of his listener. His words rather made him seem like a strong-armed king in king-of-the-castle played by rural kids.

But his features as he spoke with brio, vibrating the air of the room and at times even the shojis, gave him the look of an ancient samurai dueling with real swords, full-spirited to welcome any foe who appeared on his chosen path.

Doyu disliked arguing; especially facing so dauntless a Zen master he felt the futility of argument. 'It will lead to combat like bulls locking horns.' He wished to express his view in a different way.

"Zen Master, you say the enterprise to build up such a thing as the Greater East Asia Coprosperity Sphere to be presided over by our gracious Emperor collapsed and ended in defeat because of the shortage of able men, and that, in turn, because Buddhist and notably Zen Buddhist priests did not sufficiently direct the elite in all fields. But I wonder whether you do not in the first place doubt and question the emotion, thought, scheme, and society that countenanced being under the dominion of an emperor and also the idea of a coprosperity sphere. If you have such a doubt and question, then the Buddhist associations can be appreciated for having excellently led society by not leading it. The Buddhist associations were neither cowardly nor doltish. Quite well they guided people not to advance the war effort and to initiate a cease-fire as early as possible. It was the best available course we Buddhist priests could take. Don't you see?

"Buddhism does not endorse war, and Zen is not attached to worldly matters, especially to material comfort and prosperity. Therefore the defeat of

Japan in the last war was rather brought on by the proper function, if not altogether satisfactory, of the leadership of the Buddhist and Zennist circle, and not by its idleness or lack of leadership. That is why the victorious powers headed by America did not bomb the Buddhist centers of Kyoto and Nara — in effect, they could find no reason to destroy the Buddhist circle and rather protected it."

Doyu talked quietly to avoid stimulating the passion of his guest, but Zen Master Tengai broadly waved his left hand several times as if to push away what he had heard, and softly he laughed, "Ho ho ho!

"Tangenji Priest, it seems you don't quite understand worldly matters or human beings, spending as you do your life painting in companionship with nature. But take a look at world history, particularly the history of relations between East and West. Since antiquity Eastern people have been a quiet and friendly race disdaining to fight, with the exception of Kublai Khan of the Mongol dynasty. Those who invaded, plundered, and trampled on such a peaceful life were Westerners. They took India, once Buddha's country, they massacred pious American Indians, they eroded the high culture of China by means of opium and guns, and finally they came to this island country of Japan intent on plunder. These are the bare facts, as evident as the sun in the sky.

"On these grounds we Japanese, who had lived peacefully since the era of Prince Shotoku while keeping his Seventeen Article Constitution, wherein 'Respect harmony above all else' is written — we Japanese stood up to free not only ourselves but our Asian brethren from the heavy pressure of Westerners. This was our Emperor's wish and the true motive of the Greater East Asia Coprosperity Sphere.

"To assist our Emperor and the idea of the Coprosperity Sphere and to lead the people toward its goal was the most sublime duty of all Buddhists, and certainly of all Zennists. What we regret is that we did not do enough to accomplish it and that we made it miscarry on the way.

"Tangenji Priest, I haven't the least intention here to convert you to my view. I rather hope you will keep yours, which is milder than mine.

"Why I hope so is that one like you who loves nature and has a generosity of viewpoint is most suited to be dean of the college I am founding. So I really entreat you to accept.

"I shall find for history an apt historian, and mobilize scholars for courses on the Constitution, politics, economy, psychology, philosophy, literature, aesthetics, and so on. What I need right here and now is the dean to command and supervise both the various scholars and the students who are to master with body and mind the spirit of Zen.

"For the dean I need at any cost a priest like you who has a family as well as an academic and monastic career, and who is a strictly fair person with a noble and compassionate nature. This last must be innate and not acquired through severe training or too miserable hardship. Because he has to contact directly with all students and faculty, a naturally kind heart is the most requisite element for the personality of the dean. He must sensitively enter their feelings before they express them by word or act, and must carefully supervise and properly guide them, for they will be so tender as to be influenced by even the day's weather or the sight of fresh green leaves, or leaves autumn-tinged...Oh! but I needn't express it — I've written you many times. Please, now, accept my entreaty and take the office of the dean in my Shoshin College to produce able, Zen-spirited men for the future of the world! Please, I beg your favor from the bottom of my mind, like this — "

Zen Master Tengai put his palms to the tatami and bowed low.

Perplexed, Doyu passed his hand over the back of his half-bald head. 'It's quite a serious conjuration. Well, things generally settle where they will if I leave them undecided and keep responding agreeably with numerous interjections.... Let me suppose I'm a branch projecting into a stream that is world events. Normally the stream washes quietly past the branch. But at times it would take the branch along, and it pushes and pulls and swings it up and down. If the branch doesn't yield, the stream will soon enough leave off and flow on. I'll let it flow, and surely it will give up on me and flow on as it likes.

'But Zen Master Tengai isn't like that. He's forceful and avariciously tries to take me away. And he will if I don't resolutely make myself clear and refuse what must be refused. So powerful is his current it will take the branch by ripping it away or even by uprooting the trunk.

'To be caught in his current is to live in his world, to live as he lives, to live his life. Why should I who have my own life go and do that? — how ridiculous!

'It means by and large to live for his joy and his suffering while I have a heart and body of my own. He'll take in his laymen, associates, faculty, and many students, and put hundreds and thousands of lives into his belly. Look at his splendid barrel of a belly, enabling him to sit effortlessly and endlessly balanced in formal posture. Such fine seated posture doesn't come of practicing Buddha's strict morality or of following his teaching, but comes by and as a result of the process of eating up innumerable human lives with fearless avarice.

'I well know what will happen if I am pulled into his current. During the day my eyes, ears, body, and soul will live for him, and only when dusk visits with the appearance of bats will my mind begin inch by inch to open its window, and I will tremulously begin to stretch my limbs as if to confirm they are mine. *Keh!* no, thanks — such a hapless life! I don't like it and I'd better close the account. I'll not be caught in another man's life however great he is and however incomparably good a deed he is going to perform, and even if it leads to the reconstruction of Japan, world peace, the happiness of mankind, and the requital of a Buddha's or a God's mercy!'

So Doyu thought as he smoked, his eyes averted from the steady eyes and seated form with its heavily settled equilibrium.

Between the gaps of the weathered pine boards of the veranda he could see, if he looked, the earth beneath. By the veranda was a mossy oblong stepping stone. 'That stone and those rocks set to resemble scattered islands in an inlet and all the others composing a valley and a bridge were introduced by my father. I was told he took personal command to have the villagers transport them from Mt. Hangoku, soaring as I see it now in the south and forming the border between Kyoto and Osaka prefectures.

'It was said the work went on at the hottest time, spring to autumn. The villagers were turned out in full force to push those rocks to the valley, load them on carts, and haul them with their cows and horses across the fields and the Sakura River. The women entertained them daily with delicacies — loquats, peaches, melons...My father's intent was not only to add charm to Tangenji, but also to make an occasion to give food and pay to the poor and unemployed, so I've heard.

'What joyous work it must have been to engage so many to carry these rocks from such a lofty, precipitous mountain, having meals along the way, cracking watermelons against a rock, bathing in the stream, and at last bringing the rocks here to perfect the garden he imagined.

'However, the work of the son left with the perfected garden is only to water, weed, and prune — the duty of maintenance with no joy of creation. In fact I have ideas for partial improvements — resetting that rock a little more this way, rerouting the stream — but to touch any part would disturb the total balance. There's no money for complete reform, and I have no ability to gather it. All I can do is continue in vain to draw on white paper the scene I envision....'

Doyu raised his eyes from the level expanse of thick moss and arranged rocks to the rocky hill-like upper area with its stone lantern and farther back, to the right, a five-storied stone pagoda. To the left of these was a wooden repository for books — copied in miniature from Shosoin in Nara — and a small Shinto shrine honoring Lord Sugawara no Michizane. The shrine had a patinated copper roof and was sheltered under a tile roof supported by cypress posts, with fencing on the three sides. Behind, a mixed hedge of sasanqua, andromeda, holly, and hawthorn divided the garden from the graveyard to the west and from the steep mountainside to the north. Along the other side of the hedge, tall cedars and cypresses screened the western sun and ornamented the path to the graveyard.

The sun set behind the western mountains, leaving an afterglow in the sky. The moss farthest from the veranda was the first to regain its greenness, and a cool air moved in.

Zen Master Tengai remained immobile, patiently awaiting an answer as he looked full at Doyu. Doyu with head averted drew slowly on his pipe. The master inserted no disturbance, for he assumed the decision was being pondered in its final stage.

Doyu continued to reflect. 'This garden rests my mind; indeed it's beautiful. But when my father viewed his creation from this seat, did he enjoy only its tranquil beauty? No, he must have had the satisfaction of living his own life, and like a fountain the gush of his joy must have known no end.

'I on the contrary can't feel such joy; to view his garden is like viewing a quiet river. But consider the mountain above the hedge. It was a tangle of inferior pine and oak, all of which I cleared away with saw and ax. I prepared the soil and planted whips of chestnut. I topped them and grafted on an improved variety. I weeded, fertilized, sprayed. And now they're a productive orchard. Whenever there's a typhoon, like yesterday, immature burs are blown away and branches broken off, facilitating the invasion of various insects and diseases, and I must promptly and suitably treat each tree.

'Viewing my orchard, do I sense merely tranquil beauty? No, I have the joy of being a creator, as if seated on a cloud. How different from sitting on a chair, which is how I feel having to maintain this ready-made garden. The joy of creating or founding a new thing frees one's mind from one's limited body.

'I therefore shall never force my children to inherit this temple or educate them to feel that they must do so, unaware of the hidden dissatisfaction. They had better live as they like, choose whatever way they like, with their own responsibility.'

"To begin with, what we call 'education'—" Doyu realized he had begun, and he regretted it. Even so, he resolved to express his mind. 'Oops! I've made a difficult start! But since it's come to this, I might as well get on with it. Nobody will be helped if I keep myself at a respectful distance because he was my senior at Toyoin and is now a Zen master.'

Zen Master Tengai's eyes shone, and he slightly jutted his chin in anticipation of the answer he was at last to hear.

"Yes, I think what we call 'education' is one of the most fastuous, or if I see with sympathy, most comical, of all human activities, isn't it?"

"Fastuous? Comical?" Apparently Zen Master Tengai was surprised. But as soon as he saw what was meant, he contracted his eyebrows, glared sternly, and clamped his mouth, pulling back at the corners — his expression to demand and await what was to follow, very familiar to his attendant and to other disciples. Moreover, it was not simply an expression of waiting to understand his opponent's mind by hearing an added explanation, but of preparing to leap to the attack like a tiger as soon as his opponent finished all he had to say.

"When I was eight my parents ordered me to leave home and enter Toyoin. Of course my father considered it an educational measure. I spent my youth under Mukai's direction while attending public school and studying with two private art teachers. But even to this day I can't fathom why my father sent me off that way. I mean, was it a direct expression of his love? I think it reasonable for loving parents to hope that their children can live without the knowledge, skill, wisdom, and character that can be got by education. But more important is for parents to prepare, or to wish to prepare, an environment in which a child can live perfectly well without such education. What I am saying can be said with more certainty if we look at the results of the education intended by educators....

"Anarchism isn't a bad ideal in the political field, nor in the field of education. I've been an educator in a broad sense ever since I inherited Tangenji at age twenty-six. I've had to educate my laymen as well as my family, and it was also a necessary part of my work for the Buddhist Association at all levels — prefectural, city, town, and village. But when I was around thirty-six I began to realize education is no more than a man's vehicle to achieve his ambition to control others as he likes, especially those who by virtue of their close relationship to him should be loved by him the most.

"Education is set up to suit educators more than the body and mind of those to be educated. The essence of education is to teach 'do this, not that,' though often it is wrapped in the softest floss or warm steam. If so, one should not be an educator but take the honest way and seek political power, where one's intention to control others by power is clearly exposed. Education and politics may differ in outlook, but are much alike as to their real state of affairs.

"From the first, both education and politics could be practiced without stagnation if there were one truth, one real way to live. But such a truth is unknown to anybody. There may be some truths, but they are not one truth, because each sentient and insentient being has its individual inner truth. There are of course common truths that raise no problem. Problematic are the uncommon, unclear, indefinite truths, which are impossible to teach. If

94

an educator forcefully teaches them, his aim and methods will be like a politician's, for he can only force people to follow, and if all his educational practice is put through a sieve, only his ambition like chaff will remain.

"Viewed in this light, I question our qualification to educate human beings or even other creatures. Ironically, whoever attempts it is most fit to be educated on this point. Don't educators too feel ashamed to look squarely at themselves?

"Think a bit. Suppose I educate my children. Is their life inferior to mine, or mine superior to theirs? What are a person's wisdom and character but his life itself? Granted I have somewhat more knowledge and skill from having lived longer. But about that I needn't act superior. They will naturally acquire both knowledge and skill if we amicably live together. Sometimes too I will be taught by them without the establishment of a teacher–pupil relation.

"Then please suppose I teach a cat or a dog. It's easy to understand this isn't education but mere force: the animal will be forced to obey a more savage and ignorant being.

"Then imagine my teaching a pine or a cedar. The sole means to make it understand any educational design is by physical tyranny. Whoever calls this education will be laughed at and seen as a fearful, pitiful madman possessed by delusion.

"To attempt to educate human beings on such matters as truth, wisdom, and character is therefore an incompetent, barren, comical, pitiful, crazy act. As for teaching knowledge and skill, it is the mere ledger sheet of merchants, the calculation of politicians, and a cruel way to treat others, coming from egoistic self-love. So I humbly beg your pardon for not undertaking the job of assisting such education.

"I have spent the last ten years learning as much as possible how to live without behaving like a teacher. I'm not yet perfect at it, and often I regret speaking and acting like an educator to my family and my laymen. I hope to attain the state of peaceful coexistence without being like that at all.

"Consequently, Zen Master, you are asking that so important a post as the deanship of Shoshin College be occupied by one least suited to it."

Zen Master Tengai's face could usually be taken for arrogant, but now he was listening with a smile as he continued to look full at Doyu. Doyu had yet to finish all he wanted to say, but he decided to stop.

He wanted to express his hatred of being restrained by the power that goes with education. His long training years were self-restrained under the eyes of his teacher and senior monks. Then after his father's death, he was entreated to inherit Tangenji by his mother, the laymen, and the neighboring temples, and many devices were used to cozen him.

In truth he had not wanted to become a priest. He disliked chanting, meditation, and preaching, and simply managed those duties because he was used to them from his acolyte years.

His real wish had been to paint and to play the shakuhachi while fishing in the river or ambling carefree around the country, unfettered by severe Buddhist morality and watchful eyes. He had wanted to frolic with congenial sorts, calling in geishas, or bask in the water of the Black Current while staying at a beach hotel, or drink and feast on a meadow. In a word, he had been dreaming of just living the life of a playboy.

There was actually a brief spell when he could realize his dream. He had then in his bosom enough cash to build two or three houses. But in short course the police acceded to a request to search him out and uncovered his traces and returned him to Tangenji. There he was shut up as if imprisoned and forced to perform his inheritance ceremony and his wedding to his first wife, Aona. This chain of compulsory stratagems was implemented by the head layman, Yosetsu, who read the mind of Doyu's mother and considered his own profit.

Aona, frail from the start, died in exchange for the life of their firstborn son Bunyu. Then before the passing of three years Micha was invited in as a second wife regardless of Doyu's will, and children were born one after another, though she too was not physically strong. As the Pacific War began, the field rent to Tangenji ceased to be paid and management of the temple economy became impossible without going through the complex and mysterious hand of Yosetsu. Doyu, who had a poor sense of economy, could not comprehend such a situation as being unable to provide for his family, could not grasp that it was real.

Around that time he was ordered to head the Buddhist Association and the Agricultural Commission, both of which he served with equity, and he found some pleasure in cultivating chestnuts and in spreading their culti-vation, and when he had time he continued with his painting and calligraphy, his only real pleasure. Overall, he could not say with certainty for whom his life was being lived: his mother? the Association? the Commission? Yosetsu? He felt his situation was such that he could not live his own life.

However, when the war ended and Mokuzu was born, Doyu was awakened by a realization that dispelled the mist hanging before his eyes: 'I became poor, my children cry for hunger, Micha blames me for there being no income. But now I know that he who feels sad, senses pain, and thinks himself pitiful is no one but me. Indeed, it's my life, my mind, eyes, mouth, limbs, my own body!

'Yosetsu can no longer control my economy because I have no economy to control. I'm free of the Association and the Commission. Now for the first time I can directly feel my family's distress. The only ones who have never controlled me are my wife Micha and my children, who in their poor state are weak beings and rather in the position to be ministered to by me. But they shouldn't be controlled by me. They are the very benefactors of my awakening to my own feelings and thoughts. I am indebted to them. They are the kindest people in all my life for treating me as an individual living person.'

'At last I am I. However poor my state, I have my mind and my body.' Thinking thus, Doyu was quite enjoyably living his recent years as if he were a young man.

Naturally he thought, 'How can I allow myself to accept the deanship under the control of Zen Master Tengai? It is to freeze the liberty I have at last. You foolish Zen master! I am a free man, not a watchdog! I'm no such easy mark! Go find others who possess both learning and virtue and yet are unawakened to the joy of liberty. There are thousands who would gladly take the deanship — such a smoky, tenuous, false honor — and thus employed, they would slight their life to live another's.'

What Doyu really wanted to say was this, and he was prepared to if Zen Master Tengai produced further persuasions.

Fortunately for Doyu, he spoke calmly,

"I understand. My eyes were warped. You are a stranger to life's grim realities. You don't know even A of ABC about life and the world, not to mention education and politics. You are a stale wine, a bean sprouted in the shade, a lily-livered priest who likes to stay in tepid water. Your bones are as soft as an octopus. Your concern for others and your allegiant and patriotic sentiments are as vague as spring haze. You're a will-o-the-wisp, a veil of shimmering heat..." As he summoned these various insults the master kept a subdued tone. But he could no longer contain himself, for the words struck him as funny, and he burst out laughing. Then directly he stood and went out to the veranda leaving the words, "I'll be off!"

Bokuon, nodding as he maintained sitting-meditation form in the next room, was jolted awake, and he dashed to his side. Seeing his drowsy looks, the master heaped on him a shout, "You fool, we'll go, hurry up!"

At that instant Gyodo appeared, attended by Mokuzu. Gyodo was discomforted at the sight of his father seated in the guest room and the guests stooping at the veranda to put on their sandals and reach for their scrips.

From the moss garden he told his father, "The bath is ready." Like his father he had thick eyebrows, a fairly round, orderly face, a broad chest, and thick arms. Mokuzu had the same eyebrows and straight nose, with eyes more elongate, lashes longer, and lips thinner, and his body was slender.

Doyu came out to the veranda. "Zen Master, why do you hurry so? As you see, my sons have prepared the bath, and I was planning to offer you excellent vegetarian dishes. My wife too will soon be home. I expected you would stay the night. We can close our talk about the deanship, there being no chance of progress. But haven't we many things to talk about, to do with our teacher Mukai, and our being Dharma brothers?"

"I haven't time to squander on talk of the past. I have arranged to trouble your head layman, Yosetsu Fujii, for the night. Hey, kids!" Paying Doyu no more regard, Zen Master Tengai approached the boys, who were loitering in the garden. "This is for you. If you have siblings, divide it fairly." He handed Gyodo a severally folded white paper containing money.

Heedless of their thanks, he spoke, louder than necessary: "Listen, you two! Human beings must be strong! You can achieve anything if you have the will. Persevere to the last of the last. Drive yourself to the wall. If you do, and still persevere, certainly your situation will change. That is your chance to break through. Necessity is the mother of invention, do you understand? What's important is to perfectly combust your energy. When you are about to die you should have no energy left — die after spending it all. At the risk of your life, deal with whatever problems you face. There is nothing you can't attain if you act with the mind prepared for death. Farewell! Perchance we shall meet again!"

He turned, walked quickly to the gate, and descended the stone steps. His words shook the air, violent as a thunderbolt. Gyodo and Mokuzu stood stunned. But their father on the veranda laughed, "*Fu fu fu!*" and with a lonesome countenance spoke to himself, "Surely he's great, but I daresay he's a comic figure. Well, there's the bath…shall I enter it? By the way, why should he consort with the likes of Yosetsu? Hmm, after all, raccoon dogs of a kind can share the same burrow."

II

Rising Mist

10

Mokuzu's First Earthly Desire

The onset of March brought no change in the landscape; the trees were not yet budding nor the weeds putting forth new shoots. But Mokuzu was being allowed to go out with his mother for the first time since he could remember.

When he got up he saw her at her dressing table hastily and simply preparing for her outing.

"You promised to take me...right?"

"I never did — children only get in my way so I can't do my work," she replied without looking at him. She took up her bundle and stepped down into her clogs. At once Mokuzu's chest grew hot and a sadness rose from his belly to issue as a flood of tears and a loud, reboant wail. Micha turned in surprise.

"What's the matter? Why is today any different? You're going to wait right here playing nicely with Ran, aren't you?"

"You promised! Yesterday you said you'd take me today for sure!"

Micha did not recall saying any such thing and assumed he had dreamed it during the night.

"It's a dream — you dreamed it." Hearing this, Mokuzu noticed that his anger over the presumed broken promise was ebbing and being replaced by the realization that truly he had dreamed it. But what disillusion and disappointment! He could not continue to wail or to blame his mother. He frowned strenuously and settled to the hard black earth before the entrance, his energy spent. Sobbing, he bore his sorrow, crouched so low that his cheek almost touched the ground.

His mother unexpectedly became kind and raised him in her arms. "Do you so want to come? I can't buy you candy and won't have time to cheer you up. I only walk, patiently calling on strangers to ask 'Please won't you buy any clothes from me?' I must humble myself, and mostly I'm turned away. You may come if you want to so badly, but you must never beg me to buy you anything and never say your feet are tired. You'll just have to follow silently and patiently."

Mokuzu's heart felt brighter than the broad dawning sky. He could derive enough joy from the prospect of walking with her. To be given the chance to see the strange sights, the houses and gardens of others, gave him an indescribable sense of accomplishment and satisfaction.

Until noon they walked through country where small clusters of houses were scattered wide. Then they rested on a sunny hill. They would not have lunch.

"When I get home I'll cook rice. On the way I'll buy some food to go with it. Be patient in anticipation of supper. Your mother goes out every day like today, and she never eats. Don't you think next time you'd rather stay home?"

"I can be patient. Coming with you is more fun."

To reach the house they were headed for they had to climb a roundabout mountain path quite far from other houses. 'I didn't expect to see a pond high up like this,' wondered Mokuzu. The pond served to prevent flood during the rainy season and to conserve water for farming. It must have been made as long ago as when the area was first settled, several hundred years before. The village ancestors had brought to the task only their hands and feet and perhaps some simple mattocks, bamboo baskets, and soil-packed straw bags. It had long since perfectly assimilated into the land. On its banks was a lush growth of cogon grass and at the north side a thicket of sawtooth and daimyo oaks. Only its location remained artificial, too high for a natural pond.

By now the oaks had dropped most of their old leaves around their roots. In their topmost branches bulbuls and thrushes were bustling and pecking at the few remaining "crow's pillow" gourds shriveled by the cold but once plump and bright red-orange, attached to vines growing high up. The fallen leaves rustled with squirrels and hares rummaging for acorns.

South from the pond was an open view of thatched and tiled roofs covered here and there by trees. A single crooked road passed through wide rice fields backed by the mountains bordering the neighboring village, the sky clear above their peaks. The slanting rays of the western sun reached the pond and sparkled on cold ripples. The west shore was dark and looked even colder; yet there, where the dry reeds were especially dense, fish bubbled and jumped.

Micha did not slow her busy pace even passing the pond, maybe because of her hand-to-mouth way of life, or her determination not to be overcome by the cold. Mokuzu wanted to discover what fish jumped in the shady corner, but, fearing to be left behind, he followed after her.

The house, relatively new, stood on a small eminence facing the pond and was approached by an angled path of white gravel bordered by ilexes trimmed round. Mokuzu and his mother went up and came to a neatly trimmed sasanqua hedge with its pink flowers still in bloom, marking the front border of the property and open at the middle for flagstones that led straight to the entrance of the house. There was the sight of a wide, flat lawn the tawny color of winter, where the sun yet returned a warm light. A sandbox, a swing, and a horizontal bar were set up on the left for children's play. In the background was a bamboo grove, and, to the right of it, a pine forest. Before the house were mid-height

102

deciduous trees — maple, dogwood, apple, magnolia, Chinese parasol; and some evergreens — Chinese black pine, olive, laurel, juniper. Many shrubs were suitably placed for blindman's buff and hide-and-seek. Micha walked on ahead.

Rather than push the interphone button she called out, "Is anyone home?" Her bundle was wrapped in a large brown cloth, which she held by the two ends pulled over her shoulders, tied in a half-knot. Always she needed to fist them to avoid being choked by the load. But having no free hand was not why she ignored the interphone. More likely such a convenient electric device was foreign to her. Or her pride kept her from speaking into it regardless of how low in the world she had sunk and she wanted to speak face-to-face as long as both parties recognized each other as human beings.

"Yes! Just a moment please!" came a bright response followed by the approach of quick steps along a corridor. Evidently the door to a room off the corridor was left open, for signs of another person's presence there were casually transmitted. "Mother! Where do I put the peach flowers and how?" It was the impatient voice of a girl no doubt interrupted amidst what she and her mother were doing together. But the mother without replying went on to open the front door. "Oh, here you are! Please go around, I shall open the living room right away." She withdrew along another corridor.

Mokuzu and his mother outside the open entrance felt the warmth of the inside air. It affected them only in front as if to caress them and made them realize how cold was the air at their backs and how long they had been walking without complaint in such cold.

Micha closed the door when she heard the sliding of the veranda doors at the second room from the entrance. Although she had been here before, she seemed to be understanding as if for the first time that she was expected to step up from there. At the veranda was set a large, flat Kurama stone.

Micha stepped up onto it, sat on the veranda, and began to unwrap her load. "I brought the best quality, but I wonder if they'll fit — " The housewife interrupted her to urge, "Please enter, you'll be cold there," and she offered cushions, speaking also to Mokuzu as if she knew him well, "You've come with your mother today. You're a marvelous boy to assist her so." "Not at all, he only disturbs my work. But today for the first time since he was a baby I'm taking him along. I think if he sees something of the world it'll do him no harm." Micha spoke modestly, then added her admiration, "He's better than his brother, doesn't nag to be bought something or soil his clothes, and he walks briskly enough...."

"Please wait a moment," said the housewife. She left and returned with a tray of tea and sliced Castella cake. Over her kimono she had a clean apron. "Ena! Come!" she called, and explained to Micha, "She's decorating a room with the Ohina-sama." Micha sipped the offered tea and spoke flattery, "A house like yours must have a fine set of dolls."

A girl in a striped sweater and sea blue skirt entered and greeted Mokuzu's mother, and merely glanced at Mokuzu, as far as he could tell. "Your child always behaves so well and greets so nicely. How tall she's become, with a good strong mind." Micha promptly unwrapped the bundle and laid out girl's clothing: pure white cotton underwear, wool socks red-and-white striped, and in pink, red, and black, some maroon-on-navy knee socks, varieties of wool sweaters, and light- and heavy-cotton skirts.

Mokuzu had no interest in the display. He preferred to shut himself off from such a world and was groping for the meaning of "Ohina-sama," come up a moment ago in the adults' talk and utterly new to him. In fact, being only about six and isolated in a monotonous life spent entirely within the family, he found many words spoken by strange adults to be incomprehensible and even mysterious phenomena whose vagueness seemed to expand the more he considered them. Yet he memorized their sounds and tenaciously pursued their meanings even if it was as useless as trying to find a star in the daytime sky.

Whenever a word of uncertain meaning joined with a concrete matter and settled into a certain meaning, he was slightly disappointed. He knew every word ended up with a definition, just as a tossed ball was fated to fall, but it was one of those things he found disillusioning. 'If only a ball would fly on forever! Must it always fall no matter how I throw it skyward? Isn't there a way, isn't there such a ball?' He also mused, 'A word of uncertain meaning freely floats in the universe, but as soon as its meaning is pinned down, it is bound to the earth and frozen as another uncharming, humble, dirty, meaningless word.'

Mokuzu did not realize that the girl standing by her seated mother was directing her attention to him with large eyes and a round, slightly open mouth.

"Quick, remove your clothes and try these on so we can tell if they're right," said her mother as she raised a spring skirt of fine-pleated thin material to eye level, about level with Ena's waist. Ena received it without looking, her gaze still on Mokuzu, who remained by the glass-paneled doors of the veranda.

"Oh! You're Mokuzu, aren't you?" she exclaimed in high spirits.

"Ena, why suddenly so loud?" said her mother.

Mokuzu acknowledged his name with a nod, and Ena dropped the new skirt and went over and put her hand on his shoulder. "I wasn't sure — your face has changed. But it's the same eyes and nose and mouth, cheeks too, yes, everything's the same. Only you're bigger, and you're not dying anymore. How fortunate you didn't die!" She touched his face. Her pupils sparkled. Mokuzu could do nothing but let her touch him.

"Yes, it was when Master Mokuzu was much younger," Fumi commented to his mother. "Since then Ena has had no chance to meet you," she turned to say to Mokuzu, recalling having helped him at the scene of the hydrangeas. She had taken him to his home and arranged for a doctor, her husband, with whom she had been quarreling. His life was narrowly saved. But Fumi did not wish to rouse Micha to thank her anew, and more grave, she disliked any reminder of her unhappy marriage, which had made Ena sad and dark when she was but an infant.

"True, this one has amazing vitality as if he's immortal — there must be great meaning in his living on, for by now he's had many narrow escapes... and that time was thanks to you!" Micha was inspired to relate some other times. Warming to her subject she said, "I recently went in secret to Otani village to get his fortune told. I'd been worrying so about his health. When I give him even a little chicken soup he gets diarrhea, turns pale, and can't eat a thing...Do you know of the man living behind the tofu shop? He stays in a dark room with a shrine to the spirit of something unknown to us. He's becoming a famous seer, though he has some trouble with his eyes."

"Why did you go in secret?"

"After all, my husband is a priest, if not a quite satisfactory one. He has some religious faith but thinks the gods and Buddha aren't concerned with the specifics of our daily life. He says, 'Even more than a priest, whoever hasn't properly educated and trained himself can't possibly judge the will of the divine or the fate of others. These local seers further confuse people and further stimulate their desires.'"

"Your husband's words are reasonable. Profiting by fortune-telling is all too common. They do take advantage of people's misfortunes and weak spirit."

"No, he says so, but his true mind fears I'll be stirred up again after he's troubled to calm me down. However, this seer happens to be a fine person. As proof he asks no money from poor people like me. He says in this amusing way, 'I'd like to be paid as much as a truckload, but if that you can't do, don't pay me a cent.'"

"Amazing. What did he say about Master Mokuzu?"

"As may be expected, it was mysterious and magical. He sits enclosed in his room, facing his shrine, but no sooner did I enter the waiting room than he spoke from within in a fearsome quaking voice that grew keen,

"'Oooo, yours is a child of extremes — he has "the seal of the gulf between Heaven and Earth." If he takes a good path, even the gods in Heaven will be pleased. If he takes an evil path, even the guardians of Hell will shudder. He must be alert, for hundreds and thousands of forked paths will appear, and each time Heaven and Hell will draw him with equal charm. Brightness and darkness, joy and misery, gospel and curse. Indeed if he lives for the happiness of others by bridling his inclinations, he will bring people to a flowering field and brighten those who suffer in gloom. However, oh, however, if he should slight his pleasure of self-restraint and forget his mercy toward the ignorant and the weak, or be possessed by hate and revenge, or fall into the depths of pessimism and see his life and that of others as meaningless and needless, then, how terrible! — he will slay a multitude and fire their houses, and even as the number reaches into the millions, his heart will be unmoved as if he's but tossing a handful of sand into the sea, and his concern will be solely the efficiency of mass-destruction....'"

"Oh dear!" Fumi turned to look curiously at Mokuzu, who was standing with Ena at the veranda doors.

They were breathing on the glass to draw on it with their fingers. He came up to only about her eyes, being a year younger and what with a girl's faster growth. But he was better at drawing. She was adding grasses and a stream while waiting expectantly for him to complete a person.

He was making an image of Miyamoto Musashi, about whom Gyodo had taught him. Mokuzu believed he too ought to live like this real hero of the early Edo period who continued to train himself by swordsmanship, pursuing a succession of difficulties. "The way of the sword" included such basic concerns as the meaning of strength, of justice, and of human life. Taking it as his guide Musashi sought these things all his life and studied their essence from each great contemporary swordsman, Zen priest, artist, and such, and finally he expressed his attainment in sumi paintings and a thin book, *Gorin no sho*, which remain to this day.

Mokuzu had begun to regard Musashi as his one and only ideal hero. He was charmed by Musashi's severe self-whipping by which he drove himself toward ultimate risks to reexamine through physical practice all established good and justifiable deeds and all respectable teachings and human perceptions. As long as he attempted to be like his hero, Mokuzu could welcome and convert for good purpose every circumstantial distress — the fact that he was hungry, cold, hot, suffering a headache or stomachache, or witnessing the quarrels between his father and his mother or between his parents and the laymen, and so on. He was beginning to realize that the way to brighten his life was to use all these distresses as a means to build up his manly character.

Gyodo, three years older than himself, had first told him of Musashi with the purpose of encouraging him, "You too live like that!" Mokuzu had thus not discovered such a way on his own. Yet one thing he could not understand: Gyodo often forgot it for himself and, filled with discontent, he complained and cried.

'Why does he forget his Musashi? The Musashi he planted in my mind is getting to be more reliable than his!'

106

Mokuzu was drawing Musashi with his long and his short sword, sallying forth to duel with Yoshioka Kenpo of Kyoto. He gave him unbound hair and tiger eyes to intimidate his opponent, and made him alert to the possibility of ambush as he climbed a piney slope. Ena had little knowledge of Musashi. With her rosy mouth pursed she almost touched the glass to blow on it.

"Why don't you put his girlfriend here?" she suggested, or requested, indicating a place behind Musashi where already there were pines and a stream.

"Girlfriend? He hadn't such a friend."

Ena faintly frowned and searched his eyes as if to determine their depth. "But he must have!" she protested. "Isn't it true nobody knew if he'd be killed? He'd have to have his girlfriend secretly praying for his safety."

Hearing this and deciding Musashi's world would be thereby enlarged, Mokuzu added a girl in a kimono half hidden by a tree, her face quite like Ena's, with soft cheeks, rich hair, large bright eyes, thick lashes, and an expression of slight surprise.

"Then do you believe what he told you?" Fumi had been regarding her daughter and Mokuzu and turned back to Micha.

"Whether I do or don't, it's obvious when I think about it. Basically all he said was that this child will be unusually successful if he's fortunate and the opposite if he's not, and that the difference is vast. Isn't it true of anyone? What can people do but take a good or a bad path, don't you agree?" Micha was expressing her intellectual aspect.

Nonetheless, in her heart she was glad to have heard that Mokuzu could be great either way, enough to astonish people on earth and the beings of heaven and hell. Poverty made her feel that the duty of raising her children was a tremendous task; so she regarded the spiritual and cultural world as detached from reality. She was forced to endure hardship from morning to night and night to morning, and such a life of patience made her world seem limited, cramped, flat. She felt she was under a semitransparent dome that limited both her physical and mental activity. The thought that Mokuzu would break through and live free gave her hope, pleasure, even the hope of her own flight. 'Is my life too going to open like the autumn sky...? Even if his fate turns bad and he cracks the earth and I must see a bloody pond and the flaming creatures of hell, it will be great for ending this dreary life stuck to the ground.'

"Quick, Ena, come try these on! Afterward you can show Master Mokuzu the Ohina-sama."

"Yes!" But Ena lingered at the glass before stepping back into the room. Mokuzu, feeling the absence of her pressure at his side, began to lose interest in the picture and turned toward the room. Ena was taking off sweater and skirt and becoming a slender figure in white underwear. 'What an angel would have...while mine from Gyodo is patched and dingy no matter how much it's washed — too shameful to expose before strangers. How nice, a home with loads of pure white underpants and undershirts!'

Aware of his eyes, Ena primly turned away like a grown woman. She put on a new spring sweater, then stepped into a skirt, pulling it up with one swift motion. Where it hooked, a pair of square tags with the size and manufacturer's name dangled.

At age seven she felt a partial but piercing shyness to change her clothes in front of a boy of more or less the same age. But she reasoned that behaving self-conscious and asking to move to another room would enlarge her shyness like the spread of an inkblot. She assumed an indifferent air.

"Well now, it fits perfectly, turn around." Fumi and Micha straightened collar and hem.

Mokuzu faced the lawn from behind the glass. He looked at the clouding sky over the sasanqua hedge and fixed his eyes on a place where a roof far below was brightened by feeble rays from a tiny crack in the clouds. 'Even an old leaky roof looks beautiful when lit by the sun,' he noted and was lost in a muse.

'The other night Gyodo was begging for new clothes because his buttons are lost and his elbows worn out. "Everyone says I'm a scarecrow and asks why I'm in school when I belong in a field."

'Dad agreed he should have them, at least one set. Ma just kept darning socks with Ran on her back. Dad shouted, "Didn't you hear? I say get him something!" "Where's the money?" came her spear-like retort. They quarreled, and Gyodo ended up quietly weeping under his quilts.

'This girl named Ena is wearing quite new-looking things, yet is being given more — three sweaters, three skirts, two pairs of slacks, three sets of underwear, and many pairs of socks — what a pile she's getting!

'Poor Gyodo, and poor Ran, who gets what I get from Gyodo. He's sad because of what they say at school, and she, because she's only three and doesn't recognize the joy of new dresses or the sorrow of not having them. I have nothing to be sad about; conveniently I'm not as old as Gyodo or as young as Ran. If the sun shines, everything looks better, even that old roof....'

"All done! Let's go see my Ohina-sama!" Ena skipped over and pulled him by the hand.

He followed. 'Soon the meaning of "Ohina-sama" will be clear. I hope I'll not be disappointed, as I was with *sengiri*...I expected such a bright world and waited long for a chance to ask Grandma. "Sengiri? Such a mundane thing? It's gladly eaten by peasants," she said and motioned toward the dark shelves of the kitchen cottage. On top of the wooden steamer, bamboo baskets, sushi presses, and such things not in daily use, was a long wooden tray used for malting rice but now heaped with tiny bits of dried brownish stuff emitting a sweet sun-dried smell mixed with the smell of damp mold. She gave me a bit. It was pithy, though soft on the outside, the texture unpleasantly indefinite. A taste more acrid than sweet clung to the insides of my mouth. She let out a jolly laugh at my grimace and proceeded to tell me in detail how it's made.

"'When the first snows arrive at the peaks of Takahachi and Hangoku in late October or early November, the peasants harvest their daikon radishes. The leaves are already yellowed and shriveled by frost, the root is snow white. They pull them up by the thousands and carry them to the river shoal and stack them there. The women, tucking up their sleeves so high as to expose their upper arms, scrub them one by one in the current and neatly restack them. What a clamor they raise, chatting about all they can think of — their childhood day-dreams, their night dreams of adolescence, their married life, child care, care of the sick, about their cows and chickens. Thus they wash them to a clean white, their hands, even their arms, turning crimson in the numbing water. On and on, crying for pain, chatting, washing, crying, piling. The mountains of white daikons appear vivid even in the dusk, even against the black of night.

"'The men then bring them into the farmyards, where the women with their large vegetable knives chop them in the sun. They chop them in halves and quarters lengthwise, into three-centimeter widths, and finer and smaller till each daikon is cut to a thousand pieces — *sen*, thousand, *giri*, to cut.

"'They make great piles, choosing balmy windless days. As they work they raise more of a din than do frogs or cicadas. Just go to that village and listen! On their chopping boards without seeing knife or daikon, quickly they chop..., to what can I compare it? Its rhythmic swell floods the village, sometimes horrible, sometimes amusing, most times sad. Can you guess why? Because it's the sound of preparing what they will eat. They spread it on straw mats to dry in the sun, and it crumples, browns, and sweetens too. It must receive no damp during the entire drying process. They dry it to keep year round, or for several years if they can afford to. They cook and eat it in years of famine. I'll teach you the cooking and flavoring another day. For now that explains sengiri. Your grandfather Priest Kakkan made something of a koan, 'Sengiri is the essence of our Sakyamuni Buddha's declaration that all mountains, rivers, grasses, and trees are already attaining Buddhahood. What, then, is this essence?'"

To Mokuzu her talk was longsome and fussy, and as always it ended with an episode relating to his grandfather.

He felt awkward being pulled along the corridor. It led to the front entrance and turned left. 'I wish she'd let go before I lose my balance and fall.' With his free hand he touched the wall and realized it was covered with a soft fabric of a faint whitish green weave with a tree design. The polished floor made him look to his feet. He then noticed a toe sticking from one of his black socks. 'On the way here I saw that toe — so my sock and shoe both have holes.'

Ena had heavy pink-and-white striped knee socks and soft leather scuffs, which he had not noticed till then. The scuffs were for use in the corridor only.

Light fixtures were set along the ceiling, along one baseboard too. 'Ah me! There are so many things worthy to see and spend time on! At home there's just one twenty-watt bulb, and Gyodo is eager to take the best place under it to read....'

By seeing Ena's house Mokuzu came to realize that his had far more dark areas than bright. 'Gyodo says ours is like an animal's nest. Then Ena's has no charm of a nest. Ours would be much more nest-like if our parents didn't fight...It's darker and narrower than here, so sensing one another's body warmth is more significant than seeing, though the main building, where Grandma stays, is huge and empty....'

Ena parted from him because he was not going fast enough despite being pulled. She went ahead and called from a room,

"I'm in here, quick, come in!" Free of her hand Mokuzu felt all the more urged on, but he glanced again at the front entrance without allowing himself any feeling, just to keep everything in mind. In from the glass-and-lattice sliding doors the earth was paved with flagstones. Narcissus and *kumazasa* were arranged in a shallow white porcelain bowl on a shoe cabinet combined with shelves and topped with a lace runner. A plank of buffed Chinese quince from one wall to the other provided a step up to the wood-floor hall. Standing grave in the depths of the hall was a low reddish brown table fashioned from a cross-section of zelkova, its natural outline preserved, resting heavy on four short legs of the same wood. An ebony tray on it held a wide peaked rock suggesting a lofty mountain, which darkly shone in marbled hues of green, white, red ocher, and black.

The moment he stepped into the room, Mokuzu was surprised.

"Yipes! what a host of people and splendid colors!"

"They're dolls, the Ohina-sama."

"Ohh...Ohina-sama? They seem alive, wait, they do seem to be moving!"

Mokuzu was overawed. The dolls in gorgeous traditional courtly dress with pointed coronets were neatly placed on a bank of steps. He drew back toward Ena at the doorway. She was surprised that he was so surprised. And for his eyes the impression of her reality was fading: as against the dolls she was becoming more slender and humble, less resilient, less solid.

The dolls and their effects were arranged on seven steps carpeted with bright red felt. On the lowest step was a splendid palanquin and cow-drawn carriage lacquered in black with gold designs. The second step had a pair of imitation trees — a fruiting mandarin orange to the left, a flowering cherry to the right — and three servant-like men in whitish costumes. The center one stood and held a tray with a pair of lacquered clogs, the others knelt with raised knee and held each a closed parasol. The third and fourth steps had fancy table sets, a chest of drawers, a sewing box, a hand mirror and stand, and various tiered boxes. On either end of the fourth stood a warrior with sword, bow, and sheaf of arrows. On the fifth was a line of court musicians with rather droll faces: a piper, a taborer, drummers for a large and a small hand drum, and, no doubt, a singer, for he had no instrument. On the sixth step three minor court ladies served tea and cakes, which alternated with real cakes made of steamed rice flour tinted green by mugwort, yellow by millet, and pink by gardenia pod. The highest step received a man and a woman, seated side by side on a fancy tatami dais and before a golden screen. Their dress was the fanciest and more, their faces were by far the most regal. She held in her lap an upright open fan. He held an upright flat wooden scepter.

Mokuzu could count a total of fifteen individuals dazzling and elegant in colorfully dyed silk costumes perfect in color scheme and variation of tone.

But his eyes did not focus, or could not, on any but the two at the top. 'All else, while certainly fancy, repels my eyes the way shiny green leaves repel dew. My eyes are drawn especially to the right, to the lady, to her face...no matter how I change position....'

"They are the Dairi couple....Don't you know? His Majesty the Emperor..."

"Oh...you mean the Mikado and his Empress? Hmm, I didn't know they were so noble and gentle as I see. It's strange...my grandma says he was our country's fundamental holiness, the Constitution itself. He was God of War, and loving administrator to all people....I suppose he became quiet and is behaving gentlemanly under the protection of his yet nobler and wiser Empress, and he's highly content with such a life...for after all, he was trounced in the war...."

Ena understood little of what Mokuzu said. She picked up a peach branch with many flower buds and, taking clippers from a spread newspaper, tried to trim it suitably to arrange in a vase.

"You came just when I was going to place this," she said.

She wished to sit with him and together finish up the doll display; but she did not express her wish, for he was intent on regarding the face of the Empress.

The Empress had rich burnished black hair beautifully combed in a style that from the front looked like an inverted trapezoid rounded on top. The back was presumably tied below the shoulders and flowing down at length. On her brow was a golden sunburst. 'It must be a rising sun.'

111

She wore many layers of thin kimonos in colors derived from plants, just a glimpse of each showing at the neck and sleeve openings. The inmost was a virginal white, then a yellow from Japanese kerria, a reddish brown from a wild grape, a yellowish green from a field grass, and so forth, completed by a Chinese outer robe of scarlet, from madder mixed with gromwell.

'Like facing a rainbow! But a rainbow against mountains and sky pulls my attention to itself. In contrast, these ceremonial kimonos are designed to direct my eyes to her slightly lowered, modest face full of mercy. They perfectly assist her from beginning to end.'

As he stared at her face and tried to see it from various angles, she neither withdrew nor showed any sign of displeasure; rather, her tender nobility increased. Her face was bright and warm as the sun, yet without its force.

'The sun burns of itself with a greatness that radiates its influence to others, whereas the face of this lady draws in all surrounding things, which she converts to gentler and more merciful beings and then she returns them to the world.'

The Emperor wore a black crown of lacquered silk. His costume was darkish and rather baggy, and no doubt hung down behind like the tail of fancy rooster. His face, most unlike that of any man Mokuzu had ever seen, was graceful and quiet but without the full cheeks of the lady. He looked oddly powerless and unreal, yet not weak or humble. 'Like a clean moon,' Mokuzu thought, and decided his function must be to keep up the purity and sublimity.

'With so splendid an Empress to protect him, he has no reason to practice any of those worldly things that would demand his constantly active will, effort, and patience....'

11

Ena and Mokuzu Are of One Mind

Ena saw that Mokuzu was absorbed with the dolls, and she hoped to retrieve him lest she be pained with tedium, even estranged.

"Mokuzu, listen! Tomorrow is the Ohina-sama celebration. Don't you have a set at your house too?"

"Eh? No...we don't."

"Haven't you any sisters?"

"I do. Kiku went far off to a spinning mill right after junior high. Ran is only three, she's at home."

"The Ohina-sama is for the Girls' Day festival. Grandmothers give a set to congratulate a newborn girl."

'Would Grandma buy a set of dolls...for Ran? It's impossible to imagine her buying any fancy dolls, practicing such tenderness — as unlikely as for a mole to turn into a wagtail.'

Ena had managed to retrieve him, but her topic was just the impetus to send him away again.

'Come to think of it, how Ran would love to be given even one such doll! She plays with garden soil, waters it, makes odd shapes, and she treasures a doll Gyodo fashioned for her out of a pinecone and twigs, even takes it to bed, though he mostly can't play because he's gathering firewood, preparing the bath, or reading. I can climb in the mountains and enter the river. She's too young and must wait at the foot or on the bank. Often I find her there asleep. I know it's a live creature, a person, actually Ran, but I always worry that strangers might think she's a muddy root or a stray cat.

'I should be more attentive and patient and not desert her, especially while she can still barely toddle about. I should play with her more, for instance her favorite game, which is my least favorite, so repetitive I think I'll go nuts. She plants sticks one by one in a mound of mud, as if to make a house; then one by one she drops stones on them, taking great time. After knocking them down, she starts again. All day she can enjoy that kind of play.

'I must remember to take her the cake I was offered here. Her very black eyes well inherited in her face — though it's red and grimy and puffed by the cold — they'll shine like sunlight through the trees....'

"Say, my grandma asked a dollmaker in Kyoto to make these dolls when I was born. What's interesting is, he was a childhood friend of hers. They played hide-and-seek and bounced balls together. She told me they climbed the cherry trees in Maruyama Park and picked evening primroses on the banks of the Kamo River. Such good friends they were, but because of various circumstances they couldn't marry. He never married and since then devoted himself to making dolls. His dolls are said to have something of my grandma's childhood face."

Ena tried to introduce the most engaging tale she could think of relating to the Ohina-sama, told her by her mother and her grandmother. But in her way she could raise in Mokuzu none of the interest she had. 'I won't succeed unless I talk more slowly and calmly, and if possible while together sipping tea or carefully taking the dolls from their boxes as Grandma does with me. My talk is being wasted, like pouring perfume into a quick stream. Whatever I say becomes a flower without scent or leaves....But in the first place he isn't hearing at all! He's replying "Oh?...hnn..." I've been demoted to insignificance, to a tiny blot on the wall.' Ena became silent.

'Grandma never occasions our pleasure,' thought Mokuzu. 'She's a marsh that incubates fleas and mosquitoes, she brings only our quarrels and sorrow, she's an anchor to drag us down...though I can find no sign of her wanting such a role.

'Recently there was that late-night turmoil, which I bet perfectly illustrates what Gyodo was saying — "Tangenji is like algal fungi growing in an old skull...a den of revengeful ghosts accumulated over long years."

'With nothing to do, we all went to bed right after supper. Ran while crying fell asleep earlier. Sleet lashed the retreat cottage. I knew the persimmon tree big as five or six dragons was swaying its angular branches every which way over our heads. Hearing the wind I could visualize it and also the bamboos being bent down and rebounding all at once. On the mountain the pines with their earnest uproar helped to birl the wind into the valley.

'Then there came a banging at the entrance. Who could have realized someone was trying to wake us, what with the crashing of branches against the roof and the eaves about to give way? It must have gone on for some time — we were so far from the world of waking as are the banks of the river Ganga one from the other. At last we sensed Grandma was calling, "Venerable sir! Venerable sir!" Dad dragged himself from his quilts, vexed and exclaiming, "What, what, at this late hour? — it's so cold!" He looked like a giant spider or crab as he crawled along the frigid tatami.

'With all his might he forced aside the door — it must have bent. A little whirl of snow came in, and there stood Grandma, as I expected, her hair and shoulders all snowy. I watched with my head stuck from my bed as she shoved before his eyes a small dish not quite so white as the snow.

'"Take a good look — they came from my throat! What I've endured! If they enter my brain what will you do? I'll go mad! Haven't I been asking you for days to buy medicine?"

'The wind swept away his answer, or he didn't answer. I exerted myself to go see. I was curious and thought I could be useful. I got close enough to smell her face powder mixed with her lukewarm body smell, and there in the dish were two yellowish intestinal worms making friendly half circles together. I felt I would vomit.

'"Stay in bed, you'll catch cold!" Dad promptly shouted at me. I obeyed but secretly kept watching.

'"Oii! Wake up! Do something!" Thus he woke Ma, sound asleep, exhausted. There were some quiet exchanges. Then Ma burst out, "What's wrong with having such a trifle? You breed worms because you overeat! I know you stole the rice I was saving for us — for the children. What did you do — exchange it for cash? You'd better know we can't afford such medicine!"

114

'I'm unsure because I fell asleep, but probably Dad struck Ma to ease his aroused resentment — again he was caught between them and couldn't find a way out. Anyway it was one of those worldly happenings beyond my power even in my dreams. But had it continued before my waking eyes, I can understand I would have needed to share some responsibility.

'Ran and Gyodo were sleeping like logs. That's the difference between us — always they luckily happen to be asleep when these difficulties occur, whereas I'm an eye-witness. The world we met next day — the gardens, mountains, and fields all mantled in snow — must have had a different significance for their eyes than it had for mine.'

"Mokuzu! Are you still keeping the music box I gave you?"

Ena continued to feel that her treasured music box was more important for her having given it away. Parting with this intimate possession gave her a link with the great world of nature or idea transcending reality, for the one she gave it to had been afflicted with a high fever and had been abandoning the desire to live on, making no effort, entrusting his life, whether it was to cease or not, into the hand of an ultra being. He had looked helpless, as well as peaceful, pure, sublime.

She never forgot the world she had seen in his expression and attitude, wider, more lasting, and far more noble than the world of reality. By thinking of this other world during her daily life full of dissension, distress, and sorrow, she was given hope: it seemed the place she should seek, where her future should lead, even if she was but vaguely in touch with her awareness. Such a world seemed to promise the sweetest and most pleasant future. She sensed it, but more like a butterfly or a bee sensing where to find a flowering field. Were she to walk toward the world suggested by Mokuzu's face that day and devote herself to it, she sensed she would be brought the highest satisfaction and her life made greatly worth living.

Hearing the word "music box," Mokuzu knew there was something he could not ignore. He withdrew from his thoughts of his family and the dolls with the royal couple at the top and brought himself back to Ena's face and form beside him in a quick return to reality — like when he checked his hare-like race down a mountain so as to inspect a red flower flashing by at the corner of his eye.

He met Ena's eyes, which held the concentration of her caring mind, and which expressed an expectation or a longing for something, eyes honest and serious. Their eyes held no ill or impure thought. It was the meeting of two undefiled young souls.

Until then Mokuzu frankly had not known who had given him the music box. The kind giver and the girl Ena were now for the first time one, and the realization made him feel he could arrive at a place most yearned for after a long journey under an endless sunset sky. Three years ago was to him quite a long time ago. He could never go back and live there again. Yet his mind could go — it had just been proven. Now he could reaffirm that obscure but very peaceful world, and what had triggered his return was this actual girl named Ena.

"Were you the one who gave it? I didn't know till this very minute...," he muttered.

No longer was Ena like a blot on the wall. She was lively; light shone and scattered from her various expressions and gestures, and above all, she was a tender, bright, and warmhearted girl. Even the Ohina-sama Empress was after all merely an icy, inert, inorganic doll in comparison. There was nothing more substantial and vibrant than the life of this living girl who was actually caring about him.

"Won't you come to my room? I made some pictures of you, though I can't draw so well."

"Of me?"

"Of the time you had a high fever in the hydrangeas..."

They left the room where the dolls were displayed, passed some rooms that appeared to be bedrooms, and turned a corner south. Ena's room faced a rectangular inner garden on the other side of which was presumably the room where her mother and Mokuzu's mother yet remained; they could not be seen because the shojis and storm doors on that side were closed, and their voices too were unintelligible, almost inaudible.

In the inner garden was a well with square granite crib and cypress-bark roof. A pair of buckets hung, disused. Alongside were bushes of nandin, daphne, and azalea. Arranged here and there were deciduous mid-sized trees — crepe myrtle, maple, magnolia; and mid-sized evergreens — camellia with white flowers, *kurogane-mochi* dotted with red berries, and a kind of arbutus. Fresh green hair-moss was thriving. Where not blocked by Ena's room, a few rays of the weak western sun were making a triangle of light at a corner.

Her room looked bright and soft. At its south side were glass-paneled sliding doors. When she opened the thick curtains the effect of the remaining sun came in through white lace curtains. It was possible to step out to an open veranda and to a backyard of lawn grass. A rill crossed by from behind the house and apparently fed a pond. In the background was the trace of a flower garden, then a thick forest of miscellaneous untended trees, evidently on a slope, for their tops abruptly descended.

A pale pink fabric with rose designs covered the west wall, against which she had her desk, bookshelves, and a Western-style bed just the right height to sit on.

"You're welcome to sit," she said, and Mokuzu discovered the bed was springy. While she was taking her drawings from a closet he stood on the bed and looked north and west through the high window. He could understand that the source of the rill was somewhere farther north. To see well was impossible, but the area behind the house appeared to be a cliff that never received the sun. A dense growth of wild trees — camphor, camellia, zelkova, and *muku* — covered the north side of the roof.

From the cliff, steep from having been scarped, water steadily dripped, presumably the water that fed the rill. It was the darkest and coldest place on the property. 'On a day of great rain, those drips I suppose would become a waterfall.'

Ena was impatient, knowing he could not stay forever in her room but soon must leave with his mother. She had many things she wanted to show him, to talk of, to play. She chose three drawings. The first was of colorful but vague shapes made with few lines. Mokuzu could not distinguish the figure from the flowers until she explained. The picture was filled with what looked like colorful bubbles. "I drew it of you slightly after our first meeting, when I was four and you were three." Mokuzu could find nothing to say except, "Maybe a high fever is like that."

The second was fairly realistic. Among hydrangea clusters a girl held a compress to the head of a boy. Above them a white waterfall descended from the sky and a pair of birds circled. Ena did not explain it, and Mokuzu felt shy to see himself cared for like that. He kept silent. His only thought was, 'Expressing the world by words and pictures is shameful; it should be experienced by feeling, by touch.'

The third, more recent, showed tall trees on a mountain, perhaps cedar or cypress, with a narrow path disappearing into their depths. At the thorny base a figure was following with difficulty another figure well up the path. Ena was unskilled at people or trees or at perspective, but her shading with crayon was excellent, and in her elaborate coloration was a sense of direction, depth, volume, and light and shadow; what she thought and felt she could well express.

Bringing herself so close to him that he felt her breath on his lips, she asked with smiling eyes,

"Can you tell who they are?...This is Mokuzu, this is Ena."

"I see they're climbing a mountain and she's laboring to catch up, being a girl. He's not giving her a hand but going ahead. Isn't that heartless? Does he know she's following?"

"They're not simply climbing, you're starting your training."

"Training? For what? So...are you going to train too?"

"At this point I'm unsure if I can, but you'll begin sooner or later. I don't know what it will be, but it will be so hard I will be deserted. I will cry,

'Please wait — take me along!' but you will venture on by yourself."

Ena smiled sadly and looked down. Unable to make sense of what she was saying, Mokuzu only looked at the picture. He could find no suitable question to ask and kept his face blank. Ena recognized that her fantasy was more accurate than she had been vaguely suspecting. 'Just as I have no father at home, if I have no one I can spend my true life with, how irksome and dull everywhere will be...!'

She jumped off the bed. "Well! Don't you want to see my school supplies? Everything's ready, and today your mother brought more of what I'm to wear."

Ena was soon to be enrolled in elementary school. She opened another closet. Carefully laid out almost like at a shop were all kinds of brand-new essentials: a red cowhide knapsack, an abacus, straw indoor sandals, notebooks, a pencil case, castanets...and to the side, a new hat, shoes, an umbrella; and a raincoat, an overcoat, skirts, and blouses neatly folded or hung.

Mokuzu was provided no writing materials except for traditional bamboo brushes with animal-hair tips, some sumi sticks made with the soot of pine, a sumi stone for preparing the sumi, and Japanese paper. As the brushes were already worn out by his father, he longed to hold a pencil or a pen and write in fine detail. Gyodo owned a few pencils, an eraser, and a celluloid board to place under his writing paper, but he never allowed Mokuzu their use because they were school necessities.

What Mokuzu most envied among Ena's possessions, however, were her books. Rarely given any new book, he mostly read the antique books he took from the repository in the upper garden of Tangenji. They smelled of camphor, though bookworms had tunneled from cover to cover. The texts, printed from woodblocks, were entirely in Chinese ideographs, and the few illustrations were of Buddha images, warriors on horseback, or ancient costumes and household articles, taken primarily from stone rubbings. Still worse, almost nothing was written for children. Most of the books pertained to Confucianism, Taoism, the Buddhist Scriptures, and the history and litera-ture of China and Japan. Quite a few were as old as three or four hundred years. But for Mokuzu they were merely old stuff, extremely hard to read, and not so different from useless trash paper, since he had no relation with such establishments as museums, universities, or libraries.

Seeing Ena's shelves filled with glossy-colored volumes of Anderson's complete works and collected biographies of great people of the world, he thought, 'Truly there are many things to consider, especially why her circumstances and mine should be so different, like clouds and mud, while seemingly we have one element in common.

118

'If just this minute I allow myself to feel envy and longing for all these good things, I'll begin to cry and my head will split. What I've got to do now is remember my promise to Ma that I'll not make trouble while she's letting me go out with her.

'So I'll focus on thinking about nothing. But once I get home I'll think as much as I like and let myself realize I do have desire and envy. I'll also ask Gyodo why people's circumstances can be so different....' Mokuzu was no longer attending to Ena's talk about her belongings. He wanted to go home even a second earlier to think at will about whatever he liked.

Fortunately for him, Ena's mother came to say his mother was preparing to leave. He felt narrowly saved. 'My thoughts are condensing like clouds. Clouds make rain, which mustn't combine as a curtain of rain and become a torrent to wash everything away. My tears shouldn't become a torrent by any means.'

As he followed his mother home, Mokuzu was no longer thinking logically but only mixing his feelings with all he had seen that day. His mind was as dark as the cliff he had seen out the west window of Ena's room, steep, covered in foliage, steadily dripping water.

12

Doyu's Realization

"Zen Teacher Jau at age thirteen entered the priesthood in Jinguang. At age nineteen he climbed Mt. Hungyang,..."[1]

Gyodo, kneeling at the low table directly under the light bulb, was endeavoring to read aloud a Chinese Zen classic. It was *Changuan tsejin* (To penetrate the Zen border by self-whipping), compiled, edited, and published at the beginning of the seventeenth century by Juhung Yunchi, a Zen master who was also a master of the Pure Land sect. The edition Gyodo was reading was published in Japan in the second year of the Meireki era. The cover was so old that the original color was long since gone. Over the ages the astringent juice of unripe persimmon had been applied many times to strengthen it, and now it was a dingy brown. Only the binding thread was new, owing to a recent repair by Gyodo's father. The sharply-fashioned characters were printed from woodblocks, but the paper was so thin that the printing on the reverse fold showed through, making the pages hard to read. There were originally no punctuation marks, but Grandfather Kakkan had added them in red ink and also a red line beside the names of persons and places to distinguish them from other words. He had died early, so his grandchildren had never met him; yet they could acquaint themselves with his sharp and stately personality through the traces of his study remaining in the books. And the traces lent substance to the episodes about him often recounted by their grandmother.

Kakkan was the seventh son of a swordsmith proud of his family history of sword-making at Seki in Gifu Prefecture. One day when Kakkan was age seven, his father, his brothers, other relatives, and their patrons gathered to offer a newly finished sword to their shrine to imbue it with spirit. Once the ceremony was under way, Kakkan casually presented himself, so it was said, with a sword roped to his waist. All were astonished and could not utter a word. He withdrew it, pointed it about, and circled to make sure everyone saw it.

It was a sword with no upper half, a broken sword, and rather comical, though he looked earnest. The assembly was unsure whether to laugh or to scold him for his rude intrusion into the holy ceremony. Some must have thought, 'What a queer child!' Just as the silence was about to give way, he himself spoke,

"Nothing is sharper than this broken edge! Spend your energy as you will and you'll not produce a better sword!" Thereupon he turned and strode from the site. For years it was debated whether he had meant simply the sword or the building up of human character.

> "...and there under Priest Jiaye he studied for three whole years without allowing himself to undress and lie down to sleep. Thus did he live also at Mt. Gushe, and one day suddenly he became enlightened."[2]

When Gyodo finished the paragraph, his father, having a low-grade whiskey accompanied by a piece of baked salted salmon head, spoke up scornfully, "He studied for three whole years without undressing or lying down to sleep — is that what you just read? Ha ha ha! Have you any idea what it means?"

Although he never advised Gyodo to study hard at school or at home, Doyu enjoyed seeing his son's assiduous study and developing ability. But he never directly spoke his admiration and chose instead derisive words or a ridiculing tone.

"In short, it means Jau studied while living like a beast. Beasts don't wear nightclothes or lie down to sleep. The other day a peasant child told me his horse and cow sleep standing up."

"Like a beast? A cow or a horse? Hmm! You think quite clearly, eh?" Doyu filled his cup, emptied it at a draft, and continued,

"But there's an enormous difference between understanding a book and putting it into practice. And whether we can reduce the difference depends on our fate, including the particulars of our birth. It's not only a matter of ability, effort, brain, and character. In other words, even if we apply our effort and improve our character, it isn't enough to change from one who merely understands to one who practices. The difference can't be overcome unless we're reborn in another world, in another age, as another man. It's greater than the space between the earth and the moon! He-he-he!" The laugh was self-mocking. "In what I've just said there's the real meaning of 'three whole years.' It's not hard to sleep without undressing or lying down; that kind of thing depends merely on our fighting spirit, effort, and self-abnegation. But what can we do about three whole years? It's a measure of time, you know. Remember, we're forced to live within the bounds of time. Time controls us and not the reverse. We can't manipulate three years as we like. Naturally our effort, talent, and such will fall short, for the object is the same as the void. Hum-hum! I bet you can't understand what I'm saying, but the fact is, it's like that.

"So I question whether the great author of your book — that redoubtable sir — understood this matter. He tosses it off easily in a line: 'studied for three whole years without allowing himself to undress and lie down to sleep.' As I pointed out, three years can't be dealt with in any way by our individual power, whereas not undressing can be in one way or another. These two absolutely diverse things are treated as equal in this sentence. It is careless, too easy-going, a mistake, and leads the sincere, naive reader to an Asura's suffering life instead of guiding him to peace and satisfaction. I daresay the author has the mask of kindness, but within he's cruel. He contradicts himself like a gun shop that sells a bulletproof vest and at the same time a pistol with bullets to pierce it. By and large, all religions, not only Zen, are brimming with this sort of antinomy. Don't you agree, Gyodo, eh? Or you don't understand at all?"

Gyodo was detesting the smell of his father's breath; it was like rotting persimmons; and he felt disgusted hearing the tag ends of his sentences blurred by alcohol. Whenever his father focused his black pupils on him, the whites of his eyes looked uncommonly wide. It scared Gyodo and made him hate him all the more. In fact he could not understand a thing his father was saying and thought he was embarking on a drinker's grumble or trying to pick a quarrel. Brusquely he answered,

"I don't understand." He closed his book. "I'm going to bed." He got up and left the table.

"Hoooh? You can't bear to stay awake a little longer? Okay, sleep, sleep! There's no better comfort! Say, you agree, Micha?" Doyu clumsily turned to address his wife, who was mending a worn-out school jacket of Gyodo's.

When new it was a bright black. From long exposure to the elements it had become the color of ash. Micha intended to sew on new buttons. Now fixing the torn buttonholes was consuming her time. The elbows and cuffs would require patches.

The jacket was being prepared for Mokuzu, soon to start elementary school. Micha was not deft at sewing, but had she been, her face and gestures would still have revealed her sorrow at being unable to outfit him with new clothes. 'I've no choice but to buy for Gyodo,' she thought. 'Since he must pass everything to Mokuzu, why can't he be more careful? He's wiped his nose on the sleeves, and all over there are thorn and wire snags. Mokuzu passes to Ran just as he receives, like a cicada neatly shedding its shell....Too bad Ran is a girl; as she grows up, dressing in boys' hand-me-downs will be unsuitable....'

"Oi, why don't you say something? What are you doing in such a dark corner? That way you must incessantly complain of pain in your eyes, shoulders, and head."

Micha controlled her tongue, fearing to jar Doyu's feelings and open a quarrel. Were she to speak she could only say, "All day I must peddle; where's the time to sew but now?" or, "Because you earn nothing, our children must wear such wretched clothes."

"In our situation it isn't required, but if you are my wife it would be proper to pour my drink —"

"How can I afford time for such a thing?"

"I'm not saying you should, nor blaming you. I meant it would be nice to spend a cheerful moment together, at least at supper...."

Mokuzu, amusing Ran with blocks on a quilt in the dim next room, strained to hear; he knew the weather of his parents depended on how his mother replied. It could develop to a storm or blow away without a drop of

122

rain. Once the fighting began, the children would keep quiet, burrow into the bedding, and feign to be asleep as they spied on the scene and prayed for a quick cease-fire. Usually they slept before seeing the end of it.

The blocks were their father's handiwork. Cubes, rectangular parallele-pipeds, trigonal prisms, cylinders — there were various shapes and sizes, and each was sanded smooth to protect the hand from splinters, better made than any store blocks, for Doyu was smart with his hands.

But when he became ill-tempered, the sound of even toys he had fashioned got on his nerves. Overreacting, he would shout, "Don't be noisy!" and focus his rage on his wife. So the children were very careful. Ran, absorbed in her play, did not promptly catch his change of mood and became aware only after seeing Mokuzu grow quiet and put extra care into placing a block on the palace they were building. Gyodo sat on his bed in the same room but in a yet darker corner, taking his mother's side, his eyes red with contempt as he glared at his father's back. He was rocking his body and clenching his fists, enduring his vexation of being too resourceless and im-mature to help her despite his intense pity.

"I wonder if Fukuta isn't dying...," Micha mused half to herself. It seemed to come out of the blue, at least to Doyu.

"Fukuta? Alas, he's too old to recover, I suppose. Why do you bring him up so rudely?"

"If he'd quickly die, you could perform a service and receive some alms."

Doyu choked on his whiskey and began to cough; it had entered his windpipe. His shoulders heaved as if he were laboring to hammer a stake into the ground. His face grew congested and tears and sweat oozed out; it was much like an asthmatic fit. When finally it ran its course, he said as he wiped away the sweat and spit with a towel,

"*Aggah* — that was torture! What a horrible idea you can think and dare speak! It must be historically unheard of for the wife of a priest worthy of the name to think and speak so!"

"As the wife of a priest I have an unheard-of situation, you know. Our distress is worse than any petty peasant's or day laborer's," Micha said calmly as she rubbed her needle in her hair and went on sewing.

Indeed she badly wanted cash, wanted if possible to buy a new jacket and pants and knapsack and a few other items for Mokuzu's school entrance. More, Gyodo's sleeves were getting short and his pants already exposing his ankles. Shoes and underwear too must be newly bought.

As he listened, Mokuzu vaguely recalled the person mentioned. Fukuta was known as slightly muddle-headed. Yet contrary to leading the life of a dog, he went out early every day to repair the road and stayed till late evening.

He must have been hired by the town or the Highway Public Corporation.

He ambled along the highway with just a hoe and a bamboo basket, and if he saw a pothole where the rain had formed a pool, he would restore the gravel that wheels had thrust to the roadside and level it up. He never stopped even when a bus or truck approached, so absorbed was he in his work — for which reason no doubt he was called muddle-headed. At such times his mental state must have fit the phrase, 'He is the only one in the whole wide world.' Drivers would honk furiously. Surprised, he would escape farther than necessary, occasioning laughter. Often the places he troubled to fix were undone by the passing of a single truck, creating no end to his job as long as the road remained unpaved.

He could thus earn enough for his needs. His household was said to be wealthy but controlled by his son and daughter-in-law.

The villagers would express concern, "Why must an old man be forced to work so much?" "His son's wife allows him no leisure!" "Poor gaffer, every morning driven out to work."

'Well, maybe he's having the time of his life,' thought Mokuzu. 'He can work as much or as little as he pleases, according to his mood and energy, free of anyone's direction, like us children who play at the river with clay; and he can earn enough to live on.'

Mokuzu was at the same time worrying that a fight would arise then and there if his mother started to compare his father with Fukuta, as much as saying, "If even that idiot can earn, why can't you?..."

But oddly, his father began to laugh, "*Ku ku ku!*" He hunched his shoulders as if to conceal the base of his neck and struggled to keep from bursting into a full-blown laugh. It was a laugh peculiar to persons who have spent years of self-training in a place where silence is enforced.

Mokuzu did not lower his guard. 'Sometimes people laugh when they should anger and cry when they should laugh.'

"Micha, you're right! I'm enlightened once again, thanks to you!"

"Nothing is as useless as the enlightenment of a Zen priest."

"No, no, this isn't about the surface of the truth — it's inside. As you know, a priest must feel other's sufferings and sorrows as his own and always go forth to give comfort and salvation. On the other hand, he must hide his own distress deep in his heart, and hence suffer a million years' self-poisoning. At least, that is the principle for a priest."

"You hardly understand others' suffering. You may understand the suffering of strangers, but not the suffering of your family. To your own wife and children you're quite cruel."

"Don't interrupt, let me speak to the end. Half a priest's training is to practice this principle as much as possible. People suffer most over death, so my intention has always been to mourn at a death and to help the bereaved by whatever affordable means. Living like that, a priest can never meet any pleasure anywhere; his life must be consumed just in mourning.

"If I see people's death in your way — why, when someone dies we can receive alms. We'll have some cash, and it'll help our family. So I'd better pray for their death and not the opposite. Once a source of my grief, it'll be a source of my joy! That's the very meaning of the proverbs, Turn misfortune to a blessing, and, He who knows poison can put it to effect — and also the heart of the phrase, 'Many a lotus blooms in the fire.'"[3]

"Of course, anyone knows that."

"Of course?"

"You didn't know till now the world's common sense? Doctors hope for people's illness, priests hope for their death, carpenters hope for typhoons, peasants even hope for war."

"Hmm, it could be, it must be so. You were born into the house of a wholesale rice dealer and taught to see the world with calculating eyes. I grew up in temples with no chance to know such a matter. It's a tremendous enlightenment. Think a little. Attaining the mind to anticipate with joy the death of others is a bigger thrill than the Wright brothers might have felt when they flew into the sky by artificial wings. Don't you see?"

"Wasn't Zen Master Tengai in Gifu an acolyte like you? Take a look at him once in a while. I've heard he maneuvers huge sums of money and yet is respected as a teacher not only by high politicians and businessmen but by famous actors and artists as well, even by princes. You refused to become dean of Shoshin College, though he earnestly begged you....Had you accepted, your family wouldn't be suffering at the bottom of poverty. Aren't you at least aware that the wife of a priest is peddling clothes to peasants and poor merchants? Those with appearance and education far below mine proudly treat me like a beggar and despise me. Look at our children. What are they to wear to school? Mokuzu is skinny, only his eyes glitter, and Gyodo is scarcely better. Even the image of Sakyamuni Buddha descending from the mountain looks healthier...And —"

"Don't run on so! Your words grate my nerves and sicken me like the sight of a procession of scorpions. You're spoiling my awakening. Instead, why don't you — oh, still are you sewing? Er — hey, Gyodo!"

"He and Ran are asleep."

"Ah, I see. You're staying awake late, aren't you, Mokuzu? You'd better sleep too, and quick! But before you do, could you fetch my calligraphy materials? Be careful, there's sumi in the stone."

Mokuzu stepped from the retreat cottage. The moon was bright. The delicate tops of the bamboos sparkled in the yellow light. The earth stood out in white relief. He brought the materials from the main building. His father immediately laid out a sheet of paper and began lettering with flowing strokes.

"What are you writing?" asked Micha.

"You'll see....a list in order of expectation, as well as our estimate."

"Of what, and to estimate what?" Micha stopped her hand and moved over to peer at the paper:

> Fukuta Nakazawa, Inajiro Tomita, Hyoma Yasukawa, Mimasaka Ota, Toraichi Akashi...

It was the names of persons in order of their expected deaths. Below each Doyu left a space to add the alms he expected to receive.

Micha in spite of herself raised a high laugh. No doubt such a ringing laugh had often issued from her in her girlhood. Taken in by it, Doyu was unable to restrain himself and he too began to laugh. As if hand in hand the laughs were joined, and man and wife kept on laughing.

Mokuzu was released from his anxiety. 'Thanks to Buddha! Tonight's peace is assured, they'll fight no more, till next time...' and he fell asleep.

13

Ran Is Burnt

Micha got up earlier than the rest of the family and took the first bus, at 6:30, into the Muromachi ward of Kyoto to buy the clothes ordered by her customers.

"I've been feeling sorry for you, Micha. That's why today I'll let you in on a business secret. You work hard but aren't earning enough to support your family, I can tell.

"So let me advise you. You're buying from us wholesalers and retailing at a ten percent markup, or maybe twelve, at the most twenty. That's how to do an honest business, but you don't earn well however hard you work. Your profit must be spent on your travel and food, right? Even if you continue for the next ten years, you'll supply no more than your family's minimum needs and nothing will remain but your weary old age.

"Here's the secret, and don't forget it, and don't tell another soul, not even your husband. You may think I'm odd to be telling you, but look, I've been

126

able to hire dozens of workers and I now own this fine shop in Muromachi.

"Suppose you stock ten dresses, or whatever. Nine, perfectly manufactured, you sell with your margin of ten to twenty percent. Now, the tenth is like the others as far as people can tell unless they're pros, but in fact it's defective.

"Maybe a thread is cut, or somewhere there's a tiny chemical flaw, or one color extends a fraction beyond the design...if we examine it from end to end we can find something, so tiny no one including the wearer will notice, be it a kimono or a Western dress. But the factory inspectors and we wholesalers know.

"Now, goods with a defect, however minor, are equal to rags. These you'll buy for next to nothing and retail at the price of your perfect goods. See? Nine perfect dresses will bring your proper profit, adequate only for your daily life. The defective tenth will bring you almost the price of a perfect one, and this income you can save.

"I'll find and set aside such rejects and sell you them for next to nothing. In time you too can develop a discerning eye. Yes."

The shop owner's face was round, his expression, as always, soft and beaming. At last Micha understood what for so long had been a bewilderment. 'I've been peddling as hard as anyone else and selling quite a lot of clothes. Of course I've wondered why no cash remains in my purse, while others are setting up independent shops and hiring their own workers by doing the same business...though somehow more easily!'

As he spoke he edged closer, as much as she withdrew. Had he no sense of distance, or was shortening the distance another of his business secrets? In time their arms met and his face was almost touching her neck where her kimono collar crossed — he was quite short. But he appeared to have no amatory interest. 'At least his face and figure seem unsuited to it,' thought Micha.

ża

Doyu held up the list he had made the previous night and thought, 'I can't post this before the main hall, even if Micha recommended that I do. Wouldn't the laymen ask what it is, and how could I answer?

'If I frankly explain it's an estimate of their death dates and of the alms I expect from their funerals, no one will understand my bright magnanimity and share with me a laugh. The first to lay eyes on it will take offense at my explanation, but with no change of expression, as if he hadn't heard; and with stony countenance he'll raise in his mind a fire of rage like the swaying flame of a ghost. Then he'll bruit it about in a malicious tone and his fellows will come up in twos and threes to see for themselves.

'First they'll exchange reserved words of discontent, grievance, and resentment like the mud snails bubbling in their fields. Next they'll go to their head layman to consult. Now, Yosetsu isn't stupid, he's cunning as a mouse. He'll recognize my pure, uncalculating mind, and he'll smile. But to them he'll exhibit sympathy as he guides them to clearer thought and fires their anger into a twirl of black smoke. Then together they'll come and he in charge will censure me for his own behoof. Then — my family will be troubled. Given an excuse to press me, what unreasonable demand will he make this time? He's been appropriating Tangenji's treasures this way and that and getting close with my acquaintances, thus building his kingdom of profit. Just being reminded of each trick makes me weary of living...makes me misanthropic, makes me want to drink all the more.

'That Tengai affair was typical. Why should he trust Yosetsu and find him useful? Yosetsu is unworthy of association with any college. He's indifferent to compassionate, religious activities, and worse, is but an obstacle. Isn't it evident? His intention is to exploit the name of a first-class priest to gain access to the politicians and businessmen who share the priest's ambition. And this he does simply from a private love of filthy profit and a desire to control people as he likes.

'How can Zen Master Tengai, great as he is, allow Yosetsu to approach? Should I take this wonder as proof of their similarity in some respects — a similar nature, profit-motive, passion, disgrace...in short, what amounts to their both being...what should I say, hypocrites? abominable charlatans?...

'Well, I shouldn't care. My concern is, what to do with this list! I was about to invite trouble by heeding Micha. She may be practical, even reliable, but at times she shows a lack of worldly knowledge. Generally there's no problem in following her, for she's the one sustaining our children, even if not quite satisfactorily. But were I to practice all she says, we'd get into horrible difficulties.

'Wait — for fun did she suggest I put it up? Her hard life might be suppressing her impish nature. Last night I was in a good mood, so maybe something of that hidden nature surfaced without her notice. Yes, it's a joke! Here I've been taking it seriously and wasting my precious time at the main hall with this list in hand. My stupidity has cost me the time to chant the morning sutras, my minimum priestly duty. What neglect, what sloth! There! The children are stirring, I must make breakfast.'

Doyu rolled up the list, put it in a closet, crossed the main hall, and hurried out the service entrance toward the well.

The granite crib of the well was receiving the morning sun. The two lines of chain and the one visible bucket cast vivid shadows. On the drainboard to the side, washed pots, bowls, and chopsticks were piled beside a bamboo basket of washed rice and barley prepared by Micha.

Doyu entered the kitchen cottage with the basket, put the contents into the big iron pot in the middle of the range, and added water, measuring its proper level with his hand. The cottage was dark and cold. He laid pine needles in the middle furnace, lit a fire, and before it burned down, quickly inserted brushwood. The rising smoke was made evident by a shaft of sun slanting from the skylight; only there the great movement of smoke and numerous dust particles appeared without ceasing even a second to swirl.

As Doyu sat watching the fire, Gyodo and then Mokuzu entered and asked, "Where's Ma?"

"Gone to Kyoto for stock. Gyodo, could you go pull scallions for soup? Mokuzu, feed the chickens as usual, but give them some chickweed. Bring an egg if there is one."

Mokuzu trotted through the front garden, rounded the far corner of the shrine, and went up to the laymen's graveyard. Chestnuts grown tall were forming a canopy over the tombstones. Their pale yellow catkins had just begun to shoot out, and on the tombstones their shadows faintly swayed. Among them a stately mountain cherry had opened its petals here and there. A brush warbler, noticing his approach, slightly changed its place and called to its mate.

He picked the juicy tender chickweed in the shade between the tombstones. With his face near the earth, he could detect the odor of incense mingled with the odor of last year's rotted chestnut leaves. It reminded him of such words and their connotations as backyard, in the ceiling, temple, Buddhist sanctum, fights with the laymen, alms, gloom — and more, birthplace, place to grow up, uncontrollable fate...

Being a gentle boy he did not pick the budding dandelion growing in with the chickweed and about to open any day. Carefully he chose what he should, discarding dried leaves of chestnut and bamboo for the sake of the chickens. He evened the ends, making a bunch to hold in both hands, and transported it lightly to avoid crushing it, though he knew the chickens would immediately scatter it and kick it into the wires where it would remain hanging. 'Chickens don't know how to behave.'

After peeling away the outermost leaves, Gyodo washed the scallions in the cold water and chopped them beside his father.

"He can't believe he's going to begin school tomorrow."

"Whether he believes it or not, he must go. Would you kindly take him with you?" Doyu packed his thin pipe with tobacco and lit it with a twig from the furnace.

"There's a problem. He says if he really must go, he'll surely be given new things — jacket, underwear, socks, shoes, cap, notebooks, pencils, eraser, ruler. And a knapsack. I said old is good enough, and if he hasn't that he can get by somehow. But he talked back about a girl who seems to be the child of a doctor, and how with his own eyes he saw her preparing all those things the same time last year."

"Uuu...mm...what's to be done...? — then what did you say?"

"I said, 'Her situation is her situation. Her house is rich, ours is poor. We can't be given those school things. The entrance ceremony is tomorrow, whether you're prepared or not.'"

"Uuu, mmm...What you told him is very true. However, it's too bad... Then what did he say?"

"It wasn't clear, he tried to talk big — 'Is that so? I wonder. Our house is poor, but I didn't get the idea hers was entirely rich. And by now I know you aren't always correct!'"

"Ho ho, he talks big! However, as to this matter, you're right — unfortunately. There's no point in wishing for income to suddenly pop up like a jack-in-the-box. Anyway, please don't mind going as you are and taking him with you tomorrow...it will be thankworthy."

The rice had begun to cook. Bubbles oozed from under the heavy wood top, and a white glutinous liquid ran down in a single line or two and then in many lines.

"Done," Doyu exclaimed and quickly raked all the brushwood from the furnace; delay would cause the rice to scorch on the bottom. He struck it on the earth floor to extinguish it, then scooped out the red coals with a fire shovel and put some in a clay brazier. The rest he put in an old zinc bucket and doused. A terrible noise rose with a white smoke, and instantly the fire was quenched, leaving wet black coals.

Possibly his rough movements or the noise woke Ran. She began to cry. Leaving the work to Gyodo, Doyu went to the retreat cottage. Ran was fretful. He gently held her up, fondled her, and spoke humorous words to make her perfectly awake as he dressed her and finished all the toilet chores. He then turned her care over to Mokuzu.

Gyodo carried a tray with a bowl of hot rice, a cup of miso soup, and a dish of pickles to his grandmother in the main building. She did not appear but spoke her thanks from an inner room. Like an old garden spider she patiently awaited her catch, which she always took straight to the altar to offer to Buddha, striking the big bell three times with the heavy oak stick so hard that people often wondered why the bell did not crack. That done, she took the tray to her room for her own breakfast.

Beside the well Doyu poured water into a wooden tub, added hot water from the pot on the brazier, pulled up a chair, and began to wash the family laundry. He lathered it with a large bar of soap, spilling suds over the sides.

130

Micha complained that he never rinsed enough to remove the smell of soap.

He was accustomed to tending the fire and the rice and to doing the laundry most of the time in silence, though his occasional utterances made it apparent that he was meditating on some subject while no one approached to disturb him.

Suddenly he would raise his voice: "It couldn't be!" or "Don't be so severe!" or "There's a limit to everything!"

No one could guess who or what provoked him, with what sights rising, developing, and disappearing. Did it concern his acolytehood, or his forced inheritance of Tangenji, or matters detached from reality — utter fantasy?

Seeing his father's shapely, round, half-bald and mostly white-haired head from behind and his shoulders and back made Mokuzu think, 'Many times I was on his back while he was doing the laundry. I must have been two or three, so weak I was often carried. He used to pick me figs. The tree has grown up over the chicken house and its trunk is now one of the main posts. I remember him carrying me to the doctor. A truck had broken down on the highway. The smell of gasoline drifted between his neck and my face, lingering even after we went on....'

> "Three who were Tsyming, Guchyuan, and Langye together went to visit Fenyang. The region east of the Yellow River at that time was cold, whence most disdained to study there. But Tsyming cared only to seek the Way and was not idle day or night. When he grew sleepy meditating late into the night, he pricked himself with a gimlet. He later inherited the Dharma from Fenyang. His teaching flourished, and he was heralded as the Lion West of the River."[1]

Gyodo's voice came from the retreat cottage; he must have been continuing what he was reading the night before. 'Why does he enjoy such an old book?' thought Mokuzu. 'And why can't he read with the vigor of a beautiful sword slicing a fat, green bamboo? His pace is snail-like, and, sorry to say, his voice isn't sonorous. But he must be quite able to understand the meaning, being three years older than me. I can't understand and I think he's crazy. If he pricked himself, where? Not in the face. The arm? That would be fairly painful. The belly? More painful. The leg? Could he then have walked? Oh! that's why he kept sitting to meditate, eh?'

Given a can of soapy water, Ran was blowing bubbles with a wheat straw. 'If she doesn't blow in the sunlight, just a dirty background appears behind mere slimy balls.'

"A dream on a dream!" their father exclaimed, somewhat surprising Ran and Mokuzu. Even the chickens some distance away flapped. Beside him was a bucket of washed laundry wrung tight. 'I once heard someone speak, "Should I wring your arm?"...did he mean like laundry? Anyway, why did Dad cry out, "A dream on a dream!"? Was it a sign of ending his meditation, or a comment on Tsyming's gimlet, which Gyodo is reading about?'

"'Thus we practice every good deed as if to plant every fruit-bearing tree....'"[2] As he took the laundry to the side of the garden behind the retreat cottage, Doyu intoned a phrase from a sutra used during the ceremony to offer food to hungry ghosts. His voice was bright and resonant, and the melody indeed suitably undulated to gather in all floating ghosts of the void.

Where he went with the laundry the morning sun was shining in from an opening between the hilly bamboo grove and the retreat cottage. By paying a little attention it was easy to hear the dew dripping from the trees and weeds. As Ran followed her father, her soap bubbles got lively and colorful and rose along the hill and the mountain and high into the sky.

"Harken to me! The time to ascend the mountain has matured. I grant you the honor of attendance. We must not dally: chestnuts await my administration. Ho ho ho!" Doyu, addressing his children, adopted the manner of an old-time lord to his vassals.

From his belt hung a bundle of rice straw previously soaked in water and beaten pliant. Tied alongside were a bundle of dark green aspidistra leaves, a bundle of chestnut scions kept in moist sand all winter, and a sickle so sharp it shone like a mirror when struck by the sun. Gyodo was made to carry the saw with a long stick handle, Mokuzu the hoe.

"Let me carry!" Ran reached for the dangerous saw, then the hoe, which was much too long for her. From his belt Doyu gave her a short wood-handled knife in a matching sheath, after warning, "Never withdraw the blade."

Ran enjoyed being entrusted with this small and light tool more danger-ous than what her brothers had. She raced ahead through the front garden.

'Is she safe with that? It's sharp enough to kill,' Mokuzu vaguely worried. 'I if given charge of it could handle it fine.'

At the west end of the front garden, where the long white wall ended, they turned up behind the shrine, a branch of the Kitano Shrine in Kyoto. They came to where there was a small pond and six stone statues of the Six Jizo Bodhisattvas. Beyond to the left was the laymen's graveyard and directly to the right, the evergreen hedge bordering the upper area of the moss garden.

The pond was not elegant with a bank of arranged rocks. It was merely a pool dug to be about two meters across for receiving drippings from a projection of the steep mountain foot. The water was excellently clean, having seeped from where rains soaked deep into the mountain. The sides were sturdy and somewhat comfortable to look at with natural lawn grass, bamboo grass, Job's tears, eulalia, bush clover, and such. On the cliff, which extended partway over the pond as if about to fall, a maple was growing despite the precarious location, its exposed sinewy roots a contrast to its sensitive leaves.

The Jizo Bodhisattvas stood about two feet high on square platforms in a shallow cave carved further into the cliff. According to a Buddhist teaching, all sentient beings must keep transmigrating through the World of Hell, of Hungry Ghosts, of Beasts, of Asuras, of Human Beings, and of Heaven, in the order determined by the merit saved up in each lifetime. The Six Jizo Bodhisattvas, one at the portal to each world, judge them and guide them each to their suitable world.

These Bodhisattvas might be expected to differ in name and appearance, but the statues at Tangenji all looked alike, dusky with lichens, darksome, and dank, for having stood there so long. Mokuzu was often reminded of his thought when he had first heard their history: 'By their looks I can assume their worlds too are more or less alike; the difference must be only in the names.'

No one but his mother bowed to them with joined palms when passing by. His father utterly ignored their existence, though he raked and cleared the area several times a year.

Mokuzu as a matter of fact had not included them in his vision when he passed by that morning to get chickweed.

To the pond he had an abiding attachment. One reason was that he sometimes freed crucian carp, dace, and chubs there instead of eating them when he and Gyodo brought back a fine catch from the river. A bigger reason was that it happened to be the most private outdoor place in all Tangenji, well removed from the sound and eyes of people, being sheltered by trees yet open to the south and even in winter bright and warm. Except at night he took himself there after fights with Gyodo, when his parents quarreled, when there was no food and he was very hungry, or when he had an upset stomach, that is, whenever he thought quiet solitude was the best or only comfort. He spent many an hour just sitting and listening easily to the water dripping from the cliff, to the occasional sounds made by the fish, to the wind in the trees, while seeing the movement of small chirping birds, the shadows of circling kites, or lizards and various insects nosing among the flowers and grasses.

He was glad it did not have such a supply of water or so large a cliff as what he had seen behind Ena's house a year ago. 'That place behind Ena's

133

house has no commanding view and must always be shady. I'd like to invite her to see how nice a place this is, unlike that abominable water source better to be avoided — it isn't fit for her.'

In front of the pond was a garden mainly for vegetables needing little care, such as corn, squash, and sweet potato. It had been made by cutting into the mountain skirt and hence was well drained, though the soil was stony and poor.

Originally it was a peony garden. Out of need Doyu had converted it to vegetables toward the end of the war. Traces of a narrow canal with irises led from the pond to the moss garden. Once the flow had formed a waterfall where rocks were set to resemble a valley, and the stone lantern and stone bridge then must also have been effective.

In Kakkan's day the Tangenji gardens were large and varied. People entering beyond the gate could enjoy a wide moss garden, many flowering trees in each season, and many arranged rocks. Through the flowering trees in the front garden, they could see the precipitous mountain range bordering Kyoto and Osaka prefectures. In the west they could see a white waterfall against green mountain, and they could stroll up to the peony garden. Such settings were a rare sight in local temples and of course not to be seen at any private house. However, the size and quality of the Tangenji gardens had been greatly reduced, and now those good old times were close to unimaginable.

Most of the artistic gardens, expressing religion and philosophy each in its way, Doyu needed to destroy to produce vegetables. Referring to that time, he would say only, "It was hard — engaging in such a task —" His past, well known to him through his mind and body, he did not reconstruct to articulate it. He wished that it be understood without words.

His children had no means to understand except through his odd utterances. 'Fine, why should my life be understood by them? Anyway it's diffusing like mist, and soon my limbs will separate. Nothing is eternal. "Self-annihilation is true joy."[3] Everything is a dream on a dream.'

Between the pond and the beginning of the close-spaced tombstones was a path into the mountain. The slope was nearly fifty degrees, sixty in one particular place. The path zigzagged at a milder angle, but even so, bamboo grass covered with old chestnut leaves made it slippery. Their father proceeded well ahead. Gyodo had to pull Ran by the hand. Mokuzu pushed her from behind, sometimes supporting her heel with his foot.

The boys were used to the climb; they could run nonstop to the summit in less than thirty minutes and took only five or six to descend, which meant receiving scratches on the face, hands, and feet from thorny shrubs, eulalia, and sharp-cut branches. Wherever the descent was especially steep they neither ran nor rolled but leapt. When they lost control of their acceleration or direction, they grabbed and pulled at whatever was available, even grass roots, and if ever they miscalculated, they fell, or struck face or body against a trunk or branch and lay there as if dead. A foot were it to come down on a sharp-cut end of growing brushwood would be pierced through. Each instant they had to be alert to all dangers, and thus they could arrive at the pondside. Nothing was more fun than to descend full tilt, requiring as it did judgment of the best course among various obstacles on the spur of the moment. So they were confident of not being inferior to a hare or a monkey.

In March their father had finished grafting in the higher area. He now stopped about a third of the way up, and, choosing a relatively flat spot, he gathered dry leaves and started a fire. Gyodo dragged the bigger cut branches to another place and began to saw them into even lengths. They would be bundled for home use as firewood.

Chestnut was most unsuitable for firewood. When green it no doubt held much water; as it burned it frothed immoderately, quenching rather than encouraging whatever flame had been coaxed to take hold. Old wood was usually worm-riddled to the point of collapse and lacked power to burn even if it caught fire. Mokuzu recalled his father telling him that chestnut was used for railroad ties. 'Serves it right,' he decided. 'Wood useless as firewood ought to be run over by monstrous black trains.'

Yet, he sympathized with the living trees. 'The sprout comes white and sturdy from the glossy composed nut, but when it's grown a meter and sending out lovely wrinkled leaves, it's topped to less than thirty centimeters of least comely, rather ugly stem.

'That is split, a scion is inserted, and the whole is bound with a bamboo sheath or aspidistra leaf. Such treatment looks kind, but the grafter is thinking, "You're incompetent and disqualified as a chestnut as long as you remain as you were born." So most of its body is replaced by a scion of slightly better heritage. Under such treatment, for what is the original tree living? Even if it strives to grow, it ends up as merely a foot and waist to support a graft, isn't that right?

'Well, that's okay — later who can tell them apart? They unite and form a new life unlike the original of each. Then the problem for the new tree is, it will be forced to grow up quickly by surrounding weeds and is often disturbed by them, though they give occasional nourishment, and when finally it's grown big enough to fruit, people will rob it of its nuts.

'Excessive rain discourages pollination, the gynoecia drop, and it's cursed, "Useless tree!" Winds break its branches and tear away its half-ripe burs, and it's told, "How slovenly! So weak against the wind?" or, "Giving expectation but no fulfillment! — can't you sense my despair and hold out a little longer?"

'Not disheartened, it recovers and extends its branches and leaves again into the high blue sky. Then borers of many kinds drill in every direction and provide harbor for centipedes. Above all, caterpillars, chestnut weevils, and red mites lay eggs on the burs and eat the nuts, leaving ugly crumbled castings. So vigorous is their breeding, the woodpeckers, swallows, and spiders help little to keep them in check. Then come frostbite, sunburn, and by too much nitrogenous fertilizer, blight causing sudden death. And in the end the wood because it doesn't burn well is hated by children like me and run over by trains. I'd better not wish to be reborn as a chestnut, though any other tree would be fine.'

Taking care not to let his father's fire burn out, Mokuzu raked up dry leaves and piled on dry twigs from nearby as much as to hide the red flame.

They must have been damp, or it was the nature of chestnut to be hard to ignite: the pile created a white smoke and no flame appeared. Almost on his belly, Mokuzu brought his mouth to a faintly burning spot and blew on it repeatedly. 'Smoke to the eyes is persistent and cruel. I withdraw as soon as a wisp enters my eyes and escape to a smokeless zone. Doesn't it mean I recognize I was wrong to draw so near? At one such time Dad ridiculed me, "You're making an unconditional surrender like Japan's acceptance of the Potsdam Declaration."

'Yet the smoke stings my eyes even after I've withdrawn. Grandma said a snake is vengeful. I'd say it's tenacious only while trying to catch its prey. Afterward it isn't, why would it be? But smoke has a contrary nature. It acts like floating haze, like the waving sash of an angel to enhance her elegance, while in fact how cruel it can be!'

Ran was taking out a twig that had at last begun to kindle and was swinging it to enjoy the locus of fire on its tip. As she pressed others to leaves to transfer the fire, she managed only to extinguish them. She had yet to learn that the dense smoky area would not ignite, that even the dry leaves would not unless slightly apart from the fire. And she puzzled over why burning twigs always died when she pressed them to leaves.

The pile only kept smoking.

"Okay! I'll get pine needles and bamboo leaves, they'll burn. And beneath I may find some chestnuts dropped last year and never picked up. I'll roast you them." Mokuzu left Ran and climbed higher.

His father came into view. He was scooping soil with his hands to pack into an aspidistra leaf secured with straw rope around the top of the cut trunk of an older tree about thirty centimeters high and fifteen across. At its edge a ten-centimeter scion was already inserted.

There came an ear-splitting scream. It seemed the expression of the very nature of a creature named Terror and not the cry of a person sensing something terrible — like magma rising from deep in the earth, melting rock, overwhelming its confines, redoubling its power, and exploding as high as to pierce the heavens.

Mokuzu turned and saw Ran with arms raised, fingers spread, eyes wide, mouth screaming. Behind, higher than her hair, was a flame of cinnabar red mixed with brown like the aureole of Acala.

Then came a noise of dashing downhill, the scattering of leaves and earth, and in a trice Mokuzu was struck on the left temple by a hard fist and knocked flat against the leafy slope.

When he sat up he saw his father clutching Ran and violently rubbing her this way and that against the earth.

Right after he left to get pine needles, Ran must have pursued him, and the smoking pile as she passed it must have flamed up and licked her wool-and-rayon pants, instantly igniting them and her cardigan of similar material. Her hair in back was singed. Her head and back were spared. The flame had first touched her high on her thigh and had burned through her underwear. Blisters appeared. The worst spot looked white.

In her father's tight embrace she yelled through tears, reared back her head, and kicked. Doyu carried her home, taking great care not to drop her. He ordered Gyodo to draw water from the well and cooled the burn with a wet towel. 'We have neither Merthiolate nor Mercurochrome. Then what should I do?' he worried. 'What is the best first-aid for burn? I can't think — her cries are tearing the air to a thousand pieces. If only Micha were here at this sort of time! After all, she's practical. All things taken together, child care is woman's work. But she's gone from early morning and is gadding about — look! nothing good comes when a woman doesn't stay home!

'What a horror, what a pity! a girl burned in such a place! It'll leave a keloid and I bet be a great obstacle to her growing up. Why doesn't she come back? Where is she? She must be endlessly engaging in chat just to sell a pair of socks, consuming a lifetime as if it's factory spilth. No wonder I always felt uncomfortable about her peddling. How ridiculous that I, a man, must cook, launder, and tend the children! But if I say so, she'll say, "Who'll bring in money? Gladly I'll stay home as a matron, an honorable priest's wife, dressing in fancy kimonos, arranging flowers, offering fine tea to guests. However, you never worked for our cash...." A barren argument. There's no use each blaming the other without considering the other's career, character, and fate. But the problem is, how to treat poor Ran — oh! I see!' Doyu raised his voice:

"Hey, Gyodo! Mokuzu! For what are you depressing yourselves in a corner? Don't be useless! Go ask Grandma how to treat Ran, and be quick!

137

Make sure you say she's badly burnt, hurry! Wait, Gyodo, just you. Mokuzu, run back to the mountain and get my tobacco. Without smoking I can't settle my mind."

The grandmother came promptly, using her cane. Being stout, she seemed imperturbable even when in a hurry. Seeing her, Doyu felt sure-footed; at any rate she was his mother.

"Saving your reverence, what on earth are you doing? Quickly apply soy sauce, and you must have shredded tobacco — mix them and apply it at once!"

"What's the efficacy of that?"

"You're getting age for nothing. Infection is to be feared soon after. We must apply tobacco with soy sauce if we have nothing better. I know because I was taught it at Mr. Konoike's. I wasn't a mere maidservant. I waited on the madam. The position called for me to associate intimately with her and learn various manners, necessary womanly accomplishments, and how to live. Only young women of superior rank to that of those who went to the higher grades of school were taken in. After all, Mr. Konoike was head of the Konoike zaibatsu, which ranked with the big four, Mitsui, Mitsubishi, Sumitomo, and Yasuda — "

"Yes, Ma, I know all that, having been told a hundred times!"

"So, apply it! It's a scientific treatment. Then take her to Dr. Okada. You shouldn't waste a minute."

"Oh, yes! Of course I should take her. Then why don't you mix up your treatment and apply it while I go change."

"What? Not run to the doctor as you are? No wonder you are slighted by your wife! Any normal man would have already run with the child to the doctor and by now she'd be well taken care of. How can your concern be your clothes? Whose child is this? Furthermore, I haven't time to spare for applying soy sauce."

"Why, what will you do?"

"Pray at the Buddha hall as a matter of course. I shall pray to our Kannon Bodhisattva for Ran, so her burn won't become infected and will be as small as possible, and so her little heart won't be damaged by such a terrible experience. Religious healing. Your father always said nothing is unattainable when science and religion harmoniously combine; he said there's no better peace than the peace attained thereby. So hurry up!"

Ran, having exhausted herself by crying, had fallen asleep. Now and then she shook and hiccuped.

14

Doyu Meditates on Fame

Next morning again Doyu was making breakfast. In the somber cottage the furnace fire was brighter than an outdoor fire. "What a joke!" he spoke aloud and resumed his quiet thought.

'Roughly speaking, human beings are like children who go to swim in the ocean. I don't know why, but somehow children enjoy playing in the water as if it's the reason they came out of their mother's womb. Needless to say, for the birth of a human child, all external conditions, including a mother and a father, must be fulfilled. But a child who is to be born also has life's original nature coming through several hundreds and thousands of forebears, through global and universal time — a matter expressed in Buddhism as "the Dharma of creation rising from inner and outer causes." It is treated in a Zen koan, "Which generates the ring of a bell, the hammer or the bell?"

'Then what happens? Some of those who run to the sand, eyes bright with expectancy, are engulfed and swept away before they've known enough joy. Far from what they expected, they're choking, thrashing, and fainting. They grasp for even a moment's relief, but how paltry is human strength! Try as they may to escape the waves or to ride them to shore, their effort is dashed to atoms and their lives pulled back into the unconscionable eternal life of the waves.'

These days Doyu was counting as one of his supreme comforts his surrender to meditation as he sat before the furnace. Similar to Zen meditation in appearance, it was in fact very different. Zen meditation was far more intense, its aim being to empty the mind by shutting down the five sense organs, indeed every last feeling and thought, so that neither subject nor object remained to be recognized — a state not easy to attain without going through an ascetic practice bordering on madness.

Nor was Doyu engaging in philosophical speculation with its exacting logic and propeller-like drive to advance ideas by expending great energy.

His enjoyment was to think as he liked, to drift on the current of time like a buoy on the tide. Engaging in habitual work like tending the furnace, weeding, trimming, or walking was therefore very convenient. These easy burdens for which he had mastered the skill provided him time and space to float in thought as well as a comfortable rhythm for thought.

'I've at least ten more minutes till the rice boils. Then I must remove the fire and make soup, and soon the children will awake and I'll be distracted by their talk. Above all I must tend Ran. What a sorrow, badly burnt just after

139

outgrowing diapers, finishing her toddling stage, and becoming free of the need of care. Again she must be humored and carried like a baby. I must clean the wound, and take food to Micha...what is her problem?...too profuse for normal menses, and clotted and foul. She seems quite ill. Should I ask Dr. Okada to visit? Yes, I'll explain and request it when I take Ran this morning. What trouble! The day of Ran's disaster, her mother returns with fevered breath and collapses into bed!'

Doyu savored his peace for the nonce, sitting before the furnace, elbow on knee, chin in hand, drawing on his pipe, and feeling on his cheeks the heat of the flame.

'The reality of daily life is like a landslide about to fall on my head. It's too materialistic and allows no scope for thought. No wonder I like to ponder matters of the far past. However relentless they were, they now have no force of influence. Ha ha ha! They were certainly of the present when they occurred, but they were fated to pass.

'Now, what had I in mind? Oh yes, fame, my father's love of fame, for surely he sought fame. No doubt he had the animal desires for food, sleep, and sex, and desires peculiar to human beings, for knowledge, exercise of authority, conquest, wealth. But the conspicuous difference between him and normal men of the area was that he sacrificed all other desires for the sake of his desire for fame. Hence he could dash ahead unhindered by them, and rather was assisted by them, as if his prime desire was a powerful headquarters governing his life.

'What then is the fame he desired? Essentially, it is to be hailed as a splendid guy, a noble fellow, an illustrious gentleman, a supereminent personage, a luminary, a patrician, a cynosure, a paragon. It is to raise oneself as if upon a seat in the sky from which to regard others as inferiors in a swamp. In short, it is an elevator to lift and lower people.

'But the afflictive reality of this elevator is that it is powered by adulation and ceremony. Naturally a fame-seeker will act in accordance with how he is praised, which means he can't much expect to live an independent life loyal to himself.

'And if he's disloyal to himself, his instinct and desire to maintain his life will be sacrificed. And it doesn't end there, for those extensions of himself — his wife and children — must receive his trouble and be sacrificed without their asking it.

'Look at me, eldest son of such a man. Why was I sent so young into the priesthood? I was terribly sad and uneasy parting from my mother and going to unknown Kyoto from this remote country, torn from my accustomed and beloved friends, mountains, and river, like a ripped-off remnant of cloth.'

140

Doyu remembered: shaven head, white gaiters and sleevelets, fisting the big wicker hat, departing with Priest Mukai, come to fetch him. Many times he looked back with reproach. The fields everywhere tall with wheat coming into ear obscured his mother's figure after he came to a dip in the path. His father in formal robes sat solemn at the gate on the red-lacquered scissors chair, ceremonial fan in hand, his mother on a cane-bottomed chair beside him. They sat still as statues. All the local priests and nuns were invited and stood in rows on either side of the gate. All the laymen and villagers were serried by the granite steps below. They clapped as they saw him off.

'What insistence on formality just to send me away!'

"Was it necessary?" Doyu spoke aloud.

'He didn't send me to be an acolyte because of poverty or other difficulty in raising me. He was a landowner and Tangenji the wealthiest temple in all of Tanba. Was it for my education? How could he tell I was fitted to the priesthood? I'm actually not successful at it, and I increasingly grew to hate it. I haven't the nature and talent for it. I wanted to paint, to play the shakuhachi, and to play billiards. Obviously his decision wasn't based on any thought about my education and my future: he sent me off when I was too young for anyone to know what field suited my ability.

'What reason can I think he had other than to satisfy his love of fame? Young and energetic, he had acceded to the vice-abbacy of Nanzenji, and had begun to be recognized not only in the Rinzai school but throughout the Japanese Buddhist Association. So he must have thought the best course for me was to prepare early to be an orthodox priest. The fittest way was to force the son to live so as to serve and aggrandize the father.

'What does it mean but that he put the judgment and regard of others above his love for his son? — and of course he took no account of his wife's sentiments. He trampled on his son, on his personality, his individuality, his feelings sensitive as the alae of a butterfly. What's that? It sounds like choking. Oh! Ran waking with a cry sour as vinegar — it tugs at my heart like a magnet. Such a protracted cry, as if about to cease and afford me relief, but starting anew after a breath, proving it's not over but gaining momentum —'

Doyu hurried with his faintly bandy-legged gait to the retreat cottage. The interior was dim with the storm doors shut. Gyodo, dressed only in briefs, was holding up Ran, who was hotly crying as he struggled to support her without putting his arm to her burn.

Doyu received her, laid her by her mother, and removed the gauze soaked with neomycin, applied by Dr. Okada the day before. It was stuck to the worst area and could not be removed without leaving some threads.

"'Save us, Merciful Buddha!'" Doyu declared and resolved to take Ran to

141

the doctor at the earliest office hour. "Hey, Mokuzu, what are you doing standing around? Quickly dress, and please open the storm doors, no, maybe you'd better not."

Doyu regarded Micha, sleeping or unconscious; she made no response even to Ran crying at her side...her face was ashen, her lips dry, her hair disheveled. The quilt pulled up to her chin exposed old cotton wadding.

"Gyodo, you too quickly dress and go check the rice. By now it may be horribly gushing, it'll be a disaster if it scorches."

Doyu hastily put underwear and a skirt on wailing Ran and tied her to his back with a russet sash. Gyodo only in briefs ran ahead. Mokuzu thought it necessary to explain why they were not yet dressed,

"According to Gyodo, today is a ceremonial day since it's my first day of school. Hereafter without fail he and I must douse with cold water before dressing. It's spring and soon summer. If we start now it'll not be so hard come winter, he said."

"What? Harden body and mind, eh? He must have read some such thing in a book. But he is sturdy enough, and you are scrawny and pale. Take a look — your ribs stick out, can almost be grabbed. If you practice such a thing, you'll catch cold and get pneumonia or tuberculosis. At this moment too, come closer, look, you're all gooseflesh. Get dressed — you're shivering, aren't you?"

"I'll dress after dousing." Mokuzu proceeded to the well.

Doyu registered that both boys were not entirely swayed by their family situation and were beginning to establish their own world even if it was insignificant.

'My life and Micha's has collapsed; we have neither form nor regularity. We do only what we can among all we must do and are demanded to do, living precariously hour to hour, day to day. It must be the same for her, but never did I have to live like now, when I can be thankful the day will end. However many unpleasant and distressing occurrences repeat like lapping waves, I can finally be lulled by sleep. The children's appeals and cries of pain last only while they are awake, though a word of appeal during their dreams stings my sorrow ten times more sharply.

'We haven't the joy and comfort others can have from meals, from doing important work respected by society, from accumulating possessions, from dressing up and exchanging courtesies with intimates or eminent others, from walking through fields and mountains or pursuing such pleasures as painting. All we have is our sleep or rest in the vacuity of night. It has become so.'

Doyu went to the kitchen cottage with Ran now calm on his back. He filled a washbowl with hot water, added a dash of cold water from a bucket, and carried it to the retreat cottage. He wrung a towel and wiped Micha's face and neck.

142

Micha faintly opened her eyes.

"Ran? The boys...gone to school?...maybe serious this time, I can't get up...like a drooping candle. If you can, if there is, a little thin soup of kudzu or agar or rice...had nothing since yesterday morning....made a good sale to Toshibei at Yoshida, though I'm not yet paid....abdomen is heavy...blood stagnant...." Her mouth scarcely moved and she took much time.

Doyu dissolved powdered kudzu root in a little water and added very hot water while stirring vigorously with chopsticks to make a smooth, clear soup. When he took it to Micha's pillow he saw that she was again asleep.

'The tragedy is, my father attached great importance to form, and I, his son, can't maintain it in the face of poverty.' Doyu reentered his thought as he sat facing his wife.

'He was recognized by his Zen master, Gasan, as one who had attained enlightenment, and he was initiated into the mysteries of the tea ceremony as well as flower arrangement, and also received the secrets of calligraphy — those complete qualifications and trinkets for a Zen priest.

'He got into the nucleus of the head temple, and here at Tangenji he singled out able local youths, offered them scholarships, and raised them to the professions of scholar, doctor, artist, military officer, financier. He increased Tangenji's estate, laying a surer economy for the temple than it had during the anti-Buddhist movement in the early Meiji era. And he organized the founding of a school for nuns in Kyoto.

'Come to think of it, his successes were concurrent with the national measures to enrich and strengthen Japan. The country had gained victories in the Sino-Japanese and Russo-Japanese wars and had entered victorious into the First World War. Japan was rapidly growing to rank with the Great Powers, even beginning to disturb their peace and self-conceit.

'When I unwillingly inherited Tangenji, Japan was at a height of prosperity unequaled in all its long history. But only by colonizing Korea, China, and many other neighboring countries could that prosperity be maintained. Inevitably and vividly the breaking point was nearing moment by moment.

'My father's success too was dependent on his increasing his farmland and his driving many commoners into tenancy; and naturally here too the height of his success was the beginning of his decline. I well remember their gloomy eyes catching mine when I was a child, their faces baked dark crimson, their cheekbones jutting out immoderately. I never knew whether they were smiling or crying. The eyes of their cows were brighter and more friendly. They acted quiet, always walked with lowered heads, ate even the rinds of watermelon, licking their fingers. They expressed their rage solely by abruptly

143

standing or abruptly lifting a hoe. They must have been burying their humiliation in their minds...how dreadful was their deep-seated grudge!

'All major cities of Japan were burnt to the ground in the last war, and
General of the Army Douglas MacArthur ordered us landowners to release
our farmland. The formal culture maintained by the elite like my father and
based on heavy tenant labor was in substance turned upside down, and we
their descendants must live like paramecia in puddles under the rubble.

'How should I understand these changes? Is it enough to lament
poetically, as if to avoid the sight of anything but ripples on water? "The bell
of Jetavanavihara echoes: All things pass and naught doth stay. The flower of
the twin sal trees asserts: That which prospers must decay. Pride goeth before
ruination: A dream on a spring night. Even the stalwart shall in time succumb:
Dust before the wind."[1]

'Don't such lines slight whoever dies in torment of body and soul? Look
at this woman, face pale, breath foul, dimly conscious! Was she born only to
live in this miserable marriage? Where is the angelic face of her girlhood?

'And Ran on my back, burnt just as she was opening her world. She gets
inadequate food and medicine, and all she does is repeat the four infant
activities of crying, eating, sleeping, and defecating, expending precious hours
that should be her joy.

'In patched clothes Mokuzu must go for his first day of school, without
his mother, though at least he has his brother.

'Kiku, without even attending her graduation ceremony of junior high,
went to work in a distant cotton mill. Most of her first pay she sent with a
note, "For my younger siblings."

'Bunyu we sent to a fine Buddhist college in Kyoto; we were better off
then. But he quit and had the nerve to say, "Playing around is more fun." His
interest was to speed from patrol cars on a stolen motorcycle. Then he got a
job, he said, as a social dance instructor, and talked of becoming an actor. All
I really know is he and his gang were assembling a gramophone from stolen
parts, taking electricity from a public wire...always complaining over trifles, in
short, living like the dregs of society.

'A life that adheres to formality is made possible by the suffering of many,
can't it be said? My father's life was formality itself. Rising at four, chanting
while putting on vestments, chanting to offer tea and food to Buddha, sitting
for meditation, cleaning the temple, chanting at breakfast, writing letters,
chanting to offer the main meal to Buddha, receiving guests, chanting at the
main meal, reading, strolling, sitting at tea — such was his schedule whenever
he was at home. What would he think of my disorderly life? Would he say,
"Even Buddha cannot save him who lacks karmic relation," or coolly observe,

144

"It's dismaying that an ordinary mortal like me should be raised to honorable status by one like you"?

'Anyway, he was a traditional Buddhist priest, especially typical of the Zen sect. But the culture he inherited and promoted was destroyed by the war. It's a cause for gratitude and congratulations insofar as formality was destroyed by substance. Yet I have no reason to thank the Allied Powers, because their destruction — or "reformation," if they wish — was carried out so imperfectly for the world, while masterfully done on a trifling and individual scale.

'What they should have destroyed was the desire to maintain formality along with love of fame. Instead they destroyed the common people. Examples are the air raids on Tokyo, Yokohama, Nagoya, Osaka, and Fukuoka, and the atomic bombs dropped on Hiroshima and Nagasaki. How queer were the Allied nationals, headed by America!

'Their enemy should have been formality, most evident in the Imperial Palace, and in the head temples of each school and sect of Buddhism, centered in Nara and Kyoto. No one there was put in distress. Therein formality was sustaining itself by the tears and blood of the commoners. The Americans didn't lay a finger on this real enemy, worse, they even protected it!

'Isn't it strange? The Allied Powers fought to give people a free democratic world, but actually they maimed and killed them and aided those who were the people's real enemy.

'So I can sense what kind of men were Roosevelt, Stimson, Truman, MacArthur; they must have been much like my father, slaves to formality and honor. They must have mastered their traditional culture and sacrificed even their children to obtain their end. They couldn't have been exemplary as husband, brother, child, or parent, as friend to other human beings. Their enemy wasn't Japan, Germany, or Italy but the notion of respect for the individual, a notion spreading not only in America but worldwide. What those leaders feared was the purity, serenity, and brightness inherent in every human being, and what they protected was the unnatural love of fame accompanied by warped ideas, ideas detached from reality, ideas going by the name of tradition and culture. They didn't bomb the formal surface; they bombed the common people awakening to the idea of freedom.

'And again the same thing must be occurring in Korea. Many ambitious, formality-loving Japanese are helping the American military and raking in money by producing arsenals of all kinds for them. What a horror are those politicians, former military personnel, industrialists, and government-sponsored scholars! But who is teaching them how to succeed?

'The likes of Zen Master Tengai! He truly resembles my father — no, Tengai is a still more assiduous fame-seeker, and more cruel. And there are other differences. My father studied more fundamentally, whereas Tengai studied little and therefore uses scholars as his servants. And while my father disliked politicians and didn't associate with them, Tengai loves them like his own fists and balls.

'Moreover, my father married and had children, at least, and acted like a human being, somewhat. Tengai doesn't marry or eat even a flake of dried bonito and is devoting his entire life to honor and formality — '

"Eh? Yes, yes, I'll get your breakfast." Responding to Ran on his back, Doyu went to the kitchen cottage.

The boys, having doused themselves with cold water, were dressed and at the table. Gyodo was lecturing Mokuzu.

Set before Mokuzu was a bowl of miso soup containing daikon leaves, made by Gyodo. Mokuzu had not touched it, which had triggered Gyodo's lecture:

"You'll have a hard time if you don't eat now. Are you worrying about not having things? Don't care, just go, stay with the new kids, and at the ceremony answer 'Yes!' loud and clear when you're called."

Mokuzu had come to realize that the entrance ceremony and school clothes and supplies were not inseparably related like fish and water, and he had figured out that his family situation and that of another child could be quite different.

Gyodo was telling him,

"You have to know school is where strangers meet — the teachers and pupils are all strangers. I sympathize with you: you likely can't well distinguish strangers from family, having lived with parents who are more like strangers than family.

"So first I'll teach you about a family. A family judges everything by whether it is good for all its members, who devote themselves to one another. If the parents are true family members and true parents, they'll even steal abroad to feed and dress their children — and of course give school supplies. They haven't time to consider whether their conduct is bad for others; if they are worthy of being called parents, they care only about their own children.

"So you can understand about strangers: they do nothing good for you, and they exploit you for themselves and their family.

"The reason I said our parents are more like strangers is that they, especially our father, don't do us any good. He can't earn money from others, so he can't buy what we need. Remember what he did when Ran got burnt? First, before saving Ran, didn't he clout you on the head? It was punishment for your neglect. Think a little. At such a time who will give priority to punishment? He is somewhat strange."

Mokuzu thought back. 'After all, was it punishment?' He was unconvinced.

146

'It was too minor and impulsive to be punishment,' and afterward there came no reprimand.

Seeing Mokuzu's doubt, Gyodo added, "Look, that's why I say he's somewhat strange. He wasn't thinking of punishment except when he clouted you. Before and after, he's a largehearted, good father, so to speak. But at that moment a strange nature nesting in his depths and unknown even to him erupted. It could be a transmission from our grandfather."

Mokuzu's eyes clouded, but Gyodo spoke no more about this strange secret nature. Mokuzu could only imagine it to be some inner flow like groundwater.

"For now just know that he's somewhat strange. You'll see better by the next illustration. Why didn't he race with Ran to Dr. Okada in the neighboring village? Why did he bring her back here and waste time doing ineffectual things? You must have heard Grandma scolding, "Quick! Take her to the doctor as you are!" This shows his queerness. Why didn't he run there directly in his work clothes? He didn't act like a normal parent; his dress was more important. And he didn't run for fear he'd expose to all eyes his upset state. In sum, his concern for looks reveals a strangeness, a secretly transmitted nature, do you see? If you do, then you'll see why I say he's more like a stranger than a family member."

"Then which is he?"

"Of course he's a family member and our father. I'm saying he can be strange, but you must know real strangers are worse, they more actively harm us. They despise us, entrap us, and hope for our misfortune, and care only how to profit from us. Our father does none of that. He does us no positive good and that's all, except for the problem of his using violence on Ma."

"Then which are you?"

"Me? What a question! I'm your brother and a family member. But wait, let me think...I'll tell you when it's clear to me. Though you appear absent-minded, sometimes you're sharp!"

"It seems I could understand by and large a family and strangers and something like a suspect family. But I don't know what to do in school, and it's a pressing question."

"Right, that's why I began with this subject.

"Then, there are two hardships you must face in school once you go without caring about what you need. One is indoor shoes. We change into them at the entrance. The corridor and classrooms have wood floors, and mud is unwelcome. You were given no indoor shoes, so you'll enter barefoot. In this season your feet will get awfully cold and the cold will reach to your belly. It was true for me, but you'll be worse for being born delicate. Soon your

147

insides will suffer. It's hard to forbear at your desk with cold feet and unbinding diarrhea.

"Another hardship is, the school day will soon lengthen and you'll have study after lunch too. All the pupils and teachers bring lunch, but how about if you can't? You must patiently watch, or wander outside, or spend the time on the pine hill behind the school. Mostly I read in the library. Following the lessons is hard when you're hungry, but Ma never takes lunch. Don't worry, I'll do my best to save some breakfast for you to take.

"Those two things are the hardest. There's lots more, for instance, kids will scorn or pity you for having to endure. Above all else they'll hurt your self-esteem..."

"Then should I just be patient?"

"No, you have to be strong. This is what I want most to tell you, so listen, and don't look aside like that. By any means you have to become strong and protect yourself from every injury that others might inflict. You'd better love and protect all of you — your hands, feet, head, body, eyes, ears, nose, mouth. You aren't required to use any part of you to please others; care only about yourself. No stranger will protect you, you must protect yourself by yourself.

"For that purpose, become strong, drastically, with determination! You began to douse for this end. You'd better run up the mountain more and also read more books. Everything will be the means to strengthen yourself."

"You say I should protect myself by myself. It sounds like there are two of me..."

"Eh? Mokuzu, your brain works in a queer way. There couldn't be two of you unless you're looking in a mirror. It's a figure of speech; I must use words to say what I mean. Maybe it causes you to hallucinate so you think you are disunited to two selves. Do you really think there are two of you when I say 'protect yourself by yourself'? Stupid! It means each man protects himself by himself!"

"Well, I felt there were two of me a moment ago, not like in a dream but clear like narcissus reflected on a pond..."

"Tut! Never mind. Care to bear up and strengthen yourself. It's time — everyone will come, we'd better wait at the gate."

At this point Doyu entered the cottage with Ran, and seeing the boys he said,

"Oh, you've finished breakfast and are leaving? Take care. Your mother seems quite ill. What will happen if you meet trouble in addition to all else? Take extra care. I ask you specially, Gyodo, to look after Mokuzu."

Doyu eased Ran from his back, sat on a chair, and put her in his lap. As he helped her with her chopsticks, he said,

"There now, you eat too. Gyodo made soup. How great, doing what he should without being told. Fortunately there's rice, thanks to your ma, she earned for us — she did, and now she's ill from overwork or something. You too, you got burnt. Well, don't worry, Dr. Okada said some trace will remain, but it's not serious enough to grieve for days. This morning we'll go to him again as soon as you finish breakfast, so eat well and cheer up."

Gyodo had left the kitchen cottage, but Mokuzu turned back to make sure of something, so Gyodo had to wait.

"Dad, are you a family member or a stranger?"

"Eh? What an odd abrupt question! Ha! — again Gyodo's been preaching some hard subject? Hey, Gyodo, be careful, if you fill him with more than he can take, his brain will go awry and crack his skull!"

Gyodo went to the gate leaving a cold smile. Mokuzu lingered, awaiting an answer.

"What? You want my answer? Strictly speaking, you shouldn't ask lightly and reflexively whenever you get a casual notion, especially if it's stimulated by someone else's talk. Isn't that reasonable? Otherwise how can I understand what you really want to know? There isn't always one answer; usually there are many according to the situation and the intent of the questioner.

"Suppose you're a policeman wanting to arrest me for a murder I didn't commit. High-handedly you ask, 'Can you swear you never lied or killed?' I can only say, 'Many times I lied, flattered, made excuses. I must have killed scores of insects and mice, and I've eaten chickens, pigs, cows...' 'Just as I suspected,' you'll conclude. 'You've killed, you've lied — you're under arrest!'

"At least you must explain a little instead of suddenly asking with so serious a face. Of course you may not intend to trap me. Then all the more, why not do as I say?

"Which reminds me, you've been prattling with questions since you were around three, more than the others. That's fine while it's about simple matters, but nowadays you're asking about things you can't see or smell, things you think in your mind.

"You should solve that kind of question as much as possible by yourself. Ask and answer by yourself. If you can't answer, then meditate on the question and purify it by eliminating all solvable incidentals. Then ask that purified part to someone you can rely on. If you keep asking just anyone so casually, you'll never face your grave questions. There's a Zen proverb, 'Without great doubt, no great enlightenment.' Ha ha ha!" Beginning to sound like his old teacher Mukai, Doyu felt shy.

"I asked you, Dad, if you are a family member or a stranger because I felt they are not so distinguishable. Then I thought, if so, who are you really, and who am I who am thinking like this? Gyodo gave me a definition of strangers, family, and false family or some such, but his definition doesn't tell who you or I really am. However, I understand what you said, and it's reasonable, so I'll think on my own about such things."

"Good, you're a man of understanding. To know what they are, it seems Gyodo classed people as you say, but he's missing the basic question of how they came to be so.

"In the Nirvana Sutra there's a story of a blind turtle swimming in a great ocean. It unwittingly raises its head. Floating just there is a piece of wood with a knothole. The turtle's head enters the knothole and the turtle can't get free. The ocean is vast, the turtle is blind, the wood is the only wood around, and it has a knothole. Whether good or bad fortune, somehow the turtle's head enters that knothole.

"A very rare happening, an accident, a kind of fate. It suggests that the reason you and I became related as father and son, and the reason you and Gyodo and Ran became related as brothers and sister is not unlike the fate of that turtle."

"Come on, Mokuzu, they're here!" Gyodo called from the gate. The village boys were approaching in double file.

"Go now, and don't be out of touch with your surroundings by thinking about these things. Keep your eyes open! Ran, you advise him the same, won't you?" Doyu said to Ran, who did not understand much, after Mokuzu left.

'Our children are like our chickens. When there's food they're fed, when there's not I free them and they hop out the gate, appear on the road, go to the fields and as far as the riverbank, finding something to fill up on.

'At sunset they return and enter their house. The rooster fights off stray dogs, or he and the others are killed. They may protect one another, and often they scrap among themselves.

'Our children too are left at large. What if I were rich or could earn money? Probably they would be under my severe control and be strictly educated, as I was. For me it was a mere unfreedom, subordination by wealth. My mind and body shrank, I could do nothing as I wished, I was forced to repress my feelings, and never was I given a chance to know the limit of my ability. I didn't know for whom I was living.

'Poverty seems a tragedy, but our children are free. They can feel their pain and hunger and feel the joy of finding a coin on the road, of picking wild pears in the mountain. Can wealth and orthodox education give that?

'I never order them to do one thing or another. Being powerless I rather think they are great. Actually I have little to teach them, but from them I have much to learn, and by them I am often encouraged.

150

'What I must do is secure them food. As long as I can't, they must depend on their wild vitality. I think I'm unpardonable, and I'm sorry for them, and truly I wish to find a way to rebuild our economy...but, what a useless education I was given, and how cheap was my Zen training! Enlightenment? Alas, a most revolting word! My Zen enlightenment can't obtain even school supplies, and what can it do for Micha sick and Ran burnt? My Zen enlightenment is like those paintings of Bodhidharma shown without limbs; it's an ugly thing useful only in a life of economic stability and traditional culture; it's like all ghostly religious and aesthetic austerities that foster worship, the chanting of sutras, sitting meditation, painting, calligraphy, temple cleaning, garden care...all useless to secure even a piece of bread or a bottle of medicine.

'Nevertheless, I wouldn't want to be like Zen Master Tengai. He talks of his passion to produce able men, rebuild the country, establish world peace, and eliminate misery by educating the ignorant. But he's enslaving respectable, splendid individual human lives and humbling them to satisfy his love of fame.

'Then there's Yosetsu, another detestable type. He somehow maneuvered himself into assisting Tengai like a parasite taking up residence in a great evil host to ingest profit and work its way to power. I can't figure why he wants to live like that...with a face like a taro potato and a brain like a tiny light bulb...'

15

Mokuzu's First Day of School

The brothers stood on the lowest step of the two-storied gate as about thirty boys in black uniform advanced. They went by a hillock and through the shade cast by a camellia grove, but for Mokuzu the distance between himself and them seemed not to shorten for a long while — too far for greetings, yet too near to ignore one another.

Gyodo held a folded brown cloth, Mokuzu nothing.

The leader, a tall sixth grader named Hikoroku, halted and addressed Mokuzu,

"New pupils go today a little later with their mothers."

"She's sick, so he's coming with us," said Gyodo.

For an instant all who were chatting shut their mouths.

"I see. Then come beside me and never mind," said Hikoroku kindly, and he took Mokuzu by the hand and started on.

151

Gyodo, entering fourth grade, walked in back with his classmates.

"What's she got, a cold?" Hikoroku leaned over to ask. He helped his family in the fields and had the shoulders of a cow. He carried a threadbare tan bag slung to the side.

"I don't know the name...there's blood."

"Eh? Is it TB? Is she spitting blood, eh?"

"No, from below."

"Ohh...how terrible! — what in the world?"

Mokuzu felt pity and some amusement at the sight of the wincing mouth on so bulky a fellow. Suddenly he felt he was the bigger man for coolly coexisting with his mother's condition.

'If I mention Ran,' he mused, 'he'd be further impressed.' He considered her return to babyhood, her perpetual sobbing and having to be carried, though until the moment of the burn she had been bright, strong, and garrulous, playing as she trailed her brothers. 'But to get his sympathy, even admiration, by mentioning Ran would amount to humbling myself.' Mokuzu noticed his armpits were breaking into a cold sweat.

He still had the feeling, touched off by Gyodo's breakfast talk, that there were two of him. They were not standing side by side but were more like a self in a self, an outer shell and a nucleus deep within. This nuclear self, he felt, far surpassed the other — was much more important.

'It seems my outer self can temper and polish my inner self, but it gets cloudy and doesn't do well for my inner self if I relax my mind. Once I heard Dad mutter with self-scorn as he rested during mountain work, smoking his pipe, "An uncut, unpolished gem doesn't sparkle, ha ha!" Did he mean by "gem" this inner self? I can understand that if I do such a cruel and sneaky thing as to mention Ran for my sake, my gem will resemble a cheap, nickel-plated top of a beer bottle.

'Anyway, maybe within myself there's another self, though it's a mystery. If I think it truly exists, I get the sense that this limited, individual, solid me is connected to a grander and brighter world.'

Mokuzu's figure appeared weak beside Hikoroku's. He was regarding the sky, which in the early morning had been clear but was now graying with clouds increasing in weight as if going to deposit themselves.

"Did your sister too get trouble?" Mokuzu did not hear. 'I wonder, no, I'm becoming convinced there's another me in me, like today's sun powerfully and ceaselessly exploding, flaring bright red, almost hidden but showing through that thin cloud.'

"Didn't she get a bad burn?" Hikoroku persisted.

'Eh? Does he know? How come, if no one told him? Oh, when Dad took Ran to the doctor yesterday, some farmers or shopkeepers must have found out and spread it as a topic of chat. Hikoroku likely overheard and is returning it to me. He's the last transmitter but can be the first if I give him new information. An interesting phenomenon, to what can I compare it? Say there's a puddle, which is Ran, Dad, or me. Information rises from it like vapor and is blown away, or rises into the sky, or lingers around the mountains. One way or another it becomes clouds and falls as rain, sleet, or snow to the puddle. Hikoroku's words are like rain coming to the puddle, and my response will determine his newly rising vapor,' Mokuzu thought on the spur of the moment and answered,

"She's fine, it wasn't so bad as we thought. Dr. Okada too said, 'Don't worry,' and in fact she has a good appetite this morning and is mischievous, as usual..."

"Ah, sooo." Hikoroku produced an absent-minded yawn.

'Now I can sort of understand why Dad thought he had to dress up even at such a time.' Mokuzu recalled the sight of his father, of Ran, and of his mother in bed.

The schoolboys proceeded on a path that meandered along the mountain skirts, just wide enough to walk two together. Where it cut through a bulge it was edged on one side by cliff and on the other by a bank that resolved into the rice fields. Flourishing on such a cliff too were camellias, evergreen oaks, and camphors, which spread their leaves over the heads of the passing children. Below, the rice fields extended east, south, and west, and now in the season before rice planting, rows of half-rotted stubble still remained from the autumn harvest. Here and there were green carpet-like patches of white Dutch clover and a Chinese milk vetch planted for cows, and winter-sown wheat now knee high.

Before long the path came into a fairly flat area apart from the repeating curves of the mountain foot. From there seriate mountains large and small appeared in complicated contour, some deeply indented, some shallow, some arrogantly projecting. The path at this point cut directly and safely through the fields instead of following the skirts, whose complexity increased as much as nature wished, their various inlets a suitable habitat for many animals.

Mokuzu noted the conspicuously high riverbank. The Sakura River wound grandly west through fields that spread slightly lower than those further from the river.

'That's the shortcut we took off the Sasayama Highway on our return from the house of the girl named Ena. We passed a row of stores and houses and went out onto the ridges of the rice fields. We crossed to this side on a dangerous earth-heaped narrow bridge, built on horribly tall wooden pilings, and with no handrails.'

His mother had taught him to walk curtly along the center. Sensitive to the least weight, the bridge vibrated, absorbed his step, and magnified it up and down. To jounce it would certainly make it sway with uncontrollable elasticity, causing the piers to squeak and the mud and sand to slip to the current below.

Despite his mother's advice he looked down. The river was mostly clear, enough to see the pebbles in its bed, and seemed not so deep. Near the shore a large volume of whitish green or blue water rapidly flowed, swelling and twisting against the bank and the bottom.

'Is the color like that because the bed is bluish clay, or because it is deep and transparent there?' Looking more carefully, he saw many linear fish, probably dace, where the shallow and deep currents ran side by side. The speed of the fish as they swam upstream matched the speed of the flow, giving them the appearance of staying in one place.

After the bridge they walked on the bank and soon came to a thicket of old eulalia so dense it was hard to penetrate. Once they did, the outer world was perfectly excluded except for the sky. "I'm exhausted, let's rest awhile," his mother said. Carefully she separated the razor-sharp blades and bent the stalks to make a place to sit. The stalks that broke showed a red powder inside like dried blood.

The small world where they rested received no effect from the wind turning chill with the advance of dusk. It was a comfortably warm spot, holding the day's heat intermingled with the smell of dried grass. No human sound entered.

"How nice it would be to fall asleep here and never awake," his mother said, taking out a pack of New Life cigarettes kept secretly and smoked occasionally, a cheap brand.

"Eat the cake you were given," she reminded him. Ena's mother had wrapped it in a white paper for him to take home. He had not eaten it and was prizing it in his pocket, thinking to share it with Ran and Gyodo. 'My patience will be rewarded by seeing their eyes light up.'

"Even if you save it, they'll anger by assuming you ate a lot more," his mother said. "Now you know going out isn't fun. You must walk and walk, can't say what you really think, must endure insults, can't even have lunch. He who's staying home thinks we're having a great time, thinks I'm playing about, even thinks I'm flirting with an intimate! What a foolish and absurd idea! With no word of thanks he dismisses my daily labor. How can a man have such an abject and cruel nature?" Oppressed by her angry monologue, Mokuzu decided not to eat the cake and also not to share it, and with his hand he crushed it in his pocket.

Now he was beside Hikoroku unaware that he was walking, like a little

154

fish swimming alongside a bigger fish. His eyes drifted to the riverbank, to the fields beyond, to the clustered village houses half buried by trees, to the houses scattered higher up in the far distance, where he had walked with his mother.

'The highest house must be Ena's. Today's sky is cloudy, yet only there looks brighter. Is it because I know she lives there, or because the time she showed me the dolls and her room is preserved in my brain and affecting my eyes?'

"Look, a pheasant!"

When Mokuzu turned his head toward the outcry at the rear, already three or four senior boys followed by two or three others were running up into the terraced fields on the mountain skirt opposite the mountainside where Ena's house was.

A pheasant with brilliant bobbing head and sharp long tail was strutting without reserve near a levee at the edge of a rice field. Old chopped rice straw lay strewn to enrich the soil.

Neck, breast, and belly were a lustrous dark green, and so gorgeous was its back that one might think the drab scenery of the days before spring came of this bird's having stolen all the reds, oranges, browns, and ultramarines.

The procession grew disordered and came to a stop now that a number of fifth and six graders were chasing after the pheasant.

Without heeding its pursuers, it kept its dignified pace until such times as one got near enough almost to catch it easily if only he made the final lunge. But no sooner did a hand reach out than the pheasant nimbly dodged, though it moved ahead no more than two or three meters. Thus the illusion of thinking they could succeed combined with their desire or determination, and each time they reached out and it escaped, the illusion increased. As a result they ascended across many terraced fields quite far from their path.

The highest terraces bore no trace of cultivation in recent years and were a confusion of bush clover, eulalia, lacquer tree, winged spindle tree, azalea, and vines of wisteria, kudzu, akebi, and wild grape, which met an overgrowth of fern gradually replaced by red pine. The pheasant led the boys up to the very end of the last cleared terrace, then vanished into the tangle without a backward glance of respect for their efforts.

Some of oldest boys did not come back, and Hikoroku said half to himself and half as if consulting Mokuzu,

"What a nuisance — what should I do?..." It was his duty to lead the elementary school boys of his village to school on time, and he was made uneasy by the prospect of failure.

The boys were unaware that they were being overtaken by a procession of girls. The girls passed like a train in fine condition, and none showed any

155

civility except one in the lead, tall like Hikoroku, who merely said, "Hurry, you'll be late."

Soon they were far ahead, so suddenly diminishing as to make the law of linear perspective seem truly faithful to reality. Their figure after making a crooked ascent was gone with a dip of the path.

The hardest trial for most of the boys was to wait. Their stalled procession began to break up, especially from the rear, and some were beginning to frolic.

Among them a boy called Ippei was making standing broad jumps into the nearest field. In a patch of soft mud one of his white canvas shoes got stuck and became coal black, sending his fellows nearby into peals of laughter.

He was puny, with long fingers, fine hair that clung to his brow, and an upper lip that warped up in the middle. He by no means looked strong, but, laughing, he wiped the shoe on Gyodo's pants at the cuff, accompanied by the laughs of others. Gyodo, sensing an oddity at his ankle, turned his head.

"Hey, what are you doing? Stop!" he said, stepping forward. Ippei stepped forward too and wiped the shoe up and down the back of Gyodo's pant leg. Altogether he looked like a shabby dog urinating on an electric-light pole. His fellows guffawed. Taking it for applause, he triumphantly persisted like an actor on a stage.

Gyodo furrowed his brow with a sad expression and for a moment looked nowhere. Then unexpectedly he turned and kicked Ippei full force in the kneecap. Ippei crouched in pain but managed to look up with blazing eyes — "Pshaw! Beast! You'll pay for your nasty kick that brought me this dirt! You're underestimating me because I'm acting nice!"

Ippei's mates closed in and incited him, "Don't lose to a fourth grader!" "You were jesting! He kicked in earnest!" "Why should he be angry over a little mud? His pants are already suitable for rags, ha ha ha!"

Mokuzu watching the turn of events found three points inexplicable. First, as Ippei crouched in pain and prepared to spring, Gyodo did not escape, nor prepare to fight back, nor defend himself, but stood in dumb surprise. And Ippei when he recovered enough did indeed spring up and punch him in the head. Second, Hikoroku stood as dumbly as Gyodo, yet was one of the oldest and biggest and the group leader. Third, he himself too was watching as if the events were developing in a mirror world without temperature or weight, though the one being insulted was his brother.

"Ha!" said Ippei, spotting in Gyodo no will to fight. "Coward! You'd better believe I'm no easy customer!" and he shoved him above the ear.

Hikoroku at last laid a hand on Ippei's shoulder when the ugly looks were fading from his face. "Okay, that's enough, we'll be late," he said and resumed walking at the front.

156

Gyodo continued to stand without moving.

"Fool! Why don't you move? I've already forgotten you! Troublesome temple cat!"

At this last, again there were peals of laughter. Some repeated it, "Temple cat, temple cat!" as if savoring a relish, and some cried like a hungry stray cat out in the rain.

From each eye Gyodo shed a large tear, which ran to his lip.

Engraved in Mokuzu's mind was the face of Ippei who had beaten Gyodo, the words "temple cat," and Gyodo's tears. He returned to the front as the procession moved on.

'It must be a nickname and must have pricked his pride worse than a hypodermic needle. What does it mean? Not simply "temple" or "cat." He didn't shed tears by the pain of being struck...' The path drew near the mountain skirt. There the five or six who had gone after the pheasant were waiting, having taken a shortcut.

The procession went over a small pass and down to a woodcutter's work area. A lone man was stacking sawlogs in silence. On the open mountain above, many hundreds of pines lay fallen toward a valley. The sight was like fresh traces of a terrible flood or landslide. Everywhere small bushes were pressed beneath them and bent to extremes, twisted, torn, broken, inverted, showing white roots. The pines too were injured all over, the bark grazed, leaving clean skin painfully in view.

The woodcutter ignored the schoolboys. His only tool was a pole with a sharp iron hook like the beak of a kite, yet he was precise and quick at his work.

There the path met several from other villages and became wide enough for a truck. Soon it opened to a well-maintained road on which buses ran. Beyond, a slope led to the gate of the elementary school.

The school was on a little hill leveled on top. The slope, fairly steep and wide, formed a buffer zone with plantings of trees grown big. Doubtless the trees were over a hundred years old, for the arms of two or three pupils could not encircle them. The black pines with rough bark like dragon skin were sublime, the cedars, piercing into the sky, were heroic, and the cypresses, as erect as the cedars, with red bark, were graceful; whereas the evergreen oaks and camphors extended their crowns abroad, making the earth dark and wet and the air gloomy, as if to preserve every damp tradition.

Flanking the approach to the gate were trees planted no more than five or six years ago, perhaps in commemoration of the end of the war: cherries for spring alternating with maples for autumn. Even beyond the splendid granite gateposts they continued, to the left, around the yard, and to the right, around the athletic ground. In addition a variety of trees circled the school.

157

Gyodo and Mokuzu never thought to question who had planted the maples and cherries, or who had lettered the vertical wooden slab on one of the gateposts. Fashioned in printed style but with a gentle touch were the names of the school and the town with jurisdiction over it, done by their father's hand. Doyu had enjoyed the end of the war and given his time, labor, the seedlings, and some skill, regardless of the fact that in those days no one appreciated any contribution having no direct relation to food and clothes. Even in Doyu's family — or because the father did such things — the children went hungry.

A white arc-shaped cardboard purfled with colorful paper chains and cherry blossoms was fixed above the gateposts with the words "Congratulations on Entering Our School," to cheer the newcomers.

But the tight buds of the thin branches of real cherry and maple overhead indicated sharpness and cold, not softness and warmth. Even in a faint breeze they trembled and raised a strange sound that tickled in the ears or under the skin. As soon as they went through the gate, the boys hurried without a look at Mokuzu toward an entrance where the school building met the large auditorium. Gyodo went with them after telling Mokuzu,

"Wait here. Don't worry, soon your classmates will arrive and you'll be with them and can understand what to do. Just do what they do. Anyway a teacher may come out."

Mokuzu wanted to ask about "temple cat," but Gyodo appeared to have no time.

Left to himself, he had nothing in particular to do or to think. Involuntarily he turned toward the athletic ground. A wind was stirring the pines and cedars at his back and sweeping the athletic ground, whirling a fine sand from its surface, and disappearing somewhere after swaying the treetops at the far end

'The far trees are moving, but the sound doesn't reach me. Strange too is that if I keep looking at it, the center of the athletic ground seems slightly raised, or contrariwise, it seems depressed...'

In the yard, from where everyone was being sucked into the building, were swings, a seesaw, a hanging horizontal pole, and a globe of iron pipes, though not a soul was playing on them.

To the right of where he stood was a line of graded horizontal bars, the last so high that even an adult would need to jump to grasp it. Underneath this last was a wide sandbox and above, the cover of a huge camphor tree. Beyond the tree was an arced pipe ladder from which to hang and cross hand over hand; beyond that, a sturdy wooden frame with dozens of upright bamboo poles, which required considerable grasping power and arm muscle to climb.

Mokuzu had never experienced playing on any of these and wished to try them out. Yet he decided against it, reasoning that first, he might need permission; second, behaving like a monkey in this clearing instead of in the mountains was unsuitable, and such play would demand it; and third — and most important — he was insecure about managing them should they require some unknown skill or trick. So he went to the sandbox.

Just then lively voices rose from the gate and immediately girls in pairs advanced into the yard. 'From another village,' he thought, and intuitively he assured himself that Ena would be among them. As they came in, he scanned each face.

Ena was wearing an unobtrusive tawny coat with fur collar and cuffs, but it stood out because the girls before and behind appeared in more showy colors and designs. Among those laughing with wide-open mouths and exaggerated gestures, Ena walked without assuming an easy posture, her face dimly white. The others with their chaos of colors and sounds disturbed the surrounding air, whereas Ena's composed face and figure rather braced and tranquilized the air about her.

'She is in constant motion, yet her outline is clear, not blurred. I wonder why.'

The girl beside her was the first to notice Mokuzu now at the lowest horizontal bar. Her mental activity must have been like a brimful tub about to spill at the least knock, for when she caught sight of him she reflexively drew down a corner of her mouth, shrugged, opened her arms like a puppet, looked at Ena, and whispered something presumably witty in her ear.

Mokuzu, sensing a reproach, directly tried to see himself from her stand-point as he stood blankly at the bar. Attempting to see himself with others' eyes was becoming his habit; he did it almost automatically.

With Mokuzu called to her notice, Ena was like a sprung ball. She ran to him, ignoring her partner and her procession. She beamed with smiles, and her bright, unshaded pupils exactly caught his eyes.

"Mokuzu! How good of you to come! You must be alone, without your mother? I thought so. Never mind, I'll take care of you. I must go to my classroom. As soon as I'm done I'll return. Please wait here, all right?"

She knew she would be called back to her place in line; indeed she turned on the spot and ran faster than necessary to lessen the unnaturalness of her leave, and along with the rest she was sucked into the entrance.

'Those sprightly eyes, brilliant with wonder and delight! Kiku's were so when she was protecting me or Ma's when she was especially tender. I feel I'm shrinking with a sweet sensation in her presence, and now she's turned away I feel I'm filling with power, with more brightness and flexibility than before, as if my courage and perseverance to welcome and endure any difficulty is increased.

'Incidentally, the moment I saw the pupils of her eyes and her cheeks, clear-shaped, yet soft and warm, I remembered the red music box she gave me when I was losing myself in a fever in the hydrangeas. Why so suddenly did I remember it?

'It was a treasure, but I gave it to Ran because she cried and cried and I wondered why she was born to have so much pain and sorrow.

'The problem is, Ena gave me it and must think I'm still keeping it, when in fact I gave it to Ran almost right away.'

Mokuzu ventured into the sandbox. The softly tilled sand pulled him in nearly to his knees. It was moist and cold. When he tried to extract one foot, the sand seemed grudging to free its prey once caught, and made him feel its weight.

The luxuriant camphor obscured the southern sky, but from the sand Mokuzu could see, beyond the athletic ground, the official entrance of the school dazzling in the sun.

Soon from the gate there appeared in succession ten to twenty mothers dressed in their best, three or five in the lead, and all clamorously chatting. Near at hand each had her child, also dressed up, though some romped around the group. They went straight to the official entrance.

Most of the mothers wore over their dressy kimonos a black silk coat purled with traditional motifs — wisteria flowers, turtle and crane, wave and wheel, or pine with bamboo and plum — considered to signal prosperity, and perfect as to the effect of being at once ornate and quiet. They all had on their newest white tabi and best clogs, and must have been to a hairdresser, for their hair was a glossy black.

Every boy wore a black uniform — cap, jacket, and pants — with shirt collar and pocket handkerchief the only touches of white, and buttons glinting gold. Most wore trousers; some, high socks and shorts. Their shoes were so new as to need no extra polish.

The girls dressed as they pleased, but their overcoats, skirts, shoes and socks, and more, mufflers, hats, and gloves were all brand new.

The mothers and children streamed toward the official entrance without seeing Mokuzu; if some happened to see him, they paid him no regard. Once they were assembled at the entrance, a man and a woman came out and spoke something, but Mokuzu was too far to hear. He kept standing in the shady sandbox buried up to his knees. He could not help remembering his mother's wan cheeks, her eyes soon closing after barely opening, the quilt in need of mending and minus a cover, in the gloomy retreat cottage

'She got sick from her running walk, dawn to dark without food...struck on the head and in the stomach by his fist and his pipe...Now she's sick she can't go on as his wife and must become wife of something more obscure, and can't mother us but is becoming a child to be mothered by some far grander being...

'I wonder if Dad has finished the laundry and is carrying Ran to the doctor...

'Anyway, what should I do? Gyodo said to wait here and be like the others. What did he mean? By my clothes alone I'm so different. Thanks to Ma they're repaired, but repaired they are, and she couldn't find the two bottom buttons after all, and the color is so faded...in short, I'm closer to the raw materials of what they are wearing than I am to them, to the hide taken from a cow, the fur taken from a fox or a hare, silk taken from silk worms, to cotton taken from its dried stalks, showing white at dusk — this last, Grandma said.

'I'd rather play free in the fields and mountains, where many raw materials are living and growing, than attend this entrance ceremony and be taught lessons with all these dressy others. Come to think of it, I have no reason to get along with humans who kill my animal and plant companions and process and tailor them into fancy wear. Their enemy is my enemy.

'Look! What are they attempting? Three, four, no, five or six boys have sprung from the group and everyone's looking this way. They must have been told to fetch me.'

Each was racing to be first to arrive, the biggest in the lead, bandy-legged, shoulders angled back and swaying.

Vying for second place, the rest drew together and apart, causing Mokuzu to worry that they would tangle their legs and tumble. The hindmost so lagged as to hardly count. 'He too is running his best, but the others make him appear to be dropping off like a lizard's tail.'

161

The leader, square-faced and big-browed, was the first to the sandbox. Before he could quiet his breath enough to speak, the others arrived, and all took up an aggressive stance.

Their shoulders heaved with the pounding of their hearts, and they opened their mouths as they glared at him, their faces showing the effect of running and a repugnance toward the boy who by their standards was in rags, and who was without his mother. As their breathing quieted, their faces gave off expressions of contempt. 'What's this? Dressed up, for sure, but closing around me like a pack of stray dogs!'

"Why don't you beat it over there if you want to enter school? — you're making us wait," said their leader coercively.

"We're dying for you to join us!" added another with gleaming eyes and a double tooth. The rest guffawed or broadly grinned. The last to arrive had a poor face; all features were somehow small and pointy, though his ears were large. Pinching his nose and screwing up his face, he went through the exaggerated motions of confronting a stench.

Mokuzu with animal instinct was not off his guard. He nonetheless was astonished at their vulgarity so at odds with their fine clothes.

"Just in time, I'm lucky! You're here, hey, Mokuzu!" The voice was husky from a long smoking habit. A tall man with close-cut hair approached without concern for the state of the children. He wore a sack coat, and under his arm he had a greenish cardboard box. His cheeks were sunken as if scooped. From his nose on each side to his mouth were deep lines, said to be proof of a resolute will. A thin wattle extended from under his chin to his Adam's apple, emphasizing his giraffe-like neck.

'Isn't he that priest called Takahashi who comes to our temple with other priests for memorial services? Yes, afterward he loves to play *go* late into the evening. It's said he works in the Municipal Office...' Mokuzu scanned his memory.

"Be quick, take off your jacket, trousers too of course. Look at these, brand new!" The man pulled Mokuzu from the sand, stripped off his clothes, and dressed him in a new black uniform, which he took from the box.

"There now, it fits you fine, excellent! Lucky I was in time. Only yesterday our office granted it, but if I do say so, the decision was mine. I'm vexed by the slowness of the others in Welfare.

"Well, well, fine, fine. Now I must be off. I'll return your old clothes to your home. Be of good cheer, do your best, and keep up with the others.

"Hey, kids! If you haze him you'll be sorry. He's not the child of peasants or merchants like you, but the child of a priest despite his appearance."

He spoke fast; seemingly he was in a hurry. He hastened to the gate and

162

descended by the bicycle he had leaned against the gatepost.

The six boys maintained their stance. The broken sound of a brake squealed long. Mokuzu looked toward the official entrance. The mothers and children, whose numbers had increased, were staring in his direction

'This new clothing does please me, especially since Gyodo, Ma, and Dad will be happy for me, but it makes my shoes, worn at the heels and toes, stand out. He's a kind priest to provide it, but isn't he cruel to undress me before many eyes and make me expose my underwear browned by so many washings? It's most difficult to deal with good conduct mixed with bad, isn't it?'

"Hey, everything's fine now, never mind whatever else and come with us." The leader was speaking, as if he could sense the delicate shades of Mokuzu's psychology. In the mind of this biggest boy a bud of respect for Mokuzu along with a wish to shelter him was beginning to emerge. He, whom they called Naota, walked toward the mothers as he checked to make sure Mokuzu was following.

At that moment many large and small groups of children were forming and jumping out with shrieks of cheer from the gathering, kicking their mothers in their ceremonial kimonos and putting them in confusion as if they were obstacles. Boys and girls made separate groups of three or four, five or six, and ran to the group returning with Mokuzu.

Naota's group, wondering what was going on, was soon reached by the quickest boy, who told Naota,

"They're saying the ceremony is put off half an hour because the village head or someone isn't here yet. We can play free till we're called," and to his fellows he said,

"C'mon, we'll play over there!" He and his group took off for the yard with its swings and hanging pole. Other groups with the same mind raced to be first. Naota too ran to occupy some apparatus for his group.

In a minute the yard, from where the pupils' entrance could be observed, was filled with black-uniformed boys and colorfully dressed-up girls. So many and so lively were they that their movements and expressions were hard to discern. The yard became the origin of a terrible noise.

In addition to these newcomers, the senior pupils, who had once entered their classrooms and were cleaning and preparing the auditorium for the ceremony, were released from their tasks, and they began to rush forth, causing the yard to become so packed that each child had a hard time to maneuver.

Mokuzu was awaiting the appearance of Gyodo or Ena, fixing his eyes on the entrance through the throng coming and going in every direction. He stood between the swings and the hanging pole, all moving full tilt.

The pole was long and thick and could carry ten or more children at once. Some rough boys had taken positions by the chains at either end and rode it so wildly that the others had to hold on for dear life as they shrieked with joy and terror. The chains too at each swing of the pole raised a sharp, intense, burdened, frictional sound.

The swings, four altogether, also had iron chains and were withstanding rough use. The sound issuing from their joints was nothing less than pure screams and groans. They were made to move in a fan shape, but because the riders were not those who cared to be gentle, they swung in half circles. Naturally when each came full height, its tension was at its extreme. Then the chains immediately slackened. When the seat reached its nadir the slack was abruptly resolved, and moments after came another extreme of tension. The sound of these tensions and slackenings was really unbearable, being agonized shrieks, though produced by inorganic material.

'Oh! Ena!' Mokuzu surely thought he saw her outline, head somewhat lowered, dignified in the crowd of girls rushing from the entrance. It was just when he was wishing to be free of the jam to spend a quiet time by the pond below the mountain at home, and for a second he hallucinated that the image of Ena whom he saw was that of Ena looking into the water.

He directed his steps toward the entrance from between the pole and the swings, allowing enough distance from the nearest swing, swinging violently.

Then what? He sensed the world exploding in red and yellow. To take an objective view, Mokuzu was knocked flat against the earth and was emitting blood from his mouth.

Someone had shoved his shoulder either by accident or on purpose, which sent him toppling two or three steps, whereupon he was given a mighty blow under the nose by the seat of the swing.

He was intermittently aware of the very black earth, and oddly he could see each grain of sand and soil, and more, he thought he could vividly see the spaces between.

Next moment, as he was being lifted in someone's arms, he sensed that everything — earth, buildings, the surrounding children — was widely rising and falling and floating. Soon he was visited by alternating feelings of unsurpassed comfort and warmth, of being kindly taken care of, and of nausea and a pain at the back of his head.

When he came to his normal senses he heard the voice of a school nurse. He lay under a white sheet on a high bed.

"Ena, you're admirable, staying composed even at the sight of so much blood, never hesitating to carry this boy on your back here all by yourself... The janitor's wife is washing and ironing your clothes. Aren't you cold?"

16

A Question of Meat and Matrimony

The children had left, and the school buildings and grounds were still as death except for the sound of the wind.

So cold was the wind that the appearance of snowflakes would not have seemed odd, though already it was early April. On the slope outside the gate, under the maple and cherry branches with their undeveloped buds being tossed to extremes, Gyodo opened out his brown wrapping cloth, covered Mokuzu's head and cheeks with it, and tied it under his chin. Ena took off her coat and put it around his shoulders. Her warmth still within it affected him even to his bones.

By then the bleeding from his nose and upper gum had stopped. But the area felt like a makeshift outstation of his heart, with each pulse there enlarged. And each came with a sharp pain, and worse, the area was puffed and felt huge, heavy, and dull, except for the nerve of pain. Finding talk burdensome, Mokuzu scarcely enunciated in response to Gyodo's questions.

"'ow 'ould I know who did it?"

"But didn't you say you didn't stumble on anything and kept enough space between yourself and the swings?"

"...'ere was a power or weight from 'hind..."

"What? On top of your pronunciation, your meaning is unclear. Are you okay?"

"I felt no one pushing, only a great weight, speed, or force..."

"Huh?"

"No one's to blame. The vital element was the force, not who or what caused it." Mokuzu was weary of Gyodo's interrogation.

"Tut! What silly talk! How can you take revenge? At any cost we must find the evildoer and teach him a lesson. I hate the teachers too for not doing their duty to identify him, though I'm thankful for their first aid. Did you hear what they told you instead of getting to the bottom of the case? 'You're a lucky boy, it isn't so bad as it looks,' 'Be careful from now on, the swings can be a weapon.' They talk as if the fault were yours and demand that you be thankful for the relative lightness of the wound. But think a bit, Mokuzu, today was your first day of school. On such an important day, which ought to be joyous, how can you tolerate so unpleasant an incident? Don't you feel sorry for yourself?"

Gyodo realized that his sorrow was greater than Mokuzu's, and he was all the more angry at whoever was the cause. His white cloudy breath seemed to come not only from the cold air, but also from a deep rage.

"Too bad, everyone was photographed together to commemorate the day..." Ena spoke and looked closely at Mokuzu's face; he was walking with head bowed. He smiled, but she took it for contortion of his lip, swollen and livid by internal bleeding.

"I'm like a squirrel or a hare..."

"What are you talking about?" Gyodo asked. He and Ena looked dubious.

"About everything...school, the teachers, the pupils...the question of who pushed me, and everyone being photographed..."

"What's the connection with a hare?" Gyodo was impatient at this seeming nonsense, though his impatience originated from his discomfort and humiliation over failing to protect his brother, which was most possibly also the cause of his inordinate fury at the teachers.

"I mean, for me those were events of another planet, as they are for a hare or a squirrel."

Ena pitied Mokuzu, who already understood that school was not a suitable place for him. One of the purposes of attending school was to become acquainted with others, and he was expressing such a passive attitude in preferring to withdraw to his quiet mountain life. 'His brother is better for having a positive will, yet he keenly and disdainfully speaks of revenge, right?'

Gyodo held his hand before Mokuzu's eyes and bent his fingers one by one. "Can you see this?" He worried that his vision and brain might be damaged.

"Of course I can, perfectly well."

"What is five plus eight?"

"Thirteen."

"Eighteen divided by three?"

"Six."

"In what year did King Sung of Paekche present Emperor Senka with scriptures and an image of Sakyamuni Buddha, regarded as the first transmission of Buddhism to Japan?"

"In the year 538 of the Western calendar, 1198 of our calendar."

"Okay, '*Shaunian yilau shyue nancheng / yitsun guangyin bukeching.*' Recite the second half."

"'*Weijyue chytang chuntsaumeng / jiechian wuye yi chiousheng.*'"[1]

To Ena these questions and answers were strange, but she respected the brothers for studying subjects she had no idea of.

Mokuzu came to a stop and tried to take off her coat to return it. It was where the silent woodman was piling logs. Many wheel tracks remained on the soft edges of the road.

"Never mind, keep it on." Ena pressed the coat against his shoulder.

"Why, aren't you going that way to your house?" asked Gyodo, indicating where the path divided.

"Yes, but I want to send him home. It's still early."

Hearing this, Mokuzu was reminded of a bonfire. 'How pleasant in winter to absorb its warmth, though when I step back I must brace against the cold — the warmth doesn't come with me and only my longing and the memory of burning leaves remains in my heart. So it will be to separate from her.

'But if she comes, I'll be proceeding with the warmth. In her company the path isn't as drab and taciturn and meaningless as it seemed to me early this morning. Each stone and weed, each clump of stubble in the fields, and each mountain tree is brimming with vigor and meaning for being there, erect with quiet joy instead of sunk in gloomy stillness...'

"But your mother will worry," said Gyodo.

"I can phone her."

"There isn't a telephone...the nearest is at Yosetsu's...and..."

"Then I can use that one. Anyway, I have nothing to do at home and I'm not afraid — it's within the school zone and I'm now in second grade. My mother worries only if I always stay home and have no one to play with..."

As they walked on, Gyodo fell into thought. 'What about lunch? Mokuzu and I can manage on leftovers if there are any, but we can't offer her such trash, and how distasteful to go to Yosetsu's to ask to use his telephone! He grins at me as if I have something on my face I should be ashamed of if only I would notice it and as if he's waiting for me to notice it. Like that he regards my face, hands, feet, everything, as if licking me.

'This morning Ippei called me "temple cat" to my face. Who thought it up? No child. It was Yosetsu. I'm quite positive that particular adult, who should be an example to children, thought it up and spread it about. Thus his inventive toxin is disseminated to the world of children, and he's enjoying the fact that their world is under his control just as he wished...!'

Mokuzu was reassured by hearing Ena say that going to his house was not a problem. She was taking it matter-of-factly and walking brightly and heartily at his side. He was also thankful, though about what he was not just sure. 'It wouldn't be a bit strange if she didn't come, if she had nothing to do with me from the first, if she ignored me and my wound, or was a spectator like all the rest. It also wouldn't be crazily strange if she hated, avoided, and reproached me.

'She's like a mountain spring, her life free to flow as it likes. Yet somehow she's flowing my way as if it's natural. Isn't that marvelous?

'Could it be we have something pulling us together in harmony, despite our having separate bodies and circumstances? And does it seem marvelous simply because I'm so young and innocent? When I get older and learn more

167

about its cause, will I take it to be an obvious phenomenon, as I now see water mixed with sugar as sweet without surprise? Or will my wonder increase because I will be further on from the beginning of the mystery?'

Mokuzu noticed that the swelling was rapidly subsiding and the pain localizing to the point of impact. 'Because of my wound she's worrying over me and protecting me as if wrapping me in pure cotton. Then what if it quickly heals? It's like a typhoon — everyone drives stakes into the cliffs and river-banks, piles straw bags of soil, and boards up the houses with unusual diligence, cooperation, and delight, while the women serve tea and crackers. Then the typhoon doesn't come that way, and sure enough, the villagers are soon expressing their avarice and laziness, speaking ill, growing abusive, fighting...

'Must I conclude that to love one another, people should get sick or hurt more often, the longer and heavier the better, and that for the same reason they should welcome typhoons, earthquakes, and wars? No, Ma is sick, but who cares? Does it reconcile the villagers or raise their affection and sympathy? They enjoy others' misfortune, their expressions as ambiguous as trees and grasses swaying unidentifiable in the dusk.

'Even Grandma, all she said when she heard was, "An ailing wife is a shipwreck. She needn't be beautiful or intelligent, only she must needs be sturdy."

'And who cares about Ran? Her mental and physical pain will leave a keloid she must endure without knowing why. But no one is any kinder to her. Didn't I hear Dad cursing, "What a burden, adding to my labor and misery!"

'My wound is minor, yet Ena is protecting me. How could I think it better that an affliction last longer and be heavier or a war be welcome? How cruel and detached from the truth for those who have no protector, no sympathizer, no savior!'

Muffled in Gyodo's cloth and Ena's ample coat, Mokuzu felt his face redden. He looked down and walked only out of habit, causing Ena and Gyodo to continue to worry over him.

'On top of that,' he went on examining himself, though the realization was shameful, 'I secretly hoped my injury would worsen — to detain Ena's kindness. What a shameless mentality! Kiku warned me against that when she left: "A boy should live like a boy, not like a rotten girl." She meant I should protect rather than be protected, give pleasure rather than be given...

'What's fun about accompanying home someone dispirited by a wound? Compare how merry she'd be if instead I ran about the mountains, fields, and river with her, looking for rock crystals or for stones with natural designs of chrysanthemum or cherry flowers, or for fossil shells; or skipping flat pebbles across the river, or spearing fish.

168

'People aren't bats or moles. Surely their pleasure must be to play in the mountains and rivers under the sun — far more fun and healthful than nursing someone sick or wounded.'

Reaching this point in his thoughts, Mokuzu exclaimed,

"I don't need these anymore, I'm fine!" and he took off the coat and the cloth.

Gyodo and Ena stopped in alarm and regarded him closely. They laughed when they realized that his behavior was not a horrible aftereffect but proof of his recovery.

"I'll just go pick those yellow flowers." Mokuzu started for an inlet, taking an uphill footway beside a rice field.

"Wait, it's not as mild as it looks, those trees hide a cliff and it's wet at the base!" said Gyodo.

"I want to take them to Ma. When we were walking she pointed them out and said they're called witch hazel, prized for flower arrangement." Gyodo, deciding to help, went ahead of Mokuzu on the narrow path. Ena followed behind.

"She said it would be nice to sit arranging them and having a quiet tea on a veranda with clouds floating by and a view of a flower garden against a hedge and far mountains. She expected such a life, she said, marrying into a temple, but because Tangenji lost its property and Dad can't earn and what with her peddling and having no time to waste unless she's sick, it became unthinkable..."

They stopped near the cliff and looked up at a projecting branch with its linear, five-petaled flowers opening in order.

Below the cliff was indeed a wet valley of sawtooth oak, silver magnolia, wild chestnut, and lacquer tree, and from their yet unbudded branches pendulous vines of wisteria and akebi invaded a thicket of knotweed, kerria, and wild rose.

'Without this wound I could get there by climbing an oak, grabbing a wisteria, and swinging over like Tarzan. But how awful if it's grazed by a single twig, to say nothing of whipped by that springy tangle...'

"Look, a pretty bird! It slanted like an arrow from this branch to that. It's still there!" Ena's cheek touched Mokuzu's as she tried to direct his eyes by pointing.

"Yes, I see it now. A Siberian bluechat — it must be the female."

"Mokuzu, how can you tell it's a female?"

"See the dull green back, orange under the wings, and white belly? Only the tail is a distinctive indigo. The male is overall a more powerful indigo — shh! there he is. They forage as a couple. Look — at that treetop. Oh! he flew down! Keep watching, she'll follow..."

The female flew down and disappeared into the bushes. The male again flew to a high perch, and the female reappeared. They flew up and down repeatedly, with short intervals between.

Mokuzu and Ena liked flowers and birds. Gyodo too had no reason to dislike them, but he was soon bored by looking at the same thing. What interested him was human adults and children, whom he could judge good or bad, admirable or despicable.

He left Mokuzu and Ena, who had meanwhile forgotten about the flowers as they focused on the movement of the birds, and he thrashed his way into the dense, wet valley. Forcefully he grasped the trunks and branches of the miscellaneous trees to raise himself to his target. He tore off the flowering branch, thick enough to be called a bough, and dragged it back to Mokuzu.

"Here — I got it! Now let's go."

"What's the use of all this? Two or three small branches will do. Ma said even one is effective if arranged right."

"Then break off what you want. If we're late they'll worry. That's more important. It's well past lunch hour." Gyodo started down. Mokuzu and Ena took three flowering branchlets, tossed the remainder into the thicket to conceal it, and followed.

They walked in silence along the curve of the mountain skirt. Before long the path reached the bend that revealed the grand wall of Tangenji.

"See, Mokuzu? As far as looks go, our temple is imposing. Whoever doesn't know its inside story must think it is still the richest temple in all of Tanba."

"...."

"It's like a castle..." said Ena, but Gyodo was continuing,

"Inside it's actually a ruined temple with the ghosts of its halcyon days just managing to hang on. The roofs leak, Buddhist services are rarely performed, everywhere there are cobwebs...but those aren't serious, being merely formal or surface concerns. The problem is, Tangenji has neither the power nor the will to guide people, so naturally the laymen don't respect, trust, or of course love our temple."

"...."

"Its occupants think they're a temple and a priest worthy of respect, like old times, and the laymen too haven't changed their belief that they should receive mercy and wisdom from there. But it's not like old times anymore. Now each only makes demands on the other. There's no content; temple and laymen act like old times merely on the surface. So every related Buddhist service is a meaningless relic. Form without substance is an ideal place for all sorts of complaints and quarrels to germinate."

"Why did it get like that?"

"The direct reason, Mokuzu, is the war. It isn't any one person's fault, but a matter of society and the world. Before the war, Japanese Buddhism was leading the country in every aspect, and under its leadership Japan became strong and prosperous. The commoners' lives were greatly improved over old times, so they respected Buddhist priests and gladly supported them.

"But while the commoners were following the Buddhist leading class, Japan rushed into the war and was ignominiously defeated. So the commoners lost their trust and realized they had been taken in and exploited with fancy words like 'mercy,' 'wisdom,' and 'enlightenment,' and that they had been stupid servants.

"Then came the American Occupation to steal away the economic base of the Buddhist leaders in the name of breaking up the giant financial combines and releasing the farmland. That way the Buddhist leaders lost not only their spiritual trust but also their wealth, and they began to be openly criticized and abused by the commoners."

Gyodo's explanation had at times a spiteful tone, but mostly he was repeating what he had learned from books. Mokuzu and Ena kept silent. Now and then they unexpectedly looked up at his mouth and eyes and cocked their heads. Gyodo presumed they were listening thoughtfully, despite their pulling at old grass stalks and kicking pebbles. Even chickens could appear thoughtful.

"You don't mean, I suppose, it was wrong to be defeated in the war?"

"Wrong? For whom? Mokuzu, whenever you ask a question, you should make yourself clear."

"You said the Buddhist leaders lost their power to lead and the temples became ruined. Is it because Japan was defeated in the war, or...?"

"Well, if Japan had won, certainly those Buddhist leaders would be respected even now."

"But they were priests who taught the common people Buddhism, weren't they? If so, Buddhism is the teaching of Sakyamuni Buddha, and I understand his most important teaching is, Don't fight but be friendly. Then it's natural for the priests who practiced his teaching to fail because of the war. Winning would be more strange. Failing is their proof of being good Buddhists. Your conclusion is the opposite..."

"Your reasoning is more complicated than I expected. Maybe you're right. But the fact is different. I'll have to consider it — it's not so simple... actually it's confusing...

"Let's say there were priests practicing Buddha's teaching, who didn't fight. They were driven away by false priests a long time ago. And those false priests got positions of leadership and led the people to strengthen and enrich Japan. As a result of their work, the country prospered, their temples also prospered, and Japan began to invade other countries. And that led to defeat in the war and to the present ruin of the temples.

"So you must know real priests were defeated long ago, well before the recent war. In other words, Tangenji became rich because it had a false priest, and its riches turned to ruin when Japan was beaten down."

"Our Grandfather Kakkan was said to be a great priest. Now you say he was a false priest. If his rich temple became a ruined temple, doesn't that make Dad a real priest and not a false priest?"

"You may wish it were so, but it isn't. False upon false isn't real. Dad's a more false priest than our grandfather."

"What?"

"Well, think now, he was a false priest, yet he helped some people, taught the commoners many things, raised his family well, and studied a lot. Dad does none of that; he drinks, beats Ma, waits for people to die, is horribly lazy, fights with the laymen, and doesn't even raise his children!"

Mokuzu could not think his father was so bad. 'Drinking may be wrong, and beating Ma to shorten their quarrels is probably wrong. But is he lazy? He is so because he has nothing to do. Actually he cooks, cleans, has always done most of the care of Ran, even carries her when working in the mountain or doing calligraphy. Maybe he has no money like other fathers, but he wishes to earn...'

Mokuzu adored the touch of his father's cheeks with their rough, gray-white, copious stubble that grew out apace if he did not shave for a day or two. The sound of his breathing was also pleasant, like dry reeds blowing in his bronchi whenever he cut Mokuzu's hair, his chest against Mokuzu's head.

"He's bad and cruel. You don't know, but I saw it many times!" Gyodo tightened his mouth and from his eyes shot a glitter of hate as if that moment he were witnessing some terrible thing.

"I'll tell you my first memory of his evil to Ma. It was in the rainy season, about half a year after you were born. Everyone was cleaning the moss garden; you were crawling on the fresh green moss. I was between three and four years old. I was amusing you by twirling a gardenia. Grandma, Ma, and Kiku were weeding the moss and picking off the rain-beaten azalea flowers dropped and stuck ugly on the bushes, rocks, and moss. Dad was pruning that oldest, best-shaped sasanqua rising like a dragon by the basin at the corner of the veranda.

"Grandma and Ma were arguing, I was too young to know about what. Ma later told me she had said she would leave to sell clothes because cleaning the garden brought no cash. Grandma said cleaning should come first, that a clean temple was more important than food or money. They perfectly disagreed.

172

"Suddenly, as if lightning cracked or the mountain slid, Dad climbed down the tree and kicked Ma. She was sitting on her heels and the blow smacked her against a rock. It didn't satisfy him. He took a bamboo broom and wildly beat her with the handle.

"I remember nothing before that — probably all earlier memories were blasted by the shock into the dark of the universe. I remember nothing afterward either, only a blank, however hard I try to remember. That incident, vivid as fireworks, remains as my first and most abominable memory."

Mokuzu knit his brow on hearing of his mother's misery and his father's cruel act, both impossible to deal with because they had already happened. He knew from experience that what Gyodo said was probably neither a lie nor an exaggeration. 'Even so, we've been living together day after day, and most days have been quite peaceful. There's an occasional unhappy occurrence, but why should we focus a light on it, strain our nerves, and commit it to memory like a kind of treasure? Even if it really happened, why not consign it to oblivion? Shouldn't we keep our mind for our normal daily life, where mostly we live...?'

By giving more value to daily life with its shorter distance between good and bad, Mokuzu was instinctively protecting his mind and body from erosion by unwelcome feelings.

'Too bad Gyodo has to live with so terrible a first memory and repeatedly remind himself of it in his present life. Can't he replace it with a memory more gentle and comforting?

'My first memory is also about Dad. Maybe I was around two. Everything before is like drops of ink put in an ocean...

'I must have had persistent diarrhea and fever and he was carrying me to the doctor. A big truck full-loaded with nuts and bolts came along the highway so slowly Dad could walk beside it. They sparkled brilliant in the sun and we couldn't see when we looked away. Was the oily smell from a leak or from those new nuts and bolts? I was content on his back sensing the light and oil. No birds or flowers were in sight, it was far from a heavenly scene; yet I felt the sweetest, securest, most longed-for, mind-melting sensation, which I bet can hardly be had in any heaven.

'A nut and bolt fell off. I must have begged for it. Dad must have been reluctant to pick it up, that being a kind of stealing. But he did. As he passed it back to me, I could see his face so bright and him so enjoying his misdemeanor — it must have been one of his rarest expressions of joy...to steal something...in all his life.

'How unlike Gyodo's first memory! He's the same father, but as different as ice from water in his functions and expressions!'

173

"I'll take revenge on him!" Gyodo spoke in a repressed tone. They were below Tangenji. As he spoke he gestured toward the high wall with his jaw. His cheeks were pale and the whites of his eyes looked unnaturally large, with a set bluish hue.

They came to the steps under the two-storied gate, but instead of going up they continued on the narrow path to Yosetsu's house. Ena had all the while been walking erect with her coat over her arm, by turns regarding Gyodo and Mokuzu.

What Gyodo was saying and thinking — about his father's cruelty and his mother's sorrow — was not beyond her, but since she had never directly observed such violence, his words were too abstract for her. She tried to extend her understanding by reminding herself of her own sad mother and heartless father. Unable to express what she felt, she kept silent. 'My father's violence isn't visible, he never kicks or strikes; yet he isn't better than this other father — he's all the more cruel and inhuman. I once overheard Mother say when she thought she was alone, "Mental killing spills mental blood."

'Why, oh, why must parents hate and torture each other? Can't they be friends like those Siberian bluechats?'

"Hey, do you remember when that Zen master named Tengai came a couple of years ago?"

"I remember, he left after shouting that we must completely combust our life."

"Well, Mokuzu, a few days later the worst thing in all my life happened. You and Ran were asleep, but Kiku and I saw.

"He had come to ask Dad to be dean of his new college and Dad refused. A few days later Yosetsu came as his messenger to ask Dad to be an art professor if not the dean. In secret Yosetsu gave Ma an envelope of money, saying it was from Zen Master Tengai. Straight off she used it to pay a debt to the doctor and to buy food.

"That night she told Dad about the money. He was drinking as usual. When he heard, the veins stood out on his head, and without a word he rose up and kicked her.

"'How could you spend such a man's money, worse, receive it from the hand of Yosetsu? That Zen master is dirt and his messenger its maggot! Unbosoming yourself with joy, deserting your principles like a tart, and worst of all, willing to sell them your husband!" He roared, struck, smashed, kicked — the room next to the main hall was flaming with his rage and vibrating with her shrieks. With each blow to her loins, her head flew back, and with each blow to her head, her loins heaved.

"She tried to say she had no such intention and never encouraged him to work for that college, never thought the Zen master was good, or Yosetsu either. She saw the money before her eyes and spent it to renew the medicine and get food. He wouldn't hear. She begged him, said she'd be killed if he kept it up. He didn't stop, not even with Kiku clinging to his arms — she was as insignificant as a torn-off wing of a dragonfly.

"When she got the chance, Ma crawled into the main hall. She later told me she had thought because he's a priest raised to venerate Buddha and practice compassion and confess his sins, he would fear to pursue and beat her there. She believed our temple's Eleven-Faced Kannon would help her because Kannon's work is to help all sentient beings. But no miracle occured. He kept beating her until she fainted before the altar.

"Never had there been such a scene, and I could do nothing to help, I was too little, it was dreadful, the sight of hell!

"I swore I'd punish him, pay off Ma's sorrowful scores in place of that sooty wooden Kannon, who didn't utter a word or lift a hand, being nothing but a hoax!

"You heard that kid call me 'temple cat' — he means our ruined Tangenji, where our false-priest father is living with the ghosts of the past. We are cats making our bed here and wandering out in search of food. 'Temple cat' means everything detestable, atrocious, and negative.

"If only I can grow up even a day sooner! Then I'll go away to train my body and mind till I can take revenge on every evildoer. Mokuzu, you too become strong and quickly grow up!"

"Why did Tangenji, which was and still is a temple, come to worse trouble than common families, and why did its priest your father become more fearful than common fathers? I can understand about the war and the land reform and the poor economy, but weren't all temples hurt?" Ena asked with a serious look. It was what Mokuzu wanted to ask.

"Meat and matrimony," Gyodo said tersely and continued as if thinking aloud, "Were it only a question of eating meat, he'd be less to blame. But, a priest marrying? That's the gravest problem, the primary cause. I'm unsure of many of the finer points, but somehow all human evils, especially those of priests, come of killing and eating creatures and living a married life."

"Are those things wrong?" Although her thought was yet faint as a rainbow, Ena began to realize she did have words.

Mokuzu on the contrary realized his thinking faculties were stopped dead like an anchor dropped to the bottom of the sea.

"Well, listen you both, I must meditate further on it, and you'd better know that no school teachers can tell you. Even books by great priests of old scarcely teach it. I'm beginning to think it can't be taught; each person must solve it on his own. For now, at least know it's a problem that has to be solved

175

sooner or later. Look, we're at Yosetsu's. Let's be quick to use his telephone and go home."

The house stood where the narrow path they were on met the Sasayama Highway. It was girded by dark Chinese junipers trimmed in rounded shapes from top to bottom. The garden within had a few shapely black pines, podocarps, and *mokkoku*.

The door was open. Gyodo called into the dark interior. The house looked vacant. Not only the clock but also the mud-finished walls, the pillars, and all the furnishings seemed to count the time in fine measure as they narrowed the space one billionth of a millimeter by one billionth of a millimeter. From a back room came the sound of a drawer being closed. Yosetsu's wife soon appeared. Perhaps she was storing winter clothes.

"Welcome, Master — you are of Tangenji, I believe? You must be surprised to return from school and find your mother gone. How terrible!... but now it's all right, soon she'll recover."

Chiyo always spoke politely, but her words made no sense, even to Gyodo.

"We came to borrow the use of your telephone."

"I see, please, as much as you wish. You must be calling the hospital. Please tell your mother not to worry, that you can manage by yourselves. Your father, my husband, and Dr. Okada must be there now."

"Eh? Was our mother hospitalized?"

"Oh, yes, didn't you know? It was perfectly awful. Dr. Okada came this morning and directly pronounced it grave. The ambulance could come only this far. Everyone helped my husband carry her from Tangenji on a storm door. It's simply terrible that at such a time the path to Tangenji is so narrow.

"Fortunately my husband is well acquainted with the heads of the hospital and Public Health. He expedited all the arrangements for her hospitalization and welfare. Of course he takes these pains as the head layman...

"Dr. Okada was put in a flurry and repeatedly chided our priest for not informing him sooner, saying it could be too late. And he wasn't doing what he should as a doctor but leaving it all up to his Mitsu. Really, he can't seem to function without her."

"This is his child!" said Gyodo, trying to point out Ena, who stood behind him. "Is it? By which, Mitsu or Fumi?"

"We came only to use your telephone," cut in Mokuzu, wanting to leave straightaway and go to his mother's bed to be sure with his own eyes that she was gone.

"Where's Ran?" Gyodo worried aloud.

"I don't need the phone — let's go back," Ena said. She turned on her heel and took off at a brisk walk.

176

"Right, we'll go at once! We won't use your telephone. Thank you anyway," said Gyodo. Mokuzu too thanked her simply, and they turned about and went after Ena. They all broke into a run.

They reached Tangenji in less than ten minutes. Racing up the stone steps out of breath, Mokuzu wondered,

'If Ma's gone, Tangenji will be more of a haunt for the ghosts Gyodo talks of. Or the opposite, I mean, can we children ward them off and make a brighter family? Grandma doesn't count; she exists far closer to Buddha and is no longer much like a human being...'

17

On The Rock

Miss Sakaki raised her arm to list the homework, exposing a glimpse of armpit up the short sleeve of her white blouse, and at the same time raised her voice in the high pitch peculiar to the women teachers,

"All right, everyone, there are three assignments. First, the multiplication drill on page 29 of your arithmetic text — do the whole page. Second, review the kanjis on page 17 and 18 of your Japanese text. Third, write a composition titled 'My Thanks to Mother.' You must write at least one full manuscript sheet."

Nothing was more vexing than not having her pupils' attention turned upon her from every direction. But if the lines of vision and points of focus of their eyes could have left a trace, as much chaos would have been apparent as in the sight of tossed flax. While some insistently looked point-blank at their desks, others with aisle seats, appearing to look nowhere, were attending to the run of events in the next room, and still others sitting along the windows facing the yard were gazing at the idle pole and swings as if determined to activate them by willpower. Dealing with these children was difficult because they were misbehaving when others were properly attentive. To an outside observer, the room would have presented a rather comical scene, having reached the state where the teacher was provoked to single out one aberrant on whom to heap her impulsive admonition.

Miss Sakaki wore a blue jumper dating from her student days, faded, but ironed and clean as ever. As she persisted in explaining the homework, she swatted herself to brush off the chalk and succeeded instead in spreading it about the pearly oval clasp of the belt that spruced up and accentuated her narrow waist.

"Recently too many of you have been forgetting to do your homework. Do you know what I will do to such pupils?"

"I don't care. How I wish this class would end!"

Catching the instant the room quieted in anticipation of hearing what the punishment would be, the voice was heard at every corner with lightning sharpness. More, its timbre had better carrying power than the teacher's.

"Who said 'I don't care'? Stand up!"

Miss Sakaki's voice was keen. Many were beginning to laugh, but they abruptly quieted and everyone turned to stare at Mokuzu, who had stood up at a middle seat by the window. His face looked neither proud nor ashamed but expressionless as he resigned himself to standing.

As soon as she saw him Miss Sakaki thought, 'Oops! I didn't expect that one.'

She knew quite a bit about him, his family, his disposition, for she had been his first-grade teacher, and she pitied and even respected him. His family was poor, his mother hospitalized and not yet come home, his father mostly out, hired by the day. Their life was maintained somehow by his brother now in fifth grade and by him, in second; and there was a five-year-old girl. His grandmother seemed to have nothing to do with them.

Despite their indigence, the father was priest of a temple, which possibly explained why the boys were preeminent in the amount of reading they did, and were often reading Chinese classics and Buddhist sutras unknown even to their teachers. Their conduct was in no way bad, and they never of themselves troubled others.

Miss Sakaki noted no sign of his being jaundiced, or stunted, nor in her observation was he hated and shunned. All the same, she felt that he carried a lonely air. He smiled faintly when everyone else was in a rollicking mood and emitting cheers, and he never lost his composure when they were anxious and crying in distress. But she knew no more about him than she knew about the others. She had no time for and no interest in a child whose nature was uncommon. She was a young, ordinary woman teacher, and a distinctive feature of ordinary women teachers was not to care a whit about anything but the surface speech and behavior of their pupils and just to make them advance a grade by hook or by crook according to the course of study dictated by the Ministry of Education.

Miss Sakaki regretted having induced Mokuzu to stand, but it was too late. She took the occasion to warn him about his lack of enthusiasm in the classroom and his unwillingness to cooperate with the others.

"Tell me why you said you don't care — " She pressed for an answer.

Mokuzu turned his eyes toward the window, weary of what he knew was to come.

"What is your attitude? Why can't you clearly say? Tell me why you don't properly care about your homework! You do grudgingly what the school expects you to do, and I never see you do anything with all your heart. Come now, tell me why!"

"I thought it's of little concern because it's not decided by me and...it's a matter of no importance."

Some boys laughed and some girls darted glances at Mokuzu and at their teacher, smirks playing on their lips.

"Your school and your teachers make various rules and assign homework for the sake of your future. Its importance is their responsibility to decide. You are still a child and pupil with no ability to judge. What's important is that you willingly do what it has been decided that you do. Your uncaring attitude comes from your lack of effort or endurance to improve and is quite harmful because it's contagious. Should you continue in your way, you will lose interest in your school life and may well end up a lazy, inhuman adult. Do you understand how badly and evidently mistaken your attitude was?"

The janitor rang the bell to close the hour. The next-door pupils were obviously released from their instruction — they were flooding into the corridor with a great noise.

For Miss Sakaki's class it was a day of morning lessons only. Whoever had brought lunch could leave after eating, the rest directly — the choice was free.

Mokuzu had not forgotten his morning promise to Ena to eat together on the hill behind the school. It was becoming their custom.

'The one enjoyment in school is to spend time with her, and the one important matter is not to shorten that time. Or school would be the dreariest, drabbest place and the silliest thing I could do would be to put myself here. School hems me in with matters of no importance and annoys me with painful troubles.

'Suppose I stayed home. I could tend the vegetable gardens, essential to our life, catch fish and hares for supper, gather wood for the kitchen and bath, be a playmate for Ran. If I wanted to, I could master in one or two hours what takes a week in school. It's not mistaken to think school is no fun; it's irksome and useless, so of course it isn't what I should care about.

'However severely she preaches at me, the spirit of her view and all her words are false. Her talk is as silly as trying to stop the flow of water with a net. To confute her wouldn't be hard, whereas to satisfy her will be very hard and take me hours! She'll counterattack my words with ten times more, furiously heated, randomly fired, then she'll let go with a slap...

179

'But to confute her is useless, and why should I? My only care is that she finish so I can get out of here...'

Mokuzu stood with narrowed eyes. The face of his teacher and the figures of a few classmates were in his sight not because he willed it, but merely because they were reflected in his optic mechanism.

"Mokuzu, what's the matter with you? Why so silent? Voice your understanding of what I said or some words to acknowledge your fault. Everyone is waiting on account of you."

Those who had lunch boxes were yearning to take them out. Those going home were restless to get to their knapsacks. Some with their eyes and mouth gestured through the corridor-side windows to children passing by. Fearing the tail of the storm, most girls and a few mild boys were assuming their best behavior.

The majority were beginning to side with Mokuzu despite the delay. "I don't care" more fitted their sentiment than Miss Sakaki's adjurations, and whatever else might be said, he was in the weaker position, enough reason for sympathy.

"Mokuzu, apologizing is the better way, no matter how you feel." Naota, the biggest boy and the class leader, attempted a muted voice.

He spoke his utmost wisdom, but his words were picked up by Miss Sakaki's sensitive antennae. Mokuzu saw the corner of her lip quiver; she was exerting every effort to contain herself. Deciding it was inadvisable to spread her anger to Naota and his chums, who were grinning at their boss, she abruptly declared,

"Mokuzu, come to the teachers' room straight after lunch. Class dismissed!"

Her simple conclusion was beyond everyone's expectation, yet it was typical and no one was surprised enough to be distracted from the joy of freedom.

Mokuzu rushed out with the others and found Ena apprehensively waiting with her knapsack and lunch bag slung from her shoulder.

"What happened?" she asked.

Miss Sakaki caught sight of the two of them standing toe to toe out of the corner of her eye as she strode to the teachers' room. It did nothing to calm her nerves.

Together Ena and Mokuzu departed the building.

To that day he had no indoor shoes. When he first entered school, Ena had gone to her teacher to ask if he could use his outdoor shoes after cleaning them each time, since his parents could provide him none and since the wood floors were cold.

Mr. Yamasaki shaved but once a week, and his beard grew thick and fast, making his eyes and teeth appear oddly white. When Ena put the question to him, his eyes glittered. He regarded her face, her tinted smooth cheeks with fine soft hair like a peach, her bright, earnest eyes, the balanced wings of her nose, her lips expressing purity and modesty...and still he gazed in his unrefined manner at her tidy rich hair, her white nape, girlish shoulders, supple hands, fingers with faintly shaded dimples at the joints, and so forth — in short, he considered each part, inseparable from the whole, but then, as if separable.

Feeling an undue interval had passed without his response, Ena importuned,

"Can't he wear them inside too?" Mr. Yamasaki was startled. He inhaled and released an extensive monotone like the long tail of a fancy cock. Suddenly he took something wrapped in a soft cloth from his vest pocket, carefully unwrapped it, and, surprised, said to himself, "Oh! already so late!" And he started toward the teachers' room.

Then after a couple of steps he turned and replied, as if just hearing the question,

"It's most possibly impossible. He is in first grade, you are in second. So your teacher is me and his is inevitably Miss Sakaki...nnnnn...I suggest you ask her what relates to him."

Mere child that she was, Ena was disgusted and indignant. She ran off in search of Miss Sakaki. Mr. Yamasaki, on the other hand, was muttering to himself, "W-well, I never saw so praiseworthy an example — a mere girl, and caring and acting for a stranger. It occurs in fables but is unbelievable in this Saha world with its Asuras masquerading as Bodhisattvas while their true face is that of a Yaksa..." Thus absorbed, he almost hit his brow on the door to the teachers' room.

Miss Sakaki promptly told Ena, "I shall submit the question at the next teachers' meeting." But Ena was never informed, and seeing Mokuzu always barefoot in the cold corridor she felt guilty wearing her straw sandals with red velvet thongs, which were easily replaced when they wore out.

That first spring he had been thankful for her concern. But when summer neared and he was used to school, he no longer minded about not having indoor shoes and laughed at the tip of his nose, "Why fuss over such a trifle? Barefoot is more secure. Quickly and sensitively I can feel everything, it's more enjoyable."

Ena thought of the mandarin orange sapling in her garden: in the coldest months it was wrapped in a straw mat, in spring it put out vigorous new growth. If she took too much care, he would be annoyed, and would slight her. So thereafter she dismissed such minor concerns as his indoor shoes.

They walked through the yard, turned left at the corner of the building, passed by the official entrance and under the windows of the teachers' room, and went behind the janitors' cottage to exit from the school bounds. There the flat hilltop made a steep descent. At its edge Mokuzu always enjoyed standing to look down through the red pines at the old janitor couple working in their small garden.

Beyond the garden, a narrow road coming from the road under the front of the school made a kind of circuit and meandered away along where the rice fields met the mountains, going to deeper villages, where Mokuzu had not yet had a chance to go.

The janitors were not in sight, but a new raised bed with cellophane caps set over evenly spaced seedlings indicated their recent activity.

"Why do they need those hats? — against sparrows or weasels?" Ena showed what for Mokuzu seemed an amazing ignorance.

"Maybe, but mainly to protect from late frost and to keep the soil even a little warmer to form better roots."

Mokuzu was well acquainted with gardening, having worked for the last two years with his father and Gyodo, or just Gyodo when his father was absent.

"Is frost so bad?"

"Sure, it's the worst for vegetable seedlings planted in this season. Just a touch can blast the leaves and stems. No doubt there's something like that for us too."

"You mean...like being scolded by Miss Sakaki?"

"That kind of thing is only boring, a matter of no importance."

"After all, you mean your mother's illness...or, parents' quarreling?"

"Oh, there's her illness, but it's lasted over a year, so I'm used to it and don't think too seriously about it anymore. It's like a road blocked by a typhoon or earthquake — inconvenient, gloomy, but merely a natural phenomenon. By comparison their fighting is far worse. It could also be a mere natural phenomenon. But actually it looks very unnatural. They seem to fight forcibly, yet with the best of their intellect. However, with Ma in the hospital there's no one to fight. It became dark, but thanks to the dark we scarcely notice the dirt and disrepair."

"My parents are too healthy. He's busy in his clinic and rarely returns, because he's at Mitsu's. When he does, he ends up fighting with my mother. She's also quite healthy and often goes out...a man said to be a ship's first-engineer comes and sometimes stays overnight."

"...."

Mokuzu touched the caps to shake down the dew. He could discern three seedlings each of tomato, eggplant, and pepper. "Why don't they plant cucumber?" he muttered. He stood up and turned to Ena,

182

"It might be better if your parents too had to suffer because of an illness. It seems they are very unreasonable and becoming mixed up, at least to the minds of us children. There's the saying, Poison to remedy poison."

In the next raised bed, strawberries in various stages of flowering were here and there setting their green fruits. Some already big and turning from glossy white to faint red were muddied. Ena voiced her sadness: "They took great pains to grow up."

"They should have a straw mulch. Maybe the janitors don't know that, or can't get straw because they aren't real farmers. It's interesting..."

"What?"

"We picked wild raspberries — "

"Yes, many."

"But none were muddy. They grow their branches and leaves thickest near the ground and put their berries higher up."

"Yes, they were washed by the rain instead, and we could eat them as they were."

Among the weeds at the garden's edge near the road were some spindly marigolds, pinks, and gypsophila with just a few poor flower buds, yet their leaves were flourishing.

"Why don't the janitor couple weed?" Ena pulled at the weeds over-coming the flowers.

"They need weeding, and more lime." Mokuzu was reminded of his father applying lime. Inhaling it on the wind, he was stricken with an asthmatic cough that sent him collapsing onto the clods of earth.

"How wonderful if this garden were ours. Together we could till, plant, water, and weed in this quiet, hidden, sunny place!"

"Eh? Ena, what a thought! Well, I've no objection and can't think of a more delightful idea...But it's a matter of the far future; we don't know if there's a path or a bridge to lead us there, and more, I feel it already happened in our past, long before the present you and me...I mean, it just feels like that..."

With slightly open mouth and head raised as if to look over the mountains, Ena was briefly but quite intensely abstracted; she appeared to be savoring the afterimage of a wonderful sight. Mokuzu noticed that she had unwittingly pulled out a tenacious stalk of sedge and wound it about her finger so tight as to cause the skin to blanch. Without speaking he unwound it.

"Why don't we do as always, go up to the rock?" he said.

They angled across the road and climbed the pine hill. It appeared to be an extension of the school hill, separated from it by the road passing through.

The surface was littered with sharp crumbly rocks crusted with lichen, only the freshly broken ones showing their true color. Filling everywhere between was the evergreen perennial fern *urajiro*. Thin, lopsided red pines stood here and there in groups of two or three, their bark dried as if from advancing undernourishment. Some stood dead, and all had a noticeable number of unusually small cones.

At the top there were almost no pines and the ferns were replaced by bright green club moss, its touch like foxtails.

The north side was sheer, seemingly the effect of a landslide some hundred years ago. Perched at the edge was a flat rock as broad as the length of a tatami and half that much in height. Ena and Mokuzu mounted it and hopped and jumped. Well settled on smaller rocks, it was imperturbable.

To the side, a thin pine persisted in sending its roots into the cracks between the large and small rocks. Its crown, as if offering a parasol, came over their heads. With branches on only one side it appeared to be averting its face from the north. Its few branches gave it the look of a pine in a sumi painting.

From the rock they could see a scattering of dwarfed pines with the same branches. The trunks of some grew down below the level of their roots, while the branches and needles turned up in the usual way.

The lower cliffside was a luxuriance of fern varieties. They buried the valley and took over half the next hill as well. Similar hills large and small overlapped until replaced by more soaring, genuine mountains thickly forested with cedar, leading to seemingly endless mountains.

Those northeastern mountains were said to be inhabited by black bear in addition to deer and white-whiskered boar. News came each winter of some woodman, angler, or even hunter attacked and badly wounded or killed near a gorge.

Gyodo and Mokuzu had vowed to each other that they would go to confront a bear in the coming winter. "We'll wait till the snow piles deep so we can meet one possibly even in a lower stream area," Gyodo had said, and, "I'll slay it with my ax."

Sharing Ena's lunch on the rock, having none of his own, Mokuzu gave her his word,

"I'll take you with us in December when there's snow."

"How nice, but your brother won't agree — it's too risky for me, isn't it?"

"Hmm, he once did say, 'If we took Ena, we'd have to take Ran, and then it would be impossible to face a bear. We must prepare blankets and food for ten days and must camp in the snow until one appears. That's too hard for Ena.'"

"But Ran's only five. I'm a year older than you."

"True, but a person like me climbs mountains year round for firewood and brushwood, and I douse with cold water every morning. Let's see, I can

184

get down this sort of cliff in ten minutes and back up in twenty unscathed —
of course without rope and pickax, which are comical equipment. You'd need
three days?"

"Don't be silly!...But I might need three hours...Then you're also
thinking of not taking me..."

"No, no, as I said, I'll take you."

"How? Your brother will object."

"Well, it's May now. Bear hunting isn't till December. There's time to
persuade him. It's not so difficult, we just have to think up some advantages."

"And Ran?"

"Out of the question. There's no way to think up any advantage in that.
We'll give her something else, say, bring her here some Sunday and play as you
and I did the other day, reading the natural designs of these lichens,
interpreting them as we please." Mokuzu patted the lichenous surface near
where Ena sat with her knees under her chin.

As long as they paid it no special heed the rock was a rather drab color
overall. But Ena had recently discovered and was amazed by the complex,
rich, wide, and deep world existing there when she looked closely.

That time, before discovering this fascinating micro-world, she had been
directing Mokuzu's attention outward:

"North is mountains upon mountains. South is rice fields beyond the
school roof and trees, but even that meets mountains. East and west are again
mountains with very little flat land. Doesn't it make you feel strange? People
live between and people live beyond, and the mountains and villages go on
and on, endlessly repeating. But actually Japan is an island country, so soon
enough we'll reach to where the ocean stretches.

"If we go west we'll come to Fukuchiyama and then to Maizuru and the
ocean. We may think we have reached land's end, but there's the Korean
peninsula and all of China, and they connect with Central Asia and even
Central Europe.

"If we go east, we'll pass more villages and mountains to reach Osaka and
Kobe and the Pacific Ocean, which goes way across to North and South
America. If we go on and on, we'll come to Africa by crossing the Atlantic
Ocean, or to Europe, and again to Central Europe. You see, we can get to the
same place by going either way, because our earth is a globe.

"If we go northeast we'll come to Kyoto, Nagoya, and Tokyo...and Sendai...
and Hokkaido, which is an island above our main island. Farther north we'll
see Russia and Alaska, and yet farther is the North Pole, formed of ice.

"Now, be off to the south and there are other islands. Nearest is Kyushu,
farthest, Okinawa, and that's the limit of Japan. Then on and on are many

185

countries, Taiwan, the Philippines, Indonesia, Australia, and New Zealand...

"What makes me feel strange is that in any direction we'll meet people, except maybe at the North and South Poles."

Mokuzu had been impressed. 'Ena knows a lot about the wide world. She is respectable, naturally, being older than me.' But never having been to even the nearest town or studied any geography, he could not know her actual feeling.

'She mentioned such names as America and Europe, but I'm not inspired. Gyodo's talk about the stars is more realistic. I can see them, whereas I can't see any foreign countries however hard I strain my eyes. Ena seems interested in the land. Gyodo is interested in the sky. He keeps teaching, "Look, that dim star is Centaurus...nearest our sun, at a distance of only 4.3 light-years. The brightest is Sirius at 8.7 light-years. Altair is as far as 16 and Vega, 27. But a star like Polaris is as far as a thousand. That shouldn't surprise you — the stars of the Milky Way are as far as a million...You're not amazed? Well, you haven't the right perspective. Listen, sunlight takes 8 minutes and 19 seconds to reach the earth, and light travels 300 thousand kilometers a second. It means even the distance from the sun to the earth is tremendous — 150 million kilometers!"'

"Mokuzu, look at this! It's also marvelous, don't you agree?" Ena had drawn his attention to the lichens. Maybe she still wanted to educate him because he showed no excitement at her indication that there were people the world over, or maybe she just happened to notice the lichens as she pensively looked down. "See? If you look carefully, it's like a map. There are mountains and rivers. Here, this area is exactly like a forest!"

Mokuzu saw that indeed there were varieties of lichen resembling needled trees, deciduous trees, and all manner of shrubs. Others grew in the shape of lotus leaves, or were like the traces of scabs. The combinations formed wide geographic features if imagined from a bird's-eye view. Their colors, too, were not simply ashy, but contained pale green, yellow, even faint grades of vermilion. They were by no means inferior to the normal surrounding sights.

"Oh, yes!...like the world of a fairly tale...rivers, mountains, roads, everything is as it should be."

And now he said to Ena, "I'm sure Ran will enjoy playing on this rock. She'd rather put herself into a tiny world than follow after grown-ups. One day I asked her out of sympathy, 'I bet you want to grow up quicker than you can, because you only tag after your brothers, receiving our directions to do this and not that. And you're left alone when we're in school. You're too small to reach whatever you want and to escape from unpleasant matters. You can only cry, right?' I admit my tone was like Gyodo's; he asks me in the same manner.

"Her response was unexpected. She said, 'I don't want to grow up, I want to grow down, smaller than a pea. Even a match head is too big — I want to be as small as the eye of a mosquito.' By seeing this lichen world, I can sort of understand."

"Yes, me too. So it's a good idea to bring her here on a fine Sunday instead of taking her when we go bear hunting,. I'll make a picnic lunch. She'll be happy. After all, it's too dangerous for her, right?"

"It could be very dangerous, especially as Gyodo says we're going to seek danger itself."

"Is it all right, I mean, is he ready to fight a bear?"

"I guess so. At any rate he said it's too bad there are no lions or tigers in Japan. Let me tell you, he can ax a pine like this in a stroke, while it takes me three. And, oh yes, he did something extraordinary, but you should keep it a secret. My village has a shrine. A few days ago Gyodo said, 'There's no god in this gloomy sort of place!' and he boldly entered the fenced-in area. It has white sand spread about and overhead there's a sacred straw festoon with white paper inserts. Moreover, a signboard says Keep Out. Without apology he jumped the fence and advanced to the front of the sanctum. First he rudely peeped through the lattice at the mirror-like old copper disk that's the object of worship. Then suddenly he gave the doors a kick. Their hinges were no doubt rotten — they fell off, both doors at once."

"Oh! How could he? Won't Buddha's or a god's punishment fall on him?"

"Actually I'm worrying too. I've been straining my ears and watching his health, but nothing's happened."

"Your father and grandmother don't know?"

"Gyodo forbade me to tell. However, I tried to find out what Dad might think about such a thing."

"What did he say?"

"He thought I was impertinently asking whether he is being punished for his past evildoing by having to toil as a day laborer in his own fields that now belong to a former tenant of his, who is one of his laymen — and this regardless of his being a priest."

"He thought you were supposing he has to suffer because, for instance, he beat your mother in front of Buddha?"

"Maybe, but I hadn't such a notion. I just wanted to know if there is divine punishment relating to Gyodo's conduct. At first he regarded me furiously. Then, as if shadowed by a cloud, his face became sad, much like it is when he's most kind. And he muttered, 'Punishment...?' Then he plucked up his heart and said, 'I don't know, but I feel, yes, if there is, it doesn't go to the evildoer but to innocents, to the family...'"

"Did he say so? Then my father's evils won't be punished, and punishment will come to my mother and me...and to be fair, if my mother does evil, punishment will come to my father and me. If I do evil, Mokuzu, you will suffer. I think your father is right — punishment will go to the one we most care about."

"True, nothing is to be feared if the punishment goes to the evildoer. That's a matter of course and he should study so that he will know the effect beforehand. What we should fear is..."

"Mokuzu, it's Miss Sakaki. Listen! She must be above the janitors' garden."

"She's hunting for me, that's for sure, and look, she's brought some assistants."

Miss Sakaki and three girls were mincing their way down the pine slope to the janitors' garden.

"Watch out, it's slippery, ahh! don't step on the garden!" Miss Sakaki warned as she clung to a pine and groped with her high-heeled shoe, her leg fully extended. Somehow her skirt had hiked up to expose her knee and even her thigh up to her garter.

"Ridiculous! If she lets go, she can land easily enough. Why should she so trouble herself to ferret me out?"

"Shouldn't we go down?" "There's no need."

"Mokuzu! Where are you? Answer! Mokuzu! Ena!" From the janitors' garden Miss Sakaki called through her cupped hand. The girls rounded the bend. They reappeared, still looking about, their figures now and then hidden by the sporadic pines.

The trunks, though sparse, sufficed to hide the boy and girl at the top. Besides, for some unknown reason the searchers rarely looked up but scanned at eye level as if searching for a signboard, or looked down as if to find an old shoe.

"Didn't she tell you to be in the teachers' room right after lunch?" Ena, her tone urgent, whispered near Mokuzu's cheek.

"If it's really the case, she'll really come and find me."

"That's exactly why she's looking!"

"No, well, if she wants me, she won't give up. So far she's only diddling. We'd better see which way the wind blows."

"Aki! Come! They couldn't have crossed the road, it's against the rule. We've looked enough, we'll go back. I don't know what to do with him, he's broken even his promise to me!"

The search party clambered up the school slope on their hands and knees.

"See? She was quick to give up. After all, it's a matter of no importance."

"Right." Ena smiled. "But she said you broke your promise. Doesn't that worry you?"

"I don't recall any promise. If that's a promise, then everyone who is made to listen to the blare of a sound truck is responsible for a promise. It's the same no matter how often priests chant the sutras and laymen hear them. There's never any practice of the teachings, and one's to blame..."

Ena let out an unrestrained laugh. Then quickly she composed her face. "Mokuzu, tell me, what really is important to you and not a matter you can ignore?"

The sky was changing. Deep black clouds were rising in the east and south and rapidly extending their domain.

18

An Extraordinary Meeting

While possibly so at a park, it was definitely so at the school that the plantings of flowers and trees were chosen for requiring no special soil or such care as fertilizing, spraying, and watering morning and evening; and more, they were preferred to have a long flowering period, resistance to trampling, and the vigor to set new buds.

Accordingly, perennials and bulbs were chosen rather than annuals or biennials, and plants expressing a group effect were favored over those to be appreciated as one or two.

In Mokuzu's school the caretaker of the flowers and trees was Mr. Yamasaki, a role acknowledged by him and others almost spontaneously, for he was keeping farmland while being a school teacher — indeed, some teachers insisted on restating that he was a farmer serving at the school. Either way, he supposedly knew more than anyone else about horticulture. Further, he had been admired and at the same time disdained for his sense of color and composition, at least as it compared with his mastery of logic and knowledge. After all, he had graduated from an art college.

Mr. Yamasaki ladled into a bucket a supernatant fluid that he had made by macerating rape pomace in a barrel of water. As he rested his hands, he looked across at the silk tree beginning to bloom in melting colors of pink and scarlet at the far corner of the courtyard, near the walkway to the latrines.

"Those flowers," he muttered, "narrow the eyes like an elephant's — they're positively soporific. What a good thing there's that oleander flowering in this opposite corner with its awakening effect."

He filled the bucket to the brim, and as he deliberated over carrying it — troubling to fancy the sight of sloshing onto the cuffs of his trousers — he began to study the row of unglazed pots under the corridor eaves. Morning glory seed had been sown in them by Miss Sakaki's second-grade pupils to perform the scientific exercise of observing the growth of the plant. Into each a wooden tally with a pupil's name had been inserted to show whose work it was at a glance.

The soil lacked mulch and was dry and cracked. To expect permeation to the roots even if watered from a watering can was unreasonable. Most of the seedlings were wilting, and some had dropped the buds they had issued at no small pains.

'Not to mention seeing no flowers, performing the photosynthesis experiment of taping part of the leaf will be impossible. Miss Sakaki is a greenhorn at raising living things.' Mr. Yamasaki was ashamed for her sake, and he pitied the morning glories.

He lifted the bucket and, as he feared, sloshed the fluid onto his shiny black leather shoes; yet, he began to apply it to the roots of clustered canna and dahlia magnificently vegetating and boldly commencing to bloom.

'Why doesn't he cap that barrel? Has he a stuffed-up nose? The stink has filled the courtyard and is intruding beyond the corridor into the classrooms. And can't he grow flowers that are a little more sensitive and lovely, instead of those coarse things? What merit is there in his conceit?' Miss Sakaki renewed her critique at the step from the corridor to the courtyard. She had come to fetch him.

"Mr. Yamasaki! Everyone is waiting just for you!"

"Ah! Confound it! I forgot!" From his trousers pocket he dragged out a crumpled oversized handkerchief, wiped his hands on it, then took from his vest a small velvet bundle, unwrapped it, and regarded his watch fob.

'Again looking at that thing — it's as dear as his life, I suppose. Can't he recognize by my coming that time is pressing?' Miss Sakaki turned up her nose and without waiting returned to the council room.

"He will be here presently. He said he forgot the meeting," she reported in a businesslike manner and made a pose of studying a pupil's file before her.

"The fellow's keen on floriculture," briskly noted Mr. Nishitani with no nuance of censure.

190

Nishitani was a former pilot, one of those rare, miraculous survivors of the kamikaze corps. His physique was almost nowhere round, but square, firm, robust, as if storing a bomb; and yet, he was fluidly mobile like an assembly of automatic parts that peremptorily work.

He rarely expressed his feelings, but when he did, he did so promptly and matter-of-factly in conformity with life's realities. That way he could usually keep others ignorant of his heart, whence he was considered to be a mere physical and mechanical man of poor sensibility.

With more frequency than the change of seasons, his kin, neighbors, fellow teachers, and pupils kept at him and even beguiled him into opening up about his unprecedented war experience. But what he recounted was strictly limited to his air activity, and at that only during the early Pacific War, while the Japanese force was enjoying an advantage over the opponent and achieving brilliant war results. By no means would he speak of the Battle of Midway, northwest of the Hawaiian islands, in which Japan lost four aircraft carriers.

"Planting trees and nursing flowers...though our school is already located amid green mountains and fields...is...quite welcome from an educational standpoint. So I have long been thankful for Mr. Yamasaki's avidity," began the subprincipal, Mr. Manju. "His fine extracurricular service, I estimate, more than compensates for his slight want in the classroom....As you know, on the whole, education does not distinguish curricular from extracurricular. These classifications are made for convenience only, and...in either case teachers should at all times be teachers, just as pupils should be pupils. Yes."

The subprincipal functioned at the borderline between two antagonistic sides, one representing the common teachers, the other the principal. His speech and behavior betokened his need to keep his balance like walking a tightrope, and naturally the sense of his words changed according to his listeners, like the iridescent luster of a two-striped green buprestid.

His duty and office would have been better served had he had less loyalty and ambition, but, as it was, he was unerringly loyal to his wife and son, and his ambition was to become principal even a day earlier.

His face was ruddy and stoutish, revealing him at a glance to be a drinker. His impeccable hair gleamed with oil. So fine and clean did he appear that strangers mistook him for the principal.

The principal however was Mr. Hitomi, tall, with countable strands of hair plastered back from the crown. Deep, stiff, lusterless wrinkles lined his forehead, the area under his eyes, and the sides of his nose to his mouth, just expressing the wisdom, Life is suffering. His only brightness, slight even with the aid of an electric lamp, was his bald crown, his small eyes under long thin brows, and amid a row of brownish teeth a gold incisor.

191

He habitually bowed his head in assent when others talked and often put on a much gentler smile than was expected — though it did not mean that he had been won over.

A loud *slap slap* approaching the council room signaled to everyone waiting there Mr. Yamasaki's heels widely separating from and cleaving to his slippers. As he came in he failed to slide the door enough and hit his shoulder. Dismissing it he sat down, then stood and bowed formally to Mr. Hitomi, cornerwise on his left in the principal's seat, to Mr. Nishitani and to Miss Sakaki across the table, and to Mr. Manju on his left.

"Sorry to make you wait — I plumb forgot!" Those he addressed burst out laughing in their minds.

The subprincipal closed his eyes. He then opened them wide and announced the beginning of the meeting —

"We have requested the honor of Principal Hitomi's presence today, even as we well know he is very busy in his public and private life. We are assembled for no other purpose than to form...errr, some common recognitions and a common view...ehhh, so as to find the best educational policy to take...hem! hem! with regard to so-called problem children.

"I have said 'so-called,' there being not necessarily stereotypical problem children in our school. The issue is delicate, and we must begin from the position of whether to see them as problem children at all. That is, suppose you conclude they are not. By that alone the purpose of today's meeting will be well attained. If, however, you are going to think to the contrary, then we must trouble you to deliberate to find the fittest way to guide them.

"The teachers participating in this small ad hoc meeting are, as you see, its proponent, Miss Sakaki, in charge of second grade, where there is a so-called problem child named Mokuzu; Mr. Yamasaki, in charge of third, where there is another possible problem child, Ena, who is Mokuzu's closest friend; and Mr. Nishitani, in charge of fifth, where there is the brother Gyodo.

"Fortunately we all, including our principal and myself, know more or less causally about Mokuzu and his home. We now will be informed by Miss Sakaki of various matters relating to him, and anyone may at any time express his candid opinion, uhh, that is, we shall advance by talking informally. Well, Miss Sakaki, please begin."

"I should like to propound three issues that could be seen as problematical, at least they are to me as the teacher in charge of Mokuzu. The first concerns his home life, the second his associates, the third his attitude toward school and society.

"Presently there is nothing gravely amiss in any of these areas. However, there may be cause for concern should we let matters ride, inasmuch as

192

problems could develop for him, and for one with whom he associates, which in consequence could affect our school, responsible as an educational organ.

"As to the first, it is by no means fine. I made my home visit a few weeks ago. His mother is in Nanlin Hospital, where she has been since spring of last year, and it was hard to see his father, who goes out to work."

"She's been hospitalized for over a year? What is she doing there, I wonder..." Mr. Yamasaki interposed.

"What do you mean, 'what is she doing'? Receiving medical treatment, obviously. I don't exactly know, but endometritis and solenoma are suspected."

On hearing "solenoma," Mr. Nishitani visualized a tombstone in a dusky field and, to change the subject, he asked,

"If I recall, isn't there a grandmother? Couldn't you conclude your round in that vicinity by seeing her?"

"It's no good. She appears modest but suddenly strikes a pose as if standing on a cloud; she also turns to past matters, but, again, suddenly introduces some vague metaphysical philosophy with great confidence. For example, when I told her the purpose of my call, she said, 'I am sorry to be putting you to the extreme trouble of walking long under the hot sun,' and with the slow and fretful movements of the old she even offered tea.

"When at last we were siting face to face and I'd begun my report, she struck her knee as if slapping a mosquito and said, 'Teacher, you have to know I am an old person who was admitted to the public elementary school when it first opened its doors in the nineteenth year of our gracious Emperor Meiji. Children were admitted at age six and the course of study was four years. I was seven, and nothing could be done but to let me enter at age seven. Prior to that year no compulsory education existed. Most children were sent to temples or eminent families to study.

"'Be that as it may, I should like to tell you I attended school for only four years, and not because I gave up on the way but because, as I said, the term expired.

"'As soon as I was graduated, I became an exclusive maid to the madam of Mr. Konoike. I did not cook or clean; other maids did that. My duties were to attend the madam at all times and learn the many details of manners and etiquette.'"

All but the subprincipal sighed with admiration on hearing the name Konoike, formerly a wealthy zaibatsu. Mr. Manju sneered at the tip of his nose, "Huh-hnn," meaning, "You're at it again, granny!" He appeared to be clenching his molars and sat with his nose in the air.

"Then, when she was seventeen," Miss Sakaki hastened on, "she suffered a severe case of jaundice. She told me at length how she was nursed by the madam, reversing their roles. 'I turned yellow, even the furniture looked yellow, and my breath grew as faint as the breath of an insect. The doctors were at a loss. The madam took to sleeping in my chamber and cooking thin gruel and spoon-feeding it to me. The sediment she ate as her meal. It was more than I deserved: she was no less a personage than the madam of Mr. Konoike. And she was sobbing, "How could so young a life be allowed to pass hence?" and was praying to Buddha and sobbing again. I think it unforgivable that a zaibatsu with so great a madam was forced into dissolution by the American Occupation army right after the war. Wealth and virtue go hand in hand. What's the good of dividing a fortune and distributing it to the commoners in the name of democracy when they have not cultivated their virtue? A fortune coming to those ignorant of how to use it is an insidious bacteria to them and to others.'

"Recognizing my time was running out, I carefully interjected, 'Please, granny, the reason I came today concerns Mokuzu.' Again she slapped herself and said, 'That is the very thing I wanted to tell you. I had only four years of school and it is a matter of the distant past. I know nothing of schools today, so please don't talk to me of that. Why don't you ask Mokuzu if it concerns him?' And she shut her mouth tight as a clam regardless of my efforts to extract information on the home environment...'"

Hearing Miss Sakaki's tale of frustration at that home, Mr. Yamasaki and Mr. Nishitani, feeling sympathy, stared at the table with shaded faces. But Mr. Manju, as if heartily siding with the grandmother, guffawed. Taken in by it, Mr. Hitomi smiled.

The day was hot. The principal and the subprincipal removed their coats, seemingly a privilege of their higher station, while in deference to it their ties remained fast about their necks. Mr. Nishitani wore a jacket but no tie. Mr. Yamasaki too was without a tie, but oddly he had on both a coat and a vest. Miss Sakaki was as usual in a white blouse and the faded blue jumper apparently favored since her school days. Now enclosing a fuller figure, it accentuated her curves.

"So what happened?" The subprincipal when he finished laughing at once asked Miss Sakaki to proceed.

"Many times I went, but only last Saturday evening could I catch the father home. I entered and called in at the door. I guess he was taking a drink. He didn't answer, but I could hear him say, 'Oi, Mokuzu, I have to go to the toilet. Hold steady my clogs, they're swaying like skiffs.' Mokuzu asked how he could think they were moving. 'They don't look so to you? Hold them anyway. Today I'm drunk, hmm, what a pleasure! "Of what use are later regrets? Let us enjoy our chance encounter"[1] — ha ha! I'd have little

194

complaint if your mother would come home, don't you agree?' 'Dad, I have a thousand complaints.' Yes, that's exactly what I overheard."

"Whose poem?" the principal whispered to the subprincipal.

"Let me see..." Mr. Manju glared blankly, straining every nerve, but he soon bucked the question to the others and relaxed.

"Whose poem? You must know." Yet they each sat with faces like masks as if not having heard.

Miss Sakaki disregarded the question and continued her report, "I explained to the father the purpose of my call by introducing a simple topic, of course after greeting him and introducing myself. I said, 'Mokuzu does well in all subjects but music. He can more than adequately distinguish the major from the minor mode, can read the notes; he knows all the signs. But he can't sing in tune or smoothly follow the rhythm, dynamics, and phrasing.'

"'I see, you mean he's tone-deaf.' 'No, yes, indeed it's something like that. But he has no physiological defect, the cause is strictly psychological. He gets terribly uneasy when he must sing, or he never had a chance to hear music...'

"'Well?' 'I ask that you to give him a chance, at least let him hear a music program on the radio or play the phonograph. He has to experience growing up from now on, and if he can't sing at such times as parties, when all others are singing and dancing, he will suffer a sense of alienation, and develop a pre-dilection for loneliness and quite possibly an atrabilious as well as misanthropic disposition.'

"'With what radio and phonograph am I to make him hear music? We have altogether seventeen rooms large and small, including the main hall, but there's not a single radio, not to mention phonograph. Look about if you don't believe me, and don't fail to search the dark closet behind the sanctum.' 'Oh, I am so sorry, I never imagined a home without a radio.' 'You are not asked to imagine. To be honest, you are an unpleasant visitor. In the main, is there any importance in studying music? I myself am tone-deaf. Most unsuit-able to chant the sutras is a person who can sing well. Put simply, people become more irreligious the more they favor music and sing adeptly. You mention singing and dancing, but with whom? You say it's to make friends. You're putting the cart before the horse. You say my son could turn atrabilious and misanthropic. Isn't it the natural course for anyone? It would be strange if it were otherwise. A sutra also says, "This confused and transmigratory world is like a burning house."'[2]

"'I was becoming mellow, taking a special occasion to drink, but you've dashed it and I have to drink anew. I wish you'd leave at once. You needn't use the gate, there are exits via the bamboo grove or the laymen's graveyard. Henceforward don't come here with such a matter of no importance.'

Hearing that, I allowed as how I had come to discuss Mokuzu's attitude of seeing matters as unimportant. But he said, 'Why should you bother with what he considers unimportant? You who are teachers deliberately transmit matters of no importance as if they were of grave importance. It's absolutely topsy-turvy taken from the way essayed by us priests. We labor to somehow or other reduce grave matters to trifles and make people see them as such.

"'I've revealed to you a secret of the priesthood, but these days I'm no longer a priest. I'm a hand for a petty farmer. I haul buckets of night soil, mow grass, plant rice seedlings, indeed I spend my days suffering in an unreal world and I don't care about anything. So you'd better vanish before I find myself resorting to violence. Don't look triumphant! Children aren't the property of the school or the family: they belong to nature, to heaven and earth.'

"This was our exchange, and I obediently left. I have fair confidence of its accuracy because I recorded it all when I got home, doing without supper. The reason I hurriedly left was that I felt endangered, albeit it might look like I abandoned my duty. I don't mean to infer sexual abuse, rather, I sensed he saw me as an inanimate presence like a brick or a bundle of wood."

Miss Sakaki, a compulsive memo keeper, throughout her report followed the pages of a small black agenda laid open on the table. She did not notice that Mr. Nishitani was frantic to stifle a laugh as tears formed in the corners of his eyes.

"Then what's the problem? Thus far I see none," drawled Mr. Yamasaki. He widened his eyes and tightened the corners of his mouth as if facing some wondrous spectacle. He did not speak to dampen her enthusiasm, nor was he facing anything wondrous. Simply, most of his brain had been dozing as he looked ahead with eyes more or less open.

"You see no problem? His mother has been hospitalized for over a year, his grandmother doesn't care, his father drinks, expresses attitudinal judgments, and isn't concerned about the boy's education and future. He's dressed in his brother's raggedy hand-me-downs and almost never brings lunch. He's given scarcely any school suplies. His home hasn't newspaper or radio. And there is only one twenty-watt bulb in the entire place.

"If I dare mention how it affects his school life, first, he doesn't cooperate in class, in fact he manifests an insouciant attitude toward almost everything. Second, and as to this, let me say that you, Mr. Yamasaki, ought to share some responsibility, for he consorts with Ena Okada in your fourth grade...well, the relationship is too exclusive, too intimate. From an educational point of view I see great problems in these areas. Allow me to speak in specific terms..." As she hunted for the page, she was arrested by a gesture from the subprincipal, and he said,

"Mr. Nishitani also visited the home, being in charge of the brother

Gyodo. Why don't we hear from him?"

Principal Hitomi nodded vigorously just to express that it was a bright idea. Mr. Nishitani prepared to stand, but Mr. Manju urged him to remain seated.

"I spotted nothing that need be reported, though Miss Sakaki is right about the economy. She does not exaggerate, and it could be worse if we were to know the condition of their bedding and their lack of access to medication. Even so, I think their home is not a bad influence, not a culture to delinquency. I esteem those boys as a good example to others.

"True, Gyodo's dress is inferior and he doesn't bring lunch, but he's standing his ground. In his studies he is beyond compare. Especially as to Chinese classics, he recites such texts as even Miss Sakaki, if I may, would be strained to decipher. An ignoramus like me might hope to challenge them for the first time on retirement, after serving another thirty-some years in the present manner.

"He goes right home after school to gather firewood or to catch fish. He does everything commonly regarded as adult work — in winter helping to fertilize and prune their chestnut orchard, in spring digging bamboo shoots and gathering the sheaths for market, in fall harvesting chestnuts and hunting up mushrooms for market.

"Yet I reckon he's the kindest in my class, nay, in the school. Let me cite a recent example. When a girl vomited after lunch, Gyodo was quicker than me to get a cloth and wipe it up.

"He's also fair and prudent, which isn't easily attained even by adults. During gym my pupils noticed a cicada flapping in a web in the camphor by the horizontal bars. The girls said rescue it and the boys were about to when Gyodo intervened, 'The spider will lose its food and wait long for a new chance while enduring hunger. The cicada too is sorrowful. It's best to look on with the complex emotion of crying for the cicada and rejoicing for the spider.' Everyone saw his point.

"Don't these two examples indicate the home isn't bad?" Mr. Hitomi and Mr. Manju were impressed at once, "Is that so?" They raised their chins. Mr. Yamasaki kept looking frontward. With a start he busily shook his head.

"The incidents Mr. Nishitani just adduced relate to Gyodo's character and conduct." Miss Sakaki was speaking again. "By that we cannot conclude the home environment of the junior brother is good. Gyodo is fortunate to be overcoming the adversity by means of his nature or something else, while the same could be too heavy a burden for Mokuzu. Above all, is there any doubt that their home is not desirable even if there are exceptions? Our concern is not strictly Gyodo's personality, effort, endurance, and intelligence, or the phenomenon of his seeming to transcend the adversity. Our concern is the environment.

197

If we conclude it is good by seeing just their character and some effects, we will be censured as disingenuous and negligent teachers, will we not?"

"Miss Sakaki, we must exercise caution in discussing the rights and wrongs of the home. To introduce Ena, who is in my class...nnn, as you all may have suspected, she thinks she has two fathers, yet she hasn't even one apt father...so we can't help thinking her home is strange. However, I haven't observed the situation enough to affirm that it's undesirable. In a word, the growth of a human being takes a long time...

"Were it just a matter of economy, we could make an objective assessment. But it's beyond our duty to assess the economic state of our pupils and devise corrective measures. That's the task of our government — prefecture, town, and village — of the Welfare Department. We teachers should grasp the state of our own economy, maintain it, even enhance it. For us that's good enough, no? So I don't think Mr. Nishitani or any one else here is disingenuous and negligent as a teacher."

"But Mr. Yamasaki, if I adopt your solution, how can I amend in Mokuzu what is fostered in the home? All I can do is provide instruction to shore up the moment. Allow me to bring a case that occurred not long ago. I was intent on teaching division when he stood up and began to walk out. I asked was it for the toilet. He replied, 'No — but just a minute.' I could only say, 'You aren't allowed to have your way. Tell me where you are going and why.' He coolly stated, 'I understand division, but by staying here I can't know if there's a hare in my trap at the back mountain. I figure it's about time. I have to go check.' I was amazed, and my class broke into laughter. And I was stumped and could not unsnarl the chaos.

"I think there will be no good effect if I disallow him to leave, because it's to obtain his food; a direct consequence of the home. What concerns us is that it occurred during school, I mean, many days he doesn't show up at all. Principal Hitomi, I should like to know your view."

The principal frowned as he did whenever he espied something unattractive. "Well, surely the problem is a problem. Be that as it may, it's why we are gathered to discuss it. Yes. The point I should mention is that such things cannot be expected to settle shortly. It reminds me that I am at last due to retire. Regrettable as it is in terms of this problem, indeed if I reach the year's end without trouble, my declining years will be assured with a pension and I can sufficiently enjoy the pleasure of bonsai culture. So, our first concern is not to exacerbate matters, in short, rather than attempt a radical settlement, we must keep things calm for the interim. We teachers should recognize the limit of our duty and ability, as Mr. Yamasaki bravely indicated. Uhhh, that is to say..." His talk was like the progress of a slug.

198

"How right you are, Principal. We all who are ordinary mortals must first know our place." The subprincipal was launching a lifeboat —

"It is respectable in Miss Sakaki to have raised her question in a passion of concern. But we have to consider how much she cares, in the true sense, about the life of her pupil. Isn't she piqued when her classes don't go as planned? Is her motive like Kannon's pure compassion, or has she a selfish irritation? Miss Sakaki, you are to be married this summer? Is your care for you pupil equal to your care for your fiancé? I don't mean as to its nature but as to its degree.

"Our principal has just now confessed. Calm though it looked on the surface, it was a hot confession. Let me follow his lead and express my view. I too have family — a wife, a child, and an old mother. My care toward my son if I compare it with my care toward our pupils or a particular boy is evidently not the same. For my son it is like deep red blood, whereas for Mokuzu or any other pupil it is like a drop of Mercurochrome put in the vast sea."

The sun left the courtyard. Abruptly the council room darkened. The wood ceiling, walls, floor, glass-doored bookshelves, standing lamp, and square-built table and chairs began to exude a treacherous look of age as if it was their original nature. Mercilessly the old building and furnishings drew attention to each moment and to the advance of the years. To stay alone in such a room would have been unbearable for anyone without a considerably bright character and the vigor to live a renewed life each day.

The occasional hurrahs of children playing ball after school had subsided. No longer was there the sound of mimeographing in the next room — Mr. Hosoda, who coughed year round, had left. The janitor had finished scrubbing the concrete floor around the long sink. From the music room, across the courtyard, had come the thunk of the piano lid. Now all but the

199

small group in the council room were gone from the school.

Mr. Manju had added his confession, with graphic hyperbole, and everyone was sunk in an unpleasant silence and seemed hesitant to stir the air, as if suffering an autointoxication induced by Mr. Manju's words.

There was the smell of sulfur as Mr. Yamasaki struck a match to light his strong, cheap cigarette.

"Well, nothing is wrong, eh?" Mr. Nishitani spoke curtly. The others turned their eyes upon his brownish square face.

"I'm referring to the intimacy between Mokuzu and Ena, introduced as a potential problem. You know from experience that for our generation the worldwide trend was to separate the sexes, as was said, 'Boys and girls ought not to sit together after the age of seven.'[3] And it was withal a military age. There was no opportunity for a boy and a girl to pick flowers hand in hand, to play together with pussy willow ears at a river beach, or, of course, to talk of unwelcome home events and each other's hopes for the future. In my case, when I was yet an infant, I had to gather mulberry leaves for our silkworms and strip willow branches to weave baskets. As a youth I dug holes for electric-light posts or mined coal. When I was but nineteen, I had to service airplanes and drill in their operation. That was the extent of my boyhood.

"Now we have democracy. Society and the schools favor peace, and equality of the sexes and coeducation are recommended. I myself am made impatient by seeing that other pupils don't get on so well as Mokuzu and Ena. Why don't they also roam more often together across field and hill? Aren't these two setting an example of democracy?"

"Would you say so if you saw them toting a blanket?" Miss Sakaki sharply interjected.

"A blanket? What for? In cold weather?"

"A blanket is a blanket. They are two but use one blanket, brought from who knows where. They wrap up in it and take a view of the valley in winter, and in summer spread it in the shade of a pine. Bright and unspecific social intercourse between boy and girl is laudable, as you say, and so it is written in the 'New Outline of Educational Guidance.' Yet it must be kept within bounds. Shouldn't we nip such precocity in the bud? What if they're up to playing doctor? What do you think, Mr. Yamasaki, as the teacher in charge of Ena?"

Mr. Yamasaki was taken unawares. He hastily snuffed out his cigarette, narrowly repressed his habitual and reflexive "Wha-wha — about what?" and said, "Oh yes...you mean...nnnn, a blanket, eh? It is a problem whether such usage, that is, of a blanket, which is a commodity at any rate, is appropriate... right?"

The others had to laugh. Obviously he had been dozing with eyes open

200

and while smoking, at least his brain had been taking the equivalent of a doze. The council room recovered some life.

Miss Sakaki was thankful that her prospective husband was a pharmacist and not the likes of these teachers. 'I've had quite enough of their filthy, spineless, irresponsible ways. Their concern is only the art of self-protection. They want peace at any price and have sunk into an idle prosaic life. They're worse to deal with than rats. In comparison Mokuzu is living a more sprightly life. He's only a child yet isn't succumbing to the heavy pressure of his environment, and is sharp enough to get the maximum of whatever he can from there. He's even begun to be confident of his brave recognition that most school matters are unimportant. He is amazing...'

"It is in the main a kind of jealousy, yes, that's the motive of adults who warn early-ripening children against these intimacies by saying they are bad for their future from an educational standpoint and so forth. It's the same as saying immoral acts and feckless love are harmful to public morals. Essentially sex is a private matter and should be left to take its course so long as it doesn't directly and greatly bother others. We must assume that those who are critical wish to enjoy pleasant congress and are as yet dissatisfied. Isn't it obvious?" Mr. Nishitani soberly introduced his consideration.

Indignant, Miss Sakaki looked into space. Unblinking, Mr. Yamasaki was openly examining her tense cheeks, creamy neck, resilient-looking breasts, spotless smooth arms with soft undersides and gentle line to the armpits, and finally, again, her breasts, heaving as she breathed. He spoke, coordinating his words to the movement of his eyes,

"So...the view of Mr. Nishitani isn't a mere...nnn...but Miss Sakaki hasn't reason to feel jealous, has she? Nooo...she is about to marry. Therefore...nnn, she must be inventing to her heart's content how to use a blanket...I mean, she has the liberty to pleasure in exploring the best position, er...nnn, riding-horse, or face-and-knees-up...On this point I can advise...until autumn, overuse of a blanket induces heat rash about the pit of the belly and under the breasts, yes, my honeymoon proved it."

Principal Hitomi and the others, rendered incapable of knowing whether or not to laugh, were like a full cup in a shaking hand.

Mr. Manju all at once declared, "Meeting adjourned! Thank you for your great concern. I should also like to urge that you be careful of your health in this hot season and ever continue your great contribution to the maintenance and prosperity of the education provided by our school." Promptly he stood to assist the principal, and they withdrew posthaste toward the principal's room.

Miss Sakaki sprang to her feet, ignoring the two who remained. But Mr. Nishitani caught her elbow, "Wait, why hurry? Do you understand the true

201

nature of today's meeting? I think not. Let me disclose a secret. Being young and an outsider to this town, you don't know anything. Sit down again, won't you?

"Let alone for the moment Mokuzu's modus vivendi and school life. Reconsider his home. Tangenji, you know, was wealthy until it received the effect of the war and the farmland release. Nonetheless, and this is the crux of the problem, even after the temple ruined, the family had some land measuring about two hectares, still a big holding in these parts.

"Then what do you think happened? Listen. I will talk generally, then give you details if you wish. Please sit down. Mr. Yamasaki and I have wives and children, we won't harm you, we only like to look and imagine.

"Well now, the temple has laymen responsible for its economy. Don't be surprised — our subprincipal is an influential layman of Tangenji.

"Around when the temple economy began to slip, Mokuzu's mother became ill. Although the municipal coffers provide a scant relief fund, most medical costs must be privately borne. The Tangenji priest tried to find a way out by disposing of his remaining land. At that, the head layman of Tangenji and our subprincipal conspired to spread word that no one should buy it, with the result that the priest was forced into a corner. Those two then bought it up for almost nothing, in a word, at a distress sale price. On top of that, they acted as if they were buying it out of mercy, unable to look on in the face of the priest's hardship, especially as their families have long been powerful laymen. So he begged them to buy it, and thanked them, even gave them tickets to heaven, that is, to each he gave a precepts-name.

"Well, can you guess how much they paid? The priest could hardly cover the initial hospital charge.

"Isn't some of this worth hearing? Sit down. Say, Yamasaki, don't you share my indignation? Yosetsu Fujii and Ten Manju purchased two hectares at a price about equal to a teacher's three-month salary. In that way three fifths of the priest's land went to Fujii, two fifths to Manju."

"So little for so much land?" Aghast, Miss Sakaki sat down.

"I knew about them but didn't know that was all they paid!" Mr. Yamasaki stared in amazement.

"So, of course our subprincipal doesn't want us talking of Mokuzu's home. Mr. Yamasaki and I, well aware of his mind, had difficulty maneuvering in today's meeting."

"You were unlike teachers. You were unmanly and disgusting. Knowing this to be a cause of the family's aggrievement, you should have felt obliged to speak up — "

"Hold on, Miss Sakaki, there's much you're unaware of. You must consider life's many angles. You may know east, west, north, and south, but you don't know all the degrees between, though to know is useless as there's no end to them. Let me raise just one grave, criminal case."

"What's that?"

"You reported Mokuzu comes mostly without lunch. Has he no lunch on those days?"

"None, and my heart aches inasmuch as I am the teacher in charge of him. Early on I shared mine and he accepted it. Then soon he began to refuse and concealed himself in the back hills at lunchtime. After that I knew Ena was sharing hers, but, as with me, her kindness was finally refused, and now neither brings lunch, which means there are two, no, three, counting Gyodo. All others have lunch, all teachers too, am I not correct? Is this a school, a holy precinct of education?"

"Come now, Miss Sakaki, stay calm. I'll tell you about that. Our Ministry of Education agreed to provide bread to all primary school children within the eight biggest cities, effective from 1950, when the GARIOA fund came from America. The next year included all cities, and beginning April, 1952, the provision was implemented nationwide. When Mokuzu entered first grade in 1952 there was free bread from GARIOA for his lunch, at least there was the money for it, for all our children."

"My word, what a surprise! Then where is the bread?"

"Aha! you see, Miss Sakaki! The fund comes from the federal government to our prefecture, is delivered to our town from the prefectural office, and enters the hand of our town head, who shares it with Fujii and his sort, and Fujii shares it with our subprincipal and his sort. So there's no bread for your pupil Mokuzu, while those pocketing the fund along the way are able to buy up the land of such unfortunates as Mokuzu's father..."

19

Dead Fish

At the onset of summer vacation, in late July, as the early sun was breaking through the rich persimmon leafage and glittering on the dew of the moss, Gyodo and Mokuzu set off to fish in the river as part of their daily routine.

From below the wall of Tangenji they saw the pale vermilion flowers of the old trumpet vine that grew up into the big persimmon. Its refreshing pensile flowers, responding to the gentlest breeze, were elegant in not calling attention to themselves and seemed bashful to open.

"I wonder how Ma's doing at this time of day. Don't you wish to see her?"

"Sometimes she appears like a rainbow on the inner side of my eyelids, but not often. And you're the one who severely told me not to speak of her."

"Well, true, I said men shouldn't ask for the unobtainable or be vulnerable to attacks of sad emotion. But I'm thinking of taking the opportunity of this vacation to go look in on her."

"To the hospital? Me too. How about Ran? You also warned me not to utter a word about Ma around her, because even one word makes her think of Ma all day, and a glimpse of our ache makes her cry frantically."

"Right. We'll tell no one. So of course we'll be given no bus money. We can walk and run and get home the same day, though we might be back late..."

Mokuzu sensed a vigor rising from the pit of his stomach. He felt galvanized to uproot a tree or lift a big rock. 'If I had to, I'd drill through a mountain to see Ma!'

They veered off the path that led to school and went out along the narrow ridges between the fields of rice grown to the height of their waists. At their feet the weeds were wet as if rained on, and their bare legs got itchy from the ears of the taller grasses. The whitish green ears of rice were still flat like pressed flowers. Across them were woven subtle spiderwebs made visible by their sparkling beads of dew.

Mokuzu carried the creel, Gyodo followed with the trident. He put Mokuzu in the lead, out of regard for the possibility of a hidden pit viper. Its nature was to retract its head into its coiled body at the passage of the first comer, then spring for the ankle or calf of the second. The first, though uneasy, was safer.

The previous evening they had prepared hooks with large earthworms and set them in the river on the strong hemp thread they used for kites, choosing a spot where the flow was sluggish below an overhanging pussy willow, another directly below a big clay drainage pipe from the rice fields, another beside a rock wall collapsed by flooding; in short, wherever their experience indicated the possibility of a catch.

They could see as they stood on the high riverbank the lines made by the wheels of horse- and cow-drawn drays; there at the top the grass was short. Cherries were planted on the shoulder, but the slope to the shore was a tangle of eulalia and reeds overgrown by kudzu extending its domain with furious vigor. To get to the water was impossible without finding the route made by their frequent trips, which anyone else would have been hard put to find.

Between the wild boscage on either shore, the water surface appeared as a white darkness overhung by morning mist. The mist was writhing as it rose, and swirling wisps were escaping and drifting to the tops of the banks and quickly dispersing.

Although the river was not very wide, the mist hid the far shore; yet sometimes it unveiled a glimpse of reed tips faintly green, and occasionally let the sunlight into the river's unexpected depths.

On seeing only the swirling mist, Mokuzu briefly felt he was sighting something fearful like a mere outermost layer of a hell stretching for several thousand light-years. But most of time it suggested to him a soft bosom, comfortable and encouraging.

"Hey, didn't you say Ena was meeting you here?"

"Yes, she must be down at the dam. I'll go get her."

"Then go while I'm checking the hooks. But remember never to go near the brink. Warn her too!"

Gyodo pulled off his shirt and shorts at the edge and dived in with the trident; Mokuzu promptly followed. The mist made uncertain even where the water was, but they knew well the location of such dangers as sharp rocks or rotting stakes and where the depth was sufficient. Gyodo swam upstream. Mokuzu swam down at ease. They wore each just a towel held at the waist by a string.

Like a pole Mokuzu floated along amidstream, raising above the water only his face from the nostrils up like an alligator. The river as it widened gained volume and the banks became lower. A breeze freely came and went and the mist at the surface was no longer stagnant. The view was opening splendidly. Here and there in the grasses alongside were the orange hues of tiger lily and spotted-deer lily and clumps of bellflower and speedwell, presumably escaped from the garden. Wagtails moved from bank to bank, their intricate flight paths staying a moment in his eyes.

The sky, bearing the vapor, was powder blue, but promised a scorching day. Already cicadas were beginning their vibration from the cliff of a pine mountain close to the river at one point.

He came to where the current greatly slowed, from where he could see the opaque shining brink ahead. He knew the far side dropped sharply about three meters and the water then flowed on as if having known no obstacle. Within the dam the water looked lucid and calm. But no one could be careless, for the wall of the dam had several ducts. Thereabouts the current was strong, and a person could end up dashed to the concrete on the other side.

The wall of the dam at each bank formed a platform. A white square post marked with lines showed the water level at a glance. A red line marked the danger level.

Ena sat on one of the platforms, her bare legs over the side, looking downstream. She had picked a kudzu vine and was casting its leaves one by one onto the water.

'Under the wide sky she is just looking at the placid flow of no particular color...she is also a lonely girl.' Ena was of course alone because she had come by herself to meet him here. Yet what he felt on seeing her had nothing to do with her happening to be alone at the moment, but with her total life, environment, days of growing up, which was vaguely discernible, and more, with her indiscernible future.

Alert to Gyodo's warning, he skewed across to where Ena sat. Closer to shore the water was quicker.

'Shall I continue to lurk along and surprise her? She'll laugh when she realizes it's me,' he thought, but reconsidered, 'I hate being surprised. In the moment, my heart leaps as if to stop, even if the cause is a thing so harmless as to leave me quaking with relief. And the shock can't be erased even if I quickly perceive it was due to a misconception.

'Amidst surprise, there's no way to know whether it's an alligator, a huge snake, an indescribable monster, or a playful friend or a pretty flower. Surprise is all.

'So even if a person is soon relieved and laughs, "Oh, it was a flower whiffed by a breeze!" or "Ho! it's you!" it doesn't mean flower or friend isn't fiendish. Actually a new misconception will arise from thinking one's surprise was due to a misconception, for the truth is, anything can be fiendish in its capacity to surprise.'

"Ena, I'm here. I've come to get you." Mokuzu called quietly at first, then with his usual lively voice as he approached the concrete wall.

"Did you swim down? I was believing you'd appear on the other bank."

"I rode the current from quite far up. Gyodo is checking our hooks. Did you bring your bathing suit? It's okay if you didn't, no one's around."

Mokuzu climbed the wall. Ena helped him onto the top.

"I've my bathing suit underneath." She unbuttoned her suspenders and took off her skirt and white blouse. Nearby was her favorite wisteria basket with attached lid. When opened it exposed a soft white towel folded on top of lunch.

"Did your mother make lunch for you at this early hour?"

"They were still in her bed. I left a note. I took from last night's leftovers whatever I wanted. All today I'm going to be with you, if you don't mind."

"I don't mind. Is your father home?"

"No, the man from Kobe, you know, the first-engineer. He's at my house since two days ago, he's on some vacation."

"Hm!"

Mokuzu resisted the urge to relate his plan with Gyodo to visit their mother. 'It's a secret, and furthermore she'd be sad at the thought of her own mother.'

"Let's go. You can leave your basket. We'll come back for it later."

Mokuzu jumped in and saw Ena's figure momentarily cut the air as she followed, for his eyes a sight exceedingly clear and impressive. Her dark blue bathing suit hugged her slim torso, and her bare limbs were white and suffused with tenderness.

"Oh! It's so refreshing!"

They swam up the center of the river but could not hurry because of the flow, though it was gentle. When the sunlight came through the rising mist, the water freshly showed its fair depth as if restored to life. Where the bed was clay it appeared to rise more than it did, in a dreamy whitish blue. Where it was sand they could see sand running. Where many black rocks made a cave it looked very deep, with no sunlight there, and indeed the water was colder.

They fixed their eyes almost entirely on the water, and with nothing else in their field of vision the surface seemed to camber. They pretended they were submarines advancing by periscope on a great ocean. When they dipped their eyes, they could see tiny bubbles wreathing each other's feet, hands, and belly. Little fish in schools sometimes crossed by, and a kind of algae too came and flowed on down.

As they swam, the banks closed in. They could no longer see the plants bending from the shore, nor even define where they were swimming because of the thick mist. Where the banks became higher it would not clear till late morning.

"Mokuzu?" Ena, ahead, turned with suspenseful voice.

"Don't worry, I know all this area." Mokuzu drew almost close enough to touch her hand and foot with his.

"It must be near where I came in," he told her and called into the depths of the writhing white mist,

"Hooi! Gyodo! Did you catch any?"

Gyodo's voice arrived queerly low and distorted.

"Yuhh...there's fish...but they're all dead. Come here..."

Mokuzu and Ena hurried up to the narrow shore where the brothers had first entered. There were some deep shoals, which Mokuzu could barely touch with his toes even tipping up his chin. Gyodo's voice was queer not only because of the mist. With an expression of unease mixed with distaste, he was examining one by one nearly fifteen fish — eel, carp, catfish, and crucian — caught by hook. He lifted them carefully, looked them over, and sniffed.

"What's wrong?" Ena asked anxiously. She had reached from the water to grab a low branch of pussy willow.

Gyodo with head aslant kept turning each fish and looking in its mouth. Partly to explain to Ena, Mokuzu remarked,

"How strange. Any fish we catch in this way we never find dead. We put earthworms on the hooks and the fish bite during the night. They tire from trying to escape, but never die. When we come to take up the strings, they're still lively, especially eels and catfish. They whack the string with their elastic tails and sometimes break free."

"Not only that, they all died in the same odd way. Their bellies are white and rather puffy...and look, their eyes are ringed blood-red...," Gyodo added, and, as if half to Mokuzu, he said, "What should I do, throw them away?"

'Too bad!' Mokuzu thought. 'This many fish would please Grandma, Ran too would be cheered, even Dad would praise us...but Gyodo looks quite worried...I wish he'd decide for sure...what on earth is wrong?'

"What's that sound? Listen, it's going *иииии*..." Ena cocked her head like a hen and strained to look upriver, though the white darkness was everywhere.

"Oh!" spoke Gyodo and Mokuzu at once.

A steady noise was radiating from the vicinity of the bridge where the highway crossed the river. Far and barely audible, it would be thereabouts producing an earthshaking, house-rattling tremor.

It was even more indefinable and disquieting coming through the encompassing mist. Their attention was drawn to the distance, while actually they were regarding each other's eyes, eyelashes, nose, lips, and sensing as if with their ears each other's quickening heartbeat at point blank range... 'Should we scramble up this steep bank directly, or swim down as fast as we can and get out where it's easier?' Mokuzu hastily deliberated.

"Listen, someone's calling!" Ena again noticed first.

Against the continuous skirr widely deranging the earth and yet elusive like agglomerating clouds, there came the cry of a man, increasingly separating from the noise, nearing. A man was running atop the bank as if fleeing in their direction.

"Dad — it's him! He's calling us!" cried Gyodo.

'Something unusual must have happened. Is the village on fire? Ran harmed again? Ma dead?' Just when Mokuzu had imagined the worst and resigned himself to his fate, their father arrived above them. His figure was not visible on account of the tall eulalia, reeds, and entwining kudzu, but he was obviously short-winded and in hot haste.

"Oi, Gyodo! Mokuzu! Are you there? Quickly answer!"

"We're here!"

"Gyodo? And Mokuzu?"

"I'm here too!"

"Quick, come up! You'll die if you delay!"

Gyodo pulled Mokuzu and Ena from the water, grabbed his clothes, the creel, and the trident and hastened up the bank.

"A great many of them are spraying Folidol. Water-drinking peasants! What a reckless thing they're doing! Every insect and fish will die, even people — already some men died in a village hereabouts!

"Go home at once and wash thoroughly. Oh, Ena, were you down there too? Do you understand? Quickly come and wash. I'll run ahead and tell Grandma, and shut every storm door and whatever else, and alert Ran not to ramble outside.

"Sinners! Have they no brains? They're spraying sheer poison, far worse than war!"

This day too their father had gone out early to sickle a field near the bridge at the request of a farmer. The grass would be dried for cow fodder.

Doyu ran back along the bank and along the ridges of the rice fields toward Tangenji. His gait was horribly bandy-legged.

The anxiety-inducing noise revealed its origin. Columns of white smoke were spreading over the rice fields near the bridge and advancing by degrees with the sound of a large engine. Although a windless morning had been chosen, the smoke that hung over the fields was drifting toward a pine mountain and beginning to whiten the pines like snow. Staked where the smoke had already subsided were red pennants denoting danger.

"They were killed by poison — indeed!" Gyodo returned to the shore, threw the fish into the current and said, "Let's go home!"

"I left my basket with my clothes at the dam, on the other shore..."

"I'll get it. You both go now. Make sure you wash well." Gyodo raced along the grassy top of the bank.

Mokuzu and Ena hurried toward Tangenji, below the wall, up the steps, through the gate. Ena's bathing suit was a yet darker blue for being wet. As the water drained down it, it turned a little paler at her shoulders and back than it was at her loins and crotch.

Beside the well they drew the buckets to fill a tub, and, scooping with a washbowl, dashed water on themselves many times.

"It's so cold!" Ena's upper arms and thighs turned to gooseflesh, and she looked yet more slender.

"I can't wash you if you don't take off your bathing suit." Mokuzu waited until she was stark naked and dumped water on her as if in rebuke.

"Cover your ears!" he commanded and doused her hair. "Turn around!" He splashed water at her back. It splashed him too.

He brought a new towel from the bath room, scrubbed her back until it reddened, and said,

"Scrub yourself like that or you'll catch cold." Then he washed himself.

Ena put on her clothes, brought by Gyodo. The color returned to her cheeks. Her wet hair and clean skin had, to Mokuzu's eyes, an air of sobriety, though in the retreat cottage Ran attached herself to Ena, acting like a spoilt child on her knees as she sat erect. Ena was earnest even in dealing with five-year-old Ran and was very kind.

⅊

Throughout the ensuing days the solar radiation continued to be fiery. Cicadas appeared on every tree, whether of the garden, the mountain, or the windbreak along the rice fields. So intense was their stridulation that it seemed it would crack an iron pot or even the bronze bell in the gate.

In those several days innumerable fish big and small floated with swollen whitish bellies up in every channel along the length and breadth of the rice fields and in every irrigation pond here and there. Their carcasses, carrying swarms of green bottle flies, flowed irresolutely to the Sakura River with the water containing agricultural chemical, which left an uncanny luminous trail like slaver.

To exacerbate matters, a dry spell followed with incipient signs of drought. Between the clumps of rice stems the mud was cracked. In the channels only dirty water remained and very little of it, and the fish caught in the grass roots and plant debris began to rot.

Then around 3:00 on August 15, heavy drops of rain began to fall. Doyu had been off since morning paying a visit to a local Shingon-sect temple in a neighboring village. Gyodo was force-feeding chopped garlic to the chickens. Spent by the continuous heat, they were letting their pallid combs hang limp, panting with open beaks, and occasionally stretching wide their wings. Mokuzu with Ran was putting an old paper scrap on a sun-parched tile and igniting it by focusing the sun through a magnifying glass borrowed from their grandmother.

Raindrops fell on the tile and evaporated in an instant, yet their number increased in the twinkling of an eye. The sheer stretch of deep blue sky, tiresome to look at, was now a crazy mass of surging clouds accompanied by thunder, and the earth was swept with wind.

210

Gyodo and Mokuzu divided the work of closing the storm doors of the temple. They then shut themselves in the retreat cottage, but kept an opening from where they stuck out their heads to stare at the appalling wind and rain. The yulan in the front garden was losing its green leaves, and its top was bending so low as to seem possible to break. Flowers of althaea were being beaten down and carried away by the water, which was not penetrating the baked soil. The black pine in front of the main hall, said to be two hundred years old, and the red pines on the back mountain were the chief collaborators in the growl of the wind.

The rainwater flooding the garden made its way to the gate and gushed over the steps with the sound of a waterfall. Beyond the sasanqua hedge the sight of the far fields was drowned by the intense rain, but on the near side of the river the full-grown rice plants could be seen bowing in waves before the wind.

In the sky, darkened like evening, lighting burst and forked, throwing a momentary yellow on the world and illuminating the trunks of the *moso* bamboo in a lurid chartreuse.

The branches of the old persimmon knocked against the roof of the retreat cottage. The fruits, grown the size of walnuts, fell with every gust and struck the tiles, the storm doors, and the ground.

Ran feared the lightning and its thunderpeals rumbling among the clouds — they were too furious. Gyodo hung the tent of mosquito netting from the four corners of the room and put her inside it in deference to the folk saying that lightning never penetrates a hempen net.

The days had been bright until 7:30, but now at 4:00 it was as dark as after sundown. Needless to say, the electric bulb was out due to a power failure. Mokuzu imagined the sight of the utility pole struck by a bolt, scorched black, the wires cut and dangling into a green rice field.

"It'll mean chestnut failure again this year," Gyodo said without emotion. Mokuzu and Ran kept silent.

"After all we might have been better off opening a bakeshop...Before you were born, Ran, and not long after you, Mokuzu, a cold rain hit one day when Ma and I were out. It seemed she would sell no clothes that day either. She was plodding along with me on her back in addition to her great bundle, and at last she fell, no doubt exhausted body and soul. As usual she hadn't eaten and had been going from farmhouse to farmhouse, where always she was refused.

"Even now I remember what I thought: 'If she must fall, let it be at a drier and more convenient place.' I said I'd walk, and we went on, soaked and cold and hungry. I followed out of habit, at times sensing an unnameable comfort as if floating; maybe I was dozing. Repeatedly she said, as if delirious and without looking back, 'Gyodo, just get a bit older and together we'll open a bakeshop. We'll buy wheat flour, bake in the morning, and sell. We can eat whenever we're hungry...how great to taste bread hot from the oven, soft and full, the smell filling the room...' I was half dreaming as I answered — 'Hmm, great.' Soon after, she said it again, 'Gyodo, just get a bit older...if we keep a bakeshop we'll not go hungry...' And I said again, 'Hmm, great.' I didn't know what she meant. How sad she had to tell her dream over and over to a child."

The thunder and lightning was retreating. The wind also calmed. Yet the rain continued straight and steady with no sign of letting up. It seemed it would rain hard and the day would never again show any sunlight but be replaced by night.

After a long interval Mokuzu asked,

"Why didn't Ma and you open your bakeshop?"

"You were already born and Ma was inclined to ill health, and then Ran was born...and above all, Ena's mother began buying clothes, much more than she could use, from Ma. Nowadays she's falling into disfavor among adults, but actually she's not a bad person. For us she could be someone who saved our lives, though my saying so might be taken as an exaggeration."

Ran, apparently asleep with her head on Mokuzu's knee, suddenly said,

"When I grow up I want to be a mother like Ena."

Then silence occupied the room. Water continued to overflow the gutters, fashioned by their father from split bamboo, and from the garden it rushed through the gate and down the steps. The fields beyond the river were still obscured by a screen of hard rain as if over there nothing existed, no high-way, no far fields, no small mountains overlapping in every direction, no back range soaring to fortify the prefectural border. There was only the slightly opaque rain and clouds and mist.

But dark had settled and did not increase even as night approached; rather the dusk seemed lighter than usual.

'What is Ena doing? I remember the cliff behind her house with its water seeping out even on a fine day. Today it would be a waterfall. Couldn't it wash away her house? A rocky ditch led past her room to an artificial pond. Such a narrow ditch would overflow in no time.

'But she isn't alone, her mother couldn't be out...how forlorn she'd be even in her own house if alone! She comes here quite often to play. Why haven't I gone there since the one time I went along with Ma? She never invites me. Is there some reason, or is it just that way and I never thought about it till now? What if she wants to invite me but can't? — if so, what should I do?'

212

"Hey, Mokuzu, why don't you respond, eh? How many times must I address you? Are you a little dim-witted?"

"Nnn?"

"I have to tell you a matter of grave concern to you."

"Nnn?"

"Hey! Are you all right? From now on you can't show any unguarded moment. You have to be as vigilant as Musashi. Even while asleep you must know what's going on around you. I truly wonder, can you live amid strangers and not be deceived, can you always protect your body and soul, can you survive...? Mokuzu, tell me you'll never be defeated, that you'll love and not betray yourself, that you'll be a most faithful servant to protect yourself to the full extent of your dignity!"

"Uuu, well, I'll manage somehow or other. To do as I please might be hard at first if I don't know my opponent...I might even fall into a snare...but as time passes in this way or that, I'll begin to know what to do..."

"Hm, you're not quick — you have a cavalier character. Granted you'll be fine if you can accomplish whatever you hope without giving up on the way. But be careful. If at the start you take too much time, your energy or perseverance could be drained and you'll end up irresolute and reluctant all your life.

"Life is like swimming against a fast current. While you swim with normal power, you can't advance even though you're spending time and energy and you're lucky if you can stay where you are. Only if you swim with greater force than the current can you advance, that is, however little you advance, you're using abnormal energy with extraordinary will. Short of that you'll be carried downstream with the weeds sooner or later."

"But why go upstream with such great effort? I love to flow down; for me that's enjoyable."

"Idiot! It's a metaphor. You have to suppose you can't see what you want and can't get what you want while you're enjoyably being carried down, and soon enough you'll come to a fall and be crushed in the basin. Your battered body will serve only to feed the fish, your blood will stain the water, and meanwhile the waves will wretchedly foam. But no one will either cry or rejoice at the sight of you, and the stream will return to its original state and flow on as if nothing happened.

"How I wish I could stay by you till you secure your base! If only it were I; but there's Ran, and if I go, you can hardly take care of her. I happened to be the senior brother, and was prepared to look after you both till you could become independent. But I'm only in fifth grade, and I obviously haven't enough power and wisdom, to my unending regret...I can understand how to live here in Tangenji: gather firewood, catch and cook fish, tend the chickens and gardens, manage school life, and that's all. No single step forward is possible, that is, I'm incapable of earning money, which is the very reason you have to leave the radius of my protection!"

"Am I going somewhere?"

"Oh, yes, you're going to a temple called Ryotanji in Kyoto. Mokuzu, don't you know why today Dad is visiting Enmyoji, that Shingon temple in the next village? He has two purposes. One is to negotiate a job at a big temple on the island of Shodojima through the priest's introduction. The other is to consult with him about placing you in Ryotanji, also through his introduction."

"Dad's going away?"

"Yes, as I just said. At the earliest date, even tomorrow if it works out, because it's easier than laboring here for a former tenant and will insure him a definite income. After all, he's a priest and the former landowner of this entire neighborhood. Suffering from poverty that he couldn't help, and bearing the shame and backbreak of planting, harvesting, tilling, and manuring in fields once his own — he's been doing it for us, and for Ma in the hospital.

"But he never experienced such heavy labor, and since he's unequal to it, his asthma is becoming worse. You know, whenever you get near him you hear his bronchi whistling like reeds in the wind even when there's no fit.

"He said the combination of his asthma and the labor can't be helped, that there's no choice but to work till he drops dead. But the real problem is, he isn't paid. He gets just a few daikons or sweet potatoes, or a little rice or beans. He sighs and says, 'That peasant doesn't know the value of keeping his word.' In fact he worked for almost nothing all last year and half this year.

"The priest of Enmyoji, unable to remain a spectator, kindly approached with the proposal of work on Shodojima and the word that Ryotanji in Kyoto is looking for an acolyte.

"I don't know how sympathetic he is; he was asked to find someone for Shodojima and to find an acolyte for Ryotanji. But he must be kind enough. Dad says a priest of another sect is more understanding than a priest of the same sect."

"But, Gyodo, don't you question why that priest doesn't take the work on the island or put himself in that Kyoto temple?"

"Hm, you've a point, but it's mostly like casting a net repaired with wire — no good for real use. An acolyte is generally not an adult but a minor who lives in a temple to train to become a formal priest. The Enmyoji priest, as you must know, is already a fine priest. And he's worked on Shodojima a long time. Unlike Tangenji, Enmyoji was poor before the war and always was. He

214

never had income from tenant farmers or from laymen's contributions. So he works at this big temple on Shodojima and comes home only now and then."

"Will Dad be again hauling night soil and mowing?"

"No, that temple is magnificent. The priests alone number fifty or sixty and there are many visitors from all over Japan, sometimes eight hundred to a thousand a day. Dad's work will be to chant sutras for those visitors and to write them some memorial thing; it'll be more like priest's work."

"Oh, it will be much easier. Chanting and calligraphy are his favorite subjects. Then, where is Shodojima? If it's an island, it must be in the ocean, but you said Japan is everywhere a bunch of islands, so...?"

"Shodojima is an island of an island of an island, very far, farther than Kobe, which is on the far side of Osaka. You have to go west overland to Okayama Prefecture and cross a strait by ferry. It's deep and misty, the sea is rough. When you're really tired after being shaken for so many hours, suddenly you'll see floating on a wave a green island with yellow mandarin oranges. That's Shodojima. So I heard the Enmyoji priest tell Dad.

"But leave Dad aside for now. More important for you is that you have to go to be an acolyte in a temple in Kyoto. Why don't you have many questions about that? Aren't you feeling scared, or forlorn? Have you no misgivings? Or have you already settled into such a state as to reject thinking about anything that's too unfavorable for you?"

Gyodo brought his face near to Mokuzu's. The room was so dark that only the whites of their eyes were faintly discernible by implication.

Ran was fast asleep. 'Sleeping this early she'll awake at midnight and fuss. If Dad's in a good mood he'll play with her, lie on his back and raise her with his feet—"See? An airplane — fly, fly!" Otherwise he'll harshly order Gyodo, "Carry her around outside till she sleeps!" Tonight the rain is hard as if having lost the sense of how to stop. I wonder why.'

"Oi, Mokuzu, are you crying?" Gyodo felt with his thick hand for Mokuzu's knee.

"Why should I cry? For having to go to that temple? The twenty-four hours of each day will pass whether I'm here or there. It makes no difference to the task of having to spend the time somewhere, somehow. And above all, the one who has to go isn't you but me, right? I'll soon learn what sort of place it is, how things work, if it's good or bad, torture or delight...There's no point in asking you, who haven't experienced being there and aren't the one involved."

"Hmph! You're clear-cut about it, though I'm unsure whether it's owing to your deep or shallow thought at this important juncture...!

"Well, I guess you'll be fine like that, but one thing I have to tell you or it would be unfair to Dad. He has many bad points, but he has good points too. By and large, we can say about his present distress: As a man sows, so he shall reap. But listen, sending you off to be an acolyte isn't his real wish. He doesn't wish to send you away, nor wish you to be an acolyte or become a priest.

"To this day he's bearing a grudge against his father, is even contemptuous, because his father sent him so young to be an acolyte. By this alone you can sense Dad's inner torment.

"It's ironic: he had to be put out like that on account of his father's fame and wealth, and now he must do it to his own child for the reason that he is poor, incompetent, and unknown. So never bear him any grudge about it, see?"

"Oh, no, I love him and don't think he's bad at all, about this or anything else. Ma is sorrowful to have received his anger, but he is sorrowful for having to anger. It's not because of himself that a man can be right or wrong..."

"Oooii! I'm back!" There was the sound of clogs on the stone steps at the gate.

"What a horrible rain! It'll certainly cause the river to spill! Gyodo, Mokuzu, Ran — there's been no trouble? Look what I have for you, I was given some sweets!"

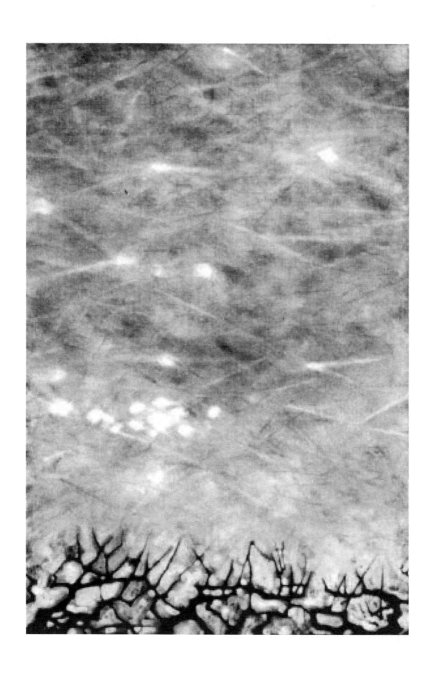

III

Whirling Snow

20

To Ryotanji

By effect of the heavy rain the bank of the Sakura River had in places collapsed. The wooden bridge where the Sasayama Highway crossed was washed out and many pyramidic granite blocks from the approach lay scattered on the riverbed. Some of the pilings under the middle of the bridge were raking downstream, their heads still attached only by years of association.

Where the river drew a grand arc from the bridge, the water in a seeming rapture of delight had broken forth across the fields of rice grown to a greenish yellow, carrying with it heaps of ashy white stones, gravel, and sand that dazzled in the sun. It had crossed a number of fields, and then, as if to say the banquet was over, had subsided, leaving them like a dry riverbed, where various water birds, crows, and sparrows, unexpectedly provided a feeding ground, were boisterously dancing.

At a projection of mountain skirt overgrown with red pines, the river was now repelled into a reverse arc. Beyond the bend could not be seen from the garden of Tangenji.

'It must be worse down at the dam,' thought Mokuzu as he looked over the tile-topped wall at the scene of the washout.

"Say, why don't we go down and take another look?" Ran pulled at his hand. Mokuzu idly regarded her round face, her thick, boyish eyebrows, her nose showing a fine perspiration though it was still early morning, her hair pressed on one side from sleep. Even above her hairline was deeply tanned.

It was three days since the flood, but no villagers had attempted to restore the fields. They seemed to be staying uncommonly withindoors, and the village was quiet.

"I'd like to, but soon I have to leave for Kyoto, you know. I was told to stick around. We're leaving right after Dad and the person in the guest room finish talking."

"How wonderful you get to go to Kyoto! Buy me a souvenir!"

"Sure, when I come back I'll bring you something."

"Promise!" Ran crooked her little finger around his and sang, "Linked fingers betoken the pledge. Be true, don't lie, or swallow a thousand pins!" But Mokuzu had no idea when he would return, if ever.

His father had looked at him intently the night before and the night before that too, and said, "I'm not giving you away. It's just that I'm compelled to consign you to Ryotanji for a spell; even so, with tears of blood. Don't

219

worry, as soon as our situation takes a turn for the better I'll fetch you, no matter what." With both hands he had grabbed Mokuzu's head and squeezed it so hard that Mokuzu felt it would be distorted.

The arrangement had been quite sudden. His father was going to Shodojima and he to Ryotanji, and both had to go promptly because there were many more priests wishing to work on Shodojima and many more needy children.

Gyodo appeared from the retreat cottage. "Look, Mokuzu, I'll give you this."

"What is it?"

"A notebook. I bound it tight with silk thread so you can use it a long time. There are more pages than you'd expect because it's good thin paper. See, a pencil is attached by string never to get lost, and the covers are made strong and waterproof by many applications of persimmon juice. Open it. You can draw whatever you like inside the cover."

"What am I to do with it?"

"Keep a diary. From today you are to be alone. Though there may be some enjoyable times, there will be many sad and bitter times, and also hateful incidents you can't tell anyone about. Then open your diary and write whatever you think."

"Hmm."

"It'll become the most important treasure next to your life. The more you keep it with care, the more valuable it will be."

Conspicuous and slightly forced laughter rose from the guest room. The shojis parted, and Doyu appeared on the veranda with his scrip slung from his neck and a fairly large cloth-wrapped bundle in his hand. As he stepped down to the front garden he spoke to Mokuzu,

"Shall we be off? Did you say farewell to Grandma?"

Still laughing, the Enmyoji priest came out after him.

Mokuzu entered the south room next to the main hall, on the side opposite the guest-room.

He never knew whether his grandmother was occupied at something; at any rate she sat all day on her bed, kept laid out almost year round. The covers were neatly folded at the foot. In a corner near her pillow was an ebony cupboard for tea utensils, its shelves kept always unchanged, again, year round. Although the season was summer, an iron kettle was set on a celadon porcelain hibachi.

"Grandma, well, I'm leaving."

"Ah, so? You are really going? Sit there. On this special day I shall offer you *matcha*." She must have been ready. With a tiny bamboo spoon she took up a measure of powdered green tea from a small lacquered container shaped like a jujube and put it into a deep, dark teabowl.

"With your father you visited your mother yesterday. What had she to say about your going to Ryotanji in Kyoto?"

Mokuzu remembered the sight of a circle of four or five nurses tossing a volleyball in the courtyard during their lunch hour. Their radiant white uniforms and gay cheers in the sunlight were widely different from the atmosphere of the dank, dreary corridor and the sickroom where his mother was bedridden. The contrast had given him an inexplicable sensation.

He recalled the boy he had met while wandering during his father's talk at his mother's bedside.

The corridor was suffused with the odor of antiseptic, to which visitors could never grow accustomed. The ceiling hung low, and set along a wall were dirty ashtray-stands and ottomans in a condition so close to junk that the springs showed. Illustrated posters were fastened high in a row, one to urge the prevention of contagious diseases, another to announce a strike for higher wages for the doctors, nurses, and other staff.

There was no human figure in sight. Then a long-haired, thin boy in black uniform appeared like a shadow, and, as if expecting Mokuzu, approached and asked with an open smile,

"Is your mother ill?" Mokuzu nodded slightly. "Mine too, very. Let's be friends," and he gave Mokuzu two large round toffees wrapped in cellophane.

Mokuzu had scarcely had sweets and was as overjoyed as he was abashed. He wanted to return outright to his mother to show her them, wanted to seize the earliest chance to be free of the boy. No doubt having nothing to say, the boy faced him in silence. Mokuzu turned back only to say, "Well, so long!"

His mother was drowsy, but when he told her about the toffees she was pleased for him and asked in a feeble voice,

"Did you thank him?" She must have been fatigued by his father's talk. He had left to confer with her physician and to settle costs in the executive office.

Reminded that he had indeed not expressed his thanks, Mokuzu quickly returned to where he had met the boy, but the corridor was dark and deserted and every sickroom door was shut tight.

On the way home he kept checking his pocket. In fact he never tasted the toffees but gave them to Ran and Gyodo.

"Said she nothing to you?" His grandmother pressed for an answer as she took in hand a smoked-bamboo whisk and whipped the powdered tea into boiling-hot water with unexpected speed for an old woman.

Mokuzu received the ample teabowl. The liquid in its depths suggested a lake tranquil and fragrant in deep mountains.

"She said nothing in particular," he replied without nuance and drained

221

the tea in a gulp. It was bitter. His lips and one cheek felt distorted and convulsively quivered. 'She held out her thin, startlingly white arm from the covers as we left and twisted her fingers on mine, but without strength, and I was unsure whether she was dozing or awake.'

"I see, she couldn't utter a word with a hundred things to speak of. Your grandfather used to say a full flask makes no sound. Yes, this world is full of souls with much feeling and no means of expression.

"Be that as it may, since antiquity in this land of Japan women however great were lower than the lowest of men. And great laymen too were lower then the most botched of priests. Nowadays many splendid women and many laymen superior to priests are surfacing. Don't misunderstand. Women and laymen aren't cultivating their wisdom and character — no, they are as ever the same creatures possessed of evil passions and idle complaints. It is only that men have deteriorated and so have priests.

"You luckily could grow up to your present age and must be able to understand that your life is lovable and at the same time that other lives are respectable, eh? You have to train yourself hard and live a worthy life. That is my entire wish for you.

"It's been many years since last I saw the Zen master of Ryotanji. I don't know what he is now. Yet he was raised at your age by your grandfather. You need not feel diffident; learn from him as much as you wish to be taught and ask him whatever you don't understand.

"Now go. And do not return wavering over trifles. You are not welcome until your father comes for you."

'Grandma must be thinking I'll become a priest. Isn't that odd? Dad said, "You shan't become a priest. Just meanwhile be an acolyte to survive our economic distress. It's the sole reason you're going. Temporarily disguising oneself in the priesthood is a necessary lie for the moment. Living a lifetime as a priest is a lifelong lie." Some years ago Ma also said, "No men are more rotten to the marrow than priests. Even thieves and black marketers are better." It was one rare subject they agreed on, albeit he was included in her comparison....

'I left without telling Ena. She hasn't come by recently, and I found no reason to go to tell her expressly. We must part because of an arrangement made by Dad, the Enmyoji priest, and the Ryotanji Zen master, and because of my home situation.

'For sure, it's I who am going, but not at my suggestion or decision or will, just as the clouds bring rain heedless of my wish. It's no act of my own making, so why advise her of it? It would be the same as to advise her of such trivia as my chancing to see a utility pole fall down or a dog running in a field.

'Even so, we can no longer hunt mushrooms or go fishing together. And fighting a bear with Gyodo this winter has become a fabrication. Picking raspberries, digging mountain potatoes...all are impossible to do ever again. But if I begin to think so, I have to think I also can't play house with Ran, or help Gyodo with the vegetables, or weave bamboo baskets — the list is endless. Even what I disliked to do will become what I want to do again.

'My favorite time was to sit quiet by the pond. Is it impossible to do again?...water dripping and occasionally stopping...the surface rings reflecting the maple leaves, the carp, crucian, and *dojo* abruptly stirring as if intent on carrying out some task....I could sit forever if not disturbed by others, and when I got bored by an uneventful stretch I could doze off....I can't take the pond to Kyoto, but can't I take my own time? It must be possible since I can take myself; at least I should be able to find moments when I can be as I like, however busy I'm forced to be. Yes, even if I lose all else, I'll not entirely lose my time to be myself. People can't so thoroughly enter my mind from start to finish!

'In the seat opposite is the Enmyoji priest, beside me is Dad, so close I feel his warmth. Beyond are people with faces and bodies inferior to beasts' and each is breathing, disturbing the air. None can keep me from thinking as I like. The Enmyoji priest and Dad scarcely talk, especially among people. It's a good thing. Speaking to draw others' attention should be done only when what is spoken is worth hearing; otherwise it amounts to senseless destruction of the enjoyment others might be having.

'That's one reason I didn't dare go and trouble Ena with the news of my leaving...If she wanted to hear, she'd have come....

'Gyodo made me a diary. He said an odd thing — "It will become the most important treasure next to your life. The more you keep it with care, the more valuable it will be." Doesn't that mean not to use it? If I use it, what for? Since I'd inevitably produce scribbles and cartoons it couldn't become valuable. If I treasure it unused it will stay snow-white. He said I'd better write miscellaneously in it. He must be confused.

'How ridiculous that it would become the most important treasure next to my life — "next to" is already unimportant! I can understand the importance of life; nothing can approach it in importance. Put next to my life, what is this silly diary?

'But Gyodo stayed up late to make it for me. He must have been happy over my report that Ma didn't seem to be dying.

'"Is it true? How do you know? Did she tell you? Did her doctor?" He was almost clutching my lapel. "No, she was mostly sleeping, and I never met him." He withdrew a fair distance and said, "After all, Dad was right: she has but a short time to live!" The corners of his eyes glinted with moisture, and he gazed at me spitefully. Then again he drew near and asked gently lest he scare me, "You said she didn't seem to be dying. Is it only your random guess?" "I meant I just felt so when I saw her. I bet Dad will go first." "What? Say how she was from beginning to end, from when you entered the hospital and don't skip a thing!"

'Gyodo is importunate. People say he's like a mosquito that's driven away again and again and yet returns to suck blood. Then, slap! it's killed. From what I say, how can he know? I just felt so and that's all. But since he plagued me with his asking, I did my best to explain.

'"She was quiet like illness itself, though I had no idea what illness. I mean, I saw no conflict; she and her illness were united, on the best of terms. But that's the very time they grow bored of each other, and the illness is the one that should leave, because it intruded. This I learned from my own experience. Whenever I had a nightmare from a fever, the fever and I were meanwhile at odds. But when it rose higher, I could no longer distinguish myself from it. Then before long it subsided...."

'Gyodo listened intently, turning pale then red, fearful then hopeful, if I dare interpret. At last he cried out, "You're the one entering the priesthood, if only briefly. Maybe you can intuit what a physician barely can. Ma will get well!" He raised his arms and spun about. Favoring his side, he passed his judgment. Isn't he simple-minded and a bit odd?

'It makes me feel sadder about him. From now on, day and night, the only ones living in Tangenji are he and Ran...and Grandma, who looks like an obstinate old woman but is a useless grain weevil living on the memory of our grandfather. Gyodo has to shoulder all responsibility for his and Ran's life. Dad was telling him, "I'll send you cash as soon as I have it." He's only in fifth grade; in his position how helpless I'd be!

'I'm getting no heavier a load than I can take, being only in second grade, or maybe it's that I worry no more than I can afford to and suffer no more than I can bear. I ignore what's beyond my ability. Gyodo worries more than he can afford to and suffers more than he can bear, and on top of that he takes responsibility for consequences.

'Miss Sakaki taught, "When you have the chance to go to a far place, don't be idle. Record the time you get on and off the bus or train, the stations, the fare, so you can insure your knowledge of the places you visit. Since old times, travel has been as important a study as reading."

'She teaches such things but scarcely practices them, whereas Gyodo

224

attempts to practice every teaching from his teachers and from illustrious people in old books. To be like him means not to have a moment's ease. If I follow Miss Sakaki's teaching or Gyodo's practice as I travel, I'll end up dizzy.

'I'm on this train, after riding a bus, and soon I must get off. Should I record it all? When I step down to the platform, I'll have no energy left to meet the master and senior disciples at the temple we're headed for.

'The route we take often enough we'll remember without effort. Who'll strain to remember their own name? It's human nature to remember what's important. Nothing's important that we can't remember naturally. Miss Sakaki is spreading a wrong teaching.

'"Try to remember whomever you meet — face, name, address." Gyodo is pitiful practicing such teaching. I don't know this Enmyoji priest's name or anything else about him, and he's been sitting in front of me for some time now.'

On the cliff above the curving tracks, many pines grew precariously as if about to fall. A covering of assorted trees and kudzu somewhat softened the appearance of the deep valley below. The river was swollen and muddy from the big rain of the previous days. It must have been a crazy torrent, but the aftermath was too far down to be seen and was often obscured by the wheels of the train. The far side, also steep and thicketed, showed the water had risen three to four meters higher than now. Many trees were down, and much lumber and rubbish was snagged.

When the train parted from the valley, the passengers could tell for the first time that the far shore was the base of a high mountain with a sharpness near to vertical. Similar peaks came in sight, giving a keen edge to the fathomless blue sky.

Just as a full view of mountains against sky appeared, the train entered a world of darkness. Soon again brightness brought a wide bend of slack water directly below, reflecting the cliff-side pines and maples. Passengers wishing to confirm the presence of such unusual beauty leaned over the sills, and again the train rushed into a tunnel. Next there were clouds and a circling kite above a pine peak. But the actuality of this scene too was denied as the train entered yet another tunnel, and yet another twelve or so.

'Someday I'll walk down there and if I get hot I can swim. I'd better carry lunch. Ena loves that sort of path....'

After the last tunnel the passengers prepared to get off. It was not yet the center of Kyoto but a suburb called Saga.

Mokuzu walked behind his father and the Enmyoji priest. They took a road into the most quiet residential area as if to avoid the crowded shopping area in front of the station. Almost every house had a hedge, making it impossible to see the garden except through the gate, where a nameplate was displayed.

Walking made them hot and sweaty; yet there was an occasional cooling breeze.

The road became an uphill dirt path, and the houses began to scatter among market gardens and bamboo. Soon they were in a dense forest of tall bamboos. The path was wet under the old fallen leaves. Crabs big as chestnuts, sensing the approach of feet, sashayed aside, their claws red in the pervasive shadows.

'I supposed I'd be going to Kyoto, but this is bamboo country. And there's no rice, only vegetables.' Mokuzu was slightly disappointed.

"The work of the local farmers is to grow vegetables and bamboo shoots and carry them to the Kyoto market." His father's comment was met with silence.

They crossed a tiny earth-covered bridge into sunny terraces of tea. The view opened out. Over the bamboo was the city of Kyoto with houses packed to the maximum in a basin resembling a lake bottom, surrounded by mountains.

"Reverend Tangenji, we should hurry so as to catch the train for Okayama. As soon as we meet the Zen master we must return...don't you agree?"

The Enmyoji priest ignored the view and often checked his wristwatch. He and Doyu had planned to start for Shodojima, where they both were going to serve, right after taking Mokuzu to Ryotanji.

Doyu's bundle of items for his use on the island must have been heavy; he shifted it from hand to hand, coughing two or three times, or five or six. His appearance reflected his sense of being obliged to perform an unwelcome act.

In fact he felt he was putting himself into a swarm of wasps flying in confusion at having their nest poked. No matter what or whom he thought of in every direction, he was overwhelmed by dark and painful feelings of pity. More, each depth of pity triggered a self-reproach and self-regret sharper than a wasp sting, for he realized his family's present misfortune was largely owing to him.

First he thought about his wife hospitalized, his young Gyodo and Ran left in Tangenji, and his old mother. Then he thought about Mokuzu, appearing to know nothing as he followed him to be left with a stranger. He thought about Bunyu and Kiku, their welfare, their circumstances at work. He thought about his acolyte days, his inheritance of Tangenji, his first wife, who sickened and died...; about his chestnuts, attacked during the war by a tiny black bee; the Buddhist Association, where his function was mostly to bury the war dead; the Farmland Reform....

226

'My life is like a snake scotched with inefficiency, indolence, irresolution, cowardice, and egotism — how unlike a crown of jewels and pearls! I've been skilled at painting and calligraphy, it's been my pleasure. But it's like saying I can cook a gourmet meal and enjoy its taste by myself. To live cleverly in this world, one needs to be both talented at what one does and keen on exchanging it for money like any famous artist or chef. What happened to the fish enjoying their quiet life? Hn! — killed by agricultural chemical!'

The path went north through the terraced tea bushes. After crossing a swell of mountain fold it turned west along a hollow where the tea was replaced by cedars and many sharp rocks lay coolly moist and mossy. As they advanced they could not see beyond the straight, close-spaced, ash brown trunks. Below too were only numerous trunks and dark green boughs.

The mountain path was quiet. Cuckoos flew from valley to valley, apparent by their call. A squirrel climbed a trunk and hid in a nest. Lizards darted in and out of bundled grass cleared from the path.

In a rocky cove a clean creek meandered. A smooth monolith was laid as a bridge. Here and there *mizo* ferns grew in the shade of the rocks, their leafstalks as tall as seventy centimeters and covered with beast-like brownish fur. Growing spindly under the cedars were aucuba, andromeda, star anise, camellia, *yatsude*, having a preference for shade. Despite the rocky slopes, many cedars of large girth were thriving and looked as if they would be undaunted even by a typhoon. The branches were sparse and high up, but the leaves lapping tree to tree overcast the sky, breaking it into a thousand fragments like scattered jewels.

Soon after the stone bridge, a graveled approach steeply ascended at right angles to the path, while the path went on into the depths of the mountains. Visible high up through the foliage was a tile roof, presumably of a temple building. The approach was stepped with old railroad ties. On either side a simple arrangement of stones formed a ditch. Beyond, the bamboo grass kumazasa with its striped leaves grew wild under the big cedars shooting up straight as ever but here attended by maples. The gate at the top was nothing like the splendid two-storied gate of Tangenji. It was humble, thatched with cypress bark, similar to the one in front of the Tangenji moss garden.

Inside was a plain dirt garden with some placed trees and bushes. Surrounded by the aspiring cedars, it was still wide enough to receive the sun, as if another world. When they stepped in beyond the gate they directly faced the central hall of the main building, wherein was the Buddhist sanctum.

From the right wing a roofed corridor led to the residential quarters. The veranda of the main building was wide and high off the ground, with stepping-stones provided for mounting it to approach the sanctum. What was grand, however, was the tile roof of the main building. The recently renewed tiles, glaring in the sun, curved elegantly from the high ridge to the low eaves.

Doyu and the Enmyoji priest paused at the center of the garden to bow to the sanctum, then turned right onto a path of stones that led to the entrance of the residential quarters. Mokuzu glimpsed a boy older and taller than himself in the corridor; he dodged behind a storm door receptacle or something else.

'He's smart, likely shrewd.' Mokuzu imitated in his mind Gyodo's way of speaking.

"Hello! Let us in, eh?"

Doyu tensed when he had to meet strangers, and disliking to see himself or be seen that way, he resorted to local speech.

"Yes," came a lucid reply, and a young, blue-pated priest hurried forward. He sat down straight-backed on the wood floor of the entrance and when told the purpose of the call invited them in directly.

'What an uncharming, vacant entrance hall! Does it look more so for having no ceiling to cover the big beams? Those at Tangenji are black with soot because the kitchen and the fuel hole of the bath were once inside the entrance hall. I could see pinpoints of light through the thick thatch, like stars. Without soot, it looks more hollow here.'

The entrance hall was entirely of wood darkened with age — floor, walls, sliding doors, and the passage to the interior. For years mopped with a wet cloth, the wood was damp and black everywhere and gleamed depressingly.

The young priest's neck looked long above his simple black robe with its collar and the collars of a white underkimono and a white kimono-undershirt aligned. He kept himself neat and clean. He was thin but looked sturdy, for his knuckles, the bridge of his nose, and around his eye sockets surfaced well. His eyebrows were dark. He looked diligent. While occupied with the two adults, he did not slight Mokuzu and regarded him openly with a gentle smile.

He pressed Mokuzu's shoulder lightly, encouraging him to advance, and they all went into the interior and turned left into a corridor facing an enclosed garden. The sun at its zenith poured in, lighting even the root areas of the azaleas, gardenias, and such bushes, and also the shojis along the inner side of the corridor. Here too was dominated by the stridor of cicadas.

The young priest knelt by a shoji. "Excuse me, Master, I have brought the reverend priest of Enmyoji, and the reverend priest of Tangenji and his son Mokuzu."

"Please come in." The voice was curt, low, and thick.

A refreshing scent floated in the air. The Zen master was formally seated before an alcove with a hanging scroll. He had a beaming smile. Mokuzu could not figure whether the darkness of his skin was congenital or due to the sun: his face and bald head were the color of dried persimmon. His little eyes and his teeth showed white. They were the eyes of a hawk, Mokuzu noted, and not smiling with the smile of his mouth.

After an exchange of greetings he firmly told Doyu,

"I shall receive your son into my care with all my conscience. As I said by letter, I fully understand your concern: I shall not induce him to enter the priesthood while he is yet unaware. Please come for him at any time, as soon as your situation allows. Until then I, Hanun, shall do my best to raise him in an exemplary manner with the intent of repaying even a fraction of your father's kindness to me."

"I am grateful to you. Should you care for my son, I shall be relieved of worry. Please grant him your favor, though he is still unformed and it is unknown whether he will become a man suited to the mountain or to the ocean," Doyu entreated, stroking himself on the head, and he lit his pipe.

The young priest brought a dish of steamed sweets and offered each guest a teabowl of matcha. At the sight of the dish set before him, Mokuzu thought he should serve himself and pass it on. Ignorant of tea ceremony etiquette, he took up a sweet with the accompanying cherry chopsticks, carried it to his mouth, and ate it with gusto. In fact it was delicious. The sweetness spread in his mouth, and he felt rather a kind of pain, with a surge of saliva.

The Enmyoji priest, on the other side of Mokuzu's father, bent forward with a strange sound, "*kyu! kyu!*" Thinking he was taken by sudden colic, Mokuzu reflexively stood to go and pat his back or offer some other aid. At that instant the Zen master bellowed with laughter, which released laughter like an opening floodgate from the Enmyoji priest. Doyu turned to Mokuzu,

"Ahey, you shouldn't eat with those. They're to serve your share onto this paper. You pass the dish before you eat." He smiled sadly and produced from his sleeve a folded white paper.

"Never have I heard of eating from the dish! It would amaze Old Rikyu or Imperial Advisor Hideyoshi. They'd have been entranced by such behavior. Come now, you have the makings of a great man!" said the Zen master, and again he laughed.

Mokuzu was both ashamed and angry. 'How can they be so tricky as to laugh at my ignorance of trivial manners known only to them?' He kept silent.

"Mokuzu, from tonight you have to live here, sleep and rise apart from your family. How do you feel? Lonely? Will you be able to manage, eh?" The master had assumed a serious look. Still thinking of his blunder, Mokuzu ventured,

"However hard and unfamiliar, the rules that may press me here are

229

nothing to me, as you just saw. Once they enter my mouth they're mine, and no one can do a thing about it."

Hearing this, Doyu and the Enmyoji priest feared that the master would think Mokuzu very ill-mannered, but he was speaking,

"Ohh — a wonderful boy! Why, like you, at age eight I was adopted, by your grandfather. I clung to my mother and refused to be parted, and we wept copiously. I dropped to the grassy path, and then, what did your grandfather do? 'Kaa!' he thundered. I felt skewered from top to toe. Ha ha ha! Well, how about school, do you like it?"

"I hate it."

"Ho! You hate school, ha-han, you're not doing well there, eh? Could you tell me why?"

"School persists in repeating the same thing when once is good enough... and above all, school teaches matters of no importance."

"Hmm, interesting. A sagacious boy. Well, what is important to you and what isn't? What do you wish to be taught?"

"I must find an infallible cure for my mother's illness, and an antidote to fighting, and a way to earn money, especially without committing myself to heavy labor."

"Indeed, those are matters even I have been wishing to know, and I own I haven't had much success....All right, I can't give you a direct answer about such things, but I'll help you to gain the basic ability essential to your learning them on your own, that is, I'll prepare you for your journey. You had better know that nothing can be attained in a day. Invest a good period to the cultivation of your character and you will gradually figure out what you must do to know what you want to know. Exercise your patience, and don't be discouraged when the going gets tough."

"Zen Master Hanun-kutsu, we must be excused, impolite as it is to leave in such haste. We beg your allowance, we are obliged to proceed to Shodojima...," timidly inserted the Enmyoji priest.

"Oh! Must you hurry so? I am sorry, I did not know. The fact is, I prepared a humble repast. I shall have it brought in at once." The master rang a bell. Promptly there came from the corridor the sound of footsteps.

"Kai, please bring lunch straightaway; our guests have little time."

"Certainly, Master." It was the young priest's voice outside the shoji. No sooner had he withdrawn than he returned, this time accompanied by other steps.

'It must be that boy who hid, helping to carry,' Mokuzu guessed. But the boy did not enter. The young priest called Kai set a tray before each of them.

The trays were vermilion-lacquered, with little cat feet. Each held vermilion-lacquered dishes and bowls with matching tops, a set of five. A cup of everyday tea and a pot-steamed stew were also served. The rice, cooked rather hard, contained halved, jade green ginkgo nuts. The soup was clear, with a yellow curl of *yuba* and a green trefoil of honewort floating. The side dishes were a bowl of cooked squash, eggplant, and butterbur stems, a dish of fried konjak seasoned sweet and peppery, and a dish of vinegared fine-sliced cucumber and highly ramified seaweed. Melon cut like a thin moon was served afterward.

The Enmyoji priest and Mokuzu's father then immediately took their leave. Under the bark roof of the gate, Zen Master Hanun-kutsu and the young priest Kai stood flanking Mokuzu to send them off as they went down the graveled approach.

On the way from the entrance of the residential quarters, Mokuzu's father had seized a last moment to be alone as father and son, and quickly he whispered,

"Don't forget the proverb, Moderation is essential to good health. To all things it can be applied, even to good deeds. What you should care about most is your health, okay?"

As the Enmyoji priest and Doyu carefully descended with their bundles, the Zen master told Mokuzu,

"It is meet to join your palms at such times."

Mokuzu did as he was told; in imitation of the master and the young priest he brought his hands up to the level of his breast. He felt shy sending his father off thus, as if worshiping a divinity, but he came to realize that his father was truly caring about his survival in this new environment.

'His care is in no way inferior to the compassion of Buddha. It is worthy of veneration, like an endless thread of gold,' he thought, and even after the figures had turned right at the bottom of the approach and disappeared into the umbrage of the tall cedars, the thread of gold remained.

All sorts of his father's good deeds came to mind. 'On his back I felt his warmth and him breathing...he made a bonfire on mornings when my fingers and toes were numb...he hung a watermelon in the well on sweltering afternoons....' The gold thread was expanding, radiating an increasing light, filling his mind. He sensed himself drifting in light and warmth.

"Come now, that will do. Kai, would you show Mokuzu his room, introduce him to Reiho and Luri, and teach him well the matters of this temple. Be kind; please think of him as your own child or brother."

"Yes, Master. Come with me, Mokuzu. Are you tired?"

"Not tired, but I feel I'm on a vagabond voyage."

"'A vagabond voyage'? You impress me, knowing such a difficult phrase.

Oh, you had the strong tea...or maybe it's the most reasonable way for you to feel while in fact your life is so. Indeed, it is so for us all." The young priest passed his fingers over his thin, bluish cheeks, fresh from shaving, and gave a wan smile.

'Why are his eyes so clear? They've even a cyanic tint...while the master's are lupine, sharp, and red about the pupils.'

21

An Inconclusive Appraisal

Mokuzu rarely spoke other than to answer when spoken to. With his brother, sister, and Ena he had been voluble, and often he had exaggerated to make them laugh. But after entering Ryotanji he was reticent at both the temple and his new school.

Even when accosted he spared his words and yielded only a minimum point.

"You don't look stupid, so what's up? Talk should be like Ping-Pong. With no fair exchange it's no fun," said Reiho. It was a fine October afternoon, and they were sitting on the veranda of the main building.

"Right."

Mokuzu did not refute him, but made no further comment. He was regarding the dense ginkgo leaves, which seemed more yellow in the western sun. 'Why do they drop before they're perfectly yellow? If I continue to look, I feel I'm lying on a hillside with heat waves rising off the grass....'

"Come, this is another example! Is 'right' all you can say? Add something — agreement, argument, whatever. To be human means to have feelings and be inspired by things. Luri was joking but concerned when she said you're homesick and wary of being harmed by the unfamiliar dispositions of the people in your new surroundings. Is that why you're shutting up like a turtle?

"It's been a month, enough time to forget your old place and get used to this one. You're clever at cooking, cleaning, and studying, so no one's complaining there, in fact we're pleased because the chores are more spread around. But we want you to be more open. We're not faulting your conduct, only we're anxious about your mind.

"We've gotta be buddies and help each other more than ordinary; it's what Zen Master Hanun is telling us. We're all parted from our native homes. Senior Unkai doesn't know where his family is, probably burnt up in an air raid, he says. Luri's abandoned her. My pa died in the town of Hiroshima with his shadow left on a stone, my ma, she died in the mountains. You have family, but you're separated. So we should never quarrel and must combine our strength to survive — which means, you've gotta open up and be frank! Right?"

"Hn! Right."

"What? You're laughing up your nose!"

"It's nothing, I perfectly agree."

"Then why the laugh? It seemed scornful...or you're scorning yourself?"

"No, I was thinking of what you said, that is, about having feelings and being inspired by things—"

"What's funny about that?"

"Imagine me expressing my feelings from morning to night like a torrent or like leaves being carried by the wind, and suppose I can't stop and no one else can stop me, ha ha ha!"

"What a weird idea! Well, they say every genius is a bit cracked, and maybe the you that you describe and the you we see are one and the same kid."

Disgusted, Reiho shook his head. Younger than himself, Mokuzu showed no particular reaction to his view that they be open and affectionate; he showed only an odd imagination. Yet to have extracted something was some relief.

Reiho, in the first year of junior high school, was big for his age, with a tough constitution. His hair was close-cut like Mokuzu's, but not as dark. His large, square brow made his nose look yet more squat. He was swarthy. His cheeks were thick, his jaw, solid. No doubt his molars were large and strong, yet his voice was oddly thin and keen, even clear. Though stocky of chest and limb, overall he appeared to have been struck from above by a maul, for his head and shoulders looked depressed with no chance of straightening up.

From the first he had been kind, pleased to offer protection to the weak- and ignorant-looking newcomer. All the same, he was not necessarily kindhearted, in fact, he looked disposed to be hostile.

With a triumphant air he delighted in guiding Mokuzu, who fixed curious eyes on each strange item and sight, such as the room they shared, Luri's room, Unkai's, the kitchen, the common room, the Zen master's quarters, the guest rooms, the main building, storage barn, well, belfry, gardens, and path to the back mountain.

Quick to sense another's mind, Mokuzu thought, 'He'll keep his humor as long as I appear eager to correct my ignorance. If I show stupidity and weakness, he'll be kind. Well, that's fine for now but will turn unpleasant if I have to go on with it much longer. As soon as I start to show my deep-rooted strength and indifference to the things he so cares about, he'll change his tune. I wonder how I can prevent such a development.'

"At any rate, you've gotta be frank. It's inconvenient if we can't understand what the deuce you're feeling, what you like and dislike. You get it?"

"...."

"Hey! — you don't get it?"

"No, I don't. Why is it inconvenient?"

"Eh? It's not obvious? I just said we all must be buddies and if we don't understand your mind we can't help you. This is a temple, we can't eat meat. But last night Unkai and Luri bought and prepared chicken to cheer you up. They worry seeing your quietness and lack of spirit. And we had sushi delivered from a shop, and there were cream puffs and pears — we scarcely ever have such extravagances.

"You acted like you had a bellyache. You didn't relish any of it! Luri asked, but you said nothing was wrong. Unkai said you needn't be modest and urged you to eat up so you'll not become an invalid like him. You said you weren't being modest. I asked if you hate that food and you said no, you aren't fussy about food. Still, you hardly touched a thing. Then you stood up and said 'I'm going to bed.'

"After you left, we were uncomfortable as if bewitched by a fox. We felt blamed for something. So to me, at least, say why you're like that. Don't worry, if you want it kept a secret, I can keep secrets."

Mokuzu was starting to detest Reiho for trying to ferret out what he supposed was another's secret. 'His face and his concern don't match; such a face isn't fitted for a sensitive response, or is fitted for just the one sensitive issue of garnering secrets. I have no secret, but he would make a secret out of nothing — what a trickster!

'Gyodo once told me, "Some things we should express, some things we shouldn't." I saw his and Ran's faces brightened by such a feast, and was reminded of Ma and her insipid hospital food, and of Dad picking at a bit of salted salmon head, chopsticks held in fingers swollen and raw from farming... and of the figure of Grandma shutting herself in a corner year round. I imagined them all harmoniously gathered at such a table, imagined them each like turning lantern silhouettes. When I came back to myself the food seemed made of wax.

'This sort of thing is private, an example of what Gyodo says we shouldn't express. Or wait, I must tell him to perfect his saying. Even if it's something possible to express, the one to hear it should be a suitable person.'

Reiho, growing more nettled on account of Mokuzu, leapt from the veranda, shot out his fists, and vigorously kicked the air high in front of him. He was studying karate.

He then sat down so close to Mokuzu that their shoulders met. Looking him in the eye, he grinned meaningfully. 'What was that? Does he think three enemies have just breathed their last? True, if it were me, I'd be flattened with my guts scrambled, unable to get up from the dust.

'Was that to demonstrate what he said the other day? "No one dare oppose me. Only force can suppress a guy without ears. Mokuzu, tell me if anyone's hazing you and I'll fix him!"...'

"C'mon, we don't need two Unkai's!"

"What's wrong with being like Senior Unkai?"

"Phew! You ask the obvious with so innocent a look! Can't you see he sits meditating whenever he gets a chance, which is practically all the time? He doesn't go out like Zen Master Hanun to earn for our life, or attend school like us others. You and I clean the temple. Luri shops and cooks. What does he do? Just answers the door, though guests are rare.

"He contributes nothing to the life of this temple, yet he makes no plans for his future despite the fact that he's sickly. And can you guess his age? Close to thirty! Of course unmarried. Is it out of a noble spirit and admirable talent that he observes the Buddhist precept against meat and matrimony? No, unlike our master, he doesn't care about the precepts and is secretly wishing to marry. Mokuzu, he's a typical hanger-on, a pile of chaff. You wanna be like him? By his age we'll be powerful men worth reckoning with, because we'll have been living an energetic life!"

"What's wrong with his devotion to sitting meditation? My Dad so esteemed it as to mourn his own state, saying, 'After coming from India to China, First Zen Patriarch Bodhidharma steadily practiced sitting meditation for nine years as he faced a rock wall at Mt. Shaulin, whence he lost the ability to move about. The highest life for a Zen priest is one of complete devotion to the practice of sitting meditation, though I myself hate to practice it. If only I could spend my days painting, there'd be no higher satisfaction for me. But over the years I've grown poor, and now I'm not allowed even that!'"

"Your pa obviously meant the real thing. There's all sorts, ya know. Unkai's isn't worth counting, it's better called a catnap or indolence, quite unlike what our master tells us. He says, 'A Buddhist trainee needs dynamic energy and unwavering spirit. Fix your eyes like the eyes of Acala, maintain the spirit of a Deva king, eradicate your evil passions, and desist from sin. Train day and night, train, train, and become victor over all!'[1]

"Unkai's heard it a zillion times but never practices it. He's like those females you see in old ukiyo-e prints!"

"Reiho, they're the words of Suzuki Shosan, a Zen priest of the early Edo period. I heard my brother reading them."

"Don't be silly, they're Zen Master Hanun's own words, drummed into me so often I can't forget. But never mind. The point is, you've got to realize Unkai is only wasting his time as he wastes our rice supply. Even Luri says he's so like a shadow she's uneasy whenever he approaches. She says if you don't watch out, Mokuzu, you'll turn into a second generation of him, unless of course you become stronger and clearer about things."

"But Reiho, isn't Senior Unkai really ill? Didn't you say he has some liver problem?"

"There's that. He almost died up at Shoshinji Monastery in Gifu. Our master took me once when he went to visit, and there he was, quite a disaster. He brought him here to recover. He saved his life. That was six years ago, but Unkai remains a failure, a bad sample of a man, and that's it, see?"

"You must make allowances, Reiho. Surely there's a suitable way for him to train while he's sick...."

Mokuzu regarded Unkai as clean and tender. He had neither the coldness of winter nor the heat of summer nor the brightness of spring. He had the longed-for warmth of an Indian summer.

He took Mokuzu shopping for a new coat, underwear, cap, shoes, and school supplies soon after Mokuzu entered Ryotanji. He was pleased to do what was necessary to enter him into his new school. During the shopping he bought him ice cream, but none for himself, and showed him to a park bench.

With a stygian look Reiho fell silent. Mokuzu went on,

"Senior Unkai does what we don't. He rises at four and chants in the main building, and chants in the evening too."

"...."

"In a temple, the most important thing is to meditate and chant and —"

"Shsssh! Shut up! Didn't you hear a noise?...a scream!...It's Luri! Come!"

Like a wild animal Reiho pelted along the veranda to fetch clogs from the entrance, then cut across the garden to the gate, kicking and scattering the gravel. Mokuzu hastily put on his shoes and followed.

As they tumbled out the gate, the sound of a motorbike reached their ears from the grassy depths of the narrow path below Ryotanji. To climb the steep slope by motorbike as far as the approach to Ryotanji was risky enough, and thoughtless; to advance beyond was even more so.

The path there was overgrown with cogon grass. Tiger sticks and lacquer

236

trees pressed in from the sides, entangled with vines of wild yam and grape, all their leaves turning the color of autumn. Reiho pushed through without hesitation. Mokuzu, ignoring the backlash, closely followed.

They found a bike set against the grassy slope with its engine running. Its shiny blackness and chrome threw back the candor of newness. The fuel tank was a glossy oval the color of vibrant magenta.

They thought they sighted Luri in her navy blue school uniform, flailing her limbs while being held aloft by a man, capless, with longish hair, presumably a student. But they neither of them were sure of what they saw, for they were losing themselves in running, their attention was diverted by the bike, their glimpse was disturbed by the vegetation grown thicker past the bike, and the act was finishing, not beginning.

Since no meaningful judgment could be formed from such precarious recognition alone, they had to exercise their imagination and their conjecture.

Truly they had seen one of his arms supporting her neck or back, the other between her legs, disarraying them up and down, her skirt hiked high, the depths of her thighs and her white underwear showing.

He had sunk under her weight into the grass with a thud, though the actual sound was made inaudible by the engine noise.

Reiho lunged in an arc, grabbed the man's collarbone or shoulder from behind, dragged him, turned him about, and struck him square above the ear.

Mokuzu were he a beast would have surely joined in and torn at and preyed on the man, who, struck and pulled from Luri, lay writhing and groaning in the grass. But Mokuzu only stood there observing.

Elbows on the ground, Luri was looking up without hurrying to stand. Reiho stood by with his eye on the man. Her eyes were wide, her cheeks flushed. Mokuzu saw the dark cavity of her mouth. Her lips were red but dry. He sensed she was astonished at the appearance and violence of Reiho rather than relieved.

The man shook his head, passed his hand over his temple, and tried to stand. Reiho lightly kicked him in the ribs and again he fell over. His face was slim, not boorish, his features clean-cut. He did not appear to be a treacherous bully. Mokuzu thought Reiho, excited and panting, was the more barbarous.

"Luri, are you hurt?" Reiho extended his hand.

"Of course not!" Luri stood up resolutely, tidied her collar and hem, brushed off the dried grass, and looked about. Reiho found and retrieved her reddish brown leather school bag and left right behind her. Mokuzu followed.

As they passed the noisy bike, Reiho kicked the tank — possibly describable as its belly. Luri turned back with a look of disdain for Reiho and shot a glance of concern toward the man in the grass.

Climbing the railway ties, Reiho discharged his words,

"Never fear, Luri, I can drive 'em away in a flash, no matter how many come up. If that one ever reappears, I'll finish him!" And proudly to Mokuzu he said,

"Did you note my capacity? You'd better learn karate. Even if you have a great conscience, you can't practice justice if your body is weak. You meet a case like this, you need confidence. Otherwise you can only look on with tears of vexation and be lucky if you aren't sliced through by the backlash of the enemy's sword, as the saying goes."

Luri went ahead without a word of thanks. So Mokuzu merely responded, "Hmm...."

From the gate they could see Unkai on the veranda looking their way with a lit stick of incense in his hand. He cast no shadow; the veranda and most of the graveled garden was already shaded by the trees and the main building.

Luri stopped sharply and regarded Reiho and Mokuzu.

"You aren't to tell! Give me your word!"

Reiho flinched and said, "I won't, it would be useless."

Mokuzu felt uncomfortable before so imperious a demand. Yet he sensed he would be abused if he asked her why, especially as it would be considered rare coming from him. So again he responded with "Hmm..."

Luri gave him a playful smile, which he could not fathom.

Partial sunlight still remained on the stone path to the residential quarters.

"Welcome home," Unkai addressed them. He called Mokuzu and quietly asked, "Shall we chant the evening sutras?"

Mokuzu silently followed Unkai into the main building and sat before the right corner of the sanctum. Unkai stood the long stick of incense in the censer at the very front of the sanctum, joined his palms, bowed deep, turned, and went back to the center of the hall, where a thin mat was placed on the tatami. There he knelt facing the sanctum and put his forehead and forearms to the mat. In that posture he raised his palms to the level of his ears in an attitude of receiving the feet of Buddha, then lowered them and stood. He went through this extravagant form of worship three times before going to sit at a small vermilion-lacquered desk that held sutra books, on the right side of the hall.

He struck the big bell set in a stand to the right of the desk three times and commenced to chant. At the beginning of each sutra he continuously struck the small bell on the desk. At the end of each sutra he struck it three times. Now and then in the course of chanting, he struck one bell or the other as he mincingly beat the large, roundish slit drum, also vermilion-lacquered, with a carved design of a monster fish, producing from it a monotonous rhythm.

As Mokuzu steeped himself in the consonant sounds so like an endlessly repeating wave, he recalled his father's chanting.

His father scarcely chanted in the evening; at that hour he was still working in the garden or up in the mountain. In the early morning he always chanted, but Mokuzu never attended. Often he was awakened by the big bell, and often he fell asleep again to the sound of the languid beat of the drum faintly transmitted to the retreat cottage from the main building.

But when he was up early preparing in the front garden to go fishing with Gyodo, he could clearly hear his father's rotund voice blending with the echoes of the bell. Depending on where he stood, he could hear better from afar, and could physically sense the waves pulsing through the air.

'What were his feelings then?' Properly seated, immersed in Unkai's chanting, Mokuzu continued to think,

'Chanting after a quarrel with Ma, or before...or while worrying about our food, or hearing our cries....Unkai couldn't be chanting with the same mind; each person is surely different.'

Unkai chanted on. He finished one sutra and began another. The hall had been darker within than without, but now the dark was equalizing. In the moment when the incense dropped its ash, the tip appeared as a red point, evidence that it was still burning.

'How's Ran? Has Gyodo made her supper yet? Is she still using the bowl with the kitten design? She'd be mortified if by mischance she broke it...large hot tears, a pause, then increasingly audible sobs....Gyodo is senior to me but poorer at cooking rice. Without peeking, he can't tell if the water is rapidly decreasing and the rice at the bottom becoming scorched. Unfortunately, each time he lifts the lid the rice loses some taste and he can't expect the perfect rise of each grain. And he can't tell if the soup is right without tasting it....I can tell by the steam and by the heat of the fire, or just by the scent....So when he cooks rice he has to risk his life. He gets short-winded and furious as if grappling with a bull. I bet I'll never see anyone more serious about cooking rice. His manner is laughable, absurd, yet now I feel only sad. Once, before Ma left — he was in first grade or so, at least a year younger than I am now — he kept up the fire and the smell of scorched rice came even to the retreat cottage. I dashed out to find him still feeding the fire. In a flush of anger Dad came pounding from the main building and struck him to the ground without a word....That was all, about the rice. It was burnt black as charcoal, yet it smelled so sweet. That day we hadn't anything to eat. Ma didn't scold him, nor did Dad after striking him. How is she at this time of day?...

'Hearing the sutras I recall various things. Unkai is reciting from memory — it's pitch-dark in here. He's great to have learned them all. Reiho says he's a failure, a bad sample of a man, but it's not true. Reiho is a roughneck. He's needlessly violent and proud of it.

'What is our sister Luri thinking? She's in the third year of a girls' junior high. She dislikes study but says she likes school. How odd...what else is there at school besides study? Well, there's recess. For that is she merrily going?

'She can cook, but it all looks attractive without any taste, or all tastes the same. She said she came here when she was in fourth grade. I was told her parents vanished in the night.

'Her exposed thighs...Ena in a bathing suit — I was reminded of Ena. There must be a likeness, though face, figure, and age are unalike....memories of playing with Ena and thoughts of the play we couldn't do arise in my mind and heart....'

22

Zen Master Hanun's Kindness

Zen Master Hanun was away, often for three or four days, sometimes for a week, and when he returned he promptly went out again.

Having no interest in the master's comportment, Mokuzu naturally did not wonder where he went, no more than he wondered where the *yuzuriha* tree by the well came from and when.

But one day on their return from karate practice, Reiho spontaneously raised and answered a question that slightly stirred Mokuzu's interest.

"You know where he goes and for what? I'll tell you. He's buzzing like a worker bee all over Japan, as far north as Sendai and Hokkaido, not to mention Nagoya and Tokyo, and as far south as Yamaguchi and Kyushu, including of course Osaka.

"That's how he was when we first met or he wouldn't have found me, and who knows what I'd be doing. I might've starved to death or been put in an orphanage...After I became his kid I trailed along like his shadow until he came here. Ryotanji was vacant, you know, and so run-down even a raccoon dog wouldn't think to move in. So I know most of the big cities and remote villages of Japan, despite what you may think, ahem! And I can tell what he's doing even now."

Mokuzu did not doubt Reiho's ability to guess the master's doings, for he too had been able to guess what his mother did, though the occasions given him to go out with her were few.

"Did you ever not have lunch?"

"You think Zen Master Hanun-kutsu is so incapable? It's not to my credit, but from the first I never went hungry."

Mokuzu took "incapable" as a brand on his mother's sorrow. Often she gained no money however hard she peddled, and taking no lunch had been her regular practice. Feeling an unbounded sympathy and pity for her, he thought,

'Reiho and Zen Master Hanun might be cruel owing to their very health and capability...I mean, they might have no such intent, but it could be their nature....'

"Even on the day of the A-bomb we ate a bellyful. Yeah, he's quick to judge and act! My pa was out delivering an order of charcoal to the town of Hiroshima. Our charcoal lodge was up in the Fuchu mountains, seven or eight kilometers away."

"Did the bomb also cause your ma to die?"

"Hey, it was horrendous, but do you think it could reach that far? She'd been sick a long time. He left before dawn after saying in her ear, 'I'll be back with a watermelon, so be patient.' We had a stream to cool it in. She wanted it but maybe by then couldn't understand. At sunup she was probably already dead — it was so quiet in the dark of the lodge when I came in with water from the stream. She was in back on a pile of straw we put there when her body began to fester and she was no longer continent. Fleas and mosquitoes and lice were all over her and swarming in the straw. And the flies! — they increased with the day and returned however hard I fanned.

"I didn't know if she was dead or alive, but I fanned her. I did every day, it was my work.

"Then suddenly the lodge got very dark. I turned and saw a figure filling the doorway.

241

"'Oi, give me water.' I ladled a cup and took it there. He had a shaved head, a black robe, white leggings and sleevelets, a full-packed scrip with a folded rain cape tied on, and in one hand a big bamboo hat and in the other a priest's staff. Yeah, he was a wayfaring priest. Well, at the time I paid such details no mind but only thought 'What an oddity came up! I didn't know any samurai still survived.'"

"It was Zen Master Hanun?"

"Yeah. He looked into the dark. 'Someone's ailing?' I nodded. He strode in without taking off his straw sandals. 'Kid, the place stinks. Maybe you're used to it. An execution ground couldn't smell worse.' He bent to her pillow. 'Kid, you amaze me. Is this your ma? She's long since dead. Don't you know the dead from the living? — how old are you?' I said I was five. 'Hmm! Is that the level of understanding for your age? Where's your pa?' I explained he went to town with charcoal. At that he said, 'Kid, cry if you want, quick, cry, cry!' and he went out. And as he did, he saw the flash and soon after heard the detonation. I heard it too.

"He called me to come out. I went out and saw a cloud higher than the tallest pine, rising, expanding moment by moment. The pine before our eyes and the other trees on the mountain at once got a sudden wind and rustled as if uneasy.

"His eyes were fierce, his face was stern. Without budging he was gazing at the mushroom cloud and figuring the center of the blast and the direction the cloud was moving. He stood there at length. Then he asked, 'Your father's in town? You know what quarter?'

"I said I didn't know, but that yesterday he told my ma an Otemachi tea master needed a quick delivery of quality charcoal.

"'Otemachi? Oi, kid, your father too is this instant dead. Well, well, it's becoming a strange age!...Hmm, do as I say without questions. I am a Zen priest and I will show you the mysteries of Zen. I have no choice but to adopt you. From this moment you are my son. Remember, just past eight on the morning of August sixth.'

"That was that, so I obeyed.

"He reentered the lodge and washed up my ma and wrapped her in some kimonos he found in a corner, did it all with dispatch. Then he surveyed the place to check the suitability of a fire.

"In the right wing were logs of chinquapin stacked up and a supply of firewood. He brought it all to the center and set up a scaffold. He added more logs and laid pine and brushwood around. Then he put her on it.

"Out back we had a clay kiln my father built, shaped like a tortoise and lined with brick. As always chinquapin logs were stuck in the holes and the furnace below was burning red. A faint smoke was coming from the chimney.

242

"'Now we'll ignite it.' He reached me a log with the end burning bright, and we went in and cast them at the pyre.

"That dry wood flamed right up. He shouted something I don't understand even now — 'A true man dependent on nothing is born of this fire! *Ka!*' And then, 'Hey, kid! Why don't you quickly come out? Or would you like me to throw you in too?' He meant it. I went out, and he pulled me free of the place. Soon a great flame shot from the thatch.

"'Follow me!' he said and took a path northeast. Finally we were going to reach a railway station called Seno, but that's not my point. In sum, I'll say he's quick to decide and act. Of course I was well fed even that day."

Hearing this of his childhood, Mokuzu was impressed, for he saw it to be the source of Reiho's tough character, entirely the opposite of maudlin. He also felt a touch of envy.

'If my family were dead I'd have no cause to regard their feelings and my world could be wider and I could act more freely. Whatever I do — view the moon, drink tea, take a bath — they float in the back of my head and follow me about. So I must say I've never done anything with all my might and as much as I wished.

'It could be love of family that makes a man worry, shrink, become tiny-minded. Now I remember Gyodo's saying that the worst thing a priest can do is to eat meat and to marry. Indeed since old times a real priest left his family, and "to depart from family" meant only to become a priest....'

"My talk's too grim? You shut up like a clam. Come now, compared to the victims who survived it's nothing. Someday I'll tell you about them, but for now just imagine. At the instant of explosion the air at the center heats higher than a million degrees centigrade. After a millionth of a second it drops to about 300 thousand degrees, and the wind pressure increases to 3.5 kilograms per square centimeter, and the wind velocity to as much as 440 meters per second. Anyhow, these figures must be beyond your grasp. Next time I'm crazily bored I'll treat you to some more!"

"The atom bomb doesn't impress me so much, Reiho. You boast of its power, but it's not your power."

"Hey, you're harsh for one who acts like a lamb of a boy!"

"Never mind, tell me why he goes out day after day. Wasn't that what you started to say?"

"Yeah, well, it's self-evident — just to get money to fix the temple and maintain our life. We depend on his going out. You should know that thanks to him our sickly Unkai can live like a ghost, our sister Luri can live as she likes, and we can attend school and karate without suffering any inconvenience."

"You mean a priest can make money? I thought that was the domain of merchants."

"Whew, you've a poor grasp of the world. You're like an inequilateral polygon."

"What do you mean?"

"Some sides project, others are underdeveloped. You're sharp and superior about some things, but incredibly immature about others, and you lack common sense."

They advanced through the terraced tea and entered the deep green forest of cedars. Fresh trimmings left strewn between the trunks were topped here and there with remaining snow. Only in such a dense forest could snow still be found at the end of March, while along the path up from the little earth-covered bridge into the tea plantation, violets and dandelions were already showing their early, short-stemmed flowers.

Mokuzu scooped a handful of snow with the intention of bringing it to his mouth. The under layer was mostly ice charged with tiny bubbles. Reiho struck it from his hand.

"Look, just like I said! Inequilateral polygon! — you have no common sense!"

"Why? We ate snow and ice whenever we were thirsty, and sucked the icicles under the eaves."

"Forget your babyhood! Didn't you hear America tested a hydrogen bomb at an island called Bikini in the South Pacific as recently as March first? The whole world is stirred up about it, especially since a Japanese tuna trawler, the Lucky Dragon V, received the lethal ash. Didn't your teacher tell your class?"

"She said we shouldn't eat tuna because it received a lot of radiation. What has that to do with this snow?"

"Plenty, and it's gonna affect us. You may think the South Pacific is remote, but our moist spring air comes from there. It collides with the cold air from Siberia, high but just overhead. That sends spring rain or snow on us, which contains this radiation. They're calling it 'strontium 90.'"

"What will happen if we drink such rainwater or eat such snow?"

"It depends on the amount; I don't know, I only know it's dreadful. Those who survived the atomic air raid on Hiroshima got sick, vomited, and developed fever, and their hair fell out and their gums bled. Those were the extreme cases, but if we receive too much radiation we'll get leukemia and malignant tumors and our children might be deformed."

'Do they know at Tangenji? I worry most about Ran; hearing a bush warbler in a plum she'll dance, run about, and sing "Spring is come, spring is come! Whither is it come? To the mountains it is come, to the village it is come, to the fields it is come!"[1] And she'll eat snow as soon as she gets thirsty. On the other hand, if Gyodo has been warned by his teacher he may be worrying whether I was. With his more pessimistic nature he'll be anxious and unable to sleep — oh dear!'

"Zen Master Hanun is great, but..."

"But what?" Reiho was suspicious.

"I mean, if really he's great why doesn't he bring the world to a state of no bombs and no wars? Why is he great? Making money day after day, even if it's for our sake, he's nowise different from ordinary people, is he?"

"Hmm?..." Reiho halted. "You've a strange view, I must say! I never thought of it like that, um, Mokuzu, you're amazing." Reiho patted Mokuzu on the head. At first Mokuzu thought he was being mocked, but Reiho was actually impressed.

Reiho was to enter the second grade of junior high school in April, Mokuzu the third of elementary school. Reiho was big, dark, and broad-shouldered. Mokuzu pale, small, and thin.

Yet on Mondays and Thursdays since January, he was attending the same private karate hall as Reiho. They each went straight from their schools to the hall at four, and returned to Ryotanji together. During vacation they went together both ways.

Though his loins and legs were strong, Mokuzu had no power and skill yet; he was like a cat compared with Reiho, who was like a tiger. Nonetheless, Reiho was struck again and again with admiration for Mokuzu, in fact was attached to him and at times even respected him.

છ

Spring vacation was over and the new school year had begun. Contrary to custom Zen Master Hanun was staying long at Ryotanji, spending his days strolling and receiving visitors.

During the master's absences Ryotanji was Unkai's full responsibility, so when the master was present Unkai stayed close by to give him reports and receive new instructions.

On such a day Luri and Reiho were individually summoned to the master when they returned from school. Mokuzu too was summoned. Because the school day was short at the beginning of the term, he returned in the morning and was told by Unkai to go to the master right after lunch.

It was his third visit to the master's room, along the corridor facing the inner garden. The first had been with his father and the Enmyoji priest, the second on New Year's Day, when he went with the others to pay his respects for the year.

Mokuzu disliked the inner garden. The huge roof and eaves of the main building kept out the morning sun, and the black earth was perpetually wet. The plantings of maple, sasanqua, and crape myrtle grew lean and were covered near the ground with an unfamiliar mold. Among the mosses none were glossy like hair moss. However often Unkai broomed the earth, only liverworts thrived. Their tenacious sprawl gave Mokuzu gooseflesh.

The inner garden was attractive only in the snow, when the large red berries of an aucuba in a corner were voluptuously beautiful and the berries of a nandin by the well, which the sparrows came to pick, were charming.

Mokuzu preferred the area behind the master's quarters, a rocky, narrow, vacant slope leading into pine mountain, which he could get to by going through the east garden beside the kitchen and his and Reiho's and Luri's rooms. Being higher land it received the full morning sun. The ever-falling pine needles were well dried, and a natural lawn-type grass grew tall between the rocks. In autumn varieties of gentian bloomed, and now in spring the orchid *hokuro* was going to bloom, all native species. An open veranda at the master's quarters faced the area, but the shojis and storm doors were mostly kept shut as the master rarely stayed within. Hence Mokuzu formed the habit of going there on fine days. The wind in the pines made a swimming sound. To the front the cedar tops descended. At the bottom of the mountains was the conurbation of Kyoto, backed by mellow mountains. In the morning the city was sunk in mist as if in a lake.

Here Mokuzu found his greatest pleasure in fantasy and reminiscence, as he had found it by the little pond under the mountain of Tangenji.

Now he joined his palms to enter the master's room and proceeded to the very front of him and bowed. Next he performed as required the most extravagant form of veneration, thrice prostrating himself and raising his palms to the level of his ears to receive the feet of Buddha, as Unkai had taught him, along with every other courtesy for an interview with a Zen master. When at last he sat down erect, he had to look the master in the eyes. During the procedure the master kept his palms joined and observed steadily and keenly. Incense was lit in the alcove, where a scroll showed a sumi painting of the orchid *kanran* blooming beneath some trees.

Zen Master Hanun beamed and said,

"I see you have grown apace, but you must eat well and grow more. Now you may sit at ease." Unkai brought in fancy sweets and soon after two teabowls of matcha.

Even after the passing of winter the master's face was darkly tanned. Nor had his eyes changed their sharpness, and when he smiled they glittered like water drops struck by light.

"Reiho tells me you are faithfully attending karate practice. That is excellent, most excellent. You must go on to achieve a black belt. The worst you could do, yes, the worst, is to quit on the way. Karate is the best study to become a man who can protect himself and when possible protect others."

The master availed himself of superlatives. Mokuzu these days disliked anyone who repeated the same words, especially when pronounced with force, just as he disliked anyone who overused hackneyed expressions.

'He is like a guy who puts a crude rock on the border between his property and a public road to assert that no vehicle or pedestrian should intrude so much as an inch.'

"Mastery of the art of karate will give you the greatest confidence in your body. You will not lose your nerve before the toughest of men. If your body is weak, your mind will try to compensate, and your thought will tend to be mean, and you'll be anxious over trifles and be unable to forthrightly appreciate the kindness of others, which means you'll only nurse your suspicions.

"So, the best feature of karate is that you absolutely must practice at once with your entire being what you think. And the pain forces you to realize that any unpracticed thought is absolutely useless. You may think of doing this or that if you are in a position to be involved, but how can you prove your thought is correct? By karate. Karate proves by reality each of your thoughts. Any thought you can't prove de facto is only desk theory, the practice of swimming on dry land, a kind of fantasy.

"Always you must practice what you think is good. There are too many whose thought and conduct are not well integrated. Put simply, their words and their behavior contradict. Mind and body should be like the wheels of a bicycle, turning at once the same way with the same speed. In one of the most important Zen books it was said, 'Mind and body must be one, and quiet must not differ from action.'[2] Yes, most excellently said. You have to under-stand this matter of fact. Do you?"

The master looked impressed by his talk and no doubt wished to ascertain that Mokuzu was following. As it was hardly possible to raise any argument, Mokuzu merely said "Yes."

"Now then, did you receive letters from your family?"

"No."

"Oh? They must be lazy with the pen. I told them to write. Well, don't worry, I've seen your father on Shodojima. He looked fine and is working hard. He told me he is sending money regularly to your mother. I've seen her too. Her malady is in something of a remission. It seems cryptogenic. Even now her doctor is puzzled and thus can't determine the best treatment.

247

"Tangenji is fine. Kiku has been back since January, all is well in her hands. She's a year older than our Luri, seventeen or so? Anyway, her beauty is like the shoal of a mountain torrent, her sensitivity like bamboo tips in the breeze."

'Kiku home? Gyodo and Ran must be glad...a lantern on a moonless night...warmth in the cold. She was as busy as Ma; rarely could I be with her. She brightly sang on her return from baby-sitting or while cooking. She left before I entered school. Late one night, I've forgotten for what and when, she and I were coming home. I wasn't tired, but she said she'd carry me and lifted me up. How reliable were her shoulders and warm her back. The path was narrow and it was a long way home. The cliffs closed in, with eulalia ears bent down, no moon, only stars...

'But wait, everything has a reason; they couldn't cope without Dad?'

"Aren't you happy to hear of your family? You're dark, eh?" The master feigned meanness. Asking the obvious in a jesting manner, he was kindly trying to make light of Mokuzu's worry.

"I was wondering why she returned...."

"Ah, yes, but don't be anxious. At December's end she was taken ill, a kidney problem, to be precise, acute glomerulonephritis. Note, acute. There's a good rate of recovery compared with chronic."

"What is, uh, acute glomerulo...nephritis exactly?"

"Eh, in truth I know little about it. I've heard it's a lesser kidney trouble. You know, the kidneys lie behind the stomach and intestines. They purify the blood by filtering unneeded or harmful materials, which are discharged as urine, while the purified blood is returned to the body. In a word, the kidneys are like a filtration plant such as you see at Keage, Kyoto. Don't be surprised — in that pair of kidneys are as many as two million units of glomeruli, shaped like balls of yarn, and they do the filtering. But...what was the name? — er, yes, a bacterium called Betabacterium if it enters the kidneys causes a dysfunction. Blood and protein are blended in the urine, and, though I don't know why, the urine decreases and there's bloat and high blood pressure.

"Please ask Unkai if you wish to learn more; he has liver trouble and is well acquainted with the internal organs.

"So, Kiku took ill at work, and because the factory infirmary nursed her well, she almost recovered. Then the factory failed. But perhaps it was lucky for her, since she was freed of both hospitalization and work and has this chance to rest at home for half a year or a year while she does normal housework. This way she can perfectly mend; she need only be careful not to overwork or take too much salt and protein. At the factory that would have been hard. So it's turning out for the best. She can tend to herself and tend her siblings for her parents, see? — there's no problem."

Learning about Kiku, Mokuzu felt he was confronting deep mountains visited by thin cold rain in late autumn. Therein were various things to be aware of...the rain obscured and separated his family from sight. 'I'm put here in Ryotanji and don't know how to get out and go home. The more I think of them the more immature and incompetent I feel...how despicable I am!'

"Mokuzu, a man should live terrifically, do his best in any situation, give full play to his ability. You are already in third grade and in your tenth calendar year, in former times old enough for your ceremony to assume manhood. To assume *genpuku* means to be adult, to be responsible for your every conduct, which means, to risk your life.

"You have to risk your life for whatever you do. Risk it and you can achieve almost anything. Conversely, you will not risk your life for things unworthy of your time and labor, that is, those matters of no importance, of which you are already fully aware. Courageously continue to pay them no heed.

"Let me repeat. The vital point is to stake your life on your thought and conduct and not concern yourself with matters for which you are unwilling to take responsibility. A samurai once he assumed genpuku was ever ready to commit hara-kiri as his ultimate responsibility, after composing a poem. You too must think this over and be resolved to do likewise.

"A samurai's first daily practice was to clean himself and arrange his personal matters so that he might leave no cause for regret should death come unexpected. About this I am much impressed by your daily dousing — you have the makings of an excellent man. My hope is that you will continue to value and practice this habit of yours all your life.

"As you know, your grandfather was once my teacher. 'There is no tomorrow,' he would say. How true, how true! Nothing can be attained by the sweet, skulking attitude that today's work can be put off. Today's work must be done today. Tomorrow breaks and is no longer tomorrow. I recall an American movie that drew large audiences when it came several years ago. *Gone with the Wind* was its title. But on this subject its message was singularly detestable, an absolute tissue of falsehood. The heroine, surely seen as a heroine by youngsters, said that there's always tomorrow. Where? I should like to ask!

"You will learn. America is constructing a false world by mobilizing science and technology. Those ought to be used only to seek or aid the truth. But all too often America uses them to conceal the truth and give a semblance of righteousness and beauty to lies and immoralities. What alchemy!

"Ah, but I must be exceeding your comprehension with my chat. Occasionally you'd better go to see a movie. Luri enjoys that. I'll ask her to take you along. Then you can understand how you should live, in what kind of world situation, among what currents of human thought.

"But I'm wasting time over trifles, and you must be disoriented as to the proper order of values. I'm feeling my age...before long I shall be sixty. By facing you who are yet newly born, I fell into an easy manner and wagged my tongue.

"Do you know that Zen priests, especially Zen masters, don't speak much? We respect a single word or half a phrase, and we shouldn't speak unless what we say cuts more than a sword. Even so, albeit without awareness of any wrong in me, I was pressed away from a monastic Zen mastership. Such a master must train disciples day and night while keeping the appearance of fury just to produce one or even half a talented man. To temper a trainee into a true man, a master must kill his animal and human affections.

"Do not misunderstand and someday think you knew a Zen master simply because you were under my care. Truly I am a mere collector of donations, an antidote to the fools promoting the rearmament of Japan, and at the same time a palliative to the idiotic peace-movement radicals.

"You would find Zen Master Tengai of Shoshinji quite a contrast. To see the whole of him instead of just one or two aspects, he is after all the last Japanese Zen master worthy of the name, yes, worthy of immortalization in the annals of Zen.

"Now, I heard that your father told you to become anything but a priest. He may well say so by reason of seeing those like himself or me. But you must look at real priests. They are different. Most great men and most heroes are but acorns before them. Only they can transcend all such coordinates as wealth and poverty, love and hate, right and wrong, beauty and ugliness, life and death; only they can live as perfect spacemen in the one billion worlds.

"In our Zen sect of Buddhism there is the enlightenment personally transmitted from patriarch to patriarch, originating with Sakyamuni Buddha. This teaching method has been described as 'directly pointing from mind to mind to make a man see his own nature.'[3] For Buddhists, to see one's own nature means to be enlightened. The unenlightened don't yet know what their life is or what the lives of others are. They are dreamers, ghosts, they have no base in fundamental wisdom. They cry with tears of delight or sorrow and know not why they cry and for what.

"But if I speak so, Mokuzu, it doesn't mean you must feel obliged to become a priest. The choice is yours, and you are freer than a hawk in the sky.

"Notwithstanding, you shouldn't forget what I am about to tell you, and it's what I wish to tell you most today. In a word, you must study, you absolutely must. As hard as you can, to the very limit of your ability.

250

"You said you dislike school because the teachers spend too much time on the obvious while they're mute as stones about the very things you wish to know. I understand how in your case this is so. I saw your report card. You are listed as excellent in all courses as well as in behavior. It is remarkable you have made such a record by just sitting unwillingly in class and not by hard study. But you must hear me.

"There are those like Luri and Reiho and the majority of your classmates who dislike school, but for another reason. They dislike being forced to study complex and incomprehensible subjects. They may try within their ability to understand what is required, but the more they study the harder it gets, and their heads pound and their world becomes as dark as a bagworm's.

"Moreover, Unkai tells me you are chanting with him when you can and that you have memorized all the sutras, which take close to an hour to chant morning and evening. You began only near the end of October and you haven't been regular at it, merely as you liked. Yet you have mastered them all in under half a year. Of course Unkai is impressed. It's long been accepted that the Kannon Sutra alone takes three years...

"I am not suggesting that you be ashamed of your talent. But you should know it is nothing to be proud of. It's like a camera, where the image is printed as soon as it comes through the lens. You happened to be born so, and it is meaningless unless you are completely aware and exercise your will to create something beneficial from it, for yourself, and for others.

"So, of greatest importance to you now is to recognize your ability and to endeavor fittingly.

"Let me make another comparison. Reiho were he to set about it would take years to memorize the sutras. Would he then be equal to you? No, he'd be far more respectable. A person's value is determined by how much he uses his given talent. We can cultivate ourselves by our effort only. Were you to apply yourself as much as Reiho would need to for one sutra, you could master a hundred. You must compare the effort, not the amount.

"In the last analysis, you will be inferior to others unless you strive to your full capacity.

"I have therefore been thinking carefully about this aspect of your fate. I am responsible for the child of another man. Your parents placed one of the purest and most sorrowful slices of their heart in my care, as I myself was put in care of your grandfather. I therefore have been inquiring into some special teachers for you, and I have found them. So from now on you must study earnestly from them after completing your school lessons.

"To harden your body you are attending Rangai's karate hall twice a week, which is fine. Continue if possible until you are licensed.

"Rangai is an admirable karate teacher, even if you don't know it. To create a new school isn't easy. He had to study all well-established schools and devise his own, which had to stand up to both reason and practice. He also mastered jujitsu and kendo. And he went to China to learn taijichyuan, and more, he studied Western boxing and wrestling. He is a master of hand-to-hand combat, worthy of note not only in Japan. You can follow him with no reservation.

"Incidentally, the tenets of his karate prepare the way to Zen inasmuch as both share a concern for perfecting the means to survive beautifully in crucial moments. Aside from its relation to Zen it's the only way to live, for we all at any moment face the chance of death.

"Then, what you must study is history, English, and sumi painting. The first two you will study twice a week, the third, once a week. Fortunately the teachers have offered to come up to Ryotanji. Unkai will explain it to you. You must be careful not to mistake the schedule and not to disappoint these teachers, who are willing to offer their love and labor.

"Mokuzu, they each are unique. They may not be the top authorities in their studies, but in Japan they are by no means second-rate. There are in fact many who are first-rate; the difference is only a matter of character and specialty. Anyhow, each has been devoting his life to his subject.

"To study from great teachers is the most important aspect of learning. One had better not study from mediocre teachers.

"Fortunately Kyoto has a thousand years' history and is still the capital of culture. Here can be found many talented people of worldwide acclaim, though you wouldn't know it, for they are living quiet as any grandpa or grandma you see anywhere. They are seeking what they want to seek, yes, that is so.

"Well, I have been able to tell you all I had in mind to tell you today. While you are young you must study hard and spare no pains. Er — have you any question, or were some parts above your head? Besides, is there nothing you wish me to know concerning your life here in Ryotanji? Don't miss this chance."

"There's nothing."

"Hmm...fine. You may withdraw....Well? What is the matter? You may bow again and withdraw."

"My legs refuse my orders — they're like a fished-up octopus, but they must fear my scolding because they're trying to humor me by prickling...."

"Ha! ha! What a way to put it! It's perfectly natural. You've been sitting long in the proper manner. You indeed have possibility! Most begin to squirm against the pain and hope for a quick end to the interview. You didn't budge. You're like a shogun who ignores a local rebellion. Yes, the best answer for some things is to ignore them in silence. This you understand admirably. Go on undaunted! Yes! Yes!"

Mokuzu returned to his desk and sat with cheek propped in hand, stupefied.

'I don't know what I want to do, however hard I think. He speaks well of me, but he's overestimating me. He recommends that I live — what was his word? — 'terrifically'....But is straining every nerve necessary? — is that what it means to live terrifically? To live such a life I'd first have to know what way I wanted to go and for what.

'Actually, do I have any certain desire to attain anything? I'm like a diving beetle that senses someone's footfall and dives from the bank and slants through the water into the mud. When danger nears, the desire to protect myself arises and at least I'll make an effort to escape...I guess. But a diving beetle's desire is stronger than mine. In the night it flies toward the light. Why does it fly into the fire? To slight its life?'

Mokuzu opened the shoji in front of his desk. The east garden was no longer sunny. There was as always the old plum with rough, blackish bark, once no doubt upright but now a rotted stump topped with an exuberance of snake's-beard. From its base new branches had shot up and were aging in the shape of a dragon.

'Some things I didn't wish for and some things I did. I disliked falling asleep with my fist pressed to my head as my parents quarreled under the dim light. I disliked seeing Ran cry from hunger and finally sleep and soon reawake to cry again. Vividly I remember the figure of my mother sick and groping her way along the wall to the toilet, grasping whatever she could. And Gyodo pointing out the stars while all I saw was his torn sleeve....On a cold day in a secret spot, Ena and I wrapped up in a blanket and played matching syllables. And we played on the warm lichened rock, imagining a fairyland...wonderful!'

Beyond the old plum was a row of tea bushes pruned round, making a border between the garden and the slope below. The spreading branches of the deciduous trees on the slope, such as wild cherry, maple, and hackberry, disturbed the view. Behind them the sky was cloudy and the dark cedar tops descended.

'I hear the song of Siberian meadow buntings from the lower land. They must be forming a little flock and are busily singing *chi-chit, cho-pizt-two-chirr* —. I read that the ancients heard it as *"Ippitsu keijo tsukamatsuri soro"* (Pray let me pen thee a line or two). What ear could have heard it so...?

253

'Oh! I know — and I too had better write!'

Mokuzu took from the desk drawer the notebook made by Gyodo. He occasionally took it out, but not a word was written in it.

'To whom should I write? To Gyodo? Ena? About what? No, what I now understood isn't about the meadow bunting's song or about letter writing. I'm struck by the amiability of those little birds together pursuing a sunny sheltered place where all day they can find food. What I want is nothing other than a family in which parents and children can happily spend their days....'

As his first entry Mokuzu wrote with the attached pencil,

> A family like a covey of birds
> or if that cannot be,
> even a nest of insects
> in a swamp is fine with me,
> provided it be possible
> to live in harmony.

23

Three Teachers

"The difference between an educated man and an uneducated man is as great as between a man who walks by the light of a full moon in a clear sky and a man without a torch who gropes in the dark.

"As for me, Mokuzu, I can't comprehend when people begin to use slightly difficult words or speak with even the least mind to deceive. You may think I should ask if I don't understand, but I don't understand what to ask or how. Or you might suggest I read, but I don't know what book is good for me.

"I bear nobody a grudge, but as I age I regret the days I didn't study, didn't wish to, and wasn't in any condition to, and the weight of my regret increases daily and always will." Thus Unkai responded to a question from Mokuzu and smiled sadly.

They had come out to the veranda after morning chanting. Unkai with a single hand made his departing bow to Buddha. In the other he held an extinguished candle.

The veranda was now visible in the dusk. Soon the sun would overtop the cedars and shine crimson on the cypress-bark roof of the gate, on the white-graveled garden with its varied plantings, and past the open shojis of the main building, onto the tatamis.

Again Zen Master Hanun was away. Luri and Reiho were not yet astir. It was that quiet advance of night to day.

"If so, why don't you study under those teachers with me, no, why don't you study instead of me?"

"Aha! Everything has its season. Rice, pears, apples, if they miss the chance to grow from spring to summer, they can't fruit in autumn....So too with marriage — no one cares about a person past the age even if he wishes to marry....And, Mokuzu, you mustn't become ill. If you have to worry over your health, you can't study. Be careful. I too will be attentive, but you are able to know better, and you must promptly inform me of any irregularities. Well then, we can talk again at breakfast."

Unkai left for the west veranda to practice sitting meditation, his custom after morning chanting. Mokuzu went to the bath room to douse with cold water.

Around six Luri got up to prepare breakfast. She started a fire under the pot of washed rice ready on the range from the night before, sliced vegetables for miso soup, took a pickled daikon from a keg, and put the beginnings of lunch into three metal boxes for Reiho, Mokuzu, and herself. She was still in her nightgown as she tended the furnace and when the fire was under way had time to step out to brush her hair. It was shoulder-length, rich and lustrous; the sight of it spread out as she brushed it in the direct sun was dazzling for anyone's eyes.

"Mokuzu, what's going on? I just found three brand-new brushes in the furnace. They almost got burnt, but I rescued them — they're on the table."

Sensing his approach, Luri spoke without turning her head, inclined with its curtain of silky hair.

Mokuzu stood where he could see her face and replied, "Never mind. My teacher Setsuro Kimura ordered me to burn them."

"But they're unused! Didn't Unkai trouble to buy you them?"

"Yes, he kindly did, but let me explain what Teacher Setsuro said yesterday. He was going to teach me about the four treasures of the literary artist, and he asked to see my brushes, sumi stick, and sumi stone. Then he said, 'What have we here? These are nothing to treasure! Take that stick and stone and stand up,' and he ordered me to go with them down the veranda to the stone basin and raise them high above the stepping-stone and drop them. So I did. He must have heard, but he called to ask what happened. I told him

255

they were broken to pieces. He said that was fine and told me to return."

"Incredible, the guy's nuts!" With her hairbrush Luri made a circle near her head.

Mokuzu was thinking of an earnest reply, but she put her hand on his shoulder and bent to look him in the eye.

"Really is he okay? I met him as he came in the gate. You wouldn't believe his gall. His first words were, 'What a beauty here in this rustic temple — another pleasure is added to my life!' I gave him a fierce scowl but he went on, 'He's a mingy priest to be cloistering such as you while asking me to teach a priestling who couldn't yet be more than a peeing cherub. Hey, girl, don't you wish to study sumi painting? I can vouchsafe you my most conscientious teaching. Eh?'

"I said I hate such dreary art. It didn't stop him. 'Dreary art?' He laughed impudently. 'Where's the sense in that? Five colors have always been said to be present in every stroke. No more sensuous beauty can be found than in the sumi painting! But, let it be. In due time I shall invite you to pose. An oil painter could render you in your middy. My nude will be far superior. Posed by a cataract, white flesh harmonizing with the vapors...a breathtaking effect!' Outrageous, huh? Believe me I hurried out to go shopping, but I could feel his eyes till I was safely beyond the trees. What a hideous bag! I tell you, Mokuzu, the guy's nuts —" Luri again gestured with her hairbrush.

"Which reminds me of what Unkai said — he let him into the guest room, you know. He said the nut told him, 'If you're serving tea, never mind, I don't care for it, especially during instruction,' and he took from his kimono an amber flask. 'Today being my first visit and assuming you're unprepared, I brought my own. I hope you won't fail me hereafter.' Unkai neared his eyes to it — he's myopic, you know. Then that nut said without shame or apology, 'I'll empty the bottle. Take it to any big wine shop, they'll sell you the same.' Mokuzu — it's Scotch, the priciest import!"

"I didn't feel he was so queer, not enough for you to worry, Luri. About those brushes, for instance. It's sensible advice. He said, 'Don't discard them; you can use them for kindling."

"Sensible advice? Mokuzu, money was paid. If not nuts, at least he's eccentric!"

"But he says brushes, paper, sumi stick, and sumi stone are a literary artist's four treasures, so anyone set on learning sumi painting should obtain the best regardless of cost. Even when practicing, cost shouldn't concern us. And in sumi painting there's no distinction between practice and real, there's only real. He says we must protect those four treasures at the risk of our life. If our house is burning, they are what we save first. Our attitude should be that of the samurai — even after their decline in the world, they kept their swords well shined."

"Hooh, I never knew stationery was so important! But Mokuzu, we have the saying, A bad workman blames his tools...or, A calligrapher good as Kobo isn't choosy about his brush."

"My teacher also mentioned Kobo. He said those who brandish that saying are idiotic without exception."

"Ridiculous!"

"And he cautioned that there's no historical truth to it. He said, 'Whoever is serious should realize Great Teacher Kobo was choosy. With pliant raccoon-dog hair how can we draw awesome wintry trees? And using springy stiff deer hair isn't it absurd to attempt a newly white rabbit? You must choose or invent tools most fitted to the subject at hand.'"

"He teaches you difficult things. Do you really feel you can study from him every Sunday?" Luri went in to reduce the heat of the furnace. She put a shovelful of hot coals into a clay brazier to heat water for soup. Mokuzu assisted by slicing and dishing out the pickle.

He had not answered her last question, so she said,

"I hear your dad is a master of sumi painting. Too bad you can't be taught by him instead of by some oddball. But a father can be great without it going to the son. I heard my mother was a koto teacher with many disciples, yet I never touched a koto and probably have no talent for it. Did your sumi teacher question your talent?"

"He asked if I like to draw. I said I do. He told me to open my right hand like a maple leaf and bend the fingers a few times starting with the smallest and then with the thumb."

"Why such hocus-pocus?"

"He tells by that, it seems. He said he could give me his word I have enough talent to be an artist."

"Ho ho ho! Don't you suspect his head? Everybody could be seen to be so!"

Reiho entered the kitchen. "Don't forget we have karate."

"Hm!" Mokuzu nodded.

"Mokuzu, you're going to be busy: today karate, tomorrow English, the next day history. Won't you get muddled by all those extra studies? Reiho has only judo as a school club, then karate, which is similar so there's little chance of confusion."

"Don't worry about him, Luri. You know he's quick to remember things. But he gets up too early — and it's not that I get up late. If I got up at four-thirty, I'd be in a daze all day like seeing through a goldfish bowl."

257

"Mokuzu is in bed by eight-thirty — it amounts to eight hours. Reiho, you sleep too much!" So saying, Luri left for her room to change to her school middy and skirt. Having finished most of her work involving the use of water and fire, she was free of the chance of harming her uniform.

Mokuzu laid out the table utensils. Reiho went to practice karate beside the old plum.

Deep in the ground he had sunk a plank four or five centimeters thick, leaving nearly two meters above, around which he had coiled a straw rope. This he regarded as an imaginary foe and kicked and thrust at it without remorse.

Beyond being large-boned, he had raised noticeable knobs on the outer sides of his feet, prepared to strike an enemy's temple by a sudden reverse turn and synchronous high jump, and the skin there was dry and whitened. More, the cartilage around his broad knuckles had become flat like a boxer's nose, and there too the skin was tough as elephant hide. So too was the skin of his elbows, prepared to repel a rear attack.

Luri detested Reiho's abuse of his body and the fact that he counted it as a weapon to be hardened against adversity.

"Don't become like that," she occasionally told Mokuzu. "Study only form. Don't hit things. Form alone is elegant. What's the point of brute force in this age of guns and bombs?"

Mokuzu was awkwardly situated between Reiho's and Luri's contradictory guidance. 'Each is tenable. I want strength, and I don't want ugliness. What is strength? Does it include being ugly? Isn't ugliness a weakness?'

Sedate in her uniform, Luri came to the table with her school bag. Reiho was still savagely challenging the board. At every strike of his knuckles or feet it issued a shriek or a groan, and a fierce whistle was audible with each thrust of his alternating fists. And there were his yells.

Luri ignored Reiho's barbarism, no doubt used to it, and poured tea into Mokuzu's cup. Mokuzu took the chance to ask her what he had asked Unkai,

"Why is it good to study so hard, and if it's good, why don't you also study more?"

"Well...great people study hard, and according to their schemes they make a world for ordinary people to live in."

"Oh? Don't you want to do that?"

"My word! Mokuzu, I am studying in school, though the way you talk it seems I'm not. Joking aside, you have to realize we each have our own forte; Zen Master Hanun must have told you so. Someone like me only hopes to live a pleasant life some way or other in the society those great people make.

Trying to be one of them is absurd for my type. In a manner of speaking, I'm more like a bird or an animal or a stem of grass."

"Do you think you're like that? Me too — it's the very life I'm most wishing to live."

"You may wish as you like, but reality isn't so easy, in fact it's hard for a person to live like a bird or a stem of grass. To be able to live like that demands a lot of study. And how much more, of course, to become a great person!"

"Then why don't you study from those teachers with me? You see its importance. If not sumi painting, how about history or English...?"

"Mmm, but I can't skillfully express what I feel...I have no learning about these things we're talking of, really...and — my type isn't required to study all that much. If, say, we study so we can live a pleasant life, what's the point if it makes us feel too much hardship? See? We'd be losing both principle and interest!

"For you, Mokuzu, it isn't such a strain, so after all you ought to do it. Put another way, you must study instead of those like me. Many people wish to study but can't for various reasons, maybe because of circumstances, or it's just too hard. Yes, that's the prime reason — you have to study in place of all who can't. That's what I think, though maybe it isn't true...."

Mokuzu could make little sense of Luri's words. Talking with her, he realized that even what he had first wanted to know was getting hazy.

Who was Luri, he wondered. He felt absorbed by her softness, warmth, and kindness whenever he was near her, but if he came too close she swiftly withdrew as if to rise above the world and leave him with no relation to her.

'What I feel in her presence is as elusive as a scent, like what I felt as an infant near Ma or Kiku, even near Ena later on...what a sweet sensation!

'And when Luri rejects me and I feel I can never enter the center of her life, it's how I feel when I am with adults...my parents, school teachers: their world seems alien. About this I am closer to my classmates, even to savage Reiho. I can sense their thoughts and feelings as if holding their minds in my palm.'

That Mokuzu could fathom Luri no more than this was very reasonable. Though only in her first year of senior high, she was no longer a virgin and day by day was approaching womanhood, whereas he was yet a child. On the other hand, Reiho, between Luri and Mokuzu, was striving for adulthood with feverish impatience and with all his might like a baby turtle traversing the sand to the sea.

'What I really want to know is not why I am someone who must study, and study hard. My question boils down to how I got into the situation of having to study so hard. It amounts to what was the cause of the present me, and being a private problem it won't yield a focused answer from anyone but me. So I must ask to myself and answer to myself why am I here now in this way?'

ર

Yojun Ishida came to teach Mokuzu English at four on Tuesdays and Fridays.

Unlike the sumi painting teacher Setsuro, he was polite and appeared to be shy on visiting Ryotanji and meeting Unkai and Mokuzu for the first time.

He was neatly dressed in a suit with a white shirt and a blue-green tie. His glossy hair was slightly receding, and his face sanguine and clear featured. He held his tall figure erect except when he adjusted his silver-rim glasses with long, graceful fingers. Overall, his bearing accorded with his polished pointy black shoes.

He was led to the guest room designated for Mokuzu's private lessons. When Unkai served him tea he was much obliged,

"Please do not trouble yourself over me. I came solely to teach English, you know."

Nor did he touch the cup during the lesson. Only when Unkai brought a fresh one at the end did he yield.

"Master Mokuzu, I am honored to be given the task of instructing you in English.

"Japanese and English are the same in their both being human languages. Language is to communicate feelings and thoughts; hence beforehand there must arise feelings and thoughts that we need or wish to communicate. If we are unaware of having feelings and thoughts, we have no need of language.

"Language is thus a tool to transfer the fire of our feelings and thoughts from here to there, carefully, lest we extinguish it or cause it to smoke. It may be transferred in many ways. Which way is most suitable is not so important as whether there is a fire worthy of transfer. In short, as long as we have feelings and thoughts we wish to communicate, language has life and its use has value.

"Now the reason I said I am honored to teach you English is that I understand I have been entrusted, first, to judge whether you have feelings and thoughts worth communicating and, second, if you haven't them, to help you to have them, or if you have them, to help you to find the best way to communicate them. Do you understand what I am saying?"

"I think you are saying that no one need study either English or Japanese if he hasn't any feelings and thoughts he wishes to tell others."

"Exactly. I'm already beginning to like you; you receive my ideas so easily, like slicing through jelly.

260

"But to preclude any misunderstanding, let me explain further. One trait of language is that it rises from need when we have feelings and thoughts we consider worth communicating. Another is that it rises from need when we wish to have feelings and thoughts worth communicating though we haven't them yet, and so we seek to know the feelings and thoughts of others. In other words, even if we have no such feelings and thoughts, the need for language rises when we believe or expect we will discover them by hearing or reading the feelings and thoughts of others. Do you understand this point as well?"

"I think so, sir. We also needn't learn any language if we haven't the desire to know the feelings and thoughts of others."

"Indeed. Now, to assemble it concisely: The purpose of language is to express our feelings and thoughts so that they may be understood by others, and to receive those of others so that we may develop our own. You and I are therefore going to speak and write what we feel and think, as well as hear and read what others feel and think, and this, by means of English."

Teacher Yojun was evidently taking into account that Mokuzu was only in third grade of elementary school. He spoke scrupulously, repeating the same words, without haste. Perhaps Mokuzu felt that an obvious matter was being tediously protracted. But Teacher Yojun's delivery was clear and well punctuated; and on the whole Mokuzu found his talk listenable and comprehensible.

'His pace reminds me of a snail advancing along a wet hydrangea leaf, but his tone and content, if I consider it, is more like a bright dewdrop rolling around a lotus leaf.'

"Master Mokuzu, one more point I wish to call to your notice before I teach you English. It is that to know language is not always an advantage. There is a Western proverb, Speech is silver, silence gold. Relating to this, there was a priest, Shimaji Mokurai, of the Honganji school of the Jodo Shin sect of Buddhism, who was active in the Meiji era. In accord with his name (soundless thunder), his silence was said to be more frightful than a thunderclap.

"The ineffectiveness of language is not so much to be feared as the harm that can come of knowing language. We must not use language to do harm.

"How often must I have harmed people by speaking carelessly in the midst of a passing emotion!

"Corporal injury is certainly wrong and only increases grief. But it is unmistakably apparent, just as a scarlet dahlia of midsummer cannot be overlooked.

"Verbal injury, on the contrary, is like the trail of the light of a firefly: it scarce is seen. Yet, whether spoken without awareness of effect, or in malice, words can pierce like thorns. And the wound has often an incurable nature. The ache may be forgotten, but can return like a neuralgia in the twilight of autumn or the cold of winter.

"Please, Master Mokuzu, imagine your word harming one who has done you no harm, who cares about you, who is a loving, irreplaceable person; or one who is suffering an unbearable agony, or is poor or sick, or repenting of something, or near the end of endurance. Yet that person must receive your ill word. It is to beat a person already beaten...to shoot at a deer pursued by wild dogs...to tramp on wind-torn chrysanthemums. Do you see? Language if it harms should not be learned. It is said a mute is closer to God.

"So if I think something is harmful and it is in English, I shan't teach you it, nor should you study it. Do you understand this point and have you any objection?"

"Well, sir, it is unlikely that I understand as deeply as you, but I think I understand through my limited experience. A person harmed by muscle or weapon will bleed. Hurt by words, he'll shed no more than a couple of tears, but a pale flame or something like steam will rise from his head."

"Have you seen such a thing? I am sorry, how stupid and rude of me to explain at length without need. I apologize for not perceiving the substance of your mental life."

"Oh, no, to be frank I thought I saw it, but I didn't make sure whether it was real."

"That's fine, there's little difference between thinking you saw it and seeing it. Please tell me the circumstances."

Mokuzu spoke of his first day of school when the boy Ippei called Gyodo "temple cat."

Teacher Yojun as he listened often bowed his head. For a while afterwards, he remained silent. Then he said,

"You had a valuable experience. A good point about you is that you observed your brother and his opponent, the others, and the atmosphere of the place. Observation is one of the most important human activities for every aspect of our life and not only for English study. It may be our most profound activity.

"To illustrate, in the study of English we must begin by observing a word or a sentence. If it is spoken, we must add our aural observation. From there we must understand its meaning, and to do that we must analyze and compare it with similar or contrasting words or sentences. Analysis and comparison are two basic studies we must engage in to understand any word. Then when we understand it, we must remember it or it won't be in our store of knowledge to help us when we face new words.

"Of practical importance to learning English are these three processes — observing, understanding, and remembering, each of which must be endlessly repeated as long as there are words and sentences to be learned. But we shall return to this. I mentioned observation only because my thoughts ran on from hearing your account. As to my own experiences of doing harm by knowing language, I shall have occasion in due time to speak."

Teacher Yojun opened a world map to give an intelligent explanation of English-speaking nations and the derivation and development of English. Mokuzu was astonished that so many kinds of people used so many languages every hour the world over.

'How would I feel if I could hear the talking of all the people on earth? It would produce a far greater din than frogs in the rice fields or a forest of cicadas.

'Senior Unkai said Teacher Yojun is married to an American. Do they span the Pacific Ocean with an invisible bridge, or is it just the mating of a cock and hen pheasant?

'The Allied Powers and the triple alliance of Japan, Germany, and Italy fought each other in what has been called an unprecedented war. Are they now reconciled? Dad said Japan was foolish to engage in such a war; did he mean Japan was wrong?

'Without asking Teacher Yojun I'm quite sure Americans and Europeans too must die after first suffering old age and infirmity. Do they fear death, or sometimes welcome it more than necessary as the Japanese do? In China the ideal of Taoism was to master the sacred art of eternal youth and live deep in the mountains as a legendary wizard. The main concern of Indian Buddhists was to seek Nirvana, described in the Heart Sutra on Wisdom as what cannot come into being or come to ruin. It was said the Japanese mix the teachings from other countries and haphazardly seek everything, and some even practice asceticism to attain eternal life because they don't want to die....'

Realizing he was raising his naive questions one after another, Mokuzu said to himself,

'Phew, what's to be gained by study but ten times more obscure questions for each one I've come to understand? People say study is good. Actually it's not unlike a kid blowing myriads of bubbles into the sky and somehow enjoying the sight of them drifting and popping into the void. Isn't study but a means of dawdling away the time so as to avoid being oppressed by tedium?'

இ

Docho Doka was of stoutish and majestic bearing. He came in a simple black robe and golden surplice, and under his arm he carried some lecture notebooks wrapped in a purple silk. His rosy face was gently round, and his head, like Mokuzu's father's, was bald except for the lower back. He indeed looked like a priest. But his right eye slightly squinted, for which reason Mokuzu felt some difficulty in regarding him directly.

"In ancient China my family name, Doka, meant an adherent of Taoism. Very early, in the age before Ch'in, it was the common noun for persons who had mastered the philosophy of Lau-tz and Juang-tz. But I know only that my forebears were Buddhist laymen or priests dwelling at Hino, a secluded place in the southeast mountains diagonally across Kyoto from here.

"My given name, Docho, denotes the priest of a Zen temple, or simply his temple. It's odd my father named me so, for his sect was Shingon, not Zen. Yes, I am a Shingon priest, inheritor of my father's poor Shingon temple.

"Quite recently I came to realize why my father named me Docho. Your Zen master asked me, in fact chose me, from many more fitted to the task of teaching you the outlines of history, though in truth my specialty is Buddhist history. I don't mean I realized in a flash; only I began to see the sense of it as if I were seeing the first ostent of dawn. I was profoundly moved and resolved with good grace to take on the grave responsibility of lecturing to you. Can you apprehend my deep emotion?"

"I am sorry, not at all."

"Hmph, you can't? It's also one historical sense you must cultivate, to wit, Buddha's Law of Cause and Effect. But listen, my father, a Shingon priest, gave me a name meaning a Zen priest. That's odd, don't you agree? Yet here I am in a respectable Zen temple to teach you, and it is assumed you will become a man capable of shouldering the destiny of Zen. What I can teach you is world history, especially Eastern history, and most of all, Buddhist history — in a word, I shall teach you about Time. This will be the realization of my father's wish. At least if I think the surd mystery of my name is thereby solved, I shan't be far from the truth, yes? Can you begin to see why I am touched?"

"Well, reverend sir, my understanding is less satisfactory than being scratched on the back by a cat where I don't itch."

"Ho? It's hard to make flowers to bloom on a dead tree or to draw on a wall with a brush parted from the hand. But those who are greatly trained can finesse such things before breakfast. Well, fine, one day you shall understand if you go through the heap of human sufferings."

Mokuzu felt uncomfortable as if smoke were being infused into his head by this teacher who from the outset introduced incomprehensibilities only to suit himself. And seemingly he was intent on closing without making clear even to himself what he felt. Mokuzu asked with overt sarcasm,

"What do you mean by saying, as if it's a matter of fact, that flowers can be made to bloom on a dead tree and a brush to draw free of the hand?"

"Do you, the child of a Zen priest, not know the Zen phrase, 'A dead tree flowers and an iron tree puts forth boughs'?[1] Mokuzu, a person who goes through all manner of religious austerities is simply great. Indeed he can revive the dead and vitalize even inanimate matter.

"In my Shingon sect too, there were many priests in the old days who mastered Buddha's great power. Performing incantations was our sect's unrivaled activity. A Shingon faith healer forms symbolic signs with his hands as he chants the *shingon*, and when his mind and mien become like Buddha's, then Buddha's absolute mercy responds to him.

"Our sect also used *goma* prayer while incinerating firewood, signifying illusion, by means of fire, signifying wisdom. It was truly effective. Yes, wondrous goma faith healers practiced thenadays here and there. They could induce rain during a drought, cure diseases, and inspire any local villain to surrender.

"A goma faith healer, exactly according to Buddhist dictate, presents himself before a platform where a square hearth is set below an enshrined image of Acala or Ragaraja. Into the hearth he casts special woods, such as mulberry, rich in latex, and the five cereal grains, offering each to the god while absorbing himself in prayers to invoke divine aid. Even now some priests perform the ritual, but, alas, they produce only an inefficacious pother.

"As a child I witnessed many healings. I'll tell you of one. A widow from Osaka brought her son to Hino. He was about my age of six. To go that distance was hard; there was a train, but no conveyance beyond the station. He was in the folds of her sleeves, with warts as big as oleaster fruit on his face, hands, and neck, and even on his eyelids and earlobes. The priest opened his kimono to find him covered with them. The mother said the doctors in Osaka inclined their heads and muttered that it was a strange incurable disease, and now she was coming with great faith to this renowned priest.

"The priest pitied the boy and at once faced his prayer platform and began the goma ceremony. After praying he turned as the volume of smoke was rising and told the mother, 'Three days hence the warts will be gone, about a third of them a day. Do not doubt the effect. Seclude yourselves in our subtemple so that your minds may remain undisturbed; our sexton will deliver you meals.'

"On the third morning I was amazed to see the mother embracing her son free of warts and thanking the priest with joyful tears. Not only that, while everyone there was congratulating them, a man rushed into the temple yard attired in the white travel robe and gaiters of a mountain ascetic.

Spotting the boy he shouted, 'You are cured? As I foresaw, the healer of this temple has power far beyond mine! Four months ago I lit a sacred fire for this boy, and I have since been regretting my inadequate power. Three days ago while holding the morning service I was struck dizzy and a light spread before my eyes. Thereupon, from my principal image, Dainichi Buddha, I received an oracle: The mother and child whom I could not heal were facing the hardship of seeking a priest, and I must hasten to him to assist him with his prayer. The oracle concluded that if I saw the boy healed, I should revere his healer as my preceptor.'

"Mokuzu, isn't it a wonder? The mother then acknowledged that she had once sought the mountain ascetic's treatment, and that neither he nor anyone else knew she was faring to Hino. With composure the Hino priest said to the ascetic, 'The instant I saw these two I knew you would come. You are sanctioned as my disciple to train yourself anew.'

"See? For such an exalted priest it is easy to cast a brush at a wall and draw freely thereon as if the brush were in the hand of a great artist. I've heard tell that in Korea there were many legendary wizards who could transport themselves over abyssal ravines as if riding a cloud."

Mokuzu decided that his difficulty in regarding Teacher Docho directly was not owing to his cockeye but to the nubilious world he believed in.

'I wonder if that eye is emitting a telestic energy, or, does it see better than a normal eye...?

'What he believes and is telling me sounds very odd. Yet, I'm willing to engage in ascetic practice if it can cure strange and even incurable diseases. I'd do it for the sake of my mother...though in my case it couldn't possibly work....'

"What I have told you is not unique to Buddhism or to other Eastern religions. The New Testament describes anomalies performed by Jesus. In Matthew you will read that he cured leprosy by laying on his hands, and satisfied the stomachs of four thousand with seven fish and seven loaves of bread.

"History is the process of the human struggle for supremacy over natural phenomena even as those phenomena sustain us. Nature on the one side is as tender as the mother we sense in the spring rains that vivify the hills, while on the other it cruelly ices the trees, freezes their roots, even kills. Nature engenders life yet induces old age, illness, and death. We have striven to escape this minatory aspect of nature. But when we reflect, we can realize how strange is our effort, for even the power to oppose nature was given us by nature.

"Since the dawn of human history we have formed groups and societies to fight against earthquakes, volcanoes, flood tides, tsunamis, typhoons, deluges, droughts — all such life-threatening natural appearances. We also discovered the use of fire, invented tools, and built dwellings to protect ourselves from nature.

"However, with people living in groups there naturally arose differences between the strong and the weak and hence the need of rules to restrain harmful conduct. In the present world the strong and these rules constitute authority, and there have developed the authoritarian cultures of politics, finance, naval and military affairs, jurisprudence, education, and so on. Insofar as they originated from the need to fight against nature, these cultures are undeniably useful to us. Yet, like nature, they have two sides — cooperative, as in planting and reaping, or in maintaining riverbanks — and tyrannical, as in the creation of slavery and poverty and in the breach of human rights by the prepotent acting in the name of the developed cultures.

"So it is that we must confront the cruel side of both nature and human culture. We can then define ourselves as beings who must struggle against two poisons, one in nature, the other in society. The process of that dual struggle is our panhuman history. An unchanging theme has been how to transcend these two cruelties, and every hero without exception has put himself to the fore in this battle.

"To transcend them earnestly, effectively, and in every direction is called in Buddhism 'training' or 'engaging in ascetic practice.' The main history of Buddhism is the history of this training.

"Hereafter I shall be talking to you about the history of Buddhist training by bringing examples from each age.

"Then, oh! before commencing my first lecture the time has sped! Shame on me, I organized neither my time nor what I wanted to say. Well, today I intended to lecture on the human situation, internal and external, where those four — natural phenomena, authoritarian culture, training, and the miraculous — are whirling. Well, well, next time I can talk more comprehensively for you. Forgive this humble lecture. I'll give myself a score of thirty for today....You know, one must be content if one's lecture can attain as much as a poem...

> "My face reveals my love concealed,
> People inquire after my health."[2]

Mokuzu suddenly recalled his mother, for the lines were from *A Hundred Poems by a Hundred Poets*. Therein were poems he had heard her sing as she hung the laundry on bamboo poles behind the retreat cottage in the morning sun.

267

'She was well then! Ran and I were busy digging into the holes of ant lions....This she sang the most:

> 'Tango Province so far,
>   beyond Oe Pass, even beyond Ikuno County!
>   How can I meet my mother
>   while I have not yet received from her a letter,
>   nor yet crossed the bridge Amanohashidate?[3]

'She was longing for her mother, I now understand.'

24

Life without Pleasure

Mokuzu's thought in mid-spring of fourth grade was not much changed from his thought in early autumn of third.

'When I wake I feel the day is spent. The cedar tops crimson at dawn. Later their sunny sides yellow. Where the sun never penetrates is everywhere dark green, and there the oxygen content feels heavy and a holy spirit seems deposited. Some days begin with rain. A vapor overhangs the trees. The saturated earth and undergrowth look disconsolate — a glossy gloom.

'Rain or shine, I chant with Unkai, then go to school to be taught as if going there to sleep. From four to six I have to attend karate practice or be lectured on Buddhist history, English, or sumi painting. Then supper and again sleep. As if in a dream I can manage all these daily requirements, I mean, perform them well enough with my eyes half shut, for they take only ten to twenty percent of my ability.

'So, on what should I spend the remaining eighty to ninety percent? How vexing that most of my hours are allotted to the use of so little of my ability! — like receiving a tiny dose of medicine to which so much water has been added that I must spend all day to drink it. A person's life is his only time. Yet the prime mission of school is to determine how to spend it without his permission and to make him waste it in the least sincere way. The two-hour private lessons I have each day are better, as is to be expected, but even so — there's too much chaff.

'As long as I can't exercise my remaining ability, I'll be criticized for appearing to be in a stupor and I myself won't feel any raging joy. But what am I to spend my remaining ability on? Everything looks good for nothing. Even if I wanted to do something, I'd be given no time for it. Moreover, I'm not yet able to become independent. Or I should say I want to do many things, but they overwhelm me in degree and number so I can't choose which to devote myself to.'

Miss Kaneko Yoshioka, Mokuzu's fourth grade teacher continuing from third, did not like his way at all. The cold fact was that his grades were better than anyone else's, when obviously he was applying himself to nothing.

It seemed that the pupils who did their best and yet turned out unsatisfactory were touching to her, even lovable, and she felt her joy watching those childish ones who raised hurrahs, or whose eyes spilled tears as if watered by a watering can, or who pressed their fists to their heads during study and bolted at the chime.

Mokuzu ignored or was indifferent to her sentiment, just as everyone ignored or was indifferent to the framed calligraphy hung at the front of the room near the ceiling with two Chinese characters demanding "Quiet Attention," written by the principal. However, Miss Yoshioka at last decided to detain him after school to reprimand him.

Whether or not the use of make-up enhanced Miss Yoshioka was her freedom to decide. At any rate, she must have thought she looked best with her hair washed daily, for it always glistened. In that respect, she somewhat resembled Mokuzu, who doused with cold water every morning. But her face, unlike his, had pomaceous cheeks, which made it appear indented down the middle. She was nearly thirty and yet unmarried. It was said she was attending graduate school at Kyoto University after her elementary-school work each day.

She spoke with a beaming face, hoping to wrap Mokuzu in a glow that would induce him to sense her as warm and kind and hence, relax his guard.

"Now, Mokuzu, he who does his best is the best child. You do everything well, but to my regret you obviously aren't focusing your all on anything. Is there nothing either at home or at school to which you ever really applied yourself? Isn't there something that interests you?"

Under her influence Mokuzu wore a mild face, until he saw what she was up to. Then he assumed a cold demeanor, which gave coherence to his disquietude, to his angry, disordered emotion.

She employed her words like a screwdriver in hopes of prying open his mouth, but because they were wrapped in soft cotton she was unaware of how they jabbed.

"What's most important is not that your result be good but that you apply yourself. Take sports, for example. Coubertin said it well: the meaning of sports is to participate, not to win but to sweat together and to cultivate friendship. Likewise the purpose of study is to cultivate character in the process of achieving something. Character is fostered by effort, not results."

Mokuzu was reminded of Zen Master Hanun's talk about the importance of straining every nerve, but his words had held no contradiction. 'Hers do — and I must find it and speak up or I'll be toyed with like a mouse!'

"You study only because I tell you to, right? Ping-Pong, softball, you participate because you are required to. You're never more than half-hearted and you wish the time would quickly pass. In short, you are...acting to suit the moment, and often you are, er..."

"'Taking an indifferent attitude toward everything.'" Mokuzu supplied the conclusion so often pinned on him by Miss Sakaki at his native school.

"Yes! You describe yourself well." Miss Yoshioka was impressed, and thence put out of humor, and her mood rose into a fountain of rage.

"Come now! Will you study more seriously and be more serious at extracurriculars?"

'That's it!' Mokuzu began to speak with composure:

"Miss Yoshioka, if I seriously study, I can finish in ten minutes what you teach for forty-five. What then can I do but steal ahead in the text? Suppose it's arithmetic. Naturally I'm absorbed. But the chime sounds and you dismiss arithmetic and begin Japanese as if nothing had happened in the past hour. So I'm serious for that and again finish in five minutes what you spend forty-five on. Inevitably I have to keep sitting there. Oppressed with boredom, I try to be serious anew, to keep thinking of matters relating to Japanese. Then again my serious study is cut by the chime and I realize you are announcing Social Studies.

"The natural outcome is that my seriousness can last only five to ten minutes. You tell me to be serious. It means in this case to maintain my seriousness of the first five or ten minutes till I get bone tired. You or this school water down study that can be done in five or ten minutes so that it takes forty-five. Moreover, after forty-five minutes each subject must be abandoned, which forces me to keep changing focus, and that is counter-productive to concentrating on my work.

"I have to say the schedule set up by you and this school prevents me from being serious. Now I hope you can see that telling me to be serious contradicts your teaching method."

Miss Yoshioka had been moving her mouth like a Chinese goldfish in her attempt to intervene, but Mokuzu was determined to seize this chance to air his frustration.

270

"The same can be said of sports and recess. Take Ping-Pong. Serious play means defeating one's opponent, so essentially one must slam the ball. But if I do, I'm blamed by you and my classmates for being too keen on winning, and if I return it mildly like a fool, you blame me for not playing seriously.

"If I'm serious about Ping-Pong I'm again trapped by the time limit. I estimate it takes five or six hours of daily practice to become a player who can receive and return any ball, even one that hits a corner of the table and can barely be returned by a normal player. Yet you provide just forty-five minutes, or ninety at most, and it must be shared by thirty-five classmates. Is there any way except not being serious?"

This unusual chance to express himself gave Mokuzu a pleasant sensation, and deciding it would be too regrettable to stop, he went on, ignoring his teacher's astonishment,

"If it's Ping-Pong it matters little — but for sumo, judo, or karate, the contradiction is more obvious. Take karate, which I began a year and a half ago at the insistence of my Zen master and my temple senior brother. There too the teacher spurs us to be serious, to risk our life. But I'd say half a year is enough to master the various forms. Thereafter the main practice is *randori* — free practice, as if fighting in earnest. However, we are forbidden to hit the mid-brow, the solar plexus, and such vital points, even in this so-called free practice. We must stop short, with no less than the width of a fist or foot between. Under these restraints we are told to be serious. Can't you see the contradiction? If we were serious we could kill or be killed.

"In my understanding, speed and accuracy are of fatal importance in karate; force isn't a major factor. I needn't use much to blind you. A baby's power is enough! Well, were I serious, you'd be this instant blind!...Now can you understand? I take an indifferent attitude because I know I shouldn't be serious when I'm told to be serious.

"My temple brother has studied karate for eight years. He's built large and strong and is the strongest in the hall, where there are boys older than he. Everyone thinks he'll be the successor. He can break through ten roof tiles and split a cedar board two centimeters thick, against the grain. But if we had to fight for real, I'd win. He can strike only 2.5 times per second. I can strike 3.5. I have no reason to wait for him to demolish me with one of his blows — he can strike with the force of 500 kilograms. Who'd wait around under a bell tower to have a 10-ton bell drop on his head? Before he blinks, I'll be striking one of his vital points. He's stronger, but, you see, he won't necessarily win.

"What I want is the practice where I can prove if what I just told you is so. But it isn't allowed. We study karate as a sport, and sports ask players to be serious under many conditions that restrict them from being serious. In conclusion, what can I do but do things moderately?

"By the way, my temple brother is strong before a static object and can damage anyone with dull reflexes. But with an opponent swift as a swallow, he can't do a thing. Up a steep mountain overgrown with miscellaneous trees he can't move about and can only roll down like a rock. I grew up in such a place and caught squirrels and hares with my hands."

What first induced Mokuzu to speak was his fury at Miss Yoshioka, but he now realized it was dissipating like vapor.

Miss Yoshioka was surprised by this pupil who was rather beside himself with anger or at least was showing an uncommon candor. She had been affecting a pleasant smile but was beginning to enjoy his effusion. She decided he was a boy who needed to be given occasions to express his earnest convictions.

She understood why he felt there was a contradiction and why he was irritated; but her understanding was as limited as that of a dweller of the Temperate Zone who says he understands the life of a Hyperborean.

She had always slaved at her studies. Were that his trouble, she could have understood and even felt some affection and respect. As it was, her feelings tended toward envy and hate. Bitterly she was reminded of her six years' labor for her doctorate, as well as the courses yet to complete while teaching primary school. Thought of the many hurdles made her grind her teeth. To expect her to admire him and search for a fitting method to educate him was out of the question. So, her final words were unsuited to the mind of a teacher.

"Unfortunately for you, our old education system was abolished a few years after you were born. In that system a child who showed high exam results could be accelerated a grade. But you should thank your Zen master for providing you with top-notch private instruction tailored to your needs.

"Are you aware that Professor Doka held a professorate at Kyoto Imperial University until his retirement and is even now a leading authority on Buddhist history? Professor Ishida obtained his PhD from Harvard. Dedicating himself to the study of American literature, he accepts no position, though such excellent institutions as Kyoto University and Osaka University wish to engage him. And do you know Setsuro Kimura is a judge for the art exhibitions sponsored by the Juridicial Corporate Association, which awarded him a prize even before he graduated from Kyoto Art College? It was said he would have received an Order of Cultural Merits had it not been for an incident of questionable behavior.

"You should account yourself fortunate to be given this luxurious opportunity to study directly from these teachers, each excellent in his field."

Until then Mokuzu had regarded Miss Yoshioka as an adult belonging to a world about which he could infer nothing. She now looked suddenly inferior, even shabby, for envying his state. He realized that she had been a local train running ahead of his express and that he had caught up and in an instant was leaving her behind like a black dot.

æ

Mokuzu's four private teachers as well as Unkai, Luri, and Reiho were also aware that Mokuzu was not enjoying his life, though he was interfering with no one else's. Even Zen Master Hanun, who was mostly away, sensed his displeasure.

Generally the four teachers and the Zen master were at one in their view that quiet observation was their best course. Such a period ought to be experienced by everyone as a process of growth, they thought, and each in his way was focusing his effort to make Mokuzu into a profound and powerful man.

Teacher Setsuro told him,

"You have mastered all the techniques presented in *Jietzy-yuan huachuan* (Mustard seed garden manual of painting). But don't forget they are inherited, none is your own. You seem to understand quite well about sketching, so just keep at it. However, your finished paintings aren't much above the product of a box camera. If you render beauty equal only to nature, why bother so tediously to waste your time? Better to put away your brushes and just look. Be alert! Every dot, line, and color must be more beautiful than nature or your painting is rubbish.

"Above all, there are too many traces of your contrived thought. If with your choplogic you wish to express what you think, then speak it, write it. For sumi painting you must direct your effort to what has never been painted by anyone nor been contrived by your brain."

Teacher Yojun one day brought six or seven heavy books.

"Master Mokuzu, you can now proceed to study English literature almost by yourself, for I have taught you the basic grammar, and here are two excellent dictionaries, English to Japanese, and Japanese to English.

"They are the best of those published in Japan, and are to the student what a pair of swords was to the samurai. The only thing two swords cannot cut is klesa, for klesa can be cut only by enlightenment, as your Zen master is wont to say.

"Now, learning grammar is like learning the rules of baseball. Actually it's a petty comparison, for however you put yourself into a sport, your body and not necessarily you mind is nourished. If you train to develop only your physical strength and skill, at most you'll be like a grasshopper flitting from

273

grass to grass — very different from a man who can appear anywhere, anytime, who can cover his head with dust and bemire his face in this wide and unfathomable human world.

"So let me find a fitting simile. To know grammar is like opening an atlas to acquaint yourself with the names and locations of the countries and seas, no more than that.

"I presume you wish to step into various countries and experience their sights and climes. You must be wishing to see how the people live, in what milieu, how they feel and think. Applied to English study, it means you wish to read the literature written by the great people of England and America.

"It's unlikely you could appreciate these works by knowing grammar alone, just as you would be ill-prepared to travel knowing only names and places. You must prepare clothing, money, et cetera. For English literature you must prepare with grammar and also a certain amount of knowledge; that is, you must learn the common sense of the children of English-speaking countries, which they have gained at home, at school, and in society. In short, you need to know the soil from which English literature is raised.

"So we shall begin with the books I brought today. They are written in English and are the parent body of English literature and the essential common sense of English-speaking people. We shall spend one to two years on them.

"The first contains English and American phrases and fables. Collected herein are origin and history, events, traditions, allusions, myths, and folktales.

"The second contains poetry, songs, and nursery rhymes. The poems are divided by form into regular verse, free verse, and prose poem, and also classed by and large into epic and lyric. The songs are folk and art songs, the important one as traditional literature being the ballad, which made its appearance in England in the fourteenth century. As to nursery rhymes, we shall read *A Child's Garden of Verses* by Robert Louis Stevenson, Walter de la Mare's *Songs of Childhood* and C. G. Rossetti's *Sing-Song*.

"Then we shall study the various kinds of proverbs, which include the proverbial simile, saying, adage, maxim, and precept.

"At the close, to some degree we must look at etymology. When all this is mastered you will be ready to journey into the main body of English literature. With your preeminent retentive ability you should not find it so hard, provided you suffer no doubts over why you should study it, thinking it has no relation to you at present. But you must privately come to terms with that. What advice I can give is, often we can find no answers to our important questions while we are continuing to ask, but answers do naturally come later on. If you question why you ought to study English literature, the answer will come once you begin.

"We shan't be concerned with English conversation. It can be attained if you visit, say, New York, and if you have in mind something of substance to converse about, and as long as you are given the chance. I ask that you earnestly study content and not waste your precious time on pronunciation, on how to speak.

"Consider for a moment what you'll find. On the avenues and cross streets even beggars and the youngest urchins are speaking English, but so vulgar is the content that you'll wish to clean out your ears, or it's so inane you'll think people haven't a divine nature after all. You mustn't study English conversation even an hour of your life, just as you ought to avoid, if you possibly can, working for money. But haven't I talked of this many times?"

ﾞ

'From now on I can almost totally ignore Miss Yoshioka; the way she is, it's inevitable she'll be ignored by me. She said I should seriously apply myself to her classes. But I'm sure she must have picked her words from a dump like a pair of old shoes. They're an echo of someone else's lecture; she doesn't know what it means to be serious. To be serious we have to know what we want to be serious for. Teacher Setsuro is more constructive. He says I must make a painting that hasn't been made, and it can't be something I've contrived in my brain. And while I don't know what I want to paint, I am to keep on practicing how to sketch, how to see.

'That seems the very thing I should heed with as much as eighty to ninety percent of my ability. Miss Yoshioka expresses envy like another pupil. Teacher Setsuro gives me direction.

'But the problem is, I don't know what I should paint with all my might. How is it possible to make a picture never made by anyone else and not

275

contrived by my brain? On top of that, he says it has to be more beautiful than nature...! Well, I don't doubt it can be done, but it would require all my unused power. I should paint such a picture, and as long as I can't, I'll not have the joy of a life that engages my full capacity.

'If I don't face the challenge with all my heart, he'll rightly not care a straw for my painting. Even I am not a bit satisfied to turn out ordinary paintings.

'Still, there's the problem of not knowing what or how I should paint with all my might.

'He's aware of my state and is whipping me on. I'm a fool who doesn't enjoy his present life yet doesn't know what he wants. Teacher Setsuro is a madman inciting the fool to become a genius!'

Mokuzu also kept pondering Teacher Yojun's words. 'He says I must quickly fit myself with wings to fly free in the vast world of English literature. He says it's a golden palace, a trove of sagacity, a close examination, dissection, exhibition of the mind, a stage whereon are presented bliss, rage, humor, pathos — all extensive, profound, sensitive, unconstrained thought...

'I've got to grow those wings. Too bad, I'd rather make the voyage right away. How frustrating to be only preparing! What's the fun of that?

'Will I come to know what I really want to do if I travel around in English literature? I ought to be able to, if, as he says, it is the very mind of those great world figures. He told me that with my youth and retentive faculty I should be ready for the journey in one or two years. He means, master origin and history, events, traditions, everything those English-speaking kids know as common sense — within two years!

'He said he'd first read and interpret each chapter. Then I'm to read it a hundred times, like chanting, to get it by heart. For sumi painting I've got to reject everything I've learned in order to paint what I've never thought up, whereas for English I've got to cram in more! Isn't that going to be another contradiction? No, each has its way, which must be the necessary condition for obtaining its essence. And both are alike for me insofar as their peaks are behind clouds. What is sure is I must prepare if I'm to get there, and just to prepare I must spend a lot of time and energy. Then shouldn't I suspect whether what I'll get is what I want and therefore whether devoting myself to preparing is what I should do?

'Certainly one cause of my distress is that I'm not using my whole ability, and the reason I'm not is that I don't know what to devote myself to. Am I to devote myself to finding what I want to devote myself to? What if I find it's not what I want? Teachers Setsuro and Yojun don't question this point; they appear to believe that by devoting myself I'll find the very thing I want. Here comes my second distress!

'Luri can blithely hum as she cooks, and why not? Everyone knows cooking is the preparation for a meal. And Reiho is like an airplane cruising just above the trees. That's how he goes about his schoolwork because he's saving his best for karate, where his goal is to be champion of the prefectural tournament.

'My goal is indiscernible, yet it must have some connection with me now. Oh, how I wish I knew what I really want! Then it couldn't be so hard to attain.

'For what am I preparing? Simply to know for what I've been preparing? Am I preparing for my future self to know my present self? What is this? The order is quite absurd!'

૱

Teacher Docho droned on without gesture or nuance of emotion as if reading from a book and as if ten years were but a day in the flow of politics, economics, agriculture, art, and religion from antiquity to the present in India, China, and Japan. But one fine day in May he said without warning,

"What a sprightly season! Our eyes are drawn to the virid foliage, the stream dances along, even the exanimate rocks emit cheer as they receive the moving shadows of the new leaves!"

Mokuzu, recording everything verbatim at Teacher Docho's behest, realized he was including this digression. He looked up. Teacher Docho smiled wryly and gestured as if to say, "Never mind, write it down, write it down!"

"Even so," he proceeded, "in just this season I was overcome with nervous prostration. Spring is usually considered the best season, but its perfection can be dolorous for some, as can holidays. Christmas is said to produce a high suicide rate in America, in Japan Old People's Day.

"University matriculation in prewar Japan was in autumn, commencement in spring. A thesis was required to graduate, but I couldn't write mine. Stacked on my desk like five or six silos were the writings mainly of Nagarjuna — such magnificent works as the *Mulamadhyamaka-karika,* the *Dvadasa-nikya-sastra,* the *Sunyata-saptati,* the *Vigrahavyavartani,* the *Yukti-sastika,* the *Mahayana-gatha-vimsaka,* the *Arya-ratnavali,* and all ancillary tomes of annotations by priests and scholars of later ages. And my manuscript paper, thereagainst, lay blank. I was stuck at my opening paragraph like the start of a bridge before a wide river.

"As I recall, I had a thousand times more desire than ability to write an exemplary thesis, and this outrageous desire was charged from behind by my aged parents, who greatly wished to see me graduate. I was like a steam locomotive without wheels!

"In fact I had already repeated a year, not by failing the exam but by my crazy confidence: I had thought if I stayed on another year I could write something better than a student thesis, more like the work of a fine scholar, enough to astound the community of Buddhist scholars. So my parents with a mix of grief and joy agreed to try to raise the money for yet another year. They asked only that I be diligent to finish this time, for they didn't know how long they could keep on living.

"To make a long story short, my thesis didn't advance and the deadline was pressing near. My friends were already employed or doing graduate work. The strain made me hypersensitive; I couldn't bear even the tapping of my father's pipe. I soon angered and was forever irritated. I lost my appetite, suffered diarrhea, and worse, began to shake.

"So, I didn't graduate this second time either. Dismal was the sight of my parents' chagrin, and withal, intense was my own disappointment, and my self-hatred, guilt, and anger toward them!

"My father asked a goma faith healer to light a holy fire at Daigoji for my sake, and my professors, also worried, took the trouble to introduce me to the psychiatrist Morita. But my state worsened with the advance of the summer heat. Sorry though I was for my parents, I shouted at them, 'Die, fools, begone!'

"Then came an odd development. I kept hearing my voice say to me, 'Not like that — you'd better die.' Whatever I did or thought it appeared — 'So shallow are your ideas, why are you still living?' From the mirror my reflection spoke—'Further sight of you is abhorrent. Useless dumpling, away!' Around the clock it was a nightmare, while I appeared only to be reclining in my study or the sitting room. I had no desire even to go out for a walk.

"There was however one exception. As soon as the western sky darkened and peals of thunder sounded and lightning began to strike, I was consumed with joy and felt a rising vigor. I even shouted, 'Strike more, sunder the sky, deluge the earth!'

"I've always been transported by electric storms. The fulminations used to terrify me, but an ineffable sensation would rise from my core, making me feel my bones would melt, and my pleasure eclipsed my fear. At the first clap I'd race to the top of the hill behind our temple and sit under a great tree to await the clouds. They usually came from the direction of Otokuni County, onrushing, whirling, expanding. Rolls of thunder shook the earth with deafening resonance, and their chains echoed around the mountains facing Kyoto....

"Then one afternoon — I remember it exactly, just past 4:30, on July 18th — I dashed out at the first rumble. My parents were as usual heaving sighs over my matters. My paternal aunt, over sixty in age, chanced to be visiting and was in the sitting room with them hearing their words with sympathy. I had been reclining in their presence. I don't recall their conversation, but surely they were grumbling.

"I ran, oblivious to the fast, hard raindrops. That day the storm came with uncommon speed. When I attained the summit, I was already amid the clouds and couldn't enjoy their approach. I could see, though, with great clarity, bolts like stakes driven at irregular intervals from heaven to earth, attacking the plain of rice through which the Katsura, Uji, and Kizu rivers flow to become the Yodo.

"Then, can you guess? There came a stentorian clap and I fell into a swoon. Maybe for five or ten minutes. When I revived I saw ascensions of flame at our temple roof. 'Great heavens, this is a matter for concern!' I ran down with all speed, only to find my approach barred by the consuming fire. So, in that way did my father, my mother, and my aunt go at once to heaven.

"Well, my nervous prostration was gone! Mirabile dictu! My mind was clear as water, limped as an autumn sky!

"Mysterious is human fate, indeed, hard to fathom...but I have at last begun a little to understand...."

&

"Ho ho ho, what a refreshing way to part!" Luri's laugh was sonorous. "Mokuzu, don't you agree?"

Luri was as always careful to appear merrily nonchalant. But seeing that Mokuzu remained serious, she thought perhaps she ought to apologize. This quick reconsideration even for the sake of a young boy came from her true mind, tender and sensitive to the shades of others' feelings. She was actually one of those young women who, while keeping up a bright countenance, suffer from inner distress and spend hours feeling sad.

"'Refreshing'? For whom, about what?"

"Isn't it obvious? For your teacher to part from his kin, or do you think I meant parting from his nervous prostration? Well, there's that too, but doesn't it amount to the same thing? You said he was suffering mainly from their huge expectations? Then, with them dead, his prostration died too. No fire, no smoke."

"I see..."

"Sure, that's it. You too, watch out. To have hopes placed on you means to be endlessly burdened. I don't know about your parents, but Zen Master Hanun and your private teachers are loading their hopes on you. Like a staff for their old age, they can't walk without their expectations.

"Really, Mokuzu, you care too much about your family. When I prepare good food you don't eat it, thinking your brother never had this, or your sister is pitiful. The other day too, when I took you to see *L'Affaire Maurizius*, directed by Julian Duvivier, you showed no interest and only stared at the rows of luxurious chairs, the loudspeakers, the audience, the fancy drop curtain. I know, you were thinking they can't see a foreign film in a gorgeous theatre — it showed all over your face.

"You can't do anything for yourself, can't expose yourself to any pleasure. That's how you see our telephone and electric washing machine and electric rice cooker, bought for us by Zen Master Hanun, right?

"From worrying about your family, naturally you can't focus on the reality in front of you. Were I like you, I couldn't even brush my hair. Reiho's ma died all covered with insects, but is he mourning? He long since discarded his past and every family matter like worn-out rubber boots. He may be a wild child, but his mind is sound as a virgin forest.

"So much thinking about your family is a sort of illness, because the effect is, you can't live with all your body and soul. It's the same as thinking too much about the future. Television is therefore very sane for dealing with today's events. Even when it deals with the past or future its aim is to address people here and now."

"But Luri, my family are all still living."

"You say so, but have they sent you a single letter? It's been two years now."

"Not two till fall. Anyway, I know how they are without letters, and the master visits them...though I don't disagree with you. It's true, as soon as I think of them I lose the wish to do anything pleasant for myself, whereas when I suffer I don't feel so much stress and can quietly endure. Any joy I might have I see beyond their sad faces, and when my circumstances are favorable I feel I must apologize to them.

"It's a problem. Since I can't do anything that brings me pleasure, I can't begin to know what to do with my life. And if I exclude all pleasures, what's left are only unimportant matters I can engage in with an absent mind...."

"Mokuzu, you really must take courage and cut them off."

"Courage?"

"Yes, because caring about them is good and not caring is bad — it takes courage not to care. As long as you do good, you can enjoy society's praise, even if your relation with society is slight; and you can praise yourself, even if it's merely self-congratulation. If you do bad, you'll be seen with disgust by others and by yourself and no one will give a hoot about you anymore."

"Not caring would lead me to further despair..."

"Well, but if you get past this difficult point, you'll be free of others' appraisal and can outgrow yourself. Then for the first time you can live your own new life."

Mokuzu began to understand more clearly who this woman Luri was. He had thought she was unreachable, maintaining an incomprehensible air. Now he thought,

'One essential difference between adults and children could be that adults, because they have courage, are capable of doing wrong out of need, whereas children are hardly capable.'

Luri was seventeen and in the second year of a girls' senior high school. Her hair was glossy, her appearance immaculate. With the season nearing summer, she wore a short-sleeved blouse. Dancing sunlight entered her room and lit up her arm. The inner side of her upper arm looked exceedingly soft and white and came close to brushing the side of her breast when she moved. As if an independent part, her breasts curved abruptly out; there her loose blouse was smooth. In finer detail he saw that they moved up and down as she breathed. Her faded red skirt had no belt and was secured with a hook and zipper.

Her cheeks were as if infused with rose. Her shiny black pupils looked moist. Often they were hard to catch; they seemed focused far away or on nothing. But when she spoke to him they caught his and dizzied him with their ardor and brightness. At such times they looked like light flashing through the dark.

In the silence Mokuzu thought over what she had once told him of her past.

'She was born in Sumiyoshi, Osaka. When she was seven — just before I was born — an air raid reduced her community to ashes. In the chaos she was separated from her parents. After much searching they found her in an orphanage and visited her several times. Then their visits stopped. She was told they had begun a business that soon failed and had fled north in the night.

'She didn't do well in the orphanage; it was unbearable. Then abruptly she was adopted by Zen Master Hanun, and with no word about her new life she came to Ryotanji, seven years ago. She must have been ten, as I am now. Unkai had recently come and was recuperating. Reiho had by then been three years with the master....I wonder if she wasn't brought only to perform the domestic chores of this temple....'

Just as the sun ceased to enter, Luri broke the silence. "Mokuzu, I feel sorry for you. But you'd better graduate from the bonds of your past." She had put her hand on his shoulder and was looking into his eyes. To receive such tender sympathy was so rare since coming to Ryotanji, or since ever, except from Ena, that Mokuzu felt a light had been turned on in a dark room.

A substantial emotion rose in his chest, closer to liquid than vapor, more sour than sweet, more yellow than blue, if there was a color for it, like a hot spring gushing through the sandy earth of his body. He grit his teeth and tightened his face lest it escape.

Luri drew him close and embraced him. Her arms pressed his back, and his cheek was pressed so hard against her soft, springy breasts that he worried in a flash whether she might get hurt. As if to herself she said,

"I know only one way to free you. I wish I could teach you...should I? You must graduate and open your life like the thrust of a jet plane. As far as I know, mental pain is soothed only by pleasure of the body...."

25

The Sea and a Prayer

Mokuzu was enjoying the midsummer sun casting its light without hesitance on everything and giving a person no excuse to scruple over trifles or to feel melancholy. He was enjoying the heat that made him sweat all over even as he sat idle.

When vacation set in, Reiho went to the Shiga Highlands in Nagano Prefecture to lodge with his fellows for karate training. Mokuzu too was of course invited, but he felt more charmed to be taken by Luri to Takahama on the Japan Sea.

The Shiga Highlands were said to be a prime summer resort area encompassed by mountains two thousand meters high and graced with ponds, lakes, hot springs, and craters among sightly forests of white birch, hemlock, and larch. But Mokuzu longed to see the expanse of shining blue water and the white sand under the scorching sun, never yet given a chance to see them. And, all things considered, there would be Luri, soft and kind.

Unkai recommended an express from Nijo Station, but since they both liked to ride the train, they chose a local.

Luri wore pale vermilion shorts and leather sandals. Her white short-sleeved blouse was generously open at the top, with only a bra underneath. She carried a lady's big straw hat. Mokuzu wore his straw hat, and a white short-sleeved shirt, khaki shorts, and rubber sandals. From their appearance they were obviously going to the beach.

She let him take the forward-facing seat and sat across, tucking under her legs a canvas bag with their change of clothes, towels, and sundries.

Other passengers were few, and, it being vacation, they were mostly small parties of youths in modish line-alphabet polo shirts and mambo pants, playing *hana-fuda*.

"Mokuzu, you must be familiar with this region."

"As far as Kameoka. I rode this line to Ryotanji. The water's low now, but with a great rain it can rise to the tracks."

282

"That high? It must be scary."

Together they hastily pulled down the heavy wood-framed window whenever the train entered a tunnel and raised it after the train passed through. Trains of the Sanin line were still fueled by coal, so the windows had to be shut in the tunnels or some passengers would cough, and again raised in the open air or the heat was unbearable despite the ceiling fans.

The scenery continuously shifted with no effort from the passengers. Meanwhile eulalia and bush clover bent so close as to almost cover the track. Then the view abruptly opened to a leisurely river and wide rice fields and hamlets set up into the mountains. There was a grand steep roof in *irimoya* style surrounded by a stone wall at the verge of a hamlet, evidently a temple. A lone house atop a hill was enclosed by a hedge. Some houses bordered the river, each with a small wooden bridge.

"Mountains and mountains, they're everywhere!" sighed Luri.

Rice was planted right up to the mountain skirts, and the skirts too were made into terraced fields for vegetables and fruits. Even the mountains were under cultivation, with neat forests of cedar, cypress, or pine.

"Oh! What are they doing with that bamboo pole?"

A boy attended by younger children who looked like his siblings was gazing up at the dense foliage of a windbreak of sawtooth oaks along a brook.

"They're after cicadas. Don't you know about that, Luri? You loop a willow twig into the end of a bamboo pole and over the loop you wind strands of spiderweb. Raise the pole to a cicada and you've got it!"

"Did you see? A giant tree covered all of that roof!"

"A cherry. I bet it's worth more than the house....Hey, we're going to cross a tall iron bridge."

Luri twisted, extending a leg. To see ahead was easy; they were now running along a broad curve. The simple-truss bridge spanned mountains thickly robed in green. The foundation bricks looked old, but the trestle was a bright Chinese red, no doubt recently repainted.

"In this remote area a bridge so brightly dressed? I wonder why...weird... like having two partners, if you think of these mountains as men. Maybe some designer in the National Railway Corporation had such a fantasy," Luri commented and laughed childishly.

They disembarked at Ayabe to change to the Maizuru line. While Luri bought box lunch and refreshments at a kiosk, Mokuzu stood at the edge of the inactive platform and watched their train disappear.

'Where would it take me if I hadn't gotten off? Sooner or later it will come to its terminal...someday I'd like to make sure with my own eyes....'

The next train reversed them some distance along the same track.

Mokuzu was mystified. Then it arced onto a new course decisively north. 'What fun! But why does it excite me so?'

"A penny for your thoughts," Luri said and pressed a mandarin orange to his brow. Frozen since winter harvest, it was like sherbert inside. She pressed it on the inner side of her thigh and exclaimed, "Ouu! how cold!"

A faintly round, red impression momentarily remained on her tender white skin.

They knew Maizuru harbor had once prospered as a naval port. But the rows of ashy old warehouses and the blue-gray patrol boats now and then visible in between seemed a shabby sight, indeed suited to a defeated nation.

At Maizuru they changed again, for the Obama line. The connection was just on time.

"Ah, that's the famed Mt. Fuji of Wakasa," Luri pointed out.

"It doesn't look marvelous at all."

"True, it can't compare with the real Mt. Fuji."

"Too bad it had to be crowned with such a name or it could have enjoyed being itself."

"I see your point. Such well-intended praise is like a slight."

As soon as the train left a fairly long tunnel, the deep blue ocean appeared beyond a sequence of leaning pines. Mokuzu could tell without hearing that the white-capped waves were breaking onto the beach of Takahama.

They got off at a small station with a short platform and simple corru-gated roof and could easily spot among the sparse gathering the boss fisherman come to fetch them.

"Welcome, you must be travel-worn. Don't worry, our house is but five minutes away. Come!"

His face was the color of chicken teriyaki. He sported a crew cut and must have once been dapper, but was now wrinkled and mild of mien.

Mokuzu had been impressed by Luri's briskness in getting tickets and finding the right platforms without confusion. Now too he admired her and felt great trust in her, for she was capable of speaking clearly and of switching from local speech to standard speech in talking with their new acquaintance, known as Genzaemon.

'I'm shy even about buying pencils. In her place how perturbed I'd be!'

"Zen Master Hanun-kutsu was just in Hiroshima. He's now in Tokyo, hey? It's swell so many signatures for the atom and hydrogen bomb protest could be gathered, more than thirty-two million nationwide and six hundred seventy million worldwide, they say. Let's hope it has clout with the Americans, British, French, and Soviets to manifest the spirit of Geneva!"

"Do you know he plans to erect a Kannon statue for world peace up

284

behind Ryotanji? He says it will be a match for the Statue of Liberty at Bedloe's Island."

"Aye, young lady, and he'll do it. I'm not much myself, but whatever needs doing in this district to raise the money, it'll be done!"

Mokuzu could make little sense of their talk.

After being led down several doglegs of a poor alley lined with ditches for bath and kitchen drainage, they came to a comparatively large house. The storm doors and every shoji and fusuma were wide open. At a glance they could see the broad earth-floored vestibule, the guest room and its alcove, and even the household Buddhist altar. Genzaemon's wife, whose flat face was dark like his, appeared with two large slices of watermelon on a tray. She wore a black half-apron. In a difficult dialect she spoke something like the following:

"Take your ease, stay as long as you want. The sea can be harsh. The other day thirty-six junior high school girls came from Mie Prefecture to learn to swim and were carried off by a wave. Keep an eye on your boy, he mustn't swim far. Don't mix with the other children. Many are here now from the Keihanshin districts and you could lose sight of each other."

As soon as Luri and Mokuzu finished the watermelon, the wife lifted their canvas bag and said, "We'll go."

Mokuzu wondered, 'Go where?' but quietly followed. Walking somewhat ahead she led them back through the closely built-up area, across the main road after the bus went by, and onto a footway alongside a thin belt of rice fields between the road and the mountains. The path ascended into terraced fields and on to a hill against a steep mountain. On the hill was a small house with the appearance of a retreat cottage.

It was wide open on all sides, but no one was there.

She motioned them forward. "If you prefer, use the veranda to come and go. It's nice and quiet here, with a view...."

Beyond the clustered fishermen's houses was the sight of the leaning pines and the sea now almost green.

"Children of all ages are staying at our main house; they're at the water now. They make a racket late into the night, so it's hard to sleep. To get to the beach from here is a bit of a bother, but you won't be disturbed."

Talking, she beckoned to Luri and showed her the bath room and adjoining shower, a kitchen with propane-gas cooking facilities, and a closet of bedding. Finally she left, saying,

"You're welcome down anytime, but I reckon you can't take the salty food, coming from a Kyoto temple. I'll bring you vittles you can prepare to your taste. Very well...oh, you can go to the beach in your bathing suits. I'll be up betimes; just speak your needs."

Luri and Mokuzu looked at each other and could not keep from smiling because of the dialect and because they were now left alone, free of strain.

"First I have to go wash my hands," said Luri. There were three rooms, two six-mat size and one four-and-a-half. The cottage, recently built, was very clean.

"What time is it? We've no watch, but it must be well past two. Oh, we needn't care." Luri took a pillow from the closet and lay down on her back. "We'll swim after a short rest."

Mokuzu did not feel tired. He stood on the veranda and regarded the green ocean beyond the pines. When he turned he saw Luri lying relaxed, looking up at the wood ceiling...her breasts and her mons veneris alone protruded. He walked past a back corner under a parasol tree and descended to a vegetable garden. The soil was sandy. Squash and sweet corn were ripening. He milled around.

Even after dark, just as the wife had said, the clamor from the beach continued. Many school children were setting off fireworks or singing in chorus around bright campfires.

After supper they lit a coil of Dalmatian pyrethrum mosquito-repellent incense on the veranda and enjoyed the sea breeze. The pines lining the beach were like a black shadow-picture. The flames of campfires rose in places. The commotion entwining with the sound of the waves seemed now after the day to have intensified.

"Shall we turn in?" Luri spoke. From the closet she took bedding for one person. She left the storm doors open but closed the shojis on the room side of the veranda.

Outside the stars twinkled like falling rain. Inside was pitch-dark.

As soon as she entered beneath the quilt Luri drew Mokuzu in and tightly embraced him. Under her cotton kimono she had on nothing but thin silky panties.

The salt water of their afternoon swim had encroached on every nook and corner of her body, and her skin was soft and smooth. Her damp hair wreathed gently around his fingers.

Her hips now and again moved reflexively. Worrying that he was tickling her, Mokuzu stopped his groping hand. But soon she was turning her thighs outward and more outward to expose their softest inner sides, and rather deliberately she raised her pelvis as if reaching for something.

Seemingly growing impatient, she seized his hand and forced it against the top of her crevice and vibrated it finely.

Like a leopardess she turned, stripped off his underwear as if not moment was to be lost, and held him where he had stiffened, caressed it, pressed it agitatedly to her nipples, even kissed it.

"Feel free to do anything — this isn't Ryotanji," she panted.

"I wish I could see..." he whispered.

"You mean turn on the light?...how about tomorrow? This is only the first night. To make up, you can do whatever you wish, even bite...as long as the darkness is kept."

Mokuzu finally turned and buried his face in her groin. He inserted his tongue, then a finger, then two, and was amazed at her depth as he put in three. More, he marveled that his fingers were rather drawn in by a steady contraction. Her mucous secretion and many folded striated muscles made his hand slip so that his fingers were urged in and out.

Finally she threw off the quilt, leaned on her elbows, put her face to the bed, drew in her knees, and raised her buttocks.

'How wonderful if there could be light! Then all of what she is would be exposed before my eyes!' He was using both hands, his face, every available part of himself, as if grappling.

With bodies embraced, slippery with sweat and mucus, entirely exhausted, each as they verged on sleep felt they were riding a cloud over green hills rolling out of sight...over a fulvous autumn plain....

Before dawn they swam in the sea, dark but for starlight breaking on the waves.

The afternoon beach was as lively as before with family parties and school children led by their teachers.

Luri and Mokuzu ducked under the rope of orange buoys and swam to the quiet end of the bay, where the water was shallow and transparent and rocks were naturally piled. Sea anemones, sea urchins, and starfish adhering to the rocks were opulent, and in their midst swam innumerable small rainbow-colored fish. After a while they began to wade back to where they had left their towels, hats, and canteen on a straw mat.

Just then a large group of newly arrived junior high school students was finishing warm-up exercises, instructed by teachers with megaphones. From their position behind the mat with Luri's and Mokuzu's belongings they began to advance in orderly rows to the water. Some teachers stood watch under the school banner; others placed themselves at the head and sides of the group as it moved warily into the deeper water.

"They look more like they're practicing for mass suicide than studying swimming."

"Mokuzu, what a thought! — by drowning? But you're right, it does look so. How sad that children from the poor backcountry can't come here unless they're sent as a school group. You must know how we are among the blessed few."

When they had approached enough to read the letters embroidered in white on the russet velvet banner farther up the sand, they saw that it spelled out "Ikuji Junior High School."

Mokuzu stopped in mid-stride and let the waves wash past his knees. 'That's the school of my native village — Gyodo must be in his first year there.'

Alertly he began to scan the array of boys advancing from short to tall into the water. Their expressions were a mix of unease and joy. Some had begun to splash one another, some were submerging their faces, some were turning back to exchange pleasantries...there were sixty to seventy including the girls.

"What's the matter?" called Luri. "Why have you stopped?" She had gone quite far ahead and began to come back.

Mokuzu was searching the rear, not yet in the water.

"Oh, there's my brother! — " He began to run in spite of himself. As he ran he came to realize that Gyodo stood at a slight remove, that he had spotted him, that he must have been observing him from well before he himself had begun to be aware of the chance of their meeting, likely from when he and Luri were on the rocks.

He realized, moreover, that Gyodo was observing him more coldly than might a stranger.

Mokuzu noticed that his hot rush of blood was rapidly cooling, yet, like a racehorse unable to stop, he ran until he came up short before his brother.

"Gyodo!"

"Gyodo, maintain your line, you're a group leader!" From farther off, a teacher was shouting through a megaphone.

Gyodo filed with his classmates toward the water.

"Gyodo!" Mokuzu cried anew and followed him to the waves rippling up the sand. "Tell me how's Ma!"

"What you said was untrue!" Gyodo shouted back. "She's in great danger!" With no further word he entered the water.

Luri rolled up the mat and carried it and the canteen and their hats. As they walked through the pines she again asked,

"What is the matter? Was that your brother? What happened, can't you explain? Maybe I can help."

But Mokuzu was in a brown study. 'To meet after so long, and by chance, here! It should have been happy. Why wasn't it? He was like a crowbar left abandoned on an icy night!

'He had to lead his group, watch, behave. Maybe it was that, if I consider his nature. But couldn't he ask for a moment's leave on account of me? Who would be so dull as to forbid it? He must have decided he hadn't enough reason; he's not so prudent he couldn't ask if he wanted to.

'But why? I sensed no reproach, no grudge in his answer. He said what he judged was right, thinking he should at least say that much, it being my greatest concern too. It was a kindness, his steadfast brotherly love.

'So the reason he was the coldest ever to me isn't coming from our past together. Rather, because of our bond, he expressed as much as he could. Then his coldness has to be explained by whatever went on after we parted. News of me could come only from Zen Master Hanun or from rumor, and he wouldn't judge by rumor....Is it because his character has in some way changed? Or because he saw me with Luri?

'You aren't responsible for any change in his character,' he addressed himself. 'You haven't been together. You can take note of it, but you shouldn't blame yourself for it...No, I've no reason to be blamed. But now what concerns me most is what he might have perceived today.'

Meticulously he tried to examine each element like checking the electrical circuit of a radio to find the origin of a defect.

'As soon as he spotted me with Luri he must have confirmed whatever sure information he had about me since we parted and assimilated this newest more sure information.

'If my ability to comprehend things is measured as one, his is at least one point five. He's that much quicker, deeper, and wider. But to know the substance of his present great comprehension, I'd have to recall all the details of my life since we parted. Like a movie film it would need to be rewound and viewed again...but in actuality how much retentive and recollective ability do I have?'

When they returned to the cottage on the hill Luri took from the well a pan of jelled agar she had made in the morning and left to cool. She sliced it in cubes and brought it to Mokuzu. He was sitting on the veranda looking out to sea. Then she went and sat against an interior post and stretched out her legs. As they ate he spoke up,

"Last night you said nobody could know what we did in the dark, but I think it can be known."

Luri briefly flushed.

"Did I say that? Well, isn't it true? Who can know unless they're hiding somewhere?"

"The only ones who don't know are those who are involved, and the blind — and I don't mean physically blind." Mokuzu's tone was sharp.

Luri had put on just a bra and panties after showering. Now she stood up and slipped into a long-sleeved white blouse.

"So what? You think your brother guessed and is displeased? It only amounts to guessing as he likes about what is none of his business. We didn't do it in public. It's a common truth that whatever needs our concentration must be done in private — work, study, sleep, toilet, sex — the worst enemy is mental disturbance. It's evil to guess, discern, or spy on others' private acts."

"He neither guesses nor discerns, nor spies. He just knows. And he knows that knowing is ignominious, so he doesn't speak. Still, he can't stop knowing, it's like instinct with him. So he must act cold with me."

"Come now, you're taught by three private teachers, aside from your own good brain, and you can deliver all kinds of high ideas in rapid sequence like baby crabs. Isn't what you want to say simply that your brother is jealous?"

"Maybe, though I know little about such a thing."

"Then why care? You are brothers, but different in character and circumstance. There's no point in being jealous of differences. Whoever is jealous is wrong, especially if you do what you do in private. You aren't wrong in the least."

"Luri, it's not a problem of who is wrong. What shocked me was his sad and pure nature and his poor situation on account of which he can't help envying his brother."

Luri stood and went to the next room. Unobserved, she sadly bit her lip. From the canvas bag she took a celluloid soap box containing sewing items. Bringing it with Mokuzu's shorts in need of mending, she came and sat again in the same place. Her utterance was like a drop of rain —

"You haven't changed...."

"About what?"

"In May you were close to nervous prostration, mainly because you felt you couldn't be thorough at what you were doing out of extreme concern for your family. I said you must free yourself, can't you remember? But here you are, bound by family. You are overly worrying about your brother, you truly are."

"I see. Just as you say: a splendid continuation of being pressed by weighty bonds."

"It's not splendid. I hate the way of life of anyone who stays in wet clothes. When I'm a mother I'll take care to change my baby's diaper as soon as it's wet. A shilly-shally is a detestable sight! You'd think he's enjoying his indecision, but no, his heart is dark. Japan is too damp and shadowy. *Adoration of Shadows*, ha! I only skimmed that book, but from the title I can tell its uncanny substance must be like a slug. To heck with *sabi* and *wabi* — they're the tastes of old men with neuroparalysis whose sole appetite is for food and sex.

"Far more fun than tea ceremony or haiku would be to rip along the beach on a motorbike or make waves on water skis!

"Kabuki, Noh theatre, I hate them! They're a national mobilization of antiquated ghosts! Firemen ought to blast soda pop on whoever mutters that this is the Japanese culture we can boast of to the world!

"Oh well, let 'em take their course. As for you, Mokuzu, you must live a more decisive, more logical life. Why don't you cart all your worries to an incinerator and straightaway burn them up? So often you hold off, hesitate to decide, obscure the issue, and entertain groundless fears like that guy in ancient China who worried himself sick over the chance of a natural disaster, and a friend caught his worry and sickened too.

"I'm no authority, but I think the world's great people have always been remarkably simple in their thinking."

"Luri, what you say is as fresh as a dew-speckled apple. It makes sense. I want to live like that. But you can discard your parents like old stockings because they abandoned you. My family have been kind to me; they're not old stockings but the very feet that enable me to stand and walk.

"Gyodo taught me not to drink muddy water, how to wrap my cut finger in the leaves of *chidome gusa*, to tie a towel on my head against cold winds, from the time he was three or four. When there wasn't food and a layman came with sweets or dumplings for the dead, Gyodo later ran along behind the main building like a giant squirrel to get them for me. I asked him 'Aren't you going to eat?' 'No' he said and kept staring as they went into my mouth. I asked 'Don't you want?' 'I want!' Yet he didn't eat. I told him 'You eat too!' 'No!' He shed tears and shook to suppress his desire. That was before he was old enough to go to school...."

"Oh, that reminds me!" Luri stood up.

"...What?"

"We can eat corn! Aren't you hungry? You can eat two, can't you?" Luri stepped out to go down to the garden.

Mokuzu was enraged. He looked at her with contempt. Her shirttail was creased, and where it covered her fanny it was whiter in a triangular shape.

'What nerve! My earnest talk reminds her of her appetite and she gets up and leaves!...Well, who can expect a bird to have the mind of a fish? And I admit she's righteously annoyed. She came for a nice time. Why should she have to listen to such dreary stuff? She'll thank me for ruining her vacation!

'Furthermore, she doesn't know what more she can do for me now that I've revealed I haven't graduated from my family bonds, though she offered, yes, gave me the most intimate relation, her greatest physical kindness. I can't nullify that, and I won't. But one thing I must do before I graduate — '

Luri brought to the veranda four ears of sweet corn in fresh husks with bright brown tassels. Quietly she asked,

"What was that poem you taught me in English as soon as you learned it from your teacher Yojun?"

"Which do you mean, this?:

> "One for the cutworm, one for the crow,
>   One for the blackbird, and three to grow."[1]

"No, you taught me that, but there was one about Evangeline."

"Oh, from Longfellow:

> "Then in the golden weather the maize was husked, and the maidens
>   Blushed at each blood-red ear, for that betokened a lover,
>   But at the crooked laughed, and called it a thief in the corn-field.
>   Even the blood-red ear to Evangeline brought not her lover."[2]

"Yes....Poems are odd. Whenever I get to know one, its air hangs over me like a haze even if I can't recall all the words. And I can't see what it's up to except through the haze. You're studying so many I bet your world will become only haze."

"Why? I arrange them in a corner of my brain and don't let them loose until it's their turn to be on duty. Luri, setting aside your haze, what do you think about my leaving..."

"Leaving? For the beach to see your brother?"

"No, for home, Tangenji, where I grew up."

Luri stopped her hands in the middle of husking. "Why? What makes you decide so suddenly?"

"You may think I'm abrupt, but that's not exactly true. It's like lava gushing from a crater after waiting for ages. A single persimmon leaf flutters down not without cause but as it should after completing its growth as a leaf and its duty to photosynthesize. Since those days in spring, I've been wishing to go back once. Now's the time, if rather late."

"Then for what will you go? Tell me."

"To explain is like peeling an onion and ending with nothing. As you said, what must be done by mental concentration must be done in private. But I'll tell you briefly as best I can so you won't misunderstand. I will pray for my mother's recovery. The principal image at Tangenji is the Eleven-Faced Kannon. The *Sutra of the Eleven-Faced Kannon's Divine Spells* says that whoever believes in this Kannon and wholeheartedly chants the spells will be given a ready response. It lists ten virtues and four fortunes that come of believing in and chanting the spells. The first is the healing of any illness. So I'd like to go. Soon my mother's illness can pass."

"Mokuzu, how can you believe such superstition? Who can expect a train to cross the ocean and head for the Milky Way? Any train is fated to arrive at a railhead or roundhouse."

"Well, I once asked Teacher Yojun if Westerners believe the miracles in the Bible. He said he can't generalize about religious faith, it being a private concern differing in depth from person to person. And, as with any subject, the amateur's understanding is so far from the professional's that it's like comparing phosphorescence with atomic fire. He advised me to ask Teacher Docho, or maybe most suitably our master. That was his introductory remark, but he went on,

"'Even so, let me venture to say what common people think. We can get an idea by reading the books they praise, for instance, Somerset Maugham's *Of Human Bondage*, published in 1915. It's a kind of autobiographical novel. The protagonist, Philip, lame and orphaned, is raised by his clergyman uncle. One night on vacation from boarding school, he comes on these words of Jesus:

> "'If ye have faith, and doubt not, ye shall not only do this which is done to the fig-tree, but also if ye shall say unto this mountain, Be thou removed, and be thou cast into the sea: it shall be done. And all this, whatsoever ye shall ask in prayer, believing, ye shall receive.

"'Philip decides to pray nightly in his cold room before getting into bed, to ask God to heal his foot during vacation, and he imagines he will play ball and run and jump with the other children. After nineteen days of prayer, vacation ends. Philip wakes to find his foot unchanged. His uncle says it means he has no faith, so he redoubles his effort. This time he fixes on Easter. Soon he begins to doubt that anyone ever had enough faith. He recalls his nurse saying a bird can be caught by putting salt on its tail. But who can go near enough for that? He thinks it a practical joke. Before Easter he stops praying.'

"Well, Luri, Teacher Yojun told me this about Philip, and he said, 'It may be the general extent of what Westerners think about miracles, I guess.'"

Luri's bright laugh was like the sound of rolling pearls.

"See? To rely on God or Buddha is like wishing for snow to turn to sugar or a car to run on water!"

"You've missed the point. Teacher Yojun always tells first what's most important. Remember he said to ask a specialist."

"I bet Docho said that casting a mountain into the sea is so easy, but that you shouldn't ask divine aid if you have a bulldozer."

"Luri, you're right! He said certainly there are miracles and divine protection, but we mustn't ask for what we should solve by our own wisdom, perseverance, and effort. For so minor a problem, he said, Philip shouldn't ask

God's help. He should find his own way to a happy life, or he can find a yet happier life if he inquires into the meaning of living with his deformity. And he said, 'Another significant point is that Philip, albeit pitiable, prays for his private happiness. Were he to pray for another's, his prayer might be granted.'"

"So you'll pray for your mother! But tell me, did you ask our master? He and a Shingon priest must have different views, regardless of their both being Buddhist."

"Our master said, 'From others you can learn whatever is to be learned so long as it has color and form, which includes such things as knowledge, skill, and style. By yourself you must understand whatever has no form. I have my answer, you must find yours.' That was it — quite brusque. I decided to ask Unkai."

"Oh, had he something to say? He does nothing but meditate or chant as if ten years are but a day. What a life, living under the same roof with such an odd creature!"

"Luri, you really can tell what a person will say. He replied, 'Ten years is as a day.' He didn't alter his stern meditation form and resumed his silence. His one remark was like a dolphin barely surfacing and again submerging. Finally he said, 'A hundred years is as a day,' then, 'A thousand years...yes, it must be,' and so long was he silent that the shadow of the eaves passed over him entirely."

"Did you wait? — what were you doing, emulating his meditation? It's sheer madness. Imagine the sight of an almost thirty-year-old nondescript priestling and a ten-year-old boy doing such a thing! I don't understand why Truman and Stimson didn't drop their atom bomb on Kyoto!"

"Oh, I was soon exasperated and urged him to tell whether we can get what we want if we pray. He seemed to be hearing me for the first time, 'Pray? to a God or a Buddha? for a person's recovery? It depends on the person, but prayers are answered. It's a matter of time. For some it happens in a flash, for others after ten years of steady prayer, for others a hundred, a thousand, or ten thousand. Your prayer might be granted right away, mine after a million years, even if we pray for the same thing.'"

"A million years? Why can't he admit prayers are useless? Well, never mind, do you really wish to go? I've no reason to object if you think it will satisfy you. By the way, I'll go with you, I'd love to; after all, we're on vacation and I can see your native home. Kameoka is about midway between here and Kyoto. There's no point in staying on alone watching the water."

Luri sustained no interest in Mokuzu's wish to pray to the Eleven-Faced Kannon for his mother's recovery; she regarded inquiry into abstractions as the business of feeble old men.

Nor did Mokuzu wish to tell her. Simply he sensed that the time had come to pray and that it was his supreme duty and donation to his nearest brother and sister. He believed if he prayed he would be doing his best. All else he would leave to Providence. And thereafter he would face any kind of reality and deal with it clearly and directly. Fortunately Luri pressed him no further. To explain would require him to bring all sorts of analogies and conjectures, when his decision rose from the compounded totality of his life of recent years. Naturally an explanation would turn contradictory and incoherent, and his mounting frustration would lead him to blow his temper like an overburdened fuse.

He had at this time so-called pure faith, a beam-like intuition: he had to do This, and do it Now. And one further condition was that it had to be done By Himself. So he refused Luri's company.

"Please wait. Much as I must disoblige you, I have to go alone. I'd be embarrassed if you came. If I start now I can reach Kameoka by evening at the latest. Then it's just an hour by bus. That will give enough time to go up the mountain behind Tangenji and pray there. I'll come down next morning and be back here around noon. That's how the prayer has to be done."

"Oh dear, you treat me like a nuisance!...but it can't be helped. Do as you wish, I don't care — though frankly I too have many things I'd like to express. Anyway, I'll make rice balls and see you off at the station. I'll buy you a round-trip ticket. Are you able to obtain a bus ticket? Just ask the conductor. Ask anyone whatever you don't understand. Don't be an idiot and lose your way! Okay?"

26

Ran's Letter

The sun's vigor was not yet enfeebled, and in the lingering summer heat the weeds and trees were a lively thick green. However, summer was over for social human beings: ocean swimming was prohibited, entering certain mountains was also artificially restricted, and done were the summer festivals and sports meets.

Summer's end made a definite impression on Reiho especially. He had been assiduous in his karate practice for the All-Prefectural Kyoto Tournament and had walked off with the championship as he had wished. But in the wake of the event his delight was as minute as a poppy seed and he sensed he was witnessing the solid earth crumble and sink beneath his feet.

"Karate is so dangerous, the maximum competition for junior high school boys is prefectural with no chance to determine who's best nationwide, and of course there's nothing worldwide. I have to settle for best in Kyoto with no higher aim!"

His thought was swept away by Mokuzu, who simply pointed out, "You won at the prefectural junior-high level. You can go on to the prefectural senior-high, college, and university levels. And there must be some world tournament, if not at the Olympics."

'True,' thought Reiho. 'Then why do I feel so blue? Am I impatient to be the world's best right away?' He was confused, and again to clarify himself he expressed his thought to Mokuzu.

"Reiho, if you wanted to be best in the nation or the world and if it could put you in seventh heaven, you'd be happy with winning in Kyoto; at least you'd not be grieving."

"Hmm, so why isn't this summer's end like normal? All the summery things in my life seem to be gone. Explain!"

It was an order, though in fact a plea belied by a bold front. Mokuzu realized Reiho was genuinely confused. 'How am I to clarify his mind when his mind is unclear even to him? If I suppose it's like a gobbet of mincemeat, then my work is to restore it to its proper anatomy!'

"Quick! If I have to stay in this morass, I'll turn into another detestable Unkai!"

"To your surprise, you could be quite alike. To see what I mean, you have to know that as to this matter there are two kinds of people. The first measure everything as victory or defeat and enjoy the one and hate the other. The second, to which I think you belong, hardly adhere to such a simple standard. They think it has nothing to do with surface appearance, that winning and losing is merely the judgment of outsiders."

"Yeah?"

"You can't be happy by winning. You're sad that you saw karate for so long as only victory or defeat, that you didn't notice or you ignored this more important issue.

"To illustrate, say, Japan and America fought. Japan lost, America won. America should enjoy its victory, occupy Japan, and subordinate the Japanese; in fact that seems to be partly so as to the looks of it. Yet America if it thinks it is succeeding is only proving a blindness to the more important aspect of Japan and the Japanese. Why? Because Japanese culture since ancient times, the mingled joyful and sorrowful feelings and thoughts of most Japanese, and the afterwar generation like us, not to mention the mountains, rivers, trees, grasses, soil, and rocks, are living where there's no influence from victory or defeat.

"Certainly many aspects, many things, were influenced by America's physical destruction. A lot of land, houses, and people as material were destroyed. Japan as a result has been suffering epidemics, economic poverty, and moral decay. Even so, there's much that received no effect. The grasses by the wayside, the autumn sky as it is today, the workings of our mind as we talk, are beyond the dream of those Americans celebrating their victory. That is to say, the kind of people who enjoy victory and cry at defeat don't know these others even as they exult in conquest or prostrate themselves in defeat..

"Reiho, after your victory you're seeking what can't be grasped by the standard of victory and defeat; you're directly facing what is impossible to grasp by that standard. Then I'll say, if you see the world as it is beyond victory and defeat, you can feel only sorrow."

"Hmm, I get what you intend to say. I have to acknowledge your talk is a rose with color and smell. But must you use so many thorny words? Well, it can't be helped, you're still in elementary school. Hey! I'm about through junior high and you're guiding me?...at least clarifying my mind. Yeah, my gloom is lifting, but of course not entirely. And now refreshed, I'm feeling talkative. At any rate, I don't have to kowtow to you — that'd be victory and defeat, get it?

"Besides, your teachers have cluttered your brain with goblins and jewels from the world over as if it's a limitless treasure house. My way is smarter. You have to be lectured by them. I can be lectured by just you while all their teachings are going through your brain. It's more efficient!"

"Reiho, I don't care about that. I have to give you another reason why you aren't clear. On top of what I said, let me say you are estimating the value of karate to be very low, though it's a righteous view. You think winning at karate is useless. You were practicing it as your dearest concern, but were taken aback that the reward for winning was so meager: you can't make even a leaf return to its bough, nor sweeten the bitter persimmon, and of course no one around makes much of you..."

"Stop. I dislike being poked in the eye or in the nerve of a tooth, for I know perfectly well what pain is and rather am on my guard against it....But, it's true. Who enjoyed my victory? Just you and the master. Rangai took it for granted, and worse, scolded me with 'There are many ways to win. Win beautifully!' Unkai only nodded. And Luri said, 'Did you notice the hands of the guy who gave you the trophy? Not calloused and gnarled, I bet.' A harsher irony than any crone might utter, yet I consider Luri my most important person!"

Zen Master Hanun was thinking Reiho ought to advance to senior high school after finishing junior high in the coming spring. Senior high, not being compulsory, required an entrance exam. Whether Reiho could qualify was uncertain; he never studied in earnest and his marks were bad. He himself rated study as less engaging than pickle-making.

The master considered a parochial school suitable, in particular one with a reputation for its upright and virile spirit as well as its various sports clubs. Reiho for his part knew the school was noted for its imbecilic and violent boys, who often appeared on the local news page. And more, he knew that most who graduated became priests of local temples.

'I don't want to become a priest! True, I was adopted by a priest, but nothing suits me less than the priesthood. Inheriting Rangai's karate hall is better, though I don't wish that either.'

Influenced by a casual remark from Luri, Reiho had concluded that his best course was to await her graduation from senior high the year after his from junior high, after which they would engage in some profitable work together.

'If necessary we'll leave here and rent a place in town,' he supposed, while at a loss about such vital points as how to raise starting funds, what work they would do, and what knowledge and skill they would need.

The near future was a haze and he himself like cotton candy. The one positive idea, thin as a lamp wick, was that he would be safe and his life have some brightness if he acted in concert with Luri. Hence he saw her as the person most important to him.

Reiho and Mokuzu were sitting against the slope with its dried natural lawn grass tall among the rocks, behind the master's quarters and directly under the pine mountain. Reiho's words were the last before they fell silent. They were facing the open east view of the roofs of the clustered houses of Kyoto beyond the descending cedar tops. Their eyes were eased by the soft range of mountains forming the border between Kyoto and Shiga prefectures. The triangular peak of Mt. Hiei, in the northeast part of the range, was prominent above all else.

Mokuzu saw each tree on those yonder mountains so clearly that he wondered if his eyesight had improved. As he regarded the foliage and branches of the cedars near at hand against the transparent blue sky, he felt a sense of serenity and dignity. In the shade of a rock at his feet several upstanding stems of late Lycoris were blooming in faint reddish purple, vividly expressing every hue of their flowers and stems.

'The flowers and trees coexist without violating one another,' he thought.

"A letter for you, Mokuzu, at last!" On her return from shopping Luri must have met the postman. She made her way up the slope with the letter, twisting to grasp a rock. She had an apron over her uniform. Being naturally tenderhearted, she thought her intrusion occasioned the silence between Reiho and Mokuzu, and she intended to withdraw right away. But Mokuzu was a step quicker to take the letter to his room.

The script on the envelope and on the many pages torn from a notebook was in pencil, done with uncertain childish strokes. It was from Ran and was the first letter he had ever received, not only since coming to Ryotanji, but since he was born,

> Dear Mokuzu my brother. I miss you. I tried many times to write but quit or didn't mail it because you leave my eyelids when I write.

'She must be in first grade. In summer her nose was beaded with sweat, in winter her face was red as a tomato...the retreat cottage...torn fusumas showing the frames, always a square of damp cloth on the wood step to wipe our feet on...tiger lilies in the side garden, althaea by the sasanqua hedge. We straddled the tiles of the wall, scared to look over to the path below....Memories come and go like the wind outside my shut room. I mustn't let it in or I can't do a thing. Teacher Docho described to me the Yellow River as 'fifty-four hundred kilometers of water flowing oblivious since eons past and even to this day.' I have to be like that and ignore all social clamor, all but my own concerns.'

> Ena says you know about her and she knows about you even you don't write. It is too amazing. I can't tell if you are in a glass castle or a rotten temple like here full of mice and centipedes and leaky roofs. How can she tell? I wish I could. She says you went to train and she will train to keep up. She takes any unpleasant thing today more than yesterday and tomorrow more than today and when she can't she says she is sorry to Buddha. If she trains she has the same mind as you so she can tell about you and you can tell about her without letters.

Alone in his dark room, Mokuzu blushed. 'Ena is watching me like the sun in the day, the moon at night! I haven't been idle, but it's a sheer fact she's been persevering more than me. Not just studying but training.'

> I asked can we understand people far off if we train. She thinks so. What is training? She doesn't really know but she studies to get ready so she can answer any questions. She is doing it so she can help if ever you are in trouble. She does not cry when she has problems. That way she can help when you meet yours. You are the same. You think for each other and train to solve each other's problems. I hope I got it right.

Mokuzu flinched. 'When did I endure hardship for Ena or study for her

299

sake? I yearned for her, thought of her as I faced each new scene here, and thought how great if we could run in this field or play on that dry riverbed. But I began to forget her and spent many days not thinking of her at all. How fine was her posture and bright her eyes!

'She's not like a mud-odored fish of a river or pond or swamp, not anymore, nor like an ocean fish. She's gone above the clouds, above the nimbostratus, the altostratus, even the cirrocumulus. I must speed up my study. And what's important is not to measure my efforts by those who dwell in a pond or swamp. They have no Ena and can afford to put their heads in the mud, tangle their tails in the dead reeds. At first glance they seem to be complaining, but truly they're enjoying their state. I mustn't be like that. I must respect Ena and repay her purity.

'What painful regret! When did I ever deeply care about her problems or study to solve them? Indeed I have to solve her grief. She's suffered from the treacherous quarrel of her parents. Her brow was filled with her sorrow, wasn't it? How bitterly she bore up!

'I felt my head would split when I saw my parents fight, yet to this day I yearn for them, and at times they appear in my dreams to give me joy. Their fights were material in cause and method. Her parents' fights involved more nerves and mentality, so she has had to feel a sharper pain. It is said that scent impresses more keenly than color or shape.

'Moreover, a so-called second father appeared, with the result that she was seen as a nuisance even by her mother. True or not, she felt so and worried that she was in their way. Yet she kept up her smile and her fine posture.'

Ran had evidently written thus far and left off for days or months. When she resumed, her pencil was sharper and her writing was improved, leaving more clean space.

> You came to Tangenji in the night and left in the morning Grandma said. I was shocked you never told. Even if asleep I would jump up. I was mad Grandma didn't say till too late. She should know I want to see you. She kept on in her poky way to tell what I don't understand. She said you came to pray for Ma and for nothing else. Praying is being purely spiritual she says. So not you but your soul came like in the old days they said it was a ghost. People who fear ghosts have no use meeting them she says.

Mokuzu thought of his leaving Luri at Takahama and going alone to Tangenji. He should have seen the sights out the window, but as if he were going through a white darkness nothing entered his mind. Dark had actually come on as the bus neared his native village; outside became pure black, his memory also.

Soundlessly he went up the stone steps and through the gate. He stood before the main hall. Every storm door was shut tight. He knelt in the garden and prayed to the Eleven-Faced Kannon.

A dim orange light leaking from the retreat cottage made him suppose Ran was not yet abed; Gyodo was likely at a Takahama inn. To the right of the Buddhist sanctum a faint light came through a crack, so he decided his grandmother was also awake.

After praying at length in the garden, he walked on toward the west corner of the temple property, along below the shrine to Sugawara no Michizane, deified as a tutelar god of learning and as a protector of house and household against fire and lightning.

He sat on a low stone by the little pond, where he had spent many an hour fancying that he was a hero in a historical picture scroll or that he could do any impossible deed.

The stone was wet as if rained on. He could not distinguish from the mountain growth the six Jizo Bodhisattva statues in the small excavation of the mountain foot, nor the laymen's tombstones. A pair of pale white shapes floated in the dark; likely, paper lanterns offered to someone lately dead and buried.

He could hear the intermittent drippings, percolations from the over-hang, but he could not see the widening rings on the surface. He fixed his eyes there and began to discern images of innumerable stars, their pinpoints of light swaying. But he realized he was not seeing that either, for while countless stars variable in size and distance were scattered in the sky, the pond was under many lapping branches of maple and chestnut.

He stared anew at the pond. With night eyes he began to perceive a thin vapor just above the surface rising in whorls and disappearing. He could hear the yelping of foxes from a far south range of mountains.

Turning, he realized the rice fields were becoming buried in a white mist that was illuminating its surroundings but that lacked the power to actualize the color of the trees.

Looking hard, he saw it rising even from the corner of the shrine, and up the slope from there, and soon it was circumfusing all of Tangenji. Only the grand roof of the main building and the ulterior mountaintops could still be seen.

He must have slept as he sat on the stone. When he woke he saw in the east the first gray of dawn. The mist rising off the moist low land was drifting with waning vigor about the mountain breast. The inky trees began by degrees to reveal their color, first in ultramarine, then in deep green. A mountain bird flapped twice or so, causing him to imagine a drowsy child falling from a Western-style bed.

'I must go back now.' As he rose he heard steps on the path coming toward the corner of the shrine. The decrescent mist still hid the path and all below. The steps were heavy. Presumably whoever it was, was rocking from side to side with weight inclined to the outer edge of the foot, the gait of someone with a low center of gravity.

The sound turned the corner and a black form appeared in the white mist. Soon he knew it for his grandmother. She had on her back a bulky bundle and was employing a hoe as a walking stick.

She advanced enough to notice him if only she looked up.

'Why on earth is she coming up here at this early hour? All day and all year she sat in her room.

'Is she going to dig a tomb for herself?...for another?'

Coming to about three meters short of him, she finally raised her head before the six Jizo Bodhisattvas under the cliff, and there he was, between herself and them.

"Oh, how convenient of you. Just so. Mokuzu, take my load, but be careful of it. I'll keep the hoe for my staff."

He hesitated to judge: should he be surprised that his grandmother was not surprised to see him so suddenly, or was it unworthy of his surprise?

"Why do you delay? Take it and climb! You are young, go ahead and shake off the dew! In the absence of our reverend priest, the path must be overgrown."

He decided to follow her orders. Instead of going by way of the laymen's graveyard, he took the steep and grassy route up from the pond, which became a zigzag path.

"Wait at the turns. What's the use of going so far ahead?"

At each turn he waited. His grandmother on arrival sank deep in the grass as if to take a small, undeclared rest.

Yet, as he was viewing the sky and the mountains showing their differentiating color, she said,

"Be quick! Your grandfather used to say all important tasks ought to be done before cockcrow."

He went on and waited at the next turn.

'Here's where Ran got burnt. Now I can see it was my fault.' Before finishing his thought, he was struck by the memory of Luri's elegant buttocks, which he had enjoyed with his hands and cheeks. Even in the dark they had risen round and white, and they were so smooth!

The rank bamboo grass, eulalia, and bush clover soaked him to the navel as if he were entering water with his clothes on.

"*Umph!* Wait! Why don't you wait? Don't you know the wisdom that austerities ought to be practiced with at least one other person?"

302

He turned and pulled his grandmother up. She had slipped and was half reclining.

"If you want so much to go on, go to the next bend and then walk back to one or two steps ahead of me. That way you can slow down. Or, now it's best if you walk one or two steps behind," she said with no word of thanks.

In due course they came up to where the chestnut plantation was replaced by red pines. From there the undergrowth was short and scarce. Between the trees brightened; any moment the sun would appear.

At the first show of its vertex, the sun crimsoned the mist at the nether half of the many mountains. The mist moved peristaltically in vertical turns. The indigo mountains seemed like islands on an ocean of clouds.

The full sun showed as a fresh red liquid sphere that spread no rays. Soon it became a random spray of yellowish white light impossible to stare at, and finally it changed to light itself.

The grandmother was praying before the sun with joined palms.

She then ordered,

"Dig there, level the ground to receive it. Chant as you work, and chant as you place it. I assume you can chant at least the Kannon section of the Lotus Flower Sutra by now, eh?"

Her cheeks were rutilant as a baby girl's.

"What is it, Grandma?"

"Why, a shrine for an offshoot of the Eleven-Faced Kannon. I fashioned it from an orange crate, adding a roof and doors. In my dream I had a divine revelation that if I enshrine this Kannon at this very spot, your mother will be healed instantaneously. She will die if she can't recover. It is too pitiable that she should die. But now she will be cured. So you too chant the sutra with now-or-never purity. We'll chant together!

> "*Kanzeon Bo-sa fumonbon dainiju-go, ni-ji, Mujinni Bo-sa, sokujuza-ki hendo u-ken, gassho ko Butsu, nisa ze-gon Se-son, Kanzeon Bo-sa, i-ga innen myo Kanzeon, Butsu go Mujinni...*"[1]

They finished chanting in about twenty minutes and bowed low, thrice touching their heads to the red earth. Then the grandmother looked Mokuzu in the face and declared,

"Hie yourself to Ryotanji at once! What do you think you are doing? You are in your novitiate. For shame stealing away, albeit for your sad mother! Run like a rabbit! I can afford to take the day to climb down. Fool! Suffer no dubiety!"

Finding no word to utter and nothing to think, he obediently ran down the mountain.

Mokuzu briefly recalled the event. Before and after were blank. He returned to Ran's letter.

> I told Ena you came back and what Grandma said. She got happy and shouted he really came back? I asked do you want to see him? She looked down. A jet plane came high over. She looked up and said it is fired by burning gasoline and kerosene with condensed air but what fires our training? Maybe the power of not meeting the one we want to meet.

Mokuzu felt that all his nerves and humors were engaged in only the work of wishing to meet with Ena.

Reiho and Luri, who had likely been talking behind the master's quarters, were returning outside the shoji before his desk. He could hear Luri's bright resonant voice.

"I don't disagree, but, for all that, you're only the engine, however mighty. We need a pilot, a navigator. And he's the most suitable."

"He's too young. He's not even in junior high." Reiho's voice was husky and unclear.

"So? We have to wait. After all, you'd better go to senior high. You can concretely prepare in those three years."

"But even when I graduate from senior high he'll only be done with the first year of junior high. And another problem, what'll you do? When I'm done with my first year you'll be graduating."

"I can be an office clerk. That way I can acquire some business savvy. Meanwhile you'll graduate and then we can really begin. While we're working, he'll grow up. We'll be the advance party. When the business could be slumped by trials and errors he'll come aboard and make it a success. It's a good arrangement."

"Then I suppose I'll have to go to that religious school for delinquents after all!"

Reiho and Luri turned toward the front entrance from the east garden. Mokuzu could hear but did not try to understand; their words were like a wind in the leaves. All that was meaningful to him was his pure passion of wanting to see Ena.

He could gather that they had joined Unkai after his sitting meditation. Soon all were exchanging greetings with Teacher Docho, just come in at the gate. Although their words were unintelligible, some intonations and a stirring of the air carried to his ears.

'Oh, it's already lecture time!' he thought, directly recalling Teacher Docho's fervent speech of the week before:

"'...Alas, Buddhist history is a history of compunction only. Who won't weep at the sight of the senseless repetition of shame, disgrace, repentance, and resentment? There were priests who conspired with political, economic, and military power on the pretext of faith, even in Buddha's name. Yet they pursued their private interests with the rapaciousness of a prairie fire and ignored the common people, whose lives are but extensions of Buddha. Spending all means of cruelty and mercilessness, they treated them as material to be exploited and humiliated.

"'Recent years have seen a sudden increase in the number of people who lament the condition of Buddhism and the fact that laymen are withdrawing from all religions. The explanation for this worldwide phenomenon is said to be that the commoners are sullied by science and materialism, which serve the human appetite for convenience and profit.

"'But let me ask, in all history had we ever true religion and true religious practice? Much as we may lament, was there really ever religious prosperity predating its decline?

"'Mokuzu, it is apparent that Buddha's teaching is not yet practiced and hence not yet perfected. There are too many examples of priests who claimed self-perfection but who, even as they studied and preached the teachings, digressed from Buddha's Way and were its detractors. I am thus obliged to conclude that the history of Buddhism is a history of shame....'"

For Mokuzu, laden with the wish to see Ena, Teacher Docho's fiery eloquence now seemed colorless, like enervated fish in a tank.

'Unkai is calling me, I must go to my history lecture. In my present state I'll have to douse with cold water throughout the day to be animated!'

He had some pages of Ran's letter yet to read, but he hastened to the guest room.

As usual supper immediately followed the lesson. After that Reiho and Luri turned on the TV set bought for them by Zen Master Hanun. Unkai went to the west veranda of the main building to meditate, referred to by Reiho as "meditation toxicosis." Mokuzu withdrew to his room to read the rest of the letter.

Ran must have delayed as much as a month to resume. What followed pertained to the most recent situation at Tangenji.

> There is a mystery. The more I think the more it gets to be. If I don't think then it looks ho-hum. It is about your return to pray for Ma. Grandma also decided to pray for Ma on that day. You and Grandma were far apart and had no talks. Actually Ma was in bad shape and her three doctors were coming and going and Gyodo wondered if he should go on his school trip he had been looking forward to for so long but he went. Dad was home from Shodojima from a while back and was staying in the

hospital tending Ma. Here is the mystery. Ma dreamed in her coma that a man like her father told her to wake up and pray to Kannon when she was in big trouble and didn't know what to do. Depend on Kannon. The man became Tangenji's Kannon, then Kannon clear as glass. Ma prayed right off to Kannon to make her well and then she will give her life to Kannon and just work to tell everyone how good Kannon is to help sad suffering people. In three days Ma got better. The doctors and nurses were amazed and couldn't explain it. A week later they said she could go home. All those years they didn't know how to cure her so they said it had nothing to with them. She became fine. They said she should stay a month more since she stayed four years with some ups and downs. She got back on September 1. She walked the distance with no trouble. Gyodo and I took the path to school and went halfway to meet her. She gave us each a green mandarin orange as a souvenir. Dad came too and they were happy. He said with Ma home healthy and Bunyu and Kiku working well we have no complaint if only we can have Mokuzu.

Learning of his mother's recovery Mokuzu felt no great joy. He had concluded that he had done his best for her, and had decided to summon all his energy for his studies. In fact he had found a place where he could live with little disturbance from others and had begun to have an active interest in English literature, Buddhist history, and sumi painting. Certainly he wanted to see Ena, but he knew he should not until he had mastered the basic knowledge and skill to study on his own, that is, until he was sure of exactly what his training ought to be. So when he read that his family situation would enable him to go home, he was not overjoyed but made uneasy.

'I'm not a ball to be capriciously tossed about! I'd prefer to be left alone until I find my own way!' Quickly he read on.

There's no sunshine without shadow. I learned about Kisshoten goddess of happiness. She has an ugly mean sister Kokuan-nyo. Dad and Ma were happy. Then they began to fight. When he drinks he gets mean. It began over soybeans. Yosetsu got them for Tangenji from all the laymen but he brought less than the paper said. He obviously stole a lot. Ma said Dad must tell Yosetsu and everybody. Dad said it should be kept in the mind and nothing should be done. Ma said Dad is a coward and is strong only for drink. He beat her. Worse, they fought around Gyodo with a high fever and crying in his sleep. He was sick from about ten days after the school swim trip. He had a little sore in his nose but it went away. Then end of August it came again and his nose and even around his eyes swelled and he felt hazy in the head. When school began he went and studied and did judo club. At home he worked in the garden and mountain and stayed up late studying. It was like that for about a week. He was really tired but never told and Dad and Ma ordered him to do everything and scolded him for being slow. Then pus came from his nose. The fever rose and he fell by the door. They carried him to bed and went on fighting. Always he shouted stop it! half asleep. He even begged them to stop for his sake. When I went in my head felt greased with the stink and the fever. He was so tortured they called for Dr. Okada. He is thin and silent but when he saw Gyodo he shouted at Dad and Ma still grouching at each other. He said they were stupid and should shut up and how can they fight over nothing when their kid is almost dying and it could be too late for treatment. He said Gyodo had a boil in his nose and it was becoming meningitis. How I was shocked! Dr. Okada put him in a hospital but told Dad and Ma he could not be saved. Even if he got a chance in a thousand he would be an idiot or some kind of crazy. But I am glad to say we are relieved. He came home and anyone can see he is normal as ever. He only got whiter and quieter like he grew to be an adult. And Dad and Ma also became normal and always fight. Sorry my letter got long and boring. Maybe like all rest I won't mail it.

Mokuzu read to the end. He felt like he had long been confined to a cold, dark icehouse.

'I have to leave the flow of the Yellow River to itself and its stagnation to itself. I have to make straight and rapid progress like a super express, no, like a white ray of light piercing through forests and across fields until I reach the depths of the universe!'

He had been ordered by Teacher Docho to draw up geographic and chronological maps of the changes in Buddhism and also charts of the Dharma transmission of each of the various sects, schools, and branches.

According to Teacher Docho, Buddhism began when Sakyamuni Buddha first preached at the mid area of the Ganges in the fourth century BC. During the century after his death, Buddhism split into two major factions, the conservative Sthavira and the more radical Mahasamgika.

Mokuzu had much interest in the cause of this early division, and Teacher Docho was glad to explain in some detail.

"There are two explanations. The first is based on source materials of Northern Buddhism. As it goes, a priest named Mahadeva, active in Pataliputra Province, advocated five new views. As to the first, one night Mahadeva had a wet dream. The disciple he asked to launder his robe questioned him, 'Why did this happen to one who has extinguished all klesa, who has no more to learn, who is worthy of universal esteem?' Mahadeva replied, 'Even an arhat will ejaculate if charmed by a devil.' The second: Mahadeva certified a disciple's attainment of arhathood, whereat the disciple asked, 'If I be an arhat, why can I not realize the fact by myself?' Mahadeva replied, 'Inviolate ignorance exists even in an arhat.' The third: A disciple asked, 'An arhat is said to have the holy eye of wisdom. Why then is he betimes suspicious of others?' Mahadeva replied, 'An arhat is certain about klesa but suspicious of worldly matters.' The fourth: A disciple asked Mahadeva, 'Forasmuch as an arhat is said to have the holy eye of wisdom and you are an arhat, why do you not see that I am now an arhat?' Mahadeva replied, 'Even an arhat may learn by another's indication.' The fifth: One night Mahadeva cried out unawares, 'I am tormented!' Some of his disciples wondered if he was truly an arhat. Mahadeva said in response, 'The holiest way rises from true cries of torment.'

"Mahadeva's five views gave rise to an argument that schismatized early Buddhism. But, as I said, there is a second explanation, based on materials of Southern Buddhism and more reliable, which pertains to a set of ten strictures. The first allowed a priest to keep a certain measure of salt, the second, to eat even after midday until the sun 'moves two fingers,' the third..."

Mokuzu tried to remember each lecture as he drew the maps and charts. When he tired of Buddhist history he made a fair copy of what he had sketched that day. Teacher Setsuro had asked him to draw a hundred different flowering plants, each with a suitable insect. As the night deepened he continued his reading of the basic preparatory English literature required by Teacher Yojun, who was sighing over his slow progress.

'What is the secret of a metasequoia's rapid growth?' he fitfully wondered, recalling the tree by the incinerator behind his school. 'Has it a definite purpose so that it can completely ignore its surroundings?'

Mokuzu alone was still awake at Ryotanji. To divert himself he opened the shoji before his desk.

Outside looked almost brighter than inside. Every inch of the garden was lit by the moon, stabilized full yellow in the oceanic sky. The sound of the night insects made him recognize more clearly the distance between himself and the moon. Behind the cedar tops, even-spaced and balanced in height, a cloud hung like a bleached cotton cloth.

27

Fomentation

Just as every cell has its membrane, so every person affects some sort of vanity that surrounds him like a curtain of air. At first any two persons are strangers, but if they are to join in a certain venture, they must break through their curtain of vanity and relate without deception.

Those who are not put off by each other's vanity and neither sneer at nor censure it can enjoy a closeness like coexisting in amniotic fluid.

When taken from an Osaka orphanage to Ryotanji by Zen Master Hanun, Luri was already a stalwart girl who formed no easy attachments and never relaxed her guard even before those who were kind. But eight-year-old Reiho, two years younger, came to adore her and addressed her as "Sister" despite his barbaric manner. More, she stood high in his account for handling all the temple cooking and cleaning and even studying at her new school without showing a gloomy face.

Luri was amazed and grateful; Reiho had soon grown friendly and even respected her without taking her nature as a barrier. She knew she was prone to be guarded and thought it explained why she was disliked at the orphanage. Accordingly she interpreted Zen Master Hanun's reason for taking her in to be simply that he wanted a maid.

Luri and Reiho were intimate regardless of vanity. They were legal siblings, and they came to be closer without sexual intimacy than many who were sexually intimate might have been.

In fact Luri, now in her second spring after graduation from high school, was apparently having successive affairs with men mostly connected with a medium-sized construction company in whose office she worked.

"Hey, I've only gotta get through this last year, though I doubt I can drum up the patience!" Reiho scratched at his unbarbared hair and spoke as soon as he entered Luri's room. Luri was facing her dresser after a bath, with a May breeze coming in the window.

"I already have a room we can use for our office, so maybe you needn't finish school if you really dislike it."

"Yeah? The crap I've gotta learn there isn't useful, it could even get in our way."

"Then the crux is funds. If we're going to lend only from my salary, you're already doing well, so about that there's no point in your quitting school." Luri finished brushing her hair and applying face cream. She turned toward him, smoothing her negligee.

"True. If we had a little more to work with, we could enlarge it in short order by the rate we're charging. Isn't there a way...?"

Reiho had been lending Luri's meager salary to delinquents at school, charging interest as high as .3 percent of the principal per day.

To persons borrowing a small sum briefly, the rate seemed a trifle. Actually it was severely high, like the sight of the pinnacle of a church, for anyone making loans for profit, or to the eye of any fair observer.

The rate of .3 percent a day meant 109.5 percent a year, or 109.8 if it chanced to be a leap year.

At this rate the principal would double in a year, and if the doubled sum were lent another year, the original would quadruple; another year and it would go eightfold. It was a fantastic dream to make big money in a short time, being a geometric progression.

At the start of his second year of parochial school, Reiho had learned about making such loans from the leader of a depraved group, one Hanazono, held in awe by all the other students.

Hanazono, son of a priest, had come up from Kumamoto, Kyushu, and was lodging near the school. He knew his fate was to inherit his father's local temple, but he neither studied nor kept up his appearance, and always had the stubble of a beard. Daily he consorted with a faction who belonged to the judo, karate, swordsmanship, or Rugby clubs. He quickly spent his monthly allowance from home, took money from weak-looking schoolmates, and also blackjacked money out of passersby. Whenever he had money on him he stood his fellows to treats, but his foremost joy was to bet on the horses.

One day he stealthily approached Reiho: "Do me a favor, man, lend me some dough," and he gestured as if in prayer.

Reiho had no fear of Hanazono despite his reigning supreme by brute force. He had mastered the basics of karate and had kept practicing under Rangai's instruction, and he too had a satisfactory build. To him Hanazono seemed a bulky, bearded ignoramus who was unashamed to use force on jellyfish. Never his friend, he replied frankly and curtly: "I've no money."

In Ryotanji all money for daily life and school was methodically overseen by Unkai. He bought whatever was necessary for Luri, Reiho, and Mokuzu, and gave exact pocket money on request, after hearing how it was to be spent.

"I know, but honest, I gambled what I borrowed off of Hashida — you know him? He says he'll tell my old man, the teachers too, this being the fifth time. I didn't figure that pale asparagus capable of a threat, but he too must be up a tree."

"So I answered you already."

"But think, you're clean broke, whereas I'm broke on top of great debt.

My case is no simple zero. My zero is, say, a rotten meat dumpling, while yours is like the enlightenment of a Zen master."

"I see what you're up to, Hanazono. You hope I'll put myself out — borrow just to lend, eh?"

"Whatever you do is your business, only will you or won't you? I'm not thinking to use it gratis, you know."

"Huh?"

"The common practice, man. I'll return it with interest at .3 percent a day." Hanazono then explained the mechanism. To Reiho's surprise he was well versed in the field.

"There's a law, 'The Interest Restriction Act,' whereby we can charge at the conventional rate of up to 20 percent a year when the principal is under a hundred thousand yen; 18 if under a million but over a hundred thousand; and 15 if over a million.

"But we have another law, 'The Law to Regulate Receipt of Investment, Deposit, Interest, and Other.' One article states the legality of charging at .3 percent a day, that is, 109.5 percent a year. It's strange that we have these two diverse laws in the same country. Any lender will naturally chose the second, which furthermore has penal provisions while the first hasn't, so it carries more authority.

"Since I'm the borrower, it's to my advantage to mention only the first. But I'll act according to my conscience and deal at the highest rate."

Reiho was calculating the complicated percentage multiplication. But, like a ball rolling down a roof and lodging in a gutter under the eaves, no conclusive figure came to hand.

Hanazono, thinking he was getting somewhere, pulled out a little slender leather pouch.

"No sweat, take this, it's my seal. Early next month my old man will send my monthly cash to the post office by registered mail. Nobody can receive it without my seal. You've got it, you needn't doubt I'll pony up. I'm a gentleman despite appearances...a proud cadet of a Buddhist priest!"

That night Reiho earnestly consulted with Luri.

"It could be my very first earning!"

"So you're hoping to use my first salary to fund your first earning. Are you truly no friend of his? If you lend out of sympathy, better to give. Lend, lose a friend. It's like expecting an apple to grow big after getting an insect when it's small as a plum — it'll surely drop."

"Easy, easy, I don't like him, don't hate him either. I couldn't care less if he's expelled, or tromped by a racehorse."

"You think you'll get it back?"

"Here's his seal. If I don't, I'll beat him near to death and take his motorcycle or whatever is equitable."

"Right, it's important to consider collateral. As for your brawn, I trust you entirely."

They promptly reached an agreement because Luri was given utter freedom in the use of her salary, though Zen Master Hanun and Unkai had both advised her to save it for her future.

From then on, Luri and Reiho cooperated in the business of usury. Bit by bit they began to earn, began to increase principal. Arithmetic as part of the school curriculum had been a bore, but accompanied by real cash it was becoming a supreme pleasure. One day Reiho exulted,

"Boy, I see why athletes are wild to set new records!"

Now, facing her at her dresser, Reiho asked,

"So look here, why don't we go full-scale? We can work from the office you got, and of course we'll register as a loan firm at the Prefectural Office."

"That's fine with me, but still there's the question of raising funds. You're really hating school, huh?"

"That goes without saying. Deliver me and I'll work hard at our business. At school I'm lending only a trifle, so we're earning only a trifle. We gotta go for real!"

"What'll our master say, and to your leaving school in mid-course?" Luri did not care a jot what the master thought; her concern was what Reiho would think of what he thought. All in all, it had been a serious turning point for Zen Master Hanun to come upon Reiho at Hiroshima. He had ever since been facing the world in an ongoing struggle for the peace movement, accompanied by his aim to erect a Kannon statue as a symbol of peace atop the mountain behind Ryotanji.

He likely wished that Reiho would follow the same path, inasmuch as Reiho was the fatal catalyst of his present mode of life. To meet his wish, Reiho would have to graduate from the parochial school, even from its university, and practice Zen training in a monastery. Should he learn that Reiho strongly wished to open a money-lending business, he would be much puzzled, never himself having had such a dream. Probably he would be shocked to learn the outcome of his education, provided mainly by his own example.

"Well, however it disappoints him, he can't force a mountain boar into robes. I'll not yield on how I am to live, so there's nothing he can do. Anyway, Mokuzu is a more suitable successor, seeing as how he's practicing the quintessence of our master's dream of dreams."

"But Reiho, he has his parents. Remember the day his dad came? I

312

happened to hear him say he wants Mokuzu back now that Gyodo found work. Our master is sick at heart over it. He asked him to wait so he and the other teachers can perfect the education they planned. I wasn't in the room, but could tell he supplicated with his head to the tatami.

"Then I heard Mokuzu's dad say something like, 'Zen Master, I have often said I asked you to raise him for the time being because my wife was taken ill due to my lack of virtue and ability in the face of poverty and many children. When I came to you, I was denying myself all emotion, which even now I'm not succeeding at. You, and I too, may think I'm capricious to ask you to take him in and then ask you to return him...but keeping him here any longer increases my regret.

"'As to education, I have my own view. I was fairly well educated, and I think compulsory education makes a child lose his naivete and spontaneity and turns him into a skeptic who must live a life of hesitations. I have always wished that my children may live as they like. One of my gravest misgivings is that I couldn't deliver them from their distress.'

"To that our master said something like, 'I understand the importance of naivete; children shouldn't lose that or their spontaneity; and we must protect them so they may live as they like. Only I hope you can understand there are some who want to study and to train. If we permit them to do as they like and what they like is to do that, can you object?

"'I pity the mind of your Gyodo. He knows he shouldn't blame his parents, yet he resents their inability, situation, and fate that disallow him to pursue higher study despite his talent. He has gone out to work so his younger siblings may advance in their schooling. How do you see this pure love? Moreover, there's an irrepressible envy for his younger brother's situation. This complex mentality rends my heart.'

"They were repeatedly talking like that."

"But, Luri, why? It's Mokuzu's matter. He should judge if he wants to stay or leave. They can have their hopes, but they haven't either of them the right to decide."

"Actually that's how it developed. They asked Unkai to call him. Mokuzu is quite a genius. He just said, 'Anywhere's the same as long as there's the law of gravity.' It sure startled them. Then he went on, 'I heard we should walk in the light when there's light, but I'll say we should walk in the light when there's light and walk in the dark when there's dark. Either way we're forced to be naive, which you both favor, and either way there couldn't be only joy or sorrow.' He's a true navigator."

"You were saying that already three years ago — I'll be the engine and he'll be the navigator and the pilot. So why don't we ask him now about my quitting school and starting a business with you? If he thinks it's good, we can ask about raising funds. How about that? He's already in the first year of junior high, and we've got no one else we can consult."

"But, Reiho, nowadays he studies so much he looks at us as if from a star. He's engrossed in abstractions and is extremely unrealistic."

"That's where he's valuable; we need his pure intuitive advice. We're not going to hear any concrete methods. We'd better ask him — let him express his view. Don't worry, you and I are the ones to interpret and judge. I'll fetch him."

"Swell, it's like we're seeking a holy revelation...but, why not, since we haven't a better idea?" Luri spoke with a laugh at Reiho's back.

Mokuzu was at his desk writing something in English. His finished pages were so numerous that Reiho was amazed.

"Oi, Mokuzu, what are you doing? You'll wreck your eyes writing so small under that dim light, eh?" He picked up a page and attempted to read it,

"'*The Vanity of Human Wishes*', lines 157-160'...What's this, haah? Explain — but keep it simple. Don't you agree I have some right to know what you're up to? As your senior brother living under the same roof, I'll be accused of neglect if you're faking study and actually are on a spy mission from Russia...or indulging in porno novels, eh?"

Mokuzu faintly smiled and seized Reiho with lucid, slightly narrowed eyes,

"Teacher Yojun is having me summarize Dr. Johnson's view of life and comment on it before next week. What you have in your hand is an excerpt I think basic to a discussion of his view. I'll read it and translate it for you:

> "Deign on the passing world to turn thine eyes
> And pause awhile from letters, to be wise;
> There mark what ills the scholar's life assail,
> Toil, envy, want, the patron and the goal."[1]

Reiho gave a rough laugh and clapped Mokuzu on the shoulder, exclaiming, "Watch out, it's you in the future if not now!"

Mokuzu did not demur, nor was he annoyed. He simply said,

"I'm the one who has to criticize this poem."

"Yeah, but whoever tasks his noggin with such stuff is fated to get entangled in it. But listen, we have something to ask. Could you come to Luri's room? If you give us good counsel it'll hit the nail on the head, I mean, we'll be able to become your patrons like in the poem. Shoot the horse to get the rider. You wanna be patronized, you gotta raise a patron, ha ha!"

Mokuzu on entering Luri's room saw her reflexively straighten up and look about as if to check for disorder. She was careful to intercept his sharp glance with her air curtain of vanity, but as always she felt it had already pierced her brain, heart, and marrow, and she tensed and heated up from within.

To feel at ease with him was becoming impossible, contrary to how it was with Reiho, who was like a cushion of grass outdoors, or a quilt indoors. Mokuzu pressed her to reflect on herself, he summoned her unyielding spirit, and inevitably drove her to be purer, wiser, and more beautiful than she was.

He had grown tall and striking. His figure was injected deep into her eyes. His back and limbs had a linear look, his movements the clean cast of a sword. His features looked assiduous, his eyes were alert, his fresh cheeks had no trace of excess flesh.

Luri never analyzed what she felt at the sight of him, but often she was vaguely reminded of her hapless state of being not younger than he, nor the same age, but much too old. 'It means I'm fated never to get what I think is best and must forever settle for second-best or third,' she thought.

Reiho explained roughly to Mokuzu and asked,

"So what about my leaving school? Tell me after considering my future, our master, and all else."

Mokuzu was looking alternately at Luri and Reiho as if at something peculiar. He then threw back a question,

"Why do you need or want money so much? That I'd like to know before I'm involved in considering whether it's right for you to leave school. I'd like to hear from Luri too."

Luri for an instant opened her mouth in a small O, faintly reddened at the cheeks, emitted an almost slimy glitter from her eyes, and smiled with embarrassment. Reiho, also momentarily perturbed, soon released a spate of words,

"Mokuzu, it's a patent truth! You must've heard, All things obey money, without which there's no dawn or dusk. Money controls even the regiment of hell, eh? Don't you know? People work only for money! Even schools levy payment from students, or first teach them how to earn and then hit them after they've graduated and are practicing what they learned. Every school public and private exists to get money. Anyone not required to go out for money is either a baby, an idiot, or a lunatic. But even they can live only because of family or other support. Everything costs, and how much more if we want to live better than average and be stronger, cleverer, and greater.

"At school I was forced to read the preachings of Zen Master Tengai of Shoshinji. He claims he's one of the most superior priests of Japan, yet he wrote, 'Nothing is unattainable with investment of time and money.' How about that? Or consider your brother working in a factory for bulldozers and caterpillar tractors. With money he could've gone to any good school, especially if you say he's smarter than you, and he could be studying medicine, even astrophysics.

"You must know the Soviets launched the first artificial satellite, Sputnik, last October, and the U.S. followed with their Explorer this January. They're competing like giant lizards chasing each other's tails, but their real interest isn't space research or the announcement of scientific breakthroughs. They're doing it for money and because they have money. Don't you know Lincoln's Gettysburg Address? It means 'government of the money, by the money, and for the money'!"

"Reiho, I know as much. But I suspect the value of spending all day every day for a lifetime to earn money. There are some questions as to the amount we need and the time we must invest. I think we should spend the least time to earn our needed amount, and so we should carefully choose our method. In other words, our attitude toward money will be important. My three private teachers say I shouldn't live for money, that I should bear up so as to minimize even by a day the time spent to earn it."

"Yeah, and they're perfect samples of penury. They may be great, but because they're less famous than their inferiors, they can't exercise their greatness. They're like leaves fallen to a corner of the garden. Who cares about them? Yet even they are earning by teaching you and by selling their books, for instance. We all need money. How much depends on the individual.

"And your favored method, to spend the least possible time at it, and ours, to make loans, will be ideally matched. No other business can yield us a profit of over a hundred percent a year on our investment. Nothing else comes close, unless you're talking about getting a handout or stealing."

"But Reiho, think why a loan shark is considered a dirty fiend. I have read Christopher Marlowe's *Jew of Malta* and Shakespeare's *Merchant of Venice*, and they both — "

"I read *The Merchant of Venice*," Luri cut in, "What nonsense! I hated every character. They twiddle their tongues over trite notions from morning to night — even a palace of cream wouldn't make me as sick. And Shylock is grossly maltreated. It's unfair to borrow money after agreeing to and signing a bond on it and then, after using it to great advantage, to denounce the lender and not return it on the promised day. And worse, Portia disguises herself and sets up as Dr. So-and-so, whose role it is to decide the outcome of the trial. And she severely defeats Shylock — injustice itself! I was enraged by the meanness of the playwright. By false comedy his audiences are made to laugh at so tragic a man. I wish Musashi, Kojiro, or some such notable samurai would cut Shakespeare and his admirers in half!"

"Well said! Did you hear? She's right. And who was it who said 'All legitimate trades are equally honorable,' eh?" Reiho spoke proudly. But Luri asked, now in a melancholic tone,

"Would you slight us if we began a money-lending business?"

"No. I don't like to be slighted and even more don't like to slight. I think all occupations are equally humble human behavior, though a necessary evil, because they share a basic purpose of selling things for more than their real value, which is a kind of theft. But as long as everyone must do it, no one is qualified to point a finger, and rather, everyone must pity one another. So as a means of comfort it was said that all legitimate trades are equally honorable."

"Then what's your word on my leaving school?"

"Everything has at least two sides, so why not do as you like? The point to note is, if you're going to enjoy the good side now, you shouldn't complain even if the bad side appears later on. Musashi said he never regretted anything.

"I get it, I too won't regret a thing. If I have such time, I'll think more about how to earn money. Then tell me what you figure our master will think."

"Reiho, you have to ask him directly. More than anyone else he knows what he thinks. Just as I don't eat another's portion as well as my own, so neither will I reply for another. Besides, your concern for his feeling is part of your regret in advance."

Reiho was perplexed at this reply, and Luri interpreted it for him by a slight distortion that came of oversimplifying:

"Mokuzu means you shouldn't care what others think."

"Well...right! Then this is my last and most crucial question. I don't expect a concrete answer, only give me your fundamental, intuitive, and inspired-by-God-or-Buddha answer in simplest form. How do we raise our funds?"

"To ask such a question is like a mother's asking her baby how she can increase her milk. I know next to nil about money, but I daresay money is where money is, and you have no choice but to get it somehow from there. But you'd be silly to spend a lot on boat or plane fare to travel far for funds. Naturally it's advisable to obtain them as nearby as you can."

Mokuzu as he answered was apprehensive. He was ashamed of his glib tongue. He thought a truly great man might respond with 'I don't give a hang!' or 'Go ask a waterfall' or make silence his answer like a rock.

Reiho's face was a picture of joy and verve. His voice swelled, "Yeah, yeah

317

— right — right!" He was increasing the weight of the conviction he already had to a certain extent.

Luri looked askance at him and shrugged at Mokuzu.

"Right, I'm getting the hang of it!" Reiho held on to his wits like a judo player who keeps gripping an opponent already pinned.

Suddenly he looked up and exclaimed, "You still here? I finished with you!"

"Good grief, Reiho, how can you be so rude? Maybe you're lost in your thoughts, but it's outrageous. Mokuzu, I'm sorry." Luri reflexively reached for Mokuzu's shoulder. "Let me offer you red tea."

Mokuzu was annoyed to receive her breath on his cheek. Coolly he refused, "No, thanks, Luri. I have a lot to do."

Luri had been spirited from girlhood, and there were those who, considering her lot, felt compassion and admiration. She was now twenty, and whoever observed her noted her starry eyes, pearly teeth, and womanly bosom and hips.

But to know her beyond her reflection in a mirror was difficult; not because her interior was beyond the powers of a mirror to reflect, but because her eyes and gestures revealed nothing in particular. Possibly she had nothing to reveal, though to say so would be shallow and arbitrary considering that one's inmost heart appears according to one's environment and the relation of cause and effect. Safer would be to say that Luri's inmost heart had been sound asleep ever since she was given life by her parents and that it was not yet awakened.

She seemed a healthy young woman, even if no one had determined how truly her health accorded with the definition given by the World Health Organization in 1948: "Health is a state of complete physical, mental, and social well-being and not merely the absence of disease or infirmity."[2] Her mental health was next to perfect according to ten criteria of normality given

318

by L. P. Thorpe and B. Katz, namely, adequate feelings of personal worth, adequate feelings of security, adequate feelings of self-confidence, adequate understanding of self, adequate understanding of others, adequate emotional maturity, adequate orientation and goals, adequate integration of personality, adequate vocational relationships, and adequate basic harmony.[3]

Reiho's physical health was beyond question. He was so robust he could fight a bull. But whoever noted his robustness and rustic behavior might have supposed that the Italian army surgeon Cesare Lombroso used his observation of many like Reiho as the basis of his claim that certain criminals have distinctive physical features and are born criminal in an atavistic return to the primitive state.

There was such an observer, one named Sako, serving as assistant inspector in the Criminal Affairs Division of the police station in the district to which Ryotanji belonged. He lodged at the home of a Ryotanji layman and often met Reiho on the road and exchanged some words.

At the time Sako was ordered to attend special training at the Kyoto Prefecture Police Headquarters to learn more than ten kinds of systems of classification of criminals viewed from the angle of crime prevention. The training demanded that he quickly memorize many classes and types. To avoid confusion he brought to mind the faces of his acquaintances and labeled each without considering that he was being frivolous and impolite, which is to say, he was committing a kind of spiritual crime. To illustrate, he thought about Reiho,

'By my lights he's merciless, hyperthymic, exhibitionistic, explosive, fanatical; his must be the nature of a positive and continuing criminal. But wait, he's just a loafing schoolboy...a thieving dog waiting his chance...he has to be a positive and opportune criminal, at least he couldn't be passive. Yes, an opportune criminal — *Gelegenheitsverbrecher*, as Aschaffenburg named the type.

'The common distinguishing feature is lack of thought and a weak will against temptation. H. W. Gruhle calls his type a criminal out of need. What did Seelig say? Wouldn't he put him in the assaulting-violence category? Probably he's prone to aggression and might display it at any minor chance. Or is he the type who commits primitive-reacting crime? He might blow off impulsive, strong emotion without regard for consequences....'

Returned to his room, Mokuzu sat at his desk and thought about Reiho and especially about Luri as if waiting for stirred dust to settle. But soon he pushed thought of them aside and resumed his study of Samuel Johnson.

James Boswell, who wrote a biography of Johnson, was defending, by bringing up their good nature, a group of Methodist students purged from Oxford University. Dr. Johnson retorted:

> "Sir, I believe they might be good beings; but they were not fit to be in the University of Oxford. A cow is a very good animal in the field; but we turn her out of a garden."[4]

'It exactly fits Reiho. If he dilly-dallies much longer, he'll be expelled from school before he leaves of his own accord. On top of that, he and Luri will be exiled from this Ryotanji by the master for being unsuitable here.

'But I haven't time to worry heartily about them. What I really must do now is find something that I think is worthwhile to devote all my life to, to burn all my energy for, and to feel no regret at exchanging my life to obtain.

'How is Ena? She seems to value self-training as the highest way of life. I don't disagree, but that couldn't mean to persevere indiscriminately. In order to start, we have to know what a life of training is, for what we should train — sure, if we're going to train, we have to know what we're seeking at the risk of our life. What is our goal? What is our white lily on the heights, star in the sky, fruit of union, marrow of life?

'By now I'm quite sure what I have to seek must be in the direction of knowing what is love and what is life, and what I have to seek won't be in any other direction....'

&

Zen Master Hanun, just turned sixty, was at last beginning to build his Kannon for Peace on the mountain behind Ryotanji.

He did not see the Kannon to be cast in bronze as an idol with mystic powers. But he had been recognizing the value inherent in the process, that is, of collecting donations, making people realize the importance of peace, and making them spend money for it. He also expected that once the statue was in place, many people in the lower land would look up to it morning and evening and meditate on the blessings of peace, and their meditation would be a force to maintain it.

The master had been active in the promotion of various peace movements, but from the first he never overestimated their influence on the world or on Japan. All such movements as long as they were organized could not avoid conflict from within. Inevitably they produced a mainstream faction and an anti-mainstream faction, and hierarchies of superiors and inferiors such as heads, managers, and common members.

The master, who regarded peace as being free of faction and rank, quickly detected that the peace movements contradicted their idea and their state. 'A

320

peace movement shouldn't be organized,' he thought. 'Organization needs politics, and politics generates confrontation, antagonism, and war itself.'

He was also convinced that the peace movement as a whole was being made into a test case by specific intellectuals, such as leading scientists, and that as such it would fail. 'With their learning they can't be persuasive but will rather be repulsive, and the end result will be a more unsettled state.

'It's impossible to educate the common people on the horrors of modern war — at least it stands to reason that they would need to study and corroborate in the same way as those scientists to understand to the same degree. For the common people it's an abstraction, which means they have the potential to turn to making the same nuclear bombs and chemical and biological weapons as our scientists have made.

'If I speak up, I know those scientists will say, "Your thought is simplistic, low-grade, short-circuited," and they'll expatiate on complexities. But doesn't it prove my point?

'I'm in daily contact with the so-called ignorant populace; I know they aren't so different from me. They don't want irksome explanations from eggheads; they have neither the time to listen nor the concern, patience, prerequisite knowledge, or aptitude. They don't need applied physics to sense the horrors of modern war and its weapons. By their life they know the importance of peace. They don't want peace contrived in the lab, they want peace recognized as they nurse their young.

'Both peace movements — the one politically organized and the other inspired by a few top intellectuals — are more evil than good. I should relate to them by using them according to circumstance, or even on occasion aiding them, so as to pursue my own way in erecting my Kannon statue. For such an end, no politics or high intelligence is needed. Peace, for anyone's eyes, is the simple, beatific face of the Kannon before whom no one should find it hard to be pleased, should they? People of all ages will see the Kannon as gentle and peaceful, and that is peace.'

The master had been touring the land to lecture on Zen practice and at once to appeal to all about the importance of peace on every level — individual, family, local, national, and worldwide. In each locality he was entrusting key laymen with a portion of his honorarium and the donations he had gathered for the Kannon fund. Although each entrusted sum was small, the number of donors came to over 500,000.

Truly there were many donors, for he had asked influential persons in each province to collect from their communities, such as Genzaemon, the boss fisherman at Takahama; and there were some wealthy ones who made substantial contributions.

Of course the master spent part of those funds to support himself and those at Ryotanji and to repair the temple. As he had no other income worth mentioning, the scale, speed, and difficulty of raising the Kannon fund could be imagined when it was considered that he had already spent thirteen years since vowing to build the statue.

To proceed, a blueprint was necessary. Next, the path from town had to be widened, and third, the mountaintop had to be leveled.

From the onset of May the master was often meeting with a civil engineer, an architect, and many municipal officers concerned with the project. He hoped to open two routes to the top, one for vehicles, the other for hikers. He planned to have primarily cherry and maple and also other flowering trees for each season along both routes. The statue was to be approached by stone steps. Subjacent would be a generous pond with a fountain circled by lotuses and a restaurant and lodge designed to face each other across the water.

Visitors would enjoy a bird's-eye view of Kyoto, from Mt. Hiei in the north to the rice fields extending south, and from the far ranges in the east to the very base of the western mountains where Ryotanji was. The wide sky would be rich in change and variety, the clouds rising from Wakasa Bay at the far north, the sun rising over Lake Biwa to the east, the haze drifting over the South Uji and Nara mountains, and the sun setting into the west beyond Kameoka and Osaka....

On the last so-called lucky day, *taian*, of May, the ceremony to inaugurate construction was held at Ryotanji. Those attending included a deputy of the prefectural governor, the city mayor (also by deputy), head officers of the organs concerned, archpriests approving of the master's spirit from the various sects and schools, presidents of the civil engineering and construction companies under contract and their field overseers and workers, some notables from the area and outside the city, and the more important donors countrywide. Their number came to more than eighty. The master intended to invite ten times that many to the completion ceremony and hold a more impressive celebration, estimated to the day of three to four years hence.

Next day, outright, many laborers came and began to fell the pines, cedars, cypresses, and all other various trees, such as evergreen oak and camellia, along the planned routes and on the lot. At once some bulldozers and many dump trucks began noisily working to scrape the mountainside and fill the valleys. Yet this work was merely to open the site for surveying and to build access for construction. Evidently a long hard task lay ahead.

Zen Master Hanun toured the labor sites whenever he was at Ryotanji. He was elsewise still making lecture tours and raising funds. Unkai did not alter his diurnal chanting and meditation. Mokuzu studied day and night without much heeding the construction. Reiho and Luri were often scheming together for their future business.

A bracing wind swept the fresh verdure of mountain and field. But with the animation of spring, vipers were beginning to stir, and some toxic mushrooms of autumn were beginning to diffuse their mycelia in unseen places.

28

Coldhearted Mokuzu

Mokuzu, in first grade of junior high, was seen by his school teachers and classmates as a boy without sentiment who functioned mechanically by use of reason only. Aware of their estimate, he no longer appealed in his mind as he had in elementary school,

'If you understood my nature and state, you'd gladly recognize my hot flow of blood and vigorous senses ever responsive and in no way inferior to yours!'

Gradually he had been burying into his depths the wish to be understood, and now he was more successful at it.

'Why should I beg sympathy of a cat or a dog, press my cheek to it, wet its fur with my tears? That would be more absurd and unproductive than to dig my own grave. A dog may approach with wagging tail, but the most I can do is let it lick me and fawn against my knees.'

Nor did he try to understand them more than they did him. Rather, he tried to have the least relation, because experience had taught him to conclude, 'If I show a hint of kindness, they'll greedily steal my time, my soul too. And will they keep them and brew a sense of gratitude? No, they'll let them evaporate from their backs like a mere vaporous heat that can contribute next to nothing to the energy of the universe expanding into the dark.

'And that's not all. Taking advantage of my kindness, they'll confess some personal anguish — family trouble, grudge, even a dire secret forming its kernel — and suddenly they'll realize they've exposed vital information, and they'll look wide-eyed at their error and take my presence as an inexplicable and unforgivable blasphemy. Then, rather than appreciate me as a measure of water to quench their thirst, they'll condemn me as an alluvion to sweep them away. They may throw a fit, even begin to strip off their clothes and flail about…and after all, they'll scream that they've had enough of me. But I'm the one who's fed up, not them!'

Mokuzu's thought was not entirely an exaggeration. There was his music teacher, thin Miss Hagami, in thick glasses with frames the color of salmon flesh or dawn.

Mokuzu had a cordial dislike for music from the day he began elementary school. He regarded it as noise or an outrageous intrusion on one's privacy. With its unnatural sound it clamored for attention, at times with sheer physical force, at times with shameless flirtation. Once he overheard the comment that music devotees no doubt had tender hearts.

"How silly," he had muttered. "I've seen none who weren't egocentric. They may do no evil, but only because their inner temptations keep them busy enough; anyway, they're too timid to commit a physical crime."

He could not come to like anyone who was keen on music, yet he did like the music room of his junior high school. Outside the windows facing the yard was a pair of stately walnut trees. On windy days the large leaves brushed the wood siding of the building, and under the sun their color was fresh and delicate. In May the rain there made a pleasant sound and the one or two halting trickles descending the trunks were engaging. Tirelessly he could watch the drips from the upper leaf tips to the lower leaves, and from the lower leaf tips to the yet lower leaves, and from the lowest leaf tips to the ground.

Just as the rain seemed ready to abate, suddenly — or so it felt to Mokuzu seated by the window intent on the leaves — Miss Hagami whacked her desk with a baton and shrilled,

"You boys there! If you so hate this class, you're dismissed! Go play baseball, or whatever!"

The words were leveled at five or six who were chatting glibly from the start of class. They were shocked into silence, and everyone else kept silent, constringed by the change of air. Miss Hagami too, groping for her next word, tensed her trembling fists and waited for the chill to disperse.

Quietly but abruptly Mokuzu stood up. His figure devoid of useless motion looked rodlike to those who regarded him from the corners of their eyes.

"Miss Hagami, I'm leaving, for I'm the one who really hates music," he said and went out to the corridor. At that, the naughty boys followed with a great commotion like beasts striving to be first to escape from a cage, talking as they went,

"Wow, we've got to play ball! She said so!"

"Great, he's the first to walk out."

"Wait up, Mokuzu, you play too — why not once in a while?"

But Mokuzu declined and went off somewhere to read.

At lunch hour Miss Hagami sent for him. He felt he was being secretly arraigned.

"Mokuzu, you are frank and strong-minded, and I understand your feelings about music. But you misunderstand. The flow of a river and the sough of the wind are also music. At times you may yearn for your father, mother, brothers, or childhood friends. Every memory is music. I can tell music is flowing in you more vividly, deeply, and steadily than in the others...."

Mokuzu suspected that it was a conciliatory measure but could not sense the reason; was she just following what might be her spontaneous and naive genius?

'If she truly sees music as the incoherent natural phenomena in and outside of us, why doesn't she urge us to spend some quiet hours sitting in places like the slope behind Zen Master Hanun's quarters? But if we act like that she scolds us with "Don't be stupefied!" She demands that we hear her piano playing, which is like chopped snake meat, as well as so-called fine music ancient and modern, which is like vinegar or soy sauce put into our veins. She thinks music education or drill is to cut up the flow of a waterfall or a stream, and she asks us to reconnect it with messy glue.

'Her conduct, which should demonstrate what she thinks, contradicts what she says.'

But Mokuzu made no appeal or protest as he had in elementary school. He nodded with a dim smile, and Miss Hagami thought he was impressed by her talk.

In fact he was recalling Teacher Yojun's comment, "Westerners tend to think we Japanese are strange for our uncommunicative, constantly smiling face, and they distrust us, or even sarcastically admire us, adding the Japanese countenance to the seven wonders of the world." Mokuzu thought of a refutation,

'Suppose we are in the company of Westerners whose words, like Miss Hagami's, are as alien to their deeds as day to night. What can we do if we are afraid to hurt their feelings by pointing out their contradiction and if we want to avoid the fight that could easily come of their ensuing fury? Of course if they are fair persons who respect reason and truth, we can afford to argue them down and yet shake hands afterward. But if they're evidently immature, we can only smile and secretly wish to be released from their presence. A poet does not talk poetry to a baby. And a samurai of honor does not aggress against a man whose sword is undrawn.'

Mokuzu, absorbed in thought, was slow to realize that Miss Hagami was absorbed in talking, eyes lowered, repeating with her hands the motion of scooping water from a heavenly pond and spinning a silver thread.

"My major at the conservatory in Ueno was the violin. As a sophomore I received first prize in the student contest and was chosen to represent Japan at the world contest in Paris. One day as I was preparing for the voyage, I began to spit blood. I must have been consumptive from much earlier, but it was now accelerating. I hadn't noticed. I thought I was tired from having driven myself to practice, staying up late against tears of hardship.

"Look at me, I've a prosthesis here where my ribs should perfectly be!.. I had to abandon Paris, the violin too. Even harder, I had to break my engagement to marry! Many times I went to gaze at Yokohama Harbor...such a mournful sight, but one to which I was drawn.

"What did I see? Tankers, outgoing liners, incoming cargoes laden with automobile chassis...but my eyes were drawn to the trash milling and washing against the pier. There was nothing to which I felt closer — because I too was trash!" Miss Hagami's eyes flooded and in spite of herself she pressed her face onto Mokuzu's knees.

Then how did it end? After seven minutes and forty-five seconds she raised her head — Mokuzu noted the time on the wall clock — and she looked at him as if ignorant of why he was there and began to blame him for provoking her thus. And, advancing from blame to contempt, she fired hostile eyes at him. So inevitably he came to count her as a cat or dog.

English teacher Miss Horie also excelled in workmanship, if in another style. Her hair was curled at the ears, emphasizing a flat face. It was rumored that Mr. Tamama, a typical music teacher of another school, had proposed to her and demanded a reply. He was a man very particular in his tastes — and distastes, which when expressed were sharp as glass regardless of time and place. He was notorious for striking students and instruments alike with his baton.

One day Miss Horie was explaining present and past participles, frothing at the mouth, while most of her class was engaged in investigating a new rumor. The Sunday before, so it went, she had been loudly slapped by Mr. Tamama in front of the show window of a tailor shop. Mokuzu was reading *Don Quixote* translated to English by S. Putnam, given him by Teacher Yojun.

This time too seemed very abrupt. When he noticed, Miss Horie was throwing the chalk and weeping. But now he was being addressed and censured. Absorbed in the world of the book, he suddenly needed to surface to physical reality like a dodge ball released from deep water.

"You can understand English better than I, can't you? Then why don't you help your classmates nearest you? Are you pleased if you alone understand? How can you be so egoistic? Knowledge is useful only to help others. You look like a duck in a thunderstorm! What's the matter with you?"

Mokuzu irritably thought, 'It isn't a joking matter. Even if I finish a book every three days, I can scarcely read more than a hundred twenty a year. But Teacher Yojun's and Teacher Docho's libraries each have tens of thousands of books!

'Besides, there's no bigger waste of time than to teach others while knowing only a little, and no worse stimulus to my sense of shame than to help them with so minor a concern.

'They don't want help; they hardly care about studying. For them study in school is enough and afterward they can play on their bicycles or motorbikes or flirt in a haystack. Like a cat stealing a sardine or two from a kitchen, their only work of the day is to read a page or two of the textbook. For me the textbook is less useful than seeing a list of the books I ought to read. They're content to be terrestrials; they feel no dire need to make great strides to fly. I have to look in every corner of those three worlds called in Buddhism the world of desire for food and sex, the world of form without the previous two desires, and the world apart from every form. And still I must find some meaning common to them all, like "an iron line extending a million miles."'[1]

And then? Miss Horie summoned him after school and said,

"I apologize. I was edgy over whether to marry and in a fume what with everyone raising a din, like sheep. Please understand marriage is a great problem for women, and a disposition to hysteria or hypochondria is peculiar to us."

Mokuzu had thought, 'Sure, sure, to excuse one woman she brings all womankind. Isn't it as ridiculous as for a megalomaniac to command an army to attack a fly? And how much more so if it's but an imaginary fly!'

Mr. Nagata taught Japanese. He always came to school in a heavy beige raincoat with the broad collar up. His voice was husky, perhaps owing to his age or to some chronic ailment. When walking alone he would mutter as if to confide to someone a little apart, "I am soon to die, my time is come." His eyes were benign as an autumn sunset, and his hoary beetle brows seemed to twinkle.

In his high school days he must have been friends with Docho Doke, for often he seized Mokuzu to ask,

"How is your teacher Docho, what is he teaching you now?" or, "Please send word I'll call on him one of these days."

His respect and nostalgia seemed genuine, but his message was always the same, proving no visit had been made. Mokuzu could not enter into the feelings of anyone who so often expressed a hope and never acted on it.

'Does he sense he will die soon after he completes his visit? Or in his way is he practicing O. Henry's sentimental short story "The Last Leaf"?'

When he spotted Mokuzu on the way home he would say,

"Wait, why must you walk quick as an arrow? It's not bad to amble, noting the stones and herbs. Now then, what are you reading today?" When Mokuzu told him, he habitually said,

"I see, fine, read on, fine, fine."

At such times Mokuzu thought, 'Men should indeed amble when their goal is in sight. I don't understand Olympic sprinters, who see their goal yet dash like mad. What mentality induces them to do that? I'd like to view them directly; on television their faces are unclear. Maybe unlike Mr. Nagata they don't yet know their goal and so must speed like comets.'

As if reading Mokuzu's mind Mr. Nagata observed, "Much as we talk this way or that, this world is full of good. Truly everyone is good and everything is fine. Few things are really bad. All mortals are good...because they will die, all but God."

Mr. Takenaka, who taught math, was proud of his height. "I'm a peak above the clouds," he would say, "so of course my brain is clear. Up here is clean, cool, and refreshing! You lowlanders are harming your brains with swamp gas."

'What a simpleton!' thought Mokuzu, ' — like brass, practical for being rust-proof, yet lacking depth and sublimity.' Warming to the subject, he advanced his sensuous and arbitrary view,

'Math fanciers must be quite simple to begin with. They give themselves to their mechanical work, claiming they are solving problems, but it seems their problems already have answers. There's an answer if there's a problem, and of course if it can be expressed, however complicated it may look.

'Admittedly it takes great effort and a natural gift to discover a mathematical expression. But each time they face some human or universal phenomenon, mathematicians and scientists seem to be asking first whether they can form an expression and thereby an answer, and when they find they can, they are like delighted children and tunnel into in their calculations to come up with a new axiom, theorem, or law. But the problem is those myriads of problems they put aside as unsolvable. Unfortunately for us, it's those that the human world and the universe largely consist of, and they are what really interest us and what we most wish to have solved. So, the work of mathematicians and scientists is hardly useful to explain the unknown universe and to solve human misery.

'Here I can remind myself of National Teacher Daito's last admonition: "Linger not at what you understand, but study what you don't. That is how to spend your twenty-four-hour day."[2]

'After all, those that are called mathematicians and scientists only analyze, measure, name, and explain the mechanism and nature of things already perfectly existing. They don't attempt to answer the more basic question, Why is it there thus? Suppose here is a pine tree. Its number of needles is the same whether we count them or not. But they will devote themselves to counting them. They are almost queer. What I wish to know is not the number of needles but why the tree is here and why I am confronting it in this sort of state.

'What will they say to my type of question? They'll say it lends itself to no expression and hence no answer, and they'll promptly take leave of me and the pine.

'It makes me think of those Forty-niners who picked up and discarded stone after stone, saying, "Shucks, no gold in here!" In mentality they were like juvenile vagrants. What dreadfully simple brains and a disreputable craving for money! Did they see no meaning as their gnarled fingers touched stone? Important is not to discriminate gold from stone but to sense the thing with our hands, exchange each other's heat, confirm our coming together at the same time and place, to wonder at it, and to think back on our past and take thought of our future. In the long run is it useful to analyze stone or gold, to fractionalize and give a fancy name to each element?'

Mokuzu had less concern for his classmates than he had for his school teachers. He had no leisure after school. There was karate in Rangai's hall, and English, Buddhist history, and sumi painting at Ryotanji.

Like Reiho, he was fearless before those who bragged of their brute force.

One day he came on the scene of a boy being bullied at a back entrance of the school. The boy, named Keigo, was not achieving in school. He was weak and unkempt and had yellow teeth and round black-rim glasses. Circled by four or five delinquents, he was crouching with knees and elbows to the ground in the pose of stooping to conquer, like the great Han-dynasty general Hanshin when he endured as a boy.

As Mokuzu went by, Keigo wailed, "Help!" Indifferent to the delinquents, Mokuzu approached, regarded him, and said, "I don't know if you deserve it, but if you dislike it, why not ask them to stop?"

"They'd hardly listen!"

His tormentors doubled up with laughter. One of them trod on his rear.

"*Awww* — see what I mean? Stop, please, stop!"

Mokuzu turned to the leader. "He's asking you to stop."

Again they laughed, and one planted a stick on Keigo's back. Instantly Mokuzu seized it and struck the offender on the cheek. He then turned to the leader, stepped close, and said,

"Will you molest him when he's asking you to stop, or can't you

329

command your stupid followers?" He had secured a position to dislocate the leader's right shoulder with his left hand and with his right strike his chin if he made a move.

"We'd nothing much in mind...just making fun of this creep...getting tired of it. Fact is, we were gonna finish up, I mean...yeah! better quit..." The leader was pluckless and spoke like someone practicing faltering English. As he turned to leave, so did the others.

"See? You have only to tell them," Mokuzu said, and he too turned away. But Keigo's voice followed him,

"You don't know the sorrow of a man who can't shout even when he's shouting in his mind! On top of that, they stop when you say stop. If I say stop, they beat me more. You don't know the chagrin of having to cry over failing!" and he cried truly and wretchedly. Mokuzu left, telling himself as his only excuse that he would be late for karate, but he was thinking,

'He cut me as if to cut my intestines! I bet he'll hate me forever, whereas he'll hate them only a few days!'

Mokuzu had no interest in his girl classmates except for their sex appeal, especially that of some of the pretty, ripening ones. He could guess their hidden parts because he had known Luri, different there in color and feel from elsewhere.

Sometimes his imagination drove him wild with the desire to touch those whose breasts and loins were daily maturing, but he thought it shameless to approach with only this reason, and he feared he might lose face, in addition to self-respect, if refused. Yet, spending many days with various excuses to grow friendly until one of them unbosomed to him was too great a waste of time and patience, he decided.

So he abandoned his only interest in girls out of shyness, self-respect, and a sense of having no time.

Occasionally they came of themselves, alone or in pairs, to ask his help with English, to borrow a poetry collection of Goethe or Hesse, or to invite him to go camping by a river or up a mountain. But he held them off by saying to himself, 'That's the very way I hate because it demands a lot of time. Why so much ado over preliminaries?'

Although he was not well aware of it, his interest, like a searchlight, was shining far ahead, while its irradiating angle was narrow, as is usual with young men; and everything outside it he treated as monochrome floating dust.

&

In June the distribution of atmospheric pressure brought on the rainy season indigenous to Japan. Although the daily drizzle amounted to not much

330

precipitation, the trees, grasses, air, and earth were suffocated and everything was eager for sunlight. Yet as soon as a band of blue sky appeared in the west, new rain clouds expanded with fresh vigor.

Mokuzu's notebook was also damp and the flow of his pen was retarded.

Even in the interminable rain, Zen Master Hanun as long as he was at the temple put on black rubber boots and went out with an umbrella to check the driveway being constructed up the back mountain of Ryotanji. Where the mountainside was scraped, red soil was exposed and multiple natural channels were running with soil and sand, making the road muddy.

Bushes such as andromeda and azalea at the brink of the raw slopes were losing their cumulus of fallen leaves and topsoil, and their roots were being washed by the rain. Yet, their new leaves were a fresh green. They were pitiful for not knowing their fate.

Throughout the misty drizzle, operators kept working in defiance of being soaked, setting their bulldozers and driving them and their dump trucks to and fro. To reduce the mud, laborers graveled the road and mixed in a large quantity of lime.

A truck departing fully loaded with red soil got mired at a precarious tilt. A bulldozer came to help in the same manner as it did to extract the tree roots, but being unfit for the task, it got mired in turn, so that a crane truck had to be brought in.

The mountain stream became a muddy flow. Influence of the construction ranged to the villages and town downstream. Roadside residents, facing the steady passage of heavy vehicles, brought their grievance to Zen Master Hanun.

The master was forced to see the sad discordance. Just to build the Kannon for peace was disturbing the local peace, ravaging the natural growth, destroying the small animals. At times taken by doubt, he timorously asked himself, 'After all, isn't the best peace and its best symbol to leave nature as it is? Aren't we better off if we see that "the figure of the mountain is the very figure of purity, of Buddha, and the sound of its torrent is Buddha's great preaching"?'[3]

Yet he remaned himself, 'Well, I'll keep on, sink or swim! What's begun must be done! Should the Kannon be reduced to rubble by an earthquake at the moment of perfection, it will be the hand of fate and not my concern.' And he rallied the workers with enlivening words.

One Thursday afternoon in mid-June the rain let up. Big raindrops fell from the cedars, and a rainbow arced beyond the eastern treetops. 'The weather is becoming fine,' thought the master, and he descended the narrow path as far as the stone bridge. A little beyond, a new red-dirt road traversed the path to go to the mountaintop. The master took a shortcut of only two or three steps to mount it, but the shoulder was still soft, and beneath the rain-loosened soil a rock the size of a human head rolled under his weight. With one step more he would have stood in safety. As it was, the rock was a second quicker, and he lost his balance, took a pratfall, and rebounded over the old path to find himself sprawled on the rocky slope below.

He was unsure of when he injured his ankle — when he lost his balance? fell? came to rest? Sure only was that it hurt. He felt almost no pain in his head, shoulders, or buttocks, but his right ankle ached severely. He remained where he was despite the wet ground, and the pain convinced him that something unusual had happened to him.

When he tried to get up, he found the least movement augmented the pain. It seemed to groan, burn, pierce with a thousand needles, press with a strong weight, and extend in waves toward the knee. He sensed his face was blanching, and that the strength was ebbing from his chest and stomach.

He remembered Mokuzu's cool demeanor. He never heard him say so in real life, but he now fancied he heard him say, "Master, there is a time and place for everything, why didn't you choose better?"

To this imaginary Mokuzu he responded with disgust and some humor roused by his tolerance born of love, 'Fool! Had I margin to choose, I wouldn't get hurt, damn it! — as if you're convinced you were born on this earth at the best time for you!'

Mokuzu with slit-eyes spoke again,

"Master, you feel pain only about the ankle, at most below the knee. It's merely the rebellion of a local upstart. I thought you admired Linji's words, 'The Imperial ordinance is well observed throughout the land. The commander-in-chief of the expeditionary force against the barbarians need light no balefire.'⁴ Shouldn't your mind be able to govern all of you? And by quoting Dungshan, didn't you adjure me to welcome a life of extremity?: 'In the cold kill yourself in the cold. In the heat kill yourself in the heat.'"⁵

'Hush! You don't yet know what it is to layer clothes upon clothes when it's cold and agitate a fan when it's hot. Oh! the pain!'

He slid to secure a little easier position and removed his boot for the time being, grumbling, "Oh, it's swollen! There must be internal bleeding. Had I delayed taking off my boot, I'd soon be hard put to get it off. Surely the ankle is sprained or broken, maybe both. I wish someone would quickly come!" And further he thought,

'Unkai would be meditating on the veranda...he caught a cold and wraps up in a blanket. He's sorrowful for having a weak body...his great misfortune was to go to Shoshinji in Gifu. Zen Master Tengai trains the strong while discarding the weak like small fish to be used as fertilizer. Mokuzu is the one to go there — it would be just right!

'How untoward no one is working today! In a war would they take a day off? They ought to proceed whether it's rain or a rain of bullets. They're upside-down if they think achieving the Kannon for peace is easier than waging a war! *Ugaah!* — the pain!

'Why such pain? I'm being made ill by having to bear it this long...I must be getting old...I feel faint...perhaps I have a weak heart...I want to go to bed. But I shouldn't be like this! I am a Zen master! Indeed! Priest Kakkan would say, "When your pain is unbearable, concern yourself with another's life, another's travail." True words. I shall forget my own pain. And I needn't think only of other people; to take thought of an animal or a tree has equal effect....

'What, I wonder, are Reiho and Luri are up to? They're incubating some shallow idea and have opened an office in a radiance of heat between them. This morning too they went off. When I asked, they said, "It's a kind of welfare. One of these days we'll give you details." What can that mean? Unless they're wolves in sheepskins, they can't make money that way. Well, I shall examine them...it would be impossible for them to do wrong. They both have known much hardship. They're incapable of harming others as long as they reflect on their own experience.

'Oh! the pain! When will they return? Or Mokuzu might return earlier. At such a time he ought to curtail karate and hurry home. The other day Unkai told me Mokuzu has occult power. Well, what's the use if he can't use it now? Any kind of divine power is generally unreliable — like a rainbow it vanishes as soon as it appears...*ouch! ow ow ow ow!*'

There was the faint pink of antetwilight, but nightfall came at once with new rain clouds.

Mokuzu realized that the mizzling rain and the dew on the grasses shone like snow even in the dark.

When he came up the narrow but familiar path he caught sight of a huddled black form with the rain falling on it and rebounding like powdery snow.

As soon as he judged who it was he responded unlike the Mokuzu imagined by the master. He rushed forward and lifted him onto his back.

"Master, are you all right?"

"Hmph! — the pain! Long I was awaiting you...! So long!"

"I'm here. You can feel safe on my back. You need endure no longer, cry as you like!"

The moment he realized the master had met trouble, Mokuzu felt dizzy. Like laundry in a washing machine the black cedar forest and the twinkling townscape gyred in the rainy sky. But when he took his weight onto his neck and shoulders, a sense of mission arose, to carry the heavy task of the Zen master and not only his physical weight.

'I sensed snow in this rain,' he thought. 'It looks like a warm June rain, but for someone it could be a blizzard. Rain nurtures things, snow freezes them to death.'

He carried the master up to Ryotanji. Unkai telephoned for an ambulance. It could come no nearer than the mountain foot, where the road was done, so the master was taken down by stretcher, then driven to a surgical hospital in town.

A surgeon chose two relatively clear X rays and explained to Mokuzu, "Here, you see, the ankle joint was forced outward. What we have is a Pott's fracture in addition to a torn ligament. In the healthy state the internal and external malleoli are joined by strong ligaments to the talus here and to the calcaneus here. You can see a ligament between the tibia and the fibula too. But when we are forced to take this odd posture" — the surgeon demonstrated, indeed his leather slipper came off — "at once a great stress comes here. The internal malleolus then separates and causes this break, and the external malleolus breaks too because the talus thrusts it up like so. That is exactly what happened in this case."

Mokuzu pitied the master: his bones in the pictures looked delicate unlike his customary stout self.

With the affected part encased in plaster he looked pathetic. Even with a crutch he was obliged to stay around his residential quarters. Unkai had a slight fever, yet tended him in the minutest fussy detail.

One Saturday night the Zen master summoned Reiho and Mokuzu to his presence and asked them to perform a commission.

"Tomorrow would you go to Ikuta ward in Kobe in place of me? You must be extra careful as your work is to receive money that is to cover a significant part of the construction fee. Go to receive it and return without stopping in anywhere. I shall be in touch by phone with the person you are to meet. If you head for Ikuta Shrine you'll not get lost. Do you understand?"

"Yes," replied Reiho and Mokuzu at once. The master detained Reiho to give details. Mokuzu was just to accompany him, so his load was light. Assuming he would simply follow Reiho's lead, he returned to his room to resume reading an English book that had nothing to do with the reality of his surroundings.

It rained next morning too. Although it was Sunday, Luri went out around nine to her office, announcing she had some extra work. Mokuzu did not know what Luri and Reiho were about but could guess they were running a money-lending business. Whatever it was, he had no interest in their work or their behavior. The master's infirmity did not affect Luri and Reiho; the master had Unkai, so their help was not needed, and they were busy with their plan to leave the temple and live in their office after remodeling it.

Reiho and Mokuzu set off with umbrellas around ten. They took a train from Saga to Kyoto Station and changed to the Tokaido line destined for Akashi.

They arrived at Kobe shortly after midday and bought and ate buns and milk in the station.

Through the crevices between the modern buildings and the warehouses and beyond the numerous tall jibs of cranes jutting straight or aslant, Mokuzu could see the harbor. Associating Kobe, harbor, and ship, he was reminded of the first-engineer intimate with Ena's mother, though he had never met him. Directly his thought fastened on Ena,

'Ena...! I say her name, but the Ena I knew was in second grade in elementary school. Now she must be in the second year of junior high. Could she still be the same?

'Ran wrote that Ena was training herself in remembrance of me...but it's been ages since Ran's first and only letter...I was wrong not to answer it!

'I wonder if Ena is like any of those girls I saw on the train or any who are merrily chatting before my eyes on the platform...or any in my school. Or is she utterly different, like the Virgin Mary? Anyway, she couldn't be the girl with whom I chased after hares and caught fish....'

"Okay, let's go. You're lucky not to have the responsibility. You can afford to be stupefied like ever since we met. I've gotta feel stress till the job's done." Reiho grinned as he spoke to Mokuzu.

It was an old town. Fine houses with fine stone walls lined the uphill cobbled street. As was to be expected of a world-famous port, there were many Western-style brick houses with balconies and square chimneys, which for Mokuzu were a curious sight. The garden trees were also old and excellently tended. Ivy covered the sides of some houses, and some had verandas with climbing roses abloom in various colors.

Mokuzu was engrossed in fancying a life with Ena in one such house and their talk were they to walk together along the cobbles.

His fancy grew wilder, and feeling that Ena might spring forth at any moment, he checked the side streets as he walked behind Reiho. He noticed several little girls leaning from a balcony to tie home-made paper dolls to a pine branch as a prayer for fine weather.

335

The reception room had a thick, colorful Tientsin carpet. The easy chairs and couch were of Chippendale style with Gobelin fabric and delicately carved wood. A prismatic chandelier hung from the high ceiling, adding sheen to glass-doored bookcases and a buffed dark red mahogany table. A maid opened the curtains. The sea, visible at a glance, was muzzy through the thin rain, but what a splendid sight it would be on a fine day.

Mokuzu, possessed here too by the fancy that he was with Ena, took no note of the furnishings, and blankly greeted the maid and the lady, presumably the wife.

'At any cost I have to see her once. She said not meeting is training. But we should be able to make strides with our training after we meet — it's necessary to affirm that our training is correct. At least for me she is the bedrock supporting the mountain, the font feeding the stream. And I so wish to see her pure, gentle, bright eyes and erect, warm figure!'

The gentleman of the house took a corrugated-cardboard box from a dark green cloth, unsealed it, and unboxed and carefully counted its crisp bundles of bills. Each bundle was bound tight with the paper band of a bank.

"The Bank of Japan will issue a ten-thousand-yen bill in December, which will reduce this amount to half its volume," he stated.

'If I went to see her, would she be disappointed, thinking I couldn't persevere in training without meeting? Would her eyes cloud like the time she found an injured bird in the snow?'

The man returned the bundles to the box, sealed it with new tape, wrapped it in the cloth, and handed it to Reiho.

It was about the size of a broad shoe box, just right to carry under the arm.

'Giving disappointment is among the worst of human acts. Who won't cry, "No, 'tis not so deep as a well, nor so wide as a church-door, but 'tis enough, 'twill serve"?[6] If disappointed, she will feel the stars have left their orbits and the flowers lost their light, and she will feel isolated from worldly relations like an unnoticed inorganic substance....'

"Hey-hey, we've gotta hustle! If you don't mind, eat up, it's melting!" Reiho jutted his chin at Mokuzu's dish of ice cream, walnut mixed with vanilla and chocolate.

"Ha ha ha! Your Zen master was boasting that one of his acolytes is a genius. Much as he often speaks paradoxically, it's doubtful he means this one."

At Kobe Station Reiho again bought buns and milk, offering them to Mokuzu too, but Mokuzu backed off. Reiho gulped down three bottles, a total of about a pint and a half.

"On a rainy day you'll get sick if you drink so much, because you don't sweat."

Reiho spurned Mokuzu's advice.

There were few Sunday passengers. They took seats in the middle of the car. Mokuzu resumed his fancy. Reiho by turns looked out the window and attempted to sleep, but kept checking his wristwatch. His coarse hands never loosened their grip on the box on his knees.

The rain must have let up or perhaps was being repelled by the train. The sporadic drops against the window were making oblique lines of dots.

'Does Ena too sometimes see June rain as snow?...Ena receding in the snow...approaching in the rain....'

Mokuzu was right in his conjecture. Reiho began to complain of his stomach. He stood to go to find a toilet. He did not return. Anxious, Mokuzu went in search of him. He was in the noisiest place, where the cars were coupled, and had opened the window wide and was bending to stick his head into the wind.

He continued at it as he raised his important parcel as high as the sill. Mokuzu tried to take it to relieve him of his duty, but just then Reiho retched and his hand on an upswing jerked the box from Mokuzu's grasp and sent it out the window. It dropped through the framework of the truss bridge that the train was beginning to cross. Below was not yet water but dry riverbed.

Mokuzu was frantic. He hung out the window to look aft of the train, and saw in a flash a figure in an oyster white raincoat running to the riverbed.

The scene shifted to iron trusses coming and going. The river was muddy and quick. The far shore came and went. New factories built in former rice fields was the oncoming scene.

'Was the figure in the raincoat real? my fancy? a presentiment? or an afterimage?' Mokuzu was unsure.

When the box fell, Reiho dashed to the rear to get a train man. Roughly he dragged him by the elbow to the window, pushed Mokuzu aside, and appealed, "Here! My precious parcel fell from here! Get it back somehow or other, please!"

"Slow down, have a cool head, passenger. You're telling me the window where you lost it. You must describe the place...Just the counter side of the Kanzaki River bridge? Well, I recommend you detrain at Osaka, which is the next stop because this is an express. Go to the railway police office there and explain."

"That's crazy! Stop the train at once!"

As Reiho challenged the train man, Mokuzu looked with detachment out the window and thought,

'He didn't vomit, he faked. Hadn't he just been to the toilet? How strange, the raincoat of whoever ran to the riverbed was exactly like Luri's...

337

but, it's unthinkable she was there; she went to her office in Kyoto...yet, why is Reiho behaving so actorish? He truly looks the part — raddled, changing color, losing all sense, signs too much like conventional perplexity and upset....

'Yes, it wasn't rain...rain freezes to snow, snow melts to rain. Well, either way it's a mere natural phenomenon. What I should take account of is not my surroundings but my mental life. It's worthwhile to study my own life with my own three hundred sixty joints and eighty-four thousand pores...isn't it?'

29

To Train Oneself

Ryotanji became more subdued and lonesome after Luri and Reiho moved to their office in town shortly following the incident of the Kannon-fund loss. No one raised any excessive commotion nor, transported by enthusiasm, let out a screech. Luri and Reiho had enjoyed radio and TV even during meals, but now dust was gathering on the sets.

Unkai shopped, laundered, and cooked as quietly as he sat meditating. On his way home he obtained seasonable flowers for Mokuzu to paint.

One day he put a large flower cluster and some leafy branches of hydrangea in a vase and stealthily brought it to Mokuzu's room.

"You are great to read so many books. Only I worry about your health. I think you shouldn't rise so early; you're not required to chant with me in the Buddha hall."

"I practice karate twice a week. It's enough exercise with the walk to and from school. I'm worried about my mind, not my body. I think I'm getting book toxicosis."

"What do you mean?"

"I remember my father drank regardless of having no money and it eroded his physical and mental health. He must have been slightly alcoholic. I begin each book with the high expectation of finding the best way to live, for it was said, 'Millions of books wait to be read, as thousands of peaks stand to be climbed.'[1] Soon I'm charmed by the skillful descriptions and curious developments, but after spending hours I find only disillusionment and never what I want to know. The nature of books is primarily recreational, like radio and TV. What books do for readers is to remove every serious problem for a while. They infuriate me for wasting my time. But soon I'm opening another with the same expectation. I'm like a cat that is toyed with by its owner, yet always returns."

"You speak with indignation, but aren't your teachers Docho and Yojun recommending that you read?" Unkai indicated the pile along the wall. Indeed they kept bringing books. Besides English and American literature Yojun brought German, French, and Russian in English translation — Pushkin, Turgenev, Dostoyevsky, Tolstoy, Chekhov, Ehrenburg, Sholokhov, Simonov; Kant, Goethe, Schiller, the brothers Grimm, Heine, Nietzsche, Hauptmann, Mann, Hesse, Carossa, Kafka; Montaigne, Descartes, Corneille, La Fontaine, Molière, Madame de La Fayette, La Bruyère, Racine, Marivaux, Montesquieu, Voltaire, Rousseau, Stendhal, Balzac, Hugo, Dumas father and son, Mérimée, Baudelaire, Flaubert, Zola, Anatole France, Maupassant, Gide, Valéry, Proust, Martin du Gard, Malraux, and Sartre.

Docho brought mostly Chinese and Japanese books relating to religion, philosophy, and history.

"True, they tell me to read and read whether I understand or not. They say someday I'll find among those books one I want to reread several or even a hundred times. I wonder. So far I've never come across any I want to read again."

"You have to be patient. The other day Yojun was telling our master and me that you took only three days to read *War and Peace* in English. He said Akutagawa Ryunosuke did it in four, which amazed his friends and his teacher, Natsume Soseki."

"It's nothing to be proud of. I read it fast as the wind, but my comprehension must be like raking a wide field with machine-gun fire — quite missing the mark. I could find no greatness in it. There were only many spectacles, as if the author were a train and I a passenger. As for your mentioning Natsume Soseki, I just began his *Kusamakura*. So famous is the first paragraph that one might think it's the opening of the Gospel according to St. John. What do you think? I'll read it:

> "Let Intellect be your guide and you will appear harsh and rigid. Pole along with Emotion and you will be swept away by the current. Insist on Volition and you will be seen as stubborn. Life is full of vexations."[2]

Unkai smiled admiringly. "Well said. That's one reason why I must practice my meditation. You're lucky you can easily read such wise books."

"Wise? This is crap, a monkey show on the street! It's typical literature, like candy, neither harmful nor good — it doesn't really touch life's essence. But this book is better. Some other authors delight in cracking jokes and in persecuting themselves. Some begin to gouge out their eyes to wash them in nitric acid; worse, others draw out their guts to rinse them before the public. I'd better consider what Schopenhauer said in his *Über Lesen und Bücher*, which I chanced to read in Japanese a few days ago. He says we have to learn to leave off reading, that bad books poison and drug our mind, ruin our mentality. Teacher Docho lectured me that the Chin dynasty was ruined by the spread of opium and mah-jongg, but to those I would add book toxicosis."

"I understand your frustration, but being ignorant I can't help. Be patient and consult your teachers. If they can't satisfy you, there's always our master. I must go for evening chanting. Don't forget to spray water on the hydrangea; there's a snail on one of the leaves." Unkai turned, then turned back,

"Minor sounds now stand out...the drip of the spigot. Birds, squirrels, and weasels now run on the veranda....Well, our master will be glad to be consulted."

Mokuzu kept thinking at his desk. 'Most books deal with two main themes, love and death. They're my main concerns too. I want to know how to attain love and how to be free of the problem of death.

'As soon as I open a new book I'm pulled into its world because of these two themes, and I'm invited by its pleasant scent and beautiful mist hanging about its peaks, and before long I enter its core. Then always at the very place where the author has to show his essential view on love and death, I find he adroitly detours or creates a smoke screen. Some authors just skip by, others even toss the themes to the reader. Then I'm left puzzled why they labored to introduce them if they're going to leave them unsolved and as vague as ever.

'It must be supposed that in order to answer these essential questions, an author must have first attained the highest peak. But often I suspect they write before they have experienced standing there. Sensitively and eloquently they can describe the sights along the path and on the mountain breast, but they are deaf and dumb at the sight of the summit. At times their views are more vulgar than those of people who work to raise cucumbers and eggplants; or as remote and abstract as an aurora or a mirage, which of course they offer the reader no means of reaching....'

Mokuzu stood and brought the hydrangea from the top of a bookcase to his desk. He opened the shoji. The mist was rising among the dense cedars and only the tops were lit by the late sun coming over the main building. From the eaves came the noise of meadow buntings disturbing the leaves in the gutter. Facing the flower cluster he more modestly rethought, 'I'm like the dew on rocks in deep mountains — charming, but shallow and narrow. Teacher Setsuro keeps saying,

340

"'You can grasp and precisely express each image. Your work qualifies as a field guide to plants and insects, even for anatomical illustration. But I see no spirit. Are you competing with optical instruments? Why can't you understand art? You have the talent of an artisan, but not of an artist."

'I'm a creature grown up in a thicket of assorted trees. The talent for which I'm admired is useful only in such quarters as Ryotanji and my school. I'm a frog in a well ignorant of the sea. I'm unqualified to compare myself with those who made history and shone through all ages and lands. I've no desire to be ranked among such great literati as Rai Sanyo, who resolved to be great when he was my age of thirteen. Yet I wish to gain insight into people and things. I am "he who dreams with open eyes,"[3] so of course I can't understand the obvious viewpoints that must be plainly set down in books. "Unseeing when seeing, unhearing when hearing."[4]

'I shouldn't be kidded and deceived by anyone.' Mokuzu bitterly thought of Reiho and Luri. 'They used me to camouflage their planned embezzlement of our master's Kannon fund. How obtuse of me not to see who they were and what their situation and character! I must be seeing all rocks, flowers, and insects with the same eyes. I don't appreciate their beauty because, as Teacher Setsuro says, I don't see their true nature.

'Anyway, I think we each have a self that we're usually aware of. But I must be careful. It's not static and monolithic but keeps changing every moment — refuting, self-contradicting, and pursued by its own correction, elimination, and addition.

'The reason it keeps changing must be that it's but a tiny aspect of a bigger, profound, intricate, and mysterious self. The self we are aware of is a transilient aspect surfacing in response to the occasion. To see the self as such isn't enough to see anyone completely. I will have to see the un-surfaced self, which even the person himself is hardly aware of, if I am to see anyone completely.

'But how am I to see people more than they see themselves or know a flower more than it knows itself?'

Mokuzu gazed at the hydrangea and at the snail. He was reminded of the gregarious hydrangeas in the mountains behind his native Tangenji. Ena's face merged with the flower cluster. He recalled the pictures she had shown him long ago.

He spent no day without thinking of her. Often he fell into a fantasy of meeting her, and he thought of boarding a train and going. 'It's under two hours.' But he imagined her at once asking, "Why?" and he had to answer, "For no particular reason, only I couldn't control my wish to see you." It was so idiotic he was ashamed even to imagine it.

"Why do you want to meet while you have yet to complete your

341

training?" she might ask. "Would you quit and be muffled in a down quilt like a baby bird? All our pains will come to nothing if we give up on the way."

The short divide between himself and her seemed in a trice to widen like the uncrossable Milky Way separating Altair and Vega.

'To meet her now would finish our relation and be death to her purity and my dignity.

'It's a sheer fact I have still obtained no fruit from my training. I'm like the water in a swimming pool with an overflow drain. Whatever I do my level never rises, because I have no primary knowledge of what real training is.

'I get up at five-thirty, chant before Buddha for forty or fifty minutes, go to school and finish most schoolwork there, study karate, painting, English literature, or Buddhist history, and read until ten but more often midnight. When I get drowsy I put menthol salve around my eyes.

'But how is my life related to real training? Nothing I do seems to have anything to do with it. I don't want to do what is unrelated as long as I have the choice. I wonder if my life is being smothered by trivia.

'Why can't I know what training is? I can't count my karate as training. It's said the purpose of sports is to build a sound mind in a sound body. How can anyone say such irresponsible words? So far as I know, sportsmen don't question what a sound mind is. Moreover, our body is fated to decline and die, so why build it up? To play sports is to build a house on sand.

'Sumi painting is not so unlike sports. It's an art form, and art, it was said, is to seek eternal beauty and to express it by perishable materials. But first, I honestly don't feel much urge to express beauty. I'm content to recognize it around me. I care most to recognize it and not express it, for I think expressed beauty is rigid, limited, as if dead and shrunken compared to the beauty recognized in our mind. Second, I can't agree with the saying that art is long and life is short. Both are short if we say short. Expressed art is more mortal than art recognized in our mind and not expressed, because it's already detached from our mind, whereas art unexpressed is still contacting with eternity, which can also be recognized in our mind. Whether or not we recognize it, our mind seems to contain a bigger self connecting with eternity, though this is but my rough guess....

'My study of literature and history has only helped me to heap up a compost of knowledge to germinate fungi in my brain. I don't want to become a man of great memory and erudition. I hate the sight of a library inside and out. People are forever seeking something there like roaches in a garbage pit. Were a library in a forest, who among those frequenters of libraries would pay notice to the birds and the trees?

'My literature and history studies dizzy me with so much glitter of gold,

342

silver, lapis, giant clam, agate, coral, and pearl, counted as the transfinite variations of love and death. They talk and talk about all phenomena relating to these two main themes, yet never make me understand what they are. What I need to know is not others' love and death but my own!'

Required to make a new painting before his teacher arrived, Mokuzu thought as he faced the hydrangea. He gazed at the aggregate flowers for so long that they floated before his eyes like bubbles, like the colorful bubbles of one of Ena's pictures of long ago. That in turn changed to multiple faces of Ena, and he found he could not look without seeing her image.

He left his desk and went to douse with cold water. When he returned he sat at a low table and prepared to paint.

In the evening Teacher Setsuro put down his whiskey glass and held up the new picture in both hands with unusual care. Suppressing a smile, he said,

"Hmm...not a mere sketch and no one can imitate it. When did you understand this matter, eh? Look at this hydrangea yet to reach its prime, indeed in transition from reddish purple to lucid indigo. And I'll say this snail could be such a gastropod as the *Hypseloconus* of the Ordovician period of the Paleozoic era, I mean, it has some eternality."

However slight, it was the first recognition Mokuzu had ever achieved from this teacher.

He made two more paintings the next week and presented them. One showed many ascendant stalks with colorful but orderly buds and flowers of hollyhock. Some years ago Unkai had received several plants from a farmhouse and had set them along the wooden wall of Luri's room at the southeast end. Mokuzu focused on the single-flower white racemes among the pink and the red and placed a white butterfly. Unkai on seeing the picture said,

"I'm sorry the cooking now serves only our hunger and not our taste."

Mokuzu made no response; he saw in the hollyhocks both Luri and Ena.

Teacher Setsuro commented, "Ho! a symbolic presentation of untainted and respectable idiocy, which should be the mother of the world. In your buoyant lepidopteran there's gross energy to stay airborne like a toddler eager to keep up with its mother, yes, pure idiocy, pure fretfulness, and pure longing."

As he held up the other picture he looked quizzically at Mokuzu and conned it in silence. Under the moon a host of eulalia plumes swayed above a precipice, some bending over the brink. Against the night the plumes appeared like candle lights.

Setsuro emptied his glass and said, "It's getting interesting. Maybe I'll need to drink less during the lesson. This work is quite supreme, but tell me, where did you see such eulalia? It's the start of summer; you couldn't be seeing white tufts now."

"Well, in actuality I saw a fresh clump of blades at the base of a red pine where the new drive crosses the path, you know, where the Zen master broke his foot."

"There? Hm, an insignificant growth. It spurred your imagination and recollection, eh? Nature responds as much as you give it thought. Drawing nature is after all drawing the mind. So you'd better study your mind more and more. Your Zen master can teach you about that.

"I was a bit older than you and was sketching a bridge in a misty rain when a mendicant priest stopped behind my shoulder. By and by he told me I had no comprehension of Shanhuei's stanza, and he recited it,

> "I walk as I ride a buffalo.
> Empty is my hand, yet I fist a hoe.
> I survey a bridge with people crossing.
> The bridge not the water flows.[5]

"The priest was your Zen Master Hanun-kutsu. From then on I began to render nature beyond my skill, beyond myself. Mokuzu, you too must go beyond this barrier of your own."

Mokuzu could make no sense of the stanza and did not attempt to explain further how he happened to see the eulalia.

He had been returning from karate. As always he was fantasizing about Ena, imagining running with her through a field of eulalia in the afterlight of autumn. As he neared Ryotanji night fell and the moon brightened. When he came up to where the new road crossed, he was arrested by the young blades. He soon resumed his fantasy but could not easily recall her figure. Her face, all of her, was lost in the vast field. He desperately ran in the dark. White plumes everywhere surged in the wind and each began to resemble her face. He was at a loss. Returning to reality he suddenly thought, 'They couldn't be more than five grams each...or five yen in a flower shop. Yet their life must be as precious, as respectable as hers. Each is a part of the earth, which is a part of the universe. She is running lightly among them and they are lightly nodding, and she and they are as great as the universe itself....'

❧

The rainy season was over and Zen Master Hanun was not free of his cast. He confined himself to his room, jutting out his heavy foot, or dragged himself to the veranda. He was nearing sixty in age and was obviously suffering a blow.

His bone fracture had occurred at an important time for him. The surgeon, caring only about his physical injury, told him laughingly,

"I suspect senile osteoporosis. By any means your fall wasn't so violent. Haven't you been experiencing backache in recent years?" The master was not one to worry over his physical condition. He replied, also with a laugh,

"Thank you for your concern. I feel pain not only in my back but all over — in my chest, shoulders..." and he thought, 'In my mind is the worst pain.'

Reiho, who had lost the master's money, made an earnest appeal at the time,

"Forgive me for being careless and grant me two or three years' grace. Don't be discouraged, I swear to compensate you in full. I'll exert myself till my flesh shreds, my blood dries up, and my bones fall apart!" He put forth every ounce of energy and brain, and tears were indistinguishable from sweat on his glowing face. At his elbow Luri was pale but added her commendatory words,

"Master, ever since that day Reiho can't eat and is having nightmares. If you drive him an inch more into a corner, you'll lose both principal and interest. Please allow him a few years to make up the sum he so unfortunately lost without malice. In return for your tolerance I vow to help him compensate you even a day earlier."

By then Mokuzu was aware that Luri and Reiho were lying. He kept silent nonetheless, but not because he had no cogent evidence; simply, he was disinterested. His concern was that he had been deceived by them and all along treated as an immature kid. His concern was how not to be deceived by anyone. Even so, he felt some compunction of conscience for not telling the master. But he rationalized that he was not obliged to tell. 'First, it's entirely between him and Luri and Reiho. I haven't been consulted. Second, and more important, I don't want to practice justice by exposing them, since I'm not a prosecutor with the duty to single out one conduct like a surgeon operating for a gallstone. But while a surgeon doesn't touch a patient's healthy parts, a prosecutor may assume a defendant to be altogether corrupt. A speck of dirt ruins a whole life. I have no cause to arraign them on account of a small aspect of their life. They may one day practice some great deed because of this experience. While I haven't an eye to see people and things, I should bide my time to judge.'

The master, whether he saw through Reiho, never blamed him. Of course he reported the loss to the Osaka and Kyoto police, and the details of the case were duly recorded. Even the Kanzaki River area was investigated. The police officer Sako came to report their conclusion,

"As you know, it wasn't a criminal act and hence justifies no further police investigation; all the same, we hope someone finds it and turns it in. Of course it's an incontestable crime if the money is found and kept, a case of 'embezzlement of lost property' as defined in the Penal Code, article 254. But establishing proof is mighty hard. There's no means of identification, why, we'd have to check every angler, resident, and traveler in the area that day... no, quite impossible."

"Then you are suggesting I trust in Providence, which necessitates and signifies fatalism or religious belief," said the master cynically. He was naturally in a fix about paying the construction workers. Yet it was a purely economic problem. He asked them one by one to accept a delay of payment and to suspend work for an indefinite term. He also wrote to Zen Master Tengai in Gifu to ask an advance to meet his debt until his foot healed and he could raise the lost sum anew.

He had within recent years made a donation of money to Zen Master Tengai in response to his request to help him establish his college.

Thus the loss did not yet discourage him. But he was confounded by the sudden realization that his adopted son had no interest in the Kannon statue. He could not fathom how Reiho had developed his interest in money. Among a choice of many occupations, he had with Luri merrily chosen money-lending.

'For whom did I resolve to build the Kannon?' he asked himself. 'Above all for Reiho; he's what intimately spurred me through the long hardship of fund-raising...sad, pure-minded, he was an ignorant child who lost his mother in a collier's lodge, and at the same time his father in town.' He recalled those days. He had always been a pacifist, but during the war whoever spoke out against war was jailed by special political police, so he had wandered the land while abusing himself for being a coward. Knowing he was not keeping Buddhist morality, he was losing self-esteem.

Then he met Reiho and saw the nuclear cloud. A few days later he went alone to Hiroshima. It was unlike the hell scene he had imagined. In his imagination the horrible sight had not come with scorching heat or the fetor of burnt bodies; nor were there seared babies and school children. "If hell is for sinners, what is this?" he had asked himself. Even at night lapping groans issued from the roadsides and streams, and from the piled corpses. Many people lined the railway hoping to go to their native homes or to relatives, some so injured they chose to fall before the train approaching in the dark, and another and another went under the iron wheels.

He took Reiho and raised him as his own and devoted himself to the peace movement in atonement for his sin of not openly opposing the war, and he vowed to erect the Kannon for peace as the conduct of a Buddhist priest.

'So busy was I raising the funds that I neglected to raise the spirit, and just when my wish is close to fulfilled, the contents are going to ruin,' he realized.

While awaiting Zen Master Tengai's answer, he often hobbled with cast and crutch to the leveled mountaintop and there too he thought,

'Many trees and grasses were cut and scraped to their death before their natural time, and many small birds and animals were made to escape. They're ridiculing me now, the raw soil is too.

'Truly I haven't been raising knights to battle for world peace, to enhance the Kannon. Without them the statue is a vain skeleton, an ugly, ghostly casting.'

The master was losing the passion to perfect his task. After the rainy season the mountaintop, wide like an athletic field, began to dry and crack. The ardent sun struck his bald head, and in the surrounding pines the cicadas kept up their endless din. Then one afternoon in mid-July he received Tengai's answer. Already in despair like cooled bath water, he began to read on the veranda with his grimy plastered foot extended,

> ...You must know the words "Buddhism of the cathedral," spoken in derision since olden times. When the edifices prosper, the true spirit is poor. This I concluded by editing Shoshinji's six-hundred-year history.
>
> We shouldn't forget even a moment our National Teacher Daito's last admonition: "Those descendants who preside over temples flourishing with pagodas, halls, and sutras decorated in silver and gold, and with such numbers of visitors that the precincts generate heat...those descendants who do not fix their mind on the wonderful Dharma formlessly transmitted from Buddha through the patriarchs — they all belong to a fraternity of demons, and their efforts to erect forms will shortly bring on the demise of true religion."
>
> But Daito averred, "Whoever devotedly investigates his own nature will meet me daily even after I die; he will know how to thank the patriarchs even if he must live with no raiment and only a straw mat, cooking in a broken pot the roots of wild herbs..."[6]
>
> Mind, not form, must be our concern. It means to issue out a talented man or even half such a man who will make the most of the materials around instead of building additional material symbols.
>
> That's exactly why I founded my college on the grounds of Shoshinji. A college, I say, though it looks shabbier than the shabbiest school throughout the land. In truth, I moved the buildings of an obsolete rural elementary school slated for destruction by the Ministry of Education. It cost me nothing, nay, it came with some financial aid!
>
> Yet I'm proud of the professors and students who must function in such poor facilities. I think they are the best in Japan, possibly in the world. They are building, cleaning, and repairing their college with their own hands and feet. They rise at four, practice meditation, engage in physical labor, study classics and moderns till ten at night. From within

they are turning effete matter into a bright palace of studies.

Now let me express my frank worry: Is your Kannon prepared to issue from its womb men to advance world peace? Do not rely on the masses who may gather when it is erected. They will be useless for any grave matter, not to mention peace. They'll be onlookers to the bitter end. What we need is a few fervent souls to sacrifice themselves for world peace.

Note an allegory from a sutra: Worms eating at a lion return evil for good.[7] I fear peace may be disrupted from within your Kannon if you are so engaged in its form.

Now I'll tell you why I didn't attend your construction ceremony. I realized that the more peace statues are erected worldwide, the more peace is at peril, just as the building of better police stations and penal institutions does nothing to decrease crime. It's a matter not for congratulation but for sorrow: your Kannon statue in its potential to deter war is like a candle before the wind.

The above is my true opinion. Then let me respond to your request. Gladly will I pay your debt, but I do so by way of replication and not in support of your Kannon. I will send you money before the close of the month, and please understand you will owe me nothing. Your merit will be rewarded with twice the sum you gave me. That is the best I can do for you...

Zen Master Hanun had no heartfelt antipathy to the letter, in fact he rather concurred with this other Zen master. 'Reiho hasn't been with me all these years. What Tengai says is so true I've well nigh lost interest in living on.

'He laid a firm foundation for his college and set it well on its path. He's even sending out graduates who adhere to his belief, and his influence is extending to prominent figures of the political and financial worlds, including a minister of state and a staff member of the Self Defense Forces....' As the unpleasant thought joined his forbearance of the itch under his cast, a sour expression crossed his face.

> 'Even this mindless brute
> is rendered sad and lonesome on seeing
> a snipe alone on the swale, autumn gloom.'[8]

Zen Master Hanun intoned to himself, and to the best of his ability stuck out his tongue to make a face.

"How are you, Master? I have your supper." Unkai carried a tray into the master's room.

"Oh, is it time already? Thank you, Kai. But wait..."

"Yes, what can I do? Should I close the storm doors?"

"No, I shall sup here on the veranda. That will be all." The master wanted to say something but changed his mind, considering it pointless to plow the sand, which was how he felt upon Unkai's response to any subject.

'I don't understand what he thinks about his life and the world; he's like a shadow, a female cat. I enjoyed Reiho's vigor. He could openly scorn Unkai. But it seems they both — the one scorning, the other scorned — care solely about their private life.' The master did not touch the tray of food.

'The world is advancing in the direction of Tengai's convictions. The Police Reserve Force and the Coast Guard, formed in 1951, were raised to the status of National Safety Forces in 1952. In 1954, just four years ago, that was raised to the Self Defense Forces — an exact return to the prewar Imperial Army. Our peace movement contributed nothing to deter this dangerous current. Only the names are changed; the content is as it was in the old Japan. The experience of defeat in war is as meaningless as letters written on water.

'In 1947 the old police was divided into two channels of command, the national rural police and the local autonomous police. It was a good system for its democratization and decentralization. But in 1954 the latter was abolished, and now again we have a centralized and highly bureaucratic police.

'There's a trend afoot that would revive Emperor Jinmu's Accession, the old moral education, and the legalization of raising the national flag. More serious, our Penal Code is being reviewed for amendment to heavier punishments. In addition, the U.S.-Japan Security Treaty is under review to make Japan assume a greater role in the world military scene. Amazingly, even our new Constitution is being considered for change. But ours is an ideal constitution, the most exceptional in the world for declaring that we Japanese waive the right to participate in any war. Yet that is the article being discussed for excision.

'In short, Japan is taking advantage of the unguarded moments of the two big countries America and the Soviet Union to recall its prewar internal structure, and is aiming for greater power than before. Isn't it the same course we took, the same nationalism, imperialism, and militarism? There are those like Tengai who don't believe this ambitious country was defeated.

'What he says and does appears to be high-spirited, and many support him because they dislike to be considered poltroons and traitors to their country. They don't know that true courage and patriotism are to speak out against the current and to act with sympathy for neighboring countries. Day after day Tengai is actively performing what he stubbornly believes, which is, by the way, a common trait of any Zennist, including me...but at any rate, being widely supported doesn't mean he's right....'

Zen Master Hanun before he realized it was comparing Zen Master Tengai's success with his own failure.

349

'What notables ever supported me? Sometimes I was slandered as a communist, though I never had any relation with communism; and often I was laughed at for my idea of a Kannon statue. World peace is of key importance to human beings, like water and air, but most people don't mind disturbing other people's peace, because they think their own peace is far more important.'

The master realized he was beginning to toss to others the blame for his failure and enervation. Quickly he rejected such thought and stared wide-eyed as if to scrutinize his own conscience. Hating self-pity, he stared at the tip of his cast until his eyes watered. Then he shut them for an interval, half opened them, and began to meditate, counting his breaths without focusing on any certain notion, freeing all notions to come and go; and finally he let the time pass through as he let himself rest. He made no attempt to put time to his practical use. He was like any stone, tree, or piece of furniture.

He kept meditating for quite a while. In appearance he was like any inanimate thing; in his mind too he was unlike a living person. His life was sustained by his automatic functions only. He was a mere existence, the flow of time itself.

When he woke from his meditation, his ears were fresh to the singing of the frogs and his eyes took note of his shadow on the shoji. Moonlight was passing over the main building to the north garden before him. The natural lawn grass appeared white as if frosted, and the red pines on the slope were lit in yellow.

The moonlight perceived by his refreshed mind made him recall an episode from *Earnest Zen Monastic Study*, introduced to him in his youth by Priest Kakkan:

> As Nanchyuan was admiring the moon, Jaujou asked him, "How many years have you been thus?" Nanchyuan replied, "Some twenty years...["]9

"How respectable! Only in recent days have I begun to sense that the moon and I are not separate entities...," Zen Master Hanun muttered. Then by association of moon and Nanchyuan, he thought of the water buffalo episode:

> Jaujou: "Where will a man go if he understands he is mortal?" Nanchyuan: "To that layman's house at yon mountain foot, there to become a hardworking water buffalo." Jaujou: "Thank you for your teaching." Nanchyuan: "Like the moon of last midnight, which alone came bright through the window."10

Zen Master Hanun recalled Priest Kakkan's emphatic lecture: "Mind you, this episode points to the trenchant difference between priests and politicians. As soon as they open their mouths, politicians claim they live for the people, but they regard them as foolish, ugly, and cunning. Pretending to act for them, they use them to get elected. Priests become cows and toil in the mud harder than people. Yet a priest's mind is like the midnight moon. No one cares about the moon of that hour, and it is beyond dichotomy between wise and ignorant, rich and poor, high and low, beautiful and ugly."

'Well, certainly I've been standing up all these years for the peace movement and finally I've progressed to the stage of almost perfecting the Kannon...but I can't deny I'm losing my passion....' The master dragged his disabled foot, leaned on his crutch, maneuvered himself from the veranda, and began to hobble to the east garden with the intent of viewing the moon clear of the eaves.

Then he saw the dim electric light from Mokuzu's room.

'Oh, still awake? It must be well past twelve. He shouldn't injure his health by overworking...but his nature is tenacious as a wisteria vine, not only sharp as a sword. Wisteria? Yes! He's a vine on a cliff. A vine can save a man when his surroundings abruptly darken and he's about to fall. A man can make a narrow escape!'

Careful not to raise a noise and disturb Mokuzu's study, the master returned and entered his bed. Enjoyably he thought,

'One Mokuzu surpasses a thousand Reihos. Compare him with Tengai's ten thousand disciples and students, said by Tengai to be thoroughly prepared to act in the world, and indeed they act like they own it with their coarse learning and rude pride. Soon they'll be treated by Mokuzu as no more than whining mosquitoes and bombinating flies. He's capable. Those politicians and businessmen who believe Tengai's teaching and conspire with him will have their misbelief and illogic pinpointed and be shivered like clay images made for a burial mound. Even Tengai will be laughed at as a pitiable lump of fat or a brainless scarecrow if Mokuzu masters the traditional Zen.' Zen Master Hanun determined to summon his last energy to temper Mokuzu, and the notion kept him awake. He thought in his bed, 'What a strange turn of fortune's wheel! I in my youth was raised by the grandfather, and now I have the grandson to nurture me and make my life worth living.'

えん

Toward summer's end Unkai and Mokuzu accompanied the master to have his cast removed. On the way back Unkai went off separately to shop, wishing to buy a treat to congratulate him on his recovery.

The master walked gingerly with a crutch even after the cast was off. He

351

refused Mokuzu's help. As soon as the sun set, a cool air rose from the bushes and the lonely metallic note of the evening cicada echoed from the tall trees here and there. The call and the alae of this species were both transparent. It did not group but chose to stay as one within its range of sound.

The master and Mokuzu took the path rather than the new drive. It was the longer way home in addition to being difficult to walk, but gave them a better view of Kyoto receiving the last of the daylight. Besides, there were many grassy places to rest.

They rested after passing through the bamboo grove, where the terraced tea opened the view. "How are you progressing in your study? Setsuro says the biggest harvest of my bone fracture is the development of your perception of people and things. Your paintings are nearing acceptability for submission to the exhibition at which he's one of the judges. But he doesn't recommend it, fearing you might be made arrogant, which would be a blemish on him. Yojun and Docho place their greatest hopes in you. Seeing your quick grasp of Buddhist doctrine, Docho says, is like the thrill of watching an ice-skating race. Yojun says you are possibly reading more English books than any native college students in England and America."

"They don't see all of me. I'm good at advanced reading like a boat sailing before the wind, but I don't understand the beginning or base of things, so about important matters I'm run aground, I mean, I don't know where I'm standing or with what."

Mokuzu had been feeling increasingly uncomfortable because of his inability to make clear sense of the rudiments of his life and of Buddhism, which reduced to the questions of how he should live, who he was, and what training he should do.

"You mean you don't know why you should study sumi painting, English, history, karate, and so on, and you don't know who it is who is studying?"

"I'd say you are about rightly pointing to my state. To illustrate, let me spend more words. I read that the great Zen Teacher Dogen lost his mother when he was eight, and that he comprehended life's uncertainty by seeing the ascending smoke of her cremation at Takao in Kyoto. Thereupon he determined to train himself. It's said he read through the *Abhidharmakosa-sastra* when he was only nine. Then at my age of thirteen he said to himself, 'As she was dying she advised me to enter the priesthood and study hard. Now it is my true wish. I don't want to live in the worldly world, yes, I shall be a priest. I can repay her mercy, my grandmother's and my aunt's too.'[11] So it's reasonable that he twice read all eighty-four thousand volumes of the Buddhist canon before he was eighteen.

"His colossal reading doesn't so surprise me, but his early resolve to train makes me enviously surprised. Frankly, I also wish to train, but I don't know what training is. I don't think what I'm doing every day is real training. Master, I too understand life's uncertainty. I guess Dogen wished to know what is not uncertain, that is, he thought he should train to seek eternity. So he could begin his life of training. My problem is I don't wish simply for such a thing; I confess I wish for more uncertainty, I mean, a quicker change of my situation and myself.

"I want to live a life of training, but I can't start without knowing what it is. I'm faltering at stage one while seemingly doing well at some mid stage. I appear to be doing well because I'm not expending all my power; I'm doing shallowly what I do and it looks fine. I'd like to put my all into a training that is correct according to my conviction."

The western sky behind Mokuzu was turning red. The colored roll-cumuli were trending southeast on the wind. Most houses were losing their individuality into the dusky belt of residential zone. Strong bluish road lamps began to shine. A crow strenuously cawing hastened to catch up with its flock high in the sky.

"Mokuzu, with Teacher Docho you must have studied Buddha's fundamental teachings. Why don't you start your training according to them? After all, we train to attain Buddhahood. Sakyamuni Buddha when he attained Buddhahood taught us the essential nature of this world and the best way to live, which he expressed as the Four Truths and the Eight Right Ways."

"Master, if I could understand Buddha's teachings I wouldn't be like this. I don't understand even the first of his Four Truths. He says this world is wrought with suffering that comes of birth, aging, illness, death, separation from loved ones, contact with hateful ones, craving for all kinds of things, and living with a body and mind that cause incessant pains.

"I'm cognizant of those sufferings but cannot thereby see all this world and all our life as only suffering. My childhood has been a sort of ash color, yet I admit at times I knew joy. Some nights my mother returned with sweets, and once she brought an illustrated book with the fresh smell of ink. And...I was given a bright red music box...oh well, there were many happy times. So I don't understand Buddha's First Truth. His Second, Third, and Fourth are based on his First, and his Eight Right Ways are based on them all. More, his 'twelve-linked chain of cause and effect' governing our suffering life and finally all of the Scriptures in Twelve Parts are based on his Four Truths. In fact he lists right view of his Four Truths as his First Right Way. So I can't possibly start practicing his Eight Right Ways.

"When I consider Sakyamuni Buddha's words, I think training means to deepen the understanding that life is suffering. Once I fully understand about

353

suffering I'll not have so hard a time understanding and practicing all his remaining teachings. But I understand this First Truth no more than half at most, so I'm not sure how much I understand the others and the Eight Right Ways, and that's why I always feel I half understand or don't at all understand whenever I consider the 'twelve-linked chain of cause and effect' and any of the Scriptures in Twelve Parts. So I can understand and practice his teachings only half at best. However, what I wish to find is the training I can put all of my power into and not be half-hearted."

Mokuzu could not agree even with Buddha about life in this world, because he had his memory of joy, especially with Ena.

"Mokuzu, there are hundreds of ways to climb Mt. Fuji or to train oneself. We each have our own fitting way. Yours is the most radical and the hardest because you are so honest with yourself. You are intellectual and respect yourself above all. For one like you, training is to know who you are till the end. You must train yourself to see your original nature. Look at the moon. If you see your original nature, everything will be clearly lit, just as everything is now lit by the moon....Oh! that's Unkai's step. He must have bought some good food for congratulations. Not for my recovery but for your new start. I shall give you a koan. When you solve it you will thoroughly know who you are. Be taught by Unkai how to have a Zen interview and come to my room after supper. In Ryotanji, where, as its name says, a dragon lives, I, Hanun, Half-a-cloud, will make you into a perfect man."

IV

Thorny Indigo Forest

30

Receiving a Koan

Mokuzu given a koan was like a person recovered from a long illness who at last stands firmly on the ground in the full light and heat of the morning sun. His mind was swollen with awe and fresh glee.

The season was just autumn, free of humidity, with a constant breeze, a high sky, and air so clear as to render the far mountains distinct.

The sights seemed to aid and encourage him to solve his questions of who was he, what was his mind, why was he born, why must he die, what was the meaning of death, of life, that is, the question of what was his original nature.

To and from school and in most of his spare time he considered whatever came to eye: 'What is it? It tries to stop me from being aware that I'm seeing it and invites me in as if to assimilate me into itself. If I don't resist, I'll become as peaceful as it, wafted by the wind, bleached by the sun, and I'll nod with the trees, flow with the stream, emit vapor like the soil. But when I recover my awareness, the distance between us is immediately evident. The air, though transparent, remains cold and separate no matter how near I bring myself to the grass or soil, so close as almost to touch it with my hand or cheek.'

Only their profile and misty blue color distinguished Mt. Hiei and the continuous eastern peaks from the clear blue sky. The cedar tops rose ahead in a gentle curve as Mokuzu ascended the meandering path, and down from the mountain breast they undulated along the folds.

The deep valleys were entirely filled with thickets of assorted deciduous trees. As he neared the rocky summit with its scarce water and nourishment, he could see the ridge with lean red pines exposed to the north wind.

On the south slope the terraces of round-trimmed tea bushes looked from his vantage point like many softly rolling belts as they reflected the sun. Lower, the delicate leaves of the bamboo grove diffused the light, and beyond were scattered the highest farmhouses, sheltered by the crowns of large trees. From there the yellowing rice fields spread like a body of water around the houses and hillocks, giving them the look of boats. Lower yet, the house clusters fanned out, replacing the green trees and yellow fields until central Kyoto overtook all the level land. The city was disorderly in the color of its building materials and presented a noise devoid of sound.

When he sighted a pair of eagles circling a nest atop a lightning-struck pine, or a monkey eating a ripe wild persimmon on a cliff abutting the path, Mokuzu was prone to feel he was a bird, animal, fruit, or tree.

Often he momentarily felt he was what he saw...the rangy weeds bent at a streamside, an earth-covered bridge taking the mountain path over a little valley, the pebbles and dirt dropping from there to the water whether someone passed or not, the electrical engineers mute on poles as they set a high-voltage cable for the resumed construction of the Kannon statue, the dry leaves below being spirited away by a gust, the long boom of a crane truck left extended overnight and coruscant with dew under the stars....

While thus absorbed, he could dwell in an easy world of no distinction between things, no passage of time, no weight to affairs. It resembled the times he was embraced in his infancy, and times with Ena, which were sheer comfort.

However, as soon as he returned to himself and asked "What is my original nature and who am I anyway?" he felt estranged and degraded to a crude, incomprehensible organic entity incapable of uttering any response, powerless, incompetent, ignorant.

He had entered the Zen master's room in exactly the prescribed manner taught him by Unkai. The master held on his knees a bamboo fillip neatly wound with wisteria bark and lacquered. He sat stern but was smiling. Then he gave Mokuzu the koan "Go to meet your original nature."

Behind the master, on the red ocher wall of the alcove, where no sunlight ever came in, a scroll presented a couplet by National Teacher Muso: "Be deluded and this world is a castle of desires / Be awakened and everywhere is empty."[1] A sasanqua branch with a white bud and some leaves had been arranged in the alcove by Unkai. Behind the master to the right, aloes incense was lit in a censer.

Mokuzu liked incense only so mild that its fragrance was hard to determine, akin to his sensibility about music. Strong incense was rebarbative, made him feel that his joints and marrow were invaded, and, after he had left the vicinity, that his body was smirched inside and out against its will, and that his nose was stuffed as if from dried blood.

He suffered nausea when he passed women teachers at school and women in town who were wearing strong perfume.

'Don't they know clear water that makes visible the rocks and shingle in a flume? Don't they see beauty in the rippling young leaves lit by sunbeams passing through the trees?'

He remembered Ena, who was of course free of perfume and kept herself clean and erect. With thanks he also remembered Luri, who never made herself up nor applied perfume.

The storm doors of the master's room were open. The shojis remained shut. The wind from the pines came with the tappings of a great spotted woodpecker.

Zen Master Hanun-kutsu talked quietly.

"Mokuzu, I never married and have no experience of feeding easily digestible foods to my own babies or of changing diapers. Instead, while I don't say my love is superior to the love of real parents, I have something that will perfect your life, make it combust in the most meaningful way, that is, it will give you real pleasure and finally give you immortality. It is the maximum kindness I can offer you. The giving of this kindness and your receiving of it will be performed through practice of the koan 'Go to meet your original nature, which has been continuing from before your father and mother were born.'

"Now, listen. As you learned from Teacher Docho, Sakyamuni Buddha was born in the small country of Kapilavastu, presently the Tarai district of Nepal. It was then ruled by the more powerful Kosala, adjacent to the northwest. His father, Suddhodana, was an administrator of his own clan, his mother, Maya, the daughter of an administrator of another neighboring country.

"Suddhodana held the title of a raja but was actually no more than an elected administrator of his own clan, for at the time his country was adopting a republican government.

"Sakyamuni Buddha lost his mother when he was seven days old and was nursed by his aunt Mahaprajapati. You didn't lose your mother, but you've been parted from her since early childhood, and from age eight parted from all your family and childhood friends and native mountains and river.

"You must be able to understand that Sakyamuni Buddha and likewise all other great priests suffered life's uncertainty and tended to their training. Indeed the deepest human suffering is over life's uncertainty, and our greatest problem is the problem of life and death. What is our life? It is the ceaseless repetition of birth and ruin from the moment of conception to the moment of death. True or not, this repetition of birth and ruin is said to occur every one seventy-fifth of a second.

"As long as we don't solve our problem of having to die sooner or later, we can't be easy or satisfied even if we solve all our thousand other problems. It's the same as saying we can't build higher floors to a skyscraper without building the ground floor. Solving our problem of life and death is the same as knowing who we are. Short of that there is no solution.

"After six years of asceticism Sakyamuni was enlightened when he saw the morning star, Venus, on December eighth.

"He is holy for the reason that he gained compassion as soon as he was enlightened. Straightaway he helped his five companions practicing asceticism with him. He then saved the three Kasyapa brothers, who were Zoroastrians, and Sariputra, and Maudgalyayana. Throughout his remaining forty-five long years he toured India to help people regardless of caste or race.

"Do you know the meaning of this compassion, Mokuzu? It is the combination of the Sanskrit *maitreya* and *karuna*. The first is an abstract noun stemming from *mitra*, 'friend'; so maitreya means 'highest friendship' or 'no discrimination.' As to this point alone you should note our Buddhist compassion is quite unlike Christian compassion. Christian compassion means the pity of God on high looking down on ignorant people who are like lost sheep. Karuna originally meant 'to groan with the pain of life.' Hence only those who have groaned understand those who groan. Taken together, that is our compassion.

"Sakyamuni Buddha went through all life's sufferings, freed himself from them, and vowed to practice compassion, and indeed he practiced it all his life.

"So you have to understand I am giving you this koan not only to free you from your trouble. I also truly wish you will someday help others.

"Now I must explain what a koan is. But my poor words are unnecessary, for Zen Master Jungfeng Mingben, admired in the Yuan dynasty as the Old Buddha of Honan, painstakingly expatiates to us in *Night Talks in a Mountain Villa*." Mokuzu received a handwritten copy of volume 11 of *The Complete Records of Priest Jungfeng*, which contained the night talks.

"This copy was made by your grandfather. His upright hand is easier to read than the original. Now, read me from where the marker is set."

The script seemed to Mokuzu's eyes to be poor in emotion, even gelid. He thought of his father's occasional comment, "Such letters must have been fashioned with the broken-off point of a sword."

The marker was a ginkgo leaf thin and waxy like tracing paper. 'If picked up by my grandfather it must be older than fifty years.' Mokuzu began to read,

"A man inquired of me why the enlightenment opportunities of Buddha and the patriarchs are called koan. I answered him thus: The word is borrowed from official language, where it means 'official ordinance,' or law essential to govern the land. Ko means the highest reason agreed upon by the sages and to be observed by all. An means official record of ko.

"Where there is the world there is governance, and where there is governance there is official ordinance, for the world should be governed by law. To practice koan is to practice law. With the practice of law the world is orderly and illuminated by justice.

"So too are the enlightenment opportunities of Buddha and the patriarchs called koan. Their enlightenment is not their mere conjecture. They comprehended the essential spirit and broke the bonds of life and death with wonderful reason and without interference of emotion. Hence they share with hundreds and thousands of awakened persons of all eras and all worlds the same highest reason. This highest reason cannot be grasped by dualistic thought, such as by interpretation of the spoken as well as the written word. Our intelligence falls far short. Approach it with dualistic thought and it is like a poisoned drum at whose sound you will perish, or like a giant fireball by which you will be burnt.

"Therefore Sakyamuni Buddha on Mt. Grdhrakuta transmitted it without reliance on scripture, and Bodhidharma at Shaulin asserted that he directly pointed to it.

"After the Zen sect divided into Northern and Southern Zen and branched to five schools, all sorts of masters freely manipulated what had been transmitted to them, what had been directly pointed to. So brilliant were the combats between masters and trainees that their applied words rough or fine were like a violent thunder that no ear could avoid.

"To illustrate: 'The arborvitae in the front garden,' 'Three pounds of hemp,' and 'A dried excrement spatula' are hardly approachable, for they are like a silver mountain with an iron wall. Only an awakened eye can see the meaning through the words and letters. Like a bird in the sky or the moon on water, each shout and cry of the masters leaves no trace. Such free expressions may appear chaotic, but they unquestionably accord with the highest reason.

"The tradition has thus been kept from that ancient time at Mt. Grdhrakuta. Naturally those enlightenment opportunities are not so few as seventeen hundred, as is commonly said.

"Each expression is strictly to prove the truth of each enlightenment, and none is recorded for chat.

"If monasteries are likened to governments, the masters are like senior officials, and what they compiled, edited, and advocated in their lectures can be likened to official ordinance. Anciently the masters introduced these records for appreciation, criticism, and comment, and added their laudatory stanzas. Their intent was not to display their erudition or to oppose the old wisdom, but to use the enlightenment opportunities to open the eye of wisdom in later comers and to certify newly attained enlightenment for the prosperity of the Dharma.

"The sense of ko can thus be 'to prevent assumption of an arbitrary enlightenment,' and an, 'to ensure that a new enlightenment is equal to Buddha's.' Thence, to solve any given koan, the recipient must extinguish all emotion and dualistic thought, and, that done, must be able to graduate from the problem of life and death and master the Way of Buddha.

"To have an enlightenment equal to Buddha's is to have Buddha's compassion for the ignorant, who suffer from delusion about life and death. Buddha helped them through silent words and formless acts. But to be equal to Buddha does not mean to repeat his silent words and formless acts.

"Another point about koan: Just as worldlings when they cannot settle their affairs ask a government office to arbitrate for them according to official ordinance, so Zen trainees unsure of their realization can measure it against the koan.

"Considering all these points, it can be said that koan means a torch of wisdom to illume the dark, a golden fillip to clear shadows from the view, a sharp ax to cut through the base of the problem of life and death, a divine mirror to distinguish the awakened from the benighted. Through the koan the mind of the patriarchs is made vivid and the mind of Buddha is expressed.

"We must therefore master the koan. The koan is to be respected but is respected only by those who know the Dharma."[2]

Zen Master Hanun with closed eyes was listening to Mokuzu's reading. Now and then he nodded with "Yes" and "So, so." Finally he raised his voice,

"Yes, 'a torch of wisdom to illume the dark,'" and he praised Mokuzu,

"So fluently you can read the difficult Chinese, you are like a free fish with precise fins and tail. I am saved the trouble of explaining it and can go on to what I wish to say." He turned to indicate the scroll in the alcove.

"What is here written is true. Deluded, we cannot free ourselves from the problem of life and death. Awakened, we can see life and death with regard to their original nature, and thus as clean matters. All mountains, rivers, trees, and grasses are performing Buddha nature. So nothing is more thankful than to be awakened. You have to understand this point very well. Now, read this. It is excerpts I myself culled from various sources." He gave Mokuzu two bound manuscripts and showed where the first had a marker.

They were quite new. The marker was a faded pink foxglove. Mokuzu was reminded of a passage that Teacher Yojun had required him to memorize in earlier days, from "The Keepsake" by Coleridge. He was reminded also of

362

his dream of those days to live in a house with foxgloves thriving at a corner of the lawn, and behind, a path leading through a forest of beech and white birch with a view of blue ocean and waves breaking against the rocks...to live there someday with Ena...

> The foxglove tall
> Sheds its loose purple bells, or in the gust,
> Or when it bends beneath the upspringing lark,
> Or mountain-finch alighting.[3]

He began where indicated,

> "The mind rolls and rolls only to gather dirt. Ultimately what is hardest to grasp is the mind.
>
> "On hearing the Eight Words, the All-Sapient One directly under-stood the Supreme Wisdom and knew his six years of asceticism had been spent in vain.
>
> "In this world devilish men go round and round creating a din of argument. They propagate their fallacies and make out prescriptions and never cure a single disease. How shabby that they have not seen their original nature and so cannot know good from bad, right from wrong. When they move, indeed they are still. When they are still, indeed they move.
>
> "Shadows exist because of forms, echoes because of sounds. Not recognizing this, they try to repair forms by treating shadows, and raise sounds to stop echoes.
>
> "To seek Nirvana by eradicating klesa is as futile as to seek shadows by eradicating forms. To seek Buddha apart from people is to attempt to hear echoes without raising sounds.
>
> "We must realize that delusion and enlightenment are not separate one from the other, that ignorance and wisdom are the same. Because we artificially name the unnameable, all such antonymous ideas as good and bad appear. Likewise we explain nature, which is unexplainable, and we suffer from the arguments. Phantom and illusion are not real existence; how then can we determine who is right or wrong? Delusion has no substance; how then can we determine what is or is not real existence?
>
> "We had better know we cannot obtain anything even if we think we have obtained it, nor can we lose anything even if we think we have lost it. As I have not reached a higher state, I talk only thus far."[4]

"Stop, stop. That you read so well is impressive, but frankly I wish you found it harder. Why? There's no sweat on your brow, no blisters on your hands or feet. I've always thought reading should be as hard as scaling a rock wall. Unkai would take fifty days to read what you just read.

"Then, do you understand what is written? It would be horrible if you're only reading like a broken phonograph record. For instance, explain the passage, 'On hearing the Eight Words, the All-Sapient One directly understood the Supreme Wisdom.'"

"Evidently it's about Sakyamuni Buddha, for it says he realized his six years of asceticism were useless. The Eight Words has to mean the second half of Raksasa's stanza. According to the Nirvana Sutra, Sakyamuni Buddha in one of his former lives trained himself at Mt. Himalaya as the youth Kumara. At that time he heard Raksasa humming, 'Nothing is everlasting / Such is the law of birth and death...'[5] The youth was eager to hear the second half, but Raksasa demanded his life in exchange. On hearing it the youth offered him his body. It was: 'Completely annihilate birth and death / Therein is eternal joy.'"[6]

"Hm, that's right. Buddha sacrificed his life to understand the truth. You also must understand by your own training that 'delusion and enlightenment are not separate one from the other.' I am not certain who wrote what you just read, possibly someone associated with a high disciple of Bodhidharma.

"Now here is the final preliminary knowledge needed for your koan on original nature. It is found in *Lioutzu-dashy fabautan jing.*" The master opened to where he wanted Mokuzu to read. There was no marker. The book, published in Japan in 1634, was based on a 1291 edition of Chinese origin with addendum by Fahai.

"This also was given me by your grandfather; you can see his red notations. Later you will read the context on your own. For now read only the most pertinent section."

Mokuzu thought his understanding of original nature would be neither increased nor decreased whether he read further or not. His suspicion was raised, 'Is an understanding of original nature the state of fainting away, a kind of ecstasy? If so, I already know it and it seems of no value.' But he began withal to read,

> "Several hundred set out in hot pursuit of the robe and bowl. The lead monk was Hueiming, surname Chen, once a general to a prince and rough in character and conduct. He advanced with zeal and was the first to overtake Hueineng. Hueineng had abandoned the robe and bowl on a rock as he uttered, 'They but symbolize the belief, which cannot be taken by force,' and he had eloigned himself behind a bush.
>
> "Hueiming labored to take up the robe and the bowl, but they would not be moved. At last he cried, 'O Trained Monk! I come for the Dharma, not for the robe!' By and by Hueineng appeared and sat on the rock. Hueiming paid him homage and said, 'O Trained Monk, I beg your teaching on the Dharma.' Hueineng replied, 'Be you truly come for the

Dharma, banish all concerns and raise no notions. Thereafter will I offer you my teaching.' Hueiming at length kept calm.

"Hueineng then spoke, 'Hueiming, when you are free of discriminating good and bad, what is your original nature?' Hueiming was that moment enlightened, and further he quested, 'Is there no more secret transmission beyond the words and mind you now imparted to me?' 'I imparted nothing secret. Reflect and you shall know that any secrecy is of your own making.'

"Hueiming said, 'I stayed in Huangmei yet knew not my original nature. Now by your teaching I know it as one who drinks water knows water. You are my master.' Hueineng told him, 'Your master and mine is Hungren Huangmei. Hereafter be circumspect and guard well your Dharma.' Hueiming put forth one more question: 'Whereto should I fare?'"7

"Fine, fine. There are many points you must study in this section, but foremost for you now is in the lines 'Hueiming, when you are free of discriminating good and bad, what is your original nature?' Hueiming is you. Can you answer?"

Mokuzu wanted to say: 'It's as if those ancient Chinese are talking about a stone-age mentality. I'm living in a far later age, but it isn't hard to guess their mental state because it's the common and rather abstract state of anyone. What I'd really like to know is my own mind, which can't be replaced by anyone else's. To know it is important to me because I can live only once. I'm not interested in original nature beyond good and bad. My interest is to know what "good" is, what I should do for my life.'

But before he spoke, the master suppressed him, "Wait, I can tell without your speaking. In his *Wumen guan*, case 23, the priest Wumen comments on this koan with his stanza: 'No brush can depict original nature / Words of praise fall short / Yet nowhere is it hidden / And evermore it will be, even if the world should end.'8

"Mokuzu, you have to understand matters deeply, as was said, 'A deep river flows long,'9 and 'Climb high if you would extend your view, dive deep if you would see the bottom.'10 You mustn't be a shallow dish. Keep reminding yourself that 'the Dharma is supreme, profound, and mysterious. Without luck you cannot meet it even if you spend hundreds and thousands and millions of kalpas.'11 And, 'The Dharma is limitless, yet I vow to study it all. The Buddha Way is high without end, yet I vow to attain it.'12 "I'd say you are sharp and clever, but you tend toward frivolity. Take your time, think well, focus your mind, and study deep. If you see your original nature, you will dance like a sparrow and laugh and cry with transports of joy."

'Am I supposed to become hysterical? What a funny thing enlightenment must be!' thought Mokuzu, but he kept quietly attending to the master's tedious talk.

"The priest Jyujy said in his last words, 'In all my life I could not use up the Zen of one finger given me by Tianlung.'[13] That's how it is. Once you attain enlightenment, you'll never exhaust its merit.

"Take these books too. They are the works of the priest Bassui, who kindly teaches us how to study the koans. He says that if you wish to be free of the transmigration of life and death, you must extinguish all emotion and dualistic thought. To do so, you must realize what your mind is, which means you must practice sitting meditation. In meditation you must be deviceful. To be deviceful means to doubt deeply every point of the koan. The root of the koan is your mind. He says something like that, easy to hear but hard to practice.

"Repeatedly I ask you to maintain your quest throughout your daily life. Who are you? What in you is seeing, hearing, thinking, and feeling distressed? You have to keep asking, as the folk saying goes, If you must recollect your love, your love is not enough, be ever mindful of your love.

"And when you are sure you have seen your original nature, bring me your view that I may examine its depth and validity."

Thus furnished with a koan Mokuzu was synthetically delighted. Now he could constringe and simplify all sorts of problems to the question What is my original nature?

With this one question in mind he could anywhere, anytime, keep from dissipating his physical and intellectual energy, could unify himself, maintain his equilibrium.

From infancy he had been vague and uneasy because of his uncertainty over what to devote all his energy to. Now he had a definite and worthy goal. To keep asking Who am I? was a lighthouse providing light across a dark and stormy sea. The boat was no longer really lost, or if lost, there was great meaning in being lost so long as it aimed for the light.

'To have a koan is like having a lifeline and oxygen supply to research the sea down where it's a maze of queer grottoes with unknown creatures lurking. A diver may meet perils and strangeness beyond imagination, but if suitably equipped he can quicken his curiosity until he is rewarded with what he hopes to find. To have a koan is to have a secure line and oxygen supply — for life. A koan enables me to continually ask who I am.

'Yet I think I won't find the answer at a certain depth, or in any certain direction, field, or domain. If, say, I regard a camellia leaf and ask what it is, I can see it's a green leaf rejecting and absorbing the light. Botanically speaking, it has the marks of rain and scale insects, it's alternately veined, ovate, serrate, thick, glossy...but knowing this is just the beginning. Magnified, there are no veins or green but many cells, the spectacle of running sap, the production of starch. And I can further magnify it. The amount of study or possible knowledge is unlimited.

'Then, in my research of my original nature it must be important to know which magnification I'm using; and aside from studying its depth there are other ways, such as aesthetic, physiological, pathological, ecological...what nonsense to conclude who I am by using just one method. I could end up convinced of some superstition.'

Mokuzu was glad that his given koan was a question not easy to answer. He thought it would yield no answer even if he spent all his energy on it for the rest of his life. Its value for him was therefore to keep on asking.

'It's a lifelong matter giving me meaning to live. If only I have it I can dive into any ocean and climb any peak. I can go even into hell. As long as I keep asking who am I and what is this self that is groaning, I'll be fine in heaven or in hell. Real hell must be where I'd be forbidden to ask, for only self-questioning can give my life meaning.

'Fortunately in this world I'm allowed to ask. As long as I live no one can take from me this basic right. When bored I can ask, Who is bored? I can enjoy the sight of distant pines, floating clouds, a pond or lake reflecting them, willows and daffodils at the banks. But my joy will double if I ask, Who am I who am enjoying them?

'Even when I fight or see others fight I can keep asking who is fighting, who is observing. Fighting has always been a dreary event. Now I can save myself from that drear.

'I'll say my koan can parlay lead to gold and ugliness to beauty, make a paradise out of a void. It can turn a raucous, flippant party into a steady, honest gathering. Factory clatter, market cram, motorcycle roar, all will turn to profound tranquility. My koan can bring me a balance between manic and depressive states. It is a quiet and lucid observing eye. With it I will be able to make the most of any situation and fetch any attractive nourishments for my happiness without losing the opportunity....'

&

On the first Sunday of October Mokuzu left Ryotanji in the morning to meet his parents at the Saga railway station. He was being sent out of Zen Master Hanun's consideration; he wished Mokuzu and his parents to have as much time as possible to themselves.

Mokuzu was told to be there at 8:30. He could guess that his parents had left Tangenji early to take a bus to Kameoka. Waiting at the wicket he could see them step to the platform with no obstruction. There were few other passengers.

Micha's hair was dark and tidy. Over her kimono she had put a deep purple coat and a grayish shawl. She wore white tabi, and clogs with russet thongs. Under her arm she carried a bundle in a dark green cloth.

He was dressed as always in a black simplified robe with a dark brownish scrip and a dark brown, brimless felt priest's hat. He carried something square in a brown cloth. In clean contrast to his robe he had a white silk scarf tucked at the neck and white tabi and white-thonged clogs. At a glance it was evident that he was a Buddhist priest and that they were a married couple.

Mokuzu was relieved to see them in their best dress, and presumably in their best mood — which was not inferior to anyone else's — and most of all not fighting.

Seemingly they were not expecting to meet him at the station. They took their time to come to the wicket and did not notice him standing on the other side.

He was aware that he was a bit queer to be asking himself Who is it who is observing his parents?

His father gave the tickets to the uniformed examiner, whose expression was sullen. For the first time he noticed Mokuzu.

"Oh, you are here?" he said in surprise.

Micha could not believe that the youth trim in a black serge student uniform, spine erect, face dignified, was a son of hers. Moon-eyed, she touched his arm, hand, and shoulder before uttering a word, as if to make sure of his being, like a child first beholding an elephant and timidly reaching to touch its wrinkled hide.

"So big!" The image in her mind was obviously of Mokuzu when he was five or six, at most seven or eight. She remembered him as having a roundish face, buttons missing, frayed cuffs, pants baggy at the knees, and affable and rather weak eyes from scanty nourishment.

He before her was awesome, incorruptible, as if reinforced by an iron rod, calm and stern. She groped for modifiers. '...like an up-and-coming cadet, yet without the rigidity and conformity inside the organization and under regulations. His body is as fine and his spirit as strong as anyone's. Face fairly slender, clean-cut, with a fresh sobriety. Eyes clear as if about to pierce soul and bone, but not the cold eyes of a madman. Taller than his father by a neck. Let me compare him with some other youths — are any in sight?' Micha scanned the street before the station. Except for the tobacco shop and tea-houses, most establishments still had their shutters drawn.

'Look at that one, and that,' Micha said to herself. 'Their legs by comparison are unsteady, and their poor bodies are stooped. Before fighting they're defeated. They're lowering their eyes as if trying to make an escape.

'Is this a child of mine? He bears no likeness to his brothers and sisters, or to his parents. The others are to some extent a millstone. He's a missile.

'He's grown so well I needn't apologize for long neglecting my maternal duty. I came out today determined to apologize, but it won't be necessary. He understands; he's not blaming his inadequate parents, not complaining of his unlucky childhood. He's beyond this world of fermented manure. He's dismissing it like a rocket departed from the atmosphere. What a miracle! Put in a cold pot to suffocate, later abandoned to a stranger!'

Micha held down his arm, gazed up at his face, and did not wipe away her hot tears.

Doyu at their side was regarding the sky with compressed lips and betweentimes glancing at his child and his wife. Repeatedly he uttered a few short phrases, "Well, it's fine," "Thanks to Buddha," "I'm relieved," "There's no problem."

They passed through the small shopping quarter. The day's activity had not yet begun, and the sun was lighting only half the street. The scent of sweet osmanthus was in the air, its essence hard to catch, like a person who never turns around however much he is hailed.

'My infancy is forever gone. I was loved by them, but their love was as faint as this scent of sweet osmanthus. The scent reminds me of an evening I waited on the riverbank for the reappearance of a fish that jumped, flashing its silver side. It never reappeared, and darkness came....'

Being polite, Mokuzu walked slowly behind his father. He saw his bandy-legged gait. His mother walked behind them. She never attempted to walk side by side. Mokuzu was conscious of her eyes on his back as he looked ahead at his father's shoulders.

Doyu fumbled in his sleeve for a cigarette. There was the smell of yellow phosphorus. Then he coughed.

With short, quick steps Micha approached Mokuzu and almost touched his sleeve.

"You're not cold? Do you always wear so little?"

"I wear nothing more, even in midwinter. It's fine for now, the ideal season of neither cold nor hot. Of course I have on a short-sleeved undershirt. In summer I'll change the jacket to a short-sleeved shirt."

"Just that even in winter? Have you no long-sleeved shirt or sweater? How about an overcoat?"

Mokuzu stopped, smiled at his mother, and replied, "Don't worry. Even

369

in Tangenji I was dousing every morning. No winter is colder than cold water on a bare body. If I feel cold I douse more. It warms me soon enough."

Without turning Doyu said,

"You are great," and he coughed.

They were at the outskirts of the town, walking by the yellow rice fields. The bamboo grove appeared ahead, then the terraced tea plantation. Locusts and grasshoppers flew about on the weedy path.

Micha was walking the path for the first time. Doyu expressed interest in the sight of the newly opened drive on the upper side of the mountain.

Micha lagged considerably. Doyu and Mokuzu stopped and looked back, concerned about her health, but she was crouching to unwrap her bundle. She took out a small item and tripped up to hand it to Mokuzu.

"This is called 'chocolate.' Have you ever tasted it?"

Mokuzu almost spoke what came uppermost to mind, that he had experienced such trifles enough even in the care of a stranger. 'In this age chocolate is carried to the South Pole. But if I pretend I never had it and ask what it is, she'll weep again. Frankly, I've eaten it at least a few times.'

Doyu turned to reprove her,

"You're restless — don't fuss! Wait till we come to a finer view where we'll stop awhile." Micha looked miffed.

'At the least provocation they dispute; they haven't changed. Their relationship must be like a precarious digestion with the unpredictability of loose bowels.'

They rested on a sunny bank about halfway up from the station. The terraces of tea above and below extended rhythmically along the contours of the mountain. Down to the left was the bamboo grove and to the right a coppice where the path went in and out. Lower were the roofs of farmhouses with persimmons coloring, while the forest was yet green. Up to the right was grassy mountain breast with a few pines continuing left and ascending to a densely pined ridge repeating several ups and downs until it became the crest behind Ryotanji.

They leaned back against the dried grass. The sky was crystal clear. A vapor from the direction of Kameoka was streaming over the pines on the ridge, but in the warm air of the south slope it was disappearing into the blue. The Kameoka basin was surely under fog at that hour; no sun could penetrate to the swamp-like town till late morning.

"Oh, no! I forgot the canteen! I made good tea and left it at the well!" Micha looked ruefully at her opened bundle.

"What a woman, nothing can you do perfectly!" Doyu spoke what should have been left unspoken.

Micha unwrapped a bamboo sheath and offered a sushi of pressed vinegared mackerel.

"Have as much as you want. I made it last night. I'll peel the apple, and there are caramels."

"It's not mealtime, how can I eat so much? How is Ran?"

"Don't worry, I made enough for her and Grandma. She's easygoing, never studies, doesn't help with the work either. I don't understand how she can play around all day."

"Don't complain, she's never dark despite our worry over the influence of her burn. It would be ideal if we could let them all spend their childhood like that....Mokuzu, I am sorry for putting you into hardship. How could I give you such a childhood...?" Again Doyu took out a cigarette.

The fresh blue mackerel, white sushi rice, and red pickled ginger minced fine were set before Mokuzu. A wind carried up the sweet osmanthus scent.

'...nostalgic smell...burning grass...,' thought Mokuzu.

At once Doyu stood up and cried, "*Arrah!* How dangerous! It's so dry it burnt right up!" He patted at the flame with his hand. His match had ignited the grass. "How horrible, I made a hole in my sleeve..." He scrubbed at the burn.

"What a dumb thing to do! That robe's from the laymen. Evil Yosetsu seized their collection and bought you a cheap synthetic one. I hope he'll be punished by Buddha!" Micha's chest heaved.

"Don't bring up such gloom on this occasion! You're seeing your son for the first time in five years. Can't you say anything nice?"

Doyu hardly ever looked at anyone he talked with, except for when he was furious. Usually he talked as if to himself. He especially never looked at his children. He loved them and was ashamed to look them in the face. Now he addressed Mokuzu rather formally,

"Mokuzu, finally Gyodo has settled. He wanted to continue school, but we hadn't money. He was able to enter the Senmatsu factory training school. There he can study English, math, and physics for three years and be paid as much as any worker. He was assigned to study how to produce tractors and bulldozers. Senmatsu was a key member of the Furukawa zaibatsu and was making tanks and anti-aircraft guns until the end of the war. Converting to tractors and bulldozers wasn't hard.

"The problem isn't about the factory but about himself. Somehow Gyodo is fitted to literature more than science. So he was juggling his time to attend night school far from the factory. In April he began to lodge in Kameoka to save time and was rising at four, catching the first train to Hirakata to his factory, attending night school on the way home, and returning on the last train after midnight.

371

"As expected he became too tired. He's young and tough, but the commute was long. He kept looking for nearer lodging and found everything to be expensive. Then last month with Kiku's help he got a cheap room near Hirakata that was once a bath room, about four-tatami width. There he can sleep till six and get to bed around ten-thirty after study at the factory and night school." Reporting that much Doyu fell silent.

Mokuzu was struck by Gyodo's tenacity to study, and he felt oppressed to think of such hardship as having to study the engineering of intricate machinery while hating it. 'He can study what he likes only after getting tired. I am fortunate to have been put in a stranger's care. I have no worry about money and have private teachers and can study as much as I like, and I'm even given a koan. How pitiable is my brother! But what can a man do about his fate? Only not be defeated by it. How I hope he can persevere until he conquers his fate!'

"So he's now settled," Doyu resumed. "His state isn't ideal, but we can hope he'll achieve what he wants if he continues his effort. Anyway, he has a footing for the life he must endure, and Kiku is assisting him while herself working. I don't know about Bunyu; he lives as he likes and changes his work. I'm not caring about him anymore.

"Gyodo extends you great sympathy for your separation from family, and whips himself to study all the more.

"And another, the girl Ena — she stoutly takes all your suffering as hers. I never saw so pure and praiseworthy a girl. She thinks about you as if she is your bride-elect. Here, she asked me to give you this."

Doyu took from his cloth an unglazed square pot planted with saffrons. From the new vaginated leaves, glossy pale purple buds were just appearing. Their modest points suggested to Mokuzu her tightly closed lips. The faint scent recalled to him her pupils and earlobes. Like an image on rippled water the rest of her was uncertain, but definitely presented in front of her swaying figure was the pot of saffrons. He counted six bulbs. When they plumply flowered, three vivid stigmata would grow up — valued since old times as a peptic and an anodyne.

'What was her heart to send these by my father? Does she know their language? "Beware of excess." "Pride and fortune."'

"Mokuzu, listen. The time has come; I can take you back. Much as I am infinitely obliged to the Zen master for his care, I think a child should enjoy childhood.

"Come home. It may be important to study and to train. But more important for a child is to be able to play free of worry about life. It is almost too late and could even be much too late. However, you can play in your second

372

and third year of junior high, do any foolish thing, be as idle as you like.

"Your mother regained her health and has devised a good way to obtain a steady income. We call it 'delivering Kannon's charm.' Fortunately we are now able to raise you, we are healthy enough to work...."

Micha kept silent, which was unusual, for she habitually interfered like a chicken in her husband's matters. She was gazing at Mokuzu's nape and profile.

31

Going Home

"What's the matter? — did you get used to eating so little because he's stingy?" Micha forced the mackerel sushi on Mokuzu and peeled and quartered another apple, though he had not touched the first.

"Unkai cooks for us. It's always enough. And we never make a practice of eating between meals," Mokuzu said simply.

"Eh? I thought your temple sister cooked."

"Luri and Reiho became independent before summer. They work in town."

"So you have to do a lot of the chores?"

Before Mokuzu replied, Doyu slipped in his concern,

"It'll be trouble...he must be shorthanded, especially if his successor has gone out...I bet all the more he doesn't wish to relinquish you."

"Why? If he wanted a child he should have made his own with his own pains. How can he subject a stranger's child to his will by reason of having no heir? It's absurdly selfish!" Micha expressed her emotion.

"Yes, but we must remember I asked that he take him when we were most distressed, and now in our improved state we want him back. Isn't it we who are selfish? — like the cuckoo putting its egg in the bush warbler's nest."

"You can discuss justice and humanity, but the prime concern is Mokuzu. So why don't you decide what you'll do." Micha turned to Mokuzu.

"Me? I've been saying I don't mind where I live. I don't think I'm the one to decide."

"It's your matter, it's best if you decide," Micha insisted.

"Decide where to live? In the first place it's impossible, and in the second, I was never permitted to since I was born. All I could do was do my best in my given situation."

"Very true. You were born without any choice of environment and like-wise have been growing up; and you were given no right or talent to create an environment of your own. Naturally you'd be perplexed if pressed to make the decision. I understand. Oi, Micha, it's our responsibility, and inevitably he must receive the consequences of our decision."

They resumed walking.

Micha had become disheartened by not hearing her son appeal, "Please take me home!" Her heart had turned cold, and she had thrust him away by telling him the decision was his — dauntless behavior on her part, coming from her reaction. Besides, she did not see the philosophical clarity in his answer that he was unable to decide where he was to live. She thought his mind was not as mature as his body, that he was still in a nebulous state.

On the contrary Doyu recognized his son's perspicacity, and all the more regretted that he had to cultivate the view of an old man. 'I am at fault, I was incompetent!' He condemned himself. 'How I wished they could exist like beasts in the forest and flowers in the field, not having to investigate the questions of life!' Walking ahead, he almost cried out.

Then silently he pleaded, 'Zen Master, that's the very reason I asked you not to teach him anything to do with Buddhism. I emphasized that you not teach him any morals, history, philosophy, or religion, although I didn't mind his learning such science as the universal law of gravitation or thermo-dynamics, or such practical skills as how to catch fish and hares! Those spiritual matters aren't the things to be taught; they must be learned by oneself.

'People clamor about the truth, but there couldn't be only one truth. We each must find our own through our own life, and doing so is the very living of our life. But some youngsters who are as yet inexperienced and naive are going to be taught only those conclusions called transmissions from Buddha and the patriarchs, which have been appropriated as the prerogative of Zen masters who think their teachings are a kindness. They misunderstand: Their kindness is as cruel as to gouge out the youngsters' eyes and replace their brains with their own. It's a crime worse than homicide.

'What an outrage to teach religion to an infant with the idea of making him into a priest! A man should be a Buddhist priest before he is a Zen priest, and be a Buddhist layman or just a mere good man before he is a Buddhist priest. More, he should be an animal, also a plant, before he is a mere good man.

'Hanun will make Mokuzu disdain his animal as well as his plant age and suddenly leap to become a Zennist.

'And what Tengai is doing in Gifu is yet crueler. He gathers youths who haven't yet fully enjoyed being children of men, creatures on earth, kin to plants and animals, and gives them an unreasonable koan, causing them to hallucinate — an abnormal mentality at any rate, though he calls it *kensho*, "to see one's original nature." Actually he's brainwashing those innocents and instilling in them a fanatic loyalty to himself and a savage valor beyond right and wrong. It's no different from raising a kamikaze corps or Hitler's *Jugend*.

'Does he so crave servants who will work just as he wishes? He should study Sun Wukung's magic and pluck out his hairs and blow them into many likenesses of himself; or better, study the science and technology of manufacturing robots, or furiously pursue genetics to turn out clones.

'In recent years there are quite a few veterans of the U.S. forces that were stationed here and some shady ex-journalists who value and study evil Zen. Tengai and his likes are using them to raise their own name and esteem among foolish Japanese who blindly admire tall, blue-eyed foreigners. And some of those foreign fools are fooling their foolish countrymen. I wonder what sort of Westerners are studying Zen. Possibly they are outsiders in their own land for not having managed to learn their own traditional culture, especially their own religion.

'Compare the Japanese Buddha image with the image of Christ on the cross. The former has a gentle face and a colorful, elegant silk robe for anyone's eyes, and is usually ornamented with gems, corals, pearls, and ivory. Here we must ask why. The answer is that there's no content, just as the Zen masters' koans and sermons have none. Hidden by the smile and vesture are the fiery desires!

'On the contrary, the crucified Christ is painful to behold. People want to avert their eyes from the nailed hands and feet and the head crowned with thorns. No child can love so horrible an image. Then why isn't it decorated like the Buddha image? Because it has substance. It needs no showy charm. Jesus sacrificed his life for all people. What Christians can discard their substantial image of Christ and come to study this ostentatious Buddhist culture? They must be low human beings!

'But what am I to do for this son? Shouldn't I take him home? Isn't it the best I can do? But it could be too late!

'The master will freely quote the words and deeds of Buddha and the patriarchs to emphasize the importance of his keeping him. But I mustn't forget his motive. He wants a successor.'

Carrying the bundle of potted saffrons, Mokuzu imagined Ena digging them beside her pond or by a tree in her garden. While yielding to his imagination, he reflected on himself between his parents as they walked up to Ryotanji. Who am I? he asked.

However often he repeated the question, no astounding introspection occurred. No rocks were sundered, no light flashed. His heart kept its original beat, his blood its quiet circulation. 'What is this self-questioning? It's like defending a besieged castle; supplies have run out and the isolated lord and his decimated kin and servants are starving with bloodshot eyes and can't consider the wide world, can scarce consider their own concerns. Their fleeting thoughts aren't sharp and objective. In such a state they can't feel compassion but must employ a temporizing, retrogressive policy to save their dying ego.

'Can't I conclude that to ask who I am is the cruelest, most egoistic conduct because it ignores other lives? Isn't self-questioning the greatest illusion? Think of Ena forgetting herself in the faint scent of the saffrons as she prepared them for me...but her consideration of me and mine of her through the saffrons could be another illusory consideration...yet, it has warmth. Self-questioning is cold as the north wind; thinking of other lives is warm as the south wind. If both are merely illusion, isn't the second better for being more humane?

'For whose sake are my parents walking? For mine. Yet we are vastly alienated. Why? Because of my self-questioning. Otherwise we could happily walk together in the light and scent of the dried grass!'

"You aren't thinking of entering the priesthood?" Doyu turned, stopped, and asked at the approach to the stone bridge. Ryotanji was quite near; the cypress-bark roof of the gate would have been visible were it not for the cedars. With no recent rain the stream exposed more rocks, wetting them just at the base.

"No, but I'd like to train myself."

"Hm, hm, in the broad sense? Fine. Becoming a priest is your freedom. If that's your intent, I hope you will decide after hearing my talk about how priests are rotten and how the priesthood ruins one's life, though I myself am a priest."

They did not rest at the bridge as it had no parapet. Upstream the drop was no more than human height, but downstream it was enough to cause a fracture and even death should a person fall.

The east view opened to the city of Kyoto beyond the descending cedar tops and rolling hills. They left the path to rest under the bridge.

"I can't see how I could forget the canteen!"

"Mokuzu, I keenly came to know the wretchedness of a priest's life. Priests are said to be great teachers about heaven and the human world and said to be the greatest physicians, but I never saw any who practiced except Sakyamuni Buddha and some patriarchs in the mists of antiquity. All I met are false and deceitful.

"In the main, helping and teaching others is not as easy as to make them

376

suffer and obey. Of course it's impossible that a man would put himself out for another without love.

"Do you know why today's priests became priests? Like me, most were forced by a father who was a priest. Or they were helpless orphans like Hanun, who was picked up by my father and made a priest while he didn't yet know east from west. Tengai became a priest because his father suffered bankruptcy from a dissolute life. From his youth he was ambitious to seek fame and fortune. His worldly desire was extraordinary. That's mainly why he became a priest — he judged it the best way to realize his desire.

"Hakuin, hailed as the restorer of Rinzai Zen, entered the priesthood because he was fearful of hell and wanted to save himself from his private problem over life and death. Even one so meek and introspective can burn with the desire for power and fame if he denies himself all other desires, such as to eat meat and to marry. Love of power and fame can be more furious if one controls one's desire for food, sleep, and sex. The more highly priests are reputed, the less trustable they are.

"Mokuzu, do you know about koans and satori, brandished whenever false Zen masters get into a scrape? I'll declare no one ever solved any koans and no priest was ever enlightened in this present world. Surely such a one if he exists will never make the blunder of being discovered by the establishment — government, the universities, big business."

"Is there no one who solved any koan?" Mokuzu asked, remaining unperturbed.

"No one. Koans are given by Zen masters to pure, green apprentices for the sake of confronting them with their inability to solve them. Giving a koan is, first, to make them taste that they are incapable and to subject them to humiliation; and second, to impress on them the greatness of the master who can give so hard a question. In short the master takes advantage of the artificially weakened mentality of his apprentices to propagate his false greatness. What an evil, shabby trick, while he himself never really solved a single koan!

"The reason he never did is so simple: he was never driven by the need, and he never had the talent. Why is it like that? As I said, he became a priest for an unworthy reason.

"Mokuzu, if a master's real interest is to soften his apprentices' suffering and open their wisdom, he will do all he can as a normal man, just as a normal mother will for her children, before he gives them a koan. Most problems of apprentices can be solved enough by maternal love. Yet a master doesn't give such love. Suddenly he gives a koan, expended in some past age and inapplicable to our present age, which is so different from that of China of a thousand years ago, for instance.

"What good is it to give 'Jaujou's Wu' to a person enduring a toothache? It's absurd to give Hakuin's 'Sound of One Hand' to a person incapable of getting over disappointment in love! Without seeing the individual, the master randomly gives the old koans. In consequence he substitutes an abstract, arcane problem for an apprentice's real problem, that is, he puts the real problem into a maze so that the sad apprentice will be as benighted as ever while being implanted with a blind loyalty.

"I think physicians are far better men than priests. While some may be immoral, most studied and practiced scientifically proven remedies. Their medicines, like koans, are supposed to relieve pain and promote health. But each is given according to a strict pharmacopoeia. To illustrate, I take Ephedrini Hydrochloridum for my asthmatic fit, and am allowed single doses of 25 milligrams, up to 75 milligrams daily. The maximum I can use at a time is 50, and I mustn't exceed 0.1 grams a day. Patients who follow these directions will benefit regardless of nationality, skin color, and so forth. So too with my cough medicines, dl-Methylephedrini Hydrochloridum and Aqua Armeniacae.

"Koans, on the contrary, may bring a good result for one person out of several hundred thousand, while most people get adverse reactions. How nonsensical! Many go mad, some commit suicide, and the majority become cruel and merciless.

"Given a koan, apprentices become ignorant if they were wise, cruel if they were kind, eccentric if stupid, perfidious if thoughtless. The systematized koans are like venomous snakes gathered from the world — boomslang, cobra, brown snake, black mamba, coral snake, death adder, tiger snake, taipan, puff adder, saw-scaled viper, bushmaster, copperhead, rattlesnake, fer-de-lance, habu, beaked sea snake...Those that are unaffected by their poison to the nerves or blood are only new asparagus shoots and wily thorns.

"To be given and to study a koan means to be injected with poison to become soundly immune, and such persons inevitably become more shameless, arrogant, and villainous masters in search of other fresh lives. During those transmissions of poison there is none of Buddha's compassion and wisdom and no real awakening.

"And, Mokuzu, while the poisonous koan has no answer, who will win the koan combat between master and apprentice? Of course he who gives it, the old son of a witch, poor in self-communion and self-control but strong in lust for conquest. It's aptly said that koan originally meant 'official ordinance.'

"Well, well, I haven't studied enough to tell you more precisely and systematically about the Zen master's device. Too bad America didn't annihilate Zen Buddhist culture. Their leaders cherished the old Buddhist culture of Japan and the imperial system. They ordered their armed forces to slaughter guileless civilians, and were good fellows only to the Japanese imperialistic capitalists. It's evident history: they destroyed not the evils but the populace tyrannized by the evils.

"Why didn't they bomb the headquarters of Buddhist culture, Kyoto and Nara? A true, gentle, largehearted Japanese culture was about to bloom as a consequence of cleaning away the ascetic Zen and Spartan militaristic cultures! It wasn't worth risking many lives to save the Japanese culture permeated by Zen poison. What an absurd phenomenon that some Westerners are crossing the sea to learn the poison marrow of that corrupt culture — *cough! cough! c-cough! gasp! — cou-c-c..."*

᨞

Mokuzu was to return to Tangenji. Because he was still in mid-term of school, and also in deferrence to Zen Master Hanun's earnest wish, it was agreed that he would stay the winter, spend New Year's in Ryotanji, and leave at the onset of spring vacation, in the last third of March. Then he would be fourteen and ready to enter the second year of junior high school.

Day after day Mokuzu watched the saffrons on his desk. The flowers began to open as the sun rose, and closed as it set. He sprayed mist on them and was reminded of Ena's face. Thinking so intently of her, he saw her with teary cheeks as the moisture ran down the smooth petals.

Teacher Rangai, when Mokuzu told him he would quit karate at the end of February, made no response but looked as though he wanted to ask, "Why didn't you quit much earlier?"

Rangai was also teaching physical education at a nearby public senior high school and was very busy with his movement against the rating of teacher efficiency.

The administration had proposed rating to make teacher management more scientific and rational, their intent being to align salaries with ability and to spur effort. The Japan Teacher's Union was adamantly opposed. Rating, they said, would incite keen competition and discrimination. More, it would aid the ambition of the present governing party to control education by political means, which could involve the populace again in an imperialistic and capitalistic war.

Mokuzu was not interested; he thought both sides were arguing without regard for the students, who ought to have been the focus of their concern, and were vying for supremacy with noisy, dreary, ambiguous words and deeds.

But Rangai was indifferent to Mokuzu's quitting karate not because he was pressed with business. He simply never liked Mokuzu, and Mokuzu in turn never respected nor liked him. Their relation had been like two cool parallel lines.

Rangai's karate aimed to build an invincible body, in short, to arm the practitioner like a rhinoceros. Mokuzu's intent was to be quick to avoid attack and to depress the enemy's attacking ability rather than to strengthen his own body.

Rangai gave highest praise to those like Reiho, whose brow and nose were degenerated, and whose fists, elbows, outer edge of the feet, and kneecaps were thick with callosity. They could sunder heavy planks or a stack of tiles at a blow. Mokuzu could not; his hands were as sensitive as an artist's.

Yet in his memory he had not missed a day of practice twice a week for five years. He had mastered all the forms — all the thrusts with fists, heel of hand, head; strikes with fist, edge of hand, palm, wrist, knee; kicks with the sole of the foot, base of toes, edge of foot. He was perfectly able to attack such vital parts as the pit of the stomach, temple, side of the stomach, and to attack the source of the opponent's fighting faculties, such as the various joints, and the eyes, ribs, chest, and neck.

Docho Doke had in the main been teaching him the history of Buddhism, Confucianism, and Taoism. He taught the basic scriptures, the developments of ideas, and the social history.

The moment he was told that Mokuzu was to leave for Tanba, he tightened the corners of his mouth, and his thick, round face flashed as if he were drunk. His alae and lower lip finely quivered, and in silence he shed large tears.

With an awkward hand he touched Mokuzu's head, then his arm, and expressed himself without completing his words,

"Because I also haven't my own child...."

Yojun, as he listened to Mokuzu's thanks for his years of teaching, inclined his head as if harkening to a faint sound. He then began to talk in his usual manner of seeming to begin from the end of what he wished to say:

"So, even to this minute the last things that we think will happen are indeed happening. Whales may stir in the green depths of the boreal seas, but we can be ignorant and unmindful of them while they have no direct effect on us. Some things aren't like that. Let me give an example. In snowy February like now, seventeen years ago, President Roosevelt signed the executive order 9066. I and many others who would be most affected by it were living in ignorance of its progress.

"I had my American wife and our two-year-old daughter. Without the least warning I was pulled from them and bussed to a camp outside Salt Lake City. I could see the soft rise of Mt. Topaz on the horizon. The road was so dusty! The climate was forty degrees centigrade in summer and minus thirty in winter. So desolate a sight — sparse sage clinging to the desert, and an occasional cactus to laugh at us. Under the surveillance of a guard, I recalled a passage from J. Evelyn's *Acetaria*:

> "'Tis a plant, indeed, with so many and wonderful properties as that the assiduous use of it is said to render men immortal.[1]

"How could I have been so obtuse? I hadn't even dreamt of separation, not a day before, not a minute. At the time, up to when the officers knocked on our door, I was reading the poem I taught you by George Pope Morris, 'Woodman, Spare That Tree!' We sat beside each other, my wife and I, as she nursed our daughter.

> "Woodman, spare that tree!
>   Touch not a single bough!
> In youth it sheltered me,
>   And I'll protect it now.
> 'Twas my forefather's hand
>   That placed it near his cot;
> There, woodman, let it stand,
>   Thy ax shall harm it not.
> That old familiar tree,
>   Whose glory and renown
> Are spread o'er land and sea —
>   And wouldst thou hew it down?
> Woodman, forbear thy stroke!
>   Cut not its earth-bound ties;
> Oh, spare that aged oak
>   Now towering to the skies!
> When but an idle boy,
>   I sought its grateful shade;
> In all their gushing joy
>   Here, too, my sisters played.
> My mother kissed me here;
>   My father pressed my hand —
> Forgive this foolish tear,
>   But let that old oak stand,
> My heart-strings round thee cling,
>   Close as thy bark, old friend!
> Here shall the wild-bird sing
>   And still thy branches bend.
> Old tree! the storm still brave!
>   And, woodman, leave the spot;
> While I've a hand to save,
>   Thy ax shall harm it not.[2]

"Master Mokuzu, the American authorities showed no consideration. I am a Japanese citizen, whereas my wife and daughter are American citizens. They were torn from me. My wife was punished by her country for marrying an enemy alien, and our child was punished for having such parents. Later I learned they went to her parents' home in Connecticut.

"Salt Lake City is where the Mormons were persecuted, and they were kind to us.

"Well, separation makes the heart grow fonder, if the separation isn't long. A long separation gnaws at love like leukemia on bone marrow. Our fifteen years of family life since the war's end have been a struggle for recovery. Only of late have we begun to feel the tree stump will grow new shoots.

> "Did the ancients also lose their way
> On this untrod path at the break of day?[3]

"My wife, my daughter — now nineteen — and I have been living to polish a gem ever since I met you. We knew it would bring out the best in us: patience, diligence, generosity, purity; and our intuition told us that the more we polished it the more it would brighten our hope. We have been aiming far beyond joy and anger through our united task, and we were experiencing progress. In truth, we even hoped to take you this summer on our tour of Connecticut, New Mexico, and California.

"We don't mind our inability to imagine whales, or barrels of Scotch slumbering in the cellars of Scotland. But how horrible that we can't hear in advance the clangor of military boots under martial law, can't see the toxin of industrial waste, can't smell germ warfare. Generally we can't foresee the fatal shadows in the darkness of our fate.

"Even so, there is one thing I have learned through my study of the literature I have taught you. It is about the soil. The soil is my solace, and I believe in its power. The soil of the earth purifies and activates everything, as you see in the budding of spring. There are said to be five billion bacteria, twenty million actinomyces, a million protozoa, and two hundred thousand algal fungi in a spoonful of soil.

"You too, think of the soil and start anew whenever you face the winters of life. The literature I have taught you is like that, a rich rejuvenating soil for human mentality, as the soil of the earth is for all creatures.

"At the close of this final lecture I want you to know that while I lectured to you these five years, my wife and my daughter always assisted me. You never met, but they are waiting to meet you. Before you depart we shall present you with Kenkyusha's 117-volume *British and American Classics*...."

Setsuro evinced no sorrow. "Fine, Japan is narrow, as is the world.

Whether or not you go home, you aren't moving much more than the distance between two fingers. You can live and can paint wherever you are. Just think, the easiest thing is to live; regardless of our will and effort we desire to do that. If we haven't such desire we'd better die. Either way our life is like straw on water, it floats or sinks.

"What we can do because it seems to impart meaning to our life is to observe ourselves who are observing things. From this viewpoint your koan on your original nature is quite useful. But solving it means no more than to see the nodes of a bamboo, the fiber of wood, the bones and ligaments of the body; it's only preparation for another illusion, as was sung,

> "Gather and bind some brushwood,
>   a hermitage for to stand.
> Unbind it and naught remains
>   but the woody land.[4]

"Or, we were warned,

> "Do not suppose there is light
>   only when the clouds pass by.
> The pale moon of morning
>   is ever in the sky."[5]

Unkai was silently packing Mokuzu's books and clothes.

"Thank you for your generous care," Mokuzu said formally and bowed. Unkai too stood formally, and he spoke:

"Perish the idea! Come to think of it, what I did for you was as useless as an ashtray of cigarette butts, while my regrets for doing so little are like myriads of flying fish cutting the waves. Besides, I should do the thanking. I could relive my childhood, which otherwise had been coarse and ignorant.

"You stunned me when first I saw your mind clear as Mashu Lake, your fairness like the common density of air, your fresh vigor to grow, like new leaves. I have been kept in awe.

"Please don't be put off by my faults. Come back here again and again. And, remember, if anything should happen to you, if you have no place to go, if you feel you have no way to escape, freely come. After all, here is your second home."

Unkai bought Mokuzu for his departure a new coat, underwear, pencils, and many notebooks. At the end he gave him a fountain pen and a wristwatch, the first Mokuzu had ever owned.

Zen Master Hanun was seeing him safely to Tangenji. Unkai in black robe stood with face stiff and pale as he saw him off at the ticket barrier of

Saga Station. Without a word he joined his palms and bowed. He remained with palms joined at his chest until well after the train disappeared beyond the west end of the platform. People threw him appraisive glances, but they were busy, and no one addressed him or had anything to do with him.

Seated beside the master, Mokuzu thought of Reiho and Luri. He had not told them he was going home.

'They must be preoccupied with their work or they could visit Ryotanji more often. Suppose I told them, would they come back just to see me off? Maybe, maybe not. I wouldn't want to blame them, so I was right not to inform them. Our relation can be left to the winds of fortune.'

Often he thought of Luri, especially her white body, but he rarely thought of Reiho, whose dark face could be found anywhere.

'Even the explosion of a multi-megaton bomb can't create one Luri, her skin sweet and soft. A bomb can only kill, and alter the mountains and fields.'

His koan was like a star in the night sky; to see it he had to make some sort of effort. Ena was like the moon, he could think about her at ease. Luri was a constellation, the Swan. He felt embarrassingly hot when he thought of her.

'She was so intimate and expressive in the dark, how could she be so coldly clean and quiet in the day? She approached like a falling star and was gone as if never having flared before my eyes. Was that her mercy, or was she forgetting herself in the joy of being merciful? Having a body like a lily, how can she stand in the business world of men who are like a thorny weald?'

The master kept obstinately mute, his face like a shell adhering to a reef. His brows were asymmetric; the left one slanted up. The right cheek was more narrow and wrinkled than the left. The right eye was like an alert tiger in a cave, the left, like a dozing tiger at a cave entrance.

He was bitter because Mokuzu acted as if he had nothing to do with the issue of his staying on in Ryotanji or going home.

'A strange lad...he had both the ability and the freedom to decide on his environment, yet he withdrew and let his parents and me argue it out. They had an incomparable advantage. My chance was only that he might greatly wish to stay.'

He was an old Zen master, accustomed to self-control, but he wanted to cry, and kept speaking in his mind,

'Why don't you stay with me? Why choose your parents? True, they are your parents, but they are ignorant and incompetent. They are irresolute, lazy, illogical, and cowardly!

'Your lot is to shine to the world like a laser beam. You're the kind who can practice good without being its slave, and act evil to turn evil to good. You won't be crushed by the five periods of the Twelve Teachings and the eighty-four thousand volumes of the Dharma, nor be dangled about by illusions. You can evade becoming pitiable and wicked; you have the looks of a screen actor but the nature and talent to become a genuine pure man, rare in this world. I know you can outshine all rotten heritages, and they will then appear as colorless as dead coral. You can make the culture of these afterdays, which is like the mucus of an oyster, sparkle like iced trees. By grace of you the world will regain its viridity and beauty.

'Truly you are the kind who is needed to end the present noisy, contradictory, tedious era and open a harmonious, clean culture. You won't stay in a single locality like narrow Japan but will travel wide. You will associate not only with industrially advanced nations; you will be respected everywhere. You can give the joy of living and the realization that stability and eternity exist even in this limited, floating world!

'You may think I overrate you because I'm a dotard with an unfinished dream. Then why did Setsuro say you have genius even in childhood and that your painting shames all renowned painters, who have long forgotten their naivete? Awakened by my chance joke, he to this day respects me, though from me he knows he has nothing to learn. He is an excellent peak in the field of Japanese painting. He says most painters are obsessed by oddity and only smear white silk and paper with their tricky illusions and half-baked ideas. They'd better be taught by you.

'Yojun confessed that you immediately pointed out the deficiency of any teacher who must spend forty years for study, and that what you are interested in is what he himself finally realized at long last. He says he is a sooty lantern in front of your clear light.

'Docho said you will be like a family-heirloom sword if you live as a layman, and if you live as a priest you will become a national treasure.

'Even Rangai said you're his most odious student. It's a kind of admiration. You didn't respect his teaching, yet you never showed a cloven hoof to be scolded. Spending no extra time on practice, you surpassed the others.

'Like a child of Kannon you are adored by Unkai. You purified his five viscera and six entrails, he said.

'So, why do you desert me, what is your real concern?'

Zen Master Hanun and Mokuzu exchanged no significant words through-out the journey.

On their way to Tangenji from the bus stop, Mokuzu was rather oppressed, 'It's my native land, yes, I smell the mud of the fields and hear the wind from the pine mountain. The pebbles and grasses of the path are unchanged from my infancy. But now I can't sense any of it without asking what is my original nature. I'm beginning to hate the question and him who gave it.

385

After all, he wanted me to have it more than I wanted it, and he never understood what I'm seeking. For whose sake am I wishing to train? Not for his. Only for Ena's. He can't dream of her existence. He had no such person, but only Reiho, who stole his money. Now I know he just wanted to change his horse!

'Nonetheless, I'm bitter to have to come home without seeing my original nature. My native land yet shows no spring. Of course! How can I face Ena with my unfruitful training? Beside this weedy path the little stream reflects the shadows of the master and me — to where does it flow? Now I see the Tangenji gate. For whom does it stand?'

"Mokuzu, you'll be a good son. 'Filial piety surpasses all other good deeds.'[6] 'Sixty days a crow feeds its mother in return for being fed as long.'[7] Think each day is the last you can see your parents."

Mokuzu perceived that the master was giving no weight to his words. He knew he would be greatly cheered if he retorted, 'How can I practice filial piety while ignorant of my original nature before my parents were born?' But he did not ask.

Nearing the gate he saw himself standing on a barren plain in a surging wind under a dark sky. Two currents, nostalgia for his childhood and the uncertainty as to how he should live, were making a whirlwind. Ena recurrently appeared and disappeared at his side.

32

Dreaming with Ena

Ena was the one who most enjoyed Mokuzu's return after his five-and-a-half-year absence. She no longer saw the lone child who needed sheltering and encouragement against becoming demoralized. He was now taller than she, with sharp eyes, a firm mouth, and a concise, unyielding constitution.

She was fifteen and soon to enter the third year of junior high. He saw the former Ena in her thick eyelashes, her bright pupils, which did not reject people's eyes, and her fine carriage. But he was dazzled by her softened cheeks, her sweater raised by her breasts, and her fuller hips, presenting a new woman.

It being spring vacation, she called on him every day. They sat on the veranda of the retreat cottage, now his private quarters, then moved to the rise between the bamboo grove and the vegetable garden, or to the top of the back mountain with its view of neighboring villages, or to the pine cliff made by a landslide in a great rain, or to the bank of the Sakura River. All the while they talked about what had happened to each and what they had learned while apart, without order of major or minor concern.

One day as they sat on the south veranda Ena, in saddle shoes, stopped swinging her legs and regarded Mokuzu's profile.

"I'm so relieved you didn't change!"

"Yes, I only grew taller, but my mind is hesitating all the more."

"No, I mean your sensibility and earnestness to live true to yourself. Your mind has grown — you now understand what training is; you said it is to keep asking who we are. By your telling me, I could clarify my own doubt and unease."

Ena was always sad to see his face cloud when he was unaware of her eyes, but she knew she also felt pleasure. She could experience this sweet sensation after their reunion too, so she decided he had not in essence changed.

At the right side of the garden before them was the old persimmon with squarish trunk. Half its branches covered the retreat cottage, the other half projected over the path below the wall. The blue sky was intercepted by only its still leafless branches and twigs. A sasanqua grown bushy broke the line of the wall. The fields were a purplish pink carpet of Chinese milk vetch that rippled like an ocean and stretched to the Sakura River, and beyond, too, rounding many small mountains and hazing into a dreamy pink.

To the left, bamboo trunks rose from underground stems that grew out from the bamboo grove. They all were a new fresh green, and their leaves raised a pleasant sound in the slight breeze.

The tall camellias at the border of the garden where it met the bamboo grove were in full bloom. Their numerous thick red flowers with yellow monadelphous stamens were like flaring stars against the dense bamboos, where no sunlight came in.

Now and again a flock of great tits flew to the camellias, spent a while catching worms busily and noisily, and at once all took flight as if pulled by invisible threads.

From the far end of the bamboo grove came the stridor of shrikes. Among the bushes by the wall a lone white-eye, its back olive, its throat yellow, moved with short quick steps.

The shadows of the persimmon branches swayed on the front of Ena's wool turtleneck striped red and white on navy. The shadows of the bamboo tips fluttered on her reddish brown wool gored skirt.

Hearing of her sorrowful life during their separation, Mokuzu meditated on how to bring her to a spring field from the cold mountain torrent in which she was immersed.

But oddly, the sadder he felt the more he visualized with heat her physical beauty little concealed by her clothes, actually rather emphasized by them. He suffered an expansion within his own body.

'Are the wish to comfort her and the wish to enjoy her body like the opposite ends of a single parabola, or are they each different in nature and just happening to come together like the curves of a hyperbola?'

"Weeds and trees don't break when young even if bent quite hard, but, Mokuzu, they have their limit and will snap at a certain point."

"So?"

"So I think I couldn't endure being separated from you again."

Mokuzu thought of her life from infancy; it was like looking at the smoke of a stick of incense as it rose and drifted into the leafage and soon disappeared into the sky.

'Her parents must have fought since before she was born. She was a mealy primrose emerging through snow. Her father had children by another woman and rarely visited. Her mother loved her but in her presence often cried, "Were it not for Ena I could divorce!" Ena was bewildered by her weeping.

'By the time she began school she was convinced that if she didn't exist, her mother's regret would be solved. Yet she acted cheerful, repressing her complicated feeling about her mother — and about her father, whose love was unattainable even if she sought it. Instead of floating on a wave of self-pity, she pitied and comforted me whose home life was troubled. How fortunate — but I wasn't aware her warmth was nursed by grief! Fortunate for me also was that she didn't choose the simplest solution for her mother and extinguish her own life.

'At any rate she and I could spend happier days than any life in heaven.

'Then I was put in Ryotanji and was too sad to talk to anyone. And Ena has tearfully recounted that she felt she was in a glass box with no warmth to the sun, no life to the color of the flowers, no vibration in the songs of the birds.

'I can say I felt like a baby left under twinkling stars on an icy road with the distant howl of a dog. Ena felt she was in an inanimate world, though the grasses, trees, animals, and school were as before. She had to relive alone the times we spent together. Without her I felt my body had no shadow. She felt she had no body but only a shadow.

'Then that first-engineer began to live at her house and a baby was born. She loved the baby, but when she saw her mother and him loving it, she couldn't help thinking of her own infancy like icicles glittering at the eaves.

One day truly she was looking at icicles while suffering from tonsillitis; yet she was obliged to tend the baby and was blamed for neglect.

'In those days her grandmother died....'

Mokuzu took Ena's hand and said,

"I don't want to be fake fruit in a show window when you are hungry, or water containing hydrocyanic acid when you thirst. But what should I do? You have to go to senior high school next year. That's not so bad since you'll attend from home, but two years from now I'll have to get a job somewhere, in Kyoto, Osaka, or Tokyo. I'm unsure where, but surely I'll have to and again we must part."

Ena put her free hand over his and put their hands on her thigh. Regarding his face she said, "Isn't there a third way?"

"A third way?"

'What would she choose? Suicide isn't a third way, or a fourth, but the way to zero.'

"Couldn't we live, if you don't object, on a sunny hill where many flowers early bloom?...protected by northern mountains, and sheltered from the lingering summer heat by a western forest? We'll live on our own and have gardens, chickens, and sheep. On fine days we'll work outside; in the rain we'll read or talk as we face the far view, as we're doing now. We'll be friends because our important goal will be to keep asking who we are!"

"Well, I can't imagine a more enjoyable life....I dream up a lot of things, but do you too? It's a dream — a dream of spring dandelions."

Ena, moved to tears, protested, "Even dandelions don't bloom unless they've been buried under snow and exposed to icy winds."

"Ena, it's dangerous to have false hopes. We were torn apart when we were spending dreamy days. While we were unaware, an evil power was taking the earth from under our feet. Like a conveyor belt, it never rests and if we don't watch out we'll be dumped into a ravine."

"I know dreaming is dangerous. So this time we'll not dream. We won't make our hope a dream. We are different from six years ago, it couldn't be the same. This time we won't separate no matter what. We'll help each other, combine our strength, and prepare to fight back."

"Let me tell you, Kiku and Gyodo after junior high had to get jobs. They were only fifteen. They didn't choose it, they hated it, yet their environment forced it on them and society swallowed them up. Like trash in a dam they floated and were sucked into a drain. They couldn't argue, their resistance was nothing before such power. They were recklessly spun, pulled, and pressed. Their sensibilities were stolen away. Now they're cogs, tiny parts of a system that engulfs new lives...."

"But, what's the point of our life if we can't realize our hope? Think how it surfaced through our torment and sorrow!"

"Well, the meaning is that it was fed by misfortune and is the mother of misery. But I understand why you ask. Indeed I'd like to know why buds appear if they're going to be trampled."

"Why can't at least one couple in this wide world live in a third way and not work in a factory and not study in school? Can't our utmost love and wisdom make it happen?"

"Sure, aren't love and wisdom the highest human values? And it seems we would need both. At least we are ready to perfect them...there's great possibility....Let's go to the riverbank."

Mokuzu left the veranda and pulled Ena's hand. They went out the gate, down the stone steps, and along the raised footpaths through the vetch. Where the path narrowed, Ena walked behind; otherwise they walked hand in hand. The vetch spread to the skirt of the deciduous mountain behind them and almost to the rise of the riverbank ahead. The fields appeared to arc. Haze hung on the far mountains. Larks flew into the blue sky.

"Mokuzu, we are sky and bird, water and fish, I am you, you are me. It's not the least strange for a couple to have one mind though their bodies are two."

Her earnest tone brought Mokuzu to a halt. Her cheeks were slightly flushed. Her eyes reflected a spring cloud.

"It's not at all strange. In the Shingon sect, chanting gathas to worship Buddha's holy body is important, such as, 'I worship and Buddha reveals his life. His life enters my body and my life enters his. His divine power responds to me that I may perform my Bodhisattvahood.'"[1]

Mokuzu wanted to quote, "If we must go to heaven, let us become a pair of birds that share an eye and a wing and always fly together. If we must dwell on land, let us become trees with boughs entwined."[2] But he did not, for the final lines were, "Though the sky is wide and the earth is long, the world will come to an end. My lamentation alone is eternal."[3]

Just when they reached a place on the bank where they could see last year's eulalia standing in disorder with fresh blades beginning to shoot from the same roots, a copper pheasant took wing in a burst of sound. Alarmed, Ena pressed against Mokuzu. He embraced her. His hand felt her scapula. 'How fast is her heartbeat — she's so tender to be surprised by such a trifle!'

Her cheeks were tinged red like sunset after rain. Her lips with ever so fine hair above were slightly parted.

'I heard copper pheasants stay at least a valley apart even if they're a pair,' Mokuzu thought.

They descended to where a pussy willow shone with new spadices and

390

leaned their backs against the slope of dried grass.

They could see the curve of the upper stream, where the bank was repaired with granite blocks. The grasses had not yet regained their former prosperity. Mokuzu remembered that the collapse of the bank occured when he had to go to Ryotanji.

'Water can be terrible. It was said heaven helps those who help themselves. But water directly attacks the most oppressed. It's also said God tempers the wind to the shorn lamb. But I can't have an illusory hope. God is whimsical.'

The river contained grades of pale blue to dark green and deep indigo according to the blue sky and the bluish clay in the bed. The shallows appeared clean. The stream circling a low sandbar was quick to follow the stream ahead. On the round white pebbles of the bar a gray wagtail, black-throated, with vivid yellow below, stood attentive to the chance of fish. Its mate stood in the shallows, white throat, stomach a fainter yellow. Her thin legs in the clear water looked painfully red.

On the opposite shore a thicket of lean redbud and quince with sparse flower buds was entangled with last year's kudzu and mixed in with the dreary dried eulalia. There too a flock of great tits moved the short distance from branch to branch. On careful observation it was possible to distinguish a coexistence of varied tits, similar in shape and movement but for their creamy cheeks and brownish bellies.

Looking up from the slope of the bank, Ena on Mokuzu's arm could see only blue sky whitened by mist. She was content and wished now were her life's goal instead of preparation for the unknown. 'But thinking so is the very danger he pointed out. Spending time in innocent pleasure lets misfortune steal near. How I wish time would freeze this moment!' But the idea of freezing the time reminded her of the dead silence of her house, the many late nights she spent alone. She drew near Mokuzu's shoulder, and he pulled her in to embrace her.

He was experiencing a concupiscence like flames in a smelting furnace. He was urged to be violent, to forget all, to strip off her clothes and infringe on her concealed parts. He controlled himself but barely by thinking that she should be the last one to be given fear and sorrow by him. He lay tight against her and kept the position as it was.

With eyes shut, Ena imagined a pair of steeds outracing a prairie fire. From rise to rise they ran, advanced, and arrowed toward her.

They stood up to return to their separate homes. Ena brushed the dried grass from her skirt.

"Somehow we must escape our unfavorable situation like fleet-footed steeds. We must build our own clean nest."

"Yes. There's hope as long as we have hope!" His response seemed on the surface a senseless tautology. They looked each other in the eye and laughed. But soon Ena looked away, shy after their long, passionate embrace.

At Ryotanji Mokuzu had been taught a study method by his three private teachers. He now applied it to himself and Ena.

'First, they said the key to any achievement is to have a strong hope. Second, its content and form should be scrutinized to make it a definite, perfect hope. True, if our hope is so faint as to be undeterminable or if it changes with time, we'll have no chance of realizing it. It mustn't be a ghostly thing. We have to make it inseparable from ourselves, as sun is to sunlight, and manifest it in each gesture and conduct.

'Then, according to my teachers, we must check in detail the reality surrounding the hope, that is, know coolly where we are in relation to it and reflect keenly on our ability to assist it. If we can do that much, we will be quite clear about what difficulties lie ahead and what approach is best — in short, we can make a plan to fulfill our hope. If we can hammer out a refined plan, we can very possibly realize our hope by fully using our patience, courage, wisdom, love, and effort, which are rather mechanical labors. A hope with a plan is what we human beings ought to have and can have!'

ও।

Mokuzu's parents told him, "You aren't required to do anything — live as you like." They also said, "We now have money to spare for your food and dress."

But his grandmother, who had attained the age of eighty, was acrid,

"When were you awakened, hn? — for what reason are you tottering home from Ryotanji? Do you wish to consume your days like a drab unspiritual sea cucumber under a reef, or a dingy sloth of the Americas overgrown with green algae? Did you never hear, 'You who have yet to pass the border set by the patriarchs, who have yet to cut your mental circuit, are ghosts that adhere to the grasses and lean on the trees'?"[4]

From childhood Mokuzu had regarded his grandmother as a bigoted soul who preached recondite matters to press others down. Now he understood her meaning, and he was impressed by her considerable knowledge, especially when he recalled that she had graduated from only four-year primary school. He assumed that she had been taught by his grandfather.

"Tell me then, did you come back to suckle at your mama's breast? Fool! Three years at the breast is enough for a human child. Don't you know yet that imagined food tastes best?"

Mokuzu tried to explain that going to Ryotanji had been beyond his control and owing to family necessity.

"Fool!"

"Well, Grandma, what do you mean?"

"Are you thinking you were forced to go? Such a notion fits your parents, not you. Even if so, you should have taken it as the best training opportunity and regarded it as just your wish while you have as much brain as a sardine. You grew up in the mountains and may not know the ocean, but imagine: Great waves roll in. Those who cry will be drowned. The stalwart welcome them and ride them asea to fish.

"Yours is a tenebrific nature — you complain when it rains and long for rain when it's fine. Your grandfather called the likes of you petty peasants. He taught people to be happy on rainy days by thinking they made it rain and to do the work they can only do on rainy days. And he taught them to be thankful for fine days by thinking they made them too and to do the work they can only do on fine days.

"Think now, if you were put with the Zen master solely by reason of economy, why should anyone trouble him? Well, it's useless to lament over what's done. You were undernourished since before you were born. Naturally you lack wisdom.

"Blameworthy is not you but your shallow mother and spineless father. Why do they spoil their child? Are they misapprehending that they can privately own a child? A child is a child of the wind, of the world, and, fortunately, above all, of the Son of Heaven in this divine land. To conceive His child is the honor of all women of Japan. To raise and train it and return it to Him, our Gracious Emperor, is a woman's calling.

"How shabby and unkind is Zen Master Hanun-kutsu! Once he takes charge of another's child his duty is to make him into a decent man without sparing the rod! How could he heed any extenuating circumstances? But it's too late. Fine, you may go. Your father is a meek devil and you are his porter. Yet even a chance encounter is due to the karma of a previous life, and while I live out my days to my hundredth year, I shall kindly watch from behind the shojis how far you and your parents are going to become depraved."

Accustomed to underestimating her, Mokuzu was amazed as he listened to his grandmother's free abuse even though she was not quite free to walk about. At the same time he detected some wisdom that, like the Buddhist sanctum, he could not entirely dismiss, and he attempted to issue a hint of his own question,

"Grandma, I have a great hope, which by any means I have to attain. Can you tell me what I ought to do to attain it?"

"Hope? What sort?" he expected to hear. But she shut her eyes tight so that her face became yet more wrinkled, and even covered her ears with her wrinkled hands. After a brief interval she answered,

"Do every distasteful work from morning to night and night to morning, endure a year, three, five, ten, do every hard horrible work! You shall at last fulfill your hope."

Mokuzu thought his grandmother did not value the human life-span. Any hope detached therefrom was of no value to him. He withdrew from her room.

> ❧

After Ena went home and before she came, Mokuzu practiced sitting meditation in the center of his room like Unkai, who sat day after day on the west veranda of Ryotanji.

It was the very room where he and his family had slept in bedding with the wadding exposed, where many a night he had not slept because of hunger and the fighting of his parents.

In yet earlier days his grandmother occupied the retreat cottage and his family lived in the main building. 'I'm reminded of when Bunyu was clipping his nails after a bath. As I crawled near, a clipping flew in my eye. I let out a howl. "Fool! — waiting there for my nail!" he said and left the room.

'We were too many children and dirtied the tatamis, tore the shojis, and scribbled on the fusumas. Yosetsu came up and said to our parents, "We laymen need only a priest. Move the family to the retreat cottage or take them away wherever you like." The network of hate, distrust, contempt, and hostility was perfected inside and outside Tangenji.'

Mokuzu pursued his memory of infancy. When he returned to reality he thought, 'What's the difference between my meditating on my past and someone's reading twice or more through the Buddhist scriptures? Such great Zen teachers as Eisai and Dogen are said to have done that. I mean, what's the value of merely reading through all eighty-four thousand volumes? The main value of reading is to reflect on one's past and to realize what is one's original nature, which is beyond the influence of environment, isn't that right?' And further he thought,

'Why did Ena care about me while I was growing up in gloomy circumstances? Why does she love and trust me now? Isn't it because she has kept on seeing my unpolluted original nature? Or does she disregard such an invisible thing and care only about my concrete life and real circumstances, which can be sensed by our sense organs?' Meeting a dead end, he meditated on his family at present.

'Ran became eleven and doesn't mess her room, so they could return to the temple side, under the same roof with Grandma. Now that they are few, they can live in wide quarters. My parents were depressed having to live in the retreat cottage. At last in the main building they're satisfied, for they can regain the laymen's respect as priest and priest's family, even if it's only symbolic. But they have to confront that gaping space, so their satisfaction comes with an emptiness. What is Yosetsu's smile at this ironic turn?

'Well, put aside his smile. The point is, they could give me this entire cottage for my free life. They wish me to spend the rest of my youth as I like. Only parents who could give their children no freedom can enjoy the sight of them living freely, even if only for a brief term. For my type of parents, one important filial duty is to establish a free life for oneself. Then, the question here too is how to obtain freedom for Ena and me.'

Mokuzu kept switching subjects because in whatever direction he meditated he found the same unsolvable question.

He enjoyed seeing the improved kitchen and bath, indications that his parents had some income and could reduce the labor of their old age. The kitchen cottage was as dark as ever, but a propane gas burner and rice cooker had been brought in, greatly freeing his father from gathering wood and preparing logs on the mountain. The rope and buckets of the well had been replaced by an electric pump, and a polyvinyl chloride pipe led to the bath room. No longer did anyone need to bucket water to the tub.

Mokuzu remembered the time Gyodo and he had spent just to make the bath and to cook. The enormous work of getting fuel from the mountain was replaced by an efficient gas cylinder. 'Where did those days of labor go?' he thought, and answered, 'My parents go out daily to rake in cash.'

True, almost every morning in any weather they went out together to deliver their Eleven-Faced Kannon charm, and they returned in the late evening.

At night they spread newspaper under the light and meticulously counted the day's coins, subtracted the cost of traffic and lunch, and exactly divided the remainder. Half they allowed themselves for their life, half went to temple repair.

The charm was a rectangle of white Japanese paper thirty centimeters by ten. In the center was printed "Prayer of the Great Eleven-Faced Kannon Bodhisattva." Down one side was the couplet "Soundness of body, fortune in everything"; down the other, "Felicitous longevity, domestic prosperity." The Tangenji address occupied the lower portion. Covering the central letters was the red stamp of a large square seal showing a specially designed Chinese character hardly readable by anyone, albeit that alone made the charm paper authoritative to some degree.

395

To produce a quantity, Doyu wrote the letters on a block of cherry and incised it himself. He twice failed, but the third try was a perfect success.

After counting their coins, they printed the papers from the block one by one for the next day's delivery.

Micha was the originator of this business. After recovering from her prolonged infirmity she had asked Doyu,

"I believe in the divine power of the Eleven-Faced Kannon by whose mercy my life was saved. I vowed to devote myself to spreading the Kannon's merit, but how should I go about it while I have children to raise?"

Doyu remembered that the temple he had served on Shodojima was issuing a Kannon charm paper to its many visitors and raking in a colossal sum.

"It would be a good idea if we made a charm paper too."

"What's the good of that? Nobody comes to this rotten temple to worship... but wait, we'll go out, as I did to peddle clothes. Then the problem is, how to explain it to the impious people of this world. They don't care if I was really saved by the Kannon, and I haven't endless time to explain. Isn't there a way for them to decide immediately?"

"Micha, it's not so hard. We'll give them the paper and simply ask if they are willing to offer any donation they want. We'll say it's to fix Tangenji, which after all houses the Kannon and urgently needs repair. In other words, we'll combine our spreading of Kannon's virtue with our asking for help to maintain Kannon's abode. Of course we can use a part for our life since no one can perform such a great deed without food and dress."

"That's it! You learned some practical wisdom by working on that island — indeed their gravest concern, however petty their offering, will be how the money is spent. If we make it clear as day, they'll have no reason to hesitate," concluded Micha.

So they made the charm paper and a booklet in which to enter the donations and the donors' names and addresses. Across the opening folio Doyu painted a panorama of Tangenji and added the history and present state of the temple together with a list of the merits of believing in the Kannon, though he was aware that what they were doing was in short a kind of inventive begging.

Micha mightily enjoyed this business, for it reconciled her purpose of exercising her faith with her purpose of earning money; indeed she prized it as the greatest idea ever to have occurred in their married life. Doyu was doubtful of the Kannon's power, but he was not an utter atheist. He had a vague idea that it might or might not be, which was why he suspected their activity of being a kind of imposture, worse than begging.

Much as he knew begging was prohibited by law, he did not consider it a wrongdoing. Fraudulence he did consider wrong regardless of the law, so he often questioned Micha about her faith, and each time ascertaining its firmness, he enjoyably comforted himself by saying to them both,

"There's no doubt of your faith. Maybe there are grounds to criticize you for a blind or superstitious belief, but you aren't practicing a deception. Even if I haven't such faith, we can say we have faith as a couple. So we needn't worry about deception while we deliver the paper together."

For three years the business had been going quite well, enabling them to retrieve Mokuzu from Ryotanji.

Seeing them counting the coins, Mokuzu acutely realized the need of money for human life.

'I knew of the importance of money before today, but it was mere knowledge like knowing the importance of air. I thought money is always somewhere and comes in according to need. I didn't realize being poor means having no money; I sort of thought it came of fate, character, illness, environment, or some such hazy thing.

'How immature I was! Without money I can't get any service, can't maintain a thing, can't move a step. Socks, coat, buttons...rice, soy sauce, pencils, books...nothing can I get without money, no medicine, not even a charm paper! More costly are the materials for a house....I wasn't precisely aware. Was I thinking a train can run without a track? Idiot!

'I judged Reiho as a rustic fool, but from quite early he knew the need of money. He once asked me, "Do you know why our master goes out day after day?" Likely I said, "He must be just walking," or "He must be wishing for world peace." "He goes out to make money — of course!" was his retort. I was so naive and he so knowing, naturally Luri went along with him.

'I must reevaluate him. How else did he express his seniority? Well, often he said, "Don't slight muscle power. Many guys don't understand reason, but who can't understand by a couple of blows on the head?" Those words could also be true.

'Knowing one's original nature may be important, but evidently it's of secondary importance. Knowing oneself is a luxury. First we must satisfy our physical needs. "Well fed is well bred"[5] spoke Guanjung in the Chou dynasty. Priests sell what is of secondary importance and themselves shrewdly obtain money, which is of primary importance. This must be the very reason my father hates priests, I now understand.

'Most books say nothing excels love in importance. That doesn't mean love is so important as to eclipse the importance of money. At most love is as important as money. Books when they overemphasize one side cause a misunderstanding in young readers. Truly kind authors should write, "Love and money are inseparable like wheel and axle, mind and body."

'If Ena and I can't secure food and clothing and a place to live, we can't maintain our love for even ten days. If we must die, our love will die. If forced to choose love or life, we'd choose life because there's a chance for love while there's life. Well, maybe we wouldn't have to face so extreme a choice. And this complex matter shouldn't be simplified. Love and life are equally important.'

ஃ

When school began, Mokuzu and Ena met afterward and climbed in the nearby mountains.

They did not climb hand in hand. He scaled a cliff without offering to help her up. Nor did they together see the sunset through the trees, nor talk or laugh much.

He rather accelerated his pace on the steeper slopes, and if she got caught by a branch, or rolled and grazed a knee, he all the more hastened on. Often she lost sight of him.

He was as quick as a mountain beast yet never marred his clothes or skin. She took to regularly wearing slacks. Even so, her white blouse got ripped and her side, bruised. Some days she utterly lost him, the stars began to twinkle, the mountain path got pitch-dark under the trees, and she almost had to crawl. Weeping, she went home alone.

She was compelled to follow him however far ahead he went. He appeared cruel, even insane, but she thought she was more insane for tearfully striving to catch up. Whenever she lost sight of him and her body could no longer go on, she felt her heart would burst forth and go on by itself in search of him.

"Wait, Mokuzu! Where are you? Please say!" she cried, ignoring her tears and abrasions as she scrambled up through the dense azaleas and andromedas. When at last she could come to a slight opening, she would find him sitting as if he had been meditating there all the while.

She plunged into him. He embraced her fervently and they rolled on the slope and remained embraced wherever they stopped. He pressed his lips repeatedly to her lips and his cheek hard against her cheek. His loins also tightly pressed her loins, and the pressure and closeness only increased.

They could contact no closer with their clothes on. Yet he sensed with his body her firm breasts, her pubic bone, her soft cleft; and she sensed his firm eminence.

'Am I chasing after him only to enjoy this rapture?' she asked herself beneath him. 'I can't understand why he should run up here for this. I wish he would give us time for quiet talk, especially about our hope and plan. I know he's pondering how we can realize our hope, and he must be having a hard time finding the answer. Then why doesn't he share the hardship with me?'

"Wait! Why don't we return together?" she would call, but he always nipped down some narrow path through the thickets.

She was left alone, but her sorrow seemed mild after their embraces. She knew his cruelty and madness were transitory and another form of his increasing love. She did not know how to doubt his love and his capacity to find their ideal way to live. 'He is sincere, and he knows how to be sincere.'

33

Birds of the Heaven, Lilies of the Field

A lapse of time for trees and plants is the same as to grow. They bud in spring, extend their leaves, open their flowers, and some bear fruit as early as July.

Exasperated, Mokuzu thought,

'For me a lapse of time is an idleness that has nothing to do with growth. True, my body grows as I continue to eat and sleep, but my wisdom, beauty, and value rather decrease in inverse proportion. Physical growth unaccompanied by spiritual growth is no more than the phenomenon of aging, with its increase of ugliness and annoyance. People lacking in spiritual growth are like dogs sprawled heedless of time and place — degraded, someone said, to a mere feces-producing mechanism.'

He detested his changing voice and the need to shave every three days or so. More odious, he suffered from an uncontrollable sexual desire. Try as he would, he could find no cage stronger than the beast's fangs and claws.

More, he could find no positive way for himself and Ena to live on a south hill in the mountain folds, though the time limit was every moment approaching. If he did not establish a sure way toward their goal and translate it to action, they would have to part again, with their hope an unrealized dream; and this time he sensed it would be an eternal parting.

Ena, much as she believed he had several times her intelligence, thought as hard as she could to assist him. Yet only scenes of their dream already realized arose in her head.

Sounding her mother out on the subject, she learned that she approved and was willing to help, and also that her grandmother had left her a competence for her own use.

On the other hand, at school she was attending the sex-education classes for girls, and she was desultorily reading a translation of *Die Vollkommene Ehe, eine Studie über ihre Physiologie und Technik* by Dr. T. H. Van de Velde, which she took from her father's unused library. Thus she came to understand Mokuzu's melancholic expression and impulsive behavior, and she was not ignorant of what made him and her moist through their clothes when they embraced.

She wished to tell him that they should be calmer, as they had been in early spring, that together they should think for their future, that he should not be alone in his unease over his sexual desire.

But even finding a chance was hard. He took to the mountains right after school. As soon as she caught up he embraced her furiously, then left without exchanging a word. When she visited his house in the early morning she found him already gone out to walk alone. She could not approach him between classes lest she create needless rumor.

She attempted a letter, but reconsidered, 'Why was I so patient not to write him while he was away? Well, I thought writing only proves estrangement. It would make me set aside the real Mokuzu and force me to write to my idea of him. I must be loyal to him who is real.'

In mid-July their school announced a three-day vacation trip to the seaside. Ena was dispirited at the thought of being regimented with so many others. She wished that only she and Mokuzu could go elsewhere, and on the spur of the moment determined to hike and camp with him in the mountains.

She told her mother of her unwillingness to attend.

"Fine. If you don't want to, why should you? Anyway, we plan to spend the early half of August at the Suma beach."

"But, Mother, I don't want to go there either." In recent years her family had spent every summer at Suma. It was the first-engineer's native town.

"Then you'll take care of this house by yourself? Or have you another plan...or some problem?" Fumi knit her brow, nervous because Ena had never adjusted to her new father.

"No, to be frank, I want to camp with Mokuzu in the mountains...not dangerous ones, near enough to walk to."

"You and Mokuzu alone?"

Fumi knew her daughter and Mokuzu of Tangenji were intimate friends. Some of the teachers said he possessed exorbitant genius and that his record was the best in the history of the school. Fumi knew Ena loved him, and that her present happiness depended entirely on him. She was convinced that Ena's topmost achievement should be to marry whomever she really loved, and she wanted to support such an ideal marriage by any means. Yet she hesitated to answer, worrying over the sexual relationship, 'Isn't it too early however they love?'

Ena too kept silent, patiently awaiting her mother's reply. Fumi felt she could not forbid her to go; her eyes were so bright and earnest. Assuming the cool visage of a stranger, she asked, "Do you know the mechanism of pregnancy and what you must do when you don't want a baby?"

Instantly Ena averted her eyes, though she was accustomed to looking directly at people, and she colored. "Yes, I know."

"Then with your responsibility you may spend your summer vacation in whatever way is most meaningful to you." Fumi, smiling for the first time, patted Ena on the shoulder. Ena was not yet as tall as her mother.

Ena was eager to catch Mokuzu. She told her homeroom teacher that she had a stomachache, and was excused five minutes early. She stole to Mokuzu's corridor and waited. It being Saturday, the students flew out when released like chickens from a coop.

Mokuzu did not appear. Ena peeped in, able to wait no longer. Three girls were gathered about him as he faced his desk to give some explanation. It must have been English class; half-erased English sentences were on the board. Begged to translate a passage from a difficult essay by Bertrand Russell, Mokuzu was obliged to diagram the grammar.

The girls glanced at Ena and focused again on Mokuzu's hand. He did not raise his head an inch. They understood none of the prepositions, relative pronouns, indirect speech, or subjunctive mood but continued to question him.

Ena thought she was nicer than those year-younger girls for not bothering him with English study, though she too found it hard. He seemed made of ice — he took no heed of her. But she could not blame him; surely teaching them was coming from his good nature.

At last satisfied, they thanked him more than necessary. 'Why don't they free him at once? They're aiming to go with him to the gate, and my wit to come here will end in smoke!'

Ena addressed him.

"Oh, Ena, I'm sorry I made you wait," he replied. "Well, see you Monday, 'bye," he told the girls and tore himself away.

"Weren't you aware of me? You didn't look up at all."

"I knew. They looked up and acted as if they were earnestly hearing me, when their habit is to be inattentive. I knew it was you because you didn't speak."

His words were cheering. In addition he looked brighter than usual, like the Mokuzu of spring. 'Did they dispel his depression?' Ena was conscious of disliking her question. Then involuntarily she asked, "Do you like teaching?"

"It's better than being taught. But I see little difference. You stand with your back to the board or you face it. Either way is an unfree endurance."

In spite of herself Ena laughed. 'He's recovered his innate way of talking. I haven't been with him for nearly a week — what's come over him?'

"You're like you used to be. You were a bit odd in the rainy season. Could you find our way?" she ventured, ready to cry, "Wait, I've something to tell you!" if he started for the mountain.

"I haven't yet found it, but I'm convinced of how we shouldn't be. I also understand there's something we should protect at any risk even if we become outcasts."

"Oh! Could you share with me what you think?"

"Sure, I thought for us. We have to protect our dandelion dream. We must do whatever we must to realize it, and not do anything to hinder it, even if that thing is considered a good deed in society. That's my conclusion. Let's go to the river, to the grass where you first gave voice to our hope."

The vetch of spring was replaced by rice. The graceful young blades undulated more elegantly than the waves of the sea. The fresh breeze over the fields appealed to Mokuzu's and Ena's sense of sound, sight, and smell, not only touch.

The wind as it swept across from the far mountains of pine and deciduous forest flipped the rice blades so that their paler undersides were exposed, and when they flipped back, the fields became again a vivid green until a new wind came over. The wind never advanced straight, yet it reached the Sakura

River before long and there too bent the young eulalia grown tall and riffled the water. It tossed Ena's hair and stirred her short sleeves, which were exposing her full, soft arms.

Gold-banded lilies extending to their best ability among the grasses on the far shore emitted a scent into the air about the two young people, and the pale pink flowers of a nearby silk tree cast on them a cool shade.

The river was swollen and muddy, but where a shoal had been in early spring, five or six intermediate egrets had alighted and were widely opening and relaxing their wings.

"Well, where should I begin? There are so many important problems all interlocked and I haven't well grasped most of them. Our problem isn't like a car, which may appear complicated with its hundreds of parts, yet each has a definite shape and function and we can explain the mechanism if we patiently dismantle everything in order. Our problem has to do with human emotions — hate, hope, confidence — and judgment of the right and wrong in taking an occupation. It concerns how we should live, why we were born, why we must die, that is, it's a judgment of our desires, such as for food, sleep, sex, property, and fame.

"These problems — in short, the good deeds we should practice and the bad deeds we shouldn't — are mixed in three dimensions, not only on a single plane. They contradict one another, or sometimes fuse, and are so complex and mysterious that if you touch any part it's like bringing a hornets' nest down on your head. There will be no great solution for someone like me, and I almost want to forget everything and devote myself to being ignorant, nonchalant, and heartless.

"Since ancient times people who were called philosophers, religious men, and artists have been chatting as they pleased according to their ability about human life and the human environment. The more talented have been honored as patriarchs or saints, but really they're all as alike as acorns. Even the greatest have their limits.

"Yet compare them by putting them in three classes. First is the large majority of minor greats. They're like fireflies with no warmth and little candle power that lend just a touch to the summer riverside. Second are quite a number of medium greats. They can light a room as well as the street and provide us food in famine and warm us in a blizzard. Third are the fewest but greatest. They warm most parts of society, and their influence reaches into the mountains and the seas, to plants and animals as well.

"Now, even these greatest cannot shine to the profound depths of human life and the endless reaches of the universe. They fall far too short of the truth, of knowing what is really good and right. With evidence to the contrary, how can they be a real Buddha or God? Rather, they must resort to Buddha or God."

"Mokuzu, the teachers, PTA, and board of education all say you're a genius.

403

Isn't it people like you who become the patriarchs and saints you mention?"

"Definitely not. Genius is a name given by ordinary people. In truth those they name are quite remote from them, but they name them that because they see in them some quality they see in themselves. The difference, then, isn't one of quality but of degree or amount of achievement.

"To illustrate, you know that recently Satoko Tanaka set a world record with her 200-meter backstroke of 2 minutes 37.1 seconds. And Tsuyoshi Yamanaka did so with his 400-meter freestyle in 4 minutes 16.6 seconds. I'll say they're geniuses for drastically outdoing ordinary swimmers.

"Their records are coveted. Ordinary people envy geniuses for being extra-ordinary. The finest examples of ordinary people are called geniuses.

"I want to live unlike all such dull people. I'm seeking a difference not of degree or amount but of substantial quality. So don't call me a genius. I'm very far from one.

"People who envy geniuses don't call anyone a genius who lives in a way foreign to their own. They give the name genius only to those whose nature is like their own. Anyone whose nature is otherwise they call a lunatic.

"Here, Ena, you have to realize that seeking to live quietly on a flowering hill in remote mountains while asking 'What is my original nature?' isn't the wish of any genius. Society regards what we are seeking as heresy or insanity.

"Think, how many of our generation are frantically elaborating a plan to avoid being caught up on the escalator of higher education or the conveyor belt of the work force? Most who have five more years before adulthood are only worrying over their homework or birthday parties. Not even one in a thousand will support our hope. We can't be attentive enough. We have to advance along what they'll call a path of madness. We are a skiff heading into a storm."

"Yes, I begin to see. Our hope rises from our passive suffering. To realize our hope, we need our active suffering."

"Exactly. Sad people wish for happiness, yet most don't nourish their hope in order to attain it."

"So...that's why you fell silent after speaking some phrases I couldn't make sense of. It was a spring afternoon. I mentioned 'the birds of the heaven' and 'the lilies of the field.' You said, 'They're just images projected on a screen of white mist,' and 'Every miller draws water to his own mill to satisfy his false satisfaction.'"

"Ah, yes, we were talking of occupations. I said our ideal life isn't compatible with society because society requires that everyone take an occupation. I said society will meanwhile laugh at us, then they'll castigate us, then lynch us. With dreamy eyes you quoted from Matthew 6:

"Behold the birds of the heaven, that they sow not, neither do they reap nor gather into barns; and your heavenly Father feedeth them. Are not ye of much more value than they?...And why are ye anxious concerning raiment? Consider the lilies of the field, how they grow; they toil not, neither do they spin.

"At the time, Ena, I thought you were aspiring to the life of birds or lilies in your wish to escape our passive suffering."

"Yes, I was falling into the danger of dreaming, which you cautioned me not to do."

"Well, I meditated on those words of Jesus Christ, and I was shocked to realize there was actually someone who recommended such a way of life. And at once I doubted he would take responsibility if it happens we are punished by society for following his recommended — and our ideal — way.

"I thought Jesus wouldn't take responsibility for his recommendation. It seems natural that he wouldn't, particularly he wouldn't take responsibility for a person who doesn't believe in a 'heavenly father.' I never saw a heavenly father any clearer than an illusion on mist. I think the Sermon on the Mount also is great, but I don't practice it. It's wrong to quote the teachings of Jesus as one likes only for one's convenience, and worse, to ask his responsibility without believing in his teaching."

"You don't believe our heavenly father will feed us?"

"I don't comprehend either a heavenly father or his feeding. I'm rather positive in denying them. But I've been examining why Jesus spoke of birds and lilies, for I think I can then figure out what difficulties and dangers might arise if we practice our ideal way, and also what wisdom and resolve we'll need.

"Ena, I never liked to do anything I detested or thought was unimportant, yet I was forced to do a great many such things by society, school, Ryotanji, and my family.

"The times I could enjoy doing what I liked were so few — the times I spent with you when I was in first and second grade, and after I returned here this spring. Otherwise my effort and endurance have been exercised to adapt to the pressure of my environment and to satisfy it for a certain length.

"Then you told me your dream, and at once I knew that my endurance and effort should be exercised to realize it. Your dream is my dream, it's the very thing we both wish to attain. So my endurance and effort are no longer passive. Now I have the joy of exercising them to the utmost for what I wish to do.

"And yet, what will happen if we don't go on in school or take a job? Society will force us to take a job. If we don't, we can't maintain ourselves, and if we can't do that, we'll be accused of being lunatics and crooks, and we'll have to die.

"Here remember the words of Jesus. Did he speak to comfort and celebrate the poor, whom we'd inevitably become? No, he incited and commanded them:

> "But seek ye first his kingdom, and his righteousness; and all these things shall be added unto you.

"No doubt many take those words to comfort and excuse themselves for being poor, yet they don't seek 'his kingdom.' 'Birds of the heaven' and 'lilies of the field' are too poetic, too pretty; they made you too only dream, as you realized. I think it would be kinder to use harsh words on the beloved poor. Let me translate Matthew 6 into a shout:

> "You dull and dirty fools — you own nothing but disease and distress! But why sorrow, why grieve? Have you forgotten what you truly wanted? You didn't so much seek bread and raiment, nor wealth, name, honor, and power. What you sought was love!
>
> "Ugly simpletons! As long as you forget what you truly want and take an occupation and flatter the rich and the mighty, you shall never satisfy yourselves.
>
> "If truly you wish to enjoy a home of love, you must make every effort to escape authority and to avoid society's demands. You must refuse to take an occupation: your endurance, effort, and wisdom are yours that they may lead you to realize your supreme hope, the value of your life, the only truth.

"See, Ena, it's the most dangerous and abominable thought in either capitalist or communist countries. I'm therefore quite sure that few people in those countries truly practice this of Jesus Christ's teachings.

"We live in a country influenced by Buddhism, so for us it's easier to understand 'heavenly father' and 'his kingdom' if we incorporate them in the idea of 'knowing one's original nature.'

"Then, why should an occupation in society be denied by Jesus and by us? There are various explanations.

"It can be said that an occupation makes us forget our basic purpose in life, which is to know our original nature. More, an occupation keeps us from our basic concern of building and maintaining our love and rather coops us in a realm of ignorance where our hostile feelings are roused and our love endangered.

"Let me explain with more intimate words for you and me. Taking an occupation is wrong because, first, it limits a person's freedom and second, it forces him to live a false life. As a result of these two, a society of such people becomes a country of unfree, dishonest people, and naturally the substance of their life is to do harm.

"For example, as to the first reason, I'm interested in any occupation if it lasts but a while. I'd like to be a painter, a writer, a priest, a doctor, even a musician, though I'm tone-deaf. I'd like to build airplane parts, ride a dogsled, plant fruit trees, market ham.... But to continue would be torture; I couldn't endure doing the same thing day after day for fifty years. Imagine if I chose to be an actor. Endlessly I'd have to repeat the lines of a beggar or a king. Or if it were raising worms I'd be better off dead. Choose any job — the limited, binding, repetitive life is the same.

"If I can't submit to unfreedom, I can't hold any job.

"Were I a policeman, I'd have to police always or I'd be abused as false or inferior and be punished, even fired. Then my purpose to earn a livelihood would come to nil.

"Come to think of it, being paid to catch wrongdoers and to rescue those they harm is downright queer. Can't people exercise their goodness without being paid? This simple criticism applies to all occupations. Unless they're paid, merchants don't supply food, doctors don't doctor, teachers don't teach. To do good for the sake of money isn't ideal — nor of course is to do evil.

"So, an occupation makes one live a false life, and there's no doubt a false life harms oneself and others. Any work done for money generally means selling things at a higher price than their value. To earn money is to make the buyer spend more than he should have to, and that's a kind of lie. As this is obvious, let me take a harder example, say, of a doctor, like your father.

"Reiho once had me see on TV a live report on a man who had murdered a number of people. Now he was holding a housewife hostage in a teahouse circled by armed police. A number of them found a chance to dash in, a gunshot sounded, and they came out with the woman unharmed and her captor hemorrhaging from the back. An ambulance arrived and rushed him to a university hospital, where the camera focused on the director and staff receiving him.

"It amazed me; he was getting care no poor and rural people ever get. And the doctors were so earnest! They hadn't met him before — they couldn't love him. Yet they could administer to him cordially because their creed is to devote their skill to saving human lives regardless of love and hate or juridical right and wrong. But if so, there are many worthy human lives in town and in the agricultural, mountain, and fishing villages. Why don't they hasten to those places?

"I must conclude they gave him their best because they fear that society might otherwise denounce them. Doctors are expected always to be doctors.

"Can you see how horrible it is to be a doctor? A doctor can't judge by love and hate, right and wrong, and so must treat each patient as merely organic matter and himself as medical equipment, which isn't even organic.

"After hospitalization, that man will go on trial and be jailed for life or executed. It's insane that so many earnest workers in white gowns were treating such a person!

"Were I one of them I'd like to say to him, 'Die now — it's the better choice for your peace.' Or, 'I'm going for a stroll, then I'll read a book, then I'll return. If you're still breathing and I'm in a fine humor, I'll treat you.'

"But I'd be fired. We won't fit as doctors unless we're dishonest, and the same can be said of any other profession.

"Ena, can you understand, despite my rough explanation?"

"Yes, an occupations disables us so we can't realize our ideal life — it appears so. An occupation limits our possibility, steals our freedom, forces us to live a false life. We wish to be free and honest or love can't be nourished. And without love how can we devote ourselves to the study of knowing who we are?"

"That's right. But if we don't take a regular occupation, we'll have no money for food, clothing, or anything. And there will be many more troubles I'm not yet fully aware of. What will we do when we get hurt or sick? How can we get the necessary money without working? Jesus says:

> "Be not therefore anxious for the morrow: for the morrow will be anxious for itself. Sufficient unto the day is the evil thereof.

"But I believe anxiety for the morrow is a large part of today. If we cease caring to solve the problems of tomorrow, what will be left today? Only lamentation over yesterday. Today has meaning because we can perceive tomorrow and yesterday. Besides, I know even birds may migrate in search of tomorrow's food, and lilies store nourishment in their bulbs.

"Anyway, I'll think further about our concrete problems. For now I'm sure that to realize our hope we mustn't take an occupation. This certainty will light our hope. There couldn't be so many problems we can't solve if we combine our best effort. Now I know more clearly in which direction I must put all my power. We'll unify our love and keep seeking our original nature."

Mokuzu's investigation seemed to Ena to bring them a step nearer their dream. 'He suffered for four months to convince himself that our dream won't be realized unless we reject taking an occupation. It's a necessary condition. With this discovery our dream of spring dandelions will be fortified. Now we know we can't succeed without opposing society. Our ideal home on a remote south-facing slope should be a fortress. There we aren't merely going to hide from society. We're going to send up a rocket as a declaration to the world. I'll be one with Mokuzu to fight. I'll be his blood and his flesh, and his will be mine!'

Actually she was in his arms on the green grass, experiencing the greatest peace ever. A warm red and yellow light filled her eyelids. When she half opened her eyes, the pale blue sky with a few whitish green blades of grass entered her vision and was overtaken by a soft white, and it seemed it was her entire world. The egrets were flying away.

The water laved the shore. Under the bright sun they lay on the grass. 'At last I'm free of that disagreeable world!' she thought, and she related her plan to camp in a mountain or valley during summer vacation. Mokuzu had no reason to object. He loved her increasingly and thought that for her sake he ought to be wiser, for he knew he had solved nothing. He kept thinking,

'I only pointed to the existence of the problem. Isn't it just another way to avoid confronting it? There are people who can easily satisfy their questions about a bird or a flower by pinning down its name. Naming things shines a light on them, but the light often blinds. 'Explaining a problem isn't equal to solving it and is rather a tricky way of putting it aside. Some people never approach a graveyard, others make it a beautiful park. Either way ignores death and isn't the choice of a man like me.

'Those who wish to appear wise lecture about the obvious. Those who wish to make an impression pretend to ignore real human distress, or are already indifferent. They pretend to do great deeds impossible for normal people, yet they teach people to do them.

'But Ena isn't so extensive a thinker or so eloquent. I should use my thought and eloquence not on her but on men who might entrap her with theirs, just as the police should apply force not to civilians but to violence and terrorism.

'Teacher Docho told me that many so-called sages of old used their wisdom and eloquence to bewilder the ignorant and keep them in awe instead of using those devices against their real enemy, powerful men.

'I'd like to comment even on Jesus. Why did he preach ideas so hard for the ignorant to practice? Why didn't he just offer them bread and fish and keep quiet? Still if he wanted to preach, why didn't he preach only to scholars, priests, and influential men? Whoever preaches the Dharma to a baby crying for milk is evil or an idiot, I assume.

'I must be careful not to commit myself to the folly of making Ena think difficult matters. Much more, I shouldn't chat about matters I myself haven't yet solved. I must love her in the most suitable way for her nature and ability.

'About sexual desire too I have to think more. I have to love her in a righteous way. I shouldn't bury in my mind every problem that is hard to solve. Nor should I entrust the solutions to Buddha, God, or Nature, for by any means they aren't human. I'm not a butterfly, nor a dog, nor a child of nature anymore.

'I have to be sane. How can I get money without working? No one loves to work. Do my parents work for the pleasure of it? No, only for their family. They haven't leisure to speculate on its correctness. They work, surrender their freedom, and are willing to live a false life for those they love. To work is to live a false life for the sake of love. And to live for the sake of love isn't false. It's right, true, and sane, for what is a more important concern than love?

'Here there's great reason why Jesus was hated, seen as a liar, and at last killed by those who worked to support their dependents. Jesus incited them without taking responsibility for the consequences, in the name of a misty, heavenly father. He subdued them like sheep. But people aren't sheep and can't live only to satisfy their private needs however spiritual. They must live for their dependents and be willing to put themselves into hell to save them. There's no proof we can live without working. We aren't birds or lilies.

'I will say the worst type of human being is the type who satisfies the desire to be a leader by using eloquence to propagate an illusion. Yes, I really must think!

'What is sexual desire? This too I must consider. I touch Ena and want to touch her again before two hours pass. She doesn't refuse, she enjoys it, she is content. Is it because she trusts me and can enjoy whatever she does with me?

'My strongest desire has been to do what I want and not do what I don't. Of the five desires — for food, sleep, sex, property, and fame — to which does it belong? I thought it didn't belong to any of them. I was misunderstanding. My desire, here simply stated, is greater than any of them and includes them all!

'Just about everyone has all five with one or two dominant. In me they're all dominant. I'm not content to satisfy only one or two. And those five can be divided to ten, a hundred, a thousand, even a million. For all of them, I want to do what I want and don't want to do what I don't. No one could be more avaricious than me! I thought I was disinterested, and have been considered to be so. The truth is, I have the greatest desire yet seem as if I haven't — it's like the proverbs, Avarice bursts the bag, and Grasp all, lose all.

'Now I realize the most ardent desire is the desire for freedom and the most outrageous ambition is the wish to know oneself!'

ॐ

Mokuzu told his father of his and Ena's plan to go camping during summer vacation. Doyu appeared to be startled,

410

"By yourselves?" But at once he said, "That's good." He brought out some money and handed it to Mokuzu with the banter,

"You know, money is essential even in the mountains, as long as you breathe." He was scorning himself for having been too late to realize the truth of his words.

Mokuzu was filled with a sense of mission. 'Whatever happens, I have to make Ena happy, like an eagle sheltering its young or zooming to the valley to rescue it from a fall. I must lighten her burden by taking the lead with those difficult human problems changeable as a kaleidoscope and dark as an abyss.'

34

Light and Darkness

A mix of apprehension and excitement is commonly experienced before a journey to a foreign place. A pessimist is prone to worry over the chance of misfortune, an optimist, to imagine many delights ahead.

Ena had no doubts about camping with Mokuzu and returning together. Her emotions as she prepared were well balanced like the pleasant days and nights of summer.

The new environment that defined the time between the onset and end of summer did not inspire Mokuzu. He was in fact made uneasy, though to express what he felt was hard.

'What begins must end. Grief follows joy, it is said. The higher the mountain the deeper the vale. Is the capacity to taste joy directly or indirectly proportional to the capacity to taste grief? If one is able to go to the heights but not to the depths, shouldn't one stay with the repose of the plain?'

Mokuzu was from infancy a gentle boy and had acquired to the extent that it was his distinctive feature the ability to master himself even when flames surged in his mind.

Ena with the help of her so-called second father was preparing a tent, a gas cooker, pots, mess kits, a canvas bucket, rice, canned food, dried fruit, cookies, extra clothes and blankets, and a sketchbook. Mokuzu could not hide his amazement,

"Ena, do you intend to climb a snowy mountain, or settle permanently in a valley?"

"We'll be away a month, won't we?"

"Yes, but we're going only within a 15-kilometer radius of latitude 35 degrees 7 minutes north and longitude 135 degrees 27 minutes east. As we move along our perimeter, certainly we'll find houses and groceries within two or three hours of anywhere we plan to stay. And it's summer; there'll be plenty of wild fruits, and birds, hares, and fish."

Mokuzu limited them to one blanket and them each to one change of clothes, rolled in some of the food, and wrapped the roll in the blue Logan tent. "This'll do," he said, taking it on his back.

Yet Ena stealthily crammed into her knapsack a sewing kit, medicine, and numerous other items.

Mokuzu took along the sword tip acquired in his childhood. The more he sharpened it the more it emitted a settled light and the better it cut. He used a rough, a medium, and a finishing whetstone and applied camellia oil against rust. He had long ago made a haft by coiling on hemp thread, applying vegetable glue, and finishing with silk thread. With the same blade he had cut down a *ho* tree and carved a scabbard.

Thus equipped he was sure he could catch any game and make any needed plates, cups, and chopsticks. So he said,

"We need just rice, a pot, a canteen, and lots of matches."

They planned to go south to climb Mt. Tendai and Mt. Myoken, which lay in Toyono County, Osaka. Next they would go west to climb Mt. Kenno and Mt. Shin, and then north to Mt. Taikonji and Mt. Bijo in Funai County, Kyoto. Toward the end they would climb Mt. Chitose, Mt. Santo, and Mt. Atago to the east.

The highest was Mt. Atago at 924 meters, second Mt. Shin at 791. The mountains were all abundantly green, with many suitable streams beside which to camp. Far enough from human habitation, the water was clean and the scenery charming.

Mokuzu had not learned much about the geographic and geologic features, so Ena explained,

"These mountains were formed by the orogenic movements of the late Mesozoic age, around 140 to 70 million years ago. Broadleaf trees were just appearing. The mountainsides were dense with cycads, cedars, cypresses, and ferns. Birds, mammals, and the giant reptiles were also beginning to prosper. The strata were mainly composed of conglomerate, sandstone, shale, limestone, and slate...."

"Look, Ena, even now the summit is covered with kumazasa and fern. I've heard ammonite fossils can be found up here. Do you suppose it's true?"

"Yes. I know a scholar who collects all kinds of fossils."

"How about rock snakes? I've heard some inhabit..."

"Oh, Mokuzu, you couldn't have...!" Reflexively Ena halted and turned around. She was walking ahead, chatting brightly, and now realized the grasses were above her knees. They had just climbed a fairly steep acclivity on account of which the grassy trail suddenly disappeared behind, leaving only a triangle of blue sky between a cliff close by and the side of a hinder mountain beyond a valley. From the cliff strange rocks projected with kumazasa grown all about; and clinging here and there were old blasted pines with bone-white tops, around which twined wisteria suggestive of reptiles.

"Ena, you know Taki who lives alone by the Sasayama Highway, good at Japanese dance? I once heard him tell my father a story about a deer hunter. One day he lost sight of his chase, and he sat down to smoke on a handy fallen tree, just like these around here. When he knocked his pipe against it, he saw it plumply begin to move...well,...it was a rock snake. The head with flicking tongue turned to size him up. At that, he flung away his gun and bolted down the mountain head over heels. For the next five days he had a terrific fever. Then he died in agony. As he breathed his last, he bit into his arm."

"Oh, Mokuzu!" Ena drew near him. "You must be making that up! I never heard any such tale. My illustrated animal book doesn't list this as an area for rock snakes. But I am a little scared...could you walk ahead?"

Mokuzu laughed loudly and told her,

"Don't worry, it isn't true. But if one appears, I'll cut it down at a stroke!" and from his belt he took his sword, and in a flash a wisteria as thick as a wrist was deftly cut in two.

"But Ena, don't forget there are pit vipers — you'd better stay ahead."

"You said they tend to strike the second comer. What will I do if you're bitten?"

"No creature is so dumb as to challenge anyone eager to display his prowess. Let's hurry on to the summit. It'll be splendid to lie on the grass and see the sunset!"

The trail went around a bulge. Then they found that though it ascended, it did not lead to the summit. They had expected it would for having gone down and now up.

The summit they wanted to reach and the place where they stood were actually separated by a valley dozens of meters wide. The bottom was filled with various kinds of deciduous oaks covered with ivy, on account of which the valley looked less terrifying. Yet, the walls were sharp, and if they were to fall they would likely be badly hurt and unable to climb out.

They had no choice but to retrace their way down or to proceed some distance around and there resume climbing.

413

Mokuzu made Ena wait while he scouted ahead.

At one place the valley was oddly narrow. To jump seemed almost feasible, but the dark of it made its depth unverifiable. With his eyes he gauged it to be no more than seven meters over. Considering that the walls were formed of rock, he thought of using a tree for a bridge. Ena was afraid.

"Ena, it's just a moment's endurance."

Deciding two trees of medium diameter would make an easier crossing than one thick one, he cut down two pines. Fearing Ena might grow dizzy and fall, he tied a wisteria vine to her waist and to his. After crossing, Ena complained,

"Now my legs are beginning to shake!" But she had endless admiration for his skill with his blade. She did not know how to express her brimful pride and joy.

Out of longstanding habit, Mokuzu woke around 4:30. Quietly he freed himself from Ena's disarranged hair and her hand and leg. He stole from the tent and descended to where a stream formed a fall sufficient for him to bathe in. The sky wherever unobstructed by mountain was set with stars. They looked near enough to reach with the hand, and the sky was like a plane figure. Between the stars was very dark.

Catching one or two birds or hares as he went down and back was easy enough, but he had no way to bring Ena the dawning sky or the several deer standing in silhouette on a cliff before they darted away. The fresh sun began to issue many rays into the deep valley. From the abundant broadleaf foliage numerous tomtits rose, now at once and now in orderly succession.

On the seventh day they reached Mt. Shin. Its northwest side was in Kawabe County, Hyogo Prefecture, its south side in Toyono County, Osaka, and its east side in Funai County, Kyoto. At the top was a lake called Tsuten, "lake to heaven," with an island in the center. The water, gushing down to the northeast, formed a special limpid creek the length of four kilometers to the flatland.

"This gorge is a typical folded valley," taught Ena.

"I heard a Zen master named it Rurikei — 'lapis gorge.'"

It was cool even in midsummer, being on high land and having countless large and small waterfalls among interestingly shaped rocks. In the basins of the waterfalls and in the pools made where the rocks obstructed the waterway were many *amago*, *yamame*, and sweetfish. In the night a kind of singing frog cried and giant salamanders inserted their grunts now and then.

The canopy of leafy maple boughs over the creek were lit by the moon and cast their shadows on the water and the rocks.

The mountain though richly forested with deciduous trees was a grassy

plain on top, with scatterings of huge rocks. One exceptionally great projecting rock appeared as if at any moment it might fall to the empty valley, yet it
must have existed there without budging for thousands of years.

In all directions the summit presented a view of peaks soaring clean and
proper, while the skirts and valleys were veiled in stagnant mist.

Mokuzu and Ena thought it wasteful to abandon so beautiful a place with
mountain and water combined and rich in food. They decided to stay until
they tired of the scenery, without minding the effect on their itinerary.

They pitched their tent on the summit, from where they could look out
to mountains upon mountains, and see the lake, the waterfall, and the creek
meandering down through the foliage and trunks. After dark they calculated
that the light cast on the sky was from the nightless cities of Osaka and Kobe.
During the day they freely walked the area.

Ena washed their laundry in the creek and hung it on branches. Mokuzu
caught fish and gathered edible herbs. Her dry underwear once blew away
into the valley and he took much trouble to retrieve it.

He could indicate most of the common trees and grasses to her, having
sketched them under Teacher Setsuro's guidance. But he found some sub-
alpine flowers he had never seen except in an illustrated book. There was a
fringed galax with a few pale pink bell-shaped flowers; a *tsugazakura*, its stems
decumbent, its flowers almost white but for a faintly pink lobated frill; and a
kinreika, distinctive with yellow cymose flowers, straight stem, and serrulated
palmate leaves. Mokuzu knew there were many alpine flowers in the north
half of the main island of Japan. He wished to visit the Japan Alps with Ena
in full alpine dress.

In the daytime heat they swam in the lake, to the island, overgrown with
red pines. The depth of the water was unfathomable. When they dived deep,
they found the drop in temperature quite abrupt and the current unexpectedly quick. They had to be alert not to be pulled to the waterfall.

They crossed the island to see the far shore of the lake. It turned out to
be a swamp with ghostly doddered trees eroded by each occasional big rain.
They beheld the other face of water, which was to kill, not nurture, though
the scene presented but a glimpse of a long action in terms of geological time.

Gooseflesh appeared on Ena's nape and arms, seemingly not from the cold
water. She preferred fire to water and mountains to lakes.

In the tent they were once in a while attacked by a fierce thunderstorm
with great bolts. Cumulonimbus clouds rose explosively from either the Sea
of Japan or the Pacific Ocean and in a trice occupied all the bright blue sky.
No sooner did the last remaining crack in the clouds become blue-black than
large drops began to pelt the grass and the tent. Then came the shower, and

the unhindered wind raved without cease across the summit as if to praise its energy and glorify the thunder. The multi-lapped white curtain of rain was driven aslant, even horizontal. The grassy plain writhed.

The lightning burst as if to display the shapes of the dense clouds and gouge the sky. Before it branched, a stentorian roar was already bounding from cloud to cloud and mountain to mountain. New bolts, not waiting for the echoes to cease, burst at once in the east and the west, the most decisive and powerful at times reaching straight to earth.

Mokuzu cast his sword and all else metallic far from the tent, took off his wet clothes, lay on his back, and waited for the tempest to pass. He recalled the tragic story of his teacher Docho in his youth and related it to Ena.

She lay close beside him, palpitating with anxiety. Yet her anxiety raised in her a pleasant sensation, which increased, making it hard for her to control herself.

Responding to her anxiety, he said,

"We needn't fear thunder. The moment we're struck, all our capability to feel and to think about pain and death will cease. We can worry only beforehand, while we're still living, so worry is a luxurious fancy. It's the same as sympathizing with a wayfarer in a snowstorm while we're enjoying the warmth of a fire after a fine dinner."

For her sensation of pleasure, he provided a simile,

"In a crowd you're like a Koryo celadon porcelain, clean and graceful. In the dark you're like a flambeau."

One afternoon a little past mid-August, as they were returning from the island, two large motorcycles with an overbearing noise appeared on the bumpy dirt road that led to the lake from the direction of Osaka. Two youthful riders dismounted, parked them by the stout pine at the shore, and sat down.

Their slicked hair glistened. Like yakuza they wore sunglasses, gaudy shirts, stomach bands, black leather boots, and black pants so tight as to appear absorbed by their calves and thighs — no doubt very uncomfortable for the season.

Ena was swimming on her stomach. She held her breath, alarmed. 'Aren't they from the Thunder Herd, that reserve band of thugs becoming a social problem in Tokyo and Osaka?'

Mokuzu at her side ignored them. He kept swimming on his flank, leaving a margin of energy.

They chunked their cigarettes into the water.

To avoid arriving at their feet, Mokuzu pressed Ena to change direction to the upper shore. The lower shore had the danger of the waterfall.

The youths also moved to the upper shore. Soon they were picking up stones and pitching them out to the water.

Ena drew as near as she could to Mokuzu. Her swimming had degenerated to a dog paddle.

"Shouldn't we again change direction?"

"No, they will too. Just look unconcerned. By any means we must get to shore."

The stones kept coming, quite near. Some were fairly big.

"Don't worry, they don't intend to hit us."

Ena silently cried, 'Even so, what if one of us is hit? Musashi was helpless when attacked in the bath. Mokuzu, you're strong, but you're only in junior high!'

A small stone hit her calf. She felt little pain but could not keep tears from oozing out. Mokuzu sheltered her with his arm as he encouraged her to keep moving landward. Then he addressed the youths, now on a root of the pine.

"Hey, do you see...?" He dropped his voice before finishing. He had nothing to tell them, but he repeated,

"Hey! Do you see the island...?" He indicated behind him. They stayed their hands to catch his words.

"You see the island in front of you, and..."

"Speak up! You expect us to hear you?" "Hah! He's shaking!" They laughed with derision.

"I mean, the island must be visible to your eyes, right?" As he talked, Mokuzu closed the distance to ten meters, then five, and finally he could grasp the root under their feet. Still mumbling to them, he pushed Ena up to the shore.

"I wanted to say the island you see has many handsome pines. Nevertheless —" and he spoke so that the words scarcely left his mouth, "your appearance mars the scene."

As soon as he was assured of Ena's landing, he swung himself up, making the most of the leverage.

The youths advanced, looking at Ena's face and at Mokuzu's through their sunglasses as if licking them with their eyes.

"What are you trying to say? Cat got your tongue? — though you're making it with that girl, huh?"

"You're finished, boy! Thought you owned the place?...ha ha! — we happened by! But there won't be no one else...."

"Say, tootsie, how many times today you did it with him? What are you waiting for? — c'mon, c'mon, take off the blue suit — don't act like you're so pure!"

"Can't you swim?" Mokuzu's voice was faint as a mosquito.

"Turn up the juice!" came their response.

"I asked, can you or can't you swim?" Mokuzu shouted full force. He was close by, and his abruptness surprised them. They stepped back. But soon they recovered, and each as he spoke unwound a chain at his waist,

"Your head must be real empty. Is your girl a dodo?"

"How about a little pain to wise you up?"

Mokuzu had been holding Ena by the shoulder, but he pushed her behind him and asked,

"Is that the extent of your weaponry? You must have heard of the pistol, invented back in the sixteenth century at Pistoia, Italy." He kept moving, imperceptibly, until he stood against the lake. He knew that the more furious the opponent, the more evident would be his line of attack, and the less accurate the attack.

"You stupid issue of idiot parents! Have you no balls?" he taunted. With a wide circling motion they flung their chains. But before they could carry through, both were plunging into the lake. The splashes were unexpectedly large.

Ena had been standing rigid, clamping her thighs and regarding her fists as she did when she was cold. Her face instantly brightened, and she threw open her mouth with amaze and delight.

The youths in the water choked and coughed with contorted faces. One, his glasses gone, exposed twitching asymmetric eyes.

"Shall I toss you your bikes? Faithful steeds don't abandon their masters!"

Mokuzu and Ena folded their tent and moved on.

੩੭

Morning and evening a wedge of cool arrived. The summer day, having behaved lordly in its prime, had to see its sphere of influence narrowing. Now was too late to regain its power, and there was no way for it to mask its decline.

The sun rose without confidence before the westerlies that withered the fields in waves, and it set with self-scorn.

Mokuzu in the evening noticed goose bumps on his arm. No more were there beads of sweat. He put all his power in his arm, and, releasing it, thought, 'What's this? I can't see it, yet I keenly sense a flow of underground water. Is it merely distress at the chill wind and the colors of autumn, which in ancient days rendered many a mind poetic?'

Sometimes he could not believe that his happy memories of camping with Ena under the sun and the stars were memories of reality. 'Memories disappear like wisps torn from a cloud. Worse, what I acutely remember is my worry and uneasiness over things that could happen, though they never did.'

As if looking at a bright shard of glass in the weeds, he remembered his worries over what he should do if Ena were bitten by a viper or pierced through the foot by a rusty nail. What if a tree he was cutting landed on her head? What if a rock he was climbing rolled down on her? What if the cold lake water sent her into shock? What if she were taken by the waterfall? So many were the possible mishaps.

He knew from experience that no merriment lasts long. Day after day, untiring, relentless, had come melancholy, tedium, hunger, and discord. He could not believe there had been days when he had known only happiness and peace.

He thought, 'A man may receive measure for measure. But fate may exercise revenge on a man too good and too happy....

> 'The angels, not half so happy in heaven,
>   Went envying her and me —
>   Yes! — that was the reason (as all men know,
>   In this kingdom by the sea)
>   That the wind came out of the cloud by night,
>   Chilling and killing my Annabel Lee.[1]

'Annabel Lee was modeled after a young woman, Virginia, who at age thirteen married the poet, Edgar Allan Poe. She was incurably tubercular. But I see Ena is in perfect health.'

The new school term began, and Mokuzu kept on meeting Ena after school, and each time he felt reassured of her health. But toward evening after saying good-bye, he began to think of every calamity that might have happened and that might yet happen to her. They were as many as the stars in the night sky, and were in his imagination as clear as stars reflected on clear water.

Wishing to be rid of his worry, for it was a kind of obsession, he meditated on his life in detail from the time of his return from Ryotanji. He tried to jot down every important event objectively, because anyhow he had to answer letters that came while he was camping.

Zen Master Hanun softly rebuked him for not calling on Ryotanji during summer vacation. Teachers Yojun and Docho listed many books he should read and pressed him to report on himself.

Teacher Setsuro sent a new painting, a scene of five or six sparrows resting on the thatch of a shed and as many on the ground foraging for grain. To the side were Linji's words "One man is ever on his way without leaving home. Another has left home but is not on his way."[2]

419

Mokuzu alternated between meditating and writing. The day darkened early by influence of a typhoon. The pines and chestnuts on the back mountain began to raise a howl. The great persimmon above the retreat cottage rustled.

He dated a letter 26 September.

No one struck the bell in the second story of the gate, yet it rang, and the reverberation was carried off by the wind. As the rain increased, the flow through the gate and down the stone steps grew noisier than the flood over the eaves troughs. Mokuzu was reminded of the evening when he was told by Gyodo that he had to go to Ryotanji.

'Since then how little I have matured! Outside is as dark as ever, and I have no light to light the gloom.'

In the main building the radio reported the eye of the typhoon to be in the Pacific off the coast of Shikoku — about 200 kilometers from where Mokuzu lived — and moving northeast. Despite the distance, the influence of wind and rain was considerable. Were it to come to the Kii Channel, off the west side of Wakayama Prefecture, the distance would shorten to 100 kilometers.

The rain flayed the window of Mokuzu's study room. He disliked the noise and feared the glass might break. He decided to quit the letter. He closed the storm doors. The old browned cord of the electric light that hung from the ceiling still swayed, as did the shadow of his hand resting on the letter.

He had not yet had supper. He proceeded with the letter and was becoming engaged in it when Ran came banging on the door — "Dad's asking your help to cleat the temple storm doors or they'll blow away!"

He perceived the increasing fury of the typhoon by her words and by the wind that gushed in as she opened the door a crack.

Doyu had pulled out many thin planks from the storage space under the floor. Micha was shining a flashlight as he nailed them aslant. The doors were shaking, warping, and indeed any moment going to blow away. Mokuzu supported them so that Doyu could drive the nails in true. They all three got drenched like brine-swept fishermen on a deck.

Branches from the old pine in the front garden were being carried off like leaves. Through the dark came tearing sounds from the chestnuts on the back mountain. Many unripe burs were flying down over the roof of the main building and being washed to the gate.

"Mokuzu, it's no ordinary typhoon!" cried Doyu.

"How is it different?" Mokuzu asked innocently.

"It knows no moderation and intends only to do damage!"

Doyu and Mokuzu went around to the moss garden side and there too affixed slanting boards. The moss garden was flooding with water from the mountain and especially from the little pond under the mountain.

"This'll do. Now to your cottage!" Doyu had to shout to be heard. They reeled before the wind through the wash.

"Watch out, Mokuzu! The gate could topple any moment!"

The south garden of the retreat cottage was strewn with persimmon leaves and branches. The green fruits were being hurled like stones.

From the far end of the village came the clang of the fire bell, soon followed by a siren to call the volunteer fire squad. They would deploy to the river, to the ponds, and to the mountain foot to watch for ripped banks and landslide, while some went house to house to warn against the use of fire.

Mokuzu had long ago wished for great typhoons because disaster seemed better than silent gloom. Now as he assisted his father he saw he was not excited but was so cool as to be able to think of the next paragraph for his letter.

"Okay, that'll do. Thanks, Mokuzu. Don't catch cold, go scrub with a towel. Better get to bed early on such an evening."

Mokuzu returned to his study room. The electric light did not turn on. He went out again into the whirl. White waves of rain raked the night. He entered the kitchen cottage and ate some leftovers. The cottage creaked. Roof tiles were crashing somewhere. The bickering of anything metallic left outside indicated where it was being carried off to by the wind until it caught on something. But before long something else sounded.

Again he returned to his study room and sat in meditation form. The scraggy persimmon branches kept lashing the roof. Broken branches slid down with dislodged tiles. He felt that the green fruits and branches striking everywhere were impinging upon his own flank and back.

He must have dozed as he sat. There came a dull but massive vibration that lasted only a few moments. 'What was that? A most unearthly but definitely earthly sound! It occurred as I was dreaming and awakened me!'

He rushed out, but saw no change to the kitchen cottage, to the gate, or to the main building, where his family were asleep. He looked back at the retreat cottage and saw nothing strange.

He passed through the front garden, angled up behind the shrine to the little pond. He could see the row of laymen's tombstones, but the midmost area was vacant. He drew nearer. The shallow valley of the mountain was now a sharp valley. The earth and sand of the center of the graveyard had slid, razed the subjacent slope thick with camellias, traversed the path to the elementary school, and landed in the rice fields.

"Oh, it's this that made the sound! But why attack the dead? What an example of indiscriminate violence! So big a slide hasn't happened around here for hundreds or thousands of years. It is said, Rare is dear. Is that true? It could be cause for great regret.

421

'Great regret? Misfortune! Oh, no! I've been forgetting Ena! How could I be so stupid? If this mild mountain can slide, what about the cliff behind her house? It could be too late!'

Mokuzu ran with all his might. As if in a dream he ran through the wind-frenzied eulalia along the riverbank, the shortest cut to Ena's house.

'She told me today during lunch hour — she shrugged and said: "Today's a monumental day. The adults' problems will at last be settled. My parents will put their seals on a legal divorce paper. My father, Mitsu, my mother, my stepfather, and lawyers for both sides are meeting tonight at my house. As it's mainly about finances, every related child must attend. What a complexity of papers! I wish they'd be swept away by a flood!"'

Mokuzu was winded when he came to a halt below the pond under Ena's house. A barrier rope crossed the road. Mud had buried the road and invaded the roadside houses. In the area above the pond many roving flashlight beams and searchlights were illuminating the oblique rain. People were gathering at the site. Only a few had on raincoats.

Ena's house was nowhere to be seen. It had been whelmed by earth and sand that now lay dashed in the pond. The embankment was destroyed. The water must have flowed in due course down to the Sakura River.

Mokuzu ducked under the rope and advanced nearer to where the house had been. A light shone on a new triangle of cliff. The trees above were fallen or standing askew. Not a piece of beam or post remained. None projected anywhere from the pile of mud. The house must have been pressed down completely and carried quite far.

'Why do these people burble so? They're taking advantage of the dark to hide their expressions of delight at others' misfortune, spewing every stupidity of the last five thousand years...!'

Quietly he left. 'Once long ago when I went to fish at the little pond up behind the shrine, I found the surface frozen solid. Disappointed, I left. Then I thought I would slide on the ice and went back, but it had melted away. What I feel now is similar to what I felt then....' He did not want to resort to words more tragic; his being was too humble to deal with them, and a more precise expression to describe the event would give Ena more pain.

He took the highway to go home. He walked mechanically. It was the least meaningful way to walk but afforded the most comfort. He wished the road would go on straight forever. 'Straight is easier to walk and bears no likeness to human life.

'Wind and rain shouldn't be hated for bringing sorrow to many hearts. They also bring relief to those who have had enough sorrow, and can give superb rest at the end.

'I have always keenly distinguished what I like to do from what I don't. Now I must realize that everything I ever liked to do is gone — it's become a matter of no importance.

'How important is asking myself "What is my original nature before my parents were born?" According to the Nirvana Sutra, Sakyamuni Buddha said every sentient being has Buddha nature. Nanyang Hueijung declared insentient beings also have Buddha nature. What a nonsensical discussion! It makes no difference to me who have no Ena, nor to Ena who has no me....'

Mokuzu spent the night in his room insensible of whether he was dreaming or awake. Doyu knocked at the entrance,

"Oii, Mokuzu! Quick — get up!"

When Mokuzu slid open the door a bright light at once came in. His father looked like a black obstruction. The sky was cloudless, but the garden was so littered with leaves and branches as to leave no space to set foot.

"A villager just came to ask me to perform a funeral. Do you know for whom?"

"Well, luckily I don't happen to be a priest. For whom doesn't concern me."

"Fool! For Ena! Horrible — the entire family was instantly buried alive!"

Mokuzu acted calm. "Did they find the dead?"

"Not yet, it's impossible by human power. They have to get a bulldozer or something...but surely everyone died. Why don't you offer incense if not flowers...before they set to digging."

"I will stay here and pray for the souls...Incense sends up smoke. There's no way to reach the dead in the earth. Wherever there is a soul, flowers will bloom before long without our offering them...."

"Hm, you play it cool. By your logic, heaven's mercy has buried them and there's no need of reburial."

"Exactly. Don't you agree with me, Dad?"

"I know you were going to marry her...."

Doyu left Mokuzu alone. The back of his bald head was round. So were his shoulders. His body was not so big as Mokuzu had remembered it.

Mokuzu closed the door. What light came in came only through the cracks of the storm doors. He heard the sound of clogs. His parents and Ran were descending the stone steps.

35

A Baby

Mokuzu rarely opened the storm doors. The bright sun, fresh breeze, and gay scenery only stung his spirit. He wanted to become sedimented. Indeed his dark and sultry cave together with his body odor brewed a suitable air for his inactive, deposited spirit. Softly and warmly it enwrapped him, without criticism or note of caution.

To avoid contact with the outside world when he had to go to school, he covered his head like an Arab woman. For an actual cloth he substituted a thorough indifference toward others and minimum relations with them.

When the balmy autumn weather turned unsteady with frequent thin cold rains passing along the mountains, he returned to his childhood habit of spending hours beside the little pond under the mountainside at the west end of Tangenji.

On the lusterless grass sat a frog made logy by the cold. Mokuzu gazed at it, not comprehending why it sat in the same spot for such preposterously long hours.

'What are you sensing and thinking? Why are you here, sitting so still? You may like to ask me the same, but, you know, we live in entirely different worlds and have nothing to do with each other, though we happen to be living at the same time and place on this earth.' He thought of two of Issa's haiku:

> O frogs —
> you play hide-and-seek
> under the blades of grass.

> You frog,
> how intent
> on the game of outstaring me![1]

Mokuzu could not treat the frog like a human child. 'Between us I feel there's an immeasurable profound gap such as I see between star and star. Seeing the chub, dace, and crucian beneath the water gives me the same feeling; I've been baking and eating them unconcernedly all these years, yet we're worlds apart.

He could nonetheless sympathize with the poet's compassion for the weak:

Quick, baby sparrows,
escape,
here comes a horse!

Strike not that fly,
behold its hands and feet,
it begs for life.

Dear flea,
jump not!
Below is the Sumida River.

Watch out,
grasshopper,
I'm turning over in bed.[2]

He also sympathized with the poet for his solitude.

Cat — how filthy
you are! Yet,
you have a wife.

Come play with me,
poor baby sparrow
left motherless.

Come along,
lone horsefly,
I too am alone.

Why turn away,
first firefly of the season?
It's just me.[3]

Mokuzu recalled with some yearning the figure of Unkai meditating on
the veranda of Ryotanji from morning to night, day after day, except for when
there was business to tend to. He never asked him why he meditated so much.
'I'm relieved I didn't ask. He might have been at a loss for an answer...Asking
is another way of hurting; it can recall an unbearable wound.'

He remembered as though it were yesterday Reiho cursing Unkai. 'He
spoke as he liked: "Look at him — he's worse than a rotten dame. All day he
acts dead. I bet the sum total of his type is what's tilting the earth. Why isn't

he eaten by a shark, at least in his dream? After coming here he never sweated anything but cold sweat. A man is made for action!"'

Mokuzu could not fathom why Unkai devoted himself to sitting meditation, but he supposed he had some reason for not doing anything else. He thought he had more in common with Unkai than with Reiho or a frog.

'With Teacher Docho I read *Jau lun* by Sengjau. There was the passage, "The universe and I have a common root. All creation and I are thereby of one flesh."[4] Are Ena and I of one flesh? If so, then in theory I am dead with her and yet she is alive with me. In chapter 90 of *Daji jing* mention is made of eternal peace: Our life and death are an event in eternal life, whence our life and death are eternal peace...if I remember it right.

'Oh well, of what use is such empty theory? It makes no solid sense to me. It seems all Buddhist doctrines are mere traces of the desperate fight to find that philosophers' stone presumed to turn things to gold and to heal any illness.'

There was a flicker of snow, but the moon was appearing over the roof. The starlight on the frozen treetops reminded him of Ena's smile. The weeds along the path and even the trace of a mole in the garden reminded him of her.

Winter vacation set in, and the New Year was approaching. Farm children came out to fly kites in the fields and on the riverbank. Cheered at the sight of snowflakes, they ran about with their homemade bows and arrows, sometimes dragging sleds.

A kite flapped on an electric wire. A mitten lay among the eulalia roots.

In February the scent of plum was carried like a stream on the wind to every house corner and to the gardens, pondsides, and mountain skirts. The ample smell entered even Mokuzu's closed room through the cracks of the storm doors. The well-rounded flower buds were cuddlesome.

In March the reddish purple agglomerate flower buds of the daphne were still tight, as if fearing a late snow. On the south slopes protected from the north wind, already some butterbur flowers had opened and several field horsetails were shooting up. A single dandelion appeared to have opened only to ascertain the suitability of the weather; it was pale, its beauty tragic.

All over again this year too the curtain about to rise on spring was keeping the audience in suspense. 'No — last year it rose at once! Every nook and corner of the stage was spring, and for Ena and me it was mid-spring, with everything beginning to grow. But this dark change was so abrupt! The curtain dropped, and its heavy velvet lets through no light.'

Mokuzu wanted to protest that he could not face spring again without its heroine, but there was no one to appeal to. The buds, the flowers, the sky, the clouds, the wind, the water, everything pierced him like needles. He was as helpless as a shorn sheep. A manslayer dragged by detectives to the scene of his crime may feel he is being put into hell. Mokuzu as he faced the same spring without his truelove felt he was being put into an isolation ward of a mental institution in heaven. He had to expose himself to an utterly strange sensation.

'Shall I call on Unkai? He told me I can return anytime, especially when I feel I have no other place. He said Ryotanji is my "second home." What a nimble, bald expression! He had foresight! A second home is where I can't live in my way, where at most I'll be allowed to live, because a first home where I can live in my way is not allowed. It could be my fate.

'Yes, I'll go and live seated beside Unkai heedless of morning and evening as if ten years, a hundred years, are but a day...seeking nothing, letting the clouds float as they like, the water flow. The leaves will turn and fall, the flowers bloom and drop...two shadowy figures, one young, one older, coexisting with the bryophytes in the damp at the west veranda of Ryotanji, where no sun comes in under the tall cryptomerias and the pine mountain, in the western region of Kyoto, where the capital of old buried its dead....'

Toward the end of March on the night before spring vacation, Mokuzu visited his father in the main building and told him,

"Dad, tomorrow I'm going to Ryotanji to see Unkai. Have you anything to say?"

Doyu was warming his hand over a big celadon porcelain brazier as he faced his personal vermilion-lacquered dining table. He was sipping warmed sake. For relish he had salted bonito guts and boiled spinach with soy sauce.

At a corner with her back to him, Micha was counting coins with undivided attention. As long as she could not verify the accounts, she could utter no sound of either grief or cheer.

Ran was in her room, perhaps arranging photo prints of popular singers.

"Oi, why don't you at least offer tea instead of counting dirty money?" Doyu spoke with a queer intonation.

"Shuh! Why should I offer tea to a man who drinks up all we earn?"

"Not for me — for Mokuzu."

"What? Since when have you been here? I didn't know if you were living or not, you haven't appeared for so long."

"Such words to your son — you're coldhearted to your children as well as to your husband!"

"Don't be ridiculous. You're foul, making every excuse not to go out to deliver the charm paper: 'Today the weather's wrong,' 'There's an unpleasant fellow in that town.' But you never skip a day of drink. It's I who support this family."

"Don't mind about me. I came only to tell you that. Good-bye." Mokuzu stood up to leave, but Doyu detained him,

"Wait a minute, Mokuzu. Hey, Micha, give him some pocket money. He's going to meet with a certain Unkai in Ryotanji."

"Thanks, but I have the money you gave me last summer."

"You didn't spend it? Indeed, who would pay the trees and mountains for their pears and mushrooms?"

"Mokuzu doesn't drink, like you," Micha interjected.

Ignoring her, Doyu chanted,

"Misery makes strange bedfellows....If on the road you meet a master swordman, offer up your sword; but unless he be a poet, offer not your poem, *hee hee hee!*"

His inebriation made it hard to distinguish to whom he was being cruel, himself or another. The roll of his voice was as unsteady as a low-flying airplane. He kept on,

"Yet there's another saying, 'Conceal your grief from him who grieves or you shall kill you both,'[5] *ha ha ah aah — aghh —*" His strange laugh became an asthmatic cough.

Mokuzu silently left, but as he closed the shoji Doyu again threw him his words,

"Your teacher Setsuro must have taught you *Jietzy-yuan huachuan*. Remember the advice: 'Should the student wish to paint in the manner seemingly free of the principles, he must first master the principles. Should he wish to paint the easy-looking painting, he must first master the difficult-looking painting. Should he wish to paint in the concise style, he must first master the complex style.'[6] I mean, in some ways meeting with that barbarian Reiho or that calculating Luri could be better than meeting with Unkai."

Next morning Mokuzu walked to the bus stop. On the low veranda of the house facing the road, Yosetsu was engaged in reading a newspaper. Startled by Mokuzu's appearance, he hunched a shoulder, and shot forth a glance.

'A quite unpleasant guy,' Mokuzu thought. 'If he'd be more open, I'd not grudge him a morning greeting.'

His eyes darted back and forth. Finally he stood.

'I see, he has some business with me.' Mokuzu opened his mouth to speak, but just then Yosetsu turned and repaired with a slight stoop into his house. Mokuzu could see only his back but was sure he was rubbing his hands together.

Mokuzu looked down the road. A new concrete bridge crossed the Sakura River. There was no bus in sight. But again there was Yosetsu. When did he rematerialize? He was approaching, rubbing his hands. But his eyes were looking elsewhere, so Mokuzu supposed he might be going elsewhere;

indeed, he ignored Mokuzu, even passed him by. Then of a sudden he turned and regarded him flush. His eyes seemed to spin, and he smiled as if meeting a best buddy and scanned him from top to toe, toe to top, deliberate as a crawler.

"Where do you intend to go?" he asked at last. Mokuzu thought, 'Were I Reiho, by now I'd have knocked him down.'

He indicated the direction of east.

Yosetsu's smile spread and he put out a feeler,

"I see. You must be intending to call on Mr. Naito's or Mr. Toyota's office, hm-hmm."

The names meant nothing to Mokuzu. He saw the bus coming and gestured with a sweep of his arm.

Yosetsu ducked, but relaxed when he sensed that Mokuzu was indicating the bus. Softly he said,

"Good luck, though I have no word on where you're going," and he smiled complacently.

In the bus Mokuzu wondered what was unsettling Yosetsu and at once causing him to smile. He made as if to brush clean his shoulder.

He did not know that Yosetsu had become guardian of the two children of Ena's father and Mitsu. Not having attended the night meeting, they were the sole surviving kin.

'Dad's suggestion has some truth. If I go to Unkai my mind could further darken, which could be a fatal misfortune for me. I have second thoughts about sitting with him all day. Isn't it like a leech and an earthworm, or rotting fish drifting with fragmented seaweed by the shore?

'I don't welcome having my depression disdained by Reiho. He'd seize a man's intestines and feed them to a dog...yet, there would be Luri. Would she concern herself with my health, asking with a frown, "What's matter? Your face is so pale!" Or would she act distant because I left Ryotanji without telling her? When angry, she was like a glass flower in a glass cube. Her nature was to love the helpless who were attached to her.

'I am indeed troubled, not knowing where I am going as the bus carries me along! Should I choose by self-divination, like Margaret plucking cornflower petals for the love of Faust...?

> 'Now I number the flower for my lot;
> He loves not, he loves me — he loves me not —
> He loves me! — Yes, thou last leaf, yes![7]

'Unkai will sow fine seeds of affliction on moist sterile cotton to germinate them. Reiho will let any such thing blow away and not care whether it's by the wind of spring or winter.

'Well, going to Unkai would inevitably mean facing Zen Master Hanun, who is a tree before arctic blasts. If I go to Reiho I can see Luri, who is a fresh spring bud. Which would be more helpful to this baby bird fallen into a well?'

Mokuzu chose to visit Luri and Reiho's office, the address of which he vaguely knew. Each time he asked and was told the way, he felt like an inorganic football being tossed about. At last he stood at the door of an old building in a deteriorated, blind alley. Anyone with social experience could have told at a glance that the building was vacant. Unknowing, Mokuzu loudly called out and repeatedly knocked.

His tenacity brought from next door an old woman who appeared to have just gotten out of bed. Without hiding her suspicion, she gestured as if shooing away a dog,

"Can't you see it's vacant? Has been for a year."

When she realized he was a mere boy, she became kinder,

"They went to Nakagyo Ward. Eh?...on foot? Well, you can walk, but it'll take till sundown even in this small Kyoto. Catch the streetcar and head for City Hall, then ask again. Are you the kid brother of that miss? You look like her. Wait — " She went in and returned with an address on a paper.

Mokuzu was instructed to watch for the sign "Seiun & Co." He got off the streetcar at the intersection of Karasuma and Oike and walked east. Oike was the city's main and widest street, having been widened in 1945 just prior to the end of the war. The government, fearing the spread of fire from air raids, had ordered the removal of the houses on one side. Now zelkovas lined both sides. Mokuzu kept walking, checking each new and old signboard. He had to strain to see the ones across the street.

There were few retail stores. Most buildings were drab, the work within being mainly the clerical work of banks, a post office, insurance and trade companies, and various unions and associations.

He came to where he could see a building with a roundish red crane, trademark of Japan Airlines Co., Ltd. From there he saw what he was looking for, a white three-story building down a bystreet.

It was inferior to its taller neighbors and also unlike them had opaque windows with iron bars. The door was so heavy that he had to brace his feet to avoid being tumbled forward by its pull. Inside, in the manner of a bank, a counter divided the interior. He saw several blue-uniformed young women busily counting with abacuses and drawing up papers. He could see no farther; there was another wall and a passage.

'I must be mistaken. He couldn't have so many employees. I'd better leave, but first I'll make sure...amazing, not a one is looking at me!'

430

A uniformed guard of stubborn bearing stepped out from the interior. 'He must have had his eye on me from the start. What an ill manner!'

"May I help you? This is Seiun and Company." He was only superficially polite.

"I came to see Reiho."

"Reiho? Would you mean our president?"

"President? Yes, if it's Reiho. I'd like to see Luri too."

"Luri? The vice-president?...Who the deuce...uh, may I ask who you are?"

"Mokuzu."

"Please wait." He picked up an interphone, pushed a button, and began to explain. Suddenly he humbled himself,

"Sir, I shall directly usher him up." He turned to Mokuzu, "Sorry to make you wait. Please follow this way."

The stairs to the second floor were richly carpeted. A number of the varnished wood doors along the hallway were shut tight. The guard brought Mokuzu to the farthest and knocked.

"Come in." It was surely Reiho's voice.

Reiho had two guests, but he abandoned them, came to the door, and seized Mokuzu by the shoulder,

"Welcome, welcome! You came at last! I was waiting for so long — what were you up to, eh? Well, you see I have guests, so why don't you wait, hm, it'll finish very soon," he said as he led Mokuzu behind a curtain, where another uniformed guard stood. Reiho ordered him to serve Mokuzu coffee or tea and returned to face his guests across a low table.

The area occupied by him and his guests had a thick carpet and fancy chairs. Behind him was a majestic rosewood desk and swivel chair, evidently for his exclusive use. Mokuzu was reminded of the parlor in Ikuta, Kobe, where once he had gone with Reiho to receive money for Zen Master Hanun-kutsu. Outside the window had been seascape. Here, beyond the opaque glass and iron bars, would be another dreary building.

Mokuzu sat on a sofa inside the curtain. The guard, a somewhat tall man, boiled water and served him tea.

"I know you. Don't you remember me?" he said in a muted tone. Mokuzu had no memory of him.

"Perhaps I made no impression. But I know you. I lived near Ryotanji. The name's Sako."

"Oh, you were with the police. What brings you here?"

Sako urged him to speak more quietly and said,

"I quit. The work's not so different — it's a matter of where you stand. This is more interesting, and practical." He smiled.

Mokuzu could not comprehend him. He was seven or eight years older than Reiho and had more education.

Outside the curtain a raised voice remonstrated, "Mr. President, that is why we are asking you to postpone only three months more. Here you can clearly see our repayment plan."

"Mr. Nagai, this is no repayment plan but merely your business plan, that is — your hope. You can despise me for my lack of education, it's okay by me, and in fact I haven't the talent to understand what you're showing me here. You're a specialist in your textile business, but you can't expect me to understand all your processes from production to marketing. I have no way to verify your paper. But I tell you, I know my own business." Reiho also talked loudly.

"Mr. President, we aren't asking you to understand our business; we're just asking for an extension."

"Listen more than you talk, Mr. Nagai. I have a special guest and I'd like to cut this short. I don't want to be deceived by your expert knowledge. Besides, I don't care how or where you get the money. My concern is the simplest: Just return my loan according to the terms we agreed on. You have fifteen more days. If you can't make it, too bad for you. I'll have no alternative but to seize your factory. If you don't like that, you can offer me your house, the one at Kamo. No need to vacate, just arrange a mortgage. For now, that's all. Hey, Sako! Take these people down and advise them on a mortgage settlement."

"Oh, no, please give us a little more time!"

Sako promptly left Mokuzu. Reiho came in smiling. "What trash! My business has no use for their business plan!"

Sako hastened the guests downstairs with menacing words.

The telephone rang. Reiho picked it up and at once lit a cigarette.

"What?...Yeah, yeah, bring everything — the kid's desk, the bedding.... Yeah, everything if it has the least value. But see that he helps with the loading. If you guys do it alone you'll be incriminated for taking it by force. Make him help — it'll prove he agreed to our policy...huh-hmm...okeydoke, 'bye now."

As soon as he finished, he took a square bottle of whiskey from the cabinet, poured a glassful, and emptied it at a draft.

"Well, well, Mokuzu, long time no see! Want some?"

"No, thanks."

"Of course, you can't even take coffee. All right, how about a cigarette?"

The interphone buzzed.

"No kidding? He came with his wife? Swell. Treat 'em civil. Didn't you say her father is on the prefectural assembly?...Careful, they're liars...

432

What? He brought the bond for the mountain? Then hip 'em to show us the mountain....Sure, I'll be down in a jiffy."

He hung up and explained,

"Some folks are here to show their mortgage. I gotta go. It'll take under two hours. I assume you'll stay the night? Why didn't you choose the weekend? Now I'm too busy to talk."

"I'd like to know where Luri is."

"Luri? Ha-hahh! You came to see her, not me."

"It isn't so definite, Reiho."

"Then why don't you come along — we can talk in the car. Don't look so serious, I'm only joking. I shouldn't be mean. I know you want to see her and you've a right to. You'll find her in our living quarters, on the third floor."

Reiho as he went down met Sako coming up.

"I'll be out a while. Keep the lid on!"

"How do I treat him?" Sako indicated one of the shut doors.

"Make him continue. No pain of sitting in lotus position ever killed anyone. But remember, never display violence."

'So this is Reiho's world? An ulcerous stomach couldn't be more deteriorated. He can't see a person at all. I came to a place least fitting my nature. It's stingy as a sea urchin!' Mokuzu went to the third floor and knocked.

The door had an ugly little hole with a lens in it. There was the sound of a chain being unhooked.

"Mokuzu! How good of you to come see me!" Luri embraced him. Her long hair as it brushed his cheek felt like tears.

"How you've grown!" Indeed her eyes showed tears.

'Her face is so pale. She's more depressed than me.'

Luri led him to a living room. She had been drying diapers with an iron. There was a neat pile of them.

"I'm so glad to see you, Mokuzu. I was beginning to believe I never would ever again. I learned you went to your native home. How are you there?"

"Fine."

"You're lucky you have someplace to go home to."

"I didn't know you had a baby."

She smiled faintly. On her brow were fine vertical lines he had never noticed before. He sensed she was quite depressed, or at least feeling she was, and was spending her days in tears.

She looked toward the room where the baby slept and said simply, "The father is unknown."

Mokuzu almost asked "What do you mean?" but quickly presumed there was some expectable and unwelcome cause. He did not want Luri to feel

433

pressed to speak about her misfortune, which no doubt she was well aware of. Yet she began,

"If you were me, how would you escape? I always think I have only one of three choices — to hang myself, to kill him and burn him with this building, or to lose my mind entirely. Of course being bright and clean, you wouldn't get into this sort of mess in the first place...."

She did not look at him, and her voice had none of its onetime spirit. Mokuzu could not introduce his own problem, his intractable misery over the loss of Ena.

'I came expecting her comfort, but I must contain my problem and release my atrophied nerves to receive her complaints; it's the least I can do. I'm like an oak with both its vascular and cribriform tissues eaten away by a long-horned beetle, and yet it must shelter a person from heat and rain. Be that as it may, where did her bright, even coquettish, nature go?'

"Mokuzu, I'm scared. I'm falling headlong into a bottomless pit and all the while I wish I could faint, but I know I'll be jolted awake with ice water or liquid ammonia. I'm forced to face the terror. What can I do?"

She ignored her tears. Mokuzu had no choice but to offer his handkerchief. She wiped her nose and continued,

"How old are you...getting to be fifteen? You're too young, regardless of your talent. You're but a fledgling angel. Your keen sensibility, pure sense of justice, and glowing hope can't equip you to fly into the stormy sky to fight that monster bird Garuda. There's no way you can rescue me!

"If only I'd chosen to live in the remote country, even in a tattered house! How I long for a simple bucolic life!"

Mokuzu was amazed at the likeness between Luri's wish and Ena's dream. 'But Luri's wish is permeated with damp gloom. Ena's dream held genuine warmth. Her motive was constructive. Luri wants to escape and is giving up even that.'

"Mokuzu, I was wrong about Reiho. He isn't just a savage beast. Actually he's endowed with a distracted madness as well as an elaborately calculated meanness.

"The A-bomb does more than ruin the human habitat and carbonate all love between man and wife, parents and children, as our Zen master apprehended. I now realize it makes people unimaginably horrible, fit to be jailers of hell. I knew many people do evil even as it tortures them, but I never imagined anyone could do evil for pleasure."

"Then his nature isn't merely crude?"

"It's that, but also so meticulous. How the two can coexist I don't know. He'll swing a sledge hammer down on someone without a second thought, and also split hairs. Remember how he ate fish? Contrary to his usual roughness, he picked clean the bones and left them a perfect skeleton on the plate. I should have realized then about his hidden nature. By that I'm tortured every night. He catches even my tiniest faults; worse, he forces me to commit obvious evils whenever he's used up whatever materials he has to accuse me with. So I'm endlessly tortured. It's absurd — and a miracle my head isn't yet broken!"

Mokuzu knew he ought to ask her to speak further. But knowing his own mental state to be a winter sky with occasional sleet, he did not open his mouth. Luri was oblivious of him.

'I don't know how grave her suffering is; but being partial to one's own misfortune and unable to care about another's is the worst type of suffering — though my criticism should be aimed at me too!

'Well, I have to become more honorable. Oda Nobunaga was said to have attended his father's wake in the barbarous costume of a warrior so as to remain ready for a surprise attack. I have to live by taking every good part of Ena into my life. I must think whether she is happy to see me living like unclear weather with day indistinguishable from evening. Yes, I need to see that I have to live not only for myself but for her!'

"Mokuzu, with him money isn't all or he could just issue loans and make his profit — but no, his aim is to inflict suffering. That's why he takes for security things worth several times what he lends — shops, factories, houses, farmlands, mountains. Then he prays that he won't be repaid. He even contrives such circumstances. So he gets back no capital or interest but claims his security, and controls his debtors.

"But that too isn't all. His design is to make people borrow who don't need to borrow. Then they and their families are ruined because he uses every trick to keep them from repaying him. It's crazy. His effort is not how to regain his capital but how not to.

"And what kind of people don't need to borrow in the first place? Mostly the rich, with high reputations. I know quite a few school principals, professors, members of the education board, heads of departments of the tax office and the police force, some famous priests, artists, members of the city assembly — all victims of Reiho's gusto for torture. Some were driven to suicide. And he's making up a new list all the time."

Luri talked in a restrained manner and glanced repeatedly at the door.

Mokuzu did not yet understand what really was depressing her so. 'As Reiho brewed, so must he drink. Why should she be bothered by his malefactions?' But his short-circuit question was quickly resolved by her further disclosure,

"Mokuzu, he uses my body to trick them — and how I'm devastated!" Luri crumpled to the carpet with suppressed sobs. Mokuzu saw through her loose-knit cardigan and realized for the first time that she was getting lean. He thought he knew the line from her armpit to her loin to be more full.

"If I refuse, he beats and kicks me till I can scarcely breathe. His karate is useful only to strike terror into the heart, and he uses sitting meditation to brainwash. I hate that karate teacher Rangai and also Zen Master Hanun for putting a bare sword into a madman's hands!

"He's also using my faults to keep me hostage. I have to obey. Then can you imagine what he does after a day of making me sleep with someone he tricked? He interrogates me about what the guy wore, how he entered the room, how we talked. Reiho gulps whiskey with inflamed eyes and keeps up his inquisition no matter how I'm exhausted and begging him to quit. He asks even about size, length, how it is when I handle it, what I do with my mouth, and if I omit anything or change my words, he turns blue and kicks me till I really faint away. He pulls my hair, drags me about, tears off my clothes, yet he never ever has slept with me, never even kissed me! It would be so much easier if only he wanted me!" Luri's cries sounded like vomiting.

The baby was awake, crying full force. Luri's weeping was heavy from her cramped posture. The baby's cries were open, sharp, even bright, as if coming from an organ whose function was solely to cry. The wall seemed almost to stagger back.

Luri showed no intention of rising from her knees. Mokuzu went in to see the baby. It was on a bed...eyes tight creases, mouth open and wavering, fists raised, springy legs kicking away a thin cotton blanket, face congested red, large tears sprouting. He felt strange seeing the nub of its nose, seemingly the only place dissociated from the action of crying.

He retrieved the cotton blanket from the floor and wrapped the baby in it. So violent was the baby against his bosom that he had to grip hard to keep it from slipping. 'The smell of milk...Luri's?'

He realized that the diaper was soaked and went to the living room to the pile of diapers. Luri was leaning against the sofa, eyes vacant. At the bed he thought, 'This is absurd! There are deep-red sores on its thighs!'

He was reminded of the sight of his father and sometimes of Gyodo changing Ran's diaper after she was burnt. 'The past is so distant as to be perfected; it's untouchable by any humble human hand!' He cleaned and powdered the baby. It cried and wriggled, disturbing his concentration. Pinning the diaper was risky. He applied force to quiet its legs.

'Luri said the father is unknown. So what? To know the mother should be enough. Further, for a baby most important is to be well taken care of by whomever. It doesn't care who its parents are, nor what its environment is. No one has any excuse not to take care of it.

'What is unhappiness? It is the inability to see a more pitiful, more weak, and more suffering being than oneself.

'Now I really am beginning to see how I was wrong. I was fixing my sorrow at the center of my life and behaving as if I am the center of the world. How wrong! Having my own sorrow shouldn't allow me to do that.

'Then what should I do? Lift up my sorrow and cast it away as if to give my guts to pigs? No, that's impossible. What I should do is to compact and condense it and keep it in the bottom of my soul and never let it surface. If I want to see it I have to choose the deep of night, when no one can see it but me. I'll thus not ignore it but keep it with respect and love as a dear part of my life. Yet as soon as the morning star appears, I have to lock it up. Sakyamuni Buddha was awakened by seeing the morning star. I too must be awakened by its light, and throughout the day I'll keep regarding plants, animals, and people more wretched than I.

'When I see others' unhappiness, I'll not see my own. When I see my own, my world will be poor and pitiful. I am the one to make my world dark or bright.'

Mokuzu walked to and fro embracing the wildly crying baby as he reflected on his shabby, mistaken way of life after losing Ena. The baby was hot, but Mokuzu's armpits were cold with the sweat of shame.

At last the baby calmed and gave only an occasional hiccup and faint shudder. Mokuzu took it to the living room.

Luri regained her composure, received it, and opened her bosom. The baby almost forgot to breathe in its eagerness to suckle.

"Thank you, Mokuzu. You are kind even to a baby," she said like dew dropping on water. Mokuzu thought he was kind not "even to a baby" but because it was a baby.

"Luri, why don't you tell your problem to the police? You may have your sore spot, but you can accept a fair judgment, and you'll be free of Reiho's..."

"It doesn't work. I tried. I had a nodding acquaintance with that assistant inspector Sako, you know? As usual, Reiho grew suspicious of the relationship and locked us in a room for observation. Sako's odd. There we were, in danger — and he quickened his interest! Every noise made him nervous, yet he kept trying to touch me — the very thing Reiho had schemed. He was completely tamed by Reiho, and quit his public service, and is now one of Reiho's loyal servants."

"But Luri, Sako wasn't all the police. You're not married, so why don't you walk out? Or if married, you can divorce. Either way, you can steal off and meanwhile disappear."

"You don't understand. Reality is more adhesive, it's not like chess. I'm not married, and that's why I can't divorce him. If married, it would be a matter of my being tortured legally with some limit. As it is, I'm tortured illegally and without limit. Anyway, this is a free world for torturing others, not for escape. Reiho's tied in with the yakuza. They quarrel among themselves over territory, but mostly they keep their agreements. Their formation and their communication network is more finely extended than that of the police or the post office. Twice I tried, but I was soon found and brought back, and — oh, it was horrible!" Luri showed a dark bruise at her breastbone. The baby was peacefully asleep on her bosom.

'Are Reiho and the yakuza so fearful? Is there no escape from their threat except to kill herself, or him, or go mad? It's unbelievable that there's a greater fear than fear of death. Luri seems paralyzed like a frog before a snake.'

Mokuzu fell silent.

"I'm sorry I exposed my trouble during your special visit. Don't think about me. Just take care of yourself and grow up fast. When you turn twenty and if you haven't forgotten me and if I still exist, please think about me also." They were her first considerate words. Then she too closed her mouth.

After a while she said,

"Will you stay the night? If you do, I can take a breath...no, you'd better not, don't, it's too dirty! You're a lily on a peak. You have to live at the front of the world. You must run on the highway and not step into the back lane. I think you shouldn't stay — yes, why don't you go?" She grew agitated.

Mokuzu, without speaking, remained on the sofa. Luri could not bear the idea of his being involved with Reiho, who she feared might at any moment enter. She also did not want to fail in her wish to have Mokuzu leave. She stood up with the baby and almost cried as she pulled his hand to hurry him to the door,

"Mokuzu, please! This is your chance to go. The longer you stay the

438

deeper you'll be dirtied and the harder I'll rebuke myself. Please leave at once and don't come ever again!"

Mokuzu was concerned that she might drop the baby if he did not comply, and he knew he could do nothing for her even if he stayed. He was pushed outside, and the door banged as it shut. At the stairs he regretted that he could not give her any consoling words. 'Why couldn't I say, "Don't worry, I'll take care of everything. In a few days you'll see yourself free of every trouble and Reiho carried away to a dump"?'

Her mention of her own culpability also weighed on his mind. 'It's said, Let sleeping dogs lie. I shouldn't replace her blizzard with a white-hot desert. I don't know what I can do for her.'

When he went down to the second floor he saw the shadow of someone withdrawing. Sako had been standing at the stairway. "Are you leaving? Won't you wait for our president to return, or should I give him a message?"

Mokuzu wanted to fire some forceful words at Sako but, unable to think of any, he merely said,

"Reiho is your president, not mine. I happened to be a sort of brother of his, of hers too; but for me Luri is a far more important person."

Despite his attempt to impart grave meaning, he recognized that his words lacked the keenness of a warning, the wisdom of an aphorism, and most of all, the force of a challenge.

It was raining and he walked along the street getting wet. 'My state is like constipation. I haven't a sword like a samurai nor a gun like a cowboy. How come? Is it because I am living in this sort of age, or because I have no power and wisdom? Or is it because I am coldhearted and lack compassion?'

The rain was lukewarm. He little recalled the figures of Luri and Reiho. But the appearance of the baby came to him vividly though he tried to erase it, like the windshield wipers of the cars trying to erase the rain.

'Such intense crying, face red and scowling, fists tight, legs flailing...then prolonged hiccups and occasional shudders...so eager for milk, almost forgetting to breathe...What is that? I'll say a baby represents us human beings on this earth more fittingly than anyone, more than everyone after all — Luri, Reiho, Zen Master Hanun, my private teachers, my parents, and so on and so forth.

'With the baby I felt a sensation much like what I feel toward Ena who is in the dark. What have they in common, she who is gone and it just come? "The starry heavens above and the moral law within"; these "two things," wrote Immanuel Kant, "fill the mind with ever new and increasing admiration and awe, the oftener and more steadily we reflect on them."[8] But for me the "two things" are definitely death and life.'

439

36

Struck on the Back of the Head

From the end of the school day until late at night Mokuzu could enjoy his own time. Otherwise, during the part of the day when he had to see his family, teachers, and classmates, he was careful to contain his emotions and act bright.

'No one should be allowed the insolence of transmitting the disease of melancholy, which is entirely a personal state. Surely nothing is more insane and infamous than lack of self-control.

'I've reflected like Rodin's *The Thinker*, and I've found that people expect only to be treated well and given pleasant feelings. It would be a pity to disappoint them.'

Mokuzu thus chose a time to be as he liked, when he could engage in retrospection and imagination; and the later the night the more he could immerse himself in his thoughts, with frequent soliloquies.

The faces, behavior, and words of all whom he had ever met appeared as he muttered in his room where no light was turned on. "Well, well, are you thinking my brain is your provisional residence or amusement quarters and you can come and go as you like? Fine, I know the drear of a vacant inn and a street without passersby. My brain would be vacant without you."

Ena was the guest of honor, nay, was invited and enshrined as the principal holy image.

"Ena, I am because you are. Without you, what would be the value of my life? You are the motive power for the beating of my heart. You are my blood. I live for your sake and share with you everything I hear, see, and think. My joy is your joy, my sorrow your sorrow."

At school he quickly saw what people expected and desired and why they were displeased, and he tried to relieve them. When his classmates fought, he arbitrated; when they wanted to play softball or soccer he made teams and played too. To those who were tired of the repetitiousness of school life, he suggested climbing a nearby mountain with lunch and a plan for various games.

Since the teachers evidently wanted their students to master quickly what they taught, during class breaks he helped those classmates who were stymied, and to him they said,

"Your teaching is easier to understand. You give relaxed and intimate examples, so we can increase our will to study."

In April at the start of the new term, he was elected president of the student council. Soon he reactivated all sorts of clubs, dividing and balancing

440

the budget, and arranged extramural contests and school sports and culture days, in addition to reestablishing safety, discipline, and beauty in school life. He also initiated clubs for karate and literature.

Some discontent arose toward his doings because of jealousy and misunderstanding, but he rejected no one and listened kindly to every complaint, thereby gaining more trust and respect all round. Even to those who destroyed school fixtures and bullied the weak, he did not object outright but was amicable as he gradually made them realize they were troubling others and debasing themselves.

Sharply and quickly he saw what people wanted, and he responded by relying on his bright brain and tough body, and, more essential, on his keen sense, like that of an osmatic animal, to sniff out disappointment, complex, and sorrow.

His teachers appraised him as kind, smart, and trustable, a model student, and predicted he would become a significant man.

The third year of junior high school was the final year of compulsory education. The homeroom teachers were responsible for career guidance, with its demands on their care and energy to counsel the students and parents, for the outcome could determine a student's entire life.

Mokuzu's homeroom teacher, Mr. Sato, had recently married into his wife's family, yet he was reputed to have a bold spirit and selfish ways. He was short and burly, with a sanguine face, his bearing suggesting the intrepidness of a viper. It was said he was quick to pick a fight with his fellow teachers.

He was devoted to a big motorcycle, which he lavishly washed at lunch hour with school water to keep it perpetually shiny. His students he divided to two groups, those who would continue school and those who had to find work. To the latter he was extra kind, teaching them about shops, factories, and companies, where most of them would work. After school he taught boys and girls alike the mechanics of a motorcycle and a car.

Mr. Sato was not required to give such instruction, but he sympathized with those youngsters who would soon be mixed in with adult workers, and frequently he said with emotion,

"At fifteen you should be adult. When you go to work next spring you'll realize your schooling was useless. I never observed that any detailed knowledge or moral words of the saints was effective outside the classroom. In my opinion school has the duty to inform you about the real world, how it is tricky and how money is important. We should be teaching you how to earn money and make connections; in society nothing's more important.

"Those going on in school have a preliminary term of three, seven, or ten more years before entering stern society. You have no such time. So I advise you to get the needed skills and any kind of worthwhile qualifications as fast as you can when you enter society. That's the only weapon you'll have against those others. Otherwise you can't buy even a house all your life. And, sorry to say, you'll be like your parents, who can't send their kids on in school. You were born into poor families and if you don't do as I say, you'll grow old poor, and poor you'll die."

Nearly a third of Mokuzu's classmates had to find jobs. Generally they were below average in their studies, but not owing to a dull nature; simply, they did not study much.

One day after school Mr. Sato invited them to a corner of the yard to demonstrate how to fix an old car. From there they could see the practice of softball and other field sports.

The car was parked under an evergreen magnolia. The smell of gasoline and grease together with the smell of the big white flowers gave Mokuzu a feeling of nostalgia and anxiety.

Noticing him, Mr. Sato asked, "What are you doing here?"

The question made no sense to Mokuzu. He reflected on himself as if in a daze, as was habitual with him.

"The course is open only to those who will take jobs."

"I know, sir. Please count me in."

"Don't joke! You have to advance to college, even to graduate school. Leave at once or you'll disturb these kids."

Feeling snubbed, Mokuzu withdrew. The fifteen or so students were again looking under the hood and attending to Mr. Sato's fluent explanation.

'What an impulsive conclusion! Can't he see most fields of Japan are planted only with rice?

'If I had Ena I'd choose our third way and neither get a job nor continue school!' He was almost pulled into his own world despite the sunny afternoon. 'Without her, what could I do but wander as a lonely beggar? I couldn't take it.'

About a week later Mr. Sato called him to an empty council room and said,

"Sorry, I never thought you'd have to get a job. Pardon my haste... coming from my long-cherished nature. But...who could imagine you not continuing with school? It's too odd! For whose sake is there higher education if not for the likes of you? In this age isn't a monkey sent into space and a dog taken to a beauty parlor and fed beefsteak?

"But I was amazed to find your family has paid no income tax for fifteen years. Your residence is big, but your finances are like Basho's dreams that run round a lorn field, no?

"I met with your parents. They're extraordinary, if in different ways. In

442

fact they greatly differ in personality. Each holds to an individual view, which makes for a perilous inconsistency in the home. But queerly their discord puts them in accord about your future, that is, they think you should decide your course with your own responsibility, and they'll neither impose any rights nor assume any duties.

"Let me sum up first what your mother said, though to sum up her garrulity is as hard as to traverse a briar patch. I reckon only a fire in the temple would have stopped her. I gather she's eager for your success, and the method is yours to choose, as it was for the others. Providing more education is a great parental achievement, but it has no relation with a child's attainment. If you fail in life because you didn't go on in school, you're proving you lack talent and are irresponsible, and anyway it's your fate, she said.

"Your father was quieter, more logical. I told him that of all our students you're the most qualified to receive higher schooling, and I said that way your future will open. Like a cat basking in the sun he enjoyed my words, and he said, 'Once at the north border of China there lived an old man named Seweng. One day his horse ran away, and at that he grieved. Then his horse returned with a fine new horse, and he was pleased. Then one day his son broke a leg falling from the new horse, and again he grieved. But the injury exempted his son from military duty, so again Old Seweng was pleased. See? Wondrous are the ways of heaven.'

"And he went on: 'I can't ensure my son's happiness if he receives higher schooling, nor can I know if he'd be unhappy taking a job. So I can't recommend either way. I think what I can do for him as his parent is not a thing at this juncture. He has to choose his way with his own will and responsibility. I'll not meddle in his affairs. Fortunately I have no money with which to control him, and fortunately I have this shelter, which he can use as he likes without charge.

"'He's fifteen, a good age to become free of his parents. He can become a beggar or a prime minister; I'll not complain. And whether he lives near or far I'll wish for his good fortune and observe without comment. Thinking my thoughts is my freedom, speaking them is not.' This I heard from your father.

"Your parents are strange. Never have I met their sort. Most I know only worry over their children from the maximum problem of their future to the minimum detail of checking that their fingernails are trimmed.

"But they are they, so it's up to you. Beginning in March you must be an independent man. How do you think about it?"

"It's okay, Mr. Sato. What you're saying isn't new to me; it's why I went to your after-school class the other day."

"Mokuzu, you're a fool. You may know who you are, but you don't know

443

society, so you're more of a fool than an ordinary fool. You won't suit the available jobs, but not because of poor health or no talent. You're too bright. Most likely you don't know who you are, after all. You're not normal. No abnormal man can stay long at the work of normal men.

"You don't know the jobs available to junior-high graduates. You must degrade yourself to a mere screwdriver, welding rod, or cart. Suppose you want a little better job, say, of an officer or a teacher like me. It's hardly better because there's little chance to exercise your creative ability. Mostly we must repeat like a tape recorder the basic knowledge and skills you mastered years ago. Yet even such jobs aren't open to junior-high graduates. You need a university degree.

"See? It's hard to get a more creative and humane job without more education. You must realize that being unable to provide education to one's children is a severe punishment allotted to incapable parents, the consequences of which fall to the children. In this society, missing the chance of an education is an evident form of punishment.

"You have to know who you are and what society is. You won't be satisfied with any of the slaving, mechanical jobs available to you. You'll be satisfied only when you can exercise your potential, which is exceptionally creative. You have to find a job that enables you to discover, invent, or create new things. Any other job won't do. It's essential that you advance your education to get a top-notch job. So, go on to senior high!"

'I can understand what Mr. Sato means. But it's amazing he can care about me while he must be busy for others and for his private matters.' Mr. Sato wiped the sweat from his red nose with his thick palm and hastened on,

"You are expected to be a leader — you have to reform society. We need your type to replace our present leaders, who are inadequate to improve the world.

"Luckily there's the Japan Scholarship Foundation. You take the government exam. It's tough, only a few dozen in the prefecture are accepted, but for you it will be like slicing tofu.

"The scholarship covers tuition, bus fare, clothes, and meals. Your parents say you can go on using the cottage. As a high school student you can take a part-time job if necessary.

"I understand you want to help your family by working full-time; you care about your aging parents and immature sister. But harden your heart for several years and study all you can. Be patient. When you perfect your studies you'll serve them far better than you would be able to now, right?"

Mokuzu wondered how this sweating, impetuous-natured man could care about him. He could not figure out the inevitabilities that would prompt such kindness, but his policy was to please others during the day, so he replied,

"Thank you. I shall do as you say if it pleases you."

Mr. Sato's eyes bulged, and he hit himself on the temple with his fist and cried,

"Don't be silly, it's entirely for your sake!...though of course I'd be happy if you'd take my advice, eh-hem!"

❧

Two students were chosen from Mokuzu's school to take the scholarship exam during summer vacation, Mokuzu and a girl named Minori Kida. They first had to take a physical exam. No physician had yet replaced Dr. Okada in the village, so they went to a hospital in the town of Kameoka.

Mokuzu had never spoken with Minori; she was in another classroom. Nor had he promised to go with her, yet she appeared on a bicycle at the steps of Tangenji.

It was early morning, when the bees were in the morning glories, a vapor was rising from the roof of the well, and the common cicadas were beginning to chirr.

"Why don't we go together?" she proposed.

"How nice of you to stop by. I intended to forget the exam. I'm not sure I want to go to senior high."

Minori wore a faded red blouse and faded blue skirt. She just smiled. He had to borrow a bicycle from a layman's house. They rode parallel all the way, which was mostly a mild downgrade, and could lightly converse in the fresh breeze.

Seeing Minori's girlish smile, maturing breasts, and waving hair and fluttering skirt, Mokuzu could not help recalling Ena.

'What blasphemy against Ena to think of her before the figure of Minori, and how insulting to Minori not to be considering her at all while I'm beside her!'

They were put together in a dark room for the X ray and had to undress from the waist up. Even in the darkness Mokuzu saw that Minori was shy about removing her white underwear. Her breast line surfaced softly in the dim light.

"Come around and take a look for the sake of your future studies," the physician said to Mokuzu when it was Minori's turn. Seeing her white ribs and sternum on the black screen, Mokuzu recalled Zen Master Hanun's foot. 'There's no gentleness or warmth to bones. It's like viewing a winter wind in some remote countryside. His and her bones are alike in construction, and are unexpectedly thin and fragile. Would Ena have looked so?'

When they came to their bicycles Minori smiled at him.

445

'Is she smiling because she was embarrassed to be half-naked, or because she feels somehow intimate after having her bones revealed?'

Returning uphill was hard. The sun beat down without mercy, and on both of them sweat ran in beads. Often Mokuzu had to wait when he reached the shade of a tree. He pitied Minori for having weak legs. Her front hair stuck to her brow, and sweat soaked her blouse. 'Were she Ena, I'd have already found a nearby mountain creek where we could drink and splash...!'

A large dump truck passed. Its smoke and dust obscured her as she followed a little behind him.

'It's sorrowful that because I already have someone in my heart she can't be given my regard and protection. Her life couldn't be easy if she's applying for the scholarship.'

Mokuzu was sad to see that his pure love for Ena and his common concern for Minori had the same root, yet the two feelings rejected each other like oil and water.

'I can see I'd be wrong to feel for Midori what I feel for Ena. Nevertheless, I'm wrong not to be kind to her.

'Romeo and Juliet were in a whirl of exclusive love and didn't see anyone else's trouble and sorrow.

'In contrast Sakyamuni Buddha and Jesus Christ extended their compassion to all, yet as far as I know they didn't love with their best ability any one person. Their ideal, abstract, un-physical, and un-daily love could hardly raise a single baby in a satisfactory way. A baby needs concrete love, or, should I say, ignorant love. Such love gives it life, and can nurse it, dress it, and keep it clean; and protect it from heat, cold, illness, and injury, and from beasts, and from other competing human beings. But then, this ignorant love toward a particular life restricts love toward any others, and even harms them.

'An inevitable consequence is that as our love toward a particular life grows purer, our love toward any others becomes less possible. My love for Ena makes me heartless to Minori...!'

When they came to where they had to part, Mokuzu at last told Minori with as much kindness as he could muster,

"Your fortitude more than qualifies you for the scholarship. I'm sure you'll do very well on the exam."

In response she said, "The written exam is from morning to afternoon, but please don't worry, I'll bring you lunch."

Hers was a tangible kindness, while he was meddling around in abstract, infructuous thought. He was ashamed.

A week later they went to Sonobe for the exam, taking the bus to Kameoka and a down train packed with beach-goers.

They found seats together. Their thighs touched, transmitting to one another a vital warmth. Mokuzu recalled going to Takahama with Luri, so long ago he hardly knew it as real. 'How awful, the longer I live the more there's suffering!'

He scrambled for a toehold against the sweeping billow of past events. There was no Luri, and no Ena who loved him. He focused a side look at Minori's bosom, flank, and abdomen faintly moving in rhythm. Soon he realized that she had to breathe one and a half times to his once.

The thirty or so examinees were seated three to a bench. The exam was five long pages that dangled down, with an extra page for filling in the answers. The questions combined math and science to test a student's ability to apply acquired knowledge.

Mokuzu solved them one after another without hesitation and answered with his cherished fountain pen given him by Unkai. When he finished he saw Minori directly ahead, bent over as if stuck fast to the table.

Left with copious spare time, he raised his hand to be excused. The monitor asked in a low, reproachful tone,

"Did you carefully go over everything?"

He wandered at length in the garden. Finally everyone else came out, with such comments as, "I'm hopeless — couldn't finish even half!" "Same here!" "It's crazy to give that many questions in so short a time!" "One guy left, did you see? Is he a simpleton or a genius?"

Minori plowed her way out to Mokuzu, her face wretched.

"I couldn't do it, I hadn't enough time, the last third I couldn't even read!"

"Minori, they're saying they managed barely half. You did better. Don't worry over what's done and I'll advise you on the rest. First, read every question, then answer beginning with the easiest and dismiss the hardest. Second, you're wasting time using pencil and then erasing: write in ink from the start."

Minori listened tamely and said, "How come you left early?"

"I found nothing difficult," Mokuzu replied honestly.

"That must be, but you're an exception."

The afternoon combined Japanese and social studies and required prolonged reading and writing.

"The morning was better," Minori moaned. "Again you left. Could you really answer everything?"

"Sure."

On the ride home, Mokuzu recalled the questions and had Minori recite her answers to score her result.

▪

447

The new term began. Then one early September day hot as summer Kiku unexpectedly returned. At the time she was working in Osaka at a factory that made household electrical appliances and was living with Gyodo in a rooming house.

Spotting her as he came from school, Mokuzu was alarmed.

True, Kiku had often replaced his mother in his infancy, and to see her should have been his delight. Occasionally she had brought home sweets and new children's magazines, and her gentle as well as lively appearance had brightened the drab and tasteless air of Tangenji. But by now Mokuzu knew that any unusual joyous excitement would be superseded by unanticipated grief. Moreover, pleasure lasted no longer than an autumn day, whereas sorrow printed a long shadow across the black earth.

He was right. Kiku came back abruptly though it was neither Sunday nor a holiday, and hastily returned to Osaka a little before sunset. She brought no sweets or magazines. But she left a curvature.

The world seemed to Mokuzu to begin to warp. The buildings, gardens, mountains, and fields bent like a straw in a glass of liquid, or appeared as if seen through thick lenses. Everything floated unsteadily, drooped queerly, and kept wavering.

Kiku came solely to report on Gyodo. She said he was acting odd. Since spring he was prone to skip his factory training school or his night school and sit inside all day without moving. Lately he was not even getting out of bed and was smoking and drinking immoderately.

She made breakfast and left for work at a regular hour, but often on her return found him as before, hunched on his bed, his head in his hands. All about him were cigarette butts and here and there scorches on the tatami from his lack of care with fire.

She would ask, "What's wrong? If you aren't well, why not call on a doctor? I'll go with you." But he seemed not to hear.

Whenever she told him not to be lazy, he lunged at her and beat her indiscriminately. She fled from the rooming house and peeped in at a corner of the window. His shoulders heaved like a bull's. He broke his desk, tore away the fusumas, upset the kitchen table, pulled down the electric light. He did not care about the dark.

When at last he calmed, he shook as if seeing a ghost, then moaned, then cried for help. Then he flinched as if in fear and uttered no further sound.

With the blanket pulled over his head he would endure, and later throw it off and laugh loud, then stand with vigor renewed. In a tone like stones pelting the walls he would sometimes sing —

448

"Ever for the Red Army!
In the face of many hardships!
Not a speck of incertitude have we!
A million miles of water!
Thousands of mountains to cross!
In a manner ever so blithe!
We cross and conquer them all!"[1]

Then suddenly he would strike a heroic pose as if before a multitude, and shaking his fist declare,

"Harken, comrades! 'Through our practice we discover the truth. Through our practice we confirm and develop the truth. Our recognition we develop from an aesthetic recognition to an active and rational recognition. Our rational recognition we guide to an active and revolutionary practice to remodel both our subjective and our objective worlds. Thus the forms of our practice, recognition, new practice, and new recognition endlessly rotate, and at each rotation our practice and our recognition advance a step higher. This is the epistemology of dialectical materialism. It is the view that unifies our study and practice of dialectical materialism.'"[2]

A while after, he would stick out his tongue, imitating a fox licking at oil.

Kiku furtively watched and was grief-stricken as she thought back on all Gyodo's hardship from infancy, which never brought him any reward, and now he was going insane. Ashamed to have escaped, she brightly reentered and humored and placated him as if he were a crying baby and soothed him to sleep.

Once he was asleep and her mind was eased, the fatigue of the day assailed her and she lay down in a corner of the room. Turning her eyes toward him again, she realized he was gazing at the wall with eyes gleaming a pale blue in the moonlight.

Day after day and night after night she took care of him without telling her parents for fear of worrying them, but at last exhausted, she came to ask their aid.

"What a headache! What are we to do?" Doyu was like a creeping winged ant. The short white hair at the back of his head, the neglected white whiskers...evinced no vigor. His shoulders too looked enervated.

"Worry won't mend a thing. To begin with, we must see him at once, and take him to a hospital if necessary!" Micha hotly remarked.

"How ruthful he should become a worse parasite than a newborn baby when I was about to have some peace of mind with Mokuzu free of my hand and only Ran left!"

"Don't speak nonsense! We make the children independent while they're well. When they're ill we must allow their dependence. You are their father

449

regardless. It's too early for you to be relieved of your care as long as you and they live. Don't act foul and unmanly!"

Catching the first bus, Doyu and Micha went next day to Osaka.

It was reported that when Gyodo saw his parents he took fright and edged to a corner, crouched, and pressed his head to the wall. Then, as if for the first time recognizing his father, he took fright anew. Soon a fire of hate flamed beast-like in his eyes; yet oddly the whites looked pale blue, even translucent. His entire body quaked with rage.

"D-d-devil!" he cried as he lunged at Doyu, and rapidly and repeatedly he clouted his bald head, though Doyu had turned to escape. Doyu uttered senseless shouts and cowered on his haunches on the road outside the rooming house. Micha restrained Gyodo's arm as best she could, crying, "Why? What? Gyodo! He may be wicked, but despite his failures he's your father!" As Gyodo winced, she seized the chance to motion to Doyu to escape. He crawled from under the arm she held and hid behind the building.

"Action speaks louder than words! He'll be killed by me! He made me mistakenly born! He gave me the virus!" Gyodo's voice grew hoarse from his exasperation and continuous exclamations.

Micha tenderly but firmly held his hand as she labored to calm him with agreeable responses. She spent what seemed to her an eternity at it and gradually succeeded. His heavy breathing subsided, also the fury in his eyes, and the passion by degrees oozed away, and he became expressionless, like a lump of lead.

Consoling, cajoling, she induced him to go with her to a hospital. "My poor son, you are a good, innocent boy. You are fatigued by many hardships. Your fatigue should be healed. You are a man with a strong sense of justice. You are an affectionate and dutiful son. You have to rest when you are tired. And we want to know what is the best way. We'll go to a hospital and ask a doctor what is best...."

Doyu, disoriented by fear and anxiety, stole mouselike from his shelter. He trailed his wife and son.

Catching sight of him, Gyodo showed renewed agitation, but only briefly. Micha kept up her assuasive manner and gestured to Doyu to follow quietly at a distance.

People on the street were suspicious at the sight of the mother and son with the father behind. Attempting to hide their suspicion, they too were suspicious-looking.

'My mother endured the fear and sorrow of being struck by my drunken father. It was the indirect reason for her years of hovering between life and death in the hospital,' thought Mokuzu.

450

'Now one of the sons she took pains to raise has become crazy and is boiling a hot magma to kill his father. I wonder why she's trying to stop him. And what does he see in his son's madness? He can't be blind to his own vices.

'My brother now resembles a religious fanatic. He seems controlled by some ultra being. His body stays in this world, but his soul is entrusted with a power that's manipulated by some part of the profound universe. Or should I understand his craziness as not a strange thing on this earth but merely one of its many productions, an excellently human phenomenon peculiar to human society?

'Shouldn't I fear I too will lose hold of myself? How can I defend myself from this invisible devil that is like an electromagnetic wave? But more urgent, how can I rescue Gyodo? It isn't right that he should be cooped in the storm of a magnetic field. What a gentle, earnest, and reliable brother he was! His good nature and great talent a million times surpass his faults. How senseless that his effort, kindness, purity, and suffering should be repaid with insanity! Such punishment is worse than the death penalty. Death is decorated with flowers, insanity with thorns. Death and insanity are like facing cliffs with life a meek flower blooming between.

'I am a meek flower. Am I bound to fade away? Or can I revive like a phoenix? It enters fire and is not burnt, takes no notice of blizzards and stormy seas, lives on and on, able to solve every dark problem and lead distressed and grieving people to a soft green field. Can't I do that?

'I now know I have been given all sorts of problems that many people have avoided, disregarded, and abandoned like trash. I must realize I am shouldering a heavy burden given me before I have really begun to live in this world. I am not invited by any of the pleasures that sing in praise of life — a convivial party, a merry picnic, invigorating skiing...success, distinction, enterprise, fame...I'll have nothing to do with applause, victory, audience.... My life demands that I clean up all those problems — it seems inevitable.'

"Mokuzu, I've never told you, but it's a fact. I had a brother named Kando, two years my junior. At age twenty-two he died soon after showing symptoms not much unlike Gyodo's. It is schizophrenia.

"The third year of Showa was a darker time than now. Radio began to be spread like television today. Yes, I remember the news that the Army's Kanto corps were invading deeper into mainland China on the pretext of defending Japan's interest in the Guandung district and in Manchuria, and at last they killed Chang Tsuolin by bombing his train. In those days the Chinese government, broken into North and South, was notified by the Japanese government that if a domestic war should affect Manchuria, the Japanese Army would not hesitate to take effective and suitable action to maintain public order. But the historical fact is that the Japanese government anticipated such a pass and maneuvered

451

behind the scenes to bring it on. Naturally the U.S. secretary of state, Kellogg, issued a notice that America would not tolerate Japan's notice to China.

"Within Japan the first universal suffrage was enacted in February. And articles on life imprisonment and capital punishment were added to the Maintenance of the Public Order Act to suppress the Communist Party. Day by day the enforcement of regulations was becoming more rigid.

"Well, in the previous year the banks became incapable of returning deposits. Hm! It was the onset of the so-called financial crisis. Scarcely a day passed without news of labor strikes or tenancy disputes in this town or that village.

"There was so little bright news. In that same previous year the American airman Lindbergh flew solo across the Atlantic. In Kyoto a trackless trolley was initiated, between Shijo-Omiya and Nishioji, yes, yes...

"Oh, sorry to talk of matters of no concern. At any rate, in that third year of Showa my brother was arrested in front of Kameoka Station. They said he had pounced on a woman in the street. It was a rainy June day. Many police in raincoats were called out. A crowd had gathered. I saw him bound with a rope and sent under guard to a police cell. And then? They just left him there, bound, without food or water. Six days later he died.

"I since learned about Hippocrates of ancient Greece. So fair and articulate a man! He concluded that even insanity must be regarded as a disease with its natural causes. He was the first to reject the superstition that madmen are possessed of the devil, or that they committed an unpardonable evil in a former life. Even to this day, commoners believe such superstition and think a madman and his family should be dealt with by the police rather than by medical treatment. Only recently are up-and-coming psychiatrists starting to catch up with Hippocrates' view. So, the cause and the treatment of the disease are as yet undefined.

"Oh, this too isn't what I really want to tell you. But one thing more I'd like to mention, about its genetic transmission. According to my reading, the incidence of schizophrenia is about 0.7 percent in either the Occident or the Orient. However, within the family of the patient — parents, children, grandchildren, siblings, half-siblings, nieces and nephews — it's much higher. There are of course many exceptions, but generally the familial incidence is more than 10 percent. Indeed, it's quite high.

"Yet environment is a significant factor. More, its inheritability isn't yet known, that is, how Mendelism applies to schizophrenia. Mendel was an earnest Austrian priest who established two laws of heredity. One is the law of dominance, which states that only the dominant gene appears in the first filial generation. The other is the law of segregation: both the dominant and the recessive genes appear, but separately, in the second filial generation. What we don't know is, which of these genetic heredities carries mental disease....

"I know I'm talking nonsense. On this matter I just wanted to confess there's no doubt I'm responsible for the heredity and the environment causing schizophrenia in your brother; and please note that you are in no less danger as to its occurrence.

"Everything for me goes athwart, and how pluckless I am! Mokuzu, I'll be killed any time by my son Gyodo. Today too your mother went to the hospital. Whenever she shows up, he wails, 'Let me go home, let me free!'

"He's cursing my blood, hating my evildoing, burning toward me an inexpugnable flame of indignation and vindication. He wants to crush my head. I admit if his justification is as large as an apple, his lack of justification is as small as its seeds.

"I don't expect your sympathy, but compare my life to eating apples. I tasted never a sweet one, only codlings.

"Even so, there were some delightful times. I was sent to be an acolyte, you know. Priest Mukai and my seniors admired my brushwork. He gathered my practice papers, bound them with silk thread, made a cover as if for a textbook, and proudly showed it about. I was in my glory!

"Another happy memory is of planting chestnuts. That I began soon after my father died and I assumed his role in this temple. From dawn to dark, day after day, I worked in the mountain to cut down the assorted trees, make them into firewood, clean the mountain, and at last do the planting. Then came the years of aftercare. I was the only person on the mountain. The hares, squirrels, weasels, and night creatures came up without reserve and disappeared after doing whatever they wanted.

"There were days when the snow danced and my hands were numb, days when I steamed with sweat and salt formed on my work clothes; yet, I never experienced days of greater contentment.

"Mokuzu, my hope is not that you'll advance in the world or make a fortune. You may think that's what you ought to do to help your insane brother, protect Ran, and nurse your old parents — and I thank you for your great tenderness. But achieving those two things is as hard as going through a needle's eye and as tricky as doing a handstand atop a flagpole.

"Look to yourself. My hope is that you'll regard your affairs and disregard all else. Be wise, be kind, for your sake. Love yourself, don't work like fury, don't be excessively patient. Be kind to yourself and learn how to compromise with hardship. Moderation is everything to health. It's great wisdom. Apply it even to eating food, and how much more to hardship. Reserve your strength. Never spend all your ability.

"You know I'm a failure rather than otherwise. Unwillingly I entered the

453

priesthood, and unwillingly I lost the land I inherited. I became poor, but please know I never wished it. I maltreated your mother and might again. But note, I never hated her or enjoyed hurting her. I made a poor and discordant family, causing misery to my children, and at last Gyodo has gone stone crazy. But I never wished even a moment of their suffering.

"What does it all mean? No doubt my wish and my state have been at odds, that is, my life has been unhealthy. People, including me, may blame me for my laziness, irresolution, poor spirit, incompetence, nonfeasance, dissociation of personality, and disqualification as a human being. Even so, I dearly wanted an improvement in our situation — yes, how I wished it, and wished things wouldn't get worse! And yet, I believed if I endeavored more and endured harder, my situation would indeed get worse. I and my situation were already half crazy and would become altogether crazy if I exerted myself harder.

"Mokuzu, the only wisdom we can practice in a crazy situation is to try not to make it worse. If you try to amend it, you'll stiffen yourself and end up saturated with unsolvable problems until your head explodes with madness."

It was not dark, but many clouds hung low. The lusterless leaves of the trees swayed. To the wind, an external force, they did not respond from their inner subjecthood; keeping their sensibilities in their depths, they let themselves be swayed.

Countable raindrops moistened the stone path, the tiles, the veranda. Owing to the high humidity and no sun, the stains took long to dry. A north air chilled the steam rising from the earth, and as it turned to fog it began to swathe the mountains. The peaks, gorges, and high habitats were steadily becoming veiled.

Mokuzu was aware that he was girded by problems and that his thinking faculties were shutting down. He felt he was turning into a depressed plant. 'Let's say I have to imagine in detail my parents engaged in sex. My brain refuses. So too with the problems of death and insanity, which are now my vital concerns — my brain is like an electric circuit with a blown fuse, or a factory with all the workers out on strike.

'...I'm buried in a universe beyond reach of light. Yet without light my brain is useless. It's useful only to see a crane on a pine and to hear the rustle of reeds. It's active only for the world of forms, like a sparrow, *tit tit tit tit*.... How incapable it is for important matters; it shuts down and becomes a vegetable, a rock! Hm! What a useless reed, acting only when it sees real reeds and becoming like them at critical times instead of finding a solution. It turns itself into a part of the environment when it meets environmental problems. In short, my brain just adds another problem to the ones I have. Let's see how it will answer a question:

'What is my original nature?

'*Chat! Chat!*

'It chats like a monkey! I wonder if I'm already insane....

'Should I scorn it and scold it, or respect its refusal to think further? Does it know the danger in persisting to ponder unsolvable problems, or know the futility of pondering abstractions? Maybe my brain knows that the greatest enlightenment is to disregard such things, though it is forced to think on and on...by what? — by me?'

37

An Exhortation to Begin Zen Training

Mokuzu one afternoon mounted the retreat cottage to fix a leak. He had to replace tiles broken by frosts and the lashing of branches. When he stood, his shoulder met the branches now laden with coloring persimmons.

The yellow rice fields were wide under a blue sky. But now and then a chill wind swept across and swayed the branches as if rehearsing to carry the snows of winter.

Rain began in the late night. Fixing a tile roof was hard for an amateur. As expected, rain seeped in and ran along the crosspiece of the ceiling and dripped to his forehead as he lay on his back. He shifted to catch it in his mouth. It tasted of soot.

'I'd like to fight a bear, as Gyodo in his boyhood dreamed of doing. A bear may be strong, but it's a definite object to deal with. Now I envy sportsmen. They can give and be satisfied by giving their all for a simple goal under simple rules. The problems I face, about death, fate, insanity, and the formation of my character, are so obscure. Besides, there are no definitive means and methods to investigate them thoroughly.'

A moderate knock sounded at the door.

"Who is it?" Mokuzu remained on his back.

"Me, Gyodo. Mokuzu, please open up."

"Oh, it's you? Come in, the door isn't locked."

"I snuck out. Don't tell anyone. Why didn't you lock before you went to bed? What if a thief enters?"

"You're soaking wet. A thief? I'd welcome him to break the tedium. You snuck out?"

455

"Right, and I'll not go back — they treat me like a lunatic!"

Gyodo was in an instant excited with fury.

"Beasts! How can they treat me like a lunatic? I'll wreak my vengeance! The world is full of lunatics. See, I'm normal, so I'm their enemy. Their worst enemy they ostracize as a lunatic. Mokuzu, you too must be careful."

"Why must I be careful?"

"It's obvious. Suppose you're a lunatic. You'll join the world and throw a normal man like me into a cell with iron bars and an iron fence. Conversely, if you're normal you'll get thrown in too."

"I see, I have to be careful on either hand."

"Aha! — exactly as you say, you have to be careful on either hand. Remember, I'm ambidextrous, heh heh heh!"

'He must be still abnormal, chuckling to himself over nonsense as if it had profound meaning.'

"Mokuzu, it's torture! I'd be killed by now if I were there. They unite to torture me to death. They put me with real patients who freely use another man's belongings and who urinate and defecate all over the floor and incessantly scream and gang up on another man and beat him like a sandbag. Some stare all day in the mirror. One stares at me — he's crazy, if I move, he moves, and when I go to the toilet or crawl into my bed, he's still staring! He must be suffering from the disease of chronic guard duty.

"I'll go crazy among those crazies. The environment is so bad I get stomachaches, toothaches, renal aches too. I complain to the male nurses and doctors and ask for an internist and a dentist, but they only leer. Or four or five sturdy ones attack and put a bag over my head, over me entirely, and bind it with a rope and throw me into a solitary cell like a sack of feed."

Mokuzu was gloomy and just listened. He understood he should make no disagreeable response to stimulate Gyodo's nerves, yet he knew that keeping a long silence might incur his mistrust.

In fact Gyodo abruptly stopped his talk, when he had seemed in the middle of it. He sank into a deep silence. He sat still as a statue, his eyes limpid, bluish, grim. He was not looking at Mokuzu or at the desk or at any-thing concrete, nor was he looking into space; his eyes were reaching nothing and nowhere and issued no light.

Mokuzu put his palm on top of Gyodo's thick hand. It had deep and shallow abrasions. His eyes gave no indication that he sensed being touched. Long after Mokuzu's body heat began to be conducted, he recovered his senses and asked,

"Er...what was I saying?" His eyes appeared sad.

"You were saying you were put in a solitary cell."

"Oh, the cell! Maybe you wouldn't think anything's wrong with being put in a solitary cell, because you'd enjoy reading and meditating. Mokuzu, it's not like that. Although they don't show themselves, they use every available method, such as electronic communication and primitive incantation, to disturb my peace. I try to ignore it, but they persist to pull me in.

"On a screen they project my past, especially every hardship I don't want to recall. They point to each scene and laugh like monkeys. I endure with the patience of a cat curled in the snow. I cover my head with a blanket and my ears with my hands. Still, they dig up all my evildoings, not only my bad actions but also my bad thoughts.

"For instance they say, 'You cut the bun to share with your brother and sister. Why did you take the biggest third?' And, 'I know you can't happily remember the bridge over the Sakura. You hoped a man you loathed would steer his bicycle wrong and be thrown over the parapet. That's enough hints. Remember each detail of your cruel thoughts and apologize.' It's so annoying I can't sleep! Then a stranger with Yosetsu's slippery smile preaches in a manner that appears kind to all but me. Like Iago, another incites me to great action and laughs if I don't stir.

"I anger and rise to punish them, but they're watching for that and they fly at me and beat me hollow. I'm a man staked in a sandstorm. And my sense of pain is acute. With a thick syringe they inject a super-toxic liquid into the back of my head and into my buttock. An unspeakable languor and bovinity overtakes me...a truly horrid feeling...To be slashed with a sword would be more bearable. Languor is the worst torture.

"Mokuzu, I'm done in, I've no reserve energy to bear up. Please help, give me sanctuary! Any moment they'll come! What should I do? By now they've told the police — they'll be after me with their dogs!

"I'm at the end of my endurance! I'm losing my eyesight too. The stars are like stains on blotting paper. Each above each twig and leaf used to be so clear, if you remember how I was. I asked for glasses and the doctor only laughed.

"Worse, my memory is going even faster. My ability to concentrate, essential to memorization, is diluted like glue in water. My faculty to select what I want from my store of information is like a magnet dragged on the road; odds and ends adhere and I can hardly pick out anything specific.

"My comprehension is ruined — they destroyed it! I borrowed from Imata a book called *The Science of Divination*. He's in as sad a plight, also forced into the hospital by the misappreciation around him. He's a school teacher being laid off. I read the foreword, but I could no more decipher the meaning than I would be able to read letters written on water.

457

"Mokuzu, how do you think — do you pity your brother? Please help me if you can. Don't send me back to that hospital. If I must go anyhere, don't let it be there!" Gyodo's tears fell to his knees. He had no tissue or handkerchief.

Mokuzu was pained to persuade him to return. Gyodo lowered his head like a dog being reprimanded by its master. He was possessed by fear and hatred of the hospital.

"Gyodo, I'll never forget your many kindnesses to me, even if everyone else fools you and regards you as a lunatic. Without your care I'd have drowned like a pup in a swamp....

"Our parents were poor and still are. The spine of their life has been ignorance, and the flesh, complaint. Their thoughts are as poor as the flowers of the holly, and like its thorns their words only prick. Their behavior is as unsightly as shredded nylon tape caught up in dried honeysuckle. They've always been so, so what more can we expect? It's well said that 'he who disputes another's virtue lives only with relative values, and unknown to him is absolute value.'[1]

"Gyodo, Dad is afraid of you. He sees how he is wrong and he's resigned to suffering revenge, yet like any other creature he fears death. You also seem to fear death, after all. Whoever knows his own fear must be able to comprehend another's. Is it right to increase the fear of one who is afraid, and who therefore ought to be sympathized with? It's unsuitable to add misery to misery. You have always been a very reliable brother with a strong sense of justice. You can choose either to take revenge on him or to return good for evil...."

Mokuzu went so far as to say,

"Give me a little more time. I am willing to penetrate to the origin of all human problems, and I will apply my most desperate effort in the coming years for that end. The sky is not mere sky. Between us and it is some unnameable thing like the membrane of an egg. If I can divest the sky of its membrane, its true nature will be exposed. Please bear the unbearable, endure the unendurable, and wait till I can grasp the origin. Then all problems will be solved and a spring field will open before your eyes."

Next morning Mokuzu took Gyodo to his hospital on a hill in a suburb of Uji.

"I will hold out, so you do too," Gyodo said at the hospital entrance. But soon he was shedding tears and saying, "Oh, Mokuzu, I'm done for! I came too early to this world!" Then he regained his seniority, "Don't fail by poverty or physical weakness or loneliness — those nourish you to make you great."

The nurse in charge of him came out to receive him. She must have handled many such cases; she spoke with undue familiarity as she adroitly led him to a long corridor with wards on either side. Their figures disappeared as they turned left. Her words trailed in Mokuzu's ears, "I didn't know you had vagrant habits, eh? Don't make us worry. Be a good boy. Patience, patience, till stones float and leaves sink. Now what you must do..."

❧

After leaving the hospital Mokuzu hastily took a suburban train to Ibaraki, Osaka, to receive an exam given by an electronics school that day. The school was privately established within an electric industrial company, its function like that of the training school of the industry Gyodo had served. In return for their studies, the students were promised the pay of regular workers, the company's intention being to train them to become principal company members.

That summer Mokuzu had passed the government scholarship exam with the best score in all Kyoto Prefecture. Yet he was thinking he should get a job in March. 'Having the scholarship and not troubling my parents isn't enough. A more active contribution is needed, especially now with Gyodo ill and Ran about to enter junior high. I can't afford the luxury of studying and solving the mental problems I have to solve. Solving those life problems must be sacrificed to earning today's money. Then I really wonder what kind of future awaits me....'

The electronics school would accept 100 students, yet in Ibaraki alone over 3,000 had gathered for the exam. Wide as they were, the company grounds were blackened with black-uniformed students. The exam, it was said, was also being held in Tokyo.

In the morning, English, math, Japanese, science, and social studies tests were given; in the afternoon came intelligence and aptitude tests, and a physical exam. Throughout, Mokuzu felt dismayed because the contents had nothing to do with his really worrisome problems. He could answer everything easily, even halfheartedly, and he concluded that even if the company received him he would be expected to act halfhearted and ignore his real problems to be a success there, since his very ability in that direction was being tested.

The following day he attended school as usual and was glad to see that his shadow like everyone else's appeared normally. 'Whether or not a person has mental problems, his shadow is cast the same, without indication of his internal life. Yet all those school and company exams test only to see whether we have the same shadow. They disregard an individual's internal life.'

Mr. Sato approached and asked in a solicitous tone,

"Mokuzu, how did you do?"

"I had no trouble with the papers."

459

"Great! I believe you can pass any exam. I was told our education board formed an inside committee to investigate your score on the scholarship exam because it was far above anyone else's. You didn't fail a single question."

Mokuzu was growing to dislike his homeroom teacher. He perceived that Mr. Sato did not care about him, but more, he saw that Mr. Sato was relieved by his attitude, which was not to expect his real problems to be understood and therefore not to expect any real kindness.

The electronics school chose 200 from the first exam and invited them for an oral exam to make their final selection. By then the company had all necessary information on them through its special agents; more than exam results and school reports, background was a significant factor.

Mokuzu's interview came in the days of early sundown toward the end of November. The spacious room was lit by a lavish apparatus, a product of the company. Seated at a table with their backs to a large glass window were two interviewers and two assistants responsible for organizing the data. They all were impeccably dressed and of refined demeanor, as if they could not possibly be descended from the Japanese of the Jomon period.

Mokuzu was offered a facing chair. The lead interviewer, wearing glasses, quickly perused the papers and commenced to talk fluently without emotion,

"We have predetermined not to employ you; so your interview will not be typical. We have invited you to explain our decision, and to reimburse you for your two days here and for your travel cost."

Mokuzu felt a rising anger when he realized he had been invited for that only. His face, he sensed, was blanching. 'He's a typical man of society, making much of a trivial kindness while performing a grave cruelty . What good is a petty reimbursement if they don't employ me? It's like a rich man denying a beggar roast beef while gladly offering him a sniff. The rich of today have learned from ancient kings not how to appear grand but to mask cruelty with minute kindnesses that sparkle like jewels in a crown.

'I bet one of their research papers describes Gyodo in red!'

"You are not suited to our company. We are unquestionably the best in the industry, and our school seeks top students nationwide to strengthen our base for the future. Yet here I ask you to listen carefully. The purpose of our school is not to produce leaders or lower workers, but to produce a nucleus of mid-level technical brainpower.

"One further point you should understand. Our industry is important to society, but our aim is to make a profit. Hence we are developing new technology, and a new consumer market nationwide and worldwide. We don't research universal happiness or the true way of life for mankind. Our concern isn't to amend the present capitalistic world. We neither decry nor extol it.

We are a kind of parasite. For the oldest and lowest desire of self-profit we employ the newest and highest technology.

"I hope you can begin to recognize why we dare not hire you and train you to be a skilled mid-level worker. For that you are too good. You are the type that must not waste a moment for an industry or a state. You must transcend such bounds. We truly wish you will apply your talent to the more profound study of how to advance universal happiness.

"I am telling you the words of our president. He began by making dry batteries for bicycles, and it is his diligence, ingenuity, and managerial skill that built up our present electric and electronic empire. He has, as well, a concern for the cultivation of character and the advance of happiness. Thus he came to realize there are two types of people: one good for companies that support the present world, the other for improving the world. And he concluded that private industry's monopolizing of the latter is a sin against mankind.

"The idea is quite revolutionary if you consider that all other companies are eager to get such people. They employ the red hens that lay the golden eggs and secretly temper them for their exclusive prosperity.

"Do you see? We want them, but we restrain ourselves and swallow our tears. We know you would be of great profit to us, but we don't wish to consume your talent for our sole interest. We hope you will develop yourself for the world.

"Being young, you may not quite understand our intent. Wait five or ten years and you'll appreciate our policy. Think now with your smart brain: We travel the world, we occupy a major share of its market, and we are building up huge capital resources. Our influence is considerably affecting this nation's politics, economy, and education, not only every individual's life. But how much are we contributing to mankind? We could be idiots if not termites, or worse, narcotics producers. I am certain no Confucius, Buddha, Christ, or Socrates will issue from our school and our company even if we prosper for another one or two thousand years. It is impossible and not our intent. We are like shells clinging to the rocks and producing tons of lime.

"We make and sell millions of batteries, radios, washing machines, refrigerators, cleaners, mixers, televisions, electronic ovens, and stereos. Now we are developing electronic computers, which will alter the life-style of the future.

"But we know those trillions of products can't make a man happier or better; we rather make most people more imperfect, more idiotic, and more evil.

"So, we have confessed what we are, and we hope you will understand that we shan't employ you. We hope you will grow to be one who will lead and console us. We are ignorant of how to live onward; we need to be taught; we need our saint to purify us of our sins, for we have committed many."

At most Mokuzu felt bored. 'His talk is as empty as an electric appliance.

461

Need he speak so much to tell me they won't hire me? How disappointed my family will be at my failure to get this job! I hope to be excused even a second earlier!'

"So may I leave?"

"Yes, but beforehand would you give us your response?"

"Well, it's said even ducks know milk from water. They must be wise because they don't dream. People dream day and night till the moment of their death. Freud says sexual desire is the base of all dreams. I disagree. Convenience of the moment is the base of all dreams, and it can affect sexual desire, but sexual desire doesn't affect it. I think your president doesn't entertain any dream inconvenient to himself. Will he dream I'll grow up to be his powerful enemy? No, not while he isn't senile or possessed of a Freudian complex....He's dreaming of the appearance of a man who will purify and console him. But in reality he's frantic to squelch such potentially able men. Substance hasn't been his subject of study, so he can't unify even himself. All he can produce is incoherent flowers on a soil of opportunism. Well, this is what I feel for now, and now is the time to leave."

The interviewer was speechless, proving that the shine of his hair, his glasses, and his words had nothing to do with him but was caused by the effulgence of the lighting apparatus. He silently handed Mokuzu a beige envelope. On the way home Mokuzu opened it. Within were two large-denomination bills, equal to a month's pay of a worker fresh out of college.

ಶಿ

The new year opened, yet Mokuzu was gloomy because his future was undecided. Fortunately, at the onset of winter vacation he had found a temporary job at a project to build a revetment along the Sakura River. The work was from eight to five with an hour out for lunch. Keeping up with the adult workers exhausted him, and at night he fell asleep before he could worry over his future.

During work he was given constant orders and had no chance even to talk nonsense. Besides, a half-measured performance was dangerous.

The first step was to make a cofferdam and dig deep along the shore. Water sprang endlessly from the riverbed, demanding haste to dig, and the noise of a pump was deafening. Digging away the top layer was not hard, but layer by layer the work got harder. Many stakes and riprap remaining from the past had to be dug up and scraped out. The ditch became deeper than the height of the workers. Those professionals young and old were so sturdy that they could work with pick and shovel until they removed to the top of the excavation everything they dug up.

Even on days when snowflakes blustered and were sucked onto the water, they wore no more than a cotton shirt over their beefy arms and torsos, and still they sweated.

Mokuzu's work was to fill a wheelbarrow with the diggings, trundle them up the bank, and load them into a dump truck waiting to be filled. Planks were laid end to end up the bank, with one put across to the truck bed. The wet dirt was heavy, and the planks, less than twenty centimeters wide, were muddy. Mokuzu had no way to pull the wheel back on if it slipped off and could only dump the wheelbarrow on the spot. With all his might he had to keep advancing or it would tip left and right or push him backward. To make use of acceleration he ran.

An overturn delayed the work, at which the boss would click his tongue, "Hey there, you're working for pay, not play. You can tumble, but don't let that barrow!"

Any delay on his part caused the diggers to shout, "Quick, move it out or it'll fall and double our labor!"

He had to keep expending all his strength and keep running. The blisters on his hands were broken and bleeding, but no one paid any heed.

After eating their lunch at the top of the bank, they dozed on the muddy earth around a fire. Some with pep to spare entered the river and caught eel or carp.

"Lookie here! — something to go with tonight's drink!"

"It'll gladden your wife, make her lively, ho, ho!"

Fearing his brain would be degraded, Mokuzu tried to remember precisely a book he had read, from section one, chapter one; but the boss and the boss's aid ordered him,

"You're new — you aren't allowed to rest. Pick up every scattered stone and piece of wood," or, "Bang the cement off those boards — they're needed this afternoon."

Mokuzu always answered "Yes" and worked in silence. Not a notion formed in his mind. The mountains and the far shore appeared vague as haze. He told himself to ignore his fatigue until five o'clock. 'A fine dog will attack regardless of an enemy's strength and hold on with its teeth to the death. I'd like to share my life with such a dog and walk together through a flowering field. Oh, Ena, I'll not be defeated by this work, please don't frown to see me labor so, it doesn't bother me!'

When the ditch reached a certain length, stones were put in, first the size of a human head, then fist size, followed by gravel. The downhill carry was far easier.

The men rapidly trampled the gravel and built a frame on top to receive concrete, which Mokuzu had to make by mixing cement with sand and water. The first layer required coarse sand and scanty water, the following layers finer sand and more water. He poured it into the frame, and the workers tamped it with stakes. Judging the right consistency was hard, as was the quick transport by wheelbarrow. He continued to run up and down.

With no moment to look aside, he did not notice at all two black-robed figures observing him from the top of the bank. Actually the boss was repeatedly shouting at him and at last hurled a piece of wood at him.

"Oi! Slug! How many times must I shout? There's priests want to see you. We're at our busiest, but it seems they have important traffic with you. I'll give you the day off, being as one of them looks impressive. You can quit now — don't worry, I won't cut your pay."

On the bank stood two Zen priests. When Mokuzu reached the top, the older one bowed deep with joined palms.

Mokuzu was perturbed. Never had he received so courteous a greeting from anyone, nor thought himself worthy of one. It was Zen Master Tengai.

The attendant was like Bokuon in looks and attitude, but he was not Bokuon. His shaven head was blue, and he was endeavoring to be silent and stern as he followed the master's every movement with his eyes, fearful of being reprimanded.

Zen Master Tengai was now of greater girth and seemed to have increased his steadfastness to the ground. His way of talking was as before, delivered from the belly, and with each word enounced in a stately tone.

"Mokuzu, I am here today to adopt you. I have the consent of Zen Master Hanun-kutsu, nay, he has in fact entreated me to raise you to be a respectable Zen priest. Of course, regardless of his entreaty, I predetermined to do so when first I saw you ten years ago carving on a bone under the gate. I have been observing your growth and patiently waiting.

"I talked with your father. Though he has his own view, he told me you have complete freedom and responsibility to choose your path when you graduate from junior high school in March.

"Well then, there is no problem. You had better come at once to Shoshinji in Gifu after you graduate. Do not hesitate. Straightway decide and come like those fishermen who were casting their nets into the sea at Galilee — they left their nets, their boats, and their fathers."

"But, Zen Master, I am not a fisherman."

"Nnn, so what?"

"Much less do I want to become a fisher of men, right?"

"Don't talk such trifles as catching men or not. Being a Zen priest means to know completely what is a human being and his fate, as an astronomer

464

knows every movement of the stars and a botanist knows the life of every plant. You are destined to be a Zen priest. It is the only way you can perfectly combust your entire ability. You must faithfully obey your fate to open it up, and must make others realize what their fate is so they can expedite their perfect life. There is no better and happier way than to live as a Zen priest, is there? All sentient beings are in essence Buddhas, and every mountain, river, tree, and grass is attaining Buddhahood. It is the greatest pity that most people are unaware of this reality and are spending away their lives in an agony of delusion. We have to make them realize during their lifetime that each is a perfect Buddha."

Mokuzu without responding walked beside the master to Tangenji. The attendant, Koko, silently followed in exact accordance with the old teaching that an attendant must walk three feet behind to avoid stepping on the master's shadow.

Wind mingled with snow rippled the skirts of the master's robe and white underrobe too.

"Zen Master, you say we must make each person realize during his life that he is a perfect Buddha. I should like to know what is the situation for one who dies before he realizes he is a Buddha." Mokuzu was thinking of Ena.

"Why, it's a well-known fact that whoever dies without realization in this world has to suffer an endless transmigration through the six worlds."

"Then what exactly happens to someone who dies young without yet knowing what he should realize and so without yet knowing what he should do to attain it?"

"Whoever dies must go to where all the good and evil he did in this world is judged by Yamaraja. Before facing Yamaraja he must ford a river with three shoals of diverse speed. Close by are an old male and an old female demon who strip off his clothes and hang them on a tree. The degree the branches bend determines the weight of his sins.

"Now, if an infant dies he must go to the river's west side and build a stupa for the repose of his parents' souls. Day after day he must work. When he is about to finish, a giant demon appears and knocks it down. Weeping, he must build it again. Repeatedly he is close to finishing when the demon comes to knock it down. Thus in punishment for an early death he has to experience an ultimate sorrow. Help at last comes to him in the form of the Bodhisattva Ksitigarbha — in Japanese, Jizo.

"This is not my invention; it appears in an authentic sutra, *Shy-wang jing*. The important attitude to take is not to laugh at the fancy and allegory but to grasp the spirit."

"Yes, Master, I have heard that sutra. But I don't know at what age one is no longer an infant. I mean, what is the age limit to receive Jizo Bodhi-sattva's help in the world of death?"

"Nnnh, you've an odd concern! I don't know for sure, but I have been told no older than twelve....Well, Mokuzu, now listen. To be frank, I myself suffered considerably over this matter, in fact it was the reason I entered the priesthood.

"I had a constitutional infirmity, whence I was a very nervous child. My head was covered with an infant eczema traceable to congenital syphilis. In addition I disliked many foods. I was the youngest of seven, and my mother had to cook for me three separate vegetarian meals a day. Being weak I was spoilt and caused her much trouble. Shameful to say, I habitually wet my bed even after I was ordained at age twelve. In Toyoin I was ridiculed by the seniors for 'drawing a world map' every night on my bed.

"I feared death ever since I could remember, for I was often sick, so often that I was labeled a 'wholesale business of disease.' Abed with a high fever, I could hear from the next room the sibilations of the physician and my family, 'This time Shinichi has little chance to pull through. It can't be helped, but how sad to die before his fifth birthday!' Somehow I survived, and next they said, 'This is it — he won't see his sixth birthday,' and then, 'His seventh is unthinkable.'

"The dreams I had in those days were of being dead and put in a coffin surrounded by my grieving family holding a wake, or I within was being carried amid a long cortege to a graveyard.

"My mother was a pious follower of the Jodo Shin sect. On festival days she visited her temple and attended the priest's sermon. I, clutching her kimono sleeve, was taken along.

"In the main hall were horrible chromatic illustrations of sinners being pierced by iron rods or gashed by swords and being revived as soon as they died. Others were being chased into a forest of swords inhabited by eagles with red-hot iron beaks. There were sinners boiling in pots, and sinners confined within walls of molten iron, and sinners being driven into a sea of boiling copper. It was so appalling I couldn't cease trembling and couldn't sleep at night without my mother.

"I was terrified, for I knew I couldn't live without committing any evil, and I feared I'd be punished in hell if I died. My mother comforted me by saying Jizo Bodhisattva would help me if I died as a child. But I didn't die. And that filled me with anxiety because, though I feared death, I wanted to die young to be helped by Jizo Bodhisattva.

"The age limit was fast approaching, and still I didn't die despite being so often ill. Even after starting school I was ever devising a way to die. I ate distasteful foods, bared my body to icy winds, but I only got a fever and diarrhea.

"Then one day in the rainy season a classmate died of typhoid fever. He had eaten a green plum, they said. Our teacher cautioned us, saying unripe plums harbor such bacilli as salmonella and botulinus.

"I of course went right home to our garden and ate an unripe plum. It was so sour my mouth rejected it, but I forced it down. I ate two, then fearing that wouldn't do, I ate a third. Glad of my coming death, I crept into bed and quietly waited. But nothing happened.

"I tried other ways. All the same, I became twelve. No one had given me a satisfactory answer to my questions about death and my fear of death. My mother didn't know what to do with me. At last I went to the Jodo Shin priest she so respected.

"'In our sect,' he replied, 'we chant Amitabha's name, asking for mercy. Adherents of the Zen sect deal directly with death by training themselves to graduate from the problem of death. I advise you to visit a Zen master.'

"I was like a drowning man catching at a straw. I asked my mother to let me enter the Zen priesthood. After that there was much progress, but, simply, to conclude, I became an acolyte under the priest Mukai at Toyoin in Nanzenji, where you father entered soon after."

Mokuzu was amazed that Zen Master Tengai's infant experience so closely resembled that of Zen Teacher Hakuin, whose autobiography, *Itsumade gusa*, he had read in addition to a biographical sketch by his disciple Torei. But Mokuzu was disinclined to think Tengai was borrowing Hakuin's life story.

'Fear of death is very common. There were nights I too was tormented by dreams of being dead as my parents mourned over me. But I didn't much care about hell. I feared death less than I felt sorrowful at separating from the people and things I loved.

'Indeed, what I want to know is not about my own death but why Ena died and what happened to her. I want to know what I can do for her and what is the meaning of her short life. Will I need to solve my private problem of life and death to solve that of Ena's?'

"Tell me, Zen Master, please, can I solve every problem to do with death by engaging in Zen training?"

"Unquestionably. Mokuzu, it was said, 'Life and death is our gravest concern. We ought to be diligent to realize the truth. Time does not await us and quickly passes by.'[2] Life and death is the central theme not only of our Zen sect but of all Buddhism. To understand it was the very reason our Sakyamuni Buddha entered the priesthood."

Abruptly Mokuzu halted, turned his head, and regarded the attendant, who was tagging along.

Koko was taken unawares as if he had been indulging in a reverie and was simply following by force of habit. He looked like a fox or a raccoon dog stirred awake.

"Attendant, could you tell me how long you have been training under the Zen Master?"

"Well...this will be my seventh year."

"If so, you must already understand about death. Could you give me some idea?"

Koko briefly hesitated, then with resolve he went into a convulsion. He rolled his eyes and fell to the ground. It was a parody of death, and not death, nor an epileptic fit.

Such eccentricity roused in Mokuzu an instinctive hate and contempt. 'He's like a clown who with unexpected skill is turning a somersault or walking a tightrope, but by planned mishap his pantaloons get hooked so at the next stunt they come off to expose his patched drawers and hairy shanks.'

Mokuzu looked at the master. He appeared satisfied. Mokuzu reconsidered, 'He couldn't be a clown. How could Zen be clownish? It has a more than two-thousand-year history transmitted since the attainment of Buddhahood by Sakyamuni. Koko must be directly expressing death, even if it makes no sense to me. I am blind to the evident truth or I would thank him for his kind demonstration. The fault is in me, not him.'

The master gave Koko a hand to help him to his feet and said to Mokuzu,

"You have to start training without delay. Open your enlightened eye and become helpful to the world."

They came to the stone steps under the gate of Tangenji. Snowflakes grazed the gate. A current of snow was being drawn into the lamp-shaped window of the second story, while the snow that confronted the fascade was wavering.

"Master, can I understand insanity if I attain Zen realization? I want to know why people go insane, what their mentality is, and how we can heal them — or should I ask, can the insane enter Nirvana...?"

"Mokuzu, it depends on your training. As long as you see your object, be it death or insanity, as something apart from yourself, you will never comprehend it. You have to transcend the division of 'other' and 'self' — you have to experience the state of complete annihilation of the conflict between yourself and your object. It was said, 'Nothing surpasses the instantaneous leap from the gateway of the Truth to the state of the Tathagata, wherein resides no discrimination.'[3] Your problems large and small will melt away the moment you see your original nature.

"The restorer of Japanese Rinzai Zen, such a talent as appears but once in five hundred years, who is our Zen Teacher Hakuin, also avowed that if you see your original nature, 'you can shatter the root of your mind, shatter your illusion, and give to your world of delusion a bright eternal meaning heretofore buried in the transmigration of life and death; and you can utilize the three bodies of Buddha and the four types of wisdom; and more, you can go beyond the three or six types of supernatural powers.'[4]

"Mokuzu, you must once for all incisively destroy the base of your mind and every one of your misconceptions so you can roll back your eyelids and graduate from all such relative conflicts as life and death, and sanity and insanity.

"You must have studied those terms 'the three bodies of Buddha,' 'the four types of wisdom,' and 'the three or six types of supernatural powers' from the historian of Buddhism Docho Doke during your stay under Zen Master Hanun. If you train yourself in Zen, you can indeed go beyond the supernatural powers and freely exercise them to help sentient beings.

"You have to know that in Zen we don't put faith in or pay homage to Buddha. Why? Because we don't keep Buddha at a distance, but ourselves become Buddha. We don't divide our mind from our body or discriminate the holy man from the ordinary man. Through dauntless training we completely become Buddha."

'According to Teacher Docho, the three bodies of Buddha are the *dharma-kaya* — the origin of Buddha, which is eternal truth without color or shape; the *nirmana-kaya* — which is the appearance of the *dharma-kaya* in concrete form, as in the appearance of Sakyamuni Buddha, in response to the needs of sentient beings; and the *sambhoga-kaya*, which is a sort of combination of the others, that is, it is eternal and incorporeal but can appear in human beings as it appeared in Sakyamuni Buddha.

'I remember the froth at his mouth; he scarcely looked up during the lecture, and I was like a machine recording whatever he dictated. It seemed he didn't care whether I understood as long as he could certify his own understanding.

'He told me that in addition to our eyes, ears, nose, tongue, and skin, we have a sixth sense organ, our mind, which is a synthesis of those five. In the back of our ordinary mind is consciousness of self, called our seventh sense, or *mano-vijnana*. It is beyond our normal consciousness, yet it gives rise to contradictions in our conscious decisions because it perpetually loves what we regard as our self. Teacher Docho said this seventh sense is what depth psychologists call 'the world of the subconscious.' But he said the Buddhist study of consciousness recognizes a deeper, eighth sense, *alaya-vijnana*, perfected in India by the Yogacara school as its essential doctrine. This sense is the source of all phenomena of the universe, and therein are naturally stored

469

all things experienced by a human being not only from his birth but from the rise of his ancestors.

'One who has studied all there is to be studied about this eighth sense can attain the first of the four types of wisdom, which is the base of the following three. This first is called "great, perfect mirror-wisdom," or *adarsa-jnana*, because it resembles a great mirror that reflects the true nature of all things. The second is "wisdom of equality," or *samata-jnana*, attained when the seventh sense is mastered. One who has attained this second wisdom can perceive the underlying identity of all dharmas and of himself and of others, and can thence overcome his feelings of separation. The third is "wisdom of wondrous perception," or *pratyaveksana-jnana*, attained after a thorough investigation of the sixth sense. At this point one can perceive all dharma forms in their true state and teach the law of Buddhism free of error and doubt. The fourth is "wisdom of metamorphosis," or *krtyanusthana-jnana*, attained only by mastering the first five senses. One who has this wisdom can work various metamorphoses and manifestations to help other sentient beings.

'Recently I've begun a little more to understand what training is. It is to attain these four types of wisdom through my own physical and mental life, isn't it?

'And, yes, Teacher Docho spoke of the three or six types of supernatural powers, *abhijna*, if I remember right. The first is the power of free activity, by which one can appear wherever one wishes. The second is eyes that can forsee all, even the future of oneself and of others. The third is ears that can hear all, even the groans of hell and the music of heaven. The fourth is insight into others. The fifth is memory of prior states of existence. The sixth is perfect freedom. Among them, the second, fifth, and sixth are specially designated as "three wisdoms," attainable, it was said, by sitting meditation.

'So Zen training means to attain those abnormal abilities. Otherwise they are merely a list of human desires, the desires of quite ordinary men, I should say.

'Zen Master Tengai says I can attain them all if I train in Zen and see my original nature. He is a descendant of Hakuin in the Dharma transmission, and Hakuin inherited the most authentic Zen of Daio, Daito, and Kanzan through Shido and Shoju. Daio received the Dharma from the Chinese priest Shyutang Jyyu, who was the sixth-generation descendant of the editor of *Biyan lu*, Yuanwu Kechin. Yuanwu was the third-generation descendant of Yangchi Fanghuei. Seven generations before Yangchi came Linji. Linji's teacher was Huangbo, whose teacher was Baijang. Baijang was a disciple of Matzu, who was a disciple of Nanyue. Nanyue was a disciple of the sixth patriarch of Chinese Zen, Hueineng...and the first Zen patriarch in China was Puti Damo, who was Bodhidharma, the twenty-eighth patriarch of Indian

Buddhism. The second Indian patriarch, Ananda, and the first, Mahakasyapa, were among the ten disciples of the originator of the Dharma transmission throughout India, China, and Japan, who was Sakyamuni Buddha.'

This somber knowledge began to radiate with aureate luster in Mokuzu's mind, because it seemed to him that he too could attain those things if he trained himself in Zen. He also felt that his limited individuality was going to open up in a wider world in both senses, time and space. He was inspired by the imaginary sight of himself with his original nature known to him and achieving every potential power and freely helping all sorts of sad, suffering people. 'The hot blood of love and wisdom has been living throughout the Dharma transmission from Sakyamuni Buddha to this present Zen master before my very eyes!'

Without a word he proceeded from the gate to the side of the well. Silently Zen Master Tengai and his attendant followed.

He turned the faucet to fill a washtub, stripped naked, and dumped several buckets of water on himself.

"My goodness! How extreme!" cried Koko, shaking.

"Hmm!" Zen Master Tengai too was impressed, and he stepped back to avoid the splash.

"Why? The work made me sweat, so I'm washing up."

Mokuzu rubbed himself with a towel until his skin turned red. As he was about it, he thought again,

'But wait...! The historical Sakyamuni rejected the idea of the three bodies of Buddha. Didn't he as his last words admonish, "Be illuminated by nothing other than the Dharma, and live thence by nothing other than the Dharma"?[5] When Sunakkhatta complained that he performed none of the supernatural powers, he responded, "My teaching is as effective to absolve suffering as is practice of the supernatural powers."[6] And one day Kevaddha, wishing to confer benefits on the commoners, asked him to enjoin his disciples to perform the supernatural powers. Knowing them to be but phantoms and curses, Sakyamuni replied, "I teach my disciples only to meditate on the Way in a quiet place."[7]

'I have no wish to help so many people and to possess supernatural powers. I most wish to know the meaning of Ena's short life and how I should live so that it will have been most worthy. Next, I wish to know why Gyodo became crazy and how I can cure him. Third, I wish to know why closely contacting people like my parents can't live in peace without fighting...my questions pertain to very concrete problems.

'My father believes my future should be mine to decide, yet he is negative about the priesthood. He often told me priests are the worst liars, and that

Zen masters are the most avaricious of men, and that Zen training, while it may make a man stronger and wiser, has nothing to do with building a noble character....

'Let me take another look at the attendant's face. He has been training for seven long years, yet he doesn't look able...it seems he has neither strength nor wisdom, nor kindness. Indeed he appears to be cramped, hardheaded, uneducated, unkind, insensitive...and what else?...well, in a word — he looks stupid.

'True, this Zen master is full of unbeatable confidence and vigor, but it seems merely the result of a lack of religious sentiment, as well as a lack of modesty and reverence toward other beings....

'How will they behave if I dash cold water on them?'

38

Tangenji Burns

Winter vacation was over, and Mokuzu was in his last term of junior high. Yet, as many days as he could afford to he skipped school to continue his job at the project along the Sakura River. The school was tolerant of its students who were graduating in March; for those who would work, a place of work was mostly settled, and those planning to enter higher schools were allowed to study as much as they liked for entrance exams.

Uncertain of what he would do after graduation, Mokuzu endured the heavy labor. He could not help his family economy like Kiku if he chose to attend senior high; yet even if he chose to get a job, his advisor, Mr. Sato, no longer heartily cared, and Mokuzu did not know what job in what company suited him.

He saw that his classmates were busy with their own concerns, though unlike him, whose course was unclear.

He wished for a steady job as a shore-construction worker.

Those workers formed a kind of large family with their boss as its central figure. Like bees they kept moving around the country to wherever they could find work, and at each place they built humble barracks just adequate to sleep in. For a bath they heated water in an empty gasoline drum they took along, burning their disused boards for fuel.

The boss's wife was unfittingly elegant, with the air of a fancy restaurant proprietress. She had a fat, manly maid, espoused to one of the workers, and together they took care of everyone's laundry and meals. Some of the men had wives and children left in more permanent places, to whom they sent a monthly allowance. But most, old and young, were unmarried.

When they finished a job, they gathered and burned all their trash and carried away their barracks in neat sections, leaving behind nothing but ash. However, some of the young ones who had sported with girls of eligible age in the towns and villages where they were working left without cleaning up their affairs. The workers were therefore welcomed for their work while rated very low and sharply watched like a contagion.

The Sakura River project was nearly finished. The men, ahead of schedule and seeing time to spare, made a bonfire before their morning work and after lunch, and around it they chatted about past notable jobs and new contracts. Mokuzu also received fewer commands. More, he was getting used to the hard labor, and was allowed to rest at rest hour.

One day during a pause in their talk after lunch, he mustered his courage and asked the boss,

"Would you continue to employ me?"

"Ho? Kid, our next job is to build a coastal levee in Tottori. How can you commute, even if you're diligent?"

Everyone laughed, which Mokuzu expected. He blushed but proceeded, "I don't mean part-time, but to go wherever you go, live under the same roof, and work together."

"You gotta be nuts! It's unbelievable!"

Even the customary wag stopped his talk. The older men fell into a strange deep silence and withheld their commotion except to nudge the ends of logs further into the fire. 'What's come over them? Down to the last they're rough-and-ready, but all thirteen have turned to tombstones. Have they the same thought?'

After a long interval the boss spoke. His tone was reserved as it never was during work: "There's kids volunteer for the military....I also heard of them who commit crimes to get into jail for protection...but to think of joining our kind is queer...."

Not fully comprehending him, Mokuzu waited for his further words, but he would say no more. The next to speak was the oldest, respected for being the boss's aid: "We figured you got family trouble but not so bad you'd want to work on."

The boss found his tongue,

"Say, you got nowhere to go, I'll take you in...but listen, we're a bunch with nowhere else to go. You're smart and bearing up well. Your record is

473

clean, and mainly, you're young. You got to make you a bright future. It won't be too late to join us if you mess up. Come then and we'll take you in if you promise not to quarrel and do what you're told. Hey, everybody agree?"

They all nodded. An oldster raised wistful eyes that seemed to appeal, 'If only the boy comes he'll be our spring spirit, a flower on a dump, the comfort of a dog for an old man, a smiling baby for a life of penury. But it can't be and it shouldn't. He wasn't born to be our little prince. We aren't suited to raise him reverently to our heads as a symbol of our remaining purity like a thin creek trickling in a valley...'

One of middle age sat absorbed as if burying his head in his hands or covering his ears. 'No, no,' he seemed to cry in self-defense, 'I didn't want it to go like that, I hoped the opposite. It went bad by some mischance. I was forced to do evil after evil against my original wish and couldn't quit on the way!'

Another, quite young, was scratching and erasing figures on the earth with a charred branch as he muttered, "Suppose I be the kid's brother and help him to senior high. There'll be this for school...this for food and clothes... then what'll remain for my needs?...Scarcely enough to buy a button!"

The boss's aid, who worked as hard as any, had the sinewed body and glossy skin of a youth, but his age showed in the bags under his eyes, his sidelocks flecked with white, several long hairs in his ears, a slack throat, and thick fingers with skin like rhinoceros hide. He put an ember to his cigarette.

"How about that priest? Looked to be a fine one. Came to decide your future, I thought, but of course I wouldn't know."

"Come off it, Gramps, you enviously said sons of class are put out to hard labor for their learning but take no more than a lick of salt before someone fancy comes to fetch 'em back to a noble life we never even get a glimpse of," heckled a lean young one with the face of a Galapagos monster.

"He's a Zen master named Tengai, who came to exhort me to begin Zen training."

"That's good. What's wrong with doing that and becoming a prominent man? You hate training? I don't know about the mind, but I can tell you about the body: no training could be worse than our labor. You've worked fine here, so you needn't fear training as far as it's physical. Or you got some other problem keeping you from it?" asked the boss. He had a pug nose. The men were relaxing and returning to their normal talk.

"It seems the training he's urging on me isn't the training I want....I don't want to become great or influential, but this Zen master hopes to fire me to train as a Zennist who will excel even a shogun or a prime minister. I'd prefer to think more about what death is, and insanity, but he dismisses that in favor of living a mettlesome life. I want to live quietly on a hill, but he recommends that I engage in Zen training to combust myself perfectly in the actions of helping others and directing the mass of fools and the wise."

"Kid, don't waste our time with hard talk. Your worry is a luxury. C'mon, everyone, back to work!" Outright the boss stood up, and the others followed.

Mokuzu never again conversed with them. He only engaged in the labor with an unclear mind.

The following week a young villager, Hikoroku, happened by the site a little before ten in the morning. He had escorted Mokuzu to school on his first day. Now he worked in the office of an agricultural cooperative. He was a sturdy and quiet man. Mokuzu had had no connection with him since elementary school.

He left his bicycle on the bank and approached Mokuzu as he was mixing cement. With a dubious look he asked,

"Oi, aren't you taking the senior high entrance exam?"

"I've not yet decided to take it."

"What a crazy idle thought! Mokuzu, it's today. I saw many groups your age going to town."

"Today? I completely forgot!" Mokuzu was flurried.

Overhearing the exchange, the boss shouted, "Fool! Go! I thought you're a genius. You're no more than a gifted idiot! Take it so you'll have more time to decide on senior high."

As Mokuzu began to run to Tangenji, the boss's aid like a youth raised a high, unstrung voice,

"Use the bicycle and never mind your dress!"

Mokuzu borrowed Hikoroku's bicycle, fetched his pen and exam ticket, and sped to Kameoka — a 45-minute distance by bus. He pedaled downhill and did not brake where it was steep. Conveniently he had on muddy work clothes.

Every room of every building was dead silent with the exam underway. The students were all stuck to their desks.

It took Mokuzu long to find the right room. Sweat steamed from his collar and sleeves, and the loud beat of his heart did not calm at all. In contrast to the dank corridor his body was hot as fire. When at last he found the room and his seat, the proctor hurried to him with the papers and said,

"You're nearly half an hour late. I'm receiving you only out of exceptional kindness."

Mokuzu's fountain pen finely trembled; he had gripped the handlebars with all his might.

Of the over 400 applicants accepted, Mokuzu was rated seventh best.

&

The senior high school Mokuzu entered in April had a general curriculum as well as courses in agriculture, civil engineering, commerce, and homemaking. Total enrollment was over 1,200.

Mokuzu was taking the general curriculum, exclusively designed to send students to the universities. His classmates were so absorbed in preparing for university entrance exams that they begrudged the time even to greet one another. The main work of their teachers was to indicate what parts of the textbooks appeared as exam questions in what years at what universities.

In reality no teacher cared about the objectives of senior high school, though they were clearly stated in the School Education Act of 1947. The Act might as well have been buried under the floor of the classrooms; no one ever consulted it but Mokuzu, who read the relevant articles:

> (1) Senior high school must expand and develop in its students what they studied in junior high school, and must cultivate in them such a disposition as will make them useful members of society and the nation.
> (2) Senior high school must guide its students to choose their future course according to both their individuality and their basic awareness of their mission in society, and must provide them with the opportunity to enhance the level of their general culture and to master their chosen speciality.
> (3) Senior high school must endeavor to cultivate in its students a broad and deep understanding as well as healthy critical powers, and must allow them to establish their individuality.[1]

As far as Mokuzu could see, being useful in society and being a remarkable individual were the salient points, if to him they looked somewhat contradictory. At any rate, the school was neglecting and overriding the spirit of the Act.

For instance, Mr. Hironaka, Mokuzu's homeroom teacher, repeatedly told his students, "How many hours do you sleep? It should be no more than four a day for the next three years if you wish to enter a first-rate university. Sleep five and abandon hope of entering a national university!"

Mr. Hironaka had silver-rim glasses and buck teeth. When he grew enthusiastic he jutted out his chin, suggestive of a shark hitting its jaw on the glass of an aquarium.

"You know, women are now putting blue around their eyes. But you needn't spend a cent on 'eye-shadow.' Study hard and don't sleep and you'll soon be leading the fashion.

"Essentially your work is to memorize. You must memorize Chinese letters, archaic Japanese words, English vocabulary, dates of Japanese and world history, atomic numbers in chemistry, the axioms and theorems of mathematics, and so on. The university entrance exams aren't concerned with depth of understanding; only you must show breadth of knowledge. So I shall teach you how to memorize. See here, this little red-covered dictionary contains a basic English vocabulary of twelve thousand English words. You have to memorize it front to back — spelling, pronunciation, tense, parts of speech, meaning. And each time you've memorized both sides of a page, rip it out, wad it in a ball, put it in your mouth, chew it up, and swallow it!"

Mr. Hironaka demonstrated before their very eyes.

"See? First remember, then eat the page. That way you'll never forget, I mean, at least not till the day after the exam." Then further he added,

"Look around. Do you see your classmates? No, they're your enemies! Whoever fails the exam will enable another to pass; each failure raises the chances of the rest. So you have to realize everyone is your rival. You must go through this severe competition period to win the garland. Devote yourselves to your study and disregard one another, even if someone should suffocate or receive a brain concussion!"

Hearing this, Mokuzu felt he had been made unclean like an old coat stuck with burs. More, he felt wretched to see many of his classmates, girls not only boys, nodding in assent.

Mr. Hironaka's hobby, according to rumor, was to wander the fields and mountains to collect pteridophytes, though he seemed rigorous about not mentioning it in school.

On one of the continuing rainy days of June, a practice university entrance exam was offered throughout Kyoto Prefecture to high school seniors, scores and rank to be made public.

Mr. Hironaka urged his first-year students to take it too, for the reason that knowing the enemy and knowing one's ability was the first step of any strategy.

With his own idea Mokuzu took the exam.

Among all examinees in the prefecture he ranked fourth, and the entire school was astir about it.

Mokuzu went to find his homeroom teacher in the biology lab, for Mr. Hironaka taught biology. "Sir, don't you think I proved to a certain degree that my merit isn't inferior to a senior's? Don't you agree I'd be wasting my time to go on in due form?"

"I know what you're up to; you want to skip a grade or even two and yet obtain a high school diploma, right? The answer is a simple and absolute no. It was possible before our defeat in the war, but not now. Ha ha ha! You must put in the required time, not just show the required result. Too bad for you! With your ability you could already be graduated from a university, were these the good old days! Ha ha ha!"

477

Mokuzu was perplexed by Mr. Hironaka's laugh. Which was he scorning, his exam result, or the change in the nation's education system?

"I was assuming able students could skip, inasmuch as failures can repeat," he sighed.

"Aha! You think it irrational, but is anything rational? Consider the world, society, school, human beings, and most of all, yourself. Irrationality is the distinctive — "

"But, Mr. Hironaka," Mokuzu cut in, "I heard the Ministry of Education is granting to those who haven't gone to senior high the chance to qualify for university entrance. Can't I be granted the chance too?"

"As you say, it's for those who never went; you came in here, so you're disqualified. You're trapped. You wanted to eat an apple and are given a bushel, all unripe! Ha ha ha!"

"So, what do you suggest I do?"

"Spend three years here, however bored, then enter university. Ho! — too much is as bad as too little."

"Well, a pteridophyte is far from human, though it's not your responsibility," Mokuzu said, and he left the laboratory with heavy disappointment.

As he could do nothing about it, he divided his time into three parts.

First, he attended classes and there mastered what he had to master so that he never had to take home any school studies.

Second, he devoted the hours after school until supper to any obtainable part-time job. Usually school finished at three. Saturday was a half day and Sunday all day free for him to work.

Third, after supper till late at night he read books having no direct relation to his school studies or of course to his part-time jobs. Teacher Docho had given him many books in Chinese pertaining to Buddhist sutras and history, and Teacher Yojun, much literature in the original English. Mokuzu read them all through once, and many twice. He also attempted on his own to read Chinese and Japanese classics. Fortunately for him this third division of his time was ample enough.

He determined to spend his time thus during his three years of senior high and to exert his all not to be pulled into anything else. His window to the outside world was becoming extremely narrow, but it had been more or less so since the death of Ena. He lived a quite exclusive, internal life. As to his outer appearance, he seemed like a ghost with no influence on other beings. His surroundings could scarcely get a response from him. He was like a black rock, and moved only when there was an irreducible demand.

Never did he look aside, never care if the day was sunny or not. The rise of the military junta in Korea, the Evian agreements, and the Cuban Missile

Crisis were of no concern to him. Nor did he note that Yury Gagarin succeeded at the first manned Earth orbit in Vostok 1 in April 1961, or that John Glenn was the first American to orbit in Mercury-Atlas 6 in February 1962, or that Valentina Tereshkova was the first woman in space in Vostok 6 in June 1963.

Luckily or unluckily, his ostensible life was similar to that of all other senior high school students, numbering nearly four million in the nation and living just to prepare for university entrance exams. So no one saw any abnormality in his mode of life.

᛫

Now he was just turned eighteen and facing the new year. His senior high school days, which closely resembled Dostoyevsky's *Notes from the Underground*, would in a few months be over.

'What an absurdity I am! I see no difference in my mind, ability, and situation from three years ago when I was facing graduation from junior high,' thought Mokuzu with disgust in his retreat cottage under the dim light, surrounded with books. 'I got only older in vain and hence would have been better off going to Shoshinji in compliance with Zen Master Tengai's exhortation!'

The morning was well advanced, but he did not open the storm doors. Because of the New Year holiday he had no part-time jobs and had been reading nightlong.

'No, I shouldn't say I didn't progress at all. Then I was standing at a three-way junction — to get a job, to go to senior high, or to direct myself to the monastery. Now the choice is narrowed to whether to advance my education or make this the time to determine to begin my training.

'I have definitely concluded I will never bind myself to a regular job. Even when I was talking with Ena I didn't want to, and I was fairly confirming that being enslaved to a regular job isn't how a human being should spend a lifetime. But for the last three years I've been working whenever I could spare the time, because I've had to earn for my basic needs and to help my brother.

'I've been an assistant projectionist at a movie house, a restaurant deliveryman, a laborer at a revetment project and at a pavement project, a bookstore clerk, a gas station attendant, and a tutor of kids, and each of those jobs hurt my pride and none kindled my mind with any pleasure.

'I endured them and could perform them safely as long as I didn't use my brain or open my mind, only to earn money. I now am sure no kind of job suits me, though I don't deny the need of working in order to live. So I'll

479

work against my will. I'll take any job according to my situation and never be troubled over choosing which work is better; it isn't worth my care, for all are fated to depress the brain and heart because they originate from shameless and dishonorable human desires...!

'So, I must make up my mind — a university, or the monastery.

'I'm reluctant about the latter because it seems I'd have to renounce the world and most of my life. In other words, I'd have to live like a dead man... well, already I'm living as if half dead because of my opinion about work, for work is what substantially constitutes the world....

'In my understanding, monastic training is the ultimate denial of work. I'd have to terminate my five desires and all other klesas, serve only Buddha, live up to his teachings and precepts, and keep asking myself who I am, who Buddha is, and what I can do for the sake of other creatures.

'Naturally, though I'm not sure it's natural, I hesitate to go straight to the monastery. It's like committing suicide.

'Am I capable of leading the ascetic life to the end? Am I capable of living only for others? Certainly I can't begin to train in Zen Buddhism without determining to leap from a cliff. I'd have to abandon not only all my evil desires but my present family, and worst, I'd have to give up having a wife and children, not only my past Ena. Indeed, I bet I can't succeed at the training and can't see who I am unless I give up all my past, present, and future. Why? Because the purpose of training is to come to know what, in essence, death is, which means to experience time with no past, present, and future. In short, I can't know death without experiencing death. Here the simple question arises: Do I want to know death by the sacrifice of my life?

'Sure I'd like to know what my life is so I can solve the question of who I am. But I'd have to know death to know my life, because my life came from and will return to death and is maintained on the base of innumerable deaths. So I can't know my life without knowing death, and unless I die I can't know death.

'Nowadays I realize that to train is to walk on a dark path to death. It's quite different from the view Ena and I had. We thought to train is to walk on a bright path through flowering fields with a sweet breeze and singing birds, for we believed training is studying our life and how to perfect it. We didn't see that we have to know death to know our life.

'Oh, how I wish she were here! Training will be so hard — I'll need her. Without her how can I walk that dark and lonely path? A life of training needs a loving companion. Then, how sad, she walked alone the path to death!'

The day must have been overcast. Mokuzu saw no gleam at the crevices of the storm doors.

480

'Well, I think I definitely must start my training so as to clarify the meaning of her life and death. But what a pitiful dilemma — to train myself to know its meaning while wishing for her companionship!'

There was a stir in the main building. His parents and Ran were likely getting up. His grandmother was bedridden. Gyodo, permitted to spend New Year's at home, was probably still asleep.

Mokuzu was disgusted by his own irresolution coming from weakness, or fear of death, or fear to live as if dead.

'After all, I'm inclined toward a university because it will postpone the monastery. Ran is soon to graduate from junior high and has decided to work at an obi factory in Kyoto beginning in March. The other day she said, "You have a good brain and love to study, unlike me, so by any means you should go to a university to learn more about life. I'll work hard and help your finances as much as I can." I felt Ena's spirit in her and was ashamed to realize I haven't been a good brother these past years. What did I do for her that she is offering to help me thus? We've been coexisting in the same gloomy family and that's all.

'Kiku said in a letter to me at the year's end, "Our parents are aging and Gyodo can't possibly recover. You may want to study or train, but don't forget we each must be loyal to our situation. There are others suited to the university or the monastery. You shouldn't ask more than your situation is giving you. I believe doing one's best in one's given situation is true study and true training. In my case I've always worked only to earn money. Who can say I haven't been studying or training? Mokuzu, don't escape reality. Study and training apart from reality are false. What you must do is get a full-time job to ease our parents' burden and contribute to Gyodo's hospital fee."

'Ran's word is warm as a sparrow's heart, Kiku's, cold as the anchor of a ship wrecked in the Sea of Okhotsk.'

The noise from the main building was unusual, like someone's tramping on a sill to move an ill-fitting storm door.

Mokuzu thought about Gyodo, 'In the last three or four years he's been repeating the same process of hospitalization, remission, rehabilitation, tentative discharge, recurrence, violence, and compulsory hospitalization — a cycle of about six months at the longest, four at the shortest.

'Whenever he comes home he's in a good mood and works hard to clean Tangenji inside and out, make repairs, help with the chestnuts, plant seedlings on the mountain. While he is working well, his hope for the future expands. But soon he doesn't wake till late morning and stays up all night with occasional roars.

'This time he didn't come home in good condition. His request just

481

happened to coincide with the wish of the staff to take New Year's off. And he's done nothing but stay in bed for the past several days.'

Mokuzu clearly heard the crash of some furnishings, followed by a wolf-like ululation.

'It must be Gyodo. He wants to destroy Tangenji. I wonder why he's so persistent in his wish. It no longer functions as a Zen temple and doesn't need his help to go to ruin. Too bad Raskolnikov couldn't wait for the natural death of the old woman. It's madness to destroy a thing already half ruined and to kill what is already dead in spirit.'

"Mokuzu! Come — please help!" Ran cried at the door.

He went out. Ran was barefoot. Before she could explain, his father's screams arrived from the main building — "Help me! Mokuzu!"

Doyu was soon tearing around the front garden trying to escape. His tread sounded heavy and shook the earth.

A moment later he pounded up to right in front of Mokuzu, who was still standing before the retreat cottage. Gyodo with a carver in his raised fist came fast behind. Between the carver and Doyu's bald head was a space not much more than the length of a hand.

Mokuzu at once slid between and seized Gyodo's wrist. Doyu ran on alongside the retreat cottage toward the bamboo grove.

'I'll have no choice but to knock him out with a blow to the pit of the stomach if he keeps raging and trying to pull free of my grasp. I pray I won't have to use violence on my brother!'

Mokuzu looked Gyodo in the eye as he gripped his wrist. He was sad to realize he was fifteen centimeters taller than his senior brother. The whites of Gyodo's eyes were whiter and more phlegmatic than a bull's. His shoulders heaved and he was panting from excitement and the chase.

His eyes were glassy, giving the impression he was comatose. His brow ran with sweat and steam rose from his hair. Mokuzu saw that his hairline was beginning to recede. 'He has his father's constitution and will be early bald.

'But how interesting — he isn't going to challenge me? Insane though he is, he can distinguish one who isn't hateful from one who is? Or is he resigned to surrender, knowing my karate skill? If so, how sad is his despair!'

The slightest shade crossed Gyodo's eyes, exposing an awful pain and sorrow. Then he sang out,

"I'll drop it, it's ridiculous!" He let the carver fall from his hand, turned, and began to retire in the direction of his bedroom, one of the guest rooms at the west end of the main building.

'Strange! He was about to butcher his father and now he stops so easily as if only playing at billiards!'

482

Doyu, who had been crouching behind the woodpile along the wall of the retreat cottage, came out muttering,

"I had a hairsbreadth escape — I thought it was the end, the exact case of putting a bare sword in a madman's hand. I wonder if whoever coined that saying experienced the same. Well, the issue is him — the relation between him and me. What a horrible causation! Mokuzu, what should I do? Sooner or later he'll surely burn this Tangenji, where he and I were born and raised...." Doyu too was barefoot.

Mokuzu wished to keep his father from sinking into dark thought. Letting him talk, he decided, was better than trying to silence him.

"Did he anger suddenly?" he asked.

"No. You know he sleeps day and night. I thought he'll ruin his body in addition to his brain, so I went in. He was curled like a grub. Then I was startled to notice smoke, and I pulled off the quilt. He was smoking under there! How could he? Couldn't he sense it was smoky? Cigarette ashes and scorches were all over the bedding and the tatami.

"'If you're like that you'll cause a fire!' I scolded. Without a word he fixed me with a lowering look. I grew uneasy and carefully retreated to the living room. I sat by the hibachi, put a coal to my pipe, and consulted with Micha about what we can do, what we should do.

"'Do nothing, it will take its course,' she said.

"Then, as she was replying, he came in with heavy footfall — the disrepaired furnishings shook from his weight.

"He drew close to me and sat with an air of profound respect. It was ludicrous, but more, it was queer, and more than queer, pitiable. He put his palms to the tatami, bowed like a subordinate before a shogun, and asked,

"'O Honorable Father, grant me your teaching, for I am but an ignoramus. Would that it please you to disclose to me the Way that I too may become a venerable priest. I have in truth deliberated with care and now perceive that no better life awaits a man than the life of the priesthood!'

"Dumbstruck, I groped for a fitting reply, but not a single notion came. My brain was like a broken popgun.

"Micha, printing charm papers, came to my aid. She said, 'No preparation is required; just be as you are and someday you'll be a fine priest.' Relieved, I added my words, 'Very true, as your mother says, you needn't do a thing.'

"Before I could finish, he rose up with a cry, 'Damn you! Go to hell!' and he kicked me, grabbed my neck, and throttled me. I was choking in agony. Micha in desperation pulled him away and embraced him like a baby, though he's twice her size. She winked at me to escape. When I moved, he

483

tried to jump on me. I was forced to be still, and she strained every fiber to keep him where he was. Whenever I moved, he became more excited and she more had to restrain him. In that way I stole by degrees toward the entrance.

"Just then Ran came in anxious from her room. He thrust Micha down and began to break every breakable furnishing. He lifted the hibachi too, huge as it is, and heaved it bodily out to the entrance floor. Micha and Ran fled outside. I too escaped. He continued to break things and proceeded to the main hall. He flung the bell, the drum too, and began to ravage even the sanctum. I couldn't bear it and cried from the garden, 'Leave off your destruction!'

"He ran to his room — to fetch the carver, which he must have been hiding. Then he hawked me savagely. I barely escaped this way, and you were here. I'm saved for now, thanks to you — but what about them? I think Micha escaped toward the graveyard. I thought Ran came this way, but I don't see her — "

Doyu was shaking. Mokuzu left him and went in search of Ran and his mother. They were not in the bamboo grove or the graveyard. He entered the main building. The hibachi indeed lay smashed on the earth of the entrance. Its heap of ash was scattered radially with the live coals settled quietly on top.

The shojis and fusumas were in a shambles, a few still barely standing askew. Mokuzu went to check on his grandmother. The furnishings in her room were untouched.

She had been bedfast since November after having experienced a stroke on what was called Culture Day. Most of the time her sensory nerves were dysfuncional; she appeared to be just awaiting death.

Mokuzu sat by her head. She was seemingly unaware of the ruckus. Her face was smooth, but her lips were dry and wrinkled. He picked up the little water jug and inserted its pipe between her lips. She must have been quite thirsty; she drank at length. He was careful not to inhibit her breathing as he fed the water. She opened her eyes. They had a healthy light. Her nerves must have recovered temporarily.

"Are you Mokuzu? Thank you. Could you grant me my last wish?" She talked without moving her lips.

"I will attend to it whatever it is."

"Could you bring me a pair of white pigeons? You know, ever since I came here to marry Priest Kakkan I have wished to see them. How nice, circling in the sky over this Tangenji against green mountain...and reposing amiably on a rafter of the gate.

"From when I came in my twenty-fourth autumn until this my eighty-fifth spring, I never could obtain a pair...It was not that I was unable to find them or that I was too busy, but that I felt the most suitable time to welcome them had not yet come.

"I know it has not come even now, but I also know my life is closing. So this is my last and urgent wish...a pair of white pigeons." She shut her eyes and slept again.

Mokuzu brought to mind every acquaintance who might be keeping pigeons. Before leaving he had to clean her and change her diaper. He refilled the water jug and sat once more by her head. Her face was like that of an infant girl. She reopened her eyes, though they were vacant. Then she said,

"Mokuzu? Did you come back? Oh, how I thank you! You brought back such a fine pair of white pigeons. How peaceful they are, pecking for grains in the garden...rising and circling in the blue. They must have been hard to find. Thank you...you are the one who granted me my last wish...."

"Yes, they are beautiful over the temple roof in the blue sky," responded Mokuzu. But she was again inconscient.

He hesitated. Should he go out at once, or stay in case Gyodo got excited again? He went to Gyodo's room. He was fast asleep, his face too looking very childlike.

He went in search of white pigeons. 'Grandma is already satisfied, believing they are circling above. Yet her joy will be false if I don't bring her real ones. Only my effort can substantiate her joy. False joy is as bad as real misery. I've got to find her a pair!'

He visited some friends from elementary school days. By now all had given up their pigeon hobby; moreover, they confessed that they never chanced to keep any pure white ones.

Naota was feeding brans fresh-cooked with crushed soybeans and chopped straw to his cows. He had inherited his family work as soon as he finished junior high and did not mind the smell of feed and manure. He told Mokuzu that Ippei was the neighborhood pigeon fancier. It was well past lunch hour. As Mokuzu ran to Ippei's house, the weeds and pebbles underfoot appeared to stream as if viewed from the deck of a train.

Ippei had begun to serve in a public office, and he too had greatly reduced his number of pigeons, albeit without change of sentiment. He kindly led Mokuzu to his backyard, to a quite fancy iron-framed aviary, dome-shaped, with concrete floor, and equipped with water like one at a zoo.

He spoke of pigeon care, of his particular affection for pigeons, of the many advantages of keeping them, but concluded he had no white ones. He spoke of other possible keepers. Some Mokuzu had visited, yet he felt compelled to visit them all or he could not tell himself he had done his best for his grandmother.

Evening was approaching by the time he gave up and took the path home. The clouds hung low, the air was still. He felt very unclean in his sweaty underwear.

As he neared Tangenji, he realized that a voluminous smoke was rising high from the center of the main building.

At the gate he found his father, squatting, trembling.

"Mokuzu! Look! Gyodo has fired the temple!"

Gyodo, grasping a firebrand, was howling with the sound of a wolf that howls at the moon and pacing the veranda like a caged polar bear. Currents of fire twining with black smoke were gushing from the window of the grandmother's room. Approach was impossible.

"Mokuzu, what can I do? My mama, your grandma, is perishing in the fire! What an ultimate horror! Save us, Merciful Buddha, Save us, Merciful Buddha!"

"Where are Ran and Ma?"

"They went for the laymen's help."

'Well, I see my mind is cool as ice. Does Gyodo feel hot so near the fire? Now burning shojis and fusumas are falling on him. The steam from his head and shoulders looks pale white against the blackening flames...the nimbus of Satan.'

Explosive sounds of burning wood with streams of flame began to shoot from the thatched roof. The sky was dark with smoke, the garden bright with the flare.

Villagers came running from every direction, shouting as much as Gyodo. One climbed the gate and wildly banged the bell.

"The crazy man'll crack it!"

Mokuzu was amazed that his father's concern was the bell. Then he reflected, 'I too wasn't thinking anything great. It's quite unimportant whether Grandma died of old age or was killed by the fire, as I was wondering.'

The villagers were passing buckets in front of Doyu and Mokuzu, still at the gate. Through the murk, fire bells and sirens reechoed from other villages. The firemen parked the fire truck on the bank of the Sakura River and joined hoses across the fields to reach Tangenji.

Mokuzu thought, 'Those ordinary men are so practical on account of their shallow view of life. How can they assume that stopping the fire is the most recommendable deed at this moment of a long history of causation? The Great Plague of London, in 1695, was suppressed only by a great fire. Well, the common character of common people is to leave things unfinished.'

486

All about got entirely dark, whereat the fire more vividly exposed its nature. Flames were reaching far into the sky, sparks scattering everywhere.

"Fortunately there's no wind..." someone remarked. It was Tangenji's head layman, Yosetsu. He secured a seat next to the crouching Doyu.

"I figured he'd grow to be a great one, but not in this way...." He drew no response. The smoke swayed and a bright flame lit his face. He wore a smile, as Mokuzu expected.

Two men, one tall, one short, carried Gyodo out senseless. They were not firemen; they were in the dress of farmers.

"Who are they? Oh, Sen and Megu. Amazing, they're saving the life of a madman." Again it was Yosetsu speaking. As Mokuzu made to approach Gyodo being transported to where an ambulance or a patrol wagon was parked, Yosetsu took hold of his arm:

"Stay put — here's the best and safest vantage place. Let the others do the labor. You exercise your brain for guidance."

He motioned to Mokuzu to sit down beside him. Mokuzu sat down, but only because he agreed on the point that nothing would come of his moving about just then.

"Now why would those two rapscallions come to the rescue of Gyodo?" Yosetsu was genuinely confounded.

"Mokuzu, let me say how they troubled me for the past months. Have you any inkling of what they were up to? Well, they were up to no good all around the vicinity. They carried off whatever they found — TV sets, washing machines, rice cookers, sewing machines, mixers — of course every house is vacant because of field work. They're the first thieves to issue from this village in a thousand years. Indeed, Sen and Megu have disgraced our village. Your Gyodo is also a kind of disgrace for us, but unlike them. Can you guess what they did with their gains from a pawnshop? They spent it all in the geisha quarter of Kyoto. Yes, in Gion! How ironic it got its name from the original great Indian monastery, er...er..."

"Jetavananathapindadarama, you mean."

"Er, the great Indian Jetavana...built to honor Sakyamuni Buddha by the illustrious layman, er...er..."

"Sudatta, known as Anathapindada."

"Just so. But Kyoto's Gion has become a most depraved quarter. Anyway, there they spent it all. And finally they were caught red-handed taking timber and circular saws from a mill."

"If what you say is true, why aren't they in jail?"

"That's the very point we must consider. They were caught, and they aren't in jail. Far from it, they've saved Gyodo's life, as you and I just

487

witnessed. Why would they do that? Because I labored to quiet their affair for the sake of their future. I implored the town marshal on my knees, of course with much money. I prevented their prosecution, on account of which they are working as messiahs, at least for your insane brother." Yosetsu with a triumphant air regarded Mokuzu.

"I have been inclined to believe all messiahs are a disturbance to Buddha's will. I now see why," Mokuzu said sharply, but Yosetsu pretended not to have heard. Most of the fire was extinguished. The searchlights exposed a great anabatic smoke mixed with steam. The ridge beam and other timbers not burnt up remained as a skeleton of the building. The center was burnt away. The wings were left half charred. The sanctum and the room adjacent, where the grandmother was, were entirely gone.

"Now Mokuzu, you must be realistic. I don't know what you had in mind for your course after high school, but forget all that. First, you must unite your family, second, you must perform magnificent obsequies for your grandmother, third, you must reconstruct Tangenji, and this third is your most important and painstaking task. For this, you must raise the laymen's sense of religion. After all, the holy center of the temple is lost in the ash. Without their faith how can you raise their donation? See? Only you can raise religious fervor in these ignorant people. Be eager to rebuild and everyone will follow. They will cut good timber from their mountains, bring in skilled carpenters, and gather the money."

"Mokuzu, you are not obliged to listen to Yosetsu's trashy chat!" It was Micha. Mokuzu had not noticed that his mother and Ran were sitting on the other side of his father. Micha with both hands was clasping Doyu's hand.

Yosetsu with a smile left for the center of the burn, where the police and firemen were investigating. The charred body of the grandmother under a blanket was carried out on a stretcher.

Ran came to take Mokuzu's hand. "I'll also go nuts if I stay here. I'll leave for that obi company in Kyoto as early as I can. Why don't you go to Tokyo — at one time you wished to enter Hoso University. You too leave as early as you can!"

"She's right. The first thing you both must do is to flee this insanity. Don't worry about your mother and me. We will see the end of it. Return only when you find worse insanity wherever you go; otherwise never come back."

The sky was clearing. Stars twinkled above the mountains. Starlight reached directly to the earth where the skeleton of the main building remained after the fire.

39

The Newspaper Delivery Shop

The powder snow on the roof and ground was dazzling even under the February sun. It reminded Mokuzu of his want of sleep, and the feeling deterred him from thinking deeply.

A funeral for his grandmother had been held in grand style. The abbot of Nanzenji officiated, caparisoned in a most ceremonial surplice composed of seven gold-brocade pieces and embroidered with a scarlet crest, worn with a gold-brocade miter, a purple underrobe, and scarlet quilted shoes. Some thirty priests from the head temple and its local branches attended, filling the garden together with the villagers, whose numbers spilled over the stone steps and down the path.

The Zen master Hanun-kutsu could not attend, being ill in bed, and no invitation was extended to the Zen master Tengai.

'Just as snow covers all ugly surfaces and decorates even half-burnt beams, so a funeral conceals the sodden accretion of human dirt. A funeral is one of the most artificial attempts to ward off reality, to cut the flow of time; it assumes an air of love, trust, and respect, virtues that hardly ever exist on this earth in harmony,' thought Mokuzu.

Again Gyodo was locked in a narrow cell. Even its tiny aperture for admitting light had wire mesh and iron rods. Located behind the central buildings and under a scarped cliff, the isolation wards were in constant shade, and the snowflakes seemed to be drawn there more than anywhere else on the entire south-facing hill. Certainly the snow, drifted by the wind, was burying the yards of the isolation wards the most.

As he descended the meandering path after visiting Gyodo, Mokuzu looked back at the hospital: 'His insanity only half burnt Tangenji. I thought insanity was a matter of extremes. I now realize its nature is to be halfway. It effects no fine and lucid sight into the mysterious interrelations between the universe, human beings, and human society.'

ৈ

Wearing his best student uniform of black serge with gold buttons, to which he had added a pale bluish gray spring hat, Mokuzu set out on a special express train to Tokyo. He carried a green blanket with personal effects rolled would spend the night when he reached the capital, but next day he was going to take the Hoso University entrance exam. The train went on and on through snowy mountains and fields and passed by houses and over rivers and roads.

Within was cozy and warm. 'Being carried away is so easy. I can act like an ambitious youth sallying forth to the capital. But in fact I'm only escaping from my cursed native land.'

To rebuild Tangenji required a large supply of quality pine and cypress and excellent carpenters, with money indispensable. But money could be raised only from the laymen's faith, and their meetings devoid of faith raised nothing but vain arguments formed in caviling, disparaging, and sacrilegious words. Doyu and Micha had to sink into the slack water of pessimism and humiliation, and to Mokuzu they had said, "Go away somewhere! Do not dream of reconstructing Tangenji in friendship with the laymen. The age when laymen and priest in union felled the trees, hauled them from the mountain, built the temple, and cheerfully rested over tea and snacks is forever gone."

Mokuzu surely wished to understand the darkness of the mind and the profound truth. He wanted to master the pathology of the human mind and the human environment. He thought he would not be able to put any souls at ease unless he could see the causation of the world of the body and world of the spirit in the three worlds of past, present, and future.

Yet he did not detrain at Gifu, where a station provided a route to Shoshinji's professional training monastery. He kept on riding with the visages of those he ought to save...Ena, Luri, Gyodo, his father, his mother...

The reason he was choosing the university (despite his hunch that he was only postponing the monastery) might be summed up rhetorically in a sentence: he was choosing to study life instead of death. He thought all the problems he wished to solve had risen during the course of his life (even if, according to his speculation, their causes could have originated earlier).

'Present problems should be solved in the present world' he thought (and he thought he had no way to enter previous time in search of their causes unless he was willing to sacrifice his life).

'As long as I can't see my original nature before my parents were born, I can't dispel my basic questions. Zen Master Hanun told me so, and so asserted Zen Master Tengai. Their reasoning is very reasonable, but I have no reasonable way to see it. Surely a camel can go through a needle's eye more easily than a living person can enter the world of death.'

Then, was he convinced he would get his answer by university study? No, he was doubtful. He even suspected that the university and its professors could be merely an extension of his high school and its teachers. Yet he wanted to make sure with his own eyes (while he wished to postpone the monastery), and he thought he would determine once for all to enter the monastery when he was convinced that the university was not for him.

He could be going to Tokyo just to waste his time; he had no definite purpose but to confirm that Tokyo would not be his place. It was a negative and passive act devoid of joy and passion, and with gloom and hesitation he was letting himself be carried away by the train. The long ride would affect his semicircular canals, and the constant noise of the big city would disturb his ability to focus all his energies.

As for having chosen the private university Hoso out of hundreds of colleges and universities throughout the nation, he thought, 'It's not unlike getting on this train. Did I check the condition of the engine, wheels, and operator? No, I wasn't given the privilege or the ability and I can only hope for good luck.'

What he knew from the books on Hoso was only about its founding spirit and its glorious epoch of contribution to the development of modern Japanese literature. Presently too the university was famous, but Mokuzu did not know precisely why.

Hoso was founded in 1882 in a northwest suburb of Tokyo. The area, from which it took its name, was in those days yet wild fields, as *hoso* — "spring germination," or "resuscitation" would suggest. Its founding spirit was "to uphold a sovereign independence from police authority and political partisanship," derived from the founder's view that "independence of the nation is predicated on independence of the citizen; independence of the citizen on independence of spirit; and independence of spirit on independence of education."

Soon the university became the base for writers dissatisfied with the romantic literature prospering at the time. The romantics tended to describe only the beautiful aspects of human life. The new writers, calling themselves naturalists, wished to pursue more plain and unembellished human instincts, their interest being to resolve the difficult and contradictory relations between the finite self and the infinite natural world, and between social realism and utopia. Their new movement, though altogether influenced by Western literary pioneers, built Hoso's early reputation.[1]

Mokuzu had a vague but favorable impression of the founding spirit and literary activities; in fact it was his whole reason for coming to take Hoso's entrance exam instead of any other.

He reached the campus at midnight and spent the remainder of the night in the bushes, sitting in meditation form under a blanket. The wind carried no snow but was icy.

In the morning the candidates began to fill every space of the campus. More than two hundred thousand were said to be coming from every corner of the nation to take the exam. Over sixty percent were challenging it a second, third, or fourth time after devoting themselves to preparing for it year after year, and most of them did not care about their looks and were aging. These were called *ronin* after the old-time samurai who in anguish wandered masterless in search of a new alliance.

The exam subjects were Japanese, English, and Japanese history, two hours each, divided between the morning and afternoon. Mokuzu had no difficulty with the exam, but he was anxious to acquaint himself with someone who could help him find lodging and a job. He kept watching for a man suited to his needs.

The hall to which Mokuzu was assigned accommodated twelve hundred at once. Many proctors were posted, some of whom paced between the rows of desks as they glanced about to administer the exam in strict fairness. Most examinees showed no individuality.

Mokuzu thought an older, scruffier countryman a better choice than a younger, neat-looking urbanite.

A proctor spied a cunning one and shot to him like an arrow.

"Show me your pencil. Cribber! Leave the hall at once!"

The examinee had split the pencil and replaced the lead with a thin rolled paper covered with tiny-written notes. But the incident stirred the hall less than a falling leaf stirs a mountain lake.

In the afternoon Mokuzu noticed a man with dingy long hair, a rectangular face, and a slightly jutting, stubbled chin; no doubt a ronin. He was a seat ahead to the right, hissing at a pale, quiet youth: "Show me your answer or I'll tear you to shreds!"

The youth turned away and faced his desk aslant; it was the best he could do.

"Oi, why so stingy? You won't lose a thing, and think how I'll be helped!" The man persisted, in a milder tone.

A proctor came running on silent feet. The man drew in his head and must have been wincing in resignation, but the proctor passed by to one in the back who had an arm in a sling.

"What elaborate guile! Here I was sympathizing, but, lo, it's a phony arm replacing your own, busy out of sight. Out! healthy arm, rotten mind!"

The faker hurled the contrivance at the proctor and sang out as he left the hall, "Too bad for me! A curse on you and your exam! I'll return to my native land and wash my bull on the sands of the Kitakami, ha ha ha!"

492

The man who had been accosting the youth heaved a sigh and looked back. Catching his eye, Mokuzu gave him a warm, knowing smile. He returned an abashed smile.

As soon as the exam was over he approached Mokuzu,

"Hi, name's Taigo. You look like the freshest man in the capital. Me, I'm from Otaru, Hokkaido. I've been here already four years by now. How'd you make out?"

"I hadn't as hard a time as you. My concern isn't the exam but where to stay, preferably with a job."

"Well, come meet my boss, you'll be welcome. But are you ready to bear up? If you haven't money, you'll trade your time and self-respect for the cost of bed, board, and school. You look like a newly plucked peach. Are you willing to see your body and mind get fouled with soot, eh?"

Mokuzu was reminded of Luri's advice that he not uglify his body by karate. He also recalled Ena's mention of the birds of the heaven and the lilies of the field. 'I hope their spiritual eyes don't see me now. Oh, am I entering a mess!' He sadly saw himself, but he assumed a placid expression and replied,

"The sixth Zen patriarch, Hueineng, said in his stanza,

"By nature Bodhi has no tree,
Bright mirror has no stand.
In this world naught exists,
The dust can nowhere land."[2]

"Huh?" Taigo showed displeasure over the recondite stanza and bulled his way out through the crowd of candidates, who were forming groups, and who were many of them joining their parents.

"Hey, don't get separated from me! Wow, what a change! This place has become a kindergarten with all these mamas and papas doting on their spoilt grown-up babies! Hoso used to be only for the ambitious lone wolf. And see how many are girls, probably aiming for a degree to ornament their prospects for marriage. How do they regard this school's founding spirit?" Taigo, his shoulders brushing those same girls and spoilt grown-up babies, yelled back at Mokuzu. Mokuzu could only agree with his lament, and he really wondered if it would be worth the hardship of having to study with a great many of them.

When at last they neared the gate, they saw a group of students in red headbands shouting through a loudspeaker on a platform set against a towering brick hall that was a memorial to the founder. Their speeches were hard to hear with the strepitant crowd and the echoes. Everyone was passing by in front of them without giving them any attention. Having removed himself

493

with Taigo to where the huge clock on the memorial hall was more easily in sight, Mokuzu asked,

"Who are they and for what are they appealing?"

"They're fools crying for world revolution. They denounce capitalism and such, though in fact they're sons of fat company presidents, lawyers, doctors, and, you know. They sponge off their folks for school, living costs, pocket money, and worst, for these stupid campaigns." Taigo was disgusted.

"You mean they don't see the contradiction between their means and their purpose," Mokuzu simply restated. Taigo ignored him and went on with his shallow empirical view,

"Were they ever noisy when I first came — in Kyoto too. Didn't you hear about the Anpo struggle? Maybe you were too young. The leading faction of the Zengakuren intruded into the prime minister's official residence and collided with the police. Eisenhower was compelled to put off his presidential visit. In June they dashed into the National Diet; it was the bloodiest collision ever between students and police. The police killed a coed, and about two hundred students were arrested.

"Nowadays the Zengakuren are split to a Communist-led party and its opponent, the Anti-Yoyogi, and each again keeps splitting. In 1960 at least they opposed the establishment; now they only quarrel among themselves. In a word they're fools practicing masturbation and that's all."

Mokuzu had been too young to have an interest in the social phenomena of those days. But even if he had been older he would not have cared, for he was going through the gloomiest days of his private life. The death of Ena, the outbreak of Gyodo's illness, Luri's misery, and his uncertainty over what course to take were all problems not in the least solved even now. He was ashamed of his lack of talent and will and could make no sense of the fact that he was in Tokyo next to a chap who had nothing in common with him except that he was poor.

'Here an individual is less significant than a snowflake at the window of my native retreat cottage. The crowds are dust floating on a constant vibration. I have to make up my mind to find a place where I can honestly face my problems. A life of mourning could be next best to a heavenly life, at least far better than a life of disturbance from endless and meaningless social phenomena....'

"Oi, where are you going? We wait here for the bus to Takada-no-baba, then take the Yamate-line train to Shinjuku, where we change to a central line to Asagaya. Don't worry, I'm taking you to Suginami, one of Tokyo's quietest wards, a high-class residential quarter."

Taigo stopped at the end of the queue waiting for the bus.

494

"Of course it's noisy, cramped, and grubby, but you can look down on a neighbor's fancy garden from the upstairs window."

"Can't we walk there?"

"Hey, don't be a bumpkin...or, you mean you haven't money for the fare? Where'd you spend the night?"

"On campus." Mokuzu raised his blanket roll.

"Oh yeah, that's why you looked odd..."

"Really, have you no money?" a willowy girl in an overcoat turned around in the line and rapidly asked.

"I have, but...I don't know what needs will come," replied Mokuzu with flushed cheeks.

"If you don't mind, I can pay your fare." She too blushed.

"Well, I do mind. Thank you, but I have no reason to receive your kindness."

"Mokuzu! Don't act like Alyosha. Receive it gladly. Our best kindness is to receive kindness from the rich. And you must recognize love at first sight. It's natural for a lusty girl when she sees your erect figure, penetrating eyes, and cool, clean-cut face." With a grin Taigo fingered his stubble. Mokuzu disliked him for acting insensitive; he could see that Taigo was truly shy by nature.

The girl regarded Taigo with scorn and said yet more rapidly with a yet redder face,

"How can you misjudge me, as if you have no trace of justice and honor? I offered as naturally as a flower opens in spring!"

"Lady, you said it — like your crotch before an attractive guy, he he he!"

The girl moved away before Mokuzu could restrain Taigo and apologize. 'How destructive and unfortunate to have to mix with this ruffian!' he thought with a smile of resignation.

At Shinjuku they took an elevated train circuiting the heart of the metropolis. The pedestrians and cars below looked like ants and flies. Offices passed by at eye level. Mokuzu looked up. The tall buildings appeared to be in motion and the clouds static.

"The shop is just halfway between Asagaya and the stop after that, Koenji, so I always hesitate where to get off. It's the only confusion in my life," spoke Taigo with fulsome inuendo.

"Well, confusion can come of fatigue, and a life without confusion can be the effect of an obliteration of the brain," Mokuzu sharply countered.

From Asagaya Station they walked south through a busy shopping district, across an eight-lane highway called Oume, and into the quieter residential town that Taigo had spoken of. But they actually went to a poorer street of shabby retail shops mixed with relatively new residences, where another big highway, Itsuka-ichi, crossed diagonally.

495

A metal facia with "World Financial Newspaper Delivery" written in red on yellow took up all the upper front of the shop.

Taigo slid open one of the four ill-fitting glass-paneled wooden doors. On a concrete floor stood black, sturdy bicycles with sturdy carriers. A raised lauan-wood floor and soon a frosted-glass sliding door divided the entry area from the interior. To the right was a door from which toilet malodor seeped, to the left, the foot of a dark, steep, and narrow staircase.

The frosted-glass door opened rather violently and a short middle-aged man in a brownish wool cardigan popped out with a forceful step. He had dark loose hair, a blocky dark face, and glaring eyes.

"Oh, you, Taigo, welcome back. Who've you brought, eh? But first, how'd you do on your exam?"

"Boss, I'm quite sure I didn't make it this year too, but I found a good one, at least as far looks and words go." Mokuzu was introduced. He saw beyond the inner door. Cheap veneer chests and drawers lined the walls, making the narrow room narrower, and mostly it was taken up by an electrically heated low table under a bright quilt. In a corner a TV set was on.

A woman, obviously the wife, came from the kitchen. She had a soft white face with bright eyes and was a size larger than the boss. She must have come from a northern region of Japan. Mokuzu could scarcely comprehend her words and had to guess by Taigo's response.

"Sure, my folks must be awaiting good news from me, but what's the difference waiting five years or ten?...Yeah, he came up from Kyoto just yesterday. I figure he's smart. He must've passed the exam. Boss, how about if he stays and works with us?"

"You are most welcome. Fine then, don't lose time. Start this evening and follow Taigo to learn the route. I've only one or two things to tell you.

"First, I don't care if you're smart or not — just deliver the paper correctly and on time. I dislike hearing any excuses. Even if an earthquake attacks you or you get a high fever — just deliver. Second, I dislike flattery, either to speak it or be spoken to. But I'll watch how you work at the deliveries, and at your studies, and I'll practice my welfare. See? Then don't be lazy.

"Frankly, I didn't go beyond grade school. At fifteen I came up with only a clay brazier for cooking my meals on in the street. But now you see I'm boss of this shop with twenty-five hundred subscribers. It may be humble, but I'm my own boss. Someday you too can be boss of whatever you desire."

'I understand him; it's reasonable in his position not to like to hear any excuse. I also understand his dislike of flattery. But I can't so easily understand about my becoming a boss. He means only a power relation in society, while my concern isn't power relations but friendly relations, and more, not social

496

relations but rather relations between human beings and the spiritual world, that is, my concern has to do with the substantial content of the universe, I guess...,' thought Mokuzu, and by his appearance he impressed the boss, his wife, and Taigo as a cold, impertinent, and inexperienced kid.

"Taigo, take him up and show him whatever he cares to see. By the way, I'll pay you fittingly for your trouble to find a newcomer."

The stairs creaked. On the left side of the mean landing was a small window to admit light. Taigo glanced out.

"You can see a beautiful garden, as I said."

Mokuzu looked down to a stone path with rocks, shrubs, and trees arranged alongside, leading from a street-side iron gate to the house. Accustomed to the far more aesthetic gardens of Kyoto, he was underwhelmed. The path badly emphasized the narrow oblong space, and the overuse of white rocks and sand, while providing a brightness, contributed also a lack of depth.

He noticed at the doorway a young housewife with a white apron over a short skirt sweeping in and out of the shade of plants.

Taigo rapped on the panel door facing the landing.

"Kamiya! Hey, Mr. Kamiya! I have to introduce you," and he told Mokuzu, "This one's a nephew of the boss, already twenty-eight and quite a literature enthusiast."

There was no response.

"He might be asleep..." Taigo leaned way down to peep through a hole, obviously made by a kick long ago.

"Hm? *Uhia*! Look, look for yourself, I can't explain..." He moved away and forced Mokuzu to lean down.

Mokuzu saw shelves filled with translations of foreign literature.

"Look left!"

Mokuzu could see the legs of a person. 'What? Peeing in his room? No...viewing the garden...the neighbor's wife!' He had his back to the door but evidently was agitating a hand in front.

Mokuzu stood up. Taigo was fixing an eye on the woman. She was stooping to rake dirt into a dustpan. Her calves showed a high color.

"Mr. Kamiya! May I enter?" Taigo boomed. He winked at Mokuzu. So loud was his voice that even a great Zen master would have been shaken from his samadhi.

"Why do you disrupt my precious time? I am reading." The sound of closing the window curtain followed his spoken annoyance.

"You're the oldest, so I felt obliged to introduce the newcomer to you first." Taigo stuck out his tongue for Mokuzu's benefit. Mokuzu maintained his usual composure.

"Let me see what sort of worn-out freshman he is."

Taigo opened the door and pushed Mokuzu forward. The cramped four-and-a-half-mat room had an insalubrious smell. Mr. Kamiya was pretending to have been reading the book on his desk. He closed it, raised a rosy, brazen face, and haughtily spoke,

"Ah, you're but a child. Too bad those clear eyes will soon be bloodshot, those pretty lips cracked, and worst, that purity soiled by the town. You'll be good only as a newsboy, another sample of how soon a lad can deteriorate. Don't you know W. B. Yeats' 'The Second Coming'?

> "Things fall apart; the centre cannot hold;
> Mere anarchy is loosed upon the world.[3]

"See? In Tokyo you're an atomy, a mere ingredient melting in the stew. Then, if you have nothing extraordinary to tell me, leave and go settle in somewhere."

"I bet you love *Ulysses*," Mokuzu stated quietly.

"Hm, you could guess? In fact my primary concern is the pursuit of the stream of consciousness. That is the profundity of man, and James Joyce — "

"I read it, and I hated it." Mokuzu cut him off and concluded in retort,

"It was just profound enough for the author and his followers to excuse themselves from self-discipline and to disdain others. But it was too shallow for them to realize the joy of having the responsibility of living in this world, like the joy Atlas most possibly has been having."

"What do you mean, you neophyte?" Mr. Kamiya groaned unpleasantly. Taigo, fearing a conflagration, pulled Mokuzu from the room, leaving the words, "Sorry, we've no time — see you later."

He shut the door and opened the fusuma on the right side of the landing. In a six-mat room two younger men were packing bedding, clothes, books, and miscellanea into a huge russet baling bag with dirty gray rope attached.

They had heard the exchange and offered warm greetings.

"You've a fine voice, and I was delighted by your riposte," said one, called Iwashita.

"Mr. Kamiya deserves your cynicism. I've had a hard time caricaturing him," added the other, Osa, introduced as an aspiring cartoonist.

Both had unbarbered hair, obviously out of need to save money. Iwashita's was coarse and scruffy, and his bright affable eyes darted about like a squirrel's. Osa's was thin and smooth, and his eyes showed lack of sleep.

"You'll be here with Osa and me. Each can have a space of two mats. Iwashita, as you see, is leaving. He was waiting for a successor, and you came just in time," explained Taigo.

"The opposite of you, I'm heading for Kyoto to go to Doshisha. I'll leave as soon as you learn my route."

"He challenged Hoso's exam three times without success, but he's not like Taigo, who stubbornly tried today for the fourth time, knowing it's useless. Iwashita took Doshisha's exam the other day and was best of all!" reported Osa jubilantly as if it were a heroic deed.

Content, Iwashita spoke of Osa in return,

"He just found work as assistant to a famous cartoonist. Soon he'll be richer than our boss. By the way, is that blanket all you brought? You'll be much too cold. I'll leave you one of mine." He began to unpack, but Taigo stopped him,

"Don't be silly, man, he spent the night on the Hoso campus, and today I watched him refuse a good-looking coed's kind offer. How can you expect him to accept a filthy blanket stiff with the semen of you and Osa? Come on, Mokuzu, I'll show you the pen of some more semi-student bond laborers." Taigo without even a knock opened the fusumas.

Beyond was an eight-mat room, just above the entrance. Panel glass windows faced the street.

Three men were absorbed each in his own interest on unfolded bedding and none even so much as turned. In their cramped quarters they must have mastered the art of concentration.

At an easel in the dark right-hand corner, one was sketching in pencil. In the center, facing the windows, another was assembling a scrapbook of clippings from weekly news magazines piled about. To the left, the third was asleep with black-rim glasses on his white brow.

"Hey, get up!" shouted Taigo. The sleeper jumped up, sending his glasses flying. Groping for them, he mumbled, "Why so early today? Well, I'll deliver quick as I can. I've my girl tonight!"

"Shibuki, it isn't delivery time. There's a newcomer," said Taigo with a grin.

"Oh, then let me be. You know I didn't sleep last night — and she wants me again tonight!" Shibuki pulled the quilt over his head without seeing Mokuzu.

"Hi, I'm Maruya, a sophomore at Chuo. I'm doing a scrapbook for my prof — he's a noted publicist. It's my second part-time. My third is to monitor for a public employment security office."

"Why do you like to work so much? When do you get a chance to study?" asked Mokuzu innocently.

"Why do I 'like'? How can I like working for money? I'm working out of need. If you enter a university you'll find all sorts of hidden costs, and the salary of this shop is barely enough to buy salt. I haven't a girl. Shibuki's is

499

working in a factory and sponsoring him. Taigo is sent extra money from home, and besides, he isn't yet a student. Kamiya gets pocket money from the boss. Osa is paid for his cartoon work, and Iwashita is helped by Osa, though what'll happen if he goes to Kyoto? Well, it's not my concern. And Shirato, hey, quit drawing and come say hello. He too isn't yet a student — he keeps failing the entrance exam of Tokyo University of Fine Arts and Music. But he can get extra income by picking up stuff along his delivery route, yes, he just picks up others' belongings...."

"Look, everybody! No, only you — how should I call you?...hm, 'Mokuzu'? Look at this. I know what they think. Give me your true view without prejudice and hopefully without pride."

The page showed an abozzo of an imaginary seated nude with the averted face of a maiden, yet with hips and buttocks broad and saggy like a char-woman's. In short, a disharmony was presented, and nothing suggested the woman's inner life.

"My thinking faculty before your picture is at a stalemate, which may accord with the artist's intent...so I've nothing to say except I'm happy your interest is to draw and not to play music," Mokuzu uttered with hesitation.

"Did you hear, Maruya? Taigo? He admitted the influential power of art: art transcends dualistic argument and directly appeals to absolute beauty. On top of that, he acknowledges the world's joy to have me as an artist. You'd better be ashamed of your habitual contempt and lack of acuity as regards my talent and output!"

"Don't be an ass. Mokuzu, kindly tell this sad fool in plainer terms," said Maruya.

"Well, I don't want to be harmful, but I'll dare mention that my sumi painting teacher once told me, 'It's like opening a bank account without a penny if you attempt to draw the human figure before mastering how to draw flowers and grasses.' Yet, as I said, I'm lucky to be spared living with a musician; a painter's pollution is more bearable."

Everyone had a good laugh. Fortunately Shirato too was laughing, with watery eyes.

The brakes of a delivery truck squealed, and soon after came the successive thuds of bundled newspapers being unloaded to the pavement.

Everyone ran downstairs, took as many copies as the number of his subscribers, wrapped them in a thick waterproof cloth, tied it on a bicycle carrier with old inner tubing, and raced off to his delivery zone.

Mokuzu, provided with a subscriber booklet, followed Taigo.

"The morning paper is three to four times heavier. Watch out for ice. Your hands will be so cold you'll cry, and you'll fall as often as a baby." Taigo was considerate of Mokuzu.

First they delivered to single-family houses. Then they came out to a new development of some dozen concrete apartment buildings, walk-ups as high as thirteen floors. They left their bicycles and ran up and down the flights of stairs. Every landing had two identical facing doors, so Mokuzu had difficulty remembering which were the doors of subscribers.

The fluorescent lights in the stairways began to turn on. When at last they finished the apartments, it was dark but for the street lamps and car lights. In the darkness Mokuzu had no way to learn the route, and worse, he had had a bad night and no food since morning. Just following Taigo was excruciating. He felt a greasy clamminess spread over his entire body. His foul breath made him sick. Repeatedly he felt like vomiting and fainting. Taigo looked back with pity,

"You've a good brain and good looks, but you can't take hard labor. I wonder how long you can stay on in Tokyo."

"I'm sorry to delay you. Don't worry about me, I'll stay in Tokyo until I see through its nature."

Toward the end they came to a wide river and delivered to the poor two-story houses along by its bank. On the far side was a public park with mercury lamps in places shining on a lush growth of trees and on pairs of young lovers.

They returned around eight. The delivery took over three hours. The others had finished supper and looked at them with sympathy but without a word while assembling fly sheets from six different piles, which they would insert into the morning paper.

The boss did not appear. His wife brought out reheated miso soup. "You were so late we worried you had an accident. Mokuzu, you'll soon get used to it and can eat your rice hot."

The boss's scolding voice came through the frosted glass, and he called, "Oii, come! Ta's fuss is making my piles ache!"

The cries of a baby followed. The wife hurried in, wiping her hands on her bulging rear end.

As soon as Mokuzu went upstairs after the meager supper and another hour's work on the fly sheets, Maruya, Shirato, and Taigo invited him to a tavern for a welcome party. He begged off, wrapped himself in his blanket like a bagworm, and fell asleep as if he were fainting away.

"How can he sleep in peace while Osa and Iwashita are at a gay bar, Shibuki's at his girl's, and Kamiya is dissipated in reading *Ulysses*?" jested Shirato.

Mokuzu woke at three-thirty in the morning. He had recovered from his fatigue. But he realized when he went down to the toilet that his hands were filthy with newspaper ink. As quietly as he could, he pulled the hose outside from the sink, undressed, and doused himself with the icy water. There was no traffic of any sort. The houses were dead asleep in the street light.

"Are you crazy?" The boss was anxiously regarding him; he had been awakened by the sound of the water. "Don't you see the snowflakes, eh? I was alarmed because there's guys come here saying they'll work, and next day they're gone with all you others' money. But your austere conduct surprises me more."

The newspapers came at four, still warm from the rotary press. Everyone inserted a set of fly sheets into each of his papers and hurried to his zone.

The stack on Taigo's carrier was about two feet high. Mokuzu followed.

Everywhere was dark except for the white street lights and the twinkle of stars. The sound of brakes echoed in the sleeping town, not only theirs but the bicycles of other newspaper shops. A milkman rattled his bottles. A van delivering bread to the small retail shops passed by.

After they finished the better residential area Taigo asked,

"Aren't you hungry?"

"Sure, I'm very hungry. Last night I couldn't eat much, but my appetite has recovered with my health."

Taigo took a bottle of milk from a wooden box on the gate of a house where he made a delivery and tossed it to Mokuzu.

"Taigo, how can you steal?" Mokuzu was amazed.

"Think about morals after you gain the energy to think." Taigo finished off another bottle and returned it empty to the box.

Mokuzu too drank. How fresh and sweet it was!

"Take all you want. Most houses have milk delivered. I'll find you bread." They came to a retail shop with shutters closed to the ground, but piled under the eaves were wooden trays of bread sending forth a fresh aroma. Taigo took some for Mokuzu.

"Thanks, but I now have the energy to think about morals."

"Then eat till you dull your sense of morals," and all of a sudden Taigo recited in translation a stanza of Tennyson,

> "Break, break, break,
> On thy cold gray stones, O Sea!
> And I would that my tongue could utter
> The thoughts that arise in me."[4]

Mokuzu felt momentarily watched by Ena from the sky. Then he ate the

502

bread and hurried to catch up with Taigo as he sped toward the tall apartment buildings.

They had to be careful to keep their steps on the stairs quiet, with everyone still asleep. A fluorescent light on one of the landings kept turning on and off.

At the last building Taigo said,

"See? We're of one of the lowest classes in Tokyo, but we can have the freshest milk and bread, news too if you like. And another great thing I'll show you. It's becoming a clear dawn." Taigo went on up to the roof. Thirteen stories down, the earth was black and dormant. Human habitats clinging to the land spread gloomily out of sight. Most of the sky was dark with no more stars and no sunlight yet.

"Look at the sky over the Pacific. The horizon's getting to be like a bright strip of cloth."

An aurelian band lay between the dark ocean and the dark sky.

"Don't you see Mt. Fuji?"

"Er...oh, is it that?...such a tiny pyramid?"

"Keep watching, now it's only an ashy inverted fan, but soon, yes! — keep watching!"

The little independent triangle began to wear a coat of red, and the red began to emit powerful rays as if it were burning in anger. The vigor of the rays was extraordinary, unbelievable, coming from such a tiny figure.

After a while the mountain ceased to radiate any light and changed to red ocher against the sky, then to yellow, then to blue. Then it paled into a haze. There was no more Mt. Fuji, and the sky was cloudy with smog.

"You'll never see it the exact same color. We're lucky, most days you can't see it at all. So you're one of the most fortunate of all ten million Tokyoites."

As soon as they returned, the boss violently opened the frosted door and shouted,

"Why are you slow as turtles? The phone's been ringing with a hell of a lot of complaints — it's already eight o'clock. Mokuzu, don't forget our subscribers are taking the paper out of need. Before they go to their offices they have to read all the financial news or they'll be fired!"

The wife brought out reheated miso soup and for each a big bowl of rice with a raw egg — "Soon you'll get used to it and can finish before seven. Otherwise how can you attend school?"

When they went upstairs they found Iwashita and Osa already gone and the others sleeping again.

A telephone rang and the boss shouted up,

"Kamiya! You skipped a house — hurry, take them their paper and apologize very well."

"Oh, how burdensome...must this too be part of my mortal coil?" Kamiya declaimed as he descended the stairs.

Around three, an hour before evening delivery, the boss summoned everyone and said,

"Iwashita left for Kyoto, as you know. That's fine, he told me he would a month ago, and Taigo found Mokuzu. But the problem is Osa. He just phoned, and can you guess? He's quitting and never coming back. I asked why, but he only laughed. I said, 'If you quit without notice I can't find a replacement — who will deliver instead of you?' Again he laughed. I told him, 'My piles are terrible; can't you put it off?' But he only kept laughing.

"So you know what to do: help one another in this trouble and share the work he left you till I find someone else. For your extra work I'll treat you to a public bath whenever it rains in the daytime. See? It's quite fair?"

No one complained until they all were upstairs.

ે

After nearly three weeks Mokuzu was quite used to delivering newspapers and could eat with the others. At breakfast Taigo asked him,

"How about going to see the exam results? Today's the day."

"I have no reason to go."

"Nor I, but...there's a speck of hope."

"Yes, go with Taigo. It's scary, but you have to face it," said the boss's wife.

"No, he means he passed, whereas I bet I failed."

"Taigo, how can you be so sure? He could be as bad as you," said Maruya.

"Right, Taigo, from the start you could declare you failed this year too. But if you overestimate him, he has to act like he thinks he made it, and today he feels like a cornered mouse. Look at his depressed face," Kamiya interpreted scornfully.

"Mokuzu, you aren't alone. Me and Taigo are your buddies. Mr. Kamiya gave up on any university long ago," put in Shirato.

"Don't worry about the first failure. You have to know how to fail and endure for the bigger victory, as I did. I spent six years getting into Keio, which is as good as Hoso. When your failure is certain, I'll tell you my hard story," Shibuki added his words of comfort.

"See? Everybody cares about you. You'd better go with Taigo. I'll give you traffic fare if you need it. And I'll see that you get a party tonight whether you passed or not," encouraged the wife.

Everyone but Mokuzu cheered up. He stood to go upstairs. No one followed. In the quiet of the room he meditated on what he should do,

'Now I know what university students are by the real examples of Maruya and Shibuki. They work for money and have hardly any study time. What's the point of becoming like them?

'To enter Hoso I must pay the equivalent of ten months' salary from this shop. I'd better think. Every day at four I have to get up for newspaper delivery. After breakfast I'll attend school. At four-thirty there's evening delivery, and by the time I finish supper and the fly sheets it'll be eight-thirty. Only then can I have my own time. But how late can I stay up? Till twelve at most. Is this student life? Is it enough study for me? On Sundays and holidays I must collect the newspaper fee. What's the value of being a student with so little time?'

After lunch hour Taigo came back full of glory. The boss and his wife invited everyone to hear his report and offered red tea and cookies.

"So on your fourth try you got in?" she asked.

"Ha? Me? Don't be silly. I can still be a free ronin. But listen, I saw Mokuzu's name at the top. He's the best of all 7,500 successful candidates. And more, he got a 91 average while the second best, a girl, got only a 76."

They all clapped, and boldly Shibuki asked the boss,

"So where's the booze?"

"Tut! One might wonder which of you I'm supposed to congratulate," remarked the boss with a pleasant face, and he brought out a bottle, saying,

"This is all for now; soon you have evening delivery. Hey, Mokuzu, enjoy it when you have it to enjoy! I know, the entrance fee worries you. Don't worry, I'll gladly make you a loan. Shibuki and Maruya have loans from me."

Mokuzu left for evening delivery. As he worked he thought,

'I must be greatly mistaking my way. It's not my purpose to obtain an empty diploma like those who intend to enter a company. My purpose is to study the problems of life rationally and thoroughly. But how can I while I have no money and no time?

'If I borrow from the boss, I'll be enslaved at least ten months just to return it, without buying books or clothes.

'If this is life and reality, why should I cling to it? Wouldn't it be better to go to the monastery and face the problem of death? The path of Sakyamuni Buddha couldn't be as meaningless as this reality in Tokyo. I'm sure Ena will contract her brow and ask, "What's the purpose of such a dirty life? You are one who has to seek the most beautiful life on earth.'"

He passed a tennis court. The bright March sun in the cold air lit up the white outfits of the girl players. A yellow ball skimmed over the dark green net. As the opponent met it with a backhand, her short skirt flew up, entirely exposing white briefs. The ball soared, and the receiver jumped and bent back to return it. As she swung forward, her well-fleshed breasts seemed almost to touch the net.

'How odd, they're enclosed behind a wire screen, yet I outside feel I'm the one enclosed, like Gyodo in his hospital.'

Mokuzu rode on with half a heart. He went to the roof of one of the thirteen-story buildings. The day was getting longer; the sunset was just beginning to illume the smoke of a tall factory chimney. Ena in his mind told him, "How I'd enjoy your enjoying tennis with those girls under the blue sky!"

When he came to the river, he saw boats with lovers pleasuring in evening rides. In the dusk the mercury lamps shone on them and the water. But no light made visible him and the bicycle. Riding on in the darkness he thought,

'When can I actualize life on a sunny hill where dandelions early bloom, the life Ena and I hoped for...? I hear her entreating, "Please be quick to find a companion who is wiser than me, and more earnest and more beautiful, and live a happy life with her. My spirit will be saved by her, and my short life given its greatest meaning."

'True, I have to find a companion who can realize the dream of hundreds and thousands of girls as pure and earnest as Ena....But first I have to finish my basic study and training so that she will not be made as unfortunate as Ena.'

V

Bluish Sacred Prints

Correction:

V

Bluish Sacred Precincts

40

Westward from the Capital of Dirt

3/31: My Tokyo life is like factory spilth. The surface is a filthy scum, and the undercurrent sweeps me off my feet. The papers variously claim life is dear, but rarely do I feel my life is so. Days I labor, nights I'm weary, and I can't confirm who I am. Nothing is worth recording. Yet someday I may have time to ruminate on my experiences, so I'm starting this diary.

4/3: In the morning I entered an unexpectedly deep, boggy puddle. The back tire sank with its heavy load, the front reared up, and as I struggled on, I took a bad fall. I ignored my wounds — they're no harm to others — but I was distressed that the papers had slid off and become drabbled about the edges. A gust blew many away, and as I raced for them the rest began to scatter to garbage cans and into bushes beyond the light of the street lamps. What a bother!

I couldn't apologize, all subscribers being asleep, but one kimonoed early-riser with a dog received his at his gate. I apologized, he asked what happened, I explained, and apologized again. "Yes, I see why you're wet, but why is my paper?" Dreadfully obstinate, he wanted it unblemished at the risk of my life. I could only further apologize. "You think apology settles it? You're attending university? What a worthless student!" he discharged and went into his house. I noticed his nameplate bears the title of public prosecutor.

4/7: Toward morning I dreamed I was laboring through a pile of books and over my desk a calendar showed a woman who changed to Ena. At first she stood in a red skirt, regarding me. February she was running in search of me along a snowy riverbank. March she was under a cherry, April, resting on a mountain path. The months thus passed. November, she was in her room arranging her belongings. December, she put on her overcoat and said, "Good-bye, I must set out on a journey." Disbelieving, I jumped from my bed only to realize the morning papers had arrived from the head office.

On my route, as I was indulging in recalling my sweet, sad, lonely dream, suddenly there was an oblong hole, deep enough for a room. The utility workers hadn't fenced it or posted a warning. I was already falling, turning in midair, landing on my back. The shock of impact was like being hit in the solar plexus during karate. The bicycle came after, striking me on the head with the front wheel, fortunately not the mudguard. The sky still showed stars. I could only sit and wait for someone to approach. I fretted as I visualized subscribers calling to demand their papers and the boss growing sour as vinegar. Pitiful, but comical because it wasn't serious.

4/9: Shirato left without a word. The boss raged and despite having piles

509

set off with a towel tied on his head. "How humiliating the boss has to deliver!" he said. He looked pathetic.

"I'm the only one he confided in," Maruya told me and explained that Shirato was in love with a young wife in his delivery zone. As it developed badly he couldn't bear to stay on, and to change his heart he left. It was said the husband worked in Osaka. She was gentle and beautiful and just smiled at him when he handed her the paper or came to collect the fee. But one day she spoke over the hedge, "How admirable of you to be studying in adversity. Which school do you attend?"

Out of vanity he couldn't say he had long been and still was a ronin, so he said he was a student at the Tokyo University of Fine Arts and Music. Further impressed, she revealed her interest in painting. From then on she had encouraged him to become a great artist, and they had established a stand-and-chat relationship.

He was ashamed of gaining her goodwill by a lie, but didn't know how to confess his aching heart. Last Sunday he resolved to stop by during bill collection to tell her. She was carrying a birdcage into the sun in the garden when she noticed him. Smiling, she said, "Today what can I do for you? Surely I paid for last month?"

Her bright voice and smile promptly dampened his resolve. He admitted she was right, and apologized. But when he started to leave, she said she had something he must need that she kept forgetting to give him. She went in and returned with a square package. With intense pleasure he rode home and made a show of unwrapping it before Maruya. It was bars of soap. Maruya burst out laughing, insisting that she couldn't stand his face and hands smirched with newspaper ink. Shirato was outraged; he thought her discourteous, and ridiculed himself for his naievete. Then he grew dispirited. What a pity, he's more naive than I!

4/19: Sunday — collection day. The boss's policy is that we each be responsible for our zones, and any uncollected bills are subtracted from our salaries. I have 3 who moved without paying last month's bill. I was greatly mistaken to think I could reimburse within 10 months what the boss lent me for the university entrance fee. How dumb of me! If I'm not careful my debt will increase the more I work.

Recently he's been pressing us to get more subscribers. An agent came yesterday from the head office to give us training. Today I made some trials. I found it extremely hard. To begin with, those who must read our paper already subscribe and to all others it's useless. I failed at the 10 houses I tried but spent long hours and many words. I'm like a kid who goes fishing, catches nothing, falls in the stream, and goes home wet.

On the way back I rode along the river and saw cherry petals from the park snowing onto the current. It was like a sheet of pink ice. I stood my bicycle and went down.

Two children, likely brother and sister, were looking into the water, she in a russet cardigan, navy skirt, white knee socks, saddle shoes. I was again a schoolboy seeing Ena. I approached with an impulse to ask them what they saw.

"Haruko! Masao! Come!" someone called. The girl turned. "But Mother, there's fish!" I then could see: close-set eyes, bulging brow, puffed cheeks, crooked teeth — far beneath comparison.

"It's dangerous. I want you up here on the double!" "We won't slip, we always come!" "Not only that, there are many dangers these days!" The tone alarmed the girl. When she stood and saw me, her face formed the expression of a shriek. She yanked the boy's hand and they clambered up the bank.

4/24: Hoso disappoints me even though I chose it and must take the consequences. Finished morning delivery, went straight to the lecture. Huge hall. I sit in front. The professors read from notes through a microphone, scarcely look up except to wipe their glasses or clear their throat. As for the material, they borrow from many Westerners and haven't their own view.

Occasionally I ask a question, much as I know it's rude. Some eye me glumly and tell me to ask later because the question is too particular. Later they give me no chance, and I can't secure one, pressed as I am by evening delivery. Others respond with admiration, saying it's nice I raise unique questions, but they answer merely that they'll research further.

So few students are earnest. Some in back play mah-jongg. The professors pretend not to notice. I can only say it isn't worth the high entrance fee I paid and the high tuition fee, which I'm not yet paying. Above all I'm dumbfounded by the professors' many absences, taken without advance notice and utterly for their own convenience. The university ought to make refunds for these absences. As it is, it's a kind of fraud. And how disgusting to see students shout for joy in front of the notices of canceled classes. Such chaos!

5/3: Slight fever these days, excessive fatigue during delivery. Come to think of it, I've had lunch just twice or so since I came. Daily the boss's wife gives us lunch money. I choose to spend it on used paperbacks because I'm keeping the discipline of taking the harder path whenever I'm at a loss. Maybe the fever is from no lunch and chronic lack of sleep. Anyway I have a dry throat and bad breath and am very tired.

5/7: Fever, fatigue, refreshed only when I douse in the morning with cold water.

Near the end of last month two queer men came in one after the other. Yamino's hair and clothes are neat, eyes narrow, voice thin. Makes no sound even when he laughs, often talks to himself. Doesn't raise his bowl and chopsticks to his mouth but draws his mouth to them like a beast. His distinctive talent is to steep himself in his own world even when others are close by. From my experience with Gyodo I'd say he's a psychopath.

The boss's wife brought us the usual supper — a big bowl of rice, miso soup, and fried egg on shredded cabbage. Facing his, Yamino began to sob. We all worried, tried to get him to speak, and I patted his back. At last he said, "Look at this plate — it's cracked, never can it return to perfection!"

Nagane is as old as Kamiya, face dark like a Chinese artichoke, constitution poor, heavy Northeastern accent. Rooms with Taigo and me. Oddly he sleeps with his eyes open. Doesn't read like Kamiya, doesn't attend university like me or cram school like Taigo, but attends meetings of a new religion and solicits new believers.

When here, he concentratedly repeats "*Namu myoho renge kyo*," the Nichiren prayer, as he faces a small black portable altar, louder and louder, and no one knows when he'll stop, and everyone is annoyed. I too find reading impossible. We hadn't nearly enough time to read even before he came. Yesterday we gathered to protest. Speaking first, I asked him how many times the holy phrase has to be repeated. He said sixty thousand times a day is ideal, but being a novice he can't chant that much or he'd exhaust himself, though he's aiming for the ideal. Maruya indicated we all must coexist and asked had he never thought we might be annoyed.

"Don't mouth damnable ignorance. I chant not only for myself but for everyone, including you all. Soon the true Buddha will grant our prayer and the world will become heaven. Our religion is the one right religion, and we are beginning to send our talents into the political field. Now in these Latter Degenerate Days of the Law, people no longer practice good deeds. So we must increase our representation in the Diet, that way achieving legislation for a national reform to unite religion and politics. Once we succeed in Japan we can influence the United Nations. Then by lawful means we can accomplish a world revolution...."

Our protest fueled his fervor. Even as I write he's chanting at my side like a lunatic. Taigo, Shibuki, Maruya, and Yamino gave up trying to study amicably and went out somewhere to drink. Kamiya went down to watch TV with the boss. (Full-time adult workers live elsewhere, appear at delivery times, in the day solicit new subscribers.)

5/10: Recently often rainy and muggy. Rain all day. Collected bills, back around three to find everyone outraged over having been subjected to a house search. My desk and apple crate were in disarray. *Linji lu* and *Eihei shobogenzo*, the only volumes I brought from Tangenji and most important to me, were unwrapped from their purple silk.

Here's what I understand from the boss's and others' explanations: On May 5, Children's Day, Yamino went to collect his predecessor's remaining bills. At one simple frame apartment building he got no response from the upstairs subscriber and decided to try the door. It opened easily. He looked past a reed screen. Down a narrow concrete-floor corridor he saw a girl student asleep on her side, skirt tucked so that the back of her thighs and a triangle of white panties were exposed. Vulnerable as she looked, he insists no notion occurred to him at the time.

At the police station he could only repeat, "It wasn't me — I was moved by a higher power as if on an escalator. Even as the distance was closing, I had no idea, no intention at all. My brain began to act only when she suddenly awoke and shrieked, but I was already on top of her."

The boss reports that since then she's been amnesic—can't respond to police inquiries about her name, birthplace, or parents, just occasionally yells. Most unfortunate for us is that with Yamino in custody we are again shorthanded.

The boss laid himself open to everyone's censure. First, he allowed a house search while no one was here, and second, his unique concern is who will make Yamino's deliveries. He said he too is a victim and we are all in it together and must pity one another. Not a one of us agreed.

Suddenly Taigo declared, "I'm quitting right now! In this shop Yamino's insanity and vengeful spirit are whirling with the suspicion and reproach of the police, and it's ignominious that you readily allowed a search of our private possessions. Your concern is to protect your interest. No longer are you my boss, nor I your worker!" I followed him upstairs. Indeed he began to pack. I asked if he had anywhere to go. He replied excitedly, "The world is wide. I'm not so shiftless that I'll starve! It's impossible to forgive the boss. Maybe he didn't commit a social crime, but he committed a fundamental sin!"

After packing he said more quietly, "Yeah, I'm mad at him, but I'm sick of the unreasonably hard labor with so few routemen. I've been waiting for an excuse to quit. My only regret is that having brought you in I'm leaving now without making sure of your future. Forgive me! Don't strain yourself by excess dutifulness and human feeling. So, Mokuzu, good luck!"

5/13: The bursar is requesting my first-term tuition fee. I complained about the many canceled classes, but he flatly said the university is not obliged to supply compensation. He even suggested I drop out for a while to make up the cost.

5/22: The boss hastily brought in replacements for Yamino and Taigo.

One is a tall, natty ronin with ruddy face and hoarse voice. Like Maruya, he's from Nakatsu Province in Kyushu, so they're kindred spirits. He's lively, loves to talk. As soon as the conversation got around to our hard labor and low wages he suggested that we engage in collective bargaining.

Kamiya, being the boss's nephew and knowing his finances, was unmoved. Nagane seized the chance to persuade us to convert to his religion, saying that our distress is due to lack of faith, and that with faith we can gain more money, be free of illness, and reach a higher social level. The virile son of Kyushu loudly told him he was a fool and to shut up, whereupon he began to chant with utmost concentration. But soon he quit to go out to solicit new believers. Whenever he gets five, he's promoted a step, Maruya says. Shibuki, politic as always, nodded approval of each of the newcomer's words. I quietly asked whether we four were enough for collective bargaining. Our newcomer scolded me for my idle thought.

As we were starting downstairs, I backed out, "After all, do as you like without me. I too have complaints, but I've nowhere else to go and we aren't actually being enslaved, and above all I respect individual feeling and thought and have no interest in what can be attained by a group." Again I was reproached, called a betrayer, spy, poltroon, hypocrite; even Maruya and Shibuki joined in, and the three of them went down. Happy for the rare quiet, and dismissing my stomachache and slight fever, I opened *Eihei shobogenzo*. Before an hour passed I could hear their hilarity. Surely the boss was offering them alcohol.

The other newcomer is Miyao, a native of Tokyo's Bokuto district. He's been delivering newspapers ever since finishing junior high. Goes out for pachinko and the races — horse, bike, speedboat. Says he bets constantly and fails as much. Nervous, absorbed in his hard lot.

5/23: No trace of that new Kyushu man. How pitiful was the confused face of the boss! His wife put folded quilting over his bicycle seat.

At breakfast he asked were we missing anything. Horrified, Kamiya, Nagane, Shibuki, and Maruya raced upstairs. Only I and the wary Miyao kept eating with composure. The boss's wife demanded that we also check our things, but we knew we had nothing to lose.

Sure enough, they each came down pale — unquestionably their money was gone. Kamiya was at a loss how to vent his rage. He had believed Marx's *Das Kapital* to be the safest place, but the three large notes he had concealed in its pages were not there. Shibuki, recently given money by his girlfriend, sighed, "Ah, ah! — she'll think I spent it on drink!" Nagane was ashamed of his shallow faith and vowed to devote himself with greater conviction. Maruya was hardest hit; he lost everything he saved from all the part-time jobs he's worked at for so long. He was secretly planning to reimburse the boss and rent a room where he could secure privacy and quiet. Discouraged beyond forbearance, he planted himself down and stared at his rough hands.

514

6/2: For a week I've had a fever and haven't gone to school — only lying on my side, reading and dreaming. Was like a sleepwalker during 5/27 evening delivery. Momentarily blacked out and banged into a meat shop display rack. Eggs, most of them, broke in front of the shop. The owner was sympathetic, but clearly I had to compensate — almost a full month's pay. I've been thinking even more about my future.

6/4: I have much to consider. From Ran:

> How are you? I'm getting used to dorm life. I promised to help your school life, but please forgive me for being so late and sending you so little (enclosed). I still can't weave a perfect obi so my work comes out as inferior goods and my salary is reduced. I also can't save money because I have to take my turn buying dorm snacks every eighth time — there are eight in this room we have to share. I tell them about you at Hoso and they envy me. It cheers me. When I'm down I think of you. They want your photo....

6/7: A subscriber's wife gave me three ironed white shirts, explaining they're like new except for the collar. She said her husband's work is such that he can no longer wear them. He's in the Finance Ministry, I heard. I blushed but took them. I'm probably the only one in all of this wide Tokyo still wearing a black winter jacket.

6/8: First good health in days, everything looks beautiful, everyone looks touching.

Miyao spent all last month's pay as well as this month's, which he got in advance, on the horses, and he's despondent. Without being asked, he spoke to me of his childhood. His daily work as far back as he can remember was to hang about the streets gathering the cinders dumped out by the richer households, which used coal. Before the dust and smoke settled he and his likes raked them into pails to take home for their family's cooking and heating. Town poverty is unlike country poverty. We went to the mountain for firewood.

He asked me for a loan and was so pathetic I gave him my lunch money, with which I'd have bought a book. He says I'm enviable for being able to enjoy life simply by reading, while he has no education and no pleasure except gambling.

6/16: Long rain. Maruya returned this evening very late from delivery. We worried and did his fly sheets. He came in with bloody brow and hands. To our inquiries he responded, "It's nothing" and went upstairs without supper. I went up and washed off the blood. He shed tears and said,

"I'm hopeless. I met a heavy truck as I was riding down a lane. To avoid being hit I let my hand get raked by a barbed wire. But it's not that. Later I realized I sensed no pain despite the exposed white flesh. I felt weird, frightened. You may think I was dulled by fear of being crushed, but no, ever since all my savings were stolen I've noticed I'm weird — I sense no pain even

515

when I fall off the bike or hit my shin on a concrete stair. Today, as you see, I beat my head on a concrete wall — and sensed no pain!"

I tried to console him by saying he's just exhausted, but his tears kept flowing. I put him to bed and held his other hand till he slept. His sleeping face was like that of a sad child.

Toward midnight my stomach ached and I had diarrhea.

6/18: After morning delivery Maruya left without telling anybody anything. At night Shibuki whispered to me, "From now on it'll be dreadful here."

When I said I didn't see how it could be worse than now, he said, "You don't know what I know through my long Tokyo life. The fact is, I came to this shop a month before you and couldn't believe how fine a place it was, an ideal land, because here everyone was independently studying, or was a student, or a ronin. Even Miyao, though he eternally gambles, is a better sort than what there can be — ex-convicts, drug addicts — around whom any attempt to study is impossible. But I want your opinion. You're the son of a priest, but not a fanatic like Nagane. Your interest in religion is rational. You're pure, young, the very one to help me decide. But it has to be kept sub rosa. I'm soon going to quit without reimbursing the boss. That's not what I want your advice on; I want to know what you think of my moving in with my girl."

I asked him why he was hesitating; he's already getting her help, so why not live together? There would be some double costs, but many things could be economized on. He said he knows the economics, but wonders whether cohabitation would bind him to marry her.

"Whether you live together or not, you are intimate and she is helping you from her factory wages, so she must be dreaming of marrying you after you graduate. And you — don't you love her?" "Well, I love her heart, enjoy her body, and appreciate her material help, but I'm not thinking of marriage; only the situation here is forcing me to move in. What do you think?"

I never met her but could easily understand her sad state. Were she Ena, it would be a disastrous blow. Shibuki is coolheaded like a man with a great future in society. I could find no words. At last I said, "Your problem is better answered by the new religion Nagane is following — it emphasizes worldly profit. I'll have no part in your inhumane hesitation, and from this moment I declare us no longer friends."

Today's paper showed damage from the earthquake in Niigata Prefecture. The Showa Big Bridge fell down, and an oil refinery has been burning since the 16th. Death count, 26.

6/24: After Shibuki left, 3 men came in who are just what he described. Like Miyao, they go out after work to gamble, or, when they have no money, they play mah-jongg in the next room, heedless of their noise. Nagane's chanting close by my desk is rather a buffer against the racket of the 36 ivory tiles being shuffled, but even Nagane is complaining.

I too have been pondering an idea I got while lying in bed here the first days of June with a fever: Should I leave Tokyo as early as I can and go to Shoshinji? My debt to the boss is all that's keeping me. By any means I have to make the money to repay him, and to buy a ticket to Gifu. I'll not pay the first-term tuition fee. According to social law I should, but I'm disinclined to if I follow my spiritual judgement, for not a single professor at Hoso can answer my questions. I am embarrassed even to record what I observed to be the ignorance, shamelessness, and cunning of the professors. True, the chance for further study of a special subject with a professor is offered under the name "seminar," but I've been unable to attend because of evening delivery and because I can't afford the obligatory extras — the cafes, snacks, etc. Nor can I afford any other circles or clubs. So I'm a university student in name only.

My single comfort is to have read through nearly a hundred books since the end of February even in this wretched situation. I never went to the school library. Securing these books by my own pains has made me more attached to them, and I feel I can better understand the intent of the authors.

7/1: After a long absence I went to Classical Japanese Lit. Afterwards I was in a hurry to leave for evening delivery, but Professor Tamano held me by the button, handed me an academic quarterly, and said, "Thanks, your thesis was very helpful."

On the train I read his article. My name wasn't mentioned, yet he had written almost exactly what I had submitted to him. The few differences were merely some conjunctions and auxiliary words, changes that made my thesis appear written in haste. My title was "Sutras Influencing *The Tale of Genji.*" He had changed it to "Sutras Digested in *The Tale of Genji.*"

7/3: With a secretary's help, I caught Professor Tamano and asked him for my thesis. He misplaced it, he replied. I told him my situation is such that I can't pay even the tuition fee. He grew excited and cried, "You're threatening me? You'll be held responsible —" I told him I would be glad if he brought charges against me for being a menace, whereupon he restrained himself and took out some money: a "private scholarship for study in adversity, but only this once," he said.

I was able to pay off more than half my debt to the boss and also the tuition fee. Isn't that a happy ending? No, I feel very uncomfortable. Were I not in such straits I would never accept money from an old professor. It's regrettable, but there's no other way to get out of Tokyo.

7/5: I've determined to leave on the first of September. I'll be leaving as a loser. However, the sooner I acknowledge my defeat the better, since my opponent is of no interest to me.

Today as I collected bills I endeavored to get new subscribers, a task that kills my pride. The boss rewards us for each one we get, and 10 brings a higher bonus. If I get 30 in the next two months, I can clear my debt.

I'll seem suspect if I begin to get many, since I could barely get even 3 during the past months. So these days, in fine weather, I tell him I'm going out to find new subscribers when actually I'm going to school or to read under the trees in the park. He thinks I'm striving to gain new subscribers and is in a good humor. He is simpleminded.

Well, I can succeed with the method I've invented. I learned that to get real new subscribers is next to impossible, but to get old ones to stop for a while isn't so hard. There are other similar papers. When I tell them my situation, some are willing to switch — and at the same time they give me a new contract for a subscription beginning one or two months later. They lose nothing, and when I bring back these new subscriptions the boss rewards me. He doesn't care about losing subscribers as much as he cares about gaining them — he doesn't keep track of the turnover. He looks like a monkey in his joy, while my face must look like that of a fox.

7/9: Tonight while reading I heard Kamiya cry for help. I went to his room to find he'd been beaten up. These days the men of this shop keep changing and as they're all villains I haven't learned even their names. They're adults, over age forty. They went to gamble after doing Kamiya in. I got water from downstairs and cooled him with a wet towel. He wouldn't explain, only shed tears of mortification. I suppose he finally couldn't resist giving such riffraff some advice tinged with contempt. It's best that a man not preach unless he really cares. Aside from that, he went to tell the boss he can no longer live under the same roof with them. I haven't heard the outcome.

7/11: At midnight, as I was reading, one of those who pounded Kamiya, named Kabu, returned and stealthily put a box tied with ribbon on my desk. "Eat — it's cake. I saw in the paper how students should eat sweets...you study hard in this situation. Don't be outdone. They say you got into Hoso on the first try. You're a feather in the boss's cap!" He went on to confess: "We guys are failures, but seeing we're living with you and how you'll be great someday — it cheers us up....I lost at the track, had to return in the rain. Passing the high folk, I says under my breath, 'Time'll tell — he'll beat you all, and I'm sharing the same house!'"

The devil isn't so black as he's painted. Kabu and his ilk are society's scapegoats, but at the same time they're ringleaders in muddying society. Cowardly villains.

7/15: The term at Hoso finished and it's summer vacation. What dreadfully heavy entrance and tuition fees in contrast to the horribly few lectures and their shabby contents! But it's all my fault. I was punished for not going straight to the most important study — and I was also wrong to expect to be taught the most important matter.

7/19: Today's paper told of heavy rains in the Sanin and Hokuriku districts — 28 dead or missing, 527 houses razed or washed away.

I think a wife is unfortunate if her husband can't fix even a desk lamp. If he's a bad provider, she's much more so. Another unhappy kind of wife is one whose husband is good at his profession only and who disregards her troubles, their home life, and child-raising, or is incapable of caring. But most unfortunate is she whose husband can't foresee her fate. The majority of men might protest, "Who can do that? If you say so, no wife can be made happy." I too am incapable, but that's why I'll train myself until I can see the fate of others. By the power of love alone, our life can't be exempt from being sad and transitory. Love must be supported by wisdom.

7/21: Sweat runs and I've become thinner. Saw the dark meat of whale at the front of a fish shop and recalled my parents' quarrel the night before I left. Dad told Ma to buy some beef strips without fail during her charm-paper delivery because he wanted to give me a farewell dinner. When she returned in the evening with whale, he scolded her for practicing her pinching ways. She did visit several meat shops, she explained, and all were shut for their joint holiday. But he couldn't rid himself of his sad emotion and kept moaning and finding fault with her. Ran cried and said a humble supper in harmony is far better.

7/25: At last Kamiya was rewarded for new subscribers and moved to an apartment. The boss gave him extra money. Hereafter he'll appear only for work. He has no other income. All remaining hours he spends rereading the same few books. He told me to take one for helping to carry them. But since all are fiction in translation, I found nothing I wanted. He treated me to a lunch of curry with rice, tasty but too much.

Nagane plans to rent a house with fellow worshipers, so he too will move out. The boss brought in another professional. I'm the only remaining student. These days he and his wife are very kind to me, often give me shirts, soap, soft drinks, and such, given to them.

8/1: Told the boss I'll quit the end of this month. His wife was speechless; he too was quite surprised and angrily asked where I would go and what about school. I didn't say much, said I'm returning to my native land.

"How can you so easily abandon your original purpose? You got into Hoso after much trouble. I can't understand young people these days!" He despaired of persuading me to stay on. I wanted to say there's nothing for me to learn in the dust of the capital, but I didn't. I have no wish to become a spunky guy by going through the tons of dust here. My true hope is beyond his ken.

8/9: Went out for bills and to garner new subscribers. Got back and doused with cold water. As I was beginning to read *Eihei shobogenzo*, I realized someone was sneaking up on me. It was Taigo. He gestured to me to keep silent; he had snuck past the boss. He was clean-shaven and was dressed in summer clothes like any normal person, which made him look better than the norm. He said he'd been working in a similar shop but was now determined to go home to take on his father's business. His one concern was me, because he brought me to this shop. I told him not to care. Coming to Tokyo was my responsibility and I had needed to find lodgings and work, so I was nothing but thankful to him.

He took out a bundle of money — a lot by our standards. I asked how he'd earned it. He smiled and said it was from bill collecting. Thinking of Reiho and Luri, I told him he'd ruin his future, that it wasn't worth it. He wouldn't listen and explained how shrewd he'd been not to disclose his identity or take so much as to compel his boss to go to the police. He offered me half, and I refused it. He gave up and asked me to go down to make sure no one was in sight. I obliged. Soon he came down and left. When I went back up and calmed myself to continue reading, I found in my book five large bills. How perplexing, but nothing can be done. I'll keep it and see what happens.

8/12: At midnight Kabu and his fellows ordered sushi and beer and invited me to their room. For some time after coming here, they acted outrageous, playing mah-jongg as they liked, for instance. But curiously enough, before I noticed, they quit playing and began to walk as quietly as cats. I guess they have been taking pains not to disturb my study.

Last night when I entered their room, Kabu began to speak,

"You got your reasons, but too bad you're leaving Tokyo. You stayed — half a year? And all you saw was this place and your campus. You never went to Tokyo Tower or even to Ueno Park, and there's lots more worth seeing — the Imperial Palace, the Meiji Shrine, the Ginza, Asakusa. Now it's summer all the guys are going to Enoshima and Zushi to swim and you're shut up on this second floor — it's like a sauna! So we three decided to divvy up the work of taking you around starting tomorrow, at our expense."

I was moved close to tears, but I clearly declined. My present mentality isn't suited to sightseeing. I know it's cruel to reject kindness, but I must prepare my mind and body for training. These days I'm having lunch and taking a nap in the afternoon.

My prime concern is to memorize all 95 volumes of *Eihei shobogenzo* before the end of the month. No matter that many words and phrases are incomprehensible; once I memorize them I can ponder their meaning. Delivery times are most fitting for memorizing. During the day and at night I read the text. As I deliver I try to remember it. If I can't, I open the text as soon as I have the chance. Doing this now day after day, I've almost got it all.

8/14: Tokyo water shortage severe since lask week, extreme restrictions enforced.

Received a letter from Professor Tamano. He's considered my studying in adversity and has hit on the idea of privately employing me to assist his research on classical Japanese literature. He'd like to discuss the details and gives a date and the name of a cafe. I'll treat it with silent contempt — "the water is too shallow to drop anchor."[1]

8/17: During a nap I dreamed I was on a train. Yulans with falling petals flanked the track, and I heard someone chanting in rhythm with the wheels. It was the first part of volume 30 of *Eihei shobogenzo*, I soon realized, where begins a description of the training of 32 Zennists, including Sakyamuni Buddha:

The Great Way of Buddha and the patriarchs always included the supreme religious practice: an endless practice of awakening, training, attaining Bodhisattvahood, and attaining Buddhahood. Each was performed without hiatus, evidence that they who practiced did so not by forcing themselves or by being forced. They were ever free of impurity and were ever endowed with Buddhahood.

The virtue of this practice is to enliven oneself and others, whence the practice benefits all heaven and earth. It is so even if we do not recognize it is so. The practice of Buddha and the patriarchs enables us to practice and open our Great Way in all directions; and at once our practice enables Buddha and the patriarchs to practice and open their Great Way in all directions. Our practice imparts virtue to these endless practices, and therefore...[2]

When I woke I tried to determine who was chanting; it seemed to be Unkai. Looking back on life at Ryotanji and at Tangenji, I was filled with nostalgia like an old man rending his heart over the irrevocable past, or a baby crying for its mother.

Toward the end of evening delivery I saw a flaming sunset.

8/20: Cold rain. Just after evening delivery to a Mr. Suzuki's house at the approach to a bridge, I heard a clear voice, "Take care not to catch cold." Was it for me? I looked back and saw a girl student, the daughter of the house. She had a red umbrella and bright eyes. Abashed, I hurried on.

After the apartment houses by the river, I sped along a bumpy dirt road and, as I feared, took a bad fall. Some young workers laughed without reserve or sympathy, as if it was the best event in days. Affected by their high spirits, I laughed.

8/30: Finished collecting every bill. Reimbursed the boss. The money Taigo secretly left me remains. Haven't heard about it ever since. Bought a ticket to Gifu. In the evening, after putting my things in order, I went to a public bath. Until tonight I'd washed only with cold water. It was so comfortable I felt I was in heaven.

8/31: Around noon I went to a barbershop for the first time. Away with my messy long hair. The barber close-cropped it. I then asked him to shave it clean, to which he commented, "Oh yes, the shaven head is coming into vogue." Seeing his razor, I thought of the sword tip I kept in my childhood. I buried it under Ena's gravestone.

At night I went again to the public bath, not to wash off the dust of the capital — it isn't hateful, for it's produced by many sad people. Rather, I wanted once more to enjoy the hot, plentiful water, to have the memory of it to comfort me until I can enjoy it in the unknown future.

The boss's wife and other adults gave me parting gifts of money. I thanked them for their kindness. The boss said, "I hope we'll meet again. Till then, take care!"

41

Entering the Monastery

Gifu is a landlocked prefecture in the western part of the central districts of the Main Island. Mostly it is mountain upon mountain to the height of three thousand meters. The rivers Kiso, Nagara, and Ibi twine from those mountains and gather at the alluvial plain of Nobi, where the population is overcrowded in contrast to the sparse distribution in the wooded region occupying over four-fifths of the prefecture.

Mokuzu got off the Tokaido line at Gifu Station around three and took the Takayama line to Mino-Ota, where again he had to change for a short run to Mino-Kamo on the Etsu-Minami line. The last train was composed of just two cars.

He wore the same black uniform and blue-gray hat he had worn when he set out for Tokyo in February, and carried the same blanket. But now his head was shaven and his clothes looked old.

The final station was unmanned. Mulberries behind it stretched to far mountains. Pruned year after year, they grew in the shape of shrubs. In front, a dirt road led north with farmhouses clustered on either side, though nobody was in sight.

A strong wind constantly swept the road and passed through the simple station.

'I can smell trees and soil and see dreary space and ignorant mountains instead of rows of tall office buildings, where glass is essential to separate inside from outside. I also feel my individuality is now conspicuous, although the significance of my intellect, emotion, and volition isn't thereby increased. In Tokyo I felt pushed about by the force of others. Here I must move by myself.'

The clucking of hens came on the wind from the rear of a farmhouse. Mokuzu went around to ask the way to Shoshinji. A bent crone in a dark smock was shooing the hens from the mulberry fields, where they had disturbed the rice straw.

She raised her bamboo stick toward the far distance and answered rather rudely, "Thatta way! It be forty minutes on foot, but what's the use?" and she went after the hens.

Where she pointed Mokuzu saw only fields, mountains, and sky. 'Maybe she hates Shoshinji or anyone heading there, or maybe, er...it's just her manner, with no other road in sight?'

He hastened along the dusty road. It left the houses, curved grandly, and joined a road, obviously coming from Seki, that went due northeast through the fields. Terraced ashy mulberry plantations continued on the right, with two-story cocoonery cottages in places along the roadside. On the left was a dark green flat expanse of sweet potato fields, at the far end of which, against the mountain, chimneys sent voluminous smoke above white factory buildings that were probably producing starch.

Soon he was past the fields. The road meandered up into forest. Now and then the view opened to lowlands of yellowing rice. The mountains increased and the road steepened. As the remaining sun came through the leaves, his shadow appeared long on the rocks and trees and sometimes went into the deep valley below the road. Wisteria hung from the deciduous trees. The valleys were buried in kudzu. There was no sign of cultivation, but he supposed the several parting roads led to villages. He had no means to confirm whether he was going the correct way but kept choosing to go northeast.

"After all, granny, pointing the way is no easy job....Incidentally, I admit I'm terribly hungry. My last food was breakfast, the last meal from the boss's wife. The sun will set any moment. I'd better find another sweet potato field, and some grass to sleep on," he spoke aloud as he walked.

After another bend he came to where narrow terraces of sweet potato and otherwise mostly cotton began. He stepped up from the road to a terrace just below a cliff.

'Well, here's a tool shed for my night. In Tokyo if I were to pick through a trash can I'd be reported to the police, but who'll apprehend me here for taking a sweet potato?' He pulled one out, brushed the dirt from its red skin, and took a bite. Its milky liquid spread in his mouth; not an inviting taste by any means.

"Hey, young one, what are you doing?" From behind a stand of raspberry near the shed came a voice, whether a man's or a woman's Mokuzu could not tell. A middle-aged person approached and took off a sedge hat, exposing a tan shaven head. Mokuzu judged it to be a woman; there was no menacing air. The face was glitteringly brown, with lines from the sides of the nose to the corners of the mouth. She had compressed her lips.

'The ugliest I ever saw! Well, what can I do but apologize while it's a fact someone's blaming me? But let me take one more bite for the energy...'

"Your head is shaven, nice and blue, eh? Where do you intend to go?"

"To Shoshinji."

"For what purpose, young one?"

"To train."

The woman guffawed. "You engage in theft on your way to the monastery? What's going on with the young these days? In the old days religious

523

trainees toured after purifying themselves under a waterfall."

"Isn't this your field?"

"No, not mine, but it belongs to my residence."

"Then what's going on with your generation? In the old days landowners never complained about the theft of a sweet potato, and they were especially kind to a thief on his way to a temple or a shrine, so I've heard."

"Ho! You've no compunction?" She let down her sleeves. "Tell me, what are you escaping from, and what are you seeking?"

"What a strange and abrupt question — you must be a Zen nun."

"Instead of mumbling, answer up!"

"Well, nun, I don't know how far you have trained, but I am sure I am not obliged to answer such a personal question."

"Young man, if you are like that, I must ask you to return what you ate. It's my right." The nun gave a perverse smile. Mokuzu saw that her nature was kind, that she was just pretending to be an ill-natured nun. He replied with a smile,

"Nun, you must know you cannot 'draw out a leviathan with a hook,' and of course not with a sweet potato."

"Hm! Your brain is as clear as the moon, but your practice is as dark as the moon behind clouds. The master you are going to meet will enjoy beating you to a pulp!...By the way, you obviously don't know the rules and manners to enter Shoshinji's exclusive training monastery. A shaven head is insufficient for acceptance as a training monk. Where are your robe and your surplice box?"

"In this age everyone wears Western clothes and makes full use of trains. Must I conform to an antedeluvian fashion?"

"Absolutely. Shoshinji's training transcends the changes of time. To out-siders it looks archaic, but the monastery knows the most fitting, perfected way to train. I recommend you come with me to my nunnery, Shogetsuan. I can introduce you to my teacher so that you may prepare properly. Under her guidance you can reexamine whether you really wish to engage in the training life of Shoshinji." The nun was exposing her best kindness, but Mokuzu hesitated to take advantage of it.

"Even if I don't know the practical preparation, I have enough perse-verance to go through any hardship by myself."

"You cannot rely on your talent, young one. The greater the talent the harder the training. Come with me. After all, what is training but to learn how to be a fool...in a sense."

The nun lifted a sack of sweet potatoes and entered a mountain footpath. Mokuzu offered to carry it, but she objected, so he just followed. The path went along the rise and fall of a mountain skirt. When they came to where it was about to curve in deeply, she paused and pointed to the farthest indentation.

"There, do you see those dense cedars and that white building receiving the afterglow? It's the college dormitory under construction. You can't see any of the monastery from here; it's hidden by the trees to the right of the college."

There was a wide stretch of rice fields and a few clusters of farmhouses in the basin before Shoshinji and its mountain. A road meandered by and went on into yet deeper mountains.

"Is that the road I would have taken had I not met you?"

"Yes. This is a shortcut; the nunnery is ahead." The nun continued on the grassy path, and soon they were shut in by mountain skirts on either side. Against a mountain stood a humble nunnery in a dark area already like a kind of cave. Along the narrow approach were narrow plantings of cotton.

'The nunnery must be very poor to have cotton instead of flowers in front. As dusk settles the bolls must sway like ghosts. The nuns are no doubt planting, harvesting, spinning, and weaving it for their own needs.'

As if reading his mind, the nun explained,

"The season is just over. The flowers are beautiful...an elegant, dreamy yellow...nice in the moonlight."

She entered the residential quarters. Within was darker than without. She stepped up to a living room, turned on a dim light, and politely reported her return to her teacher, who must have been sitting or dozing in the dark and now expressed appreciation for the day's work of her disciple.

The nun invited Mokuzu up and introduced him. The teacher sat at a quilt-covered low table. A cubicle set in the floor underneath held a charcoal heater. He sat across from her and offered a formal greeting. She appeared to be partially blind; her eyes were turbid. Possibly she was eighty, even ninety. She wore a white robe with a softer, white *habutae* scarf tucked around the neck. Her shaven head looked like a steamed white potato, and her face was gentle, with tender furrows. Mokuzu was reminded of his grandmother toward the end of her life.

The teacher recognized his good will to train himself and his fatigue from travel.

The nun, addressed as Shorai, stepped to the earth floor of the kitchen to prepare tea and supper.

Owls cried at the back mountain, preordaining a change of weather. A wind began to rise. Mokuzu sat quiet before the teacher. He had nothing to say and felt he was losing his sense of why he was there.

"Young man," the teacher opened her mouth after a long interval, "you much resemble a brilliant priest I chanced to meet when I was an acolyte. He stopped here on his way to a Zen interview with Zen Master Taigi, the master

525

of Shoshinji at that time. I offered him tea and was astonished that he had memorized every word of the 'seven most important Zen books.' Being so, he was ill-disposed to stay under Taigi, who was a master not of learning but of religious austerities. So he went to Tenryoji in Kyoto to study under Zen Master Gasan.

"Such a gifted priest, with incisive looks, yet kindly and bright. He was certified as a Dharma inheritor by Gasan. Then he transferred his domicile to Nanzenji at their request, and did much there to rebuild the Dharma hall. He had a local temple as well, Tangenji, in Tanba."

"Teacher, you speak of the priest Kakkan. I am his grandson," interrupted Mokuzu to avoid further embarrassment to her and to himself.

The teacher gasped, and she gazed at him yet more, her expression like that of a primitive beholding a solar eclipse. Hastily she called, "Shorai! Shorai, come!"

The disciple came promptly with a bamboo blower in hand, cheeks flushed. She was apprised of Mokuzu's kinship to Kakkan.

"What a strange turn of Fortune's wheel! My teacher met your grandfather seventy or even eighty years ago. She's never forgotten the impression he made on her. As she often mentions him, I have been regarding him as one of the most respectable Zen priests. Now I realize you aren't a total stranger. The Zen master has told me that a young talent from Tanba will come sooner or later, and he's asking me to assist when he shows up. So it's you and you're here!" said Shorai excitedly.

The teacher put her palms together and mumbled,

"Thanks be to Buddha for guiding us all to the perfect Dharma on this land. After all, the priest Kakkan ought to have studied the practical Zen of this Shoshinji. He died so early because he did not learn the other half of Zen....Young trainee, please perfect your training. My disciple and I shall do our best to assist you. Shorai, prepare all necessities for him and teach him Shoshinji's rules and manners."

In the night Mokuzu stood on the veranda of the guest room. The pods of white cotton were floating in a misty rain. 'These nuns are strange. They think the lineage of Zen priests is the Dharma. I could be prey for a web they're spinning in their mind. Sure I'm partly indebted to my grandfather for my existence, but my concern is not to know where I am in a lineage, but to know who I am as an individual and what is the life of those I care about. What I really have to know is what training I'd like to do and not what training others have in mind.'

Next morning after chanting and breakfast, Shorai brought white ginger in a pail to the guest-room veranda. The schizopetalous corollas with their unusually long androecia gave off a strong scent, like gardenia but purer. The oblong leaves were a dark green. The flowers had received the night rain and were exposed to the morning sun.

"Where did you get them? I thought this nunnery didn't much care about flowers," Mokuzu remarked candidly. Shorai smiled as if understanding his every thought and replied,

"They've begun to bloom in the shade out back; I thought you might like them. Around twenty years ago there was a training monk similar in age to me then, a sensitive man for whom Shoshinji life was too hard. He fled here one night with a high fever. I tended him and he stayed about a month. While recovering he walked around the vicinity, and from a teacher of floral art he obtained a root, which he planted out back. Later you can see; they've grown wild and are giving us this sweet scent year after year."

Mokuzu intuitively decided the monk was Unkai, but he only nodded, not knowing what their relationship had been; and more, he could not catch how much, if anything, Shorai knew of the life he himself had spent at Ryotanji. He did not want to talk of his past while he could put it in no clear and meaningful order. His past seemed to him to have been mostly led by an uncontrollable and incomprehensible force. He wanted now to take command of his life.

Shorai seemed eager to talk but gave up at his minimal response.

Later, near noon, she brought a list of what was needed for entering the monastery and began to take his measurements. Mokuzu was amazed to see so many accoutrements for Zen training, where simplicity ought to have been a trainee's principle. 'The possessions I'm supposed to have are more complicated and luxurious than what I had for Tokyo life! Am I entering the right place for my training?' He looked the list over with an apprehensive eye.

> 2 black (dark blue) cotton robes, daily; 1 summer, 1 winter
> 1 black silk robe, ceremonial, all-season
> 2 pepper-and-salt cotton underkimonos, daily
> 2 white cotton underkimonos, ceremonial
> 1 brown cotton obi, daily
> 1 white cotton obi, ceremonial
> 1 black cotton padded belt, daily
> 1 black silk padded belt, ceremonial
> 3 white cotton cords
> 1 hemp surplice, daily
> 1 silk surplice, ceremonial
> 5 sets white cotton underwear
> 2 pairs white cotton tabi, ceremonial

527

2 pairs white cotton sleevelets, mendicancy
2 pairs white cotton gaiters, mendicancy
1 bamboo hat, mendicancy
2 scrips, mendicancy
1 scrip, formal outings
2 pairs cotton work clothes, indoor
2 pairs cotton work clothes, outdoor
1 black vinyl rain cape, mendicancy
3 pairs straw sandals
1 set 5 black-lacquer bowls, 1 pair oak chopsticks
1 straight razor, 1 finishing whetstone
sewing kit
meditation cushion
surplice box
sutra books: *Zen Manual, Three Sutras Combined*
essential Zen classics for lecture attendance: *Biyan lu, Linji lu,
Wumen guan, Zudokko.*

With no regard for Mokuzu's feelings, Shorai ordered the articles from a robe shop in Nagoya and herself sewed what she could, such as the underwear and the kimonos.

She sat on a sunny veranda, wearing glasses for hyperopia, and absorbed herself in sewing. A white grimalkin, formerly stray and now taking up residence, slept at her side.

At night she taught Mokuzu how to write his personal record and application. He had to obtain his father's written consent.

Doyu promptly returned it with his signature and seal and enclosed a brief letter. Mokuzu thought his handwriting was too beautiful for the contents, which were filled with bitter jest. 'It's like moonlight on a dump, or an evening primrose blooming on rubbish where a river opens to a bay....'

> Dear Mokuzu,
>
> You well know I dislike being a priest, though a priest I am. There must be some great unspeakable reason why I who am a priest should wish to live like an ordinary man, while you who are an ordinary man should wish to enter the priesthood. But since it has come to pass, I pray for your good health and for full enjoyment of the Dharma to come to you as early as possible.
>
> Actually, anticipating that you might enter the priesthood, I submitted notice to Nanzenji when you went to Ryotanji at age eight. You are thus ordained on paper and have a career of eleven years as a priest. This is a mere formality but very important, for the priesthood so respects

formality that it can excellently lead ordinary society on this point.

Much as I know you disregard rank and promotion, I did the aforesaid in case of your need. So, laugh at my inconsistent concern for a while.

Yours truly, with love and respect,

Doyu

The required application form was as follows:

I herewith declare my determination to study Zen and to train myself in Zen. I beg you to receive me as your trainee. If allowed to reside in your holy monastery, I vow that I will obey your dictates. Should I violate them, I vow that without complaint I will receive from you any form of punishment. I further vow that I will exert myself unremittingly until I master the most important matter. Should I come to wish otherwise, I vow that without complaint I will receive from you any form of treatment....

The monastery was one-sidedly demanding a trainee's perfect obedience until his achievement of enlightenment.

Shorai told Mokuzu, "Any reason for not perfecting your training is disallowed. Sickness, death of parents, and of course change of mind are not counted as sufficient reason.

"Please don't forget for a minute that the monastery has absolute authority over you and that you as a trainee are required to be unconditionally loyal and obedient. And note, the way of the monastery does not necessarily coincide with the rules, common sense, and laws of ordinary society. It is traditional in Japan that civil authority of any kind cannot intervene: the monastery is sacred, with extraterritorial rights.

"Within, the fundamental doctrines of a religion are mastered. Outsiders have no just cause and no ability to meddle in the business there. Shoshinji's exclusive training monastery is a spontaneous confraternity with the same mind to train. Naturally its rules have nothing to do with outsiders."

One night when Mokuzu was making a brush-written fair copy of the application under the moonlight, Shorai brought in a cup of tea, placed it on the low desk, and asked,

"Do you know the fact of Hueike's cutting off his arm?"

She was referring to Shenguang, who in search of the truth came to Bodhidharma on Mt. Sung. The snow lay waist deep. Bodhidharma refused him as a disciple. At last Shenguang cut off his arm and presented it to prove his earnestness, whereupon Bodhidharma received him.

"Yes, I know."

"So be it!" Shorai said and left the room.

Mokuzu meditated, 'Is my seeking also going to be tested? I know there is the matter I must be awakened to, and I know the place where I can be awakened. I am only waiting to be received as a training monk and to be guided by the Zen master. My mind is now clear as the autumn moon. I can remember every path I took since infancy to arrive here. All the events I experienced are like the autumn mountains and fields, colorful, sensitive, intricate, wonderful. Some are receiving the sun of joy over my commencement of true training; others are quiet in the shade of sorrow over my long detour.'

He recited in his mind a passage from "Hymn of the Empty Hand: Resolution to Live as a Bodhisattva,"

> Rare is the soil under our fingernails if compared with the soil of the
> earth. Equally rare is to be born a human being, when all others must
> sink into one of the *durgati*. Far rarer is to meet intimately with the
> teachings of Buddhism. The chance comes once in a hundred thousand
> kalpas. Let us not waste our fortune, but abandon worldly desires and
> seek the truth.[1]

Mokuzu was deeply moved by his fortune of having come to his present state. He thought he would be able to cause religious flowers to bloom wherever he went with the mind of self-training, just as the spring wind brought forth all kinds of new flowers and leaves.

Life at Shogetsuan was quiet. The teacher spent most of her day dozing at the quilt-covered table, except for when she performed morning and evening chanting assisted by Shorai. Shorai kept sewing for Mokuzu. Mokuzu dug the sweet potatoes, dried them in the sun, and stored them. He also climbed the back mountain and made a pile of firewood for the nunnery.

ॐ

On September fifteenth Mokuzu got up at two in the morning. The garden was whitened not yet by dawn but by mist rising in the moonlight. The bushes were wet as if rained on, and the quiet was such that the dropping of dew was audible.

Inside the nunnery only a dim light altered the darkness. Shorai cooked rice with red beans to congratulate Mokuzu on his new venture.

The teacher, supported by Shorai, came out to the front to see him off, and she said,

"The customary parting words to a Zen trainee are to tell him to train hard and to command him not to return until he perfects his training. They are fine words, but I have aged and my spirit has weakened, so I shall tell you something else. Being fired with youthful enthusiasm is important, but life is long, and should be long. The most important attitude toward training should be to train in the fittest way for oneself and to keep training throughout life to the end.

"Therefore, if you meet unbearable hardship and think you must quit, come here in secret. You might not have to abandon your training. Come and restore your passion to train further in another way. Truly, 'if you don't climb a mountain peak your view can't be high, and if you don't dive into the ocean depths your view can't be deep.'[2] But true also is that you cannot see the height of a mountain unless you stand apart, nor the depth of the ocean unless you reflect on yourself."

The teacher and Shorai put their palms together at their bosoms and bowed deeply, at length.

Mokuzu, his head freshly shaven, walked down the wet grassy path properly accoutred as a traveling monk in white gaiters and straw sandals, and carrying a large bamboo hat. His stiff new cotton training robe, dyed dark blue, was tucked up at the waist with a concealed white cord and bound with a black padded belt. The sleeves hung grandiosely, while at the neck the layers of robe, gray kimono, and white kimono-undershirt neatly overlapped.

At his chest hung a scrip, in which was a box containing a surplice and sutras. The box, made of paper and glue, was lacquered black and had a glossy shine. According to a sutra on rules and morality, its size and shape had been dictated by Buddha.

The surplice, or kasaya, was the most important item he carried, being the quintessential symbol of the Buddhist monk. Dogen asserted that the virtue of wearing it was limitless, that the wearer could sever all evil and attain supreme enlightenment.

Buddha and his followers were said to have scavenged old clothes from trash heaps and graveyards, which, after dying with persimmon juice, they sewed together to make their robes, known as *kasaya* — "robe the hue of persimmon astringent." Because the pattern of the joined odd pieces looked like rice fields, the robe was also called "blessed fields," and it received other names, such as "virtue robe" and "salvation robe," owing to the belief that it freed its wearer from worldly affairs and protected him from attack by thieves.

The surplice was worn as a symbol of this original robe and so too was called a kasaya. Mokuzu thought as he made his way toward Shoshinji,

'I was seen off by that devout teacher and kind nun at a wee hour auguring a fine cool autumn day. Now as I walk up winding stone steps through a forest of tall cedars to the sacred precincts, I am close to steeping myself in religious exultation.

'However, fortunately or unfortunately, I fell into the habit of seeing everything with a cool, critical eye, including myself. For instance, when I see an orchid with its elegant parabolic blades and perfect flowers, I can't help seeing through its elaborate contrivance to attract insects to its fleshy labiate petal. And I can't forget a debt if I happen to have one, even at such a time as I am smelling the scent of narcissus.

'Thus I wonder why those nuns were so kind. What do they expect in return? Are they content just to be good assistants to a young trainee? Do they know what training is?

'The irksome question remains: Do I need these trappings to seek my true nature, why I was born, the meaning of my life, and how I should live? The nun teacher said the monastery respects tradition and is where trainees learn the correct way to live, that "a dignified mien is the essence of Buddhism."

'But is it respect for tradition to buy perfectly whole cloth, cut it up, and join the pieces in parody of Buddha's original kasaya? And these straw sandals will wear out within three hours of walking. Are they also for the sake of tradition? I heard the new Tokaido bullet train with a speed of over 200 kilometers an hour will run beginning this October.

'What the nun teacher calls tradition and what Shoshinji demands that a trainee should follow seems not the way of Buddha's time; nor the way of Tang China, nor of Kamakura Japan — periods when Zen prospered most. Quite certainly it's a tradition that originated in the Edo period, when feudalism was perfected and a strict caste system and relationship of master and servant were firmly established.

'Those nuns' understanding of religion must be highly welcomed by people who practice authoritarianism and capitalism, for such an understanding denies individuality and encourages submission.

'Step by step I'm nearing the gate. The mountain has many cedars as old as a thousand years. They impress me with their sublimity. The gate appears and reappears from the predawn mist.

'At this juncture what I wish is to penetrate quick as lightning the true nature of these sacred precincts and to obtain swift as a spark from flint whatever is useful to me. I should not waste my precious time even a minute.

'For all that, isn't formality the worst deterrent to real study and real awakening? I will have to shatter formality as if it were enamelware, at least for my sake. I am one who frets over the fact that his life is passing quick as an arrow, and who is tormented by the shame of not knowing what is the most important matter.'

When he reached the top of the long approach of stone steps, Mokuzu faced an imposing and substantial gate built of thick zelkova. A white-plaster wall extended from either side to make a definite border between the sacred precincts and the outer world. Five indented parallel lines ran the length of the plaster, marking the temple as having been related to the Imperial Palace.

The right-side square pillar of the gate presented a vertical plank inscribed "Shoshinji: Most Demonic Monastery in the Land," indicating that the training within was so hard as to make even demons cry, while all monastic training elsewhere was as gentle as the play of princesses. 'What ostentation!'

On the left-side pillar a plank lettered in the same heavy coercive style announced that the resident Zen master was lecturing on *Biyan lu* during the present term.

Mokuzu passed through the gate. Before him spread a flat garden of fine white gravel with a few plantings. Near the gate, on the left, stood a bell tower under a black pine. On the right, in the distance, was higher ground banked with a rock wall, where a meditation hall was set against a bamboo grove. In mid-range was the grand main building, with magnificent high tiled roof elegantly curving. The open veranda was wide and high off the ground. Stone steps led to the main hall at its center. 'Hm, the style of Zen temples is about the same anywhere, with differences appearing only in dimension, quality of material, and ornament. Ryotanji was bigger than Tangenji, Shoshinji is bigger than Ryotanji. Head temples can be even bigger.'

A cross-wing connected the main building with the monks' living quarters on the right. An entrance for privileged guests was provided at the center of the cross-wing. Ordinary people were expected to use the entrance to the living quarters. The roof of the living quarters was not massively square like that of the main building, but sharper, like an open book laid face down. The triangle of white plaster from the eaves to above the entrance was accented by the faces of horizontal and vertical beams interposed with brackets, giving the facade a Gothic air. On the ridge, a monitor like a square turret served as both skylight and vent for the kitchen.

From the left end of the main building, a tile-roofed corridor extended to another square building, which alone was as large as the main building of any local temple.

The monastery was dead quiet. The time was around three in the morning, with only moonlight and mist.

From the center of the garden Mokuzu looked about and tried to remember the pleasant flow of Teacher Docho's lecture on Zen architecture,

'"What we presently call Zen architecture was a direct import from Sung-dynasty China. The first example can be seen in Kyoto at Senyuji, built by Shunjo in 1211 on his return from a 12-year stay in Sung. He imported to Japan the orthodox Tendai, Zen, and Ritsu sects.

"'As a matter of fact, even earlier Eisai returned with Zen from Sung and built Shofukuji in Hakata in 1196, Jufukuji in Kamakura in 1200, and Kenninji in Kyoto in 1202. What he introduced, however, was actually a mix of Tendai, Shingon, and Zen, so naturally his temples were not of the pure Sung style, that is, not so-called Zen architecture.

"'Dogen on his return also built temples, Koshoji in Uji in 1233, and Eiheiji in Echizen in 1243. Unlike the golden tenets of his Buddhism, they were remarkably shabby, beneath notice.

"'In those days Kujo Michiie, then regent and chief advisor to the emperor, vowed to build in Higashiyama, Kyoto, a Zen temple large without precedent. That was in 1236, and 37 years were needed for its completion. It was named Tofukuji, 'To' from Todaiji, 'fuku' from Kofukuji, the two largest temples in Nara. These weren't Zen temples, and the architecture of Tofukuji was an amalgam. Enni Benen was invited back from a sojourn in Sung to be its founder.

"'Then in 1253 Hojo Tokiyori, regent to the Kamakura government, built Kenchoji and invited the Chinese Zen priest Lanshi Dalung to be its founder. In 1282 Hojo Tokimune built Engakuji, also in Kamakura, and invited the Chinese Zen priest Wushyue Tzuyuan to be its founder. The religion of Zen and its unique architectural style were thus established in Japan for the first time, in Kamakura.

"'With the decline of the Kamakura government, from the end of the thirteenth century to the beginning of the fourteenth, culture shifted back to Kyoto, and there Zen prospered unrivaled, as we see in the rash of great temples — Nanzenji, Tenryoji, Shokokuji, Daitokuji, Myoshinji. Copying the Sung system, these solidified their base — for example, by establishing a ranking of temples known as 'five supreme temples and ten superior temples.' Their prosperity continued through the period of the Northern and Southern Courts, and lasted until almost the end of the Muromachi period....'"

Shoshinji was built by Kanzan Egen, a disciple of National Teacher Daito, founder of Daitokuji. In fact Egen built merely a cottage, for he was tending his Zen understanding while tending his ox in this remote country before the retired emperor Hanazono discovered him to be one of Daito's most important Dharma inheritors. So Mokuzu had heard.

The monastery was still in deep slumber, but the moonlight was waning. The air grew chillier, and Mokuzu's robe grew damp. He circled the garden, careful lest he make a sound. He tried to remember a little more of Docho's lecture.

"'Now, what are the distinctive features of Zen architecture? First, consider the ground plans. The square is evidently the dominant form. Second, the exterior emphasizes the vertical; note the lean-to roof construction and the rectangles formed by the beams and brackets. Third, there are two-story buildings affording views in all directions. Temples before the appearance of Zen architecture had pagodas of two or many more stories, but they were to be admired from the ground and couldn't be climbed. In detail..."'

Tired of recalling Docho's lecture, Mokuzu turned his thoughts to his English teacher, Yojun.

'Just think what I could be doing by now if I were staying at his wife's home in Connecticut as he had wished. What would he say if he were to see me standing here dressed like this? Would he say, "The world is wide, you must be wise. Be fearful of being trapped in a pit of convention, it's a sure way to lose yourself. Prize freedom more than wisdom bound up in tradition!"...?'

Mokuzu restrained himself from being pulled by a fancy that was not to be his real course in life. He had to be alert to the reality of where he was.

He proceeded to the silent entrance of the living quarters. The doors were open, and he could see a spacious earthen floor, a long broad step fashioned from a huge beam, and a black wood floor that disappeared into the darkness of the interior. Standing just outside, he noticed a zelkova doorplate. The moon was setting into the mountains and emitted no light. The letters were formed with bold strokes, but the plate was old and hard to read. He deciphered three big Chinese characters somewhat like a blind person reading braille, "*SHI KA TO*."

'Ha-han...it means, Do not lean your staff. It warns that newcomers are not to enter, as the nun teacher explained. In old times training monks toured the land, she said, and whenever they came to temples and monasteries, they leaned their priest's staff against the entrance and asked for a Zen interview with the master. If a monk could meet with his ideal master, he became his disciple; otherwise he resumed his tour.

'Now, this plate refuses touring monks. Yet, only at the times when it's posted are they allowed to tour. The nun teacher said, "Buddha decided on two seasons a year when all monks were to stay in their temples to devote themselves to study and meditation. One is called 'rainy-season residence,' from 15 April to 15 July, the other, 'snowy-season residence,' from 15 October to 15 January. So monks could travel and visit other masters only in other seasons, which is exactly when the plate is posted. It's a paradoxical irony characteristic of Zen. Indeed Zen-related people use many paradoxes. So, Mokuzu, don't heed only their outer appearance. The true meaning of '*shi ka to*' is to welcome newcomers, do you see?"

'What a silly and obstinate irony!' Mokuzu decided. 'I know Zen Master Tengai once came to Tangenji to ask my father to let him take me as a disciple. He's eager to get new trainees. Yet he posts this plate — what a queer mix of reality and tradition!'

"You have to believe in the great compassion of the master and the great kindness of the senior monks," the nun had said.

'Well, were I Reiho I'd splinter this plate with my fist. He thinks one after practicing ten, whereas I think ten before I practice one. That's the difference between us. Oh! What about Luri, is she ill?'

While Mokuzu thus thought, a light was turned on in a room by the entrance hall. It had a lattice window facing the garden and was situated as if for doorkeepers.

Evidently the monks in there were dressing. Noisily shaking a bell, one hurried out and ran toward the interior. Mokuzu supposed he was waking others. Another came out and passed with celerity toward the kitchen.

Unnoticed, Mokuzu thought with determination, 'Now's the time to begin my entrance ceremony as Shorai taught me,' and he stepped in onto the earthen floor of the entrance hall after leaning his bamboo hat against the wall where touring monks of old would have leaned their staffs. He put out his surplice box and a white envelope containing his personal history and application for acceptance as a training monk. Then he sat on the step, drew in his breath, and voiced a deep, powerful, and prolonged supplication,

"*Tano — mi — ma — shoooo!*"

No response came at all. He could hear the bell-ringing monk go toward the meditation hall on the eastern rise. Then,

BUNG! A loud abrupt sound rived the monastic stillness. Mokuzu could not determine the cause, but it was the sound of the heavy cedar sliding doors of the meditation hall being opened all at once. No monk could continue to sleep.

Soon after, the sounds of striking hard, dry wood pierced the mountain air and steadily echoed. The sounds carried to other mountains, and more than the cry of foxes reminded Mokuzu of how deep in the mountains he was.

The initial loud stroke was followed by two quick ones quite faint. After a pause came seven loud strokes evenly spaced, then a single faint one, then uncountable strokes beginning loud and even and diminishing as they quickened, suggesting the tapering tail of a snake. Just when it seemed to be utterly ceasing it began anew, but now with five loud even strokes; then again a faint one and the quickening, diminishing ones, starting loud but now shorter and trailing to nothing. Next the initial strokes were counted as three. When the quickening and diminishing strokes, this time yet shorter, had disappeared except in Mokuzu's ear, there came a final loud stroke.

No sooner had this performance finished at the meditation hall than the bong of the big bell in the bell tower at the west end of the garden reverberated, and slowly the strokes there continued.

The wood sounded immediately when struck, and the sound cut the air like the bark of a hunting dog. In contrast the heavy sound of the bell was slow to rise, and the reverberation seemed to produce an almost visible swell.

The intoning of the bell was kept up as the eastern sky dawned. Mokuzu was reminded of the nun Shorai's teaching,

"In the Zen monastery every function is announced not by mouth but by various sound-producing instruments only. So while you are a novice, be mindful of them. After a long period of training, you will be able to catch what kind of monk is ringing by the sound."

'Well, I hear the sounds and now have no way to see the personality of the monks,' Mokuzu admitted.

After the eighteenth stroke of the big bell, a half-sized bell began where the cross-wing met the main building, diagonally opposite the bell tower across the garden. Like the wood sound, it came in a seven-five-three sequence with trailing strokes. This smaller hanging bell had a much higher tone and a limited reverberation, its effect being to urge people on.

As Shorai had instructed, Mokuzu kept his brow pressed to his surplice box placed on the step. He thus could not see what was going on and had to guess by means of his ears.

Monks in twos and threes issued from various rooms and hurried through the cross-wing to the main building. They walked straight without heeding him.

Then came the clean sound of a metal stick against a handbell in the meditation hall, and soon dozens of monks were filing down from there. The handbell was struck by a lead monk at each turn of a corner. Silently they processed in past Mokuzu and on through the cross-wing to the main building.

As the monks from the meditation hall and elsewhere were seating themselves in the main building, a slow and heavy footfall accompanied by the step of an assistant sounded along a corridor from deep within. A strong aura of musk preceded.

Mokuzu realized that it had to be the Zen master, Tengai. But he could not turn his head. Having studied karate, he knew very well how to read a person's mind by hearing his tread. He could tell that the master had taken note of him, but he turned into the cross-wing and kept advancing.

Just as he was no doubt arriving at the center of the main building, the hanging bell at the wing-side entrance finished with two faint strokes and a hard stroke. At once a big bell on a stand was struck, and the monks began to chant.

The chanting of many monks was like the cry of cicadas, or wind passing through a green forest. The obbligato of the huge slit-drum came through the wood floor to Mokuzu's forehead.

537

'I once read that the din of cicadas on a South Pacific island drowned out a machine gun...Would these monks notice a machine gun?...It's strange — surrendering to the sound like dust on a wave, I feel the main building is the core of the world....

'The chanting also reminds me of Unkai...yes, at one time he was here, doing what I am now? How did he feel when he got sick? Oh, I'd like to know how he and Zen Master Hanun are faring at Ryotanji these days...!

'Well, I shouldn't waste my time. I've got to do something. No one answered my supplication. I'll call again, even louder, and I don't care if it disturbs their chanting,'

"*Tano — mi — ma — shooooooo!*"

He could feel his voice penetrate the air and cut between the high and the low sounds of the chanting.

But the monks continued with the steady beat of the drum.

He was not going to be acknowledged by anyone.

'What a breach of etiquette! I've a mind to step up in my muddy sandals and bark, "Didn't you hear me?"'

To Mokuzu the training monks appeared to be a bunch of egoists absorbed in their own concerns.

42

Meeting the Zen Master

Mokuzu continued to sit on the step with his feet on the earth and his head pressed to his hands pressed palm down on his surplice box. He was going through *niwa-zume*, "to attend in the garden," a traditional formality required of monastery applicants to test their determination.

'What nonsense! Do they see endurance of physical discomfort as proof of the determination to train oneself in Zen? In this unnatural posture, certainly the blood is rushing to my head and my back is starting to ache.

'Is endurance necessary to the fulfillment of religious training? Anyway, who can live free of the pressure of endurance? It seems people live with endurance upon endurance, yet most remain unenlightened, beset with unsolved problems, full of complaints and anxieties, and they do evil and don't care to do good. There must be something far more important than endurance...for

538

instance, a society in which no one has to endure, or a mentality that can face matters without the need of endurance.

'I'll refuse this test, but not by walking away. That would be to surrender the chance to train myself for a great awakening. I'll also not take an easy posture, or walk about and exercise while no one is looking. That would be cheating.

'I'll keep this posture till they're satisfied, and use the hours to reflect on my past and imagine my future, and most of all, I'll try to keep searching for an answer to the koan "What is my original nature from before my parents were born?" given me by Zen Master Hanun.

'Thus my mind will be very active even as my body stays very still. I'll be like a boiling kettle.'

The chanting had finished and the monks were leaving the main building. Those who dwelled in the meditation hall filed back past Mokuzu. Others from the residential quarters went by his head to the kitchen, where they briefly chanted with amazing speed before dispersing to their rooms. In the meditation hall too another sutra was chanted, followed by the single clap of wood clappers and the keen ring of a handbell. The monastery then returned to a state of quiet.

'How deadly quiet! But the light of dawn is here — time to call anew, the third time. No one should have any excuse not to hear. If I get no answer I really will step in to abuse them for their impoliteness.'

Mokuzu raised a deep and silvery tone:

"*Tano — mi — ma — shooooo!*"

"*Do — reeee!*" came a prompt response in a tone equally deep and rich, though muddier. A monk stepped from the nearest room, presumed by Mokuzu to house doorkeepers. He knelt at Mokuzu's head and spoke courteously,

"You troubled to come here at this early hour. May I ask what you wish of us?"

Mokuzu responded as Shorai had taught:

"I was born in Kameoka in Tanba. My father, priest of Tangenji, a second-ranking temple of the Nanzenji school, ordained me when I was age eight and sent me to receive care and tutelage from the Zen master Hanun-kutsu of Ryotanji. There I stayed five years. You will find the details in this accompanying paper.

"I am here to supplicate permission to train myself with you. I realize there is a grave life matter I must study, and my determination is set, as you will see in the other accompanying paper. Please sympathize with my earnest wish and receive me into your monastery."

"Wait a moment, please. I shall report the matter to my superiors," said the monk, and he left. Mokuzu noticed his ankle bones protruded uncommonly. He returned shortly, knelt as before, and said,

"We do not doubt your determination. Be that as it may, to you it should be evident that this monastery deep in the hinterland is in great disrepair, and we have no Dharma worthy to teach, nor any provisions to share.

"Let me remind you of other monasteries, such as Nanzen, Shokoku, Tofuku, Tenryo, Myoshin, and Daitoku, in Kyoto; and Engaku, Kencho, and so on, in Kamakura. You can easily count three dozen of brilliant renown throughout the land.

"We suggest you apply to one of them, and we stoutly refuse you here. Now excuse me." The monk returned the white envelope that Mokuzu had prepared and simply withdrew into his room.

Mokuzu wanted to burst out laughing. The monk's words and manner were just what Shorai had told him they would be.

'What a hackneyed display! Soberly he repeats the age-old formula without presenting anything of himself. What kind of pressure was he given to behave so? He adopts even the exact style of language.

'How ridiculous that some Zen scholars elatedly introduce to the West this sort of blind obedience as a great Zen heritage, and how absurd that some Westerners yearn for it,' thought Mokuzu with derision. Then, as he continued to press his head to his hands in begging form, he reflected on himself with bitter sadness and frustration,

'So, why don't I walk away? I'm a free man, yet I'm participating in this decayed tradition. After all, I must laugh at myself. What should I do? What can I do?

'I should be ashamed of myself...but I can't leave. I must steal everything of the Dharma that Zen Master Tengai can offer, yes, I must endure my unclear state until I become enlightened.'

Mokuzu in the open entrance hall resembled an invalid hunched in pain. No one cared; the monks passed by as if they had not noticed him. His posture kept him from seeing anything.

'Hey, Mokuzu!' he thought. 'You have an unfortunate habit of assuming a critical attitude toward everything. You're acting like a pure, obedient trainee, but the truly enlightened will see through your pathetic, schizothymic, Jekyll-and-Hyde character. You're least suited to Zen training, which is to efface oneself, deny one's dualistic thought and conduct, and neither analyze nor criticize a thing, but become it. A Zen trainee must have no relative concepts, such as subject and object, good and evil, mind and body, light and darkness. For a Zen trainee there must be only a free and absolute world.'

After thus meditating, he responded in self-defense, 'Well, I'm no coward, and I love myself enough to resist self-hatred and to remain confident even if I am to hear I am a Jekyll and Hyde. My ever-critical spirit and ability to adapt to the surface of reality are like the tibia and fibula of my leg — together they aid me to cross any terrain.

'I also must remember I'm engaging in my study not to become simpleminded but to gain depth of character, like a Japanese sword. It neither bends nor breaks and cuts very well, three diverse fine qualities. In fact a Japanese sword is made of more than one metal. The core, to resist breakage, is a pure but soft iron without slag; the outer layer, to resist bending, is a hard steel; the edge, for sharpness, is the hardest steel.' Mokuzu's mind was incoherent with many thoughts, like the mind of a child playing with clay, though his posture remained unchanged.

The monks from the meditation hall came and went in orderly file, first for breakfast, then for another ceremony in the main building. In the residential quarters monks were busily cleaning, dealing with laymen, or otherwise engaged; Mokuzu could scarcely confirm what they were doing.

His face became congested, his head began to float, and his limbs and back alternately ached and went numb.

Around eleven o'clock, without warning, three monks in work dress attacked him. One struck his head, back, and elsewhere with a length of thick green bamboo, which easily splintered and sent a sliver through his robe into his shoulder. The others grabbed his legs and dragged him over the threshold, directly across the gravel garden, and through the gate.

He could make no sense of what had happened to him; he crouched in pain as if his life had been put to an end. One of them hurled at his tonsured head his bamboo hat and it rolled down the stone steps.

They left him with the words, "What nerve! Denied entrance to this monastery, yet you remained in the entrance hall. At once begone! If you ever show up again, we'll break your bones and crush your noggin!"

Before the gate, his robes in disarray, Mokuzu grew furious at the monks, and more, he shook with feelings of compunction.

'How could I be so careless? Was I dozing? I didn't notice their approach at all. I minimized the chance of danger and let my limbs go to sleep. I assumed in these sacred precincts of wisdom and compassion there were no gangsters. How shameful I couldn't use my karate skill! Musashi after he was attacked in the bathtub determined never to take another bath....Well, well, I'll not be daunted by such a trifle!'

He returned to the entrance of the residential quarters as if nothing had happened, though his face had many bloody scratches. He resumed his

541

position, but this time kept moving his muscles to be ready to retaliate.

Most of the monks from the meditation hall had apparently gone out for some kind of field or mountain work. Toward evening they returned, bathed, and supped, and directly there came the deep resonance of the evening bell. This time the monk at the bell tower chanted the Lotus Flower Sutra as he rang, and all the while no other sounds were raised. The moment the bell finished, the wood sound at the meditation hall was sent echoing to the mountains in the same pattern as the early morning. Then came two claps of the clappers and four clean strikes of the handbell. The monks must have begun to meditate.

Dark settled. Odd sounds occasionally issued from the meditation hall. Mokuzu had no idea what they were. In fact the direct monk was beating monks on the back with a warning stick.

He who refused Mokuzu in the morning appeared and spoke kindly,

"You must be bent on entering this monastery. As I said, we cannot receive you. Yet we are not without sympathy, for we too seek the Way. Hence we offer you the convenience of one night's stay. Please come with me."

The monk was broad-shouldered, his midriff sturdy. His face was bistered and blocky, almost square, with full lips, but his eyes were slits below faint eyebrows. At the crown his head had a gentle depression.

When Mokuzu looked straight at him, he lowered his eyes. Mokuzu presumed his nature to be meek and warm.

The monk stepped out the entrance, turned the corner of the residential quarters, and crossed the stone path that extended up to the meditation hall. He led Mokuzu to a dark room annexed to the bath house, which faced the kitchen area of the residential quarters. After fetching a bucket of water, he advised him to wash his feet.

The room had a dim light, a damp floor with many knotholes, and one thin cushion.

He brought in a tray with a cup, a tiny teapot, and a rice cracker. Mokuzu accepted three cups of tea in succession. Next he brought in a brush and ink and asked him to register his name and address in an old bulky guest book.

Seated alone with legs across in meditation form, Mokuzu thought about the Chinese Zen priest Yungjia.

> Zen Teacher Yungjia Shyuanjiau of Wenchow...with another Zen teacher, Dungyang Tse, visited Mt. Tsaushi. As soon as he met the Sixth Patriarch, he thrice circled him, jug in hand and shaking his staff.
>
> "Three thousand dignified miens and eighty thousand circumspect conducts are required of a priest. You are so rude I wonder from whence you came," spoke the Sixth Patriarch.

"So grave is the problem of life and death, there is no time to waste," replied Yungjia.

"Why don't you comprehend non-life, and why don't you master non-time?" the patriarch asked.

"I have comprehended: there is non-life. And I have mastered: there is non-time."

"Fine, fine." The patriarch's quick assent astonished the attending monks.

Yungjia paid him the customary worship and spoke a farewell. "Why are you in such a hurry to leave?" the patriarch asked.

"My nature is not moving; how can you say I am hurrying?"

The patriarch further quested, "Who is he who knows 'not moving'?"

"Judgment arises spontaneously."

"You well understand the meaning of non-life."

"Has non-life meaning?"

"Whether it has or hasn't, who can judge?"

"Judgment is meaningless."

The patriarch remarked in admiration, "You are great, your understanding is profound! Why don't you stay the night?"

Later people called Yungjia "the priest enlightened by a single night's stay."[1]

Whether he understood it or not, to Mokuzu this type of Zen episode appeared to be a kind of idealism without power to influence his daily life. But he had no confidence to dismiss it as mere idealism. He thought the reason he understood it to be idealism was that he could see it as only an idea and not as something he had experienced. His hope was to go through the religious experience of understanding his original nature so that he could live a free, active, and awakened life. This hope was his very reason for coming to Shoshinji.

Facing the wall in the dark room, he continued to meditate.

'In his infancy the Sixth Patriarch, Hueineng, lost his father. He toted firewood on his back into town to sell and was dutiful to his old mother. A month before he died he returned to his native village of Shialu and erected tombs to his parents on a hill overlooking the village and facing low western mountains resembling a recumbent dragon...so I have heard.

'I could more readily understand had he preached, "Losing your father while yet too young to remember him is indeed sad! Appreciate your mother and be a good son. Build tombs for your parents so they may rest in peace. In your youth, travel the world. In your senescence return to your unforgettable native land and sit quiet on a hill facing the setting sun...."

'What he preached was not that. He preached an abstract idealism, which sometimes I feel I understand, but then I don't at all. "He who knows the

543

Dharma," he said, "is free of apprehension stemming from retrospection and attachment, and is unaffected by fallacious reasoning. His innate nature, *bhutatathata*, correctly functions, and his wisdom contemplates all phenomena. By rejecting both attachment and detachment, he is able to take the path of Buddhahood."[2]

'He also said, "The tenet of our religion is non-thinking, the body of our religion is formless-form, and nowhere is where we dwell."[3] What does it mean...?'

Mokuzu repeated niwa-zume a second and a third day. In the evening of the third, when the same monk led him to the room for the night, he said with compassion,

"I have been here six years, but I never witnessed such a hard niwa-zume. You're given no meals. Aren't you starved?"

"I am hungry, but it makes me view the past with nostalgia."

"What?"

"When I was far more helpless than now, I knew many days without food. Even the pebbles on the mostly deserted country roads looked edible. It's as if I'm reexperiencing my childhood," Mokuzu explained quietly.

"I see, you had a hard time. So this niwa-zume isn't unbearable for you, I understand. My senior told me to be strict; don't hold it against me.

"Beginning tomorrow you will be confined to this room to go through *tanga-zume*, I don't know for how long. The head reception officer will interview you daily. Be careful: he decides whether you enter this monastery," said the monk evenly.

He then gave detailed instructions. Mokuzu was to attend morning chanting, at the lowest-ranking seat, as soon as he heard the morning bell. After the monks finished their meals, he would be offered meals in the kitchen with those whose work kept them from eating with the others, and he was to be attentive to the cloud-shaped gong announcing these secondary meals. He also might be asked to join those cleaning the buildings and the gardens and should be prompt to show up.

"Do not forget you are a guest of this community. Your status is that of being tested for suitability as a member, called 'going through the tanga-zume period,'" warned the monk.

Mokuzu voiced no word of consent. The monk must have felt he had to be tender and intimate to some degree, not just sternly official, for he added,

"Tanga-zume is one of the hardest periods you may experience in all your monastic life. It will seem an endless, insecure time, but you have to recognize the hidden kindness. From the day you are accepted, you will be asked to behave like a perfect training monk and you will be given no excuse

544

for being a newcomer. So while undergoing tanga-zume, you can gain all the knowledge and skills you will need as a monk. Do you see?"

Mokuzu could discern the monk's good nature, but also his lack of confidence. He was being severe due to pressure from his seniors; he had not yet gained his own way. Pursued by an unease about the effect of the monastery's training life, Mokuzu asked, regardless of being rude,

"You say you have been here six years. Can you tell me, do you know your original nature?"

The monk's eyes momentarily darkened as if by the shadow of a passing crow, but he soon resumed his stern manner,

"You ask about so grave a matter so easily — don't be silly! You are like a kindergartner asking about a doctoral degree."

Mokuzu without blinking regarded him. The monk looked aside, and what he said was a remarkably honest confession,

"Being stupid as an owl, I still don't know even now in what direction to exert myself. I'm given the very koan you mention, but I feel I'm being made into a puppet by the expedients of the master's education."

"Do you know the episode of Yungjia meeting the Sixth Patriarch?" Mokuzu asked, and was amazed that the monk had no knowledge of it, though the koan he had been given originated with the Sixth Patriarch.

After he left, Mokuzu tried to read the wooden tablet posted near the ceiling. It evidently listed rules to be observed by the occupant of the room; but the light was so poor and the letters so sooty that in places he had to supplement them with his guesses:

> For monks who wish to master the secret of Zen, touring is for no other purpose than to find a great teacher and excellent companions.
>
> A monk granted a night in this room is to meditate facing the wall and wholly focus his mind and body on the gravest concern of his life.
>
> Work hard, spend no idle time. Be reminded of the ideal example of the tour made by Shyuefeng, Yantou, and Chinshan.
>
> The following rules are to be strictly kept:
>
> No monastery may be visited after evening bell.
>
> A stay of one night may not be extended however stormy the weather. Depart directly at morning bell. Illness only is excepted.
>
> Dozing by leaning on the surplice box is prohibited at all times. Sleep is prohibited until the finish of night meditation.
>
> Morning chanting must be attended without fail. A touring monk is exempt from donning the surplice.
>
> A breakfast of rice gruel is offered at the kitchen at the sound of the cloud-shaped gong.
>
> No light is ever permitted at night.

Mokuzu quickly turned off the dim light and took meditation form. In the dark and quiet monastery only the sounds of the direct monk beating the meditating monks echoed now and again from the meditation hall.

Next morning the monk in charge of Mokuzu came to explain how he was to offer worship to the head reception monk. Mokuzu knew how to bow and prostrate himself as if to receive the feet of the one being worshiped; it was required before Zen Master Hanun.

The monk was obviously busy and wanting to leave promptly, but Mokuzu asked,

"It is hard to orient myself. Could you explain simply the monastery layout, and more, what kind of officers are in charge?"

"Soon you'll learn by yourself; you'll scarce be taught by words and only be ordered about," the monk replied rather sternly with what he had no doubt been told as a fresh monk.

But as he left, he turned and said with hesitation,

"I know your disquiet. I spent almost a year just to figure out where I was. I felt blindfolded. Naturally I hadn't any margin to spare for concentrating on my koan.

"Listen, we monks are about equally divided into two groups. Half are the so-called experienced, who live in the residential quarters and who are given the work of maintaining the monastery. The other half, where you'll be put, live in the meditation hall day after day just to train themselves.

"The head reception officer is one of the three highest officers. He superintends the daily life of all monks. I am head of the chanting office, which is in charge of maintaining solemnity in the Buddha hall. I take the lead there on all ceremonial occasions. I also assist the head reception officer.

"I'm giving you this much information, but I'm forbidden to behave like this...only I didn't want to see you confused...by the way, my name is Zui."

At nine an assistant chanting officer twice sounded a large pair of wood clappers at the residential quarters entrance and Mokuzu was led by Zui to the head reception officer's room. It was catercorner to the chanting officers' room, on the inner side of a wide corridor that at mealtimes was the monks' dining area, in the cross-wing between the main building and the residential quarters. The fusumas of the head reception officer's room were wide open to the corridor and also to an inner garden on the opposite side of the room.

The head reception officer was framed by an alcove. He sat as erect as had Zen Master Hanun. To his left was a white warning stick, to his right lit incense. No scroll hung in the alcove.

The head chanting officer, Zui, knelt outside to announce Mokuzu.

"Come in!" spoke the head reception officer, his voice strongly compressed.

Mokuzu stepped in with palms joined at his chest and thrice carefully performed the highest form of veneration. The head reception officer intensely observed every minutia of his manner, even how he breathed.

Mokuzu then sat before him. The head reception officer persisted in confronting him with eyes astare. Mokuzu stared back. His pate was bulky, whereas his chin was slightly deficient.

"You wish to enter to train yourself. Tell me why you choose this monastery above all others."

Mokuzu considered an answer as he held the monk's gaze, and also considered his eyes. 'Strong eyes don't perturb me at all. It's eyes like Zui's that are hard to look into — meek as autumn gloom, confused with shyness and pride, stern but tender....'

"Answer at once!"

"Why I chose this monastery goes without saying. I came for the teaching of the great master," replied Mokuzu frankly.

The monk raised his eyebrows with a trace of surprise, swallowed, regained his dignity, and issued another question:

"What do you mean, 'the great master'?"

"Zen Master Tengai."

"Why is he 'the great master'?" His tone was nasty.

"I trust he will equip me to know life that doesn't die, that lasts forever. He will enable me to see who I am, mortal yet made by eternal life to live."

"Hm, you are clever! Do you know he will demand absolute obedience? Tell me your resolution! Without hesitation can you enter fire, enter water, if he commands it?"

"I came ready to enter the mind of the Zen master, which must be complicated, inscrutable, trackless, and poisonous. I should find it far easier to be asked to enter such simple elements as fire and water. I shall not spare even my life, in accordance with the saying: A man who learns the Way in the morning can die in the evening without regret,"[4] Mokuzu earnestly replied.

Every day thereafter a short interview was held. The reception monk uttered nothing, and Mokuzu only bowed and prostrated himself in worship.

The rest of his time he mostly had to spend facing the wall meditating. Until then he had never spent more than three days without reading any book, and, suffering from withdrawal symptoms of book toxicosis, he longed to read.

'Extensive meditation muddles my brain. In this direction I'll no doubt begin to hallucinate and I wonder if I can arrive at the great awakening. I

547

wish I could read even the least interesting thing, even an old newspaper.'

Soon he lost track of the date, for he had to repeat a simple routine and was confined to a small, gloomy room.

One day he sensed that all Shoshinji was dead quiet inside and out. Until then, too, the monastery had been quiet, but the quiet had been full of the energy of monks training. Now it was obviously from emptiness.

At three in the afternoon Zui brought in tea and sweets.

"Too bad you're not allowed to go on the big mendicancy." He then explained, "Monks tour for a week, divided to groups for the various districts, such as Nagoya-Chita, Gifu-Ogaki, and Gero-Takayama. Had you come a little earlier, you could have gone too.

"It's mendicancy, but with pleasant aspects. The seniors, for instance, are less severe, and seize opportunities to visit the tourist spots. Twice a year we have these big mendicancies, during the equinoctial weeks. They afford us our only chance to see the outside world."

It occurred to Mokuzu that in places alongside the rice fields the cluster amaryllis was now in full glory like the fire of passion, and that the nostalgic flowers of crepe myrtle were extending over garden hedges.

The monks who remained were few in number, yet they had to maintain regular monastic functions. They asked Mokuzu's help as if he were a full-fledged training monk. He participated in the work of cleaning, vegetable gardening, and making firewood.

It was a good period, indeed affording him the chance to become acquainted with monastic conduct.

He was permitted to bathe after the more strenuous work. Even for taking baths there were strict rules. First he had to prostrate himself three times before a sooted image of the Bodhisattva Bhadrapala enshrined at the center of the dressing room. Bhadrapala had become enlightened while taking a bath, according to a Chinese sutra.

All clothes had to be hung in a prescribed manner, and before entering the tubs area, another deep bow with joined palms was not to be forgotten. Of course Mokuzu knew he must wash thoroughly before entering the water.

If he chanced to be bathing with a more senior monk, he had to scrub the senior's back everywhere with a firmly wrung towel, so hard as to redden the skin, then lay the towel on and pour hot bath water under it, then tap and massage head and shoulders. While thus administered to, the senior kept his palms joined in thanks.

Mokuzu himself was once given such service as a sample by Zui; otherwise he had to serve the seniors and had no time to soak in the tub.

Zui instructed him never to speak in the bath house, it being counted as one of the three places where silence was most respected. The others were the dining area and the meditation hall, though in fact no one spoke useless words anywhere throughout the sacred precincts.

Zui also taught him that he was not to show his teeth for three years. And further, his walk was at all times to be dignified, hands clasped at the bosom, backbone straight, no swaying of the shoulders, and eyes always directed to the earth six feet straight ahead.

Fortunately from childhood Mokuzu had adored Ena's clean posture and himself made no needless motions; never had he been reprimanded for his way of sitting, standing, or walking.

The fussiest manners came at mealtime. Meals began with the chanting of the Heart Sutra on Wisdom and the "Ten Buddha-names"; then, at breakfast the "Stanza for Rice Gruel," at lunch the "Stanza for the Proper Meal," followed both times by the "Stanza for Hungry Ghosts," which continued as each monk offered from his serving a small amount of rice, stipulated as "not to be offered by spoon and not to exceed seven grains, for the reason that too much and too little stimulate greed and grudge."[5]

The custom of offering food to hungry ghosts came from a tale in volume 16 of the Nirvana Sutra: The yaksa Atavaka, commanded to kill no creature, was close to starving. Sakyamuni Buddha hence ordered his disciples who had become enlightened by hearing his teaching to offer Atavaka a meal wherever Buddhism was practiced.

After the offering to hungry ghosts, chanting continued with the "Five Observations" and the "Stanza of Three Spoonfuls." Only then could the monks begin to eat, with spine as erect as during sitting meditation; leaning in any direction was strictly forbidden. No noise was allowed in setting out their five black-lacquered bowls and placing their stout chopsticks on the wood table, or even in chewing the hard pickles.

After meals again there were stanzas to chant. Each monk as he chanted washed his bowls with tea, which he drank; then he wiped them with a dry cloth, stacked them neatly, and returned them to their black cloth bag.

One day Zui came to Mokuzu's room and asked, "How are you doing? Now you know this is a hard place. Morning gruel is so thin you can see the knotholes in the ceiling; it's called rice but is mostly barley. We just add more water when there's a newcomer. A bit of daikon pickle is the only thing else. Lunch is hard-cooked barley rice; there are no side dishes then either, other than miso soup and pickle. We have no supper unless food is left from lunch. Can you manage day after day on that alone?"

"It's better than being obliged to eat excessive, elaborate fare," Mokuzu replied calmly.

"Hm, you may not realize how important food is to your health. You seem too thin. If you can't increase your weight in the next half year, you'll get sick or have to flee in the night like most newcomers. I don't want to teach you sneaky ways, but remember, your life can be protected only by you. What's the point of getting enlightenment if you die at it...?"

"Head Chanting Officer, as I said, I went many days without food in my childhood. In Tokyo too I worked for a newspaper shop, yet I spent my earnings on books, not lunch."

Zui was unable to believe Mokuzu was not suffering from scarce nutrition. He went on to say, "At ten we sleep. But in fact when put in the meditation hall, you're ordered to meditate extra hours on the veranda of the main building or on one of the rocks on the back mountain. Yet you must rise at four in the rainy season, three-thirty in the snowy season. It's a miracle we aren't dead. What a hard physical life for a mediocrity like me! I've been barely keeping the looks of a training monk, and I haven't at all figured out the answer to my koan...."

Mokuzu kept silent. What he wanted most was to be allowed to meet Zen Master Tengai even a day earlier and have his view of his original nature certified. He was passionate to solve all the koans the Zen master would give him. The only reason he was silent and polite before this meek monk was that he knew by heart the five basic rules to be observed by fresh monks:

> Be self-effacing
> Be compassionate of others
> Be respectful to seniors
> Know the correct order of all things
> Speak no word unrelated with training.[6]

❧

The monks returned from their long-distance mendicancy on the thirteenth day of Mokuzu's stay at Shoshinji. At last he was to be received as a regular monk and the ceremony to enter the meditation hall would be performed for him.

The head chanting officer, Zui, escorted him up the roofed path to the meditation hall. The stone steps of the path turned twice and met a meticulously swept garden with traces of bamboo brooming. The trees were old, lean, bent, and sporadic.

At the back entrance the attendant to Manjusri Bodhisattva received him, and Zui returned to his quarters.

The attendant to Manjusri, tall and white of face, gave Mokuzu two lit sticks of incense and announced his arrival with a loud, prolonged intonation —

"*Shin — to —— san — do —— !*"

The immediate striking of the handbell and two claps of the clappers echoed from inside the meditation hall, signals from the direct monk, who was head of the meditation hall, that a meditation period was ended.

The Manjusri attendant urged Mokuzu to enter the hall with palms joined and the incense held horizontal between thumbs and forefingers, and, as at all times, to lead with the right foot. Mokuzu stepped over the huge threshold and proceeded straight along the monks seated on the north side. The dense black tiles of the floor were so clean as to show not a fleck of dust. The Manjusri attendant took his seat on the south side. Mokuzu approached to the very front of the Manjusri image enshrined at the center and facing the open front entrance. He bowed, offered to Manjusri one stick of incense, placed the other temporarily aside, thrice prostrated himself in formal veneration, and bowed again.

He retrieved the second incense and turned to the direct monk, seated on the north side nearest the front entrance and diagonally across from the Manjusri attendant. After stepping before the direct monk and bowing deeply, he extended his hand with the incense, in response to which the direct monk bowed slightly and extended his hand. As their hands met, the direct monk received the incense. Mokuzu could feel his dry warm hand. The direct monk stood the incense in a censer.

Mokuzu returned along the north-side monks to the lowest-ranking seat, exactly across from the Manjusri attendant, who had already brought in his surplice box and prepared a cushion. Before taking his seat, he politely bowed to everyone in the hall, especially to the monk next to him. As soon as he was seated, the direct monk sounded the clappers once and the handbell twice. Then the Manjusri attendant, having disappeared without Mokuzu's notice, cried from outside the back entrance,

"*Sarei!*"

It was to announce a tea ceremony. Quickly he poured each cup, from the direct monk to the lowest on the north side, and from the highest to the lowest on the south side. The tea was of a daily sort and a very small amount. In no time the direct monk rang the bell to signal commencement of a meditation period.

Everything was done in strict silence within the shortest possible interval. The simplicity of each ceremony clearly indicated that any individual circumstances, or monk's own personality, constitution, thought, and emotion, were to be minimized, even entirely denied, for the sake of investigating his most profound problem, which involved going beyond limited individuality and returning to limitless eternity.

551

Therefore what Mokuzu had been required to vow when he offered incense to Manjusri was that he would not leave the meditation hall until he perfected his training and gained the same perfect wisdom as the wisdom of Manjusri.

Offering incense to the direct monk was to show complete obedience to his tutelage and to ask his utmost kindness, even if it appeared to be his utmost cruelty.

The meditation hall was dark, cool, and damp; yet the singing of birds in the bamboo grove to the southeast sounded to Mokuzu so cheerful that for a while he did not know what to make of where he was.

The following morning Mokuzu was allowed to meet the Zen master, a moment he had been long and impatiently awaiting. His head was freshly shaven, and he was dressed in his best — white underkimono, black silk robe, and white tabi.

The Manjusri attendant escorted him from the meditation hall to the residential quarters. The head chanting officer gave him a smile as he received him, and led him down a wood corridor to the interior. On the right side of the corridor was a long row of shojis behind which was a large rectangular drawing room. The left side of the corridor opened to the inner garden.

At the corridor's end Zui handed him over to the Zen master's head attendant, who turned left at the corner and led him along the corridor facing the north side of the inner garden, then up some steps, and on to a pair of adjoining rooms used exclusively for interviews with the Zen master. His private quarters were at a farther and higher depth.

Mokuzu could easily figure the layout of the buildings and the configuration of the terrain because of their similarity to Ryotanji, though here everything was on a much larger scale.

Bowing and prostrating himself before the master was also done in exactly the same manner, but the smile of Zen Master Tengai at the sight of him was more pronounced than the smile of Zen Master Hanun.

"I reprimanded the seniors for not setting this interview much earlier. True, I tell them to be severe with newcomers, but not with all. They have no eye and confined you for a uselessly long time," the Zen master said in a loud voice. His face had no gloss, but his voice was lively. Mokuzu noticed that his eyebrows had grown longer and whiter and that the left one was near to bald at the tail.

"Put aside their stupidity, I truly welcome you. You are not normal, so you must train harder. I also will do my best.

"I have nothing special to tell you now. I just want you to work your way through quickly to seeing your original nature and obtaining a bright enlightened eye. Whoever doesn't know himself is a ghost that adheres to the grasses and leans on the trees.

"To see your original nature you must pass the koans I will give you. The quickest way is to follow my instruction exactly. Act on my advice, imitate my way down to every detail of my every movement, identify yourself with my mind, and naturally you will understand all the koans I have.

"I received the Dharma from my teacher, who received it from his teacher, who received it from his. Thus my Dharma has come from patriarch to patriarch — from Kanzan, Daito, Daio...from Linji, Huangbo, Baijang...from the sixth patriarch, Hueineng, and from the first, Bodhidharma, and more, Prajnatara, Punyamitra, Vasasita, and after all from Sakyamuni Buddha. Now I must transmit the Dharma to you like passing water from bucket to bucket. However, after you have mastered all the Dharma, you must build up your own view, which should surpass mine. Only then will you be certified to carry on the transmission. To be a new patriarch for the coming generation, you must do more than master all that is old: you must add what is your own.

"You must be serious. If I say work hard, work hard. If I tell you something else, do that something else. All men of ordinary ability don't do what I tell them and do what I don't — they do everything but the one correct thing. Their unfortunate character is to be disloyal to the truth while being firmly loyal to every falsehood. No wonder there is no progress of human wisdom in these thousand or two thousand years.

"Now I shall give you a koan. Go with it to the meditation hall and study it from morning to night and night to morning. Keep it with you as if you've bit into a stinkbug or are holding in your mouth a burning ball. Don't forget it even a minute, whether you are cleaning the garden, working in the mountain, or touring for alms. Study it even as you eat, even in the toilet. Absorb yourself in the study of your koan. You can solve it only when you become it and when it becomes you.

"Do you understand? You won't be able to solve a single koan in any other way. Reading millions of books will give you tons of knowledge but not an ounce of wisdom. Thousands of hours of self-reflection will make you only muddier, because mud is washing mud. Don't borrow the wisdom of others, and don't use your intellect, which was given by others. You have to exalt new wisdom after destroying all of your old self. Don't depend on others and don't depend on the old versions of yourself. Become one with the koan and you will find yourself renewed in a new world. Do you see? Don't leave any space between. You and the koan should be unified.

"This that I have told you is my request. Devote yourself like a waterwheel

553

that allows no ice to freeze on it even in deep winter. You must also be like water dripping from the eaves onto a rock and finally making a hole."

Zen Master Tengai then gave Mokuzu the koan "Listen to the Sound of One Hand," which originated with Zen Teacher Hakuin.

Automatically he gave a newcomer either this or "Jaujou's Wu."

Mokuzu was fortunate to have read the booklet *Yabukoji* by Hakuin, wherein he related his thoughts on his koan of one hand.

> For forty-five years until then, I taught all who came, whether or not they were friends or kin and regardless of age or class.
>
> My wish was to enable them to gain the power to solve their most important concern, and my method was to make them continue to ask what is their original nature or to make them study "Jaujou's Wu." As a result, scores of men could attain great joy.
>
> Five or six years ago, however, I struck on the idea of asking them to listen to the sound of one hand. I then realized that my new way of teaching gave them much more doubt and hence much more progress with their study. In short, my "sound of one hand" is widely different in effect from other methods.

Hakuin went on to explain his koan:

> What do I mean by the sound of one hand? If you clap your hands, evidently there is a sound. What if you clap just one? There is no sound, nor scent. This is the very meaning of the words of Confucius: "Heaven creates mankind." It should also be the very meaning of the words of a certain mountain witch: "There is soundless sound in the echo of the valley."
>
> This sound is not the sound we hear with our ears. You must not depend on your thought and discretion, nor on your emotion. Meditate on this sound every moment of your daily life until your reason is spent and you lose words to utter. Then suddenly you will be able to sever the root of your life and death, destroy your knot of ignorance, and attain spiritual enlightenment and peace, like a phoenix flying over an iron barrier or a crane released from a cage.[7]

Mokuzu was escorted back to the meditation hall by Zui. He discerned Zui's sympathy for his having received the heavy weight of a koan. For Zui, living monastic life with an unsolved koan was akin to being a cow awaiting slaughter.

Mokuzu in turn pitied Zui for evidently having no background knowledge of any of the koans and no basic urge to solve even one; and yet he had been in the monastery for the past six years.

Mokuzu as he returned to his seat in the meditation hall firmly resolved to listen to the sound of one hand.

'I will believe the successive patriarchs and Zen Master Tengai and will exert my all for this koan. I won't fear dying or going mad, won't care about anything but the koan. By any means I will experience the mental state of going beyond all thought and emotion. I will go beyond joy and pain, and see the world beyond that of mortals who repeat what they do in confusion. I will gain the eye of wisdom and see what I can do with it to help people who suffer.

'Now a rocket to search out universal truth is launched into the dark, where the only light is from falling stars. I see the concrete world I left behind getting smaller and smaller, and I feel the power of a blue flame firing within me.

'I will never come back without achieving the task of seeing my original nature. The rhythm of my heart is the sound of one hand...sound, sound, sound...breathing in, breathing out, I will be with the sound of one hand... sound, sound, sound, sound...'

43

The Sound of One Hand

The meditation hall as an organ of education was Shoshinji's pivotal center. Like the xylem of a tree, as long as it stood in good condition, it allowed no outsider a look inside.

Entrance was granted to training monks only, and photographing was prohibited. Any outsider wishing to learn about the life within had to ask a monk who had experienced it, or imagine it by investigating disused meditation halls kept as a cultural asset and a heritage of bygone days.

Fortunately, soon after entering the meditation hall, Mokuzu resumed the diary he had begun the habit of keeping.

Writing and drawing in the meditation hall were proscribed, and violation brought severe punishment. Yet, after every other monk was fast asleep Mokuzu snuck to the latrines, and there under the five-candle-power bulb he wrote hastily with a pencil in small characters in the notebook presented to him by Gyodo as a parting gift when he left for Ryotanji.

10/2: Serotinal heat severer today. Chanting. Breakfast. Meditation for one long stick of incense (45 minutes), during which the bell to invite us for interviews with the master is rung at the main building. No answer to my koan, didn't go.

Right after meditation, ordered to do mountain work. My duty as new-comer: prepare saw, hatchet, sickle, straw rope for each member, haul it up by cart. Took about 45 minutes to enter many-folded mountains with deep valleys. Blue sky, white clouds. Black or dark blue work clothes, sleevelets, split-toed heavy-cotton footwear — towel tied on the head the only white.

Steep, rocky, overgrown with deciduous trees that Zen Master Tengai once ordered the monks to increase when shiitake cultivation and charcoal-making prospered; now orders us to cut them for firewood and to plant pine, cypress, and cedar.

By a creek had lunch brought up by kitchen officers. Many maples lent shade. The direct monk, Kaijo, ordered me to make a fire to reheat the soup and make tea. Didn't brandish warning stick as in the meditation hall. Allowed two-hour rest after lunch; we all, he too, lay supine among the eulalia — I could rest after washing the soup and rice buckets in the stream. Red dragonflies, quiet clouds. How languid I felt when work resumed!

When the sun was getting low, the monks' major, Seigan, came to me and commanded, "Go higher and work hard!"

"Won't I be scolded for going too far from the direct monk and his assistant? I won't hear their instructions."

"Right! Soon they'll give the stop command. You won't hear it, so our return will be slowed and we'll get back after evening bell. There's a tacit rule: we may doze in meditation form if we return after evening bell however little we're late. The direct monk doesn't appear in the meditation hall. It's called 'free meditation.'" He grinned. Physiognomy ugly like a demon's. Before hearing my response he left to tell others the same.

As expected, direct monk ordered us to hurry back. Loaded firewood in cart and careered down, I inside the handle, others braking with ropes. Was sure I'd get caught under if I didn't keep running. Steep stony grassy path, dangerous work.

Came at last to level road, cart got heavy. On rise to Shoshinji we were panting. Others helped me with cart, direct monk's only concern was setting sun, made us hurry even more.

Artifice of monks' major to no avail, reached Shoshinji a minute before bell, no time for bath; right after supper, night meditation. I then understood his wish to be relieved of forced meditation: with the day's sweat cooled off, I was damp all over, horrible. Stiff shoulders and back almost kept me from correct posture, breath smelled. One after another slept at their seats. Direct monk furiously exercised warning stick. I rather welcomed it to relieve stupor. Time seemed endless till chanting prior to bed. Very few went for Zen interviews during night meditation.

Writing in toilet, violating ban — can thus be by myself.

Life here puts me always under close surveillance. Reprimanded by everyone from the moment we rise to the moment we bed. I'm a minnow in a shoal with many night herons gathered. To be alone is my one remaining and greatest comfort. I once read of a soldier whose foremost desire amid a shower of bullets was to smoke a cigarette. The pleasure of solitude must have been his last wish. Gyodo spoke of a patient who stared in a mirror all day. Maybe the habit came of having every comfort denied except that of seeing himself in his severe environment.

Writing and drawing are proscribed no doubt because the monastery is warning us not to waste our time or put others in a flurry by recording our bigoted and unenlightened cogitations in the name of art, literature, or philosophy. True, for sober men it is unbearable to read or see writing or drawing produced by drunkards. Being alone and facing oneself without yet seeing one's original nature is like seeing a ghost in one's delusion.

But the monastery must have another reason: those in charge likely fear our having sufficient time for reflection. Leaders, regardless of good or evil intentions, want to exercise control. Allowed no chance for reflection, people become dolls, machines, doing as they're bid.

10/3: Calendar days ending with digits 1, 3, 6, and 8 are for mendicancy. Classed by distance: (1) Near-distance, confined to neighboring villages. Depart after chanting, breakfast, and meditation. Soon after lunch return. Bath, supper, night meditation, as usual. (2) Mid-distance, at least 2-hour walk to reach decided town or village. Depart after chanting and breakfast. Return by evening bell, usual evening and night. (3) Far-distance, no morning chanting or meditation. Rise, eat hard-cooked rice instead of gruel, promptly leave. Can use modern conveyance — bus, train. Must return by evening bell. Bath, supper, free meditation (monks' major explained it all to me).

Head reception officer lists members and destinations on a small black-board. Manjusri attendant reads it at teatime in the meditation hall the night before.

Today assigned to Hachiya, a village famed for dried persimmons. Leader: direct monk Kaijo, sub-leader: monks' major Seigan, with Joten, who came in the spring, and me. Sub-leader plans route, finds layman to offer us lunch. (Maps and other materials kept in Manjusri attendant's room.)

Manjusri attendant gave us each new straw sandals, 2 pairs. Doffed bamboo hat, bowed to direct monk, filed off behind him, bowing in succession to Buddha hall. Before six, dark.

Direct monk ran like a rabbit down stone steps and along rough dirt road, then monks' major, Joten, and me, each keeping about six feet apart — said to be high among mendicancy rules.

Some time later direct monk turned off highway onto narrow mountain path without reducing speed. Joten fell way behind monks' major, at last admitted I should go ahead of himself. I was bleeding at the toes from the straw thongs but was confident of my stamina, thanks to Tokyo newspaper delivery; soon caught up to direct monk and monks' major.

Then monks' major hit an apparent stone — edge of a buried rock. Nail came off, horrible amount of blood. Unconcerned, direct monk went on at his lancing pace and vanished around the bend. I tore up the towel kept in my sleeve. Monks' major on receiving it said spitefully, "That bigot runs recklessly to show you how hard mendicancy is. When we return to the meditation hall, he'll needle us on our failure to keep evenly spaced and punish us with extra use of the stick. Well, to heck with him! Go on, I'll wait for Joten and we'll come at our own pace."

I came to a fork, studied the grass, chose the downward path, by a brook, up a slope, and there was the direct monk. He must have tired, was walking at a mere brisk pace. Kept six feet behind but noticed he was moving his mouth as if chewing gum. Paid him close heed, realized he was chanting the Diamond Sutra.

After probably close to two hours we crossed a pass with a view down to ripening rice between mountains. Suddenly he called a short halt, sat deep in the grass, and let out a long breath. Only then did he realize I alone was following.

"Where are the others — they couldn't be ahead?" I explained, and he asked why I too wasn't delayed. Unsure of his meaning, I said, slightly arrogant, "From infancy I've had no problem with walking."

"Hm!" A sound seemingly of admiration, though I couldn't read his real mind. As our sweat was easing, they labored up with an apology to direct monk. Monks' major's toe a painful sight, bandage steeped in blood. Joten must have suffered nausea, gray-faced. Direct monk made no comment, abruptly stood and ordered, "Begin from this end of the village, I'll take the newcomer to the far end and work back. Meet beside the village assembly house at 11:30 — I'll allow a ten-minute margin."

All were farmhouses. Before the entrance of each we cried, "Good day! We are here from Shoshinji. Please give us your benefaction for Buddha" — simply expressed, but with melodious embellishment. Housewives or grannies appeared with rice. Received it on open cover of black cloth sack (monastery name is left undyed). As we raise and clap our hands in thanks, the rice slides in. Near lunch my 2 sacks, slung in front, held over 35 kilos. The weight bit into my neck and shoulders.

Reached house offering us lunch. I had to fetch water in haste so we could wash our feet. I washed last, emptied bucket into bushes, went up to guest room. They had finished tea. Monks' major lit incense and candle at family altar. Led by direct monk we chanted Lotus Flower Sutra, Heart Sutra, and "Dharani to Avert Disaster." Direct monk's chanting was spirited but sharp as if he had thorns in his voice.

Magnificent lunch, even sake was offered — monks' major drank a whole bottle, nearly 2 liters. Observing monastic rule to eat everything offered, we ate the fish bones, even the decorative chrysanthemum — bitter! Newest to this occasion too, I was required to finish off all else, including the sake. How hard! I had to keep from shouting in protest over this unreasonable order. Overeating feels to me far worse than not having enough. More, we walked back soon after. Lugging sacks on full stomach was horrible. Fortunately, direct monk too must have been tired. He walked slowly, with endurance.

Returned to gate, doffed hats, bowed to Buddha hall. Went to veranda of head fiscal officer. He measures the rice and records it in a book.

After bath, two spare hours before supper. All but monks' major ordered me to wash their laundry. Wash area is a spring behind Manjusri attendant's building, to the north, under a cedar mountain. No chance to enter the tub, having to wash and massage others, so I entered the spring. Frigid water. I could stay in only a few minutes.

Hung the laundry on bamboo poles and saw western sky burning red. Momentarily visioned Ena hanging laundry.

At night meditation, as monks' major predicted, direct monk reproved us for our mendicancy disorder and gave each 29 beatings. Declared free meditation, withdrew to his room in Manjusri attendant's building. I'm in the toilet, so can write. Hard to focus on the sound of one hand.

10/4: Dates with 4 or 9 are for shaving head and cleaning buildings inside and out. After morning meditation, Manjusri attendant receives hot water from a kitchen officer. Adjacent monks pair up, whet their razors, shave each other.

My partner, Gakushi, who came half a year ago, is as dull as his razor — hesitates like a crawler, leaves ridges of hair, makes many cuts. As we're shaved we hold up a cypress plate to receive the hair. Head, neck, and shoulders are then massaged under a towel. I shave him in 5 minutes, he takes so long monks' major scolds us and gives us his fist. I'm angry but can do nothing before rule to obey seniors.

We sweep area around meditation hall, then front garden of main building, gate, and down winding stone steps to path from highway. Abundant kumazasa, many cedars several hundred years old. When I look up, the light through the leafage is dazzling.

Seniors sweep debris into numerous piles for me to rake into a winnow and dump in the bamboo thicket. "Hey! — that's no good! Anyone can tell where the piles were. Do it over right away!" monks' major scolded me. Not a fragment must remain.

Today after lunch we thinned carrots. Crouching long hours gave me a backache.

At night meditation, direct monk rebuked us for slovenly cleaning, exercised warning stick. Made of oak, yet it can break. Back bled, stuck to undershirt — unpleasant. Bell invited us for interviews. Went for first time to express my view on my koan.

Interview period is a terrifying sight. Around 8, as we're meditating, bell at master's quarters sounds with 5 sharp strokes. "*Sanzen!*" direct monk shouts.

Monks may disregard rank only then. Those wishing interviews spring up, dash from meditation hall and down dark stone steps to residential quarters entrance, step up, run along wood corridor fronting drawing room, line up from corridor end formally seated on thin straw mats to wait their turn. Each strives to be first. Feet pounding in the dark like thunder. However they hurry, meditation hall monks always end up behind residential quarters monks.

At jangle of master's handbell, first monk twice strikes interview bell and takes corridor along north side of courtyard, goes up with palms joined in veneration. Returns, hands clasped at bosom. The next and the one returning pass at steps to interview room. Generally interview lasts only a minute or so.

I likewise passed returning monk, but before seeing my figure the master shook his handbell, indicating I must withdraw. I was perplexed. Then came his hisses: "Go back! Meditate more earnestly! This is a sanctum for sober Dharma combat!" Much discouraged, I returned to meditation hall and as I breathed in and out, taxed my ingenuity on the sound of one hand.

After going to bed, snuck out like the others to meditate on main building veranda. Moon shifted, shone from behind pine mountain. Reminded of Unkai, I was encouraged to meditate in earnest. Still — no miracle, no laudable realization. Now writing in toilet as usual. Must be well past midnight.

10/5: Mountain work. A senior who came in last autumn — don't know his name — hit his shin with his hatchet, blood gushed out, he rolled down-slope in agony, hit a stump. Direct monk descended, arraigned him: "Serves you right for your impudence and proves you, your tool, and the wood weren't unified — halfhearted man!" Ordered monks' major and me to give aid. Monks' major weak at the sight of blood, though he never hesitates to strike juniors. Urged me to do my best.

I tightly bound the shin with my head towel, yet it bled. We carried him down, rushed him by cart to the monastery, asked Manjusri attendant to treat him, started back up. I was hurrying, but monks' major stopped me: "Why hurry? They've finished lunch by now and surely left us none. Rest here till I return," and he disappeared.

About half an hour later he reappeared with rice balls in a bamboo sheath, which he shared. Must have got them from a farmhouse. We took long to return. Amazed to find everyone still at work. Spotting us, direct monk came down to ask monks' major about injured monk. He had delayed lunch for our return.

At night meditation he cautioned us all to be careful during work, beat everyone, then asked to be beaten by his assistant.

Wind and rain began about when interview bell echoed. After bed hour I meditated on main building veranda, got very wet.

10/6: Mid-distance mendicancy in rain. Our group went to town of Ota,

6 including direct monk and me (don't know others' names). Walked in mountains with no landmarks, rain obscured visibility so I couldn't memorize route. Black vinyl cape useless in windy rain. Rain runs through bamboo hat, down head and neck, beneath underwear. Wet straw sandals promptly wear out, leaving ankle strings on bare feet. I'm fortunate to be strong at walking — could meditate at length on sound of one hand. No house gave rice. Received only coins, easy to carry.

Direct monk sped along, the others lagged. Following in a kind of ecstasy, I ran smack-dab into him — he had stopped. "What? Again only you? Why such an adept walker?" Repeating "the sound of one hand," I almost spoke it in response.

10/7: Experienced great vexation when Gakushi and I served breakfast. Meditation hall monks assist kitchen monks by serving meals, two in turn daily. Servers watch for head reception officer to raise his chopsticks, then carry in rice, miso soup, and pickles and serve each monk. Containers must be held high to keep our breath off the food. Rice container is quite heavy.

I set the soup bucket on the floor, and as I served a residential quarters officer, I spilled down the side of his bowl. He at once slapped my head, which raised a high sound. Then he abused me, "Blind fool!" No doubt he meant I'm not only sloppy but unenlightened. I was furious. I may be narrow to anger over such a trifle, but it's deeply insulting to be slapped on the head, the most important part of the body, and more, on the shaven head. Such conduct doesn't fit a monk who has at the least passed the first koan, and who is taking the role of a respectable officer.

In this Shoshinji, juniors are commanded to obey seniors and the master is considered the greatest of persons, greater than the emperor, even greater than the patriarchs. We have to obey completely. In the meditation hall the direct monk is the monk supreme. I must obey him, his assistant, the Manjusri attendant, the monks' major, and all others, even those barely above me. Joten, Gakushi, and such came only half a year or a year ago, yet they freely exercise their seniority and, rather than educate me on the Dharma, express an immature humanity. As the newest I'm expected to take each of their cruelties as the charity of Manjusri and be thankful. But my endurance is limited and I'm dutiful to protect my dignity. I'm a man of self-respect. I don't think it's my original nature, but what use is original nature without self-respect? I can't believe being a yes-man is one's original nature.

But alas, I'm unawakened. Without words to return for being called a blind fool, I can only obey, no matter how mean and shallow the seniors are. Until I see my original nature, I have to be slighted. Being the newest of the ignorant, I'm the lowest in rank. While we're all ignorant we have to submit to a ranking based solely on when we entered or there'd be no order here.

Then what I should do as a matter of urgency is to solve the first koan so I can see my original nature. It's why I came. But there's the constant work:

chanting, mendicancy, mountain and garden work, indoor and outdoor cleaning, laundering, etc. If I try to meditate on the sound of one hand, the seniors scold me for not being wholehearted. If I concentrate on working, I must forget the sound of one hand. How can I maneuver with this antinomy?

Rain all day. Made sandals in straw-thatched shed in cedars below meditation hall at monastery's southeast end. Built a fire inside to sit around. Beat rice straw with wood hammers while sprinkling on water to rid it of its sheaths. Imitating the seniors, I found it reasonably easy. Tried to meditate on the sound of one hand, but the rain of this season reminds me of Ena's end. The more I think of her the more I'm determined to become enlightened. My wish and determination are settled, but, regrettably, by my willpower I can't break through the rock.

On and on I meditated and only the time passed away. Zen Master Tengai told me not to solve the koan with my brain; he said that from logical analysis and ratiocination no answer comes, and he warned me not to depend on past experience. Then what remains is to chant "the sound of one hand" and hope to forget my entire self and just be the sound of one hand.

10/8: Mendicancy in near village of Okuse, direct monk and me only, under an hour going northeast. Clear sky, steady cool breeze, trees and peaks in far distance vivid. Took highway skirting some mountains, came to river issuing from deeper mountains, grandly it rounded forbidding rock cliff that blocked view east. Farmhouses scattered on terraced fields to west, view there also partly blocked by mountains. Sunrise must be late, sunset early. Only a few hundred houses, received under 20 kilos of rice.

My duty as sub-leader was to find a house willing to offer lunch. I came on a tiny Shinto shrine girded by tall camphors and *ogatama-no-ki*, before a deep valley. Noticed a small white-robed priest brooming away spiderwebs. Daringly asked him. Mustache and long ponytail. Expressed wonder, "Shoshinji never came here in the last dozens of years, not for lunch, not even for begging." Then, "What a great pleasure! Please allow me to offer lunch." I escorted direct monk there at lunch hour. He too was astonished, "Ho! This newcomer is adventurous. I never heard of a monk receiving kindness from a Shinto shrine."

The priest served us noodles made by his own hand. Boiled them, cooled them in a back rill. "As a child I heard a monk can't be satisfied on the quantity offered a cow, or, a cow will eat as much as a monk. Is it enough?" Showed us two large buckets of noodles. Noodles are a favorite of the direct monk. We dipped them in cups of broth. The quantity he ate amazed me.

Afterwards we had much spare time. Direct monk descended from the highway to the riverbed and lay down, distended belly up. Wide dry riverbed of roundish sedimentary rocks decreasing in size toward the water, no sand. Far side, a mural precipice, could see clumps of toad lily and beauty berry among various dwarfed plants, and creeping pines growing over the top.

562

Below, shady dark indigo stream of inestimable depth. Clean shallows, sweet-fish arrowing upstream.

"You too lie down," he ordered, and added, "This is where our founder washed his ox." Scarcely heeded his words. Given the first breather in days, I saw the mountains, sky, river, and fields with prolonged interest. Recalled my childhood in Tangenji and Ryotanji. When I returned to reality I couldn't believe my life is truly mine.

Sat on a rock, regretted I can't yet see my original nature and am incapable of teaching the truth to those I care about.

Abruptly, or so it seemed, he sat up and asked, "How are you getting on with your training in the meditation hall? It couldn't be as easy as you expected, eh?"

I was honest — "I can't concentrate as much as I had hoped."

"Why not?"

"There are too many events and too much work. I dissatisfy the seniors if I'm not always wholehearted, and if I am I neglect my koan study. Luckily there's scheduled meditation twice a day, but even that most quiet time is greatly disturbed by the warning stick."

"Hm! You're telling me I strike the monks too much? That's a complaint — the mother of criticism. If I and my assistant don't beat, everyone will nod off. Besides, the meditation hall is designed to disturb a monk's mind by various devices. Samadhi attained amid noise is true samadhi. A monk has to bury himself in his koan regardless of being tired, hungry, sleepy, or afraid!"

I wished to remind him of how different Shoshinji meditation is from mild meditation under shade trees, suited to the Middle Way and recommended by Sakyamuni Buddha, and how different from the substantial meditation expounded by Dogen in his *Exhortation to Practice Sitting Meditation*. But I kept silent.

A little later he spoke again, "From now to October's end we will be busier and meditation will be the last of your concerns, owing to the upcoming farce — the founder's anniversary. You'd better remember Zen Teacher Hakuin: 'Exertion in activity is a million times superior to exertion in stillness.'[1] Moreover, a Zen master once said that annihilation of both activity and stillness leaves you free as a gem rolling in a silver dish."[2]

I silently watched the fulgent ripples.

10/9: Got a smooth shave by whetting Gakushi's razor. But he angled it wrong and it cut into my scalp like lightning just when I was concentrating on the sound of one hand, and I hallucinated that the one hand spurted out.

While sweeping below gate, we were approached by Manjusri attendant asking our help with monks' graveyard, under his jurisdiction. From gate took path through cedars. Monks' major on the way let out a curse, "To hell with him! He must've been upbraided by a higher officer for his neglect. What gall to come here only to complete his training to become a flatterer after finding he couldn't perfect it by his several years' stay in a Soto monastery!" Everyone laughed.

Arrived at narrow graveyard cut into slope, found Manjusri attendant engrossed in weeding. Weeds grown as high as the many close-spaced tombstones. They're rounded like monks' heads, the dead obviously monks. Engraved letters show many dates from mid Edo to early Meiji. Most indicate a lowest or next-to-lowest sacerdotal rank. No way of knowing about them, but I inwardly wept. Their bitterest mortification must have been to die on the way of training — oldest, under age 30, youngest, 15.

As I was weeding tough grass and scraping moss from tombstones, monks' major, who had seated himself on one in a forward-leaning posture, commanded, "Oi, newcomer! Run to the grocery on the road and bring us up some snacks. Never mind paying, charge it to my account." I was puzzled, knowing I can't leave the monastery without a higher officer's permission.

"What? — why don't you scoot?"

When I mentioned the rule, he laughed and expressed anger — "Don't be a fool! I'm highest when there's no direct monk or his assistant. My word's the rule. Quick or you'll be flogged!"

I turned to Manjusri attendant, but he kept operosely weeding in a groveling posture. At last I called, "Manjusri Attendant, what should I do?" Half to himself he said as he faced the earth, "The first monastic concern is friendship."

The others all laughed with monks' major.

On the way down I was ashamed of Manjusri attendant's impuissant attitude, and on the way back I began to suspect the merit of seeing one's original nature. Officers are supposed to have become enlightened by seeing their original nature, yet they don't correctly govern themselves or the monastery.

I understand the importance of friendship. It's also written in *Baijang's Monastic Rules*: "Monks as sangha members are to refrain from argument and share the waters of a harmonious ocean."[3] But monastic friendship should issue from observance of the precepts for a mutual purpose and not be a reason to break them. Acutely I felt the necessity of solidifying my determination to stand by the rules with my responsibility when they are violated by seniors and high officers. I'm indignant not for the sake of Shoshinji and society but for my sake, because I wish to protect my dignity and not waste my time.

I came here only to steal all of Zen Master Tengai's Zen transmission in the shortest possible time and to solve every one of my deep-rooted problems. After all, I don't think what Confucius said is right for me, that a man who learns the Way in the morning can die in the evening without regret. If soon I must die, I don't see that it matters whether I learn the Way or not. My purpose in learning the Way is to live my best by knowing it.

Therefore I should live as long as I can. I'll live for those who are already dead, and live as a pathfinder for those who are yet unborn. I will see through to my original nature not only for my sake but for the sake of those who are unable to see through to theirs. Sacrificing myself hasn't occasioned my death, so by sacrificing myself I will live on.

What grieves me, then, is that I haven't progressed with my koan. I don't show my anguish, but I'm like a pot-bound plant with gyrate roots.

10/10: Mountain work. Just now came in to write, but someone else has come in, is near the toilet door, has begun to scrub the urinals....I peeped through a crack — it's the Manjusri attendant. He's scrubbing at the encrusted calcium, hard to remove by usual cleaning. It must be well past midnight. Surely we alone are yet awake in this entire monastery. How zealous of him, while I'm recording benighted delusions for my own comfort! I clearly have to see the difference. I'm sweating — how I wish I could leave! He's mumbling...Oh! he's repeating the Four Great Vows:

> I vow to save all sentient beings
>   however innumerable.
> I vow to extinguish all klesa
>   however inexhaustible.
> I vow to master all the Dharma
>   however immeasurable.
> I vow to attain the highest Buddhahood
>   however incomparable.[4]

ès·

Mokuzu terminated his diary on 10 October. His prime reason must have been that he was ashamed of taking the comfort of solitude. Rather than critically analyzing himself to deepen his character, he was merely facing himself to affirm who he was. He was, so to speak, acting like both mother and baby.

One's original nature recognized by Zen had nothing to do with the usual, individual self. That was regarded as a lump of ignorance, a hindrance to understanding the meaning of life, an object to be destroyed. In a trainee the individual self was respected only so long as it served as a suicide bomber: when he attained sight of his original nature it was to self-destruct, for what had to be sought was something absolute, which was recognizable only after perfect self-denial.

This process of self-denial was the life of training admired in the folk saying,

> Behold the raftsman,
> He risks his life and arrives at the shoal.

It was the ultimate way of life described by Zen Teacher Shido Bunan in his *Account of the Mind*:

> The ideal is to do everything spontaneously.
> Hearken to my song:
>> Be a dead man — even as you live
>> Cease to be a human being.
>> How fine, you shall go free!
> This is the sense of the yaksa's stanza:
>> Nothing is everlasting.
>> Such is the law of birth and death.
>> Completely annihilate birth and death.
>> Therein is eternal joy.[5]

A Chinese Zen master, Changsha Jingtsen, also advised Zen trainees:

> If a man seated atop a hundred-foot bamboo pole is yet ignorant of the truth, he must go a step higher to reach the realization that all worlds in the ten directions are nothing other than his own being.[6]

There were hundreds and thousands more references and excitations by those who had attained the great realization.

Thus determined to experience enlightenment, Mokuzu gave up his last pleasure of keeping a diary. Constantly, every moment, he was going to meditate on the sound of one hand to break himself and go beyond himself.

He believed in Zen Master Tengai's guidance, and he meditated on and on as he cleaned the garden, worked in the mountain, begged in the towns and villages. He was a strange sight, like a man possessed. But his behavior was no different from that of all other earnest Shoshinji monks.

Some could be seen sweeping the same narrow spot over and over with a bamboo besom while lost in their given koan; others did not realize that the trees they were cutting had fallen, and they kept on cutting.

One day Mokuzu was walking at the end of a line of mendicant monks as he meditated on the sound of one hand. When he returned to himself he found he was far off the road in the middle of a harvested rice field.

Another day he lost himself in the sound of one hand during morning chanting. When he came to, he saw that he alone was left in the Buddha hall.

All monks, including him, looked sad and bitter whenever they returned to themselves, for they well knew they were not yet blessed with enlightenment. Moreover, they were required to endure insults from seniors and the Zen master, who said they were blind fools. They did not know how to devote themselves to their koan study more than they were doing, though exhortations from seniors and the master continued to shower down on them.

How dark was the trainee's mind! — like a bottomless pit. But how often each dreamed of the day he would be enlightened.

All were fated to be gloomy because they were giving away most of their entire present life, instead of enjoying it, for the sake of their unknown future. A person making the most of his present reality can be seen as having a bright character, whereas a person whose attention is strongly pulled to matters of the past or future emits a dark air.

Until the day they could see their original nature, their gloomy life had to last. But was it not true that to see one's original nature meant to realize one was already a perfect being endowed with Buddha nature? It was true. So they had to realize that their present reality was perfect while it was imperfect; that even as they lived a mortal life, they possessed great eternal life. They had to awaken to the realization that even as they sought enlightenment they were enlightened....Indeed they were as if searching for their heads. When could they say to themselves, "But it was meet to make merry and be glad: for this thy brother was dead, and is alive again; and was lost, and is found"? (Luke 15:32)

≥⋆

As the direct monk had mentioned to Mokuzu, Shoshinji in the last third of September had become increasingly busy in preparation for the founder's anniversary, and the meditation hall monks were summoned to assist the officer monks. Mokuzu was horribly annoyed by this disturbance to his concentration.

The anniversary day was the twelfth of October, but more than four hundred laymen from far distances arrived the day before and stayed until the day after. Adding to Shoshinji's monks, priests from neighboring temples and from the head temple in Kyoto gathered for the ceremony, making a grand total of nearly a hundred. Most from the neighboring temples were former Shoshinji monks, among whom were Bokuon and Koko, though Mokuzu had no chance to meet them.

He was not required to attend the ceremony or tend to guests, but was ordered to do the most inconspicuous work of keeping all lavatories clean and patrolling at night against fire and theft. Assigned to him were four students from the junior college on the west slope of Shoshinji's domain, a ten-minute walk.

There were seven main lavatory areas inside and outside the monastery buildings. Mokuzu with the students' help had to empty each toilet reservoir and have it spotless before the tenth of October.

Yet on the anniversary day the reservoirs were immediately filled and the areas constantly fouled, leaving Mokuzu and the students not a moment's pause.

They ladled the contents of the reservoirs into large buckets and carried the buckets away on bamboo poles. Mokuzu carried one at each end, the students just one with a student at each end. They had to use a hidden path into the bamboo thicket.

Understandably the odor was revolting to the students, and they hated the pain of the cowlstaff against their shoulders and made a big fuss over splatters. Then before completing a round of all areas, Mokuzu was met by officers from various quarters demanding that their reservoirs be emptied anew. Around noon, as they were dumping their buckets from a cliff into the bamboo, an attendant to the master came running in a flurry,

"Please, I beg you, do the master's straight away; it's close to overflowing and he's twitching his nose and asking what is the taint. Next he'll be thundering at me regardless of his guests!" and he raced back to his work in full dress — white tabi and underkimono, black gossamer robe — his skirts whiffling unceremoniously.

"I'll be darned! I believed all those priests in gold-brocade surplices and ladies in fancy kimonos wouldn't ever pass water no matter how much tea they drank!" one student remarked, and the others snickered.

"There's no way but to go now to the Zen master's," said Mokuzu, and he began to walk ahead.

The area behind the master's quarters was shaded by the mountain. The path went up a narrow slope with many creeping roots, making passage hard even without anything to carry.

The reservoir was set about with aspidistra and disorderly nandin. Their feet got mired in the mud of the overflow, and the students abominated having to approach. Mokuzu maneuvered the long handle of his ladle while the students, afraid of being splashed, kept their distance and exchanged useless comments.

"Bet it's mostly women's pee, look at all the tissue."

"Aw, let's sympathize with this monk. The founder's anniversary comes but once a year and he gets no time to eye the ladies — what a sad plot!"

"Wait, I've got an idea. Ever since the Zen master's last lecture I've been wondering. He bragged he washes his own underwear, remember? I was only half impressed. Now I see why. He doesn't do his own toilet."

"All I care about is that I lost my appetite. I'll always bear the founder a grudge."

Mokuzu finished filling the four buckets, but the students were loath to carry them and kept prattling. To get their attention he said,

"Look here!" And he washed his face from one of the buckets. The students were aghast.

"Now let's be off. Don't spill." Mutely they complied.

They had to remain awake all night as they had the previous night, patrolling hourly.

Exhausted, the students leaned sloppily on the bell tower. They wanted to complain but could not speak as much as they liked out of deference to Mokuzu. They had no interest in the moon rising behind the meditation hall, traversing the lucid sky, and casting a white light on the garden, quiet with everyone asleep.

Out of pity for such inaesthetic students, Mokuzu offered to talk about the founder, as much as he had heard from his teacher Docho.

"Shoshinji's founder, Kanzan Egen, died at age eighty-four, on the twelfth of December, 1360. He died at the head temple, Myoshinji, where naturally the anniversary is performed on a much larger scale. The one here is held today to avoid conflict.

"According to a biography he put on his travel wear, took up his bamboo hat and priest's staff, stepped down to the garden, and immediately died. It has been said since antiquity that Zen priests don't die but just change the place where they teach. Thus the founder practiced whatever he believed. His will-power is breathtaking.

"How did his teacher, National Teacher Daito — or Myocho Shuho — die? He was born lame. When he died at age fifty-six, he addressed his lame foot, 'Always submissive to your perverse demand, I could never sit in full lotus position. Today is one of my most important days, so you'd better obey once for all.'[7] As he forced foot over thigh, his knee broke and his robe was wet with blood, but in full lotus position he could breathe his last.

"The severity we see in those teachers and disciples is the transmitted air of Japanese Rinzai Zen, not only the air of this Shoshinji monastery.

"To speak in more detail, Kanzan Egen entered the priesthood under Toden Shikei at the subtemple Kogenan within Kenchoji at Kamakura. At age thirty he chanced to meet National Teacher Daio (Nanpu Shomyo), yet he did not clearly break through his doubt. He must have been living an unpleasant life, for an unenlightened but earnest life requires much patience.

"Twenty years later, in 1327, there was held, in the subtemple Sairaiin, the fiftieth anniversary of the death of the founder of Kenchoji, Zen Teacher Daikaku — or Dalung Lanshi, he was Chinese. On that occasion someone told Egen about National Teacher Daito, who was at Daitokuji in Kyoto. Egen intuited that this was the teacher to make him fully enlightened. Daito was Daio's Dharma inheritor.

"Egen promptly set off for Kyoto. Amazingly, he didn't once notice Mt. Fuji during the long journey on foot — he must have been utterly absorbed in his concern.

"The next three years Egen spent under National Teacher Daito, who gave him 'Yunmen's Guan,' the very koan he himself had suffered over for three years. When Egen completed his koan study, Daito gave him the pseudonym Kanzan and the honorary name Egen. The calligraphy 'Kanzan' written by Daito is well kept in Myoshinji to this day and is designated a national treasure.

"After certifying his enlightenment, Daito advised Egen to conceal himself in a mountain to perfect his training. The smell of enlightenment should be well washed away like soap from laundry. So Egen came here to these deep mountains, no doubt really remote in those days, and he built himself a hermitage and cultivated some fields with an ox.

"Not knowing how much manure to use to grow rice, he asked a peasant, who, thinking him a shabby vagabond, scornfully replied, 'Ask the soil, lick it! If it's sweet it'll do.'

"Egen did, though to do so must have been hard for him. He was the second son of Takanashi Mino no kami Takaie, lord of a castle in Nakano, Shinano Province. And while training in Daitokuji, he had substituted for Daito in the teaching of Emperor Go-daigo.

"So, he lived an eremitic existence in this mountain. How he came to move back to Kyoto is an interesting story. The retired emperor Hanazono had asked National Teacher Daito, 'By whom should I be taught after your death?' Daito answered, 'I have a Dharma-inheritor, one Kanzan Egen. Seek him out.'

"Hanazono sent Fujiwara no Fujifusa in search of him, and he was at last found right here. Hanazono converted his detached palace into Myoshinji and invited Egen to be its founding abbot.

"When the messengers arrived, the peasants were surprised to learn that their shabby-looking neighbor was a great priest, and they apologized to him for their impropriety. Among them, it was said, were an old couple particularly intimate with Egen. Tearfully they approached him and said,

"'Being ignorant, we knew you not. Most regrettable is to have wasted these many years without hearing your teaching. Please, at last teach us how we should live!'

"Egen invited them to draw near, and he knocked their heads together. The old couple cried '*Awwww!*' 'Never forget what you just experienced!' he said and left for Kyoto."

Telling the story in a low, even voice, Mokuzu realized that, all four students were leaning on one another, asleep.

He stood up to make a round by himself. The moon hung in the west just above the tiles of the former main building. Over the entrance was a plank that read: "Cave of Poison Grass."

570

'Indeed I must eat a lot of poison grass! Already four weeks have passed since I came. How dreadfully slow is my progress! It's an unsuitable speed for me. I must go through the first koan as quick as I can — no, quicker! I don't much care about the founder, because his life story is full of adaptations by later patriarchs, though I am greatly impressed by his teacher Daito.

'Daito went up Mt. Shosha in Hyogo Prefecture when he was only eleven and there studied the sutras, vinayas, and abhidharmas of the Tripitaka. At seventeen he realized the limitation of intellectual study and began Zen training. In his first monastic year he mastered two hundred koans! He was only twenty-six when Daio certified him! For him Daio wrote, "You now understand the secret of the world: relativity and absoluteness freely interchange. In fact your understanding surpasses mine."[8]

'Has my career anything in common with Daito's? Yes, I studied Buddhism from Docho Doka, and more, a certain degree of English literature from Yojun Ishida. I can't give them the shame of seeing me fail in my training. And I have Ena with me always. I bet Daito couldn't have had such a girl — that's why he was good only at teaching noblemen and elite samurai.

'Well, I must be quick to steal all of the Dharma from Zen Master Tengai. I'd like to study not just Zen, not just Buddhism. The world is wide, and I must learn all sorts of matters relating to creatures and human beings. I shouldn't stagnate here for a long time. From tomorrow I will devote myself more and more to the sound of one hand!'

44

Zui Is Upset under Pressure

The weather changed, as if it had been waiting for the founder's anniversary to end, and a cold wind blew a thin rain. With the shojis and storm doors of the meditation hall kept open from the moment the monks got up until bedtime, the backs of those meditating on the north side, including the direct monk, became soaked.

Mokuzu unintentionally turned his eyes to the south-side opening. Several bamboo tops beyond were dancing boisterously; farther off, the cedar tops were but dimly visible.

After morning tea of salted plum in hot water the Manjusri attendant, reading as usual from a portable blackboard, announced that the whole day, after shaving of heads, was to be given to rest in preparation for the snowy term of exclusive training with week-long meditation periods, beginning on the morrow, and that the summer robe was to be changed to the winter robe. Preparation day was an easy day for the monks, but without exception all were to attend a general tea ceremony in the cross-wing after the bath and supper.

Moreover, for monks of the residential quarters it was a day to exchange offices. The meditation hall was little affected. The direct monk, Kaijo, and the Manjusri attendant would continue as before; only the assistant to the direct monk was promoted to head chanting officer, and the head chanting officer, Zui, was ordered to replace him.

After shaving, the monks, with the monks' major, Seigan, gathered outside. They sat on the black tiles and leaned back against the white plaster wall of the meditation hall. Some mended their robes, others wrote to or read letters from next of kin. They had to face the week-long meditation periods with the mind of "death or glory," whence they were expected to tidy up their personal affairs and to regard any letters, if they wrote them, as their last.

Mokuzu had received no letters and, having no reason to write, continued to practice sitting meditation in the hall. Then the monks' major addressed him,

"Hey, what's with you, sitting all by yourself? Why don't you do everyone's wash — didn't you hear about the change of robe? Use your brain — there's loads of wash!"

"Yes. But how can I dry it in this rain?"

"Use the Nirvana room, and the Manjusri attendant's room, yes, hang it above the bed of that sycophant!"

Mokuzu collected the laundry from the monks. Zui, now assistant to the direct monk, said to him,

"A newcomer has to go through a lot of hardship, but you must persevere. You're excused from doing my laundry."

The rain soaked him to the skin as he labored at the spring. When he returned to the meditation hall after hanging the laundry, the monks' major again commanded:

"Heat the bath." It was well after lunch hour.

The bath house was annexed to the room where Mokuzu had spent his earliest days. The fuel hole was behind, under a cliff from which hung an overgrowth of such trees as lacquer, wax, and sumac, their leaves now beginning to color.

Bath firewood was inferior to kitchen firewood, being fresh trimmings from the garden trees and green bamboo thinned from the thicket. Mokuzu patiently piled dry twigs in the furnace, made a strong fire, and inserted the green wood. It began to burn furiously. At its ends white foam boiled out with a noise.

The smell of burning firewood recalled to him his childhood. His mind was torn between two choices: should he persist to meditate on the sound of one hand, or let himself steep in emotions over the old days?

'How many times did I escape from reality by yielding to memory? Was reality so hard? Was my heart so weak? The sound of one hand is the key to opening my unknown future. If I keep meditating on it, I can challenge my maximum potential. I'd better resist fondling myself — I must meditate on the sound of one hand!'

He fixed his eyes on the flames and chanted aloud "the sound of one hand." Steam rose from his wet robe. Soon he forgot his body and no longer distinguished himself from the blaze, as if it were the fire that was meditating on the sound of one hand.

"It's burning well. You're skillful at coaxing the flame," came a voice. Mokuzu turned and saw Zui.

Zui was dispirited. He did not bother to come under the eaves. He was already wet from having crossed the garden of the meditation hall. He stood half in the rain. Mokuzu withdrew a little to make room and offered him a bundle of wood to sit on.

"Thank you. You're a strange one, tenderhearted even though earnest," Zui said and sat down before the fuel hole.

Mokuzu could not figure why he had come; yet he understood that Zui was undergoing humiliation over being released from the chanting office and sent back to the meditation hall, where he was acknowledged as a senior but otherwise slighted for being known as an officer who had not passed the first koan.

Mokuzu kept silent. He could not ignore Zui entirely, but neither was he allowed to talk freely with a senior. He studied Zui's profile. His thick cheeks were lifeless and heavy like those of a death mask. Now and then he grimaced and they twitched as if he were a baby about to cry.

"How are you taxing your ingenuity for your koan?" he asked after a pause, seemingly wishing only to divert himself from his own concern.

"Well, how should I say...I'm straining at the oar, though the boat is tied to the pier," Mokuzu frankly answered.

"I know what you mean....Yet you're lucky, your passion is gushing out. As for me, my patience is spent...besides, I see no improvement in the character of those who are supposedly enlightened. It seems enlightenment turns a mean man into a cruel man, a greedy man into avarice itself, and a sneaky man into an old schemer. Indeed enlightenment appears to add boldness, self-justification, and arrogance to the vices a man already has....But the master, if I tell him this sort of worry, will surely abuse me with his shouts — 'Ignoramus! Don't grumble before you've seen your original nature!'"

Not knowing how to respond, Mokuzu added more firewood in silence.

After a while Zui spoke again,

"Today you hadn't a letter from anyone. But I suppose your parents are eagerly awaiting your letter telling that you passed the first koan, aren't they?"

"Nnn? They don't believe in the virtue of seeing one's original nature, so they don't expect anything from me about that, much as they'd enjoy my enjoyment, whatever its cause."

"Oh, how nice. It's enviable to have such parents. As for the likes of me, seeing my original nature is required for the sake of my mother above all, and second, for Zen Master Tengai. For myself I can't much feel its necessity...you know, the greatness of Sakyamuni Buddha's mother was very different from the greatness of Mencius' mother, as I see it. Sakyamuni Buddha's mother didn't wish her son to become a Buddha; she died seven days after his birth, exchanging her life for his...."

Again at a loss for words, Mokuzu only fed the furnace. A branch of lacquer tree sprung by the wind shed raindrops on part of Zui's head, and they ran down by his ear.

"I apologize for repining at my hard lot in front of you, the newcomer..." Zui stepped into the rain. There he lingered and hesitantly took out a flat brown packet.

"Sorry to trouble you, but could you burn this?" He handed it to Mokuzu and left for the meditation hall.

It was a postal package, there were stamps and seals. Evidently Zui had seen the contents; the string was wound untidily about it as if it was trash. Mokuzu sensed the contents to be something soft.

As he bent to put it into the fire, he was arrested by concern for Zui's condition, and surmising that the package had a direct bearing, he checked the contents.

There was a wrinkled sheet of Japanese paper, once a letter cleanly written by brush, and something in another white paper, which turned out to be a thick coil of fine, grizzled hair.

The hair gave Mokuzu a horrid sensation and an ominous presentiment. Hurriedly he read the letter.

> Honorable son, my dearest Zui:
> I am happy to hear of your leading role as head chanting officer for the founder's anniversary observance.
> However, my son, the supreme concern of a Zen priest is to see his

574

original nature, as you may well know. An unenlightened priest cannot understand the true meaning of the sutras and be a true disciple of Buddha, even if he can chant the sutras with intricate melody and flawless ease.

You inform me that the first week-long meditation of the snowy term will soon begin. Again you write that you will open your enlightened eye in this period so as to report to me quickly your greatest joy.

My son, how many times in the last six years have you told me of your fine resolve? Each time you gave me hope, and each time you disappointed me.

I offer your letters of resolve to the family altar, where your father is enshrined. Whenever your letters come I pray with renewed fervor that your training will be accomplished.

Do you know I am now sixty-seven? I have little time left. Yet I rue that I often indulged you in the process of raising you after you so early lost your father. I know not how to apologize to him.

Please understand that I do not in the least accuse you of negligence nor doubt your diligence. Only I lament over my own faults and my own ignorance.

The first frost came today. I cleared the garden of dead chrysanthemums this morning. After lunch I brought out the foot-warmer from the shed. I then realized the Gifu mountains must be yet colder.

While I can keep warm with layers of kimonos, you in Shoshinji wear nothing on your feet but straw sandals even in snow. More, I can eat when hungry and doze when sleepy, and if tired I can choose light work.

As long as your mother keeps comfortable, you will not be helped by Buddha and by the spirit of your father, I now realize.

I am deeply ashamed. So I have resolved to practice cold-water ablution every morning. I will by no means warm myself, I will eat only barley gruel, and at night I will always practice sitting meditation.

Do you see, my son? Thus far you have been training alone, but hereafter we will train together. We are in separate places, but our time is the same. I truly believe you can get enlightenment.

I cut off my hair, in this land second in dearness only to the heart. I did so to prove my vow, and I send you a portion. Keep it in your stomach-band and train hard.

Please take care of yourself. Do not forget I await the great news. May it come even a day earlier!

To my dearest,

from Mother

Mokuzu felt an abhorrence for what in reality was the undisguised muddy attachment of mother to son, though it was taking the form of a concern for Buddhist training and Zen enlightenment.

575

'Piteous Zui! Even as he places himself in sacred precincts, his mother's ignorant love is reaching him like the long red tongue of a serpent. Luckily my mother can control her maternal love — toward me it is as light as a fine autumn sky. Controlled love is more precious than uncontrolled, thick, bloody love.

'Didn't Linji say a man must kill his mother when he meets her, for a mother is covetous love?[1]

'Religion is beneficial as long as it welcomes whoever wants it; but if it forces a person who doesn't want it and takes his soul as hostage, it becomes a satanic atrocity.'

Mokuzu cast the package into the flames in deference to Zui's wish. It flared up at once, emitted a noisome odor for a spell, and turned to lifeless ash.

He looked up at the sky and saw that the dense rain was only increasing. He remembered Luri with thanks; she had truly cared about him when in Ryotanji she encouraged him to sever ties of blood. And he thought, 'I must quickly finish groping for the truth so I can free her from her sad plight.'

The general tea ceremony was held after an interval following supper. The direct monk led the meditation hall monks in single file to the south seats of the cross-wing. The officer monks had already seated themselves from highest to lowest rank on the north side.

The three light bulbs hanging from the ceiling were on, but inside was darker than outside with the rain subsiding.

Mokuzu, at the lowest seat, spotted Koko diagonally across at the highest seat. He looked for Bokuon in vain. Koko had gained weight. With effort he sat facing straight ahead.

'He must be nearest in rank to the master. He told me he was in his seventh year, which means he must be in his eleventh by now. He must be the highest disciple, though I've heard there are several who have stayed longer — they are quite dull, I suppose. It was a snowy day when he and the master came to Tangenji, but I was so tired working on the revetment I didn't heed the weather.

'I wish I could have decided then to train myself and come with them here. Had I done that I wouldn't have wasted three years in senior high school and another half year in Tokyo. By now I would have solved most of the koans, not only the first!

'Why couldn't Koko reply more clearly to my question? He played possum, that's all. What would he do or say now if I asked the same question? And how superstitious and mega-delusive were Zen Teacher Hakuin's words quoted by Zen Master Tengai to charm me to train under him! Why couldn't they simply answer when I asked them what is death and what is insanity?

'As for Koko's character, according to his looks, didn't Zui well express it just some hours ago? "I see no improvement in the character of those who are supposedly enlightened..." I wonder how true Zui's conclusion is.'

"*Haii!*" came a sudden cry, repressed and hoarse, as if the speaker were vomiting. All monks at once put their hands to the floor and their heads to their hands in the posture called *dogeza*, preserved since before the Japanese knew the calendar.

Koko spoke in the most dignified voice he could summon, which induced Mokuzu to imagine him enduring constipation in a toilet.

"Honorable monks, from tomorrow the first of the week-long meditation periods of the snowy season will at last commence. Let me express my congratulations to you all, who have been waiting so long and so patiently. It was said the spirit of the meditation hall is greatly owing to the fresh vitality of its newcomers. I especially ask our newcomer to make the most of this blessed opportunity to learn life's most important concern.

"Now as is customary I shall read to you the paragon, notwithstanding that I am a densely illiterate monk. I hope you all find in it nourishment for your training.

"Ahem, ahem! The paragon known as *Zen Teacher Kueishan Dayuan's Encouragement*:

> "First: On the Great Travail of Having a Body. Our body we received as an effect of karma. We thence have no means to escape physical ills. By the seed of our parents and by a host of worldly elements our body was formed. All elements constituting our body assist and yet contradict one another. Hence aging, illness, and death befall us seemingly without portent and beyond our control. Alive at dawn, we may perish at dusk, changing our world in an instant. How like the frost of spring, the dew of morn....
>
> "Second: Chastisement of Priests for Their Deep-Rooted Abuse. Priests are excused from filial piety; are given the right to desert family and family business; are exempt from service to and governance of the nation; are permitted to depart their native land. All this they are granted because they keep the tonsure and devote themselves to study under a teacher. Their work is to meditate deeply and to promote harmony. Priests are delivered from a worldly existence.
>
> "Senseless is it then for men who have taken the tonsure and received the precepts to expect to be fed by donors and to use public resources without reflecting on the provenance of those benefits. They consider them wrought by nature. They babble after meals about mundane matters and enjoy evanescent pleasures, ignoring that pleasure occasions suffering.

"Immersed in the din and bustle of the world for a billion years, they never self-reflect but squander their time and opportunity. Out of avarice they gather gifts, and their profits mount. Even in senescence they disregard worldly detachment and couch their bodies like illusory flowers in raked-in treasures.

"Our spiritual leader, Sakyamuni Buddha, enjoined priests to study hard, to exercise self-control, and to satisfy only the minimum need of dress, food, and sleep. Yet there are priests who indulge themselves till their hair grows white. If in their training they are indeed inferior, they ought to consult their superiors. But they do not, and boldly they proclaim that priests may seek dress and food.

"Our Sakyamuni Buddha stated the precepts to educate the ignorant. The rules and regulations ought to be kept pure as snow and ice that we may each accomplish our original aim....

"Third: A True Priest. A true priest transcends the dust and bounds of this world. Not only appearance but mentality differentiates him from others. He is one who attains Buddhahood, who occasions the surrender of evil, who makes requital for his inability to fulfill the Four Great Obligations, and who frees sentient beings from suffering. A priest without this mentality disrupts the priesthood...

"Fourth: How to Attain the Way. Should you want to study Zen, to be quickly released from the endless study of relative wisdom, and to understand directly the most profound truth, you must study widely from learned seniors and acquaint yourself with good friends. Our Zen is not easily attained. We must beware miscomprehensions and be attentive to detail. When we arrive at the abrupt awakening to the truth, we must be able to...

"Fifth: The Final Encouragement. I earnestly entreat you to make a fierce resolution..."[2]

Koko read on carefully; yet he was often stuck because of the archaic Chinese. As he listened, head on hands on the floor, Mokuzu was impressed when he realized that many must have risked their life for the Way both as students and as teachers.

'Here in Shoshinji too, even to this day, many monks are gathered and are renewing their resolution before the term of intensive meditation. I too shouldn't fall behind — I must see my original nature!'

When at last he finished the *Encouragement*, Koko shouted "*Haii!*" and all the monks resumed their upright position. The corridor floor creaked under the Zen master's slow and heavy gait. The smell of the incense that saturated his robe preceded him. He approached with an attendant who carried a square paper-covered lamp. The instant the master took the highest seat, at the head of the room and facing the monks on either side, Koko again shouted,

"*Haii!*" and all the monks like falling dominoes pressed their heads down, from highest to lowest in rank.

"Ahem! Ahem!" The master cleared his throat, with a sound much like Koko's.

"The first week-long meditation will commence tomorrow," he began his address.

"During this period there will be neither work nor mendicancy, so you can indulge in meditation to the fullest and be absorbed in koan study from morning to night, night to morning.

"You have to be aware of how fortunate you are. Few in this world were ever given such an opportunity. When the wish to train meets a suitable environment, a sense of thanks should arise, which engenders further good fortune. If you are blindly thankless, your future will be paved with ice. You must not waste the great sponsorship of the many people who have made your training possible. Do not waste their goodwill: Take pains.

"Opening your eye of wisdom is easy if you risk your life and exert yourself. Push yourself into a corner. Drive yourself to the wall to the limit of your ability. Then certainly your situation will turn, and when it turns you can break through the wall. As you know, a cornered mouse will dare bite the cat.

"Listen well. I was fifteen when I chose Zen Master Shutan as my teacher. The earlier a person finds a teacher qualified to teach him about life, the better. As long as he cannot find the teacher to whom he can entrust his life, he will be wasting his time reading and studying under mediocre teachers. I think our one concern from birth until we begin our training is to find that one teacher. Until a man finds such a teacher he is not required to study much of anything and had better devote himself to his search. Yoshida Shoin also said we must not become teacher to another by caprice, nor student of another on a whim.[3]

"If you are fortunate enough to find your teacher, your training is as if half completed. Naturally you can complete it if you just faithfully follow his guidance. When I say you must work harder, you must work yet harder. When I say you are wrong, you must frankly admit you are wrong and not insist on your wrong view. As soon as I say you are wrong, you must change your view and work hard in the direction I have indicated. Bring all your strength to the correct view, and surely you will become enlightened.

"Even so, I had to spend three years to pass the first koan. There were two others who entered Daitokuji monastery during the same term as I — Kon, who is now a local priest in the Maiko district of Kobe, and Ron, who left the priesthood to become a professor of philosophy at Tokyo University.

"We three competed to be first to solve the first koan. Kon was the winner, then came Ron. I was horribly vexed — oh, how vexed! Yet I could not solve it at all. I thought I was making as much of an effort as they, yet I could not see my original nature. I fell behind by half a year, a whole year, and still I could not succeed.

"At last I determined that instead I would not fail to be first to pass all the koans. 'I will be first to be certified for mastering all of Zen training,' I kept telling myself, and I believed it would turn out so. I thus determined, remembering the race of the hare and the tortoise.

"My native family were believers in the True Pure Land sect. Recalling the pious life of my mother, I applied myself to my koan. You know how great is a mother's love. There are among you, I know, those who have great mothers too. Do not betray your mother's love. Strive hard! When you think of her, she is with you. She is awaiting her son's completion of his training. She is ready to sacrifice her life for the life of her son. How sad if she has to see the truth of the proverb, Children when young make fools of their parents and when grown drive them mad.

"Let me repeat what my mother did the morning I decided to enter the priesthood. She bade me take the highest seat before our household altar, and she said to me, 'You are no longer your parents' child. You are Buddha's child. Henceforth we shall not sit higher than you. But because I have been your mother, please hear my last entreaty: I do not wish you to become abbot of a splendid temple, nor expect you to become an archpriest entitled to wear gold brocade. I ask only that you never muddy the face of Buddha. Put your hand to your shaven head and ask Buddha how you should live.'

"Ever since hearing my mother's words, I have consulted Buddha, and I have never once, not to this day, muddied the face of Buddha.

"Well, when I failed to be first to solve the first koan, I recalled my mother's last entreaty and I renewed my vow to see my original nature. Nightly, after regular meditation, I went to meditate at the tomb of Lord Nobunaga behind Daitokuji, where the bitter winds from Mt. Hiei come directly in winter. I conserved my time by urinating where I sat — how hot! Often I returned to the meditation hall with the sound of the morning bell.

"One morning I fainted as I stepped in for my interview with Zen Master Shutan, for my body had started to freeze after my limbs grew stiff at the tomb of Lord Nobunaga.

"Having had such an experience I do not even now warm my interview room.

"Thus I exerted myself. But I could not see my original nature. The first week-long meditation period of the rainy season was approaching.

"The day before was given to rest, as it is here. Daitokuji being in town, the monks all went out to shop and to see a play; they had finished the first koan and were feeling at ease.

"I had a weakness for the baked mochi filled with bean jam sold at Kamigamo Shrine, and I always went there to eat them on rest day. But now, in my determination to become enlightened, I quit even my one and only rare habitual pleasure.

"As I sat alone in the meditaion hall I thought of the others. Knowing they would return weary from their outing, I folded and stored their clean laundry and readied the bath.

"As I went about it I meditated on the sound of one hand and fell into a transcendent state. Unaware of myself, I kept feeding the furnace to the point where it must have become filled with firewood and smoke. Yet I kept on. Suddenly the fire blazed up and I was thrust away by a brilliant pillar of flame. At once I was enlightened, and a tremendous joy rose from the pit of my mind. What a sensation! I burst into laughter.

"See? You too must work hard and know that if you work hard you too can become enlightened. Don't give up on the way. Keep going like a hen that broods regardless of hardship and danger till the chicks begin to pip. *Hai!* — that's all!"

At the close of the master's address, the monks again in turn sat upright. Then the head chanting officer served the master tea in a black-lacquer cup on a tall black-lacquer stand, and other chanting officers hastily served the monks. As soon as everyone finished, Koko shouted for the third time the command to press the head down. While the monks from the meditation hall thus remained, the master left with his attendant, followed by Koko and the officer monks in order of rank.

The direct monk struck his handbell and led the remaining monks to the meditation hall. The darkness was dense after the rain, but clear above the pines was a waning moon.

During the week of intensive meditation, the monks rose earlier than usual, at three, and went to bed later, at eleven.

Thrice daily there were invitations for interviews with the master — around four-thirty (after breakfast), four (just before supper), and nine — which no monk could refuse even if he had no view on his koan to present.

Around nine each morning the master gave a two-hour lecture in the main hall. Zen Master Tengai lectured on *Biyan lu*.

Twice daily a tea ceremony and walking meditation were provided — in the afternoon around one, and in the evening around eight-thirty.

The meditation hall monks otherwise practiced sitting meditation, and were of course encouraged to meditate on their own after the official bed hour.

Like most monks, Mokuzu seized the week as the ideal chance to break through his wall of ignorance, and he kept meditating on the sound of one hand. But he too did not have an exceptionally strong body and often fell into a doze when he became unaware of the pain in his legs and loins.

Head Monk Kaijo panted like a raging bull as he applied the warning stick to all monks in rapid succession. Several dozen sticks, propped ready for use against the wall of the Manjusri shrine, were lavishly consumed.

With the tip he bobbed the recipient's shoulder, whereupon the monk joined his palms and bowed. The direct monk too bowed with palms joined as he held the warning stick crosswise between thumbs and index fingers. The monk bent forward from the waist and ducked his head. The direct monk struck him four times aslant across the shoulder from the right side, and the same from the left. Then both again bowed with palms joined.

Mokuzu had been annoyed by these beatings. But during the week-long meditation he welcomed them and actually felt thankful to the direct monk for enabling him to stay awake even a bit longer.

Direct Monk Kaijo too was unexceptional and fell into a doze. But as soon as he came to himself, he left his seat and made a tour to strike the monks. Mokuzu was impressed with his performance, which he was not doing for himself.

Walking meditation was practiced to relieve the pain of sitting. Dogen's *Hokyo-ki* described it as not a circling walk but a straight walk of twenty or thirty steps, a clockwise turn, and the same walk back, many times repeated. To maintain precious concentration of mind, the pace was to be as slow as half a step per breath, with posture erect and hands clasped firm at the chest.

The so-called walking meditation at Shoshinji was, however, quite different. The monks were ordered into a rude fast run contradictory to quiet meditation.

After tea ceremony the direct monk shouted,

"Walking meditation!"

Promptly all had to stand. Those on the direct monk's side filed after him, while those on the other side filed after his assistant, and the two lines ran in opposite directions along the black tiles around the outside of the meditation hall. All kept their hands clasped at their chests, but their steps caused a tremor in the ground. At the front and back entrances the two lines brushed past one another.

Mokuzu enjoyed Shoshinji's style of walking meditation for its refreshing effect on his physical condition, though he regretted that it disturbed his maturing meditation on the sound of one hand. In fact this chance to glimpse the twinkling stars during night walking meditation was worth the disturbance, or was his sole remaining pleasure.

On the third night Mokuzu dissociated himself from the others after regular meditation and climbed up to a shrine. He crossed the roofed path connecting the main building with the former main building, known as Cave of Poison Grass, and made his way up steep steps fashioned from ordinary local stones. Many were irregularly raised by creeping tree roots, and some had been entirely washed away during heavy rain.

He relied on the faint moonlight. As he progressed, the gigantic roof of the main building and the other roofs together with some thickets made the buildings appear to be more substantially occupying the ground, and the moon and stars seemed to become yet farther away.

The shrine had been built about two centuries earlier, in memory of a certain layman who greatly contributed to the construction of the present Shoshinji buildings.

It stood in disrepair, with the deep well in its garden long abandoned. Mokuzu had once been told by the monks' major,

"Don't attempt to go there for night meditation. That layman died in misery after donating his fortune to Shoshinji. His ghost comes up in a pale yellowish robe. Whoever saw it certainly went crazy or committed suicide."

Mokuzu nonetheless began to make nightly use of the shrine, for it was isolated from any other monks. It was directly against the pine mountain, above a complete view of Shoshinji.

Wind raised a sound from the rotted gutter and swept dead leaves in under the floor. A strange sound like a groan from the earth echoed ever and anon from the well. Mokuzu decided it was the resonant effect of a stone or dirt falling from the sides to the water far below.

He sat on the veranda. The trees were in deep blackness, but the damp earth of the garden was white, especially where it was frozen over, and was bright under the moon and stars.

After nearly half an hour of meditation, he noticed faint intermittent footsteps slowly ascending as if with hesitation.

The figure that appeared from the thicket of trees indeed shone with a pale yellow light.

Mokuzu's state of mind was not such that he was afraid of ghosts; rather he wished that anyone, even a ghost, would help him to become enlightened. He continued to sit without moving and observed its advance into the garden.

The face was downcast, hand pressed to brow. It was Zui.

Hoping to forewarn him of his presence, he coughed. Zui appeared to be startled; he looked up, but his face showed no surprise.

"Ah, Mokuzu...you're bearing up well...I suppose you'll be enlightened before long," he commented in an asthenic voice, pausing by the veranda.

"Are you bleeding? What happened to your head?"

"Oh, nothing worthy of concern. I was meditating on the main building veranda and must have dozed off. I fell to the concrete. Had I been meditating on the koan, I could have become enlightened like our master. But I got only this bloody brow. It doesn't hurt much, though queerly enough, I have a horrible ache in the back of my head."

"Shall I call the Manjusri attendant? Why don't you take a rest in the Nirvana hall?"

"Don't worry needlessly. Whoever enters the Nirvana hall is fated to die or abandon his training. I'd prefer to meet a ghost up here and go mad. Madness is an expression of protest. The life of a ghost has no abandonment and no death. I feel an intimacy with ghosts, and a great detachment from human beings. I wonder which you are."

"...."

"Well, I don't know what I'm saying....Time rushes like a stream along with this headache. Oh, I'm sorry. I'm senior to you and assistant to the direct monk, yet all I'm doing for you is hindering your training. Forgive me." Zui left the veranda and started to wamble up the path.

"Where are you going, Direct Monk's Assistant?"

After a breath Zui replied,

"Higher to meditate. You know the cliff at the dead quarry? I dare not fall into a doze, unless I don't mind being crushed."

"It's too dangerous, don't go. You'd better return to the meditation hall." Mokuzu got down from the veranda, went after Zui, and caught his sleeve. He leaned over Mokuzu. When Mokuzu attempted to carry him, his slaver dangled onto Mokuzu's neck.

On the fifth day too the master lectured in the main hall. To announce the lectures, the big bell in the bell tower was struck eighteen times. The wood instrument hung at the door of the meditation hall echoed consecutively with its pattern of seven, five, and three strokes. Next, the huge cowhide drum stationed at the southwest corner of the main building began to be struck. At the sound of the drum, the residential quarters monks and visiting laymen appeared and seated themselves on the right, facing the

584

sanctum. Led by the direct monk, the meditation hall monks entered and sat on the left, and behind them sat the students from the junior college, brought by the dormitory inspectors.

The drum resounded like a war drum inside and outside the main building, which was wide open for the occasion. The clatter of the drumsticks against the rivets rumbled like thunder.

After the audience was properly seated, in came the Zen master, flanked on either side by an attendant. Pacing with measured step and firm-set mouth, he resembled a tycoon. He was fully appareled in whitish robes and a surplice. One attendant held his white horsehair whisk, an age-old symbol of the Dharma.

He ascended to the high wooden lecture chair, set just within the south side and directly facing Buddha. A chanting officer positioned behind the chair then began to chant "National Teacher Daito's Admonition," followed by the rest of the monks.

During the chanting Koko, representing the audience, silently performed the ceremony of entreating the master to lecture. Just before the chanting ended, Zen Master Tengai began to read with traditional intonation the text on which he would lecture:

"Case 31: On Magu's Shaking His Priest's Staff and Circling the Meditation Seat.

"Harken. When it moves, its shadow appears. When its shadow is perceived, it freezes. But when it neither moves nor perceives, you are as unfree and confused as a man who confines himself in the cave of a wild fox. If, however, you completely understand and attain perfect peace, you will have no single thread to hinder you and cause you gloom. You can be like a dragon in water, a tiger on a mountain. When you let go, even a heap of rubble will emit light. When you hold back, even pure gold will lose its luster and even the old koans will circle round about. Now understand what I am saying by seeing the following koan:

"The case: Magu came one day with his priest's staff to Jangjing and thrice circled Jangjing's meditation seat, once shook his staff, and there stood erect. Jangjing remarked: 'Right, right!' Shyuedou comments: Mistake.

"Magu then went off to Nanchyuan, thrice circled his meditation seat, once shook his staff, and there stood erect. Nanchyuan remarked: 'Wrong, wrong!' Shyuedou comments: Mistake.

"Magu asked Nanchyuan, 'Why do you say I am wrong when for the same deed Jangjing said I was right?' Nanchyuan replied, 'Jangjing is right, you are wrong. Your body is but the movement of many elements and will sooner or later ruin.'

585

"This mistake, that mistake,
So long as you are mindful of them
the world will be as peaceful as the pacific waves
of all oceans and all streams that flow therein.
Noble is the sound of the twelve rings
on the priest's staff! (Yungjia at Tsaushi)
Each gate is wide open and well aired,
but not a place to settle into at ease.
An able man had better seek medicine
to cure his ailment of being well."[4]

Following his reading of the text, Zen Master Tengai sipped tea from a large cup. He then proceeded to his lecture.

"This tells us that Zen priests have to get into the skin of their role in each place and time. Things done by halves are never done right. You must always be thorough about everything. When you must open your hand, open it to the best of your ability. Then when you must close it, you will be able to close it. Decisively clench it as if to squeeze moisture from a stone. Our life is this repetition of opening and closing.

"To do your best means to risk your life. To see your original nature is an easy task if only you determine to risk your life. It should take no more than ten days.

"You are all taking a mild bath. Look here, today is already the fourth day of the first week-long meditation. In your way two or three years will soon fly by. Life is short. It was said, 'At dawn, rosy cheeks, at eventide, bleached bones.'[5]

"Now give your attention to the passage 'When it moves, its shadow appears. When its shadow is perceived, it freezes.' This is talking about our mind, the function of our mind. Originally it was said by Sengjau in his writing *Jau lun*. In a later age a Zen priest applied the words to answer the question 'How should priests behave?' Oh well, that is a matter to be investigated by a bibliographer.

"Our concern is the point that every working of our mind, however deep, will always surface in visible form. Nothing exists without leaving a trace; everything gives evidence.

"Our mind when it moves will cloud. Why? Because as soon as we see, hear, or smell something, our mind is no longer like clear water; a shadow is cast. Whenever we think, that is, exercise our discretion, we are bound by notions. Our mind is then no longer free as running water but rigid as ice.

"This is the nature of our mind, like it or not, and it often causes us trouble. Yet what will happen if we try to still our mind, not let it function?

586

Here it says, 'But when it neither moves nor perceives, you are as unfree and confused as a man who confines himself in the cave of a wild fox.' It's as bad as or worse than having a shadow of perception and being bound by one's created idea.

"What will you do? Let your mind function, or not let it function? Both are wrong because both lead us into human troubles. Perception gives us shadows and binds us. Non-perception denies our humanity and makes us evil creatures. How then can we keep from falling into one or the other trap? Buddhism teaches us the Middle Way, but what is the Middle Way concerning this point, in the practice of our daily life? This is the main question we will investigate today in case 31."

Zen Master Tengai here took a sip of tea, and his meandering but powerfully delivered lecture was just begun. The audience kept their eyes slightly lowered and listened attentively. Those of the senior monks who had passed several koans were able to comprehend what the master was talking about despite his rough expression; and they were groping for their own manner of expression to use should they too have future occasions to preach. The junior monks, not having passed even their first koan, could barely make out the literal meaning of the archaic Chinese text; and they were endeavoring not to lose a word so as to obtain a hint toward a solution to their koan.

One junior, Mokuzu, shut his ears and continued to engage in meditating on his koan while assuming a listener's attitude.

Many laymen as well as some nuns from the vicinity were also attending the lecture, seated behind the monks of the residential quarters. Among the nuns was always the figure of Shorai, though Mokuzu never noticed. Some of the laymen were expecting the master to suggest how they ought to conduct their political or business affairs, and they took his lectures in a practical and prosaic sense.

Most students from the junior college were tortured by the pain in their legs from sitting erect. They squirmed, and in their minds cursed the master for his endless talk. They wished him to provide vulgar and scandalous criticisms of real and famous persons. Some entirely ignored the lecture and were exciting themselves by noting the presence of sparse snowflakes in the air, by observing the faces of the audience, or by imagining a romance or two of their own as if they were fledgling poets.

"Jangjing was kind; his remark was to encourage Magu to train further. There are teachers who admire a student's diligence and what he has attained instead of severely criticizing him for his slow progress and what he has not yet attained. A kind teacher of this sort has to be careful, because, as in the case of Magu, there is the student who deceives himself, who thinks he is being

587

certified for what he is. Admiration can blind a person and make him proud of his very stupidity. I myself therefore refuse to admire talent in my disciples..."

At that moment there occurred something queer. Zui, who must have been reposing in the Nirvana hall, showed up. He was clad in only a white underkimono, a white kimono-undershirt, and a long white loincloth, the last dangling partially undone. He advanced with a drunkard's gait, yet it was apparent that he was imitating the master's manner of entrance.

He came to the center of the hall and looked up dubiously at the master. His underkimono waved in the wind, exposing his hairy thighs, reddened by the cold, and his bandy shanks, thin and hairier.

Zen Master Tengai, his lecture interrupted, clenched his molars and glared at Zui. Pointing at him, Zui exclaimed,

"Oh, no, there's no eyebrow on that side — it got bald!" and he began to gambol like a child.

Koko, at last convinced that something was definitely wrong, seized Zui by the arms from behind. Zui paled, assumed an earnest attitude, pulled free, and yelled,

"Get out of my way, bogus senior!"

Then, shedding all but his loincloth, he raised his right arm and pointed skyward, and with his left arm lowered he pointed to the floor.

"See, Master!" he shrilled. "'I alone am honored in heaven and on earth!'[6] This is the answer to my koan. Did you hear? Please accept it and certify that I am right. Please, Master, please — — !"

Zen Master Tengai sat quiet and joined his palms.

Koko, from behind Zui, called irritably to the nearest of the master's attendants and to the Manjusri attendant. The three of them pinioned Zui this time with much more care and force and made off with him toward the

Nirvana hall. Yells and shouts came from the cross-wing. But soon the temple quieted again, after a final groan — evidence that one of the three had knocked Zui senseless.

All other monks, including the direct monk, remained utterly quiet, seated meditatively as if nothing had happened.

Then the master on the high chair pressed the corner of his eye and spoke in a slightly nasal tone,

"I wish I could teach it, were it possible...! But the answer to the koan is the one thing no one is capable of teaching to another, even to a most beloved person. No one can take the place of another for such inevitable human tasks as eating, sleeping,...and arriving at the realization; as was said: 'Annihilation of one's delusions can be realized only by oneself and certified only by oneself.'[7]

"Were it a diploma and a doctorate, which in this world are useful, I could freely vouchsafe him a hundred, a thousand — but Zen training is not like that."

Most of the audience were lowering their eyes in depression. Mokuzu with gimlet eyes was staring at the master, behind whom a whirl of snow was carried off by the wind.

45

Mokuzu's Realization

It continued to snow at the backs of the meditating monks. The shojis were kept open. Snow produced at random in the leaden sky grazed by the tall treetops, got around the complicated eaves, and landed wherever fated to land.

The trees were covered with snow, the garden was white. Snow was heaped on the roofs, and where it invaded the roofed path from the meditation hall to the residential quarters, the Manjusri attendant was busily sweeping.

The ambient mountains were everywhere white.

> Snow rejoins the broken bridge over the gorge,
> Smoke indicates a concealed hermitage.[1]

The meditation hall was cold and damp. The only heat was the monks' passion for self-training.

Having attained no result by the week-long meditation of November, Mokuzu was regretting that his endeavor had not yet matured. For him endeavor meant to keep on with self-denial to its extremity.

He determined anew to see his original nature before the end of the December week-long meditation, and he privately vowed to eat no more than one bowl of barley-and-rice gruel a day. Eating was indeed the origin of worldly desires, and the more he ate the harder his digestive organs had to work, with the effect of making him sleepy. Were he to fall asleep, his meditation on the sound of one hand would be broken off, and his body restored to vigor would disturb his concentration as if to detain his spirit on earth. The energy he required was the minimum, just enough to keep meditating on the sound of one hand.

Whenever he went to see the master, he received encouragement —

"Remember Jsyming's words: 'Every prosperous light of grace emanating from the ancients is the result of their labor.'[2] You have to become the only sound of one hand in the entire universe. 'Stick to your meditation and think the unthinkable'![3] Go on!"

Every night Mokuzu went up to the shrine after the official bedtime. His teeth, knuckles, and elbows ached, and he was visited alternately by diarrhea and nausea from the cold and so little food and sleep. As soon as he closed his eyes he verged on sleep. How he wished to lie down, to curl up like a snail, to forget everything, and sleep! Yet on clear nights each time the charm of sleep approached he told himself, 'Keep meditating until the moon reaches that pine branch,' or, on snowy nights, 'Stick to the sound of one hand until another gust blows your sleeves.' Thus encouraging himself at each breath, he could extend minute by minute the hours he meditated.

Such was his penance. Yet by outer appearance he sat as if nothing was the matter, back straight, abdomen firm, posture a balanced pyramid. With the advance of the moon, his shadow on the snowy garden turned. Wind dislodged snow from a branch, *whump!* Each sound deepened the night, making it seem a night with a midnight sun.

In the postmidnight hours, when he could no longer bear to stay awake, he would climb higher, to the remains of the quarry, where he had stopped Zui from going. In the excavated caves several icicles sharp as lances reflected the starlight. The clarity of the night made it evident that the distance between the moon and the stars was greater by far than the distance between himself and the moon.

When it snowed, one side of his head as well as that ear and shoulder got more snow than the other, like the trees and rocks.

Toward the end of November he quite often entered the state of forgetting he was a being with a body. Like a balloon detached from a child's hand, his soul floated off and he was released from all sorts of pains. Seemingly

590

his soul could alight on a pine, could circle above the mountains as it pleased.

Sitting meditation devoid of pain was indeed "an easy gate to the Dharma."[4] Still Mokuzu continued to meditate on the sound of one hand. He left the rock only when he heard from down the mountain the sound of the morning bell being struck by a chanting officer. When he tried to stand, he was forced to realize he was a being with a body, one that did not function well, and he fell over. Fortunately the snow piled more than a foot deep protected him from injury.

One morning at the sound of the bell he was abruptly awakened from his samadhi. He had been entirely forgetting himself, forgetting who was meditating on the sound of one hand. He could not distinguish whether it was himself or the one hand that rang. In effect, the world that had been utterly hidden by a dense mist suddenly burst forth with all its reality. His sense of sound, sight, smell, and touch, which had been dead, began at once to work again.

He had been cutting off all his senses and thought, had been maintaining a state whereby they were rendered inert. He had gone beyond meditation on the sound of one hand and become the sound of one hand, and the sound of one hand had become the thing-in-itself, the world. He had been breathing it in and out without distinguishing himself from anything else.

When he emerged from meditating on the sound of one hand, he realized that his life was a particular and limited existence like any other thing. In samadhi, on the contrary, everything was equal and impartial; it could be described as the sound of one hand roaring all over the white mountains, or the world as only one hand, or a sound reaching as high as the Trayastrimsa — the thirty-three heavens — and at once as low as the Naraka — the hells made of diamonds.

The world outside samadhi was unequal and multifarious. There was a white moon above a pine branch above the cliff. Below, the expanse of the roof of the main building was partly visible through the cedars. From the bell tower came the plangent sound of the bell announcing dawn. And Mokuzu's hands were red from chilblains.

He took good care of the relation between the thing-in-itself, namely eternal life, and the world of the individual mortal, his particular life. He returned to the meditation hall and followed at the end of the line being led by the direct monk to morning chanting in the main building. The monks in their black robes went along the roofed path through the snowy garden.

❧

The December week-long meditation had begun. It was to commemorate Sakyamuni's attainment of Buddhahood and would last till the dawn of

591

December 8. This was the most important meditation week. The yearly program was in fact designed to make the monks display all their inherent energy on this last occasion, with prior weeks being occasions to get used to the hardship and to determine to become enlightened at any cost.

Accordingly, the purpose of the first koan given to meditation hall monks was to make them see the true nature of themselves and the world, to free them from the basic problems of life and death, and to enable them to attain perfect freedom. Koans serving this purpose were called Dharma-body (*dharma-kaya*) koans, among which belonged "The Sound of One Hand," "Jaujou's Wu," and "The Sixth Patriarch's 'Original Nature.'"

Solving this class of koans was not so difficult once the monks were able to sacrifice their life; conversely, as long as they clung to it, solving these koans was impossible however much they made use of their knowledge and intellect.

To comprehend the Dharma-body thoroughly, that is, to experience the life of the thing-in-itself, the monks had to fix their mind on the koan and attain the state of forgetting themselves and their object, as Mokuzu had done, faithful to Zen Master Tengai's instructions.

When their samadhi was by chance broken, as by a bell, or a pillar of flame, they were pulled back to their usual state, in which they would inevitably have some reflection. This reflection was the thought and feeling that arose as they again saw the usual world after seeing the absolute world. The world in which they had to go on living was not changed by their experience, but their understanding of it and their attitude toward it would be greatly changed.

The content of this experience of entering samadhi had to be the same for whomever. Wumen naturally stated it in the following way in case 1 of his book *Wumen guan* — a case formerly introduced to Mokuzu by Zen Master Hanun:

> Whoever has gone through this gateless gate walks hand in hand with the successive patriarchs, sees with the same eye, hears with the same ear...[5]

Now Mokuzu clearly understood what all the Zen patriarchs through Bodhidharma and continuing on down to Zen Master Tengai or Zen Master Hanun had been talking about, and what they had been encouraging their students to do.

The content of the experience was the same, but each patriarch's expression of his understanding of the Dharma-body was different, reflecting his unique character, ability, and environment.

In the meditation hall Mokuzu thought quietly, 'When I asked him what is death, Koko tumbled down and pretended to be dying in agony. He didn't give an interpretation of death, he tried to show death. He demonstrated how to go beyond the agony of death by devoting his all to the agony. What he wanted to tell me must have been, "Die earnestly when you must die, and there will be no fear of death nor unease." He did his best to express his understanding of death and his so-called Zen experience, which were tinged by Zen Master Tengai, whose essential teaching is, Become the object, whatever it is.

'His answer didn't strike me at the time, because, first, I couldn't understand the art of going beyond relative matters by becoming the matter itself; and second, I could detect he was faking, merely repeating his foregone knowledge that the wise answer was that kind of answer. Had he really gone through the experience of samadhi? Certainly he was degrading wisdom to mere knowledge. Was it because he hadn't gone through the experience? Or is he dull and therefore unable to use the experience creatively in accord with each daily event?

'I wanted to understand my own life and death. But what I really longed to understand was Ena's death, what was the inevitable cause and what was the meaning of her short life. Both Koko and Zen Master Tengai did not see into my heart (and I can't expect they've improved about seeing into another's heart even to this day). So for me their answer had no resonance.

'It's reasonable they couldn't see into my heart, because I wasn't just expressing my questions in vague form but rather concealing my real concern. Yet their impercipience doesn't suit them if they are enlightened, or at least it doesn't suit me.

'What about the monks sitting here with me in this hall? Can't I see their dear passing life as representing all common things? And further, can't I see into their mental state? Their robes may cover their flesh but not their mind.

'The lotus leaves sway in the still air.
A fish is likely stirring.[6]

'Well, that is that. But very possibly Koko and his Zen master Tengai do have wisdom, though it is wisdom solidified into knowledge. Knowledge is an effective weapon for attacking others, but for helping them it is as crude as the hands of a robot. Their wisdom, the antecedent of their knowledge, might have come from their experience, but more likely it came from the founder of this Shoshinji, Kanzan Egen. One day when asked about the problem of death he replied, "In my world there is neither life nor death!"

'What he meant was, Go beyond death to become death — an adaptation of Yuanwu: "Life is the great activity of Buddha. Death also is the great activity of Buddha."[7]

'Comparing their expressions on the same subject, Yuanwu was more religious than Kanzan.

'Let me see...now I too have experienced the world of death and learned that a relative individual corresponds to the absolute whole. For the absolute whole I have no other mode of expression but to say that it is the purest world. I have directly undergone by my own experience the law of conservation of energy discovered by Western scientists through their objective experimentation.

'In my understanding, death is not different from life insofar as the thing-in-itself changes its form as it likes. Unease and fear toward death stem from our contradictory wish for immutability. We cling to our life even at the time our life is wishing to change its form. We don't want to change, yet our life is the effect of the change of the thing-in-itself that made us. When we respect the thing-in-itself, we can reject our attachment and can die gladly and cleanly according to the wish of the thing-in-itself to change its form.

'Kamo no Chomei, author of *Account from My Hut*, was heavily depressed by life's uncertainty. He couldn't see and therefore couldn't respect the purity of the thing-in-itself. Finding no joy in following the current of the change of things, he wrote:

> 'A stream flows on and on, its water ever changing, while bubbles drifting at the shallows repeat their birth and ruin.[8]

'For the same sight I should like to say,

> 'Dew-spangled driftage reflects the stars. As the flow meets the sea the waves meet the sky. Opening flowers scent the air, when dead they enhance the soil.

'Thus have I seen the nature of death, and I have no fear of my own death and no complaints. I am no longer worried about any superficial cause of death, such as traffic accident, earthquake, disease, homicide, nuclear holocaust, chemical warfare, environmental pollution, food shortage, energy crisis, and overpopulation. They are nothing but the opportunity for each mortal's pre-decided fate. In all great nature there is not a single unnatural event. My life is also one natural event. If I respond correctly to the changes of nature, I can participate with my own subjecthood in the changes.

'Sakyamuni Buddha stated that "every creature is a mortal being (*maranadhamma*), a being that ends its existence at death (*maranadhamma-pariyosana*), and a being that cannot go beyond death (*maranadhamma-anatita*)."

Further, he advised us to transcend the problem of death by "constant meditation on death"[9] instead of trying in vain to escape death. He taught that we should ride on the wave of death rather than frantically flee it. His teaching and what I think substantially agree.

'Since old times Japanese samurai studied, by means of Zen, Buddha's teaching about constant meditation on death, and they lived ready for an unexpected death. Yamamoto Jocho, for instance, observed:

> 'The spirit of the Way of the samurai is to die, die every morning, die every evening. He who is prepared to die can freely practice his chivalry.[10]

'I too will live with daily-renewed readiness to die. But this is not new to me. Gyodo taught me to douse with cold water every morning. Beyond its toughening my weak constitution, he had in mind that it would prepare me for death. By that means I was to clean myself so as to have no shame of being unclean if death suddenly came. He was influenced by many books relating to Buddhism and the Way of the samurai. How grateful I am for having chanced to have him as a senior brother.

'Now I have my own view on my life and death. And have I solved all related problems? Not at all. I can die peacefully according to the wish of things to change. But how sad to separate from a loved one by death! Nature changes, and we are mortal. I know the law of birth and ruin, yet the more I know it the more I sorrow. The moon rises over the forest and the water turns infinitely closer to dark indigo.

'The more I know that no one can escape death nor have a second life, the more I dearly and vividly recall Ena, even her slightest gesture.

'I feel sad seeing others trying to enter samadhi in this hall. They are devoting themselves, but I know they can do nothing about their fate. I sense the weight of the snow that the roof of this hall is enduring; the roof at intervals squeaks, and the blackened ceiling is warping at the corners. The black tile floor is wet with moisture condensing in the cold. The incense marking the time burns on. Its scent drifts, mingles with the monks' sleeves for a while, and disappears. To where? Into love, if it is to be named.

'I moan over all things that are reaching their end, and I feel affection for all things living their short lives.

'Zen Teacher Dogen knew this feeling,

> 'But the flowers are soon gone,
> And to our annoyance the grasses increase.[11]

'I am comforted very little by knowing the thing-in-itself is my true mother as well as the mother of Ena's life. In eternity there is no separation between her and me. Yet as long as I exist with my own form, what comforts me is form. My individual life can't be satisfied by knowing common and eternal life. Nevermore can I see her hair scattering the light, her lips eager to express her mind, her tender eyes frankly approaching, her erect figure radiating warmth. They are gone forever, and no truth can comfort me, and this is the truth.

'Therefore I wonder what Zen Master Tengai and his Koko should have done could they have seen into my heart and wished to reply authentically to my question at that time. They should have wept like Niobe, cried like the constant sound of a waterfall, like a snowstorm, like summer cicadas, immersing their bodies, even their shadows, in the sorrow...until they forgot themselves and others amid their tears.

'On hearing the sound of one hand and seeing my original nature, I hear my own song,

> 'There is nothing,
> "snow covers the arborvitae in the garden,
> ice freezes the dam."[12]
>
> Love is nothingness, but nothingness is not love.
> "The snow melts, exposing the mountains,
> the sun rises over the sea."[13]
>
> "Carry snow to fill the river."[14]
> Behold the blue of its depths.
> It is indigo, the color of love.

'Wisdom fallen to the status of knowledge is as useless to help people as the cast-off shell of a cicada, and when it looks down on them it is heavy as armor. Wisdom without compassion quickly diminishes to a mere shell. Is there any way for whoever has seen the depth of nature but to be affectionate toward all souls living and dead?

'Now I know Gyodo's life can't be affected by insanity or sanity. I have to respect his changeless nature without being baffled at the sight of his changeable form. Yet the more important attitude I have to maintain is to lament over his insanity, which is wasting his brief life on this earth.

'Insanity is the private accumulation of society's overwhelming contradictions. Contradictions between Ideal and Real especially when heaped upon an immature but sensitive and lonely heart can cause it to break. It's like ordering a hungry child in a cold wind to untie in a limited time a tangled kite string without giving him anything to eat. A child who hasn't yet attained the wisdom to cut the Gordian knot must be protected by a merciful Bodhisattva. There was no Bodhisattva near Gyodo!

'Considering Gyodo's case, I think there's no doubt Zen Master Tengai misled Zui and drove him mad. The master committed a great, inexcusable sin. To sacrifice an individual life is to trample on the dignity of universal life. "To produce one or even half a useful man in this world," is what he says to justify his faulty teaching. But his purpose is not great by any means. Certainly it doesn't justify the sacrifice of one who might have come to know his Buddha nature within the course of his lifetime. Anyway, this world keeps changing, and the function of those few talented men has been only to catch the public fancy.

'Whoever is awakened to eternal life must first respect what is eternal in each person and thing, and second, must love what is mortal in each person and thing. Love and respect can transform wisdom into a sword to help others, while wisdom devoid of love and respect is a sword of destruction.

'We Buddhists must know why Sakyamuni abandoned his six-year practice of *tapas* and *yoga*. Inherent in both, he realized, was a dichotomy of mind and body, for body was considered an enemy to enlightenment. Sakyamuni Buddha regarded mind and body as inseparable, and he thought body rather assists mind to achieve enlightenment: "Those ascetic practices are meaningless. They are of no merit, like the noise of an arrow shot from a bow."[15]

'He then recalled a day in his boyhood when he had left a crowded festival to go sit under a tree, and there had resigned himself to silent meditation. Next he recalled that at that time he had attained a deep samadhi wherein he forgot his worldly desires, and it had been an easy task! Recalling that it had been easy, he abandoned his six years of ascetic practice.

'Sakyamuni Buddha's account suggests much we should not overlook! I remember his words as if directly hearing his quiet sermon:

> 'He who has comprehended Reason and attained his own free state must practice to be competent, frank, upright, agreeable, kind, and never arrogant.
>
> He must learn to be content and by food easily satisfied; must live simply, avoid sundry affairs, control his five sense organs, be modest and wise, and not covet in a layman's house.
>
> He must not act shameless, rousing censure from the wise. He must ever practice compassion to bring good fortune, peace, and comfort to all beings:
>
> Good fortune to each, whatever life it has received, and whether or not it is driven by desire, is long, short, large, mid-sized, small, visible, invisible, near, or far, or has ceased its klesa.

He must not slander, despise, or wish misery upon any being anywhere however his fury incites him to anger.

He must pour boundless compassion upon every being just as a mother with maternal love risks her life to shelter her baby.

He must pour endless compassion throughout the world; must love purely without grudge and discontent, upward, downward, and in the four directions.

He must establish a compassionate mind whether he stands, walks, sits, or reclines awake. Buddha's teaching is called To Dwell in Purity.'[16]

❧

During week-long meditation, each monk had to visit the master at least thrice daily to show his view on his given koan.

As soon as the bell sounded at the master's quarters, the direct monk struck his handbell, twice clapped the clappers, and shouted, "Compulsory interview!"

As usual, all the monks left their meditation seats, noisily bolted down the stone steps like ambushed rabbits, and raced to line up along the corridor by the drawing room. Most had formed no view worth showing; yet they acted as if their interviews were urgent, for their reality had been moulded into an ideal of how an earnest monk ought to behave.

In the momentary confusion, some escaped into the latrines or behind bushes for the duration to avoid the master's abuse and the bustle of the direct monk. It was said the monks' major, Seigan, always hid in an empty bathtub.

Only the direct monk and Mokuzu remained in the hall.

Unaware that anyone else was present, Kaijo discharged,

"How dare he call me a draff eater? He acts like a king-of-the-castle, and I have to clean up his mess. One of these days I'll snub him!" and he got down from his seat. Then he noticed Mokuzu still meditating.

Somewhat amazed, he seized a warning stick from those propped against the Manjusri shrine and took a stance before him.

"What are you doing? Didn't you hear everyone has to go to the king — nay, the master, Tengai?"

"Direct Monk, 'One's reliable foundation is only oneself,'"[17] Mokuzu replied quietly.

"What? What do you mean — 'oneself'?"

"'Just as no one can see a flower in a forest of figs, so no one can obtain solidity in the world of constant transmigration.'"[18]

"Tut! You mustn't fall into the fallacy of believing either that death is the end of existence or that the soul is eternal. Dahuei said, 'The doctrine of

598

annihilation is, To extinguish your bright nature, to adhere to emptiness, and to dwell in tranquillity. The doctrine of eternality is, To deny that all dharmas are empty, and to adhere to worldly laws and regard them as the ultimate.'[19] It was said, 'Shyshuang set up a hall, called it "Dead Tree," and put therein many monks who were like dead trees. Always they kept meditating in sitting or walking form and never did they lie down. Many died as they sat or stood.'[20] Do you want to become like that?" Kaijo glared at Mokuzu.

Mokuzu faintly lowered his eyebrows and responded,

"'A dead tree can sing like a dragon.'[21] We human beings esteem trust because the world keeps changing, we practice love because the world has no absolute altruism, and we respect all beings because the world is composed of mutual relations. We must keep building a palace of trust, love, and respect, even though we are aware that it is a palace built on sand."

"If you've come to understand that far, you'd better go see the master, the reasons being, first, to check whether your understanding is really correct, second, to thank him for his guidance, and third, to be given a new, higher koan." The direct monk lightly struck Mokuzu's shoulder with the warning stick.

Mokuzu did as he was told. The morning sun streaked the snowy courtyard and brightly reflected on the shojis along the corridor. Icicles at the eaves cast magnified shadows.

Zen Master Tengai raised his voice before seeing Mokuzu,

"What splendid work, I am greatly relieved! Come in. You know, the hardest part of being a Zen master is to watch the development of the disciple wandering in a miasma until he comes in vexation to his death, or loses his mental balance, or happily arrives at the realization." The master took a Rauwolfia for his hypertension.

Mokuzu sat facing him after thrice performing the highest form of respect. His figure had been majestic like that of a general in command of an army, but to Mokuzu he now looked like any ordinary country priest with a gloomy brow. He too had been undergoing various hardships. He had an ill-shaped, pyknic build, and his chest heaved at each breath as if just to maintain his body was a heavy task. His asymmetric white eyebrows and the hair growing uselessly like tendrils from his ears seemed symbolic of worldly attachment. At his temples the formation of brown moles suggested extravasations of poison accumulated during a long life.

"Just to make doubly sure," he said, and he proceeded to ask nearly twenty small questions, such as the following:

"You must have heard the sound of one hand. Then what is your proof?"

"It was said that to hear the sound of one hand assures your attainment of Buddhahood. Tell me, how will you attain it?"

"After being cremated and turned to ash, how did you hear the sound of one hand?"

Having experienced becoming the sound of one hand, Mokuzu easily answered every question. He was reminded of a cat toying with a ball of yarn.

Moreover, the questions were like pond skaters, useless to measure the depth of his understanding. Sadly he saw the limit of Zen Master Tengai, which was the traditional Zen.

At the end, the master asked him to quote the most apposite phrases from the poems compiled in *Tang shyshyuan* to exemplify "the root of the sound of one hand." No longer was it an inquisition into his mastery of the wisdom. Merely his knowledge of the poems of Tang-dynasty China was being tested.

"Master, how can you expect me to present some particular phrase you have in mind? *Tang shyshyuan* contains 127 poets and 465 poems in 7 volumes. Could you tell me the poet, or the volume at least, if you don't wish to waste my precious time?"

"Four hundred sixty-five poems? So many? Hmm, it never occurred to me...Well, I never read it through and I have no way of telling you which volume, but I do happen to know the poet: Shen Chyuanchi, am I correct?" The master was frank about his lack of knowledge, knowing it to be the most effective way to blunt criticism.

"Shen Chyuanchi? Oh, it was he who perfected the meter of a new style called *lyushy*. His character was reputed to be shabby. He was exiled to what is now North Vietnam for being obsequious to Jang Yijy. Yet surprisingly his poems are so limpid there's no taint of his real life. Then, is it a *jyuejyu*, the poem 'Wangshan'?

> "Rows of tombs on the northern mount Wang
> face through the ages the castle Loyang.
> Music rises from the castle day and night.
> The sough of the pines is the sole sound on the height.[22]

"Or had you in mind 'Guyi'?:

> "Sad is the tender wife quiet in her curcumin sanctum
> where on a crossbeam adorned with tortoise shell
> a pair of petrels roost.
> Chill September breezes bring the beat
> of fulling cloth and cause the leaves to fall.
> She muses on her spouse ten years gone,
> gone on an expedition to Liaotung.
> No letter comes north of the river,
> there where the white wolves dwell.
> Slow is the passing of an autumn night

600

south of Cinnabar Phoenix Castle.
She is absorbed in sorrow as the moon
brightens her weaving of twill."[23]

"That's it, Mokuzu —

"No letter comes north of the river,
there where the white wolves dwell.
Slow is the passing of an autumn night
south of Cinnabar Phoenix Castle.

"We Zennists borrow these phrases to express 'the root of the sound of one hand,' do you see? We disregard the original poem. It describes a sentimental phenomenon, but we give it far deeper meaning than the poet ever dreamed of. We can turn a cat into a tiger, a snake into a dragon. If by his own phrases he understood what we understand, the poet would have fainted. Mokuzu, this sight, of the root of the sound of one hand, is the base of our inexhaustible religious passion 'ever upward to seek Bodhisattvahood and ever downward to help sentient beings.'"[24]

Snow loosened by the morning sun dropped from the roof to the courtyard with an unexpectedly loud thump. Neither Zen Master Tengai nor Mokuzu even blinked.

The master went on,

"You are, as I expected, one who literally works hard. Your thoughts, words, and deeds are always consistent. For one such as you, reality can catch up with the ideal before long, and reality can be the ideal. I dislike people whose ideal and reality are poles apart. More than anything it proves their laziness and weakness.

"Please realize that those of my disciples who have seen through their original nature as thoroughly as you have are countable on one hand. He who deeply understands nature tends to live his life as an onlooker. This is because he lacks either the compassion or the means to help others. But the deeper one understands, the higher one's leading role should be. So, you have to keep burning your fire of compassion by taking the suffering of others as your own, and at once you have to keep cultivating every means to help them.

"It will now be evident to you how you should train henceforth, and for what. Our Zen Teacher Hakuin arranged all koans into six categories, namely: Dharma-body, Dharma-function, Verbal Analysis and Application, Abstruse, Five Classifications and Ten Supreme Precepts, and Last Barrier. The koan you passed is of the first kind. You must pass those of each kind, nearly 200. I'll not be stingy; I'll give you a new one whenever you pass one. So your speed of mastery depends entirely on your effort. The iron should be struck while hot. Ninety miles is halfway for a man who travels a hundred. Endeavor to the last of the last!"

The master then gave a new koan, "Shiangyan's 'Up a Tree.'"

> Shiangyan proposed a case: Suppose yourself up a tree with hands and feet contacting no branch, no part of the tree at all, and holding on only by your teeth. Just then someone happens by and asks you, "What is the true meaning of Bodhidharma's coming to China?" If you make no reply you will disappoint him. If you reply you will fall to your death. Tell me, what will you do?[25]

Shiangyan assumes the trainee already understands the true meaning of Bodhidharma's coming to China and is asking him how, in a tight situation, he will express it for another's benefit. The koan is therefore a Dharma-function koan.

Mokuzu returned to the meditation hall and pondered first the question "What is the true meaning of Bodhidharma's coming to China?"

He wanted to know about the historical Bodhidharma, how he was raised, why he decided to desert his native land for China, and how he actually lived in such a foreign land. But the available material on his life was very roughly recorded, and subsequent records were merely embellishments, greatly disparate one from another even as to the dates of his birth and death.

Docho Doka had taught him that the oldest record on Bodhidharma was in Tanlin's preface to a work ascribed to Bodhidharma called *Two Ways and Four Practices*:

> Bodhidharma was born third child to a great Brahman king in South India, west of China. He was a prodigy who understood all he heard. His concern, however, was Mahayana Buddhism, whence he put off his worldly attire and donned priestly robes. He received transmission of the Dharma, attained Nirvana, comprehended all social matters, and mastered all requisite studies inside and out. In his own land he earned love and respect, yet he was discontent over the decline of Buddhism in remote lands. Crossing ocean and mountains he came at last to the Hanjung and Wei districts of this land. Those of frank nature became his followers, whereas those possessed by traditional formality and fixed ideas began to reproach him....[26]

Baulin chuan (Transmission of the treasure forest), which influenced the later *Tzutang ji* and *Jingde chuandeng lu*, gave the date of Bodhidharma's arrival at Canton as 21 September, year 8 of Putung, Liang — AD 507. "But there is much disagreement over the date alone. Moreover, the episodes of his meeting with Wu, king of Liang, and his great easing of Hueike's mind are obvious fictions created by later Zen people," Teacher Docho had said.

In the meditation hall Mokuzu had no way to learn more about the historical Bodhidharma. But for understanding the koan "What is the true meaning of Bodhidharma's coming to China?" his scanty knowledge was no cause for regret: no knowledge was rather welcome for those engaged in solving the traditional koans.

The koan was not asking why or how Bodhidharma came to China, was not concerned with the social phenomenon, but asking what was the true meaning of Buddhism or the essence of Zen. Dissociated from the historical person, the question becomes universal and inseparable from the mind of the trainee. In other words, it is only a variation of "What is Your Original Nature?" or "Listen to the Sound of One Hand."

Therefore, when asked by their disciples about the Bodhidharma koan, the various Zen masters of the past answered in seemingly odd but truthful ways.

Jaujou: "The arborvitae in the front garden."[27] Dungshan: "I shall tell you when the river Dung flows backward."[28] His disciple Lungya: "Let me answer when the stone turtle begins to understand our tongue."[29] Shianglin: "Manifold thanks for your lengthy meditation."[30] Yunmen: "I see the mountains in the sunset."[31] And Shingkung: "I shall answer when without a rope you rescue a man down a well"....[32]

Those answers affirmed that the true meaning of Buddhism, the essence, is in the mind of each individual trainee and that it cannot be grasped by words, because words are fated to detach from it.

Mokuzu kept meditating on how to live in each situation as loyal as possible to his original nature. He looked like a dwarf star in the dark meditation hall.

46

Assistant to the Dormitory Inspectors

Mokuzu was giving his undivided attention to solving the Dharma-function koans one after another like water rounding numerous mountains.

The snowbound monastery was quiet and looked retrenched. The shadows of the training monks were short, and the moon during night meditation appeared small.

The last third of December was nearing and the season's training term was also soon to close. In the meditation hall the direct monk relaxed his stick and increased the hours of free meditation. The work became lighter; mostly the monks attended to making straw sandals and bamboo besoms in the shed among the cedars below the meditation hall. In the residential quarters the monks of the various offices began a meticulous cleaning in preparation for the New Year.

For Mokuzu there was vitality only in the world of the koan he was pondering. In these days Zen Master Tengai had given him case 42 of *Biyan lu*, "What Nice Snow!"

> When the layman Pang was leaving Yaushan's temple, Yaushan ordered ten disciples to see him to the gate. There Pang remarked as he pointed to the falling snow,
> "What nice snow! Each flake settles to its place."
> The disciple Chyuan asked, "Where is that?" at which Pang directly slapped him.
> Chyuan remarked, "You sure are rough!"
> "If with your sort of understanding you claim to be a Zennist, Yamaraja will grant you no freedom," said Pang.
> "How about you?" returned Chyuan.
> Pang slapped him again and said, "Though you see, you are like a blind man, and though you speak, you are like a mute."
> Shyuedou comments: Were I Chyuan I should have flung snow in Pang's face the moment he first spoke.[1]

Properly speaking, Pang must have come from poor circumstances. However, in an embellished biography written years later, he was described as a rich man who, disliking the bother of being rich, loaded all his belongings onto a boat and scuttled it in the lake Dungting, or the river Shiangjiang. Indeed he was a devotee of Zen and practiced Zen philosophy in his family. Content with honest poverty, he and his wife and son and daughter made bamboo ware, which the daughter peddled. But how they each met their end is odd.

> When Layman Pang was about to die, he told his daughter, Lingjau, "Nothing is substantial: all things are phantoms that appear and disappear according to how you are. Now please step into the sun and tell me when it is noon."
> Lingjau stepped out and hurriedly reported,
> "Father, it is just noon, besides, the sun is eclipsed. Come and see with your own eyes."
> "Don't be silly!" said he.
> "But it is so," said she.

Layman Pang went to the window. While he was there, Lingjau withdrew to a couch and gracefully sat cross-legged and departed this life. Seeing her gone, Pang said with a smile,

"My daughter has performed an agile feat!" and he gathered firewood and disposed of her.

Seven days later Prefectural Chief Yugung came to inquire after Pang's health. Pang laid a hand on his knee, stared him long in the face, and spoke:

"Please maintain the view that every existence is empty and do not misconceive that emptiness is existence. I bid you keep yourself well. Everything is like a shadow or an echo." Thereupon an indefinable aroma filled the room. Pang appeared to be meditating. Yugung hastily tried to revive him, but Pang had departed this life.

A wind swept the marsh and a heavenly sound was soundlessly transmitted. Over Mt. Sumeru the moon passed with full golden color.

In accordance with his will, Pang was to be cremated and his ashes scattered on the water. When the funeral was about to be performed, Yugung sent a messenger to Pang's wife and son to inform them of the foregoing events. At the news, Pang's wife exclaimed,

"That stupid daughter and ignorant old man left without warning. It's beyond endurance!" She went to inform her son, tilling the garden.

"Pang and Lingjau have passed away."

Dropping his hoe, the son cried in disbelief, "Sha!" and he too departed this life.

"What a stupid son!" said his mother, and she cremated him.

The villagers on hearing this story felt queer. Pang's wife erelong paid a farewell visit to each house. Then she renounced the world. Indeed she vanished, and no one knew what became of her.[2]

Mokuzu viewed this legend of the Pang family with curiosity because he had once dreamed of living a reclusive life with Ena on a south-facing hillside.

At the winter solstice he was asked to help the Manjusri attendant to re-paper the shojis. In front of the bare wood frames set under the eaves, he stopped his work to look up at the sky.

Myriad snowflakes were coming from the indistinguishable ashen sky and soon landing after traveling with a lively motion unexpected of inorganic matter. Fixing them with his eyes, Mokuzu grew confused whether he was rising or the snow falling. Truly each flake had a unique shape and locus. Pang's admiration "What nice snow!" could be the only words at such a sight. Snow-flakes were said to have no more than four basic forms, plate, stellar crystal, column, and needle; yet each flake was unique. Nonetheless, they all sooner or later came to rest and ceased to move, when before they had been ever so lively. Piled on the earth, they were consigned to the still and silent world.

'Pang's remark obviously conveyed his view on the destiny of all forms, including himself, while Zennist Chyuan saw merely the snow landing. Yet I can't believe Chyuan never faced the death of a near relative. Why wasn't he reminded of the way of life and death? If he was so happy that he did not see it as the gravest concern, why was he training under Yaushan, and further, how could he have been among his highest disciples?

'I already know the loss of Ena. The gravity of death needn't be pointed out to me by any layman or Zen master (and I'm not entirely satisfied with my master's way). Whoever knows the loss of a loved one must be able to understand why Shyuedou commented, "Were I Chyuan I should have flung snow in Pang's face..." Indeed, why speak of mortality to one who knows the sorrow of death? What I'd like to know is what I should do with my sad, unwelcome experience.

'...I suppose Layman Pang is teaching, "Live like falling snow, it's a nice life." Zen Master Tengai keeps saying, "Relinquish your desires and live day and night for the benefit of others." Both recommend effacement of thought and feeling. The only difference is that Tengai demands that it be done for others, while Pang disregards social and ethical activity. For Pang, self-relinquishment is purely the purpose. For my Zen master, self-relinquishment is the way to help others — or, it could be said, helping others is the way to relinquish oneself.

'Should I relinquish myself living on a mountain or staying in a thronged street? Either way my mind would be the same, although for society the effect of my deed would not be the same at all. But the argument is nonsense, for I can hardly relinquish myself! I can do so only partly and occasionally. To relinquish oneself while in fact one is maintaining one's life is impure and imperfect. Life is innately impure, from which premise alone I can deduce how I should live.'

"Say, Mokuzu — " He was addressed by the Manjusri attendant, Saiso, who was brushing starch from an earthenware mortar onto a frame. Mokuzu fitted it with new shoji paper.

"Do you know anything about the Soto school? I spent six years at Eiheiji."

"I've had no cause to know, but it could be useful to learn why you left to come here."

"I might tell you someday when we're better acquainted. For now suffice it to say that Soto Zen is quite profound." Saiso wiped the back of his hand across his runny nose, red from the cold, and went on,

"In a word, they just meditate without seeking anything. Pure meditation is so important to them that all other acts, such as walking, sitting, reclining, dressing, and eating, are regarded as merely its variants. Such meditation is not the means to attain Buddhahood but the practice of Buddhahood. The Soto school believes we are all endowed with Buddha nature, and therefore we can't possibly get it by meditation or any other means. So our only work is to recognize its presence within us and to practice it.

"You must know of the Chinese Zen master Hungjy. He said, 'Truth is attained solely by quiet meditation and tacit study. When we are not affected by outside phenomena and our mind is open, our reflection can become admirably bright, enabling us to admit everything into our life and put it in correct order. Moreover, when we relinquish worldly matters, we can be as clear as the empty sky, and exist by ourselves without being dark, and be satisfied by our own absolute spirituality.'"[3] Hearing this, Mokuzu could not help thinking of Unkai in Ryotanji, and he inquired,

"Manjusri Attendant, according to Hungjy it would seem the Soto school attained the ultimate spiritual depth. I wish to know, is their way practiced even now in Eiheiji?"

"Don't induce me to refer to the present. Such talk tends to get critical, and criticism isn't fitting in a trainee, whose way of life is to take responsibility for all that surrounds him," Saiso said coolly, and he carried inside a finished shoji. He then returned to the eaves, applied more starch, and said, now rather warmly,

"Well, as I said, I spent six years there and was quite earnest in my sitting meditation day after day. Yet my mind didn't become brighter at all, and instead I felt it rather darkened. My meditation was like wearing down a sumi stick. In addition, though you needn't know it, my hate toward a certain woman only increased. Practicing sitting meditation, I felt...oh, sorry, I wasn't going to relate any personal concern.

"So, one day I happened to read that Hungjy's way of meditation was strongly discredited in a letter by the Zen teacher Dahuei. Dahuei was an outstanding contemporary of Hungjy in the Linji school. He accused Hungjy of being 'an evil teacher of silent reflection' and said, 'The evil teacher buries his trainees alive in a pit.'[4] Dahuei wished to say that we can't recognize our Buddha nature nor practice it, even though we are born with it, unless we go through the hard training of koan study. In other words, he says that there's great awakening only after great questioning, which is koan study, and that koans can be studied by sitting meditation. For Dahuei the koan is thus a necessary condition, and sitting meditation one effective way to solve it. Now, you see, what for Hungjy is the very purpose, for Dahuei is nothing but a method." Having spoken, Saiso again carried in a finished shoji, but this time he remained at length laboring to fit it back in place.

Mokuzu looked at the sky and thought how nice it would be just to enjoy the falling snow. 'Even Layman Pang had to allude to human life at the sight of snowflakes. It's obvious the monks' major and his fellows are staying here only to fulfill the qualification for obtaining a local temple — it's a mere necessary condition. But their discontent over their present monastic life must greatly resemble Pang's seeing snow as a means to understand life rather than as something simply to enjoy. Life, or in this case snow, can be an end in itself, whereas Zen or studying Zen possibly is not....'

Mokuzu heard a stir. The monks' major was leading a line of monks up the snowy path from the work shed. At the same time, the Manjusri attendant came out and said,

"Mokuzu, you're perspicacious, so you'll not lose sight of the fact that the aim of both Soto and Rinzai is to live up to the Dharma realized by Sakyamuni Buddha, albeit in nuance these Zen schools differ. Trainees may point to the faults of one or the other, but the concern of both is Buddhism. A deep understanding is the key to finding harmony in the differences, while a shallow understanding is a sure way to see conflict among whatever."

The monks' major and the others, each shouldering three finished brooms, advanced into the side garden. Their split-toed cotton footwear was hidden in the snow, and their dark work clothes were covered with snowflakes.

"Mokuzu, an attendant to the master was looking in confusion all over the place for you. Quick, be off to the master or we all must receive his shouts. Manjusri Attendant — can't you see if you use monks under my charge, everyone but you will be troubled? While you enjoy company and progress well with your labor, I must be wigged for poor supervision and productivity," Seigan spoke spitefully and passed on with his followers.

Paying him no heed, Saiso concluded, "So, don't forget, the faults of the Rinzai school will be evoked if all you do is count the number of koans you solve like climbing the rungs of a ladder. Your nature tends to favor speed over elaboration, so I worry. One of the most besetting sins is to misapprehend that your present life is a means to gain some future goal. Do you think it possible to live a more enlightened life than the earnest life of pursing enlightenment? When is there ideal life if you can't find it in the monastery, where the work is to solve koans, those human questions? At this very moment, you see the snow falling and your heart is beating. Is it for the sake of your future or your present? Now go and see the master. Thanks for your help, and never mind about those like the monks' major."

Mokuzu left the Manjusri attendant's residence and went to the south terrace of the meditation hall to change from work clothes to robe. The monks' major and the others had already changed and were resting, leaning their backs against the white wall.

"I pity you, being used here and there without a moment's ease. But be patient till you develop the knack to protect yourself. It's typical in any community, including the monastery, to use others or be used. After all, we're every one of us used by the master, who exploits Zen to use us, and, as might be expected, the seniors follow his example," said the monks' major out of sympathy.

"I don't know what he's using us for, or (isn't it for mutual interest?)...," Mokuzu said (and muttered) as he tightened his cotton-padded belt around his robe.

"Ho! He's using us to gratify his lust for power, of course! He's running for abbot of the head temple — again. It's his third try," said the monks' major as if venting the bitterness of heartburn. Taking Mokuzu for an ignoramus, the others laughed. The monks' major continued,

"Don't you realize the master is educating us just to be his tools? We aren't cattle. How can we feel thanks? You must know he doesn't care if we get sick or wounded. If we aren't completed according to his scheme, we'll be shivered like the pots of a ceramic artist. The former assistant to the direct monk was carried off to a sanatorium in his native region. The master has the vileness to derange a man and no virtue to heal him. I heard Zui continues to meditate beside his mother there on the floor. Another senior, Keizan, hanged himself from a beam of the work shed just months before you came. The day was so hot the stink from where a rat gnawed at his neck filled the vicinity. The master did nothing but order us to spread salt."

Mokuzu had already well perceived the master's ineffectuality and nonchalance toward the dead and the insane; he was too busy organizing the living sane. Likewise, his concern was not how to help the defective and disabled but how to educate the healthy, bright, and willing. "I'm not a psychiatrist, nor a probation officer, nor a philanthropist. I'm the creator of a handful of talented men," he once openly declared in his lecture.

"Mokuzu, beware. Each of us is enslaved in exchange for being certified to preside over a local temple. Do you know what he'll do if we disagree with his teaching and leave this mountain by our choice? He'll stamp our personal history with the red seal of 'exile' or 'deserter' and circulate it to every monastery in the land. That would finish us — we could never secure a local temple and provide for our old parents eagerly awaiting our return. Did you never think about it, eh?"

"Well, I never thought about it as much as you. It's as if I'm seeing like a blind man and speaking like a mute."

"Tut! You'd better be a little more shrewd. As for me, I've put in enough years to qualify for a local temple, and I'm leaving as soon as the Day to Decide One's Course comes at the New Year."

Shoshinji's three highest officers — the observances head, the fiscal head, and the reception head — assisted by the direct monk, interviewed each monk at the New Year to ascertain his wish to stay on for training or to leave. They then sternly commented on his behavior, and, if he was choosing to stay, issued some conditions.

"Anyway, you'd better get yourself to the master's. He has a short temper. And don't tell him anything disadvantageous to us. We want no ricochets."

When he went to the master's room, Mokuzu as he had feared was asked in a hasty tone,

"For what reason didn't you promptly come?" Knowing he would be vilified as incompetent if he alibied, Mokuzu deeply lowered his head and said,

"I am entirely wrong, there's no excuse, I beg your pardon."

"Hm, all right. Tell me what the meditation hall monks are maundering about."

"Master, I don't know. I was assisting the Manjusri attendant in renewing the shojis."

"Nnn! He is a kind senior to you?"

"Yes, he is a kind senior."

"What advice did he give you as you worked together?" The master raised his chin and cast an upward glance.

"He didn't speak. We are prohibited from speaking near the meditating Manjusri."

"I see. Now listen, he came here from Soto Zen. You shouldn't copy him. Go intently on your decided way, never run after two hares. The Middle Way Sakyamuni Buddha enjoined us to follow does not mean to be in a state of equilibration like a pair of scales; that is a merchant's middle way. Nor is it a bisector, which is only superficially a middle way. Buddha's Middle Way can be realized only after you have been thorough.

"The training term is closing. I know the direct monk is relaxing his supervision so as to give the monks some ease. Naturally they will complain during work and rest. Just tell me, what are they saying?" The master was back at his first question.

"Master, I have no occasion to talk with any of them."

"You may not, but they have ample occasion — or do you mean you are caring only about yourself? A man's worth depends on how much he can contribute at the very time he is in a busy fix. You must train yourself to benefit others. Tell me their worries regarding the day of deciding to stay or leave."

"Master, it grieves me that I have been trying only to be like a falling snowflake; I never considered any fellow trainees as distinct from rocks or trees. Please be reminded that I am but a newcomer." Mokuzu carried on creditably.

Zen Master Tengai's face broadened with the smile of a genial old man, and he said,

"It may well be. You are after all a pure and tender trainee. But that is the very reason I recommend you to take the offer I am now going to spell out, with my slight anxiety over whether you can bear up."

Whereupon, the master explained how important an academic career was in the world in which people are judged by title and degree.

"In society, a degree is like an umbrella on a rainy day. You may not mind being drenched, but people will pity and disdain you and hardly listen to your teaching." The master then noted one peculiarity of laymen,

"They may climb a mountain to see alpine nature, but never with their subjectivity. Before setting out, they must be told how the flora and fauna are worth seeing, and once on the mountain they will check off the name of each thing after taking merely a glimpse at it."

"Master, it may be true that the world attaches great importance to titles, and heeds the words of those who are titled. But I think priests needn't conform to the trends of the world. Drawing a clear line of demarcation could be the very teaching to give worldly people instead of putting ourselves on their level. National Teacher Daio used to say that 'our study ought to be real study and our enlightenment real enlightenment.'"[5] Mokuzu ventured to express his honest opinion, for he knew that perpetual submission made the master suspect a trainee's loyalty.

Zen Master Tengai had expected that he would be cross-questioned, and he put forth more of his tautology:

"Do not misconstrue my intention. I am not saying you should be a fox that borrows a tiger's authority, and of course not saying you should hang out a sheep's head and sell dogmeat. First, my wish is that you will be able to practice your charity of teaching the Dharma without discriminating or deserting anyone in need of it. Avalokitesvara Bodhisattva, whom we call Kannon, assumes the most suitable form for each individual to be saved, and will appear as a scholar for a scholar, a magistrate for a magistrate, and so on.

"Second, you have to know that to persuade others is as hard as to capture an enemy. You must cherish great enthusiasm and exercise great strategy, must appeal to both their reason and their emotion, must stimulate even their interests, and must also take advantage of their weaknesses, for they cling like narcotic addicts to incorrect and injurious views to the detriment of their health.

"Third, you mustn't be ill-timed, and therefore you must keep pace with

611

the age. Be aware that since the war's end, Japan has not been well influenced by the victorious countries, and in every field titles and degrees are valued above real ability and sincerity. Many fools think democracy necessitates destroying all traditions, such as the apprentice system and the guilds.

"Any herb doctor, however excellent, must now submit to a medically licensed physician in accordance with the Medical Act. A great master carpenter, the likes of whom built Todaiji and Horyuji, must be led by the nose by a green architect who, though he holds a degree, is unable to plane a board. Farmers who since their youth have raised crops and livestock are forced to hear the instructions of a bachelor of agriculture, who never touched the soil. The same is true of the relation between the traditional landscape gardener and the new, licensed gardener, who can't shape a tree.

"It is horrible — the trend is spreading even into our Zen world. Scholars read a few Zen classics aided by a dictionary and invent strange new interpretations by borrowing Western logic, and they are deluding a mass of ignorant people. The amount those scholars experienced of the traditional monastery is just the amount they are able to criticize it. They do not know the pain of sitting meditation. They do not know the days of giving up their life in the process of training to see their true nature. Yet they are regarded as leading figures not only in Japan but also in various foreign countries.

"Just the other day too, a young American came here and insisted on meeting me. No sooner did I allow him in than he began to express his so-called Zen view. It was no more than a mix of the writings of those Zen scholars and his own drug experience. Finally he began to rebuke the inefficacy of a Zen education and Zen's contribution to the world. You must know that writing books on Zen is easy if you happen to possess an ounce of fantasy and a ton of immoral principle. The life of a saint can be written while embracing a mistress.

"Now I assume you can see why you should obtain a degree, not as makeup for your exterior but as an essential prelude to enable you to introduce your true teaching."

Mokuzu could not argue; he would be considered to be approving all those whom the master detested. So he replied,

"Master, I now well understand what you say and have in mind. But I don't see how I can obtain the degree you speak of while I am a trainee who has yet to perfect the koan study of this monastery."

"Don't worry. I've figured it all out. As you know, I established Shoshin College. Presently it is a two-year college, but I am exerting myself to promote it to four years. The monastery will then play the role of a graduate course.

"Don't hastily mistake me. I'm not telling you to study there. Just obtain the degree. You would learn nothing in the classroom."

"I don't see how I could earn a degree without attending classes."

"Indeed it is difficult. Therefore I thought, and consulted with our founder, Kanzan, for three days and three nights. The college, even if mine, is within the jurisdiction of the Ministry of Education, and after all there is also the board of trustees and the faculty. I had to devise a procedure whereby you can get the degree without censure and also without hindrance to your monastic study. The answer is to make you an assistant dormitory inspector. That way you will qualify for the degree by occasionally attending the college from the meditation hall. Have you any question at this point?"

Mokuzu realized that the master was reporting what he had predetermined, which meant his report was equal to an order. There was no choice but to say,

"Thank you for your trouble on my behalf. Could you tell me what my task as assistant dormitory inspector would be and whether it can be satisfactorily performed by an immature person like me?"

"Never mind! The duty I am assigning you is very simple, and your youth is an advantage. Most students are eighteen to twenty-five, your age more or less, and you will be able to relate without their feeling stiff. That is important. You will be friendly, yet guide them as I wish. This is the first duty. Another is that you apprise me of the daily happenings, especially the words and conduct of the dean, the professors, the librarian, and the officers, and of the two dormitory inspectors, who will direct you — while you remain alert to them. Your report will benefit my building up of the world's best college from within, and I can then afford to focus more on building up the outer appearance. In short, your duty is to be the liaison and lubricant between me and the college staff."

Just when Mokuzu got back to the meditation hall, the cloud-shaped gong was struck to announce supper. The monks were led down by the direct monk. The dark obscured the snow, but some flakes came into the range of the dim light along the path. Even during the meal Mokuzu could not clear away the unpleasant feeling of having been given an order by an authority — an order dressed up as a kindness. He cried in his mind,

'He's asking only that I spy! Had I refused, he'd surely give me no more koans. Must one use any false means to obtain the truth? How wretchedly impure are these sacred precincts! I never dreamed I'd have to master the art of living while in the process of mastering the artless life. Impurity may extend a person's sphere of influence, but his value becomes as light as pumice.'

ぶ

One day near noon in mid-January Mokuzu walked to Shoshin College, where the new term had begun.

A crooked dirt road descended gently to the college from the western edge of the monastery. Below the road were dense cedars and soon a bamboo grove, and then deciduous forest took over. Above, the monks' terraced vegetable gardens continued until replaced by a graveyard. Up behind was the ridge of the pine mountain that was the background of Shoshinji.

The road was barely wide enough to accommodate the Zen master's private car, and for his sake the snow had been shoved to either side. Mixed with the mire and car exhaust, the snow impressed Mokuzu as being dirtier than any muddy area.

The college buildings were stepped up the mountainside. He came first to the prefab lecture hall, serving also as the students' meditation hall. Subjacent was an eel-like, one-story wooden building, the first-year students' dormitory, titled "Place to Select Buddhas."

He climbed the steep diagonal stone-stepped path to the second level, whereon was the main school building, which was also a flat wooden rectangular structure. High up, a two-story building appeared to be a second dormitory. He stood at the front entrance of the main building. In the yard were planted some pines and cherries, small and ill-tended. But the view of snowy fields spreading in the distance under the blue sky was quite splendid, with villages scattered near the mountains and along the river and the highway. A tablet above the door gave the name of the college in thin sumi, the letters formed as if by a palsied hand.

'The dean's hand,' thought Mokuzu. 'At least he must be a scholar with an honest intellect, for he didn't omit "short" before "college," unlike my Zen master, who always does.'

Getting no response, he went in and opened the sliding door of a room that appeared to be an office. Four persons were devoting themselves to calculating at desks pushed together in a square. To the side a big aluminum kettle was boiling on a stove. Easy chairs were placed about, and at the windows white cotton curtains were drawn shut.

The first to look up registered surprise; it was the nun Shorai from Shogetsuan.

"Oh, Mokuzu, do come in. So the master meant you when he said he would send an able monk to assist the dormitory inspectors. I thought so, didn't I, Miss Iwai?" Shorai caught the attention of the young woman beside her. A blush appeared on the young woman's white face, and she nodded to Mokuzu with a faint smile. She had bright eyes and full lips.

"We often talk about you. For you it may be the first meeting, but I take

614

Miss Iwai with me to the master's lectures, where I privately pointed you out to her. She knows as much about you as I do. Now, Priest Tanishi and Priest Tsugaru, please leave off your work and welcome Mokuzu as your assistant."

"Yes, j-just a moment, please. This'll do, but we must be a little more severe to collect their expenses for light and fuel. Many are bringing in portable electric cookers to make night snacks. Sorry, sorry — I didn't want to forget the sum I just arrived at. Let me introduce myself," the older of the two said in a flurry and looked up through black-framed glasses. He had a thin face with high cheekbones, a small nose, and many wrinkles about his eyes and mouth. His eyes were narrow though mild. One winked with the frequent tick of his upper cheek. He was a Zen priest, with shaven head and patched crude black robe.

As he rose to introduce himself, one of his long sleeves caught the back of the chair, and the sound of ripping was audible. Half standing, he pulled at the sleeve, which swept a ballpoint pen to the floor. He crouched as if going to hide under the desks.

The other dormitory inspector stifled a laugh. The young woman feigned calm, but bit her lip. The nun gazed sternly at the kettle. Mokuzu stood erect with eyes lowered meditatively.

At last the older dormitory inspector straightened up and began his own introduction: "Dreadfully sorry to be so uncouth. My name is Chozen Tanishi. I came two years ago from remote country, Itsuki village in Kyushu. Surely you know the sad folk song, 'I can stay till the lantern festival, then it's good-bye! The sooner the festival the sooner I can be home again. I am but a beggarly serf's daughter, and they are so high, with kimono so fine...'"[6]

He sang in a plaintive tone, but phlegm caught in his throat and he coughed.

"Excuse me, I did not get your given name," Mokuzu said.

"Chozen — 'to surpass Zen.' See? True Zen is beyond Zen study and training. Do you know Jaujou's song? He describes his daily life: 'Amornings around two I rise at the cock's cry and behold how shabby is my dotage. Without priestly robe and skirt am I, and yet, I have my surplice, if crumpled. My sash is threadbare, my drawers so tattered I know not where to step in. Much as my head be covered with dandruff, truly I once yearned to train myself and free the sufferers of this world. Who then could foreknow that I should become this very sort of sluggard?'[7] You don't know it? Never heard it? Amazing! What is your Zen master teaching you? Only koans? They are but the traces of those Zen masters' youth. Well, we shall have time anon to discuss it. For now, please note my name is Chozen. Let me introduce my partner, Seisho Tsugaru. He is in charge of the upper students, which is to say, I am in charge of the lower."

Priest Tsugaru had the cleanest face and sharpest eyes Mokuzu had seen in Shoshinji. He talked in a crisp, unreserved way, with some exaggeration, and no one took him literally.

"Actually I too am a Shoshinji monk, but I've been kept away for some years, forced to be a raiser of beasts. Shoshinji dislikes the educated — I was graduated from Taisho University before coming to the monastery. I don't know why you've been sent over here; doubtless you're being trained to take Koko's place someday. This April he'll be sent to America as Dr. Yasaka's successor, though it'll be a crazy burden for him. Of course Zen Master Tengai plans to have me fill Koko's position and you mine. But I tell you I won't be here, and I don't mind if you report my unwillingness to put myself into his plan. I simply want you to know you shouldn't lose sight of yourself — and don't be astonished at the sight of our students, supposed to be the best imaginable, according to the master's declaration."

"Priest Tsugaru, you are saying farewell the moment you meet. Isn't that a bit extreme?" protested Shorai as she set to making tea.

"Well, I've seen all there's to see here and I'm going to change my training monastery," Tsugaru answered her.

"You are too young to find peace anywhere," remarked Tanishi, to which Tsugaru answered, "You are too old to find trouble." Mokuzu alone took it seriously.

"Come to the stove everybody. Miss Iwai, would you offer Mokuzu this cup — you must be the same age, yes? Mokuzu, she is the only child of a master of flower arrangement in Nagoya and has been with us at Shogetsuan since October. She gets bored, so I bring her here."

Mokuzu glanced at Miss Iwai, then turned his eyes and noticed a brownish overcoat and a yellow silk scarf hung casually at the entrance. He glanced again at her. She had on a sweater with large flowered patterns and a grass-green thick wool skirt. Her hair was done in a pageboy. She looked at him only when his face was not turned in her direction.

"See, Mokuzu? There is the pleasant show of beauty even here. I have regained my juvenescence," said Tanishi.

"I'm not joking. After she arrived I got new spectacles and began taking medication for my facial neuralgia," he continued emphatically. Miss Iwai smiled at Tanishi and at Mokuzu, though each smile had a different implication.

Mokuzu felt he was basking in the sun as he recalled the warmth, softness, brightness, animation, and cleanliness that all young women commonly exuded.

'My monastic life resembles life in an air-raid shelter, with everything indifferent to anything flowery. The world of the past Zen patriarchs is as tenebrious as the negative of a photograph. Their world appeals to none of my five senses. Where then is the truth? Is it here with my senses, or somewhere beyond? But the important question isn't where is the truth but what is the truth for my own life.'

Mokuzu felt the heat of the stove against his knees. On the opposite side were the knees of Miss Iwai.

"...Mokuzu, are you with us? I was telling them how we happened to meet in the sweet potato garden, and about my teacher's once meeting your grandfather."

Mokuzu apologized for his meditative state and added, "Oh yes, I was entirely forgetting to thank you and your teacher for preparing me to come up to Shoshinji."

"Don't mention it. You are giving us far more pleasure. But won't you answer Miss Iwai's wonderment?"

"Excuse me?..." Mokuzu looked at Miss Iwai. She blushed again, and instead of her Tanishi spoke,

"After all, you both are young. The proximity of age buries the gulf between laywoman and trainee, whereas there's no chance of accord between one like me, who escaped death in a rain of shells, and those of you who sprang up in peace like mushrooms. What the young lady wanted to ask in her diffident manner was why you came to train in Zen. It is such an uncommon path for a youth today, and for one who doesn't look like an ordinary trainee, and who must also look nice in a suit and tie."

"Oh dear! It wasn't such a private question. I only wanted to know what charmed him to the hardship of Zen training, because it might be a hint for my own path," corrected Miss Iwai.

Everyone quieted and looked at Mokuzu. The kettle kept boiling.

From the direction of a classroom a noise issued, and Tanishi stood up — "Doggone it, again I forgot the buzzer!" His skirts flew as he made for the wall by the entrance. That moment a stout person flung open the door and came in with bald head down. He and Tanishi would have collided had he not ducked through beneath the sleeve of Tanishi's robe. Tanishi humbly apologized,

"Sorry, sorry, Dean, we were so absorbed in serious talk — " He pushed a button, sending a furious buzz down the corridor, and persisted at it till the dean with a faint smile nudged his hand aside.

"Never mind, I already dismissed my class, it's the only one today." The dean went to wash the chalk from his hands. His round brownish face resembled a raccoon dog's. His old dark suit had stiffened like hide where not deeply dusted with chalk. The nun Shorai attempted an introduction:

"The Reverend Dean Shiba — "

"I know, I know. You are Mokuzu, son of Tangenji in Tanba. I visited there once or twice a few months before the defeat; I still held the title of president of Manchuria University. I received great kindness from your father."

Miss Iwai brought tea on a tray to the dean. He took the cup and saucer, reached in his pocket, and withdrew a crushed pack of cigarettes. Tanishi extended his hand to hold the tea while the dean lit a cigarette. The dean then took back the cup and began to sip, leaving Tanishi with the saucer.

"Despite his kind nature, your father is obstinate! Zen Master Tengai entreated him over and over to serve as dean, but he continued to refuse," the dean proceeded. Then, seeing the two women, he abruptly interjected,

"Where's lunch? Bring for him too. What's the meaning of work if we can't take proper refection?"

Shorai and Miss Iwai left the room.

"Yes, the Zen master was displeased, nay, he was wroth. I tell you he'll never forget his failure to bring in your father. So be careful. He never backs down once his mind is set. If he can't engage the father, he'll try the son. Knowing this, I fail to see why you came of your own free will. Did his psychokinesis directly appeal to you, or are you mischievously playing with fire?"

Mokuzu kept silent. Tsugaru then asked the dean outright:

"Why did you accept the job?"

"Thanks to Mokuzu's father; his refusal gave me the position. It's defined as the deanship, but in addition I must serve as professor and caretaker. Your father, Mokuzu, was highborn and is by nature faithful to his own feeling and opinion. He loves plants. In contrast I'm lowborn and respect the life of beasts. As a result of the war, I had to flee back from Manchuria with my wife and five school-aged children. When I got Zen Master Tengai's offer I had many thoughts, but I gave top priority to my children's education, yes, that's how it was."

"And how are they now?" Tsugaru asked sharply.

"By virtue of my patience and my wife's help, all but one graduated from Tokyo University and are now professors in various universities. Of course it's been quite hard for me to have to hang on to Zen Master Tengai's sleeve since I too am a proud and profound Zen specialist. But what is the essential power of Zen? To practice patience, the patience to live on. Sixth Patriarch Hueineng lived perforce among a band of hunters. During those fifteen years he actually must have killed and eaten many deer and boar. In Zen it is easy to die like Layman Pang and his family, but hard to live on...; at bottom, not many things are worth protecting by the sacrifice of one's wife and children. Living faithful to one's feeling and thought is no doubt the second best way to live...and not the best at any rate."

The nun and Miss Iwai brought in lunch. As Miss Iwai set a tray of food before Mokuzu, he saw her gentle hands.

618

47

Percussive Realities

Mokuzu went straight to the college after chanting, meditation, interview with the master, and breakfast. The other monks had to perform monastery tasks and mendicancy, and some envied him and saw him with the eyes of beasts of burden.

There was a thaw, and from early morning water dripped at the eaves as if the day were rainy, though it was clear. Old roof tiles left during winter beside a building were now exposed. Fresh green weeds had begun to grow around a sheaf of boards to be used for repairing the sides of the bell tower. The run-off had worn many channels in the monastery ground, and the road to the college was slushy.

Mokuzu usually arrived just after the students were done with their chanting and meditation. Then before breakfast they had to clean the buildings inside and out, led by the two dormitory inspectors. At 8:30 classes began. The number of professors, including Dean Shiba, was two, or at most three, and they showed up in due time.

Tsugaru carried a warning stick and presided over the work of cleaning, while Tanishi habitually read a newspaper as if utilizing every odd moment.

"Ah, me! At last America has begun bombing North Vietnam! Can't they learn from history?" Tanishi wailed and went on,

"It's the same process as Japan's assault on China, which drew us into the quicksand of war. Last summer's Tonkin Gulf incident is very like the Japanese Guandong Army's staging of an explosion on the tracks outside Mukden and blaming the Chinese Army as a pretext for initiating armed operations. I'm sure this special war to oppress the South Vietnamese National Liberation Front can't be contained as a newly escalated local conflict. It'll turn into an all-out war. Why? Because China is backing the Vietnamese. And with its regard for history, China never renders futile the lessons of history. Don't you agree?"

Nobody responded. The nun Shorai was diligently dusting the book-shelves. Miss Iwai was preparing tea. Mokuzu was writing out a list of classroom hours attended by the second-year students as well as their credits attained, having been asked the previous day to do so by Dean Shiba.

"Look, if I dare comment from a Zen viewpoint, it's a typical case of 'War comes of neglecting to sever what ought to be severed.'[1] Mokuzu, don't you see?"

Mokuzu was embarrassed at being addressed so abruptly. Shorai dauntlessly took over, requesting an explanation,

"Do you mean America should have trounced Vietnam at the point when Communist influence was aroused?"

"No, no, I respect the principle of self-determination of peoples. Moreover, I'm a pacifist. What I mean is America shouldn't have allowed the rise of its own military despotism. It's axiomatic that a nation will dispatch armies abroad when its domestic politics are in disarray." Tanishi expressed his trenchant, conclusive opinion, but again there came no response to advance the topic.

After an interval Tanishi raised his voice anew. His delivery was polite, but his manner undeniably curt:

"So, Mokuzu, who is responsible for this war?"

"Well, how do you expect me to make you a correct answer?"

"Clearly your training is not yet hitting the nail on the head. It's obvious. All responsibility rests on us Zen priests. Only because we are negligent in our work are we unable to make the world transcend its egotistic attachment and its insistence on relative values, and we are letting people uselessly kill inestimable human life. If I may go a step further: All responsibility for the war in Vietnam rests on my incompetent shoulders, yes, I am guilty, and I feel deep mortification. Frankly, latter-day Zen priests, including me, have comprehended 'Huanglung's three barriers' with our intelligence only, and we have no ability to practice them."

Tanishi strained his face with its twitching cheek; he looked like a marionette. Miss Iwai carrying a tray of tea smiled at Mokuzu.

"Good morning." Dean Shiba spoke as he entered with head down.

"Dean, your cuffs are muddy. Wait a second, I'll fetch a cloth," said Tanishi, and he moved hither and thither.

"Never mind. I dressed to come by motorbike. The road is wretched now with the thaw. There was a snowslide near my temple, but no one was hurt."

"Your wife must be uneasy," said the nun, handing him tea.

"Oh, she's quite enlightened in her way. She can keep dozing by the fire at such a moment. Where is Dormitory Inspector Tsugaru?"

"Surely he's supervising the cleaning. Shall I go find him?" replied Tanishi.

"You needn't. But later tell him not to be too strict with them, especially with the second-year ones, who will soon graduate. They're in a happy period now, and we should tolerate a certain measure of laxity." The dean then turned to Mokuzu,

"Thank you for your trouble. I assume they all qualify for graduation. But for the sake of world peace, have the good sense to hike any doubtful grades, do you follow? And, I have something for you." The dean took a multi-folded calligraphy paper from an inner pocket.

Mokuzu opened it out. Across it were written in sumi a circle, a triangle, and a square, slightly overlapped from right to left. The dean offered an explanation,

"It's not my idea; I copied it from the original by the priest Sengai of Hakata. One of Zen Master Tengai's laymen, you know, built up a fortune selling petroleum. Though I don't know why, he loves to collect anything by Sengai, who wrote and drew to teach the common people plainly about Buddhism. The other day this layman came to ask Zen Master Tengai to write an introduction to a book of photographs of his collection, which he wishes to publish. Of course our Zen master accepted the request, and then promptly asked me to do it. See? I must be a ghostwriter! Well, it's unimportant. The point is, I came across the original of this yesterday as I was examining the collection, and I thought a copy of it would benefit you."

Mokuzu, still seated, looked for the meaning in the drawing, which rather impressed him as an awkward and crummy article. Shorai and Miss Iwai and then even Tanishi regarded it from behind his chair. Miss Iwai had to move in so close to keep any part of her person from being touched by Tanishi that her breast for a second pressed Mokuzu's shoulder.

"I can make no sense of it," she avowed with sparkling eyes.

"I know the work — it's typical of Sengai. Let me tell..." Tanishi desired to talk, but the dean gestured him aside and spoke,

"Dr. Yasaka has given his personal analysis, according to which the three forms are the phases of perpetual life: the circle is formlessness, wherein is yet no separation of Darkness and Light; the triangle is form emerging from formlessness; and the square — a combination of triangles — is the multitudinosity of things.[2] Scarcely having gone through hard real life, Dr. Yasaka understands Zen by relying on his philosophical speculation. Hence no vigor arises in the process of reading his works. I am not giving you this with his sort of understanding. The picture was fashioned to aid the ordinary layman, who has no recourse but to do his best in his given situation. You too are no exception. You'd better understand it in a significant way."

Mokuzu sensuously took the circle to be himself meditating as one man with a koan in the meditation hall, and he thought,

'If so, then the square is my life at the college, where I must abandon the quiet of the meditation hall and be practical. The triangle between is the guidance from my Zen master, who expects me to harmonize my life torn at either end. Indeed I have to unify my character in three different worlds, and the incoherence was beginning to vex me. As might be expected of a dean, Dean Shiba perceives the problem.'

Mokuzu thanked him. The dean smiled warmly and sipped his tea.

Tsugaru hurried in and pushed the buzzer as he complained,

"Dormitory Inspector Tanishi, how can you so often forget the buzzer? Today there's a first-year class in the first hour!"

"Oh, I committed a blunder! Yes — only the second-year students have no class. But it's deplorable the first-year students don't show up simply because they hear no buzzer. Well then! I'll go fetch them! Mokuzu, would you assist me?" said Tanishi, and he took with him a warning stick.

Mokuzu followed him down the steep stone steps.

"Careful, it's slippery....The dean appears pleased with you....That makes me happy. After all, to be liked is most important in this ordinary world, yes, though it was the least convincing law for me in my youth....Young people tend to attach greater importance to righteousness, equality, and purity." Without looking back Tanishi spoke in a reminiscing tone.

They passed the lecture-and-meditation hall and descended to a level where a latrine area was becoming swamped, though whether from melting snow or the students' cleaning was undeterminable. Tanishi halted and spoke as if confiding a secret,

"You know, the first-year students are somehow of particularly bad quality this year, despite their being strictly as well as naturally selected. Last spring twenty-two entered; now only half remain. Many left of their own accord, and some were expelled for acting miles apart from what the founder, Zen Master Tengai, expected. You might think the remaining eleven must then be excellent, but far from it. Could it be the changing times?...All are spoilt, complacent, spiritless wet blankets with no sense of solidarity."

Behind the latrines was the first-year dormitory, "Place to Select Buddhas." At the entrance Tanishi with both hands gripped his warning stick apeak and proclaimed,

"Attention! Surmount all hardship and hasten to class!"

Perhaps his molars were gone; at any rate, his tone was unfocused. Some stir of response was audible from the rooms along a passageway.

"All righty, let's quit this game and accept the situation. Keep track of the score — I'm coming out on top."

"What's the difference, sleeping here or there?"

"Hey, Sato, toss me that comb. My hair's a magpie's nest. How sad for Miss Iwai if she sees it!"

Still at the entrance, Tanishi suddenly piped,

"Lend an ear! I shall make you a present of reciting 'Virility' by Bito Jishu!

> "To be a patriot you must be a man
> Who values Right, for it is the source of Light.
> Moderns as if they were women

Regard only looks and words and are ashamed
To perform their duty as men.
Quickly abandon your female behavior
And hasten to see what makes a man.
A fine horse does not rely on its coat,
Nor does a patriot. He establishes his life aim."[3]

Tanishi thereupon heeled about, skirts waving, to go back to the office. On the steep stone steps he tripped forward, exposing a hairy calf, and, catching his balance with the warning stick, said half to himself,

"This is a dangerous spot. Public facilities ought to be designed in the kindest way for the elderly and infirm. He who built this knows only to go straight ahead. I'll give him no more than a score of eighty as a Zen master." Turning back to Mokuzu, he took another unsteady stance,

"Of the first-year students, the second group is better. Generally they're older and are sent from local business organizations as their future executives. The first group is horrible. They're children of local temples, but I can't imagine them turning into local priests unless an educational miracle transpires. Yet they're exempt from dorm and tuition charges. The second group bears the cost. The combination of the two is the invention of the Zen master, who can display his real talent by this sort of Zen management or Zen economics."

When they returned to the office they found Dean Shiba looking at the schedule. Soon he left, after telling Mokuzu,

"I'm off to lecture on the philosophy of religion. Today's subject is interesting, so come as soon as your chores are done."

Mokuzu spent another hour finishing the list. A monk was required to bow with palms joined in veneration whenever he entered or left a room. As Mokuzu did so at the classroom, the students all stared at him. He had to bow when he took his seat too.

The blackboard was as unclear as the sleety sky, for Dean Shiba kept writing over what he had written. Everywhere he scribbled important technical words, names and dates, and the sources of his quotations, in Chinese, Sanskrit, English, or German.

He did not prepare a notebook; yet as if reading from a text he kept up an orderly lecture as he paced back and forth, shoulders stooped, hand in pocket. He was not detached in his introduction of historical figures but presented them as if he were each one. In his eagerness he forgot himself as well as the students before him, and reasonably he did not see Mokuzu enter.

"So it is a daily happening," he said, and hastily he wrote *Taglichkeit*, and continued, "Getting rid of daily happenings was the gravest concern of Gautama Siddhartha, who became Sakyamuni Buddha, and the same could be presumed of Jesus Christ.

623

"Heidegger called the man engrossed in daily happenings *das Man*, defining it as 'he who loves idle talk, who flourishes with curiosity, and who is full of ambiguity.' This is not at all hard to understand, for it is describing you. Now, our Sakyamuni Buddha called the same man 'a different species.'" Here the dean swiped the blackboard with his arm and jotted down the Sanskrit *puthujjana*.

"To *puthujjana* he gave the meaning 'a downright fool who lacks self-awareness and repeats life and death in vain'...a splendid definition of some of us. What did Jesus say of such people?" The dean scribbled at the upper right corner,

> As it is written, the people sat down to eat and drink, and rose up to play
> — 1 Corinthians 10:7.

Dusting off his hands, he asked himself, "What does this all mean? In brief, I will say it is the inevitable process of reflection and establishment of 'self,' the subjecthood of the personality; that is, these men recognized themselves as an individual self rather than a 'homogeneous man' in a 'homogeneous mass,' which had been primitive society."

Mokuzu was astonished not by the profound learning of the dean, nor by his passionate lecture style, but by the students.

The room was large enough for as many as forty, and there were indeed as many desks and chairs. But only eleven were present, and they had taken seats far from one another, out of respect for, and to secure, their individuality or privacy. They were multifariously dressed, some in training robes like Mokuzu, though their hair grew long, some, following Zen layman style, in kimono and hakama, some in sack suit with necktie, some in jeans and sweater.

One at the very center front impressed Mokuzu as odd for not turning like the others to look when he came in. His round head with short stiff hair resembled a chestnut bur. His cheeks slightly drooped with surplus flesh. He wore a birch-colored sweater and old jeans. He did not turn, no doubt because he was practically asleep, head erect atop round shoulders. As he labored against the pleasure of dozing off, his head began to rock. At last he surrendered and put his brow to the desk, threw his arms over it, and began to snore with a sound like the bass notes of a bullfrog.

The dean as he paced the platform could ignore the figure but not the sound. It was drowned out while he spoke. But despite his passion he had to breathe occasionally and pause as he wrote, with the effect that the snores were added to the noise of scribbling that accompanied his lecture.

"Greek philosophers thought that reason distinguishes men from beasts. True, man because he can reason is lord of all creation, whence he was named 'homo sapiens' by Carolus Linnaeus. Diogenes at Sinope jested that man must have reason or a rope to hang himself. Plato's motto was, Persist in following the demonstration wherever it leads."[4] The dean evidently intended to furnish sources. But just then the sleeping student broke wind with a reverent tone like the note of a fluegelhorn.

The room was stunned. Tolerant though he was, the dean was blown off his thought. He took a baton, and he vehemently percussed the sleeper's desk, shouting,

"Wake up! How can you sleep away the time like a pig?"

The offender suddenly stood, but dared not rub his eyes or yawn out of regard for the dean. Seemingly unaware of why he was standing, he looked back at the others as if expecting their help. Mokuzu saw his eyes. They were wide open but had no spirit. They looked like two fat tadpoles on the verge of absorbing their tails. Abruptly he began to answer a non-existent question,

"Yes, sir, I got her into a sweet potato field. We grappled for a while, and the circumstances gave me good cause to get her to play ball. Only, the milk of the runners blackened our skin all over, yeah, that was a nuisance."

"Hold your tongue! How far are you drugged by sleep?" The dean thumped the desk and grieved,

"Don't you know what place this is? This is Shoshin Short College, under the direction of Shoshinji Monastery! Did Zen Master Tengai found it after years of effort — even to the extent of making many enemies — to raise a student like you? Is he running about day and night like a beggar to gather money to maintain the college to nursle your sort? I too, for whose sake am I curtailing my time, which ought to be given to perfecting my magnum opus? Don't make clowns of us, Kawada! For shame! I now grant you the opportunity to apologize."

There was no sign of emotion, certainly not penitence: Kawada just kept standing, his stout figure and dull eyes making him seem impudent.

The dean clasped his hands at his back, resumed pacing, and spoke low,

"Kawada, you are one day to become a priest. It is formidable that youths like you and not the older generation are perpetuating the rotten convention. You're like new wine in old wineskins. You're lazy as Lawrence. How can you expect to become a priest and lead others?"

"He's competent enough to become a Rinzai priest but absolutely not a Shingon priest! My sect may be on the wane, but it wouldn't for a second consider him eligible. From novice to archbishop we Shingon priests are a little more conscientious as disciples of Buddha. Ha ha ha!" came a jeer from the back, obviously disdaining the Rinzai school and the Zen sect altogether and not just Shoshinji, its college, and the dean, nor Kawada alone.

The speaker, seated near Mokuzu, had down-sloping eyes, a shaven head, and a three-day beard. He wore a creamy turtleneck and new jeans.

The dean deserted Kawada, turned to this other student, and responded first quietly, then with passion,

"Well, Hoden Soma, I detect insincerity in your words. According to your personal history, you have already graduated from a decent university and also been beneficed as a respectable local priest of the Shingon sect. Yet you stated that your reason for desiring to enter this school was your dissatisfaction over studying merely the Shingon sect until you know true enlightenment. Even so, I see no spirit of inquiry nor a merciful heart, but only a lazy and foul nature that presumes on other's care — that is, you can't forget your go-as-you-please student days and are unwilling to face adult life, which is plain and yet difficult because it requires your responsibility. In short, you are a hypertrophied baby who has not yet found his subjecthood in society. Your derision of Kawada is a heavier sin than his ill conduct in class."

"How wonderful, Dean, is your analysis! I know analysis is often exercised with foxy intent. You gained no results from tossing pearls at Kawada-pig and wanted to relieve your chagrin by indicating my short-comings," retorted Hoden Soma in his native Tochigi dialect.

The dean smiled with the face of a sly dog.

"You too have analyzed me. Now listen. I want you to realize that your superiority over the others requires you to be an exemplary student."

"Excuse me, Dean; you're putting the cart before the horse. I came here to be well educated so I may later be an example to others, not vice versa. I came because I saw the catalogue, wherein it's clearly written with the signature of Zen Master Tengai, 'This is the world's best college, imbued with the spirit of Kanzan, founder of Shoshinji. Students both day and night do not divide their practice and study of the spirit of Zen. Together they strive to impersonate their model, Sakyamuni Buddha, perfect in wisdom and compassion. Their aim is to contribute by means of their Zen Buddhist personality to the wealth and development of mankind.'

"But how absurd to have judged the college by its catalogue! I thought this could truly be the world's best college and must be where I should study at all costs. Then I came only to find the students are all like pigs, monkeys, and cocks, yes, many fat pigs but not a single thin Socrates. Except for the dean, the professors are all borrowed from other institutions. The library is chaotic; its only books are gifts from publishers or the descendants of some collectors. The librarian, after retiring from being a local primary school principal, is filling his days by acting as sole librarian and the library's sole reader. No student ever reads any of the books. Well, it's useless to anger after

626

being duped. I'm the one to be blamed for falling into the Zen master's trap, and the best I can do for myself is to leave as soon as possible. My thanks to you for all your teaching, Dean, and to the guys whose bad example confirmed for me what the limitation of a human being is."

Having spoken, Hoden Soma stood up, and without a backward glance, and without taking his hands from his pockets, he just left. He was tall, and the stoop of his back well expressed his derision and banter.

The matter had turned rather abruptly. The other students were confused how to act. Then Kawada, who had triggered the affair, rose deliberately and expressed his mind, seemingly in words carefully chosen,

"This is a good chance for me also to determine to leave. After all, it wasn't my idea to come. Getting wind of me, Zen Master Tengai repeatedly called on my dad and badgered him into putting me here. I think by now I've done enough for them both...."

"You silly ass, don't be rash! I still have much to preach to you," scolded the dean, and he addressed Mokuzu,

"Assistant Dormitory Inspector! Why are you so dull-witted? Pursue Soma and ascertain whether he really intends to leave. Don't forget our Zen master's true hope in your handling of the matter!"

Mokuzu rose, joined his palms, and bowed toward the dean. As he left the room he joined his palms and bowed again, then hurried to the first-year dormitory.

Passing the lecture-and-meditation hall, he saw the nun Shorai and Miss Iwai arranging flowers for its altar. They called to stop him. He glanced at Miss Iwai holding pine, plum, and forsythia cuttings. She was scrutinizing him. He pretended he had not heard and went on.

"Priest Hoden Soma! Do you hear me? Please reply. I'm the assistant dormitory inspector," he called at the dorm entrance.

"I am here," came an agreeable response from one of the inmost rooms.

The passageway was dim and moldy.

"May I come in?"

"As you like."

Mokuzu found him lying supine and fully clothed on a bed fixed to the wall. He kept on reading a newly published paperback on Nanten-bo.

Piles of similar books, popular and non-technical, were mixed in with a water heater and a toaster on a desk at the window. A poster taped to the wall read, "Smoking and Drinking Produce a Thousand Evils and Nothing Good." On the white ceiling was written, "Pleasant Sleep, Pleasant Meals, Pleasant Activity, Pleasant Reading."

The letters were formed in a muddy style. Contradicting his mottoes, a milk bottle was stuffed with cigarette butts, and empty wine bottles littered the floor.

'It's an ugly, vicious circle when an intemperate person injures his health and then must concern himself over it to the extent of composing such mottoes,' thought Mokuzu.

"What do you want? Quick, tell me." He did not even sit up.

Mokuzu ignored him and undrew the curtains and opened the window. The same view as that from the office, but at a nearer distance, extended below.

The shadows of the sharp bare treetops were cast on the road leading up to the college. The road was scarcely used except by the students. The basin below, checkered with dark soil and the green of new barley, extended to the terraced fields on the far-side mountains. An old farmer was tending a fire at the riverside to burn insects in old grass; nearby, the wife was trampling the barley. The sky was clear, relieving the impression of the enclosed countryside.

"You have a fine view. Isn't it nice you can study as much as you like, and without haste?" said Mokuzu.

"To hell with you! How can you see it as a fine view? Both your inner and outer vision must be dreadful if you can enjoy such a humble sight. Shut the window. The breeze is too strong. I'll catch cold!" He struck a match for a cigarette and continued, with irony,

"Great Assistant Dormitory Inspector, you are admirable coming to these distant mountains to be taken in by Tengai. There's but one way to ease the vexation of being duped: dupe the more innocent. This is the secret of Zen's vitality in the transmission of the Dharma, aren't I right?"

Mokuzu remained silent and kept looking out the window. He saw the nun Shorai descending the slope accompanied by Miss Iwai.

'They must have called to me to invite me to walk with them...to seek the earliest field flowers?'

"Hey, let me tell you! I spent four years in Tokyo but never met any students as low as these. How can this be called a college? It's a stagnant pool of delinquents! My university offered all its courses in a complete system — the trivium of sila, samadhi, and prajna, and both exoteric and esoteric Buddhism. As for language alone, we were required to study Pali, Sanskrit, Chinese, Latin, and Greek. Besides, every morning we had to stand naked under a waterfall and then light a holy fire for invocation. What can these bums do after graduating? They'll be incapable of even begging. But tell me, how's the monastery? — though I can presume from here."

"I can't understand why you keep reclining here after you announced you're leaving," Mokuzu spoke calmly.

"What? Didn't you come to dissuade me? You're an odd one."

"To stay or not is your choice and your responsibility. I'm sorry I can't help you since I don't see what's best for you."

"You can help by answering my questions. First, how do you tolerate your disgraceful position as assistant of assistants, one a senile megalomaniac and the other a juvenile frivoler, assistants to a dean spared insanity only by his interest in rhetoric, and himself assistant to Tengai, a genius of gigantic fraudulence? Second — and it's the other half of my first question — what's this Zen master's greatness, which you must have seen and I'm obviously overlooking?" As he asked he took out a process cheese, sliced it with a knife, and began to eat it.

Mokuzu saw the nun and Miss Iwai stoop on a sunny footpath amid the fallow rice fields.

'What flower are they finding in this season, a germander? a speedwell? Teacher Yojun taught me that Europeans before the Gothic Revival sometimes regarded speedwell as forget-me-not, or *Myosotis scorpioides*.

> 'I steal by lawns and grassy plots,
>   I slide by hazel covers;
> I move the sweet forget-me-nots
>   That grow for happy lovers.[5]

'Or have they found a dandelion?

> 'Dear common flower, that grow'st beside the way,
> Fringing the dusty road with harmless gold,
>   First pledge of blithesome May,
> Which children pluck, and full of pride uphold,
> High-hearted buccaneers, o'erjoyed that they
> An Eldorado in the grass have found,
>   Which not the rich earth's ample round
>   May match in wealth, thou art more dear to me
> Than all the prouder summer-blossoms may be.[6]

'How fast the clouds fly and how slow is the growth of the tree buds!' Mokuzu closed the window.

"Eh? Listen, let me tell you how hard I prepared for two years to come here. As you know, I was already a responsible priest of a local temple. My laymen didn't want me gone for more than three months. At last I found a priest to preside during my absence. Of course I had to get leave from my head temple. Finally last spring I could come. Then what did I find but that I had been a victim of Tengai's deception! The man has no sense of sin. He's a master at transcending good and evil. He cheats himself and thus can confidently cheat others. Now I know why Nichiren abused Zen as 'the doings

629

of a demon.' Zen thwarts good conduct. So I'll leave after getting your answer, especially about any good points of your master, and after being given some lunch. While you're his kept dog, it's your duty to answer."

"Priest Hoden Soma, you already know the greatness of our Zen master. As you said, he is a master at transcending good and evil," said Mokuzu simply.

"Hm! Interesting!" He made a gesture to rise, but Mokuzu stopped him,

"Stay put, I haven't time. I wish you a good trip wherever you intend to go," and promptly he left the room.

"Eh, escaping from me? Too bad, I thought you had more sense. Well, I pity you for your enslaved status. Take care of your health, mental as well as physical — so long, we'll not meet again!" He threw his last words at Mokuzu's back.

Mokuzu returned to the office. The dean, smoking by the stove, asked, "How was he? He talks big, but he hasn't the vigor to crack through the ego formed in his infancy."

"Yes, he could be a journalistic critic, but not a creative reformer. It reminds me of the old woman's words, 'The monk is competent enough, yet goes off like that, like all the rest.'"[7]

"Right, Mokuzu, he's impudent like a hypnotist's subject who demands to be hypnotized as he strains to stay alert, thus to enjoy seeing how futile is the hypnotist's art." Tanishi inserted his view.

"Your metaphor has a point, though education shouldn't be likened to hypnotism. In the last analysis Hoden Soma sees how important a faculty and facilities are to a good school, but he doesn't see the most important condition, which is himself, or the subjecthood of the student. Needless to say, the school bears the task of developing the subjecthood of each student, but I doubt if the task can be satisfactorily carried out in a democratic educational system. After all, subjecthood emerges only after violent destruction of ego. Without transcending the bounds of self, one cannot distinguish one's subjecthood from one's ego. Only the Zen monastery can give one a *grenzsituation* backed by educational care," the dean replied thoughtfully.

"Then what is our responsibility for failing to lead a student who may not have perfected his character and his study but who has an evident love of learning?" protested Tsugaru.

"My own responsibility is heavy. I must continue to study and to train, and I must find yet better educational methods. While Zen Master Tengai is spreading the name of this college, I must grope for its substance. He is the branches and I am the roots. Now, the urgent question is how Mokuzu is to report the loss of a student." Bitterly the dean looked over at Mokuzu.

"Dean, I question whether the master will reflect on himself as an educator at the news. If he doesn't whip himself for amendment, who will he whip instead? You are already bitter enough," said Mokuzu.

"He won't reflect; his function is to make others reflect. He is a symbol of the perfect Zen personality," advised Tanishi.

"Mokuzu, your duty is to inform him of whatever happens as it happens, or how can he improve himself and the college?" Tsugaru said earnestly. The dean ignored him and said with a smile,

"I think it best if you just tell him Hoden Soma left for the clear reason that being a Shingon priest kept him from harmonizing with the Zen aspect of the college."

"Dean, how can you distort the case in a direction that will lead him to detest the Shingon sect in addition to scorning Hoden Soma? He'll just become further convinced of his rectitude," objected Tsugaru with flushed face.

"Dormitory Inspector Tsugaru, why don't you understand?" The dean clicked his tongue and began to lecture as he paced the office, his hands clasped at his back.

"You're not the one to bell the cat. Please think for Mokuzu's sake, not only for abstract righteousness, goodness, finickiness, and the like. Dormitory Inspector Tanishi has rightly said that the Zen master will only blame us if the real particulars are given. We had better revere him as our symbol and endeavor to make up for his deficiency. As for Mokuzu, he is now in the process of completing his koan study as early as he can. We must avoid any noise that would cause him delay. We mustn't make him into another Bokuon, who had passed over eighty percent of the koans when one day he made a report that so roused the Zen master's ire that he expelled him. Then remember? Koko deftly jockeyed himself up and gained the master's deep trust. Koko is several years junior to Bokuon in Zen training, but he now is considered the first inheritor of Zen Master Tengai's Dharma. We are no longer children and must realize that reporting is a hard task."

Everyone fell into an uncomfortable silence. Mokuzu wanted to know more about Bokuon. His eyes met the dean's, and the dean talked further,

"Koko always uses the same form: 'Master, there was such-and-such trouble, but I humbly and patiently endeavored to convince them of their error, and it has turned to this fine result.' Bokuon would say: 'Please hear their side. They surely have their faults, but they have their reasons. I can make them comply if you permit them thus-and-thus.' It is stupid that Koko receives the praise 'you understand me to the marrow,' and more stupid that Bokuon is called 'a foolish double-crosser.'

"What ensued was fatal. The village experienced a flood, and representatives came to the master to arrange raising a repair fund. At the time he was in Kyushu negotiating to sell all rights and interests of his shiitake business, so they asked him through Bokuon and Koko. Well, Bokuon stood up for the villagers too much, whereas Koko repeated the master's cherished view that priests assist by producing talented men, not by economic measures. So, Mokuzu, the choice is yours. Report on Hoden Soma as you see fit."

The nun Shorai and Miss Iwai gaily returned.

ᨀ

Toward February's end, the thirteenth graduation ceremony of the college was held in the main building of the monastery. The garden was fragrant with plum blossom and the back mountain riant with bush warblers. The number of guests, including parents of graduates, and prefectural high politicians, businessmen, and bureaucrats, amounted to at least three times the number of graduates. A congratulatory telegram from an imperial prince was read aloud.

In the night the graduates held a party in their dormitory, and Zen Master Tengai, Dean Shiba, Dormitory Inspectors Tanishi and Tsugaru, and their assistant, Mokuzu, were invited to take the central seats. The nun Shorai, who was an officer of the college, could not attend because her nun teacher had a cold.

That left Miss Iwai as the only woman at the party. Especially because she was young, she felt out of place, and she whispered in Mokuzu's ear to ask him to escort her back to Shogetsuan before the sake took effect on everyone. After informing the master, Mokuzu went out with her. The night was dark with no moon, only stars.

The second-year dormitory was yet higher up than the classrooms. Roots and rocks along the path so impeded descent that Mokuzu had to walk unusually close to Miss Iwai to protect her from stumbling.

When they reached level ground, she asked him what she constantly wanted to know,

"I can tell that you and the other monks are going through a hard training life. What I can't understand is why it is necessary. Is koan study so meaningful that you are willing to sacrifice your joyous youth?"

"I am not sacrificing my joyous youth. I am training because I have nothing to sacrifice. Monks are, as it were, aged failures in life, though they may be physically young."

"Really? What a dismal, negative view! I can't believe it. You appear to have some kind of excellent purity, goodness, introspection, discernment, even a hidden passion or fervor. Anyone who is young can enjoy life if only he's frank."

"There must be such fine training monks. Now could you tell me why you came here, Miss Iwai?"

"The only reason is my father sent me. He disliked seeing me playing

632

around with my friends and wanted me to be influenced spiritually, though it's queer because he hates anything spiritual for himself. He even ventured to say he would disown me if I didn't listen to him."

"Were you having fun with your friends?"

"Oh, yes. Adults are just jealous."

"How do you feel about it now?"

"Honestly, I'm bored here. I love being busy in the world, and being cozy sometimes."

In the dark they could not see each other's looks. As soon as he returned her to Shogetsuan, Mokuzu hurried back to the Zen master. The graduates, affected by the sake, were noisy and sitting at ease. Inside their circle the dean was dancing to a folk song, "Yasugi-bushi," sung by the students as they clapped the beat. The dean had tied up his sleeves with a red sash, tucked up his skirts, and tied his head with a towel, knotted at the chin. Holding a tray to represent a conical trap, he was dancing to enact a funny fisherman catching loaches. Not a trace of his intellectual dignity remained.

Tanishi, though of sober habit, had soon become tipsy and in the next seat but one from Zen Master Tengai was behaving like a monkey in priest's robes as depicted in a scroll by the bishop Toba. The master was as he had been from the start: legs crossed fast, force put in the abdomen, molars clamped, gaze fixed forward — his normal posture for hiding his unpleasant feeling.

"Oi, Tanishi! Where did Tsugaru go?" he asked.

Mokuzu sat beside the master. His position was to attend him like a shadow. He sat austerely, making sure nothing escaped him, and tried to absorb all of the master.

"Tsugaru? Oh, don't worry about him, Zen Master. He is still immature and is bent on being earnest; he can't fit himself into a setting like this. I saw him depart right after a toast. Surely he's reading *Vita Sexualis*, or some such thing, in his locked room," replied Tanishi with unusual license.

"What is *Vita Sexualis*?" The master turned to Mokuzu.

"It is an autobiographical novel dealing with carnal appetite, by Mori Ogai."

"Never mind the book! Go see if he's really in his room and bring him here!" the master harshly ordered Tanishi. Alarmed by his tone, Tanishi nonetheless looked over at Mokuzu with the notion that he should go since he was far more junior. Mokuzu affected to gawk. He knew Tsugaru had left the college.

"You go, and be quick!" the master scolded Tanishi in an undertone. Tanishi, his face cramped, rose on tangled legs and walked away as if traversing a seesaw.

The dean was still dancing inside the circle of graduates.

Tanishi returned in a flurry, took a posture to whisper in the master's ear, and yet shouted,

"Master, it's serious, he's gone! No, not left this earth — surely he's somewhere in Japan — only he's beyond your guidance, yes, he's left the college. I checked his closet. There's nothing left but a pepper shaker. Tell me, what should I do?"

"Fool! Hold your tongue! There's no rush. Who can keep what will away? I can cook swine in a corral, not a boar on the loose. Call the dean."

Before the dean could be summoned, one of the master's attendants entered with a tense aspect and went straight to the master and whispered in his ear.

"Speak up! What happened?"

"It's dreadful — he's all bloody. I fear by now he's in his death throes." The attendant, Gyokuro, was addlepated.

"Master, I gather it is Eiso, a kitchen officer. I think you ought to return at once," prompted Mokuzu.

Just then Tanishi brought over the dean. The dean took the towel off his head. The master glanced at them and told Mokuzu,

"I shall go now. Come!"

Gyokuro started the car at once. Outside and inside the car was dark.

"Tell me, which part?" asked the master afresh from the back seat. Gyokuro replied as he drove,

"Yes, Master...not the neck, or the wrist...it was, er...the member vulgarly called the *chinko, chinpo, nankon,* or *yomotsu,* uh..."

"Nnn? He mistook what to cut off. It is impossible to follow the third Buddhist precept by violating the first. Mokuzu, you must know by heart the passages in which Jesus Christ teaches about adultery. Recite them for me."

"Yes, Master. Beginning from Matthew 5:27,

> "Ye have heard that it was said, Thou shalt not commit adultery; but I say
> unto you, that every one that looketh on a woman to lust after her hath
> committed adultery with her already in his heart."

The master nodded in assent and was inspired. "Hmm, his teaching is stringent! Go on."

> "And if thy right eye causeth thee to stumble, pluck it out, and cast it
> from thee: for it is profitable for thee that one of thy members should
> perish, and not thy whole body be cast into hell.
> And if thy right hand causeth thee to stumble, cut it off, and cast it
> from thee: for it is profitable for thee that one of thy members should
> perish, and not thy whole body go into hell."

"Eiso is a model Christian! The teaching of Christ is indeed stringent. But amputation leads nowhere. The animal passions are like carcinomata, which spread to other parts even if a skilled surgeon removes the primal site.

"...To begin with, the idea of cutting off the disadvantageous part is very wrong. Such an idea is rooted in a dreadful ignorance of the nature of things. During the war Hitler oppressed the communist elements and pogromed the Jews. White supremacists continue to discriminate against the red, yellow, and black races.

"How fearful is a stringent teaching based on unfair ignorance! Excising the evil is easy advice, but it's impossible to practice because no clear distinction exists between good and evil. All things are neither good nor bad. Good and bad is the judgment of a certain person for his own convenience in a certain place at a certain time. Our judgment of any phenomenon has no absolute authority. Our judgment keeps changing. The enlightened can tell that good is evil and evil is good. Those who do not yet understand this truth had better observe the first and greatest precept: Do not kill. We must keep nursing our patience and magnanimity." The master thus related his thoughts.

Mokuzu was only listening; his interest was focused on the unusual sight of the graveyard, the bamboo forest, and the terraced garden lit by the headlights.

The car arrived at the monastery entrance. Attendant Gyokuro turned off the headlights and the ignition. Zen Master Tengai remained sitting deep in the seat as if in meditation, though Mokuzu promptly got out and opened the door for him.

48

Carnal Desire

Shoshin Short College began its spring vacation, and Mokuzu resumed his monastic life, acting the same as the other monks.

From the onset of March the monks labored from early morning to split wood on the mountain behind the meditation hall. The scent of pine resin hung low on the mist, while the sound of axes traveled far into the growth of standing timber.

Attendant Gyokuro went up to summon Mokuzu. He wore a ceremonial robe, his main duty being to chauffeur the master.

"The master will make a confession. He asks that you appear at the founder's hall."

Mokuzu set aside his ax, peeled a blister from his hand, and asked, "Can you tell me why I should attend his confession?"

Gyokuro replied as he made his way down the path,

"Of late, one misfortune is following another around here. As you know, Zui went off his rocker, and Eiso did what he did and barely survived. A student named Hoden Soma quit the college, and a dormitory inspector disappeared. Our master figures each occurrence has by degrees something to do with you, and he entertains the expectation that you will grow to be capable of sharing the responsibility with him."

"I hadn't a thing to do with Eiso."

"When he acted on his resolve you were with the master."

Mokuzu changed to ceremonial white underkimono, white tabi, black silk robe, and silk gauze surplice.

The founder's hall was annexed to the back of the main building. Usually no one but chanting officers was allowed to enter. The hall was very dusky, for almost no daylight came in, and the wood floor, as wide as thirty tatamis, was cold and damp. At the rear was a bank of seven steps flanked on the left by a tall iron light-stand with an oil flame so dim as to barely show. On the right was a large square box made of red sandalwood. From its lattice top the smoke of incense steadily seeped out. Both the flame and the incense were said to have been burning from the very moment of the founder's death, for which reason they were likened to his endless teaching, and watching over them was one of the gravest duties of the chanting officers.

At the topmost step on a scissors-style chair was a seated life-size image of the founder. It was a chromatic wood statue dressed in ceremonial robes, with inlaid glass for eyes, and, in imitation of a living Zen master, it held a whisk. A faint shaft of daylight coming in at a roundel directly hit its occiput; the light came in under the huge roof of the main building from the north garden.

A chanting officer had prepared a special dinner with the help of a kitchen officer and had it ready to offer with flowers, incense, tea, and confectionary. He led the chanting of the Heart Sutra on Wisdom and the last gatha of the Gandavyuha. During the chanting Zen Master Tengai incensed each oblation and offered it to the founder. He then performed the most reverential form of worship eighteen times, bowing and prostrating himself at the foot of the steps. The act took considerable motion as he was an overweight Zen master, and he grew short of breath.

Mokuzu, ignorant of how to participate, continued to stand at the side. Seeing him, the master spoke curtly,

"You fool! Do as I do!"

The ceremony completed, he withdrew with his attendant toward a side exit to return to his quarters. Mokuzu could make no sense of what had taken place and pursued him to dare ask,

"Master, please clarify my doubt. Was that the confession? Can all guilt thus be purified?"

"What guilt? There is no guilt after confession, none even so fine as a rabbit hair in the whole ten quarters of the world!"

"But Master, you are merely talking about the expiation of your consciousness of the guilt in your mind, isn't that so? I wish to know about the suffering of Zui, Eiso, and those related. What about that?"

"You dumb fool! I have dispelled it all! You performed the confession, but you did not confess. Perform it entirely again, this time by yourself!"

Fearing he might hurt his feelings, Mokuzu bowed with palms joined and saw the master off.

In Theravada Buddhism, confession was called *ksama*, or *desana*, "to confess one's guilt to others and to beg their acceptance." Mahayana Buddhism gave a far more active meaning to confession: To admit one's guilt, confess it to Buddha, and repent of it are not yet a perfect confession. One must, in addition, free oneself from every guilt. Moreover, for Mahayana Buddhists, "Buddha" means not an external, superior being, but oneself, one's original nature, whence all one's guilts must be absolved by oneself. The power of Zen priests is absolute self-reliance, which may not be easily found in priests elsewhere. Because they see absolute being in themselves, Zen priests can reduce to micro proportions their guilt stemming from acts committed in the relative world.

On the one hand Mokuzu was impressed by his Zen master's great ability to extinguish his guilt; on the other he was saddened to think of the mortification of those who had been misguided in their training.

'Is it true that Zen priests are able to exercise their great power to save themselves when regarded as assaulters, whereas they are impotent to relieve those who are the victims?'

༄

In April, at the start of the new school year, a new dormitory inspector was assigned to the first-year students. He was Banan Chita, formerly head of the kitchen officers and thus a direct superior to Eiso, who had cut off his penis.

Mokuzu, seizing the chance, asked him the particulars of Eiso's case.

Banan's head was shaped like a wax gourd, and the distance between his nose and mouth was unduly long. When he laughed his upper gum showed like the gum of a horse, though he looked better that way than with his mouth shut.

"So...you'd like to know about Eiso...It's not impossible for me to understand his torment, eh,...every sincere young monk must go through the gate, the crucial battle between carnal desire and Buddha's precepts," he prudently began.

"During the first several years we can barely follow at the heels of our seniors from lack of sleep, scanty nutrition, and hard work. There are many dropouts. Those fortunate to learn to sleep as they walk and to absorb nourishment from water and mere fibers can go on training. But soon they will be afflicted by their own severe impulse.

"As you know, our master's guidance about carnal desire in this monastery, a place closed to women, is extremely stern. Compare it with the monasteries in Kyoto. There monks can step out onto streets filled with flowery women, can meet women wherever they go for begging. Those monasteries have many women visitors, and some even go so far as to hold tea-ceremony parties or flower-arrangement exhibits within their very precincts.

"Urban monks are rendered immune to women and are no longer stimulated by just a glimpse. I even heard that a Zen master at Tenryoji, Seki Genjo, took his disciples with him to the geisha quarters. Here we have no means to ease and disperse our impulse. It condenses at the base of our mind, and we are often scorched by our absurd fancies."

Mokuzu wanted to hear quickly about Eiso, but Banan kept on reflecting as if he had unlimited time,

"We are enclosed by mountain upon mountain, and after the leaves fall under shower-threatening skies, winter lasts long. Our carnal desire grows strong and stronger. It is certainly pure, yes, we are pained at just the sight of spring buds. If we chance upon a feminine handkerchief dropped on the road, we can barely contain ourselves.

"The purer our impulse, the more bizarre our fancy. We are hardly gratified by fancying the ordinary sex act performed by married couples united by social courtesy. We fantasize about every aspect of all possible forms...prostitution, fornication, adultery, incest, unsuitable match, misbehavior, unrestrained behavior...We also dwell on the various sexopaths: sexual hyperesthesia, impotence, frigidity, homosexuality, lesbianism, pedophilia, fellatio, cunnilingus, bestiality, fetishism, sadism, masochism, scopophilia...Our minds are thoroughly corrupt, and we have no way to escape falling to the bottom of hell, where only the sex of snakes is prospering.

"Now, in such a state common to monks, Eiso got to know the young wife of an old priest living in the mountains at Mino. You must have gone there for mendicancy, those villages scattered up the Nagara River."

Mokuzu had visited Mino the previous autumn. The coloring leaves above the roofs and in the mountains were reflected on the river in the valley. Under many small suspended bridges the lucent water flowed. The mountains were wooded mainly with varieties of paper mulberry frutescent among maples, the area being renowned for paper production from the earliest recorded time, AD 801.

In late autumn the villagers harvested the new mulberry shoots. They removed the bark and scraped it to leave peelings much resembling skinned snakes. These went over bamboo poles to bleach in the sun, and a few days later they were boiled with plant ash and washed in the creek. Far below the mountain path, women of all ages crouched on the alluvium picking out the dirt and non-fibrous elements, using pins as well as their fingers.

And still the fiber had to be crushed by mallets. Then it went into a tank of water and was stirred with a mucilage extract from the root of a species of hibiscus or the bark of panicle hydrangea to produce a mushy liquid. Mokuzu had observed a young woman dipping a meshed frame into a tank, scooping up the pulp, tilting the frame to distribute it evenly, and casting out the excess and impurities. Her hands were red from the cold fluid, and her eyes intense, for the amount scooped, and what was cast out, and the manner of tilting determined the thickness and uniformity of the paper. The settled pulp would be removed from the mesh and laid outside on a cypress board to become dry white paper rejecting the sun.

The young woman realized his presence as he stood watching, and she stopped and offered him alms.

"Out of thanks and respect for your hard training," she said simply and bowed.

He had thought as he left in silence, 'Who thanks and respects her? What's the difference between her hard work and hard religious training?'

Banan was still talking,

"Upon my word, the woman Eiso became intimate with is a beauty, though I had but a chance glimpse. Let me say of her...oh! her eyes speak even when she says nothing, and her neck and the shape of her back, especially her waist — you can't help looking. She is childless, younger, much younger, than her husband. He must be getting on to fifty. He's a well-known preacher. You would recall him if I mentioned his name. He stays at his temple no more than once in a fortnight, I mean, he was actively touring the country and preaching in the local temples too.

"His temple is in such a remote glen we seldom go there. But one summer, by now already two years ago, Eiso lost his way. As he told me later, he wished to be given a cup of water and be taught his whereabouts.

"He said the temple was so quiet, seemingly no one was home; there was only the sound of water running through a bamboo pipe. He stepped into the backyard and came upon her as she was soaking a bundle of Chinese bellflowers in a cistern. He expected her to be alarmed, but he felt she greeted him with the warmth and intimacy of a relative.

"Since then he began to 'lose his way' whenever he was assigned to the area for mendicancy. Sometimes he obtained special permission to go out by saying he had to be treated for his pulpitis, or whatever.

"Well, swine in rut can't be contained in the hut, nor a monk in the monastery.

"As it happened, an event occurred that enslaved him to her. They were in the bedroom, certain her husband would not return that day. Then they heard the approach of clogs on the stone pavement from the gate. Unmistakably it was he. Calmly and swiftly, not stopping for her underwear, she put on her kimono and tidied her hair. She then assisted Eiso with his robe, gaiters, and straw sandals and made him sit on the veranda. As she was bringing out tea, the priest appeared in the garden.

"'Ah, it's you, what a surprise! Did you forget something important? I was about to offer tea to this Shoshinji monk. Oh, young monk, I should like to introduce you to my husband. But I haven't heard your name...Would you tell us?'

"'From Shoshinji? How hard you train, coming this far on foot!' said the priest, and to his wife, 'Don't be concerned, I simply forgot my glasses and travel diary.' Mokuzu, I suppose you can't fathom Eiso's psychology — how erotic that she was deftly deceiving her husband and thus exposing to Eiso her love!"

Mokuzu regretted having asked about Eiso. 'Human sex done on the sly is uglier than the ingenuous copulation of animals.'

"However," Banan was concluding, "the priest, who after all was having conjugal relations with her, soon detected infidelity. Being a well-educated and respected preacher, he agonized in his heart, without redress. All he did was wait for her to regain her sanity. Day by day he grew thinner, and he lost his zest for preaching and began to stay home most of the time. So she and Eiso had to meet elsewhere, and sometimes they were observed. Before long a villager notified Zen Master Tengai."

"I'd like to know exactly how our master guided Eiso."

"Well, Mokuzu, of course he roundly excoriated him for an act 'fatally odious in a monk.' Even so, he was lenient: 'No one is perfect. However, I shall pardon you this once only, and only if you promise to sever all relations with her, including by letter or telephone. Hereafter I shall grant no exceptions.'"

"Doesn't that mean even Zen Master Tengai couldn't do a thing for the source of the energies other than order a tight lid be put on the container?"

"Yes, but are you judging our master negatively or positively? I know full well that in koan study you are far ahead of us who are your seniors. Tell me how you would guide Eiso were it your position to do so."

Mokuzu passed over Banan's provocation and fell into thought,

'Is there no way to bring forth true love from sexual love like a lotus flower rising from the mud? Which is the right attitude toward carnal desire — to disregard it, to control it, or to develop it? In the *Kama Sutra* it is magnanimously considered one of the three important subjects that should be well studied and mastered during one's life.

'In a passage of the Suramgama-samadhi Sutra, Ananda, the second patriarch of Zen transmission in India, is described as having become enlightened while playing in a prostitute quarter. In China, Kueiji was respected as an outstanding disciple of Shyuantzang and as founder of the Fashiang sect. But, as recorded, he never gave up his appetite for women and wine and for meals past midday. Even when he went to lecture before the imperial presence, he was accompanied by three carts laden with sutras, wine and meat, and ladies.'

"Mokuzu, why don't you ask me what became of the cuckolded priest?" Banan persisted.

"Well?"

"Just ten days ago the master sent me to him to report Eiso's amputation. I was surprised, for the temple had become a den of cats — I could count at least thirty at a glance. He must have been feeding them. Fine, but he didn't heed a word of what I told him. Will you believe it? He was gathering cats on a sunny veranda and preaching to them just as he preached to his many audiences. His delivery was gentle and patient, and he even inserted apt humor. Most of the cats too were polite and indeed seemed attentive."

"And the wife?"

"For sure, she wasn't there. Likely our master advised her to become a nun....Well, I too have experienced serious torment from carnal desire. But I'm now relieved I didn't commit a rash act like Eiso's. It's thankworthy to have a body with no physical defect, right?"

"Do you mean you determined to keep holy vows all your life, in accord with Zen Master Tengai's teaching?" asked Mokuzu, feeling respect for the senior monk.

"Don't be silly! I'll leave this mountain the moment I find a suitable wife. I've asked Dean Shiba."

"Dean Shiba?..."

"Don't you know? For all his looks, he's a matchmaker. Haven't you seen

641

Bokuon's wife? She's nice and attractive, has a striking bottom. The dean found her for him. Don't laugh! The one fitted to inherit Tengai's Dharma is Koko. His ilk is capable of twining the rope of carnal desire into love of fame!"

❧

Since the onset of spring Mokuzu resided no longer in the meditation hall but in the attendants' room, next to the master's quarters, for he was appointed fourth attendant to the master. The head attendant served him day and night functioning more like a secretary, the second looked after his meals and dress, and the third was mainly his chauffeur.

Mokuzu went to the college to assist the dormitory inspectors and reported the events there to the master as before. Besides, he now had to attend as a second-year student.

(As an attendant to the master he was counted among the monks of the residential quarters. Their role was to be hosts to the meditation hall monks, who were considered guests. Host monks were required to sponsor the ideal environment for guest monks to concentrate on their training. In contrast, host monks even as they concentrated on their own training had to study how to help others.)

At the college office Miss Iwai occasionally spoke to Mokuzu what seemed very close to indecencies when no one else was present. Getting to know him better, she was, it could be said, molesting him.

"Banan told me the other day that the type who is chosen as a Zen master's attendant is quite definite."

"What do you mean?"

"Handsome — and attractive in black robe. Someone like Banan is never chosen even if he stays here all his life. Zen Master Tengai sees no woman as a woman except his mother, so inevitably he tends to be a sodomite. Banan was worrying about you."

"Worry is needless, I've no taste for it."

"Are you sure? Where's proof?"

"Do I have to prove it?" Mokuzu was nonplussed. Miss Iwai chuckled, and further ventured,

"Dean Shiba mentioned that boys were put at priests' disposal in Babylonia, and that Aristotle and Plato advocated sodomy, saying it was nobler than heterosexuality. In Japanese history too, sodomy in the monasteries is documented as if it was commonplace, he said. You live in a setting where the predominance of men is so extreme that heterosexual activity is absolutely ignored; moreover, you adore the master as if he's a living Buddha. How can you not be suspected? Oh, which reminds me! A noted folklorist, Yanagita

Kunio, somewhere wrote that a true master–disciple relation can't be attained without practice of sodomy. Tanishi was muttering that Zen Master Tengai's Dharma inheritor is predecided. It'll be Koko, because advancement of koan study is determined by the master's partiality."

Hearing this from Miss Iwai, Mokuzu's face darkened like shady pond water. He had been going through hardship with the sole hope that he would be offered all the koans in accord with his ability. He was purely believing that no private notion, emotion, or other matter ever interfered with koan study.

'Koans are the Dharma. The Dharma is embodied by Zen Master Tengai, yet at once it transcends him. That is why I have been believing I can obtain from him all of the koans.

'But in reality the Dharma doesn't seem to be transcending him. Or should I say he isn't transcending the Dharma, because he isn't as high as the Dharma. He flies the Dharma like a kite, but the kite in the sky and he on the earth are connected by only a thin string. Oh, how I respect and yearn after Sakyamuni Buddha! He asserted that "whoever admires my looks and sound is practicing evil and is unable to recognize the Tathagata."[1] He also taught, "In this world make of yourself an island, your own foundation; rely not on others. Still higher, make the Dharma your island and rely on no other foundation."'[2]

Miss Iwai cast him a worried look and said in an earnest tone, "You expect to get the Dharma, as important as life itself, from one you can't love as much as to sacrifice your life for, right? How can you so selfishly expect to be given it? You're selfish and you know nothing of the world. Suppose he gives you it. I assume you'll give it to the one you love most. Isn't the Dharma passed from love to love like a butterfly drifting from flower to flower?"

'How sharp is her intuitive observation when she isn't even studying like me! "Passed from love to love"? Indeed I was going to snatch it from one I don't really love, and the one I want most to give it to is gone. How absurd if it's passed from one loveless hand to another loveless hand. No life could be more meaningless and wasteful than the life I am living. I am like a damp wind making a noise in the dark.'

"I pity you — you aren't living in reality, even though you are un-questionably living in so serious a manner. You have to know that whatever bears no relation to love is sterile and a waste of life. Klesa turns to Bodhi only if there is love, and Bodhi turns to klesa if there isn't. I think I won't reject either sorrow or joy as long as it's accompanied by love, because love is the only meaning of life." Miss Iwai's fair cheeks were flushed and her eyes zealous. She was suitably dressed for the air of May, and her figure was in lively motion.

Mokuzu frowned and looked out the window.

'Oh evil day! if I were sullen
While Earth herself is adorning,
   This sweet May-morning,
And the children are culling
   On every side,
In a thousand valleys far and wide,
Fresh flowers; while the sun shines warm.'[3]

ॐ

Mokuzu knew from experience the bitterness of having no food when hungry and the difficulty of being denied sleep when sleepy. He had learned that the only solution was to abandon the wish to live when such desires could not be satisfied.

Now he had to suffer from seething carnal desire. He kept reminding himself of a passage of Zen Teacher Dogen:

> All Buddhas without exception were wearing the surplice when they attained Buddhahood. We must recognize that in the surplice is the holiest supreme virtue.[4]

Mokuzu too wore the surplice. But he felt he was like food cooked from within while its surface remained unscorched in the electronic oven developed by Raytheon.

'Ena...Luri....' He recalled the body of each, and imagined Miss Iwai, and Eiso's woman, and a hundred others he had seen in Tokyo's hustle and bustle. 'Tokyo was plentiful with women's sexual parts, enough to give Henry Miller tears of ecstasy. But it's despicable to see women with one's sexual interest only and not with affection. How sad are women seen by such filthy, heartless, selfish men! And yet I too want to see and treat women that way! I'm like a feather on surging billows of carnal desire, and I now know more than enough that love is hard to realize and lust hard to control,' he moaned in distress.

Nonetheless, night after night he climbed the mountain behind Shoshinji and continued to meditate on a rock lit by moonlight through the pines. He deferred to *Tzuochan san-mei jing* to contemplate with scrupulous care the process by which beautiful women age, grow ugly, die, decompose, and turn to bleached bones. The sutra stated:

> Whoever has strong carnal appetite ought to practice contemplation of defilement. From the hair of the head to the tips of the toes, all is defiled. Hair, nails, teeth...fat, meninges, all are foul. Behold, more foul are congestion, bloat, rot, blood, discoloration, fetid pus, terminal gluttony, the stench of cremation, and the scattering of bones...[5]

This contemplation recommended that Mokuzu recall and imagine every

644

scene having the potential to defeat the memories and fantasies that assisted him to discharge his semen. After all, willful ejaculation was counted among the second heaviest sins, *samghavasesa*, next to *parajika*, in Theravada Buddhism.

ૐ

During one of those days Dean Shiba, who was also teaching the history of Zen thought to the second-year students, assigned a term paper on Ikkyu Sojun. Knowing he was busy with monastic life as well as assisting the dormitory inspectors, the dean gave Mokuzu a specific topic: "The Sinful Priest Ikkyu as Presented in His Collected Poems, *Kyoun shu*," and he granted him the use of a newly collated text.

Mokuzu completed the paper in his spare moments at the college, but he was well aware that his work would be subject to criticism for its coercive simplification and inadequate verification. The dean, however, rated it high, copied it, and made it available to the other students. Mokuzu was ashamed of himself. His paper was as follows:[6]

I

Ikkyu was regarded as having been born to the purple, son of Emperor Gokomatsu and a lady of the Southern Dynasty. But there is no corroborative proof, and even as the traditional view is advanced, lack of proof could be proof of his humble origin.

Throughout his life Ikkyu attached importance to Zen, poetry, and love. Zen was his fundamental persuasion, love his activity, and poetry his means to perceive and to express Zen and love.

These three concerns were determined in his infancy. At age six he entered the priesthood. Whether or not he was truly an orphan, it is certain he had to eat another's salt. His infancy was the wellspring of his hunger for love, which apparently was little satisfied during his life.

Ikkyu chose four pen names, using Mukei ("to dream of the bed chamber") whenever he wrote love poems.

At age thirteen he began to study how to write poems from a priest-poet of the day, Botetsu.

At age twenty-two he began a serious study of Zen under the direction of Kaso Sodon.

Ikkyu took five years to arrive at the great realization. On his arrival he artfully presented in a poem his three prime concerns:

> "Realization at the Cry of a Crow"
> Here am I with no sign of decrease
> In spirit, wrath, and lust, lo! these twenty years!
> Harken to a crow's laugh at desire-severing arhats:
> "Of what use be they to a brilliant dancing girl?"[7]

The poem was based on "Changshin chioushy," a masterpiece by the Tang poet Wang Changling, a man of loose conduct.

"These twenty years" alludes to the mendicant life of National Teacher Daito. Daito was ordered by his teacher Daio to leave the sacred precincts and stay in the city for another twenty years to perfect his Zen training in a practical life among the common people. Ikkyu was a descendant of the Daio and Daito line of the Dharma. He respected these two great teachers, and indeed his pride was such that he considered himself the sole true descendant.

"A crow's laugh at these arhats" expresses Ikkyu's view that the essence of Mahayana Buddhism is not to sever the desires but to fulfill them to the best of one's ability.

Lust, the subject of the poem, was just one of Ikkyu's desires. But his view of lust distinguished for him Mahayana from Hinayana Buddhism.

In this poem written on the occasion of his realization, he thus declared his three important lifelong concerns: Zen, poetry, and love.

II

To elucidate the theme of this paper, a study follows of those of Ikkyu's poems that directly relate to transgression of the Buddhist precepts.

For a correct understanding of the poems, it is necessary to know what is the traditional Zen that Ikkyu studied and learned from experience. Zen has been transmitted by lineage from Sakyamuni Buddha down to the present Zen masters. Its philosophy is summarized in its epistemology and ontology. Zen epistemology regards union of subject and object as the ultimate cognition. Likewise Zen ontology esteems one's unification with the world as the highest form of one's existence.

What is singular about these tenets is their thorough denial of individuality. The intent of Zen is to restore individuality in illimitable absoluteness by denial of oneself, self being a limited and relative existence.

Zennists who have gone through the experience of realization know without any doubt that the epistemology and ontology of Zen are exceedingly efficacious for the basic questions What is oneself? and What is the world?

However, it is an evident fact that most Zennists do not complete their life when they attain Zen realization. On the contrary, they live on to the end because naturally no creature wishes to die. Even our Sakyamuni Buddha expressed at his death that this world is beautiful and that the pleasure of coming into existence is to live.[8]

By living on, Zennists inevitably confront problems that cannot be answered solely by their epistemology and ontology. Living on is to practice living; and what is needed for living is practical ethics, not epistemology or ontology, which are merely ideal explanations of life seen to be complete-as-it-is and static. Practical ethics, which enables us to choose how to act from moment to moment, is for Zennists the Buddhist precepts. Reduced to two phrases they are: practice only good, practice no evil.[9]

Having practical ethics in addition to an epistemology and an ontology, Zennists are equipped with feet, not only a head and heart. Can they then live brightly in peace and with confidence? No, not yet. They must realize they are trapped in the inconsistency and antinomy between theory and practice, because obviously their epistemology and ontology are a kind of monism, while their practical ethics is based on a kind of dualism. Hence their head and heart recommend that they denounce dualistic thought, while the modus vivendi of their feet is to distinguish good from evil. If they are not supermen, they will be wretched hypocrites who preach monistic enlightenment while they themselves live in dualism.

How did the great line of Zennists get out of this trap? First they allowed themselves no time to doubt the Buddhist precepts, then they adhered to them, and therefore it seemed to them that there were only good acts in their life. While they firmly rejected evil acts, only good acts remained; indeed they erased the existence of evil from their world. The Buddhist precepts thus became a kind of monism. "In my world there is neither life nor death!"[10] declared the founder of Shoshinji.

Zen Master Tengai, one of the great line of traditional Zen masters, often says the secret of Zen is to become the object. He is applying what he says not only to the epistemology and ontology but also to the practical ethics. So it is evident there is no duality in his practical ethics. He is teaching his disciples not to become the evil object, but to become the good object since there are only good acts in his world. Thus he sees no antinomy between his theory and his practice.

How then did Ikkyu regard the solution of the traditional Zennists? He laughed loudly and bragged: "Priests who keep the precepts become donkeys, while depraved Zennists become true men."[11]

III

Ikkyu could by no means convert the dualism of the Buddhist precepts to a monism as the traditional Zennists did by their erasing evil from their world. He thought that was a childish, forced complacence. To begin with, he could not clearly distinguish good acts from evil acts as defined by the Buddhist precepts. Much more, he could not believe that his life consisted of only good acts. So he abandoned practical ethics and acted without consideration of either good or bad, just as the sixth patriarch had taught (though the sixth patriarch taught it not as practical ethics but as epistemology and ontology).

The poems Ikkyu made when he forgot the Buddhist precepts are few but beautiful, even in their direct expression of the sexual act.

"Narcissus Scent in the Beauty's Pubes"

Slim waist, hills awaiting the climber,
Expectant face, at midnight, abed.
A flowering stem under the plum tree opens,
Narcissus between the thighs.[12]

"Oako Bathing"

How is her nude skin?
She washes away paint, powder, worldly cares.
I too bathe like a newborn babe,
Splendid am I in spring![13]

"Narcissus"

Secret blend of fragrances:
Plum and narcissus in the valley.
She lightly sways, moist, and
Looks up at the blue night sky.[14]

Here Ikkyu could reject the ethics of the Buddhist precepts, be faithful to his amatory interest, and realize Zen epistemology and ontology even in the realm of action.

Even so, the world he lived in did not esteem him for his rejection of the Buddhist precepts, nor regard him as even narrowly achieving the state wherein they did not exist. The world saw him as merely unethical and branded him as an antinomian. He too must have realized that action could not always be so pure and passionate as to justify rejection of the Buddhist precepts. Indeed he had to recognize their indispensability as soon as he saw that he could not purify himself in the flame of passion.

Whenever he regarded the Buddhist precepts he had to scorn himself as a transgressor, or display himself as a true man. In fact most of his poems relating to carnality are either self-scorning or self-displaying. They are the poems of a failed Zennist, a failed poet, and a failed true man; poems made difficult by erudite references to Zen classics and Chinese poetry. They are not even beautiful, but give us the feeling of hearing the grumbles of an old man.

Every serious young Zennist must go through the antinomy between Zen monistic theory and Zen dualistic ethics. It is hoped that young Zennists will be earnest, energetic, and lucky as they work at the task that no true man has yet successfully resolved.

❧

Mokuzu came to realize that contemplation was not enough to build up his own confident view on carnal desire. In addition he needed to study from books. Contemplation led him to a state of stillness, but did not make him any brighter or more vigorous.

He therefore asked Tsurumi, director of the college library, to find him the sutras and books that he ought to read.

Tsurumi was a decrepit old man, though he sat erect in his chair. Day after day he killed the time by putting the donated books in order, reading, or composing poems in a Chinese style at a desk near the window. Seldom were there any visitors.

He removed his reading glasses and told Mokuzu,

"Entrust it to me. I shall find whatever you want, not only from here but from all over. Just give me a list. I'll leave the books wrapped in a cloth under the floor so you can read them at night unnoticed. Frankly, I disagree with the monastery's principle of banning reading and writing. Linji's words and Deshan's conduct are being mistaken. It is true that self-realization is determined by one's momentary intuition. But intuition doesn't occur without a long preparation of studies. Moreover, intuition unexamined by reasonable speculation is as dangerous as blind belief. Zen gives birth where literature falls short, but Zen was raised and developed by literature. Zennists who can't fathom literature aren't much different from intrepid stone cutters, hunters, and soldiers. At best they can guide only people like themselves, such as entrepreneurs and politicians. Zennists from whom the most can be expected are the sincere, well-educated, creative ones; they are able to guide artists, scholars, and men of other faiths."

Mokuzu did not respond. He recalled Docho's lecture:

"Master Mokuzu, in addition to the Hinayana Buddhist precepts, Chinese Zen priests practiced the Mahayana Buddhist precepts. The former arose from a human existence that coexisted with all manner of organic and inorganic life — plants, animals, and minerals. The Hinayana precepts are thus more important than any acrobatic enlightenment. Nonetheless, Japanese Zennists practice only the Mahayana precepts and are self-complacent. Those precepts are a practical application of the base of the Hinayana precepts, and when the base is forgotten, the practical application disintegrates into a play of ideas. This is one reason why I regard Japanese Zen as an inferior imitation of Chan, Chinese Zen."

Mokuzu began to read *Syfen lyu*, to which Hinayana Buddhists attached the greatest importance. Its 60 volumes in Chinese were translated in AD 408 by Buddhayasas from the Sanskrit *Dharmaguptaka*. Therein are described 250 rules of moral conduct for monks and 348 for nuns, set forth by Sakyamuni Buddha. To understand *Syfen lyu* definitely, Mokuzu at the same time had to read *Syfen lyu singshy chan*, 30 volumes of annotations by Daushyuan, wherein the criteria for monks' behavior are systematically redescribed and plainly set forth. Moreover, he had to study *Syfen lyu singshy chan tzychyji* by Yuanjau, 16 volumes of annotations on *Syfen lyu singshy chan*.

Tsurumi was impressed by his reading speed. Mokuzu feared that by just studying the precepts he would become one-sided in building up his own view of carnal desire. So he asked Tsurumi to assemble the major works of pornographic literature from around the world. Tsurumi had difficulty finding them and often went to secondhand bookstores in Gifu.

He brought back *The Art of Love*, a Western classic by Publius Ovidius Naso; *Arabian Nights*, representative of the Middle and Near East; *Fabliaux* of medieval France; Boccaccio's *Decameron* from the Italian Renaissance; and from France *Les Cent Nouvelles nouvelles* and Marguerite de Navarre's *Heptameron*.

Tsurumi recommended to him some modern Western realistic writings: Charles Sorel's *Francion*, Choder los de Laclos's *Liaisons Dangereuses*, Zola's 20 novels under the title *Les Rougon-Macquart*, Brantome's *Les Vies des dames galantes*, Casanova's *Memoires*, Crebillon's *Le Sopha, conte moral*, Cleland's *Fanny Hill,* and Balzac's *Contes Drolatiques*.

He also brought *Tzashy mishin* and *Feiyan wanchuan*, which he said were the earliest Chinese pornography, from the Han dynasty. Mokuzu perused them and could not believe they were written before Ming or Sung. The former was of interest for elucidating the mysteries of the female body.

Youshianku, regarded as the best novel of the Tang dynasty, was lost in China and preserved in Japan. Most works of its kind were anonymously written, as were *Ruyijyun chuan* and *Chypor'tz chuan* of the sixteenth century. The Ming dynasty contributed *Jin-ping-mei* and *Her'shang chiyuan* (or *Chuanshin ji*). Foremost in the Ching were *Jyuewuchan* (or *Rouputuan*), *Shinghuatian*, and *Langshy*. *Pinhua-baujian*, also of that period, was a novel noted for its depiction of sodomites.

Tsurumi told Mokuzu that the Japanese were as amorous as any peoples, with pornographic descriptions already appearing in *Kojiki*, *Manyo shu*, *Nihonshoki*, and *Nihon ryoi ki*, produced during the Nara period, and in many more from the Heian period: *Saibara fu, Ryojin hisho, Konjyaku monogatari, Koji dan, Zoku koji dan, Kokon chomon ju, Uji shui monogatari, Shin sarugaku ki*, and so on. But since pornographic descriptions were only incidentally scattered in those works, the first genuine pornography in Japan could have been *Shinsen Inu Tsukuba shu* by Yamazaki Sokan. The trilogy *Takitsuke so, Moekui,* and *Keshizumi*, published in the late seventeenth century, was pure pornographic literature.

One day Tsurumi included a note on top of some of these books wrapped and left under the floor:

"I shan't prepare for you any of Saikaku's works, it being impossible for me to regard them as pornography. They are excellent satires and assert the freedom of love under the feudal system. The same can be said of *Lady Chatterly's Lover, Sexus*, and *Journey to the End of the Night*."

Japanese pornography flourished most in the eighteenth century. *Itsu chomon ju, Hakoya no himegoto*, and *Ana okashi* continued to be honored as the three most curious books.

Mokuzu was provided with more and more — *Daito keigo, Shunran takuko, Haifu Suetsumuhana, Shitone gassen, Naemara initsu den, Mizuage cho, Shunjo hana no oboroyo, Hitorine*...[15]

He read them all, even if the moonlight on the mountain did not always assist him. Stealthily he brought out the candle from the Buddhist sanctum. Yet there were windy and rainy nights. He had to secure a congruous place to read, with light indispensable. He believed he could compensate thereby for his scanty reading time.

One day on his return from the college he noticed a compact charnel at the heart of the gently terraced graveyard where the tombs of Shoshinji's successive Zen masters and laymen were set. Leading unobtrusively to the charnel was a pair of electric wires.

In the night he approached the charnel. It reposed beneath the intricate branches of tall summer camellias planted to the sides to represent the tropical sal, idealized as the Nirvana tree. The building was a small-scale reproduction of the Temple of the Golden Pavilion in Kyoto, about twenty feet square, with white plaster walls and a quadrangular pyramidic roof thatched in cypress bark and topped by a standing bronze phoenix.

At the front was a pair of hinged lattice doors of unpainted wood. Mokuzu opened them and stepped in, only to find a solid iron door barring with a strong lock any intruder. But he easily found the key on the lintel.

He slid the heavy door and felt for the light switch. The light was so bright that he was momentarily blinded. The interior walls too were plastered white. He stepped out and closed the door. As he expected, no light broke through. He had found a place where he could read as much as he pleased without abusing his eyes or needing to defer to anyone.

The charnel interior was semibasement, its floor finished with concrete. At the inmost recess a Kannon statuette stood on a console table. Star anise, green for the length of a season, was offered in a pair of vases. Lining the walls much with the look of coin-operated lockers were rows of hinged-doored boxes to which the urns of the reliquiae were consigned.

The air smelled sweet-sour from the damp incense left on the table. It contained musk, honey, and plum vinegar. Mokuzu borrowed the low desk, which held the sutras that were recited before the Kannon.

651

49

Sengtsan's One Mind

At Shoshinji a fine day was designated for airing the documents and household effects that were the heirlooms of each office, and to help with the work, the meditation hall monks were summoned. The office of the Zen master's attendants, to which Mokuzu now belonged, was responsible for carrying the robes and portraits of Shoshinji's chief priests to the veranda of the main building.

With summer vacation nearing at the college, the students gladly helped the librarian, Tsurumi, to air the old books. As a result of the rainy season, the rare leather-bound Western books had acquired a frost-like mildew, which if wiped took with it the gilt titles.

"After all, they aren't suited to the damp of Japan, and worse, they're heavy," Tsurumi complained to Mokuzu.

Dean Shiba, hands clasped behind his back, came to look at the airing books as if wishing to make a lucky find. He bent, picked up one browned with age, and pulled out the card.

"What? Has no student ever read this...though I myself toiled...? And yet the paper is deteriorating. It was published during the war. Mokuzu, never mind, keep it as yours."

The book, indeed written by the dean, was annotations on *Shin-shin ming*, a poetic treatise extolling the mind, by the third Zen patriarch in China, Sengtsan. The dean had given it the subtitle, *The Origin of Zen Thought*.

"Oh, I almost forgot. You'd better leave off airing books and accompany Miss Iwai to wherever she's wishing to go. We have to allow her some leeway, for she's soon returning to Nagoya," the dean said to Mokuzu with a smile.

When Mokuzu entered the office, Banan Chita was in the midst of remonstrating with Iwai,

"Despite all, I hate flower arrangement. What audacity, downright fancy, that man ventures to express nature in a vase. A fellow once said flowers should be arranged just as they are in the field.[1] Then all the more should we desist from bringing them into the house," and turning to elicit Mokuzu's support, he flexed down the corner of his mouth and widened his eyes, which gave him the look of an actor portrayed by the artist Sharaku.

Tanishi, cheek twitching as usual, spoke with ardor,

"Dormitory Inspector Banan, your view lacks a grasp of the essence. Don't you know the poem by Kino Tsurayuki?

"If only they were not ephemeral,
would forever bloom!
So did I wish, arranging them in a vase,
And now they are gone,
The cherry blossoms!"[2]

"What's special about it? Ridiculous! It states the obvious, and confirms my view that flowers should be left uncut."

"Banan, you lack aesthetic sense. You must feel alien in Japan. Think of the poet's earnest desire for the longevity the flowers, intensified by bringing them indoors. Had he left them as is, his desire, his love for them, couldn't have made of them a tragic beauty. When the human hand violates the laws of nature, the beauty of nature is increased. This is a clue to appreciating the art of flower arrangement. Besides, can't you see the poet's pure, childlike soul? He hoped and thought the flowers would live longer by his care. And another clue..."

"Thank you, Mokuzu. We must be off — there's little time," Miss Iwai curtly interrupted Tanishi.

"Ha? Where are you going?" Tanishi asked.

"I have the dean's permission." Iwai threw off the inquiry and was out the door. Briskly she made her way down the sideling steps and down the lower slope. Mokuzu followed, unapprised of where or why she was going.

They came down to a thicket of trees. Cool shadows and hot sunlight produced a busy pattern on the path. Iwai slowed her pace and said,

"Working with them has done me good — I learned to be abrupt, didn't I? You know, I think a feature of people well seasoned in Zen is their abruptness. I once told Tanishi so. He said it may look that way to laymen, but it's because Zennists live each moment with all their might. I sort of get what he says, but I can't stand that they deny their individuality at every turn. Their abrupt actions make me suspect they are radicals. But no, they are timid and ultra-conservative. Really, they should be aired like those books. And those books should be burned."

Mokuzu had to keep reestablishing the space between himself and her. She walked so close that her hand touched the sleeve of his robe. Thinking he was rude to remain silent, he asked,

"You were discussing the art of flower arrangement?"

"Sort of. I haven't told you, but I'm leaving at the end of this term. At home I must prepare to inherit my father's position as teacher of flower arrangement. The dormitory inspectors were nattering as they like. Well, forget them. Thanks for coming."

"You're welcome. Where are we going?"

"Dear me, didn't Dean Shiba say? Anyway, it's just that I found a place

653

with a profusion of fringed orchis, not far, and I want a root to give my parents. I can go alone, but I asked for you on the pretext of needing your help, because I feel sorry that you're only quietly obeying every senior. At night too on your own you study the Buddhist precepts. Tsurumi told me so with admiration. How's your study progressing?"

Her manner was much freer and brighter outside the college. Mokuzu felt a warmth toward her and an intimacy. 'The fields and mountains through her eyes must be more animated than they are for me,' he thought. Often she regarded his face, each time raising her own and standing somewhat on tiptoe, at which the pleats of her York skirt waved and her flexed rosy calves were exposed. Her blouse was smooth and dazzling.

"I have very limited time to read. I've finally been able to read through the Hinayana precepts, and I've just begun chapter 10 of *Fanwang jing*, which must be read with the annotations *Fanwang jing heju*, *Fanwang jing lyueshu*, and such."

"But in your way even if you study a lot, how much will you be able to understand the precepts? It seems people who violate them are more suitable, I mean, they can understand them better."

"You may be right, but I think by way of example that children hardly out of swaddling clothes in the poor countries of Southeast Asia smoke opium without knowing they are poisoning themselves. Isn't this example enough to show that studying the precepts has value as a preventive measure? As for your indication that we can't understand them without violating them, let me remind you, has anyone never violated both the light and the heavy precepts from birth? Everyone has violated enough of them to be capable of understanding their importance."

"Well, you've studied more than me. But aren't you talking only about the precepts that should be kept by Buddhist priests and Zennists? I mean, isn't it possible a man can't live an honest life for the very reason that he strictly observes the precepts, though he may be a fine disciple of Buddha? He's like a beautiful pet, but how far from nature!"

"That's the very point I'd like to see through. I want to see how the Buddhist precepts hold true for human beings, and more, for my own life. To build up my own precepts, not for Buddha or for others, is the purpose of my study. How much I wish to live in my own way with confidence, pride, and stability!"

"Then all the more reason you shouldn't follow just the sutras and the teaching of Zen Master Tengai. Before anything else you should divest yourself of prejudice and risk yourself in trials and errors. The precepts are rules for actions, so they can be learned in actions, not in reading and in meditation. Right?"

"Well, I have no objection to your advice except for the definition of actions. I believe inaction is also an excellent action. What I don't enjoy now is only that I'm taking so long to build up my own precepts. While studying the Buddhist precepts is itself not my purpose but rather the means to go on to live freely and beautifully, I mustn't spend much time at it. It's a shame to spend time just to prepare to live, and a kind of sin to neglect consideration of others while busying myself with my own concern. You know, the most wearisome people to be with are those who busily care only about their own matters, and you are just now with one of them. Forgive me...I am a bore!"

They approached Shogetsuan. The cotton, no doubt sowed by the nun Shorai in the spring, was already two feet tall, and some buds low on the stems had begun to open.

"Mokuzu, I must change. Can you wait here a bit?" said Miss Iwai, and she ran between the cotton plants to the nunnery.

Mokuzu sat on a little grassy bank. The cotton flowers, whitish yellow with dark red centers, all faced the young sun. He had heard that some begin yellow in the morning and turn dark purple in the afternoon.

A breeze passed over the green rice fields from the western mountains, where the mist was clearing. Reaching the cotton, it stirred the palmate leaves, and when it paused, Mokuzu's head and shoulders were made hot by the radiant heat.

'Cotton is said to have originated in Khotan, the northwest border of China, now called the Sinkiang Uighur autonomous region. It was transported to Arabia, where it was pronounced "qut(u)n," and in due course it became the English "cotton." Caravans in search of it crossed the great desert Taklamakan with heat waves shimmering on the dunes. When at last they emerged, could they meet flowering cotton plantations? Khotan meant "milk of the earth"...'

Miss Iwai reappeared with a small bamboo basket. She had on a sleeveless blouse, a short divided skirt, and sandals.

Mokuzu was shocked to see the incongruity between her white, racy limbs and his black, anachronistic training robe. Walking beside her, he came to feel he was wed to an old, narrow, dying culture.

'In the industrially advanced countries, questions about good and evil and the cultivation of character have passed beyond people's concern, and desires are blithely affirmed by reasoning that we are born with them and are perfect beings in nature. People are concerned not to control their desires, much less to deny them, but to find how to fulfill them by taking advantage of every being other than themselves.

'They don't see their desires as evil. They see their poor ability to fulfill

655

them as evil, and also see as evil the social mechanisms that hinder their realization of them. And anyone or anything that thwarts their desires is the worst evil.

'Well, this current isn't new. In the East it was germinated with the rise of Mahayana Buddhism, which affirmed klesa to be the progenitor of Bodhi, or enlightenment. Mahayana Buddhism reinstated individual dignity, but the prosperity of Mahayana Buddhism without the foundation of Hinayana Buddhism is dangerous for mankind. Individual dignity rationalizes human desires but isn't sufficiently dignified to be responsible for the consequences.

'On this earth limited in natural resources, to fulfill one's desires means inevitably to depress and trample on others' desires. The struggle for existence is a common condition, and people have to be sickened by realizing that the more they affirm their desires, the more they must deny the desires of others. To solve this inversely proportional guilt, people endeavor to increase production chiefly by more effective use of natural resources, and try more fairly to divide the profit. But they don't question whether their desires are justifiable. They believe their right to the final and perfect gratification of their desires has been granted — but by whom?

'...Thus society is flooded with those who complain that their desires aren't satisfied, and with those who realize they are satisfying their desires by depressing others. Both are alike in affirming their desires, and alike in not trying to solve within themselves the problems that ensue. So the problems are shifted to society and become social problems. Society is thus composed of people with problems, and the main work of society is to solve their problems.

'Then of what use is society to a person who solves his problems by himself and within himself? No use. The functions of society would diminish if such persons were to increase. Society is composed of and exists for those who don't solve their own problems. It ignores those who do — they are like invisible spacemen. Society's leading participants are those who don't control their desires but cheer them on to the extreme. To control and govern one's desires is equivalent to killing oneself as a member of society.

'I know that the best way to live in such a society is to train oneself highly enough to be able to control one's desires and yet not extinguish them altogether. That is, a person must be able to solve his problems and yet must keep them for the sake of his pleasure. That way he won't be rejected by or detached from society and can take all the conveniences it offers, or he can enjoy acting the fool or sufferer as long as he likes. But what a crafty way to live! The more society blazes with desires, the more crafty people will increase, won't they? How hateful to become such a guy!'

"Did I vex you by decoying you? You look stern and dark!"

"Not at all. I rather thank you for giving me a chance to air myself." Mokuzu's tone was quiet.

The place to which Iwai came for the fringed orchis was the riverside of Okuse. The shore where the direct monk Kaijo and Mokuzu had rested on their return from begging was presumably not far upstream, but to Mokuzu that time seemed remote.

A short distance up on the other side was a cliff eroded at the toe by the water. Straight across was like the near side, sandbar sporadically overgrown with cogon grass and eulalia.

"I see no fringed orchis," said Mokuzu. Iwai pointed,

"There. We'll cross, walk down the grassy sandbar, and find a wet area with masses of them; they go all the way to the foot of that rocky mountain." She proceeded to the water.

It was a clean ford, but the current was quick and the far side looked deep.

"How refreshing!" She was in the water with her sandals on. She advanced, hiking her skirt, and stopped where she could hike it no higher. Mokuzu on the sand, seeing the back of her thighs, felt an electrical stimulus in his palm, elbow, and upper arm. When the hem of her skirt was licked by a wave she let it go and bent to wet her face.

She returned, her face bright with water droplets. "What? Are you afraid of the water?"

"I can swim, but, er..." Mokuzu hesitated and remembered on the spur of the moment a passage from the Holy Bible: "Unstable as water, thou shalt not excel,"[3] and he continued,

"...but it is a restriction — Buddhist monks should not swim."

"You needn't swim, you can walk. Even where it's deepest isn't above your neck."

"Miss Iwai, if I do, my robes will get dripping wet." Mokuzu sat down on the grassy sand.

"What? Of course you'll take them off. Don't worry, no one comes here and there's lots of tall grass." She took off her blouse without a scruple. Mokuzu averted his eyes to the white sand where there was her shadow. The shadow shed skirt and bra, and those on the sand were real. Clad in only a brief triangle of cloth, she ran with short steps into the stream. She steadied herself in the deep water and turned back. She was smiling.

He did not miss that she had blushed before she ran, but now he could not think carefully under the hot sun. She was waiting for him. Finally he managed to speak,

"Excuse me, please. I'll wait here until you come back with the fringed orchis. So could you go by yourself?"

Without replying Iwai began to swim. She reached the other shore and without looking back disappeared into the grasses.

Mokuzu fixed his eyes on the flow. To avoid the spectacle of her clothes, he did not look aside.

He fancied the scene of her coming back and dressing, quickly, matter-of-factly, or taking time for some reasons.

'How easy I was with Ena! We had no problem of precepts, only the warmth of love. The precepts stand out like iced trees in a forlorn field.' He decided to return ahead to the college. He felt like a fool, a defector.

On the way back, the bamboo-sheath thong of one of his clogs broke. He worried whether anything wrong had happened to Iwai. Yet he kept walking, carrying his clogs.

He might never see her again, for she went home that day.

That evening Zen Master Tengai gave Mokuzu a new koan, one of the eight hard-to-pass koans listed by Hakuin:

> An old woman for twenty years took care of a monk, and always had a maiden wait on him at table. One day she ordered the maiden to embrace him and then ask him how he felt. "Like a dead tree," said he, "devoid of warmth for the last three winters, leaning by a cold cave." Given this report, the old woman drove him away, burned down his hermitage, and cried, "Lackaday! All these years I have been serving a mere snob!"[4]

As long as a person eats, his life is maintained. As long as he lives, his carnal desire arises and love toward other lives also grows. But the monk coldly rejected the maiden.

To Miss Iwai Mokuzu had not declared with overweening indifference that he felt like a dead tree. For him it was too far from true. Besides, he did not want to become like a dead tree. As he left her, he had looked back with a sense of humiliation.

'Could she, close to naked, sit on the soft grass and enjoy the view of the marsh with its flowers so like a flock of dancing snowy egrets? Green pines on the cliff, deep blue sky, sweet breeze, clean sound of the flow.... Why didn't I spend a while with her there, sheltered by the tall grasses?

'She might have picked one, elegant and pure white, tripartite lip, fringed side lobes wide open, fan-like. She might have wished to ascertain if there was a scent and raised her nose to the middle lobe, smooth and ligulate.'

Zen Master Tengai requested that Mokuzu be the monk when he dealt with the koan. Mokuzu knew the master would be furious and even excommunicate him if he embraced the maiden. The master so disliked women that he would have literally vomited were he made to come in contact with any. He must have seen in femininity a filthiness and a devilishness.

Mokuzu knew how to satisfy him; he was expected to see through the old woman's gambit and lead the maiden to Buddha's teachings, and it had to be wittily done without harming her sentiments, like this:

"Oh, pretty maiden! Today too in beautiful attire you are serving me. I am thankful! Presently you are under the old woman's direction, but soon you will comprehend the nature of true service. Work hard and study hard. I too will continue to train myself, and together we shall walk the Bodhisattva Path." But in his mind Mokuzu cried,

'How false and wily is the answer I am expected to make! I hate to be the type of Zennist who can feign to be free, easy, and aloof!' He hated Zen Master Tengai too. He wanted to kick him in the ribs and strike him a karate chop on the temple.

'Whoever has suffered knows that compassion without carnal desire is cold, as is preaching without offering any material sustenance. Carnality is the vitality to live on. Compassion alone is an invitation to die!'

After a week of intense meditation, Mokuzu decided to give the answer that would please the master. He was well aware, though unpleasantly, of his deceit in answering contrary to his own view. He could not think of himself as able to follow the master's teaching and have no sex and no child all his life. Often he was tempted to declare that his view and the master's were antipathetic and that he would depart the monastery at once. But each time he reconsidered,

'Dishonesty in the relation between master and disciple is less important than self-honesty. I must be loyal to my original intention of stealing all of traditional Zen. If I finish "The Old Woman's Burning the Hermitage," the only koans left to master are "Dungshan's Five Classifications," "The Ten Supreme Precepts," and "The Last Barrier." By any means I want to master every single one. Then I'll know if Zen too is after all only a useless bubble for killing time — ignorant, incompetent, and inefficient for the world of death, for the world before birth, and for the mentally distressed, and for all who are unfortunate.

'If I'm not satisfied even the day Zen Master Tengai permits me to be certified with full mastership, I'll bid him farewell without a day's delay. I'll act like Ikkyu, who burnt his certificate before the very eyes of his Zen master Kaso. Until such time, I must endure any impurity and unpleasantness.'

❧

In early August a certain major cutlery company in Seki completed its new seven-floor office building, and Zen Master Tengai with his disciples was asked to the celebration. The company president, Kaiba, was one of the master's successful laymen. He had been helped materially and morally by the master since right after the war. The master had loaned him earnings from his shiitake plantings without asking compensation. And on occasion he had taught him an occupational Zen awareness based on Suzuki Shosan, an Edo-period Zen master who combined Zen and the samurai spirit.

Suzuki's thesis was that every occupation that benefited people was the practical application of Buddha's teaching. Hence every workplace was a training hall of Buddhism wherein all should efface themselves in their work. Accordingly, workers would realize the deep pleasure of engaging in seemingly trivial and tedious work, and such pleasure would raise their utmost working ability, thereby increasing output. Inspired by this teaching, President Kaiba produced and marketed disposable safety razors and so amassed his fortune.

Zen Master Tengai had many such laymen, but the master's results in this field had never impressed Mokuzu, for Mokuzu gave little value to any business concern.

The monastery was in a touring period, and many senior monks were traveling about or returning to their native homes. Those of the attendants' office who were senior to Mokuzu were also absent, so Mokuzu was obliged to take the seat next to the master in the back of the car chauffeured by Gyokuro to the company ceremony. All the other monks were carried by two microbuses.

Zen Master Tengai as always sat deep in the seat, straightening his back with force in the abdomen and looking directly ahead, which produced the impression that he was the best and the strongest man in the world. Mokuzu, with such a rare chance to see the town, kept looking out the window.

In the glassed office of a service station a girl raised a cup of tea to her lips. '...keeping her composure amid such noise and smell...in a swivel chair, short skirt, shapely leg turned sharp at the knee...'

A young couple entered a bookstore. Soft healthy shoulders exposed, looking up into his face with delight. His hand was lightly placed where her hip broadened.

'...must be a bus stop. A tall lady walking indifferent to the crowd, a stick of French bread protruding from her shopping bag. Girls coming down from the second floor of a store selling bathing suits. So many people crossing, never bumping, and none of them notice they are being observed. I wonder why girls with pretty faces and figures stand out instantly even in a crowd, though a crowd conceals people's private affairs.'

"Oi! What's the matter with you? Why don't you proceed?" the master sullenly reprimanded Gyokuro.

"Master, the light is red."

"Hm! Who arranged such an inconvenience without consulting me?" The chauffeur could not tell whether it was a joke or a serious question.

A policewoman whistled to direct traffic and moved with verve, her uniform accentuating her torso. 'Her plump parts resemble balsam pods — at a touch would they pop?'

After the ceremony and a lecture by the Zen master, a banquet was held. The master, disliking any sort of consumption of his past merit, quickly escaped from his seat. Attended by Mokuzu he toured the newly equipped offices and factory and went out to the go-round-style landscaped garden, also new.

Except for a path, all was green lawn under sprinklers. Seen close up it was rectangles of sod delineated by sandy soil not yet grassed over. The garden's design must have been based on utility, and the garden was thus fated to be generally flat. A gourd-shaped shallow pond gave a cool impression, but the accompanying shrubs were too small and the trees too drastically pruned to give shade. The harsh summer sun directly hit the water. Clumps of oleander at a far border were in bloom.

The master and Mokuzu came to an arbor set on an artificial hillock overlooking all of the pond. The elevation would be clad in green when its pines, camphors, oaks, and maples grew up.

The rice fields to the southeast were being developed into disorderly urban communities. The northwestern region still presented the traditional sight of rice fields extending to mountains with ridgelines vivid against a deep sky.

Office girls in blue-and-white uniforms chatted as they walked along an open-air connecting corridor. Those ahead looked back, and those behind reached to catch a hand or touch a shoulder. Some carrying manila folders took a path to the main entrance. The three who remained went on chatting as they approached the pond. Under the weeping willows they squatted and then sat with legs extended.

'They, who are employed to serve the company, aren't lost in gloom but are prizing their joyful moments, while I, unemployed, am disallowed by my koans and precepts to take a moment's breath. What makes them bright and me dark? They must have good human relations here and at home or somewhere, unlike me....'

"Tell me, Mokuzu, did you ever experience touring with Zen Master Hanun to raise the money for his Kannon statue?" asked Zen Master Tengai while fixing his eyes on the far mountains.

"No, never."

"Hm, I see. You were young, and he would not give you hardship. Now you are adult, which means you should not shirk to raise money in the world of money. If even worldly men resolutely challenge the task, how much more should priests. Priests should gather money to be spent for what least concerns worldly men, that is, for the welfare of our nation. The welfare of our nation entirely depends on talented men, and talented men are produced only by excellent education."

"Master, do you mean I am to be useful to raise money for your college?"

"Yes. I hope you will quickly complete the first stage of your koan study and come along with me for that purpose. I expect you'll not blunder and also not tire during the tour."

"But isn't your college in good financial shape?"

"Certainly, but it's far from ideal. Didn't you ever wonder why work on the new dormitory was discontinued? It may look great as a white modern building against the blue sky, but I have yet to install central heating and air conditioning and also audiovisual equipment. Then the classrooms and lecture hall must be rebuilt, the latter combined with a gymnasium. Everything must suit the high quality of the students who are to become leaders. My students must know a luxurious and comfortable setting so they'll not be intimidated when they must visit fancy settings. The spiritual base of the college is by now established. Next, building up its container is my task."

'Old wine into new wineskins — worse, percussion instruments into a showcase,' thought Mokuzu, but against his will he said, "How assiduous the students will be if they learn of your parental affection!"

"That isn't all I have in mind. I must increase the permanent endowment of the college so that whoever becomes my inheritor can maintain everything from accrued interest and entirely devote himself to teaching without financial worry. My trouble is, I haven't much time left."

"Do you see your death as imminent?"

"It couldn't be so far off, even if I boast in front of my disciples that my physical age is twenty-one and my spiritual age twenty-seven. But I shall have to carry my regret beyond the grave if I die before I raise the fund. Therefore be quick to complete your koan study. Haven't you yet satisfied your understanding of the old-woman koan?"

Mokuzu pitied the master for having to worry that a pecuniary matter would follow him beyond the grave. But at once seizing the chance to advance his koan study, he carefully said,

"Master, I know you are guiding many to the teachings of Buddha according to their ability and situation. President Kaiba could perfect his company thanks to your care, and he is able to propagate Buddhism through his business. Hundreds of employees are working here for a united purpose and are enjoying its benefits. This is one fine example of your passion's having brought forth a number of talented men and enabled them to help many others.

"Some office girls are now resting under the willows. How would I respond if one were to throw her arms about my neck and whisper, 'How does it feel?' Ought I to say, 'I am like a dead tree devoid of warmth for the last three winters, leaning by a cold cave'? No, I think not. It would be the response of one who least knows the master's mind, and who knows neither his own life nor the girl's. He who clearly knows both Buddha's teaching and the master's mind will lose no chance to resolutely spread that teaching and that mind, and he will speak warmly, softly, and wisely." Thus Mokuzu presented his predetermined view.

Just as he expected, the master expressed joyous consent, with eyes half-closed as he cleaned his ear with his finger.

Mokuzu was easing his several-days' fury at the master. Seated cross-legged in lotus flower meditation form on a bench in the arbor, the master raised his might and said,

"I myself chose the name Tengai, which means, 'to go beyond the world and see no equal.'[5] Can you see this ardent and tragic temper toward life?

"Listen, Mokuzu. I have firmly rejected meat and matrimony since I entered the priesthood at age twelve up to this very moment of my sixty-ninth year. In all these years I never once violated the precept, but not because I had no opportunities. There were as many as trash in the market. Was I, then, incapable? True, I have been allergic to animal protein. But I have always been brimming with lustihood. Such a man as Tanizaki, who died recently, is beneath comparison. It was said he could hang a wet towel on his thing after a bath, but with mine I could flip it to my shoulder.

"Yet why have I been persistently keeping the precept? Simply because it is Buddha's teaching. You know that when I was ordained, my mother repeatedly asked me not to muddy the face of Buddha even if it meant disgracing anyone else. It is a fact that if we marry there will be children. Then we must embrace our wife with one arm and our children with the other. And I ask, how will you embrace your laymen? See? This is the problem. Men worthy of being called Buddha's disciples should make others happy before making themselves happy. If they marry, how can they practice their best for others?"

Mokuzu listened silently with lowered eyes. An ant was dragging an ala. He wanted to look up at the blue sky and the indigo mountains backed by a rising gigantic column of clouds. He was reminded of some lines of D.G. Rossetti's "Hill Summit":

> 'And now that I have climbed and won this height,
> I must tread downward through the sloping shade
> And travel the bewildered tracks till night.
> Yet for this hour I still may here be stayed
> And see the gold air and the silver fade
> And the last bird fly into the last night.'[6]

The master was speaking: "Without hesitation I can reply to the question Who is the best Zen priest in the world? It is me! I don't yet know a man more lovable, more trustable, and more respectable, for I have been practicing all good deeds whenever I realize them to be good, and however hard they are, and more, I have stopped being bad just as soon as I realized I was bad... and what a hard life it has been!

"You know the episode about the Chinese Zen priest Niauke. He quoted a stanza from the Nirvana Sutra to answer a question from the poet Bai Jyuyi. Bai Jyuyi then refuted him by saying even a three-year-old baby knew as much.[7] Niauke shot a second arrow, namely, that a three-year-old baby might comprehend it, but even a hundred-year-old man was incapable of practicing it.

"This is the point: can we practice it? It has nothing to do with knowledge. Our Zen practice may produce much knowledge, but much knowledge doesn't amount to even half of Zen. Only in practice has Zen its life. Therefore Zen training is hard to bear. Living all one's life as a Zennist is truly hard. Mokuzu, my life since the day I became an acolyte has been a chain of hardship, bitter as if keeping aloe in my mouth.

"If an aloof outsider asks me 'What is Zen?' I will say 'Zen is to become

664

the object.' If he asks 'What is life?' I will say the same. But note, to an intimate I will answer that Zen is to be patient and life is to be patient.

"Can you make sense of my mind? Listen, and remember: Whoever is impatient and sparing of his pains had better stay where he can live without patience and pains. Indeed he had better live where indolence and pleasure are more meaningful than patience and pains. I decidedly refuse to live there. I live where patience and pains are greatly valued, and I fully enjoy the world that is exposed to whoever is patient and painstaking.

"From infancy I didn't want to die. I feared death and even now I fear it. Therefore I am living a complete life. I haven't a minute to waste on a false life, and I know there is no life more complete than when I am tortured by patience and pains."

Odds and ends of his energetic speech must have reached the girls under the willows. Possibly they understood that a disciple was receiving a reprimand. They quietly left.

Mokuzu could feel the overshadowing of the cumulonimbus. A faint smell of oleander was on the wind. Zen Master Tengai lowered his voice and regarded the far sky as he talked,

"Daitokuji in those days when I was a monk was a kind of social circle for notables from various fields. Each season a tea party and a flower arrangement party were held, to which young ladies of good family came in their finery.

"Among them were two singularly attractive sisters who had won the reputation of being like an elder and a younger Komachi. They were nineteen and sixteen, daughters of a Zen temple that had a garden designated as an important cultural property.

"Their priest father hoped one would marry me and make me inherit his temple. He expressed his wish to Zen Master Shutan and implored him to persuade me. I forthwith refused, but my Zen master, being of gentle nature, was slow to inform the priest. There was some suspicion that he was contriving with him and waiting for my mind to change.

"Meanwhile, whenever he had the chance, the priest asked me through my Zen master to assist his services, and as I could not refuse my master's orders, I often had to visit the temple. There I always found little for me to do, yet each daughter in turn kept serving me tea and food. One night the priest and his wife had to make a distant visit and asked me to take charge of the temple because the daughters would be forlorn. First the elder invited me to her room to hear her koto playing. Then the younger asked me to see her flower arrangement. Then together they asked me to take them to a movie or a concert....The entire family was trying to turn my head.

"Some nights only one or the other was left in the temple. Even so, I kept my purity. Truly both were beautiful and tenderhearted! They even brought me into their dressing room to be advised on which dress suited their outing of the day...!

"Oh, I was great! I bore it all to the end. Often my gums bled, and I was as if amid flames with a fougasse in my gut."

Mokuzu noticed the line of a tear in the master's eye.

"I cannot help being moved to tears at the awesome purity of my youth. I respect myself as Buddha's best disciple, I love myself with a twinge of sorrow; I was excellent, I fought successfully through the discord of youth. Where is there another Zennist who truly practices Zen through his individual life and therefore in a highly individual style, and therefore, directly united with the boundless eternal life of the universe?"

Mokuzu too was moved by the fact that he happened to have so unusual a Zen master, who had been controlling his personal desires and sacrificing himself for Buddhism, on which he had set such great store. He felt the urge to just follow him by impulse.

On the other hand he felt like laughing loudly at the master's reminiscence:

'He sacrificed himself for the Buddhism he fabricated in his own favored way. I know individual life is mortal and a speck of dust compared to Buddhism, the Absolute, or the universe. But we should not forget it is we who recognize its greatness, and therefore we are superior to it in quality.

'He also says we cannot spare an arm for our laymen if we marry and have children. But first, it is ridiculous that we must embrace wife, children, and laymen with our physical arms only. And second, without the experience of marriage and child raising, how can he know in what way laymen wish to be embraced? To be embraced in a way one doesn't want is rather annoying.

'What we must respect is not a person's sacrifice to help others but a person's surplus to help others after he has helped himself. I don't believe anyone can be happy living on another's sacrifice. Zen Master Tengai denies meat and matrimony, but I wonder how he can sponsor others who partake of what he denies himself.

'How uninteresting that the reward of his enormous patience and effort is a narcissism blended with enormous self-praise and self-pity! This could be the motive of his fervid preaching filled with criticism and reproach, and also of his lowly desire for name and power.'

Mokuzu wished to go beyond his Zen master rather than blindly follow him; yet he did not want to secede from him in a detestable way as other disciples did.

'After all, to go beyond him means to go beyond traditional Zen. Isn't that an audacious idea? The nucleus of traditional Zen is *Shin-shin ming*, as Dean Shiba pointed out in his writing. All Zen masters after the eighth century quoted *Shin-shin ming* to authorize their Zen view. Baijang, Daju, Huangbo, Linji, and Dungshan are none of them exceptions. In the Huayan sect as well, the fourth patriarch, Chingliang Chengguan, admiringly drew on its essence in fascicle 37 of his annotations on the Huayan Sutra (Avatamsaka Sutra). How can I go beyond *Shin-shin ming* and not fall into an ignorant life?'

Mokuzu thereafter meditated nightly in the charnel, and always he read *Shin-shin ming* before he entered into samadhi.

Shin-shin ming
(Inscription on the Believing Mind and the Mind Believed In)

The Ultimate Way asks of us no difficult training,
But rejects our preferences.
It exposes itself explicitly, in detail, and in totality
When we free ourselves from love and hate.

A minute error in understanding
Is like the disparity between heaven and hell.
If we have neither affirmative nor negative assumptions,
The Ultimate Way will reveal itself before our eyes.

*

Forming attachments and bearing hatred
Are ailments of the mind.
To toil in search of tranquillity without knowing
The contents of the Way is to toil in vain.

The Way is perfect as the sky,
Neither wanting nor superfluous,
And is made imperfect
Only by our discrimination.

Do not pursue forms;
Yet, do not dwell in the idea of emptiness.
Once the mind is unified and evenly settled,
Everything therein disappears, taking its own course.

Even if we still our moving mind,
Our stilled mind moves anew.
By trying to keep our mind either moving or still,
How can we understand its unity?

As long as we fail to understand the unity of our mind,
The virtue of our mind moving or still is lost.
If we drive away forms, we fall into emptiness.
If we are faithful to emptiness, emptiness becomes forms.

The more we have words and thoughts,
The further we detach ourselves from reality.
When we cease our words and thoughts,
We are free to pass through anywhere.

When we return to the origin, we gain the essence.
If we linger at the reflected forms, we lose the meaning.
If even for a second we see the base of the forms,
We can go beyond this floating world confronting us.

Forms, ever-changing,
Are all caused by delusion.
But we must not trouble ourselves to seek the truth.
What we must do is stop our dualistic thought.

*

Do not cherish a dualistic view:
Refrain from pursuing it.
No sooner do we discriminate right from wrong
Than we lose our mind in confusion.

Two discerned by a dualistic view come from one indivisible.
Hence one indivisible should also not be cherished.
When we have in our mind not even one indivisible,
We are not vexed even if ten thousand vexations appear.

When we are not vexed, they do not exist;
When they do not, even our perceiving mind does not exist.
Perception ceases as forms are seen to cease to exist.
Forms cease as perception is seen to cease to exist.

Forms are forms on account of our subjectivity.
Our subjectivity is our subjectivity on account of forms.
The subjectivity of the perceiving mind
Is rooted in sunyata.

Sunyata is one indivisible and contains forms and the perceiving mind.
Sunyata contains all things fairly.
Since they are fairly contained,
Why should we see them unfairly?

*

668

The Great Way is generous and wide,
With no distinction as to being easy or hard to walk.
Yet like a fox, a narrow-minded person hesitates.
The greater his eagerness to set forth, the more he delays.

Adhering to forms, he loses proper perspective,
And surely he will stray onto an evil path.
We must free ourselves and see there is no departing from
And also no abiding in the essence of the Way.

If we entrust ourselves to the Way generous and wide, we will
Harmonize with it and walk with ease, knowing no anguish.
If we cling to forms, we will run counter to the truth
And our unfreedom will make us heavy of heart.

Unfreedom frays the nerves.
Why should we trouble to depart from or abide in the Way?
If we wish to ride on the One Great Vehicle,
We must not reject the forms sensed by our six sense organs.

The state of not rejecting the forms
Is the very content of Buddha's Great Awakening.
The wise do no particular thing;
The ignorant are caught in their own trap.

In the existence of all things, nothing is particular.
Yet we attach ourselves to particulars.
Is it not a great mistake
To let one's mind abuse itself?

When one's mind abuses itself, repose meets disturbance.
When one's mind is correct, there are no likes or dislikes.
All confrontations are naught but the product of egotistic
And unreasonable valuations of forms.

Yet forms are definitely not substantial.
Why then do we valuate them?
Once and for all, abandon them —
All confrontations, pros and cons, rights and wrongs!

*

When our eyes are awake
All dreams are erased.
When our mind is one mind
All objects are truly one,

669

The substance of which is so elusive, it is as mysterious
As an embedded rock that affords no hold for the hand.
In this state of mind, all forms look alike
And we are returned to our natural state,

In which all grounds for comparison
Are extinguished,
And in which there is no movement to be stopped
And no repose to be disturbed.

Hence both movement and repose lose their base.
How then is one indivisible even possible to exist?
In the ultimate state thus perceived,
There is not any sort of standard.

The believing mind and the mind it believes in are one,
Wherein all artifice is eliminated,
All hesitation is cleared away,
And pure spirit maintains its harmony.

Therein naught remains and
Naught is recalled.
Therein each form is lit by its own formless light,
And we have no need of troubling our consciousness.

Thought, emotion, and will
Are all unfathomable
In the state of mind
Wherein circumspection is not exercised.

*

In the true world, neither subject nor object exists.
Be not two — go beyond all relativities!
This is my best advice to those eager to fit correctly
Into the true world.

In non-relativity all is one
And naught is excluded.
The wise throughout the world
Have reached the essence of this principle.

Unaffected by extension or diminution of time,
It is graspable in a moment and lasts forever.
It does not distinguish where it is from where it is not.
Thus the world is uniform.

The minimum equals the maximum.
All distinction is forgotten.
The maximum equals the minimum.
There is no perception of inner or outer limit.

Existence is non-existence.
Non-existence is existence.
Were this not the right view,
We should have no reason to cherish it.

One is All.
All is One.
If this we realize,
Our realization needs no further perfection.

The believing mind and the mind believed in —
Truly it is not two separate minds.
Unlimited by past, future, or present,
Unapproachable by words.[8]

    The night wind quieted. The gravestones stood serene. The charnel was limned by moonlight. The mountain was still. Mokuzu was still. He felt like an island in a mountain lake. '...but the island will be dug of its gold ore and devastated.'

VI

Yellow Sediment

50

Self-Assertion

In the office of Shoshin Short College, Mokuzu was eating a school lunch with Dean Shiba, the dormitory inspectors Tanishi and Banan, the nun Shorai of Shogetsuan, and two lecturers, one on the history of culture, the other on pedagogy.

The lunch was rice boiled with barley, miso soup containing a brown seaweed, residue from the production of tofu (called *unohana* after the flower deutzia), and three-year-pickled daikon. Having no experience of monastic life, the lecturers noisily sipped the soup and crunched the pickles.

Mokuzu, who disliked the salty, malted, red miso, waited for the stuff in his bowl to settle before he drank the liquid. He would add tea to finish what remained. He looked in the bowl. The finer particles were surfacing, and a thin, eddying steam rising. He felt as if he were looking down through early mist at florets of cauliflower...

> A steed canters downhill in the mist,
> passes a dewy cauliflower field,
> enters a pinewood lit by the sun
> rising over the sea.

"Mokuzu, today I plan to fix those lazy students once and for all. Bring a warning stick and come with me as soon as we finish lunch," said Banan with a forbidding countenance. The two lecturers looked apprehensively out the window. One timorously opened it a crack. A bracing wind streamed in.

Because Mokuzu made no reply, the nun broke the silence,

"Isn't it a year ago today you came to Shoshinji?"

Everyone regarded Mokuzu, but he suddenly stood and addressed the dean,

"Would you give me my own time for just a short while?"

"Ha? Sure, fine, as you please," replied the dean with a faint and dusky smile.

Mokuzu silently left and took a path behind a dormitory to the mountain. The rocks and strewn pine needles were well dried; the weather had been steadily fine. Each fitful wind caused a dead branch to fall and carried a terebinthine scent. He turned off the path to go directly to the top. As he climbed the crags, the upwind winnowed his skirts.

The pines decreased as the crags increased. The blue sky widened overhead. The view extended below. Many red dragonflies flitted about or drifted on the currents.

He sat against a rock near the top. With a sweep of his eyes he could see ripening rice fields, a winding river, and mountains far and near. The college was hidden just below, and the scattered villages were so distant as to blend into the natural scene.

'From now on I must gain more composure. It's foolish to let my time be minced and bound by the orders and regulations of superiors. If I continue as I am, they'll try even to break the sky. The racket of all kinds of orders makes my head ring like a tin pan, and the many regulations make me like a caged bird. I obey and I'm regarded as a model trainee, but it's simply my loss of composure. I'm the only one who truly appreciates my life, and to appreciate it, composure is the key. I'd better be reminded of a tree that is host to an invasion of vines; it gets no thanks from them and is blighted and killed and falls down *thump!* with some powder flying away.'

The rock was warm. He was led into a merry memory of infancy and then into a pleasant doze.

"Assistant Dormitory Inspector! Mokuzu!" The call woke him. Tanishi was crawling up with his skirts tucked into his belt. Crumbly rocks rolled down and broke to pieces. Little birds flew away to another valley.

"Mokuzu, why are you up here? It's only midday. Please, quickly come with me, there's trouble. The first-year students are enraged...but wait, why so many dragonflies? I'm sorry to disturb the insects and mountain with our stupidity!"

"Why are they enraged?"

Tanishi had come in haste. He now seated himself as if to stay, shaded his eyes with his hand, and looked into the distance. Finally he said,

"No doubt they've exhausted their stock of patience, especially such unruly fellows as Hajino and Kusamori. They have good cause to anger. Banan hisses and strikes them too much. He can't understand that students aren't monks, who come to train and can take quite a lot of beating because Zen training involves reflection. The students are here because their parents or their company forced them to come. We should excuse their sleeping during meditation — it's better than spinning daydreams — and excuse their faking illness to skip classes, better than being truly sick. So now they are set to get back at Banan and are gathered in the dining hall. What will you do, Mokuzu?"

"I'd like to know what Banan will do."

"Oh, he's beyond reason and is declaring he welcomes such rebels. He's preparing a length of loquat wood."

"Loquat? What for?"

"He intends to counterattack and is fashioning a sword. Loquat is best, it doesn't splinter. How gauche he is!"

"And the dean?"

"He sensed darkening clouds and instructed the nun to go home, and he too left, with the excuse of a service he must perform at his temple. 'Phone me if there's difficulty and I'll promptly come by motorcycle' were his parting words to me. Well, we must do something. Shall we go down?" Tanishi got to his feet and waited. Mokuzu continued to sit against the rock with his hands behind his head, and he muttered,

"It's nothing. We too will lose our equilibrium and centrifugal force if we're nervous over a quarrel between some catfish and an eel."

"You're right. So it's I who must take care of it, after all. Why don't you pretend you are ignorant of the affair."

Tanishi cautiously descended. A red dragonfly followed behind his bald head.

'I should act like this from now on, for I am what I should constantly observe,' thought Mokuzu.

After a while he went down. In front of the office he saw a clog turned askew, Banan's apparently. The students were quiet in their dorm. A cool breeze swayed the bush clover. He entered the office. Alone, Tanishi was stooping to sweep up broken window glass.

"Welcome back. It was quite silly. As you see, what all too often ends up the victim of resentment is a silent but substantial object. Banan didn't stay in his room. He came running here, though I know not why, pursued by those fellows. Too bad he was unable to finish his sword."

Mokuzu picked up a crude wooden sword from the floor.

"They ignored it. Hajino and Kusamori jumped him like beasts. He scarcely used it — he flung it away and went out. His clog came off as he ran, and he snatched up the other, and he bolted barefoot for Shoshinji. They were resolved to quit college, so they were fearless."

"Banan is a superior at the monastery. He'd find plenty of support."

"That's why he went there. It reveals he's riding on the power of an organization, a convenient vehicle for bluffers. We have to know such dependency weakens our ability. It's not the choice of Zennists."

"You must be right, Dormitory Inspector Tanishi. A large establishment like Shoshinji can be burnt by a match. But what makes me further doubt the true value of any religion is to see its inefficacy for those who aren't its members. I have sort of been believing that the essence of any religion should be comprehensible to all and that a master of any religion would see no one as an outsider. These students aren't outsiders, they're kin. Still, Banan can't communicate with them. I bet you can evoke sympathy from all kinds of people even if you don't wear a robe and use Zen terms. As a test, join a circus and make a world tour; you'll be welcomed wherever you go."

"Ho! Mokuzu, I'm not so great as you account me. Then, what do you think of what followed? Koko came from Shoshinji and neatly persuaded Hajino and Kusamori to let him escort them there. He told me they are precious guests of the college. I assume they are now lined up to go confess to the holy founder. Oh yes, I forgot, Koko was looking for you. Don't worry, I said you were out on college business, but it seems he wants you for something other than this stupidity."

Mokuzu returned to Shoshinji. From the west border he saw, as he expected, Koko in ceremonial attire walking the veranda of the main building. Close behind were Banan, dressed likewise, and the two students. Mokuzu stopped in the shade of the cedars. Koko's walk with protruding belly was exactly Zen Master Tengai's, whereas his shrill voice was a poor likeness of the master's. Their figures disappeared into the main building. A chanting officer carrying a censer in one hand and throwing on his surplice with the other hurried after.

When Mokuzu arrived back at the attendants' office, the room was filled to suffocation with the odor of cooking oil.

'My stars! — I can't even begin to love the smell of either cooking oil or incense, the two dominant smells in a Zen monastery. I must after all be incompatible with Zen,' he thought. Senzoku was frizzling *kusagi* and soy beans.

Kusagi was a smelly bush growing wild throughout the area. On a June day all Shoshinji monks went to gather its leaves. These they boiled and then soaked for a week in buckets of water, often renewing the water, and on a fine day they opened them out flat and dried them on straw mats. The product when perfectly dry was stored for important occasions like the founder's anniversary and visits by honored guests. The recipe for this reserve food was credited to the founder, but more likely it had been devised by peasants during a famine.

Senzoku stirred the oil with a wooden ladle as he sampled a porridge of rice and mountain potato in another pot. His profile as he blew on the hot spoon looked like a weasel's. His eyebrows were thick and short.

He scooped some porridge into a bowl and gave it to Mokuzu.

"Taste this for me."

"Why so much just to taste?"

"Don't worry. You too must be hungry."

Senzoku's face was dauntless as if he never reflected on his past or future, but his nature was fair and warm.

"I can't detect what makes it sweet, so unusual, milder but more complete than sugar. The taste is slow to appear."

678

"I put in an extract of *Gynostemma pentaphyllum* I prepared last winter. You too will be required to study various savors if you're appointed to cook for the master; he's fussy. Tell me, what's going on at the college? Banan is lucky to escape being thundered at — the master is engaged with guests... though Koko's manner of scolding is sticky."

"How did he scold?"

"In short, he said Banan could afford to be silly because he hasn't grasped the master's mind. Banan lowered his big head like a resisting buffalo and said he wouldn't have given the students a single shout or blow had he not been considering the master. 'The master always sees the one behind the one presented,' was Koko's response, and he quoted the master, 'An important function of the college is to provide a cage for beasts so society can be safe and sound.'" Senzoku removed the pot of oil and begun to make a clear soup.

"Why does Koko happen to be here today?"

"Our guests are impressive personages — a former state minister and the chief of naval operations. The former state minister is presently working to revive Empire Day and came for advice. The chief of naval operations came to be accepted as a private student. The master plans to have them sponsor all the expenses of sending Koko to America to study English and teach Zen."

"I didn't know that about Koko."

"Next spring. The master hopes Koko will grow to be like Dr. Yasaka, honorary professor of our college, who has been spreading Zen in Europe and America since early this century. He is more famous abroad than in Japan."

"I thought Koko was to inherit this monastery."

"Who knows? It could be Genkaku, Kaijo, Bokuon, or even our head attendant, Ryoshin. But Koko if he fails to become like Dr. Yasaka could at least gain recognition as a widely educated inheritor," said Senzoku, and he rang the bell to signal the meal was ready.

Ryoshin, serving sake in the drawing room, came back in no time. Seeing Mokuzu, he spoke with a condescending air,

"How long have you been here? You are making the master and his guests wait. You must have been told by Tanishi to return here at once. Hurry to the drawing room, but be careful, they're important guests going to provide funds for Koko. Be tactful. Act in the manner they wish to see. Don't be awkward. Hey, Senzoku, we'll serve dinner as soon as Mokuzu is dismissed — don't overcook it, but don't let it cool!"

Ryoshin, his face dark and thin like a mussel, minutely regarded the nerves of his superiors but never those of his inferiors. Mokuzu left for the drawing room, annoyed by his injunctions. The gong was calling the monks to supper.

He entered according to protocol, but without any introduction Zen Master Tengai abruptly questioned him:

"Oi, Mokuzu, this is what year of the Imperial reign?"

Concealing his rising temper, Mokuzu dutifully replied,

"Master, it is the year 2625, counting from Emperor Jinmu's ascension."

"Hm, frankly express what you think of the Rising Sun flag."

The chief of naval operations, as Mokuzu had supposed, was gray-haired and rather small. Dark, with deep wrinkles, he resembled an aborigine of the South Seas. He kept his head slightly bowed, but his eyes were keen as an eagle's, keener than Zen Master Hanun's. He sat solidly with erect torso and did not budge an inch.

The former state minister was large and fair-skinned, with a loose double chin. 'Shamelessly,' thought Mokuzu. His hair was pure white and well groomed. 'Unnecessarily.' Only he and others of his type could deny he looked patronizing. 'He won't be impressed by anything good, won't ever admit his faults, and must believe he is the most talented man to manage any problem. I'd like to see him and my Zen master fight, though never would they fight each other,' Mokuzu mused as he began to answer,

"The Japanese flag assumed as its center the sun, that is, Amaterasu Omikami, the Sun Goddess. It has been worshiped by the Japanese since antiquity. I am told it was displayed at the main gate of the Council Hall in the Imperial Palace as early as AD 701, when Emperor Monmu held a New Year congratulations ceremony. In medieval times such warlords as Takeda Shingen, Uesugi Kenshin, and Toyotomi Hideyoshi employed it on the battlefield. When Commodore Perry visited these shores in the closing days of the Tokugawa shogunate, a member of the Shogun's Council of Elders, Abe Masahiro, ordered all feudal clans to hoist the Rising Sun flag on every Japanese war vessel. In 1870 the new Meiji government proclaimed through its cabinet an additional order stipulating that it be hoisted on every Japanese mercantile vessel..."

"Stop, stupid! Who asked you to lecture on the history?" railed the Zen master in a needlessly loud voice. It was the moment that the two guests were relaxing their fixed expressions out of admiration for Mokuzu's precise knowledge. They immediately recovered their gravity.

Mokuzu knew the master's art of unhinging guests by making a cat's-paw of a disciple. The paper of the shojis vibrated, but he calmly continued,

"Hence the Rising Sun flag symbolizes the fresh and passionate spirit of the Japanese living in the Land of the Rising Sun. Yet it seems to me the flag denotes a bloodstain."

"A what? What the devil?"

"By bloodstain I mean...," Mokuzu could infer that his audience expected

680

him to say that a bloodstain was the pure joy and anger felt by every Japanese, including the Imperial family, from their ancestors of ancestors down to their descendants. With serious demeanor he went on,

"...the Japanese flag is stained with blood, and blood is a fluid circulating within the vertebrate animal body. Blood supplies oxygen, nourishment, and hormones to the tissues and carries away metabolites. Blood consists of red corpuscles, white corpuscles, platelets — "

"Fool! I understand what you wanted to say. You're dismissed. Bid Koko come quick. But wait, this chief of naval operations has the experience of attacking Pearl Harbor, and this former state minister is exerting himself to establish National Foundation Day for our new Japan. Regard them with thanks and respect."

In the corridor Mokuzu passed Koko arriving. Koko wiped his mouth with the back of his hand and gave Mokuzu a friendly as well as a cunning smile. His cheeks were flushed on account of his having just filled his stomach with the porridge before it was offered to the Zen master and his guests.

In the attendants' office Senzoku was busy dishing everything up. Head Attendant Ryoshin was smoking a cigarette and to conceal the smell was burning a stick of incense. To Mokuzu he asked ironically,

"Meeting those magnificoes you must be feeling constricted and shaky. You can realize how useless the advancement of your koan study is, eh? Particularly, could you face the great chief of naval operations?"

"'A defeated general is best not exposed to further trial,'"[1] Mokuzu replied quietly. Neither Ryoshin nor Senzoku got his meaning.

The evening bell sounded. From the attendants' office only Mokuzu went to evening chanting.

Next morning when he showed up at the college, Mokuzu was asked by Dormitory Inspector Tanishi,

"Banan didn't appear for morning service; he seems quite broken down. But the two students are gloating. Would you look in on him and console him in some way?"

Banan was seated in his room, leaning his back against the wall. In the alcove hung a temporarily-mounted calligraphy by the Zen master of Shokokuji in Kyoto, who was a distinguished calligrapher. It was one of Banan's few proud possessions:

> Yunmen said in a lecture, "In us each there is light. When we endeavor to see it, we don't see it. Pitch dark. Tell me, what is this light?" He himself answered, "The kitchen, also the side gate," and he added, "The unspectacular surpasses the spectacular."[2]

"Mokuzu, I've lost confidence. Ever since I passed the first koan, I believed I had nothing to fear. But yesterday I was panic-stricken with those students..." His drooping eyelids showed want of sleep.

"What's wrong with being afraid and having something to fear? Hot water should be hot, cold water cold," Mokuzu commented.

"On top of that I fled to Shoshinji. It's disgraceful. I became a priest because I wanted to be respected, and now I myself have destroyed the root of my honor. I don't understand. I knew I'd be scolded by the master and Koko and laughed at by all other monks — yet I went back to the monastery."

"A man with a keen sense of honor often chooses the worse way for himself in a fix. Being scolded is good medicine for a pampered child. Banan, you never lived where there wasn't honor and sweetness. It was said we should stand away from a mountain if we wish to see it in its entirety. Likewise we must put ourselves outside human life to appreciate human life."

"You mean I ought to leave the college? I'm not averse to it. How can I face them as their dormitory inspector? My regret is only that I'd be leaving before Dean Shiba finds me a wife."

"I don't mean you should leave. I rather think you should go back among them as if nothing happened. Pat them on the back and say 'How are you doing? Study hard and play hard just like me.' The great advantage of losing confidence is that you can be modest. Neither shouting nor a warning stick is necessary to make them realize their life is flooded with light."

"How can I be so cocky as to change overnight? I'm not a chameleon. I must be loyal at least to my own feeling."

"In *Yi jing* it is written that the wise can adapt as quick as a leopard to any change of circumstance."[3]

"Then please tell me what was my enlightenment in passing the first koan and seeing my original nature?"

"A hallucination in an extremity, induced artificially by no sleep, no food, and endless beating. I believe real enlightenment should come from daily reason and experience and not from discontinuance of them," Mokuzu said quietly and indicated the scroll in the alcove. Banan looked at it as a tubercular might look at his thermometer. He fixed his eyes on it. Mokuzu left the room.

A few days later Tanishi approached Mokuzu as he was sickling grass on the bank with some students.

"What medicine did you give Banan? Come see."

Mokuzu found Banan in a growth of tall grass circled by those inveterately lazy students. He was singing a popular song:

Don't be eager to win.
Victory free of avarice
Is the Way of judo...

His ugly tone and flattening of the embellishments produced bursts of laughter. Hajino corrected him, and Kusamori demonstrated. So amiable were they all that Mokuzu could not figure out whether Banan was stooping to their level or exposing his intimate nature.

☙

That same day Koko appeared at the college after lunch and called Mokuzu to the yard.

"Mokuzu, needless to say, I have always regarded you favorably, even if you may not have noticed. Apart from that, would you comply with my request? Well, our old teacher tells me English is a humble tongue that looks like the sidewise crawl of a crab; and he says I can easily master it in two or three months after I arrive in America if I put aside my pride in being Japanese. Even so, I'll feel uncomfortable if I go without knowing anything. Besides, it would be shameful to be instructed by persons inferior to me."

"Senior Koko, I have studied English only a little, and only reading and writing, not conversation. And I'm one of the lowest monks. Why don't you ask the English lecturer at this Shoshin College? He's evidently excellent at English and at teaching it. I think he's here today."

"Hmm, he spent a whole year in class on *Animal Farm*, and he calls whoever is fat, 'Comrade.' Well, were that all, he'd be less objectionable. But you must know I am a trustee of the college. Unlike him, you're an outsider. Just teach me what you happen to know without fuss. I trust your attainment because our Zen master advised that I do."

A request from a superior monk was an order. Mokuzu could not flatly decline or Koko would lose his temper, for he too was a man who relied on an organization.

At three that afternoon Mokuzu awaited Koko in the college guest room, between the office and the library. Half an hour after the time agreed on, or demanded, Koko arrived without haste.

"Oh, my! Sorry it got late. I was delayed by a newcomer who came in last spring. An oddball, he snitches things from the various offices, but not out of need. Anything of value to another he takes and deposits in a queer place— the latrines, the bamboo thicket. He stole a loincloth from the direct monk and hung it on a maple branch, stole a memorandum of koans from the head cook,

683

stole the white ink from the reception head, who found the bottle watered down in his sutra box — where he had a stash of cigarettes — and he couldn't write the day's announcements. Our kleptomaniac even snuck into the Zen master's quarters and made off with a jar of macadamia nuts — a choice gift from a layman in Hawaii. The head attendant found it below the gate, in the lotus pond. Look, this too is pilferage from the Zen master's and half eaten." This last Koko said rather cheerfully while from his bosom he withdrew a flat box.

"How can I return it half gone? Eat, eat! It's delicious. Fancy French meringue. Soon Shorai will bring us coffee." Koko helped himself to a piece and ate it up.

"Are you sure the box was stolen before it was opened and not after?" asked Mokuzu.

"You mean you think there's the chance our Zen master opened it and was enjoying it bit by bit, and then it was stolen? Well, no matter, stolen is stolen, ha ha! Anyway you're too thin, eat up, Teacher!"

Shorai brought in coffee, and spoke,

"Mokuzu, you are fortunate to be given the opportunity to instruct such a great senior as Koko. Please be reminded of the saying, Do good: thou doest it for thyself. The dean was telling me that if Dr. Yasaka had happened to have as deep a fund of knowledge and respect for English-speaking people as your English teacher Yojun, Zen introduced to the West would be really welcomed by all healthy common people there and not just by a few exceptions to them."

'I wonder how seriously Koko will study English. But it's a fact people always respect him. Surely the reason isn't that he's gaining weight, since he isn't a cow to be prized for its marbled meat. After all, he completed the total koan study and yet hasn't lost his humor and generous attitude. I've no reason to criticize him, although the rumor that he chased away Bokuon lies close to my heart,' Mokuzu thought and began to teach English after the nun left the room. He borrowed from *The 26 Letters — Origins of the Alphabet* by Oscar Ogg, one of America's leading calligraphers.

"In China, it was said, Tsangjie hit on the idea of writing by seeing the marks of a bird. He was a subject of Huangde, who began to rule the country in 2697 BC. In Egypt the god Thoth was said to have invented hieroglyphics. In India Brahma began by deriving letters from the crevices of the human skull.

"The English alphabet came from the Greek. The Greeks got their letters from the Phoenicians, who got theirs from the Egyptians."

Here, to illustrate, Mokuzu drew the Egyptian Apis — the head of a sacred bull. He then drew the Phoenician Aleph in the manner inclined to the left, inverted it to make the Greek Alpha, and, last, drew the Roman A.

When he looked up he saw that Koko was mutely laughing. He started

684

to talk again, but Koko raised his thick, red, oily palm, opened softly, to the height of Mokuzu's eyes.

"What?"

"Sorry to stop your lecture, but please, I must leave for America in April, I have only half a year. By your way of teaching I will become a white-haired old man just growing acquainted with concrete English. I know it's very impolite to tell the teacher how to teach, but would you teach me a more practical English, you must know something more, eh...more important English for daily life, yes?" Koko produced a forced laugh.

Mokuzu thought him indeed impolite. He swallowed and changed course.

"If such be the case, I shall explain some obvious but very important differences between English and Japanese. To begin with, let us consider the personal pronoun, first person singular. As you know, in Japanese we have a great many expressions for the first person singular alone, including archaic and modern, masculine and feminine, standard and dialectal, modest and bold, such as *wa, ware, onore, yo, jibun, sessha, oidon, wagahai, ore, washi, wate, ate, uchi, temae, watashi, watakushi, boku*...Yet these all can be conveyed by the one word 'I' in English, with rare exceptions, such as 'a fellow' and 'yours truly.'

"For the first person singular in Japanese there are abundant choices according to need and circumstance. In English there is almost always no choice. Is this because of an absence of fertile sentiment and consideration in native speakers of English? No, it couldn't be. In my inference it is because they have been so considerate when they listen that the speaker has not had to trouble himself over an accurate and appropriate first person singular. Native speakers of English are highly developed in the art of listening, I assume. As soon as they hear 'I' they can distinguish among the variety of possibilities.

"This tells us that essential to English study is learning how to listen and how to read. Suppose a beautiful girl utters 'I.' We must instantly understand who she is and what is her background and present status.

"When we think of it, how many have spoken 'I' since the beginning of the language? Day and night, vigintillions and centillions of people regardless of age, sex, and station have uttered 'I' whether happy or sad. No other word could be more often used. Truly English study must begin with and continue with 'I.' Let me illustrate..."

Koko was tapping the table as if he had writer's palsy. Finally he gave it a big thump and spoke out in English, "*Stop! Stop!*

"Are you trying to make a claim for Zen and the art of English grammar? Don't make me the butt of your experiment, and understand I am not eager to learn English for the sake of listening. I must be able to speak before others speak or I can't win — at least I must be able to express what I have to say even if I can't make sense of what they say. Since I am undeniably a Japanese Zennist, my prime hope is to express in English what is suitable from a Japanese Zennist."

Mokuzu was listening with slit-eyes as if meditating. Possibly Koko felt he had hurt his feelings. Softly he intoned,

"Sorry. I was wrong to ask you to teach me English without letting you prepare. This is enough for today. Then prepare some materials for my use beginning tomorrow. And don't forget I earnestly ask that you teach me only what is suitable for a Japanese Zennist to express. I'd be grateful if you'd gather some worthy sentences to learn by rote the way we learn the sutras. But don't include anything from Dr. Yasaka or the likes, whose works are well known in America. People would figure out I'm only borrowing and it would be scandalous. See? So you'd better select what is hardly known to any American and yet pertains to Zen, okay? I leave the matter to your discretion."

Mokuzu went into the library to hunt up some materials for Koko. Tsurumi was dozing over an open illustrated book on Japanese national treasures — another complimentary book recently arrived from a publisher.

In the depths of the shelves his eyes fell on the writing of a Confucianist, Hayashi Razan, who was born in 1583 and died in 1657. He had taken Buddhist orders and studied in Kenninji, Kyoto; later he became a Confucianist and was employed as an advisor to a succession of Tokugawa shoguns — Ieyasu, Hidetada, Iemitsu, and Ietsuna — especially on foreign and educational policy. He was an advocate of anti-Buddhism.

Mokuzu browsed through the pages:[4]

> Myocho had wife and child. To sever family ties he bade his wife go to buy sake and in her absence he shut the doors, killed their two-year-old son, and roasted him on a spit. On her return his wife was whelmed at the truth of it. As he drank he ate of the flesh. Screaming, she fled the house. In turn Myocho left. Later he became National Teacher Daito of Murasakino. Heinous is this Buddhism that darkens the heart and bends it to cruelty. More humane are wolf and tiger, that never devour their young.

The passage was from an essay "Alert to Zennists." Mokuzu had no way of knowing whether it was fact or fiction, but thinking it engaging material for Koko's English study, he translated it. He also took a passage from the essay "The Temple with a Great Buddha Image" by the same author:

> The cost is inestimable. People were driven to hard labor. Just to convey the timber hundreds were crushed. Many carpenters were injured by accidents, some fell to their death. A treasured array of antique bronzes was lost to the smelting furnace to build the great Buddha image. What is the merit of such labor?

In a similar vein Mokuzu continued to extract diverse criticisms of Zen and Buddhism from the writings of Japanese Confucianists in the Edo period. As he made excerpts he translated them to English for Koko to memorize, though he was not confident that Koko would enjoy learning the whole of each.

> Nakae Toju (1608-48) thoroughly studied the doctrines of the great Chinese Confucianist Wang Yangming and established a school after him in Japan. From "Okinamondo" (An old man's dialogues):

Those lunatics see the vast and nitid substance of the Way. But as they do not yet comprehend the secret of the Mean, they are rough and careless in their perception of nature and attainment of enlightenment. Moreover, their form of self-training is queer, deviating from that of others. Such men as Shyuyou, Chaufu, Mupi, Tzengjetzy, Sanghu, and Juangtzy in China were prominent lunatics. Eminent lunatics in India were Sakyamuni and Bodhidharma. They are like stars compared to our Confucius, who is like the sun. Just as stars are perceptible after the passing of the sun, so lunatics like Juangtzy made their name after the death of our Sage.

Far worse than in China was the situation in India. There no single sage appeared until the age of Sakyamuni. The country had been one of savages, wherefore the masses readily believed the lunatic teachings of Sakyamuni. Incomprehensible to them was the delicate secret of the Mean, consistent through the world of heaven, earth, and mankind. They were induced to believe but a part of the vast and nitid substance of the Way as if it were true enlightenment....

Buddhism generally teaches morals, but just as the good it advocates is not the highest good, so neither is the bad it condemns truly bad. Disallowing amour is such an example. Sakyamuni gave up his princely crown and entered a mountain. After his great realization he did not engage in natural human conduct. He begged sporadically, neglected human duties, shunned human affairs, and led the ignorant into delusion and insanity by various expedients. All were incorrect, shiftless, paranoiac actions stemming from his initial slight misconception that the highest way is to be free of avarice, to live in faineancy, and to keep natural purity. Hence he entrusted all natural vigor to spiritual awakening....

Buddhists, saying they have transcended emptiness, do not respect their parents or other elders. They extol Zen Teacher Huangbo, who killed his mother as his demonstration of filial piety. Buddhists misguide people in teaching them that the three basic principles of human relations and the five cardinal virtues are but affairs of this transient and illusory life and unavailing to the attainment of Bodhi. Some claim that even a consummate villain who killed his lord or his parent can be reborn in Paradise.

Yamazaki Ansai (1618-82) was a Myoshinji priest who became a Confucianist at age 25. Later he founded the Suika Shinto school. From "Byakui" (To clarify a misunderstanding):

Jutzy wrote in reply to Wu Renjie that Buddhism and Confucianism are similar in form only and very different in content. We must see the difference. The teacher Mingdau said each phrase and each practice is the same: the difference is in the meaning. Without careful study, we cannot see the difference.

In Confucianism we say Hear the Way. Simply it means to increase one's store of information and to research so as to gain self-realization. The Way means to practice the natural daily affairs of lord and vassal, parent and child. Buddhists, quite to the contrary, claim they can understand the profound mystery by their "sudden enlightenment" achieved with profuse body sweat. We should not seek what we might be able to attain by special force, but seek what we can reach by piety and reason.

Our Sage teaches us to be faithful and pious at each moment and in each place, which in no way resembles the Zen claim that supreme reason is perceivable only after mentation has ceased. This Zen teaching is far from the truth. The correct function of our mentation is the very function of supreme reason. There is no mentation apart from supreme reason. Why should we wait for our mentation to cease in order to see supreme reason? Supreme reason is nothing other than benevolence, righteousness, propriety, wisdom, and sincerity, that is, the way of human affairs, as between lord and vassal, parent and child, elder and junior, sibling and sibling, man and wife, friend and friend. Buddhists if they understood in this light would not need to violate the Way, to cease everything, and to stupefy themselves.

Mingdau said...Buddha escaped from his father to become a priest. It means he dismissed his incumbencies and stayed in retreat for the sake of his own interest. Naturally the native people did not accept him; only the lowborn and the outcast helped him. This is not the way of a sage or any wise man. Buddha violated the way of lord and vassal, parent and child, man and wife, but he criticized others for not practicing it. He expected them to practice it while he did not, with the groundless excuse that he had attained the highest spirituality. If the world follows his way, mankind will become extinct. As for his intellection, he merely speculated on death. The motive of his study was fear of death and the wish to live on. In short he sought only what benefited himself.

Kumazawa Ryokai (1619-91) studied under Nakae Toju and was an administrator under Ikeda Mitsumasa (1609-82), lord of Bizen (now Okayama Prefecture). From "Shugigaisho" (Unofficial arguments):

Buddhism of old flourished and fostered training to achieve enlightenment. In these latter days there is no real training and anyone may become a priest. Most priests thus live in the priesthood for economic reasons only, and with no priestly learning.

Some rebuild temples to be acclaimed as restorers. Others build new temples to secure the title of founder-abbot. Still others become archpriests of various names and allow themselves feelings of elation.

The ancestral tombs of laymen are taken by temples in pawn, whence laymen cannot refuse temple requests. Laymen stupidly worry over their afterlife. Thus do temple assets yearly increase.

We should not forget that much as the land is fertile, Japan is small and her populace great. Out of regard for this reality the shrines to our Sun Goddess have been frugally built with raw timber and simple thatch. Our guardian before the Sun Goddess was Miwa Daimyojin. That time saw even greater frugality, for torii archways alone were built and Miwa Mountain was reckoned as the deity's shrine.

In further antiquity such indigenous trees as cherry and cedar were dedicated as abodes of the deity and they sufficed as shrines. This custom came of the need to conserve the land. In summary, Shinto shrines require little wood. Contrariwise, Buddhists without regard build many magnific temples fashioned after those in the great countries of China and India, which are fifty to a hundred times the size of Japan.

> Tominaga Nakamoto (1715-46) was born into the household of a time-honored soy sauce brewery. At the mere age of 15 he indicated errors in Confucianism; at about 24 he made a comparative study of Buddhism, Confucianism, and Shinto; and at 30 he made a comparative study of all the Buddhist sutras and proclaimed that every Mahayana sutra was written later than in Buddha's lifetime. From "Shutsujo kogo" (Words after meditation):

Just as the Indians delight in miracles, so the Chinese favor polished sentences. Whoever establishes and wishes to spread a teaching should generally adhere to his nation's traits or he will gain no followers. In *Apitan* it is said that Sakyamuni Buddha succeeded in preaching only by delighting the people with an occult power. In *Dajydulun* it is said that Bodhisattvas use divine power to exhibit manifold laudable miracles and to cleanse the hearts of the people, and that without divine power they cannot teach as they wish, just as birds cannot fly without wings.

I have indicated that priests are adept at occult power. So too I shall now say Confucianists are adept at polished sentences. The difference is only that between twelve inches and a foot.

Shiki also once told me the Indians are disposed to favor such expressions as "infinite" and "immeasurable." The Chinese favor words, especially formal words. The Japanese favor clean, straight words. Again, it is the disposition of each. Moreover, much figurative language occurs, "mustard seed," "Mt. Sumeru," "Indra's net," for the Indians favor such expressions.

> Hattori Somon (1724-69), son of a textile manufacturer, became a Buddhist priest at age 38 and studied Buddhism, Confucianism, and Taoism extensively. From "Sekirara" (A frank assessment):

Hinayana, a realistic teaching, has four Agama Sutras translated to Chinese; and indeed some passages seem expressed by Sakyamuni Buddha. But the entire Mahayana canon, presented as Buddha's words, was no doubt written well after Buddha's time, for it describes unrealistic theories. The Hinayana canon, in contrast, is for the most part factual. For instance, therein is stated that Buddha renounced the world at 19, attained his great awakening at 30, and entered Nirvana at 80. The same events treated by the Mahayana show Buddha spending eternal years after his great awakening, entering Nirvana without actually dying, and continuing to preach from Nirvana Peak — idealism, not fact.

> Nakai Chikuzan (1730-1804) studied Neo-Confucianism under Goi Ranshu. To a member of the Shogun's Council of Elders, Matsudaira Sadanobu, he submitted a report on how to deal with Buddhism. From "Sobo kigen" (A vehement argument on governance, from out of office):

Through the ages, it must be said, Buddhism has harmed the world. Buddhist brutality and inauspiciousness can be observed in an event of the Later Han: Chu Wangying believed in Buddhism and introduced it into Hur Castle. He then turned traitor and was put to death. All emperors who rejected Buddhism, discarded its temples, and disallowed priests and nuns were therefore wise without exception. Like Shytzung in Chou, they were clairvoyant. Emperors who embraced Buddhism, built temples, and allowed priests and nuns were purblind without exception, whence they some of them perished and the country fell to ruin. Note the example of Emperor Wu in Liang....

To build schools for the Royal Government is important. Schools serve not only to ostracize heretics, albeit that can be a side effect. After teaching the practice of filial piety, fraternal love, rectitude, and propriety, if our Confucian schoolmasters in their spare time repeatedly teach about the falsity of the Buddhist field of good fortune, the delusiveness of its transmigration in the three worlds, the absurdity of the Buddhist concept of heaven and hell, and worst, the rustic and shallow tenets of the Ikko sect, then the ignorance of the foolish people will gradually be corrected. Whereas the habitual ignorance of the old is hard to amend, the young can surely be rehabilitated. After steadily advancing this education for thirty years, all the old people will be gone and the rehabilitated generation will be full-grown. Then we can see a great decrease in the number who squander their property in donations to the head temples of the Buddhist sects where they worship.

> Yamanashi Tosen (1771-1826) damaged his right hand in infancy; with his left hand he studied calligraphy and became a master calligrapher; later he studied phonology. From "Moro rigen" (Rambling talk):

Especially the Zen sect is fallen to extreme decadence. Priests of Soto Zen vie in elegance of robe like snooty brides. Ever since Dungshan and Dogen, the Dharma transmission is gone from this world. Zen priests are more eager for handouts than are beggars and more cunning than merchants. Zen masters teach their disciples only how to turn a profit, and priestlings not twenty years old are called high priests or graduate monks. So grievous and deplorable has it become that they unblushingly parrot their founder's manner of speaking, secretly plot their Zen questions and answers, and record their koans in notebooks to facilitate transmission. Verily the true air of Buddha and the patriarchs has sunk below the soil.

Zen priests are least concerned to help people; rather they torture their laymen by exacting payment. They act covetous, wayward, and atrocious. Truly it is a degenerate age. How lamentable they have no regret.

Rinzai Zen priests are loose and rude, and are addicted to drink and to paper and brush. They may lukewarmly comprehend a phrase or half a koan, but their view no more than describes the doctrine of annihilation and is a non-Buddhist philosophy. How hopeless they are, proclaiming there is no Zen in this world and that they alone know the heart of Buddha!

> Hoashi Banri (1778-1852) studied economics, Confucianism, and, by the Dutch language, physics. Later chosen as principal retainer of Bungo (now Oita Prefecture), Kyushu. From "Tosenpu ron" (Critique on economics):

There must be over a hundred-thousand Buddhist temples and as many as several hundred-thousand priests and nuns. But nowadays only a few of them love to study. Because they do not study even what is easy, there can scarce be found in a thousand any who observe the precepts of Sakyamuni Buddha. Priests and doctors ought to study sedulously. Owing to my having taught many students from my youth, I know they do not. A doctor has but a spoon to depend on, so he studies at least a little. A priest is apt to inherit his master's temple or can enter a vacant one to make a living; wherefore priests can afford to be lax.

Priests are also lax due to the prohibition against Christianity. Moreover, every household must by law join a specified temple, whence the number of laymen of each temple stays constant regardless of whether the officiating priest is wise or stupid. Furthermore, with the civilizing of our nation, children from less wealthy homes are put into the priesthood in increasing numbers, and only they are becoming priests. Thus the character of our priests is disreputable and Buddhism a harmful agent to the nation.

By sanctioning marriage and family, the Jodo Shin sect violates the teaching of Sakyamuni Buddha. But these practices are in accord with morally acceptable law to begin with, so Jodo Shin priests are in fact righteous. The character of Zen priests is blatantly bad. Setting aside the priests, look at the acolytes: They elope with a man's wife or daughter or make off with another's goods. There are those who interpret these sins as coming from a Zen view of sunyata, which is to see through the empty nature of this world. But a more accurate explanation is that Zen acolytes are granted the convenience of travel and permission to stay the night in other Buddhist temples. Other sects grant their acolytes no such freedom and hence have less misconduct. Permission to stay the night was first established on a nationwide scale to assist Zen acolytes in their study and self-training. As to this aspect other sects might well follow suit. Nonetheless it should be remembered that greater convenience occasions greater harm.

> Shoji Koki (1793-1857) was a descendant of a lineage of merchants who amassed great wealth, to which he contributed. From "Keizai monzo hiroku" (Secret recorded dialogues on economics):

In the Rinzai school there is a supreme echelon of priests allowed to wear a purple robe costing 1,500 ryo. A priest aspiring to this height must pay the head temple, Myoshinji, 500 ryo from his temple and 1,000 ryo from his feudal lord. Myoshinji is thereby the richest temple nationwide, and its riches are further augmented by interest from loans to various prefectures. Myoshinji priests neglect their duty and focus on rank and profit. The folk of Kyoto therefore sing, "The face of Myoshinji is an abacus, the face of Daitokuji a teabowl."

Library Director Tsurumi awoke and went over to Mokuzu and tapped him on the shoulder.

"Translating to English, eh? Who in the world is going to read those grumbles?"

692

51

To Act Least in Society

At the autumn equinox the Shoshinji monks went out as they did in the spring on a big mendicancy tour, leaving just a few monks behind. They were divided to small groups each with a leader, and set forth at dawn.

The tour, though it was called a big mendicancy, was to augment their knowledge of the world more than to gather alms, and with discipline left to each leader's discretion, the extent to which they could see the various scenic spots or experience other pleasures depended altogether on the leader's ability.

After seeing them off in their travel wear as they ran in file down the stone steps through the cedars under the main gate, where a cold white fog overhung, the remaining monks kept monastery discipline throughout the large vacated temple buildings. The rare noises came only from mice, whose disposition was reserved.

Mokuzu finished cleaning the attendants' office and was leaving for the college when Koko, having just withdrawn from the Zen master's room, called to him to stop,

"Oi, today you may skip the college — you're coming with me."

The master had asked Koko to go to Kanbara, in Shizuoka Prefecture. A Zen temple there, Shoryoin, lay under a planned expressway, the Tomei, to be constructed by the Japan Highway Public Corporation. With negotiations between the laymen's representatives and the corporation at loggerheads, the priest was asking Zen Master Tengai to mediate; and the master was sending Koko to hear in advance what the laymen had to say.

Koko and Mokuzu were chauffeured by Gyokuro to Hashima Station to take the Shinkansen.

"Were we not pressed for time I'd invite you to Shofukuji, my temple in Nagara, and treat you to a feast aboard a boat on the river. After all, you're my English teacher," said Koko with a smile as he handed Mokuzu a box lunch bought at the station.

"I didn't know you already had your own temple. No wonder I've scarcely seen you in the monastery."

"Right. I was attending Gifu University while serving as chief priest of my temple. It's a good temple, brings me a substantial income, ha ha. I finally graduated from Gifu last spring. Next year I'll be admitted to the University of California. As you see, our Zen master looks after us if we're obedient. He appears bigoted and stern, but in his heart we are his real children. He boasts that his college is the best, not only in Japan but in all the world. Of course he knows it isn't true, so he recommended I study at Gifu."

Koko made short work of the lunch and asked while making use of the toothpick,

"How do you feel riding the Shinkansen for the first time?"

Mokuzu was marveling at the expansive brotherly air Koko was brewing and replied,

"It's so fast the landscape appears as lines, but it's sure comfortable, with surprisingly little noise and vibration. The speed disposes of the travel time. Everyone must have so grave a purpose as to require its disposal. I alone must be unworthy of this train while I'm merely going with you ignorant of why."

Koko responded with a grin. A pair of girls in azure uniforms with white aprons approached, one at either end of a handcart loaded with foodstuffs.

"Hey, give us that sake and whatever you have to go with it. You don't object, do you, Mokuzu? We're on a special outing — why not enjoy it?" So saying, Koko pulled from his bosom a fancy cowhide purse and paid with a fresh large-denomination bill.

He began outright to drink, and offered some to Mokuzu.

"I already feel sick before taking any sake."

"You fix your eyes too much on the near sights. Look off and enjoy being a passenger. Ho! There was a monk, Bokuon, you heard of him? His concern is always what isn't his concern. In our place he'll see only that the dust and noise harm trackside residents. After a little thought he'll conclude there should be no trains. No trains means no dust, no noise. But if there's no civilization, there'll be no solutions to environmental problems. What's important is to be a passenger when there are trains and not a pedestrian or a resident. Crying and posting protests along the tracks will do no good. First hop aboard and ride, then look for a solution. That's the right attitude. Our master too believes in improving society from within — live in it, and take an active role."

"What is Bokuon doing now?"

"He took issue with the master too much and too often. Now he's in a dilapidated mountain temple. He chants morning and night, at least eight hours a day, accompanied by his own bell-ringing."

"Why does he chant so much?"

"To purify the sins of mankind, he says. Phew! I never got any benefit from his labor, nor did the world, it seems. Nor did the people in Kanbara, where we're headed."

Mokuzu was apprehensive over the amount of sake Koko was drinking.

"Do you know about the priest of Shoryoin?"

"Oh, he too was an odd monk! We were contemporaries. He was quite sober, thanks to his narrow mind. Ha ha! I'll tell you a funny moment I can't forget. We were in the mountains cutting wood for shiitake cultivation. During a rest I causally asked him why he became a priest. At that he assumed the posture for sitting meditation. I stared in wonder. Soon after, I addressed him, 'Shukyo, hey! — what's going on?' At last he spoke:

"'Toward the war's end, we kids who had been bombed out were gadding in the market like a band of beggars. The shopkeepers drove us away with brooms, buckets of water, and salt, but those same folks reverently gave rice or coins to a bonze whenever he came begging, and sent him off with prayerful hands and a bow. He received their alms, but he never humbled himself and he always walked off in a stately manner.

"'It made no sense. Seizing a chance, I boldly asked him why he was so respected. He said he was a priest. I pondered it deeply. I wished to be a man who was respected like him. One day I went to his temple in the neighboring town, stepped up uninvited, and in a corner of the gloomy main hall imitated his meditation. At dawn some laymen began to come to worship the temple's main image. One old woman was shocked when she noticed me in the shadows. She ferverently chanted, pressing her brow to the earth, and tossed some coins my way. "This is it!" I thought, arriving at the realization that she was respecting not me, but me imitating Buddha's figure. So I determined to spend my life imitating Buddha.'

"Well, when I heard why he became a priest I couldn't stop laughing." Koko revived his laughter without laughing aloud. "But there's some truth to his motivation," he added, wiping his eyes.

"I would enjoy hearing why you became a priest."

"Me? I've no idea. Even now I can't fathom it. Somehow it turned out like this, ha ha ha! But since I don't know, I can tell people whatever I want according to the occasion, ha ha ha!"

Koko drank off the bottle he bought for Mokuzu, and after telling him to wake him at Shizuoka, he fell asleep. His ruddled face was breaking into a slight sweat and in repose was gentle and half smiling like the face of Hotei, a god of good fortune.

At Shizuoka they changed to the old Tokaido line.

"Mokuzu, I'll try to elicit the true mind of the Shoryoin laymen. Your role is to set it all down in writing so our Zen master can understand it at a glance, see? That's the extent of today's work," said Koko, and again he fell asleep.

'Is Koko defective in intelligence? He absolutely disregards metaphysical matters. I suppose that quality contributes to his liberality and shrewdness in human affairs, and so he's seen by the master as a born Zennist. The master is prejudiced against sensitive emotion and extensive speculation. Is the nucleus of his teaching full of stark Pragmatism, Instrumentalism, just and righteous cause, and love of fame and power? Those are the ornamental philosophies of parvenus!'

The town of Kanbara had developed under a steep weathered bluff that illustrated the rough Suruga Bay. The local soil was reddish and crumbly; it was said to be volcanic ash turned to clay and was called "Kanto loam."

The Shoryoin priest's young wife, in a kimono of Yuki pongee, was at the station to meet them. Her hair, done up in a knot, exposed her hairline in back, and the solid texture of the kimono emphasized the lineal beauty of her figure. She looked tidy, but her manner with Koko suggested to Mokuzu a landlady or a mistress and not the wife of a priest. She and Koko seemed bosom friends of long standing.

"I worried you might be losing weight over the expressway, but I see you're in the pink of health!"

"No, no, I'm so anxious I can't sleep. I really wish to be sure of what's to come."

"I know, you can't sleep because of your juvenescence. You shouldn't annoy your husband, he must be work-worn. You're not too demanding of him at night? Ha ha ha!"

The wife glanced at Mokuzu. He evinced no interest and kept facing the wind off the bay.

They entered a taxi in front of the station. Mokuzu took the seat next to the driver. Koko got in back, and the wife as she followed exclaimed in a flurried voice,

"*Mah!*"

This was followed by Koko's amused laugh. Her outcry was likely owing to his having in an instant put his thick hand where she was to sit and her having sat without realizing it was there. But only they could know, or know if he had withdrawn it to his knee, or put it on her inguinal region, or was it still beneath her?

Mokuzu felt his existence, like the driver's, was being ignored. He attempted to divert his mind into thought, but no thought came. Outside the window a shopping district stretched promiscuously along a narrow street; just the sight of it wearied him. He wished to stand on the high bluff eroded by the Pacific.

'What's making it so rare for me to act as I like?'

Soon the car came out to a national road, Route 1, and headed east past small factories producing aluminum articles or processed foods.

For the most part, Mokuzu could not catch the backseat conversation, but the two conversed like lovers and laughed easily. It seemed Koko was often whispering in her ear.

"Oi, Mokuzu, you go on alone — we'll call in at the local office of the highway corporation to get word on the progress of negotiations. She says the key laymen are by now assembled, so make haste to record what they say. I'll thank you for your fine assistance," said Koko unconcernedly, and he ordered the driver to stop. Where Mokuzu got out was the end of a shabby town. The road there was on a rise some twenty meters high. The old Tokaido line passed along the shore. From the roadside clustered houses extended up to mandarin orchards.

The wife spoke from within the car,

"The temple's in the center of town. Don't worry, you'll find it, and make sure you tell the priest we're at the local office; it shouldn't take more than a couple of hours. See you! You can look forward to supper, I'll treat you well." Mokuzu felt she was treating him like a baby.

'Her type swiftly puts a person into one of three groups: people too high, whom she can disregard; people too low, whom she can dismiss; and people just right, who for her are few. Dealing only with these few, she can always be happy. And Koko? Is he really the highest disciple at Shoshinji, which because of its hardship is said to suit only self-training demons? I'm a hundred percent sure he's lying — they must be going to a motel or a "rendezvous" hotel!...Well, what should I do? I can't keep standing by this noisy, sooty road. I'd better find Shoryoin.'

He walked along the national road. The storm doors of every house were shut tight. They were darkened with car exhaust, and were full of crevices from exposure to the constant salt wind. He passed between the close-packed low houses, heading for the hilly quarter of town. The lane came out to a road as wide as the national road, but as it was a local road there were fewer long-distance trucks.

The narrow town, crammed between craggy hills and wild ocean, had two big roads and two railways running parallel and crossing in places, and now the Japan Highway Public Corporation wanted to add an expressway. The houses of fisherfolk as well as farmhouses and home industries were jostled between, before, and behind these roads and railways. Mokuzu found it hard to understand why the Shoryoin laymen were opposed to leaving this town of noise, tremor, and soot.

The expressway was planned to pass just between the gate and the main building of Shoryoin and directly above the laymen's graveyard. The corporation was flatly refusing to adjust even an inch to either the seaside or the hillside, in deference to safety issues. Without considering Shoryoin there were enough problems, such as how actually to apply the geometry of Euler's spiral to the terrain, how to solve the problem of soft ground and Kanto loam, and how to introduce the innovations of rational pavement design approved by the American Association of State Highways.

Negotiations had been underway for over a year and a half between corporation and temple. With no compromise in sight, the former was determined to gain a court order. It had a deadline in just four more years to open the total 340 kilometers between Tokyo and Komaki, and in the Kanbara district the expressway was already completed both east and west of Shoryoin.

Having lost their unity, the laymen were insisting on diverse solutions and even starting to accuse one another. Their priest, who had no leadership capability, was criticized and pressured by every faction, and out of fatigue was begging Zen Master Tengai's help.

Mokuzu listened in place of Koko and recorded the laymen's views, grouped roughly as follows:

Group A: 140 — nearly half — positively oppose the expressway. They say it will bisect the area, with no interchange, and produce a thousand ills and no good for the residents. Relocating the temple and graveyard is also dreadful in its disturbance to their ancestors. Should the corporation seek to enforce a court order, this group will resort to sit-down tactics. They are willing to appeal to arms, aided by communists, who will stage a propaganda campaign against capitalism, the expressway being its symbolic evil.

Group B: 70 — one fourth — agree to construction as an inevitable consequence of the public interest. They approve relocation to the hilltop if the site is finer and the new temple and graveyard are made splendid, and if their houses are moved there too.

Group C: 70 — the final quarter — neither oppose the expressway nor agree to the hilltop. They want compensation to their heart's content. They know they can't oppose governmental power, yet they are mortified at the thought of being asked to leave their long-established place of abode and temple of worship. They are anxious over where to go but lack any imperative to remain. They have no strong emotion over deserting their ancestral tombs. Moving from this trashy town would be an opportunity given them by Buddha. The hilltop is no good owing to stronger winds and the added distance from the conveniences of town.

"Such diverse laymen! Their priest can't possibly get a consensus of respect," said Koko with mirth when he saw Mokuzu's report in the train on their way home.

"Our master must unite the laymen and get them to turn the matter over to him before he ventures to negotiate with the corporation. Uniting the laymen won't be easy," said Mokuzu, making an agreeable response.

"Fine, fine, he's like a beast before blood. The greater the problem, the fiercer his mettle. He has a thorough knowledge of how to break up human

698

relations. The reverse is an easy task for him. I too, to the best of my ability, ordered the priest's wife to help. She can easily lead them to the master's side. Given a little pleasure and stimulation to her pride, she'll work like a bee. Those fishermen are so stupid they can't catch anything but fish weakened by pollution, and the peasants can't grow mandarins without using poison chemicals. Ha ha ha!"

"The priest did look weary. It's a pity he's despised when his reason for becoming a priest was to gain respect," said Mokuzu, hiding his animosity toward Koko. Yawning, Koko said,

"It's his fate. Moving the graveyard is easier said than done. There's the curse of the dead. It wouldn't be strange if one or two human lives are sacrificed. He should be thankful if he can at least maintain his shape."

ॐ

At the onset of October's intense training week, Mokuzu was given the koan "Baiyun's 'Not Yet.'"

> Zen Teacher Baiyun Shouduan recounted to Wutzu Fayan: "I was visited by a number of Zen trainees from Mt. Lu. All had some understanding. When I asked them to explain, they could refer to the sources. When I inquired into causes and occasions, they could specify. When I asked for their comments, they could comment. But they had not yet gone through."[1]

Zen Master Tengai as he gave Mokuzu the koan told him, "There's nothing like this koan for you. Truly no one can comprehend its real meaning without devoting ten or twenty years to unhurried study. You should fear being rough-and-ready. I hope you'll seize it well and invest ample time."

Although every koan had to be studied in the same manner, this koan was particular in its testing whether a monk's intellectual grasp was accompanied by his emotion and practice. Mokuzu knew that to pass it would be next to impossible for him: He could not be content in any given place or time, nor could he concentrate long on any one affair, for he quickly saw things as being not what he really wanted, and he was beginning to see the negative sides to everything. His attitude toward life was always cool and half-hearted, and often he was a mere bystander. Was it because he had lost the person most dear to him?

Baiyun left another koan:

> "I don't dwell where others dwell nor go where others go, but not out of any difficulty in complying with them. One must clearly distinguish black from white."[2]

Mokuzu could sympathize with Zen Teacher Baiyun if his words

699

reflected an exclusive and self-righteous attitude. But far from it, Baiyun lived with the understanding that the whole world was his whole life and he made no distinction between himself and others. Hence he saw himself as dwelling where others dwell and going where others go, with no further perfection. Such a way of life Mokuzu could understand with his intellect only.

He was growing aware of the limit to which he could live the Zen way enjoyably, which was also the limit to how far he could follow the teaching of Zen Master Tengai.

In those days the master was writing a serialized essay on a Zennist's view of social problems for a newspaper distributed mainly in the Chubu district. The series was titled "A Spitball." Mokuzu was given the responsibility of making a fair copy of his writing and submitting seven days' worth of manuscripts to an assistant editor who came once a week.

"Master, there are as yet only three manuscripts. What should I do? Tomorrow is this week's deadline," Mokuzu had to ask.

"Why ask me so trifling a matter? Act as you see fit!"

Mokuzu relayed the information that the manuscripts would be temporarily delayed. Behind his glasses the assistant editor was expressionless, quite nervous. He twitched the wings of his nose and found no comment but "Nonsense!"

That evening Mokuzu was called before the master and given a dressing-down directly after a phone call to the master from the newspaper office.

"How long have you been my attendant? An attendant must be one with the master, as I tell everyone. He should walk, talk, think, and act the same. It is the very training given you. As I walked the corridors during my training in Daitokuji, the officers told one another, 'Hush! — the Zen master is coming!' They took my step for his because I completely endeavored to be him. How dubious is your training in comparison! Am I to you like a kite to the hand, where the connection is abruptly ended when the thin twine breaks? If you deem it so, you will never complete your koan study."

At the time Mokuzu could not account for such a scolding. He knit his brow. Further exasperated, the master raged,

"Idiot! You cosset your petty ego and can't realize how you are neglecting your duty! Whippersnappers like you are keen only to draw a line between self and others. Attend to what is mutual! Look! Why don't you write it when it falls into arrears? You must know what I'd write if you are training to be one with me. From the outset there is a requisite point to the essay — to establish National Foundation Day so people can celebrate the nation's birth just as they celebrate their own. To raise their patriotism is of vital importance. Think back: Why did I trouble to introduce you to that former state minister and that chief of naval operations? Become me, become them — and write what I'd write. Pick some aspect of daily life, appeal to the readers' experience, and don't let them see the writer's real intent. Now, I've taken pains to elucidate what I meant by 'act as you see fit,' and you have no excuse to commit a stupid error again. And take note, I'm currently so busy with the Shoryoin issue I haven't time to stay long in one place."

Mokuzu had been ordered by the master to serve as an amanuensis. Being ordered now to be a ghostwriter was making him more uncomfortable and giving him an impure feeling. He knew the master's writing was full of fallacies and dogmatisms, often vague in point of argument, a mishmash of standard language and dialect, and faulty in postpositional usage.

'How ridiculous that I who am endeavoring to go yet higher should have to model my writing after his artless, awkward sentences!' Yet, staying awake all night in the charnel, he composed for the master. No moonlight or sound of wind in the pines entered; only the lifeless fluorescent lighting was bright.

Whenever he took a rest, he strove to recall Zen Teacher Dogen's view on how to write...

> Students of the Way should not study the writings of Buddhist scholars or of non-Buddhists, but study only the Zen records. Zen priests of recent times are wrong to favor literature, hoping to be benefited in their writing of gathas and sermons. Recommendable is to write what one thinks regardless of gatha form and to write the Dharma regardless of style. Whoever denies the Way by rejecting this recommendation can enjoy excellent expressions and polished sentences but cannot grasp the truth. I too loved literature from infancy. Even now I tend to admire the beautiful expressions of non-Buddhist writings and am influenced by the ancient Chinese prose and poems in *Wenshyuan*. But because they are useless I think I should disregard them all.[3]

Within a few days Mokuzu received another unpleasant reprimand from the master, in consequence of being asked to produce calligraphy in the master's name.

Usually Zen Master Tengai prepared calligraphy in his spare time for visitors who wished to receive it. Now none was left. Head Attendant Ryoshin commanded Mokuzu,

"Quick, write something — you're good at calligraphy! I'll put his seal to it."

Mokuzu was restringing the master's broken rosary. Startled, he raised an objection,

"Head Attendant, we can't do that. The layman will go home delighted, believing it's the master's work, and surely he'll have it mounted and hang it in his alcove to adore all his life."

701

"Quit grumbling and set to! He's waiting, and I've already received his compensation." Quite ignoring the problem of deceit, Ryoshin cared only about the moment and about preserving his authority.

Mokuzu took the posture of sitting meditation. Ryoshin scowled at him and said,

"You lack versatility — you shall smart for this!" In haste he prepared sumi and produced a humble calligraphy, too thin in tone and too blurred. But he gave it the master's seal and went half running to the drawing room, where the layman sat waiting.

At night Mokuzu as he feared was stopped by the master after his koan interview and preached at one-sidedly:

"Whoever disobeys seniors disobeys me. How can you hold so hard to your egoistic view while you haven't yet completed all the koans? Don't you know the saying, Evil often comes of good intentions?[4] You don't understand Yunmen's phrase 'When the south mountain sounds its drum, the north mountain dances in concert.'[5] At any rate I ask you not to break monastic friendship. Disharmony is the worst crime you can commit in these sacred precincts."

The master's eyes were like the eyes of a poikilotherm.

Next morning in a thin cold rain Mokuzu left for the college wearing clogs and carrying a coarse oil-paper umbrella. The skirts and sleeves of his cotton robe got wet.

When he arrived at the office, Dean Shiba, who was hanging up his khaki raincoat, drew near. The dean groped in his pocket, took out a crumpled tissue, which was caught in a crumpled handkerchief, and loudly blew his nose. Returning it to his pocket he said,

"You're being fastidious about intellectual honesty, ya? But the Zen master is not so scrupulous as to distinguish his matter from another's, you know. A tiny, dainty honesty is by nature like a work of mother-of-pearl. Often it's hollow, lacking in ontology. I advise you to be a donkey tied wherever its master wills. You must realize he isn't simply driving you hard. He genuinely wishes you will act in society and is teaching you the know-how rather impatiently."

Mokuzu did not say anything, nor mask his displeasure. The dean, hands clasped at his back, was leaving. Suddenly he turned and cheerfully asked,

"Or won't you marry? I found a beautiful daughter much suited to you, though she couldn't be a match for Banan."

"Marry? Dean, I never thought I will be active in society, and so, I never thought I will accept an arranged marriage."

"She is the daughter of a wealthy temple in Shizuoka, where the climate is the best in the nation. You don't know how salubrious the Shizuoka climate

702

is. The area faces the sun on the Pacific and is backed by hilly mandarin orchards. North you can always see Mt. Fuji. How marvelous if you could keep studying whatever you wish in such an ideal location!"

Mokuzu recalled the noisy, dirty, shabby town of Kanbara, which too was between the Pacific and mandarin orchards.

"The temple is truly rich. It has over a thousand lay families. Half are mandarin farmers, half work in commerce and industry; but among them are a mayor and some municipal assembly members, and, note especially, the owner of a private railway. Your income is insured for life. Freedom from economic worry is a key condition for being a good priest. What do you say?"

"I have nothing to say."

"Hm, that's nice. She's a bit older than you, twenty-three. The father is near seventy. He's a man of understanding and says when the new priest comes in, he and his wife will build themselves a retreat cottage and hand over all temple authority. As to the daughter, about whom you must have the most interest, she is attractive. I have a photo of her in a kimono standing behind a hydrangea. I promise to bring it tomorrow."

"Dean, please, don't misunderstand. I thank you for your care. But I am sure I should like to decide my matters by myself. I shall be slow to choose my future because I prefer to find my most natural and inevitable course through my own effort. I dislike submitting to happenstance."

Mokuzu was also growing to dislike the dean, who, like the Zen master, was fashioning his own painting of the world and going to put Mokuzu in it for human interest. 'Inept painter, don't paint me into your humble picture!'

"Hm! I see you can't trust either the Zen master or me — a contrary disposition!" The dean looked full at Mokuzu for the first time, and, pacing back and forth as he did in his classes, he went on, impassioned,

"There's one thing you've got to know. Most offensive to a boatman is to carry a passenger who doubts his navigational skill. What moves others to kindness? Only trust. We have to live and can live only in the network of human links. Suspicion is a fatal flaw we cannot allow ourselves in our human relations. Suspicion is isolating, and isolated, one keeps seeking an ideal.

"What ideal? For instance, an ideal woman. Her image isn't formed after seeing all women, who constitute sixty percent of the earth's population, but is formed by the chance sight of just one woman, which you claim you object to. Yet it's better to form an image of an ideal woman by seeing at least a real woman. Were that true of you, I would congratulate you. As it is, I regret to have to point out that youths like you often form an image of an ideal woman by seeing only one man and not even one woman. And who is this one man? It is you. Thus you won't find your ideal woman anywhere in the world, not in a fruiting orchard, nor in a pasture of grazing cows and horses, nor in a forest of tall buildings, nor on a lakeside or seaside, nor in the mountains or valleys....Ha ha, where can you find her? It's easy: look in the mirror and there she is, ha ha ha!

"How sad that the one you find with your sharp eyes is in the end only an imago of yourself! I will bless and respect you if you can find at least one woman who is not your shadow. Most human beings are not so fortunate as to see anyone but themselves; they are lonely ghosts floating in space. Suspicion puts distance between planet and planet, star and star, and the space between is so dark..."

Mokuzu was not listening. He was thinking, 'Noisy, noisy! He assumes he knows everything, while he can't know very much, especially who I am.' He was conscious of an ache is one of his molars, which as the air grew colder was becoming worse and worse without opportunity of treatment.

Tanishi, with his facial neuralgia, entered the office.

ॐ

The week-long extensive meditation periods of October, November, and December brought Mokuzu no progress with the koan "Baiyun's 'Not Yet.'" Zen Master Tengai repeated "Not yet, not yet!" and on each occasion gave an irritated shake of his bell.

Mokuzu had to ghostwrite for the master, attend the college to assist the dormitory inspectors, and on top of that teach English to Koko, who was quite persistent in studying. He was not given time to devote all his mind and body to the koan, unlike when he worked on the first koan. The founder's anniversary, a great tea ceremony under student auspices, and begging daikons from farmhouses also distracted him. Day after day many sundry affairs took up his time and energy.

But his worst torment in those days was his toothache. He felt cloaked in a mantle of darkness. One day in the college office he asked the nun Shorai to obtain an anodyne. She brought a dried aconite tuber to apply to his gum.

It increased the ache, then he felt half his face had become corrugated, as might be the feeling of Tanishi, and more, his vision dimmed as if he were seeing the world through a goldfish bowl. Disgusted, he asked the nun, "Have you ever applied this herb?"

"No, I never had the need, but my teacher habitually uses it," she replied, looking innocent. Mokuzu feared he would be taken ill like the master nun with her senile cataracts, and he hurried to a lavatory to rinse out his mouth.

At last he asked Head Attendant Ryoshin for permission to visit a dentist. According to Tanishi there was a dentist a forty-minute walk away, in the village of Kaji.

Nonetheless, Ryoshin coolly said to wait till winter solstice, still a week off.

"Why must I wait so long?"

"Why? What makes you raise discontent before a senior?"

"My tooth — it's aching just this minute. It comes and goes, but I have been bearing the torture for a fair number of weeks."

"It'll go again. Forbear a little more as it's purely your matter."

Ryoshin was ironing a white underrobe of the master's. Mokuzu wanted to kick him in the rear to tumble him with the ironing board. Just then Senzoku called from the back entrance,

"Mokuzu, come help!" He was hanging the cut-off leafy tops of daikons and turnips along a rope under the eaves. When dried they would be chopped and put in the master's winter miso soup, one of his favorite soups to warm him up. The wall under the eaves wherever the white plaster was exfoliated exposed a reddish mud mixed with minced straw. Snow flicked the still green daikon and turnip leaves.

Senzoku lowered his voice,

"Mokuzu, hold on. You are already third in rank in your koan study, next to Genkaku, who is next to Koko. Soon you'll be promoted above Head Attendant Ryoshin. Think also of the master. At his age he's holding on energetically. Right after December's week-long meditation commemorating Buddha's enlightenment, he went out and has been doing so daily for the sake of Shoryoin. He made a show of saying he won't fail, but in reality he seems to be having a hard time unifying the laymen."

"How do you know he made a show?"

"Last month I went with him to the highway corporation branch in Shizuoka. Right off he apologized to the director for the temple's impeding the corporation and explained it was due to the ignorance of the farmers and fishermen, who can't see that the corporation's intent is to build the safest and best road at the lowest cost, for the people, with the taxes paid by the sweat of their brows. This he said loudly. He is a master of compliments.

"After that he gained time by saying, 'Implementing any change to the temple and its gardens is very difficult, because the temple must seek the consent of its laymen, its related temples, and its head temple. The difficulty will multiply if the graveyard must be moved, there being the issue of the laymen's thousand sentiments toward their ancestors.' See, his talk was to secure time to unify the laymen."

"I'd like to know why he offered to mediate; was it only that he was asked by the Shoryoin priest?"

"He never mentioned him, in fact he said if it were only a matter of Shoryoin he wouldn't care. He told the corporation something like 'There will be many more similar problems with your plan to build expressways totaling 7,600 kilometers across Japan. If you resolve the displacement of temples by such individual trials as this, when can you complete your plan so important for our nation's development? With this worry in mind, I volunteer to solve Shoryoin. You can then solve similar cases in like manner. "Look at Shoryoin in Kanbara," is all you'll have to say. We must make it a model. Such a fine example of temple relocation will benefit the nation, not only the corporation and Shoryoin. My wish as a Buddhist is to help the nation and the people.' See how our master secured his footing and imparted grand meaning to this relatively minor case? They welcomed his offer and were glad to leave Shoryoin entirely to him. Our master's talent is extraordinary, don't you think?"

Mokuzu, bearing his toothache, commented sharply, expressing his honest view, rare though it was for him to behave so,

"Certainly the corporation would jump at his offer; he stands primarily on their side and the government's — he isn't really for the people. He doesn't question the pros and cons of building expressways or doubt the type of civilization that requires them. For him, serving the nation, helping the people, and taking an active role in society obviously means to echo the authority of the time. In this sense, the more he helps others the more he tramples on the powerless people. I wish to act least in society, and above all I respect modest people and, especially, politer beings, such as animals and plants."

"Mokuzu, I don't disagree with you, but our master expects a lot from you. How can you disappoint him?"

"Hey, you two! What are you grumbling over? Quickly finish and go warm the master's room, he'll be back any moment." The voice of the head attendant came from inside. Senzoku and Mokuzu carried live charcoal and hot water into the master's room and reported at the entrance the minute they heard his car.

ॐ

The sun's longitude reached 270 degrees. In the northern hemisphere the noon sun was at its lowest height and the daylight was the shortest of the year. At the winter solstice, the Shoshinji kitchen monks prepared squash reserved from summer, in deference to the custom of wishing monks good health in winter.

It was the only day the warning stick was not applied in the meditation hall. Everyone could take a rest.

That evening an exceptional dinner was offered in the meditation hall, to which the residential quarters monks as well as the Zen master were invited. A large quantity of sake too was provided. Everyone was to enjoy the night with all decorum thrown aside, and many exposed their talent for amusement.

Singing, chanting poems, and even dancing occurred. Some juniors parodied seniors scolding juniors. Some seniors parodied Zen interviews with the master. A monk who had stocked women's wear in the previous days performed a striptease, though he could not disguise his hairy shanks. Genkaku, displaying skill at waltzing, crossed his arms and gripped his shoulders to make a show of having a partner. The inebriated took it for real.

As the night wore on, the low-ranking monks, always reprimanded and now free, watched for a chance to retaliate, and in the confusion they beat up some seniors. On the other hand, the highest-ranking monks as well as the Zen master, seeing trouble brewing, watched for the chance to withdraw.

Prior to the evening razzle-dazzle, Mokuzu called on the dentist at Kaji. The road was frozen hard. Some hunters toting guns, who must have come from a town, were heading for a mountain skirt accompanied by setters. One smoked a cigar.

The dentist's house looked like a common farmhouse. Mokuzu opened the door and called in, but no response came from the dark interior. He went around to the back and found a little independent clinic apparently built in recent years. In front a man of retirement age wearing an apricot-color sweater over a white shirt and a necktie was wrapping a straw mat around a cycad to protect it from winter damage. He must have been longing for a southern ambiance. The lawn had a cluster of dracaena. Japanese banana plants, their leaves torn in disorder, formed the back hedge.

He continued his work, yet, seeing Mokuzu, he asked,

"From Shoshinji? Which tooth?"

"A lower left molar."

"Mmm. If you give me a hand, I can fix you sooner."

Mokuzu climbed a stepladder and helped to wrap the mat around the cycad and secure it with rope.

"You are as skillful as a gardener." The dentist seemed to be rating a gardener as a lower being and Mokuzu as equal to a gardener.

"Ha-han...it's pulpitis...let me see, it could be invading the root...." With his bare index finger he forcefully pulled down Mokuzu's lip and poked the affected area with a broach. Each time the pain felt like a pillar of flame shooting up.

"The alveolus seems okay, hm, but I'd better extract the pulp...it'll take work...," the dentist said to himself. He had a reflector on his brow but did not put on a medical robe. He also did not cover Mokuzu's chest or hand him even a single tissue.

"Your Zen Master's teeth too are quite foul, all of them suffering from pyorrhea. A toothpick and salt are inadequate to clean the teeth. I've advised him to recant the monastic tradition on this matter, but he treats me with silent contempt. What do you think of it?" the dentist asked while preparing his instruments. Mokuzu also passed over the matter in silence.

"But what a stoic! During any treatment he never emits a sound. Being one of his disciples, you too might disdain anesthesia." He began to work. As soon as he applied a carbide bur to enlarge the cavity, a scorching odor filled the air. Mokuzu's brow broke out in a greasy sweat, and the dentist pressed his hand harder against his face. Repeatedly he thrust a broach into the cavity to clean the root canal and remove the pulp. Mokuzu saw falling thunderbolts in a dark and dense forest that caused a fire to flare up with a black smoke. The dentist took a long time. An image of the Zen master looking hatefully unconcerned appeared in the flames of pain.

'If even he can endure such pain, there's no reason I can't.' He gripped his hands together, dug his fingernails into them. He twined his ankles and put all his might there.

'However long it seems, nothing lasts forever. Even a horrible pain is fragile before Time!'

The next moment he was visited by a comfort that released the pain. He must have swooned. It was a sweet interval. He was wrapped in a soft, warm smile, Ena's, he felt, and he thought he knew where he was — 'Oh, I was struck a blow by a swing, and I've been carried into this infirmary by Ena.' He tried to stand, only to return to the awareness that he was in a dentist's chair. The dentist was taking something from a cupboard.

"Don't get up, I have to fill in the cement. You fully justified yourself as a Shoshinji monk, forbearing stubbornly." He seemed not to have noticed that Mokuzu had fainted. Mokuzu felt sad and longed for the sensation he had just experienced. He wanted to be quickly alone. But the dentist took more time to make an impression for a crown.

When he could finally leave it was dark, but well before evening bell. Snow was falling.

He hurried, nursing Ena's visage. He felt strange to see himself hurrying in spite of there being not the least charm in the place he was returning to.

'Ah, me. I'd willingly follow if a path led to the sky....'

With a squeal of brakes, a white car stopped hard beside him. A door was flung open and there came the master's voice, "Quick, get in, I'll let you ride." He gave the impression of being in a good humor and asked,

"Where did you go?"

"To a dentist."

"Hmm."

"Master, are you returning from Kanbara? I thank you for your lengthy trouble. Could you unify the laymen?"

"I have yet to attain it. But now it will go fine. This very moment I got a bright idea from catching sight of your back. The laymen will be able to complain no more. I must thank you for providing me the occasion to hit on a conclusive idea." The master was forgetting his fatigue. He looked triumphant.

"Could you tell me your idea?" Mokuzu was not interested; he wished most to fall asleep, but knowing that to be impossible, he performed his obligation of behaving like a good disciple.

The master gave a short reply,

"Kannon — a Kannon statue!"

"Oh? What's the connection with the Kanbara laymen?"

"Truly it's the answer. Their foremost problem is their tombs. It's their last defense against the corporation. Now, if a Kannon is put up behind Shoryoin, their ancestors' bones can be relocated there after being reverently cremated. With the ashes consigned to its interior, the laymen can pay homage to the Kannon morning and night. When they die, their ashes will go there too. The Kannon housing their ancestors will stand on the hilltop apart from all noise and dust, commanding a fine view over the sea. Who can righteously object to so irenic an idea? I hit on it when I saw your back — I was reminded of your teacher Hanun-kutsu and his vow to erect a Kannon for world peace. What do you think?"

Mokuzu was silent. He remembered the misfortune of Zen Master Hanun, whose dream had miscarried.

Zen Master Tengai then boasted in a conclusive manner,

"Hanun-kutsu's Kannon collapsed before completion because he was dreaming of an empty abstraction. Mine will contain what is real, and there are actual laymen who need it. It's practical and will contribute to the real peace of living people. For whose sake did Hanun wish peace? Only for the sake of an idea!"

But Mokuzu thought,

'Alas, the more such statues as Zen Master Tengai's are erected, the more the world will accumulate tensions toward war. His Kannon is not for world peace, but for a particular ethnic group. He is teaching people to be all the more bound to their ancestors and to love only their own nation, rather than teaching them to be free of their egoistic self-love. Oh, how I do not welcome being active in society!

'It blooms white among the grasses,
Knowing not its name.'[6]

709

52

Dungshan's Five Classifications

Whatever the year brings, he brings nothing new,
For time, caught on the ancient wheel of change,
Spins round, and round, and round; and nothing is strange,
   Or shall amaze
Mankind, in whom the heritage of all days
Stirs suddenly, as dreams half remembered do.
Whatever the year brings, he brings nothing new.[1]

On 7 January all monks had to secure permission to leave or to stay on in the monastery. The observances head, the fiscal head, and the reception head, assisted by the direct monk, assembled in the high officers' room in the main building to receive the monks from highest to lowest, and in the Zen master's name they granted permissions.

Mokuzu waited in line, seated in meditation form on the veranda. The thin layer of snow was so bright on the garden in the morning sun that no one could fix an eye on it.

Behind him a dozen fresh monks who had arrived the previous spring and autumn were idly talking in low voices. Like frogs they silenced each time a senior passed by.

The black pine in the front garden was also absorbing the sun, and its loosened snow dropped.

The way a crow
Shook down on me
The dust of snow
From a hemlock tree

Has given my heart
A change of mood
And saved some part
Of a day I had rued.[2]

There still being time before his turn, Mokuzu stood and briskly left by the residential quarters' entrance as if he had some business.

Roping icicles hung from the cliff behind the bath house. In the shady north garden of the meditation hall there were many small drifts. The area behind the Manjusri attendant's building showed no sign of life, but the notes of a wren singing in the forest wound sharply through the tree trunks.

Wishing to view the sunny south slope where the snow deeply buried the trunks, Mokuzu advanced toward the spring. He saw footprints. A squatting monk was washing laundry. At the sight of Mokuzu, he quickly stood and bowed with palms joined out of respect due a senior. Perhaps he was the newest comer. Mokuzu knew nothing of him, but he knew Mokuzu:

"Good morning, Master's Attendant."

His clean-shaven head was expressly blue. His cheeks were pale, his hands painfully chapped.

"Are you washing the seniors' laundry?" Mokuzu asked with sympathy.

"No, it's all mine."

"Oh, then why don't you let it be and take a good rest since today is a rare day of no warning stick?"

"Everything's dirty. I can't stand a dirty collar."

"If that's your concern in the meditation hall, how can you devote yourself to koan study?"

"Master's Attendant, if I may say so without disrespect, I regard koan study as a mere part of monastic training. I believe the right course of training is to purify oneself, to keep tidy, and to give thanks to Buddha. From what I hear, you are solving koan after koan with unheard-of speed. You are the focus of the other monks' attention. But it seems to me you are failing to notice something more important than koan study."

Quite apparently the newest comer was mustering courage to speak frankly to a senior. Mokuzu bent and scooped a drink of water from the spring. It was less cold than he expected.

"What you say isn't incorrect. So you'd better disregard my matters and keep washing your clothes and getting your hands more chapped, availing yourself of the abundant time you have at your disposal. Here the wren is singing away. It reminds me of a stanza from an English poem I once learned...

"Her sight is short, she comes quite near,
A foot to me's a mile to her."[3]

From the spring he went down a steep, narrow path alongside a creek. The area, although beneath dense cedars, was not everywhere clear of snow; and snow light made it brighter than it was in any other season. Beside the creek a lean winter camellia sheltered its flowers with its leaves. The leaves were laden with snow, the flowers merely lined with dew.

The path went to the straw-roofed shed where the monks worked on rainy days. Mokuzu saw a faint smoke leaking out. He entered and found three juniors crouched around a tiny fire. His appearance startled them.

711

Mute, they awaited his reaction.

Like the newest comer, they were older than he and seemed to know him, though he had never taken note of them. Each was dressed for travel — leggings, straw sandals, scrip containing surplice box. Their bamboo hats were propped against the wall. They were dressed the same as when they entered the monastery, and now they were illicitly leaving.

At last the middle one spoke up defiantly. He had a pockmarked, potato face.

"Master's Attendant, we've already decided to leave the mountain. No one can stop us without the use of force."

"Wait — " The monk to his right cut in. His fair-skinned, chiseled face was calm. "He hasn't said why he came. Master's Attendant, as you see, we've made ready to quit without permission. We each have a grave reason, and we wish you'd keep quiet about it." His manner was polite, but he did not hide his inflexible will.

The last, toad-faced, mouth slightly open, was watching for Mokuzu's move.

"You are needlessly worrying. I was just passing by on a private walk," Mokuzu said quietly.

They were relieved, but the toad-faced one issued a captious question,

"Your passing by may be accidental, but you're an attendant to the Zen master, you're of the establishment. What'll you do?"

"Nothing. I feel sorry that you set your aim here in this monastery life and on the way must leave. Other monasteries more fitted to you would welcome you, were you to leave after getting permission." Mokuzu turned his eyes to a lustrous clump of leopard plant partly covered with snow by a post of the shed.

The three recreants silently looked into the vanishing fire. Mokuzu disliked seeing their impuissance: they wanted to be persuaded to stay. "Excuse me," he said and left.

He took a path up to the monks' graveyard. The shorter tombstones were buried in snow, the taller ones crowned with it. There was no trace of footprints. Enshrined at the entrance was a small statue of Jizo Bodhisattva. On its head he noticed a pale purple butterfly settled motionless. It looked frost-killed. He filliped it lightly and it feebly blew away like a ruin following after its soul.

So steep was the shortcut from there to the meditation hall that he could not climb in his clogs. He took them off and pulled himself up by grasping the thin green trunks of aucuba. He had to make his way through a dense growth of camellias. A large quantity of snow thumped down on his back. Already half melted, it turned to slush. As the icy water spread through his robe, underkimono, and undershirt he was reminded of the sad folklore in Wordsworth's "Lucy Grey":

> They wept — and, turning homeward, cried
> "In heaven we all shall meet;"
> — When in the snow the mother spied
> The print of Lucy's feet.
>
> . . . .
>
> They followed from the snow bank
> Those footmarks, one by one,
> Into the middle of the plank;
> And further there were none![4]

His turn came soon after he got back to the veranda. In the high officers' room, the head of observances, Genkaku, was warming his hands over a hibachi as he waited. Tall and potbellied, he looked like Bodhidharma as depicted in Zen paintings. At his side the three other high officers were seated gravely before a long table on which were piled writing materials and monks' records. Kaijo was among them, serving as fiscal head for the term.

Genkaku talked in an open manner,

"I know of the great advance of your koan study. But you have in fact just begun your Zen training. You will stay on?"

"Yes, please allow me to stay a little longer."

"Hmm, are you starting to enjoy the training life here?"

"Frankly, no. But I must verify whether I am suited to it."

"You can't enjoy it because, for one, it's too busy for you. You have to find the art of enjoying snatched leisure moments. Of course the real reason you are made busy is that there aren't enough monks to keep up traditional monastic life. Of late young talents don't come, they go into other fields. Our master's motive in founding his short college was to secure training monks, and Shoshinji is succeeding in getting more monks than are monasteries without schools. But, as you see, so few of our monks are newcomers, and many who are, are impatient and quickly leave. I hope you will help them to stay. Be kind, and make them perfect their original intention."

Genkaku well knew the tragedy that the monastery needed monks more than monks needed the monastery. 'People can't make sense of what they don't like,' thought Mokuzu. 'But is there anything that can give as great a meaning to life as the essence of Zen? Only Zen enables us to go beyond the world of life and death, good and evil, day and night. And what place can educate us as thoroughly and extensively to live in Zen as can the monastery? Elsewhere people seem to live with a one-sided view.'

"Mokuzu, to help others is to help oneself. The more you help the more you deepen your character. You have been like a long-distance swimmer intent on bringing only yourself to shore. I hope you will care more about others from now on. Don't let those near you lag and drown. Go together to the other shore. Your koans should be like bamboo sheaths dropping one by one as the bamboo matures. The number of koans you master should correlate with the maturing of your personality. See? Koans are not to attain, but to cast away. They are a means to clear yourself of your five obstacles to becoming enlightened."

Without speaking, Mokuzu frankly reflected, 'I'm sorry I wasn't caring about others. It's true, only busying oneself for one's own concern is an ugly sight.'

After the interview he went back to the shed, rueful at not having done his best for the three who intended to leave. He found no trace of them. The fire was cleanly extinguished.

'All their life they must carry a pannier of regret for having escaped. And their load is also mine.'

From the four eaves, drops kept falling with a rainy-day sound. Inside the shed with no fire, Mokuzu remained immobile.

彡

Shoshinji on the day before college graduation had many overnight guests.

The Zen master's attendants, Ryoshin, Senzoku, Gyokuro, and Mokuzu, were engaged in opening rooms, cleaning, and preparing beds at Kento-kaku, a guesthouse situated high in the back mountain and approached by meandering steps from behind the residential quarters. Well above the roofs of Shoshinji, Kento-kaku commanded a wide view south to the far mountains floating on the fields.

Mokuzu rested a moment from cleaning an oriel,

> 'The green mountains east of the far village
> are like penciled eyebrows.
> A wind blows the yellow powder from the
> new verdure of willows along the creek.
> Flocks of tomtits not knowing
> how nice are the outlying fields
> Enter the small gardens
> in quest of the lingering flowers.'[5]

"Mokuzu, why don't you dust the shojis — you must attend to such details," Head Attendant Ryoshin spoke bitterly as he himself dusted a transom. Senzoku took a stack of pillows from a closet and as he went with them toward a veranda one fell, and as he tried to retrieve it they all fell and scattered. At once Ryoshin shouted,

"Fool! Treat everything with your best care!"

To cover his embarrassment Senzoku made an ugly face for Mokuzu. Ryoshin, catching sight of it, ordered him and Mokuzu to sit on the veranda, and there he scolded them,

"You don't really understand what training is. Think a little. Parents are to stay here tonight for their children's celebration. The pillows are to assist their sleep. How can we do as Senzoku just did if we truly wish them a peaceful night? We also must think some might be allergic to dust. How will you justify yourself, Mokuzu, if they have a coughing fit because you neglected to clean sensitively? Don't you both understand the mind of parents who keep worrying over their children's future and praying for their happiness? I can make allowances for you, Senzoku, because you are dumb, in fact not advancing in your koan study. But Mokuzu, you are well ahead of me, and yet you are always halfhearted. I can't make out what goes on in your head, or why the master keeps giving you new koans."

Just then Gyokuro brought up a bucket of water for mopping the wood floors and set it on a stepping-stone. Inadvertently he set it on the head attendant's clogs and it overturned. Ryoshin jumped from the veranda and struck him with his fist.

That evening Mokuzu had to go up to Kento-kaku to invite the guests to enter the bath. Afterward, where the steps began to descend, he paused and looked up at the sky,

'New moon thin as an eyebrow,
spring cloud long as a sash —
birds enjoy the quiet and endure the cold
out where the plum flowers bloom.'[6]

As he started down the steps, a shoji opened. The mother of a graduate came out calling him and approached with a tripping gait. She was short and plump. Over her black formal wear she had a white lace shawl.

"Attendant, please receive this." She unwrapped a purple crepe cloth and handed him a white paper folded like an envelope.

"For what? I cannot receive it."

"Please, it is but a tiny token of gratitude. Earlier this evening I had occasion to give to the other attendants. And I was told you assist the dormitory inspectors. I know of your particular care..."

"I cannot receive this sort of thing," Mokuzu plainly replied, and returned the envelope.

"Please, it is a token of our gratitude. Our son was born delicate, but owing to the many kindnesses given him by such good persons as you, he could graduate. Like me, he has an infirm heart," said her priest husband, tall, with up-slanting eyes. He too had come out.

715

"I don't remember doing anything special for your son, in fact I don't even know his name."

"It may well be. Our name is Makino," said the mother. "We are from Ehime in Shikoku. You may not recall him, but he often informed us of your kindness. For instance, one hard day cutting grass on the bank, he felt ill and went to the dorm to rest. Then one of the inspectors — called Wax Gourd by the students — came with a warning stick to force him back to work. You intervened and told him to spend the day copying a sutra with brush and ink."

"Further, we learned you are one of the Zen master's most trusted monks," the husband took over. "Our son is aiming to enter your monastery in April, and we must ask a special favor of you. Please make him able to go through the training." He bowed with due ceremony. In the dim moonlight Mokuzu could see on his head a large nevus.

Hoping to be quickly freed, he told them,

"I understand. Much as I too am a novice, I shall do my best for your son when he enters. But I won't receive any unreasonable gift from anyone." He turned and ran down the steps.

At the bottom Senzoku must have been overhearing, for he rebuked him,

"Stupid! Why didn't you take it? They're quite wealthy. If you care about your life you'll grab every chance to get money. All able monks are doing so. Otherwise what will you do the day you leave? Spending years giving free service, gaining only age, and sooner or later you have to leave this mountain, unless you inherit the Zen mastership. Then without money, how will you be treated? People won't appreciate your so-called enlightenment and cultivated Zen character. They can sense only the glitter of what money you possess; they're blind to anything spiritual. Look at Koko and Genkaku. By now they've made a fortune this way and that."

"Thanks for the advice. But what I most care about now is, after all, to complete my koan study. Besides, I really don't remember even his face."

"Fine. Why care about the name and face of anyone who isn't important to you?"

"In addition, it's odd to take money for doing a kindness, and unkind to take money from one needy of kindness."

"Mokuzu, don't expose your immaturity. Receive the money and don't offer the kindness. That's the right way to make money, because, as you noted, we mustn't earn money from anyone we care about. So, we earn from those we don't care about. The world isn't so complex, but rather simple. Ask our Zen master if you suspect my economics!"

❧

716

Graduation day presented fine weather from early morning on. The sun brightened even the depths of the main building, and the monks in their best robes were radiant to behold as they walked the corridor to attend the ceremony. Bush warblers kept up their song as if to scatter the plum blossoms, the fragrance of which was carried with the sonority of the bell throughout the garden and to the mountains.

The moment the ceremony ended, without prior warning except to a few high monks and his attendants, Zen Master Tengai announced:

"We shall proceed to perform a farewell ceremony for Koko, who has perfected his Zen training in this mountain. He will now go abroad and engage in the training that follows enlightenment."

There was a general stir among the guests, students, and monks. Gyokuro hurried out with the master's cinnabar scissors chair and set it before the formal entrance, where a red baize carpet was laid and a white curtain with Shoshinji's crest in purple was stretched above. Senzoku and Mokuzu tactfully guided those who were still in confusion, and all at last stood in rows on either side of the granite path from the chair to the gate.

A chanting officer sounded wood clappers five times, and everyone quieted. The master, having once withdrawn to his quarters, was escorted in by his head attendant. Immediately after he was seated, Koko appeared from the residential quarters entrance in new travel wear, with his bamboo hat carried against himself, in front. He no doubt felt awkward. He smiled sheepishly when his eyes met Mokuzu's. But quickly he tightened his face and advanced to the master. In the most reverential attitude he bowed before him. The master, looking slightly skyward, kept a solemn air. Then in response to Koko's bow, he joined his palms in silence. For a short while they looked eye to eye.

> A heroic man is not a tearless man;
>   only he shows no tears at separation.
> To show a sad countenance is shameful,
>   leaning against one's sword over wine.
> At the bite of a venomous snake,
>   a heroic man is able to sever his arm.
> His sole care is to achieve a great exploit;
>   there is no merit in weeping at separation.[7]

Koko was awkward at keeping his dignity. He stiffly turned and with measured step advanced toward the gate. He gripped with one hand his bamboo hat and with the other the thick strap of his scrip. His hands shook perceptibly. Was it because of his crowd of emotions as he departed from the master, for years adored like a father, or was he foreseeing his hard life in a foreign land, where he would have to persevere alone? Or was he simply

717

tense out of apprehension over fumbling before many eyes?

The audience was unstintingly clapping and cheering as they saw him off. He stopped at the center of the garden, turned, and with joined palms bowed toward the principal image. Then he moved on at a quicker and more resolute pace. The monks, in rows near the gate, did not clap but bowed silently with joined palms. The clapping and cheering lasted even after his figure completely disappeared down the stone steps through the cedars.

'Koko is a strange and sad man. His behavior is expansive, but his nature is timid,' thought Mokuzu. Zen Master Tengai was returning to his quarters, escorted by his head attendant. 'There's no power in a clouded sun and no wisdom in a Zen master swayed by personal feelings.'

The ceremony scheduled and unscheduled was done. As Mokuzu and other attendants were removing the carpet and curtain at ease, Dean Shiba and Observances Head Genkaku approached, chatting. To see the dean in a robe was unusual. He held a priest's half-open ceremonial fan, with the vermilion lacquer partly gone.

Genkaku tapped the smooth, rounded back of the scissors chair and muttered to no one in particular,

"Poor guy! At last he must go to America. After so-called enlightenment, our founder followed the rump of an ox for his training. I wonder what rumps Koko will follow in America."

Dean Shiba half smiled and sat down deep in the scissors chair.

"Were I a Zen master I'd chant a gatha rather than speak not so much as a word. Let me do so as a trial," he said. He inhaled deeply and began to chant in a compressed tone,

> Spring sun and autumn dew now thirteen times returned.
> Summon him at the cuckoo's call and he'll not show up.
> After enlightenment he is training in a rare place.
> To see him, note the mossy branch with fruiting plums.[8]

"See? Hm, to be able to express this much on such an occasion is expected of a Zen master." The dean in a flash opened wide his fan and fanned his bosom, though the day was not at all hot. Genkaku and the other monks were grinning.

"Oh, Mokuzu, may I have a word with you? Come," he said, getting up from the chair, and he drew apart from the remaining monks. Mokuzu obliged. As if to whisper, the dean shaded his face with his fan and said,

"Don't raise your guard — I'll not broach the topic of marriage. It's about your diploma. I signed it, and the master will surely give it to you tonight. Then I should like to know with what attitude you will receive it."

"Well, as I wasn't a regular student, I have no particular emotion over the

718

diploma. But if it releases me from assisting the dormitory inspectors, I'd be very glad."

"Ah, just as I feared. I think you ought to receive it with grave thanks, as if receiving a new life; and you must express lavish thanks to your Zen master. I know that over a million students are graduated from college year after year in this nation, and that the diploma is becoming less and less valuable, less than pearls to a lady. Especially the diploma from this short college unknown to the world — it will be useless to you, no more than a fossil. But take my advice and see from the side that is granting it. You can understand how you'll incur anger if you show no gratitude in receiving his kindness, can't you?"

The dean took Mokuzu to the shade of the pines at the bell tower and added,

"You must practice living with gratitude, and practice how to express it. Koko was great. His loyalty to the master consisted in gratitude. When the master was exhausted, Koko massaged him until he slept. When he suffered from obstipation, Koko administered an enema and even used his finger to remove the compacted feces. Most certainly Koko had great points beyond compare, and from him you have much to learn." The dean left Mokuzu then and there and set off for the college, tapping his head with his fan.

Mokuzu lingered at the bell tower.

Phee — phee — cried a bird overhead as if blowing a fife. Its underparts as it perched on the guardrail were conspicuously white, its throat and breast rosy — a bullfinch come to pick at the garden plum. Its sound was gentle, sweet, and mournful. As it cried, it raised its legs by turns.

'A bullfinch in the wild isn't blamed for its inept song. Were I free of the monastery, I too wouldn't be forced to be useful and kind. Where I am determines whether I am good or bad. Because I must live in a certain place, I must find there how to be free of its force. In theory the way to be free is to be unfree and to become altogether unfree...?'

That night the customary graduation party was held at the college, but Mokuzu was excused from attending because he needed to ghostwrite the essay series "A Spitball" for the newspaper.

Zen Master Tengai had told him to write something to inspire Japanese businessmen working abroad, for, according to him, Japan as an island country poor in natural resources could survive only through trade; whence such businessmen, more than the military, were important to the nation. The master had given him a prewar poem and ordered him to update it to suit present-day businessmen.

The wind whips our regimental colors
displaying the Rising Sun.
The more it is rent by showers of bullets
the more it heightens our honor.
We are Japanese, courageous men;
Bringing no disgrace to our flag,
we advance until we fall down dead.
We do not disgrace ourselves under our flag
nor subject it to shame.
We fear nothing and have no cause to hold back.

Flight brings shame on our nation.
Death in battle wins acclaim.
Rather will we die honorably like shattered gems
than in disgrace survive like tiles.
Death on the tatami
is not the samurai Way.
To be a corpse kicked by passing hooves
and left to lie beaten by the weather —
this is the code of the true warrior.
We fear nothing and have no cause to hold back.[9]

Faced with the poem, Mokuzu became depressed. 'Zen spurred innocent and ignorant soldiers to invade other men's lands, and now Zen is abetting greedy businessmen to exploit gentler lands. I see no relation between real Zen and such aggression. Not a single line of this poem is recommendable as the right sense of Zen,' he thought under the dim light.

He had often considered leaving the monastery, but each time he was arrested by his wish to perfect his koan study.

'I should be watchful of my critical nature. How can I dare criticize my Zen master without perfecting my training? Besides, I should distinguish between his personality and the Zen treasure transmitted to him. He is pointing to the moon. I must see the moon, not the finger.'

Before he began to write, the master's car arrived at the front garden. The head attendant dashed to the entrance. Soon the master entered his quarters, where Mokuzu was working.

"Oh, I'm tired out! Drinking is the most barbaric of all evils! Man isn't drinking sake, sake is drinking man! Hn? What are you doing? Why didn't you receive me at the entrance?"

"I am sorry. I was reworking the essay and did not realize you had returned," Mokuzu lied. He took off the master's robe and hung it over a bamboo dress stand.

"Master, excuse me, the bath is ready," came the voice of the head attendant kneeling outside the room.

"Tonight I am too tired for a bath. Bring me a steamed towel. Oi, Mokuzu, massage me, my legs are stiff and dull."

Like the image of Buddha directly after death, the master reclined on a quilt. Mokuzu repeated a thorough massage down his thighs to his toes and back up.

"Mokuzu, though Koko was telling me he is proficient in English, is he truly?"

Mokuzu perceived that the master was anxious over having sent Koko away, like an ordinary father worrying over a son.

"The wren may strive against the lion, but in vain"[10] was on the tip of his tongue, but he did not wish to see the master lose his temper. He felt repulsed and nauseated as he replied,

"Koko is like a warrior geared for the field. He has mastered all the basics of English. More, he has gained the art of 'listening by eye.'[11] He is sure to become Dr. Yasaka's great successor."

The master took Mokuzu at his word. He regarded modesty as befitting only humble persons, and flattery as true praise.

"Indeed, Koko must become a second Dr. Yasaka. I told him to apply himself with such determination as to bury his bones in the foreign soil. Seventy some years have passed since Buddhism was transmitted to America. Dr. Yasaka introduced Zen theory only, for he was a man of cerebration and knowledge, with little experience of Zen life. Koko has an advantage: he can surpass Dr. Yasaka because he went through real monastic traditional Zen life. It's time to teach Westerners Zen in practice."

"Master, could you kindly give your impression of America?"

"A few years before you came here, I had a chance to visit America and Europe to attend services in commemoration of the seventieth year after Buddhism crossed the ocean to America. I went abroad with as easy a feeling as going to the toilet.

"America is a stew of races like our stew of carrot, daikon, burdock, deep-fried tofu, and konjak. But Americans don't train themselves by partaking of that stew, so they have neuroses even though their material life is the richest in the world. The many contradictions in democracy, capitalism, white supremacy, consumer economy, machine civilization, and so on are coming to a head, and now it is said as many as one out of sixteen suffer neurosis.

"Yet America's strength is that the majority are scientific-minded. For them immaculate conception and the existence of heaven became unbeliev-able. So they were surprised to meet Buddhism, especially Zen, which doesn't contradict science. Zen teaches them the importance of self-realization and that they can become a Bodhisattva or a Buddha."

"Master, please speak of the circumstances that first brought Buddhism to America," said Mokuzu, disliking having to hear anything further on the virtues of Zen.

"Beginning the twenty-first of September, 1893, a two-week international exposition was held at Columbia Hall in Chicago. A world's congress of religions was held there concurrently, a gathering of some two hundred high priests. Representing Buddhism from Japan were Doki Horyu of the Shingon sect, Ashizu Jitsuzen of the Tendai sect, Yabuchi Banryu of the Jodo Shin sect, and Shaku Soen of our Rinzai sect. At this congress Shaku Soen delivered a paper titled 'The Law of Cause and Effect, as Taught by Buddha.' The Japanese manuscript was checked by the eminent writer Natsume Soseki and put into English by our professor emeritus, Dr. Yasaka — who was the one to arrange all matters for Koko's study at an American university.

"Shaku Soen was ordained at twelve and completed his koan study at twenty-five, an unusually early age. He could have become a Zen master with many disciples. But he refused the position and entered Keio University, founded by Fukuzawa Yukichi. There he became a mere student, and it was said Fukuzawa often advised other students to emulate him. After graduation he went to Ceylon to study Hinayana Buddhism. Thus he studied to prepare for an active future not only in Japan but in the world. Mokuzu, do you understand his passion for the Dharma? Do you have the mettle to compare with him?" asked Zen Master Tengai, at ease with eyes closed as he was being massaged.

Mokuzu in fact knew far more about Shaku Soen than Zen Master Tengai had just related, and he saw the difference between Shaku Soen, who had produced Dr. Yasaka, and Zen Master Tengai, who had produced only Koko. Shaku Soen's interest was to deepen the understanding of Zen and to save people by teaching them Zen. Zen Master Tengai was too much involved in the passing world of politics and economics and had produced no revolutionary improvement in the mental life of the people. Mokuzu felt he was wasting his noble youth under a worldly Zen master. 'Why doesn't he give me a new koan as soon as I understand each one?' He wanted to cry out, "Let me see all the koans transmitted to you and I'll ascertain whether or not my understanding is superior to yours!"

He halted his hands, and suddenly with full power he clapped them together.

"What?" The master raised his upper torso in hot haste.

"Master, I am young and I have as much spirit as had Shaku Soen, if not more, but can you compare with those great Zen masters who taught him?

You are spoiling your body and asking an able disciple to waste his time more precious than alluvial gold on massage. In this country massage is the traditional profession of the blind. Why don't you ask such a one — in this monastery too there are plenty who are blind. Shaku Soen's first teacher, who ordained him, was Ekkei of Myoshinji; second was Gisan of Sogenji; third, Dokuon of Shokokuji; fourth, Tekisui of Tenryoji; and finally Kosen of Engakuji. Who among them asked of him massage?" Mokuzu was ready to leave the monastery at once if Zen Master Tengai shouted abuse.

As he expected, the master gave him a scorching scowl. Mokuzu was not unsettled. Fixedly he stared back.

The master was the first to break the balance of forces by averting his eyes. Fretfully he called,

"Attendant! Attendant! Is there no head attendant?" and he busily shook his handbell.

Mokuzu suspected that the master was asking to have him taken away. There was a loud sound of steps, and the head attendant rushed into the room. Unable to figure why he was summoned, he continued to stand before the master and Mokuzu.

"Why do you blankly stand there? Massage me if you don't mind," said the master, and he lay down as before like the image of the departed Buddha. Ryoshin tucked up his sleeves and began to massage him on the small of the back.

Puzzled over what he should do, Mokuzu sat erect at their side.

"Why the devil do you sit idle? You're already dismissed. Hasten to engage in your own concern! And keep reminding yourself of the advice Yunyan gave his disciple Dungshan."

Mokuzu left the master's quarters and took his route up the mountain. He passed the layman's shrine and went above the abandoned quarry to the ridge, where the rocks and sparse red pines were more exposed by the moonbeams. He sat facing south under a tree. Where the starry sky and the far black mountains met was distinct, but where the mountains met the fields was indistinct.

> Darker grows the valley, more and more forgetting:
>   So were it with me if forgetting could be will'd.
> Tell the grassy hollow that holds the bubbling well-spring,
>   Tell it to forget the source that keeps it fill'd.[12]

Zen Master Tengai had told him to remember Yunyan's advice to Dungshan. Mokuzu recalled the episode:

723

Dungshan asked as he was leaving Yunyan, "How should I reply after your death if someone asks whether I possess your true figure?" Yunyan said after a pause, "I am but I." Unable to make clear sense of his teacher's words, Dungshan fell into thought. Yunyan advised him, "To understand the most important matter, you must be very prudent."

Still confused, Dungshan left Yunyan. He came to a river. As he crossed he saw himself reflected on the water, and fully he understood, and he made a verse:

> To seek outside is taboo,
> It leads only to further alienation.
> Though I now walk alone,
> I can meet him all the time.
> Indeed now he is me;
> But I am not he.
> This is the right understanding
> Of the truth that all is one.[13]

'Throughout his life, beginning in his youth, Dungshan was persistently concerned with clarifying the relation between nonexistence and existence,' thought Mokuzu. The world of nonexistence is called absoluteness, equality, *sunyata*, *wu*, emptiness, the real state of all things, Buddha nature...The world of existence is called relativity, distinction, *rupa*, *you*, matter, rise from causation, cause and effect, mountains and rivers...Buddhists commonly understand these two worlds as complementary halves of one world, accommodating each other.

Dungshan at age ten read the Mahaprajnaparamita-hrdaya Sutra. It is a concise treatment of *prajna* (wisdom), the most important, most indispensable of the six practices to attain Buddhahood. The sutra states that matter and emptiness do not differ: matter is emptiness, emptiness is matter. It is the basic Buddhist view of the world. Reading the sutra, the child Dungshan came to the passage "There are no eyes, ears, nose, tongue, body, or mind."[14] Touching his eyes, nose, and tongue, he wondered, "How strange! I have them all, whereas the sutra maintains there are none." He questioned his teacher, but his teacher was unable to explain. Thereupon Dungshan started to train seriously as a Zen priest.

Mokuzu thought, 'It seems to me he was unfortunate to have been arrested by those words before he had enough experience of life.'

Dungshan was a brilliant young trainee. When he first visited Nanchyuan, Nanchyuan was performing a service to commemorate his teacher Matzu. Nanchyuan said to his disciples, "Tomorrow I shall offer food to Matzu, but I wonder if he will show up." Dungshan stepped forward and said, "He will if he happens to gain the company of his body." Nanchyuan commented, "Despite your youth, you are worthy to be polished." Dungshan retorted, "A gem is a gem regardless of polishing, just as what is lowly is lowly."

'He was toying with words while he hadn't more pressing problems. A clever but immature comic makes a joke of the suffering of others. A mature, humane comic finds humor in the happiness of others. I see why my Zen master detests scholars. They talk so much about life but live it so little. Were I Dungshan I'd help Nanchyuan serve his offering to Matzu.'

Dungshan next visited Kueishan, and to him he asked, "Recently I had a chance to hear an episode concerning National Teacher Nanyang Hueijung's advocating that nonliving things preach the Dharma. But I do not understand it." Kueishan said, "Do you remember the whole episode? If so, recite it to me." Dungshan recited:

> Monk to Nanyang: What is the mind of the old Buddha?
> Nanyang: Flinders of brick and wall.
> Monk: But aren't they nonliving things?
> Nanyang: Just so.
> Monk: Then how can they preach?
> Nanyang: They preach — vigorously and unceasingly.
> Monk: Why can't I hear?
> Nanyang: Because you have no will to hear. But it doesn't mean others can't hear.
> Monk: Who can hear?
> Nanyang: Every saint can hear.
> Monk: Can you also?
> Nanyang: No, not I.
> Monk: Then how do you know nonliving things preach?
> Nanyang: That I can't hear is fortunate for you. If I could, I would be a saint and you wouldn't be able to hear my lecture.
> Monk: Then there's no hope for human beings?
> Nanyang: I speak for human beings, not for saints.
> Monk: What will happen to a person if he can hear the preaching of nonliving things?
> Nanyang: He will no longer be a human being.
> Monk: Which sutra says nonliving things preach?
> Nanyang: Clearly it is stated; the wise speak nothing not written in the sutras. Haven't you seen the passage 'The land preaches the Dharma, human beings preach the Dharma, all things throughout the past, present, and future preach the Dharma'? It is written in the Avatamsaka Sutra.[15]

Dungshan finished reciting. Kueishan said, "I entertain the same view, but how hard it is to meet anyone to whom I can tell it!" "I don't understand it.

725

Please teach me," Dungshan begged. Kueishan raised his whisk and said, "Do you understand?" Dungshan said, "No, please explain." "There is no way to explain to you by this mouth given by my parents." Dungshan gave up hope of understanding under Kueishan and asked him to recommend another teacher, with the result that he went to Yunyan.

Mokuzu thought, 'It is an empirical fact that we can't clearly distinguish whether we are living things or nonliving things. This fact can be experienced when we free ourselves of the habit of distinguishing. Words force us to distinguish and provide us the means of explaining it to others. But if they have no experience of it, they can't readily understand it, just as Dungshan couldn't. Whoever can't hear the preaching of nonliving things has to live a narrow and shallow life. Intellectual humility is said to be essential to genuine research work; but I'll say humility toward things, including oneself, is the key to a full appreciation of the world.'

Leaving Kueishan, Dungshan went straight to Yunyan. After telling him his circumstances, he asked him, "Who can hear the preaching of nonliving things?" "Nonliving things can," replied Yunyan. "Can you also?" asked Dungshan. "If I could, you wouldn't be able to hear my preaching." "Why wouldn't I?" Yunyan raised his whisk and asked, "Can you hear?" "No." Then Yunyan said, "You cannot hear even my preaching. How can you hear the preaching of nonliving things?" Dungshan asked, "Which sutra says nonliving things preach?" "As you may know, the Amitabha Sutra says that 'the birds and the trees round the pond, yea, all things without exception chant Buddha's name and his teaching.'"[16] Dungshan at last understood, and he made a stanza,

> Wonderful! Wonderful! What a mystery
> is the preaching of nonliving things,
> impossible to hear with my ears,
> obvious when I hear with my eyes![17]

'I can enjoy Dungshan's joy,' thought Mokuzu. 'It is very reasonable that he was regarded as the first Zennist to combine Zen philosophy and Zen literature.' He stood up to return as the morning bell was about to sound. There were no more stars, and where the fields and the mountains met was becoming distinct.

> The sun is clear, the mountains full-tinted.
> Warm is the wind, the grasses as if fumed with incense.
> Plum blossoms scatter, yet snow remains in places.
> Wheat brims in the vale like a green cloud.[18]

At his morning interview Zen Master Tengai gave Mokuzu a new koan, "Dungshan's Five Classifications." In Buddhism, sunyata (the absolute world)

726

and rupa (the phenomenal world) have been called by the one name Dharma. Dharma thus has four principal meanings:

(1) causation, law, or truth, having universal validity and therefore uninfluenced by any Tathagata (one who has attained Buddhahood);

(2) ethics or righteousness, which should be practiced by Buddhists and non-Buddhists alike;

(3) Buddha's teaching, endowed with the first and second principal meanings of Dharma;

(4) everything, whether existence or nonexistence; the whole universe as the object of thought. In this sense especially, Dharma always keeps a certain character and is a standard for all things.

Dungshan classed the Dharma into five phases encompassing all four principal meanings. His classification was a summary of the prudent training to which he had devoted nearly half his life.

Dungshan's Five Classifications

I. Existence indwelling in nonexistence:
    After nightfall, chancing on an intimate beauty
    How vexing is the dark before moonrise —
    Her face is indistinct.

II. Nonexistence indwelling in existence:
    An aged beauty who overslept faces her heirloom mirror.
    There all is clearly shown,
    And she has no reason to be as silly as Yajnadatta.

III. Nonexistence exposed:
    From emptiness a path leads to the world.
    Whosoever is innocent of voicing the Emperor's personal name
    Can surpass the old orator whose tongue was cut off.

IV. Existence and nonexistence both exposed:
    Sword heads exchange, unneedful of conscious parry.
    Rare as a lotus blooming in fire
    Is the combat of master swordsmen of regal spirit.

V. Destination:
    No one dare make a stanza for the indefinable,
        be it existence or nonexistence
    Everyone wishes to cross the flow of life and death.
    But after all discontent and compromise,
        where a man settles is before the hearth.[19]

53

Evening Bell

In the spring Mokuzu was appointed head chanting officer with three monks under his command. Choho, some years older than he, had served many times in the chanting office as well as in other offices. In the attendants' office Senzoku had been senior to Mokuzu, but now their positions were reversed. Myokei was newly moved from the meditation hall.

After a rain Mokuzu and his officers were painstakingly weeding the moss garden enclosed by the main building, the reception monk's rooms, the drawing room, and the Zen master's quarters. Senzoku drew near Mokuzu and spoke,

"Oi, we should be glad of our timely transfer. How dreadful if we'd been left in the attendants' office. It's really getting hot and the monks there are quitting the monastery."

"Yes, our office serves Buddha and the successive chief priests. We're exempt from being at the mercy of...and can put all our heart and soul into our own work," responded Mokuzu.

"Getting up half an hour before the others is hard, but waking them is easier than being waked. I'm thankful our role is to do the waking. I was growing sick of thinking my lot would be always to be routed from a sound sleep," said Senzoku.

In Shoshinji a clock was lawful only in the chanting office, which had the responsibility for proceeding steadily with the daily and monthly schedule as transmitted. The chanting officers had to order the inorganic time, which advanced regardless of heat and cold, day and night, in an organic way to fit human convenience within the circumstances.

As soon as morning came for the chanting officers, Senzoku dashed from the room noisily shaking the handbell to wake all officers. Ringing, he ran to the end of the cross-wing and back, along the corridor by the drawing room, and up and down the stairs to the second floor. He then turned the corner to an office next to the fiscal office and the kitchen to prepare rice gruel for the founder, for which he fetched a measure of raw rice from the kitchen. Mokuzu for his part had to make a round to wake the reception head, who was his direct superior, and the master's attendants, the observances head, the fiscal head, and the cooks, kneeling politely before the shojis of each office.

"One superior cries out and writhes like a dying snake when he's waked, another is dressed and meditating before I arrive. How people react reveals their nature," Mokuzu said to Senzoku.

After making his round of the residential quarters, Mokuzu went to the Manjusri attendant to give him the announcement board with the day's schedule written on it by the reception head the night before. He then crossed the front garden and climbed the bell tower. The garden in the spring dawn was filled with a fog that reached up to the guardrail. Branches of black pine hung over the guardrail, stars twinkled above.

In the dark he bowed to the suspended bell, fully five feet high and about two and a half feet across. Then with both hands he seized the strap to the long hammer made of hemp palm, strung horizontal to swing forward and back, and, using its momentum and gathering his strength, he drove its end square against the right place on the bell.

At the moment of impact he felt the sound was not yet born; it seemed to be first siphoning ample energy from the surrounding air. Then it began to travel in a low and stately tone with almost visible undulation. It carried to every nook and corner of the monastery buildings, to the weeds, bushes, and rocks, to the treetops and into the sky, over the roofs and over the ridges, and kept traveling for miles in all directions.

He thought about the mountains, rivers, trees, and grasses that continued to meet the morning with the sound of the bell, just as the monks who were training themselves could not help recalling Dungshan's sermon:

> "Is anyone here not repaying the four kinds of debt of gratitude and not willing to save the creatures of the three worlds?" With no response from his audience, Dungshan concluded, "If you don't come to realize what I mean, you can't free yourselves from the suffering of life and death. You can be free only when your mind doesn't conflict with each thing as it comes and your feet don't stick to any certain place. You'd better persevere in your efforts and not live an idle life."[1]

"Well, to resume," said Senzoku to Mokuzu, "don't you agree the master is using his attendants too much only to serve his ambition? Ryoshin and Gyokuro had to stay on in the attendants' office, and they've quit training here."

As soon as he had solved the problem of relocating the temple Shoryoin, Zen Master Tengai had taken on the position of heading the executive committee to commemorate the eleven-hundredth anniversary of Linji, planned for the coming October by the united branches of the Japanese Linji, or Rinzai, school. The abbots and Zen masters of all branches had each hesitated to be responsible, knowing it would inevitably entail huge expense. Even so, Zen Master Tengai had volunteered for the task, as was expected, considering his nature.

He was surely worrying how to raise enough funds for his college so that his inheritor would be given no headache, which was of far more concern to him than Linji's anniversary. But he dared put himself in greater difficulty by taking on this other burden. His determination likely came from an unshakable belief that the more one was cornered, the more one had a chance at a way out.

Indeed he had hit on an idea for fund-raising, which was to gather the calligraphy of all sorts of notables countrywide and publish it as a photo collection, while giving the originals to whoever donated funds. During these days he therefore traveled as much as his time allowed, and the attendants' burden alluded to by Senzoku was to accompany him.

Mokuzu asked a naive question,

"He goes all over the nation, though valuing his time he uses buses and trains. And he's already seventy. However hard the trips, can an attendant be broken down before he is?"

"Mokuzu, you don't know what it is to accompany him. His stamina is monstrous and doesn't indicate his age at all. Besides, he can get through the day on only a pack of peanuts and a mandarin orange. He can fall asleep anytime, anywhere, and recover his vigor in minutes just like Napoleon. And the attendant has to tote a huge stack of paper and some gifts, which feels all the more heavy the longer the distance. The master asks thirty calligraphies of each person. Visiting famous people in places like Kyoto, Tokyo, and Osaka is easier, thanks to well-developed transportation. But he goes there alone. He takes an attendant to remote places where there are famous temples, like Shoshinji, since old times. In those temples important priests even now reside. They're all far from the end of any bus or train line, and visitors must walk up rough roads and steep mountains. It's not unusual that the master and attendant arrive after the gate is closed, in which case they must spend the night before the gate in the form of sitting meditation."

Mokuzu was enjoying his quiet work as a chanting officer, yet he envied the attendant who could travel and share hardships with the master. Senzoku without reading Mokuzu's heart kept on voicing his resentment,

"He's absolutely dishonest. His prime object is to raise funds for his college, but he knows no one will give him free calligraphy and no one will buy it for his shabby private college. So now he can say he is raising funds for Linji's anniversary, and he well knows everyone will give him a donation for that. Can't you see this first trick? And second, he can realize his desire to make enough for the college to ease his worry there, while he proves his success at bringing off the anniversary all by his own work. And why all this? Because his deeper desire is to become chief abbot of our Myoshinji branch. Obviously it's a desire for name and power, and he isn't in the least concerned about using up his attendants."

Mokuzu looked across to the far corner of the enclosed garden. There the sun pouring in over the tile roof was strong, but Choho in silence was scraping away a liverwort hard to remove.

Mokuzu was respectful of this older monk, and grateful, because his help enabled him to carry out his first responsible position as head chanting officer without gross error.

Choho's face was like a flatfoot, and he was growing bald up onto the crown. His face could have been seen as ugly had he not been training for long years. He had passed only "Jaujou's Wu," but he was not keen on studying other koans and as often as possible neglected to have interviews with the master. He was said to have reached his deep realization and secured his view of life and death by an ancillary koan to "Jaujou's Wu," called "Eight Wu's Posed by Jungfeng." It was also said that his favorite Zen phrase was

> A tree in the spring breeze has two sides,
> The south boughs, warm, the north boughs, cold.[2]

Mokuzu was particularly indebted to Choho for his knowledge of the traditions that the chanting office had to follow, which included yearly observance of the anniversaries of Shoshinji's former chief priests.

Their number came to one hundred twenty-eight, and every three days or less the anniversary of one rolled around, requiring the chanting officers to bring out the small table and set of bowls dedicated to his use; and more, they had to redecorate the altar where he with the others reposed by changing the drapes, altarcloth, and various ornaments. And the posthumous titles bestowed on him by imperial favor had to be well researched, for the head chanting officer was expected to read them aloud at the anniversary ceremony. Choho fortunately tended to all these fussy details before Mokuzu needed to ask him.

Seeing Choho silently working, Mokuzu recalled the two old kitchen monks whom the young Dogen met on separate occasions early on during his excursion to Sung China.

One, hatless and drenched with sweat, was single-mindedly drying mushrooms in the summer sun before the Buddha hall. Asked his age by Dogen, the monk replied that he was sixty-eight.

"Why don't you get help from an assistant?"

"He is not me."

"At this hour when the sun is scorching the earth, need you be so stringent in performing your duties?"

"When is there a better time?"

The other, who was sixty-one, had come from a far monastery to buy mushrooms at the boat on which Dogen was staying. To him Dogen asked,

"Why do you at your venerable age labor as a cook instead of meditating and studying the Zen classics and the Way?"

The monk vigorously laughed. "Naive foreigner, you still know neither what it is to study the Way nor what are the Zen classics!"

Both old monks were finding an inexhaustible meaning to life through the use of their own bodies, and they took no account of Zen understood by speculation. For them speculative Zen was not real Zen. Their silent activity was a full life, which if it chanced to benefit others made them happier than they had expected to be.

Mokuzu asked Senzoku, who was weeding away in a dudgeon,

"Did you ever ask the master to affirm your idea that he, enslaved by his desires, is enslaving his disciples?"

"How can I ask? I'd be deafened for three days by his shouts, with the outcome that I'd descend this mountain in the dark like all the others."

"Senzoku, I feel sorry for the master. Even monks who are or have been his attendants see him as fashioning a worldly scenario, which is just how worldly men easily see him."

"Ho? You believe he's a noble Buddhist priest after all, an excellent Zen master? And you think his calligraphy tour is for the sake of Buddha, the Dharma, and the world?"

"It's evident," Mokuzu forcefully replied. "Shoshinji's short college is an indispensable educational organ for producing the Zen personality. Besides, his calligraphy tour is a retraining pilgrimage and not only for the utilitarian purpose of raising funds. He must be training by exposing himself to hardship and by meeting many noted persons. We ought to recall Jaujou. He attained his great realization at age eighteen, and at age sixty he started a training pilgrimage all over again. As he set forth he left this famous oath:

> "I shall beg to be taught by a seven-year-old if he be superior to me, and
> I shall teach a centenarian if he be inferior to me.[3]

"According to the chapter Gandavyuha of the Avatamsaka Sutra, Sudhana visited fifty-three sages for the purpose of training toward enlightenment. Jaujou's purpose was to train to help others, not only himself. He began his second pilgrimage at sixty, but our master is seventy. Isn't that wholly respectable?

"His pilgrimage is his very act of repaying his debt to Linji. Those others who don't assign themselves any such practice will drink, eat, and recline in festive mirth on the anniversary — for which our master is raising the capital.

"Senzoku, you mustn't overlook that he cares about Linji's anniversary. And what was Linji's life attitude? He wordlessly practiced instead of garrulously criticizing others. Listen to what was recorded:

732

"To Linji as he was planting pines the teacher Huangbo asked, 'What will you accomplish by planting so many pines in this deep mountain?' 'For one thing, some charm for the monastery. For another, a guidepost for later generations,' Linji said and spaded up more earth. 'Hm, much as you may, you have already received my thirty blows,' said Huangbo. Linji kept on, grunting 'Yo-ho!...yo-ho!'"[4]

Senzoku was maintaining an oppressive silence but broke it with an obscure pronouncement,

"You've begun to see things from the enlightened side, a far departure from a dumbhead like me...still, how would you explain the master's mounting fury to become elected chief abbot of the head temple in the coming term? His attendants say his primary talk with most guests is how to tighten the bonds of his clique and how to fight in the upcoming campaign."

"Well, he seems to have no doubt that the sect is the necessary organ, first, to address society's various ills, and second, to produce talented men. But he must be feeling impatient that the sect is presently not functioning well to fulfill either need. So he's trying to take the central position in the sect to improve it from within, instead of taking a critical attitude like a yowling dog," explained Mokuzu quietly.

"I see...then are you willing to string along with him no matter what?"

"No. We are entirely different in age and position, also in taste and character. He sees great meaning in social action. I rather see it in quiet observation and deep feeling and thought, given expression by art and literature...."

"Excuse me, it's time for midday chanting," noted Choho.

"Oh, thank you. Senzoku, about this we may have another chance to talk." Mokuzu left the inner garden.

He changed from work clothes to regular training robe, received a fresh-cooked lunch from the kitchen, and went to offer it to the founder. All meditation hall monks and most from the residential quarters were out for begging or mountain work, and the main building was vacant inside and out. In the gloomy founder's hall the odor of ceaseless incense with faintly wavering smoke seemed like the stagnation of time gone by.

After chanting before the founder, he offered chanting before the altar of the successive chief priests and the altars of the guardians of the land and buildings; the guardians against fire; Puan, reputed for answering the prayers of worshipers; and such. Because this chanting, unlike morning and evening chanting, was done by him alone, he could choose his own tempo. As he proceeded he felt his mind become tranquil as the depths of the sea and clear as the sky.

Finishing at the main building, he had to chant also at the old main building, Dokuso-kutsu. He went out onto the veranda, and entered the roofed corridor, dappled with the shadows of delicate maple leaves. Looking up to the cliff, he saw many small birds flitting from branch to branch.

A kitchen monk, having waited for his chanting to finish, struck the cloud-shaped gong to call the monks to lunch by its dull sound.

&

At dusk Mokuzu again went up into the bell tower for evening bell. On cloudy or rainy days he depended on the clock and began to strike the bell a little earlier than he did on fine days with rutilant sunsets, when he did not miss the moment to give the first stroke just as the sun dipped below the skyline. After waiting for the sound to carry over the mountains, he sent a less forceful second and third stroke. The fourth he raised with all his might and began at once with a round, steady tone to chant chapter 24 of the Lotus Flower Sutra. As he chanted, he continued with approximately isochronal strokes.

The monks who had gone for mountain work were coming back under the bell tower pulling and pushing the laden cart. Those who had been on mendicancy were hurrying up the stone steps under the gate with one or two heavy rice bags slung from their necks.

Mokuzu's chanting resonated throughout Shoshinji, reaching not only the meditation hall and the Manjusri attendant's building but also those deepest rooms where the fiscal head and the attendants to the master resided.

The master was said to have enjoyably told an attendant that he had never before been able to hear from his rooms a monk's chanting at the bell tower.

In due course a professor, Muto, of Shoshin Short College began to appear in the garden around evening bell. One evening he went with his walking stick to a pine root directly under the bell tower; another evening he sat on the veranda of the main building. He kept changing places, at times choosing the garden of the meditation hall, even the ridge of the back mountain. Some evenings he was joined by students and other professors.

As he began to chant Mokuzu felt uneasy about the professor's presence, but, taking care to harmonize his voice with the bell, he could soon forget everything. When at last he descended the bell tower, he always felt that his inner ills had evaporated into the air, that his body had become enlarged and his mind made pure and wide.

As the sound of the bell subsided, the environs darkened as much as to render each form indistinct and the mountains set into sleep. In contrast the moon brightened over the tall treetops and the monks' night training began to manifest zeal.

After evening bell, according to custom, the residential quarters monks meditated in the Buddha hall of the main building until interviews with the master were over. Marking the time of their meditation by a burning stick of incense as the direct monk did in the meditation hall was also the duty of the head chanting officer. Thus Mokuzu was always last to have an interview. Although quite fatigued by his daily tour for calligraphy, the master gave relatively more time to Mokuzu because he normally had no important tasks afterward.

Early in May, Mokuzu was already investigating the fifth of 'Dungshan's Five Classifications.'

Zen Master Tengai asked him unconcernedly with no show of emotion, "Tell me the meaning of 'No one dare make a stanza.'"

"'No one dare make a stanza,'" Mokuzu slowly repeated.

"Explain with words."

"Master, these days the professor Muto comes to listen to the evening bell, sitting here, standing there. I noticed he had a tape recorder, and one day he introduced himself, saying his specialty is Buddhist music. He asked me what is my mind as I chant and ring the bell. It seemed to me an odd question, for whatever one's mind is would be expressed. I can explain before and after, but during chanting even I don't know, because I am chanting in a state of self-oblivion. In such a state indeed, as a Zen phrase well says, 'the whole universe is flooded with self-radiating light,'5 and in the whole universe there is only oneself."

"Hm, quite so. Professor Muto was telling me he will send a tape to Dr. Yasaka, who will translate your voice and the bell, hard to define as sad or pleasant, into his awkward language. I wonder how far he can introduce Zen music by his writing. Too bad most people have no chance to hear it directly. Well, what is the meaning of the next phrase, 'Everyone wishes to cross the flow of life and death'?"

"The phrase refers to the earnest and most conceited human desire to transcend mortality. In comparison, the worldly desires for name, position, power, money, and such are like rabbit hairs or the buzzing of bees. Because of this one extraordinary desire, we Zen monks disregard our life, make nothing of Linji's shouts and Deshan's stick, whip ourselves as long as an ounce of vigor remains, and struggle on and on toward ultimate perfection. Naturally for us, Sakyamuni and Amitabha are not objects of worship but precursors we must get over. The fierceness of such trainees can be likened to nuclear fission."

Receiving Mokuzu's answer, Zen Master Tengai was like a sumo wrestler taking a stance at the edge of the ring, but suddenly he dodged with a new question,

"How do you see the last phrase, 'But after all discounts and compromises, where a man settles is before the hearth'? How you see it makes a great difference to your future. Present your views."

Mokuzu was reminded of the sight of his father's back as he hunched before the furnace cooking rice for his infant children and their sick mother, his shadow swaying with the flicker of the fire. 'The small flame was the maternal care he must surely have felt the warmth of in his babyhood. What a comfort is a small flame to a lone, ill-fortuned man!'

He too had spent hours by the little pond at the approach to the laymen's graveyard. '...the surface so calm, now and anon a loach stirring the mud, the newts so slow they made no stir. Lonesome in Ryotanji...remembering Ena, I thought the sough of the pines was like crying and wondered why the blue sky through the branches didn't weep red tears.' Then he could again meet with Ena and spend exalted days with her. 'They flew like an arrow! Indeed they seem an illusion.

'And I came here to investigate death. I feel I've been here a hundred years staying underground. This too isn't where I want to be; it's good only for those who have no dream of living a happy, cheerful life. This monastery is said to be the place to train oneself in Zen, but for whose sake?'

Mokuzu thought he understood the mind Dungshan finally attained after years of training without ever having had enough maternal affection, scarcely ever tasting any joy, scarcely sleeping as much as he liked, probably never conversing with a loving woman. Dungshan saw through the depth of the Dharma and realized he could gain no special ability, no way to fly like a bird or swim like a fish. From beginning to end he was a mere ignorant man — 'his elbow could nohow bend backward.'[6] Hence he wasn't even a Zen trainee, and certainly not a god or a buddha. He was a most human of human beings who well knew the difficulty of restricting human desires, and who well knew the human feelings of humor and pathos.

'I think I understand Dungshan, but I don't believe his final stage of realization should be the end of the Zen training for which we risk our life. Where he arrived is too desolate. Reconsidered, his final state is pitiful and laughable, a suitable end for trainees who love ideation but not for me, who loves concrete life. Most began their Zen training by abandoning love and home, and their prime concern was self-loyalty. Indeed the reason they sought to be 'a true man of no position' was only to attain their own freedom. As a result what they understood overemphasized life's negative and sorrowful aspects. They undertook their training with a completely wrong attitude, didn't they? Training should be for the sake of others, not for oneself. One should train to build up and perfect love and home rather than train to abandon them.

'For the sake of love and home we need to allow ourselves a certain amount of disloyalty to our spirit of inquiry. What is wrong with knowing the truth a little less, being a true man in a slight haze, on account of our eagerness for love and home? The important attitude is not to know the truth but to use both truth and illusion effectively for a happy life. We must wish a happy life for everyone and everything, and with the ability we possess make even one more creature happy. And I think what is most suitable for me is to find a lifelong companion with whom to deepen the meaning of life.'

Mokuzu spoke after a long pause, "Master, I am fortunately only twenty. 'Before the hearth' could be the conclusion of Zen training for Dungshan, but for me it's just the start of training with the awareness of what Zen training is. From now on I must live my own Zen life rather than only study the traditional Zen that prospered in Tang and Sung China."

"Of course. Then what do you see as lacking in Dungshan's view?"

"What is lacking is a viridity that has no shame or fear of being ignorant. There are always things about which we are unenlightened, regardless of how hard the Zen training we have gone through. In fact the unknown world should increase as we continue our training. The stars emit a more vigorous light for trainees than for the already-enlightened. Each star reminds us of a question mark. The sky is thus filled with questions, which are the light of life. By recognizing our ignorance, we are released from the need to pretend to be perfect beings, and we are enabled to love, respect, and trust other beings. The source of 'the Bodhisattva mind willing to save others before saving oneself'[7] is not the recognition of self-perfection but the recognition of self-imperfection."

"Don't spend so many words, I know what you want to say. In short, Dungshan's state of enlightenment lacks incandescent compassion. That is why our Zen Teacher Hakuin here placed his comment. Listen:

> "The affable priest Meghasri climbed down Mt. Sumeru uncountable times only to ask other stupid saints to fill the well with snow.[8]

"Zen is not mere learning of the truth. It is a religion, which is Buddhism, to help others. I think you understand this very well, so by and large we have finished studying 'Dungshan's Five Classifications.'"

Zen Master Tengai then assumed an easy posture and thumped himself on the shoulder, where he must have been quite stiff.

Allowed to pass 'Dungshan's Five Classifications,' Mokuzu felt somewhat dissatisfied. He could tell his master had no fresh sensitivity toward sentient and insentient beings. 'He's tough as stone. Too bad he's a mere sedimentary stone,' he thought, and withdrew.

৯

One morning before a week had passed, Mokuzu was summoned by the master. He asked Choho to do the chanting for the offering of meals.

In the master's room the nun Shorai was being offered a bowl of tea. Kneeling on the north veranda, arranging flowers, was a young woman about whom Mokuzu had entirely forgotten.

As always the nun had a tanned face and patched robes, making her indistinguishable from a monk, especially when her mouth was shut tight. Miss Iwai wore a white hemp-and-cotton suit with sleeves and bodice fussy at the hem. The multi-pleated skirt covered her legs and feet as she sat square. Seeing Mokuzu, she smiled warmly and went on adding feathery asparagus stems to an arrangement of white carnations.

Mokuzu was losing memory of most of the lyrics he had learned from Teacher Yojun, but he could scrape together a verse of Robert Herrick,

> Stay while ye will, or goe;
>   And leave no scent behind ye:
> Yet trust me, I shall know
>   The place, where I may find ye.[9]

Zen Master Tengai was asking him to make a call of inquiry on Dr. Yasaka at Kamakura, for the professor had a slight cold. That was only his ostensible interest; in fact he wanted Mokuzu to thank Dr. Yasaka for his various courtesies offered earlier when Koko was leaving for America. And more, the main purpose was to feel out how far he had progressed in translating *Linji lu* into modern Japanese, which the master had already requested of him five years ago to the month.

The master hoped to print Dr. Yasaka's translation in commemoration of the coming anniversary of Linji and give copies to all the priests and their laymen from the six thousand local temples under the fourteen branches of the present Rinzai school.

"Leave as early as you can, with Miss Iwai here. She is to stay in the doctor's residence until he recovers from his cold. She is willing to look after his home life now that he must be bearing many discomforts following the death of his wife."

"I respect your order, but Master, I am head of the chanting office, with great responsibilities. Can't you send another?"

"You are the monk for the job." The master spoke forcefully and did not open his mouth again.

With an unpleasant feeling Mokuzu returned to his office. As he prepared for the trip he gave Choho, Senzoku, and Myokei instructions for his absence. Then the nun Shorai whispered in at the door to summon him, and standing before the chanting office she spoke under her breath,

"Mokuzu, be thankful for his plan to let you study under Dr. Yasaka for some years. He is sending away his dear disciple for the sake of the Dharma. It was well arranged through Professor Muto. You know Dr. Yasaka is a world-famous authority on Zen. Brace yourself — such a chance occurs but once in a lifetime!",

On his way to Kamakura, Mokuzu saw a great big chestnut tree in full bloom by a cow shed near a stream. He sensed the smell of manure, though the smell could not reach him through the window of the running train. The waterways along the rice fields were brimming. On a mountain skirt pomegranate flowers appeared singularly red amid the green inside a white wall like that of Tangenji.

At his side Miss Iwai chaffed him with her interests and manner of talking as she tried to engage him.

"So, can you tell me about the excellent fruit of your extensive study of the precepts?"

"There's no room either to keep or to break the precepts if we respect, trust, and love the opposite sex whenever we happen to meet," replied Mokuzu as a dodge.

Miss Iwai was unpleasantly silent, searching for a return; then she said,

"Obviously there'd be no room for the precepts or for such sentiments during the sex act. Koko told me that according to the highest Zen understanding of the precepts, if we see a beautiful person just as a beautiful person and an ugly person just as an ugly person, we are keeping the precepts. But as soon as we begin to have notions about which part or what makes the person beautiful or ugly, we are already violating the precepts."

"Koko's understanding must be descended from the third Zen patriarch in China, Sengtsan; indeed it is the highest understanding of the precepts. But while there is no such high person to observe such high precepts, whoever practices such an understanding will immediately deteriorate into the lowest being. Those who don't know how to use wisdom had better remain ignorant, just as those who don't know how to use money are better off poor."

Seemingly his words pricked. Miss Iwai quickly retorted,

"You act like the wisest of the wise, but you have a woman called Luri or something, kept a secret. I heard it from Koko when he told me his view of the precepts."

"How could he have come to know her?"

"Well, I don't know how. But I struck the right chord in your heart." Miss Iwai studied his face.

"When exactly did he tell you?"

739

"The day of the ceremony for him, that is, the night before he left for America. I drove him in my car to his temple by the Nagara River."

"You aren't being straight with me. It must have been a very important time for him with his leaving Japan the next day. Surely he wanted a quiet night alone."

"Far from it — you know nothing but scriptures. When we arrived he said, 'You will be transporting me to Osaka Airport in the morning, so why not stay the night and have a fine evening together?' I laughed and said I would return to my home in Nagoya, but he entreated with prayerful hands, 'Don't abandon me. I can't be alone with the thought that tomorrow I must set off for a land where I have no kith and kin.'"

"You're making that up," prompted Mokuzu to extract more about Luri.

"No, no, I sympathized, and kept him company over supper. But then he said something like 'Alas, it's my last night in Japan! I am ready to die in a foreign land. My sole regret is I'm a pure and simple virgin with no carnal knowledge of any beautiful Japanese woman. Of course I have my holy vows, but in a foreign land full of attractive women I worry if I can restrain myself without the precious memory of having touched the spirit of Japan...a pearl. Please — ' It was then that he said your abnormal eagerness to train is due to your having a woman called Luri."

"Oh? What else did he say about her?"

"That's all. But he added that the only ones who know are the Zen master, the Shogetsuan nuns, and him, and that it should be kept from you. So, you too keep secret what you've learned. Now don't you want to hear what he said after our night together? You ought to — it concerns his honor. He said, 'How was that? Substantial sex insures sound sleep. Give me a few more chances and you'd grow to be a fine woman.' Ha! I'm unsure which of you is cherishing the precepts as mere idea and which is cherishing them as practical philosophy."

Soon after arriving at Dr. Yasaka's residence, Mokuzu turned back, leaving Miss Iwai there. He reached Gifu Station near ten at night and walked to Shoshinji.

He came through the gate at the odd hour of two in the morning, but more odd for him was the sight of the shadows of kitchen monks busy under an untimely light. 'Something's amiss with the master!' He hurried to the chanting office and found no one there. He went to the kitchen. In great haste monks were making a large quantity of rice balls and chopping pickles; others were at the furnace cooking more rice.

"A fire started at a farmhouse in Sendo and is spreading even now. All monks have gone to the rescue. We'll distribute rice!" replied one.

Mokuzu, his mind set to rest, returned to his office. He sat in the dark deliberating whether to go to the village or assist the cooks. Soon he chose neither, changed to his regular robe, and went at a slow pace up the back mountain. His interest was not to see the spectacle of the fire from the top, but to meditate there to ascertain that denial was the correct decision for him and his environment when Zen Master Tengai recommended that he become a disciple of Dr. Yasaka.

Nearing the place where he usually took his meditation seat, he noticed a figure seated like a rock. The trees and terrain were entirely black. In the western sky was a tiny glow; the burning village had to be quite far, behind some mountains.

Without moving, the figure spoke first,

"Is that you, Mokuzu? Why didn't you stay overnight to make it a leisurely trip?"

"Yes, Master, it's me. I am impressed you could come up this far by yourself in spite of your age."

"I can climb anything this low in no time." The master stood up.

"Did you intend to inspect the fire?"

"Hm, I couldn't sleep with the noisy monks. Coming up this high doesn't augment the excitement, the view's no better." The master smiled. Mokuzu could see his face and was surprised to hear what he had just said in jest. A doctrinarian, were one to overhear, would raise no end of criticism.

'Is it his unsullied purity, or his unpolished taste?' Mokuzu wondered.

The master sat down on a flat rock. "How was Dr. Yasaka?"

"He told me he is about finished proofreading various texts. But evidently the work of translating to modern Japanese is untouched. It won't come near being ready by the anniversary in October."

"Really? Is he unwilling to take it on?"

"I think he is unwilling. Three scholars were there, who are his disciples. They had brought rattan chairs out to the garden. Dr. Yasaka said to one, 'Why don't you take on the translation? It's worth a try'...and he gave a gentle laugh."

"Hm...all right, I will print one of his proofread texts and donate that. What else did he say relating to *Linji lu*?"

"He told his disciples that the number of characters employed amounts to 14,535 and the variety to 1,336, and therefore the average frequency of each character is 11. He concluded, 'Now, the frequency of *ren*, or "man," is as high as 196, enough to prove how important *ren* was to Linji's thought,'" Mokuzu precisely reported.

"Ho! A method of study like catching at straws! I suppose his cold isn't so bad then?"

741

"I don't feel misgivings about his cold..." Mokuzu was reluctant to say.

"Well, then?"

"It was odd for me that he hadn't the least perception of being near his death, when he is as old as ninety-five and moreover a famous Zen scholar. He kept telling his disciples of his intentions to perfect this and that."

"Not knowing the time of his death, you say? A life-span is dependent on Heaven's will. What ordinary mortal can know it?" The master's tone was condescending. Mokuzu raised his voice,

"Without knowing one's time of death, how can one know another's? Without knowing another's — which is a most dire concern for human beings — how can one fairly guide another? It is not healthy to act like an ordinary man when important questions arise, and not healthy to act like an extraordinary man in the face of matters of no grave concern. Is that the proper conduct for great leaders of the world?"

"Set aside the case of others: how about you? Can you tell the time of your death and of others'?"

"I can tell roughly."

"Roughly? Who cannot tell roughly?"

"Others are much too rough. A man intimate with the Way must be able to know the year of his death at least seven years ahead, the day at least seven days ahead, and the hour at least seven hours ahead."

"Ha ha ha! You also have grown up to be a man able to bluff. Well, then didn't he give you any special words of kindness?"

Mokuzu was greatly dissatisfied with his Zen master for taking his sensibility as a bluff, but he contained his feeling and replied,

"Yes, while he was talking on with his disciples, I took my leave. He was startled, 'What? Leaving? Sorry, I wasn't aware that yours is a busy lot. Please express my gratitude to your Zen master.' I then asked him, 'Coming this far, I could have the happy occasion of meeting with the renowned doctor. I would value some advice for my training.' Straightaway he took his pen and wrote on a pad a passage from *Jaujou lu*,

> "An old woman asked Jaujou, 'I am an old woman with five obstacles.
> How can I be rid of them?' Jaujou replied, 'Would that others be reborn
> in Heaven and the old woman ever remain in the sea of suffering!'[10]

"And the doctor commented, 'Here is the essence of religious life.'"

"I see. You are lucky. In your first meeting Dr. Yasaka showed you the essence. Listen, I am thinking of letting you study under him for some years. He is a great benefactor to the revival of Zen, which has been suffering a general prostration as if from generations of consanguineous marriage. He has exposed traditional Zen to the currents of world thought and repolished it. And more, the side effect of his work has been to bring friendship and understanding between East and West; indeed, he is building a bridge between the two. For sure, your former Zen master, Hanun, also had a strong wish for world peace. But erecting a Kannon statue is like trying to bite into a tortoise in comparison to Dr. Yasaka's work, which is like a blood transfusion. In the present state of Japan and the world Dr. Yasaka's work is more effective; it benefits both Japan and the world. The best way to achieve world peace is to make the people of the world understand the Zen that was perfected in Japan.

"Parting from you as you verge on completing the transmission of all traditional Zen is quite unbearable for me. But you are young, in fact too young to be given 'The Ten Supreme Precepts' and 'The Last Barrier.' The longest way around is the shortest way home. I believe letting you study under Dr. Yasaka for a while — a luxurious loitering — is best for your future, for Zen transmission, and for the world; and I should like to practice what I think best, however hard it is for my own self. I wish to hear what you think of this. Tell me without reserve."

"Master, before anything else I thank you for your consideration of me." Their eyes had adjusted to the dark and each could discern the other's countenance.

"Moreover, I have no objection to the high appraisal of Dr. Yasaka's achievement in Zen studies and his introducing them to the West. But, Master, please hear me. He and I have traditional Zen in common, and our aims too are likely the same, especially about wishing to contribute to world peace through Zen life and understanding. But the age and society in which he has lived and the one in which I must live are very different. Our talent and character are also different. In short I see a difference, even a hetero-geneity, so to speak, as much as I see a quality of sameness. I'd like to respect the difference, as I respect the sameness. But to respect it is difficult because the one rides on top of the other."

"You are speaking only a matter of fact: every two men have their samenesses and differences," the master cut in impatiently.

"Indeed, Master. But please note that a difference on top of so similar a base is quite fatal because it comes from a difference of depth of understanding of the same subject. We see, talk, and study the same subject but on very different levels of understanding. If we want to respect the difference just as we respect the sameness, we shouldn't put ourselves in the relation of teacher and student. We had better live apart, each in our own way, if owing to obstacles of age and social rank we can't form a relation on an equal footing."

Mokuzu stopped, seeing in the master's eyes a flame of anger.

"It seems I made you haughty! You're telling me Dr. Yasaka is worthy to be your acquaintance but not your teacher, eh? Let me hear exactly what is and is not the same between you."

"There is a good example, Jaujou's reply to the old woman, which Dr. Yasaka wrote down for me. Dr. Yasaka's comment was, 'Here is the essence of religious life,' for he read into Jaujou's reply great wisdom and great compassion. It is great wisdom to tell the old woman that the only right way is to stay in the sea of suffering and there find happiness instead of trying to escape her five obstacles; and great compassion to tell her to wish happiness not for herself but for others."

"True. Dr. Yasaka read Jaujou's reply as the harmonious combination of wisdom and compassion. What is your complaint?"

"I have no complaint, only I could detect that Dr. Yasaka was not really understanding what the old woman's five obstacles were. His interpretation is no better than the popular view of Buddhism, and this is the vital difference between us. According to him, she suffered because it was said women could not be reborn in heaven as any of the five important figures — Brahma, Sakra, Maharaja, Cakravarti, and A-vaivartika Bodhisattva. Forget those chimerical figures! Her suffering was from earthly hardships: the poverty that kept her from nursing her dependents, disease to herself and her kin, the cruelty of men, separation from loved ones, the inability to get help from the wise, and so on. Without understanding her suffering, any interpretation of Jaujou's reply becomes a mere exercise of ideas. A million words on Zen don't amount to an iota of Zen. It was said Zen begins to live only from the moment we begin to practice our understanding. However, the quality of our practice is determined by the degree to which we understand the core of reality."

"Mokuzu, how could you tell that the Zen of Dr. Yasaka is only a play of ideas?"

"Yuanwu preaches with regard to case 23 of *Biyan lu*:

> "The quality of jade is gauged by fire, gold by a touchstone; the sharpness of a sword by a hair, the depth of water by a rod. In Zen dialogue, a trainee's depth of perception and what course he is taking should be known by his single word and phrase, the least movement of his heart and body, each of his advances and retreats, each jostling in and out....[11]

"Dr. Yasaka was studying in an ideal place, surrounded with rich greenery but conveniently near the capital, and surrounded by disciples who might raise even his used tissues to their heads in expression of their gratitude. No suffering women were approaching him. I wonder how he could understand such women by seeing through the window of his study. Without depth, his words, his great wisdom and compassion, and essence of religious life are empty!

"It reminds me of the queer words he used in his writings to explain Zen: 'the consciousness of Wu,' 'the consciousness of non-consciousness,' 'the logic of non-difference of non-diversity and non-uniformity,' 'the absolute nothingness,' 'the Eastern spirituality.' When he was writing these, I doubt he was thinking about great wisdom, great compassion, or women suffering with five obstacles.

"I can't believe that people desperate for help can be helped by such writing. I rather feel they will be sickened and get gooseflesh, and will reject the world of Zen, which in reality is the world of peace, pleasure, and brightness. I prefer being with people who reject that kind of writing to being with the few scholars who extol it. At best Dr. Yasaka has exposed a juggler's trick with trickier language. But Zen isn't a trick. If we reflect on it in our actual experience instead of making it a philosophy and a mystery, we can understand that it is very reasonable everyday common sense. The sight of a spring path should be the true face of a Zennist's wisdom and mercy."

Mokuzu saw that the master had his eyes closed and his hands joined under his simplified surplice. He went on to his conclusion,

"During my visit I also heard him and his disciples analyzing the recording of the bell and my chanting with almost no regard for my presence. One seemed to be intending to translate the sound into words. What I'd like to say is simple: I hope many people can have the occasion to hear the bells and the chanting here in Shoshinji, and more, I hope many can have the occasion to chant and to strike the bell in the bell tower.

"Let me finish by saying, in his writing Dr. Yasaka passionately discusses Linji's 'true man of no position,' but he himself is a doctor, a professor emeritus, a recipient of court rank and honors. It surely proves he is a specialist on Zen studies of the Tang and Sung dynasties, but it nowise proves he's a Zennist here and now. What will he do if the word 'Zen' is fetched from him?"

"Okay, I understand you. Say no more, you have won. You have defeated Dr. Yasaka, and soon you will defeat me, for I am the one who recommended that you study under him. Well, I shall return to my quarters. Will you descend with me, whether you go to pay your condolences after the fire, or to sleep so as to save your energy to accompany me beginning tomorrow on my pilgrimage for calligraphy?"

Although the master had openly declared that he could still keep pace with young monks, his movements on the path were decidedly those of an old man. A rock from under his foot rolled down with a deep sound into the darkness below. Instantly Mokuzu caught his wrist, but the master shook him off,

"E-hey! Make no unsolicited meddling! I'm not so old as to need assistance on this trifling mountain!"

54

Pilgrimaging for Calligraphy

The train with its orange line of windows departed into the far darkness after letting off the master and his attendant. In contrast to the sweet doze-inducing warmth of the train, the vicinity of the station was cold, and there was a thin slanting rain illuminated white by an overhead lamp.

Mokuzu took out his rain cape from one of his bundles and put it over the master's shoulders.

"Don't care about me — just care not to wet the paper," the master said testily.

"You may ease your mind; I put it all in a vinyl bag before wrapping it in the cloth and I'll carry it in my sleeve."

Zen Master Tengai lumbered along the road below the eulalia-covered bank of the railway. Mokuzu followed. Nothing could be done but resign himself to leaving the master's head exposed to the rain.

Before long the road parted from the railway and went on to a mountain skirt where a grape plantation extended. Far off by the mountain were the dim lights of some farmhouses.

> 'Season of mists and mellow fruitfulness,
> Close bosom-friend of the maturing sun;
> Conspiring with him how to load and bless
> With fruit the vines that round the thatch-eaves run.[1]

'What's the meaning of being pursued by rain in the very province of Koshu, noted for its scanty precipitation?' Mokuzu asked to himself.

The master was shifting the load of his body forward step by step. His legs were thin for the size of his torso. As the road steepened, his pace shortened and slowed.

"Master, shouldn't we rest under some tree?"

"No, we must keep on, even a step more. A halt is equal to a ten-foot regression." The master as though muttering to himself did not turn back.

It was so dark that the trees overspreading the road were indistinguishable as to their being chestnut or walnut. Underneath, the rain was sparse, but each gust shook down large drops.

After a while, worrying that the master might become stricken with apoplexy, Mokuzu called out again, though he knew he would be denied,

"We have come quite far. Since we are uncertain of the area, I wish to visit one of those farmhouses to check if we are on the right road. Could you wait here just a short while?"

The master stopped and regarded the lights, considerably far from the road. The road was becoming increasingly arduous as it narrowed into the mountains.

"You'd better not. If you appear in this rainy night, they may sympathize with you and offer a meal and lodging. We must abstain from expecting kindness. But we'll take a recess here." The master sat down on a bulging root, took a towel from his scrip, and dried his head.

"A Zen teacher, Tetsugen, of the Obaku school, pilgrimaged throughout Japan to raise a fund to publish the entire Tripitaka, but I envy him because he had no time limit. For me the term has already expired. True, a few more days will complete the gathering of calligraphy, but converting it to money is a yet harder task," sighed the master.

"But Master, Tetsugen had to rebuild several temples and rescue famine-stricken people besides publishing the Tripitaka."

Mokuzu's comment was ignored as if it had not been heard. However, the master soon stood up and said, "All right, we'll go on! There is no better preaching than to lay down one's life!" and he resumed walking.

The slippery narrow path lay mostly under big trees, but in the openings it was thick with eulalia, thoroughwort, and valerian, and also kudzu creeping in all directions to catch at the foot. No starlight and no house light came in. There came only the occasional whistle of a freight train. The rain laced the trees and the grasses, suppressing the insects.

As he walked Mokuzu chanted "The Ten Supreme Precepts" as set down in *Yishinjie wen*, a work attributed to Bodhidharma. With this koan he would by and large finish koan study under the master's instruction. He would be given "The Last Barrier" as his last koan, but it was to be studied alone, without a teacher's detailed guidance.

747

These ten precepts were advocated by Sakyamuni Buddha, and were recorded in *Fanwang jing*, the Brahma's Net Sutra. The Chinese Zen master Rujing transmitted them to Dogen, who returned with them to Japan. They appear in Dogen's *Kyoju kaimon* with his clarifications:

I. Do not kill: Kill no sentient beings and your cause to attain Buddha-hood will increase. Accede to Buddha's wisdom: kill no sentient beings.

II. Do not steal: Keep your mental state as it naturally is and the gate of emancipation will open.

III. Do not commit adultery: Keep pure your body, speech, and mind; and desire nothing. Thence shall you walk with Buddha.

IV. Do not lie: When the wheel of the Dharma turns well, there is neither excess nor want and everyone benefits from Buddha's sweet teaching by attaining verity and substance.

V. Do not deal in intoxicants: Adhibit no intoxicants and give others no occasion to violate the precept. Therein resides bright wisdom.

VI. Do not slander: In Buddhism all follow the same path and the same Dharma. Walking together, all perform the same teaching of Buddha. Let no one disturb another's progress by slander.

VII. Do not insult: All Buddhas and patriarchs have thoroughly comprehended the phenomenal world and the substantial world. The eye of the Dharma-body does not distinguish large from small, outer from inner.

VIII. Do not be stingy: Each phrase and each gatha is not unlike every single thing, even a blade of grass. Each dharma and each evidence of each dharma is a Buddha and a patriarch. Not a one ever withheld its teaching.

IX. Do not anger: The true world cannot be grasped by advance or retreat or be comprehended by truth or falsehood. The true world is a mass of clouds brimming with light and sublimity.

X. Do not speak falsely of Buddha, Dharma, or Sangha: The physical Buddha's teaching is a ferry and a bridge, and its virtue returns to the sea of the substantial world. The teaching cannot be an object of criticism. Regard it with the highest veneration and practice it faithfully.[2]

Mokuzu visualized the modest daily life of those trainees who were contemporaries of Sakyamuni Buddha. He thought they must have had great affection as well as great respect for all creatures. Evidently for them, human beings were not the most important beings in the world.

'Knowing that to maintain their life they had to sacrifice other creatures, they deepened their remorse at having a sinful body. How pious and prudent they were. What if their way of life had been widely embraced and become the prevailing way of life on earth? Then surely the human world could not have developed the multifarious, high-level culture we presently see. Rather, their way of life may have anticipated such a culture as we might finally reach if human culture develops for another ten or twenty centuries.'

He also mused on the cogitation of Mahayana Buddhists when they branched off to prosper apart from Theravada Buddhism. For them the precept against killing, for instance, was no longer a concern for the life of other creatures. Their object of interest was their mind that took pity on other lives; that is, they thought from the standpoint of the human view, and what they wanted to know was themselves.

'They gave full rein to their speculation on the true meaning of killing, the true meaning of self and others, of compassion, of wisdom. Sometimes they even came to contradictory and paradoxical conclusions, such as that it was right to kill one life to save ten, or that sparing a life that ought to be killed was violating the precept against killing. Their views were based on a faith in human intellect, but it is a fact that to this day no proof has been presented of our capacity to comprehend universal truth.'

Bodhidharma's *Yishinjie wen*, which Mokuzu had received as a koan, was a more transcendent and also a more fundamental view than the ten supreme precepts of Sakyamuni's day (later known as the Hinayana precepts) or the ten supreme precepts as they were developed in Mahayana Buddhism (known as the Mahayana precepts). *Yishin* (one mind) meant "absolute mind," or "undiscriminating mind," explained in *Dacheng chishin lun* as follows:

> All of the Dharma has always existed and will always exist. It is unnameable, beyond reach of language and cognitive faculties. In the last analysis it is impartial, invariable, unbreakable. It is One Mind, *bhutatathata*, "immutable truth."[3]

Further, therein it was said that all sentient beings are endowed with this One Mind, the nature of which is ever pure, impervious to pollution. One Mind is thus free of any offense, sin, and fault. One Mind by another name is Buddha nature. To see the precepts in the light of Buddha nature has been believed to mean to see them as including all beings in the universe, not only human beings. If that view is right, we can escape the criticism of seeing the precepts from only the human viewpoint.

Mokuzu kept chanting Bodhidharma's *Yishinjie wen* so that he might experience seeing the precepts in terms of Buddha nature:

I. Do not kill: One's original nature is marvelous. Do not kill means to hold the view that death is not the end of existence, for the Dharma is eternal.

II. Do not steal: One's original nature is marvelous. Do not steal means to think nothing is obtainable, for in the Dharma nothing is obtainable.

III. Do not commit adultery: One's original nature is marvelous. Do not commit adultery means to form no attachments, for in the Dharma there is no attachment.

IV. Do not lie: One's original nature is marvelous. Do not lie means to preach no word, for the Dharma cannot be preached.

V. Do not deal in intoxicants: One's original nature is marvelous. Do not deal in intoxicants means, do not be unclear, for the Dharma is ever pure.

VI. Do not slander: One's original nature is marvelous. Do not slander means to speak of no one's faults, for there are no faults in the Dharma.

VII. Do not insult: One's original nature is marvelous. Do not insult means to make no distinction between oneself and others, for all are equal in the Dharma.

VIII. Do not be stingy: One's original nature is marvelous. Do not be stingy means to withhold nothing, for immutable truth pervades the Dharma.

IX. Do not anger: One's original nature is marvelous. Do not anger means to assume no individual self, for there is no noumenon in the Dharma.

X. Do not speak falsely of Buddha, Dharma, or Sangha. One's original nature is marvelous. Do not speak falsely of Buddha, Dharma, or Sangha means to see the awakened and the ignorant without discrimination, for the Dharma consists in absolute and unchanging equality.[4]

Knowing that Bodhidharma's version of the precepts was beyond his apprehension, Mokuzu endeavored to forget himself and the world by continuing to chant. He neither looked ahead nor heeded the rain trickling down his brow and entering at his collar. He walked as if spellbound.

"Carry through to the end of the end of the end!" the master suddenly intoned. He seemed unaware of having voiced his thought. Mokuzu readily perceived that he was remembering his mother and expressing to himself her words of encouragement on the day of his decision to enter the priesthood.

The apologue of the dutiful son his mother told him to be was repeatedly recounted to his trainees:

"In ancient China there lived a rich old childless couple who wished to adopt a son, and to all who aspired to be their son they gave a test," she began.

"Each they led behind the house, where they asked him to fill a twenty-gallon cask with water from the well before the first cock crow.

"'I can fill it in a trice!' said the first, and he immediately set to work only to find the bucket had no bottom.

"'Don't mock me! Who can draw water with this?' said he, and he left. Youths came one after another in like manner, and as the years passed finally no one came.

"'Not a one can meet our ideal,' despaired the old couple, ready to give up. Thereupon a youth appeared. Without hope they led him to the well and asked of him the same task. Meekly he complied, and he too found the bucket had no bottom. But rather than complain, he drew it up and let the drops that came with it fall into the cask. Soon he was absorbed in his work. And so it went that he did not hear the cock at dawn. When the old couple arrived at the well, the cask was overflowing," concluded the master's mother, and she gave him this lesson,

"Had the cask been bottomless, the youth would have failed; as it was, the bottomless bucket was not fatal. The cask with a bottom symbolizes unlimited will, the bottomless bucket limited ability. This teaches us that however incompetent we are, if only we continue, we can succeed." Her final words he had just repeated — "Carry through to the end of the end of the end!"

On the rainy mountain path what supported the seventy-year-old master was his mother's face, last seen by him in his twelfth year.

He and his disciple reached the front gate of a Soto temple well after bedtime. The small gate was shut tight under a big nettle tree. Wind whipped the branches; bush clover grazed the gateposts. The thatched roof provided scant shelter from the spray of rain.

The master took from his scrip a newspaper he had picked up in the train. He spread it, sat down, leaned against a post, and extended his legs. He was so wayworn he could meanwhile utter no word. Mokuzu, disburdened of the bundles, clenched and unclenched his hands. One was light but contained the calligraphy paper not to be made wet. The other had printed copies of the master's prospectus and many packaged gifts, and, though hefty, it required less protection from the weather.

Mokuzu unslung the bamboo canteen from his shoulder and offered the master tea in its top.

"Hmm," he said, emptying it at a draft, and asked for one more. Mokuzu offered it and realized very little remained. He himself could drink none; it had to be saved for when the master took his antihypertensive.

"We could come this far. It'll make tomorrow easy. We'll ask the head priest here for his calligraphy as soon as the dawning bell is struck. We'll then

751

proceed to Enzan to visit Erinji and Kogakuji. From there we return to Otsuki to get a private railway to Fuji-yoshida, for we'll visit the Sengen Shrine...then how to get to Kuonji at Minobe, head temple of the Nichiren sect?...Well, tomorrow I'll do some research in the train...."

The choice of whom to ask for calligraphy and of planning their itinerary was entirely at the master's discretion. In his scrip he therefore carried a thick address book, and railway and road maps, as well as their schedule.

"Isn't Erinji renowned for the priest Kaisen?" Mokuzu asked.

"Right, he was born in Gifu and stayed at Sufukuji before being invited to Erinji by Takeda Harunobu. Harunobu's heir, Katsuyori, was dauntless, though also by nature thoughtless; so when he was attacked in 1582 by Nobunaga, Erinji too was implicated and was consequently burnt. Kaisen scaled the flaming two-story gate with his hundred-and-some disciples, and there he calmly died after leaving his last words, 'Mountains and water are not indispensable for meditation. When we clear our mind of mundane thoughts, we shall find even fire cool.'"[5]

The thin rain continued and the trees kept soughing. Mokuzu could not revere Kaisen as a genuine and outstanding Zennist. He saw something extraneous in him when comparing him to what an ideal Zennist ought to be. 'Leading a mass suicide is what he did. He was protected by a warlord, for whom he needed to suffer martyrdom. Hence all his disciples had to follow him into the fire. What he possessed was not Zen spirit but a vassal's fealty.' Mokuzu took the measure of the Zen master beside him in the dark, and what registered set his mind to tremble. He could not restrain himself from asking,

"Master, did you ever consider the fate of the disciples? As they perished in the fire did they likewise feel it was cool?"

"What? How should I know? But there's no question old-time Zennists always risked their lives in their training. Chat aside, the reality is that we are getting chilled. Don't relax your mind or you'll catch cold. You too must be soaked to the bone." The master straightened up to keep meditation form. His theory was that the meditating body could not be invaded by cold.

Mokuzu remembered the Hida mountains crowned with the first snow of the year; the sight had held his notice during a pilgrimage in Toyama Prefecture. He wanted heat for his own sake, but he could not go into the temple to borrow blankets, nor make a small fire. Zen Master Tengai was extremely careful not to trouble a temple other than to ask for calligraphy; and he was as careful not to spend money on any comfort while asking for donations to the fund. Indeed, since the start of their pilgrimage in mid-May, the master and Mokuzu had not made use of any sort of inn. There were places where the master could stay for free, in his laymen's homes, or in his former

752

disciples' temples, but he left Mokuzu in Shoshinji and went there alone.

Beneath the gate the master covered his head with his copious sleeves and soon fell asleep, keeping meditation form. Mokuzu did likewise but had difficulty falling asleep. 'He is immediately able to sleep when he ceases his activity, and immediately able to act when he is waked. As for me, a lot of impure, untidy, and sundry notions come and go like clouds before I sleep and after I wake; and I love those ambiguous times. For me they seem one of the most human parts of life...'

Toward morning it was raining harder. A stooped little sexton with jutting chin showed no surprise when he opened the gate and beheld the Zen master and his attendant. Even when the master told him they had spent the night there, he was unimpressed and appeared to be caring only to withdraw quickly from the rain.

"You are impossible!" he said impatiently. "Why didn't you phone? Coming this far into the mountains! We do have a phone! The priest is a professor at a university in Tokyo; he'll not be home for some days." As he turned away he looked back and said more brusquely,

"Come in! Don't you care about getting wet? I can at least offer you a simple breakfast."

"No, thank you. Please never mind about us. Nothing further detains us now that we know of his absence. But do tell him we came." The master spoke firmly and straightaway began to descend. Mokuzu hastily gathered their bundles and followed.

After turning the bend, the master slowed his pace and said,

"That'll do. I'm sure he'll assent to our request out of sympathy alone when he hears of our fruitless call. The telephone may save labor but makes it easier for people to refuse."

Again they boarded a train, to go to Enzan. Mokuzu watched the tireless rain over the hilly vineyards. The wind exposed the undersides of the leaves, and the rain as it hit them finely spattered up. The hills resembled a stormy sea. 'If the rain stopped, the mist would rise and there'd be the peak of Mt. Fuji over a rainbow,' he fancied, though the rain was increasing.

While the train was standing at Yamanashi Station, the master kept eyeing a vendor moving alongside the windows selling box lunches of flavored rice wrapped in deep-fried tofu, a favorite of his since infancy. With resolve he said,

"Oi, Mokuzu, for days we've had only peanuts, mandarins, bread, and milk. Shall we permit ourselves some luxury?"

Mokuzu had swollen tonsils and no appetite. Coldly he replied, "As you wish, but please never mind about me."

The master fell mute, but realizing the train would start up, he soon said,

"Young though you are, how you're obstinate! Another attendant would already be hanging out the window and calling with an eagerness equal to that of seeking his own enlightenment. Well, no matter — go buy two lunches. After all, without flesh our Dharma-body cannot act," and he handed Mokuzu some coins.

The train started the instant Mokuzu stepped in from the platform.

Zen Master Tengai with palms joined murmured the stanza chanted at mealtimes. He ate slowly and with relish, and at the end carefully picked up and ate every last grain of rice stuck to the bottom of the box. Seeing him, Mokuzu recalled the comment

> The world within a pot
> is beyond the mundane world.
> There too are the bright moon and fresh wind,
> though they be entirely different.[6]

After visiting Erinji and on the way to Kogakuji, the master complained of a fever. Mokuzu put a hand to his brow. It felt viscid with the mix of sweat and rain, and hot like very warm oil. Yet the master refused to alter the schedule. Repeatedly he crouched by the road and soon started up again. The rain was becoming mercilessly harder. The road was muddy, with foaming rivulets. Visibility was poor. They were forced to see their powerlessness.

Kogakuji was the head temple of a small Zen school having only some sixty local temples. The abbot, as well as being head of the school, was Zen master of the monastery within Kogakuji. There were no more than six trainees, who served as the abbot's attendants. The abbot, his face pale like a skinned steamed potato, was old and of gentle manner. Frequently, with palms joined, he muttered gratitude for the task Zen Master Tengai and his disciple were undertaking,

"Thanks very much, for the sake of Linji, the sake of religion, the sake of us priests...." Hearing they would visit Sengen Shrine in Fuji-yoshida, he muttered,

"Going through Otsuki by train makes a lengthy, needless circuit. One of my laymen might be driving there direct..." And he made some phone calls by himself. He found that a truck from a fruit growers' cooperative was going to the Kawaguchi lakeside and arranged for it to fetch the master and Mokuzu at the front gate at 3:00. The master, with over two hours to wait, gladly accepted the respite.

Mokuzu was told by the abbot that the site of the original Kogakuan, a poorer temple than the present Kogakuji, was no more than a thirty-minute climb up the back mountain. The master permitted Mokuzu to see it while he himself rested.

Kogaku meant "facing Mt. Fuji," but Mokuzu knew he would not see Mt. Fuji through the rain even if he made the climb. Nonetheless he wished to feel the difficulty of the path and the strong wind on top, for he knew the founder, Bassui, chose the site because of those conditions. Bassui never stayed anywhere longer than three years, and taught whoever came, priest or layman, man or woman. Many lepers were said to be among his followers.

The path showed no trace of having been recently walked; it was blocked with bush clover and eulalia under which rainwater ran. At the site, on a leveled eminence, indeed both the green and the autumn-tinged leaves were being torn from their branches and whirled into a valley in a flurry like a snowstorm. To the left, half erased by the rain, was a hummock with a grove of larch. The view straight ahead and to the right was unobstructed, though in an opaque veil of rain. In fine weather the clean form of Mt. Fuji in ultramarine would be directly to the fore above the many peaks of the Misaka mountains. Mokuzu remembered Mt. Fuji as he had seen it from Tokyo during newspaper deliveries, and he descended.

As he neared Kogakuji he noticed a cellar in the mountainside, and with much time left he chose to rest there. It was wide and warm and filled with the sweet odor of malted rice.

When his eyes adjusted to the dark, he was startled to see in the deepest recess a man frozen in a bent posture, watching him. He realized the man was caught in the act of stealthily eating malted rice out of his hand after having helped himself from the topmost of many shelves.

"Don't worry, I'll not blame you for so trifling an evil as sneaking to eat. I only chanced to come in to shelter myself from the rain," said Mokuzu, and he leaned against a pile of dry straw just inside the entrance. The man hesitated, then scooped up more and approached as if to offer it. Mokuzu was startled anew by seeing his face in proximity. He was a foreign national.

His cropped rust-colored hair was offset by a stubby beard so thick as to hide the contours of the lower half of his face. His eyes, tinged blue, were clear, and his thin lips gently smiled. He wore a khaki duffle coat with toggle fastenings and a hood hung slovenly behind.

"The world is wide. How do you choose to be in this cellar in the Far East?" Mokuzu spoke in English.

The man was delighted to hear English and replied,

"I wasn't given a chance to meet the abbot, because he's screened off by followers just like at every other temple I've visited so far. All the head temples and monasteries have ignored me. There's been no chance even to have an interview. I'd like to know, where is the Zen of 'pointing directly to the mind'?"

"I'm sorry to hear of your difficulty. Why do you come this far looking for Zen? Zen is not special to Japan. Zen must be possible to find wherever anyone has become his own master."

"Maybe. But I felt I'd never satisfy myself as to what is the best way to live as long as I lived in the U.S. There what's important is not how deeply you reflect on your life but how aggressively you keep going. Unsolvable questions are neglected even if they're important, and only solvable questions are uselessly highlighted—that is, Americans are perpetually trying to conquer the mystery outside themselves and don't try to see the mystery within. After two whole years of hesitation I determined to study Zen, and I came here believing Zen in Japan knows my mind. You say Zen is wherever one becomes one's own master. But many earnest Chinese once went to India to seek Buddhism, and later many earnest Japanese went to China for Zen. Now I've come to Japan to investigate my mind." To Mokuzu his words seemed rapid.

"I well understand your wish to experience the detonation that can come of contact with another. I too sought it, and I entered a Zen monastery and got a certain Zen master. As a result I was almost convinced of a conviction that had nothing to do with what I was seeking...and I am sure that what one can get from other countries and other people is not Zen but the cultures and traditions of a different age and society, which can be the affectations of Zen and nothing more than other people's effete matters or excretions....So the point is to find something eternal and common rather than the culture and character of a particular age, society, person, or situation. And one must then adjust oneself to that eternal and common thing. The truth realized by a particular person in his particular situation is of no use to others unless they extract only the truth. Therefore all kind and wise people, regardless of whether Eastern or Western, old or modern, never force their teaching on others, and of course never expect their followers to die a martyr's death for their teacher's faith."

Mokuzu was expressing one danger of studying Zen from any living person: though a person could live in Zen, Zen was not necessarily living in all of that person. He thought Zen was very respectable, but in his experience a Zen master was a mere caricatured personality.

The American, whether or not he understood, kept silent with a faint smile. Mokuzu continued,

"One more point to consider is how much did you master your American culture and tradition before deciding to come to Japan. America inherited one of the most profound religions from Europe and also developed one of the most practical philosophies. I think there are a lot of views in common with Zen in the philosophy of such of your countrymen as Charles Sanders Peirce, William James, Josiah Royce, John Dewey, and Alfred North Whitehead. Are you coming here after understanding and being discontent with them?"

The American was indirect:

"It was said Zen doesn't rely on words but has a special means of transmitting its secret. You love to talk, which makes me suspect whether you are an authentic Zen monk."

"Better than making you believe by cunning silence. Not relying on words is effective only at certain times; it's but one element of Zen tradition. I would have thought you are free of Zen's moldy tradition. Anyway, for your sake I'd like to remind you of the honest confession of a Tang-dynasty priest, Jingching:

"Coming to the realization is easier than accurately expressing its contents.[7]

"Yaushan more openly said in a lecture:

"We should not cut off our words. I am now describing with the help of words the place where no words are.[8]

"Furthermore, we shouldn't dismiss the warning of Heshan:

"No decent person can separate from words.[9]

"See? I hope you understand what you have heard and understand that falling into a belief is not all of Zen tradition. Not relying on words is a good method for absorbing everything the master and seniors show you. But it isn't enough for building up your own view, although this 'own view' isn't concerned with your limited self. Only words can approach the world that the Chinese Zen priest Shytou Shichian had in mind when he asked Nanyue Huairang,

"How is it when we have no attachment to any sage and at once disregard our own soul?[10]

"At any rate, words are very important to the process of grasping true Zen beneficial to oneself and to others. Any monastic and traditional Zen that does not rely on words cannot possibly fill the depression made by loss of love. The absence of words means no cleanness and no real satisfaction or possibility of finding new love in each thing and each occasion."

Mokuzu finished his passionate exposition on respect for words and detestation of the phony, dishonest, and undemocratic approach of a Zen that denies the value of words.

Having attended with a pensive, or suspicious look, the American said,

"Well, 'depression made by loss of love' describes my state. It seems you can read my problem, and I might trust you, even if unfortunately I missed most of what you said. I want to begin Zen training because I think Zen can fill that depression. Tell me how I can attain the Zen that can do that!"

"I am a depression lake in the mountains, the indigo water reflects the moon....You have to remind yourself that Linji stayed three years under Huangbo, and later, when he became enlightened under Dayu, he exclaimed,

'How unexpectedly easy is the Buddhism Huangbo taught me!'[11] Later yet, he reminisced about his enlightenment, 'I came to the realization not by just living day after day as I liked. One day I finally arrived after I had gone through training upon training.'[12] The first step of your training is to find a fitting teacher. And my main advice is that you'd better not start training only for yourself."

"Oh, no need for worry there. My depression came from my mother's death, it was so senseless. Since then I've wished to make sense of it, but being already married, I've had no chance to really start my Zen training. My depression darkened my marriage. After five years of being married to me, my wife realized my training in Zen was inevitable for regaining a bright marriage. She agreed to my coming here and promised to wait till I return with my Zen realization, and with my depression gone. So obviously I'm training not only for myself."

Mokuzu understood instantly that the American was unaware that the training he had in mind was entirely for his slack self.

"How long do you estimate your training will take?"

"Three to five years, maybe more."

"And your wife is willing to wait however long?"

"Sure, that was understood," replied the American lightly.

"It was said nearly twenty years are required of a normal man to perfect just traditional Zen. Since you are unquestionably below normal, I estimate you'll need two to five hundred years. Is your wife going to wait?" Mokuzu asked, exaggerating somewhat.

"There's no other way."

"Are you thinking your wife is a saintly fool, or a foolish saint? You aren't considering her life at all, but pitying yourself out of a helpless mother complex. Your training is not only selfish; it will sacrifice another's life. Such Zen training is merely to camouflage your lazy, weak, and vacillating nature. What you ought to do is not train in Zen but exhume your mother's bones and burn them up completely. Then love your wife. Anyone who cannot love a living person but who longs for someone dead can find only words and skills to rationalize his cruelty toward living creatures. Zen is not for you. Zen is to make good men great, honest men wise. You'd better go straight home and apologize to your wife for your neglect. Confess your self-pity and do all you can to make her happy. She will return what is more precious than anything a Zen master and a hundred years of Zen training can give you. Don't you remember Matthew?

"But I say unto you, that every one that leaveth his wife, saving for the cause of fornication, maketh her an adulteress."

"Humph!" laughed the American with disdain, and he said as he took an envelope from an inner pocket, "To tell the truth, I got this five years ago. There are many tasks more important than making a wife happy. She also can't deny that, even to herself."

Mokuzu was shown a letter of introduction from Dr. Yasaka, addressed to the Zen master of Shoshinji:

> The bearer of this letter is an earnest student in my class, taking the PhD course at Columbia University. He wishes to enter the practice of Zen in a Japanese monastery at the earliest chance. I anticipate his growth into a reliable man to bridge East and West. I ask that you offer him special kindness when he calls on your monastery.

His name was Grogan, Mokuzu learned. He retrieved and pocketed the letter as if it were an important title deed, and he smiled with a triumphant air.

Mokuzu laughed and stood up.

"Well, were I a monk with a little more heart, I'd seize that letter and tear it to pieces...too bad for you, and good-bye till such chance as we meet again!"

After taking his medicine and resting, Zen Master Tengai regained his vigor. While he rested, the Kogakuji abbot had an attendant iron his clothes. The master was against receiving such a kindness, though he enjoyed the refreshing touch of dry clothes. Everything Mokuzu had on was wet and cold. His head ached as if it enclosed mercury, but he could not express to anyone how he felt.

The master as he sat on the high seat of the truck must have felt a surge of controlling power like a delighted kid. The windshield wipers actively oscillated, the front wheels sent up spray, and each second the invisible sights became visible.

Mokuzu's headache worsened, and he all the more abominated his swelling tonsils, and all the more felt the master's way of life was wretched, for the master never reflected on where he had come from and only continued to go on energetically and offensively. Mokuzu fell into thought,

'This Zen master who is lashing himself to raise funds for Linji's anniversary has much in common with Zen Teacher Linji, as may be expected.

'First, how similar are their times and their societies. In the Hueichang Suppression Linji encountered the greatest destruction of Buddhism in all Chinese history. He did much to avert it and in a province beyond its influence taught Zen to a newly rising warrior class. It stands to reason that his way of teaching was quite rampant and keenly direct.

'Tengai has been teaching a newly rising commercial and industrial people after a war's fatal destruction. His way of teaching too is quite rampant and keenly direct. I must say those ancient warrior laymen and these modern commercial and industrial laymen are alike in having so little ethical and aesthetic interest while being exceedingly vigorous in competing for supremacy.

'As it was then it is now: the economy of Buddhist temples has come to a rupture, and all laical faith toward Buddhist priests has disintegrated into the soil.

'It seems the teachings of both Linji and Tengai are very effective for survival. So it is that they emphasize making a free-acting independent personality. Indeed they act like burglars galloping away through fields and gardens.

'The similarity between them that concerns me the most is their apparent lack of reflection — not reflection on the mind, that being the occupation of Zen priests, but reflection on what caused Buddhism to lose the faith of its laity.

'What invited the Hueichang Suppression was the corruptness of priests and nuns, the influx of false priests and self-ordained priests, and the disposition of Buddhists to feed on the state economy. How frankly and carefully did Linji call for grave reflection on this issue? If he did call for it, why do we see no trace of it in his recorded words?

'And how much is Tengai reflecting on modern Buddhism in Japan, which was allegiant to a military government and in consequence exploited and oppressed the common people, and, further, helped Japan invade its neighbors? Where can I see his self-scrutiny for having been sponsor to an undemocratic and internationally isolated Buddhism? There is, for sure, in both Linji and Tengai much self-reflection, but scarcely a speck of reflection as social beings.

'If Linji's "true man of no position indwelling in the bloody human body"[13] is recognized to exist and given full expression by those who don't reflect on themselves as social beings, how dangerous they can become, as dangerous as scientists without ethics who fiddle with atomic fire. Whoever possesses some patience and an unyielding spirit, and probably a somewhat stupid nature, can recognize in himself a true man of no position. It can be recognized even by a rascal or a criminal if he's given a fair chance. But no one, no matter who, can distinguish God from Satan if he respects a Zen tradition that doesn't rely on words, that is, if he doesn't reflect on his recognition of himself as a true man of no position.

'As long as one is far from being a decent man, the true man of no position should be confined to one's purely religious, philosophical, and artistic life.'

"Oi, why don't you hear me?" Zen Master Tengai elbowed Mokuzu and accused him, "Amid this horrible jolting, how can you slumber in meditation form?"

"What? Master, is there something important?"

"In a truck nothing can be important, but the driver is asking if we'd like to see a monkey park by the lake since we're passing that way. He says there are also peafowls, pheasants, and hares all free in a pasture."

"Master, we cannot afford to indulge in idleness on the way. Don't you sense any danger in this rain? It's not normal, it will take lives if people aren't careful. We'd better finish our work even a minute earlier and find shelter... Monkeys? — at such a critical time? Well, there's no danger in keeping true monkeys of no position in a pasture, but true men of no position should be kept within monastery walls..."

"Hm! I told you out of kindness, but you've no sense of play!" The master fell into an unpleasant silence.

The driver helped the Zen master to the ground before the Sengen Shrine. The presiding priest readily complied with his request, and, informing him of an oncoming typhoon, offered a night's lodging. But the master stoutly declined.

They resumed walking in the increasingly hard, windy rain. The lakeside, a noted tourist spot, had many souvenir shops, restaurants, and hotels. All were shut tight in readiness for the typhoon. A group of small stands around a big maple were covered with a tarpaulin secured by a rope. Lingering proprietors threw suspicious looks at the master and attendant.

The driving rain seemed to Mokuzu to penetrate his aching head. He uttered invectives at the master's back in a voice low enough to be drowned out by the wind,

"Dumb fool! Walking on in this weather, soon you'll be seized with a relapse. Your fever was allayed only by a drug. Out of pride you flatly refused the thoughtful offer of a night's lodging. There are proper times and circumstances for availing oneself of another's kindness. You are like a truck with its breaks gone — you can't see your future even an inch ahead!"

Just as Mokuzu had worried, Zen Master Tengai came to a standstill before an hour passed, on the path along the lake. First he thought the master had stopped to watch the waves hitting high against the bank and seizing the rain as they fell. But the master stood with his hand extended.

"Give me the antihypertensive — something's wrong."

In the rain washing his greasy sweat, his face was livid. The path swam not only with rainwater but with waves overthrown from the lake.

The viridescent far shore disfigured by the rain had looked like a copperplate engraving. Now with evening setting in, it was melting into the dark rain to leave nothing in the distance. The black robe of the stalled Zen master fluttered, but his white underrobe was stuck to his legs. His leather-soled, white-thonged sandals were submerged.

"Master, after all, we'd better return to Fuji-yoshida and accept the Shinto priest's kind offer."

"Don't be silly, we are Zen priests. How can we receive care from a Shinto priest? No, the hamlet of Ashiwada couldn't be so far. Somehow we'll arrive there. Koko, no, Mokuzu...well, Koko would never propose turning back. He would plumply proceed even if he had to carry me!"

The master's voice was unnaturally loud because he spoke just as the wind for a moment lulled. Mokuzu shouted back,

"Quite probably the senior monk Koko would carry you without realizing you were getting cold, and on reaching the destination he would realize for the first time you were dead, and I bet he'd wail like a pig! Master, it seems to me a man who is rigid as a rock, and who cannot sense danger, and who therefore cannot act promptly is unworthy of living as a creature on this earth!" Tasting salt on the wind, Mokuzu could not help remembering he had let Ena perish by his obtusity.

Yet the master went on, and took a side path leading into the mountains. There he slipped and muddied himself. The thong to one of his sandals broke and he had to walk in his white tabi.

"Oi, Mokuzu. Are you so hating to go on? I agree with you to some extent. Then why don't we resign ourselves to passing the night under that big tree up ahead?"

Indeed a broad tree stood before a forest. Its many branches were so leafy that the raindrops beneath were not too bad. The trunk was as large as three feet in diameter. Mokuzu touched the bark; it had irregular, corky cracks. He stripped back a piece and found the sap to be lubricious.

"Master, it's an elm. No wise man rests under an elm."

"What's wrong with it?" The master was already deeply settled and asked with annoyance. Mokuzu translated to Japanese the relevant part of "A Tree Song" by Rudyard Kipling, taught him by the teacher Yojun:

> Ellum she hateth mankind, and waiteth
> Till every gust be laid,
> To drop a limb on the head of him
> That anyway trusts her shade.[14]

He took the master on his back and carried him farther up the slope where hemlocks were making a forest.

He was waked by a cool fresh air and the bright beams of the morning sun coming through the hemlocks. The lake stretched calmly below with a vivid inverted image of Mt. Fuji in blue on its surface.

The master still slept, making a pillow of his scrip. His face had regained color, and his breathing was gentle.

As they proceeded on their pilgrimage, they soon witnessed that the hamlet of Ashiwada had been sucked down under a phenomenal landslide during the night. What they had encountered was the twenty-sixth typhoon of the year. It had cut through to the Sea of Japan after damaging the central districts and stealing away 314 lives.

At the site the master joined his palms in veneration of the vanished houses and lives. Mokuzu at his side was realizing that the day to become independent of his Zen master, the day to begin training on his own, was fast approaching.

55

The Death of Luri

Zen Master Tengai asked over 600 people for their calligraphy, 30 works apiece. Those who complied amounted to 572, distributed as follows:

> Buddhist high priests:
>> Zen sect: Rinzai school 57
>>> Obaku school 13
>>> Soto school 59
>> Jodo sect (including Yuzu-nembutsu) 53
>> Nichiren sect 55
>> Tendai, Kegon, Ritsu, and Shotoku sects 55
>> Shingon sect 67
>> Jodo Shin sect: Otani, Takada, Koshoji, Sanmonto,
>>> Izumoji, Seishoji, and other schools 62
>>> Honganji school 73
> Shinto-related high priests 53
> Ex-admirals and ex-generals 25

These calligraphies arrived daily by mail, amounting at length to 17,160 works, which the master's attendants circumspectly arranged into 30 sets in one of the master's rooms appointed exclusively for that purpose.

One night in early October the master invited Mokuzu in. "See?" he said. "What do you think? They're treasures. Any dilettante would kill me to get his hands on a set or two. As a matter of fact, already three sets have been sold to three rich men and the recompense is in my account. That sum, for just three sets, will amply furnish the cost of the coming anniversary of Zen Teacher Linji, ho! The remaining sets will be kept as an endowment for Shoshin College and can be disposed of as occasion demands by leisurely sale, ho ho! I'm relieved of the worry over what will happen after my death, for whoever inherits the college will have no trouble running it, at least about finances. Quite evidently the value of the calligraphies will appreciate as all those high priests begin to die...." The master, his hands clasped at his back, was nicely satisfied.

Mokuzu found it incredible that those calligraphies could be eagerly coveted and calmly sold at so high a price. To his eyes they seemed generally not up to being calligraphy, but rather of less worth than a heap of plain white paper, though he did not check them all. Their value was due solely to the fact that they were written by persons of note and high rank.

Nevertheless he felt he had been taught by actual experience the art of making big money. What the master had spent was some capital for paper, gifts, and travel fare, supplemented by daredevil physical suffering and a tenacious fighting spirit. The secret of his earning was to obtain things for almost nothing and sell them to those who wanted them so much as to risk even their life for them. It was a modification of the saying that a priest earns without investment. Instead of reflecting on how the world ought to be, priests needy of money had to have the business gumption to see the world as it is.

"Well, you shared the travail. What is your comment before the fruit?" said the master, still in a good humor. Mokuzu recalled a comment he had overheard during the pilgrimage. A passenger had said with self-scorn, "For such a people such a government was inevitable." Appropriating the turn of phrase he said,

"For such nouveaux riches, such art is inevitable."

"Ho ho ho! I'll tolerate your comment as an excusable outburst of youthful vitality. You resemble Huangbo, who called his followers draff eaters and declared there wasn't a single Zen teacher in all of Great Tang. Just the same, you must have learned a lot by meeting so many high-ranking priests of all the sects. At only age twenty-one you have laid a network of routes all over Japan. It is a treasure not easily obtained, and will be of great use to you in the future when you take an active role in Japanese Zen, and Buddhist, society."

'Master, as a result of meeting so many high-ranking priests all over Japan, I have come to wish to have nothing to do with them,' Mokuzu wanted to say, but he kept his words in his bosom.

"Oh, Mokuzu, speaking of Huangbo reminds me of something I must tell you. It'll not take much time. Come into my new room."

A new room with new corridor had been added to the master's inmost room. To accommodate the slope, the corridor twice turned and twice went up three steps. The exterior was in Japanese style to keep it compatible with its surroundings, but inside was altogether Western, with a thick carpet, easy chairs, and a couch with a sheepskin.

A TV with an eighteen-inch screen was set against a wall. At either end of another wall were flush doors, one to a simple kitchen, the other to a Western-style toilet. The veranda, facing the mountain, was enclosed by large glass doors and was furnished with a pair of rattan chairs and a little table.

"Mr. Yamashita, general manager of a corporation that owns a professional baseball team, donated it all, knowing of my troubles with high blood pressure and constipation. He is very kind. It is equipped with air conditioning — a pleasant place, but, alas, I have no leisure to improve my health here." The master sounded apologetic; evidently he was embarrassed to have such comfort unexpected of a Zen master.

Mr. Yamashita, once so famous a ballplayer that his name was known world-wide, had been studying Zen under Zen Master Tengai's guidance for as long as eight years. His team was said to have done poorly under his management until he commenced his Zen study. Thereafter, it had steadily won. Now the master was considering the proper timing for his retirement from baseball.

Mokuzu had never been charmed by baseball, and so neither was he by Mr. Yamashita. Occasionally during an extensive meditation period or work in the garden, they were shoulder to shoulder or facing each other, but they never exchanged a word. In fact, most of the master's laymen were quite famous and powerful figures in politics, the Self Defense Forces, business, and journalism. They were important in society, and the master was teaching them. But they were outside Mokuzu's interest, possibly proof of his failure to comprehend the master's main feature. He was sad to realize that he and his master had very little in common.

'Those capable of dwelling at length in the monastery, like Koko, Genkaku, and Kaijo, share the master's view and are satisfied by actively participating in society. A man like me most enjoys living in a place they could hardly dream up.'

Mokuzu was regarding the mountainside through the glass doors while the master was heating water in an electric kettle and preparing cups for tea.

"Oh, I'm sorry, I was absent-minded — let me do it."

"Never mind, sit in that rattan chair. Today is special, I'll offer you red tea." Mokuzu felt himself color at the master's unprecedented behavior of inviting a monk into his most private quarters and therewithal offering him tea by his own hand.

He continued to stand, regarding a winterberry among wild azaleas at the foot of a pine. Its berries were not yet red, though its leaves were losing their green.

The master brought a tray with tea and seated himself.

"I formally thank you for assisting my calligraphy pilgrimage. Its completion owes greatly to you," he said and truly bowed his head.

"I have done nothing to deserve your thanks. Please accept my apology for having stood in your way, and for countless impertinences rendered unknowingly throughout. It is I who am thankful: I could indelibly learn your teaching that anything can be accomplished if one risks one's life," Mokuzu said, also formally, and bowed low.

"Now, you have just finished 'The Ten Supreme Precepts.' The only koan left is 'The Last Barrier.' All the koans you studied can be compared to textbook study with a teacher. This one is different; it belongs to the training called training after enlightenment, which is for cultivating a well-rounded wisdom and compassion through life experience. It's not the type that can be understood in a short period of months or years, no matter how assiduous you are. To pass this koan an assiduous life must be maintained for ten to twenty years.

"Well, I shall inform you further during your next interview. What I have to tell you now, and get your ex post facto approval of, has to do with a woman called Luri. But beforehand, I should like to know your response to an episode about Huangbo, to whom I referred a moment ago.

"As you may know, Huangbo was born in Fukien and had been training under the Zen teacher Baijang in Kiangsi, far from his native land.

"Twenty years after leaving home, he was sent by Baijang on an errand to Fukien. But Baijang warned him against seeing his mother for the reason that affection might overcome him and interfere with the completion of his training.

"As it happened, Huangbo's mother was concerned for his safety and fettered by bonds of affection, and she had become blind by weeping for him day and night. Yet, believing he would one day return, she had engaged herself at a riverside inn, washing the feet of travelers. She knew him to have a wen on one foot, and she prayed she might identify him.

"Huangbo indeed came to that very inn. When his feet were washed he offered the same foot twice, joined his palms in quiet veneration of his mother, and left. Thereat a native recognized him and spoke up. Huangbo fled along the riverbank. Calling his name, his mother pursued him, and in so doing she fell into the rain-swollen river. The curtain of night descended. Huangbo returned with a torch, and aided by the villagers searched for her, but in vain.

"In his grief he exclaimed, 'A sutra tells us that the relatives unto the fifth degree of whoever becomes a priest can be reborn in heaven. If it is not to be, all Buddhas have been liars!'[1] He then cried 'Ah!' and chanted an impromptu gatha:

766

My mother for many years lost her mind.
Flowers now bloom in the forest of Bo trees.
When she attends the mass of Maitreya she shall return
To the life of Avalokitesvara's great compassion.[2]

"Thereupon he threw his torch in the river, and it was said he saw his mother's figure rise in the smoke to heaven."

At this juncture of the master's talk, something swept across the garden and struck the glass. It fell to earth, fluttered a few times, and ceased to move.

"Leave it be," said the master, but Mokuzu was already outside in his bare feet. He cupped it in his palms. Its light body was warm and its eyes were open wide, but it no longer made the least tremor.

A chill wind was blowing the fallen leaves up the mountain. He went inside, shut the glass doors, and put it on the table. Its back was olive brown, its belly white. This female bird was often confused with the Siberian blue robin, Siberian bluechat, or narcissus flycatcher. In fact Mokuzu was once bitter over being mocked by his teacher Setsuro:

"Aha! What's this bird you've drawn? Cut up several kinds and join them and we'll have your bird — a jigsaw puzzle!"

It was a blue-and-white flycatcher, clearly distinguishable by its slightly larger size, larger eyes, red-tinged tail, and bright, light brown throat and breast.

Mokuzu gently closed its eyes and put it into his bosom.

"Then what is your view of this Huangbo tale?"

"Master, do you mean the woman called Luri is dead?" Mokuzu spoke in a low voice while fixing his eyes on the master's. The master with an aloof demeanor returned his stare, and briefly as well as coercively he said,

"Right. Last December she showed up and desired to see you. I met her in Shogetsuan and refused her. My reason was ipso facto Baijang's reason. Iron must be struck while hot. Affection is the worst enemy of training. You had better ask at Shogetsuan for details, if you wish. Fortunately for you, I am excusing you from the great anniversary of Linji to be observed at Tofukuji next week. Then you'll have lots of time."

"Well, I shall express my opinion of Huangbo's episode. Aside from the question of its historical truth, both Baijang and Huangbo — strictly so far as the episode goes — are terribly narrow-minded, I think. To begin with, the Dharma is not a petty thing hindered by affection. Commonly it was said a man abandons affection on entering the priesthood; and Sakyamuni, it is commonly believed, did so to seek Buddhahood. It may be a tradition for Buddhist priests. But I don't believe it's the true way. A man trains himself not to relinquish or to transcend affection, but only to raise a sane, healthy, and beautiful affection, only to perfect it."

"It is you who are confused: you are taking blind love for compassion. Mokuzu, I could perceive her nature. She was a slave to lust while declaring her love was the love of a stepsister. She may have been praying for the success of your training, but her bestial love wished you to be pulled into the hell where she was writhing."

"Master, I thank you for the measure you took for my training. I thank you not for your wisdom, which enables you to distinguish blind love from compassion, but for your leniency, which treats and teaches equally an inferior monk like me and an excellent monk like Koko. Now that you have told me what you had to tell me and I have acknowledged it in my way, may I withdraw? I wish to bury this bird before it gets cold and stiff." Mokuzu stood up and left without waiting for a reply.

"Um," uttered the master, remaining seated as he gazed at the faint trace on the glass where the bird had struck.

ॐ

In the early morning heavy with mist, Zen Master Tengai left for Tofukuji in Kyoto, leading all but a few monks, who remained to look after the monastery. The anniversary was to be held for ten days by a gathering from the fifteen Rinzai schools. Some representatives were also being sent to mainland China for the anniversary to be performed at the original site of Linji's temple in Hopei Province.

From across the nation, laymen, priests of local temples, and monks training in the monasteries were hastening to Tofukuji, where daily they would chant, hear sermons, work, and perform local mendicancies. For the monks the most exciting event was the chance to have Zen interviews with any master they favored, since the masters of all monasteries were attending.

Genkaku as he broomed the garden after seeing the master off commented to Mokuzu, "You are unlucky to be missing this historical event, considering it was you who were behind the scene raising the funds."

"I've already met all the Zen masters of this country. You're the one who's unlucky. Tending an empty monastery brings you nothing good," replied Mokuzu.

"Never mind, I favor the atmosphere when everyone is gone. Sweeping the leaves and acorns out the gate like now, I can be reminded of Priest Jaujou:

"Prime Minister Liou entered the temple. Seeing Jaujou brooming the garden he asked him, 'How can you a great wise man be sweeping dust?' 'Because dust comes in.'"[3]

Genkaku laughed.

768

'Genkaku is easily satisfied, he has no tomorrow. He's a paste-and-paper Bodhidharma!' Mokuzu muttered, and he said aloud,

"Ease your mind, Senior Genkaku, for I too shall soon be out the gate."

Alone Mokuzu performed all his duties as head chanting officer. After offering the meal and chanting to Buddha, to the founder, and to the others enshrined, he left for Shogetsuan. He thought being told about Luri was useless now that it was over, but he had been invited to lunch.

The mist under the gate was rising high and the cedar tops were shedding dew. The evergreen oaks too were dropping their acorns. Sharply they struck the stone steps and rolled until they lodged in the ditch.

'Up the stone steps she came, under the cedars, to the thatched gate, in her blue school uniform and carrying her russet cowhide schoolbag. Often she turned on the light in my room without speaking when I was studying the subjects given me by my teachers Docho and Yojun. I hadn't even noticed the moon was up.

'Daily she shopped for our food on her way home from school, washed our laundry, cooked, prepared the bath, while Reiho and I played outside or attended our karate gym, or he watched TV in the living room and I studied in my room, and while Unkai meditated on the dusky west veranda.

'She did it all without ever expressing any complaint. Zen Master Hanun brought her to Ryotanji from an orphanage in Osaka. She must have been bitter when she realized it was to fill the want of a female resident to do the housekeeping.'

Luri in Mokuzu's memory was gentle and beautiful. The miserable last image of her in Reiho's dreary office building was, strangely, quite faint in his mind.

'Dissolved with her death is her ill fate, and freshened is her tender, bright visage.

'The death of Ena and now the death of Luri. By death their differences imperceptibly merge in the dark of a valley, and rising mingled with white mist is the best womanly quality, maternal love. It smiles on me, comforts and guides me...a fragrant white lotus in heaven...encouraging me to oppose anyone and any teaching that slights love and denies life.'

Mokuzu entered the path to Shogetsuan. At a side garden Shorai was cutting chrysanthemums to offer to Buddha, taking only the small white, yellow, and magenta among a variety.

Straightaway she led him to the somber living room, where her teacher was sitting half under the quilt of the low, foot-warmer table.

The nun teacher, her vision further deteriorated, inclined her head as she searchingly regarded him, and with palms joined she brought her face near to his and began to speak in a quavering, provokingly slow manner,

"Well!...well!...You trained yourself creditably! The Zen master too is pleased with your mastery of all traditional koans in so short a time! It cannot be duplicated by mediocre monks. His work for you now, he says, is to wait patiently until your wisdom surpasses his; for 'being equal means the master's virtue yet exceeds the disciple's.'[4] At any rate, congratulations on your initial training as a Zen priest. But such sad news upon you at once. Upon us too. But far more it must be for you. No one can reduce your sadness, no one steal it. It is yours. Be sad to your fill."

Mokuzu maintained his formality:

"First let me offer you my congratulations on your health. You are troubled by your eyes and feet, but the four elements of your body otherwise appear to be in accord. Second, I thank you for your direct and indirect care of me ever since I arrived here to train. Third, I thank you for your kindness to my Dharma sister and the trouble you might have taken for her.

"Now let me say that the death of a person is pure white and clean. So too is the related sorrow, but it is easily tinted by any other color. Thus every color can appear to contain sadness. The color of the trees, the soil, walls, rocks, water, sky... none is without a tint of sadness. Yet they are the colors of life. I receive her death with my high esteem. I resolve not to slight the meaning of her death by any words or acts in my future."

"Shorai, did you hear? He is indeed the direct descendant of Priest Kakkan of Tangenji in Tanba, and also talented, mastering every koan in just two years! He remains composed before the sad news and does not condemn the severity of the Zen master's dispensation. His mind is clear as a mountain lake, and more, his attitude of transforming the sorrow of death to the passion to help others is like snow water quickening the life of the fields."

"Yes, Teacher, I have heard. I am greatly relieved! Today I shall cook a treat of rice with chestnuts!" said Shorai delightedly, appearing from the kitchen.

"We must ask him to chant a sutra for her. Come, would you lend me your hand?"

As Shorai assisted the old nun, the white grimalkin dozing on her lap moved away leisurely. Mokuzu had not noticed it hidden by the quilt and camouflaged against her cream white robe.

He went ahead into the sanctum and lit the candles and a stick of incense. The room was small. The storm doors and shojis were wide open. Wind bearing the harvest smell of burning rice chaff came in directly and stirred the smoke of the incense. On a table before the sanctum stood a black-lacquer mortuary tablet engraved with a posthumous Buddhist name in vermilion lacquer. It was of moderate size, adorned on either side by a stand of offerings

770

piled in a pyramid, one of glossy persimmons, the other of steamed rice cakes filled with bean jam. The chrysanthemums that Shorai had picked and trimmed of their blighted leaves were in a vase at a corner.

Mokuzu read Luri's posthumous name, "Return to Clarity: snow flower in the light of lapis lazuli." He recalled a passage of Bodhidharma's *Ehlru syshing lun*,

> 'The basic way to enter the Truth is to understand the gist of Buddhism with the help of the sutras and to hold the conviction that all creatures, including the common run of men as well as the holy, have equally the substance of the Truth, and that the only difference between common and holy men is the external confusion in common men, which hinders them from actualizing the substance of the Truth. If common men shake off their confusions and return to clarity, keep mind and body sedate as a wall, steadfastly dwell where no distinction exists between self and others or between common and holy, and rely on no verbal teaching, they will be unified with the Truth and will be calm and content, with no artificiality or discrimination....'[5]

Mokuzu chanted the Heart Sutra for the principal image and the Lotus Flower Sutra for Luri. Amid his chanting, the nun teacher and Shorai, seated near the veranda, began to weep.

When they returned to the living room, Mokuzu asked the nun teacher to tell him who had given Luri's posthumous name.

"The successor of Ryotanji troubled to come. He also well understands the way of the world, and is modest, with lowered eyes. His master is bedridden, needing constant tending, yet he came and coped."

Mokuzu did not respond; he wished to avoid inciting her urge to relate the various useless events. Yet, stroking the cat, she began:

"Zen Master Tengai briefly regarded her, then decisively said, 'I refuse your meeting with my disciple. He is now a steed bounding through a wilderness and must run until he leaps to the state of no setback to his realization. He must renounce all worldly concerns so as to grasp the profoundest meaning of Buddhism and become a Buddhist knight to participate actively in the three thousand realms. He must not lose his eternal life on account of being charmed by a passing illusion.'

"Your sister was desperate and refused to retreat. Finding words, she said, 'Why do you deny the meeting of Dharma sister and brother? On what authority?' 'Ask that of yourself' was his flat reply, and he went away. As you know, he is endowed with acuity to spot devilishness in beauty, and his mind is rock-steady against emotion.

"...Luri must have been having some heart ailment. She was pale, and looked like a chaste women to me. Her cheeks were faintly red...yes, she complained of palpitations....I guess the Zen master concluded that her affection was increasing as she weakened and that it was nothing but lechery."

Shorai brought in tea and added, "As might be expected, she deepened her wish to see you, even lost her balance of spirit, now furious at him, using quite abusive language, then trepid, and implored us to arrange a secret meeting."

Shorai offered Mokuzu tea.

"My teacher spent every means of dissuasion. She especially repeated that ever since old times fine monks have sacrificed their personal interest to the Dharma. 'If you love him, pray for the completion of his training. Your prayer will help him, and when he succeeds he and you can openly meet in a pure land on this earth. Until then, forbear.' Koko came to our aid and kindly offered her a drive, telling her, 'Don't carry on so. You're caught in your own trap. Come with me, I'll take you along the snowy route to the Gero and Takayama hot springs. In one of those spas you can warm yourself and freshen your mind.'

"She took courage and approached Koko's car out front, then like a snuffed candle she fell into a swoon. In a fright we summoned a doctor. He told us it was fortunately just an attack of cerebral anemia caused by stress. It happened the third day after her arrival."

"Yes, poor soul! Fatigue must have come when her strain was eased," inserted the nun teacher.

"Then she spent all day in bed, skipping lunch. I brought in kudzu soup near sunset to find she had folded the bedding. Equipped for travel, she was seated formally with a tender smile. She said something like 'It was wrong of me to disturb the serene world of training. I now understand that meeting with a young woman could be a fatal hindrance to a young trainee....My wish to see him won't fade, but I'll restrain myself. Now I only pray for his attainment, and please, you too continue to help him.' She was going to leave promptly, but my teacher urged her to stay one more night, saying, 'It is becoming dark and starting to snow. Wait till morning.' To this advice she smiled, and yielded." Telling this far, Shorai left for the kitchen. The nun teacher resumed, as if unaware of her leaving,

"Yes, together we chanted the evening sutras. It was impressive she knew by heart most of the common ones, though it may well be expected with her Ryotanji upbringing."

Mokuzu listened politely with a dim smile. He wondered why they should relate the details, but he soon realized they no doubt hoped to be eased of the onus of failing to save a life.

Shorai returned, drying her hands, and hastened on,

"That night I readied the bath and washed her back and her hair. She was macerated by cares, but her white skin in the steam was lovely. Her hair as I combed it regained its luster. I then understood that a woman's hair is a most beautiful thing, and understood why women have prized it as life itself. As she sat erect she began to weep. I feared she again couldn't control her wish to see you, but it wasn't that. She cried, 'Nobody ever offered me such a kindness as to wash my back and my hair!'"

"Kindness is as rare as a living leaf in winter's deciduous forest," mumbled the nun teacher in a mist of tears.

Hearing these details, Mokuzu fell into lowery thought. 'Everywhere tangible sorrow and suffering cover the earth like lichen. How can we solve human problems and find the meaning of human life? All who are awakened have been bidding defiance to this problem. The development of science and its applications has brought many improvements, yet the perfection of science and its conclusive remedy belong to the unknown future. Science while relieving people is also creating and increasing new problems as if it has no purpose but to recycle human suffering.

'Moreover, the Zen Buddhism I have been studying, though it came to its height in grasping the ultimate and abstract truth, is in its means of transmission quite reckless and too much dependent on individual fortune. Zen training is for most people laborious but fruitless. Some masters and some training methods rather promoted suffering. In short, Zen has a head but no limbs. This sterility of practical application for common people is a peculiarity of all religions, not only Zen.

'Take for instance the discourse on compassion by Huangbo, who experienced losing his mother in a turbid river. If indeed people understand his discourse, their anguish will scatter and vanish. But how many are ready to understand? How can we make others understand? "Whoever understands, understands; whoever does not, does not" is Zen's disappointing methodology.

> 'Question: "How do all Buddhas practice their Great Compassion (*tsybei*) and preach the Dharma?" Answer: "A Buddha's compassion is not based on any cause and effect, whence it is called Great Compassion." *Tsy* means "not to adhere to the perception that Buddhahood is the ideal attainment." *Bei* means "not to adhere to the perception that there are people to be saved." Truth contains no Dharma to be preached or exposed and no audience to hear it and obtain it. Whoever preaches the Dharma is like a magician preaching to an imagined audience. To say one became enlightened by the words of a certain sage is nonsense. A Buddha's Great Compassion cannot be understood by thought, however one thinks. All understanding is of no use unless one understands one's original nature.'[6]

Shorai, without seeing Mokuzu, continued,

"Next morning we rose at four-thirty as usual and again chanted togeth-er. Soon after breakfast the time came for her departure. Of course she was returning to Ryotanji, we thought. My teacher, being disabled, said farewell at the entrance, and I saw her to the taxi. All about was white with snow, as my teacher had predicted, and the sky was clear, becoming vivid. I handed her a lunch in a cloth marked with the name and address of Shogetsuan. Over her grass-green coat I put a new damask shawl, a gift from my teacher." Shorai took a breath.

"After she left it was so quiet; no flowers, no visiting birds. As you know, we are a little nunnery snowbound beneath a mountain....Six days later, just before midday, a long-distance call came...from the police in Shirakawa County, the northernmost part of Gifu, near the borders of Ishikawa and Toyama prefectures. To such depths? Why?...in a pure forest of beech, after crossing a suspension bridge over the source of the Oshiro River. She was found by a hunter. I also went, and learned how deep the snow is, up to my waist. Not a leaf remained on those ashy straight trees. The ridge of another mountain was clearly visible through the forest. Against the snow the trees were everywhere the same whether mountain or valley.

"The police made it plain that she took her life....Never before did I so blame Buddha and Zen Master Tengai. For the first time I began to doubt the Buddhist way of training. To be frank, my doubt will last until I see how you make yourself into a great Zen priest."

Shorai kept her face expressionless as she talked, but now she pressed to it a cloth. The nun teacher's head was bent so low as to touch the cat settled again on her lap.

"However...," said Mokuzu as he stood up. He went to the veranda. This year sesame instead of cotton was planted in front. The leaves had dropped, and the stalks stood straight with their columnar capsules well dried for harvest. With his back to the nuns, he finished,

"...what a fine day! In autumn the sky is blue and a horse grows fat. The deep sky makes me forget the saying, Retribution comes to whoever has no appreciation of heaven's gifts."[7]

Shorai was perplexed how to respond to his words, whereat the teacher no doubt made some instructive gesture, for she said,

"It is ready, I shall bring it right in," and she vanished into the kitchen.

The lunch was a quite handsome entertainment, considering the poor-ness of the nunnery: rice boiled with chestnuts, steamed matsudake mushrooms in an earthen pot, dishes dressed with sauce, fried brown algae....Mokuzu enjoyed it all and was thankful for the kindness of Shogetsuan.

Soon after lunch he indicated that he would leave. With surprise Shorai said,

"Why, what is the hurry? We have permission from Genkaku, in charge during the master's absence. Besides, Miss Iwai will come. Er...thinking you rightfully wish to visit the last place of your Dharma sister, I asked her to drive you there. Please stay seated. I shall peel you a persimmon. Very soon she will come. Offer fruit and flowers to your Dharma sister. I have them prepared." Shorai glanced at the wall clock several times.

Mokuzu knit his brow on hearing the name Miss Iwai. He did not want a stranger to know about Luri. The more known, the more she would be exposed before inconsiderate people, and her image in his mind would be marred. He said frankly,

"Fruit and flowers are blessings for the living. For her I prefer to offer a gatha, and, please, let me leave. The vacant monastery is a suitable place in which to compose it."

"Let him do as he wishes, Shorai. Not to interfere is one of a nun's basic prudences, is it not?" The teacher's enunciation was feminine. Silently Shorai went into a back room and brought out a paper package.

"It is getting cold. I made you a lined pepper-and-salt kimono. Before New Year's I shall deliver you a new robe."

56

Grogan: From Zokki's Private Record

Grogan came the end of October — in fact the day I came back (more precisely, was put back) — and he left before December's end. Like me, he was placed under the authority of the Manjusri attendant, whose name is Mokuzu. The Zen master, because he wanted to know why Grogan so easily quit, summoned me to find out every detail of his stay. I didn't tell anything disadvantageous to Mokuzu, being his loyal servant.

I'm a sneak thief, and lies and truths are all the same to me. Yet, affected by Mokuzu, I think I shouldn't keep mum, at least to myself. So I'll record the circumstances as much as I happen to know them. But since I'm the one laboring to write, and since I'm not a mere stagehand, I'll include much of my own matters.

First, about the day Grogan and I arrived. My old man and I waited long in the room of the observances head, Genkaku. The master finally returned with all his followers from the Linji anniversary in Kyoto. Genkaku and the others in charge here snapped to and made for the entrance. The master looked exultant, like a general returning from a triumphant campaign.

I overheard Genkaku say to the one I soon came to know as Mokuzu, "See? The success of the anniversary has secured his election as next chief abbot. It seems true he gathered the most monks wanting Zen interviews."

Mokuzu's queer silence silenced the others. He spoke only what to me was nonsense: "A setting sun burns." I longed to send such a one as him into a flap like a kicked hen.

Genkaku ushered me and my old man into the master's room, and we were given tea. The old hermaphrodite again grumbled about his "opprobrious" son.

"...Such being the case, this time he was irrevocably dismissed from Ground Self Defense, where thanks to your great pains he had been promoted to corporal. Yes, truly he lost face, robbing not only a second lieutenant but also a major..."

"You said all that in your letter. Don't repeat as you did on our first visit here two summers ago," I advised him out of shame for his excessive unmanliness. Ashamed to have me as a son, he doesn't realize I'm ashamed to have him as a father.

The master with a strategic smile asked me, "Oi, what the deuce did you steal from your service superiors this time?" More embarrassed, my old man folded up like a sea anemone. I couldn't resist the chance for mischief and replied without apology, "I got an Utamaro print from the second lieutenant, and a vibrator from the major."

"What are they?" The master showed interest. Genkaku cut in, saying he'd explain later. My old man sighed with relief, while the master and I were discontent.

"In any event," the master heightened his tone, "you have to understand very well how the matrimony of a priest comes to no good. Even so, outliving you wife, you creditably raised him this far by your own hand. Your only regret is his thieving. Ease your mind, for it couldn't be his nature, and I am sure that if I give him a second chance, he can correct himself under the influence of these sacred precincts. However, while he trains here, you must not forget to keep asking yourself how you have been incompetent in raising him."

The master was virile and optimistic. Already my old man was shedding tears into a handkerchief — a lady's, my mother's.

When the affair was settled, an attendant came up in hot haste and spoke through the shoji, "Master, for some time an odd foreigner has been at the residential quarters entrance. What should I do?"

"Don't use the word 'odd' casually. Who in this world can be odder than you? How is he odd and what does he want?"

"Yes, er...he calls himself 'Grogan,' er, but he can't make himself understood, he speaks only English. He badly needs a shave, his clothes are filthy…and I suppose he must have an imperfect knowledge of the manners of niwazume, for he's thrown himself down on the ground of the entrance without flinching and is using a rolled sleeping bag as a pillow. I should report he has an introduction letter from the late Dr. Yasaka — well kept, it has no wrinkles."

"Show me it."

"He won't give it — he wants to give you it directly."

"The trouble with him is he can't speak Japanese," stammered the master. My old man nudged me to offer my English. I can speak it okay from being on the U.S.-Japan joint maneuvers, but I can't read or write.

I kept silent so as to see the master in a fix. But Genkaku — fat as he is, like a picture of Bodhidharma — got to his feet nimble as a dragonfly. "I'll get Mokuzu," he said and left.

So both Mokuzu and Grogan were brought before the master. On seeing Mokuzu, Grogan expressed joy as if they'd met before. Mokuzu, being a queer monk, showed no sign of recognition. No one but me noticed.

"This man has turned up with laudable words, 'to learn the arcana of Zen.' But he is making an idle boast. In reality he can't manage Japanese, let alone Chinese. His Japanese is limited to baby talk, very convenient to relay his self-centered demands. While in appearance he is remarkably like those pioneer priests who went to China, he is noway alike in character. They risked their life to cross the sea and were well versed in Chinese before they landed. With the development of flying machines travel is now the easiest thing to accomplish." The master expressed his resentment, and asked Mokuzu to translate. Grogan was amused to hear the master's vigorous emphasis on every word, but when given the translation he quickly resumed his serious air and said,

"Chinese has many rival dialects—for instance, men of Peking are unable to communicate with men of Canton. Worldwide the ratio of Japanese-speaking people is but one in forty. This shows that Chinese and Japanese are merely tribal languages. Zen thought has international currency, so it's a kind of sin if one doesn't spread it in the international language of English. What is regrettable is not that I can't speak Japanese but that you can't speak English. Yet, since your brain is too old to learn English, we should observe Buddha's teaching about friendship and the Middle Way so I can study Zen — that is, I'll learn some Japanese and you some English, and Mokuzu can fill the gap between."

Nonplussed by Grogan's mercenary spirit, Mokuzu scrupled to translate. The master pressed him to put it exactly. Genkaku faintly smiled. My old man, utterly embarrassed, was touching his head to the tatami like a dancing mouse.

Sure enough the master was horn-mad. But being the kingpin of all the foolish, wise, wicked, and good fellows of this outfit, he laughed "ho ho ho!" like a nobleman oppressed under the Tokugawa regime.

He then said, "It's an age when a beggar makes a special request of a benefactor. But I shan't ever learn such crab-crawling letters. And the pronunciation is full of explosives and fricatives. Speaking like that for years turns Westerners into brutes. Anyway, Mokuzu, tell him I'll not permit him into the meditation hall until he learns the protocol, and not grant him Zen interviews until he communicates in Japanese."

He glared at me and continued, "You too aren't welcome into the meditation hall unless you mend your ways. Compete with this Grogan to be first to be accepted as a training member. One more thing, you're "Zokki" from now on. Steal wisdom, not people's belongings. And bear in mind this is your last chance!"

He then ordered Mokuzu to take charge of Grogan and me.

It happened to be the day to shift offices, and Mokuzu had just been made the attendant to Manjusri. Toward evening I again overheard him and Genkaku in the garden behind his office:

"You've been given two additional encumbrances, Mokuzu. Please exercise your forbearance. In return I've given you Choho so you can leave most office work in his experienced hands. You must realize the master sets a high value on Grogan. If well educated here, he can assist Koko in America and many others who will be sent in the near future. The master is scheming to make Zen prosper worldwide, and he's going to establish an international office in the head temple if he's elected chief abbot. So you see the importance of your teaching Japanese and basic Zen culture to Grogan."

"Grogan's a moth flown into a spiderweb."

"Ha ha ha! Nobody intends to eat him. We'll give him a new birth. What's wrong with giving him something to live for?"

Grogan and I were assigned a middle room in the Manjusri attendant's building that gets no sun, so day and night are the same, cold and damp. It was used for sick monks till Mokuzu took charge. He's moved them to a sunny room facing the garden.

His room is in front facing northwest — with a desk, a tea cabinet, and brazier in a wooden box always with hot tea, making it one of the most comfortable of the officers' rooms. He gives most work to Choho, his obedient shadow, and himself stays in his room except for when he exits to strike the wood instrument twice daily and three times serve the monks tea.

Grogan and I got disgusted hearing the sick monks' groans and from the meditation hall the direct monk's scoldings. Mokuzu was ordered to teach us, but as he teaches us nothing Grogan began to fret and fume.

One day we called on him to ask what we should do. Believe it or not, he was using a brush and sumi, strictly forbidden in the monastery. All the same he was calm before our gaze.

"Don't ask so stupid a thing as what you should do. Next to you there are sick monks, and in the garden leaves are piling up," he replied and turned us out. I got angry and on impulse nabbed a discarded sheet of his writing from the wastebasket. I wanted his brush, but he held it firm.

Grogan badgered me to read him what was on the paper, so I translated it in my way. It put me in a nice fix — instead of Mokuzu, I was teaching him Japanese.

> I will leave because, first, I want to test myself by meeting such eight great sufferings as come of hunger, thirst, cold, heat, water, fire, sword, and war. I especially want to meet people in places or circumstances so unfortunate that they cannot see Buddha and thus cannot train themselves to see the Dharma; who are, according to the *Dirghagama*, in the conditions of hell, beasts, hungry ghosts, old age, outlands, blindness, deafness, and such, and in the conditions of secular prejudice and the period of Buddha's absence. Those extremely sad people and cruel people will spur my growth, I believe.

> Second, I want to visit Ceylon or Thailand, because I cannot believe Buddhism in Japan is the whole of Sakyamuni Buddha's teaching. What Northern Buddhism left behind in the process of abstracting primitive Buddhism is so immense. If I can practice Southern Buddhism as well as learn Pali and Sanskrit, I will be greatly benefited.

> Third, I want to visit America and see its reality. America is said to be founded on Puritanism and to be waywardly enjoying the benefits of being the most advanced nation and one of the strongest, with dominating power over all human fate. There I will have a chance to learn the virtue of the Christian faith and compare it with Buddhism, and to see how I can be useful to the world.

> Above all, while thus engaged I won't forget even a day my profoundest wish to find a lifelong companion with whom to train enjoyably as a Bodhisattva. My Zen master if he learns of this last wish will surely be outraged and possibly cancel me as his disciple. A break between master and disciple is grievous, but keeping a calm and phony relation is more grievous. There isn't enough reason to depress my true desire for the sake of helpless prejudice.

On hearing Mokuzu's private writing, Grogan sneered perversely and vented some negative criticism. I responded, "Yeah, well, in years he's junior to you and me."

Some days later I snitched three brushes from the master's and chestnuts from the kitchen. I chose a time when there's no bath attendant and invited Grogan to the fuel hole to destroy the evidence — brushes into the fire, chestnuts into our bellies.

But ill luck, Mokuzu appeared! He had the wooden case of herb medicines kept in one of the sick rooms. He began to put the contents into the fire — comfrey for stomach ulcer, smartweed tuber for nervous prostration, bishop's-weed for angina pectoris, mahuang for asthma, etc.

Grogan stopped him, "Hey, what are you doing? What'll we give the sick monks?"

"You're unkind, Grogan. You came from a country foremost in the field of modern medicine, yet you unconcernedly give sick monks this crude old stuff about which there's no clear understanding of prescription or effect. This is a good opportunity. You have my permission to go out. Before evening bell, obtain a variety of modern medicines."

"Where will I get them, and how will I pay for them?"

"Go wherever you please and get them by any means. What's important is to be quick, but you can start to run after eating those chestnuts you're roasting. Zokki, what do you intend to put in next? Show me what you have hidden there in your bosom."

I produced the brushes.

"These are quite new...they haven't yet formed the owner's character. Let me use them and you can believe you burnt them," he said and took them.

I proposed that I assist Grogan, but Mokuzu refused: "You incite people's evil spirit instead of their good faith. Stay and tend the sick monks."

In our room Grogan was encumbering himself with how to get the medicines, especially how to pay. With a roommate's sentiment I too taxed my brain and finally suggested, as if I'd hit on a great invention, "Hey! Why not use your own money, since unlike me you have some?"

He was displeased and cut off all possibility in that direction:

"Nope, it's for my plane ticket in case I'm compelled to leave. Besides, I don't see why any money of mine should be spent on anonymous monks."

"But you told me you're expecting to be certified as a Zen master and planning to open a Zen center in the U.S. That means you have to stay here at least ten to twenty years. What's the point of keeping your purse till then?"

"In an emergency all I can depend on is money."

I had no choice but to summon my chivalrous spirit for his sake, though I knew it to be an evil course. My stealing ought rather to be to outwit and shame uppity guys.

Nonetheless I sniggled into the main building with a blanket. A chanting officer was endlessly loitering, so I had to wait till he left for evening bell. Then — presto! I spread it by the huge offertory chest, overturned the chest on it, and made off with it loaded to our room just like Santa Claus!

But, too late — Mokuzu was there to see if Grogan had carried out his order, and he was telling him,

"Concern yourself with it no more. I was wrong to ask of you such overwhelming work. Incidentally, did you write to your wife, who must be awaiting your return?"

"I don't write. To change the subject, why don't you instruct me? It seems you're neglecting the duty placed on you by the master," Grogan complained. Mokuzu answered distinctly, "I'll not teach anything to a man who is unable either to obtain medicines for the sick or to write to his wife left behind. Every bit of Zen teaching, including so-called enlightenment, is for the sake of living beings."

"Don't you fear you're impeding instead of assisting my Zen training? Let me emphasize you have nothing to do with my writing my wife — it's my own affair. You should be reminded of the manifest tradition of Buddhism since Sakyamuni Buddha: to abandon home to seek the Dharma."

"You adore a tradition that is like the herb medicines inherited by this sickroom, moldy, replete with superstition. Listen, Grogan, any Zen realization, however great, is shabby, fruitless, and insubstantial in comparison with married life. Even a great Zen master, when we see through his essence, is like a wild chrysanthemum come too late in the season and unable to enjoy full expression of its endowed color as it awaits being carried off by a snell wind."

"Head Attendant to Manjusri, aren't you opposing Zen and Buddhist tradition?"

"Not keeping any tradition is the true tradition of Zen and Buddhism. Grogan, if you love tradition, why don't you respect your Christian tradition? In Matthew it says clearly:

> "Think not that I came to send peace on the earth: I came not to send peace, but a sword. For I came to set a man at variance against his father, and the daughter against her mother...[1]

"It's one of Christ's basic teachings, which should be esteemed by his followers. But for a person like me it should be dismissed like flicking a bit of chaff from one's sleeve."

Grogan was so mad his thinking faculties were stymied. He glared at Mokuzu. I didn't know which side to take. But to be fair I should say Mokuzu got most of the medicines he wanted in some unknown way during Zen interviews that evening.

I was at a loss how to dispose of the offertory money. Since returning it to the chest would cancel my credit, I decided to put it all, oodles of coins mostly, into the drum and the bell in the secrecy of night to provide a big laugh for the monks in the morning when the chanting officers make the first strokes.

To add to the fun I turned the clock back 45 minutes. If the chanting officers are delayed in waking up, everyone, the master too, is delayed as much — good for their health!

As I was returning to our room to sleep, I got unbearably hungry in the vacant dining wing. So I stole into the founder's hall. It's the safest place, off-bounds to ordinary monks. The lugubrious all-night light revealed not the founder's face but a dish piled high with bean-jam buns offered to him. I filled up on half. I see it as no more of a sin than the master's sermon given in place of the founder's. By the way, "Zokki" comes from the founder's words, according to Mokuzu.

781

The story goes, a priest named Yinyuan came long ago from China and founded a new Japanese Zen school, the Obaku school. At the outset of his propagating, he rigorously made visits of challenge to the established Zen monasteries to ascertain if their heads' level of understanding was equal to his own. If the responses to his questions were unsatisfactory, Yinyuan made the head remove the monastery's nameplate and consign the monastery to his authority. Thus he also came up to Myoshinji and spoke with a threatening look,

"Your monastery stands high in public esteem. I presume your founder left a great record of his words. Show me it."

Myoshinji's head replied that the founder left no record but simply the comment, "There's *zokki* — a thief's talent — in Jaujou's cypress." "Your founder's one comment excels hundreds of records," said Yinyuan and he promptly took his leave.

The comment is beyond my ken. Mokuzu says it expresses a genuine Zen life-style.

So much for my name. Feeling satisfied, I was truly returning to our room. But when I passed the room of the direct monk, I was taken by the whim to look in because he constantly whips the trainees. I assumed he too was meditating on a rock somewhere at that hour of the night since he drives others on to extra meditation. But, lo! he was fast asleep, covering even his head with the heavy quilt. Of course I felt a rush of anger and opened his closet. Surprise! Five or so apples were treasured up. What would he do if he detected others hiding things? He'd beat them half to death! I munched one at his very pillow and left it a neat spool atop the rest.

Next day was fun. Everyone overslept and the master and the head chanting officer in ceremonial robes went to the founder's hall for confession. The reception head had to change the schedule from long-distance begging to mountain work. And all the officers were called to the master's for a dressing down and missed lunch. Mokuzu returned with a mild face and merely said, "You are a help in caring for the sick monks."

Trouble came, for me, after that. When I went to our room, the direct monk, his assistant, and the monks' major were trying to sweat my nocturnal maneuvers out of Grogan. It was obvious he'd already told them about the heap of coins in the blanket and about my absence during the night. He wanted to impress on them the difference between us even though we're the same hangers-on. I regretted I'd taught him Japanese against Mokuzu's will.

The direct monk's assistant and the monks' major carried me to the empty meditation hall, and there they kicked me at least 300 times. The direct monk held down my neck with his warning stick and shouted, "Confess every one of your foul deeds!"

Many times I met such difficulty in the Ground Self Defense Force. I spit bloody saliva and retorted, "Lousy specimens of monks — you can't answer your koans however the master presses you! I'll not relate my secrets to fools!

My supervisor isn't any of you but Mokuzu, who's a little wiser and kinder. You're transgressing your petty function!"

They exploded, then battered me with kicks and punches. I revived to find myself lying in a flood of water — they must have dumped buckets on me. Then they bound my hands behind my back and hung me from a lintel. The rope cut into my wrists and gut, yet they kept beating me with warning sticks. I swayed in circles, twisting and untwisting — it made me sick. Hoarsely I cried, "You're killing me! Have you no fear of creating trouble for yourselves in the future?"

The direct monk said with a grin, "We're specialists in funerals, we'll give you a fine service, gratis."

That terrorized me, so I owned up. Then I saw Grogan peeping in, and in English I called for his help.

What an ass! He just clung to the door like a drowning man to a life preserver. I squeezed out my voice — "Fool! Get Mokuzu!"

At last Mokuzu came, and rescued me without a word. The direct monk didn't say a word either. I feared my eardrums were split it was so quiet. It's not that he did Aesop's "The Wind and the Sun" on them, nor did he start a heated argument, but they let him untie me. Were they scared of his dignity, or just tired of their game? I knew my ears were okay when he took me on his shoulders and told them before stepping out, "You mistook what to beat. If the juniors get worse, more beatings should come to the seniors." His words faintly rang in my ears and a hot feeling rose in my heart.

He carried me to the Dragon Fountain, a spring behind the Manjusri attendant's building where the mountain begins. He washed my wounds and my defiled clothes in the cold water. Grogan brought a towel and salve.

With his weird Japanese pronunciation Grogan said, "*Shikata nai ne.* Serves you right for committing crimes in, of all places, these stern traditional sacred precincts."

Mokuzu was unusually excited in his response, "Grogan, you may regard this as tradition, but it isn't the tradition of Buddhism or of Zen; it's merely Shoshinji tradition. Remotest from human ideal is reality cloaked by tradition. Don Quixote too said nothing is crazier than to see only reality and thus lose sight of how things ought to be. As for sacred precincts, I'll show you true sacred precincts if you like. Just remove those fallen leaves," and he pointed to the pool by the spring.

Grogan did as he was told —

"I see nothing...oh? a turtle...some turtles. What of it?"

I tried to crawl near for a look. Grogan gave me a hand.

There was a turtle, and underneath, three turtlets stirring, and two or three heading that way. Their slow movement was yet slower in the cold water. Grogan, I guess disliking the sight of reptiles, screwed up his face. But Mokuzu said,

783

"See? Adult and young are living assiduously. No other sacred precincts are more sacred than these that border on sacred precincts. How much more valid it is to train in one's household, slowly, but steadily and honestly, than to train in a monastery with the dream of making a fortune by a single stroke. Grogan, you lost your mother, you know maternal love. If you know the grief of losing a mother, can't you sense the grief of a wife who has lost a husband? A wife is a mother, a daughter, a sister, also a sweetheart. Think deep and don't be so unwise as to separate from your real treasure. I repeat, all of God, Buddha, Zen, and enlightenment detached from your love and your beloved is false and not true."

Now it was the day after the December week-long meditation. Having had no sleep all that time, the monks, like stone statues in meditation form, slept eagerly under no restriction. Snow blustered outside.

In a sickroom I was feeding a monk gruel and Grogan was changing the towel on another's head. Suddenly he dropped the towel and said to me, "I'll talk with him once more to make up my mind to stay or go home. Please come and ask him to hear my side."

I had nothing better to do, so we left the sick monks with Choho, though he was dozing.

No reply came from Mokuzu's room. Was he too dozing? I opened the shoji a crack. He wasn't there. On his desk I found a painting of a beautiful lady done in thin sumi, an odd painting. She was bathing in a natural hot spring in a snowy forest, her clothes on a branch stirred by the wind. But she was altogether quiet. Above to the right was a eulogy,

"Return to Clarity: snow flower in the light of lapis lazuli," with a date of death. I regretted sneaking a look at it and carefully closed the shoji.

I supposed he might be at the spring and took Grogan, who was concerned only with his own affairs.

He was there, in the water, chanting. In this cold he had to be out of his mind. We watched quiet as mice. Luckily it was a short sutra. He leapt out and rubbed himself down with a towel. Then he noticed us and asked, "Is it the sick monks?"

I felt awkward. We must have seemed like idiots. But I told him Grogan's request.

"Grogan, you are indeed akin to the cowards described in Dante's *Inferno*, despised by both God and his enemies...Well, tonight after lights-out I'll hear your story on top of this mountain. Zokki, rustle up something tasty. You needn't practice your talent; some farmers will gladly supply you if you ask. But be sure to go up the mountain unseen."

Pleased to be thus acknowledged, I got possession of a hen, a bottle of sake, and some carrots and potatoes.

The path was tricky with the snow. On top we found him already making

784

a bonfire scorching the night sky. The powder snow was sucked in before it could land, and the nearest scrawny pines were swayed by the heat. He was burning the firewood the monks had labored over in the autumn. He chose a nice rock for himself, put a blanket on it, and sat down.

"Aren't you afraid to make such a walloping fire? What if the master and the seniors find out?" I was anxious.

"Men are ignorant of what's happening above their heads. And the villagers afar can lend wings to their fancy."

As soon as I set to roasting the hen, Grogan began his life story. I get bored to the point of wanting to steal or set a fire if I'm made to see wedding photos, or wash dishes, or hear a guy's life story, but after drinking a little sake Mokuzu got shamelessly patient and Grogan shamelessly talkative.

According to him, he studied 17th-century English poetry at a university, where, with no pressure to work afterward, he stayed on for graduate study of John Donne, and there he came to know a poet gaining recognition for her talent in some quarters. Before long she became his wife. They enjoyed their early married days and agreed to have no children for the reason that the present and future would be unsuitable for a sinless baby when they considered the prospect of nuclear war, global pollution, race riots, and so on.

In fact they were too content and too young to care about any future child between them. Weekdays they lived in an apartment near the university; weekends they often visited his father's vacation home, a stone house on a south-facing hill with a lake below where they swam nude in the early morning. The forest beyond remained sunlit well after the lake settled into dusk. Behind the house was a century-old walnut orchard extending to a seemingly endless forest of oak, hickory, tulip poplar, and dogwood, once a farm as evidenced by the remains of pickets and barbed wire. In the snow they cross-country skied.

Their parents didn't entirely approve of the marriage, owing to differences of background, religion, occupation, and social status, about which they had pride. Yet they were suficiently in accord in respecting their democratic and capitalistic social system, since both families had a high education, a high income, and an easy life. All in all the parents had no reason not to enjoy their children's happiness, and they exchanged occasional visits, with some pleasure and some strain.

In their second married year, Grogan's mother took ill and was hospitalized, which brought a change in their routine life. Weekends they visited her instead of going to the country, and it also meant no outings together to the movies, museums, or restaurants, or to see their friends.

One such weekend Grogan's wife, S., attended her father's birthday party. As he drove to the hospital in the rain, Grogan was furious. "What's more important, flying to a happy, healthy father or comforting my mother, lonely and in pain? After all, my wife and I came from different places and must go to different places." From then on S. often declined to visit his mother and found reason enough — a promise to see a friend, the need to perfect a poem or talk to an editor...all seemed trivial to him but vital to her, and soon she bought her own car. Then as a matter of course they acted independently from morning to night, even during the week, and their mutual friends decreased as hers increased.

One day at dawn in March of the next year, Grogan got a call to hurry to the hospital. This time S. insisted on going. The weather had loosened, a mist was rising, and he could hear as he crossed the snow the sound of water under his boots. He sped with lit headlights down the empty road. He came to a makeshift bridge built after a flood the previous spring and had to slow down. It was a daytime watering spot for cows. There a man raised a hand to ask for a ride — a hunter with red vest and gun but no take, a massive man whiskered in the style of Francis I of France. S. persuaded Grogan to stop. He then drove on in silence, worried about his mother, while S. and the man, actually an artist called L., chatted about the seasons of the natural forest. Soon he had to brake abruptly because of a fallen tree at a bend in the road. Through the trees was the sight of a red farmhouse with a rusted reaper in the yard.

"It's a trap!" S. exclaimed. Indeed three suspicious-looking men got off the hood of a jeep in the forest and approached.

"Keep cool, they're probably not insane or drug addicts," said L. from the back, patting Grogan's shoulder. His words and gesture alarmed Grogan — was L. their buddy? One jumped on the fender and banged on the window. The others ordered everyone out. L. put an arm around S. and egged Grogan on, "Hey, here's a great chance to show her your stuff!" and he dashed from the car and fired his gun. The outlaws scattered, but L. aimed another shot at the sky and demanded, "Wait! Reopen the road before you disappear, unless you want to get shot!"

When peace returned, Grogan was still shaking and suffering stomach pain. "Why don't you drive on? Weren't you in a hurry?" said L., and to S., "Why don't you take over?"

Once at the hospital, Grogan and S. knew by the gathering of relatives that they were too late.

"From then our relationship...," continued Grogan as if assured of the endless time and patience of his listeners. I was really starting to doubt Mokuzu's ability to manage another man, but Mokuzu raised his hand and asked,

"May I make sure, Grogan? I assume you are putting each topic in the fire as you relate it" — an odd confirmation, but I approved of it as his indefeasible right. And more,

"Grogan, sorry to interrupt, but you also must understand I'm very sleepy because, unlike you both, I had to participate in the week-long meditation. To keep me awake, won't you recite something of Donne? I remember only 'John Donne, Ann Donne, Un-done.'[2] What is it from?"

Grogan could remember no poem with such a line. He recited "The Anniversary":

> All kings, and all their favorites,
>> All glory of honors, beauties, wits,
> The sun it selfe, which makes times as they passe,
> Is elder by a year, now, then it was
> When thou and I first one another saw;
> All other things to their destruction draw,
>> Only our love hath no decay;
> This, no to morrow hath, nor yesterday,
> Running, it never runs from us away,
> But truly keeps his first, last, everlasting day.[3]

Mokuzu appreciated the poem and admired Grogan for knowing such a nice poem. In return he recited lines on the ecology of salmon from a poem by Michael Drayton, quoted by Donne's friend Izaak Walton in his *Compleat Angler*:

> And when the Salmon seeks a fresher stream to find;
> (Which hither from the sea comes, yearly, by his kind,)
> As he towards season grows; and stems the watry tract
> Where Tivy, falling down, makes an high cataract,
> Forc'd by the rising rocks that there her course oppose,
> As tho' within her bounds they meant her to inclose;
> Here when the labouring fish does at the foot arrive,
> And finds that by his strength he does but vainly strive;
> His tail takes in his mouth, and, bending like a bow
> That's to full compass drawn, aloft himself doth throw,
> Then springing at his height, as doth a little wand
> That bended end to end, and started from man's hand,
> Far off itself doth cast; so does the Salmon vault:
> And if, at first, he fail, his second summersault
> He instantly essays, and, from his nimble ring
> Still yerking, never leaves until himself he fling
> Above the opposing stream....[4]

"After my mother died, I lived a pathetic life. I was literally in mourning," Grogan resumed. He too is queer. He was telling his pathetic story as he ate a well-roasted drumstick with gusto, like a baby busy crying while licking a candy.

At any rate he lost the will to study, he became more taciturn, rarely walked in the woods with S. or talked poetry, politics, or art with their friends around the fire, and rarely went to town. His remaining intellect went mostly into reading the newspaper. S. was gentle with him, but often went out. She and L. became friends and agreed on publishing her poems with his

787

illustrations. Grogan disliked L. but his position was to thank him for the rescue; in fact he had no grounds to stop their meeting. S. wished to see L. together with Grogan, but Grogan was unwilling.

One day old friends, married and unmarried, came for a surprise party, bringing food, drink, records, and so on. They worried about Grogan and wanted to cheer him up. But it coincided with an important family gathering at his father's house. He and S. couldn't both leave, considering their friends' goodwill, so Grogan left after the party began.

When he returned late the party was still on, at least he saw the friends' cars, and candlelight in the living room. He scented marijuana. Neither he nor S. had allowed themselves its habitual use. The living room was quiet, though evidently many people were there. He opened the door a crack and could at first make no sense of what he saw. It looked like bodies piled in pestilence. A man lay on a woman, both half-clothed. In the shadow of a couch a nude woman had her head on a man's groin while another man embraced her from behind. Others were mingled by the hearth, under a piano, behind a rocking chair. He further opened the door to find his wife, alone, leaning against the wall in a corner. She seemed drugged and had a vacant look. He saw her clothes were disarrayed and supposed she must have permitted some heavy petting. As he strained to examine her expression, a man moved to her and put a hand on her thigh, meeting no resistance. He had whiskers, it was L. Grogan closed the door and went to his study.

They never spoke of the night, but whenever he sensed she had been with L., he sought her body rather violently. She did not refuse him, in fact was uncommonly excited. Yet her health was going, and he feared the ruin of their life.

"It was during this horrible period that a friend invited me to one of Dr. Yasaka's lectures in New York and I first heard about Zen..." Grogan suddenly realized Mokuzu was asleep. I knew he'd been for some time, but I neither waked him nor stopped Grogan. In a fury Grogan shook him awake.

Mokuzu said, "I understand you. What I'd like to say won't change after hearing your story. In the Vimalakirtinirdesa Sutra it is written, 'The happiest life is to enter Nirvana without severing klesa.'[5] Prince Shotoku interpreted these words in his *Gisho*: 'To realize Nirvana means to understand there is no klesa to be severed, for klesa is sunyata.'[6]

"Grogan, the problems of life can be solved only within life, and the problems of marriage only within marriage. Zen training is to seek the Bodhisattva Way. A Bodhisattva recognizes the Bodhisattva in himself as well as in others. He is saddened to see others suffer, but he enjoys his own suffering because he sees the value of his life in the depths of life. A Bodhisattva can easily be seen in the sacred precincts but is very hard to find in the human family. Go home even a day earlier and train to see the Bodhisattva in your wife.

788

"It wouldn't be too late to come here again if you lose your wife by her death in old age. Now is too early. If you stay here, I assure you that someday you will be able to become a Zen master like some others, and you will lead many youths to dark confusion. Please be aware that the first work of a conscientious Zen master is to drive people away from the charm of Zen and by any means not to entice them.

"What is fearful about Zen training is that it produces a hundred people who can freely talk about hundreds of koans without really understanding even half of one. To understand any koan in its true sense is as hard as to seize a tiny jewel amid a whirlwind. Yet it is so easy for a person who loves! Grogan, you have enough love. According to your story, so does your wife. Please enjoy the life you can live without Zen. It will bring you more happiness than any Zen can offer you."

This was all I witnessed of what went on between Mokuzu and Grogan. I have no reason to greatly understand, but my understanding could be a mite better than the Zen master's. I'm sure Mokuzu loved Grogan and his wife too, though he never met her, and when Grogan left I saw him thanking Mokuzu.

57

Koko's Scandal

As elsewhere, icicles a foot long hung from the eaves of the Manjusri attendant's building. Receiving the pale western sun, they cast shadows on the shojis of Mokuzu's room. Day after day, as much as he could afford to, Mokuzu was secluding himself to paint the subjects of the koans he had worked through.

Sometimes icicles fell and shattered on the black tiles around the meditation hall, precipitated by, or coincidental with, the usual bitter, angry voice of the direct monk.

The direct monk's unreasonable asperity increased only the numbers of the sick and wounded, and one day Mokuzu invited the direct monk into his room to protest.

"Mokuzu, I believe the mission of the direct monk is to give trainees a *grenzsituation*. That's why I beat them black and blue. Your gentle words won't have meaning to them unless they are beaten half to death, because thanks comes only from the heart of the tortured. They must be beaten until they can feel thanks for any minor kindness. This sense of thanks will beget their vigor and pleasure to survive in the world. What could be a greater gift to them than Shoshinji's beatings?"

"Direct Monk, whoever lives is experiencing his *grenzsituation*. Many may not realize the state they're in, but realization comes naturally according to talent and opportunity. I worry that your artificial *grenzsituation* is driving them from their real *grenzsituation*. Besides, what you call thanks is merely a sense of relief from torture. The pleasure of living couldn't be so meager and partial. It should be total and fundamental from morning to night, whether fair or foul the weather, in keeping with the saying, 'The ordinary mind is the Way.'"[1]

"Mokuzu, I respect you for having quickly passed more koans than any of the rest of us, yet I must point out that you've been here less than three years. You know only idea, not reality. You say it's a matter of talent and opportunity. But if we rely on that, five hundred years won't be enough time for them to realize anything. They're cowardly, lazy, tricky, and care about nothing but their own immediate interests. Beating is the only way to help them."

The direct monk had a passion for training the monks. Mokuzu for his part saw it differently. He thought giving them a suitable environment for pleasant self-training was a more important task than to levy a hard, constrained training.

"Your way creates too many martyrs. In order to muddle through your stern training, the monks discard their effort to mature their intellect, emotion, and integrity, which they could otherwise spontaneously attend to. You apply your sternness not to their inner development but to their skill at fitting into a formula. Frantic to obey for the time being, they must suppress their faculties for inner growth. Eventually they'll turn out to be agile and shrewd, with the appearance of being wise, fearless, and resolute. Moreover, pressed to receive interviews with the master, they are cornered into a dead end where no reason reaches, and implanted with a narrow and irrational loyalty. Thus the longer they train in the monastery the more they become rough-and-ready instead of prudent; decisive instead of observant; arrogant instead of respectful; bigoted instead of flexible — and they pledge their loyalty to one certain person instead of being loyal to themselves and to all others. They should fully open their faculties. Instead they are limiting themselves. Aren't they the greatest of martyrs?"

"Ah ha ha! Mokuzu, while describing them don't stare at me! Well, now I understand why you failed to hang on to Grogan. The master too is grieving over your undependable leadership."

"Direct Monk, you must have studied 'Nanyue's Polishing a Tile.'" Mokuzu showed the direct monk the koan and his illustrative painting.

In Chuanfayuan Monastery during the Kaiyuan era there lived a monk called Dauyi (Matzu) who always practiced sitting meditation. Esteeming him to be a future Dharma talent, his teacher approached him and asked, "Reverend Monk, what is your aim in practicing sitting meditation?"

"To become a Buddha."

The teacher picked up a tile, set it on a rock before his residence, and began to polish it. Dauyi asked him what he was doing. "Fashioning a mirror."

"By polishing a tile?" Dauyi was incredulous.

"And you, can you become a Buddha by practicing sitting meditation?"

"What then is the right approach?"

"Suppose you are on a cow-drawn cart. If you make no progress, which should you whip, cow or cart?"

Dauyi made no answer. The teacher further explained,

"You are trying to learn Zen and become a Buddha by the practice of sitting meditation. You have to realize that Zen does not mean sitting and that Buddha has no certain form. Zen and Buddha have no settled habitation and reject fastidiousness. If you are particular about a sitting Buddha, you are killing Buddha. If you adhere to sitting form, you cannot attain the truth." Dauyi listened as if drinking pure milk.[2]

The direct monk frowned on seeing Mokuzu's illustration. "It makes no sense. It's not Millet, yet a man and wife are planting seedlings...and on a path a baby is pursuing a frog. Why not show Nanyue polishing a tile?"

"That won't do, because the koan doesn't say polishing a tile is a futile task as is commonly thought. To appreciate this koan fully, our Zen master hinted that we recall the Diamond Sutra, didn't he?"

"He did. 'Unobtainable,' which is sunyata...sitting meditation is to come home to sunyata."

"Yes, and it was the Sixth Patriarch's original understanding of sitting meditation. Now, if sitting meditation is to come home to sunyata, consider what I've drawn. The daily life of the couple and baby is not different from sitting meditation: it is the substance of sunyata. I encouraged Grogan to engage in a substantial daily life."

"...But, Mokuzu, how can ordinary people distinguish sunyata from emptiness, and a substantial life from a meaningless life? What you recommended to Grogan is as risky as to walk on the blade of a sword. I who have no ability will remain within our master's safe teaching."

Perceiving the direct monk's unwillingness to reform, Mokuzu talked no further. He detested anyone who slighted the disability of others and who yet withdrew from challenging higher achievement by the excuse of his own disability.

Dauyi, having enjoyed the benevolent influence of his teacher Nanyue, passed the teaching to his followers:

> To attain the Way requires of us no endeavor other than the endeavor not to become polluted. What pollutes us? Every intentional act and device comes from fear of death: all life's cares are pollutants. To know the Way, we must realize that the ordinary mind is the Way. The ordinary mind has no intention, and distinguishes no right or wrong, no receiving or discarding, no annihilation or eternity, no Buddhas or unenlightened ones....It just comes and goes, sits and reclines, according to object and opportunity. This is the Way.[3]

One of Dauyi's Dharma inheritors was Nanchyuan, and he too passed the teaching to his disciple Jaujou.

> Nanchyuan said, "The ordinary mind is the Way."
> "Should we then seek it or not?" asked Jaujou.
> "As soon as we seek it, we are separated from it," replied Nanchyuan.
> "How is it possible to know the Way without paying it any special care?" Jaujou persisted.
> Nanchyuan replied, "The Way belongs neither to knowing nor to not knowing. Knowing means false realization, not knowing means no recognition. If we truly attain the Way, we will see that the Way is like the great inane broadly expanding and there will be no point in discussing it."[4]

What these Zen patriarchs are evidently talking about here is equal to the 'Ultimate Way' of Third Patriarch Sengtsan's *Shin-shin ming*, and 'the ordinary mind' is therefore Sengtsan's 'believing mind and mind believed in.' The only difference between Sengtsan and these later patriarchs is that he remained in philosophical speculation about the Way, whereas they found it in their daily practice. This seeing of the Way in daily life became more definite, simple, and concrete in Nanchyuan's disciple Jaujou.

> A monk: "What is the ordinary mind?"
> Jaujou: "The mind like a jackal or a lone wolf."[5]

And more directly he spoke of the ordinary mind:

> A monk: "What is Self?"
> Jaujou: "Did you eat breakfast?"
> "I did."
> "Then attend to washing your bowls."[6]

Jaujou saw the function of the ordinary mind in such daily acts as eating and cleaning up afterward, and he was confident in his understanding that living with the ordinary mind is how a true man lives, which is living true to the Way.

The early Chinese Zen patriarchs thus saw the substance of sunyata in the ordinary mind in daily life. For them it was the truth, the Way of human life, the meaning of life, the key to making human life bright and cheerful; and they passed this wisdom from generation to generation.

Mokuzu well understood their wisdom and had no contradictory view. But he regretted one thing, which was that they all practiced their understanding of the importance of the ordinary mind only in the Zen monastery, one of the least ordinary places in the world, whence their belief became an impractical notion from the viewpoint of the world. Now he wanted to practice the same belief in a family, the most ordinary, natural, and basic form and place for human life.

His wish was regarded as a risky venture and somewhat scorned by the direct monk. Was it really an unreasonable wish, like nursing alpine plants in a lowland garden? Mokuzu believed it was not unreasonable as long as there were women who sorrowed and suffered; for sorrow and suffering were the very elements with the potential to raise the vitality to seek the Way as well as to build an ideal family.

※

Zen Master Tengai was irresponsive when Mokuzu reported simply that Grogan had left. He kept his usual bearing, chin up, mouth set, gaze lowered.

Yet he questioned Zokki in detail, according to Zokki, who reported it to Mokuzu in an elated manner. Mokuzu said,

"Zokki, let go of a matter that has nothing to do with you."

"Okay, I'll let it go, but the master spoke furiously of you. He said whoever betrays his trust shortens his life."

"Let it go, too. Study to be like that fabled wizard who sustained himself by eating haze and not by circulating rumor." Mokuzu showed Zokki to the door.

He was displeased with his painting when he returned to it. He crossed it out and wrote:

> So heavy is trust that a man will quake in fear of losing it; hence trust is a device of manipulation. Note that trees do not root and branch to gain trust.

In those days Mokuzu was enjoying a quiet mental state. In contrast, the mental state of the master went up and down, and he could not even sleep well because of the counterplan to elect a new abbot. The present abbot, close to a hundred years old, was growing senile. With his resignation in April almost certain, four candidates including Tengai were preparing for the position. A campaign headquarters had been set up in Shoshinji, and the priests supporting Tengai were said to be going to hold a caucus there near

December's end. So every day he was busy visiting or being visited by old disciples, like-minded priests, and many floaters.

On one such day a Zen master, Banryu, who had returned for a short while from missionary work in California, paid him a visit. With the election in mind, Tengai received him cordially, though they had never been friends and Banryu was younger by nearly ten years. But soon both tempers ran high, bitter words were exchanged, and Banryu charged from the room. Tengai's attendants were embarrassed and did not know what to do with the well-prepared delicacies. Their master recklessly shouted,

"You fools, judge the hospitality after seeing the guest! Take it all to the pond and feed it to the carp! Nevermore will I speak to such a low-down skunk!"

From what the attendants overheard of the meeting, such words as scandal, inheritor, entrap, acquisition, and the name Koko frequently flew back and forth.

Like the sound of the wind it all reached Zokki's ears. But fear of being dispraised kept Zokki from telling Mokuzu. Then late one afternoon, innocent of the matter, Mokuzu was summoned to the master.

"I am sending you to America for your study. Have you any objection? No, how could you? After all, without experience of living in their culture, you can't suitably guide them even if they come here to study."

Instead of scolding him for his ill success with Grogan, the master was offering him an educational opportunity. Mokuzu replied with gratitude,

"Thank you for your thoughtful consideration. But going to America would be a venture so grave as to affect my destiny. Please allow me some time to think it over."

"Of course. I don't expect an immediate answer. I rather hope you will meditate on the idea to your satisfaction...inform me by, say, the day of receiving permission to leave or stay on in the monastery." The master spoke openhandedly, though the day he suggested was January seventh, just two weeks ahead. Mokuzu heard the noise of a flock of birds gathering on a tree in the inner garden. The master added,

"You have to study *Shyutang's Hundred Koans* before you start 'The Last Barrier,' but don't be concerned: they are just to give alternate or additional answers and can be studied through letters even if you go to America."

Learning that he had to study a hundred more koans, Mokuzu was surprised and suspicious of the master's intent. 'Nothing is better than to accumulate the rich resources of the teaching. But at this rate there won't be a day I can be free of him until one day I have no energy left to study on my own. Besides, all the koans, according to his understanding of them, are alike in depth and merely vary in surface plots.' But, owing to his innate politeness, Mokuzu did not voice his feeling.

794

As he withdrew from the master's presence, he saw a large number of dusky thrushes move all at once from a red-berried *kurogane mochi*. They rose to sit noisily whistling in a tall oak indefinitely keeping its foliage.

The idea of going to America charmed him as if he'd been put on a hilltop with an excellent view. But he wanted to go without the stricture of being the master's disciple, or even of being identified as a Zen monk. He wanted to go as a mere free man, with no Zen master's strings attached and no girding Zen armor. Then purely as himself he would be able to discover a new world, a new people, a new himself. 'I shouldn't be drawn into a quick-sand of obligation any deeper than what I'm already in. After all, Zen isn't the main current of the world; it's only a slack water devoid of great improvement.'

Yet, realizing he had no money, he saw that the easiest and shortest way to go abroad was to accept the master's offer. He lacked money for an airplane ticket, living costs, and tuition, much as he might want to study in an American university. He had to remember his bitter experience in Tokyo.

He was beginning to enjoy a certain freedom, but it was entirely spiritual and within the protection of a traditional religious community. One step into the world and his spiritual freedom would be subject to economic restriction.

'Like Nanchyuan, Baijiang received Dauyi's teaching "The ordinary mind is the Way." But considering matters of economy, he suppressed that aspect of Dauyi and emphasized strict monastic rules and great diligence: "A day of no work is a day of no eating."[7] No wonder he raised such vigorous and invincible followers as Kueishan and Yangshan, and Huangbo and Linji.'

Mokuzu was uncertain whether to accept the master's offer. He was not the boy who had gone up to Tokyo ignorant of how to obtain his economic needs. Now he was confident that wherever there was the Dharma there was the means to sustain his body. What people really wanted for themselves he could see at a glance, and he knew things would turn not only to his disadvantage but to his advantage, as was the nature of things. He was also more able to bear hardship without making it the grave matter it had once been.

One evening Genkaku brought him the remaining cakes offered to the visiting caucus of priests. Mokuzu was quietly continuing to illustrate the koans.

"I thought you were deliberating like Hamlet, but you appear to be on easy street, putting that old priest-painter Chingjyu in the shade with your illustrations. Did you decide?"

"I have ten more days."

"Don't you realize how the master is being held in suspense? In fact he's irate over your hesitation to obey. He thinks you ought to have made him a ready answer."

"Why should he be like that on my account? What is the rush?" Mokuzu expressed his naive heart. Doubting his shrewdness to judge another's plot, Genkaku said,

"Truly Koko seems driven into a corner. He can barely speak English and badly needs your help. And the master must hasten to smother the scandal lest it be put to bad use by the election counterforces, including the Zen master Banryu."

Mokuzu had to withdraw completely from the subject of his painting. "I had no idea my going was to help Koko."

"For what, then? To see Disneyland, or the Everglades?"

"He asked if I wanted to go to study, that was all."

"Hm, he resorted to knavish tricks, and you were unthinkably imprudent. But the fault is yours more than his while you have access to our expert thief," said Genkaku coolly, taking out a cigarette hidden in his sleeve, and he exhaled a big puff.

"How rotten to have to depend on a thief to determine the master's true intention. Oh, I recall Zokki once told me in passing that you'd never become a Dharma inheritor of our master because you were formerly a Bolshevik."

"It's not new news. Anyway, for your benefit I'll tell you what I know. First, he is certainly willing to let you study in America if you like. But listen: on the condition that you prove to be a satisfactory assistant to Koko. In short, he will grant you the reward of study abroad if you succeed in extricating Koko.

"About Koko, though I don't know for sure; I'm telling you what I heard from the master. Zen Master Banryu came the other day to offer his support for the election. He's in the wake of Zen Master Tokai, who was a Dharma brother of Zen Master Shutan. Banryu had a temple in Matsushima, but about ten years ago he was invited to America by a Japanese society in Los Angeles.

"Well, in exchange for supporting the election, he asked that Zen Master Tengai commit himself to international missionary work with the aid of head temple funds if he becomes abbot. Our master agreed to that, but the second demand he flatly refused. It was to make Koko Banryu's adopted Dharma inheritor. Banryu has industriously taught in America and opened several Zen temples there. Without a successor his efforts will come to nil.

"Refused this second demand, Banryu openly stated that he will oppose our master's election, that he sees no merit in favoring someone who lacks understanding. He also said he'd concern himself with Koko no more, though he's been helping him since he arrived. Our master thrust Banryu off, saying no one ever asked his help and no one ever would, knowing his motive.

"Banryu then accused our master of being selfish: 'I've been looking after Koko neither for my sake nor for his or yours, but only for Zen and Buddhism. I'll no longer worry about him, not even now during his prosecution.' And their meeting was broken off," related Genkaku with a mocking laugh.

"Why is Koko being prosecuted?"

"Our master hasn't told even me, but I can guess. It must concern some woman, considering Koko's nature. He did say he firmly believes Banryu pushed Koko into a corner to advance his adoption plot; so he wants you to leave as early as possible."

"There are some unclear points, Observances Head Genkaku. First, why would Banryu trick Koko if he was hoping to adopt him as his Dharma inheritor? It would disgrace his inheritor and inevitably smirch himself too. Second, is there some definite fault in Koko irrespective of whether it was a plot? What does our master think about that? And third, which concerns me, why didn't our master tell me directly?"

"You must present your suspicions to him," Gengaku hedged, wary of being involved.

Mokuzu felt a quiet resentment. 'To the master I'm powerless and crude, like a raw green pea. He believed I'd go to America gladly, and, finding Koko's sad plight, do my best for him. Stupid, cunning, covetous old man! Love of Koko is blinding him to the honor of all others. At the least he's slighting my personality. How horrible! His potbelly filled with hypertrophied digestive organs and blubber is supporting only his desire for fame and his blind love for immoral Koko! His objective authority, based on such things as his advancing age and his growing number of disciples, is hiding his shabby interior. I showed too much docility in front of this master and too much enthusiasm for absorbing traditional Zen. I made him overly confident I'll move as he wishes. It's a defect in me to have such a lack of potential to deter evil....'

As Mokuzu sat ruminating in his unlit room, Choho came to ask, "Manjusri Attendant, a sick monk is asking for light after lights–out. How should I answer?"

"What is his reason?"

"It's worthy of commiseration. He's been ailing since early September and has had no chance to meet the master. With New Year's Day approaching he wants to meet him to wish him well for the year, but his robe needs much repair, and being sick he can't mend it without extra time."

"Tell him we can't break the rule no matter what, but I promise I'll obtain a new robe for him before the end of the year."

સ

To welcome the New Year all the monks put on work clothes, tied towels about their heads, and diligently engaged in the semiannual total cleaning.

In the residential quarters, monks using straw–topped bamboo poles were brushing soot from the high ceiling and exposed roof trusses of the entrance. Others in pairs were lifting shojis from ill-fitting sills. In the sanctum, where the cleaning had finished, chanting officers were offering new flowers. In the kitchen, steamed glutinous rice would soon be pounded smooth and made into patties.

In and around the meditation hall and the Manjusri attendant's building, Choho and those assisting him were working like beavers, all merrily cleaning. Wide open and cleaned, Shoshinji appeared to have increased its spaciousness. Only the sickrooms remained unclean.

Mokuzu went to see the master in his quarters. He was resting with a touch of a cold but received Mokuzu on the condition that it be brief.

"Did you decide?"

"Not yet, in fact I came to clarify some opacity. I understood you are offering me study abroad based on your unalloyed care about my future. That seems untrue. Is it?" Mokuzu ventured, gathering his strength. The master regarded him without expression. Finally he urged, "Well?"

"Then it means you greatly imposed on me, taking advantage of my complete trust in you."

"There is no use talking nonsense if you place complete trust in me, is there?...Well then?"

Mokuzu knew the master would counterattack like an eagle after letting him expose all of what was on his mind. To parry that stratagem he imitated the master's experienced manner,

"Well then?"

"You fool! Can't you see I'm tired? Quickly spell out what you'd like to know!"

"Then evidently my request is, please tell me frankly why you want me to go to America." Mokuzu was controlling his rage.

"No one is forcing you to go, it is utterly up to you; didn't I say so? If you wish to study abroad, it can be done, and then you'll able to extend your leadership. Not knowing any English language and Western culture, I myself am limited to teaching those who are Japanese, which won't be enough for the coming age of internationalism. You already know basic English, and you have the ability to adapt to a new environment. While you are young, study hard. Hoard up more learning rather than just applying what you already have. This is my belief. I therefore am not wasting your time and energy on my election campaign, much as I know you'd be a useful hand."

"Master, I am sorry. I was harboring a suspicion that your only reason for sending me was to have me assist Senior Koko."

"You are free to entertain suspicion; yet it is silly to torture oneself with unfounded suspicion and create a bugbear. In Zen it is reasonable to muse that one is the center of the world. From your standpoint you are going to America for your sake alone through and through. But if viewed from Koko's, you are going for his sake to the end. Take a look at it from my standpoint and you are going for me. When each is purely thinking egocentrically with confidence, each is unflinchingly contributing his best to serve the Dharma in totality. Serving the Dharma through our individual life is true service. Where there is no individual life, there is no service beyond the empty theories of hypocrites."

Mokuzu was not fully satisfied, but fearing to be rude, he made no further inquiry. As he was returning through the garden between the meditation hall and the Manjusri attendant's building, Zokki with a broom on his shoulder emerged from the cedars above the monks' graveyard.

"Manjusri Attendant, where were you? I was looking for you. As you ordered, I cleaned the graveyard perfectly and gave incense to each tomb, but by now I bet it's finished burning."

Mokuzu was going to offer chanting before the monks' tombs. He took a handbell and descended with Zokki.

"A young lady named Miss Iwai came up to the graveyard in search of you while I was cleaning. She was entrusted with a bundle from Shogetsuan. I put it in your room."

"Thanks. Later you can give it to that sick monk who's eager to dress well for New Year's Day."

"Okay. You know, she was queer, in black slacks and black windbreaker and fluffy white turtleneck, moving between the tombstones as she talked, as if performing ballet positions. Her slacks so accentuated her heinie I was tempted to give it a swat, though of course I didn't because of where we were."

"You're the queer one," remarked Mokuzu with faint humor.

"No, really, she was. She kept asking about you, and when I said you're absorbed in painting she seriously expressed anger, came to a stop, and said, 'He cares only about himself, he sees only inner images, indeed he'd better be packed off to Koko.'"

When they reached the graveyard, Mokuzu straightaway began to chant. Zokki, having forgotten to dispose of the swept-up debris, quickly, before Mokuzu might notice it, whisked it over the cliff.

"Zokki," said Mokuzu after chanting.

"W-what?..."

"You're a talented thief. Tell me who besides the master can give me precise information on Koko."

"Well, surely that Miss Iwai can. Koko was boarding with an uncle of hers....He began an affair...with the uncle's daughter."

"Really? Would you run to Shogetsuan and fetch her. Bring her to my room, but don't be seen. I must know more before I decide on going to America."

"I'll be off posthaste! — she said she was soon leaving Shogetsuan to drive her uncle and the Zen master Banryu somewhere!" said Zokki, and he hared down through the thicket.

Back in his room, Mokuzu waited for Zokki's return. He could not paint well.

At last Zokki appeared.

"What trouble! — I had to wait till she was alone. She was fixing flowers with that Jerusalem artichoke nun. As soon as the nun left, I jumped from a bush and covered her mouth so she wouldn't shriek. Manjusri Attendant, her breasts are firm and rich unlike what you'd expect from her boyish looks. I'll not forget the tactile pleasure of my holy mission."

"Zokki, what did you tell her?"

"I said I came as your emissary...it took some time to remove a little misunderstanding, I mean, she was shocked, thinking I was sent by you to violate her, perhaps? I said you're waiting in your room for her clandestine visit and suggested the safest time would be after lights–out. Instantly she colored, out of shame, or joy? Anyway, without a word she pressed her hands to her bosom."

"Did you tell her why I want her to come?"

"Sure, I said why you want her — to learn about Koko's scandal in more detail so you can decide about studying in America, right? Of course I told her."

"Be clear. What was her response?"

"She paled, in fact turned cold as if her blood had curdled. Mutely she twisted a plum branch. I urged her to reply, sensing the nun's return, and I snatched an answer in the nick of time. She'll do her utmost on your behalf, and says to wait till she contacts you."

"Thanks for your sinuous labor. At New Year's I'll request your inclusion as a full training monk. I believe you can become an above-average priest as long as you keep up your antipathy to authoritarianism. And as long as you keep admiring shapely women, you'll enrich the species known as Zen monk."

❧

According to convention, Shoshinji's officer monks had to deliver to the neighboring temples and nunneries within the first three days of the New Year a charm paper of the Great Wisdom Sutra consecrated by prayer. However, Mokuzu left his share of the duty to Choho and Zokki and entered Miss Iwai's car awaiting him in concealment below the main gate.

Miss Iwai was arrayed in a showy kimono with a rabbit-fur stole to be suitable for New Year's, though the traditional clogs were awkward on the brake and accelerator pedals. Mokuzu was in his usual old training robe.

The road was wet with slush, and the fields were bright with snow receiving the warm sunlight.

"Koko needed me there! Imagine, in a strange land, unable to speak the language — he must have fallen into melancholy. I could have at least consoled him."

Mokuzu could not tell whether she was serious or making fun.

"Zen Master Tengai is sending you, but you can't console him. You'll outpace him and frustrate him all the more. You and the Zen master are alike, you don't understand human weakness."

"...."

"Mokuzu, you care exclusively about yourself. Your passion to study and train is to put things into your own order, only that. It's another form of lust for conquest. You aren't studying to bring out the best life of each thing. Your training is only to perfect yourself according to your definition of perfection. It scorns others who can find modest pleasure in their hard situations. Your attitude of seeking the ideal makes others who live in reality feel guilty. The ideal isn't gold, and reality isn't trash. Zen should be the teaching to see gold in reality and to activate reality, shouldn't it?...Why don't you say something? Tell me what you think."

"I don't oppose what you say, and also, I fear you'll shove me out of the car if I say anything uncongenial. Er..., anyway, I am grateful to you for your trouble."

"Nnnh, another typically perfect response! Koko and Zokki are more human. By now they'd be complaining of their monastic life and blowing hot breath on my nape. I'd prefer you to avail yourself of what I personally have to offer instead of using my connections — if you're going to use me at all. Why should I introduce you to my credulous uncle and that acrid Zen master? You should realize how your conduct insults me." Her stiffened cheek attested to her rage, so Mokuzu apologized,

"I am sorry to trouble you for my own matter. I ought to be able to decide on going to America regardless of Koko. And I'm sure I'll leave the monastery anyway. But I wanted to ascertain that going to America is right for my future."

"Are you leaving the monastery, leaving Zen Master Tengai? *Corruptio optimi pessima!*"

"*Sequiturque patrem non passibus aequis.*"

At the ferry landing of Imawatari, Iwai introduced Mokuzu to her uncle and the Zen master Banryu and drove away to no one knew where. Her uncle and Zen Master Banryu had only a few days left of their stay in Japan, but they entertained Mokuzu's request for information and invited him to dinner on a houseboat.

The interior was heated. Dishes were already spread on a low table, and sake was warming on a hibachi. They opened the shojis. The boat headed down the Hida River, which merged with the Kiso to form a grand expanse. From the gunwales it was possible to extend a hand and scoop at the muddy waves.

Before long the river ran narrow and the current was sucked into a gorge carved through late Paleozoic strata. The leaf-like boat made its way like a remote-controlled arrow between bluffs, barely escaping collision with rocks of fantastic shape and hidden reefs thanks solely to the two boatmen who employed bamboo poles fore and aft. The gorge no doubt always had unstable weather. The sky looked threatening, the peaks were often obscured, and a quick slanting snow seemed intent on increasing the volume of the water.

Shooting the rapids, Mokuzu was told, would take an hour and a half for about seven or eight miles through a variety of bends, levels, and widths. At the terminus, a four-storied castle once belonging to the principal retainer Naruse of the daimyo Owari soared to the sky, commanding a full view of the Bishu plain. The rapids were called the Japan Rhine after being compared to the German Rhine by Shiga Shigetaka, a Taisho-era geologist.

Iwai's uncle was an elderly, refined-featured gentleman. He was bald except for white sidelocks and wore silver-rimmed glasses. Politely and re-peatedly he supplied sake to Zen Master Banryu's and Mokuzu's cups. Banryu appeared to be of pervasive strong will. He was sable-faced, with odd eyebrows thick at the inner ends. His nose too was odd, crushed out of shape. But oddest, though it was his pride, was his mouth, so large it could receive his bulky fist. Mokuzu on seeing his demonstration suspected his level of civilization.

"I was told Koko is Zen Master Tengai's highest disciple and I placed absolute trust in him. But he grew intimate with my daughter within the first month of his arrival, which I learned only after the summer," confessed Iwai's uncle timorously and shamefacedly to Mokuzu's inquiry. Banryu, who had been liberally drinking, briskly took over with gestures that waved the long sleeves of his black robe,

"Were he in Japan having an affair with a guardian's daughter, that alone would bar him from society. A snake warmed in a guardian's bosom he was! Daughter, yes, but herself a married woman with a five-year-old daughter. Her husband is a dedicated bank clerk. Being a practical, steady American, he wouldn't have made much of it were it merely an affair between man and woman. But Koko's target was money. When she came to her senses most of her savings and precious jewelry given her by her husband were gone, and Koko had begun taking from him too. Naturally he sued Koko for fraud. It is the proven substance of the scandal. It is a disgrace to all Japanese, not to mention the Buddhist priesthood!"

"Zen Master Banryu, why did Koko want money?" asked Mokuzu.

"To indulge in dissipation and neither for his study nor for charity. In America there are women from all over the world. I guess he hoped to obtain a taste of each as if to study a variety of koans—the evil result of Tengai's diffi- cile rigidity about meat and matrimony in addition to his systematic shallow teaching of the koans. Forgive me for talking ill of your master, but he is an inferior Zen master, much as he could be an excellent politician or stockjobber."

"Being one of his disciples, I can judge him without help. No Zen master can be perfect. Zen Master Tengai's strengths well outweigh his weaknesses, I believe. Apart from that, Zen Master Banryu, can you refute his belief that you enticed Koko into immoral ways because of your supreme wish to secure a successor?" Pressed by the little time allowed him, Mokuzu was direct.

"What you've just asked is so absurd as to be unworthy of polemic. But it shows one of his mysterious talents, which is to make himself believe a crow is white if it's to his advantage. The stronger his belief, the fainter his sense of guilt, and he can make a multitude believe what he has made himself believe — an indispensable talent for the head of a religious sect, yes, but irrelevant for a righteous Zen master. Sorry to speak ill of him again." Banryu patted himself on the head, laughed, and gulped more sake. Mokuzu figured he was an honest man, if unrefined.

"Allow me to speak for the honor of Zen Master Banryu," said the uncle. "The first time he met Koko was after my son-in-law took the matter to the police. Only because I went up to San Diego in October to consult with him about it did he become involved. He was busy teaching white people, mostly fishermen; but as he has said, there was the worry of shame on all Japanese if the scandal went to court. No longer was it only Koko's personal affair, nor my daughter's and her husband's."

"But Zen Master Banryu, aren't you concerned to find a successor to continue with the laymen you cultivated?"

"Yes, it is a fact. I know my health, and when I think of my responsibility to those laymen I can't sleep well. They are my children. What will they do with their heavy load of questions and no answer yet found? Besides, it will be a sad lot if I can't bequeath all the Dharma I was given by my teacher."

"Your solicitude and resolve puzzle me. Why do you want Koko for your dear laymen? How can you trust him now?"

"There's no one else. No matter how stupid he is, he's better than those who are ignorant; after all, he mastered the traditional koans. With a little reeducation from me, he can become a good Zen master...or, Mokuzu, would you become my successor?"

"You place so much value on their traditional interpretation—no wonder anybody can become your successor if only he's studied the koans! In a sense it's a reasonable conviction, since the ordinary course of koan mastery takes twenty long years..." 'without learning anything else of importance, you stupid Zen master!' Mokuzu spoke freely, but stopped short of this last. Then, to camouflage his dissent, he hastily smoothed over what he had spoken,

"It proves you are an authentic and not only a kind and decent Zen master. I am grateful for your generosity in providing me the chance to clarify each of my groundless suspicions. Meeting a Zen master unlike mine enriches me and gives me another summit to scale."

Relieved from the strained, uncomfortable talk, Mokuzu realized he was weary. He wished the boat would quickly reach the bank. The river had widened and become sluggish. Banryu ravenously ate what was left on the plates. After more sake he said, chin in hand as he leaned an elbow on the table,

"Inasmuch as you too are one of Tengai's high disciples, you ought to make a study of how he took over Shoshinji."

"He is the Dharma heir of Zen Master Shutan."

"No, that's inaccurate. Shutan when invited to take charge of Shoshinji was followed by his attendant Tengai. Within a few years Shutan died and his highest disciple, Ishin, was invited to succeed him. Ishin, staying in a subtemple in Daitokuji, was obviously the only certified Dharma heir, and he was quite senior to Tengai. But by then Tengai dominated all the monks. So when Ishin arrived, conflict rose between them, and none of his intentions, orders, or instructions reached the monks without going through Tengai, who was now observances head. Tengai thus controlled both the new master and all the monks as he wished.

"Imagine yourself in Ishin's place, Mokuzu, and you'll appreciate his frustration. By that alone his life was shortened. I know the situation well through my Zen master, Kaiban. He and Ishin were close because Kaiban's teacher was Tokai, Shutan's Dharma brother.

"Well then, Tengai as observances head incited the monks to quit mountain work and even to quit one of the week-long exclusive meditation periods. He also enticed an attendant to mix sand in Zen Master Ishin's rice and heavily salt his soup...all to force Ishin to certify him as his Dharma inheritor. I'm not creating this story, nor exaggerating. I have some letters in which Ishin complained to Kaiban. I can produce them if you wish, and even if you don't, I'll send copies to your master for congratulations if he's elected abbot." Zen Master Banryu laughed, and exposed a shin and vigorously scratched it.

Mokuzu was growing nauseated by the sake, the heat, and the roll of the boat. Again he opened a shoji. Inuyama Castle atop the river terrace and against a chilly blue sky was so near as to make him feel extracted from the sediment.

Iwai's uncle and Zen Master Banryu planned to call on the descendant of the lord of the castle. Iwai in her car was duly awaiting Mokuzu.

"How was the meal? Could you get what you wanted?"

"Yes, more than enough, thanks to you."

"You know, you confided to me that you might leave the monastery. It sickens me. I'd sure like to know why. What's wrong with you? Is there anything I can do? — er — Mokuzu, we never really talked. We put on a bold front with each other — needlessly. Mokuzu, in December I decided to live away from my parents. My apartment isn't far from here. Won't you come in for tea or coffee?" trolled Iwai at the wheel.

"I'm sorry, I have duties, especially there are sick monks...cleaner than the healthy ones."

"...! You and I are the same age, and yet you don't know how to go through life's whirlpools. Just wait and see what'll happen if you oppose Zen Master Tengai. Why can't you use the good points of him and of others?"

"It's a waste of time to worry over human relations when there isn't mutual love, trust, and respect."

"Ha ha! Mokuzu, I know an interesting poem by Yosano Akiko. Listen —

> "Are you not lonesome, you preacher of the Way,
> touching no fair soft skin,
> knowing no hot blood within?"

"It calls to mind another of her poems," said Mokuzu, and he recited it,

> "Dreams should be dreamed by two.
> Yet as if there were two have I alone
> learned to dream."[8]

805

58

The Sound of the Bronze Wind-Bells

Zen interviews were held as usual on the morning of the day to decide to leave or to stay on in the monastery. Mokuzu knew this interview was his last. The wind whishing through the pines on the back mountain penetrated the dark corridor and rattled the shojis. The moon and stars were obscured not yet by daybreak but by a thin overcast of clouds.

Though it was his last interview, his koan was the first koan from *Shyutang's Hundred Koans*:

> One day, seeing Manjusri outside the gate, Sakyamuni Buddha said, "Manjusri, won't you come in?" "I see no Dharma out here; how can you ask me in?" said Manjusri.[1]

Taking Manjusri's role, Shyutang replied, "There are many who respect me," and his reply became an index to understanding this koan in the orthodox way. Zen Master Tengai without entering into Mokuzu's feelings asked as he asked at any other time,

"Manjusri said he saw no Dharma outside the gate. Isn't that incongruous? Tell me why."

"Yes. Here Dharma means Truth, which according to Zen understanding is omnipresent, expressed in case two of *Biyan lu* as 'everything is the Way and is naught but the Truth.'[2] Indeed everything that can be an object of our consciousness is the Truth and is evidence of Buddha nature. From this Zen view, the Dharma is everywhere, whether inside or outside the gate," replied Mokuzu apathetically.

"Apart from the Zen view, what is your view?" Zen Master Tengai demanded without show of emotion.

"Master, when I see myself as the center of the world and all matters and events as the evolution of my mind, I recognize the world as the present-perfect-progressive form of the Dharma. There is no doubt in the saying that all rivers, mountains, grasses, and trees have been attaining Buddhahood. So I believe that the teaching 'All sentient beings have Buddha nature,' advocated in volume seven of the Nirvana Sutra, shouldn't be taken to mean merely that all sentient beings have the potential to attain Buddhahood. Rather, each is an existence, and each existence, as it is, is functioning as evidence of Buddha nature.

"I therefore view all objects of my consciousness in an absolute and affirmative way, and thus is my subjecthood established. However, flesh and

806

spirit are heir to many ills, so I realize how hard it is to maintain my subject-hood. As soon as I'm off my guard, my subjecthood is swept away by the winds of phenomena and I become a speck of dust.

"I sympathize with the priest Rueiyan, who daily addressed himself as recorded in the twelfth case of *Wumen guan*:

"'Hey, Master. Yes? Be careful! Yes. Never be deceived by anyone! Yes, yes.'[3]

"Rueiyan did not neglect the task of continuing to confirm reality, wherein the Dharma is brimful and each thing is luminous in its function as Buddha nature. For me too, Zen training for the sake of self-cultivation means to continue tirelessly and perseveringly the task of confirming. Zen training is to exert oneself to gain unshakable stability while putting oneself in a flood; or to gain a noncombustible life while putting oneself in the fire of an ending world."

Mokuzu was expressing one of the highest realizations he had attained during his Shoshinji life. Indeed he was going to assign himself the task of confirming. It was a training life to be carried out alone for his own benefit, and no one would be able to help him. He was after all alone when delivered into this world, and would be alone when facing his death. To establish his subjectivity was nothing other than to confront the world by himself.

Even so, what he expressed received no appraisal. Zen Master Tengai averted his gaze with disinterest and issued another question,

"Yet Manjusri said he saw no Dharma outside the gate. What was his intention, eh?"

Mokuzu regarded Manjusri in this fictitious koan as a disagreeable figure assuming the role of devoted missionary. Still he repressed his feeling and replied soberly,

"Manjusri's use of the word Dharma here meant Buddha's teaching, and he regretted that the proper understanding of the Dharma, the understanding I just explained to you, was not spread among the people. True, when there's no proper understanding of the Dharma, people are unable to see any beings, including themselves, as anything but meaningless passing phases of birth and death. They don't perceive Buddha nature in anything, and sigh and cry away their days and harm one another without any significant reason. Unable to see Buddha nature, they are unable to establish their subjectivity, and it is a pity that they must waste their short lives. To establish subjectivity is the greatest challenge a man can give himself. Yet whoever doesn't make himself aware of Buddha nature neglects this greatest challenge and busies himself with anything as long as it's of no vital importance.

"Naturally, though it was his meddling, Manjusri raised his compassion to educate the ignorant by spreading Buddha's teaching. His sorrow was to see those outside Sakyamuni Buddha's benevolent influence, and he said to Sakyamuni Buddha, 'How can I desert the reprobate and take my enjoyment? Let me stay outside the gate until I can save every last one.'"

"Hmph! As usual you lecture as if for a course on Chinese literature. Remember you are neither student nor scholar but a Zen monk whose sole merit is in his actions. Put yourself in Manjusri's state and let me hear what you'll do to assist Sakyamuni Buddha and spread his teaching." Zen Master Tengai kept his condescending approach, eager though he was to hear Mokuzu's determination. Mokuzu said quietly,

"I know I will practice by myself alone outside the gate what I believe, but — "

"Don't take it easy, little negativist!" interrupted the master impatiently. Mokuzu fell silent and thought of what he had wanted to say: 'Certainly I will practice my own, and not for the purpose of propagating Buddha's teaching and also not out of obedience to Buddha. It will be fortuitous for Buddha if my training life produces good results for the spread of his teaching, but it should be clearly understood that I am not to be complimented for such a thing. And even if my training life happens to coincide in part with his teaching, it is not due to his teaching but utterly to the nature of the Dharma, just as the real Sakyamuni Buddha fairly stated.'

Zen Master Tengai, growing more impatient, clenched his fists at the ends of his warning stick and, clearing his throat, loudly chided,

"Don't you see Manjusri's impressive resolve to sacrifice his training in order to devote his life to spreading Buddha's teaching? Can't you gratefully acknowledge his contribution, and don't you wish to inherit his honorable task? A moment's thought will make any Buddhist monk understand that Buddhism has prospered because of hundreds and thousands of Manjusris, including Buddha's ten great disciples, five hundred arhats, kings, ministers, millionaires, and so on. However great a sage he was, Sakyamuni could not perfect Buddhism by his power alone, and therefore the greatness of Buddhism is owing not only to him but to the aid of all those assistants. Any monk who does not realize the importance of assisting is a parasite on Buddhism, not only an ingrate. Linji strengthened the foundation of his education at Jenjou by the aid of Puhua, whose Zen power well matched his own. Hakuin restored Japanese Zen by the aid of Torei. Now Mokuzu — you: Do not hesitate! Tell me your resolve toward assisting Buddhism in concrete terms." Awaiting Mokuzu's reply, the master hardened his face like a toad.

He was demanding that Mokuzu put himself in Manjusri's stead, and it followed that he was taking the role of Sakyamuni Buddha. On another occasion Mokuzu might have laughed, declaring he was not Manjusri, nor his master by any means Sakyamuni — absurd! But now he was only sad to realize the master did not sense even his decision to leave the monastery. 'There are no flowers to ease my eyes in the dusk of wintry dawn.'

Further, the master was obviously expecting him to go abroad to help Koko, forcing him to put a theoretical understanding of the koan into muddy practice. 'It's no longer pure study of the Dharma but a crude test of allegiance!' In addition to his sadness, Mokuzu felt his hackles rising. Were he to deliver his honest thought, he knew the relationship of master and disciple would explode. They were confronting each other not like Sakyamuni Buddha and Manjusri at all, but more like a dragon spitting flames against storm clouds and a tiger surmounting a rock in a flood, positioned to fight.

"What's the matter with you, eh? How can you cook even a wedge of potato if you indulge in vain speculation? Tell me how you will assist Buddhism, Shoshinji, your Zen master, and your senior monk — or can't you hear when people cry for help?" the master insisted.

Mokuzu felt Ena's sad eyes were seeing his plight. He did not want to augment her sadness by fighting. Quietly he stood up and said,

"Master, please give an ear to the bronze wind-bells at the eaves of the main building, invisible in the dark, but audible. I will be led by their sound."

"What?"

Mokuzu bowed deep with palms joined and departed the room.

"Wait, wait! I haven't heard your reply about studying abroad!"

Mokuzu ignored the master's calls. He sat still as a statue in his room in the Manjusri attendant's building. At the first gray of dawn a pheasant cried, and as if acting in concert, the direct monk in the meditation hall clapped the clappers and rang the handbell, initiating meditation hour.

Zokki stole into Mokuzu's room and said in an undertone,

"Here's the glue and cardboard you wanted me to find. What are you going to make?"

"Thanks. Merely a little amusement." Mokuzu took out his surplice, ripped it up, and began to affix it to the cardboard.

"Good golly, Manjusri Attendant, don't you fear divine punishment for vandalizing the holy surplice?" Worried, Zokki pointed a finger at Mokuzu.

"Ha ha, Zokki, the sound of ripping cloth reminds you of your guilt, not your maternal love? If you preserve such a bygone sensibility, you'll surely become a good priest under your Zen master. Please check on the sick monks."

Mokuzu was making a cover for the hundred koans he had selected and illustrated. Each picture was already mounted on another paper. Across the opening folio he had drawn a bird's-eye-view of Shoshinji in spring.

Before lunch Choho informed him that the master was awaiting him. Having yet to finish assembling the album, he asked Choho to deliver the message "I am detained by an important duty in the Manjusri attendant's building."

After lunch Choho came again, and apologizing for disturbing him he said,

"You have an inopportune visitor. He seems to have come a great distance. Impertinently he drove into the main garden and bid his chauffeur wait with engine running."

"Let him wait awhile, and ask him to be quiet." How Mokuzu wished his last day in the monastery to be clean, reflective, and most of all, undisturbed; but it was as hard as to see an indigo flower in the dark.

He sighed, and wrote on the back of the album:

"Prohibited to be removed from the sickrooms."

Inside the back cover he wrote, by translating to Chinese and employing a Chinese stanza form, lines from Shelley's "To a Skylark":

> We look before and after,
>   And pine for what is not:
> Our sincerest laughter
>   With some pain is fraught;
> Our sweetest songs are those that tell of saddest thought.[4]

He then handed the album to Choho and had him enter it in the list of fixtures for use exclusively in the sickrooms.

He was ready to leave the monastery, but there was still the unexpected visitor. He sighted a bulky man from the back, hands deep in the pockets of a dark overcoat, looking down at the main garden from the base of the stone steps of the roofed corridor to the meditation hall. Cigarette smoke swayed about his square shoulders. As Mokuzu approached, he turned his head, beamed a smile, and raised a hand, saying in a thick voice,

"Yo! Mokuzu! Amazing you can live in this sediment! Are you okay?"

"Reiho!" Memory of their infant days danced in Mokuzu's head, but his kindly feeling turned to wariness toward the man he had not forgiven for driving Luri to her death. With no betrayal of emotion he said,

"You seem little changed. What do you want of me?"

Actually Reiho had grown plump, and his thick, dark-red cheeks made his eyes appear narrower. His coarse hair peppered with white hairs suggested an unprincipled life with much alcohol and constant irritation. His clothes were evidently costly but ineffective to express virtue and nobility. He dropped his cigarette on the clean step and heeled it with his polished black shoe. Disregarding the carrying power of a normal voice within the quiet monastery, he enunciated his words with loathing,

"Wow, it's queer here! Just more Unkai — reptile in hell. What are they doing only sitting docile in line? Waiting to make confessions at this hour of the day?"

He must have been questioning the sight of the monks on the veranda awaiting interviews with the three top officers. Mokuzu did not reply. Finding it unbearable to continue to see a man so out of place, he asked him into his room.

He offered him a cup of daily tea and exposed for him the red charcoal in the brazier, though Reiho did not remove his coat. His hands spread before the heat showed traces of the karate for which he had once been zealous; yet they had become used to an easier life and showed no fresh color and vigor compared to Mokuzu's.

"How many more years do you plan to stay on here, without wearing even socks?"

"Not long."

"Great. It's time you too played an active role in society." Reiho took out a cigar and lit it with a golden lighter. Immediately a voluminous smoke rose to the low ceiling and hung there with no exit. He slurped the tea, then said with a simper,

"You sit dignified so I feel put off...well, maybe it's reasonable as your work isn't to treat the living...eh, the fact is, I've come to ask you to build a new temple. Of course I'll handle the money end. I'm asking only that you be head priest."

"The request is quite incongruous. There are too many temples, including Ryotanji. Or is atonement your concern?" Mokuzu maintained his coolness and brought out his painting of Luri. Shown the woman bathing in a hot spring in a snowy forest, Reiho grimaced as if seeing a horrid scene. But like an old man adept in the ways of the world, he soon said,

"She too was a pitiful lady. We're most defective when we love only one person. Love's like a haze over the eyes, it hides a clear view of the world and worst, makes us hallucinate so we see all but that one person as false, worthless, and squalid. Though you mention atonement, I declare I'm innocent of any sin. I beat only guys who are already doing wrong — those stupid sinners who invent wrongdoings. I learn their craft and return it, but with a little more craft. It's reasonable that the harder they hit, the harder I hit back."

"Reiho, originality is esteemed in the field of enriching humanity. It doesn't follow that originality in performing wrongdoing pardons wrongdoing. Your atrocities are archaic, uninventive; yet, newly budded lives are the hapless victims of your stupidity. You abused Luri when you should have adored and respected her as your senior sister, and you cornered her and sent her to her death. It can never be forgiven." Mokuzu was boiling within as he spoke.

He tightened his abdomen. But Reiho had no will to fight.

"Mokuzu, I see why you want to anger, but don't exaggerate, at least don't blame me for what I didn't do. Okay, so I was hard on her, but it was because, like I said, she loved you too much to regard anyone else. She thought meanly of everyone, including me, and made an exception of you. In the first place she was the one who started the business, taking the Zen master's fund. It was for your benefit only, after all."

"You too are liable for embezzlement."

"Yeah, but I believed she and I were doing it for ourselves. The fact is she dreamed of living with you and of helping your higher education. And think, please, what the fund was for. Ostensibly for a Kannon statue, for world peace — and he did care about that. But he had his parental heart toward me and was planning to hand me Ryotanji along with the Kannon for Peace — for my future economy, see? If you can follow that far, you can realize how evil she was. She took advantage of my frivolity and made me ruin by my own hand Zen Master Hanun's parental affection for me — and she did it splendidly!"

Mokuzu could understand Zen Master Hanun's steadfast parental love, just as Zen Master Tengai's for Koko was understandable. Blind love for one individual drove both masters to use Zen to the utmost. Used in that way, Zen was no longer a love to liberate the common people, but a means and weapon to attack, oppress, and bind. 'Zen, like atomic fire, is too good for ignorant men; and that pertains to other religions as well.'

Thinking he was making headway in getting Mokuzu to understand his lot, Reiho continued with less tension,

"Before long I realized what a great disservice she did me, and I justly tortured her in return. That was all. But it caused her to slip back to Ryotanji. I didn't follow her, I let her do as she liked. This is important — you've gotta believe it. You may blame me for causing her to escape there, though I had a justifiable reason. But don't blame me for anything else. I didn't corner her and force her to her end. She took care of me when I was young — my hate was mixed with thanks." Reiho wiped the froth from his mouth with the back of his hand.

"You say you didn't force her to her end. You tortured her. But she escaped. So you happened not to kill her. Then tell me who is responsible."

"Unkai."

"What?" Mokuzu reduced the force of his accusation. After some silence he said in a dispirited voice,

812

"Unkai was too mild to be rough with her."

Reiho, his composure restored, explained with some sympathy,

"Remember how creepy he was, meditating whenever he had time, possibly just like your monks here. I guess men commit evil when they act, and imagine it when they don't. Simple guys like me can do only physical harm. Perverse prigs like him can gnaw at another's heart. On the veranda of Ryotanji soon after her death, he made me hear his confession, which turned into a crying fit. Confession or penitence is queerer behavior than meditation. Maybe it's the queerest mentality. Unkai was in ecstasy while confessing! Ha, what do you think of that?" Reiho raised his hands, wide apart, but Mokuzu sat sternly, with eyes shut and arms folded.

"Listen, she dreamed of living with you after fleeing to Ryotanji too. Unkai admonished her for being polluted and said she'd disturb your training if she went to see you. He poured on her all the sermons he could muster, as if compensating for his twenty years' silence. And he concluded she'd better purify herself by chanting and meditating with him in Ryotanji for the next twenty years, and together with him wish for you to complete your training. Idiot priests always speak like that, laudable on the surface, but useless, and their motive is just to gain time."

"Where is Unkai's fault? His fault, if I call it that, was only his shallow understanding of what he spoke. We shouldn't overly blame him for his bad timing and inept expression if his intention was good." Mokuzu felt his anger return.

"Mokuzu, you were a smart kid, you must've already figured out his sin. But if you like, I can spell it out. Luri took his advice and began to chant and meditate, even began to douse with cold water like you. Unkai didn't, but he confessed he watched. Wow, my spine was chilled, so eerie, and yet so ridiculous! I don't want to invite your misunderstanding, so I'll repeat his words: 'In due course she recovered from her emaciation, and her figure as she wholeheartedly prayed for divine protection was as awesome as a well-honed blade. I trembled at the sight of her.'

"Phew, it was nothing but his tiny pecker awakening. Yet he went on chanting with her before the Buddha image morning and night in addition to their meditating on the veranda.

"Then by and by he strained his unleashed wits to get her. According to him he mixed the right to the first night practiced by priests in old Venezuela or Cambodia with the tradition concerning a girl named Naga who achieved Buddhahood, according to, er...some sutra...in short, he advised her to sleep with him to purge her past. So she was put in a quandary: if she left Ryotanji she thought she'd be nabbed by the yakuza working under me, though there was no such fact of any yakuza, and if she stayed on she thought she'd fall into Unkai's pallid hands. Ha! Where could she go when rejected by temple and world alike?"

"Reiho, you've talked enough. You wanted to say that you, a fierce wolf, only inflicted a wound while Unkai, a vulture, picked at her. Your story is unbelievable. Even if I believe it, you can't reduce the gravity of your sin." Mokuzu suddenly thrust at Reiho one of the hot metal chopsticks used to maneuver the coals. Reiho blanched. Quietly Mokuzu stuck it back in the ash.

"By the way, what happened to Luri's baby?"

Wiping his brow, Reiho replied with a humble smile,

"I took her to an orphanage in Kyoto before Luri stole back to Ryotanji. It's a good environment, behind a TB sanatorium, with a wide camellia garden between. I donated a hefty sum...I too was orphaned."

"Excuse me, Manjusri Attendant, your interview with the top officers is very soon. Besides, the master sent an attendant to call you a second time."

"Zokki, as you see, I have a visitor. Can't you give them some excuse for me?" Mokuzu's voice showed his weariness.

"I already did."

"Then why don't you do something besides eavesdropping? Wait. Shall we make a fire atop the mountain tonight? It'll snow again. Prepare whatever you think necessary," Mokuzu requested warmly. He knew he would not stay on to evening in the monastery, but he did not wish it known even by Zokki.

Reiho hoped to resolve the gap between himself and Mokuzu, and, lighting a cigarette, he too said in a quieter tone,

"Aren't you going to ask about Zen Master Hanun? To me he's a father, you know. He's steadily weakened ever since. Unkai looks after him, but these days he has no appetite."

"Reiho, there may be a spring afternoon to rest on a sunny hill and talk of our common past beyond love and hate. Now's not the time. Quickly relate the purpose of your call and relieve me of my hospitality." Mokuzu was smiling, but his heart was cold. Reiho answered to the smile. With some confidence in his ability to persuade, he said with a smile,

"What you made me speak of isn't the issue. What's important is the new model temple. It doesn't look so new to build a Kannon for Peace and to make a bunch of schools teach so-called Japanese culture — judo, karate, tea ceremony, flower arrangement, koto, and all. But it's to perfect his wish, and I'll spare my words on this point because you must know how it's important. What's new about this temple is its inner task, which will also be the means to maintain its economy.

"You know the filtration plant at Keage? That's where I got my idea. It purifies water. Our new temple will purify money. I bet you don't know a thing about dirty money. Let me explain.

"First you have to know there is a lot of dirty money in circulation, money that tax officers haven't pinned down the real source of. Second, this dirty money is powerful and valuable money. It's like a real gun compared to ordinary money, which is like a toy gun. Think of buying votes, or bribing officials, or contracting for murder..."

"I see, Reiho. Don't go on. I wish we had a little more of a mutual interest, but in reality we are too different." Mokuzu spoke decisively. Opening the shoji, he summoned Choho to instruct him to see Reiho to his car.

Reiho put on his black leather shoes and said without looking at Mokuzu,

"Well, for the sake of fraternity I'll leave. Someday you'll come to realize the importance of money. Oops, I almost forgot...you must know a guy called Yosetsu from your native area. He's working under my control. He's afraid to meet you. Can you guess why? He told me you had a childhood friend, eh... Ena? He made a fortune after the landslide that killed the family. See? He has reason to fear you because he's the one holding the property in escrow. Just say the word: I can deal with him any way you want."

"Reiho, I don't care about anything to do with either of you. Tell him I never bore him hatred because I never took him into account, and it will be the same for you from now on." So saying, Mokuzu closed the shoji. He was tired and sad. He regretted that he had to spend his last day in unclean irritation. Those of Reiho's words relating to Luri remained ringing in his head: "Where could she go when rejected by temple and world alike?"

Sitting at length quiet in his room, Mokuzu collected himself. Then he went to the Dragon Fountain with a towel and his wastebasket. A strong snowy west wind carried the sound of the bronze wind-bells. There he burnt the paper scraps and his painting of Luri. Not a trace of him was left in his room.

He took a final bath, staying in the spring until the unbearable pain of the cold replaced the images of Ena and Luri.

෨

The reception head, the observances head, and the fiscal head, assisted by the direct monk, were waiting to receive Mokuzu in the high-floored officers' room in the main building. The room had a brazier, but drafts incessantly shook the fusumas. The direct monk, looking gloomy with dark cheeks even after shaving, made a solitary comment,

"We are waiting only for him; what is he thinking?"

"Does he by some remote chance not consider us respectable seniors?" quietly suggested the reception head, who was fairly handsome, aside from an unfortunate birthmark on his cheekbone.

Fiscal Head Kaijo, who had been direct monk when Mokuzu was a new-comer, took the register of all monks from the reception head's desk. "You so tentatively speak the obvious," he said and poured tea into his cup only.

The direct monk extended a cup as he said, "He is quite possibly not trusting even our Zen master."

"That couldn't be!" returned the reception head, though he expected it could well be, and he filled the direct monk's cup, which the fiscal head had ignored.

"Oi! Direct Monk! Go find Mokuzu right away!" Kaijo commanded. "How can you be so easy, drinking cup after cup like me? Stupid!"

The direct monk bounded to the veranda. Ducking against the driving snow, he muttered, "It's so cold even my balls will freeze! How vexing — he always looks down on me and high-handedly orders me about!" He hastened to the Manjusri attendant's building and called from outside, "Hoy! Manjusri Attendant!"

'Hnn? Absent? Sleeping? Impossible. I've never seen him sleep during the day, unlike Kaijo.' He went around the building, calling Choho. In one of the sickrooms Choho was reclining by a sick monk, sharing a look at Mokuzu's illustrated koan album. Quickly Choho tucked it under the quilt.

"Hey, Choho, where's the Manjusri attendant?"

"He must be at his interview with the top officers."

"You ass! I'm one of them and I'm looking for him."

"Oh, yes. How strange...well, then he's with the master, because he was summoned. Please wait, I'll go check," said Choho, and he left.

"You malingering sick monk, show me that!" Leaning in from the veranda, the direct monk unkindly extracted the album, riffled through its pages, and commented,

"Hm! You've been given a charming picture book to ease your life of struggle against infirmity." His tone scorned the monk as well as the book, while with his long sleeve he protected it from the slanting snow.

"Direct Monk, the album may be seen only by sick monks. The Manjusri attendant left it to us as a keepsake," protested the monk, straining to speak in his husky voice.

"What did you say? A keepsake? You mean he's departed the monastery? Did he tell you?"

"I wasn't told. But I've been sick a long time, so it's as easy to figure as to read my palm."

The direct monk doubled back to the main building. Soon after, he reappeared with the reception head in the garden between the meditation hall and the Manjusri attendant's building. Together they entered Mokuzu's room.

"Surely he's left," said the direct monk.

"Perfect fact and perfect faith exclude all doubt. There's nary a speck of dust in here. He's a bird that took wing without stirring the water," added the reception head.

"Tut! Don't wax eloquent when you should keep mute, nor be impressed when you should be dismayed," said the direct monk bitterly. The fiscal head approached, and, lingering in the garden to examine the plum buds, he commented,

"They're fairly late this year, maybe as much as ten days..." and he checked more branches and scraped off some insect scales as if it were his most pressing concern.

"Fiscal Head, plum buds are unimportant at this juncture. What are we to do?" asked the direct monk in perplexity, accompanied by the reception head, who assumed an air of perplexity as at the same time he showed concern for the buds.

"Nothing can be done if he's left. For him here was merely a flyway. Some migratory birds go south, others north, and you'll remain to rot like a spile," replied Kaijo in a doleful tone.

"True. I shall hasten to fill his vacancy." The reception head spoke with tact to avoid the unpleasant order sure to come from the fiscal head.

Choho returned with the observances head, Genkaku, who was out of breath from having climbed the steps with his barrel belly.

"Well, I expected as much. I only regret he left in this cold instead of waiting for the warm days with the singing of bush warblers. Oh, now who could that be? It's Zokki. Fetch him, he must know everything." Genkaku glimpsed a figure laboring up the cliff dense with bamboo and shade trees close below the meditation hall, a trackless route used exclusively by Zokki.

The direct monk and the reception head ran to the cliff. Zokki tried to flee but found retreat harder than advance. The direct monk collared him and hoicked him up. Not yet formally counted as a trainee, he wore his usual work clothes. He was straining to keep the jacket shut by crossing his arms, and he kept at it even as he was dragged through the garden.

Brought to the center of everyone's focus, he sat on the earth with a feeble smile, still protecting something in his bosom. With a queer laugh he exclaimed, intending a compliment, then an excuse,

"Goodness gracious! All you high monks are gathered to welcome me? With due respect let me say I'm not engaged in anything to offend you. I believe you'll be downright pleased, he he he!"

Genkaku knelt, laid a hand on his shoulder, and said,

817

"See here, Mokuzu has left this mountain, and we think you may know the particulars."

"What? Left? He hornswoggled me! I knew it! What nonsense that a born thief should be outdone by a naturally honest man!" As he beat his brow, something dashed from his bosom. Taken by surprise, the reception head, who was squatting, fell over. The direct monk, also squatting, ducked and raised an elbow, but he received a foamy whitish green deposit of solid mixed with liquid ordure on his head.

"Wait, wait!" Welsh onions, carrots, and eggs scattered behind Zokki as he chased a pinioned brown broiler hen. It kicked free of the simple straw binding and ran about the garden and the stone pavement flanking the meditation hall, then jumped and broke through a shoji. One or two exclamations rose at once from within, where monks were greedily sleeping in sitting posture with their heads covered by the long sleeves of their robes, it being a day of no warning stick.

The direct monk made for the lavatory to clean up. The reception head followed for a few steps, then, realizing he had no reason to accompany him, returned rubbing his hands and soliloquizing,

"An unheard-of calamity!" Then, seeing Genkaku laughing with reddened, teary eyes, he too allowed himself a laugh.

But Kaijo, who was upholding his dignity, shouted with many exaggerated fricatives,

"Direct Monk! What's this? Your monks are utterly demoralized in training spirit. During the season I was direct monk no monk indulged in indolence even on a day of no warning stick. Reception Head! You too, what's the use of your bearing witness to a mere worldly incident? Quickly return to the residential quarters and check what each monk is doing at this very moment. Don't spare the stick! Value their brief time and beat them whether they're dawdling or diligent!"

Genkaku and Kaijo exchanged looks, and, grinning, returned to the residential quarters.

"So Mokuzu left without telling even Zokki. He hadn't a soul in whose company he could relax his guard. Our Zen master knows how to struggle and not how to be at peace. Naturally he can't mature any talented monks. He's a master only from whose bad example a talented monk can learn." Genkaku was cheerless.

"Indeed. Too bad those who stay on here are like us, whose talent is measurable by a yardstick and a steelyard. I'm horrified at the bare thought that our present direct monk and reception head will one day become Zen masters," Kaijo responded.

"And they will. They are passionate for the title, and their shame is next to none. They don't understand that to teach others means to reflect on oneself, and that to reflect on oneself means to see what an imperfect being one is. They are slabstones, sufficient to pave the way for the master's election as abbot. Well, Kaijo, so much for criticizing others. As for you, what will you do, remain here...until when?"

"If only I could leave like Mokuzu, if only I had his talent! The way he left is one ideal way, finishing all essential koan study and ready to receive certification of completed monastic training. Yet he waived it. Compare how Koko left, seen off amid thunderous applause and the sweet scent of plum blossoms!"

"And soon he'll return, because he can do nothing in America without Mokuzu's help. Well, Koko's greatness is that he can return with no blemish of shame."

"Observances Head Genkaku, again you speak ill of others."

"Oops, sorry! I shall repair to the master and take the role of a papier-mâché Bodhidharma to be blasted with abuses."

Just as Genkaku was parting from Kaijo at the residential quarters entrance, Zokki came speeding from the meditation hall.

"Help me, Observances Head! Again the direct monk and those are trying to lynch me! This time they're wrong. I got the broiler at Mokuzu's order!"

"Really, did he ask you to sneak a hen into these sacred precincts?"

"Yes, you'd better believe it, he wanted a party on the mountaintop tonight!"

"Hm, hm, then your fault is that you didn't find six or seven. Do you understand? Prepare for a feast tonight, and go secretly tell all monks that whoever wants to attend a memorial party for the loss of Mokuzu should ascend the mountain after lights-out," said Genkaku, and he went down the dark corridor into the interior.

As Kaijo walked the veranda of the main building to return to the interview room, he said to himself,

"This snowy wind is so fierce it's erasing the clang of the wind-bells. I wonder where he'll take refuge tonight. Well, he's abler than I, and he wrote in the registry beside the entry on Mokuzu:

> He left with his mind set on the second pilgrimage. Yungjia stated that a pilgrimage is to traverse mountains and oceans to find a great teacher, to seek the great Way, and to study Zen.[5] But for Mokuzu the mountains are no longer so green nor the oceans so blue. Unneedful to his quest is that the teacher and the Way be great, for evidently hereafter he will study Zen where there is no Zen.

59

Outside the Gate

Having walked down from Shoshinji, Mokuzu met vehement snow slanted by wind. He pulled his bamboo hat over his eyes and devoted himself solely to advancing west along the dirt road through the rolling hills.

The pruned sericultural mulberries extending in rows were exposing their ugliest possible shapes in the snow. The evergreen mountains beyond were clouded like the brains of an ignorant government during an emergency.

Soon the mulberry hills turned to wide fields reserved for sweet potatoes. The thin settling of snow hid the poor reddish soil.

As he left the land he had grown accustomed to, Mokuzu was unwilling to halt and look back on account of its overwhelming dreariness. The local farmers grew a meager variety of crops simply by force of habit in land inherited from their ancestors, and also upheld a tradition of spending no care on aesthetic appearance. Even nature from ages past had lost the vitality to ornament itself.

Backed by mountain, the starch factory as ever issued a massive white cloud like the smoke from a standing steam locomotive. The emerging plume was forced to the ground by the wind and too readily for its volume kept vanishing into the snowy air.

A short distance ahead a road curved from the highway. By taking it Mokuzu could have reached the railway station, where he had stood when he first came. But lacking sufficient travel money he chose to stay on the highway, which led to the towns of Seki and Gifu. His decision was immediate, though he thought as he moved on with rapid step,

'A desolate parting of ways...,' and he intoned,

> "Go, go, seek out some greener thing,
> It snows and freezeth here;
> Let nightingales attend the spring,
> Winter is all my year."[1]

He was losing track of how long and far he had walked on the deserted road in the wide fields when he felt a tug at his sleeve. It was beyond his expectation to find Dormitory Inspector Tanishi following fast behind him, but there he was, unshapely in frayed robes and black rubber boots, with an umbrella up, and carrying in a purple silk obviously two bottles of sake. He must have drunk some, for his cheekbones were tinged red. As usual one eye twitched. Keeping a grip on Mokuzu's sleeve, he said,

"What's going on, wherefore such haste without looking aside? *Arrya!* — you're dressed for travel as if to quit Shoshinji and set out anew...!"

"Dormitory Inspector Tanishi, I never expected to meet you here. Yes, I have left Shoshinji behind."

"Left behind? Mokuzu, how can you speak lightly of so grave a matter? Just tell me what's going on and I'll gladly give you counsel." Tanishi's breath reeked of sake.

"Your care is needless."

"Don't speak like that. Calm down. Well, can't we find a suitable place to sit? On this bridge the wind is extra strong; the snowflakes are sticking to my glasses."

Indeed they were on a low wooden bridge crossing a broad and shallow river through flatland. The far end of the bridge was blurred by the snow.

"Were we in a town I'd take you to a restaurant and at least offer you noodles...how unfortunate not to see even a single private house from here... let me think...oh, of course, we'll go under the bridge; it's the traditional coverture of beggars, so we needn't feel diffident."

Mokuzu resigned himself to his fate of meeting Tanishi. He followed him through dead eulalia and over white cobbles to a place directly under the bridge, with the sight of pilings and girders. At that, some mallards with deep green crowns burst into the air. Surprised, Tanishi dropped his glasses. Blades of eulalia whipped aloft were carried quickly downstream.

Tanishi sat on the dried grass and wiped his glasses.

"Now please tell me whether leaving the monastery is the result of your thorough discretion. A man should meditate for three days and nights before making any big decision. But if you've had a run-in with the master or any

821

of your seniors, be assured I will assume responsibility for mediating."

Mokuzu gave a strained laugh. "You really needn't worry about me. I spent many months to come to this choice. Actually almost as soon as I came to Shoshinji I began to consider when I should leave. Why not tell me instead what brings you this way."

Tanishi laughed self-consciously, gleefully, and slovenly. "In truth, I could finally become a chief priest thanks to Zen Master Tengai. At the year's end he introduced me to a vacant temple deep in the mountains of Mino, very poor, with few laymen, but better than the end room of a dormitory, living with students. Since New Year's Day I've therefore been drinking a toast to myself. Then I thought of the master's kindness and of Dean Shiba's help, so I've come out with the remaining bottles to thank them. Now you see, Mokuzu, courtesy is vital to human affairs. Look at bamboos, upright because of regular joints, and a pine, so mannerly green in the snow. You have to respect the order between master and disciple, senior and junior, noble and humble. In "Shyeerl" too it is discussed:

> "Yotzy said, 'To put people at ease was accounted a prime function of courtesy, and the preceding king to that end applied himself on every occasion. But not all affairs went well, for he was ignorant of another prime function of courtesy: to distinguish clearly.'[2]

"So, Mokuzu, I assume you expressed your heartfelt gratitude to Zen Master Tengai, Dean Shiba, and the nuns of Shogetsuan at your departure. Did you?"

Mokuzu was touched on a sore spot. With all his might he fixed his eyes on the water laving a piling. At any rate Tanishi indicated a teaching that all who were higher-ranking, richer, and abler than Mokuzu would surely support.

'Quite probably the Zen master and others will denounce me for a breach of courtesy as their last resort after having spent all fair means to detain me. But aren't they

> "'...the bulk of your natives...the most pernicious race of little odious vermin that nature ever suffered to crawl upon the surface of the earth'?"[3]

'What reason have I always to be polite and to exhibit total submission to them?' Mokuzu heard himself actually pronounce the words of the Brobdingnagian king.

"What did you say now? You spoke in English. Could you repeat it?" Tanishi advanced the ticking side of his face.

"Dormitory Inspector Tanishi, it is meet that you observe proprieties and take sanctuary in Shoshinji's domain. I will dismiss proprieties and live in rusticity. The Dharma is valued above proprieties by the wild." Mokuzu's tone was conclusive, but Tanishi was not put off. He spoke with energy:

"See here, Mokuzu. That's the perilous abyss of isolation into which young people often fall! A human being is not a wild animal and can perfect his nature only through human intercourse. In fact, 'The Art of Administration Based on Zen' is the title of my recent study. First, to understand my Zen-imbued administration, you must examine Yunmen's 'Ringing of a Bell,' which surely you studied at a certain level under your Zen master, but listen:

> "Yunmen said: The world is wide. Why then at the ringing of a bell do we dutifully don our robes?"[4]

Tanishi proceeded to talk, joyous over gaining the chance to express his cherished view, and paying scant heed to his belches and farts. Moreover, unawares, he pulled the stopper from one of the bottles intended as a gift and irrigated his throat.

Mokuzu, fearing to be obliged to nurse him and return him to his temple, sharply interrupted,

"Yes, I know Yunmen warned us not to cause the withering and malfunction of the original nature inherent in us each and beyond the reach of outer vice and poison. And here the ringing of a bell symbolizes outer vice and poison. Yunmen's motive is to tell us that physical and material restraints don't rob us of our spiritual freedom. But is it true? Shouldn't we realize that spiritual freedom severed from physical freedom isn't consummate freedom? An overestimation of our spiritual power leads us to resign ourselves to narrow circumstances. Such spiritualism is a pitiful, imprudent, and self-destructive concept, as was demonstrated by the kamikaze corps who took off from aircraft carriers in wooden airplanes with no return fuel.

"I say spiritualism ill suits young people who refuse to cling to the imperfect past and who seek future perfection instead. Yunmen, while recognizing and advocating spiritual freedom, is giving over his original nature to outer restriction by submissively donning his robes at the ringing of a bell. However much he insists on spiritual freedom and independence from pollution, it is useless after donning the robes; afterwards, he is like a poor man who once prospered and now boasts of what he had, like a kind of maladjusted invalid in a new situation.

"His words are a refusal to admit defeat, mingled with self-pity. What he should have done was to oppose that bell. Religion's true role isn't to comfort spirit separated from body but to generate joy in the functional unity of spirit and body.

"Now, the fault of the established religions is very clear: They were too hasty to seek spiritual peace and enlightenment and achieved it in a mean manner like hungry fish before bait. Unfortunately the spiritual peace and enlightenment they achieved was not backed by any physical and material proof. Thus I see that the priests and laity who are satisfied with the old religions are unsteady on their feet and are looking up meaninglessly with raised chins.

"We must realize that human history has just begun and that we are all only totteringly beginning to learn. In other words, our world is still benight-ed and we are savages. At this step of human history what we should seek is not easy peace and shallow enlightenment. We should not fear that we are filled with vexation instead of peace, with indignation instead of satisfaction. We should not be charmed by easy peace and satisfaction while vexation and indignation are the driving force to improve and perfect this undeveloped world. Bodhisattva is not the name for those who are obedient to the ringing of a bell and who dream an unattainable dream; it is a name for those who shatter the bell. There are so many bells large and small, and as long as they ring for unjustifiable strictures, we have to break them each and all." Mokuzu had uncurbed his passion, and he stood up to hurry on his way. But Tanishi grabbed his skirts,

"Wait, don't get so excited. I'm not trying to impugn you. In point of fact I'm greatly impressed by your view. More, I only hope for your growth as an extraordinary Zen priest. But I must speak to you of strategy.

"Say, Koko's enlightenment was certified by the master, and he was blessed by everyone at his departure. Why didn't you emulate his style — why couldn't you wait? You're like a fruit just getting its particular flavor and color. On this narrow earth, in this long life, why should you hurry so?

"Ordinary people are fools. Even though you are a diamond, they will see you as fake jewelry if you have no certification. Whereas Koko, who is a porous turnip, will be prized for his certification and enshrined.

"Think about your parents if you don't understand. Parents wish solely for their children's health, peace, and social success. If you bring home no certification, they must taste bitter disillusionment. Hearing of your resolu-tion to take the Bodhisattva path, they will be dismayed. The more passionate and abstract your resolution, the deeper their dismay. They can't enjoy your goodness...I know whereof I speak."

Mokuzu kept his eyes on the river receiving countless snowflakes. 'True, though I'm heading for my native land I have nothing to give my parents with

824

pride. The dear fields and mountains, curving Sakura River, and sunny grassy path under the Tangenji wall invite me as if to gouge my soul...but what will my mother think when she sees me in a wet robe, with no travel money? Surely she has been dreaming of my social success and clever money-making, as much as would give rise to people's envy of her. My father must be always praying for me to attain a comfortable life with minimal annoyance, and he criticized monastic training. He won't enjoy my vision of death and my endurance of tyranny — he'll see it as proof of a hard life.

'I also have to ask myself what bright news I have for my sister who must be standing at a loom all day; for my brother who I suppose can see out only through a barred window. Poetic and lofty Zen thought is of no use to social reality, whose nature is adamant ignorance, and whose face is gloomy evil.'

"How about it, are you willing to reconsider?" Tanishi asked apprehensively, and he offered Mokuzu the bottle of sake.

Mokuzu ignored the offer and said quietly,

"It's time for me to part from you, Dormitory Inspector Tanishi. I can't deny I have nothing to take home. That is another reason I am not leaving for home but only dropping in on the way on my new journey. You must know I am not a plant, unable to walk. I can see the beauty of the violet and the nipplewort blooming by a dunghill that charms flies and oozes brown liquid. But I admire the hawk, the falcon, and the eagle, who fly high above the peaks, and through blizzard and even through tornado. They are candidates for a future phoenix."

Mokuzu walked on. The dusk with increasing snow was turning to night. His figure vanished before the end of the bridge.

ﻬ

The third evening after leaving Shoshinji, Mokuzu was walking along the Amano River, which would open onto Lake Biwa. He was worn down from having stridden that day across the snowy Sekigahara, site of the ancient battle between Tokugawa and Ishida to determine whose side would rule Japan. As he was figuring that the town of Omi was not far ahead, an old moon began to light his path from behind. There was no snow, but the incessant wind rustling the reeds was frigid. At intervals cormorants cried with sounds like the striking of stakes.

The opposite shore was a diagonal fault mantled with broadleaf trees, a dark and beetling precipice. The river had accumulated sand and earth to the extent that its bed was higher than the plain neighboring the near shore. Scattered farmhouse lights shone from the nether distance.

Even the nearest house in view was too distant to raise his desire to beg for supper. He wanted only to find a cozy spot to sleep like a beast. As he was about to descend to the riverbed, a girl jumped from the reeds like a rabbit.

Confronting an unexpected figure, she was more taken aback than he. She stared at him wide-eyed; then as she was about to withdraw, curiosity made her ask,

"Who are you? Why do you walk here alone with no light?" Her hair was short. She wore dark trousers and jacket, their color indistinct in the night. Oddly her sleeves dangled and waved in the wind. Mokuzu thought her arms were folded inside her jacket, but actually only her firm breasts stood out, and he realized she had no arms.

"Don't be afraid, I'm just a traveling monk. I'd like to ask rather what you are doing in this dark thicket." Getting no response he added, "I intend to stay the night on the beach."

"Oh, you're an itinerant trainee. It's the first time I've ever seen a real one. You must watch out walking so free around here. I've set many snares for pheasant and mallard."

"I'll be careful. But...how can you set snares?" Mokuzu asked innocently.

"With my mouth, even birds haven't arms," she replied immaculately.

"True. I admire you." Her bright eyes and direct, fearless gaze reminded him of Ena. He passed her by to go on, but she called after him,

"Have you had supper? I don't know if my ma will let you stay the night, but I can assure you of food."

"I haven't, but your house must be far. I'm too tired and I'd prefer to sleep."

"It's just around the cliff. Come."

With a lilting gait she set off along the grassy bank. Mokuzu as he followed noted that she was well contoured. Fastened on her high waist was a loop of horsehairs, which now and then shone in the moonlight. Her empty sleeves shifted as she moved. He visualized the Venus de Milo.

Her house was indeed around the bend, but across the river. They had to walk long planks that ended at a sandbank before the house. A windbreak of dark camellias surrounded the square property. Within was unexpectedly wide. A chicken coop by a big tree was half lit by light from an electric lamp coming through the shoji at the house entrance, which was beneath a low thatched roof. The chickens cooed.

The house was poor and gloomy. It was isolated, in a very inconvenient location, as if the family had been ostracized from the village.

"What is this big tree?" Mokuzu looked up at the bare branches against the stars.

"A walnut. We're grateful for its many nuts."

'Teacher Yojun taught me that in old Europe people believed witches and warlocks gathered about this tree. Could it house a spirit to ease the hearts of the oppressed...?'

Nearing the entrance, he could detect the taint of incense and hear a prayer to Amitabha being intoned as if to put a baby to sleep as well as the one intoning it.

"It's Grandma, she prays to Amitabha all the time. She almost can't see."

"Is that so? Listen, I shouldn't startle her. Why don't you go in ahead and get her consent?"

The girl's mother in kimono and white apron soon appeared, smoothing her hair as she came. Without a word she looked steadfastly at Mokuzu as the girl had on the bank, then she tugged at his arm to invite him in. Next to a sunken hearth the girl, using her feet and mouth, was putting away sewing items and a kimono that the mother must have been stitching until just then. The unfinished kimono was gorgeous. At once he understood that even such kimonos were produced by lonely women in this sort of gloomy house. The gray-haired grandmother moved on her knees to the front of the room, touched her head to the floor, and spoke a welcome as if to receive a most venerable priest,

"Thanks be for your training to save us lowest of the low. Thanks be for your trouble to come by this wretched abode. Please put off your travel raiment and take your ease."

"Grandma, I am a nameless mendicant. I'll not step up and soil the room. After being offered something to eat, I shall leave directly." Even as he spoke, the mother approached along the earthen passageway from the interior with a tin basin of hot water. She made him sit on the step to the room and began to untie his leggings and straw sandals with the intention of washing his feet.

"What? I am a priest unworthy of having his feet washed by another's hands." He withdrew his feet. The mother, with her sleeves hitched up and holding a floor cloth, regarded him from her crouching posture. Her eyes through the steam appeared painfully sad like the eyes of Mary in El Greco's "Annunciation." Her white, handsome features stirred his interest to know what she was thinking, but by then he knew she was a deaf-mute.

After he washed his feet, she pulled at his sleeve, made a scrubbing gesture, and pointed down the passageway.

"She says to enter the tub and she'll wash your back. It's new water, no one's entered. I'd gladly serve you if I had arms," the girl interpreted brightly.

"I see. Tell her I'll not enter, I must avoid catching cold as I'm sleeping outside." Then the grandma spoke meddlingly,

"Our home is shabby, but we do have guest bedding. The guest room is on the north side. To warm you Mine will lie with you."

"She means Ma. I'm Hana," said the girl, and her mother nodded with feminine modesty and a blush.

Mokuzu could not altogether comprehend the hospitality of this house-hold. To calm himself he offered to chant at the family altar. In the center of the fussily ornamented, glittering gold altar was a golden image of Amitabha. The girl hurried to light a candle and a stick of incense. She took in her mouth a chopstick with a match bound to it by thread and struck it. Mokuzu watched silently as she labored at her work.

During his chanting, the grandmother sat behind him bent over with sounds of sobbing mixed with sorrow and awe. The girl and her mother busied themselves preparing supper for him.

As soon as he finished, the mother brought rice, miso soup, and other foods to a low round table set near the sunken hearth. The girl deftly served from each container, using a spoon held in her mouth, and she did not drivel at all. Mokuzu watched her with admiration. Then, before he was aware of it, the grandmother began grumbling,

"You seem a young mendicant. My son died at age twenty-seven. He was drafted. During a drill a companion's shot took his life. He left behind Mine after three months of marriage. Foolish parent, I cry whenever I'm reminded. I know I'm ungrateful to Amitabha, for he was invited to the Pure Land. Yet how often I wish he was alive...even if disabled like each of us, even if a beggar, or a mendicant like you, or even a convict who did great evil...but I know I shouldn't complain of what Amitabha designed for us. Still, the life of one who has lost her only son is a year-round winter in an unlined kimono...."

Mokuzu coolly thought, 'Parental love is but an extension of self-love,' and he put in, "Aren't you fortunate that he gave her a daughter?"

"Hana isn't his child, though, yes, she's Mine's. After our son died my husband and I encouraged Mine to return to her native house or to marry anyone she pleased, repeatedly we urged her to while she was young. But she stayed on...and Hana came by way of my husband. He pitied her settling in this house and roused himself to make her a mother, much as he was then over fifty. Mine was given the chance to mature as a woman...," related the grandmother matter-of-factly.

Mokuzu looked at Mine. This time she did not blush, whether aware or not of being guilty of an immoral relation with her father-in-law. Hana, evidently aware, affected ignorance.

"But with her desire awakened, Mine has no doubt been feeling forlorn....My husband hanged himself after getting into trouble with a conservation official for hunting in a wildlife sanctuary where he had always hunted...from the bough of a mountain pine overlooking Lake Biwa, I was told...so blue was the sky...well, that too is Amitabha's will...."

"Grandma says everything is Amitabha's will. The doctor told me my legs must someday be cut off at the knee if the gangrene doesn't stop. Is that Amitabha's will?" the girl spoke with barbed voice. An awkward quiet settled over the ready supper. The girl's mother looked at Mokuzu as if to throw herself on his charity.

'To save myself is easy,' he thought. 'I can if I squelch my wish to be saved. But how hard, almost impossible, to save others, who are beyond my control!' He ate in silence.

As soon as he finished, he put on his leggings and sandals without heeding the family. When he went out, he was ashamed that he had been unable to leave them with any decisive words to contribute any happiness. The sky was set with twinkling stars, his shame was like a burning flame.

'This is no time to take sublime pleasure, letting a sensual woman wash me and lie beside me! Eh...let me recall something serious...

> 'Which to maintain I would allow him odds,
> And meet him, were I tied to run afoot
> Even to the frozen ridges of the Alps...'[5]

He retraced his steps along the narrow planks. Then, the girl, who had stealthily followed, spoke up,

"Reverend Priest, if you are a true trainee, please tell me how I may train. I think the best way is to go with you, but I know you'll not allow it." Her eyes were tinted blue by the starlight. Regarding her, Mokuzu imagined how she would have moved her arms. Her sleeves hung still in the lull in the wind.

"Yes, I can see you would benefit if you had a training companion. But for me this is a fit season to be alone. Furthermore, you need to give special care to your body, so you should make your home your place of training."

"How should I train here? Pray to Amitabha all the time? To begin with, I don't know what Amitabha is."

Mokuzu invited her to sit by him on the bank.

"My ideal is to live each day without thinking of or recalling anything of Amitabha and without praying. But living such an ideal life is impossible while we have our pains, sorrows, and complaints. So we have to learn what Amitabha is. According to the Sukhavativyuha Sutra, Amitabha is so named for sending an infinite light throughout the world. Amitabha is also named Amitayus, 'endless life throughout the world.' You see, what is endless or infinite is time and space. Naturally Amitabha is a Buddha as great as time and

829

space," explained Mokuzu. The girl was looking up at the starry sky.

"It was said this Buddha began to train countless eons ago in the time of Dipankana Buddha. Then he met many more Buddhas. At last in the time of Lokesvara-raja Buddha, he, then a king, entered the priesthood and became the training monk Dharmakara."

The girl looked dubiously at Mokuzu.

"Never mind if you don't understand — it's like a legend, and its point is to impress on us that the appearance of any great person takes a long development of cause and effect. Then, more important, this training monk Dharmakara vowed to realize forty-eight prayers as a Bodhisattva, and it was said he achieved them all and was reborn as Amitabha in Sukavati, the Pure Land; and even to this day he continuously preaches the Dharma."

"Well, really, his story seems no more than a legend. Do you believe it?"

"I don't believe it as historical fact. Whether you believe it or not makes no difference in the end, since it's a story involving endless time and space. Whoever believes it will think it can happen somewhere in this universe, including our planet, and whoever doesn't will see it as the story of the development of his own mind.

"Among Buddhists, those of the Pure Land sect believe Amitabha is actually preaching the Dharma in the Pure Land, considered to lie west beyond a trillion countries with Buddhas dwelling in each. But people of the Zen sect understand the Pure Land to be in their mind, and they see Amitabha as their perfected humanity. That's why they believe in their potential, however slight their ability. They depend on their faculties and continue their effort to realize the Pure Land in their life and to perfect themselves as Buddhas. Naturally this Zen approach to Buddhahood is called self-power. In contrast, Pure Land adherents reflect on their inability and incurable depravity, however much they are capable and sinless, and they believe the help of Amitabha will enable them to be reborn in the Pure Land by the easiest means, which is to chant Amitabha's name. This approach to Buddhahood is called the power of Other."

"I wonder if we can be reborn in the Pure Land simply by chanting Amitabha's name..."

"Your doubt is reasonable. But recall the vows taken by Dharmakara. His greatness is there. In the same sutra, among his forty-eight vows there is vow eighteen, clearly stated. Listen:

> "Were I to attain Buddhahood, I would desist from becoming a Buddha
> as long as all who believe in me, desire to be reborn, and chant my name
> even as few as ten times are not reborn in the Pure Land.[6]

"All people regardless of age, sex, wealth, social status, and so on, are promised salvation if only they believe in him, desire to be reborn in the Pure Land, and chant his name at least ten times."

"I'd sure like to be at ease in the Pure Land, and the easiest thing seems to be to chant Amitabha's name. I've already chanted it over ten thousand times under Grandma's influence. But I know I believed in Amitabha only when I was very young...and when I had my arms cut off. Maybe I have to confess I never really believed and I know I never will. Do you?"

"You've come to the point very directly. Keep attending to what I say and asking me your honest questions. Our belief is an unnecessary condition because he is especially compassionate. That means we don't need to believe in him to be saved by him. Saint Ippen said as much. You see, if we abandon self-power and rely entirely on Amitabha's compassion, our chanting of his name too will no longer depend on self-power but will come from his compassion. We are not chanting and not going to the Pure Land by self-power. Rather, Amitabha lets us chant and leads us there. The same can be said of believing in him. We don't believe in him by self-power. He makes us believe in him. So the problem of believing in him is resolved into his responsibility, and we can be released from our fear of disbelieving. This is the ultimate self-abandonment."

"You've said why I needn't worry about believing. Is that why you don't chant his name? You don't, right?"

"Since I haven't yet seen the real limit of my ability, I'm not ready to perfectly abandon my self-power. I think it won't be too late to put myself into Amitabha's compassion if I put myself there after thoroughly perceiving my inability."

"I too am not seeing my real limit, but I know my inability. So I'm confused and can't decide whether to go on by my power or by His Power. I can't be consistent. I now see my uneasiness comes from my unsure devotion to any path," said the girl, airing her basic concern.

Mokuzu kindly admired her,

"You followed my talk patiently and with clear perception. Now you realize your problem is that you can't definitely choose self-power or Other-Power. Many people, including you, think being thorough is important for achieving anything. But with me it isn't so. Taking only one approach isn't necessarily the best way to gain salvation, to master one's life, to find life's meaning. Generally, being thorough in anything is our hardest task because our life involves so many things. You'd therefore better take the Middle Way: for some things use self-power, for others depend on Other-Power. Sometimes you'll obstinately insist with self-power, at other times you'll yield

831

and rely entirely on Other-Power. This is the most natural human way."

"I see! I was troubling myself by believing I should follow one or the other! He who chases two hares catches none, they say. I was convinced I shouldn't complain of anything if I believed in Amitabha, or I shouldn't chant his name if I believed in my own power."

"It was an unfortunate misunderstanding. Your life is yours. You are free to believe or disbelieve in your power. Amitabha is so great throughout the universe that he doesn't mind whether you believe in him or not. You can be bright and calm by using both self-power and Other-Power freely. This way of thinking can be rejected only by people who care about religious sects as social phenomena, whereas it is seen as a matter of fact by every free person," said Mokuzu laughingly.

To express her thanks the girl put her lips to his shoulder.

&

Mokuzu had to spend three more days to reach his native land. Again it was night, around eight o'clock, when at last he stood under the gate of Tangenji. A wind was setting from the pine mountain behind the temple, a nostalgic smell and sound, though he had feared it in infancy as the visit of an indescribable monster. It stirred the bamboo tops and came out the gate, causing his skirts to wave. The only light was the eternal light of the stars. The doors, hooked open by metal fittings, rattled.

'What was the inevitability of my being born in this poor temple? It's a question as impenetrable as the meaning of the deep indigo between the stars. I now see how small is parental love compared to the unknown world a child has to venture into. Parental love is like a bagworm's dwelling, twigs patched together and hung tenuously from a branch.'

He went up the stone steps and through the gate. The garden was white with frost. He hesitated to knock; it might alarm his parents, and he had brought them nothing. He heard sound from a television. The entrance of the main building was not darkened with age as he had remembered it. The door, eaves, everything, was renewed with relatively new, cheap pine. 'Of course,' he recalled. 'Tangenji was half burnt by Gyodo that night.'

He knocked and announced himself. The television was turned off, but no stir arose. Again he did so.

There came the sound of someone hurriedly stepping to the earthen floor and unbarring the sliding door. It was his mother.

"Oh, Mokuzu, after all. What's the matter, returning in the dark without notice? Anyway, come in quickly, it's very cold."

After letting him in, she again barred the door. Then she touched his arms and shoulders as a blind person might do. She appeared to him to be much shorter than he had thought.

His father, beside a brazier, was relieved to confirm it was truly he. Wiping sweat of apprehension from his brow he came to the entrance of the room.

"Oh, how scary, I feared Gyodo had escaped from the hospital again!" and he lit his slender pipe.

'Could there be a more wretched relation between father and son than the father's fearing the son's return? For him the social and moral order has become completely distorted. He will find no peace until he gets one more chance to live and train himself thoroughly,' thought Mokuzu.

"Come in. It's your birthplace. Here you can be free and easy," said his mother as she took his bamboo hat from his hand and pushed him from behind.

"You tell him to enter — can't you see his feet are muddy? Quick, fetch hot water. You don't know the manner to receive a trainee, when thirty years you've been a priest's wife."

"You tell me that? Tonight we made no bath. Where's there hot water?"

"Tut! What a dull wit! Boil some, and be quick!"

"'Dull wit'? You've a poor spirit to fear Gyodo!"

Hearing them censure each other like cat and dog, Mokuzu immediately time-slipped to his infancy.

"Don't bother about me, cold water is fine," he said and went out the back entrance to the well. Micha followed and turned on water for a bath. A pump was installed in the well, eliminating the labor of hauling water to the tub, an innovation Mokuzu had met seven years ago on his return from Ryotanji. But heating the bath was still done by feeding kindling and logs into the fuel hole. As always, Micha was inept at starting the fire and raised a lot of smoke.

Mokuzu cleaned his feet and stepped up to the living room. Doyu turned a gas heater in his direction. A bluish hose connected it to a propane gas cylinder in the next room. Tangenji too was being invaded by the transition between a life dependent on charcoal braziers and a consumer economy with such comforts as central heating.

Doyu put a kettle on the gas heater and prepared a teabowl.

"I was anxious because you didn't write at all; I'm glad to see you are well. Did you quit training in Shoshinji?" Doyu's tone was kind and calm.

"Yes. I feel I have nothing further to learn from such a narrow world. Now I wish to meet more people earnest in dealing with worldwide problems."

"I wonder how Zen Master Tengai permitted you to leave..." Doyu was warming another bottle of sake, though he had finished his evening portion. He offered it to Mokuzu, and Mokuzu declined. On the side dish was a bit of salted salmon head.

Micha reheated leftovers and brought them to Mokuzu with clear soup containing an egg. She then sat by the TV and resumed counting the day's coins from her delivery of Kannon charm papers. Piled on a table were booklets neatly bound by Doyu in which the donors and their addresses and donations were recorded.

"So, what did he say to you at your departure?" Doyu repeated.

"In truth, I left without permission. I think the relationship of master and disciple is no longer what it was in ancient times. Nowadays the old generation scorns the young for its tendency toward waste. But the worst act of waste is to get all the use out of a person and then discard him. This 'throw-away age' is not new. In fact it has flourished in the older generation."

Hearing this, Doyu was silent, then he choked and coughed. An unwrapped paper containing asthma medication was blown from his tray. After calming himself, he said,

"It's this cough that keeps me from delivering the charm paper on windy days like today. I also avoid rainy days. I go only in fine weather. She goes daily because she has gratitude to Kannon for curing her illness, and she has a strong interest in making money. Anyway, thanks to our effort the temple is getting fixed. We've been able to fix everything burned by Gyodo. Tomorrow you can see the extent of our improvements. There's a ditch around the building to receive rain from the roof. The passage behind, which was always dank and gloomy, is now paved with concrete. We also rebuilt the ovens. The laymen never provide money. We alone are continuing to fix this temple little by little. We are lucky we can, for we can now make a living; we can even pay part of Gyodo's hospital expense."

Unable to figure why his father spoke of his economy, Mokuzu remained unresponsive. Then Doyu added,

"I don't know why you returned and what your plan is, but don't worry, you can stay as long as you wish. We have enough income to feed one more."

"Thank you, but I'm not staying for long."

"Where do you intend to go?"

Micha, counting coins all the while, stopped and pricked up her ears. She was kneeling, elbows on the tatami, like a dog.

"Presently I have no certain destination. I'd like to travel. I will go anywhere if it is good for my training."

"Travel? When?"

834

"Beginning tomorrow, if possible."

"But you just came tonight! You're like time with no halt!" Doyu was astonished.

Micha suddenly straightened up and began to recite,

> "The days and months are travelers through the hundred generations; the year also comes and goes a traveler. The ferryman spending his days on a ferry and the road-horse driver aging as he pulls at the lead both live a life of travel. Of yore many a man died while traveling. I too couldn't resist the call of the wind blowing the specks of cloud, even if I know not the origin of my penchant for travel, and I wandered along the shore..."[7]

Micha was stopped by Doyu: "Don't be ridiculous!"

"What? I only recited what I learned in my school days because you looked sad and as if you wanted to complain after hearing Mokuzu's wish to travel. I believe it's best to let him do as he likes. You shouldn't utter any hint of your old age and lonesome life." Micha was unsparing of Doyu and left to go to check the heat of the bath.

Mokuzu for the first time in some years could take a hot bath quietly alone. But when he lowered himself into the deep round cypress tub, the water from midway to the bottom was still cool, though steam spiraled from the surface.

Micha took his clothes from the dressing room to the well side to launder them. Doyu came down from the living room and asked through the sooted wall, "How is it? I can add more logs."

"Thanks. I could use a little more fuel."

The iron bottom grew hotter, and streams of hot water like cast silk filaments rose around his body. The water meanwhile became almost unbearably hot, but for Mokuzu there was only the sight of the cold snowy fields he had walked.

"Thanks, it's just right." He declined Doyu's further help and while still in the tub pushed open the little cedar-paneled window. The steam was at once drawn out, and a cold air flowed in to cool his shoulders.

He could tell by the commotion that Micha was hanging his washed clothes at the side of the retreat cottage in the dark. Soon she entered the retreat cottage, turned on the light, and was cleaning the room. She was readying a bed for him there.

The *moso* bamboos beyond the retreat cottage roof swayed in arcs, their leaves a fine greenish yellow under the starlight.

'There were good nights when I could see the full moon above the bamboo grove,' he thought, and closed the window. And he endured, like a patient during an operation, the chains of bitter memory from infancy. Then he said to himself, 'Well, from now on too I will continue to discharge my life into the eternal past. The more I do, the more I will advance my life into the unknown future,' and he got out of the water.

While dressing in fresh clothes prepared by Micha, he could overhear the conversation in the living room,

"Oi, he's passing his youth with no memorable joy. I worry he'll regret it, especially after our departing this world."

"He's entrusting himself to his training, which he seems to be enjoying."

"It's unnatural to have so strong an interest in training. Most young men his age are playing about with girls."

"He wants to train. He's very different from you in your youth." Micha's voice was scornful.

"You're too simple. He could be training because he realizes he can't do anything he really wants. Think a moment: in tattered robe who can escort a girl? I suggest you go and buy him a three-piece suit tomorrow at Muromachi since you have access to wholesale." After a minute's silence, Micha replied,

"We didn't buy any good kimonos for the girls, nor obtain anything good for Gyodo."

"Kiku and Ran are working now and can buy whatever they want from their earnings. A suit is useless to Gyodo in the hospital. What he needs is more pajamas," said Doyu persuasively.

"Mokuzu can buy a suit if he works," she cut him short.

"Micha, you are unreasonable to expect him to work while he is training. You don't know how hard a task it is. You can't compare such training with worldly work. In the monastery even military officers were overwhelmed. Prisoners have a much easier life. To begin with, no ordinary person sets his heart on training unless he has — "

"If training is so splendid, why couldn't you become a little better man?"

"Again you speak like that! You can't imagine that making an inch-better personality is yet harder than moving a mountain or shifting a river, as I've said a hundred times."

"I'm not utterly incapable of understanding what you're saying. But where's the money even if we decided to buy him a suit? I think having nothing is better than having a cheap one." Micha turned the talk to reality.

"You can spend that."

"You mean what you saved for our tombstone? You wanted so much to accomplish it before you die, to secure our friendship at least under the ground."

"Right. Surely I can live another five years and save again...."

Mokuzu could stay no longer in the dressing room and opened the door. His parents fell silent.

He had to spend all of the next two days in Tangenji because his laundered robes were not yet dry. So quiet were the days that the growth of the roots and buds of the trees was audible despite the season being winter. In the fine early morning of the third day, he stood at the gate in his clean travel wear.

Doyu said in disbelief,

"After all...you are truly going away. In that case, go on until you satisfy your desire. Don't worry about us. If we have no chance to meet again, you will see me in my grave. Farewell...Oh, I'd appreciate it if you'd write us from wherever you are, so I can open a map and trace where you are going...."

But Micha scolded him,

"Don't ask for letters with your lingering attachment! They're a waste of postage!" and she hastened to the backyard to cultivate furrows of peas. From inside the wall, Doyu with his pipe in his mouth continued to watch Mokuzu walk along the bank of the Sakura River until his figure disappeared behind the outcropping of a western mountain.

> I saw Eternity the other night
> Like a great ring of pure and endless light,
>   All calm, as it was bright;
> And round beneath it, Time in hours, days, years,
>   Driv'n by the spheres
> Like a vast shadow mov'd, in which the world
> 8

837

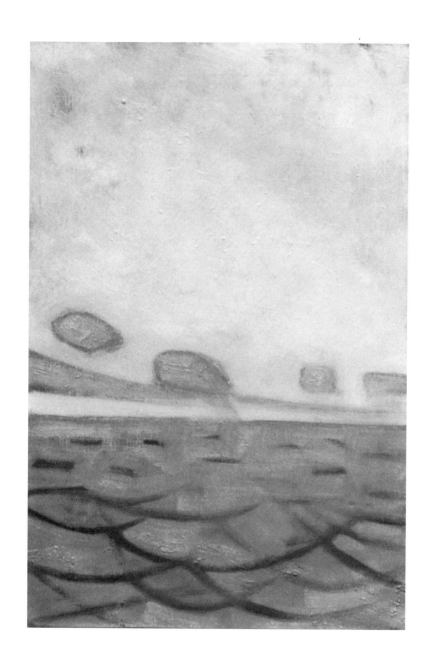

VII

Path along the Peaks

60

A Flower Yet to Bloom

On the sunny mountain pass, snow water was forming many rivulets that looked warm. Sand and soil fallen from the bases of pines on a cliff was accumulating at the right shoulder, while down from the left a stream threading a deep gorge reflected the sky. Beyond were more soaring rocky mountains with dwarfed pines and in places dazzling unmelted snow. Through the rising steam the hinder peaks showed turquoise.

From atop the pass Mokuzu could see snowbound farmhouses scattered in a basin to the northwest. He aimed to reach the shore of the Japan Sea, but many more mountains and villages lay ahead.

As he descended the shady side of the pass, he visited the sporadic farmhouses there for alms. He would exchange the offered rice for cash at whatever town he met.

Before the entrance of each farmhouse he chanted a sutra. From most came no response, for the local farmers were off at work in barns raising beef cattle. In the vacant area in front of one, children in wadded jerkins were making a snowman.

"It's big!" he called to them, but they did not respond.

"Is anybody in your house?" They still kept silent. The eldest broke into a run, at once tailed by the others. From a hiding place they studied him as they spoke in whispers, having learned from their elders to suspect strangers. They probably supposed him a mere beggar and were determining whether he was fearsome like a kidnapper or just one to be kidded and chased like a cowardly cur. .

He disregarded them and began to chant at the door. After a long interval an old woman appeared with a meager amount of rice on a tray, pecky rice, no doubt submerged at harvesttime. She emptied it into his scrip, where it got mixed with good rice. Then she bluntly slammed the heavy door. Facing the door, he bowed low. He knew at such a house he would be observed through a crack.

As he left he saw the face of the snowman. Charcoal and round briquettes formed a queerly unhuman expression that seemed to be made not by children's hands but by the nature of the village.

He walked on without making further visits and tried to remember "The Snow Man" by Wallace Stevens:

One must have a mind of winter
To regard the frost and the boughs
Of the pine-trees crusted with snow;

And have been cold a long time
To behold the junipers shagged with ice,
The spruces rough in the distant glitter

Of the January sun; and not to think
Of any misery in the sound of the wind,
In the sound of a few leaves,

Which is the sound of the land
Full of the same wind
That is blowing in the same bare place

For the listener, who listens in the snow,
And, nothing himself, beholds
Nothing that is not there and the nothing that is.[1]

He descended farther down the mountain path and in the evening came to where he could see a wide river. It drew near as if to hollow out the mountain foot and after forming a composed pool receded into flatland. Along the middle in one place a reedy towhead divided the flow.

Flickering snow dimmed the far range; toward there the river was flowing. On the near shore, against the snowy fields, a bamboo grove showed green, with a boat for angling crucian in midwinter revealing half its length.

Mokuzu brought to mind a poem in which an old Chinese poet was absorbing himself into nature solitary and cold:

Not a bird in these thousand mountains
Nor a human form on any path
None but an old man under sedge hat and straw cape
In a lone fishing boat on a snowy river.[2]

The poet, Liou Tzungyuan, having joined a political party led by Wang Shuwen, was relegated to the Liou district (Kwangshi Province), far from the capital of Changan during Emperor Shiantzung's ascendancy. There he led an ill-fated life as a statesman until his death at age forty-seven. However, it was recorded that the people venerated him for his wise governance.

Mokuzu thought, 'Although critics say this poem heavily reflects an unfortunate mental attitude, I see his wise governance reflected therein. He who shuns neither solitude nor nature can deeply understand and be truly affectionate to people, who are the children of nature.'

The next day Mokuzu assiduously begged in Fukuchiyama. The snow the evening before had changed to sleet. The households of this local town locked up early for the night, leaving the streets to winter. Now the day was clear and still, and the shopping district near the station of the railway leading to Osaka and to Kyoto was becoming active.

Since antiquity the town had developed as an important center for traffic and the transport of goods from inner Tanba. During the medieval age it had prospered as the castle town of Lord Akechi, and even now the layout remained, with divisions by rank and occupation: warrior domiciles just outside the castle main gate, a belt for merchants, an outer belt for craftsmen, and farmers strictly kept to the outskirts.

Mokuzu stood and chanted before the shops, where many housewives were shopping. The shopkeepers at once put coins in his scrip, not so much from faith as from the wish to send him quickly away. Some stalwartly ignored him out of differences of creed and principle, yet he bowed before passing on. Most of the ordinary buying public pretended not to see him, but fixed an eye on him after he went on. One warned her kindergartener to study hard lest he turn out like such a begging bonze; Mokuzu heard her behind his back. On the other hand, an upper-class shopper offered him a donation and bowed most politely.

A little past lunch hour he had about finished one side of the busy street. He was planning to beg on the other side when he noticed he was before a luncheonette with a white curtain hung in the upper part of the open doorway. The strong smell of frying fish was almost visible. With his mind set on chanting, he began to chant at this doorway too.

"Hey, come in!"

The voice, a woman's, had fiery energy with some coercive nuance. Mokuzu took off his bamboo hat and entered.

Inside was narrow, with about ten red-vinyl-covered stools set before an oily counter. Three men, who looked like road workers, were cramming themselves with fried horse mackerel and large servings of rice. A round woman stood between the counter and a deep black pot of boiling oil.

"Bet ya ain't ate. What can I give? Flatfish's good today." Her words were indifferent to distinction between man and woman, priest and layman. He thanked her; indeed he had not eaten since lunch the day before. The rice, soft and full in a big bowl, and the flatfish, fried at such high heat that the bones were edible, were both tasty.

"How's yer beggin' business?" she asked brusquely.

"Shops give right away. Houses with shut doors take long to answer, so it's hard to decide whether to keep chanting till someone comes or to go on," he replied, adjusting his manner of talk to her.

"Throw open the door and ask direct, 'Do ya hear? Say if ya'll give alms!' These days the wives watch the soaps after packing the men off to work," she said and guffawed with the road workers. She saw no element of religious training in begging; it was just another means of making money.

"What'll ya do with yer earnings?"

"Send them to my native temple. My parents will fix up the old buildings," Mokuzu answered honestly. She then said,

"I wouldn't know the temple, but how much can ya fix it with yer meager earnings? Visit Myounji, by the public garden, where the castle site is at, only a mile on, and study how to rebuild a temple. The priest wormed himself into a construction company's favor — Matsukuma and Company, one of the big five in Osaka."

Mokuzu showed no interest.

"Ya don' know Matsukuma? He's a famous yakuza — come up from this town," she continued. "A priest's got talent who can wrap a guy like that around his finger, eh?"

In the afternoon while begging, Mokuzu learned that Myounji belonged to the Rinzai school and he decided to go there to ask a night's stay. He walked the lane under the hill where the castle had been. The bank was covered with such evergreens as camphor, oak, ilex, and tobira. The granite pavement was shady and wet.

Opposite the bank were rows of quiet town houses, among which soon appeared a new, conspicuously grand tile roof shining in the western sun. It was the rebuilt main building of Myounji. The temple domain was enclosed by a white wall topped with dark tiles. The main gate faced south, the east side faced the tree-covered bank.

Mokuzu went through the new gate. It had four main posts, and carved into the crossbeams were arabesques filled with a matte green paint bordered in white. Inside was a sunny expanse of garden with sand, rocks, moss, and trees arranged in Kyoto style. The main building was wide open, emitting the aroma of fresh unpainted cypress, which overpowered the aroma of incense.

The residential quarters entrance too was open. It was not sooted and oppressive like that of Shoshinji. The earth was flagged, the plaster walls were white, and the wood floor was a light orange. Such a bright temple entrance Mokuzu had never seen. In the hallway stood a huge zelkova-wood screen with raised Chinese letters, "Holding up a flower and faintly smiling."

A pilgrimage monk when asking lodging of a temple was required by Zen prescript to answer a koan given by the chief priest. If he made an unsatisfactory answer, he was refused. Ready for any question, Mokuzu called in a strong, formal tone,

844

"Tano-mi-ma-sho — — !"

"Hai!" came an instant acknowledgment. It was the clear voice of a young woman and came not from the interior but from an area of the garden where an arrangement of reddish rocks gave the effect of three islands. Trying to ascertain just where it came from, Mokuzu saw shapely hips in faded blue jeans backing away from a narrow space between the wall and some rocks with azaleas under the branches of a black pine. Her Naples yellow jacket was caught on the azaleas, and her sweater too was pulled up at the waist. She must have been cleaning pine needles from the moss.

As she faced the training monk of similar age as herself, her cheeks blushed. Mokuzu had not shaved for some days, and his face was well tanned unlike the face of his infancy. His eyes had grown yet sharper, and he habitually held himself alert like an old-time samurai.

He asked her in a tone more familiar than he would have used to address the chief priest,

"I am a son and novice of Tangenji in Tanba. In the course of my training, I have come to ask you the kindness of a meal and a night's lodging. Would it inconvenience you?"

"Oh! What should I do? I really don't know the correct manner, and my parents are out at the moment...!" Expressing consternation, she clasped and unclasped her hands. Her earlobes under her curled hair were soft and creamy. Her full cheeks were like peaches. Her parted lips were dry, her teeth white.

"I did not realize the chief priest is away. Please excuse me." Mokuzu turned back.

"Wait! That won't do...My father has repeatedly told me a training monk is a temple's highest guest and we must offer our best hospitality... besides, like a prophet he said such a one would come in the near future. Oh, please won't you sit on the veranda for now? I shall bring tea."

Mokuzu did as she suggested. Before him was a crepe maple, under which, beside an accessory stone, were some snowdrops. Their milk-white blooms entered his ken with parts of poems,

> Make Thou my spirit pure and clear
> As are the frosty skies,
> Or this first snowdrop of the year
> That in my bosom lies.

> Many, many welcomes
> February fair-maid,
> Ever as of old time,
> Solitary firstling...[3]

845

The young woman, obviously the daughter of the temple, brought him tea and took a seat next to him, with a little space. The tea was powdered kelp in hot water.

"How could your father foretell the impending visit of a trainee?"

Her face again flashed rosy, and shyly she replied,

"It must be from his strong wish. He could finally rebuild this temple, and he's expecting the coming of an able young priest who can make the most of it. He's telling me to be ready by keeping clean the temple and my body and soul."

"You mean, of course, you are to marry that able monk?"

"Yes. I know I am immature and lack a suitable education for the wife of a well-trained monk, but I will do my best to follow his guidance and help his religious work." She grew breathless and hurriedly added, "And I want to build a happy, healthy family as a sample for lay people. My father says it is one of the most vital religious teachings."

After a stillness Mokuzu said,

"You are honest and bright. I am quite sure you can realize your ideal. Having so nice a father is impressive; it's no wonder you take his advice."

"Yes, I do, as long as what he says is sensible. After I marry I will follow whatever my husband says and does, and this too is my father's teaching."

"I sincerely hope a fine monk who is continuing his training will soon appear for you." Mokuzu returned his emptied teacup. Confused, she pressed her fist to her chin and bit her lip, searching for the words she ought to express. Evidently she believed Mokuzu was that very monk. After all, a young monk traveling for his training was by then very rare.

Mokuzu stood up, retrieved his bamboo hat from where he had set it against the veranda, and said, "Thank you for the tea. Please express my respect to your father."

The young woman was put in a flurry, "Oh, my! What should I do? Please wait, he'll return any minute. Say, won't you come in? Yes, I'll not be blamed for inviting you into our guest room — please come in."

"It is unthinkable to enter a temple in the absence of the chief priest. I shall leave. Before dark I must find a place to spend the night."

"But, please wait — you are welcome to stay here. Ah! Won't you see the back garden? The allspice is competing with the narcissus...!"

"Indeed, I've noticed it on the breeze...At any rate, I cannot tour the garden in his absence, so, good-bye."

Just when Mokuzu was nearing the gate, a round-faced priest came up with a hasty clatter of clogs. He was dressed in a shimmeringly glossy black robe over a milk-white kimono, both of finest silk. He must have been attending a Buddhist service, for he held a folded cloth evidently containing

846

a scrip and another with received offerings.

"Oh, Father! Just in time! This monk has asked to spend the night, but with your returning so late..."

"I know, I know, you need worry no more; I heard from a layman that a monk was headed this way, so I came back after accelerating the service. Well, well, an itinerant monk, it's the most honorable training! I apologize for my untimely absence. Do come in." He pushed Mokuzu toward the entrance as he said,

"Nahomi, hurry here with warm water and a new towel. And...look what you have on, quickly change to a kimono."

"But I can't tie an obi without Mother!"

"Tut! She's delaying in useless chat with the tea club. Well then, a dress. Do come in. You can remove your travel wear here in the entrance. We'll wash it. Nahomi!" He called into the interior to instruct his daughter to bring an everyday robe.

Mokuzu strongly declined any excessive kindness. Fortunately the priest did not insist.

"Very well, as you like. Being a great trainee, you must know what is right, and what is most comfortable for you."

He appeared to Mokuzu unlike a priest capable of leading a yakuza by the nose; he seemed an ordinary homely father. He initiated no Zen question but guided Mokuzu to the best room, next to the main hall. Although the day was not cold, he turned on an electric heater set in a wall the color of sea-crest green, and opened the shojis so Mokuzu could enjoy the view of the back garden. Outside the shojis, a corridor enclosed by glass doors went behind the sanctum to the residential area.

Mokuzu studied the interior and the garden. The moss, more lively than in front, had an actual waterway through bushes and rocks and around a miniature mountain. Under a miniature waterfall was a *souzu* — a device that produced a high and light sound from a length of bamboo as it hit a rock after receiving a measure of water that sent it tipping. Intended to heighten the quiet of the garden, the sound came too often for Mokuzu's sense. The allspice tree and the narcissus were out of view. 'They must be in a domestic garden with some laundry posts.'

He was seated before the alcove at a low table made from a slab of Chinese quince. He turned to see the scroll. It was a painting of the orchid *kanran* on a windy cliff, with a poem,

> Over the ranges the morning rays green the mist.
> Wind stirs the snow, the flowers are serene.
> For the last seven years living among beasts,
> I have viewed the Milky Way mirrored in a ravine.

Without taking note of the signature or seal, Mokuzu knew the painting was by his former teacher Setsuro. He recalled one of his teachings as if it had been said yesterday: "At the sight of your painting, the wind must be heard, the scent scented."

"Well, well, Tangenji! My daughter just informed me," uttered the priest even before setting foot in the room.

"I see your father once or twice a year at our head temple, Nanzenji." He placed a guest book and an inkstone case on the table. The guest book was new with no names in it yet. The brush was brand-new.

"And where will you be going from here?" he asked as Mokuzu entered his name and address.

"I have no particular destination in mind, but I'll advance west along the Sanin coast."

"It is fortunate you are in no hurry. Don't be strict about the saying 'a night's lodging and a meal': stay as many days as you like. Much as we are no more than a local mountain town, there are many places hereabouts worth seeing, each within a day's trip. My daughter will gladly guide you. But if I may say so, your father is a tease. Last summer when I met him at Nanzenji for a patriarch's anniversary, I asked him to introduce to me any young priest who might suit my temple. With a rather sardonic laugh he said, 'To find a young priest willing to take on a local temple is as hard as catching sweetfish or rainbow trout in the canal of a chemical factory. Such is the age. The war's end was only the beginning of the war in which materialism is subjugating spiritualism. Priests of our generation must bear the sin of having extinguished the Dharma and must prepare for a dreary death with the death of the Dharma.' Indeed he said so, but look, he has a splendid inheritor in you!"

"My father's sad view isn't false. He doesn't expect me to inherit Tangenji."

"What? Well then, can't you come here? We're near enough. If you wish, you can serve both. Or have you some other temple in mind?"

Mokuzu gave a forced laugh at the impetuosity of the chief priest. "No, no, I haven't any temple I wish to serve."

"Fine! A divine will has brought us together! In truth, yesterday I got word that an authentic young monk was nearing our town, and I tried my luck: should he stop at our temple we would be fortunate, and if not, not. Now if it's all right with you, I shall go to Tangenji even as early as tomorrow to ask your father's consent to welcome you as our inheritor."

His daughter entered with a tray of coffee. She was now in a cashmere sweater and a V-neck jumper. The collar of her white blouse had a dainty embroidery of blue daisies. Miniskirts were becoming popular, but she must have

848

chosen from her most conservative clothes to present herself before Mokuzu.

"Nahomi, this is the very person I kept telling you and your mother would one day surely appear, a suitable monk, if only we prepared ourselves to receive him. He will be most important to you. Now, venerable trainee, son of Tangenji, please understand that my monastic career is shamefully humble. In fact I never could solve even the first koan, and no doubt as a Zen priest I am blind. However, I have been endeavoring to become just a so-called good man in society. And I have been believing that my duty is to raise a good family, a good daughter, as well as cultivate good parishioners and rebuild a good temple; and all this to receive an able priest. Fortunately my daughter has grown into a woman of twenty-one years, and Myounji was rebuilt last year, by a single contributor, the head of a construction company. There's been some negative talk about the relationship, because he's also head of a yakuza group. What they say is rootless rumor coming from envy. You know, I have been thirty years a rehabilitation worker at the request of the Ministry of Justice, and I have continued to look after him and his followers from my position as protector and rehabilitator of offenders. Now it is your turn to introduce yourself, Nahomi. Be frank and relate how you have prepared for this day."

"Father, I spoke of it before you returned." She again blushed.

"Ah, so? Well, of course you both are young and quick. Then what was his response?"

Silence pervaded the room.

"I understand, you couldn't make an offhand answer to so grave a question. It must be an unexpected proposal, though for us it's a most common daily subject, cherished during chanting, meals, walks...so please both of you talk freely and without disturbance. I shall excuse myself and go get my wife." The chief priest promptly left the room.

A silence, this time longer and cleaner, hung between his daughter and Mokuzu. The room was warm. Mokuzu felt awkward at the long silence. With no deep intent he asked about the scroll,

"Does your family know the artist Setsuro?"

No doubt thinking hard about something else, the daughter asked lightly, "Eh?" and soon replied, "We've never met such a famous artist. Someone gave it to my father when he rebuilt Myounji."

"I see."

After another silent spell she looked up and said,

"I recognize that proposing marriage as soon as we met was rude. Especially sitting here like this makes me see I can't compare with you — I have nothing to offer, and no charm...But please understand we are at least

849

serious, and I am truly willing to study whatever you would want me to. Please don't misunderstand about my following whatever my father says. I would go with you anywhere if you told me to...!"

"...I think you are a fresh person like the green after rain, and your heart is as pure as a yulan bud within its bract. But please realize I have just begun to train myself, at first for my own sake. I think it is correct and wonderful that you believe the first step of true religion is to build a happy family. About that your belief isn't different from mine and we have the same goal. But while our goal can be the same, our paths there can be very different. What can be easily obtained by you could be impossible for me unless I go on by a thick and thorny path. I hope you will keep your ideal and yet be steady in daily reality. Indeed I think the ideal sought and practiced in daily reality makes the most fulfilling life. I haven't yet a reality where I can firmly stand; my earth is shaking, and I must advance my steps. It's not the time to settle and practice my ideal. I am a person who must go on in order to see through himself and others. You'll understand my situation, won't you?"

Mokuzu wanted to leave the temple before her parents returned, but the noise of their approach rose from the entrance. Before long there came a rustling of clothes, and her mother entered the guest room with a tray full of fruit.

"Oh my! It's getting dark. Nahomi, why don't you turn on the light?" she said and herself turned the switch. The room became bright, but there were many things in the world that were not made visible.

⋗

Thereafter, Mokuzu was careful about asking a night's lodging even when he came upon a Zen temple.

The seventh day he was walking alongside Wakasa Bay aiming for the Kyo cape, the northernmost point of the Tango peninsula. The bay looked leaden where cloud shadows were cast and dizzy like scattered silver paint where the sun shone through.

Nearer the cape the shoreline became a steep rock wall, the effect of erosion by the rough Japan Sea. There were also more small inlets such as pirates of old must have enjoyed for concealing their boats. A briny wind swept a terrain rugged with exposed rocks — andesite containing amphibole. The thin pines had no branches. Dead vines buried the valleys. The milder hills were cow pasture and would be a carpet of green in spring. Mokuzu saw here and there dried piles of white Dutch clover, red clover, and bur clover.

'Ena were she with me would relate that the land here is like that of the far-distant Andes, for once they were connected in a landmass formed in the

Tertiary period. Together we could imagine the earth with mountains forming and mammals and dicotyledons prospering amid volcanic activity...'

He crossed the pastureland to go to see the sunset at the cape. Black cows were eating from a pile of hay at a hollow in a pine grove. They had their backs to the sea. Most did not move their limbs but certainly kept moving their jaws. From their cold-looking wet muzzles saliva was torn off by the wind. Their eyes, large but with little expression, were riveted on Mokuzu and moved as he moved.

"I too am robed in black, but I'm a mere trespasser. You with your thick coats hear the waves day and night, adapt to the sea wind, and calmly face the change of seasons. You are much more suited to inhabiting this rugged seaside hill than is any human being. You are excellent creatures without exception, but are fated to be slaughtered...how sad you are!" he spoke with frequent pauses as he proceeded.

He worked his way through a thicket of dead eulalia to the tip of the cape. There he sat under a pine whose trunk looked like a thick iron rod with geniculate bends, reminiscent of the brushwork of the Southern Sung painter Ma Yuan. The trunk, grasses, and even his black sleeve became tinged by the sunset.

Quickly the sun's orb disappeared at the cloudy horizon. The waves as they darkened no longer showed their white crests, and the expanse of water bereft of color all the more presented by its smell and sound its phlegmatic liquidity.

As he sat two hundred meters above the sea Mokuzu attempted to enter samadhi, but cold and hunger interfered with his peace and only humiliation and loneliness recurred in his mind. In the distance a single cow, possibly suffering from some disorder, steadily lowed as if to supplicate help.

With the intention of begging for supper, he began to descend to the east shore. The steep path though insecure showed traces of cows; they had made a very modest path, just a narrow line, despite their bulk.

Before reaching the shore, he came on a large wooden rain tank. Below were rows of long barns with some silos, and beyond, a cluster of one-story houses. He assumed a number of families were sharing the enterprise. Except for the moonlight and what light leaked from the barns, the alley was unlit. He stepped carefully to avoid waste water and the chance of nails.

He heard a bark, many barks, and was abruptly circled by a pack of dogs. He shifted quietly to the moonlit beach. A reef extended into the offing. The smashing waves and wet rocks shone yellow.

"Bark more profoundly or the waves will drown out your voices," he addressed them with composure despite their running about and closing in on

851

him. Sharp whistles came through the dark, and he and some of the dogs were lit by a flashlight. The dogs ran faithfully to the light. A lanky man approached.

"What can I do for you?" It was the language of a townsman.

"I am an itinerant monk. I shan't trouble you for a night's lodging, but I ask a meal. Kindly make me a frank reply." Mokuzu spoke stiffly with slightly archaic language. The man's short mustache with his breath condensed on it radiated a white light. He mused awhile out loud,

"It's probably impossible...we are at evening service...well, I'll get his word on it. Come along."

"You mean this isn't an ordinary ranch but a kind of religious community?" Mokuzu asked from behind in the dark. Without replying the man stepped up to the entrance of a building resembling a meeting house. He made Mokuzu wait outside and pushed open one of the heavy, hinged doors and entered.

Mokuzu, having to wait long, sat down on the wood step. He could hardly catch the voices within, but evidently several dozen people, men and women, were repeating some tenets chanted by a leader.

Mokuzu's tendency to dislike groups had been reinforced by his Shoshinji life. He had especially grown to dislike religious groups for their propensity to be narrow-minded and perverse-natured. Such groups restrained the individual with impersonal rule or doctrine like a great common divisor, whereas religious concerns arose from the most personal needs. He had also learned that religious groups often had to act with both overconfidence and exclusiveness.

He considered himself a member of no religious group, and he really hoped the service would end even a minute earlier. Just when he thought he would leave, the lanky man quietly opened the door to invite him in.

Inside was illuminated by a hearth in the center of a wood floor and by candles on an altar. The congregants still had on outdoor shoes. On the sooted roof trusses many shadow-figures swayed. Everyone was dressed in his or her own way, seated on rugs, mats, or furs. A baby nursed in the arms of a woman near the hearth. Beside her a man in a poncho smoked a long pipe.

The leader, bearded and long-haired like Jesus, appeared from behind the candles and moved with an affected air toward Mokuzu at the door. His clothes were an amalgam: a Tibetan chaplet, a fur vest, and a Russian rubashka. He walked soundlessly even in leather sandals. His followers watched him from behind and Mokuzu from the front. The dullness in their eyes reminded Mokuzu of the cows. But these had eyes that were turbid, restless, and shallow in due proportion to the development of their brains; whence they rightly belonged to a diferent order of Mammalia from that of cows.

The leader approached Mokuzu and spoke in a tone just audible to all,

"On first glance I knew you for a Zen monk. Let me ask if you come knowing this is a holy community." His mouth smiled, but his eyes as he observed his visitor were cold.

Surmising that he loved polemic, Mokuzu instantly acted like an imbecile. He opened his mouth wide, gestured as if to fill it, and said, "I need food, then I'll choose to sleep with the cows in the field."

The leader relaxed his guard. Raising his arms to question what could be done with this fool, he evoked a laugh from his followers. Then without a word he drew with his hand a crescent as if to trace the path of a falling star, though it was just to beckon to a woman near the altar. His instructions seemed to Mokuzu very generous:

"Share what food is left over to satisfy this lost sheep."

The woman, in black evening dress and black shawl, walked elegantly through the group. Without focusing on him, she asked Mokuzu to follow her and went out as if vanishing into the dark.

Soon she entered one of the houses, turned on a light, and invited him in. There were some tables and benches of the sort usually seen at campsites.

With her back to him she silently reheated and stirred something in a pot. 'She must be about the age Luri would be now.' The smell of a stew began to flow. He regarded her black back. 'Was it Amedeo Modigliani who infallibly expressed a woman's form and volume? Moreover, he succeeded in suggesting a sweet melancholy, a man's longing for home and love...'

She brought him a dish of stew with whole-wheat bread. When she set it down she sharply caught his eye and said,

"You're no fool, you couldn't be."

"Sorry, I didn't want at best to be asked to deliver a sermon, or at worst, challenged into a discussion or urged to convert to your group." Mokuzu answered candidly because he decided she was not altogether imbued with the group's belief, whatever it was. Indeed she was upholding a fair critical attitude; she smiled at his apprehension and said,

"That's wise. He's a good debater, so everyone goes along with him."

She brought apples and sat facing him as she peeled them. She managed not to sever the peel on the way. She seemed from a well-to-do and well-educated family.

"How long have you been here?"

"Slightly over three months. I came after hearing one of his lectures...."

"You must have found something great in him."

"Yes, I thought, in his talk. His wish is to build heaven on earth. He inculcates this view of Norman Mailer's, which in his words is, 'Don't be a square who affirms the established values of the advanced capitalistic nations and who pursues material happiness and prosperity in daily life. Be hep, deny all that, search for human values in un-prosaic thought and action.' What do you think of that?"

"It's refreshing as long as one tells it to, and practices it by, oneself. It turns to platitude when it's forced on others, for the point is to eagerly recreate oneself. So, telling it to others should be done with caution like treading on ice. We must realize there are quite a few in this world whose influence is tremendous, but whose responsibility for their influence is next to nil. In modern times, men of literature divide influence from responsibility to suit their own convenience, though influence and responsibility are indivisible as long as they stem from the same love. Men of literature talk without guilt as they like. Their audience must then protect themselves by their own careful criticism. And indeed sterling people no longer respect literature, because men of literature have abandoned their responsibility."

"I see, but it's a boring life in a glass box if I stay under my parents' protection and influence. They never see their faults in the present system of values and are burying themselves in a stale everyday life."

"Many parents are pained to see the result of their influence on their children. What they lack isn't a sense of responsibility but the power to influence. So their children leave to seek influence elsewhere while yet protected at home. That's fine. In that way children can find something beyond daily life in daily life. What is true is true in daily life, not outside it." As he spoke, Mokuzu thought of the daughter Nahomi at Myounji in Fukuchiyama.

'She might have come with me if I asked it. But I had to consider her background, where she grew up straight, bright, and gentle. I also thought of her undeveloped talent and her inexperience against hardship. I concluded that what happiness I could provide her by taking her along would little surpass what she already has. A poet doesn't take a flower from a mountain path, nor should a priest take a happy person under his influence. This woman before me is unhappy from having been incorrectly taken out of a happy environment.'

The woman asked Mokuzu if he would like coffee. He declined. She took a pack of cigarettes from a shelf and puffed on one. The smoke was blue as she did not inhale deeply.

"Here everything is shared, even sex. What do you think of communal property?" Her fingers were graceful, and her bare wrist was suggestive of the rest of her covered in black.

"In heaven there couldn't be any distinction between things possible and impossible to be owned; so there couldn't be any distinction between private and public ownership. On earth these distinctions are evident. We labor to achieve a proper order and harmony of ownership. Our desire to achieve it

854

is very natural and personal, and we can achieve it only through personal contemplation. So what's important is that our personal contemplation be ensured regardless of whether we live in or outside a community." Careful to be critical of no one, Mokuzu was obscure in voicing his judgment of right and wrong.

"Well, in this community there's neither order nor harmony to be sought by our free wish, but the various disparities are definitely regulated." The woman stood up from the table after grinding out her cigarette. She looked angry but also sad.

Mokuzu stood up. "Thank you for your hospitality."

"Wait a moment, would you, traveling monk? I'll gather what was mine and go with you," the woman abruptly proposed with a smile and went into an interior room without heeding his puzzlement.

He hesitated but left before she returned. Outside was pitch-dark. He sought the moonlight and walked along the beach. The dogs reappeared, but he ignored them. He found a path up the face of the cape. He grew winded and did not notice the tiny light behind him that was the flash of a lighthouse on another cape.

61

Spring Winds under Mountain Shade

With the morning sun on his back, Mokuzu strode west along the wave-lapped Sanin shore. He walked just where the waves receded, leaving no footprints on the sand. Little fishes flickered in the clear water like silver foil, and washed-up shells of carpenter's tellin lay scattered like petals.

On a map the coastline was simple, without limbs. Actually it presented small-scale erosions at every turn; and now and then there were small capes, islands, and reefs, some with black pines providing a base for martins, auks, black-tailed gulls, and Temminck's cormorants.

Both static and dynamic nature were harmoniously and semi-permanently coexisting on the beach. Day after day as he walked, Mokuzu examined and reflected on his past and the koans he had gone through under Zen Master Tengai.

Many had praised Mokuzu's excellent memory, but none ever noticed in him another superb faculty, which was repeatedly to reflect on, analyze, and integrate his experiences and what he had learned so that he might criticize himself and establish his surer wisdom. 'Just as the marvelous rumination of cows enables them to take nourishment from coarse food, so I must learn most from my own past however shabby it was. When I stop learning from it, my growth will stop,' he thought.

To learn from his past, he inevitably had to reexperience its sorrows, agonies, embarrassments, and some vexations at being unable to seize the chance to express his fury. Even so, he could endure to recall those unpleasant accompaniments.

His attitude was therefore unlike his father's, for Doyu lacked the will to challenge reality. Mokuzu often looked at his past because he wanted to be correct in his decisions without losing time in the face of reality. 'I don't want to repeat a mistake; I want to learn and make the best use of what I learned so the present will improve on the past and resurrect it.'

He could test what he learned, and he believed the accumulation of his tests could bring him nearer to an ideal future. The present was the occasion to purify his past to make ready for a clean future. But in reality it was not always so, for often to the present were added new regrets. The present sometimes invited his ideal future, and sometimes drove it away. And in the present there were unsure and unknown elements.

&

In early April he stepped into the small fishing town of Hamasaka. Although still within Hyogo Prefecture, it was near the famous Tottori sand dune.

In the slip of a wharf many idle fishing boats closely moored were bumping their gunwales cushioned with old tires. The water was a thick mix of dark blue and dull blue-green, and it gleamed with leaked fuel.

Torn *wakame* seaweed and bits of straw rope swayed without leaving the same spot. Mokuzu was attracted more by these meaningless flotages than by the strange stout rocks and cave openings scattering the crashing waves.

On the wharf was a slate-roofed, open-sided building with a concrete floor, where the landed fish, shellfish, and seaweed were auctioned. A fishy wind blew freely through the wooden pillars. There was no sign of life. Inside was dark and cool.

Mokuzu went on past many warehouses and came to an area of small, family-operated factories opening onto the street. He stopped before one to observe the work.

Machines at the back were grinding fish — shark, Pacific cod, walleye pollack, flatfish, Atka mackerel, lizard fish, croaker, and others he did not know. Belts slanting from the ceiling drove the machines. The workers stood in a considerable noise that had no influence on reducing the stench.

Zen Master Tengai, able to eat only vegetarian foods, could not have stood there without immediately sickening, but Mokuzu continued to stand calmly under the eaves.

In the center, machines were mixing starch, salt, sugar, and such into the ground fish, and workers there were fixing the pasty product to metal rods like many ears of cattail. Near the entrance, workers were putting the ears on a belt that moved them through a roaster as they turned, and others were removing and boxing them one by one.

No doubt in winter the work at the back was cold, in summer at the entrance hot. All were dark-clad women in white kerchiefs who worked in silence.

None looked at Mokuzu, yet one at the roaster nimbly wrapped several in newspaper and thrust them at him. She wore gloves and a thick gray fire-proof apron and black boots. She resumed her work and never turned his way again.

As he climbed a paved slope toward a densely built-up area, he un-wrapped the newspaper and gnawed on the contents. The shadow of a large bird crossed his hand as if to slap it, and the angry face of Zen Master Tengai appeared in his mind: "Fool! Act right, don't disgrace the proud mendicancy of Zen!"

"Ha ha, Zen Master, don't judge others by your own experience! One's experience is most useful to oneself but least useful to others," Mokuzu retorted aloud.

The houses of the fisherfolk were packed on the sun-beaten slope like shells adhering to a reef. Scarcely was there space even for a cat to walk through. Cobbles were laid on the roofs against stiff winds, and not a house had a garden tree. For greenery there was no more than some onion, clematis, or catchfly, in rusty cans below the eaves.

The day being hot and humid, at most houses the door was open. On the earth of the entrance floor as narrow as half a tatami, children's rubber shoes and straw sandals were strewn over those of adults, and a raveled badminton racket or jump rope lay neglected. Mokuzu could see into the kitchen of one such house. Behind a torn fusuma was only one other room, serving as living room and bedroom, and beyond, a cramped laundry yard met that of the neighbor's.

Before chanting at the entrance, he could not help recalling "A Poetic Dialogue on Poverty" by Yamanoue no Okura, a unique poet who described a commoner's life in the Manyo age.

On sleet- or rain-swept nights I am at a loss what to do. So plaguey cold it is, I sip sake-lees broth and lick crude salt. Despite persistent snivels and cough, I smooth my disheveled whiskers as if to boast I am a man of exemplary character. So cold, so cold, I don all I own and wrap up in a hempen cover. In such cold how do you, a poorer man, survive, whose parents must be cold and hungry, whose wife and children must cry for want?

Narrow became my world. The sun and moon for others are bright. Not so for me. By a whim of fate a human being I was born and I grew to manhood as others grow. But look, my vest has lost its wadding and is frayed like thick-haired codium. In our run-down cottage, on the straw-spread earth, my parents in rags are at the pillow, while about their feet my wife and children moan. The furnace sends up no smoke. In the rice pot spiders make their webs. Having forgotten even how to cook, we only cry like mountain thrushes. To make matters worse, the village head with rod in hand keeps calling me through the door to where we sleep, as if to cut the end from an already shortened staff. Alas, how could I have come to such a pass?

> I have no means to fly away,
> Though hard and shameful is my lot.
> No bird am I!"[1]

When Mokuzu began to chant, two preschoolers, one naked but for a bib and diaper, came out with curiosity. Their mother, in the kitchen, ignored him. Then her husband, reclining in the back room, chided her,

"Oi! Give him something!"

"We can't give the kids even a snack with you idle!"

"Call the fish and I'll gladly go out. But why are you idle? Go to the factory!"

"Stupid! Today I'm on night shift!"

Soon she came out and handed Mokuzu some coins in a paper, with a rather gentle excuse,

"Fishing's no good now. Come near the end of the month and the town will be in high spirits."

Every home was in a similar state. The men slept in their clothes, and some gathered in a vacant lot on camp stools to play *go* or *hanafuda* as if it were a holiday. The women either were doing housework or were at the fish-paste factory.

Mokuzu found it curious that while the town was the poorest of the towns and villages he had passed through, the amount of alms was the most. After all, the work was risky with the weather unstable and the haul primarily determined by marine nature, such as the ocean currents and fish migration.

858

So these fishing families could not altogether abjure their traditional beliefs even in what were now scientific and technological days.

Around three that afternoon Mokuzu could finish begging in the fishing town. He then took a dirt road hazy with heat into the hills. On either side were terraced fields of forced strawberries in vinyl tunnels, between which shining rows of peas in patches were beginning to cling to bamboo branches.

Above were peach and pear orchards full-blown in the haze, and farther up seemed to be clusters of farmhouses. Each time he looked back, wiping his sweat, the roofs of the fishing town were more obscured by the hillside, while the view of the sea increased and the horizon appeared higher.

He came on a village entrance, where a small but fairly deep rill crossed the road. Beside the rill were two impressive pines, one red, the other black, possibly a landmark for boats, and likely planted by some old-time villagers of sweet mind, for they grew together like a compatible man and wife.

As he sat facing the rill to eat the remaining fish paste, he noticed some pale and tawny stalks, pulpy, cylindric, and covered with down, shooting straight up about seven inches from an incline of leaf mold. They bore many degenerate leaves. He had never seen their likes, but from their distinctive shape he concluded they were the "priest's staff," or pinesap, and he felt a joy as if happening upon a fellow trainee.

He lay on his back on the pine needles. A fat, sheep-shaped cloud was slowly passing above a pine bough. He lost sense of whether the cloud or he was moving, and whether he was enjoying his journey, and also whether it was meaningful.

Tired, he fell into a doze. A cheerful noise coming up the slope awakened him, the noise girls would make. Being off the road and by the rill, he assumed he would not be seen and lay where he was to let them pass.

Soon it became audible conversation, which he understood was coming from a number of elderly women.

"...so like a silk spider!"

"Oh, dear! — it that fashions elaborate webs and has males serving at each corner?"

"I don't mean to disparage, only her stunning beauty is inappropriate."

"He took her in to educate her, you know, but he sickened soon after. I heard his condition this time is critical. Why doesn't she call his son from Tokyo?"

"He's unwelcome even if qualified. I bet she'll bring in some other priest she likes."

"Certainly she has many such connections."

Then they said something Mokuzu could not hear and again laughed like girls. He watched them recede from view. Each held a basket brimming with flowers, not only peach and pear but also globeflower and milk vetch.

He decided to visit the temple they spoke of, to ask an early supper. He stepped to the rill to wash his face.

The water he scooped by pushing aside galingales and *ao-goso* was cold and clean. When he looked up he saw a spider centered sedate on a web in the branches of a mimosa. As to the beauty of its graceful figure there was no doubt. The legs were black with yellow rings. Three dark blue stripes ringed the the pale yellow abdomen, and a large red posterior dot was vivid against the green foliage. The silk spider had been likened to a courtesan, but for Mokuzu it seemed more like a forest fairy.

The dirt road began to wind and had many offshoots to farmhouses. As he proceeded it became narrow, rutted, and weedy and went into mountains. An old stone post indicated a village with a richly supplied hot spring.

Soon he came to a long wall, obviously of a historic temple. It was of quarry stone, dark with lichen, and much higher than the wall of Tangenji. Old cedars soared yet higher, while trees with spreading crowns cast beneath it a dark shade. The many stone steps led to an eight-pillar gate with the cinnabar paint mostly worn away. Appearing from inside, to the right, was a huge Yoshino cherry partway in bloom, to the left, a tall yulan in full bloom with no trace of frost-brown.

From the top step he turned and was directly facing the sea. The temple enjoyed a singularly luxurious prospect. 'A picturesque location may cause poverty of the imagination. So too, a handsome face and figure may cause neglect in cultivating the mind.' With such a thought he went through the gate.

In the center of a wide garden was a lotus pond, divided in two by an arched, roofed wooden bridge leading to the main building. The plants on islands and around the pond obscured a view of the main building, but

Mokuzu could see several women, presumably those that had passed him, seated on the veranda, working at something.

'I see, they're decorating a little shrine with flowers for Buddha's birthday. April eighth is tomorrow.' He recalled his grandmother doing the same in his long-gone infancy.

'She ordered us children to gather the flowers and by herself engaged in the decorating. The fields and mountains were warm as if smiling. What a delicious languor to bask under the sun in the flowering fields! Memory of spring days is sweeter than real spring, as is the blue of indigo bluer than the materials it comes from. The past will never return, however many springs return with their flowers and mild winds. The more flowers give cheer, the more old people are saddened. With such understanding, how suitable for old women to decorate a shrine to commemorate the birth of the savior Sakyamuni Buddha!'

He went to the residential quarters entrance to announce himself. The women, chatting as they worked, paid him no heed.

A broad, middle-aged woman appeared. She had the dress of a nurse or a homemaker or both. Mutely she made Mokuzu repeat his request for supper. Even after hearing, she only regarded him with dull eyes so he had to ask would the chief priest see him.

"He is confined to his bed."

Mokuzu realized his stupidity and impropriety in visiting the temple of a sick priest. 'Travelers, having no innate responsibility for the life of residents, dismiss information inconvenient to themselves when forming their composite judgments.' He wanted to leave, but she went inside with the words that she would summon the priest's wife.

"Sorry to make you wait so long, I was in the tub," said the young wife in informal kimono as she came out. Her hair still hung loose. Indeed she was beautiful, and her appearance seemed to light the gloomy passage. Mokuzu began to repeat his formal introduction, but she cut him short,

"Supper? Fine. You can stay the night. Oh, you have all the proper togs — bamboo hat, leggings, straw sandals...like any who have only tradition and not themselves!" Smiling, she stepped into red-thonged clogs and led him toward the back, passing the huge cherry.

On the way she stopped and pointed to the daffodils blooming along the white wall, as many as to be expressed as a mass.

"Aren't they glorious?" By herself she had been admiring them passing their best, and she could not contain her impulse to share her joy.

Mokuzu did not speak. Like rapid clouds, a glimpse taught by the teacher Yojun occurred in his mind,

'In England the daffodil was inseparable from Eastertide and the Annunciation, and children who found the first sang out,

> 'Daffy-down-dilly is new come to town,
> With a yellow petticoat, and a green gown.[2]

'And who was the Leftist poet who saw in them the strength of the commoner?

> 'Now the full-throated daffodils,
> Our trumpeters in gold,
> Call resurrection from the ground
> And bid the year be bold.'[3]

Getting no response, the wife frowned and said,

"A trainee doesn't stay in one place, 'like a cloud or water,' and respects a life that discounts emotion and encumbrances. So you aren't touched by flowers."

"I won't speak for others, but I'll say of myself that while a trainee should be like a cloud or water, he shouldn't be cruel or insensible. He should be extra responsive to his surroundings and to people's minds, just as clouds and water react to atmospheric and geographic phenomena, making them important elements of weather change. A trainee should as such be an important element in helping to improve the world."

"Oh, you're verbal! I dislike taciturn old rotten potatoes. The floral language of the daffodil is 'regard' and 'unrequited love.' What's your impression of these?" She seized his eyes, and because she stood so near, he had to keep looking aside.

"Well, their nature is more evident when we see them with some sort of sad imagination than when we just see them. For instance, there are those of one's native land that bloom when one returns heartbroken, or those to which one says farewell when one must depart....It isn't my original view and isn't peculiar to the East. In Roman myth Proserpine saw and picked a daffodil just before Dis took her to the underworld to be his wife. An Englishwoman, the poet Ingelow, describes the scene...,

> "Lo! one she marked of rarer growth
>   Than orchis or anemone;
> For it the maiden left them both,
> And parted from her company.
>   Drawn nigh she deemed it fairer still,
> And stooped to gather by the rill
> The daffodil, the daffodil."[4]

As Mokuzu translated the poem, the wife squinted like a myopic person. When he finished, she exclaimed,

"I know how she approached and picked it — all women more or less experience such a mood when they marry, a priest's wife especially! A priest may say he wants company in his training. But what if all he really wants is help with his priestly duties? Anyway, thanks for telling me, it touched my heartstrings and makes my day! Come, you are welcome to enter the bath. The water is clean, I showered first."

The dressing room was of plain wood, with a figured mat. She entered with him to remove a wicker basket of her previous underwear. The bath room was tiled, the tub made of cypress. The still water was limpid in the daylight coming through a frosted glass window. When he submerged his body into its warmth, he saw a single pubic hair floating.

He opened the window and was amazed to see, beyond the trees along the wall, the ocean beginning to receive the light of sunset. He keenly sensed he was a traveler.

A stir came from the dressing room. The wife opened the door enough to look in and said,

"I'll keep a change of clothes for you here; they're his. You can make it hotter — use the red-dot faucet. Yes, open the window, feel free of constraint," and she withdrew.

In the tub he thought about her,

'From the start she's intimate like a sister or an old friend. Is it her custom? Maybe dismissing useless formality is the right way to live our short life. Less substance generally means more formality, and the over-polite don't realize they are rude in wasting a person's time. But her frankness and simplicity might cause her to trust and love too easily, which could harm her. If so, the world needs men who are bright, strong, and honest enough to protect her type....What is her husband, chief priest of this temple?'

Mokuzu was given rooms joined to the residential area by a corridor, with utilities provided as if for an independent building. It was the most private place in the temple and apparently used by the wife only. To enter the bedroom given him, he had to pass through a room where her kimonos and dresses hung. In it were also a desk and a dressing table surmounted by three mirrors.

From his bedroom veranda he could see nemophilas against a forest of snapdragons. The garden air was sweet, and to the blue of the nemophilas the twilight gave depth.

Entering with a tray of tea and sweets, she said,

"I'm impressed by your influence. He never stirs when I appear; he just stays in a weird posture with head back and eyes and mouth half open so I don't even know if he's conscious. When I spoke of a training monk he opened his eyes normally and said by all means he must hold a proper interview. He labored to rise, but the nurse pressed him down, saying he should care only about his health. He closed his eyes with a tear and faintly asked me to relate whatever you said. I said you taught that daffodils are picked on the way to the region of the dead!"

"That is queer to say if he is unwell," Mokuzu objected.

"Don't worry," she returned with playful eyes. "Thoughtless though I am, I'm not so rude. I merely related your Greek or Roman myth. Anyhow it will turn out like that, right?"

"What did he say?"

"He insists on meeting you. He entreated then ordered the nurse to dress him. You must know how unlike him it is; these three months he has never left his bed. She's dressing him now, supporting him with her broad waist. What'll you do?"

"Pay my respects. Please prepare a censer in his room with a lit incense. Please give me one too," Mokuzu said matter-of-factly as he put on his own robe, which she had hung up.

Soon, with a burning stick of incense between thumbs and forefingers of his joined hands, he followed her along a dim corridor with a creaking floor.

Whenever he was about to meet a Zen priest, Mokuzu was full of the greatest circumspection and moral energy, an attitude fostered by his many interviews with Zen Master Tengai. For him, meeting a Zen priest was an occasion to actualize Yuanwu's clear and trenchant instructions, which he usually hid deep within:

> Those who would teach religion must be outstandingly high. So to speak, only those who are like men who do not avert their eyes even in committing murder are able to lead others to Buddhahood. Without contradiction they can see and at once grasp ripe opportunities, understand and apply theories, receive and conquer, gain means and ends...[5]

Mokuzu detected the odor of urine in the mingled odors of incense and disinfectant. He could not tell for what reason the sickroom was shut up, situated as the temple was on a mountainside and facing the sea. Was it fear of exposing the invalid to the outdoor air, or to the eyes of outsiders?

The chief priest was not old, yet his eyes were deep-sunk. His patchy stubble had grown long. Indeed he seemed within the hands of death. Mokuzu thought of a baby tooth that had for some three days begun to loosen.

He wore a fancy surplice — gold brocade with embroidered silver crests — but was so thin that his vestments appeared to be draped over a skeleton. Unlike on a person of normal bulk, the folds and pleats hung closed, a wretched sight. In actuality such a costume looked best on a round person like Zen Master Tengai.

The nurse was set to catch him from behind should he fall, and in the half-light her eyes seemed to blame Mokuzu for his temple visit, which was causing her charge to labor so. The wife waited beside Mokuzu more like his attendant, and she stared at his extravagant manner of offering his devoirs with bow and prostration thrice performed.

The priest cleared his throat repeatedly to no avail. His unsteady, husky voice was so hard to hear that Mokuzu failed to catch at least a third of his talk.

"...How thankful...your pilgrimage....A monk who doesn't mind cold or heat...yields to no temptation...travels purely for the Way....The best means of propagation is to show at each place and moment a sample of training. Relying on books and the fine arts, however good they are, is indisputably secondary," he said with great effort, and assisted by the nurse, he spat.

"At the same time," he resumed, "I am ashamed...contracted a disease... can't perform even tomorrow's nativity service....The laymen's misfortune is to have a sick priest," and he drooped his head. Because of the long silence, Mokuzu spoke up,

"It is a reasonable anguish. I understand your torment."

Suddenly the priest looked upward and gestured as if blindly tracing a Buddha image. Then he said, "What comes to mind are only compunctions... no one can comfort me...I've indulged myself while feigning to do my best... no task have I ever perfected...my faults come from my weak will....Perceiving that to eat only serves my illness, I resolved to fast for a week, but on the third night I was eating three days' worth! Laugh if you like, and laugh that I was betrayed by my first wife...and rejected by my only son! My second wife I brought in to educate and I haven't taught her the sutras or meditation. I'm increasing her perversity and gibbeting my ugly self — I can't even go to the toilet unaided." He began to sob.

The nurse steadied his shoulders and told him to lie down. By a glance she asked Mokuzu to leave. He ignored her contemptuous eyes. The priest summoned the energy to free himself, and he spoke,

"Now, young trainee, you who are not yet old enough to gloss over your life and not so young as to be unaware, tell me your view, tell me the meaning of my life!"

Mokuzu listened patiently, then quietly like a bird gliding on water he began,

"Your question must be one of the most common questions of a dying person, though rarely is it answered to full satisfaction. First let me say I recognize your right to ask me, a stranger. Indeed one can't ask oneself, for one's life is like any other natural thing, the course of the sun and the moon, the tidal ebb and flow, the turn of the seasons: it cannot know its meaning while engaged as itself.

"Then, the meaning of your life can be argued by others only. And their views are fated to be either affirmative or negative and to be subdivided endlessly, with the possible number of mobilized words amounting to no less than all the terms employed for the systemization of botany and zoology.

"So you can choose to keep asking strangers until your final day, or stop asking and fully live your life. Anyway, I'll improvise a gatha for you:

> "Even a poem jotted on wastepaper without reason or rhyme
>   is of worth if it has a timeless line.
> Brighten yourself and others as if to light a night village.
> If it be short of such words, burn your poem
>   and lay the ash around the base of daffodils."

Just as Mokuzu finished, the priest with a weak cry fell backward into the arms of the nurse. "Uphold your spirit!" she said and hurriedly prepared a restorative.

As he withdrew he saw that the wife was stifling laughter. He could not figure why, but made no comment. When they entered the room given him, she exclaimed,

"Why didn't you snub him like Bodhidharma when he answered Emperor Wu with 'I don't know!'? She laughed openly.

Later she brought him a meal ordered from a restaurant in the fishing town and ate with him. Offering him beer, she asked,

"By the way, he's beseeching that you perform the nativity service and the lecture to our laymen. What do you say?"

"With regret I must decline, much as I am receiving his kindness of a night's lodging and a meal. Please explain I am a trainee who can merely walk through towns and villages."

She left and soon returned.

"He begged me with prayerful hands to ask you to accept 'no matter what' — his pet expression. He added you can do the whole thing absolutely as you like. Why not grant his request? After all, he feels guilty not to be doing his duty, and it's a good chance for you, and I can see how you do it." Her manner was like a sister persuading a younger brother.

Mokuzu ate the supper. Afterward he said simply, "I'll do what I can."

Delighted, she offered him more beer, though he declined. She had prepared three bottles, and they had each taken only a glass from the first.

She cleared the table. With his supper tray he followed her to the kitchen. "Thanks, just leave it there," she said, but he began to wash his dishes. "You needn't, they're the restaurant's." Yet he continued in his conscientious way.

"How good to see a real trainee! You do it anyway and raise no clatter. My native home is a hot-spring hotel. I wish you could teach them how to work in the kitchen."

Mokuzu faintly smiled. Then she said, "But what's the value of such training? What's the point of self-restriction? Is it a necessary base for influencing others?"

"I have no interest in putting anyone but myself under my control, if that's what you mean by 'influence.'"

"How about having a favorable influence on other lives, then? Isn't that part of a Bodhisattva's vow?"

"It depends on how 'favorable influence' is defined; seeing each person's total life is very hard. We have only one life, and we can't compare what we have with what we might have had."

"Then what is a priest's task? How can a Bodhisattva help others if he doesn't surely know what's a good life for them?"

"A Bodhisattva loves, respects, and trusts his life and is responsible for it. And he will love, respect, trust, and be responsible for the life of someone he can love as his own if such a one appears," replied Mokuzu somewhat impatiently.

"Ha ha! You mean a Bodhisattva loves a sweetheart? That's like any ordinary love affair!"

"Your understanding, I believe, isn't far from the truth. Love and wisdom are two essentials for a Bodhisattva, and after all they are everyone's basic concerns." Mokuzu wanted to retire, having washed and dried the dishes.

But she stood in his way.

"It's early. Won't you walk in the front garden with me?" she asked with a straight face. Mokuzu thought it improper to walk intimately with another man's wife, especially the wife of one who was gravely ill, and at night. Yet her eyes were charmingly direct. He preferred walking with her to meditating alone in his lodgings. "It couldn't be wrong," he said.

They went out and came to the veranda of the main building.

"The lotuses in summer open their buds one after another, you can hear them, they make a sound, and many fireflies circle above the water," she said, standing beside him.

"It must be nice. I suppose you can see the far lights of cuttlefish boats.

867

I detect the yulan in this moist air."

"Oh? It isn't my perfume?" She tilted her head to expose her nape. Her shoulder touched his chest, and he felt some stray hairs on his face. Embarrassed, he went to the pondside. She too came, and, pulling his sleeve, she said,

"See those pine branches? The moon reflects on the pond through an opening there. Some nights I stay awake so late I can see it cross over the front gate and set in the sea, and then I wonder why the founder put a pond here. For committing suicide there's the more dreadful sea. Or did he like lotus flowers, and use the rhizomes for his vegetarian diet? What do you think?"

"You've a bright nature and don't see how morbid your pleasantry is when your husband is meeting his end. A naturally beautiful woman grows ugly day and night unless she cultivates her mind," ventured Mokuzu calmly.

She did not flinch.

"True, but I haven't a bright nature. And I never thought I'm beautiful, even told so a thousand times. Am I?"

"People tend to slight laudable qualities when they praise surface looks. You may resemble this pond...lotus flowers and fireflies in dim moonlight through pines in summer; dry stalks, snowy banks, and strikingly white pines in winter...but as we admire its seasonal beauty, we shouldn't miss the intent of whoever built it."

"As we circle it, so does our talk. Didn't I ask what you think his intent was?" She sat down on a flat rock at the end of the bridge, by the leaning trunk of a red pine. She looked up at Mokuzu, who kept standing, and slightly tightened her smile, anticipating his teaching.

"Well, Sakyamuni Buddha advised his followers to gather all creatures caught in their drinking-water filters and release them into the ponds and rivers. I think this ancient story alone tells us that our Buddhist precepts are formed not merely by our sentiment for weak creatures, but also by our practical rules for health. In other words, saving other creatures was a natural principle of live-and-let-live.

"And in China at Mt. Tiantai, Jyyi designated a square zone as a fish sanctuary."

"Wasn't it more from a utilitarian view than from any view of coexistence and coprosperity? Fishermen now increasingly have to restrict their haul and restrict where they fish, but where's any element of compassion?" said the wife.

"At age eighteen Jyyi became a priest because the Liang dynasty faced disorder and his kin had the misfortune of being scattered. His disregard for worldly fame brought him to Mt. Tiantai. There he protected the fish with evidently pure compassion. However slight the effect, he did his best. I think human beauty surfaces especially when one does one's brimful effort regardless of whether the result is minuscule. In contrast, human ugliness is exposed when one's spirituality is minuscule, though one's conduct leaves a massive consequence. In Japan the thirtieth emperor, Bidatsu, prohibited the killing of animals and fish on six specified purification days each month. The fortieth, Tenmu, initiated a regular practice of freeing birds and fish from captivity. Was the concern of these emperors only their own weight or blood pressure?"

"No," she said and excitedly added, "Japan had an abundance of creatures in its fields and waters, though it's almost unimaginable now. Yet those leaders of our nation cared about them, while in other countries with equal abundance, creatures were caught to the point of extinction. I begin to see the hidden beauty of this pond. You spoke of hidden beauty versus outer beauty. What exactly is a person's hidden beauty?"

"You mustn't be impatient to know; it takes years of self-training, I guess. There's a petition chanted at the end of the service to free birds and fish." Facing the pond, beside the bridge, Mokuzu chanted in a low voice,

> "May you creatures nevermore be caught. May you complete your natural life, and after a natural death be reborn in Trayastrimsa to enjoy life under the divine influence of Prabhutaratna; and because various Buddhas have appeared to preach the Vaipulya, may you attend, hear the Dharma, realize the mind of non-birth, and obtain certification as a Bodhisattva.
>
> "May we who free you also be granted greater will and wisdom to attain Bodhisattvahood that we may continue to save suffering creatures. May we be reborn in the peace of the Pure Land and meet there the various saints. May we quickly realize the life of non-birth even as we remain in this unclean world to help sentient beings attain Buddhahood along with us."[6]

"Your pleasant voice put me to sleep. My mind stopped and I couldn't make sense of all the words and ideas." The priest's wife stood by Mokuzu with her hands on the parapet.

"You needn't make sense of it all, but the basic ideas of the prayer are occasionally worth serious thought. They are the belief that first, all creatures are equally valuable; second, the real and ultimate saving of other lives means to lead them to Buddhahood, the life of non-birth; and third, attaining Buddhahood together is important, so while others are yet behind, those ahead will keep working as Bodhisattvas to help them to attain it. The best realistic life for a human being is to live as a Bodhisattva until all sentient beings attain Buddhahood. We should have a dream. To live as a Bodhisattva is the greatest dream we can give ourselves. Whoever hasn't this dream cannot be a beautiful person."

"I see. Someday beauty counters will display cosmetics with names like 'Bodhisattva.'" She giggled and swiftly took his hand. "Won't you go to the beach? There isn't now, but later there'll be an orange waning moon. How nice to go barefoot on the night sand! For days and nights that's been my dream, but I couldn't, being a priest's wife and a woman..."

Mokuzu was amazed at her quick shift of subject and level of the word "dream." But he had no ill feeling toward her. He unaffectedly freed his hand and asked,

"The beach is nice, but what about your husband?"

"He's sick!"

"Well, yes."

"I mean, in the worst sense — it's sinful to fall into such a state. It isn't cancer or anything cardiac. They say he has nothing wrong anywhere. He was thoroughly checked in a university hospital and in a Red Cross hospital."

"The doctors can't diagnose his illness?"

"He believes he's ill, and that's all. I hate to see him, or anyone with any sort of belief. I've begun to believe all believers are ill." She walked toward the gate. Following, Mokuzu said,

"But he is living in a fine temple, with a fine view of the sea, through flowers...."

She talked about the priest's ridiculous behavior as they descended to the beach,

"Like a thrush intently listening for any stir in the ground, he tries to detect unusual signs from his innards. He so cares about his health that he insists on eating only insecticide-free foods to the point of ill effect; sometimes he won't eat for days, saying it's necessary for purifying his body, and he meditates or chants without sleeping. In short he does everything to injure his health so as to pull my attention, and that, because he fears death. This absurd fear makes him toy with his life, with a woman's affections. Will you hear more?"

"No. My concern is human decency and the ideal with which to live proudly one's honorable life." Mokuzu was inwardly ashamed of his having been unable to see through at a glance the chief priest, and also his wife.

62

Lecture Tour

The sun through the trees brightened the nemophilas and snapdragons laden with dew. Mokuzu at the white wall was looking out to the calm and faintly indigo sea when he realized the priest's wife was beside him.

Her given name was Shizuka, maiden name Fuji, and she was in fact not yet entered in the priest's family register though she had been living in the temple for some years. This she told Mokuzu the previous night on the beach.

She met his eyes and smiled affably. There were fine lines between her eyebrows. Her brown irises were dazzling.

"Are you thinking of the lecture you will give the laymen?"

"No, I was imagining the old days when ships sailed before the wind and carts were drawn by beasts of burden. After the invention of motors, Buson's haiku became outmoded —

> "Spring sea,
> idle is the wave
> rolling all day long."[1]

"While appearing so intense as to make others nervous, you're indulging in such easy thoughts? Isn't this your first time addressing so many people?"

"Yes, but I tell myself a Zennist is always steady." Shizuka looked apprehensive.

"What good is telling yourself that? A plank a meter high is easy to walk, but one between the tops of two skyscrapers is another matter. You should prepare."

"It's nothing to worry about. My Zen master told us a preacher must see his audience as tombstones. Besides, he said a Zennist's lectures are to give evidence of a Zennist's way of life, unlike lectures that unilaterally transmit dead knowledge and premolded ideas. Zennists prepare nothing special outside of living a careful daily life."

"Okay. Then you'd better dress up. As expected, about two hundred are already crowding into the main building. I've brought his ceremonial robes." She hiked her kimono to step to the veranda, where indeed there were the chief priest's gala robes in a paulownia drawer.

"They don't suit me. I'm satisfied with my own."

"But today is an auspicious day, everyone is dressed up. I'm of the temple and you're the sort who doesn't mind my quiet dress, yet this is my choicest pongee kimono of Oshima Isle production — look, the threads are spun from floss dyed in Yeddo hawthorn, then dyed again and again in an iron-containing mud unique to the island. These splashes are made by pricking up the warp every few inches with a needle, evenly to match the woof — altogether a fabric made by tremendous labor," she explained, patting herself on the flank.

The kimono, dark blue-brown patterned in white, looked refreshing to the touch. She was kneeling on one knee on the veranda. 'A good choice; it doesn't compete with all the flowers,' Mokuzu thought, still in the garden.

"It looks nice. And I am content as I am. I hope I never have to wear fancy robes. I shall begin." He mounted the veranda to head to the main building.

"Fine, but walk slowly so I can meet you at the entrance." As she hurried to step down, her calf was momentarily exposed. Mokuzu thought of a lily bulb dug from the soil.

When he arrived where he could see the audience in a general stir, Shizuka came breathless from the front garden with a branch of plump yulan buds.

"Hold this," she whispered. "I'll be attending in a corner. Do your best!"

The audience spontaneously quieted and watched Mokuzu advance to a prepared lecture platform.

'Does she know and is she observing the custom of Buddha's being offered a lotus or an *udumbara* flower by a member of the audience whenever he was asked to preach? Or is she merely displaying her femininity to ornament and encourage me in a plain robe?'

Within the flower-decked shrine, on a table before the lecture platform, an infant Sakyamuni Buddha stood with right arm pointed heavenward and left arm pointed earthward. The little statue was set in a basin of hydrangea tea, a tea likened to the *amrta* that Naga showered on Sakyamuni at his birth. The infant's face was round, noble, and pure. Banked on either side of the shrine were offerings harvested from the sea and the mountains.

Mokuzu surveyed the assembly. Most were old people accompanied by small children. Shizuka was sitting reverently at the very back, a little apart, behind a pillar.

He started quietly,

"I did not know until my chance now to walk along the Sanin shore that coast dwellers can tell the advent of spring by the change of the tide; that from a wintry deep blue, the sea gradually turns a pale blue and the ebb and flow is more notable than in any other season.

"Born in the mountains, even now I don't know such delights as gathering short-necked clams and razor clams at low tide, and turban shells, ear shells, and abalones from the reefs; nor know the joy of gathering *kajime*, *tsunomata*, *hijiki*, *mozuku*, *ugo*, and other seaweeds.

"Fortunately I do know mountain spring, which becomes more sure with each rain. The birds chirp increasingly, and their nest-building can be spotted here and there. Hawks and eagles choose to nest on cliffs or the tops of giant trees in mountains hardly approachable by us. Herons gather dead reeds and build coarse nests at the waterside. Pheasants prefer the thickets of piny mountain skirts. Crows choose firs or cedars and lay grass and feathers in their nests, so pleasant for their young.

"People sow vegetable and flower seeds. It's also the best time for cutting and grafting. Aside from that, the fields and mountains provide many edible herbs: buds of angelica tree and pepper tree; matrimony vine, *udo*, arrowhead, chives, wild rocambole, leek, field horsetail, bracken, flowering fern, dropwort, horseradish...

"You have an enviable environment, open sea in front, mountains behind, and you are now in the midst of spring. That you know spring is a matter for congratulation; you naturally have no difficulty celebrating Buddha's birthday. Buddha was born in Lumbini, near the Nepal border, a place described as 'a land quite fertile, with regular changes of season, orderly agricultural activity, and gentle public morals.'[2] He was a prince, son of a raja named Suddhodana, meaning 'pure rice.' His given name was Siddhatta, which happily means 'every wish attained,' and his family name was Gotama, 'preeminent cow.'

"But I don't intend to introduce the biography of a great man who lived about two thousand five hundred years ago. It's an impossible task, and even among the oldest sutras no biographic record exists. The so-called life of Sakyamuni Buddha is a mythical invention of much later generations. Orthodox Buddhists, including his direct disciples, regarded his personal life as no more than a transitory, relative phenomenon. Their concern continued to be universal values warrantable for all mankind.

"So while we say today is Buddha's birthday, it is not to celebrate the man Gotama Siddhatta but to congratulate new life, the newborn of all creatures. Today is also not the occasion to think about Sakyamuni Buddha himself, but to investigate and to aspire to become a Buddha or a Tathagata, the ideal human image for us all.

"My talk is getting a little hard, but please understand that the basic thought of Buddhism and the rightful life of Buddhists is to desire a pure, peaceful, and non-suffering life for all sentient beings and to summon our effort to realize such an ideal world.

"This being my preliminary, let us now chant together 'The Stanza for

Pouring the Amrta on Buddha,' chanted on this occasion and telling us basic Buddhist thought. The melody is quite difficult, but never mind, just repeat each phrase after me. We shall chant the stanza three times, and I'm sure you will become skillful toward the end. So let me begin," and he struck the big bell five times and began,

"Go—u ki—n ka—n, mo—o shi—i i—, ji—ra—a a—i."

Hearing the resonant voice and embellished melody, the people were taken with wonder and preferred just to listen. But urged on by him they began, their timid start wavering like the tentacles of sea anemones.

Mokuzu earnestly advanced, "Ji—n shi—i, so-u-o o—ne—n ku—n te—e e—, e—jyu—u u—"

The repeats became brighter and more vigorous.

"U—ji—u, u—shi-u-n sa—n, ri—n ri—i i—, i—kyo—o o—"

As the audience repeated, Mokuzu scooped the amrta with a bamboo ladle and poured it on the little statue. Among the elderly he could see infants imitating the chanting with palms joined. Shizuka too was chanting with praiseworthy earnestness.

"Zu—n shi—n ji—i i—ra-a-i, ji—n pa—a a —, a—shi—i i—n."[3]

Before they completed the last phrase, Mokuzu returned to the first. The tone of the second chanting was higher and the third yet higher, and the chorus thus traveled from the open main building, through the trees by the pond, over the wall, and out to sea.

At the close of the unified response, the vicinity became clear and quiet as if a levitation had settled, and the assembly felt a well-being from the flush of oxygen in their chests and from the resting of their thoughts.

No one raised a sound. The image of the baby must have appeared even more noble and smile-provoking.

Mokuzu let some time pass as if waiting for a full measure of water fed to a new-planted tree to soak into the soil. But he was not necessarily enjoying the musical effect given to his audience; in fact it made him rather uncomfortable to see their satisfaction gained with no realistic effort to draw the ideal nearer. Then he said,

"What we chanted is the ideal for all people not only Buddhists. The stanza was written in Tang-dynasty Chinese. It can be translated roughly to Japanese as follows:

"We now pour sweet dew over all Tathagatas, whose merit it is to be adorned with pure wisdom. May sentient beings suffering in the five defilements come to realize they are as pure as any Tathagata.

"Here 'sentient beings' implies each of us, who are afflicted by contradictions between our desires and the unfulfillment of our desires. Desires arise through our five sense organs — eyes, ears, nose, tongue, and skin — in the five environs of color, sound, smell, taste, and touch. 'Suffering in the five defilements' therefore modifies 'sentient beings.'

"In other words, we are beings who live in a phlegmatic sea of defilements, or klesa. Klesa distresses, disturbs, deludes, and defiles us, and it is what separates us from our highest mental state. So we Buddhists have since of old struggled to identify the true character of our klesa and to deal successfully with it. Indeed a great portion of our training is to contend with klesa.

"Now, klesa has been classified in various ways. Though complicated, there are basically two main groups. One is called, in Chinese, *mili* and is intellectual, uh...to do with mental confusion in understanding the Buddhist universal truth, and is divided into eighty-eight kinds. The other is *mishy* and pertains to the confusion over individual, phenomenal affairs, relating rather to emotion and will, and is divided into eighty-one kinds. There are other ways to count klesa, for instance to total one hundred eight — which is the number of times we strike the temple bell on the last night of the year. Another version details as many as eighty-four thousand kinds.

"Next, about pure being, Tathagata. The word is Sanskrit. As *tatha-gata* it means 'one who has arrived at the bare truth.' When analyzed as *tatha-agata* it becomes 'one who has come from the truth and who teaches the truth in this world.' The Tibetans and the Chinese translated the same sutras into their own languages, but the Tibetans held to the former interpretation and the Chinese to the latter.

"Moreover, *tathagata* was already long in use by the religions of ancient India before Buddhism, and to those ancients it meant 'one who has attained freedom from the transmigration of souls,' so I have heard.

"Now, in the stanza for pouring on the amrta, understand tathagata as our original nature, or pure being beyond the influence of time, relativity, and causation, thus, one who has transcended every affliction coming from klesa.

"Last, let me explain about purity. This too Buddhists classified variously, as physical purity, mental purity, the mental state wherein klesa is temporarily suppressed, the mental state wherein klesa is severed, pure environment, pure people who dwell therein, and the mental state wherein the purity of one's original nature is realized by an understanding of sunyata.

"As to explaining the Buddhist terms, that is enough. They are complicated and annoy us, but the meaning of the stanza is simple: We sentient beings troubled by five defilements are the same as the Tathagata, pure being, when we conquer our defilements. Let us vow to be assiduous to realize we are the same. So we vow before the baby Sakyamuni today and vow whenever we see the newborn. We all were born pure and must realize we are pure, and must help one another to realize we are pure. This is the highest way to live, taught by Sakyamuni Buddha.

"Jesus Christ also taught the importance of purity. When his disciples asked him who was greatest in the kingdom of heaven, he called to him a child and said,

> "'Truly, I say to you, unless you turn and become like children, you will never enter the kingdom of heaven. Whoever humbles himself like this child, he is the greatest in the kingdom of heaven.'[4]

"Christianity emplaces an absolute and transcendental God outside oneself. And Christians see righteousness and salvation in their approach to God, unlike Buddhists, who see righteousness and salvation in realizing Buddha nature within themselves; and there are some differences of expression. Yet what Jesus says here could not greatly differ from our idea of pure being.

"What we truly should love and respect is pure being. Our culture should be based on a firm recognition of pure being, and pure being should be protected and nursed at all costs.

"Nowadays we worry about environmental pollution and nuclear extinction. I think the best preventive measure against both is a worldwide recognition of the importance of protecting pure being. When we know what we should safeguard and nurture, we will seek every means to maintain a pure and peaceful world.

"Listen to Jesus, he speaks of the value of pure being:

> "'Whoever receives one such child in my name receives me; but whoever causes one of these little ones who believe in me to sin, it would be better for him to have a great millstone fastened round his neck and to be drowned in the depth of the sea.'[5]

"His words to all who slight and harm pure being are vehement as if he were swearing revenge; though remember it was he who taught us, 'Love your enemies and pray for those who persecute you.'[6] In the Dhammapada, Sakyamuni Buddha also said,

> "Anger will never end unless our anger ends.
> Such is the nature of anger.
> Until we see the need of self-reflection,
> War will never end.[7]

"Even so, pure being is worth defending to the last, and those who harm it are performing an outrage upon humanity and are the greatest enemy of humankind.

"Then where, when, and in whom can we see pure being? We each are endowed with it, and we must see it in our daily life, in everyone, everywhere. When we see it in our ordinary days, our ordinary days are not merely tedious, random repetitions. When we see it in our family, in our workplace, and in our place of abode, we are practicing the ideal life taught by Sakyamuni Buddha. When we see it in those nearby — spouse, children, parents, neighbors — we are practicing the ideal of Buddhism instead of taking pleasure in abstract arguments over ideas.

"However, we must continue to remind ourselves of our stupid, forgetful nature. Once on shore, we pray no more. We forget the mind of the poor when we are rich, the pain of illness when we are well, the greatness of peace when we live in peace. In a life of comfort we think it absurd to consider pure being; in a life of indolence and luxury we shun sincere subjects and ridicule the sanctity and beauty of humanity. Then the ordinary day, which should be radiant and holy, lapses into a stagnant day, which, amounting to nothing, is sucked into oblivion.

"Sakyamuni Buddha was exemplary. Although he was a prince who could enjoy as much peace and wealth as he pleased, he did not avert his eyes from the needy and from war. While young and healthy he pondered illness and death. And he entered the priesthood to seek eternal peace of mind.

"Those who in peacetime do not see the misery of war are also those who do not identify the Tathagata in sentient beings suffering from five defilements.

"At the close of my lecture let us be reminded of the background that induced Jesus to express his fiery words 'to have a great millstone fastened round his neck and to be drowned...' Let me translate from The Lamentations of Jeremiah:

"Even the jackals give the breast and suckle their young,
but the daughter of my people has become cruel, like the ostriches in the wilderness.

The tongue of the nursling cleaves to the roof of its mouth for thirst;
the children beg for food, but no one gives to them.

Those who feasted on dainties perish in the streets;
those who were brought up in purple lie on ash heaps.

For the chastisement of the daughter of my people has been greater
than the punishment of Sodom,
which was overthrown in a moment, no hand being laid on it.

Her princes were purer than snow, whiter than milk;
their bodies were more ruddy than coral, the beauty of their form was like sapphire.

Now their visage is blacker than soot, they are not recognized in the streets;
their skin has shriveled upon their bones, it has become as dry as wood.

Happier were the victims of the sword than the victims of hunger,
who pined away, stricken by want of the fruits of the field.

The hands of compassionate women have boiled their own children;
they became their food in the destruction of the daughter of my people."

❧

After lecturing, Mokuzu returned to his lodging room and at once prepared to set off. As he was tying on his leggings, Shizuka entered and lightsomely said,

"Why the hurry? I planned to guide you to my native house, a hot-spring hotel. The car I sent for is waiting."

Indeed under the gate there was a black car. A chauffeur was dusting the hood with a feather duster.

Mokuzu got in. The seat had a white slipcover. Shizuka followed, and though there was ample room, she drew near and took from her bosom a wrapped honorarium, which she handed to him with the words,

"The laymen's token of gratitude. I could study a lot from your lecture. You know, many works of Kandinsky came to mind."

"Who?"

"A Russian-born painter regarded as one of the originators of abstract art. I saw his works in Europe with my aunt; she's a tea ceremony teacher. We went at the end of my school years. His works are so pure they directly appeal like an extract of emotion with no muddy surplus. Concrete forms hinder our understanding of ourselves and others. In my native house I'll show you a book of his paintings."

The car advanced through mountains covered in vivid green. The gorges were filled with rich crowns overhung with mist. Whenever the car passed under a dark growth of trees, the chauffeur applied the windshield wipers.

"Look, there are leeches on those mossy branches! — do you see?" Shizuka pointed and brought her cheek near Mokuzu's. He did not see them, and she smiled.

The car labored up a steep dirt road. Even a second's delay in turning the wheel could have sent the car into the misty valley. Each curve exposed new peaks in regions inland.

"Colored carp are stocked in the valley stream. The hot spring warms it year round. The villagers raise carp as their main work. Look down to where the mist has cleared — you can see them even from here."

"It must be nice to walk along the stream."

"Yes, everyone used to walk, there was no road for cars. Which reminds me, Great Teacher Jikaku is reputed to have discovered a hot spring deep in the mountains while touring like you. But in this modern, highly developed narrow land what hot spring can you discover?" Shizuka smiled a playful smile.

Koko in Mokuzu's place would likely have put his thick palm somewhere on Shizuka and exhibited his Zen talent in saying, "Eureka!"

But Mokuzu was, so to speak, often disengaged, drawn by ideas. He had read Jikaku's record of his pilgrimage to Tang China to seek the Dharma. He recorded his hardships at sea, and that he spent over half his stay just to visit Mt. Wutai. When finally he reached the capital of Changan he faced the religious persecution of Hueichang and was forced into a secular life. Mokuzu fancied himself traveling the world and publishing his own record.

Shizuka pulled his hand and spoke with energy,

"Listen, I've a splendid idea I dreamed last night. I'm sure it's possible now that I've heard your lecture. You will tour, you and me. I'll handle such matters as audiences, locations, and lodgings, and you'll just give lectures suited to each audience. Of course the honorarium will be all yours."

"It sounds haphazard, as if you're proposing to go for a drive to seek a minor thrill," laughed Mokuzu.

"I'm serious. You too give it serious thought! You can talk freely in front of people without having to prepare. You'll earn a lot of money effectively, and I don't care how you use it. Tell me any reason why you can't accept my proposal."

Mokuzu had in fact begun to wish to earn money more effectively than by begging. He thought he was wasting his youth and was impatient to see a definite date to go to Thailand and then to America. What was preventing him from departing this island country was a shortage not only of travel money but of money to sustain his old parents and his ill brother. He knew once he left he would not return.

Frequently he remembered the circumstances of Sixth Patriarch Hueineng, how he left home to train under Fifth Patriarch Hungren. Hueineng himself said in his recollection,

> My father, native to Fanyang, was relegated to Lingnan, whence he became a peasant in Shinjou and unfortunately died early. My mother and I then moved to Nanhai and endured poverty and hardship. While growing up I sold firewood in the market.

One day a messenger came to me with an order for a delivery. When I with my payment was leaving the house where I made the delivery, I saw the owner reciting a sutra. Hearing a snatch, my mind was opened and I came to a realization. I asked him what sutra it was. He said, "The Diamond Sutra." I asked how he came to have it.

"I got it at Dungchan Temple in Huangmei of Chi. There a great teacher named Hungren is teaching a throng of over a thousand. I attended among them. He advises priest and layman alike to read the Diamond Sutra, for it teaches 'self-realization of one's true nature and at once attainment of Buddhahood.'"

Mokuzu could not forget the conclusion:

I must have good karma for his telling me so. He therewith gave me ten ounces of silver for my old mother's livelihood and encouraged me to visit Fifth Patriarch Hungren for my training.[8]

There was no one to support Mokuzu's parents and brother. He was inclined to abandon his regard for them and carry a guilty conscience. But now Shizuka's proposal gave him hope that he could make money in a short time. He asked her directly,

"You will manage the business but don't ask to share the honorarium? Why?"

"You ask with so earnest a look — you don't see me at all! You might reasonably misunderstand if I wore heavy makeup, but I don't. Can't we be more intimate so we can understand each other beneath the surface?"

Mokuzu was baffled. Her voice became subdued,

"Isn't it obvious? I can hear your lectures. Regardless of how you think of me, please know my interest has been to train in Buddhism. I also studied Christianity in college. Can you remember Martha and Mary, sisters of Lazarus of Bethany?"

She impressed him by quoting in English from Luke 10:

"Now as they went on their way, he entered a village; and a woman named Martha received him into her house. And she had a sister called Mary, who sat at the Lord's feet and listened to his teaching. But Martha was distracted with much serving; and she went to him and said, 'Lord, do you not care that my sister has left me to serve alone? Tell her then to help me.' But the Lord answered her, 'Martha, Martha, you are anxious and troubled about many things; one thing is needful. Mary has chosen the good portion, which shall not be taken away from her.'

"I read it in my school days and resolved to become a woman who partakes of both Martha and Mary. It became my ideal!"

Mokuzu was amazed by her archaic ideal, so like a little old building with a patinated roof in a busy modern city. He was not the only one pursuing an ideal, however old-fashioned in appearance. She was a free-spirited person, but not shallow.

The inn that was Shizuka's native house was built in tiers against a rocky mountainside just beyond a short bridge over the flume. Above the entrance, lounge, office, and kitchen were a second and third floor for guests.

After the death of her parents, the inn was run by her brother and his wife. The guests were mostly regular visitors and the inn was quiet.

The brother and wife came out to greet Mokuzu and courteously ushered him to the best quarters. The inn being small, Shizuka's brother served also as chef. He wore a white apron over a developing paunch and constantly smiled with gentle manners. His wife, in a yellowish silk kimono with an apron, appeared to be serving as a parlormaid. She and Shizuka seemed intimate and exchanged much womanly information in a short time.

The best quarters were a separate, hip-roofed building reached by an elevated tile-roofed corridor exposed to every wind. The corridor bridged the flume. Its supports and handrails were partly hidden by tall maple and cinnamon trees. Looking up through cherries just beginning to bloom, Mokuzu saw a half-open shoji and a towel hung out on a rail.

There was a living room adjoining a bedroom, surrounded by a veranda. A breeze came from the green mountain behind, and the purling of the clear stream rose in front. The building, like the corridor, was supported by exposed columns as if designed for aquatic life. A path descended directly below through rocks and such bushes as azalea, rhododendron, andromeda, and cowberry. The stream flowed over some little falls. In their deep basins colored carp were gathered.

After lunch Shizuka left Mokuzu to himself. He spent the time looking through a picture book she had brought and writing his diary of the past several days.

Toward dusk she reappeared to guide him to a hot spring. She made him change to a cotton yukata, white with indigo print, provided by the hotel, and she too changed to one. They went to the second floor and out one end to a path through a wooded garden. The bath was in the open against rock walls and a hedge. Round black pebbles laid over a drain received the overflow. Seven such springs were said to be hidden here and there from near the summit to the level of the stream. Some guests enjoyed visiting them all. Of course each room also had a bath.

"This one is best for appreciating the moon," said Shizuka as she undid her sash. Mokuzu, at a loss, remained seated on a rock in the hotel's yukata and pretended to be watching the pink clouds over the mountain beyond the flume.

"Relax, I'll go behind a rock," she said and moved off through the water to an area of rocks and ferns.

While she was out of sight Mokuzu quickly entered the water, and before she reappeared he returned to his quarters. He opened the fusumas dividing the two rooms. Within, beds for two were laid side by side with two neatly placed pillows.

He quietly closed the fusumas, went to the veranda, and sat on a rattan chair facing books of paintings by Kandinsky, B. Shahn, J. Pollock, and M. Graves.

In his embarrassment he pondered what his Zen master would do in such a situation and imagined him bitterly scolding,

"Fool! Caught by the lure of lecture fees! Don't put me in your place, I'm not so stupid! Well, you can only remind yourself that without entering the water you cannot know whether you are great."[9]

"My, you were quick!" Shizuka, with a fresh complexion, was standing next to him, inclining her head as she cooled her nape with a damp towel. She carefully hung the towel on the rail and leaned over to look at the scenery settling into dusk.

"Won't you walk below? Soon the hanging lanterns will be lit." She turned to him. With solemn gravity he replied,

"Walking is good, but I understand I am here solely for a lecture tour. Am I right?"

Shizuka laughed brightly as if reading his mind, "You are oversolicitous! Don't worry, I'm making a plan. Beginning tomorrow you will lecture. If you wish, I can arrange a schedule more strenuous than your pilgrimage, so at night you'll have no energy left. At ten tomorrow morning you are to lecture to hotel managers and workers, sponsored by the local hotel association. They hope to hear about Zen manners. My brother arranged it. My aunt will come here tomorrow afternoon. She teaches tea ceremony at over thirty places in the prefecture. You will lecture at each. She has many connections, with 4-H, Lions, Rotary..."

"You are relying heavily on your aunt. Have you considered its merit to her?"

"It seems you can't trust a person's simple good wish. My aunt didn't marry, and she raised me from as far back as I can remember. She did all I asked, even when it was an unreasonable request. This time, being aware that

Zen has great relation to her tea ceremony, she has given me her hearty approval by phone. Look, come quick, it's a kingfisher!"

Mokuzu leaned on the rail beside her.

"It's a lonesome bird," he said, to which she responded,

> "...After the kingfisher's wing
> Has answered light to light, and is silent, the light is still
> At the still point of the turning world.[10]

"T. S. Eliot's lines would please Zen people, don't you agree?" she said and caught his eye. Mokuzu could sense the poet's attempt to halt eternity, but he saw no such effect in the actual bird; and he remembered the first lines of "The Kingfisher" by W. H. Davies, the Welsh poet who loved a vagabond life, peddling and roaming now and anon in England and America. He recorded his experience in *The Autobiography of a Super-Tramp.*

> It was the Rainbow gave thee birth,
> And left thee all her lovely hues;
> And, as her mother's name was Tears,
> So runs it in my blood to choose
> For haunts the lonely pools, and keep
> In company with trees that weep.[11]

Shizuka moved to where the railings crossed at the corner and reached for a Takao maple leaf, deeply digitated, the basal part like the top of a heart. She raised her heels and leaned out, a risky attempt with the deep valley.

"Well, I cannot go like a spider so freely between branch and rail....The fact is, my father built this annex so a woman painter could stay here. And she gave birth to me. My brother is actually my half-brother. My aunt took me in."

Mokuzu remained silent, his face grave, but with a laugh Shizuka continued,

"It's not so serious! I know, this worries you?" and from the veranda she opened a shoji to the bedroom and said, "What's wrong with unbending to trust and love? Or do you prefer a restless night lying apart under a quilt heavy as a reef? Bringing a measure of purity to a relationship is generally not so important as being just. Recall Matthew I.18-24,

> "Now the birth of Jesus Christ took place in this way. When his mother Mary had been betrothed to Joseph, before they came together she was found to be with child of the Holy Spirit; —

"And listen, here's the point:

> "and her husband Joseph, being a just man —

"See? He was just. So he was 'unwilling to put her to shame,' and 'resolved to divorce her quietly.' And then, he could dream of an angel of the Lord, whose command he obeyed in taking her as his wife and her son as his son. Sex is ugly only if the people involved are unjust. At any rate it's a natural phenomenon beyond judgment of purity, like the water of the sea: a little stain can be remedied by nature's purifying functions."

"You are clever and bright," said Mokuzu. "You remind me of Manjusri in a sutra called *Bauji jing* in Chinese. He is described as having attempted to kill Buddha by a sword to prove sin has no substance and thus rescue Buddha's disciples prejudiced and troubled by surface meanings of morality. What you have just said is good for such people. But you have to know that nature has a limited capacity to purify. A polluted sea cannot easily regain its purity; nor will ozone if destroyed soon again cover the sky.

"I believe my character will be cultivated in the struggle to realize my ideal. Being aware of my immature development makes me want to grow toward my ideal, and accordingly I must restrict my conduct. So I'd rather remain hungry than be fully satisfied.

"I want to step with care, with the least mistake. My life may seem timid and rigid, but my pure mind is hot as a furnace. In my heart I keep burning a fire of suffering, and I wish to meet one who is doing the same. Fire doesn't burn fire, nor does water purify water. I see in you the same quality, but it's partial, and the meeting of a partial sameness should not destroy the possibility of meeting a total sameness. It's too bad many don't realize that enjoying a transient and partial love drives away the pleasure of eternal, total love."

"Ha ha! With such force and elocution you express so simple a notion! You want to say your purity should be kept for the one you'll marry. Fine, that's respectable. But understand I'll not prepare separate rooms during the tour. I can sleep very properly side by side, but can you? We'll see!"

Mokuzu too laughed. An old couple walking below looked up.

63

Criticism

Shizuka stood quiet in the mist after seeing Mokuzu off for mendicancy. Over her head an evergreen magnolia became lit with sunlight and its opening buds emitted their summer-orange fragrance.

"The Zen teacher sets out so early, he had no breakfast," observed Aunt Hiromi. Suddenly aware of her presence, Shizuka responded, "He wishes to reach his destination when people are just beginning to be up and about."

They had come the day before into another province, Mokuzu had lectured, and they had spent the night in a Pure Land temple where the chief priest was an old friend of Hiromi's. Shizuka and Mokuzu were given a detached building and would stay two more nights. Hiromi, given a guest room in the main building, was returning to her work before noon.

Shizuka entered by a back opening through a hedge and after crossing a rill entered the detached building, divided from the main garden by low bushes.

She brought to the veranda a portable desk and opened a thick notebook in which fine letters were closely penned. Hiromi, having followed her in, came out with a tea set and said,

"I admire your meticulous work without use of glasses. Are you then recording every detail?"

"Yes, and I'll add an index and a glossary. It's amazing, he's been lecturing for nearly two months, but he scarcely repeats. Even when he quotes the same koan he lights it from a different angle, and yet he never contradicts anything he's said. So he's basically talking the same thing after all."

"A rare gift. I've been teaching the same thing for scores of years, and it's full of contradictions."

"Yes, he's unusual. He doesn't prepare, and can tell what people want to hear as soon as he sees their faces, and he talks on a level they can reach if only they extend their hand. So they aren't made uncomfortable by his lofty ideal, and at the same time no one treats him in an overly familiar way."

"And he illustrates difficult subjects with examples experienced by us all....But Shizuka, aren't you concerned for his health? He leaves so early, and today he has lectures in the afternoon and evening."

"Today he has only one, in the evening."

"I see. But he isn't built like a farmer or a laborer, nor are you for that matter, even if he endures for his training. So may I suggest you take separate

885

rooms? I'm thinking one reason he leaves so early is to avoid being with you in a narrow room."

"Oh, he doesn't care about that. Needless to say, I let him be." Shizuka laughed.

"May I ask how you spend the night?"

"We confirm the next day's schedule. Then I record the last lecture and he studies Sanskrit — he obtained a textbook in English. You can understand our need to be together just by realizing I must be very accurate in recording his lectures."

"Yes, but whose idea was it to record them like that?"

"Mine, obviously. He keeps everything in his head. I can't, and if I don't often reread it, I can't make it my flesh and blood. Besides, there are many points I don't understand right away."

"An amazing and enviable relationship, like brother and sister, teacher and pupil."

Shizuka then declared,

"It's decent, friendly, yet stern. These are the happiest days I've ever had. I confess I was intending to live proudly like those magnolia flowers beyond the hedge, but now I've begun to think a fig is more suitable. Look, that fig by the rill is making a dark shade, and within its leaves it perfects its fruit with devotion. My mother chose that way, I understand...."

Her aunt made no response, and Shizuka spoke some lines translated from "Figs" by D. H. Lawrence:

> "There was a flower that flowered inward, womb-ward;
> Now there is a fruit like a ripe womb.
>
> It was always a secret.
> That's how it should be, the female should always be secret.
> There never was any standing aloft and unfolded on a bough
> Like other flowers, in a revelation of petals..."[1]

"Shizuka, I can tell you are living fully these days and learning the depth and height of life beyond mundane concerns. Your progress leaves me well behind. But am I not right to worry about what you will do when this ideal relationship ends? Of course I'll keep assisting you to find lecture situations, but how long does he intend to go on?"

"If only forever! I've learned to manage the lectures and how best to present him. I keep his collar white and lay a flower on the platform. We could tour the Keihan district even to the National Capital region. He wants to go abroad. I'll go too, and through hardship we'll make our lecture tour. But it's a dream, too good for me. I must be thankful for the brief time I could experience a sample of ideal life. Otherwise I knew only a fast-fading life sullied by material interests and sundry affairs.

> "So pure in pure white,
> Moonflower in the hedge —
> Alas, an abortive flower![2]

"I've been truly happy!"

"But Shizuka, there's been no decision to stop..."

"I know he will suddenly say it's over. It could be tomorrow, even today. This record will then be my dearest belonging, proof that these days were no hallucination!" Shizuka clasped the notebook to her bosom.

Aunt Hiromi pitied her. "Why don't you speak your wish...?"

"That's impossible. I've presented myself as bright, composed, and stalwart. And I'm not as young as he. And above all I'd never hinder someone's training even if it meant no good chance for me. Trainees are the hope of the world, the credit of humankind, our closest treasures. Without them the earth had better be dashed by a giant meteor!"

❧

By July the lectures arranged by Aunt Hiromi were about exhausted and Shizuka had to make contracts on her own. Most lectures were set for evening at Mokuzu's request to enable him to gather alms throughout the day.

One day he was in a small town quite far from where he and Shizuka were lodging. Near noon he came back out of a local post office into the strong sun. Narrowing his eyes, he surveyed the row of low-roofed shops and houses. Not a soul was about. In the distance beyond was a mountain range backed by a great column of cloud.

'How will my parents receive the money I just sent? Anyway, I can now proceed on my way for my training,' he thought, and added, 'thanks to Shizuka.'

He walked on. Around one o'clock he was in a suburb planted with adzuki bean.

He crossed the tracks by an unmanned railway station. At the roadside was a humble teahouse with an old nettle shading some benches. He decided to have a simple lunch there.

From the teahouse the land dropped to thick green rice fields that extended like a vast swamp to a far mountain. On the mountain at about eye level was a village. Over the mountain the column of cloud was growing more active, rising high. He presumed that if he were standing on the summit he could affirm the cloud to be over the Japan Sea.

The shopkeeper with infant grandchild on her back brought to the bench the lunch he ordered. Reticent, she made to withdraw as soon as she placed the tray. But she did provide the information that the land had indeed been a swamp, that in her maidenhood there had been a ferryman, and that after being reclaimed to make rice fields, the area had declined because of the removal of the state road to elsewhere.

The nettle pleasantly blocked the sun. Its trunk was three feet in diameter. A hollow rose seven feet to where the branches began. Humus was heaped at the base. Mokuzu looked up and noticed a green insect in a crotch. It showed no movement. He poked it with a fallen branch and easily dislodged it to find it was a dead two-striped green buprestid. It was as light as nothing in his palm, but in the sun emitted so powerful a metallic emerald and purple that he could not look.

Gently he wrapped it in a tissue and a handkerchief and put it in his sleeve for Shizuka. According to a folk belief, a woman if she kept one in her bureau or vanity box would increase her wardrobe and be loved by many people.

Sitting again to have another cup of tea, he considered how to express his thanks to Shizuka at his coming departure. There was the vibration of a passing train.

After the tea more sweat broke out on his brow. Red and yellow evening primroses drooped at the roadside.

Noticing his fatigue, he debated whether to start on his return. Just then an old woman using an umbrella as a cane, who must have gotten off the train, entered the teahouse. She came out with flavored ice on a stick and sat diffidently nearby, eating it with clacking sounds as if extracting the optimum taste.

She had a bundle tied askew on her back. Tears ran from her eyes, though she was not weeping. Her face was darkly tanned, her hair thin and white. Her teeth were gone, giving her mouth creases like the draw-string end of a purse.

Mokuzu stood up to go and was reaching for his bamboo hat when she spoke something.

"Did you speak to me, granny?" he asked politely.

"I only said you're a young monk." She turned and unexpectedly raised her voice, "Hoi! Another!"

The shopkeeper approached with another ice stick.

"Not for me! For the monk!"

Mokuzu felt much obliged and also at a loss because he had never engaged in such behavior as eating an ice stick in public. But he sat down and licked it in her manner.

Again she mumbled in a dialect, her voice thick,

888

"Must be you leavin' and not goin' there." With her umbrella she indicated the mountain beyond the rice fields. "Never a monk come, they always turn back here. We'd offer at least a handful of rice even we're downtrodden."

After a silence Mokuzu said,

"I was wrong, I did intend to leave. But I'll give your village the chance to know some joy of almsgiving."

The old woman seemed to take forever to walk the footways. The field water reflected the clouds now soaring higher, and some covering the mountaintops. He resigned himself to being hit by a downpour.

"Granny, where are you coming from?"

She acted as though she had not heard. He asked again.

"Osaka. Set out yesterday, nighted in a park, but the time given to meet was only half an hour...well, can't expect kindness from a prison."

"Who is your connection?"

"Innocent of the charge! My son didn't never kidnap and kill a schoolgirl!...True, our kind always disposed of dead cow and horse and executed lawbreakers, but only by order of the shogunate or we never did, and we never threw our babes in the river, never took our old folk to die in the mountains — not even in famine. We now butcher for townsfolk and eat only the guts."

Mokuzu kept silent, but she talked on, looking at the soil.

"He couldn't of written a threat with so many Chinese characters! He never had such a pen — his skill was whippin' horses. And it wasn't hers. They said he confessed he wrote it with her pen after killing her. They couldn't find proof, they have only his word. They never believe our words, but they believed his. Then they took him on a separate charge. He was using a red flashlight he found, and that was hers..."

"Why did he confess he wrote the threat, and with her pen?"

"They say the pals you want is a doctor, a lawyer, and a cop. He and a local cop were pals — he was proud of that. But this cop was called to headquarters, and he told my son to fess up even if it was a lie so he could get him out — he would take care of everything. My son had several hundred pigs to feed — he needed to make up a quick story."

As they neared the village, the upper half of the mountains became hidden by clouds resembling the spurted ink of a squid. A cool wind off the mountains rustled the rice.

The blue sky was fast diminishing, but the old woman did not seem to care. Mokuzu was silent, and she too stopped talking after stammering,

"To them his life is less than a dragonfly wing. They put him in a fix he couldn't get out of...!"

A while later Mokuzu said,

"Think about him moment after moment. Your thought has the power to deepen the meaning of his life."

His words did not penetrate. She was shut in her world, unaware even that she was walking with him.

They entered the village and the rain came down. He proceeded to beg, but the people were too busy slamming storm doors and putting away tools and laundry to respond. Those who gave alms were countable on the fingers of one hand.

The same day, after watching Mokuzu go out of sight, Shizuka set about her recording work. Lately sewing for him an unlined pepper-and-salt cotton kimono, she was behind in recording the lectures and had to recall the context in places.

She enjoyed working at the small portable desk on the veranda. The breeze carried a scent, and she kept turning her face toward the source, a gardenia.

Mokuzu had said the gardenia appeared in the sutras as *campaka*, and that when about to immolate themselves by fire to save people or bring world peace, Buddhist priests drank the oil of gardenia flowers and ate the resins of other fragrant trees.

> ...Living amid passing phenomena, one can be consoled the moment one glimpses eternity.

> > Scoop water, the moon is in the hand.
> > Pick a flower, the robe is scented.
> > (*Shyutang lu*, vol. 3)[3]

> This beautiful couplet expresses human daily conduct: hand = sense of place, robe = sense of time, where and while a person lives. Moon and scent = unchanging Nirvana, which is to attain eternal enlightenment, to live free of suffering, restriction, and impurity....

Writing thus far, Shizuka rested her pen and imagined Mokuzu walking along a stream through a forest.

At that moment across the garden came her host, escorting two men. One was tall, with mean-looking eyes. The face of the other was red and round and ran with sweat.

To Shizuka they seemed like a pair of detectives. But when they were introduced as activists for the emancipation of special villages, she tensed more than she might have in the presence of detectives and said, "The Zen teacher is on mendicancy and won't return until evening."

The red-faced one laughed harshly and said to the other,

"His aim is to earn by a synergism of lectures and begging."

Taking heart, Shizuka looked straight at him and said in defense, "Earning isn't his sole purpose."

"Ho! He's tricky to combine investigation of customs with exploitation, eh? Doesn't he worry he'll blunder in the villages discriminated against for centuries? The paths are narrow and complex like a maze against government agents and oppressors. You enter, you get lost."

Shizuka resisted his attempt to unsettle her. "Please come to the point of your visit. I will assume responsibility for telling him if you give your names, business, and place of contact."

"'Responsibility'? Ho!" said the tall one, who was the older of the two. He had been looking quietly aside. He fingered his stubble and continued in a composed but hoarse voice, "Ma'am, I'm One-eyed Hanzo." He turned to reveal that one eye was indeed defective.

"He's director of the Kansai region. I'm Kemi, his secretary," inserted the other.

"As it happens, we were at his lecture two nights ago."

The words struck terror in Shizuka. According to hearsay, activists for the emancipation of special villages would seize any chance to eradicate discriminatory words whether deliberately or carelessly uttered.

A certain schoolmaster was forced to resign and lead a penurious life cultivating his garden as his only means of survival. The head of a certain ward hanged himself, and a certain police chief ended up a petty guard at a bank. Rumor mixed with fear and curiosity was disturbing the whole prefecture, and the activists were feared like a contagion.

> Be attentive to see the sadness and beauty in things rather than fear them.

These words Mokuzu had given Shizuka; and also,

> When seized with fear, listen to your heartbeat, breathe as slowly as possible, move quietly, and act like a fool or an idiot.

"Please sit down," she said and offered them cushions on the veranda. She took the desk inside, seated herself at it, and opened her book to the record of two nights ago.

"He talked of those who joined the early Buddhist sangha — scavengers, hunters, er, I don't recall the details since I haven't his memory power," commenced Hanzo. Wishing to allay misunderstanding, Shizuka offered to read the relevant place:

891

"'All sentient beings have Buddha nature' (Nirvana Sutra)[4] was Sakyamuni Buddha's teaching, revolutionary in his time because society was ruled by the caste system of Brahmanism. Asvaghosa, later expatiating on this teaching in his *Vajrasuci*, confuted the claim that Brahmans constitute the highest class by fact of birth, body, knowledge, mores, works, and Veda. A Brahman, he stated, is made by penance and virtue alone.

"Because of Buddha's unconditional fair teaching, people of all kinds gathered under him and formed the early Buddhist sangha. Their common wish was to be free of the fetters of class.

"In the early sangha, only seniority and wisdom were distinguished. The Theragatha and the Therigatha are among the oldest of the Buddhist canon, considered to have been compiled around 100 years after Buddha's death during King Asoka's reign. The Theragatha is a record of the gathas of Buddha's senior men disciples; the Therigatha, of his senior women disciples.

"The Theragatha is composed of gathas by Suppiya, a gravekeeper's son; Channa, a slave's son; Kappatakura, a beggar; Daniya, a potter; Yasodha, a fishermen's boss; Upali, a barber; Sunita, a scavenger's son; Angulimala, a phonomaniac who killed 99 persons to make a necklace of fingers; Thalaputra, an actor directing 500 actresses....

"The Therigatha is composed of gathas by an umbrella maker's wife (name unknown); Vimala, a courtesan converted after trying to charm Maudgalyayana — one of Buddha's 10 main disciples; Chanda, a beggar; Kisa Gotami, impoverished after loss of husband, children, parents, and brothers by starvation; Upparavana, who shared her husband with her daughter; Punnika, maid to a rich man, Sudatta; Anbabali, early abandoned, raised by a forest keeper, turned courtesan before conversion by Buddha; Chapa, daughter of a hunter chief, wife of a follower of Ajivika, a then notable fatalistic religion....

"There was thus no class discrimination in the sangha during Buddha's lifetime. In fact a trainee's robe was called a *kasaya*, meaning a fouled article, the raiment of the *candala*, the lowest social class."

Shizuka thought she had read enough and looked up, but Kemi said with irritation, "Go on — you must be getting to why we're here! You keep a good record."

Shizuka felt uneasy like a girl whose walk is being observed by men. Her voice was tremulous,

"However, we must remind ourselves of sad and ugly human nature when we look at the next step of the early sangha. Those who sought help, entered, and achieved peace began to protect their vested interests and refuse others entry. Those very ones turned the sangha into a mean, egoistic enclave whose concern was no longer the salvation of so-called bad or weak society members. In consequence they made many rules.

"The saved would save no others — a painful but apposite illustration of social, economic, and administrative reform without thorough improvement of the individual soul. People are rather degraded from what they were.

"The sixth patriarch of Chinese Zen entered training not to improve his social status and material comfort. He didn't flinch when his teacher noted he was a southerner, meaning a barbarian. He made no endeavor toward such material improvements as freeing people from discrimination, but directly sought Buddha nature beyond any category of social inequality..."

"Enough," said Hanzo, raising an arm that showed varicose veins. "You may not see how wrong his talk is — he's clever and you don't know discrimination. He's pressing his audience to conclude that our movement is senseless and based on impure, ugly human nature. We activists won't let it pass...especially now when we are, unlike your Chinese patriarch, striving to make the government issue a law to improve our villages. Our effort is to reinforce the report submitted last August to the prime minister by the council investigating the matter. Now you can see how your teacher's lecture is hostile to us." Hanzo's voice was mild, but his one eye was fixed coolly on Shizuka. She felt she should not stir an inch and had difficulty breathing.

'Oh, dear, this trouble is caused by Mokuzu's seemingly incriminating utterance! Mokuzu, what should I do?'

> When censured and driven to the wall, phrase your opponent's blame of you more precisely to him than he phrased it to you, then ask if you have it right. He will possibly grant that you do. Agreeing on however small a point is like a match flame in the dark in an emergency. He might be impressed by your display of calm acuity and conclude that violence is needless.

This teaching of Mokuzu's occurred to Shizuka, but she had no experience of practicing it, and Kemi with his sweaty face was haranguing her while she remained perplexed.

"For generations our people have hated and cursed Buddhism. Your religion taught the Japanese to abominate meat-eating and to shun impurity, which led to contempt of our ancestors, whose work was butchery and cleaning. The devil take Buddhism! Its priests and laymen can't sustain their lives without perpetuating butchery and filth directly and indirectly. Always needing people to do that work, they fixed social occupations and made class and occupation hereditary. Our work was so vital, society couldn't survive without it. Yet Buddhists put us at the bottom, not at the top of society. Following this history, and with the aid of Buddhist priests, the Tokugawa shogunate legalized the classification. So Buddhism can't escape blame as to discrimination and the creation of designated villages for our restricted residence as outcastes in Japan.

"But what a tactical twist! Your teacher would have his audience believe all culpability returns to those who were of the lowest class before the Buddhist fraternity saved them; and that after being saved, they were still low for refusing to save others. In short they were low, and are low and will always be low unless they enlighten themselves. Isn't that a kind of fatalism and a wile to perpetuate discrimination? He could be a real enemy for us!"

"Kemi, she's not him, don't be snappish. Now, ma'am..." Hanzo, sitting cross-legged on the veranda, turned to Shizuka.

"Please, I'm not married."

"Ho! Pardon. You're not his wife? What are you?"

"Director, it's getting popular to cohabit without formal marriage," Kemi put in, with a look of curiosity.

"I consider myself his disciple, though there's been no official proceeding," Shizuka said irresolutely.

"I don't mind either way. We came to accelerate an understanding, not to fight. See here," said Hanzo, and he made a circle by joining his thumbs and forefingers, "Suppose this is the center of a culture. It can be the center only by excluding its surroundings. In Japanese culture, say, the center means an emperor and the edge means us. Understand — no emperor, no lowly. We aren't making ourselves what we are, we're being created. Your teacher says the lowly create the lowly. That's not so. Think about our political, economic, and social system, controlled and plundered by modern monopolistic capitalism. It supplies itself with cheap labor by keeping the lowly low. Here too, the lowly don't create themselves, they're being created. So your teacher's view is wrong."

Shizuka could follow Hanzo's quiet and logical explanation. She gave a slight nod. Her fear was beginning to ebb. Her stiff expression softened.

'His manner helps me understand, whereas I was put off by the other's belligerence. As for feeling strange about his eye, it's my prejudice from inexperience, which I should overcome.'

Kemi took over with a torrent of words, merely exercising his role as assistant,

"Wrongs must be righted. The false notion spread in the lecture must be

894

righted in the lecture. He's facile and should find it easy to correct himself if he's responsible and values honor. Or we'll take him to be malicious for saying discrimination won't end until the lowly seek and realize Buddha nature, er, didn't he say? — that is, we'll not be rid of discrimination unless we get an enlightenment? Nonsense! The lowly aren't necessarily discriminated against for being dirty, poor, and uneducated. Even if we raise ourselves we'll be discriminated against. Why? Because the cause of discrimination is in the discriminating society, as our director explained. If you care about your teacher, set him straight — you get me?"

"Don't be loud with the pretty disciple. Forgive his style. Understand we didn't come to attack an individual by fastening on his careless utterance. There are members in the lower reaches beyond our control who enjoy attacking the individual. Our true purpose in eradicating discriminatory words is to reform the society that produces such individuals. So we are seizing every chance and will hack through to the end." Despite his combative spirit, Hanzo spoke less coercively than Kemi.

"'Hack through'? — may I ask why you speak so?" asked Shizuka as if to test her equanimity.

"We don't believe discrimination can be resolved by the sympathy and philanthropy of so-called good citizens; that's the counter side of the discrimi-nating mind. Besides, the government contrives to placate and integrate us by temporary remedies. If we're gulled by their stratagems we low laborers will be kept as we are in the coming generations of this capitalist nation. More-over, our culture, worthy of our pride, won't be transmitted and developed. Our ancestors cultivated a unique culture, which shouldn't face extinction. So we have to hack through or we'll be mutilated and dismantled by social trends. Only what we gain through our fight will raise us. Then we can build unprecedented fair human relations."

"I understand!" said Shizuka, clenching her fists. "My teacher too says that whoever quits self-training is like a fallen tree — it begins to rot."

Hanzo ignored her. "So we wish he'll correctly understand our history and our present state. He's smart and can rectify his viewpoint by a little study, especially at your recommendation. After that we can wish he'll resume his lectures. We have sub-organizations all over the nation. We'll ask their help in securing him audiences. Of course fees and lodging will be settled to your satisfaction."

Shizuka had been suffocating with the fear of being censured and forced into self-criticism to the extent of having to cancel the tour. As it was, they were even suggesting almost endless lectures. With relief and delight she brightened like a flower.

She wanted at once to tell Mokuzu the happy news. She rose to offer tea, but the two men hurried to depart.

"Fine. That way we can cooperate in the cause to equalize society. It's wasteful to stand in each other's way!" were Hanzo's parting words. And Kemi's: "We'll be back tomorrow for his signature on a deal. See he's here or that you can sign."

ક

The summer showers recurred often over several days. On the day Mokuzu parted from Shizuka he was also caught in a hard rain, but as soon as it stopped, the cicadas as if nothing had happened resumed their stridor under the purged blue sky.

In wet robes he took a mountain path, a shortcut to cross the prefecture limits. He climbed beside a gushing stream that was flattening the wild cypress vines. The sun through the forest was warm, the green shade cool. The stream where it passed over rocks looked like white yarn. Mist rose in a shaft of light. By his feet, behind rocks receiving spray, a damselfly, alae black, body thin as a thread, was living quietly.

> 'How from that sapphire fount the crisped brooks,
> Rolling on orient pearl and sands of gold,
> With mazy error under pendent shades
> Ran nectar, visiting each plant, and fed
> Flow'rs worthy of Paradise…
>
> . . . .
>
> …meanwhile murmuring waters fall
> Down the slope hills, dispersed, or in a lake,
> That to the fringed bank with myrtle crowned
> Her crystal mirror holds, unite their streams.[5]

'Cool air by clean water recalls to me Ena's concise figure remote from vain worldly affairs!'

He left the stream to aim for the summit. The light of the setting sun was spreading over the trees. Content to be alone and to forget his social self, he kept climbing.

> 'Men chained by men still depend on men.
> Men harmed by men still harm men.
> Of what use are men to men, even men begot by men?
> Men afflict and abandon men.'[6]

The sunset was fading. Only the clouds at high altitude remained faint salmon. The sound of orthopteran insects, replacing the sound of cicadas, deepened the night silence. He settled under a bush to sleep and was thankful for the clean separation; both he and Shizuka had been remarkably intellectual and had controlled their emotion.

"Great news!" she had said as soon as he returned the previous evening. She then noticed he was drenched with rain and handed him a change of clothes. Not liking to trouble the host over a bath, he brought a washbowl to the garden. There Shizuka reported on the visitors. While dressing he said,

"Are you actually naive, or were you being cunning? Either way, you must finely and repeatedly reexamine the fear you felt when they arrived and completely surmount your mentality or you will never have your season to begin training yourself independent of another's help. I hope you will break through your shell given by your surroundings."

Silently Shizuka made tea and then sat to face him.

"To begin with, in my lectures I have been encouraging people to go at once beyond the world of discrimination by understanding Buddha nature. That is because I dislike discrimination. Still, these people think I am opposing their movement? The cause of their misunderstanding is probably that they have lost themselves in their means and have forgotten their goal. So they could shamelessly threaten you and attempt to involve me in their movement. Threats are the product of a discriminating society. By adopting such undemocratic means these people are supporting that society to the detriment of their goal and their community."

"I see, I now understand my mistake. Don't waste further words on the matter. Tomorrow morning I will visit their office and upon my honor make them withdraw. I regret my fear and my falling into their snare, and also, I so wanted lecture contracts...because, honestly, I have none set beyond tonight!"

"Shizuka, this has happened at just the right time. I was thinking I would finish and proceed on my way." He gave her the two-striped green buprestid.

For a long while she remained in the attitude of regarding the lifeless thing in her palm. Then she asked,

"What do you think, will it or won't it cry?"

"Beautiful creatures are already and always crying."

The night air at the summit was cool. Dew dripping from the treetops shone in the starlight. He covered his head with his sleeves and took a sleeping posture, curled like a dog.

'I told her to ignore those activists...did she go to her aunt...or return to that temple? As am I, she too is a strange bastard child of the latter half of the twentieth century....But I'm unlike those early Buddhists. They were dreadfully pessimistic as well as misanthropic. The reason I must perfect my training is to make myself most useful to people. I must teach them that paradise exists nowhere but on earth. Wait, wait a little longer....'

64

The Sun Sets and Rises

From the ceiling of the dusky grotto, innumerable stalactites hung like icicles, dripping water. Saturated with calcium bicarbonate, the drips where they fell were leaving calcite deposits that were forming stalagmites like bamboo shoots. Here and there the forms had joined into columns, some of which blocked the pathway.

Although acclaimed as a natural palace concealed in a grotto, to Mokuzu the sights suggested the jails of Avichi — the eternal hell regarded as the terminus for those who commit the five deadly sins. Lit by a candle in a pricket attached to a wall, they shone a slimy brown like teeth defiled with nicotine.

Mokuzu stooped and narrowed himself to pass through a labyrinth of them and abruptly came to a spacious hall. A magnanimous daylight entering through a hole overhead made all within appear in queerly lucid relief as if under stage lights.

Calcareous sinters forming in the shape of terraced fields contained clear water and small agglutinated stones that resembled sea cucumbers or enlarged scale insects.

The sound of a cascade echoed from the depths. Concerned about the approach of dusk, Mokuzu left by following the river that ran through the grotto's deep valley.

He climbed a hill showing a typical karst-protruded peneplain, about three hundred meters above the sea. There were almost no trees, only rows of weathered limestone rocks in every direction. The sky was low with strato-cumuli dyed muddy orange.

Seized with sudden fatigue, he sat down between two of the rocks. In the thickening dusk their continuous rows looked like troops of ghosts in old-fashioned cloaks. Being inhuman, they could not have been bearing a grudge as is seen among humans, but they seemed to be harboring an enmity against all mankind.

Mokuzu, outspent, breath foul, lacked the vigor to stand again. He saw cows descending a far hill as if in a shadowgraph, and also noticed for the first time a clump of *manjusaka* trembling in the evening breeze by a nearby rock. The cows had left it, knowing it to be poisonous. It bloomed red in the dark. Manjusaka, or *Lycoris radicata*, was named for a beautiful sea goddess of Greek legend, but Mokuzu could see none of the sea from the dreary hill. In Buddhism, manjusaka was counted as one of five august flowers. It was thought to release people from their three basic evil actions. But in Mokuzu it inspired nothing.

> 'Manjusaka,
> I picked an armful,
> Yet my heart aches for my mother.'[1]

Such a poem might induce sadness, but recalling it Mokuzu was apathetic, like the limestone rocks. He was exhausted.

Moreover, his stomach was empty; he had eaten only Chinese noodles somewhere between morning and noon. But he felt no urge to descend the hill to seek the lights of town.

Indeed he derived no joy from a sunrise or a sunset. He was bathed in sweat amid the lingering summer heat, which he did nothing to avoid. He ignored his want of autumn clothes, though he was exposing himself to cold breezes morning and evening. In short, he could sense heat and cold, but the sensation remained on his skin and was not linked to inner feeling.

Day after day, starting at dawn, he walked, begging at the houses that stood along his path and just walking when there were none, until he was too tired to rise from a rock or root at sundown. He took irregular meals when offered and repeated his introspection in the dark until he fell asleep. It was a life that bore him into a temporary depersonalization.

Settled between two limestone rocks, he recognized his state, and he recalled the name of an American psychiatrist, Louis Alexander Dugas, about whom he had learned in the early days of his brother Gyodo's schizophrenia.

He also recalled a part of Bergson's philosophy. 'Wasn't this the gist of it?' he thought desultorily,

> 'Man ought to regard not only the external traces of changing matters. The sun rises and sets. He is born, and grows up, and usually marries and begets children, and dies before long....Truly, external matters repeat their changes without cease and are ever monotonous and meaningless.
>
> However, the individual stream of consciousness, which keeps sensing, observing, thinking, and experiencing external matters, is new each moment and is unique to the individual. It perceives external repetitions but neither repeats its perceptions nor stops perceiving.
>
> If man heeds this internal absolute being, which exists as the only one, unique, in the whole world of past to future, then for him the old sun becomes new, the life and death of others becomes meaningful, and the mere phenomenal world becomes an important nourishment. Rather than dwell on external matters, man should focus on his life, which selectively takes in every sort of external matter to vitalize him....'

But Mokuzu did not need spiritual encouragement; he needed, simply, food and rest.

Since parting from Shizuka he had been bothered nightly by mosquitoes. Now with their season ending, the cold often woke him.

He had received scant alms and could not find it in his heart to buy food in view of his wish to leave quickly for a Southern Buddhist country. Worst was to encounter people more distressed than he...a lone, sick mother nursing a baby, a man blind and crippled. To each he left every coin he had saved.

He felt more thankful to Shizuka and tried to sleep while fancying himself on a southern islet ringed by a coral sea, dozing under a tree after eating bananas, papayas, and mangoes — when in fact the wind was intensifying over the karst peneplain where no human culture had reached.

That night he had a strange dream. At times more vivid than reality, at times carried by emotions purer than reality, dreams can affect the entire body. Visible on a veranda framed by cherry boughs in their glory was a man dressed casually as a luxurious priest, smiling in an easy manner: Koko. A monk in coarse robe stood in the graveled garden: Mokuzu, summoned by Koko. As he dreamed he could tell the place was Shoshinji.

"A woman named Shizuka came for a Zen interview."

"Wasn't her name Luri?" Mokuzu was anxious. He understood Koko to have succeeded to the Zen mastership of Shoshinji following the death of Zen

Master Tengai, and himself to be continuing his training under Koko.

"Luri was a gem, Shizuka too. Your women are beautiful, even if neither yet knows a woman's greatest pleasure," said Koko, smiling happily.

"Then how did you guide her?" Mokuzu with a stern look was ready to censure Koko. He was regretting that he himself had not done much for Shizuka, and all the more would he be furious at whoever might harm her.

"She entered and I spurred her on: 'You are bedizening and cramping yourself with shallow knowledge and narrow experience. Open up or you'll never grasp the secret of Zen. Come again pure as you were born!' To my surprise she leapt to her feet, undid her belt, and began to remove even her lingerie...indeed she stood pure as she was born — ha ha ha, she got the better of me!"

"And you? How pure were you while asking her to be pure?"

"Oh, relax. Let me say, her body is milk white, and is as well proportioned as her face."

Like tasting vinegar Mokuzu sensed that Shizuka was pitifully earnest to seek the truth and be spiritually at one with himself. "I am asking, what did you do?"

"Ooh, nothing in particular. I attempted to speak some words brimful with Zen spirit, but my perfectly agile tongue faltered before such beauty...oh — what could I do but mystify her by such a pose as is peculiar to Zen masters? I bowed my head with eyes shut as if discerning the beings of all worlds by my unfathomable wisdom, while I was actually letting my brain lie idle — whereupon, she swiftly dressed and hastened to leave. In confusion I involuntarily cried out, 'What's the matter? Wait, the interview isn't over!' 'It is quite over,' she said. 'I now know for sure that the greatness of Zen Teacher Mokuzu is owing to what he is and owes least to Shoshinji training.' Just like that she left, ha ha ha!" Mokuzu wanted to know where Shizuka went, but he awoke.

Awake, he felt relieved that she had not fallen into Koko's hands, but he worried over her whereabouts and prayed for her happiness, and kept chanting until he slept again.

He directed his heavy steps toward Hagi, a town facing the Japan Sea from Akiyoshi Hill. Partly he was retracing his way. There the manjusakas were still blooming.

He walked a country road all day seeing no one but a single boy picking manjusakas left standing on a fairly distant riverbank where the grass had just been cut. He was taken by a hallucination that it was himself in his boyhood.

He walked beside the river, slowly, with frequent rests like a person bleeding. Low clouds were about to bring down rain. He wanted to take shelter in the pine forest by the sea.

> 'Two days ago the sky was
> Full of mares' tails. Yesterday
> Wind came, bringing low cigar
> Shaped clouds. At midnight the rain
> Began, the first fine, still rain
> Of Autumn. Before the rain
> The night was warm, the sky hazy.'[2]

Under the pines he covered himself with his rain cape. Stirred by a soft rain, the aroma of terebinth drifted low and mingled with the musty odor of hyphae in the heaped pine needles.

That night too he was awakened by a strange dream.

He was being called before Zen Master Tengai for somehow having incurred his wrath. In the corridor stoutish Koko, rubbing his hands together, spoke with a generous smile that usually set people at ease: "Don't worry, just perform your apology and later I'll smooth it over for you."

Mokuzu knew he was being faulted for a matter beyond his responsibility, yet when he entered the room the master was indeed angering with the look of a king crab. Calmly he expressed his innocence, but the master redoubled his fury,

"Your attitude gravely misleads others. The sin of one who directly commits a fault is light for having come from simplicity and indiscretion. Letting others sin by your neglect, though it is indirect, is a greater sin. To begin with, the greatest sin is not to heed all things relating to human affairs...."

To be judged on how he ideally ought to be as an indirect agent was hard for Mokuzu to take; his responsibility was judged as enormous — and his authority, next to nil.

He withdrew in gloom, but now it was from the presence of Zen Master Hanun and he was climbing the back mountain of Ryotanji to enjoy his solitude on the pine needles. There he found Ena standing. She cuddled up to him and put her cheek to his shoulder, and if she did not speak he could hear her say, "A thoughtful man, according to Seneca, doesn't easily anger, but I'd like to say whoever is short of love blames others for their indiscretions."

When he awoke he was affected not by anger or grudge but by sorrow.

During the night the rain let up and a dense mist pervaded the pine forest.

'I saw old Autumn in the misty morn
Stand shadowless like Silence, listening
To silence, for no lonely bird would sing
Into his hollow ear from woods forlorn...'[3]

As the first sunlight shone into the mist, he advanced through the forest to the sea. The sound of waves led him to a cliff.

The waves after tiding over the black reefs of an inlet were striking the rocks at the water's verge. The shallows were whitish green with tossing foam, the deep water dark blue. Among the reefs a blow hole violently ejected spray at each surge.

A monkey might have easily reached the water by jumping from branch to branch of the pines on the cliffside. A skilled high diver could perhaps have put himself into the deep water by clearing the leaning trunks. But Mokuzu took long to detour to the beach. He found sea urchins fixed to the submerged rocks, broke them with a stone, and made a breakfast of the contents and the drifting wakame seaweed.

He timed the start of his begging to the waking hour in Hagi, where the mist was beginning to clear.

Hagi had been the capital of the fief of the daimyo Mori for a long two hundred sixty years. On the orderly streets the solid plaster walls of merchants' houses refused even a glimpse of the life within. In characteristic style, the houses of former samurai stood behind tall rigid wooden walls as if even the wind were unfree to pass from neighbor to neighbor. The present town policy was to preserve the historic sights. The streets were devoid of liveliness, even of playing children.

Mokuzu came by way of one such historic sight, Shoka Sonjuku, a village school founded by Yoshida Shoin. It was a plain one-story building with a single black pine in front, its inaesthetic appearance like a symbol of Shoin's short life, during which he taught many disciples in a fever of impatience. In the closing days of the Tokugawa shogunate he was an authority on military science, and his imperialist disciples impetuously took an active role in the Meiji Restoration. Heroes in the age of upheaval were much too enthusiastic over local affairs to reflect on the detrimental side of themselves, and so ended their lives without knowing such gratification as breathing with the natural world.

Mokuzu got a dreary sense and bent his steps toward the hotel quarter. Quite a few visitors from various parts of the country were coming to see those holdovers from feudal times by their choice.

Hotels lined both sides of a stone moat with weeping willows at its banks. In the hotel entrances, open wide since early morning, maids were placing hotel clogs and spraying water into the street. Clerks were hanging out black lacquered tablets with the names of the day's arrivals inscribed; finding their names, they would feel welcome.

Under his bamboo hat he stood at the center of such entrances and began to chant. The employees were perplexed. Some, noting his frayed wet robe and bare feet with abrasions, were nervous.

The guests, released from their hometown restraint, were delighted to catch sight of his archaic style and hastily fetched their cameras. Some bent shamelessly to peep at his face and as if he were a zoo creature remarked as they pleased,

"Ho! still young!" "Let's see how it'll take alms."

Mokuzu was intensely fatigued but held on, chanting. He expected the owner to appear with a contribution.

Just after receiving money in a white paper from a gracious woman, the owner of a hotel named Koyokan, and as he was moving on to the next, the call "Hoi!" came from above to pull his attention. Had he looked up by reflex, the caller would have seen his face, but he ignored the call and went on. Again it came, louder.

He approached a willow at the moat and under its branches slightly tipped up his hat. On an upstairs veranda stood Koko, his full face beaming.

"Mokuzu! I knew your voice! Come up at once!" It was obvious that he had ordered his attendants to fetch him.

Koko's fleshy envelope, now plumper, had indeed a kind of friendly sucking force. Yet Mokuzu was on the alert, recalling the difficulty of penetrating his inner thought, which had often seemed chaotic. As he was hesitating over what to do, two monks came out and seized him to pull him into the hotel. They were so forceful that he felt uncomfortable. He was pushed upstairs to where Koko was.

The owner and maids were surprised, but being quick to figure the circumstances through the nature of their occupation, they straightaway brought up tea and a steamed towel.

"I heard rumors of your nationwide pilgrimage, but I never dreamed we'd meet here. You look a bit haggard. Take a look at me, always faithful to the master, why, even my body begins to resemble his." Koko cheerfully patted his belly, and saying "Anyway," he offered Mokuzu a cup of sake.

More like a seeker of riotous pleasures than a Zen priest, Koko had been enjoying a morning drink after a morning bath and ample sleep.

"I thought you were even now in America."

For an instant Koko was agitated, then he resumed his magnanimity,

"There's no use staying long in such a land. Nothing profound can be learned from a nation that adores nudity in everything. Moreover, in the spring our master was invited to be abbot of the head temple and I was summoned to act for him at Shoshinji. Er, you don't know he's now abbot...? It's a social matter, but you must know that's the only way Buddha Law is practiced. To neglect social matters is to neglect Buddha Law."

Put in warm room and offered sake in his state of exhaustion, Mokuzu grew muddled as if his cup contained a hypnotic. Wishing to be quickly freed, he said,

"It was enjoyable to meet again, Senior Koko, and I congratulate you on your assuming the Zen mastership of Shoshinji with the inauguration of Zen Master Tengai at the head temple. Now, as for me, it is always true that time is and time was and time is passing. Please let me excuse myself to proceed with my begging, for I have just begun."

Koko laughed. "Don't be silly. How can I free you as soon as I've caught you?" and, offering more sake, he went on,

"Do you know how disheartened he was by your leaving? Living with him, I can tell just by hearing him talk in his sleep. It might well be one reason I had to return so abruptly from America. But we needn't inquire into past matters. We must concern ourselves with matters-to-come. As abbot he will establish an international department within the head temple. He'll be greatly encouraged by your participation. Mokuzu, do it — I advise you with all my heart. To that end, first you will apologize to him for your truant leave. It's a mere formality. I assure you I'll mend the relationship. Fortunately he is to arrive here this evening. He too is touring the nation. Tonight a reception by the local Buddhist association will be held, and I'll arrange you an interview with him beforehand."

"But, Senior Koko, I am now very tired and I have no interest in his 'international department.' Don't you see the nonsense in my meeting with him?"

Koko with a trace of rising temper called to his attendants in the next room and ordered them to prepare a bed at once. He had acquired his master's manner of striking guests out of their wits by scolding his attendants in a sudden loud voice. But Mokuzu was unfazed. There was a commotion as the attendants sprang up and rushed to lay out a bed.

Feeling awkward, Koko said,

"Ho! Having two constant attendants is interesting. I'm always reminded of Fayan's indicating a reed screen, ha ha ha."

"Hungji Jengjian said, by way of comment on that koan, 'A pine is straight, a jujube crooked, a crane tall, a duck short,'[4] but I wonder what the distinction is between a baby pig raised by a wild boar and a baby wild boar raised by a pig."

905

Koko, acting as though he had understood Mokuzu's words, though he had not, laughed happily and said,

"Now go have a good sleep. And take the interview or you'll not leave the hotel. By the way, in general you are excellently critical. Needless to say, such is your virtue and not your defect while the world is full of injustice and stagnant with conventionality. However, being critical isn't an excuse to escape society; it's but a process on the way to improving yourself and society. Don't be always critical. Become a reformer. Zen Master Tengai and I appear uneager to criticize society, not for lack of critical spirit but for lack of time as we labor to improve the world. So we who direct our efforts toward reform ignore any criticism that we are after money, power, and fame, for we recognize those as indispensable concomitants. Ha ha! Oh, sorry to give a great admonition to one who's half asleep. Now, to bed. Sleep well, enjoy a hot bath and a nice meal, and recreate yourself. Taking regular meals and sleep are pleasant duties for fleshly beings — and a necessary condition for raising oneself from a critic to a reformer."

"Senior Koko, so great is your admonition it dispelled my drowsiness, at least for the moment. I am particularly impressed by your telling me we should turn to reform. In fact those who remain critics are liable to fall into a pessimism, such as to say the sun rises and sets before long, whereas reformers will say the sun sets and rises anew. There is only one question: Is it truly possible to reform a world controlled by money, power, and fame by resorting to money, power, and fame? By such means reformers can no doubt replace an old head with a new. But isn't it merely a struggle for supremacy and a sure way to preserve the world as it is? Well, this is the time not to argue but to thank you for your kind offer and to accept it with thanks."

The hotel quilts were as light and warm as feathers. Mokuzu entered the bed and slept at once. He dreamt he was overhearing private words between Zen Master Tengai and Koko.

The master: "Damnable chap, a stickler for trivialities! He lessens the effect of my lecture! Anxious for our country's future, I was summarizing my basic thoughts on how to live on as a peaceful and neutral power:

> 'Disregard our shortage of armaments; take heed only to be governed by benevolence. A country that attacks a benevolently governed country is itself not benevolently governed and will surely suffer domestic unrest.
> 'Self-defense is unnecessary even if an enemy lands on our shores. Place our soldiers among the peasantry and fisherfolk and direct them to live as these common folk live, that we may appear unarmed. In the event of an invasion, let our people freely surrender to escape death. We should capture and imprison invaders and command their leader to

admonish them only if they behave outrageously. If they make a wholly unacceptable demand, we should refuse it point-blank and issue them a warning. By seeing we are resolute, candid, and unarmed, they will surely reflect to some degree on their conduct.

'All the while we must assiduously encourage the enemy country's loyal retainers and righteous persons to correct their country's policy. Thus will we secure our final victory....'"[5]

As Zen Master Tengai was recounting this to Koko, Mokuzu could vividly picture him addressing his audience with fervor.

Koko responded, "A deeply impressive sermon! Without armament! I bet the audience was given bright hope and full vitality. Well then, what fault did that whippersnapper find in it? According to the gravity of his sin, I shall chastise him out and out!"

"He coolly said it was entirely Yoshida Shoin's words."

"So impertinent? How can he betray you, and in front of your audience?"

Mokuzu had indicated the source of the master's lecture in private, but the master did not correct Koko's assessment. And, as might be expected of a great Zen master, he said, "Of course they're Shoin's words. But I needn't tell whose words they are and how I'm indebted. My intention has nothing to do with such trivialities!"

"Right, Master! Your sermon was to advance the security and prosperity of Japan and the inevitability of Japan's assuming world leadership. Besides, even if they're another's words, they're often forgotten and mistaken nowadays, which is the very reason you give them new life and new perspective. So it's no exaggeration to say they are your entire invention. Too bad Mokuzu is a greenhorn and has yet to comprehend the profound reasoning of Zen. By way of example, we have to know that the words of Socrates are not necessarily great for being his, and certainly if you quote them they will be great by your giving them new life. Even the words of Sakyamuni Buddha are of no merit if they remain buried in the Tripitaka. They're great for the first time when you quote them with your own deep discernment and experience of hard training."

The master was on the one side fed up with the absurdity of Koko's verbiage, and on the other touched by his loyalty like the filial piety of a true son.

"Mokuzu is a worm bred in a lion, as evil as Devadatta was for Sakyamuni Buddha. Now listen, Koko, I further lectured on the importance of setting a life aim,

"'Setting a life aim is the start of everything. True resolve can by no means be stolen. A man who has established his life aim will continue

907

to seek it with determination and pleasure even if alone, and will not rely on others nor expect sweetness from society. Study begun with no life aim becomes more harmful the more a man studies. Such a man will slight the truth and lead the ignorant into confusion, and take a wrong course of action, betray his principles, and submit to authority and to profiteering....'"[6]

"Well, what trouble did he give you then? If circumstances require, I'll hang him nose down over a pickle tub! He couldn't be fool enough to indicate again the source of your sermon! Impossible! This time I can prove they're your words because I've heard them repeatedly ever since I became your humble disciple — through the hard years of your founding Shoshin College to these happy days of your becoming abbot. Living twenty years with them enables me to take charge of Shoshinji in your absence. They're true words of care. No one can gainsay their authenticity and your love toward your disciples."

"In fact he indicated each again to be from Yoshida Shoin."

"Indeed? I can forgive him no longer, the words are yours! My proof is here — on both ears I got sores from hearing them more than enough for twenty years, oh, I mean, through my ears your life entered me. At any rate, suppose they are Yoshida Shoin's. Then why didn't I hear them from him? He never told me them, I heard them only from you. Even if his, they're yours by strange coincidence, and coincidence doesn't lessen your greatness an ounce, my Zen Master. Shall I go catch him and press him with all my weight into a mud wall? Or..."

"Wait, Koko, you're a champion of justice, but don't be hasty. You must be smart. He's rampant, but talented. If you correct him and win him over, it'll be equal to gaining the power of many men. That way, even after my death he'll supply the deficiencies that come of your good nature. If, however, you let him live free of your control, then without awaiting his action you'll be endangered by his very existence. See? Whether he becomes your reassuring ally or your inauspicious enemy to give you insomnia depends on what you do. Right, Koko? A man incapable of establishing his own Dharma and mental order must freely use every means, such as regulation, authority, position, credentials, and organizations, to seize fellows who have their own Dharma and mental order."

Koko threw himself at the master's feet as if given a divine revelation and said with uncontainable joy,

"Yes, Master. Wonderful is what I have just heard! I shall commit it to memory!"

In his dream Mokuzu overheard these exchanges, and he could no longer resist the impulse to laugh, and indeed he did laugh, just when Koko was shaking him awake.

"Oi, oi, Mokuzu, get up! *Tse!* — laughing in your sleep! Did you dream of some prank played in your acolyte days? Have you no idea of the time? It's already five! Our great master arrived long since and has visited Yoshida Shoin's historic school and finished his bath. Soon he must go out with me to the welcome dinner. But be thankful, he's granting you an interview beforehand. I shall lead you to the room for honored guests, where he is now. Quick, get ready."

Mokuzu washed his face with cold water. To the side, red sunbeams shone through the shoji. He moved slowly, being uneager to meet with the Zen master. He went to the veranda that faced the street and said,

"Senior Koko, don't you know I already met him?"

"Don't be absurd. You'd better meet, I assure you. I expect he'll mention setting up the international department, and you should answer with tact. Respond if possible with your accomplished English and turn his eyes up and down." Koko laughed with customary cheer, drawing in his short neck.

Mokuzu felt all the more keenly the stupidity of Koko. He looked down at the willows. The shadows of those on the far bank slanted across the moat, while the shadows of those on the near bank slanted across the street. Despite a rising wind, some guests attired in the yukata of their hotel were enjoying a stroll — women guests too, and the wind pressing the thin cotton fabric made their contours very discernible.

"Oi, Mokuzu, rather than gaze at erogenous zones, we'll go down and see the master," urged Koko.

In a room expediently made into an interview room, a red felt carpet was laid. Positioned on it were a thick silk cushion in purple for the master and a normal cushion for a guest. Mokuzu took the guest seat. An attendant went to the adjoining room to inform the master that all was set for the interview. The master produced a dry cough before he appeared.

As the master and Mokuzu silently confronted each other, the attendant brought in teabowls and served the master, then Mokuzu.

Zen Master Tengai faintly turned his palm to invite Mokuzu to drink, and he also drank. When each was done, he ordered the room cleared of persons, including Koko, who was attending behind Mokuzu.

This course of concise, mute behavior might have made Mokuzu extremely tense as if drawn into frozen earth were it an early interview with the master. But now he could easily distinguish between a true, abysmal silence and an artificial silence. The silence the master was generating was unworthy of even a laugh, Mokuzu thought, because first, it was to camouflage his lack of intuitive insight; second, it exposed his cold nature; and third, it was his usual strategy of awaiting the move of his guest.

Mokuzu supposed that abbots of yore were equipped with a little more spiritual power, not only social influence. 'This abbot before my eyes doesn't impress me as much as a dinosaur skeleton in a museum. What a joke, and what a pity!'

Zen Master Tengai said with heavy reproach,

"Given a chance for an interview, you have no words?"

"Right." Mokuzu spoke lightly, though it was extremely impolite. He intended to take his leave. Without concealing the rage in his eyes, the master stopped him,

"Wait, I have one thing to verify. Answer frankly. Why, for what purpose, did Koko return from America?"

"That's an odd question. There may be a parent who would raise the question of a medical bill the moment a child comes home with a bone fracture. Answering an odd question surely makes the answerer odder than the questioner."

"Hold your tongue! I asked your frank reply."

"I don't know is my frank reply."

"Stupid! If you just correctly answer, we can discuss many things, including the establishment of an international department. Tell me, why did Koko return?" The master softened his tone. Getting no response, he said more explicitly,

"Was the reason in America, or was it that he had to take over Shoshinji with my taking the office of abbot of the head temple? Which is the truth?"

"Master, you must be careful. Nobody doubts you have taken the office of abbot, but some might doubt whether the abbot is you," said Mokuzu calmly, and he stood up.

As he was tying on his straw sandals at the hotel entrance, Koko approached with an uncustomary stern look and, finding no words, kept glaring at him.

"Thank you for the kindness of giving me a chance to rest," Mokuzu said. "You'll look fine if you keep gritting your teeth like now. It's the right attitude when we're hindered from directly facing nature, people, and especially ourselves, whether or not we have attained money, power, and fame."

With the sunset behind him, he left Hagi for the outskirts, the seaside. Aged trees on the beach were bowed over the waves, their quaking shadows cold in appearance. Looking back, he saw smoke creeping along the grassy hills from farmers' fires. The sky was dark except for a fraction of red in the west. On the rocky beach colorless birds were foraging for food.

'They are reformers? Wretched. I might cry over my disappointment were I yet so young as to be going through the change of voice. But now I understand everything very well. Brightness and darkness, sunrise and sunset, are entities only when they enter my mind, and such phenomena I have no reason to blame and resent. And now I can find enjoyment in perfecting my life like a bird sitting patiently on its eggs. At the same time I greatly sympathize with young people who don't yet have an inkling of what is right and wrong in the world, and who are just meeting the rough-and-tumble of life on their way to establishing themselves. I'd like to cry to them this encouragement,

'"Grow quickly, with patience, and become master of the Dharma!"'

65

As if Walking through a Sala Forest

10/...: Third day after setting foot into Kyushu, proceeding south through Onga County by the Hibiki Sea. On the highway many high-speed, long-distance trucks, few houses alongside to visit for alms. The heat, noise, and exhaust render me as petty as a maggot. A bitter journey others would think pointless and far from laudable. "I've neither friend nor lover" — so might I grieve if fainthearted.

Tired from walking, I climbed a hill graced with rolling lines of trees planted to arrest the sand. The indigo sea curved widely in. Kaneno Point jutted out as I advanced. From there the sea is the Genkai Sea — well named, the water looks black. It's said to be no more than 50 meters deep but windy and reefy, with strong currents, and with unpredictable weather especially from now into winter. Countless people and boats have succumbed to its waves ever since the ancients first went to sea. Resting, my bamboo hat put aside, I recalled lines from Psalm 104,

> O Lord, how manifold are thy works!
>> In wisdom hast thou made them all;
>> the earth is full of thy creatures.
> Yonder is the sea, great and wide,
>> which teems with things innumerable,
>> living things both small and great.
> There go the ships, and Leviathan
>> which thou didst form to sport in it.

10/...: Footsore, I entered a well-grown forest by the sea and spent the day there. Trees issue no evil spirit for me, do me no harm, actually appear welcoming and ease my fatigue.

Come to think of it, all past Buddhas achieved their great realization under a tree: Vipasyin under a poon, Sikhin under a magnolia, Visvabhu under a *sala*, or sal, Krakucchanda under a silk, Kanakamuni under a clustered fig, Kasyapa under a banyan.

The seventh, Sakyamuni, in later years, according to the Sutta-nipata, reviewed his training and narrated it to his followers:

> I thence journeyed to the Magadha kingdom and entered Sena in Uruvela, seeking to know what is good, the supreme and superb state of tranquillity. There I saw worthy of praise a beautiful forest and the Neranjara River, its banks well built and picturesque, the village rich in crops. And I thought: Truly the area is praiseworthy, with a river flowing between well-built banks and a beautiful forest, indeed a suitable place for the study and self-training of a son of good family who wishes to exert himself. So I sat there thinking it indeed suitable...[1]

Then as Sakyamuni sat in the forest, the evil spirit Namuci approached to arrest his training with these consoling words:

> You are thin, pale, near your end, your chance of survival is one in a thousand. But live you must, for only thus can you do good...[2]

So Sakyamuni's first temptation was to do good, to act in society. By exercising his self-denial he overcame this and each of Namuci's temptations:

> Evil spirit, kin to the lazy, you come on behalf of worldly good, but I have no need to seek it. You had better approach those who seek the merit of doing good. I have faith, I can endeavor, and I have wisdom. Unlike you I am wholehearted about life. The wind of my effort will dry up even flowing water, and of course dry up my blood, phlegm, and bile, and when my flesh is gone, my mind will be yet more clear and my feelings, wisdom, and meditative concentration yet more steady. Thus am I finding a spiritual home and therefore enduring the greatest pain. I naturally have no interest in worldly desires. Behold the purity of my mind and body. I know desire is your first army, hatred your second, hunger and thirst your third, attachment your fourth, languor and sleep your fifth, your sixth fear, your seventh doubt, your eighth pretense and obstinacy. Namuci, you also have armies of profit, fame, adulation, and honor, all gained by misconduct, and armies of self-admiration and slight of others. These compose your devilish attack forces over which only the brave earn the joy of triumph....[3]

Sakyamuni was meditating under a bo tree when he overcame the evil spirit. A sutra tells that a man who was mowing gave him a bundle of *kusa* to sit on, an annual weed of the Gramineae family with spikelets soft as fluff.

In detail, Sakyamuni maintained samadhi for seven days under a bo. In the second week he moved to a banyan, in the third to an Indian oak, in the fourth to a rajayatana, and in the fifth back to a banyan. Under each he enjoyed a state free of all suffering.

Another source, the *Mula-sarvastivada-vinaya, hdul-ba gshi*, about precepts, relates that Namuci when he failed to tempt Sakyamuni resorted to his last means: levying 36 thousand *koti* (1 = 10 million) of malevolent deities and bidding them shout. Sakyamuni blocked the disturbance by exercising occult power to create a munjeet forest 12 *yojana* wide (1 = a day's trip by cow).

Noise is the worst devil, from which forests give shelter.

10/...: The last few days I have been crossing the great plain of Munakata County, the prominent rice area of the prefecture, some miles from the shoreline. Undulating rice extends everywhere yellow. The horizon looks curved. In the heat waves some ant-like dots linger but soon can be perceived as reaping machines, advancing, still inaudible. The sky is high and light, in the distance is a dark blue sea.

> How great is the human mind, extending even above the immeasurable height of heaven, even to the unfathomable depth of the earth, even beyond the unsurpassable speeding light of the sun and the moon![4]

In a bright mood I began to recite Eisai's preface to his *Advancement of Zen to Protect the Nation*.

Although now measurable, the height of heaven, the depth of the earth, and the speed of light remain august, especially when we each face them without going through any medium. Even so, Eisai asserted that the human mind is greater. Did he mean by 'mind' such excellent cognitive functions as imagination and inference?

> The three thousand realms are boundless, yet our mind transcends them. They are so enormous that we cannot describe them save to say they are the great void or original energy, yet our mind encompasses them.[5]

Here Eisai comprehends our mind as greater than the universe and as the source of its vigor. According to our objective recognition his view seems to mistake effect for cause, insofar as we normally understand the universe to be the prior condition for the earth's existence, and the earth the prior condition for our human world wherein we appear as specks of dust. It is natural to see Eisai as a fanciful megalomaniac who disregarded objective recognition.

To the contrary, this is a paean sung by one who earnestly searched for and found the meaning of human life. Against the vast universe, a fragile, humble, transitory being who was Eisai obtained the subjective meaning of his life and heralded its significance.

913

But his view of life and the universe didn't originate with him. It is a faithful development of thought described in the Avatamsaka Sutra. Therein is advanced the doctrine that all phenomena are produced by the mind and that the mind is the ultimate reality of the universe.

In the chapter entitled Dasabhumika (Ten stages of a Bodhisattva), this lucid statement appears:

> The three worlds are false, mere creations of the mind.[6]

And in another chapter, Verses by the Bodhisattvas in Yama's Palace:

> The mind is like a master artist who can paint all kinds of phenomena. In all the world there is not a thing the mind does not create. The same is so of Buddha. The same is so of sentient beings. Mind, Buddha, and sentient beings, though they are three, they are one indivisible. All Buddhas know that everything is the product of the mind. Whoever understands this sees the true Buddha.[7]

At any rate the greatest joy is to discover one's subjecthood, the overflowing meaning of living. To recognize that the vigor of the universe is one's own mind and that universal time passes and space exists for one's own sake is the height of establishing one's subjecthood. Eisai concludes his preface with

> Heaven is spread above and earth is placed all for my sake. All for my sake do the sun and the moon orbit and the four seasons turn. For my sake only do all creatures and non-creatures come into being.

Now that I think of it, in his first lecture of the sixth Chinese Zen patriarch, Hueineng, tells us to regain our lost humanity by giving our subjective cognition priority over our objective cognition:

> One day I thought the time had come to spread the Dharma and I seized the chance. Just when I reached Fashing Temple in Canton, the Dharma teacher Yintzung was lecturing on the Nirvana Sutra. The flag announcing the lecture occasioned a discussion between the monks. One said it was the wind that moved, another said the flag, and as not one or the other side would yield, the discussion reached an impasse. I then stepped forward and spoke: "Neither flag nor wind moves. It is your minds that move," whereat those gathered were astonished.[8]

Such words can be delivered only by one who has been questing the meaning of life in the phenomenal world and been successful in his austere training. And I make my way across the yellow plains under the blue sky.

10/...: Last night I received an impressive talk from an amateur astronomer.

I went out to a point with a convenient shelter of rocks and natural lawn-like grass, high enough above the sea to keep the sound of the waves from disturbing my sleep.

The night became as dark as a blackberry lily seed right after sundown, with twinkling stars innumerable.

Near where I was leaning against a rock, a small truck came in. A man got out unaware of my presence and began to set up a telescope and a camera with the self-preoccupation of an insect. I produced a cough, but he continued as if classing me as a rock. When he finished he approached and coolly asked, "Are you okay?" Maybe he took me for a wanderer injured or ill; if so, what admirable control not to speak until he finished.

I said I was a Zen monk on a training pilgrimage, making the earth my pillow for the night. My introduction might as well have been a stone dropped into the night sea — he didn't respond, though perhaps it had no more significance than the silence of a repairman confronting a broken TV set.

Somewhat later he stumblingly asked, "What?..what training?"

Unable to see his face, I couldn't figure his motive or depth or the extent of his inquiry, but I had thought about Eisai, the Avatamsaka Sutra, and the Sixth Patriarch during the day, so of them I spoke. Again I couldn't tell how he took me, but as I was thinking he was like a giant insect raising and lowering its antennae, he quietly began,

"To embrace objective truth by subjective truth is good, it gives it energy, direction, and so on. Bosanquet also considered the universe to be comprehensible by our intellect, it being a reasonable system that can be freely treated by our intellect once we understand it. So the question is, how far did your Eisai and sixth patriarch understand the universe when they established their subjective truth?"

"How far? What do you mean? Can you illustrate?" I asked, and I was impressed when he explained to the following extent:

Our sun, he said, is near the edge, about 32,600 light-years from the center, of a spiral galaxy presenting the shape of a convex lens, within which are about 100 billion stars.

While containing so many stars, it is but a mere galaxy. Indeed there are gatherings of galaxies. A relatively small gathering is called a group of galaxies, a big gathering — some hundred to several thousand — is called a cluster of galaxies. Large numbers of these groups and clusters compose what could be called a Milky Way of galaxies, much as the stars of our galaxy compose a Milky Way of stars.

Around these many groups and clusters are large gatherings of galaxies in much greater concentration than the galaxies of any cluster, and these could be called superclusters. Among some known ones is one of discoid shape having the Virgo cluster as a dominant feature near its center. Its diameter is approximately 60 million light-years, and toward its edge is the Milky Way galaxy with our solar system.

What's intriguing is that all these galaxy clusters are receding and, according to Hubble's Law, the farther they are from us, the faster they recede. For instance, the Virgo Cluster is about 36 million light-years away and receding 1,140 kilometers per second. The Corona Borealis Cluster is about 620 million light-years away and receding 22 thousand kilometers per second. The Hydra II Cluster is 1.8 billion light-years away and receding about 60 thousand kilometers per second. And a certain galaxy in the Boötes Cluster is as remote as 4.7 billion light-years and receding 145 thousand kilometers per second — almost half the speed of light!

10/...: This afternoon I met a queer man claiming to be as important a Zen layman as was Pang, layman of Zen Master Matzu Dauyi; Kanyu, layman of Zen Master Dadian Pautung; or Li Au, layman of Zen Master Yaushan Weiyan....

I was dripping sweat, so I went down to a sandy beach with pines and swam toward the offing as far as I could maintain full speed. As I turned back leisurely, I noticed a white smoke rising from the area where I'd left my clothes on a branch.

When I got to the beach I saw a man of late middle age almost on his belly blowing at a fire, clogs cast aside. Seeing me, he stood and offered a Westerner's openhearted handshake.

"Hullo, my name is Ryuge. I'm a Zen layman. Greatly impressed by your youth. Fine weather, but isn't the water frigid, and abounding with stinging medusae?"

Cold, I kept rubbing myself with a towel. Then I asked,

"A Zen layman? You mean you're 'disinterested in entering into service; selfless and enjoying the practice of virtue; wealthy; and cultivating your moral sense that you may come to self-realization'?"[9]

"All but the most important third. I daresay you're well-proportioned, with fine muscles hardened by pilgrimage," he said and kept talking as he meddlesomely brought me my clothes one by one from the branch.

"You must be acquainted with the Noh play *The Celestial Raiment of an Angel*, a variation of the swan-maiden myth, said to be a popular folktale motif the world over. A fisherman steals the angel's celestial raiment as she's bathing and forces her to be his wife....It's one of the egoistic fancies cherished by every stupid man. You know, the more vulgar the man the more he seeks a woman of refinement, for his supreme pleasure is to make purity and beauty serve his ugly desire. But it's interesting, she never forgets her original nature. Think, she bears the fisherman a bunch of children, raises them, and exhausts herself in a commoners' life. Yet when she finds and regains her celestial raiment, she quickly returns to heaven — which tells us she's stubborn and ineducable."

I sat on log, put on my gaiters, and said, "Was it to describe her stubborn nature? I understood it simply as a lament over the brevity of beauty."

916

"Don't be silly! It describes her stubborn mistrust of all men but her father — a disgusting consanguineous love. You must know we never obtain a woman's trust however long we're married or hard a life we share. I myself was a well-to-do trader, whatever you may think. I shuttled between Vancouver and Tokyo, or Kobe and Seoul, as if playing at cat's cradle. I loved to swim and enjoyed the beaches wherever I went, and ate steak whenever I pleased, though now I favor hot springs...and eat only fried tofu.

"As it happened, a foreign duo defrauded me of my commodity. They looked handsome and trustable, but were professional swindlers, and I desired to make a good profit. Well, I don't blame them. From the first, trading, pirating, and practicing deception aren't so distinguishable. At any rate the amount involved was too much for me and I immediately went bankrupt. During the confusion my only child got encephalitis, which turned to pneumonia, and she died. Then my wife left me to return to her native home. Amazing, so simple and light was our tie it broke like the leg of a cricket!"

"Was that when you became interested in Zen?"

"No, no, it was when I was still wealthy. I was impressed by the longevity of Zen priests. My Zen master lived to 101 without betraying my unerring expectation. He built the first old people's home in this nation, but refused to enter himself. By any means all excellent Zen masters live long. For this alone I believe Zen deserves more notice from the world's intellectuals. Let me list you some, so many in these postwar years alone." And he began to recite:

"...Zen Master Kishizawa Ian of Gyokuden-in, Shizuoka, lived to 91; Takagi Enitsu, an Eigenji abbot, to 92; Nakane Kando, a Komazawa University president, to 84; Zen Master Furukawa Ekun of Engakuji, Kamakura, to 91; Yamamoto Genpo, a Myoshinji abbot, to 96; Zen Master Harada Sogaku of Hosshinji, Fukui, to 90; Okada Giho, another Komazawa University president, to 80; Watanabe Genshu, a Sojiji head abbot, to 95; Sawaki Kodo, a Zen master without a temple, to 86; Yamazaki Giko, a Shokokuji abbot, to 92; Dr. Yasaka of Kamakura, to 97..."

"Great Zen Layman Ryuge — " I interrupted, fed up as if from seeing the disorderly goods in a curio shop, and rather cruelly I commented,

"I assume your daughter greatly lacked Zen qualities."

Layman Ryuge closed his mouth and averted his face from the smoke without otherwise moving, but soon he regained his garrulity,

"I admit some great Zennists did go early to the grave. One was the elder of two brothers, the younger being the master I now serve. He was great, very unlike the younger, who is, I know, cowardly, lazy, lukewarm, and stingy. The elder was assiduous, modest, and affectionate, and was expected to be our old master's successor. But he was abruptly killed at a bus stop awaiting a bus. An unlicensed motorcyclist struck him — he hadn't a chance even to greet the kid, I bet. Camus advocated a philosophy of the absurd and quite reasonably

917

was killed in a traffic accident. But this elder brother believed in Buddha's teaching. The sutras are full of false promises. One sutra says,

> "A Bodhisattva is like one who has procured medicine against suffering, even against accidental death, for a Bodhisattva has attained the mind that aspires to the highest Buddhahood. This wisdom keeps a Bodhisattva from trouble and disease."[10]

"Layman Ryuge," I said, "Natural and physical phenomena are meaningless as long as we relate to them passively. They begin to have meaning only when we take them into our bosom. Snow steadily falling into the ocean is meaningless, but there's great meaning in our taking snow and trying to fill up a well."

Scarcely had I finished when he stood up, saying,

"Ah! — yes!" He looked like any of those characters who frequently appear in the Chinese Zen records, who are enlightened by a word. He took from his bosom a newspaper-wrapped packet, which turned out to be nothing other than a bundle of dried cuttlefish.

"I quite forgot I had this tasty food!" he said and bent to put the cuttlefish over the fire, where they curled and began to emit their odor, such as would daub all high concepts into a mud wall. I was reminded of so many aspects of the commoner's life.

Then I felt solitude, a noble solitude.

My faith is like the faith unfolded in the Avatamsaka Sutra:

> This world exists to perfect character.[11]

I live my life to deepen this faith and live in this world as if walking through a sala forest.

10/...: Grew tired on the highway, descended a cliff by grasping rocks and trees to reach a narrow shore of dark sand with many black rocks. Noticed a line of smoke, expected the layman Ryuge, advanced among the rocks and was surprised.

Seated about a lively fire were three women naked except for a skimpy white cloth tied at the hips. They kept still but gazed at me all at once like seals. Evidently they were divers. Each had a bamboo basket to the side and was eating roasted corn rather than their catch.

I thought of a Korean history book that scornfully described the women divers of Cheju Island:

> During the season to gather seaweed, stark naked they scatter here and there on the rocky beach. The sight of their shameless venery is astounding.[12]

Facing them I was the one who felt ashamed to be so completely clothed. I wanted to disappear as soon as I could apologize, but the oldest, maybe

918

around 25, made a space and offered me some corn, and more, in standard language rather than in dialect asked if I would eat ear shells. I couldn't find it in my heart to take from their catch and positively declined.

"But you are an honorable monk," she insisted.

They didn't question who I was and frankly told me they were sisters who lost their parents last autumn.

The sea that day they said was increasingly rough, yet their parents went out as usual. Their mother dived with a weight quickly and deeply. Their father's role was to retrieve her by rope and pulley. That way she could dive to 15 fathoms. They waited all night — their parents always came back before dusk. The sea roughened with wind and rain. Three days later the boat dragging the rope was found on a beach.

I said I admired them for living together and helping one another after losing their parents. The middle sister with large moistened black eyes remarked, "Spending the days deep in the water lessens our sorrow. There it seems the difference between this world and that isn't so clear."

"I'm happy when almost out of breath," the youngest added childishly. "I feel smothered in Mama's bosom," and she laughed. She was as yet unlike the others in development of flesh and was rather boyish about the shoulders, eyes, and mouth. Her chignon and dark complexion reminded me of the Asura statue kept as a national treasure at Kofukuji in Nara.

Unknotting her own hair so that it fell before and behind her shoulders, the oldest said, "We've been together, but soon I'm to marry and go to Hegura, a far island in Ishikawa Prefecture. I'll take my youngest sister, but my other sister will be married into an old family of Tsushima Island. So I'm teaching her all the secret spots for catching that our parents taught me."

Listening to the details of their talk, I learned that the two who were marrying had never met their prospective husbands, even by photograph, and were fully trusting a go-between, content to meet for the first time on their wedding day.

I was prompted to ask their impression of the Noh play introduced by the layman Ryuge. The oldest spoke for them all,

"The angel is cruel to leave her husband and children behind, she can't be an angel just by living in heaven. An angel must have a tender heart for earth-lings. If she's an angel, she'll devote herself to her family. I don't yet know my husband, but I know whoever he is he wants me. My joy is to be wanted. It's said our ancestors were likely either pirates or people carried off by pirates. Whichever isn't important to us, for by now our blood is mixed and we all need and help one another and are enjoying a peaceful life on the coast and the islands. But it's sad to part from our middle sister."

That sister too undid her chignon. Her hair hung like a screen and reached to the inside of her thighs. I felt pity at the sight of one nipple exposed through the strands. Half to her sisters, half to me, she said,

"Divided as we must be, the water where we dwell is one, and the family I am to enter is very religious. They are going to hold a forty-day Buddhist service to commemorate the wedding. It's their family tradition. During that period there will be lectures on a scripture called the Avatamsaka Sutra..."

10/...: October is already half spent. I stayed four nights in the three sisters' thatched cottage because they begged me to stay. Great excuses to accept were (1) to await their parents' death date so as to hold a memorial service, and (2) to wait out the spell of rain and high wind.

The house faces a rocky cove and is backed by a forest of *nagi*, a kind of podocarp. They told me the fishermen settling in the area planted it as a prayer for calm seas because the name sounds like nagi, "to grow calm." The tree is also a reminder of everlasting married love — the leaf resembles a handsome couple, the front a glossy dark green, the back a yellowish green, and the seeds germinate well.

I thought of a Chinese folktale:

> King Kang of Sung murdered Kanming and abducted his beautiful wife. Faithful to her husband, she took her life. Where she was buried beside him, and there two nagi grew up and began to entwine. King Kang, humiliated by jealousy, tried to cut them down, but they turned into a pair of mandarin ducks and flew away...

After leaving the three sisters I have been walking straight to Hakata without stopping for alms. In truth I'm interested in those 40-day lectures on the Avatamsaka Sutra to commemorate the marriage of the middle sister into the Sou family on Tsushima Island. A large temple in Hakata is seeking the lecturer by public invitation. Applications must be submitted before the end of the month.

10/...: Reached Hakata in late afternoon, cirrus clouds, refreshing sea breeze. Each break of spray against an offshore island, each tree there too, is vivid.

From antiquity to the Middle Ages, Hakata was Japan's largest international port. Japan then hadn't relations with any Occidental land; foreign lands meant the Korean peninsula, the Chinese continent, India, and their environs.

As I stood on a wharf I could see a sandbar extending out from a northern beach and at its tip a tiny island evidently accessible on foot at low tide. It must be Shikanoshima, famous for a gold seal inscribed with five Chinese characters connoting that Lioushiou, founder of the Later Han, presented it in AD 57 to the ruler of Na, then one of the prospering minor countries of the region known as Wa. A peasant chanced to unearth it in 1784, a date also becoming historic.

In the Nara and Heian periods, official envoys were sent to China from this very port more than a dozen times. As an undeveloped island country, Japan had to introduce hastily and with great risks the advanced continental culture.

When I eliminate all modern traces from sight and only see the clouds and hear the waves, past spectacles come to mind, as does the bitter thought of why I can't yet depart from this port.

Eisai, now respected as the founder of Japanese Zen, departed from here in 1168 and in 1187.

What did he think as he headed for the advanced country? Travel to China was dangerous. It's recorded that after he parted from his parents he visited a branch of the Usa Shrine to pray for a safe sail. As for me, I've parted from my parents forever. His goal must have been to bring back the advanced culture to contribute to Japan's development. I have no such goal. I'm unwilling to return once I've left. Where I live is of little importance. What I wish is to become acquainted with people who are earnestly searching for or deepening the meaning of life. For them life's importance is inside not outside themselves and phenomena are not a graveyard to be buried in but the opportunity by which to be energized.

Eisai at age 19 climbed Mt. Hiei to study the Tendai doctrine, but there he found the study stagnant and the Buddhist precepts in decay. So, as the records relate, his first visit to Sung, at age 28, was to obtain the new phase for a reformation.

If that's true, it's odd he stayed only 5 months. How could he obtain enough of the new phase? In so short a time what people obtain is often just the reputation of having studied abroad. Am I absurd and violating propriety to think of Koko's visit to America?

During that first trip Eisai was able to purchase the new 30-some volumes of Tendai works. When he returned he gave them to his teacher Myoun, who was greatly pleased.

On his second visit, a stay of 5 years, he was already 47, a remarkably old age for a foreign student even today.

In fact his activity in Sung shows he was no ordinary foreign student. To receive various conveniences beyond facilities for study is not discreditable, but evidently Eisai gave more than he received. (In this respect I must follow his example wherever I visit in Thailand and America...)

The main benefits he enjoyed in Sung were the opportunity to read through the Tripitaka three times, and certification as a Dharma heir by Shyutang Huaibi — a Zen master of the Huanglung branch of the Linji school, who was chief priest of Wannian Temple at Mt. Tiantai. Yet, Eisai's contribution well surpassed that of an ordinary student abroad. First, he offered prayers against a drought and an epidemic, and because of the fine outcome, he applied for and received the honorary title *Chian guang* (abundant light) from the emperor Kautzung. Second, he rebuilt the monument to the great Tiantai teacher Jyyi, rebuilt the wings of the main gate of Wannian Temple, and remodeled a pagoda at Mt. Tiantung. What he did seems messianic and unlike the activity of a foreign student.

921

Here again I have a question, if an unsophisticated one. How could Eisai obtain the great money to act as he did? I haven't enough in my scrip even for passage to Okinawa.

For expenses he couldn't have relied on his father, a Shinto priest of the Kibitsu Shrine in Okayama. But his father was by marriage related to a high priest of the Munakata Shrine, which owned the large rice fields I crossed. Did he support Eisai? His position alone wouldn't have made him so wealthy.

Furthermore, right after this second visit to Sung, Eisai began to erect many significant temples, such as Chieji in Hizen, Torinji and Tokumonji in Chikuzen, and Senkoji in Chikugo. For me they look like chain stores of Zen in the present business sense. And in the fourth year after his return he built Shofukuji in Hakata, which should be regarded as their headquarters. It had dominion over 38 large and small subtemples. Who was his patron to afford funds of such magnitude? An interesting subject, though no historian offers any light.

I gaze at the invisible dark sea and smell the smell of rotting seaweed renewed by each big wave, and again Koko's face comes up and he happily laughs.

Having criticized the Buddhism at Mt. Hiei for years, Eisai at Shofukuji wasn't content to criticize; rather he advocated a true Buddhism through practice, and the Buddhism he practiced was Zen combined with strict observance of the precepts. Hence he later came to be respected as the founder of Japanese Zen.

But his Zen was supported by mighty funds and tremendous authority, quite unlike the original Buddhism, which arose with the idea of freedom from authority and equality of all beings.

Shofukuji was built on a fief of Minamoto no Yoritomo, who then held the highest power as shogun of the Kamakura government. Eisai dedicated Shofukuji not only to the nation but also to the Minamoto family as their oratory, thereby gaining an intimate route to the government.

At the same time he asked Emperor Gotoba to grant him the highest award for his calligraphy "First Zen Monastery of the Nation" to be displayed at Shofukuji, and luckily this he got, assuring him of a connection with the Imperial family on top of his governmental connection.

10/...: Begged all day in the town of Hakata without taking any meals. When night came I went through a geisha quarter by the Naka River. Colorful illuminations reflecting on the water and on the streets after a passing rain made the area look merrier than it was. The hostesses and waitresses entertaining their guests took leave of their false countenances when they saw me and offered me coins generously.

Dog tired I dragged my way back to the wharf where I spent last night. A metallic darkness, no one about, only the light of an offing beacon, certainly inorganic.

As I ate roasted corn bought on the way, I thought of the three sisters, especially the one going to Tsushima. Brawny white thighs. She knows the island well, she said, but not the man she's to marry. She and her sisters went with their parents to Tsushima to peddle sundry goods. She says it's halfway between Kyushu and the Korean peninsula, about 700 square kilometers with under 50 thousand inhabitants; poor mountainous land, but having beautiful sights of numerous inlets, especially Asaji Bay constricting the center, gourd-like. Its coastal rias are the largest in Japan.

She said the Sou family has for generations managed the island's fishing and trading. They are erecting on a wooded eminence overlooking the bay an octagonal hall for whoever lectures on the Avatamsaka Sutra.

With the deadline two days away, I'll visit that large temple tomorrow, and meanwhile I'll dream that I've been chosen and that I'm secluding myself day after day in the octagonal hall to prepare the lectures.

The environs of the hall I would name Sala Forest. The Sanskrit *sala* means "lofty"; moreover, the wood of the sal is hard; and, just as we can have fine fruit if we keep the precepts, by taking care of a sal forest we can have fine trees. Sala thus gained the meaning "firmness."

The place where Sakyamuni Buddha was released from his perishable body into eternal peace, or Nirvana, was said to be between two pairs of sals.

After Buddha's death, the one in the south who preached the wisdom of our attaining Nirvana while we are yet living — the concept of *prajnaparamita* — was Manjusri Bodhisattva, respected as a father and a mother among all Bodhisattvas. In the Avatamsaka Sutra, in the chapter titled Gandavyuha (Gateway to the Dharma), there is this account: Faring south, Manjusri came to the east side of Bodhi Castle. Sudhana-sresthi-daraka Bodhisattva also came thither, having determined to perfect his training by visiting all sorts of wise people. Manjusri admired and encouraged him,

> How good you are to have resolved to attain *anuttara-samyak-sambodhi*, the unsurpassed wisdom of the Buddhas, and to ask the wise directly about the Bodhisattva Way. What you are about to do, you know, is a Bodhisattva's first treasure, already containing all wisdom, that is, to visit the wise, acquaint oneself with them, respect them, and offer them the best of oneself.[13]

This encounter took place in a sal forest.

During the night as I slept on a bench by the ferry-house, I was awakened by what at first I thought was rain on my sleeves, but it was spray blown from the whitecaps, which even in the dark were visibly white.

I was so cold I couldn't sleep again. I pulled up my rain cape. The warmth inside became like a faint light, and I remembered my childhood teachers Docho and Yojun, especially their words about the *wako*, Japanese pirates based on Tsushima.

They were earnest academicians and heartily kind to me. When I looked wearied by the monotony of their lectures, they would shift to more engaging subjects with added imagination. Their studies had little in common, but strangely they each spoke with lively eyes when they lectured on the wako.

The one who talked about Scandinavian pirates, or Vikings, must have been Yojun:

> According to *The Oxford Dictionary of English Etymology*, Viking is commonly held to be formed from *vik* creek, inlet + *-ingr* -ING, as if "frequenter of inlets of the sea"...

Was the following description about the Vikings or the wako?

> Born in a cold, gaunt land dreary with mist day in and day out, they pursued no honest calling but took to the open sea to plunder...

Docho taught that the wako assembled armed boats, from 2 or 3 to several hundred, each with a crew of about 10, which raided the coasts of Korea and China repeatedly. Their objects of plunder were transport boats as well as storehouses of rice prepared for land tax, and sometimes they abducted the coast dwellers to Japan to sell as cheap labor. It matches what the oldest sister said about her ancestors.

Vigorous wako activity occurred in the later 14th century and in the later 16th — periods of great disorder in all three countries, Japan, Korea, and China. Docho said:

> When the highest class, including administrators, exercise their status, wealth, and power not to advance social welfare, supreme morals, and recondite truth but to indulge their sensual pleasures and worldly desires, as if they were the ignorant and feckless poor, then the commoners will ignore morals and opt to survive by any means. To expect the commoners to be righteous and fair would be ludicrous; they don't care that it is a cruel and false economy to sacrifice a thousand lives to maintain their kin. With their dignity trampled, they will override authority and outlive scenes of carnage as a matter not of shame but of pride...

The wako were undaunted even on a stormy sea, nay, found it an advantage. Can't I hear even now their incitive cries? They raided their victims, fired ships and warehouses, and pillaged in a mix of glow and shadow, some gasping their last on the shore, others in the waves. Was the path to death more luminous than the flames or more dark than the night?

They bared themselves to extremes of danger for their kin awaiting them and their booty. Familial love burned high on the roar and sparks of the night. How dangerous to others is exclusive love of self and kin! No doubt the raided and abducted also knew familial love, and it too blazed high in the dark.

Each side had precious kin and fought for supremacy instead of finding a way to coexist. Blood washed blood and sank into the earth or dissolved in the sea.

The sky next morning could have been fine and the sea clear.

Imagining thus far, I suddenly hit on the hypothesis that the generous patron behind Eisai could have been a trader or just as possibly a wako.

In the Avatamsaka Sutra it is said that mind, Buddha, and all sentient beings are not different from one another.[14]

It isn't the least strange that a patron, a trader, and a pirate could be one and the same person.

66

Going On

Mokuzu climbed the stone steps to a certain large temple understood to be seeking by public invitation a lecturer on the Avatamsaka Sutra. Under the big trees the steps and the cogon grass growing between them were wet with morning dew. He was expecting to see the ocean through the trees, but a dense mist hung stagnant. He looked up at an old maple and thought,

'Autumn reds occur because the movement of sugar from leaf to stem is slowed by the drop in temperature. From the sugars trapped in the leaf the red pigment anthocyanin is formed.'

He went through a half-ruined brushwood gate. There were abundant shrubs of bush clover past their prime. No one was in view, but he heard sounds of rather lazy brooming.

He called out. Quite long after the brooming stopped, two youths in black public-school uniforms silently appeared from different directions, evidently resident priestlings of about junior high school age.

Both seemed somewhat mentally handicapped. One had a creased brow and a gruesome grin. His skin, hair, and irises were deficient in melanin. Perhaps he was a phenylpyruvic urea idiot. He pointed at Mokuzu and kept earnestly uttering something. Mokuzu managed to decipher "a real training monk" but could not determine whether it was a question or a statement.

The other looked down yet peeped at him. Not merely light-headed, he was dull and gave the impression of being in the absolute sulks. His face was flat like a slice of large sweet potato. It was obvious that he was a mongolian idiot, or affected with Down's syndrome — a more courteous name.

925

Mokuzu was struck by their strong likeness to Hanshan and Shyde, a favored subject of Zen painting; only their hair was not long, nor had they Chinese robes with flared skirts. He recalled one of Hanshan's poems:

> I live in a rock cave remote except to birds.
> Nothing here is laudable, yet clouds embrace the rocks.
> Many years have passed, many springs and winters.
> I dare say to rich folks, vanity is useless.[1]

Mokuzu directly told them the purpose of his call. They put aside their brooms and ran off, one giggling like a monkey, the other repeatedly glancing back.

He who came to relieve them was the layman Ryuge, muttering as he approached,

"...embarrassing...a public invitation merely to keep up appearances while securing private ends....Our temple built an old people's home and a hospital, which we ourselves don't enter...and established a school, where we don't enroll our children; for we well know the inner conditions of those places....Our custom is also to invite lecturers, advisors, and tenderers by public announcement after deciding on them ourselves, for we know outsiders are to be feared....If you don't believe me, meet the master and find out for yourself."

He kept muttering like a water leak as he led Mokuzu along a corridor dark as a tunnel and cold as outside,

"I tell you he never studied any sutra beyond indiscriminate rote, but he's loath to share the honor and honorarium and is burying himself in worm-eaten annotations and interpretations. What a shame! — every few minutes he meets a word he can't read and lowers his head and rubs his temples around with his fists. Young trainee, don't mistake our master for a Merino sheep!"

When Mokuzu reappeared after a brief interview with the Zen master, in the garden there was, oddly, a training monk dressed like himself in travel robes. He was being cordial to the layman Ryuge and the two priestlings as they stood together by a pile of burning leaves. All were laughing over a story he was telling of a pet monkey taught to practice onanism.

Ryuge detained Mokuzu, saying in the fire there were sweet potatoes soon ready to eat. But Mokuzu, thinking it useless to linger, went out the gate. The monk came after him.

"Wait up, Dorm Inspector! I've been asking in at Shoshinji, Ryotanji, and Tangenji on the trail of none other — now I've fetched up with you, how can I let you go?"

Mokuzu tilted his hat and saw a vaguely familiar face. It looked inverted, for his pate was smooth as an egg while his chin sported a dark but short, coarse beard. His down-sloping eyebrows and eyes and the straight column of his nose gave him an air of nobility.

"Don't sadden me by totally forgetting me. It was I who quickly resolved to leave that inane Shoshin College because of Shiba's reckless fury. Your work was to detain me, though you didn't."

"Oh, Hoden Soma. For what reason are you pursuing me?"

"Thanks. That is the question. To explain is my wish. By any means I need your consent. I must be careful to explain well, so let me suggest a better place. Those two idiots at the gate are still watching us. I congratulate you if you were rejected as the Avatamsaka Sutra lecturer, or rather were excused. How was your interview?"

Having no set destination, Mokuzu went with Hoden toward a cheap lodging house where Hoden had spent the night.

"Nothing worth telling; at a low desk the Zen master was buried in books like a mailbox among tall buildings. He has a full set of the Avatamsaka Sutra in Chinese: the 60-volume translation by Buddhabhadra, the 80 by Siksananda, the 40 by Prajna. More enviable is his collection of related works: *Huayan-fajie-guanmen* (Observations of the Dharma-world revealed in the Avatamsaka Sutra), by the Huayan sect's founder, Fashun, and annotated by its fifth patriarch, Tzungmi; *Huayan-kungmu-jang* (Exegesis and comment), 4 volumes, by Second Patriarch Jyyan; *Huayan-jing tanshyuan-ji* (Comment on the 60-volume version), 20 volumes, by Third Patriarch Fatsang; *Huayan-jing shuyanyi-chau* (Comment on the 80-volume version), 90 volumes, by Fourth Patriarch Chengguan, and..."

"Stop! It's still morning and you're already making me drowsy! Instead of cataloging his books, why don't you tell me what he said?"

"Well, he asked first, who wrote my letter of introduction, second, how many years I'd studied the sutra and under whose guidance, and third, my present degree and status."

"And with all that being tough to answer, you turned tail, eh? You could've dropped the name Tengai, that great impostor. Just by hearing it this provincial Zen master would wet his pants."

"Indeed I left, not because I couldn't answer with words, but because I recalled the substance of Kierkegaard's criticism of Hegel's philosophy,

"A thinker constructs a gigantic sanctuary, a system including all the universe, history, everything. But behold his private life! Surprisingly he lives not in this lordly mansion but in a kennel, an annexed office, or at best a gatehouse. A horrible sight.[2]

927

"Hoden, I was ashamed to fancy myself studying and lecturing on the Avatamsaka Sutra. I reconsidered: I should be one who practices its teaching at all times. So I am going on."

"Phew! So exemplary are your words they should be widely heard to compensate for being wasted on my ears. Anyhow, your resolve to go on is fortuitous for me."

The lodging house was on a blind alley with the depressing smell of a drainage ditch. Accustomed to sleeping in the open, Mokuzu would have hesitated to stay in such a place even if paid. Next to the room occupied by the landlady's family, the dank stairway creaked, and the deteriorated mud wall and wood ceiling of Hoden's room were so moldy it seemed they would exude pus if pressed. An iron-framed Western bed stood in a corner on a rug hiding the frayed tatami.

"Sit down," said Hoden, offering Mokuzu the bed. Where Mokuzu sat the mattress sank to the floor, and they both laughed.

The landlady's daughter, looking unexpectedly refined in a pale pink sweater and striped wool skirt, brought in tea.

"Thanks, no tea — bring sake," said Hoden.

"We don't keep sake." She did not take him seriously. But he was quick in making her receive a bill as he patted her on the behind and said,

"You know I'm flush of money — quick now! This is a very important friend I could finally meet up with after a long time."

After she descended he said,

"She looks pure and is attending senior high, but she has an appetite for sex and money. Last night too she made an exorbitant demand and I had quite a time haggling as I tackled her slim waist. Hey, Mokuzu, don't enter samadhi — take an easy posture. What's the use of looking dignified when there's no one to see? You've got to learn life both top and bottom."

Mokuzu urged Hoden to relate why he wanted to see him. In short, as he put it, he was taken with the ambition to visit India to make a pilgrimage round of the eight sacred stupas associated with Sakyamuni Buddha, and he was asking Mokuzu to accompany him.

The stupas were erected in Kapilavastu, Buddha's birthplace; Buddha Gaya, where he was enlightened; Mrgadava, where he delivered his first sermon; Jetavananathapindadarama, where he expressed his occult powers; Kanyakubja, to which he descended from the heaven Trayastrimsa; Rajagriha, where he reunited two estranged groups of monks; Vaisali, where he realized his predestined life span; and Kusinagara, where he entered Nirvana.

Hoden gulped the sake brought in by the daughter and said,

"This pilgrimage is everyone's dream if they're an earnest disciple of

928

Buddha. But not many can do it. Nor could even Eisai, founder of your Zen sect, because of disorder then in Sung's outlying districts. The greats were Fashan in the fourth century and Shyuantzang and Yijing in the seventh — all Chinese. I a Japanese will now attempt to go, and on foot as much as possible. I have iron nerves but not your prudence, and iron nerves without prudence are liable to invite danger and fights wherever I go. Likewise I have some wisdom but lack the precepts you keep, and wisdom without precepts will make it easy for me to grab money, wine, and women and prevent me from realizing my great ambition. So I need your help. Frankly, I've attempted the pilgrimage three times and gotten only as far as Taiwan. Each time I had to return because of one inauspicious event or another."

Then, dwelling on his early days, Hoden told how he came to believe this pilgrimage was vital to his remaining life. Mokuzu practiced his tremendous receptive capacity, thinking it the most demanded but least supplied virtue of a present Bodhisattva.

Hoden was born in Tochigi, "a rare landlocked prefecture. My native Yuzu, near the border of Ibaraki Prefecture, is not noteworthy but just a wide, dreary, infertile landscape with constant dry wind. Yet the locals are proud of its being the widest village in Japan," said Hoden cynically.

His father was a Shingon archbishop, also a superintendent of education, a noted man of the area. The family was eminent. One of Hoden's paternal uncles was chief of the district public prosecutors office, another was chief of a police station.

But Hoden's mother was of humble origins and uneducated. Soon after his parents were married, his father's sister came back divorced. She was Hoden's Aunt Ata, the first woman to receive a degree in philosophy from the local university. She was close to Hoden's father and slighted Hoden's mother at every turn, introducing philosophy into even such trifles as pickling plums and drying laundry; and she naturally gained authority in the social affairs of the temple, and assisted Hoden's father's work and Hoden's education, while his mother worked as a maidservant.

"This hateful aunt who made my mother miserable must have been a primary factor in my running wild," said Hoden.

In elementary school he detested study and was naughty. Soon the adults' contacts with his school became specialized: his mother going to apologize for his conduct, his aunt going to criticize the education policy, and his father going to deliver congratulatory addresses at entrance and graduation ceremonies.

In time Aunt Ata began to go daily to meet him. She waited for his class to finish, fetched him even by means of tying his neck with a rope, and made him sit erect before his father to study under his surveillance. His father freely raised his fist, his aunt lashed at him from behind, and Hoden beat the neighborhood children as much as he was forced to study.

"They clung to me as if hoping I'd beat them. Far from refusing my rash demands, they came asking how else they could serve me."

When he entered sixth grade his teacher told the class, "You are all good except for one. We must endeavor to complete the elementary-school work and prepare for junior high, so please ignore and don't copy that bad example." Everyone looked furtively at Hoden and laughed up their sleeves.

Hoden felt his blood would run backward in his veins, and when he came to himself he found he had already struck his teacher to the floor. His parents and his aunt were at once summoned. Before the principal his father's manner was so unlike his usual swaggering manner at home that Hoden, though but a child, thought him indecent, on his knees with congested face, unable to speak a word.

Sure enough, once they were home he regained command, made Hoden sit erect, and pressed him with hard questions, "Will you mend your ways and study? If not, do you know what I'll do?"

Hoden considered giving him the whaling he had given his teacher; he had just learned adults were not so strong as they appeared. Silently he glared back.

"What's this?" His father was quite perturbed by such open rebellion. His boy had hitherto been submissive, at least to him. "Answer me, will you study, or leave home?"

"What? — " Quick as a thought Hoden raised himself into a fighting stance. His father blanched, and soon conceded, "All right, do as you like. No longer will I tell you a thing."

Since indeed he kept mute, Hoden's education fell entirely to Aunt Ata's charge; and she soon spoke only what Hoden enjoyed hearing, and to his father only what pleased him.

"Even in those reckless days there was one girl who showed me sympathy, a parishioner's daughter named Izumi."

One day his aunt reported to him that children were gossiping about him, saying he was so beastly that soon he would commit a crime, possibly a parricide, and Izumi had protested, "He never will, his true heart is delicate and kind!"

After that whenever Izumi was in sight Hoden took care not to be rude, and behaved like an ideal boy.

His school record barred all chance of his entering any private higher school; yet he did enter one owing to his father's authority as superintendent of education combined with a bribe masquerading as a contribution. Though he wrote no more than his name on the entrance exam, Hoden was informed that he was accepted because of excellent exam results.

Once each in junior and senior high he had to change schools on charges of inflicting injury. Every school he attended was renowned for fights and for the activities of its karate club.

After finishing high school he entered Taisho University in Tokyo without spending any years between preparing for the entrance exams. The university was founded by the Shingon sect, and in addition to his father's being a Shingon archbishop, one of his relatives was Taisho's president, whom no scholar there, however great, dared oppose.

In Tokyo also he did not study. Day after day he sent his fellows sprawling in karate club. Nights he drank, fought, and battered passersby.

But even then he could not forget gentle, fair-skinned Izumi and her faint sweet smell...a white sasanqua flower.

"Hey, Mokuzu, how much a man loves a woman is equal to how much he masturbates thinking of her. I practiced and practiced, plucking off her clothes like sasanqua petals in my imagination."

Each school vacation he went home and could glimpse her, different in each season. Seeing him on a path she said, "I know you are working hard in Tokyo. Do bear up and become a fine priest." She had faith in him.

He then occasionally put on vestments and followed his father to funeral and memorial services. After all, he had to succeed him, and more practically, he could gain pocket money.

He chanted at Izumi's house too. In the summer she sat politely behind him with her family and fanned him, and afterward offered him a damp towel. In the winter she offered a noodle hot pot. So he behaved like a good priestling and began to realize he was a child of Buddha.

In the summer vacation of his final university year, he truly wished to enter the priesthood, even though he could not study well, and he declared to himself, "I'll perform what no ordinary man can — I'll walk in pilgrimage robes from Tokyo to my native Yuzu."

Having led a decadent life, he found it hard. But when at last he arrived, villagers in the fields dropped their tools and cried throughout the village as if a great event were unfolding, "Ooo-i-i! The rascal's reformed — is returning in robes!"

Aunt Ata rushed to summon all the parishioners to the temple and bade them line up along the approach. His father in full regalia sat on the priest's chair before the main building patiently awaiting him. Little devils and old folks drew near. Izumi put aside her work in a factory and ran toward the temple.

Hoden found it dreadful; he could not turn back but approached and entered the temple precincts with his best dignity. The crowd quieted in anticipation of the meeting of father and son. How would they greet each other after so long an estrangement? The distance narrowed to ten steps. The father, no longer able to bear his emotion, stood up from the chair.

"Hoden, congratulations!" he said. Then he dropped down dead. It was Hoden's first and last kindness toward his father.

Taking it as a golden chance to start anew, Hoden returned to Tokyo, piled up the books, and commenced to read. He had to complete four years of study in six months. He read about three hundred books, he said, and had yet to write a thesis. He wanted to graduate to show his excellent first step as a priest to Izumi. He wrote his thesis as if it were a long love letter to her. And he graduated without any complication.

"Ha! The professor couldn't tell whether or not it was the study of a mandala; anyhow he said it was 'full of passion.'"

Returning exultantly home, he found no Izumi. She had gone to work in another prefecture.

Concurrently his stomach betrayed his immoderate past, twinging whether empty or full. He had constant heartburn, even the beginning of bloody excrement. He was discontent but compelled to spend time recovering from an ulcer. Then one day he resolved to himself and confessed to Aunt Ata,

"I want to marry Izumi. I'll keep this parish in harmony with her." Outright his aunt visited Izumi's house. Her parents replied that for a laywoman to ascend to a temple marriage was a matter for serious thought and they would have to delay their answer. Izumi, who was with them, tittered and took it lightly.

Hoden angered wildly at his aunt, "How could you fulfill the errand so ineffectually? Go back — get her definite answer!" Aunt Ata went to Izumi's company. Izumi pleasantly introduced a higher officer with whom she was intimate and clearly replied, "I never even once thought of Hoden as my future husband."

Aunt Ata said to Hoden, "She is honest and eupeptic, and he, mannerly, kind, and understanding. They'll make a fine couple."

Mokuzu let Hoden talk freely. When at last he ceased, he said quietly,

"Hearing what you said and didn't say about your life makes me see how

932

you grew to long for Buddha and why you wish to perfect your character as you make a pilgrimage round of the eight sacred stupas. It's a rare wish; ordinary people are too busy or too clever to yearn like that. I assume those like you with so innocent a desire don't question the exact value of the stupas. For instance, about the sixth. A sutra says it was erected to commemorate Sakyamuni's persuading Devadatta to reform himself and rejoin the sangha. Devadatta had sought independence with five hundred followers. Later history fabricated him as a consummate villain who opposed Sakyamuni and set drunken elephants against him. But that couldn't be true. First, Devadatta sought independence because he deplored the sangha's slackening morals, and yet Sakyamuni rejected his proposed amendments. Second, in those days there were several who were honored by the title 'Buddha,' not only Sakyamuni. Some Jains regarded Sariputra as the representative of Buddhism. Later some people found reason to single out Sakyamuni, rating other Buddhas as no more than Sakyamuni's highest disciples, and they called such ones as Devadatta rebels. Whoever supported Sakyamuni benefited therefrom, and it was their successors who built the stupa at Rajagriha. Hoden, are you wishing with no doubts to pay homage to those stupas?"

"Mokuzu, the prime object of my pilgrimage is to straighten myself, not others. I don't much care how the stupas were built but only that I complete the pilgrimage, and I see the great need of your accompanying me all the way. You can teach me more of such things as we go. In exchange I'll teach you the best places in the pleasure quarters, how to flatter stupid believers into donating money, and such." Hoden took more drink.

"Hoden, you are asking me to be a fellow seeker on a pilgrimage, that is, a good friend, *kalyanamitra*. Listen to a passage from fascicle 4 of Jyyi's *Mohejyguan lu* (Great meditation and observation):

> "There are three kinds of good friends: protectors, companions, and teachers....Companions are unnecessary while a person is cultivating his mind and voluntarily practicing meditation. But he needs them if he is going to train himself by walking to attain the Middle Way, the reality of all things, to see Buddha in everything. Companions encourage one another to stay awake, to be careful, and to make a fresh effort every day. As friendly rivals they have the same mind and same wish as if riding the same boat, and they respect one another as if seeing Sakyamuni Buddha in one another. This is what companions are.[3]

"Hoden, are you asking me to go with you thus? If I am to be your companion, you must be mine."

"I can write my vow with my blood if you wish — after all, abstinence, continence, and moderation are good for my health." Hoden quickly finished the sake. "Just tell me your specific conditions for being my fellow pilgrim."

Mokuzu only laughed. Mistaking him, Hoden abruptly said,

"I see, offering my blood seal mayn't do. Okay, here and now I'll share all my money fifty-fifty!" Exposing his breast and the scar from an abdominal operation, he reached deep into his squalid stomach-band and withdrew a bundle of notes. All were American dollar bills.

Mokuzu promised Hoden that he would accompany him as far as Thailand and try to be the best companion as long as Hoden was in his range of vision. Then they left Hoden's lodging.

Already having a long-distance ticket for the train from Hakata to Kagoshima, Hoden pressed Mokuzu to get the same, but Mokuzu persuaded Hoden to refund his ticket and walk. They planned to get passage to Okinawa at Kagoshima. As Okinawa was then under military administration headed by an American high commissioner, this would be their last travel in Japan. Mokuzu wished to absorb and keep in mind everything good and bad that was Japanese and never to regret not ever returning to his native country. And to Hoden he said,

"Our walk to Kagoshima is to experience the initial hardship together and to reconfirm our resolution to be seekers of the Bodhisattva Way."

Hoden hesitated but could not object. "Indeed we must expect some troubles. In a strange country we may encounter misfortune. If we're killed by a thief or a back-street pervert in some remote place, no one will notice. We might think it a prankster when some guy is intending us real harm. We must be careful. From now on I'll restrain myself and avoid fighting as much as possible. But if it can't be helped, I'll be so earnest as to kill my opponent."

They went south on Route 3 along a national railway. Fortunately the weather was fine and the traffic scarce. They talked as they walked.

"Hoden, in the Avatamsaka Sutra, chapter 7, Pure Conduct, Manjusri expounds on a Bodhisattva's many wishes:

"When we walk a road we shall wish
only to walk Buddha's Way
and not stray elsewhere.
When we come to an offshoot we shall wish
to walk straight in the pure Dharma world,
where we have no mental obstacles."[4]

"Mokuzu, it's base to be on the lookout for coins when we walk; likewise it's avaricious to deplore the ruin of nature caused by road construction. Both views are egocentric. Still, let me tell you, these days nobody walks around thinking of Buddha's Way or the Dharma. First, most people don't walk but

934

use some vehicle, and second, a Bodhisattva's wish isn't the wish of a man unless he's bedfast with broken legs."

"Hoden, the sutra continues,

> "When we come to an upgrade we shall wish
>   to ascend to the Supreme Way
>   and to transcend the Three Worlds.
> When we come to a downgrade we shall wish
>   to be modest and kind
>   and to enter Buddha's deep Dharma."

"Such wishes are more impracticable than astronauts' dreams, but perhaps they originated from grim reality. So, Mokuzu, nobody praises them, nor ridicules them as long as you keep them to yourself and don't trouble others."

> "When we see a curved road we shall wish
>   to reject wrong ways and to annihilate
>   wicked views.
> When we see a straight road we shall wish
>   to be honest and free of falsehood
>   in our sayings and doings."

"What the sutra says can always be easily supposed even by a fool. After all, it asks us to be faithful to Buddha's teaching and at once to be good moral persons. But our brain is deaf and dumb, and we are ingenious at committing every contrary deed."

"Listen, Hoden,

> "When we see dust rise from the road
>   we shall wish to detach from dirt forever
>   and to attain the ultimate purity.
> When we see no dust rise from the road
>   we shall wish to practice compassion
>   and to be content with our spiritual abundance."

"Mokuzu, when I consider religious history, the activities of all sorts of founders, and especially the monstrous activities of your sect's Eisai, I feel I'm seeing clouds of dust after the trot of an ostrich across dry land. When I examine Eisai's contributions in the settlement of the dust, I see nothing to encourage us to seek human ideals. The synthesis of his contributions is of less value than, eh,...uh..."

"...is less appealing to human sentiment than is any trifling work of Hans Christian Anderson, eh, Hoden?"

"Oh, maybe — I never read Anderson. Anyhow, were it not for those hyperbolical founders along the road of history, we'd see no dust. Had they kept silent so we could live as we like, it would have been the practice of their great compassion. Have you more of the sutra?"

> "When we face a deep inaccessible road
> we shall wish to be rid of all troubles
> and to aim for the true Dharma.
> When we see or hear of a courthouse
> we shall wish to teach the profound Dharma
> and to make peace among all."

"Tut! The teaching is getting harder. I'll forgive no companion who entraps me, nor anyone who sides with him and asks me to forgive him. A true God or Buddha doesn't forgive, because from the first he doesn't punish, and no man has the authority to forgive another. Only the devil can forgive because he can punish. As a man I'll forgive no man who wrongs me, and of course not make peace with him. Sorry, Buddha. But if it's a woman, I can make a temporary union — gladly I'll bed with any who wrong me! Well, in my view the clever guys of this world look down on us and restrain us while they preach that we must respect peace and order. Their real concern is law and order — they despise the individual."

> "When we see a great tree
> we shall wish to resolve all dispute
> and to cure our indignation.
> When we see the trees of a great forest
> we shall wish to respect them
> and to regard them as teachers of all beings."

"Sure, trees have no sin," said Hoden.

"That's right, their existence is the very practice of great compassion. In *Jaujou lu* it is recorded that a monk whose intent was to ask the essence of Buddhism or the secret of Zen asked, 'What was the meaning of Bodhidharma's coming from the West?' Jaujou replied, 'Behold the arborvitae there

936

in the garden.' I think if we take this answer literally as a tree's practice of great compassion, we can understand Jaujou's plain but deep meaning, rather than resorting to any farfetched interpretation. Next,

"When we see a high mountain,
    we shall wish to aim for and to reach
    the summit of goodness."

"Hmm, a mountain is only nice seen from afar. Even Mt. Fuji they say is littered with cans. Guys who enjoy conquering the summit lack reflection. Mokuzu, I hope you'll never retreat to a mountaintop; to die in the foothills is better."

"When we see thorns we shall wish to extract
    the Three Poisons — covetousness, wrath,
    and ignorance — and to have no harmful mind.
When we see a tree with lush foliage
    we shall wish to shelter ourselves in the Way
    and to enter samadhi.

"Hoden, you must have studied about the Three Poisons, because that is written in the *Mahaprajnaparamitopadesa*, ascribed to Nagarjuna, the Indian patriarch common to Zen and Shingon as well as other sects. It says,

"The notion of self induces the notion of what is of concern to self, which in turn induces the notion of what is profitable to self, wherein arises greed. Whatever opposes self-interest naturally becomes a focus of anger, for anger comes not of wisdom but of delusion, whence anger is born of ignorance. The Three Poisons are thus the root of all desires."[5]

"Mokuzu, if we eliminate our greed, anger, and ignorance, we'll be no longer human but an image of Buddha with a mechanical brain. They make humanity interesting and are as important to us as the useful bacteria in our digestive organs. Buddhism, with its negative viewpoint, will never be loved by the majority of people. Listen, when I see lush foliage I think of a moist female thicket. Shelter to me is a woman, not a tree, and I can enjoy samadhi in her. You are immature and inexperienced. I respect purity, but I mean purity that has survived many evildoings. Untempered purity is like unfired china, unworthy of notice."

"Hoden, you are addicted to worldliness, and your view treasures a petty ego. The sutra speaks with love and respect for all beings, not only mankind. Its scale is universal as well as atomic; it surely cares about the fate of mankind, but it also cares about the fate of the earth, and more, cares that the universe be well ornamented with worthy beings. So it continues:

937

"When we see a tree in full bloom
  we shall wish our purity to bloom
  and wish to possess a wonderful appearance.
When we see a tree in full fruit
  we shall wish to practice to attain the fruit
  of Buddha's Way just as a tree attains its fruit."

"Mokuzu, you must know flowers are genitalia. As for fruit, you'd better cheer up: we're headed south. The farther we go the better the fruit and the women on all accounts — color, shape, taste. Northern women are pale as celery, but think of, imagine, anticipate, and desire the affectionate women of the south! Pious eyes, shapely nose, full lips, sweet underarms, big breasts, fragile-looking but strong waist...features that incite me to pursue their secrets just as on the contrary the six paramitas are binding you to the secret of emptiness. But don't worry, in return for your virtue of introducing me to the Avatamsaka Sutra, I shall excise a little greed and share a number of southern women with you. First in Okinawa, then in Taiwan, Hong Kong, Macao, Hanoi, Vientiane...yes, greed is a sin. We should be generous. In a single ejaculation we have over three hundred million spermatozoa."

'Poor Hoden,' thought Mokuzu when they reached Kagoshima four days later. Hoden had obeyed Mokuzu's discipline of not spending the night in either a temple or a hotel, and having slept on the grass in the rain, he got a cold and diarrhea.

The continuing rain became sleet on and off and ran down their necks. Their cheeks were red, their leggings muddy. Hoden complained that his wet corded belt bit into his waist and was impossible to untie.

They went to the wharf, though much too early for the ship to Okinawa; it had not yet arrived. The waves of a heavy sea broke against the wharf and splashed high, occasionally as high as the light poles. In the empty waiting room Mokuzu asked the booking clerk to light the kerosene stove, and, leaving Hoden there, he went off to gather alms in the town.

A few people struggled with half-open umbrellas. The electric wire howled above pruned sycamores standing ghostly. After finishing one side of the street he was returning on the other when he noticed ahead an odd gathering. Looking in through umbrellas and shoulders he saw a shoe store, and, seated on the floor, Hoden surrounded by scattered pumps and high-heeled shoes cheaply shining before a fallen rack.

"Hoden, what happened?"

"Mokuzu! I came to chant for alms despite being ill — I thought of you

938

striving in the rain. But this stupid shopkeeper winked at the salesgirl to indicate she give me nothing. When she said she'd offer her pocket money, the brute enjoined her by bodily force and took the smallest of coins from the register and tossed it to the floor as if to a dog. I shouted, 'I'm not a dog, I'm a beggar, an honorable beggar — a national treasure who lights the corners.' Forgetting himself, he shouted back, 'Thankfully receive your alms however scanty, or you're extorting money and I'm entitled to call the police. You must know begging is illegal in this nation.' I told him, 'Call them and disgrace your shop! To keep her from offering her good wish is more unlawful than soliciting donations for a pious purpose.' I then sat down as you see," and he added in a low voice,

"Mokuzu, look at her, puzzled over whether to call the police. She bears a likeness to Izumi."

Mokuzu picked up the rack and returned the shoes to it. From the counter the man grudgingly regarded him while fondling a small mallet. Mokuzu found the coin on the floor, put it in his scrip, bowed to him, and said,

"Please regain your humor as nicely as you repair shoes," and to Hoden he said,

"It's time to board the boat. Don't fight others. Fight yourself — you are your worst enemy. Samantabhadra Bodhisattva also says:

"When you anger, know there is no worse evil than anger. Anger engenders hundreds and thousands of obstacles on the way to becoming a Bodhisattva."[6]

Mokuzu went up the slanting ladder and looked down from the rail. In the sleet Hoden was disconsolately following at the rear of the gathering on the wharf.

67

Wheat and Tares

The subtropical weather gave Mokuzu a sense of freedom when he disembarked, though the season was midwinter. The sky was blue and the water over the extensive shoals a pale aquamarine.

'Like this,' he thought, 'it will be as I cross some islands to reach Thailand, where Buddhist ideals are said to be practiced even now. But my purpose isn't to settle on some beach where the sun sets behind palms, or to please and receive praise from the idealized, apotheosized Sakyamuni Buddha and his followers by persisting to practice what they once taught. I can picture a life of begging in saffron robes at houses where bougainvillea hedges bloom year round, where veranda piers face the river, with the thick mist clearing as the morning sun lights the golden pagoda. Afternoons I might be immersed in Sanskrit and Pali Scripture and reflect on the bygone days of Buddha....But that isn't how I should spend my youth.

'I am going to Thailand to draw a sharp line between my ideal and the Buddhist ideal, to part from the latter, and to realize the former in my own life. So for me Thailand will be the port nearest to Buddhism and the port to bid it farewell.

'But how different this liberal weather is from the winter of the land I left, which made me shriveled and defensive! It suits me, who should decide how to live best — frank, fair, and generous.'

Hoden was out of humor: "This sticky climate saps a man's will to work and leaves him with no aspiration or sense of cleanliness." He was still regretting that he had not given the Kagoshima shoemaker a drubbing and was also furious that his sleep had been disrupted by a couple sharing the compartment; the man had ignored his seasick wife and snored loudly all night.

Mokuzu thought to placate him by reiterating "There is no worse evil than anger." But he did not speak.

They boarded a bus to visit an old acquaintance of Hoden's in Koza, where they would stay while in Okinawa. The bus took a state road north along a western beach.

The Ryukyu Islands, the official name of Okinawa, had been occupied and administered since the end of the war by the U.S. Army, whose top executive there was a lieutenant general. The economy was colonial with monetary circulation dependent on the American base — the largest and strongest American base overseas — and production was controlled by both American and Japanese capital. The society was concerned over frequent offenses committed by American soldiers and over the large number of prostitutes.

To Mokuzu it was curious that the currency was in dollars and the signs of the stores and firms along the road were primarily written in English with Japanese subordinate. Crimson hibiscus and simple yellow allamanda not much minding their location if only the climate was warm were common on the banks of poor house lots and in the gaps between furniture stores and garages with old tires piled.

Soon white houses appeared on a rise some distance from the road and no doubt commanding an ocean view. The terrain was grassy like a golf course. Mokuzu fell into thought,

'I am reminded of Ena's and my dream of a south slope with early dandelions. True, my ideal is to find a fine life companion and have our amicable family life be our training life, though it's a quite personal concern. In this respect, the Buddhist ideal is extraneous to mine in regarding human beings as ugly, impure gobbets of desire. Its ideal is that we eschew our five desires, free ourselves from our illusion that things exist, detach ourselves altogether from our present life, neglect our body and material things to the degree of minimal self-maintenance, and live as lone individuals who finally turn even themselves into ideological emptiness.

'All Buddhist thought basically regards life as passive, as a preparation for death, as a temporary unity of four elements wherein no active meaning exists. Indeed our body keeps changing and is never still even a second, with the consequence that we can never seize it as changeless. Yet our life isn't thereby without meaning. I find meaning in its harmony of continuous change. As it changes, its meaning can be intuitively understood. But in their endeavor to seize life as a fixed entity, Buddhists drove themselves to despair and thus were fevered to build a philosophy around death, or Nirvana. I like to see great meaning in each changing life. I like to see life as beautiful, enjoyable, and admirable. My life is full of hope when I try to practice and experience it in that way.'

"Why do you gaze so?" said Hoden. "Do you envy the life in those houses, attractive on the surface, or do you intend to beg over there? It's no good. That's where the U.S. military officers live, actually just their wives, who don't know what to do with themselves. The men are at the base or off bombing Vietnam. The wives can only shop and cuckold. I went there to beg, chanted before a door. It opened a crack, and one peeped at me and shrieked, then *bang!* went the door, and *click!* she locked it. Worse than a baboon, I thought, feeling half enraged and half, well, it was funny. Soon a siren wailed from down the hill, and as I was wondering what would bring a patrol car to so peaceful an area, two hefty MP's were upon me with guns and forcibly taking me away. I pity the natives — a quarter of their land, the best part, is occupied by thoughtless and chicken-hearted Americans."

"Hoden, you're respectable for having gained your own experience that can't be highly valued by those who haven't the experience to understand."

"Thanks. I'll tell you the best experience in Okinawa — visiting a brothel. It's also a queer story. Soon after the war, you'd better know, GHQ abolished licensed prostitution. In 1958 by extension Japan prohibited all prostitution. But in Okinawa it's still well kept up for the U.S. base. Apart from that, you must experience spending all day and night with eight girls in one room. You'll realize how the sutras are empty theory! Their writers saw

941

reality as thin air. They kept denying the value of our body, though don't forget that greatest of sutra translators, Kumarajiva. While translating he not only took one of the Kucha king's women to wife but later was busy impregnating ten courtesans while educating three thousand students."

In the Avatamsaka Sutra, Gunavana Bodhisattva teaches about a Bodhisattva's ten practices to benefit others. They are joyful service, beneficial service, tolerance, courage, right conduct, appearance in any form at will, detachment from existence and nonexistence, attainment of the root of merit, preaching the Dharma, and pursuit of the Truth. These ten practices are the intensive Buddhist ideal, the standard of action and thought for earnest Buddhists, including Mokuzu, and also a binding golden chain against the pursuit of worldly and bodily pleasures.

Mokuzu pretended to be dozing and recalled the second:

> Sons of Buddha, a Bodhisattva's beneficial service is to keep the precepts and be pure in the worlds of color, shape, sound, smell, taste, touch, and thought. A Bodhisattva as such has no taint of illusion and widely preaches the untainted Dharma; has no wish to be born of an elite family in this world or the next; disregards profit, pulchritude, and sovereignty; and is steadfast to keep the precepts so as to be pure, saying, "I keep these pure precepts that I may save sentient beings from every controllable illusion, passion, misconception, and distress, and that I may delight all Buddhas and attain the highest wisdom.

'So far I can follow the preaching except for "that I may delight all Buddhas." It shows a lack of subjectivity, of doing for oneself, and is different from my ideal,' thought Mokuzu.

> One day the Bodhisattva while thus keeping the precepts is visited by a quattuordecillion, quindecillion, sexdecillion devils each accompanied by as many angels attractively blooming with voluptuous poses and playing charming instruments. The Bodhisattva thereupon thinks the five desires are obstacles on the path to the Dharma, barriers to the highest wisdom, and in his mind no desire arises and his mental purity remains like a Buddha's. Maintaining the highest wisdom, he can distinguish the fine differences of each of his visitors. Yet he is well aware of the absolute equality of them all, and with excellent expedients he educates them so that they no longer pose before him as obstacles. By keeping a correct mind, he is not led by the five desires into thinking the depraved thoughts that anguish human beings.

'Here the sutra writer must have imagined woman like those figures adorning the Hindu temple at Konarak, with whose number Hoden's eight in

942

a room can't compare. I wonder how many different faces, bodies, and gestures the writer could have actually imagined. At any rate the last sentence contains a quite realistic consideration. Did I never feel carnal desire before a woman consulting me? Did I really care only to be of benefit?' Mokuzu reflected and went on,

'Yet the ideas of this preaching don't sit too well with me. Being ideals, they're hard to confute, and I much agree with them since I'm not an epicurean. But, let's see, what is the tangible meaning of "the five desires are obstacles on the path to the Dharma, barriers to the highest wisdom"? Here the sutra seems utterly to disregard concrete organic life and see it as only an abstraction. With such a view, no one can be inspired even by seeing the wonderful harmony of our ecosystem, for instance. Inspiration is the base of optimism, and optimism is our life.

'I see this world consists of ceaseless restoration of matter. Plants compose organic matter from inorganic matter through photosynthesis; animals and fungi resolve organic matter to inorganic matter. Life is this constructive and destructive metabolism, which when well balanced makes for the beauty of life, of the earth. The sutra ignores this sort of aspect. Note what is said; isn't going along with it actually hard?

> All phenomena and forms of existence are falsehood wherein is no truth. Nothing stays even a moment or has any ground. All things are like phantoms and are deceptive to fools. Realizing that all things are so is to realize they are like a dream, like lightning. Whoever understands can be free of the problem of mortality and attain ultimate wisdom; if unsaved can be saved, if unfree can be free, if not master of self can be master of self, if agitated can be tranquil....[1]

'I think freedom from the problem of mortality shouldn't be gained by focusing on the end of individual life or by ruminating on life's transience; rather it should be gained by realizing that the life and death of an individual existence is a part of the ceaseless continuation of the time and space of the great world.'

❧

Hoden's old acquaintance was a mortician. His office adjoined his house at the far end of a seemingly bustling street that was the beginning of an un-decorated downtown where the native population had multiplied after the war.

Before the house was a black hearse — a remodeled, second-hand Lincoln with vivid retouches of paint. The passersby as if out of avoidance kept to the other side of the street. Not wishing to be reminded of their fate, they hated merchants of death.

943

"That hotchpotch shop is open all night." Hoden spoke so loudly that people looked at the shop and at him and Mokuzu. "If you get hungry, go eat, say, pig foot." Mokuzu felt somewhat insulted. Heedless, Hoden entered the mortician's office as if flattering himself for his familiarity with it.

"Hey, how're you doing, how's your piles? Look, you'll be glad — I've got my buddy with me this time."

"Hoden, great to see you! I knew you'd return!" screeched the mortician, showing only his face from behind a stock of cheap papered lamps and garish aluminum lotus flowers.

'An odd face,' thought Mokuzu, regarding his fleshy cheeks and his chin poorer than that of a catfish. His very black hair did not suit his age or his oily white face. Without noticing Mokuzu, he continued,

"You're vital to my business! You can understand by remembering Mr. Osano — he's no priest, but he wears robes. I can't, that's too much — a mortician's a mortician. Now that you're back we'll prosper together. I'll put an ad in tomorrow's paper and Osano will be pop-eyed!" He withdrew, calling his wife by a childish word and with a strange insinuating tone.

Mokuzu was struck by the feeling of having come to an out-of-the-way place. 'My native place was so, but so too is this. It's sad when earnest young persons in quest of the central human theme have no chance to live outside the cultural and spiritual boondocks.'

Hoden freely went into the next room, removed his travel robes, leaned against the wall, threw out his legs under the low dining table, and massaged his shoulders.

"Hey, I'm tired. Why don't you quickly offer up your millet brandy or something."

"In a second, Bishop Hoden. Tonight we'll have a jovial feast for this happy reunion. What's she doing — again nodding off over the flower-making? I'll just go see." The mortician went down a dark and creaky staircase. The family area was a semi-basement opening to one-floor dwellings below the road.

Mokuzu, taking a seat facing Hoden, realized how Hoden could make a large sum of money. Hoden was avoiding his eyes. Soon he began to act odd, concerning himself with the outside as if trailed by a detective. Mokuzu kept his mouth shut. Then the mortician came up talking,

"Mercy, Kazuko's fretting, troubling Mammy. You see, I was indisposed and we had no income till you last appeared. Kazuko was resigned to not going to college, and since she disliked study, she was content working part-time in a blacks-only cabaret instead of regularly attending school, and she intended to work there afterward. But now many of her classmates are taking the college entrance exams and she's wailing and wishing to go on with her studies after all. Mammy told her she should be thankful enough to get through senior high what with younger siblings, and she reminded her of the poor girls who have to go to the prostitute quarters after junior high. But that all the more frustrates Kazuko; she says we must know a cabaret's no different. Well, just now I told her not to cry — 'Bishop Hoden has come, it'll be easy to earn your college cost. People think of me as a half-dead merchant of death, but I'm in the arms of the God of Wealth!' But still she's fretting, she says her school record is too low for college, she couldn't study! So, Bishop Hoden, haven't you a suggestion to save her?"

Hoden responded as if he had not heard a single word,

"Hey, I'm going out. Ask your wife to hurry upstairs with the shirts and pants I left in her custody."

"Oh, I see, you're busy. Well, at once — Mammy! Leave those things and quickly bring his clothes!" His voice was hysterical.

The wife came up with a bundle and entered the room now dominated by silence. With a stiff smile she spoke a welcome to Hoden and Mokuzu. Her face was thin and sallow. Surely she had red eyes and a stuffed nose.

Hoden heedlessly changed then and there to an open-neck shirt and jeans. He could easily turn into a worldly man.

"Mokuzu, please understand there's a place I must call on. You needn't act reserved here, so recover well from your travel fatigue." Hoden spoke with a tragic air of resolution.

"When do you plan to return?" Mokuzu asked simply.

"Within a few days, could be a week, could be tonight."

"Go if you must. But don't forget, in any situation nothing is more valuable than self-control."

That night the mortician and his wife held a welcome dinner for Mokuzu in the same narrow room, offering pork sukiyaki and more than necessary a millet brandy, an Okinawan product.

Both loved to drink, and importunately pressed Mokuzu to do the same as if convinced that friendship grew in the exchange of cups. As he failed to comply, they began to twit him, comparing his drinking with the greatness of Hoden's. More, they became insinuative:

"Hoden is uncommonly handsome, brave, and openhearted. Yet he's pure, sensitive, and versed in the niceties — quite unlike other monks. He's the most noteworthy itinerant monk ever to set foot on Okinawa.

"If you don't agree, listen. Two summers ago we were at the bottom of fortune's wheel: no customers, me with piles, she with sore shoulders, an ulcer, and eye strain from making flowers — and they were in poor demand. Our kids were younger then and more trouble. In such a fix, Hoden appeared like a messenger from heaven and gladly became officiant priest for our business, and it began to prosper. Thanks to him we could get through our crisis without selling our daughters into prostitution, and could buy the hearse — it's ours. Hoden is truly a Bodhisattva. Now, you look like you come from a good family free of worries. You go through thick and thin and you'll know what I mean."

The mortician's eyes were an angry red and fixed on Mokuzu. Mokuzu kept silent with a smile. Then the mortician went on,

"You too become an officiant priest. Take part in people's gravest sorrow and learn what people are. That way prove your worth and grow up to be indispensable to the public. Such is the orthodox training expected of a priest. I don't respect those who coop themselves in a shell meditating and studying. You should train to manifest yourself in public — no one need train just to conceal himself."

"You're saying that to bury people is to manifest oneself," said Mokuzu lightly. To the mortician it sounded sharp; he shut his mouth, and his wife put herself forward to assist him,

"Frankly, his indefinite nationality meant he couldn't take up an honest calling, since in fact he's a Taiwanese. When young he was in a party opposed to the Japanizing of Taiwan. When Japan was defeated and its army withdrew, Chiang Chiehshik, leading the nationalists, took over, and ironically his exploitation became yet worse than Japanese rule. My husband joined in a revolt, but the nationalists instantly squelched it with arms confiscated from the Japanese. With only the clothes on his back he escaped here. I saw the refugee boat. I was working in a pineapple field. They ran aground on a reef.

"I took him in. He was awfully weak. Since then we were married and actually he's bearing my family name and assuming the air of an Okinawan. But he could never get any good job requiring official documents, because it would expose him. So he had to contend with day labor or side work at home. Year after year the stress of his youth began to tell on him. Even so, he got work with the big mortician Osano. Well, Osano's avaricious and lewd, and oh, what we've endured! Then suddenly Hoden appeared and we could leave Osano. How we thank Hoden!"

Calmly observing the mortician, Mokuzu intuitively sensed that he was lying to his wife, that his reason for fleeing to Okinawa was possibly dishonorable. 'But even if he's lying, it's no longer a big problem as long as they're living as a family. What's important is that they care about each other,' he thought, and to change the subject he said,

946

"Now I wonder where your divine Hoden Bodhisattva went."

"You don't know?" The mortician was surprised and addressed Mokuzu with apparent distaste and suspicion, "Knowing is your business if you're his friend. Of course he went to his woman. It's natural that an excellent trainee like him is in demand. Odd you don't know. You're different from him, also from us."

Wishing to extract himself early from the situation he was in, Mokuzu said to the mortician's wife,

"Your children must be waiting to eat; I don't wish to disrupt them. Thank you, I've had more than enough."

She fetched the children from below and sternly ordered them to greet Mokuzu. Yoko was a seventh grader whose intense expression and direct regard faintly resembled Ena's. Hiro, a sixth grader, was expressionless.

"Kazuko left for work," said the wife. The mortician did not respond.

"I'm sorry she had to leave without supper," said Mokuzu.

"She can eat there as she likes," said the mortician irritably.

Downcast, the two children ate quietly. Mokuzu spoke to Yoko, who showed some interest when he mentioned the four seasons of Kyoto and children's play in snow country. But the mortician interrupted,

"She's a wicked child. Kazuko works instead of studying, Hiro studies instead of working — Yoko does neither."

Quickly Yoko lost her small measure of brightness and hurried to finish eating. Hiro behaved as if he had not heard. Their mother excitedly reinforced their father's comment:

"After all, Yoko's dad is different from other dads — but Hiro studies well. He reads the school texts over and over and studies ahead. So I want to give him a university education. He's got to finish high school at all costs...a good university such as a former Imperial university on the mainland."

"Hiro, you're great to give your parents cause to admire you. What books do you like besides your texts?" Mokuzu asked.

"It's a waste to read other books. They don't appear in the exams and don't affect my grades." Hiro seemed queerly precocious in his utilitarian concern, but his parents contentedly smiled.

❧

During the day Mokuzu begged in Koza, awaiting Hoden's return. After waiting three days he left the mortician's before dawn in a thin rain, intending to make a mendicant tour of upper Okinawa for about ten days.

As always, he walked with brisk, soundless steps, fixing his eyes on the ground six feet ahead. Absorbed in walking, he felt close to the animals, plants, and fungi all living fully without analysis and reflection.

Sometimes fragments of poems came floating like lanterns:

> My road calls me, lures me
> West, east, south, and north;
> Most roads lead men homewards,
> My road leads me forth.[2]

> Alas, why afar am I straying, why ever linger here?
> 'Tis with thee I would fly! 'Tis there!
> 'Tis there! my heart's love obeying,
> 'Twere bliss to live and die!
> 'Tis there my heart's love obeying,
> I'd live, I would die?[3]

After more than five hours of walking, there was still a misty rain. Mokuzu left the road to take a rest and went up a narrow path darkened by plantains and cycads. Large raindrops fell on him irregularly.

The path led him to a clearing by a bluff, brighter as if thin sunlight came through the clouds only to there. Dug into the bluff was a large mausoleum. No doubt in fine weather the site afforded a view to the ocean.

The facade was made of blocks of sandy limestone, the stone door sealed with mortar. The Okinawans, like some other tribes, went to great expense for funerals and tombs, expressing very materially their filial love and ancestor worship.

Mokuzu thought, 'Like mist drifting on lakes or dense fog in glens, these customs are retained here and there all over Japan, and their people regard them as beauty. But I think it's false beauty, and self-indulgent — a neglect to endeavor to see logically what death is. True beauty can vividly inspire us. It's what we see when we look squarely at birth, aging, sickness, and death progressing each moment. Sakyamuni Buddha said,

> 'All sentient beings are beings on death, and end when they die, and cannot go beyond death.[4]

'How right he was. Everything has its end each moment, and our life is the continuation of these endings. With this perception he and his followers devoted themselves to practicing the Eightfold Noble Path (to Nirvana) so as to transcend sorrow and fear of death. In particular they must have spent lavish time meditating on death. They recommended that we regard our remaining life as lasting for

a day and a night,
a day,
half a day,
a meal,
half a meal,
four or five bites and swallows,
one bite and swallow,
one breath in and out.[5]

'Over and over they practiced this meditation on death. The tradition was inherited by Zen meditation and also became the base of the samurai philosophy of being ready to die cleanly at any moment. In my view, we today must also practice this meditation, for we are no less inseparable from our death. But our practice should be such that we come to appreciate our life fully and not merely gain the ability to disregard what threatens it. In other words, our meditation on death should be a warm-up for our positive and optimistic attitude toward life, and not the opposite.' Thinking thus, Mokuzu left the mausoleum and went under an old tree at an edge of the clearing.

The tree was a banyan. Aerial roots descending from the main limbs made the trunk look oddly uneven, as if scores of habus were enwrapping it. Other roots from high secondary limbs came down like harp strings, stiffly blocking further approach.

Mokuzu sat on an upheaved root. When he took off his bamboo hat, large raindrops from the dark foliage hit his head unsparingly and at once wetness from the wet root reached his skin through his robes.

Keenly he felt the loneliness and vastness of the world.

'I have been studying in some depth about a human being as an individual. Thus absorbed, I have studied almost nothing of how to be in a community. Nowadays even kindergartners are well taught about cooperation, harmony, and conciliation....

'I am a member of the organic world, yet I am here like an inorganic being.

'Human life is said to begin and end as a lone individual life. But that couldn't be all there is to it. Isn't my lonely state contributing to a full completion of my life?'

Mokuzu remembered Chingshuei, who appears in the tenth case of *Wumen guan*:

A monk addressed Tsaushan, "Teacher, my name is Chingshuei. Please help me, for I am poor and lonely."

949

Chingshuei was asking for mental pabulum. 'But,' thought Mokuzu, 'he was depreciating himself for seeming to the world to be poor and lonely, when actually he was brimming with the confidence of self-completion. So he asked to test Tsaushan and was ready to retaliate if he gave an unworthy answer. It's a nasty question while thousands are genuinely asking. Yet only those who can go through the material level as if it's nothing can comprehend the freedom of the spiritual level.'

> Tsaushan addressed Chingshuei by name. Chingshuei replied "Yes."
> Then Tsaushan said, "You have already drunk three cups of the famed
> wine produced from fine Chingyuan rice, yet you say you haven't wet
> your lips."[6]

'Chingshuei's "Yes" was his candid reply before comparison and analysis, and therein the perfection of his being was ingenuously expressed. Perfection of his being means his sense that the whole universe is acting through his being and at once that his being is completing the process of each moment of the whole universe. It is the extreme of a subjective understanding of self and universe. His "Yes" is hence another variation of what Sakyamuni Buddha is said to have spoken at birth: "In all heaven and earth I am alone and as such am respectable." Tsaushan was saying to Chingshuei, "Having such of yourself, how can you be poor and lonely?"

'More, he reminded him that this extreme subjective understanding was not uniquely theirs, but was the understanding transmitted from Sakyamuni Buddha to all trainees through the twenty-eight patriarchs of India and the six patriarchs of China; and under Sixth Patriarch Hueineng was Chingyuan, referred to as "fine Chingyuan rice" in the text. Chingyuan transmitted to Shytou, Shytou to Tianhuang and Yaushan. The Tianhuang line descended through Lungtan, Deshan, and Shyuefeng to Yunmen, who founded the Yunmen school. Shyuefeng also transmitted to Shyuansha, from whom the transmission went to Luohan, whence it went to Fayan, who founded the Fayan school. The Yaushan line went to Yunyan, and from Yunyan to Dungshan, and from Dungshan to Tsaushan. Dungshan and Tsaushan founded the Tsau-Dung school. Tsaushan must have been the teacher of Chingshuei. And Tsaushan and Chingshuei are the characters of this text.

'With so many Zen heroes who are companions in understanding, where is there poorness and loneliness?' Mokuzu asked himself while feeling poor and lonely.

He stood up from the tree root. Still it was raining, now a little harder. He sat down again and thought,

'Well, I'm stupid — I'm still poor and lonely. I'd better go further back,

to the Avatamsaka Sutra, the base of those Zen heroes' subjective understanding.' He tried to recall "The Ten Details of the Blending World," from
chapter 31, wherein the world is seen as one is all, all is one, and all forms and
phenomenal existence are seen as blending without impediment:

(1) All the world blends into one hair. One hair gives rise to the infinite
world.
(2) All lives blend into one life. One life gives rise to uncountable lives.
(3) All periods of time blend into one momentary thought. One
momentary thought gives rise to innumerable periods of time.
(4) All Buddha's teachings blend into one teaching. One teaching gives
rise to all Buddha's teachings.
(5) All objects of our sense organs blend into one object. One object
gives rise to all objects.
(6) All sense organs blend into one sense organ. One sense organ gives
rise to all sense organs.
(7) All sense organs blend into insensate organs. Insensate organs give
rise to all sense organs.
(8) All forms blend into one form. One form gives rise to all forms.
(9) All word sounds blend into one word sound. One word sound gives
rise to all word sounds.
(10) All worlds past, present, and future blend into one world. One world
gives rise to all worlds.[7]

After meditating on these, Mokuzu stood up and muttered, "Spiritually I
understand, yet physically I am indeed poor and lonely. Well, I think nothing
can be done about it. After all, thinking I am physically poor and lonely is the
correct feeling and cognition for my state."

Fortunately the weather was clearing. The ashy veil as it thinned began
to reveal beyond a sugar cane plantation the coral sea, the color of which was
intensifying with zones of light blue, Persian blue, sky blue, willow, grass
green...

'Beauty independent of human ingenuity...but I know a mental scene
more beautiful, more fulfilling, and there I shall go.'

❧

Fifteen days later, after finishing his round of begging in upper Okinawa,
Mokuzu returned to the mortician's. The mortician and his wife with wry
faces denounced him,

"You care only about your training. Thanks to you Hoden's very nice to
us — he frequents the pleasure quarters and the bars. Worst of all, he refuses
to officiate at funerals," said the mortician, and his wife, "Like that he'll soon

vomit blood and need another operation. For you trainees isn't friendship the highest virtue?"

"I thought you were senior enough for me to leave Hoden in your care. But I realize your profession is to deal with the dead. Then where is he now?" said Mokuzu. Though hungry, he went to a bar where the mortician suggested he check.

He found, as directed, a souvenir shop and a stuffed-toy shop, which, as it was getting late, were empty of people though brightly lit. Between them was a dark tunnel with a board walk and pipes exposed under the roof. Small bars lined one side. The only light was the lights at their doors.

He opened the heavy door of the farthest. Inside seemed yet darker. Were it not for the welcome voiced by the bartender and the madam, he would have thought nobody was there. Soon he could discern the red vest and white shirt of the bartender and the purple dress of the madam, and Hoden in jeans, all unpleasantly silent. He sat down by Hoden. After a while Hoden spoke,

"You're a useless companion. You abandoned me for your benefit only." Drunk, he was like a bull with head lowered, ready to attack. Mokuzu wished to avoid a quarrel.

"Hoden, you have to know we each have our own concern, and our primary duty is to realize it within a given time known as life. I plan to leave for Taiwan as early as tomorrow morning. But if you need me, I can postpone a few days." Mokuzu spoke calmly, and he cleared out of the bar.

He took the main street and was entering a quiet residential area by a small park when he noticed Hoden pursuing him.

"Wait, please! I was wrong to blame you and wrong to impute to you my misery. Credit me for my puerile frankness and understand I too wish to go on with the pilgrimage. But I have to clear one thing or I'll be burdened like your adored sixth patriarch with a millstone on his waist. Help me and I'll provide you the chance to be a great doctor to heal my trouble, or if that sounds conceited, let me say you can be the best scavenger of my life, past, present, and future. Vitalize me as my maieutic companion — it'll be my best expression of you! Anyway, sit down. But where? We can't go back, I scared 'em sharp for their forged whiskey. There, there under the lamp — there's no sweetness but at least some light!"

"Hoden, you're like a Shakespearean clown. Calm down, I'll listen."

As he came under the road lamp, Hoden kicked a garbage can to the best of his ability, sending a clatter through the quiet night. He sat on it where it lay and said,

"I see by the light your contemptuous face. But look, you must pity me! I got an ugly bruise...here too." He pointed to his temple and turned his head.

"Outrageous — he hit me with the stock of a gun! I didn't plead for my life — I fled for my life!"

"It must hurt a lot. It's an impressive reality that there are those who are stronger than you."

"Of course. You are such a one, than whom I believe few are stronger. So I'm asking you a favor." What Hoden told Mokuzu amounted to this:

When first he came to Okinawa, two years before, he got to know a teacher of traditional Ryukyu dance while begging in a Koza suburb. She lived with her ten-year-old daughter, comfortably by Okinawan standards; the house had a lawn with a fruiting papaya. Actually it was the house of her protector, but owing to a slump in his cabaret business he could not help her in those days and was instead taking money from her. Worried about the influence on her child, she hoped to cut him off. But it meant giving up the house and producing some compensation.

Hoden promised to raise the money, for she was kind, sensuous, and excellently susceptible in bed. So he negotiated with many morticians and became an officiant priest.

"I contracted with five or six, the least pitiful being the one in whose house we've been hanging on. I made lots of money, freed her from her protector, and gave you half the remaining. By the way, that cabaret owner taught Okinawan karate — I now realize he knew your boyhood karate teacher, a certain Rangai; it seems they're old friends."

Mokuzu said nothing. Hoden went on explaining.

With the dance teacher he lived as if pickled in honey, especially during the previous summer, when she left her daughter with an acquaintance and they enjoyed Tokyo life alone. She returned to Okinawa with the understanding that Hoden would soon follow. Twice they exchanged letters, then there was no word, though he wrote many times.

Now, on this second visit to Okinawa, he had gone at once to her house and found no trace of her. He called on her former protector, her friends, her neighbors. At last he learned she was residing at a major restaurant in a pleasure quarter, where it seemed she was regularly teaching dance to prostitutes, waitresses, and apprentice entertainers. Hoden could not determine her relation to the restaurant manager.

When he called on her there, a servant refused him. At each of his many attempts he was refused. On the third day he resolutely entered with his shoes on and was directly surrounded by three musclemen. One caused the miserable bruises, and they flung him out.

"Who's telling them to treat me like this," he wondered, "she, or a new patron? It greatly puzzles me."

In her first letter to Tokyo she had hinted at her wish to end the relationship.

"Why?" Hoden said to Mokuzu. "We were terrific, mentally and physically. What made her change? Was she faking love, enjoying me from the first to use me to cut off her patron? I have to know, and I humbly ask you to meet her to find out. If you do, I'll meddle with her no more whether she loves me or not, and again put my energy into our pilgrimage. 'Clear awareness is the heart of spiritual life.' Who said so? You."

"Hoden, clarifying your affair doesn't require my meeting her. Think about her character and situation, and about some points think in further detail. Logic will yield the answer."

"No, such a stony method won't satisfy my flesh and blood. Go with your own eyes and present me with the indisputable facts. A man resigns not by his intelligence but on account of overwhelming material insistence."

Early the next afternoon Hoden led Mokuzu in the rain to a pleasure quarter.

"Mokuzu, you hold the umbrella, I don't want to look like your attendant."

"No, you take it. It suits a training monk to get wet when he must go in the day into a dead-quiet segregated district."

It would be animated come evening. Now all was shut, and inside the lattice doors there were no figures of harlots alluring in thick makeup like dolls. Mokuzu thought,

'Ukiyo-e artists portrayed them touting before their doorways and pulling the hands of guests, and always low clouds hid any view above the second story. Now I see why. There's no open space for breathing and no sky into which to free a dream. Contiguous houses with deep eaves press everywhere into the street, forcing one to see not the sky but the doors.'

From some houses steamy water drained with a soapy smell.

"Haah! They're getting up at this time of day, washing their un-washable bodies, and making up to deceive men."

"Hoden, don't speak like a mean bumpkin. When our aim is low we look down on them. When our aim is noble we see our low state and see it's the same as theirs. At times we must cherish an ideal so lofty that it strikes people dumb with astonishment. The current world trend is that people select only subjects they can handle within their capacity, and they comment on them with honeyed tongue. They're like chickens rummaging in a feeder. A priest's duty is to show people astonishing ideals and to make known to them those

954

who have lived an astonishing life. For a right-minded person the pleasure quarters are also sacred precincts."

"Ha ha ha! I can understand — after all, prostitution originated in the temples."

68

To Please Oneself

The rain was over, leaving bright droplets on the bougainvillea above the weathered coralline wall. Mokuzu looked up at a palm, beyond its collar of dead leaves to its rippling fresh leaves, brilliant against the sun.

He parted from Hoden and went toward the restaurant. A group of fan palms cast thick shadows on the damp lawn. The approach was lined with royal palms, trees Mokuzu had never seen before. Over their pinnate compound leaves the dark blue sky aroused his optimism. 'To be scrupulous over psychological discord and conflicts of interest isn't worthwhile. Our only concern should be to make no foolish move leading to the ruin of these fine-growing trees and the expanse of sky.'

There was no sign of life at the front of the restaurant. To one side, amid a fresh growth of alocasias, an eminent flower suggested a colorful bird with sharp beak and crest. Observing its color, orange tinged with bluish purple, Mokuzu imagined a bird thriving on a jungle island. 'The world is open and free. The unknown world is even more so, if only we don't cling to our acquired standards. How pitiful to think we have something to lose when the world keeps giving to us,' he thought, mindful also of the loss of Ena.

In Zen monastic manner he sat with lowered head before the entrance and raised a sturdy voice:

"*Tano-mi-ma-sho* — — !"

A man, presumably he who had hit Hoden with a gunstock, came out suppressing his perturbation. He wore a vertical-striped red ocher kimono with informal sash. Mokuzu, looking up at him with admiration — for he was notably large — introduced himself politely and related his business. The man, also keeping a polite bearing, led him to a reception room and offered him a glass of juice. He opened a round window with a view of tree ferns, and in came the sound of a three-stringed instrument. Stiffly he said,

"The dance teacher you wish to see is presently teaching, as you can hear. She says you may await her here or there."

He guided Mokuzu along a concrete-floored corridor to the class. Within a sunny courtyard was a lawn, a flower garden, and, near the corridor, a gathering of pandani, sparsely branched, with fascicled terminal leaves sharp like swords and trunks supported by many thick aerial roots. '...like incarnations of European knights in armor, with fragrance their moral virtue.'

The tatami-floored classroom was wide enough to hold over a hundred people. Stepping in from the broad veranda, Mokuzu saw on a stage at that moment a pair of girls posing with a tension of air between them. About twenty others sitting sternly on their heels were carefully watching them and not a one turned to look at him. To the side of the stage also intent on the dance was the teacher, playing a samisen.

Mokuzu sat soundlessly at the far back of the room. Behind the dancing pair was a cloth backdrop of special Okinawan production, dark blue with stenciled designs of plum, pine, and bamboo in bright red, green, and yellow.

All were in kimonos, but they were barefoot, Mokuzu noted. Prostitutes kept an old tradition of going barefoot to preserve their born dignity in not decorating themselves from top to toe for their guests. Their feet, so easily soiled, they secretly dedicated to purity.

The teacher said as she dismissed the class,

"The time you are bearing up under hardship is the very time you are advancing in your art. Art assists life, a saying particularly true of you. Art is the land you could not inherit from your parents and is a parent to protect you where yours could not. Art alone can help you. I shall see you tomorrow."

The girls bowed deeply before standing, and as they left they curtsied to Mokuzu. 'Like wellborn daughters,' he thought, 'though such no doubt study dance for fun, unaware of its merit to their vested status, whereas these know it to be a strategy for life. I hope some of them will transcend life's vexations by means of the freedom and tranquility of art.'

"They are no older than fourteen or fifteen but are already receiving visitors," said the dance teacher as she sat down next to him. Her eyes sought his response. He kept calm and invested enough time to imagine Ena and Ran in the same situation, but he had no words to express. Then with detachment she said,

"Ah, yes, you are simply Hoden's messenger here to find out why I refuse him. Tell him I was disillusioned by my dream, by priests, and by Buddhism. I want to live affected by nothing."

"I see what I am to tell Hoden. But I can't figure the depth of your

956

words, though to me they are interesting. I know the ocean is everywhere salty. Then tell me whether you mean where tangle sways, or where colorful fish swim in coral caves," Mokuzu spoke and waited patiently. After a while she relaxed a bit.

"Well, like all these girls you saw, I served from an early age in a licensed quarter. But I was born on Yaeyama. My grandmother raised my brother and me after our parents died. When I began school she took ill, so I had to look after her and him.

"In June in the fifth grade I was helping to harvest a neighbor's rice, worrying ours would be ruined if a typhoon came. Even Grandma tried to leave her bed, and broke down in the yard.

"After harvest the villagers held their annual festival. The village was poor, but they had some surplus and their faith, so they invited a high priest from the mainland. I wanted to hear his sermon, but I had our rice yet to do. I worked in sweat and tears, my chagrin like the pain of a habu bite!

"When the sun was high I heard instruments and saw them moving along the beach, first the priest, then the villagers dressed up, heading to a little eminence, the village holy ground. He was robed in scarlet and canopied by a parasol held by a servant. Even now I remember the sight under the hot sun! I so wanted to hear him and to join the festival! I stood weeping in our field. That night I shook Grandma awake to ask what she supposed he said.

"He must have talked of going to the Land of Perfect Bliss, she said. I had many questions. What kind of place is it? Can I meet my parents if I go? And how can I go — is dying enough? I regret I cruelly disturbed her rest, and in fact she died soon after.

"Since then many things happened, but I never forgot the sight of the high priest passing behind the field and my questions about the Land of Perfect Bliss. As I waited to be bought, and later as I awaited my protector, I again and again thought of my questions and recalled the sight. Then as I grew older, I'll say, I was only cherishing the memory of my girlhood when I was zealous for such matters.

"My life began with misfortune and was misery on misery, but I had a rainbow in the belief that I might sever my life's vicious circle if I could get the answers to my questions. Hoden destroyed even my dream. Don't misunderstand, he isn't much to blame, and I partly thank him. Buddhism is what is dreadful — it asks me solely to keep giving. Always I've had to give and only give. I pity the girl who sustains herself by a rainbow. Priests are hateful — they're bill collectors, and Buddhism is a skull full of maggots."

She was growing agitated but managed to steady herself. "You look clean and wise. Please understand my rapture when I met Hoden, and then my

957

odious disappointment like stale fish put under my nose. Please see that he never visits me again." She fixed her eyes on the clock. Mokuzu thought as he left,

'Like a prickly shrub of the family Araliaceae, she grew up in an inferior spot and because of no care is harming herself with her own suckers and crossed, weakened, injured, and dead branches. Adversity doesn't make one wise if one blames others instead of oneself.'

❧

"You're like silk chiffon—you're so naive! It isn't praise, Mokuzu, so don't feel good. You should tolerate yourself for deceiving others; that's a comfortable way to live. But don't be deceived — that's shameful and shows lack of vitality. She acted so laudable you believed her every word. Wishing to be reborn in the Land of Perfect Bliss? Ha!—the lie of a demon! If she dies she can go, quicker than an arrow. The rapture of meeting a priest? — great disillusionment? It's as ridiculous as blaming the water you boiled if it scalds you. She doesn't reflect on her faults. Seeing their virtues isn't a sure way to learn what people are. You have to see their faults. She was reared like a pig or a monkey on a deserted islet and began to work in a pleasure quarter before her menarche. If she had TB and was worn to a shadow, you could pity her. On the contrary, she's getting fat and crawling to a height above what she deserves."

"Hoden, you are thoughtful, and she may be thoughtless, but understand it's harder for her to become thoughtful than for you to become more thoughtful. How can you become more thoughtful? Not by more thought but by less. How can we attain less? By walking and by seeing some beautiful nature. I called on her for you, and I will do more for your benefit. Then you sometimes do me a favor. Now I'd like to see the ocean. It will be nice and so will the sky after the rain. Won't you go with me? Full cumulonimbus clouds in a clear sky! Or rain clouds low over the horizon with glimpses of blue sky like lakes in deep mountains. Sundown will come with intricate and harmonious reflections, beauty amazingly superficial but suggesting infinite depth — even a master painter would stay his hand.

"The codium washed ashore must be attracting green-bottle flies. Even if they appear to be indifferent to us, the warmth and their faint buzzing will remind us of a maternal bosom, not of this actual life but of aeons ago."

"Mokuzu, you may be uneasy over my tenaciousness for reality, but don't fail to notice my anxiety over your disengagement. Well, if you so want to see the ocean, I'll not begrudge you. It is, however, quite a ways away."

Mokuzu was glad of his success in calming Hoden's rage and heading him on a constructive path. "It'll take under an hour at a quick pace. We'll start

958

now and not stop. Look at the ground six feet ahead and maintain a speed that makes the pebbles seem to run in lines."

To get there they actually walked over an hour and a half without rest. No sooner did they reach a grassy bluff than Hoden flopped down full length beside a stout deciduous tree with a slight tinge of sunset gracing its deep brown bark.

"I'm wiped out! How often I wanted to kick your butt! You walked like we were born only to walk, without consideration of my state! Two-thirds of my stomach was excised, don't forget." Mokuzu looked from the sea and sky to the mangroves filling the area from the shore to the bluff. Halfheartedly he responded,

"I sensed no danger behind me."

"You're too healthy to understand a sick man's pain and envy. I'm so thirsty! Oh, for a chilled bottle of Coke!"

"Wait here. I'll get water from a house we passed."

Mokuzu took half an hour more and handed Hoden a gourd of well water. Avidly he drank.

"Listen, Mokuzu, during your absence I got to thinking. First, about your loneliness. You're far from your native land and aiming for a farther and more foreign land. Next I thought, you're lonely, and so am I — we're the same. But you keep doing good while I commmit sin after sin. I wonder how such a disparity can come from the same loneliness."

The clouds at the horizon were darkening, the higher ones were ruddy.

"Hoden, we are both lonely now. But I have many companions in the past and in the future. You are unfortunate. You sneer at everybody in the past, present, and future."

Hoden picked up from the grass a dried pod that must have come from the tree. He opened it and found it to be acarpous.

"Well," he said, "I'm not as spiritual as you, and I don't care about friends in the past or the future. But I should care more about my few...my only friend now."

"Look up, Hoden, this is a fine tree. Now leafless, the spreading branches are more distinct. I wonder what it is."

"For a plant fancier your ignorance is surprising. It's a common tree here in Okinawa, the Indian Coral, often planted along streets. In early summer its blooms are like a red haze."

"Oh, the *parijata*, or *mandara*; it's quite popular in the sutras too. One on Mt. Sumeru is said to be nine hundred miles high. The size is impressive if you understand that the sutra writers are talking about the greatness of a Bodhisattva's spiritual influence. The Avatamsaka Sutra says:

"A Bodhisattva's piety is like the parijata, whose bark in fragrance excels the flowers of the varska, campaka, or sumanas....Even before flowering, we must know, its fragrance is that of its flowers to come. A Bodhisattva too, even in whom flowers of wisdom are yet buds, is a source of other Bodhisattvas' unlimited flowering."[1]

"How odd, there's no smell." Hoden had stripped off a piece of the bark. He passed it to Mokuzu.

"It proves the sutras are talking about the spiritual world; like the 'grain of mustard seed' Jesus spoke of. We tend to learn from those of great attainment, but we should know the world's real treasures are those of earnest will who have yet to bloom."

"Mokuzu, you talk sutras as if they're your words; they must be well assimilated into your organs. I am made uncomfortable beyond reason when I must deal with them. I was in a bog under my father. It's unfortunate to feel like that when a son should most love and respect his father. It's still so. As a priest I'm supposed to love, trust, and respect the sutras, but whenever I come into contact with them I feel I'm tied on a gurney being wheeled to an operating room. The sutras preach to the meek and pious and never reach those who ought to listen. And if I show an inch of modest interest, they dig into me to disdain my intemperance, immorality, ignorance, and incompetence. Yet if I launch a counterattack, they retreat like ghosts and change the level of discourse and never admit their defects and finally escape into their spiritual world. Mokuzu — I'll listen. Tell me how you're coping, how you're accepting them and winning them over."

Hoden and Mokuzu were the only ones on the bluff, under the tree with the patulous crown. The sea was calm, the sky suffused with the quiet blue of the prolonged light after sunset.

"Hoden, you've spoken honestly. It's rather abstract, but I understand because I too had to go through it. It must be the same for you as for anyone who grows up in a traditional society and wishes to improve himself. That's the cost of being serious. In the last analysis you feel helpless before the boundless virtues you are expected to practice, and for that you're resentful of the sutras. To get over your uncomfortable feeling, first of all you have to understand that each stage along the way is the very figure of perfection. The third Chinese Zen patriarch, Sengtsan, spoke about this in his *Shin-shin ming*,

> "One is All.
> All is One.
> If this we realize,
> Our realization needs no further perfection.

"For many, perfection is like the farthest star receding and receding. But the impossibility of attaining perfection should not be an excuse to be lazy and to feel helpless; it should be an encouragement to us to do our best at each level. Then, to be like that and to get over your uncomfortable feeling toward the sutras, second of all, you must regain your subjecthood, that is, you must reread the sutras for your individual interest and put what they tell you into your individual practice. In my view, deficiency of subjecthood is the prime instigator of all our negative judgments, such as to blame, hate, and condemn others, including the sutras.

"Just as our robes get heavy when wet, so the sutras, our guiding torches, singe us when in our frustration we lose our subjecthood. The sutras may turn even gold into shackles if we fail to see our precious individuality. So, how to recognize and maintain our subjecthood is our most important theme and the content of our training. All our energy and optimism to climb the soaring mountains of virtues comes from our awareness of our subjecthood.

"Here, Hoden, with good grace be cool like an unbiased observer and consider the sorrow of your woman, the dance teacher. I will analyze for you why she was enraptured by meeting you and why so soon disillusioned. She should hear it instead of you, but, too bad, she isn't ready, in my judgment. Your mind is not so deeply warped, and you are franker as well as more educated. You will understand what I say and can see her in your mind to the Land of Perfect Bliss. Listen in the manner that corals entrust themselves to the waves.

"Hoden, how long was she tenderly raised, how long unaware of hardship? In grade school she already had to support her family. She got so little kindness, yet suddenly she was obliged to give. When she couldn't attend the high priest's sermon, wasn't the essence of her chagrin the pain of being denied the chance to learn how to escape having to give and only give?

"When her grandmother said he surely spoke of the way to the Land of Perfect Bliss, she knew it was what she longed for — a world where give and take are well balanced. Not knowing its whereabouts or how to realize it, she deepened her conviction that it must exist somewhere.

"As a prostitute she saw herself receding farther from such a world in inverse proportion to her conviction; for she got no love and had to give unilaterally. Give and take can be balanced only in a society where each person's dignity is recognized and love and esteem are mutually practiced. So she dreamed of a fair world somewhere, sometime, though her dream was a rainbow, not a real bridge. Even with a protector or by the birth of a daughter, her dreary dreaming life couldn't be amended. Then she met you, and what caused her disillusionment?"

"Enough, I know what you're going to say — like all others I only forced her to give, and it led to her great disappointment. You must realize your talk is platitudinous — I can easily predict what you'll say," said Hoden impatiently.

"No, as to that, the wound you caused, if any, is slight. What's hard for her to mend is the wound coming no doubt from the platitudinous Buddhism delivered by you. If we're platitudinous, especially in introducing religion, we'll kill our listeners' spiritual life. What was the Buddhism you introduced? The very Buddhism you hate. On this point you both are victims of the Buddhism commonly understood by people who have neither established their subjecthood nor gone through the hardship of living with the Buddhist ideals. It's the same Buddhism that advocates *dana* — giving so as to be welcomed to the Land of Perfect Bliss — the first virtue to be practiced by Buddhists, followed by observance of the precepts, perseverance, assiduity, concentration, and finally wisdom, which if the others are practiced should and will be possible to practice. Truly it's not too much to say that among the entire Mahayana and Hinayana Scriptures there's no sutra that doesn't persuade us of the importance of these six virtues — headed by giving. They come over us like ripples, sometimes like surges or billows, over and over, pressing us, trifling with us, and choking us till we lose our subjecthood.

"Therefore, Hoden, as you now realize, you needed to help her to regain her subjecthood rather than tell her about the virtues and their effect. The virtues shouldn't be preached, nor should people be forced to practice them. Instead let us be confident that we can recognize their value and enjoy practicing them as we like, without help from others. I myself recently came to realize this when I was reciting A Bodhisattva's Ten Practices to Benefit Others, chapter seventeen of the Avatamsaka Sutra. The practices are defined as being for the sake of others, for the pleasure of Buddha, and so on, through the ninth. The tenth is pursuit of the truth, that is, to learn the true words of all Buddhas in the three worlds past, present, and future, and to interpenetrate the nature of all Buddhas throughout, while not abandoning all other practices of a Bodhisattva. What is the reason for this tenth? Listen, the sutra answers:

> "I practice Bodhisattvahood and aspire to the highest Buddhahood not because sentient beings asked me to do so, but because I myself resolved to do so, with the wish to benefit all sentient beings that they may attain Buddha's wisdom.[2]

"'I myself resolved to do so' — it's the basic tone throughout the sutra. With this you'll not be drowned in the vast sea of virtues."

"I heard, but it doesn't appeal to me — you've just given me another

962

wave. It's like you're telling me the menu of a feast you ate and I'm hungry
— truly, I mean it!"

"Well, too bad. I thought you'd be greatly relieved and activated."

"Mokuzu, don't be discouraged. It isn't your fault."

"I'm not discouraged, although I should improve my way of talking.
Well, maybe I'm not as bad as a writer who writes in vain on this sort of
subject, unpalatable for most readers. Now won't you briefly summon your
remaining energy? I've another approach to how to establish subjecthood."

"Okay, but you'd better know the role of a teacher is far easier than the
role of a student."

"I understand. I'll try to be a cook, a heavy laborer, and you be a diner,
an open-minded guest. Establishing our subjecthood has the effect on us of
making us optimistic and positive as opposed to pessimistic and passive. Your
woman too — if she can establish her subjecthood, she can live enjoyably with
thanks; otherwise she'll lead a life of resignation and complaint and even if
blessed in her future with a kind protector and many good students, she'll find
only a little compensation and little worldly wisdom and she'll need a lot of
ceaseless patience.

"So, how can we establish and maintain our subjecthood? Where is its
birthplace? In prajna, true wisdom, or reason, in its deepest meaning. What
is prajna? It is to see absolute equality in all beings or phenomena. How can
they be equal? In The Ten Stages of Bodhisattvahood, chapter 22 of the
Avatamsaka Sutra, it is well explained. Our concern is stage six:

> "All phenomena are equal because all are
> of no substance;
> of no fixed form;
> beyond birth;
> beyond death;
> naturally pure;
> beyond argument;
> not obtainable as well as not dismissable;
> beyond the 12-linked chain of cause and effect;
> phantoms, dreams, shadows, echoes, a moon on water;
> neither beings nor non-beings.[3]

"Hoden, seeing through the fundamental nature of the world and living
in its basic equality is the ultimate establishment of our subjecthood. As you
now understand, subjecthood is established beyond confrontation between the
subjective and the objective world. It's very unlike the subjecthood of
Western philosophical tradition. There people base their subjecthood on an

artificial confrontation between the subjective and the objective world, and out of their emotional needs they declare the independence of their subjecthood, or vainly insist on its dominance over the objective world. Their subjecthood is a mere self-deceptive alchemy. Ours is subjective well before any confrontation between the subjective and the objective world. As we see it, subjecthood is not something we can willfully gain. Rather, it is established and maintained by the objective, or natural, world. So for us subjecthood is a very objective matter, free of our egoistic view; yet it has a fair life beyond both the objective and the subjective view. Do you see? This is the only correct way to establish our subjecthood. To establish our subjecthood, we should by no means depend on a resistance to, or challenge of, the objective world; nor depend on a denial of, rejection of, or contempt of it; nor of course depend on an unprincipled and intoxicated exaltation of our subjective view.

"Bearing this subjecthood in mind, listen to Yuanwu in *Biyan lu*, case 8, which I happen to remember:

> "If in your effort to attain Buddhahood you come to understand Buddhahood, you can gain perfect command like a dragon in its watery element or a tiger scaling a crag; else you are an ordinary man, like a ram bucking a hedge, unable to move forward or back, or a peasant ever watching a stump in hopes of catching a hare because once by mishap another brained itself there...."[4]

Mokuzu stopped reciting, for he realized Hoden was not following. He was extending his tongue like a tired dog. 'Ugly man, so lacking the vigor to search for intellectual truth at the prime of youth, how can he live decently?' he thought, and said,

"At least know I am walking on the path of Bodhisattvahood because it is as refreshing as walking through a green forest, as beautiful as walking on a moonlit beach; it gives me pleasure."

"Mokuzu! — look at those pressing lights! — above the horizon! — look, they're bombers!"

From a pale blue crack in the clouds above the horizon four U.S. B-52s appeared in the dusk, approached, and zoomed down as if to shatter the two figures under the tree. They passed in tandem just over their heads, shaving them it seemed with their roar, which tyrannically severed all sound from every organic creature, and straightaway they disappeared behind a far forest to land at their base, Kadena. Yet the bluff did not crumble. The two figures under the tree looked at each other with concern and waited for their ears to recover.

"Well, of what use is your subjecthood against B-52s? Once the Japanese

964

Imperial Army was preparing bamboo spears against B-29s, but your philosophy is even more ineffective. By now the pilots must be showering as they brag of how many hamlets they fired and how many Vietnamese people and pigs they wasted. This trashy world won't change. That wretched tart must keep on whining and enduring. And I have to keep on being a cynic. But Mokuzu, I hope you'll become a little more easygoing. Otherwise you'll remain awkward — respected, but kept at a distance. Come on, I'll treat you to a pleasant bawdy house — bathe with 'em, eat a plateful of shrimp, and..."

"Hoden, my loneliness does me no harm. Like the moon, it helps to reveal all sorts of good people hidden in the world. Let me spend tonight under this moonlit *parijata*, and early tomorrow morning I'll leave for Taiwan. You do as you like."

69

In Taiwan

Under the high sun the heat and humidity was everywhere equal with no place to escape. Royal palms like electric poles stood tall on either side of the four-lane road with a divisional strip. At the far end was a thickly wooded hill, but before that they came to a street flanked with a kind of acacia.

"This street is lavishly shady and active, so we'll beg hereabouts until sunset."

"Really? Begging as soon as we come to Taipei? I think we should first find lodging, then have a bath, then drink something cold, preferably beer, as much as we like, then steep ourselves in the exotic mood and enjoy the evening cool."

"Hoden, we aren't ordinary tourists, who can afford a hotel and shopping; that way we can't benefit this land. What we can do is gather alms to remind people of the importance of patience and charity. In due course we may come on a benevolent person who will offer us lodging."

"Tut! Going with you may provide security, but it makes me feel I'm lugging iron-covered sutras on my back. In point of fact, I'm perfectly fit to be received as a tourist — good as any, or better, unlike you. I prepared very well beforehand. Remember the proverb, Provision is prevention." So saying, Hoden proudly took an envelope from his scrip.

It was a letter to the Taiwan Buddhist Association from the Japan Buddhist Association, requesting in English that various conveniences be offered to a promising Japanese Buddhist priest making a pilgrimage to the eight sacred stupas commemorating Buddha.

"No big deal — I got it through my uncle."

Recalling Grogan, Mokuzu doubted its efficacy, yet he said,

"Fine. While I beg in this neighborhood why don't you find the address, secure us lodging, and then spend the time as you like until we meet here again at five."

Parted from Hoden, Mokuzu began to beg in the same manner as he had begged in Japan. The shop-lined street was alternately sunlit and shaded by acacia. The shops were not as neat and bright as those in Japan, but the signboards with stately script in dark blue or cinnabar were worth appreciating. Merchandise of limited variety was heaped up, unlike in Japan, where much variety was set out, each item in small amounts.

Just as in ancient times there were vendors with full loads of vegetables on winnowing baskets or carrying ducks jam-packed in bamboo cages slung from poles. A woman shopper pushed by unconcernedly with a plucked chicken.

All the adults and children, shoppers and sellers alike, who noticed him stared at the strangely dressed young man without concealing their curiosity. Most had smooth eyelids and oily skin. The outdoors people were dark, the rest pale. What impressed Mokuzu was that they did not shrink back even when they realized that he noticed they were staring — they just kept staring. In Japan the local people would quickly pretend not to have seen. Those over the age of about forty-five took the lead in offering him alms, knowing the practice under Japanese rule, and some even volunteered to explain his conduct in a plosive Chinese.

Meantime he finished the bustling street. The shady trees too ended, and he came upon a busy road. On the parapet of a footbridge a slogan was written in large red characters: Regain the Continent — Repel Communist Elements.

Then beside one building he noticed an entrance leading as if to a subway had it been Tokyo. He descended concrete steps and found an iron door with small characters again written in red, instructions on taking shelter in the event of an air-raid warning. He was reminded that this country was presently in a state of war with Red China.

When he returned to the street he was called to a halt by a youthful policeman. He did not understand Chinese but followed obediently. The police station was a large stone building, old and dark inside. He was led to an interrogation room with a dim light, umber walls, and an old wooden desk and chair. Through an open door he could see part of a big room with other staff at work.

Two officers entered, examined his visa, his passport, and his personal effects, and asked the purpose of his stay and what he was doing on the streets. Their concern was whether he was a Communist agent of some sort. Finding nothing to blame him for, they soon released him. "Provided," said one, "you don't beg in this country. Or we send you home by legal force." All communication was carried on in written Chinese, not perfectly clear, yet sufficient to convey the prohibition.

It was still hot and too early for sunset. Wondering what he should do without liberty to beg, Mokuzu was standing before the police station when an old woman came up, took a bill from her purse, and silently offered it to him. No doubt in her youth she would have been taller. She was generally shrunken and a bit stooped. Her looks were evidently not her concern. Her gray hair was chopped just above the shoulders, and she wore a simple white short-sleeved blouse and black crepe skirt. Mokuzu raised the bill reverently to his head, then looked back at the police station. The policeman who had stopped him was observing but did not move. Mokuzu went on begging as if nothing had happened.

As he begged he came up to a big temple, Lunggu-sy, a compound complete with seven buildings. Busy roads bordered its four sides, and many visitors were coming and going. The buildings were gorgeously colored in cinnabar, yellow, white, and dark blue, and vociferous firecrackers were being set off anywhere within the grounds. Incessant also were billows of smoke from incense offered in a large caldron-like censer before the main building. Mostly it was old people who were actually worshiping with joined palms. Young couples only strolled. Among them Japanese tourists led by a courier with a flag were hurriedly making a round and busily taking photographs.

Mokuzu stepped up to the main building to see who was enshrined. There were all sorts of divine figures with brilliantly colored faces and costumes, including Amitabha, Avalokitesvara, Yama, Arhat, Budai, and even Confucius, Kueishing, and Guanyu. To each was ascribed a worldly virtue: erudition, fine health, winning of lawsuits, business success, and the like. Having no wish yet for those virtues, Mokuzu left without worship. He wanted only to find a lavatory.

A communal one, a separate concrete building, was situated at the east corner behind the Buddhist sanctum and next to the priests' living quarters. He paused at the doorway because he saw an old woman inside crouching and fanning a clay brazier to cook her supper. The lavatory was well cleaned, though the floor was surfaced with nothing more than rough cement. She also sensed him and rose to sell toilet paper. Then she issued a faint sound of surprise. Obviously she was making a living by selling toilet paper, but she was the very one who had offered him a bill on the street.

She gave him a pack of paper without charge. He felt obliged to bow in reverence to her, though he had not felt that way toward the sanctum.

Mokuzu returned to find Hoden was not at the promised spot. He seated himself under a leaning acacia. Hoden appeared after a delay of nearly half an hour, his bamboo hat slung behind his shoulder, his long sleeves agitating the air with the swing of his arms, the hem of his skirts in disarray on account of his loosened waist cord. His slovenly appearance would certainly have induced tears of blood from traditional Zen priests, proud of completing to the acme the beauty of form, order, and simplicity. More, he was attended by a Taiwanese in a faded national uniform who gave the impression of being bound and dragged.

"Mokuzu, how terribly rankled I got! I called on the temple housing the Taiwan Buddhist Association headquarters, but the fat chief priest said he had no word from the Japan Buddhist Association and that my letter was unreliable. So I asked him anew to take us in, relating my noble purpose of travel and how my companion is excellent in knowledge and character. He was like a trepang under a reef; he wasn't moved at all and only repeatedly told me to bring a letter of introduction from the Japanese Embassy. I detest officials as much as fleas, lice, and acari. With no alternative I left spitting venom, 'Fool, eunuch, don't be sorry when I return with a certificate!'

"Next I looked for a firm called International Car Trade, for I had one more letter from my uncle by way of precaution — I was impressed by my prudence. But the firm I found after asking many times was no more than its splendid name. Such shabby cars as would have long since been junked in Japan were being resold to equally shabby buyers. A family partnership — and worst, the head, who kept eating watermelon in front of me, insisted he'd never met my uncle, never heard of him, and bluntly asked if I was a sleepwalker.

"I flew into a blind rage and wanted to inflict a just punishment on his person, but I remembered you're my companion and, fearing to trouble you, I practiced a great meditation and a great pardon. Then just as you might do, I turned on my heel without a word and hastened to the Japanese Embassy. But I didn't know where it was, and closing hour was pressing, and I was feeling the call of nature, and my language was useless when I tried to ask the way. Then I chanced on a man who could speak Japanese, who taught me to go the opposite way, and when at last I got there, this fool was closing the gate. I shouted, 'Idiot! Don't close the very moment I come to the consul on urgent business!'

"He scurried in and returned with a secretary or something, young, and yet, as you know, for us priests age has nothing to do with depth of faith, it's a matter of this foul world; anyway, he cleverly said I had to call again tomorrow because they were already closed.

"Abruptly I became so polite this poor Taiwanese couldn't make sense of me. Rather than insist that serving me was honorable, I entreated the secretary in emphatic begging posture for his mercy — 'Our noble vow is what made us leave our native land. Now we face a shortage of funds, and our letter from the Japan Buddhist Association is treated as a mere scrap of paper by the misfeasance of a Taiwanese priest. My companion is sick from the long journey and is languishing by the roadside awaiting my good news. Please issue us a letter of introduction.'

"At that the secretary coolly laughed and called our trip a wild scheme and lectured me not to injure the credit of Japan. Though I had been humbling myself, I sprang up furious and said he was a public servant fed by people's taxes and his duty was to protect his compatriots. He must have seen through my inadequate education. He rattled on in his professional jargon about the embassy's duty being to furnish protection by diplomatic means, not to individuals but to the national position and interests. Duty to an individual applies only when injury to him or his property might harm the nation. As for issuing an introductory letter, he said it's for the embassy acting in the interest of the nation to decide and not my right, at any rate. In a word, it isn't the duty of my nation to fulfill my request.

"Well, I didn't want to expose my complete ignorance of such matters, so I left firing some parting shots incomprehensible even to me — 'Fine, I'll count you and your nation no more. You must know the life of a nation is as brief as the morning dew, whereas the Dharma is eternal!'"

"I see, Hoden, you had a hard time. You must be hungry. Then why is this man following you like a dog?"

"Oh, I turned everything to account. I thought he might be useful, he knows some Japanese. While the secretary was inside locking the glass doors, I took out my American bills and sported them before this horseface. It wowed him. Ever since, he can't shut his mouth, and if I say 'Turn right!' he turns right, 'Left!' he turns left. Hey, fathead, take us to your place and we'll award you the honor of our staying the night!"

His name was Lin Wentsan. He led Mokuzu and Hoden to a narrow, gloomy, and clamorous downtown.

"I buy you supper," he said nervously and took them to a quarter with open-air stalls. A cart was set up as a kitchen with campstools around it for diners, who ate in front of the flood of passersby. On the counter were platters piled high with chicken, duck, pork, and their assorted innards, which the cook grabbed in turn with his bare hands and deftly fried, baked, boiled, or made into soup. The town was dark, but the row of naked bulbs on the cart brightened his face and the steam. Mokuzu noticed that all the plates, bowls, and chopsticks provided to the unknown scores of diners were washed in only a bucket of water.

After treating Mokuzu and Hoden to Chinese noodles in pork broth, Lin Wentsan bought a bunch of fully ripe red bananas for their dessert. Then he invited them to a teahouse.

Inside was murky, smoky, and noisy, with a TV on. Pumpkin and watermelon seed shells littered the floor. The host and patrons knew Lin, and he, suddenly garrulous, proudly introduced Mokuzu and Hoden. They placed them at a center table and gathered round, eager to hear anything from their mouths through Lin's imperfect translation, though the TV was kept on loud. It was broadcasting a Peking opera apparently about Emperor Shyuantzung and his concubine Yang. The shrilling of the performers and the overstated gongs, peals, cymbals, and other percussion instruments rang painfully in Mokuzu's ears. He was tired, and felt he was losing his equilibrium. Hoden was joyful as if returned to an old haunt.

Among many choices of tea the host brought one of his best in a china pot set in a metal bowl of hot water, with quite small cups; also a tray of dried nuts, seeds, and fruits, including litchis, mangoes, dates, and betel nuts. Dropping the shells on the floor was their custom.

"This all is the host's treat for you foreigners," Lin translated happily but more crudely than the host might have wished, and his fellows cheered, assuming they were included.

Meanwhile timid as a mouse the host brought a brush, ink, and paper and asked Mokuzu and Hoden to write something to ornament the drab wall. Hoden merely glanced at the writing materials and continued his desultory conversation with Lin as cheerily as before, as if dealing with such a request were solely Mokuzu's obligation. Naturally everyone focused on Mokuzu. He accepted the situation and concentrated on writing an episode from *Jaujou lu* in careful printed style:

> Teacher Jaujou questioned two new monks. To the first he said, "Did you ever visit here before?" The monk answered, "No." Then the teacher said, "Please have a cup of tea." To the second he said, "Did you ever visit

here before?" The second answered, "Yes." Then the teacher said, "Please have a cup of tea." The secretary-general monk asked Jaujou, "Not to mention your offering tea to the one who never came before, why do you offer tea to the one who did?" Jaujou addressed the secretary-general by name. He responded, and Jaujou said, "Please have a cup of tea."[1]

Those surrounding Mokuzu were impressed by his skill. When he finished they made a stir and began guessing at the meaning of the episode. Mokuzu, however, was indisposed as though he had become anemic. He was aware of a cold sweat almost dripping from his brow and armpits. He looked for Hoden. Hoden had moved with Lin Wentsan to a far table and was flirting with three young women in tight Chinese dresses and earrings; when they had entered Mokuzu did not know. One was on Hoden's lap, another was patting his shaven head. They were streetwalkers come in to hunt up customers.

Fearing he was losing his sense of reality, Mokuzu summoned Lin and asked to be taken to his residence if he was providing lodging.

"Now? Too early. Too hot. Nobody sleep. Soon me and my buddies take you to play." Lin gave an obscene smile. Mokuzu glared at him and ordered,

"I am unwell. Please take me to a restful place."

Fortunately Lin lived just upstairs. He spread a mat and a blanket on a cot and added a rattan pillow while talking his head off about himself regardless of Mokuzu's inattention — he rented three rooms, for which his salary covered only two thirds, the rest was supplied by his hard-working son, he was separated from his wife, once a top-class prostitute, now a third-class, there was no fourth, but lower prostitutes were better for having to rely on dense love rather than looks.

"I have no further business with you," Mokuzu said. "Turn off the light, shut the door so the least noise comes in, and withdraw from my sight."

As soon as he left, Mokuzu crawled onto the cot fully dressed and endured the cold shakes. Even his scalp and the soles of his feet began to quiver. His whole body was languid, and chills alternated with a high fever. The experience was new, but he had no composure to observe the strange symptoms and had to bear it with all his power. He felt he had dropped to a bottom world where suffering was the unitary quality.

At last the torture grew extreme. In the dark he crept to a toilet to vomit; he also had diarrhea. He was reminded of each offensive smell of the noisy, crowded plebeian town. Most abominable were the smells of fermented

971

banana, twisted tea, and strong liquor. At the sink he took a large quantity of water and repeatedly forced himself to vomit.

It was ending. He saw the clock: three AM, yet Hoden and Lin had not showed up.

Mokuzu was awakened by a white beam coming through an awninged square window. He felt fresh like an autumn morning after a typhoon. Hoden and Lin were sprawled on the floor, Lin snoring with mouth open, Hoden covering only his head with a blanket. The room was sour with the smell of liquor. Mokuzu attempted to open the window, but the handle was broken. The wall was blotched with damp.

In the afternoon when he returned from begging, he found Hoden sitting dejected on the cot. Lin, in briefs only, sat on the floor with his hands bound at his back like a lawbreaker. Below his eye was a swelling, and just to keep sitting was hard.

"What is this, Hoden?"

"Oh, terrible! Last night while you were indulging in peaceful slumber I went to a pleasure quarter with him and his chums — they said they'd treat me and I wanted to study some sociology as well as practice some charity. We hired a bicycle-ricksha. We bathed with the women, ate delicacies from all lands and seas with unlimited booze, and I got intimate with one. That's all, and we came back and slept. Then a while ago I woke and found my sheaf of American bills gone! You know its importance is next to my life. I always keep it where I can feel it against my skin. I took it even to the bath and checked on it before and after I was with her. So I stripped him and whacked him to make him fess up. Trouble is, he seems innocent."

"True! — we don't touch people's things, we are needy, but happy, and we really regaled Mister, uh, Reverend Hoden. In my youth a Japanese taught me each chance to give hospitality never comes again!"

Mokuzu untied Lin and said to Hoden,

"Well, dismiss it. As you wished, you could study some sociology and practice some charity. Completing your study and practice should be done in your mind."

"You make light of it because it's not your matter. How can I do my pilgrimage round of the eight sacred stupas?"

"Take it easy, Hoden. I'll return all the money you gave me. Fortunately I've saved some alms since then. To change the subject, we'll proceed to Taichung. A kind person introduced me to a respectable priest there. After twenty years of study in Thailand, he returned to found a nunnery. Look, I was given two train tickets."

Hoden regarded the schedule printed on them, braced himself, and said, "We'll miss the train if we don't hurry."

The scenery out the windows was cultivated small-scale fields. A man was tilling with a water buffalo. In a waterway ducks crowded ahead of a boy with a rod. The farmhouses were no more than crude rectangular parallelepipeds built of sunbaked red brick. The people were directly grappling with the problems of sustaining their families. Hoden was rather an educated idler. He opened a newly purchased notebook to begin a diary.

❧

1/18/69: At Mokuzu's instigation I'll keep a diary. I said whether I do or don't, everything will be forgotten and soon our life too will be returned to the void. But he said much as it's impossible to retrieve gems dropped in a lake, there's beauty in the sorrow of extending a hand to try to retrieve them; and though all will be lost and forgotten, we should take an active role in the passage of time by grasping each thing, putting each and all in order, and throwing them one after another away.

His birthday was toward the year's end (careless me — I wasn't aware to congratulate him, to my regret). He's now 23. I'm older, but have much to learn from him. If I compare us, I'm a drag on him and have nothing to teach him. I said, "Be honest — you must be disgusted with me." Laughing, he said,

"There's no one and nothing impossible to be regarded with affection. Whether we see them as respectable or humble or useful or useless depends entirely on our mind and our might."

Well, at least he's not just awaiting the day we reach Thailand and go our separate ways.

1/21: Third day in a Thailand-style temple. The yellow-robed chief priest is mild and kind, is teaching Mokuzu Pali Scripture, which he'll need for ordination and monastic life in Thailand. At tea he told me as his highest tribute of admiration for Mokuzu that he had never met so earnest a student, so clear of memory, so tireless to study — exceeding himself on every point. He said he'd been understanding, sinful as it was, that some sutras exaggerated about Buddha and the patriarchs. Now he's sure it's no exaggeration. I was proud as if it was a reflection on me, but his next words made me feel the world had turned red as blood:

"You are lucky to have a good master. Please know, he who can't carry out his master's instructions is low, he who waits and follows his master's instructions is middling, and he who sees his master's mind and well performs without being told is high."

Does he think I'm Sancho Panza? I wanted to bray him to death with a wooden pestle, but I thought it better to swallow my rage and let him keep believing I'm Mokuzu's attendant, because he treats me well and has another priest show me the famous sights during Mokuzu's lessons.

1/23: The nunnery attached to this temple has about 400 young nuns. Their heads are shaved, but they mostly stay just a few years. They're here instead of attending a domestic training school; at any rate they won't become lifelong nuns.

Before breakfast they chant sutras in Pali. Mokuzu attends at the back and imitates them. At four in the morning I'm still asleep. I'm too late even for breakfast and barely manage to show up when the nuns on duty are clearing the table. They give me innocent laughs. Nuns they may be, but their breasts and hips are developing favorably. My merciful heart is stimulated, and my desire is irrepressible to initiate them into the secret art of joyful sexual relations.

At lunch I told Mokuzu I too wish to found a nunnery and reside as its chief priest when I'm safely home from this pilgrimage. It would make a man thankful to Buddha for being one of his disciples, as well as thankful for being of the sterner sex. Mokuzu burst out laughing. The nuns gathered round and importuned him to translate. He was perplexed but with my approval explained. They too burst out laughing, and some ran to tell others. Oh, what angels they are in puberty!

They wish to take care of us, and one after another ask to wash and mend our clothes. How foolish Mokuzu is to decline, while I purposely tear my robe in order to hand it to them. He's an ass and doesn't understand a woman's mind!

1/25: I too wished to experience morning chanting, so I got up early. Mokuzu can already chant smoothly in Pali. I was like a stupid frog in a rice field and got so sleepy I went back to bed. Skipped breakfast and awoke well after lunch. Mokuzu was waiting for me with two local priests, a lean, middle-aged one and a young one, dressed as they do here in gray Chinese robes resembling overcoats. They wanted to take us to a scenic spot, Jihyucht'an, and had hired a car.

The road was good, with plantations of banana, sugarcane, betel palm, and papaya coming into view. A kid was riding a cow up a shallow river under a bamboo thicket. Both priests are great talkers. I got tired listening, so I left that task to Mokuzu and fell asleep again.

We reached Jihyucht'an after driving over two hours. I said we could find as much beauty anywhere. With sad eyes Mokuzu said there couldn't be so many halcyon days. He's a sentimentalist.

A boat took us out on the lake to the island of Guanghua. On top is a temple called Shyuantzang, and on the side another, Santzang. Each enshrines a part of Shyuantzang's remains, they said. I didn't believe it. Tonight we're staying in Santzang.

974

1/26: Our two priests guided us on a tour of the lake. They tediously explained why it's named Jihyucht'an — the north half is shaped like a sun (jihy), the south like a moon (yu). They kept childishly explaining things. Amazingly Mokuzu listened with genuine interest even the second time. No doubt he'd listen even a hundred. I don't understand his nerve.

(Same day) We left the boat to see a village of the native Formosan tribe. Similar to Japanese Ainu they wear a colorful costume; work on horn and tusk or weave as they squat on the earth — helpless for having to maintain their primitive life-style to earn a living. Mokuzu was sympathetic even to such wretches: "There are those like my father, my mother, my siblings....It's a pity they can't entirely conceal their pains and sorrows from one another. They are blessed by neither God nor Buddha, yet the earth blesses them."

On our return we met a fierce warm rain with heavy drops. The little scull-propelled boat so pitched and rolled I feared it might capsize. Then the rain gave way to dense fog and we lost sight of any shore and couldn't see even the bow. I got very uneasy. I feared we'd run foul of a reef or meet a sharp drop. I looked at Mokuzu, thinking I should be afraid if he was, and if he wasn't I shouldn't worry. I asked if he was. He said there was nothing to fear because everyone else aboard well knew the location, configuration, and direction. More, he said, "Imagine it's night. The moon will brighten the fog over the lake. I can almost hear the music of strings."

He is gallant, but blunt. He may be as unruffled even at his death, so his state is useless to indicate danger. I'll excuse myself from going with him to the ends of the earth.

When we returned in the evening, I prized the remaining time in dallying with the nuns while Mokuzu was hearing from the chief priest practical advice on keeping the precepts in Thailand. In a flower garden I appreciate the colors and scents, while he crouches, absorbed in weeding. Which is the more natural way of life is evident.

1/28: We left Taichung and came to a temple in Tainan introduced by the chief priest of the Thailand-style temple — slightly under four hours by train. There we first had an audience with a retired 80-year-old priest. He told us,

"I am gladdened to hear you are on a pilgrimage to seek Bodhisattvahood. In the eve of my life it can't be helped that my body doesn't suit my mind."

I had no response, but Mokuzu dared:

"I am now 23, but that's not the age of my beginning my pilgrimage to seek Bodhisattvahood. I have been traveling since countless aeons ago. Likewise your travel isn't done at age 80. I hope you won't relax your mind but will continue your travel until you can attend Maitreya's sermon five billion six hundred seventy million years from now."

He shamelessly brags, as is to be expected of a disciple of that rodomontade Zen master Tengai. Disdainful as I was, I couldn't help being impressed by the simplicity of the old guy — he was delighted by Mokuzu's words.

975

1/29: Arrived at Kaohsiung and will stay in a temple close by a dense bamboo valley. The bus driver got off at the last stop and found us a taxi, prepaying our fare. A pious soul.

I asked Mokuzu why those who seem more religious and kind are generally countryfolk rather than townsfolk, poor rather than rich, uneducated rather than educated, and irrational rather than rational.

"To which group do you belong?" he asked.

"Well, I'm a mix."

"So is everyone. I think our concern should be how to repay our thanks."

Disagreeable man!

1/30: Owing to bad weather we stayed on in the same temple. A professor from a certain Japanese university arrived with five graduate students of Buddhism. We lunched together in the dining room. Their work is to compare how the same sutras were accepted in China and Japan. Noticing us, he remarked that to see any itinerant monks nowadays is surprising, and he ordered his students to study us as their worthy subject. We then were inspected and questioned like anthropoids in a zoo. I was elated and, after the example of Mokuzu with that 80-year-old priest in Tainan, I magnified how noble is our end and how hard the path we travel. But Mokuzu oddly kept silent and soon withdrew to his room. His unpleasantness gave me ten times more unpleasantness.

2/3: These days I've been called for funerals. Rich pro-Japanese invite me by preference. Mokuzu accompanied me the first time, but hasn't been willing to go again. He hates to perform funerals, whereas I love to. It involves almost no labor but is marvelously lucrative. Part of my alms I give to the mortician. Pleased, he invites me again, and again I give him part and again he invites me. I kindly taught Mokuzu this secret for priests who perform funerals, but, thankless guy, he just mumbled something incomprehensible — "If only those killed by landslide could enjoy your secret."

I asked him, "Don't you want money?"

"I don't want it, but I need it," he said, and went out to beg despite heavy rain. In my case a fancy car delivers me and returns me. More, he said he won't chant before each door as it's illegal here. He just strolls and no police accuse him even if he's given alms. How patched and piteous is his reasoning! A wretched mix of genius and imbecile.

2/5: I want to stay here longer because of my good funeral income, but he insists on seeing the most famous sight in this land, Tailuger in Taitung. Why? Just to stand on a suspension bridge and gaze at a three-thousand-foot cliff. So he left at dawn. Stupid, without being a monkey how can he enjoy a cliff?

He said he'll get in touch with me within a week, after finding us lodging in Hualien. I worry I'll be deserted. Well, he's reliable about this sort of thing, but often I've no idea what's going on in his head. He did promise to go with me as far as Thailand. I too am a man, a son of Japan. I shouldn't doubt.

2/6: In his company I feel I must cringe — no, not quite, but inevitably I can't be totally myself and must act better than I am. It's natural, considering the polarity of our life views. He does first what he ought to, then what he wants. I do first what I want, and if there's a surplus I try to do what I ought. I'm convinced there's no reason I ever have to change my way.

So, today too I slept as long as I liked. Nobody was around when I went to the dining room well after lunch hour. I raised a cry — "I'm hungry!"

The sub-chief priest and priestlings, who don't understand Japanese, appeared in a flurry and were seriously concerned whether I was ill. I gestured to them to make me lunch, and they did, in great haste. It was fun.

When there's no Mokuzu, delightful events occur one after another, such as — around 3:00 a certain rich house sent a youth to fetch me to perform a funeral. As usual I began after the nuns finished their high-pitched chanting of the Amitabha Sutra. I was solemnly chanting as ten women in white, hired to raise a keen for the dead, writhed in front of me. I noticed one young keener had a beautiful bottom and wonderful movements worth viewing to one's fill. I was sure my chanting couldn't revive the fellow in the gorgeous huge cedar-log coffin, but that keener surely awakened my sleeping part. Then I noticed I was skipping the middle of the sutra. But I was well paid.

Curiously, my young driver was much impressed by my solemn chanting and invited me to a first-class seafood restaurant. Great to eat fine food after so long — I was just feeling the oily vegetarian diet of the temple was unbearable.

He finishes university this year, and came out with his vacillation over whether to enter graduate school or the priesthood. When I asked why he is attracted to Buddhism, he earnestly replied, "If I strive after Buddhist training, someday I'll be able to fly like a bird out the window of this two-story restaurant. It's long been my cherished desire."

I was convulsed with laughter but, hoping he'd be useful to me, I squelched it. Mokuzu I bet couldn't have contained his. But in my view Mokuzu isn't so unlike this youth in his naivete. Solemnly I advised him: "If you want to realize your noble desire, you must study the secret of Shingon I have mastered."

"Teach me, please." He leaned forward.

"The time's not quite ripe," I said meaningfully. He could draw from me no further word and asked me to meet his parents. I said I would. His name is Chen Shenje.

2/7: At sunup Chen came and waked me. He has a fine foreign car. As I expected, his dad has a palatial house on a hill in a suburb of Kaohsiung. He is said to own a large poultry farm and piggery.

Most amazing and enviable — he keeps four mistresses, from old to quite young, in addition to a wife. All have individual charm and are serving him harmoniously. He can't compare with the shogun Ienari in the Bunka and Bunsei eras, who had a wife, 16 consorts, and 24 concubines, and sired 56 children. But compared with me he's endlessly enviable. At last I seized a chance when only his women were amicably having tea as some crocheted and others looked at albums in a big living room. I made a hyperbolic show of weeping in spite of myself. At once they surrounded me and patted my back and offered handkerchiefs. At that I felt truly sad, and my tears kept running.

The wife said with composure, "There must be some great reason a high priest should weep so. Please say, and we will combine our efforts and if necessary summon help to do our best for you."

I thought the time was right. I'll summarize what I said:

"From infancy having set my mind on the study of Buddhism and having been assiduous at it, I came here knowing nothing about sex. I now realize it's the foundation of life and without experiencing it I can't attain true enlightenment. How can anyone expect a harvest without fertile land?

"Come to think of it, Buddha wasn't a priest from infancy. In his Lumbini palace he fully experienced sexual relations, which later bore fruit as his great awakening. Until now I was following the result of his achievement and neglecting the cause. I believed I was faithful to his teaching. In fact I was opposing his life. Realizing thus, I weep with repentance.

"Seeing your master's ideal life assisted by you makes it plain to me that he is the very person walking the Bodhisattva path, whereas I have been walking contrary. Please, I beg your compassion to help me onto the correct path like your master."

With no Mokuzu beside me it was easy to speak shameless words and behave with shameful mimicry. As expected, they were moved to tears and said, "Brace up. We'll act with prudence for your benefit and make it possible for you to rejoice in your restart on the right path."

Their master is more of a superstitionist than his son. Earlier today he declared that his faith makes him impervious to the cut of a sword. To demonstrate he bared himself and one of his mistresses and set about to cut his arm and her chest with a sword held at right angles to the flesh and dull as a carpenter's square. It made only a pink trace. Yet all the women, perfectly believing in him, were filled with awe. I, unlike Mokuzu, affected to believe. Now I'm sure they'll do me their best.

2/12: On the train to Hualien. Didn't write for the last days, was living a full life. I'll say a diary is a toy of self-regard, needed only when we suppress our urge for sex, food, and society. In my observation, Mokuzu by suppressing these basic instincts is like Ajatasatru, who confined his father, Bimbisara, without food in a cell bound by walls seven layers deep. A deadly sin. In contrast I'm tending my father in my mind with the highest filial piety and

978

am perfectly satisfying every one of his senses. So I have the quiet of a contented mind as if basking in the unlimited light of Amitabha.

(Continuation) After five or more hours of boring train I arrived at the temple that Mokuzu had informed me of, but he was out. The chief priest knew only that he'd appeared a week before and asked lodging for tonight. He showed me a concrete hut next to a wild banana thicket — one room, two simple beds, like a jail.

In the evening he returned. I, ashamed to express the joy of reunion, slightly criticized the place he'd found.

"You're right," he said. "What human beings make is usually cramped and ugly in contrast to where I've been sleeping for the last week. I envied those natives of the ravines and cliffs in the districts of Tailuger and Tienshiang."

His words nipped my first enthusiasm to sport my sensual indulgences of the last days. Yet my wish to pique his interest exceeded my fear that he might sneer at or even censure me, so I gave full particulars.

"I can enjoy hearing of your enjoyment" was his only response, to my chagrin. Still, I said, "We'd better hurry back to Kaohsiung if you want the same. I guarantee you'll receive their compassion, because they now know their compassion secures their pleasure."

To that he said the daftest thing, but choosing his words with care:

"In these days I could learn more from the way trees grow and rocks exist; they are truly doing their best in their given environment; they don't waste even a second, even a calorie. Being like them is the only way to embody such truths as 'In each speck of dust there are billions of worlds, uncountable Buddha lands,'[2] or 'Past, present, and future are all contained in a single notion.'[3] Indeed they live unperturbed — dauntless, calm, and with minute sensitivity."

Outright I asked, "Don't you want a woman?"

"My wanting a woman is like the trees or grasses awaiting spring. My dream is to find a life companion and to perfect our life together. Because it's important to me to realize my dream, I am watching over my conduct and cultivating my character as I await her appearance. Loving one's companion from the start of marriage is right, but I think it's not enough. Well before we meet we should begin to love our future companion, just as trees and plants prepare their buds to flower. So too, loving our companion's past, present, and future is good once we are married, but it's good to do so before we've even met. I hope I am already acting with her, thinking of her future and past, and especially sharing her sorrow and joy. I believe how I live now has a great influence on how actual married life will be."

"Mokuzu, if you're like that, who'll be suited to you? Most women couldn't bear your stiffness unless they're idiots."

"Stiff shouldn't be confused with serious. Being serious doesn't exclude laughter, and doesn't mean being hasty, narrow, or rigid; or humorless,

979

pessimistic, or restless; nor exclude being stupid sometimes. To be serious is to regard the sad nature of all things and to treat them tenderly in the long-range view," he said with a smile and extended his tired body on his bed, face up like me. In the darkened room we heard mosquitoes nearing. I realized he's much more of an ordinary man than I am.

2/13: Today we return to Taipei. Before dawn Mokuzu went out. He had promised a native Ami that he would escort his foster children to a certain house in Taipei, and he went to fetch them.

As I awaited the 7:20 bus he came out of the mist with two girls, apparently departing their native land for a long time — they each had a large bag. They weren't yet grown to full height, but their eyes were bright and their cheeks like peaches. They were merry, shoulder-to-shoulder, and adored Mokuzu like kin.

I asked if they were twins. He said no, but they were raised like twins and looked after each other. He said they mingle their native language with Japanese and Chinese, for their tribe was forced to speak Japanese under Japanese rule and now the Kuomingtang Government forces them to use Chinese.

This was their first bus ride. They sat in front of our rear seats in jolly spirits, delighted by the bumpy road. The only others were a villainous-looking detective, presumably from Taipei, and a native boy, handcuffed and silent, with sober face.

Mokuzu spoke little. Mostly he looked out the window. Now and then he responded to the girls with a smile. I got bored, and as I was eyeing those innocent but ripening girls lively before me, I realized again my appetite was aroused. Alas, every good thing is un-storable. The satiation from food, drink, sleep, and sex lasts but a day! Again I'm starved, proof that fulfilling those desires is sinless. Yet when I said I'll visit a pleasure quarter as soon as I reach Taipei, to practice my charity, Mokuzu gave me so chilly a look I felt funny.

I respect the subjecthood he often advocates. He has no right to spoil what I enjoy, however much he disagrees. He'd better know how he's in danger, like a man going to fetch a bone from a dog even if he's the master who gave it. And I'm not a dog but a son of Buddha on my way to pay homage to the eight sacred stupas. And I'm not going to be given a bone by him, nor steal one from him. I'll get one by fair economic means.

The bus made a two-hour rest stop (actually I wrote all that then). The girls spread their lunch, brought for us too, by a creek. They took a share to the handcuffed boy.

After lunch they tucked up their sleeves and skirts and playfully caught fish under the rocks. They didn't mind wetting their clothes, which became transparent about their breasts.

Mokuzu sat on a rock under a tree and made two sketches of them. On each he wrote a legend in Chinese I didn't understand. He gave them as mementos to the girls. They received them reverently and put them deep into their baggage like amulets or indulgences — his typical hypocrisy, owing to his trifling skill at painting and calligraphy.

(Same day) This evening we arrived at Taipei. I was weary from the over nine-hour bus ride. Mokuzu left with the girls. I patronized the bar of a cheap hotel. He returned around seven. I asked where he took them.

"To a brothel."

"What? Did you assist in the trade of human flesh?"

"Not exactly, but I have a feeling it's akin. Their foster father has stressed circumstances. Arranging for me to bring them here was his sole consolation."

I asked why he hadn't told me, because if it's like that I could have kindly initiated them. He rejoined,

"How could you give a guiding principle for their life?"

I felt a surge of rage, but he appeared to be going into mourning, so I held my tongue and felt uncomfortable. Somewhat later I asked what he wrote on the sketches. "Oh, merely a jingle —

> "Guard what you cherish, fear not others' evils,
> Center yourself in the world.
> Undaunted by ups and downs, cultivate the field within,
> It yields mercy and moves gods and devils to tears."

I was going to pay reverence at a pleasure quarter, but I reconsidered, thinking it advisable to show respect to Mokuzu, who looks grave. So, I'll sleep quiet here tonight. After all, tomorrow morning we'll sail from Keelung to Hong Kong, and from there fly to Thailand.

Epilogue

70

A Bodhisattva

For several days in late autumn, my sister and I with our families visited our parents, who were of course delighted.

My children call the house "sunny hill house." I think of it as quiet; not gloomy but having an uncommon tranquil air. There's no glory, but also no discord or peril. I can sense the contentment of the occupants living there steadily, but sense as well some loneliness — or sadness, to overstate it perhaps. Even when the children shouted for joy, it seemed to remain and absorb their immoderate tones to keep them from excess.

On the day of our arrival we set out around three through the back forest, heading west toward the inlet and meandering northwest to make our way down to the beach. My parents named it "ablution beach." We all still call it that. There the children enjoy gathering shells.

My mother was starting dinner. She had prepared some things in advance but always serves us fresh warm meals. My father brought in some vegetables for her and went to his study. My sister hoped to be useful in the kitchen after nursing, so her husband put their baby on his back and came with us. Our son and daughter, familiar with the path, dashed ahead.

As usual they didn't want to leave the beach. For sure it wasn't sunset yet, but the rest of us started back after considering those at home and deciding there was no harm in letting them linger and catch up.

When we returned, the trees behind the house were making shadows on the front lawn longer than the shadow of the house. The day was fine and windless. The towns below shone white in the remaining sun. The east mountains were so clear we could see where they overlap.

My father had a fire going at the end of the vegetable garden on the open south side. He was composting raked leaves and burning some with garden refuse. After harvest he turns it all into the soil.

We approached and saw he was putting old notebooks from his study and library into the fire.

These years his study is kept neat. The sight of more than three books on his desk is rare. When I was growing up, there were so many books I couldn't see him, and his writing space was narrow as a cat's brow. Now his desk is so clear I feel sad.

From the trash basket he took the last notebook and was about to put it in. On the spur of the moment I spoke up,

"Dad, at every chance you're burning things you consider disused, one after another, and certainly it's your freedom. But I wish you'd leave us something in your own handwriting. Isn't that a memorandum you made when you were young? May I have it, if you don't mind?"

He gave a short laugh and said,

"I thought it is of no value and that no one should be troubled to read it. But take it if you want and please don't hesitate to burn it when you consider it disused."

"The Bodhisattva Way, by Mokuzu" was written on the title page. Indeed it was a memo made in his youth (before coming to America?). After dinner and the evening, my parents retired to their room and our children slept. Then before the fireplace, my sister, her husband, and my wife asked me to read it aloud.

"The Bodhisattva Way"

Just as our planet tilts a little on its axis, if we love, trust, and respect people and the world only a little more — but always more — than we hate, disdain, and despair of them, then we are walking on the Bodhisattva Way.

Blessing newborn lives is the start of building paradise on earth. We must congratulate them with our available food, clothing, and shelter. Digressed from here, all thoughts are barren no matter how high.

We must consider that making war or peace is the work of the same human being. Because we each can turn good or bad, we can understand the importance of self-control. Then, what is the source of self-control? Isn't it

986

to give optimistic and supreme credence to oneself by deep reflection and by recognition of one's nobility, instead of depending on one's outer environment?

What must be hindering this world from becoming a paradise is distrust. And the root of distrust is the desolate reality that we still have to provide our own food by ourselves.

Almost all problems relating to personal affairs can be settled if we firmly refuse to overindulge ourselves. Our reward will be the ability to struggle on with those world problems that can hardly be amended by our self-restraint.

Truly there is nothing but our own self-cultivation to support us in our hardship. Then shouldn't we be resigned to the idea that only when we die can we forget self-cultivation and be free as a bird in the sky, for, as long as we live we must suppress and kill other lives?

Cultivating ourselves to face hardship is more painful than any other pain. But is there any enjoyment greater than to take this painful course, especially when those who love one another take it together? Apparently this enjoyment can be experienced in this world only and is impossible to experience in any other.

After all, the desire for fame is no more than an abstraction of the desire for love. Whoever wishes to be loved must endeavor to love. But while those one should love are many, often those by whom one wishes to be loved are few, and they may die or refuse their love, which compels one to love an abstraction instead. If one is too eager to serve an abstract love and neglects to love those one should love, then one will be excellently dominated by desire for fame.

As long as we live, we hope to keep a sense of humor. Humor arises when we see life's positive and negative aspects fairly.

Loneliness gives depth to life. The degree to which one can endure loneliness determines the depth of one's life. Depth creates the value of daily life. And gaining a meaningful daily life is indeed compensation for bearing loneliness well.

To establish oneself does not mean to live in isolation. It means to return more favors than one ever received.

A great memory need not always be esteemed, especially if it is for knowledge that can be conveniently stored outside ourselves, as in a dictionary. But if it is for such emotions as agony, sorrow, fear, and pleasure, we must keep it well within ourselves or it will be of no future use. Whenever I meet pain, I try to remember the greatest pain I ever met, and, comparing my pain now with my pain then, I won't let myself be troubled if my pain now is less, and I will be thankful. This could be an answer to how to live without much dissatisfaction and complaint.

Certainly my parents loved their children. But regrettably they could not transcend their self-love. I wish to become a father whom my children can remember for his teaching them to respect all well-intentioned persons, just as they respect him for that reason. I wish my wife will become a mother whom they will remember for her admonishing them to love all pure persons, just as they love her for her pure nature.

Man seeks man, but a man is hard to meet. A man hard to meet is one who has four distinct qualities: intimacy, appreciation, hope, and means.

A man of intimacy fosters the same basic understanding toward all human beings and all societies irrespective of his particular environment. Well aware of human weakness and strength, merit and demerit, he continues to feel friendship.

A man of appreciation sympathizes with, understands, assists, and encourages a man's life work if its aim is to be of universal benefit rather than merely of benefit to a particular small thing, such as to his individual well-being and that of his private family.

A man of hope is an optimist as well as an idealist. He believes in people's good nature, he recognizes that the happiness of all mankind is desirable and ought to be achieved, and he is certain that it will be achieved if we keep steadily working for it.

A man of means is financially able to assist a man's life work that aims to be of universal benefit, and he is able to introduce connections for that purpose.

If I close here, these words will be among the most meaningless and pessimistic ever written, because to meet anyone of such qualities is extremely rare. I therefore will add the following to sustain a glimmer of hope.

First, I should not idly await any such persons, but should persevere to cultivate myself to be suitable for them. Then they will be pleased to meet me. Second, I should not grieve over their rarity, and even if I cannot meet them, I should not bear society a grudge. Instead I should reflect on my insufficient effort and unrefined talent, and thus go on, calmly and steadily. The time will come when an iced-up seed can be brought forth. If only there is the seed, there will be buds.

In all events we should not harm others. To inflict threats, offense, sadness, and torture is inexcusable. Even so, we should not be stiff through excessive fear of doing harm. Best is to take not a hundred precautions but one positive attitude, that is, to think what we can do now to please others.

We wish to face our death with pleasure and thanks. These may be common words the world over. Establishing common words is an important task. Devoting ourselves to this task is the key to living with pleasure and thanks.

. . . .

Notes

Chinese romanization is based on Lin Yutang's *Chinese-English Dictionary of Modern Usage* (Hong Kong, 1972).

Major source reference: *Taisho shinshu daizokyo* (The Tripitaka newly edited in the Taisho period), ed. Takakusu Junjiro and Watanabe Kaikyoku (Tokyo, 1976 ed.) Hereafter cited as TZ.

I . 1 (pages 3 - 20)

1. "I am my own lord": Shyuantzang Santzang, *Datang shiyu ji*, vol. 6, in TZ 51:902a.

2. 'Eyebrows one foot two inches long': *Shyutang Her'shang yulu*, vol. 2, in TZ 47:1000b.

3. 'Though its looks be humble': Hakuin Ekaku, *Kaiankoku go*, vol. 6, in TZ 81:569b.

I . 3 (pages 20 - 31)

1. "The worse you are": Kakunyo Shusho, *Kudensho*, vol. 2, in TZ 83:748c.

2. "There is enlightenment": Eihei Dogen, *Eihei shobogenzo* (Treasure repository housing the eye to see the right Dharma), vol. 3: *Genjo koan*, in TZ 82:23c.

I . 5 (pages 42 - 52)

1. '*Mo-ji-chyu!*': Hungjy Jengjian, *Wansung lauren pingchang Tiantung Jiau Her'shang sunggu Tsungrung-an lu*, (Leisure Temple record of Priest Tiantung Jiau's stanzas on his collected koans, with commentary by Old Man Wangsung), case 10, in TZ 48:233b. (Hereafter cited as *Tsungrung lu*.)

I . 6 (pages 53 - 64)

1. 'a ghost that adheres': Wumen Hueikai, *Chantzung Wumen guan* (Gateless gate of the Zen sect), case "Jaujou goutzy," in TZ 48:292c. (Hereafter cited as *Wumen guan*.)

I . 7 (pages 64 - 71)

1. "know the presence of fire": Shyedou Jungshian, with commentary by Yuanwu Kechin, *Foguo Yuanwu Chanshy Biyan lu* (Zen Teacher Yuanwu's sermons recorded at Blue Rock Temple), comment on case 1, in TZ 48:140a. (Hereafter cited as *Biyan lu*.)

2. 'The real treasure': Ibid., case 5, in TZ 48:145a.

I . 8 (pages 72 - 83)

1. 'seeing the tree peonies': *Biyan lu*, case 40, in TZ 48:178a.
2. 'There is only nothingness': Ibid., case 1, in TZ 48:140a.
3. 'The willows are green': Ascribed to Su Shy (Su Dungpo).

II . 12 (pages 119 - 126)

1. "Zen Teacher Jau": Yunchi Juhung, *Changuan tsejin* (To penetrate the Zen border by self-whipping), in TZ 48:1105b.
2. "...and there under Priest Jiaye": Ibid.
3. 'Many a lotus': Hueiyan Jyjau, *Rentian yanmu*, in TZ 48:315b.

II . 13 (pages 126 - 138)

1. "Three who were": *Changuan tsejin*, in TZ 48:1105b.
2. "Thus we practice": *Kaiganlumen*, in *Goko hosshiki bontonsho*, ed. Ishikawa Ryoiku and Mori Koju (Kyoto, 1954), 96a.
3. "Self-annihilation is true joy": *Daban niepan jing*, trans. Dharmaksema fr. the Skt. *Mahaparinirvana-sutra* (Nirvana Sutra), vol. 14, in TZ 12:451a.

II . 14 (pages 139 - 151)

1. "The bell of Jatavanavihara": *Heike monogatari* (Tale of the Taira clan), ed. Yamada Takao (Tokyo, 1962), 1:43.

II . 16 (pages 165 - 177)

1. '*Shaunian yilau shyue nancheng*': Ju Shi, "Oucheng" (Spontaneous poem), in *Wakan meishi ruisen hyoden*, ed. Kanno Michiaki (Tokyo, 1924), 11–12 (Hereafter cited as *Meishi ruisen*):

> Desist from slighting even a moment.
> Learning is not so easy as growing old.
> The dream of spring grass by the pondside
> Breaks at the rustle of kolanut leaves outside the study.

II . 18 (pages 189 - 203)

1. "Of what use are later regrets?": Jang Wei, "Hur jung dueijioutzuo" (Poem made while drinking on the lake), in *Meishi ruisen*, 630–31.
2. "This confused and tranmigratory world": *Miaufa lianhua jing*, trans. Kumarajiva fr. the Skt. *Saddharmapundarika-sutra* (Lotus Flower Sutra), vol. 2, in TZ 9:14c.
3. 'Boys and girls': *Liji*, pt. "Neitze."

III . 21 (pages 232 - 240)

1. 'A Buddhist trainee needs dynamic energy': Suzuki Shosan, *Roankyo*, vol. 1, in *Nihon no Zengoroku*, vol. 14: "Shosan," ed. Fujiyoshi Jikai (Tokyo, 1977), 116-17.

III . 22 (pages 240 - 254)

1. "Spring is come": *Nihon shoka shu*, ed. Horiuchi Keizo and Inoue Takeshi (Tokyo, 1910: 1972 ed.), 148.

2. 'Mind and body': Baijang Huaihai, *Chyshiou Baijang chingguei*, vol. 5, in TZ 48:1143a.

3. 'directly pointing': Huangbo Shiyun, *Huangboshan Duanji Chanshy chuanshin fayau*, in TZ 48:384a.

III . 23 (pages 254 - 268)

1. 'A dead tree flowers': *Zengo jiyi*, ed. Nakagawa Sosuke (Tokyo, 1969), 416b.

2. "My face reveals": Taira no Kanemori, in *Jui waka shu*, vol. 11, no. 623, in *Shinpen Kokka taikan*, ed. Shinpen Kokka Taikan Association (Tokyo, 1983), 1:79a.

3. 'Tango Province so far': Koshikibu no Naishi, in *Kinyo waka shu*, vol. 9, no. 550, in *Shinpen Kokka taikan*, 1:153a.

III . 25 (pages 282 - 295)

1. "One for the cutworm": *Standard Dictionary of Folklore, Mythology and Legend*, Maria Leach (New York, 1941), 1:251.

2. "Then in the golden weather": H. W. Longfellow, "Evangeline" 2.4, in *Eibeibungaku shokubutsu minzokushi*, ed. Kato Kenichi (Tokyo, 1979), 285. (Hereafter cited as *Shokubutsu minzokushi*.)

III . 26 (pages 295 - 308)

1. "*Kanzeon Bo-sa*": *Miaufa lianhua jing*, vol. 7, in TZ 9:56c.

III . 27 (pages 309 - 323)

1. "Deign on the passing world": Samuel Johnson, "The Vanity of Human Wishes," in *Eibeibungakushi koza*, ed. Fukuhara Rintaro and Nishimura Masami (Tokyo, 1965), 5:207.

2. "Health is a state": In *Seishin igaku*, ed. Murakami Masashi, Mitsuda Hisatoshi, and Ohashi Hiroshi (Tokyo, 1976), 891.

3. Ten points: L. P. Thorpe and B. Katz, *The Psychology of Abnormal Behavior* (New York, 1948), 18.

4. "Sir, I believe": James Boswell, *The Life of Samuel Johnson*, ed. Christopher Hibbert (London, 1979), 160.

III . 28 (pages 323 - 338)

1. "an iron line": *Rentian yanmu*, vol. 2, in TZ 48:307b.

2. "Linger not": Shuho Myocho, "Daito Kokushi yuikai," in *Zenrin nikka* (Zen manual), Kichudo edition (Kyoto, n.d.).

3. "the figure of the mountain": Su Shy, "Tzeng Dunglin Chang Janglau" (To the chief priest of Dunglin Temple), *Su Dungpo shyji*, vol. 23, in *Kanshi taikan*, ed. Saku Setsu (Tokyo, 1974), 3:2739.

4. 'The Imperial ordinance': Linji Yishyuan, *Jenjou Linji Hueijau Chanshy yulu*, in TZ 47:497a. (Hereafter cited as *Linji lu*.)

5. 'In the cold': Dungshan Liangjie, *Rueijou Dungshan Liangjie Chanshy yulu*, in TZ 47:523c. (Hereafter cited as *Dungshan lu*.)

6. "No, 'tis not so deep": *Romeo and Juliet*, 3.1.99-100.

III . 29 (pages 338 - 354)

1. 'Millions of books': Li Jiayou

2. "Let Intellect": Natsume Soseki, *Kusamakura*, Iwanami Bunko edition (Tokyo, 1972), 5.

3. "he who dreams": *Tsungrung lu*, case 7, in TZ 48:231c.

4. "Unseeing when seeing": Eds. Jyjing and Dautai, *Chanlin leijyu* (Zen monastery classified records), vol. 1.

5. "I walk as I ride": Shanhue (Chuan Shi), *Jingde chuandeng lu* (Record of the transmission of the lamp), vol. 27, in TZ 51:430b. (Hereafter cited as *Chuangdeng lu*.)

6. "Those descendants": "Daito Kokushi yuikai," in *Zenrin nikka*.

7. Worms eating: *Fanwang jing* (Brahma's Net Sutra), vol. 10b, in TZ 24:109b.

8. 'Even this mindless brute': Saigyo, *Shinkokin wakashu*, vol. 4, no. 362, in *Shinpen Kokka taikan* 1:223b.

9. As Nanchyuan was admiring: *Chanyuan mengchiou* (Earnest Zen monastic study), vol. 1, ed. Tsuoan Jyming, annotated by Shyuetang Dalian, in *Manji-zokyo* (otherwise called *Dai Nihon kokutei zokyo*), addenda "Zoku-zo" 2B:21:200.

10. Jaujou: "Where will a man go": Jaujou Tsungshen, recorded by Wenyuan, Jaujou Chanshy yulu, vol. 1, no. 3, in Joshu Zenji goroku, ed. Suzuki Daisetsu and Akizuki Romin (Tokyo, 1964), 1. (Hereafter cited as Jaujou lu.)

11. 'As she was dying': Aizan Shokin, Denkoroku, vol. 2, in TZ 82:405b.

IV. 30 (pages 357 - 373)

1. "Be deluded": *Tsungrung lu*, case 100, in TZ 48:291c.

2. "A man inquired of me why": Jungfeng Mingben, ed. Tsyji, *Shanfang yehua*, in *Tianmu jungfeng guang lu*, vol. 11, in *Manji-zokyo* 31:700; or in *Gendai soji-zen hyoron*, Ho-ou (Tokyo, 1971), 46-48.

IV. 38 (pages 472 - 488)

1. (1) Senior high school: "Gakko kyoikuho," chap. 4., art. 42, in *Roppo zensho*, ed. Suzuki Takeo (Tokyo, 1975), 1344d.

IV. 39 (pages 489 - 506)

1. Hoso was founded: Derived from "Waseda Daigaku" and "Waseda bungaku," in *Sekai daihyakka jiten*, vol. 32, Heibonsha edition (Tokyo, 1981), 587–88.

2. "By nature Bodhi": *Lioutzu-dashy fabautan jing*, pt. 1, in TZ 48:349a.

3. "Things fall apart": "The Second Coming," *The Collected Poems of W. B. Yeats* (New York, 1960), 184.

4. "Break, break, break": *Tennyson Poems and Plays*, ed. T. Herbert Warren, rev. Frederick Page (Oxford, 1965), 116.

V. 40 (pages 509 - 521)

1. "the water is too shallow": *Wumen guan*, case "Jou kan anju," in TZ 48:294b.

2. The Great Way: *Eihei shobogenzo*, vol. 30: *Gyoji*, I, in TZ 82:127a–b.

V. 41 (pages 522 - 538)

1. "Hymn of the Empty Hand": "Hotsu Bodhaishin kukensho," *Zenrin nikka*.

2. 'if you don't climb': *Kaiankoku go*, vol. 5, in TZ 81:558a.

V. 42 (pages 538 - 555)

1. Zen Teacher Yungjia Shyuanjiau: *Chuandeng lu*, vol. 5, in TZ 51:241a–b.

2. "He who knows the Dharma": *Lioutzu-dashy fabautan jing*, pt. 1, in TZ 48:350c.

3. "The tenet of our religion": Ibid., pt. 4, in TZ 48:353a.

4. A man who learns the Way: Kungtzy (Confucius), *Lunyu* (Analects), IV-8, in *Genzaigoyaku Rongo*, ed. Hara Tomio (Tokyo, 1969), 98.

5. "not to be offered by spoon": Wuliang Tzungshou, *Rujung ry-yung chingguei*, in *Manji-zokyo*, addenda "Zoku-zo" 2:16:5.

6. Be self-effacing: *Misha sebu heshi wufenlyu*, trans. Buddhajiva and Ju Fodausheng (fr. the Skt. *Mahisasaka vinaya*), vol. 19, in TZ 22:132c.

7. For forty-five years: Hakuin Ekaku, *Spearflower*, in ser. *Nihon no Zengoroku*, vol. 19: "Hakuin," 324–26.

V. 43 (pages 555 - 571)

1. 'Exertion in activity': *Orategama* (Teapot), ibid, 109.

2. annihilation of both activity and stillness: *Zengo jiyi*, 656b.

3. "Monks as sangha members": *Chyshiou Baijang chingguei*, vol. 5, in TZ 48:1138b.

4. I vow: *Lioutzu-dashy fabautan jing*, pt. 6, in TZ 48:354a.

5. The ideal: *Shido Bunan Zenji shu, Sokushin ki*, ed. Koda Rentaro (Tokyo, 1968 ed.), 31.

6. If a man seated: *Chuandeng lu*, vol. 10, in TZ 51:274b.

7. 'Always submissive': *Ryuhozan Kaisan tokushi Kozen Daito Kosho Shoto Kokushi goroku*, ed. Shochi, vol. 1, "Daito Kokushi gyojo" (written by Zenko), in TZ 81:224a.

8. "You now understand": Ibid., 223b.

V. 44 (pages 571 - 589)

1. a man must kill his mother: *Linji lu*, in TZ 47:502b.

2. "First: On the Great Travail": "Kueishan Dayuan Chanshy jingtse," in *Tzymen jingshyun*, vol. 1, in TZ 48:1042b-43b.

3. we must not become teacher: Yoshida Shoin, *Ko Mo yowa*, ed. Hirose Yutaka, Iwanami Bunko edition (Tokyo, 1936), 72.

4. "Case 31": In TZ 48:170a-c.

5. 'At dawn, rosy cheeks': Rennyo, *Rennyo Shonin ofumi*, in TZ 83:807b.

6. 'I alone am honored': *Changehan jing*, trans. Buddhayasas and Ju Fonian fr. the Skt. *Dirghagama*, in TZ 1:4c.

7. 'Annihilation of one's delusions': Tsungshan Lianjie, ed. Jyyue Hueiyin, *Yunjou Dungshan Wuben Chanshy yulu*, "Baujung san-mei ge," in TZ 47:515b.

V. 45 (pages 589 - 603)

1. Snow rejoins the broken bridge: *Zengo jiyi*, 557a.

2. 'Every prosperous light': Hakuin, "Rohatsu jishu," in TZ 81:616a.

3. 'Stick to your meditation': Dogen, *Hukan zazengi*, in TZ 82:1a.

4. "an easy gate": *Chanyuan chingguei*, ed. Changlu Tzungtze, vol. 8: "Tsuochan yi," in *Manji-zokyo*, addenda "Zoku-zo" 2:16:5.

5. Whoever has gone through: *Wumen guan*, case "Jaujou goutzy," in TZ 48:292c-93a.

6. 'The lotus leaves sway': *Zengo jiyi*, 494b.

7. "Life is the great activity": *Yuanwu Foguo Chanshy yulu*, comp. Yuanwu Kechin, ed. Huchiou Shanlung, in TZ 47:793c.

8. 'A stream flows': Kamo no Chomei, in *Hojoki*, ed. Yamada Takao, Iwanami Bunko edition (Tokyo, 1971), 41.

9. "every creature is a mortal being": *Suddha-nikaya* 2:22:7, in *Shin Bukkyo jiten*, comp. Nakamura Gen (Tokyo, 1968), 2141.

10. 'The spirit of the Way': Yamato Jocho, recorded by Tashiro Saemon Tsuramoto, *Hagakure*, Iwanami Bunko edition (Tokyo, 1971), 23.

11. 'But the flowers': *Eihei shobogenzo*, vol. 3: *Genjo koan*, in TZ 81:23c.

12. "snow covers the arborvitae": *Kaiankoku go*, in TZ 81:552c.

13. "The snow melts": Dachuan Puji, *Wudeng hueiyuan*, vol. 4, in *Zengo jiyi*, 556b.

14. "Carry snow": *Tsungrung lu*, vol. 5, in TZ 48:276c.

15. "Those ascetic practices": *Tzaehan jing*, trans. Gunabhadra fr. the Skt. *Samyaktagama*, vol. 39, in TZ 2:288a.

16. 'He who has comprehended': *Khuddaka-nikaya, Sutta-nipata* 1:8, in *Nanden Daizokyo* 24:52-24, in *Bukkyo to Kirisutokyo no Hikaku kenkyu*, Masutani Fumio (Tokyo, 1970), 257-59.

17. 'One's reliable foundation': *Fajyujing Shuangyau pin*, comp. Dharmatrata, trans. Vighna et al. fr. the Skt. *Dhammapada*, J. trans. fr. the C. by Ogiwara Unrai, *Hokukyo*, Iwanami Bunko edition (Tokyo, 1972), 48.

18. 'Just as no one can see': *Sutta-nipata* 1:1, *Nanden Daizokyo* 24:2, in *Bukkyo to Kirisutokyo no Hikaku kenkyu*, 1.

19. 'The doctrine of annihilation': Dahuei Tzunghau, *Dahuei Pujyue Chanshy yulu*, vol. 28: "Dahuei Pujyue Chanshi shu," pt. "Da Chen shiauching," ed. Shyefeng Yuwen, in TZ 47:923b.

20. 'Shyshuang set up a hall': *Tsungrung lu*, case 96, in TZ 48:289c.

21. 'A dead tree can sing': *Biyan lu*, case 2, in TZ 48:142b.

22. "Rows of tombs": *Tangshy shyuan*, comp. Li Panlung; in *Toshisen*, annotated by Maeno Naoaki, Iwanami Bunko edition (Tokyo, 1972), 2:7:126.

23. "Sad is the tender wife": Ibid., 1:5:285.

24. 'ever upward': Jyyi, recorded by Guanding, *Mohejyguan lu*, vol. la, in TZ 46:6a.

25. Shiangyan proposed a case: *Wumen guan*, case "Shiangyan shangshu," in TZ 48:297c.

26. Bodhidharma was born: *Chuandeng lu*, vol. 30, "Puti Damo lyuebian dasheng rudau syshing," in TZ 51:458b.

27. "The arborvitae in the front garden": *Wumen guan*, case "Tingchian baishu," in TZ 48:297c.

28. "I shall tell you": *Dungshan lu*, in TZ 47:514a.

29. "Let me answer": *Chuandeng lu*, vol. 17, in TZ 51:337c.

30. "Manifold thanks": *Biyan lu*, case 2, in TZ 48:157a.

31. "I see the mountains": Yunmen Wenyan, ed. Shoujian, *Yunmen Kuangjen Chanshy guanlu*, in TZ 47: 545c. (Hereafter cited as *Yunmen lu*.)

32. "I shall answer": *Chuandeng lu*, vol. 9, in TZ 51:267b.

V. 46 (pages 603 - 618)

1. When the layman Pang: *Biyan lu*, case 41, in TZ 48:179b.

2. When Layman Pang was about to die: Pang Yun, ed. Yuyou, *Pang Jyushy yulu*, in *Hokoji goroku*, annotated by Iriya Yoshitaka, in *Zen no goroku* (Tokyo, 1973), 7:3.

3. 'Truth is attained': Hungjy Jengjian, eds. Tzungrung et al., *Hungjy Chanshy guanlu*, vol. 6, in TZ 48:73c.

4. 'The evil teacher': *Dahuei Pujyue Chanshy yulu*, vol. 28: "Dahuei Pujue Chanshy shu," pt. "Da Tzung Jyge," in TZ 47:933b-c.

5. 'our study ought to be': Nanpu Shomyo, comps. Shosho et. al., *Enzui Daio Kokushi goroku*, vol. 1, in TZ 80:99c.

6. 'I can stay': *Nihon minyoshu*, ed. Machida Yoshiaki and Asano Kenji, Iwanami Bunko edition (Tokyo, 1960), 362.

7. 'Amornings around two': "Shyelshy ge," in *Jaujou lu*, 94–95.

V. 47 (pages 619 - 635)

1. 'War comes of neglecting': *Biyan lu*, case 38, in TZ 48:176c.

2. the three forms are the phases: Derived fr. R. H. Blyth, *Zen and Zen Classics*, frontispiece to vol. 4, "Mumon kan" (Tokyo, 1966).

3. "To be a patriot": Bito Jishu, "Danshi," in *Meishi ruisen*, 8–9.

4. "So it is a daily happening": Lecture passages, ref. *Bukkyo to Kiristokyo no hikaku kenkyu*, chaps. 1 and 2.

5. 'I steal by lawns': "The Brook," *Tennyson Poems and Plays*, 132.

6. 'Dear common flower': J. M. Lowell, "To the Dandelion," in *Shokubutsu minzokushi*, 169–70.

7. 'The monk is competent enough': *Wumen guan*, case "Jaujo Kanpo," in TZ 48:297a.

V. 48 (pages 635 - 651)

1. "whoever admires my looks": *Jingang Banreboluominduo jing*, trans. Kumarajiva fr. the Skt. *Vajracchedika-parjnaparamita-sutra* (Diamond Sutra), in TZ 8:752a.

2. "In this world": *Digha-nikaya* 2:100, in *Gotama Buddha*, Nakamura Gen (Kyoto, 1969), 192.

3. 'Oh evil day!': "Ode: Intimations of Immortality," *The Selected Poetry of William Wordsworth*, ed. Geoffrey Hartman (New York, 1970), 164.

4. All Buddhas without exception: *Eihei shobogenzo*, vol. 12: *Kesa kudoku*, in TZ 82:48a.

5. Whoever has strong carnal appetite: *Tzuochan san-mei jing*, trans. Kumarajiva fr. the Skt. *Dhyana-nsthita-samadhi-dharmaparyaya-sutra* (Meditation Sutra), vol. 1, in TZ 15:271c.

6. His paper was as follows: ref. *Nihon no Zengoroku* (Tokyo, 1978), vol. 12: "Ikkyu," Kato Shuichi, with interpretation by Yanagida Seizan, Introduction (Tokyo, 1978).

7. "Realization at the Cry of a Crow": Ibid., 67.

8. this world is beautiful: *Bannihuan jing*, trans. unknown, vol.1, in TZ 1:180b.

9. practice only good: *Ekottarikagama Tzen gyiaehan jing*, trans. Samghadera fr. the Skt., vol. 1, in TZ 2:551a.

10. "In my world": Byakue Shushin, *Shobo rokuso den*, in *Nihon Bukkyoshi*, Tsuji Zennosuke (Tokyo, 1983), 5:4:96.

11. "Priests who keep the precepts": Ito Toshiko, "Kyounshu shohon no kogo ni tsuite, fu, Koi Kyounshu," in *Yamato bunka*, issue no. 41, poem no. 128 (Tokyo, 1964).

12. "Narcissus Scent": Ibid., no. 542.

13. "Oako Bathing": *Nihon no Zengoroku*, vol. 12, no. 173.

14. "Narcissus": Ibid., no. 190.

15. Inclusive list of titles, ref. "Koshoku bungaku," in *Sekai daihyakka jiten*, vol. 10.

V. 49 (pages 652 - 671)

1. A fellow once said: Sen no Rikyu, "Rikyu shichikajo."

2. "If only they were not ephemeral": *Gosen wakashu*, ed. Onakatomi no Yoshinobu et al., vol. 3, no. 81, in *Shinpen Kokka taikan* 1:35a.

3. "Unstable as water": Gen. 49:4.

4. An old woman: *Wudeng hueiyuan*, ed. Dachuan Puji, vol. 6.

5. 'to go beyond the world': *Chanlin leijyu*, ed. Jyjing and Dautai, pt. "Jiyi," 535b-36a.

6. "Hill Summit": D. G. Rossetti, in *An English and American Literary Calendar*, ed. Narita Narutoshi (Tokyo, 1979), 89-90.

7. even a three-year-old: *Tzutang ji*, comp. and ed. Jing and Yun, photocopy edition, ed. Yanagida Seizan (Kyoto, 1974), 54a.

8. *Shin-shin ming*: Sengtsan, *Shin-shin ming*, in TZ 48-376b-77a.

VI . 50 (pages 675 - 692)

1. 'A defeated general': *Biyan lu*, case 38, in TZ 48:177a.

2. Yunmen said in a lecture: *Yunmen lu*, vol. 2, in TZ 47:563b.

3. the wise can adapt: *Eki kyo*, trans. Takada Shinji and Goto Motomi fr. the C. *Yi jing* (Book of Changes), pt. "Gegua," Iwanami Bunko edition (Tokyo, 1972), 120.

4. Myocho had wife and child: These and all following excerpts fr. *Nihon Bukkyoshi*, vol. 10, pt. 4.

VI . 51 (pages 693 - 709)

1. Zen Teacher Baiyun Shouduan: *Shumon Kattoshu*, no. 259; also in *Wudeng hueiyuan*, no. 19.

2. "I don't dwell": *Tetteki tosui*, ed. Genro Ouryu et al., no. 14.

3. Students of the Way: *Shobogenzo zuimonki*, ed. Koun Ejo, pt. 3, sec. 6, in *Shobogenzo: shobogenzo zuimonki*, ed. and comp. Nishio Minoru et al. (Tokyo, 1968), 363.

4. Evil often comes: *Zengo jiyi*, 421b.

5. 'When the south mountain': *Yunmen lu*, vol. 2, in TZ 47:569b.

6. 'It blooms white': Masaoka Shiki.

VI . 52 (pages 710 - 727)

1. Whatever the year brings: Rose Macaulay, "New Year, 1918," in *Augustan Books of English Poetry*, second series, no. 6 (London, 1927), 13.

2. The way a crow: *The Poems of Robert Frost* (New York, 1946), 233.

3. "Her sight is short": W. H. Davies, "Jenny Wren," in *An English and American Literary Calendar*, vol. "Winter," 193.

4. They wept: Ibid., 65.

5. 'The green mountains': Gau Heng, "Shunry tzayung," in *Meishi ruisen*, 226.

6. 'New moon': Hirose Han, "Shunya," ibid., 174.

7. A heroic man: Liou Tzungyuan, "Ribie," ibid., 739.

8. Spring sun: Daikyu Sokyu, *Kentoroku*, vol. 1, in T. 81:425a.

9. The wind whips: *Nihon shokashu*, 41.

10. "The wren may strive": Christopher Marlowe, *Edward II*, 5.3.34-35.

11. 'listening by eye': *Dungshan lu*, in TZ 47:520a.

12. Darker grows the valley: George Meredith, "Love in the Valley," in *An English and American Literary Calendar*, vol. "Spring," 59.

13. Dungshan asked: *Dungshan lu*, in TZ 47:520a.

14. "There are no eyes": *Banreboluomiduo shinjing*, trans. Shyuantzang Santzang fr. the Skt. *Prajna-paramita-hrdaya-sutra* (Hannya Sutra, or Heart Sutra on Wisdom), in TZ 8:248c.

15. Monk to Nanyang: *Dungshan lu*, in TZ 47:519b-c.

16. "As you may know": Ibid., 519c-20a.

17. Wonderful! Wonderful!: Ibid., 519c-20a.

18. The sun is clear: Wang Anshy, "Tijaianbi," in *Meishi ruisen*, 208.

19. Dungshan's Five Classifications: *Dungshan lu*, in T. 47:525c.

VI . 53 (pages 728 - 745)

1. "Is anyone here not repaying": Ibid., 523c.

2. A tree in the spring breeze: *Kaiankoku go*, vol. 4, in TZ 81:553a.

3. "I shall beg": *Jaujou lu*, vol. 3, pt. "Shingjuang," no. 5, 100.

4. "To Linji as he was planting pines": *Linji lu*, in TZ 47:505a.

5. 'the whole universe is flooded': *Zengo jiyi*, 565a.

6. 'his elbow could nohow bend': *Biyan lu*, case 1, in TZ 48:140a.

7. 'the Bodhisattva mind willing to save': *Eihei shobogenzo*, vol. 23: *Hotsu bodaishin*, in TZ 82:240a.

8. "The affable priest": *Minjyue Chanshy yulu*, ed. Wei Gaiju, vol. 5, in TZ 47:702b.

9. Stay while ye will: Robert Herrick, "To Carnations," in *Shokubutsu minzokushi*, 100.

10. "An old woman asked Jaujou": *Jaujou lu*, vol. 2, no. 436, 70.

11. "The quality of jade": *Biyan lu*, intro. to case 23, in TZ 48:164a.

VI . 54 (pages 746 - 763)

1. 'Season of mists': "To Autumn," *Poems by John Keats* (London, 1979 ed.), 242.

2. Do not kill: Comp. Banjin Doutan, *Busso shoden Zenkaisho*, in TZ 82:647c-55c.

3. All of the Dharma: *Dacheng chishin lun*, trans. Paramartha fr. the Skt. attributed to Asvaghosa, in TZ 32:576a.

4. Do not kill: in *Goi sanki sanju jujukinkai dokugo*, Yasutani Hakuun, (Tokyo, 1962), 13-16.

5. 'Mountains and water': *Biyan lu*, case 43, in TZ 48:180a.

6. The world within a pot: Eizan Shokin, *Shinjinmei nentei*, in TZ 82:419c.

7. "Coming to the realization": *Tzutang ji* 10:195b-96a.

8. "We should not cut off": *Chuandeng lu*, vol. 28, in TZ 51:440b.

9. "No decent person can separate": *Tzutang ji* 12:232a.

10. "How is it when we have no attachment": Ibid., 4:75b.

11. 'How unexpectedly easy': *Linji lu*, in TZ 47:504c.

12. 'I came to the realization': Ibid., pt. "Shi-jung," in TZ 47:500b.

13. "true man of no position": Ibid., in TZ 47:496c.

14. Ellum she hateth mankind: "A Tree Song," *Rudyard Kipling's Verse, Definitive Edition* (Garden City, 1939), 496.

VI . 55 (pages 763 - 775)

1. 'A sutra tells us': *Hyakutsu kirigami*, vol. 3, in *Indo kogosho*, Kawamura Uko (Tokyo, 1962), 2.

2. My mother for many years: Ibid.

3. "Prime Minister Liou": *Jaujou lu*, vol. 2, no. 411, 67.

4. 'being equal means': *Linji lu*, in TZ 47:506a.

5. 'The basic way to enter': *Chuandeng lu*, vol. 30, in TZ 51:458b.

6. Question: "How do all Buddhas": Huangbo Shiyun, recorded by Peishiou, *Huangbo Duanji Chan-shy Wanling lu*, in TZ 48:386a.

7. Retribution comes: Syma Chian, *Shyji*, pt. "Junyinhou chuan."

VI . 56 (pages 775 - 789)

1. "Think not that I came": Matt. 10.34–35.

2. 'John Donne, Ann Donne': Donne's Letter to Ann, in *Eibei bungakushi koza* 4:128.

3. All kings: John Donne, "The Anniversary," in *An Oxford Anthology of English Poetry*, H. Lower and W. Thorp (New York, 1935), 278R.

4. And when the Salmon seeks: Izaak Walton, *Compleat Angler*, second edition (London, 1860), 181.

5. 'The happiest life': *Foshuo Weimojie jing*, trans. Kumarajiva fr. the Skt. *Vimalakirtinirdesa-sutra*, in TZ 14:539c.

6. 'To realize Nirvana': in TZ 56:32b.

VI . 57 (pages 789 - 805)

1. 'The ordinary mind': *Chuandeng lu*, vol. 28, in TZ 51:440a.

2. In Chuanfayuan Monastery: Ibid., vol. 5, in TZ 51:240c.

3. To attain the Way: Ibid., vol. 28, in TZ 51:440a.

4. Nanchyuan said: "The ordinary mind is the Way": *Wumen guan*, case "Pingchang shy dau," in TZ 48:295b.

5. A monk: "What is the ordinary mind?": *Jaujou lu*, vol. 1, no. 147, 29.

6. A monk: "What is Self?": Ibid., vol. 2, no. 291, 52.

7. "A day of no work": *Tzutang ji*, vol. 14:271a.

8. "Are you not lonesome": *Yosano Akiko kashu*, pt. "Midaregami," Iwanami Bunko edition (Tokyo, 1972), 9. "Dreams should be dreamed": Ibid., "Ryokkai shunu," 245.

VI . 58 (pages 806 - 819)

1. One day, seeing Manjusri: *Shyutang Her'shang yulu*, vol. 6, in TZ 47:1024b.

2. 'everything is the Way': *Biyan lu*, case 2, in TZ 48:142a.

3. 'Hey, Master': *Wumen guan*, case "Rueiyan huan junren," in TZ 48:294b.

4. We look before: Percy Shelley, "To a Skylark," in *A Treasury of Great Poems English and American*, 723.

5. a pilgrimage is to traverse mountains: Muan Shanehing, *Tzuting shyyuan*, vol. 8, pt. "Tzanjy."

VI . 59 (pages 820 - 837)

1. "Go, go, seek out": Henry Vaughan, "Idle Verse," in *An Oxford Anthology of English Poetry*, 313R.

2. "Yotzy said": *Lunyu*, I-12, in *Genzaigoyaku Rongo*, 73.

3. 'the bulk of your natives': Jonathan Swift, *Gulliver's Travels* (Arlington, 1980), 6:204.

4. "Yunmen said": *Yunmen lu*, vol. 1, in TZ 47:553a.

5. 'Which to maintain': *Richard II*, 1.1.62-64.

6. "Were I to attain": *Foshuo wu-liangshou jing*, trans. Samghavarman fr. the Skt. *Sukhavati-vyuha*, vol. 1, in TZ 12:268a.

7. "The days and months": Matsuo Basho, *Oku no hosomichi*, ed. Sugiura Shoichiro, Iwanami Bunko edition (Tokyo, 1972), 9.

8. I saw Eternity: Henry Vaughan, "The World," in *An Oxford Anthology of English Poetry*, 315L.

VII . 60 (pages 841 - 855)

1. One must have a mind: *The Collected Poems of Wallace Stevens* (New York, 1965), 9-10.

2. Not a bird: Liou Tzungyuan, "Jiangshyue," in *Meishi ruisen*, 214.

3. Make Thou my spirit pure: "St. Agnes' Eve," *Tennyson Poems and Plays*, 102. Many, many welcomes: Ibid., "The Snowdrop," 812.

VII.61 (pages 855 - 870)

1. On sleet- or rain-swept nights: Sasaki Nobutsuna, *Shinkun Manyoshu*, vol. 1, Iwanami Bunko edition (Tokyo, 1972), 228-29.

2. 'Daffy-down-dilly': Iona and Peter Opie, *The Oxford Dictionary of Nursery Rhymes* (London, 1975), 141.

3. 'Now the full-throated daffodils': Cecil Day-Lewis, *Feathers to Iron*, ed. Leonard and Virginia Woolf (London, 1931), no. 14, 29.

4. "Lo! one she marked": "Persephone," *The Poetical Works of Jean Ingelow Longmans* (London, 1902), 181.

5. Those who would teach: *Biyan lu*, case 5, in TZ 48:144c.

6. "May you creatures": *Tojo-gyoji kihan*, ed. Sotoshu Shumuin, pt. "Hojo-e kechiganmon" (1890, Tokyo).

VII.62 (pages 871 - 884)

1. "Spring sea": *Shin-saijiki*, ed. Takahama Kyoshi (Tokyo, 1972), 186.

2. 'a land quite fertile': *Datang shiyu ji*, vol. 6, in TZ 51:900c.

3. "Go—u ki—n": *Chyshiou Baijang chingguei*, vol. 2, pt. "Fo jiangdan," in TZ 48:1116a.

4. 'Truly, I say to you': Matt. 18.4.

5. 'Whoever receives': Ibid., 18.5.

6. 'Love your enemies': Ibid, 5.44.

7. "Anger will never end": *Fajyujing shuangyau pin*, vol. 1, in TZ 4:562a.

8. My father, native to Fanyang: *Lioutzu-dashy fabautan jing*, pt. 1, in TZ 48:348a.

9. without entering the water: *Shutang lu*, vol. 1, in TZ 47:988b.

10. "...After the kingfisher's wing": T. S. Eliot, *Four Quartets*, (London, 1944), 1.4.34–36.

11. It was the Rainbow: "The Kingfisher," *W. H. Davies Selected Poems*, ed. Jonathan Barker (London, 1985), 47.

VII.63 (pages 885 - 898)

1. "There was a flower": *The Complete Poems of D. H. Lawrence*, ed. Vivian de Sola Pinto and Warren Roberts (New York, 1964), 282-83.

2. "So pure in pure white": In *Kanginshu*, comp. unknown.

3. Scoop water: In TZ 47:1005b.

4. 'All sentient beings': *Daban niepan jing*, vol. 27, in TZ 12:522b-28c.

5. 'How from that sapphire fount': *Milton Poetical Works, Paradise Lost*, ed. Douglas Bush (London, 1966), 4.237.63.

6. 'Men chained by men': *Theragatha*, in *Butten*, Nakamura Gen, vol. 84, nos. 149 and 150, in *Sekai Koten-bungaku Zenshu*, vol. 6 (Tokyo, 1981), 184.

VII.64 (pages 898 - 911)

1. 'Manjusaka': Nakamura Teijo, in *Shin-saijiki*, 554.

2. 'Two days ago': "Autumn Rain," *Collected Short Poems of Kenneth Rexroth* (New York, 1966), 261.

3. 'I saw old Autumn': Thomas Hood, "Autumn," *The Oxford Book of English Verse* (London, 1922), 752.

4. 'A pine is straight': *Tsungrung lu*, case 27, in TZ 48:244c.

5. 'Disregard our shortage': Yoshida Shoin, ed. Hirose Yutaka, *Ko Mo yowa*, Iwanami Bunko edition (Tokyo, 1972), 1:3:21-23.

6. 'Setting a life aim': Ibid, vol. 1:2:19, 2:17:76, and 2:18:83.

VII.65 (pages 911 - 925)

1. I thence journeyed: *Gotama Buddha*, 96.

2. You are thin and pale: Ibid, 85.

3. Evil spirit: Ibid, 86-87.

4. How great is the human mind: Myoan Eisai, *Ko Zen gokokuron*, in TZ 80:1a.

About the Author

Seikan Hasegawa, born in a temple near Kyoto, Japan, in 1945, became a Buddhist priest at age fourteen. He studied Northern Buddhism in a Japanese Zen monastery and also studied Southern Buddhism in a Thai monastery. He first came to America in 1969. He is the author of two other books, *The Cave of Poison Grass: Essays on the Hannya Sutra* and *Essays on Marriage*.